Andrew Pyper was born in Stratford, Ontario in 1968. He is the author of international best-seller *Lost Girls*, selected as a *New York Times* Notable Book of the Year and currently in development by John Malkovich for a feature film adaptation. The film rights to *The Killing Circle* have been sold to the award-winning producers of *The Last King of Scotland*.

Andrew Pyper lives in Toronto.

www.andrewpyper.com

By the same author

Lost Girls
The Trade Mission
The Wildfire Season

SHORT STORIES
Kiss Me

ANDREW PYPER

The Killing Circle

HARPER

HarperCollins*Publishers*
77–85 Fulham Palace Road,
London W6 8JB

www.harpercollins.co.uk

This paperback edition 2008

First published in Great Britain
by HarperCollins*Publishers* 2008

ISBN-13 978 0 00 716508 7

Printed and bound in Great Britain by
Clays Ltd, St Ives plc

Mixed Sources
Product group from well-managed
forests and other controlled sources
www.fsc.org   Cert no. SW-COC-1806
© 1996 Forest Stewardship Council
FSC

FSC is a non-profit international organisation established
to promote the responsible management of the world's forests.
Products carrying the FSC label are independently certified
to assure consumers that they come from forests that are managed
to meet the social, economic and ecological needs
of present and future generations.

Find out more about HarperCollins and the environment at
www.harpercollins.co.uk/green

For Heidi

LABOUR DAY, 2007

I didn't know my son could tell directions from the stars.

Corona Austrina. Lyra. Delphinus.

Sam leaves noseprints on the passenger window as we highway out of the city, reciting the constellations and whispering "South" and "East" and "North" with each turn I make.

"Where'd you learn that?"

He gives me the same look as when I came into his room a couple nights ago and found him slingshooting a platoon of plastic Marines, one by one, on to the neighbour's roof. "I'm a terrorist," he had answered when asked what he thought he was doing.

"Learn what?"

"The stars."

"Books."

"Which books?"

"Just *books*."

With Sam I know I'll get no further than this. It's because both of us are readers. Not by passion necessarily, but by character. Observers. Critics. Interpreters. Readers of books (most recently the later, furious Philip Roth for me, and *Robinson Crusoe*, told in bedtime snippets, for Sam). But also comics, travel brochures, bathroom-stall graffiti, owner's manuals, cereal-box recipes. The material doesn't matter. Reading is how we translate the world into a language we can at least partly understand.

"North," Sam says, his nose returned to the glass.

The two of us peer at the slab of shadow at the top of the rise. A square monolith jutting out of an Ontario corn field like the last remnant of an ancient wall.

"Mus-tang Drive-in. End of Sea-son. La-bour Day dusk-'til-dawn," Sam reads as we pass the sign.

He leans forward to study the neon cowboy on a bucking bronco that is the Mustang's beacon, directing us in from the night roads.

"I've been here before," he says.

"You remember that?"

"The sign. The man on the horse."

"You were so little then."

"What am I now?"

"Now? Now you're a book-reading, star-gazing young man."

"No," he says, grimacing. "I'm eight years old. And I just remember things."

We have come out here, widower and son, to watch the last movie show of the summer at one of the last drive-ins in the country. The last of the lasts.

Tamara – Sam's mother, my wife – died eight months after Sam was born. Since then, I have found a parental usefulness in moviegoing. In a darkened cinema (or here, in a darkened corn field) Sam and I can find an intimacy without the dangers of talk. There's something distinctly male about it. The closeness fathers and sons find in passive, mostly silent hobbies, like fly fishing or watching baseball games.

The guy at the admission booth pauses when he spots Sam in the passenger seat. Tonight's main feature – a spooky Hollywood thriller currently raking in the last of the easy summer dollars – is R-rated. I hand the guy a bill that more than covers full price for two adults. He winks and waves us on, but offers no change.

The place is packed. The best spot left is in front of the concession stand, well off to the side. Sam wanted to try further back, but I know that's where the high school kids go. Pot and smuggled rye, teenaged boys and girls and all the things they get away with. It's not concern for Sam's moral education, but the nostalgic envy that being so close to these crimes would cause in me that makes me stay up here with the rest of the respectables.

"It's starting!" Sam announces as the flood-lights cut out.

It leaves me to pull our chairs and mothballed sleeping bag out of the trunk with only the light of the commercials to see by. I slide along the side of the car keeping my eye on the screen. This, for me, is the best part of the whole drive-in experience: the vintage ad for junk food. A dancing hot dog, leering milkshake, a choir of french fries. And there's something about the tap-dancing onion ring that always breaks my heart.

I set up Sam's chair, then my own. Snuggle up next to each other under the sleeping bag.

"En-joy Our Fea-ture Pres-en-ta-tion!" Sam says, reading the screen.

The parked rows await the sky's final turn from purple to black. A single honk to our right, a minivan rollicking with sugar-freaked little lea-guers, brings muffled laughter from the vehicles around us. But there's something nervous in these sounds – the bleat of alarm, the reply of hollow mirth. To make this impression go away I try at a laugh of my own. A dad laugh. And once it's out, I inhale the familiar mix of gas fumes, popcorn, burnt hamburger. Along with something else. Something like fear. Faint as the perfume a previous guest leaves on a motel pillow.

The movie starts. A scene of introductory hor-ror: a dark figure pursuing its prey through a field at night. Flashes of desperate movement, swinging arms and boots and jangling keys on a belt. Jump

4

edits between the killer's certain stride and the other's panicked run, fall, then sobbing, crab crawl forward. A brief shot of hands dripping with what may be oil, or wet earth, or blood. A close-up scream.

We don't know who this person is, this certain victim, but we recognize the context of hopeless struggle. It is the dream all of us have had, the one in which our legs refuse to carry us, the ground softened into black syrup, taking us down. And behind us is death. Faceless and sure, suffering no such handicaps.

We're so close to the screen that to look at anything else forces me to turn all the way around in my chair. An audience of eyes. Looking back at me through bug-spattered windshields.

I sit forward again and tilt my head back. The autumn dome of night, endless and cold, lets me breathe. For a moment. Then even the stars crowd down.

"Dad?"

Sam has turned at all my fidgeting. I force myself to look straight ahead at the actors on the screen. Enormous, inescapable. Their words coming from every direction, as if spoken from within me. Soon the film becomes not just any dream, but a particular one I've had a thousand times.

I'm standing before I know I'm out of my chair. The sleeping bag spilling off my knees.

Sam looks up at me. Now, his face half in shadow, I can see his mother in him. It's what gives him his sweetness, his open vulnerability. Seeing her in his features brings the strange feeling of missing someone who is still here.

"You want anything?" I ask. "Tater tots?"

Sam nods. And when I reach my hand out to him, he takes it.

We shuffle toward the source of the projector's light. The blue beam and the glimpsed orange of matches lighting cigarettes in back seats – along with the dull glow of the quarter moon – the only illumination to see by. And the same dialogue broadcast from the speakers hooked to every car window.

It's him.

What are you talking about?

The thing that lives under your bed. The eyes in your closet at night, watching you. The dark. Whatever frightens you the most …

Somebody opens the door to the concession stand and a cone of light plays over our feet. Sam runs to stay within it. Pretending that if he touches the unlit gravel before he gets inside he'll be sucked into another dimension.

Which we are anyway. The Mustang's snack bar belongs to neither Sam's generation nor mine, but to whatever time it was when men wore ties to buy cheeseburgers. Just look at the posters on the walls: beaming sixties families stepping from their fin-tailed Fords to purchase treats for adorably ravenous Beaver Cleaver kids. It's almost enough to put you off the food.

6

But not quite.

In fact, we need a tray. On to which I pile cardboard boats of taters, foil-wrapped dogs, rings so greasy you can see through the paper plate they sit on, as well as a jumbo soda, two straws.

But before we can leave, we need to pay. The girl at the till is speaking into the air. "No way," she says, hang-jawed. "No *way*." And then I notice the cord coming out of her ear. The little mouthpiece thingy under her chin. "For *real*?"

"I'll meet you where we're sitting," Sam says, grabbing a hot dog off the tray.

"Just watch for cars."

"They're *parked*, Dad."

He gives me a pitying smile before running out the door.

Outside, after I've paid, the sudden dark leaves me blind. A tater tot leaps off the tray and squashes under my shoe. Where the hell did I park anyway? The movie tells me. The angle I'd been watching it from. Up a bit more, off to the side.

And there it is. My ancient Toyota. A car I should really think about replacing but can't yet. It's the lipstick and eyeliner Tamara left in the glove box. Every time I open it to grab my ownership certificate they spill out into my hand and she is with me. Sitting in the passenger seat, pulling down the visor mirror for a last-minute smearing. When we'd arrive at wherever we were headed to, she would turn to me and ask, "Do I look okay?" Every time I said yes, it was true.

I keep my eyes on the Toyota's outline and stumble toward it, right next to the van of little leaguers. Quiet now. Their attention held by the movie's suspense.

Why is he doing this? Why not just kill us when he had the chance?

The tray falls from my hands.

It's not the movie. It's what's in front of my car that does it.

There's our fold-out chairs. The sleeping bag.

Except the sleeping bag is lying on the ground. And both chairs are empty.

A couple of the minivan kids are sniggering at me, pointing at the unsheathed hot dog on the ground, the dixie cups of extra ketchup splashed gore over my pants. I look their way. And whatever shows on my face makes them slide the door shut.

I drift away from the Toyota, scuffing through the aisles between the cars. Slow, deliberate scans in every direction. Poking my head into the vehicles and noting the hundreds of North American lives in recreational progress – the dope-smoking kids, gluttonous adults, the couples slumped under comforters in the backs of pick-up trucks.

But no Sam.

For the first time the idea of calling the police comes to mind. Yet it remains only an idea. Sam's been gone three minutes at most. He has to be here. What *might* be happening is *not* happening. It can't be. It can't.

"Sam!"

My son's name comes to me from someone else. An alarmed third party.

"Sam!"

I start to run. As fast as I can at first. Then, realizing I won't make it the length of a single row, slow it to a jog. A pushing-forty man trotting his way through the parked cars in the middle of the main feature, rubbernecking this way and that. It's the sort of thing people notice. A teenager in his dad's convertible wolf whistles as I go by, and the girls bunched into the front with him offer an ironic wave. Without thinking, I wave back.

When I finish zigzagging all the rows, I start around the perimeter of the lot. Peering into the shadowed fields. Each line of corn another chance of seeing Sam standing there, hiding, waiting for me to find him. This anticipated image of him becomes so particular that I actually spot him a couple of times. But when I stop for a second look, he's gone.

I make it to the back of the lot where the light from the screen is dimmest, everything bathed in a deep-sea glow. The corn rows seem wider here, and darker. The roof of a distant farmhouse the only interruption on the horizon. No lights in its windows. I try to blink it into better focus, but my eyes are blurred by tears I hadn't felt coming.

I thought you were a ghost.

I was a ghost. But ghosts don't get to do things. It's much better being the monster. The kind you don't expect is a monster until it's too late.

I bend over and put my hands on my knees. Sucking air. A pause that lets the panic in. The horrific imaginings. Who he's with. What they will do. Are doing. How he will never come back.

I saw someone. Looking in the window.

Did you see who it was?

A man. A shadow.

I have already started to run back toward the concession stand when I see it.

A figure disappearing into the stands of corn. As tall as me, if not taller. There. And then not there.

I try to count the rows between where I was and where the figure entered the field. Seven? Eight? No more than ten. When I've passed nine I cut right and start in.

The fibrous leaves thrash against my face, the stalks cracking as I punch my way past. It looked like there was more room in the rows from outside, but now that I'm within them there's not near enough space for a man my size to move without being grabbed at, tripped, cut. Not so much running as swallowed by a constricting throat.

How is whoever I saw going any faster than me? The question makes me stop. I lie down flat and peer through the stalks. Down here, the only light is a grey, celestial dusting. With my open mouth pressed against the earth, it's as though the moonlight has assumed a taste. The mineral grit of steel shavings.

I teach my body to be still.

The thought occurs to me that I have gone mad between the time I left Sam and now. Sudden-onset insanity. It would explain crashing through a corn field at night. Chasing something that likely wasn't there in the first place.

And then it's there.

A pair of boots rushing toward the far end of the field. A hundred feet ahead and a couple rows to the left.

I scramble to my feet. Moaning at my locked knees, the muscles burning in my hips. I use my hands to pull me ahead. Ripping out ears of corn and tossing them to thud like another's steps behind me.

Every few strides offers a peek at the farmhouse in the distance, and I cut sideways to stay in line with it. As if I know this is where the figure is going. As if I have a plan.

I lift my head again, scanning for the gabled roof, and catch the figure instead. Rushing right-to-left across the gap. A glimpse of motion through the silk-topped ears. Darker than the night stretched tight over the corn.

I launch forward. Blinking my eyes clear to catch another sight of it down the rows. But what *was* it? Neither identifiably man nor woman, no notable clothing, no hat, no visible hair. No face. A scarecrow hopped off its post.

Now when I shout I'm no longer addressing Sam but whatever it is that's out here with me.

"Bring him back! Bring him *back*!"

There's no threat in it. No promise of vengeance. It's little more than a father's winded gasps shaped into words.

11

All at once I break through into the farmhouse's yard. The grass grown high around a rusted swing set. Paint chipping on the shutters. Smashed-out windows.

I go around the back of the place. No car parked anywhere. No sign that anyone has come or gone since whatever bad news ushered out the people who lived here last.

I stop for a second to think of what to do next. That's when my legs give out. I fall to my knees as though moved by a sudden need to pray. Over the pounding of my heart I listen for retreating footfall. Not even the movie voices can reach me. The only sound the electric buzz of crickets.

And the only thing to see is the Mustang's screen. An ocean of cornstalks away, but still clearly visible. A silent performance of terror so much more fluid and believable than my own.

It's as I watch that it comes to me. A truth I could never prove to anyone, but no less certain for that.

I know who has done this. Who has taken my son. I know its name.

I kneel in the high grass of the abandoned farmyard, staring at its face. Forty feet high and towering over the harvest fields, lips moving in silence, directly addressing the night like a god. A monstrous enlargement made of light on a white-washed screen.

The part all actors say is the best to play. The villain.

PART ONE

The Kensington Circle

1

VALENTINE'S DAY, 2003

"Love cards!"

This is Sam, my four-year-old son. Running into my room to jump on the bed and rain crayoned Valentines over my face.

"It's Love Day," I confirm. Lift his T-shirt to deliver fart kisses to his belly.

"Who's *your* Valentine, Daddy?"

"I suppose that would have to be Mommy."

"But she's not *here*."

"That doesn't matter. You can choose anyone you like."

"Really?"

"Absolutely."

Sam thinks on this. His fingers folding and unfolding a card. The sparkles stirred around in the still wet glue.

"So is Emmie your Valentine?" I ask him. Emmie being our regular nanny. "Maybe someone at daycare?"

And then he surprises me. He often does.

"No," he says, offering me his paper heart. "It's you."

Days like these, the unavoidable calendar celebrations – Christmas, New Year's, Father's Day, Mother's Day – are worse than others. They remind me how lonely I am. And how, over time, this loneliness has burrowed deeper, down into tissue and bone. A disease lurking in remission.

But lately, something has changed. An emerging emptiness. The full, vacant weight of loss. I thought that I'd been grieving over the past three and a half years. But maybe I'm only just now coming out of the shock. Maybe the real grief has yet to arrive.

Sam is everything.

This one rule still helps. But in the months immediately following Tamara's death, it was more than just a focus. It allowed me to survive. No one-way wants, no *me*. Not permitting myself to dream had got me halfway to not feeling – easier conditions to manage than feeling and dreaming too much.

But maybe this has been a mistake. Maybe I was wrong to believe you could get along without something of your own. Eventually, if living requires being nothing, then you're not even living any more.

* * *

16

Tamara's last days is something I'm not going to get into. I will confess to all manner of poor behaviour and bad judgment and broken laws. And I am prepared to *explore the nature of memory* (as the cover bumpf on those precious, gazing-out-to-sea sort of novels puts it) even when it causes the brightest flashes of regret. But I'm not going to tell you what it was like to watch my wife's pain. To watch her die.

I will say this, however: losing her opened my eyes. To the thousands of hours spent gnawing on soured ambitions, petty office grievances, the seemingly outrageous everyday injustices. To all the wasted opportunities to not think, but do. Chances to change. To see that I could change.

I had just turned thirty-one when Tamara died. Not even half a life. But when she left, a cruel light was cast on how complete this life could have been. How complete it *was*, had I only seen it that way.

We bought the house on Euclid just off Queen as newlyweds, before the arrival of the yoga outfitters, the hundred-dollar-haircut salons, the erotic boutiques. Then, the only yoga being practiced was by the drunks folded up in store doorways, and the only erotica was a half-hour with one of the ladies pacing in heels at the corner. I could barely manage the downpayment then, and can't afford to sell now. Not if I want to live anywhere near downtown.

Which I do. If for no other reason than I like to walk to work. Despite the comforts offered by all the new money washing in, Queen Street West still offers plenty of drama for the pedestrian. Punks cheering on a pair of snarling mastiffs outside the Big Bop. A chorus of self-talkers off their meds. The guy who follows me for a block every morning, asking me to buy him a prosciutto sandwich (he's very specific about this) and inexplicably calling me Steve-o. Not to mention the ambulances hauling off whoever missed the last bed in the shelter the night before.

It is a time in the city's history when everyone is pointing out the ways that Toronto is changing. More construction, more new arrivals, more ways to make it and spend it. And more to fear. The stories of random violence, home invasions, drive-bys, motiveless attacks. But it's not just that. It's not the threat that has always come from the *them* of our imaginations, but from potentially anyone, even ourselves.

There's a tension in the streets now, the aggression that comes with insatiable desires. Because there is more on offer than there was before, there is more to want. This kind of change, happening as it's happening here, fast and unmanageable, makes people see others in ways they hadn't before. As a market. A demographic. Points of access.

What all of us share is our wishing for more. But wishing has a dark side. It can turn those who were once merely strangers into the competition.

* * *

18

I follow Queen all the way to Spadina, then lake-ward to the offices of the *National Star* – "*The New York Times* of Toronto" as one especially ill-conceived ad campaign called it. This is where I started out. An angry young man with no real grounds to be angry, quickly ascending from copy-editor to the paper's youngest ever in-house book critic. My unforgiving standards buttressed by the conviction that one day all those tall poppies I had scythed to earth would see I had a right to my declarations. One day, I would produce a book of my own.

From as far back as I can remember I felt I had something within me that would find its way out. This was likely the result of a solitary, only-child childhood, throughout which books were often my only friends. Weekends spent avoiding the out-of-doors, curled up like a cat on the rug's sunny squares, ripping into Greene, Leonard, Christie, mulling over the out-of-reach James, Faulkner, Dostoyevsky. Wondering how they did it. The making of *worlds*.

What was never in doubt was that I would be among them when I grew up. Not their equal necessarily, but participating in the same noble activity. I accepted that I might not be good at it. At first. But I could sense the hard work that had gone into my favourite works, and was prepared to devote myself to slow improvement.

Looking back on it, I must have seen writing as a sort of religious practice. A total commitment to craft and honest disclosure no less holy for its god-lessness. There was the promise of salvation, after all. The possibility of creating a story that spoke for me, would be *better* than me. More compelling, more mysterious, more wise. I suppose, when they were still alive, I believed that writing a book would somehow keep my parents with me. And after they were gone, I simply changed my articles of faith: If I wrote a good enough book, it might bring them back.

But no book came.

Instead, after university, I started typing my way up the ladder of small-town weeklies and specialty magazine freelancing ("The New Dog, The New You" for *Puppy Love!* and "Carrots vs Beets?: The Root of the Problem" for *Sustenance Gardening* being two prizewinners in their fields). After I got married and was hired at the *National Star*, I thought about my book less, and about a flesh-and-blood future more. Children. Travel. But the niggling idea that I was thwarting my destiny with domestic comforts couldn't be wholly escaped. In some private corner of my soul, I was still waiting. For the opening line. For a *way in*.

But no line came.

Two things happened next, oddly related, and at the same time: Tamara became pregnant, and I cancelled my Sunday-only subscription to *The New York Times*. The articulated reason for the latter decision was that I barely found the time to peel apart its many sections and supplements, never mind read any of them. And now, with a baby on the way – it was a *waste*.

The truth had nothing to do with saving time or trees, however. It had to do with my coming to the point where I could no longer open the Book Review of the Sunday *Times* without causing physical pain to myself. The *publishers*. The *authors' names*. The *titles*. All belonging to *books that weren't mine*.

It hurt. Not emotionally, not a mere spanking of the ego. It hurt in the same way kidney stones or a soccer cleat to the balls hurts – instantly, indescribably, critically. The reviews themselves rarely mattered. In fact, I usually couldn't finish reading the remotely positive ones. As for the negative ones, they too often proved to be insufficient salves to my suffering. Even the snarkiest vandalism, the baldest runs at career enders, only acted as reminders that their victims had produced something worth pissing on. Oh, to awaken on a rainy Sunday and refuse to get out of bed on account of being savaged in the *Times*! What a sweet agony *that* would be, compared to the slow haemorrhaging in No Man's Land it was to merely imagine creating words worthy of Newspaper of Record contempt.

Then Sam arrived, and the bad wanting went away.

I was in love – with Tamara, with my son, even with the world, which I hadn't really liked all that much before. I stopped trying to write. I was too busy being happy.

Eight months later Tamara was gone.

Sam was a baby. Too young to remember his mother, which left me to do all the remembering for the both of us.

It wasn't long after this that I started believing all over again. Waiting for a way to tell the one true story that might bring back the dead.

The demotions started some time after my return from bereavement leave. The dawning millennium, we were told, was ushering in a new breed of "user friendly" newspaper, one that could compete with the looming threats of the internet and cable news channels and widespread functional illiteracy. Readers had grown impatient. Words in too great a number only squandered their time. In response, the Arts section became the Entertainment section. Features were shrunk to make room for celebrity "news" and photos of movie stars walking, sunglassed, with a barbell-sized latte. Memos were circulated directing us to fashion our stories so as to no longer appeal to adults seeking information and analysis, but to adolescents with attention-deficit disorder.

Let's just say they weren't good days for the Books section.

Not that the ruin of my journalistic career happened overnight. I had slipped down the rungs of respectability one at a time, from literary columnist (gleeful, sarcastic trashings of almost everything) to entertainment writer-at-large (starlet profiles, tallying up the weekend box-office results), a couple months as "junior obituarist" (the "senior obituarist" being five years younger than me), before the inarguable end of the line, the universal newspaper grease-trap: TV critic. I had tried to talk my section editor into at least putting "Television Feature Writer" under my by-line, but instead, when I opened the *Tube News!* supplement the following weekend, I found that I didn't even have a name any more, and that I was now, simply, "The Couch Potato".

Which is accurate enough. These past months of professional withering have found me spending more of my time on various recliners and mattresses: my bed, in which I linger later and later every morning, the chair in my therapist's office, which I leave shining with sweat, as well as the sofa in the basement, where I fast forward through the lobotomized sitcom pilots and crime dramas and reality shows that, put together, act on me as a kind of stupefying drug, the bye-bye pills they slip under the tongues of asylum inmates.

No shame in any of this, of course. Or no more shame than most of the things we do for money, the paid positions for Whale Saver or African Well Digger or Global Warming Activist being so lamentably few.

The problem is that, almost unnoticeably, the same notion from my childhood has returned to me like a lunatic whisper in my ear. A black magic spell. A devil's promise.

Maybe, if I could only put the right words in the right order, I would be saved. Maybe I could turn longing into art.

There is something unavoidably embittered in the long-exposure critic. It's because, at its heart, the practice is a daily reminder of one's secondary status. None start out wanting to *review* books, but to *write* them. To propose otherwise would be like trying to convince someone that as a child you dreamed of weighing jockeys instead of riding racehorses.

If you require proof, just look at the half-dozen souls keyboard clacking and middle-distance staring in the cubicles around mine. Together, we pick through the flotsam that the waves of pop culture wash in every morning. The CDs, DVDs, game software, movies, mags. Even the book desk. My former domain. Now responsible for assembling a single, ignored page on Saturday. But still a better place than where they've put me.

Here we are. Off in the corner, no window within stapler-throwing distance. A desk that my colleagues call the Porn Palace, on account of the teetering stacks of black video cassettes on every surface. And it *is* porn. It's TV. An addictively shameful pleasure we all seem to want more of.

There's a box of new arrivals on my chair. I'm pulling out the first offering – a reality show where

I'm promised contestants in bikinis eating live spiders – when Tim Earheart, one of the paper's investigative reporters, claps me on the back. You'd never know it, but Tim is my best friend here. It occurs to me now with a blunt surprise that he may be my best friend anywhere.

"You got any *Girls Gone Wild*?" he says, rummaging through the tapes.

"Thought you were more of a documentary guy."

"Wife's away this week. Actually, she might not be coming back."

"Janice left you?"

"She found out that my source on last week's Hell's Angels story was one of the bikers' old ladies," Tim says with a sad smile. "Let's just say I went more undercover with her than Janice was comfortable with."

If it's true that his most recent wife has taken off, this will be marriage number three down the tubes for Tim. He turns thirty-six next week.

"Sorry to hear that," I say, but he's already waving off my sympathy.

"Drinks tonight?" he says, stepping away to re-join the hectic relevance of the news department. "Wait. It's Valentine's, isn't it? You got a date?"

"I don't date, Tim. I don't anything."

"It's been a while."

"Not so long."

"Some would say four years is enough to –"

"Three."

25

"*Three* years then. Eventually you're going to have to face the fact that you're still here, even if Tamara isn't."

"Trust me. I face that every day."

Tim nods. He's been to war zones. He knows a casualty when he sees one.

"Can I ask you something?" he says. "You think it's too late to ask out that new temp they've got down in Human Resources?"

It happened again on the walk home.

More and more these days, I'll be in the middle of something – dashing to the corner store, pounding out the day's word count at my desk, lining up for coffee – and the tears will come. So quiet and without warning I hardly notice.

And then today, walking along the sidewalk when I would have said "Nothing" if asked what was on my mind, it started again. Wet streaks freezing on my cheeks.

A rhyme pops into my head. An unconsoling sing-song that carries me home.

> *I'm not well*
> *I'm not well*
> *But who in the hell*
> *Am I going to tell?*

By the time I get through the door, Sam's already finished his dinner and Emmie, the nanny, is drying him from his bath. Another irretrievable moment missed. I like bathtime with Sam more than any other part of the day. A little music. Epic sea battles waged with rubber ducks and old toothbrushes. All of it leading to bed. To stories.

"I'll take him," I tell Emmie, and she opens the towel she has wrapped around him. He rushes out of his cocoon and into my arms. A soapy angel.

I get him into pajamas. Open the book we're working through. But before I start reading, he studies me for a moment. Places a palm against my forehead.

"What do you think, doc? Am I going to make it?"

"You'll live," he says.

"But it's serious?"

"I'm not sure. Is it?"

"Nothing I can't handle."

"I don't want you to be sad."

"I miss your mom sometimes. That's all. It's normal."

"Normal."

"More or less."

Sam purses his lips. He's not sure whether to buy my pinched grin or not. The thing is, he needs me to be okay. And for him, I'll stay as okay as I can.

He yawns. Squirms in close, his head against my throat so that he can feel the vibrations of the words to come. Jabs his finger at the pages I hold open.

"Where were we?"

* * *

27

Once Sam is asleep it's down to the basement office. What Tamara used to call the Crypt. Which is a little too accurate to be wholly amusing. A low-ceilinged room that was a wine-making cellar for the previous owner. Even now, I can catch whiffs of fermented grapes. It makes me think of feet.

This is where I watch the tapes. A notebook on my knee, remote control in my hand.

I'm just three minutes into the spider-eating bikini babes when I hit Pause. Dig out of my pocket the ad I clipped from today's classifieds.

Tell the Story of Your Life

Open your soul. Bring your buried words to the page in this intensive workshop with Conrad White, published poet and novelist. *Truly write. Write the truth.*

I've never heard of Conrad White. Never attended a writers' workshop, circle, night class or retreat. It's been years since I've tried to write anything other than what I am contractually obliged to. But something about this day – about the taste of the air in this very room – has signalled that something is coming my way. Has already come.

I call the number at the bottom of the ad. When a voice at the other end asks me what he can do for me, I answer without hesitation.

"I want to write a book," I say.

2

People read less today than they used to. You've seen the studies, you've got teenagers, you've been to the mall – you know this already. But here's something you may not know:

The less people *read*, the more they want to *write*.

Creative writing workshops – within universities, libraries, night schools, mental hospitals, prisons – are the true growth industry in the ink-based sector. Not to mention the *ad hoc* circles of nervy aspirants, passing round their photocopied bundles. Each member claiming to seek feedback but secretly praying for a collective declaration of brilliance.

And now I'm one of them.

The address the voice on the phone gave me is in Kensington Market. Meetings to be held every Tuesday night for the next five Tuesdays. I was told I was the last to join the group. That is, I called it a group, and the voice corrected me.

"I prefer to think of it as a circle."

"Right. And how many will there be? In the circle?"

"Just seven. Any more, and I fear our focus may be lost."

After I hung up I realized that Conrad White – if that's who answered the phone – never asked for my name. I also realized I'd forgotten to find out if I should bring anything along to the first meeting – a pen, notebook, cash for the donation plate. But when I dialled the number again, it rang ten times without anyone answering. I suppose that now the circle was complete, Mr White decided there was no point in picking up.

The next Tuesday, I walk up Spadina after work with my scarf turbaned around my ears. Despite the cold, most of the Chinatown grocers still have produce tables outside their doors. Frozen bok choy, starfruit, lemongrass. A dry powdering of snow over everything. At Dundas, nightfall arrives all at once. The giant screen atop the Dragon Mall casting a blue glow of advertising over the street.

I carry on another couple blocks north, past NO MSG noodle places and whole roast pigs hanging in butchers' windows, their mouths gaping in surprise. Then dash across the four lanes of traffic into the narrow lanes of the market.

Kensington means different things to different people, but for me, a walk through its streets always gives rise to the same question: How long can it last? Already some of the buildings are being turned into "live/work loft alternatives", promising a new "urban lifestyle" for people who are seeking "The Kind of Excitement that Comes with Walking on the Edge". I take out the tiny dictaphone recorder I always carry around (to capture any especially biting phrases for the next day's review) and read these words directly off the hoardings around the latest condo project. Some shoppers have also stopped to read the same come-hithers. But when they see me whispering into a tape recorder, they walk on. Another out-patient to be politely avoided.

On a bit, the old Portuguese fishmongers are lifting the slabs of cod and octopus off their beds of ice and waltzing them to the walk-ins for the night. The street still busy with safety-pinned punks and insane, year-round bicyclists, all dinner-time bargain hunting. Or simply congregating in one of the last places in the city where one can feel a resistance to the onslaught of generic upgrading, of globalized sameness, of money.

And then it strikes me, with an unsettling shiver, that some of the people bustling around me may be here for the same reason I am.

Some of them may be writers.

The address for the meeting brings me to a door next to The Fukhouse, a bar that, as far as I can see through the grimy window, has every wall, table surface, and both floor and ceiling painted in black gloss. Above the sign, on the second floor, stout candles flicker in the windows. If I wrote the number down right, it's up there that the Kensington Circle is to gather.

"Anarchists," a voice says behind me.

I turn to find a young woman in an oversized leather biker jacket. Her shoulders armoured with silver spikes. She doesn't seem to notice the cold, though below the jacket all she wears is a threadbare girls' school skirt and fishnets. And a raven tattooed over the back of her wrist.

"I'm sorry?"

"Just thought I'd warn you," she says, gesturing toward The Fukhouse's door. "That's kind of an anarchist clubhouse. And anarchists often don't take well to those not part of the revolution."

"I can imagine."

"Not that it matters. You're here for the circle. Am I right?"

"How'd you guess?"

"You look nervous."

"I *am* nervous."

She squints into my face through the looping snow. I have the same feeling I get when the customs officer at the border slides my passport through the computer and I have to wait to see if I'll be allowed through or placed under arrest.

"Evelyn," she says finally.

"Patrick Rush. A pleasure to meet you."

"Is it?"

And before I can tell if she's joking or not, she opens the door and starts up the stairs.

* * *

The room is so dark I can only stand at the entrance, hands feeling for walls, a light switch, the leather jacket girl. All I can see for sure are the candles oozing wax over the two distant window sills, the snow outside falling fast as TV static. Though I followed Evelyn up the stairs, she now seems to have disappeared into the void that yawns between the doorway and the windows.

"Glad you could come."

A male voice. I spin around, startled. This sudden movement, and my boots slipping on the puddle of snowmelt over the floorboards, makes me lose my footing. Someone releases a coquettish gasp. In the next instant I realize it was me.

"We're over here," the voice says.

The dark figure of a stooped man passes in front of me, drifting toward what I now can see is a circle of chairs in the centre of the room. Boots kicked off, I slide over to one of the two unoccupied places.

"We're just waiting for one more," the voice says, and I recognize it only now as the same as the one on the phone. Conrad White. Never-heard-of author and poet, now taking his seat across from mine. The sound of his lullabye voice also brings back the feeling I got when I first spoke my desire to write a book. There had been a pause, as though he was measuring the depth of my yearning. When he spoke again, I wrote down the details he gave me without really hearing them.

His words seemed to come from somewhere else, a different time altogether.

All of us wait for the voice to begin again. If there really are six of us sitting here, we are still as dolls. Only the faint tide of our breaths to be heard, taking in the vapours of red wine and incense from the rug beneath our chair legs.

"Ah. Here he is."

Conrad White rises to welcome the last member of the circle to arrive. I don't turn to see who it is at first. But as a second pair of feet step deliberately forward (and with boots left on), I sense some of the others shrink in their seats around me. Then I see why.

A sloped-shouldered giant steps forward from out of the darkness. At first he appears headless – there's a ridiculous second when I glance down to his hands to see if he carries his own skull – but it is only the full beard of black wires that obscures most of his face. Not his eyes though. The whites clear, unblinking.

"Thank you all for coming. My name is Conrad White," the old man says, sitting again. The bearded latecomer chooses the last chair – the one beside mine to the left. Though this saves me from having to look at him, it allows me a whiff of his clothes. A primitive mixture of wood smoke, sweat, boiled meat.

"I will be your facilitator over the next four weeks," Conrad continues. "Your guide. Perhaps even your friend. But I will not be your teacher. For writing of the truest kind – and *that*, I'm assuming, is what all of us aspire to – cannot be taught."

Conrad White looks around the circle, as though giving each of us the opportunity to correct him. None do.

He goes on to outline the ground rules for the meetings to come. The basic structure will involve weekly assignments ("Little exercises to help you *feel* what you *see*"), with the bulk of time spent on personal readings from each of our works-in-progress, followed by commentary from the other members. Trust is crucial. Special note is made that criticism, as such, will not be tolerated. Instead, there will be "conversations". Not between ourselves, but "between a reader and the words on the page". At this, I feel a couple of heads nodding in agreement off to my right, but I still don't look to see who it is. Somehow, so long as he's speaking, I can only look straight ahead at Conrad White. It makes me wonder if it's not only shyness that holds my stare. Perhaps there is something more deliberately occult in the arrangement of our chairs, the candles, the refusal of electric light. If not enchantment, there is definitely a lightheadedness that accompanies his words. A vertigo I can't shake.

When I'm able to focus again I pick up that we're now being told about honesty. It's the truth of the thing that is our quarry, not mastery of structure, not style. "Story is everything," the voice says. "It is our religions, our histories, our selves. Only through story can we hope to become acquainted with experiences other than our own."

In a different context – a room with enough light to show the details of faces, the hum of institutional central air, EXIT signs over the doors – this last promise might be overkill. Instead, we are moved. Or I am, anyway.

Now it's time for the obligatory "Tell us a little bit about yourself" roundabout. I'm terrified that Conrad will start with me. ("Hi. I'm Patrick. Widower, single dad. There was a time I dreamed of writing novels. Now I watch TV for a living.") Worse, he ends up choosing the woman sitting immediately to my right, someone I have so far sniffed (expensive perfume, tailored leather pants) but not fully seen. This means I will be last. The closer.

As each of the members speak, I play with the dictaphone in the outside pocket of my jacket. Push the Record button, Pause, then Record again, so that I create a randomly edited recording. It's only when they're halfway round the circle that I realize what I'm doing. Not that this stops me.

The good-smelling woman introduces herself as Petra Dunn. Divorced three years ago, and now that her one child has left for university, she has found herself "mostly alone" in the midtown family home. She names her neighbourhood – Rosedale – meaningfully, even guiltily, as she knows this address speaks of an attribute not lost on any of us: money. Now Mrs Dunn spends her time on self-improvement. Long runs in the ravine. Charity volunteering. Night courses on arbitrary, cherry-picked subjects – Pre-Civil War American History, The Great Paintings of Europe Post-World War II, the 20 Classic Novels of the Twentieth Century. But she became tired of seeing "different versions of myself" in these classrooms, "second or third time around women" not seeking to be edified but asked out by the few men who prowled the Continuing Studies departments, men she calls "cougar hunters". More than this, she has felt the growing need to tell a story concerning the life she might have lived if she hadn't said yes when the older man who would become her husband offered to take her to dinner while she was working as a bartender at the Weston Country Club. An unlived existence that would have seen her return to her studies, a life of unpredictable freedoms, instead of marrying a man whose free use of his platinum card she'd mistaken for gentlemanly charm. A story concerning "A woman like me but not …"

And here Petra Dunn pauses. Long enough for me to steal a look at her face. I expect to see a woman in her fifties who's been silenced by her fight with tears. Instead, I'm met with a striking beauty not much older than forty. And it's not tears, but a choking rage that has stolen her words.

"I want to imagine who I really am," she says finally.

"Thank you, Petra," Conrad White says, sounding pleased at this start. "Who's next?"

That would be Ivan. The bald crown of his head shining faintly pink. Shoulders folded toward his chest, his frame too small for the plaid work shirt he has buttoned to his throat. A subway driver. A man who too rarely sees the light of day ("If I'm not sleeping, either it's night, or I'm underground"). And lonely. Though he doesn't confess to this outright, he's the sort who wears his chronic bachelorhood in the dark circles under his eyes, the tone of defeated apology in his voice. Not to mention the shyness that prevents him from making eye contact with any of the circle's women.

Conrad White asks him what he hopes to achieve over the course of the meetings to come, and Ivan considers his answer for a long moment. "When I bring my train into a station, I see the faces of all the people on the platform flash by," he says. "I just want to try and capture some of them. Turn them into something more than the passengers on the other side of the glass who get on, get off. Make whole people out of them. Something I can hold on to. Some*one*."

As soon as Ivan finishes speaking, he lowers his head, fearing he's said too much. I have to resist the impulse to go to him, offer a brotherly hand on his shoulder.

And then I notice his hands. Oversized gloves resting atop his knees. The skin stretched like aged leather over the bones. Something about those

38

hands instantly dissolves the notion of going any closer to Ivan than is necessary.

The portly fellow beside Ivan introduces himself as Len. He looks around at each of us after this, grinning, as though his name alone suggests something naughty. "What I like about reading," he goes on, "is the way you can be different people. Do different things. Things you'd never do yourself. If you're good enough at it, it's like you're not even imagining any more."

This is why Len wants to write. To be transformed. A big kid who has the look of the stay-at-home gamer, the kind whose only friends are virtual, the other shut-ins he posts on-line messages to inquiring how to get to Level Nine on some shoot-the-zombies software. Who can blame him for wanting to become someone else?

The more Len talks about writing, the more physically agitated he becomes, wriggling his hefty hips forward to the edge of his chair, rubbing the armrests as though to dry his hands of sweat. But he only gets *really* excited once he confesses that his "big thing" is horror. Novels and short stories and movies, but especially comic books. Anything to do with "The undead. Presences. Werewolves, vampires, demons, poltergeists, witches. *Especially* witches. Don't ask me why."

Len shows all of us his loopy grin once more. It makes it hard not to like the guy. His passions worn so plainly, so shamelessly, I find myself almost envying him.

Sitting beside Len's nervous bulk, Angela looks small as a child. Part of this illusion is the result of her happening to occupy the largest chair in the room, a wing-backed lounger set so high the toes of her shoes scratch the floor. Other than this, what's notable about Angela's appearance is its lack of distinction. Even as I try to sketch her into my memory I recognize she has the kind of face that would be difficult to describe even a few hours from now. The angles of her features seem to change with the slightest shift, so that she gives the impression of being a living composite, the representative of a general strain of person rather than any person in particular.

Even what she says seems to evaporate as it drifts out into the room. Relatively new in the city, having arrived via "a bunch of different places out west". The only constant in her life is her journal. "Except it's not *really* a journal," she says, and makes an odd sound with her nose that might be a stifled laugh. "Most of it is made up, but some of it isn't. Which makes it more fiction than, like, a diary, I guess."

With this, she stops. Slides back into the chair and lets it swallow her. I keep watching her after she's finished. And though she doesn't meet eyes with anyone else in the circle, I have the notion that she's recording what everyone says just as deliberately as I am.

Next is Evelyn. The deadpan pixie in a biker jacket. I'm a little surprised to learn that she is a grad student at the University of Toronto. It isn't her youth. It's the outfit. She looks more like Courtney Love when she first fell for Kurt than the fellowship winner who can't decide between Yale, Cornell or Cambridge to do her Ph.D. Then the answer comes: her planned dissertation will be a study of "Dismemberment and Female Vengeance in the 1970s Slasher Film". I remember enough of university to know that such topics are best handled by those in costume.

We're now all the way around to the latecoming giant. When Evelyn's finished speaking, there's a subtle positioning of our bodies to take him in, more an adjustment of antennae to pick up a distant signal than the directness required in making eye contact. Still, all of the circle can steal a look at him except for me. Given his proximity, I would have to turn round and tuck my leg under to see him straight on. And this is something I don't want to do. It may only be the room's unfamiliarity, the awkwardness in meeting strangers who share little other than a craving for self-expression. But the man sitting to my left radiates a darkness of a different kind from the night outside. A strange vacancy of sympathy, of readable humanness. Despite his size, it's as though the space he occupies is only a denser form of nothing.

"And you?" Conrad White prompts him. "What brings you to our circle?"

The giant breathes. A whistling that comes up through his chest and, when exhaled, I can feel against the back of my hand.

"I was called," he says.

"'Called' in the sense of pursuing your destiny, I take it? Or perhaps a more literal calling?"

"In my dreams."

"You were summoned here in your dreams?"

"Sometimes –" the man says, and it seems like the beginning of a different thought altogether. "Sometimes I have bad dreams."

"That's fine. Perhaps you could just share your name with us?"

"William," he says, his voice rising slightly. "My name is William."

My turn.

I say my name aloud. The sound of those elementary syllables allows me to string together the point form brief on Patrick Rush. Father of a smart little boy lucky enough to take his mother's looks. A journalist who has always felt that something was missing from his writing. (I almost say "life" instead of "writing", a near-slip that is as telling as one might think). A man who isn't sure if he has something to say but who now feels he has to find out once and for all.

"Very good," Conrad White says, a note of relief in his voice. "I appreciate your being so frank. *All* of you. Under the circumstances, I think it only fair that I share with you who I am as well."

42

Conrad White tells us that he has recently "returned from exile". A novelist and poet who was publishing in Toronto, back just before the cultural explosion of the late sixties that gave rise to a viable national literature. Or, as Conrad White puts it evenly (though no less bitterly), "The days when writing in this country was practiced by unaffiliated individuals, before it took a turn toward the closed door, the favoured few, the tribalistic." He carried on with his work, increasingly feeling like an outsider while some of his contemporaries did what was unimaginable among Canadian writers up to that point: they became famous. The same hippie poets and novelists that were in his classes at UofT and reading in the same coffee houses were now being published internationally, appearing as "celebrity guests" on CBC quiz shows, receiving government grants.

But not Conrad White. He was working on a different animal altogether. Something he knew would not dovetail neatly with the preferred subject matters and stylistic modes of his successful cohorts. A novel of "ugly revelations" that, once published, proved even more controversial than he'd anticipated. The writing community (as it had begun to regard itself) turned its back on him. Though he responded with critical counter-attacks in any journal or pamphlet that would have him, the rejection left him more brokenhearted than livid. It prompted his decision to live abroad. England, at first, before moving on to India, southeast Asia, Morocco. He had only returned to Toronto in the last year. Now he conducted writing workshops such as these to pay his rent.

"I say 'workshops', but it would be more accurate to speak of them in the singular," Conrad White says. "For this is my first."

Outside, the snow has stopped falling. Beneath our feet the bass thud from The Fukhouse's speakers has begun to rattle the windows in their frames. From somewhere in the streets of the market, a madman screams.

Conrad White passes a bowl around to collect our weekly fee. Then he gives us our assignment for next week. A page of a work-in-progress. It needn't be polished, it needn't be the beginning. Just a page of *something*.

Class dismissed.

I fish around for my boots by the door. None of us speak on the way out. It's like whatever has passed between us in the preceding hour never happened at all.

When I get to the street I start homeward without a glance back at the others, and in my head, there's the conviction that I won't return. And yet, even as I have this thought, I know that I will. Whether the Kensington Circle can help me find my story, or whether the story is the Kensington Circle itself, I have to know how it turns out.

3

Emmie has Wednesday mornings off, so it's my day to work from home and look after Sam on my own. Just four years old and he sits up at the breakfast table, perusing the Business and Real Estate and International News sections right along with me. Though he can hardly under-stand a word of it, he puts on a stern face – just like his old man – as he licks his thumb to turn the grim pages.

As for me, I comb the classifieds to see if Conrad White's ad is still running, but can't find it anywhere. Perhaps he's decided that the one group who assembled in his apartment the night before will be all that he can handle.

Sam pushes the Mutual Funds Special Report away from him with a rueful sigh.

"Dad? Can I watch TV?"

"Ten minutes."

Sam retreats from the table and turns on a Japanimation robot laser war. I'm about to ask if he wouldn't mind turning it down when a short piece in the City section catches my attention.

A missing person story. The victim (is one a "victim" when only missing?) being one Carol Ulrich, who is presumed to have been forcibly taken from a neighbourhood playground. There were no witnesses to the abduction – including the woman's son, who was on the swings at the time. Residents have been advised to be alert to any strangers "acting in a stalking or otherwise suspicious manner". While authorities continue their search for the woman, they admit to having no leads in the case. The story ends ominously with the police spokesperson stating that "activity of this kind has been shown to indicate intent of repeated actions of a similar nature in the future".

It's the sort of creepy but sadly common item I would normally pass over. But what makes me read on to the end is that the neighbourhood in question is the one we live in. The playground where the woman was taken the same one where I take Sam.

"What are you *doing*, Daddy?"

Sam is standing at my side. That I'm also standing is something of a surprise. I look down to see my hands on the handle of the living room's sliding door.

"I'm locking the door."

"But we *never* lock *that* door."

"We don't?"

I peer through the glass at our snow-covered garden. Checking for footprints.

46

"Show's over," Sam says, pulling on my pant leg and pointing at the TV.

"Ten more minutes."

As Sam runs off, I pull the dictaphone out of my pocket.

"Note to self," I whisper. "Buy padlock for back gate."

It's the weekend already, and Tuesday's deadline requiring a page from my nonexistent work-in-progress is fast approaching. I've made a couple stabs at something during the week, but the surroundings of either the Crypt at home or the cubicle at work have spooked any inspiration that might be waiting to show itself. I need to find the right *space*. A laptop of one's own.

Once Tamara's out-of-town sister, Stacey, has come by to take Sam and his cousins to see the dinosaurs at the museum, I hit the Starbucks around the corner. It's a sunny Saturday, which means that, after noon, Queen Street will be clogged with shoppers and gawkers. But it's only just turned ten, and the line-up isn't yet out the door. I secure a table, pop the lid on my computer, and stare at a freshly created word-processing file. Except for the blinking cursor, a virgin screen of grey. Its purity stops me from touching the keys. The idea of typing a word on to it seems as crude as stepping outside and pissing into a snowbank. And the dentist office grind of the cappuccino machine is starting to get on my nerves. Not to mention the orders shouted back and forth between the barista kids behind the counter. Who wouldn't raise their head to see what sort of person orders a venti decaf cap with half skim, half soy and *extra whipped cream*?

I pack up and walk crosstown to the Reference Library on Yonge. The main floor entrance is crowded, as it always is, with the homeless, the new-in-town, the dwindling souls without a cellphone who need to make a call. Through the turnstiles, the building opens into an atrium that cuts through the five floors above. I choose the least occupied level and find a long work table all to myself. Lean back, and think of a single word that might stride forth to lead others into battle.

Nothing.

All around me are tens of thousands of volumes, each containing tens of thousands of printed words, and not *one* of them is prepared to come forward when I need it most.

Why?

The thing is, I *know* why.

I don't have a story to tell.

But Conrad White did, once upon a time. Seeing as I'm in the Reference Library, I decide to take a break and do a bit of research. On Mr White, ringleader of the Kensington Circle.

It takes a little digging, but some of the memoirs and cultural histories from the time of sixties Toronto make footnoted mention of him. From old money, privately schooled, and author of a debatably promising novel before going into hiding overseas. As one commentator tartly put it, "Mr White, for those who know his name at all, is more likely remembered for his leaving his homeland than any work he published while living here."

What's intriguing about the incomplete biography of Conrad White are the hints at darker corners. The conventional take has it that he left because of the critical reception given his book, *Jarvis and Wellesley*, the fractured, interior monologue of a man walking the streets of the city on a quest to find a prostitute who most closely resembles his daughter, recently killed in a car accident. An idealized figure he calls the "perfect girl". To anyone's knowledge, Conrad White hasn't written anything since.

But it's the echoes of the author's actual life to be found in the storyline of *Jarvis and Wellesley* that gives bite to his bio. He *had* lost a daughter, his only child, in the year prior to his embarking on the novel. And there is mention of White's exile being precipitated by his relationship with a very real teenage girl, and the resulting threats of legal action, both civil and criminal. A literary recluse on the one hand, girl-chasing perv on the other. Thomas Pynchon meets Humbert Humbert.

I go back to my table to find my laptop screen has fallen asleep. It knows as well as I do that there will be no writing today. But that needn't mean there can't be reading.

The edition of *Jarvis and Wellesley* I pull off the shelf hasn't been signed out in over four years. Its spine creaks when I open it. The pages crisp as potato chips.

Two hours later, I return it to where I found it.

The prose ahead of its time, no doubt. Some explicit sex scenes involving the older protagonist and young streetwalkers lend a certain smutty energy to the proceedings, if only passingly. And throughout, the unspoken grief is palpable, an account of loss made all the more powerful by narrating its effects, not its cause.

But it's the description of the protagonist's "perfect girl" that leaves the biggest impression. The way she is conjured so vividly, but using little or no specific details. You know exactly what she looks like, how she behaves, how she feels, though she is nowhere to be found on the page.

What's stranger still is the certainty that I will one day meet her myself.

4

Tuesday brings a cold snap with it. A low of minus eighteen, with a wind-chill making it feel nearly double that. The talk-radio chatter warns everyone against going outside unless absolutely necessary. It makes me think – not for the first time – that I can be counted among the thirty million who voluntarily live in a country with annual plagues. A black death called winter that descends upon us all.

Down in the Crypt I dash off a column covering two new personal makeover shows, a cosmetic surgeon drama, and five (yes, *five*) new series in which an interior designer invades people's homes and turns their living rooms into what look like airport lounges. Once this is behind me, I get to work on my assignment for the evening's circle. By the end of the day I've managed to squeeze out a couple hundred words of shambling introduction – *Tuesday brings a cold snap with it*, etc. It'll have to do.

Upstairs, as I heat up leftovers in the microwave, Sam comes to show me something from today's paper.

"Doesn't she look like Mommy?"

He points to a photo of Carol Ulrich. The woman who was abducted from our neighbourhood playground. The one snatched away as her child played on the swings.

"You think so?" I say, taking the paper from him and pretending to study the woman's features. It gives me a chance to hide my face from Sam for a second. He only knows what his mother looks like from pictures, but he's right. Carol Ulrich and Tamara could be sisters.

"I remember her," Sam says.

"You do?"

"At the corner store. She was in the line-up at the bank machine once too."

"That so."

Sam pulls the newspaper down from my eyes. Reads me.

"They look the same. Don't they?"

"Your mother was more beautiful."

The microwave beeps. Both of us ignore it.

"Was that lady ... did somebody hurt her?"

"Where'd you hear that?"

"I can *read*, Dad."

"She's only missing."

"Why would somebody *make* her missing?"

I pull the newspaper from Sam's hands. Fold it into a square and tuck it under my arm. A

52

clumsy magician trying to make the bad news disappear.

Conrad White's apartment is no brighter, though a good deal colder than the week before. Evelyn has kept her jacket on, and the rest of us glance at the coats we left on the hooks by the door. William is the only one who appears not to notice the chill. Over the sides of his chair his T-shirted arms hang white and straight as cement pipes.

What's also noticeably different about the circle this time round is that each of us have come armed: a plastic shopping bag, a binder, a sealed envelope, two file folders, a leather-bound journal, and a single paper clip used to contain our first written offerings. Our work trembles on our laps like nervous cats.

Conrad White welcomes us, reminds us of the way the circle will work. As his accentless voice goes on, I try to match the elderly man speaking to us with the literary bad boy of forty years ago. If it was anger that motivated his exile, I can't detect any of it in his face today. Instead, there's only a shopworn sadness, which may be what anger becomes eventually, if it shows itself early enough.

Tonight's game plan calls for each of us to read what we've brought with us aloud for no more than fifteen minutes, then the other members will have a chance to comment for another fifteen. Interruption of responses is permitted, but not of the readers themselves. Our minds should be open as wide as possible when listening to others, so that their words are free from comparison to anything that has come before.

"You are the children in the Garden," Conrad White tells us. "Innocent of experience or history or shame. There is only the story you bring. And we shall hear it as though it is the first ever told."

With that, we're off.

The first readers are mostly reassuring. With each new voice trying their words out for size, the insecurities I have about my own tortured scribbles are relieved, albeit only slightly. By the halfway point (when Conrad White calls a smoke break) I am emboldened by the confirmation that there are no undiscovered Nabokovs, Fitzgeralds or Munros – nor a Le Carré or Rowling or King – among us. And there are few surprises, in terms of subject matter. Petra has a bit of *As the World Turns* meets *Who's Afraid of Virginia Woolf?* husband-and-wife dialogue that captures certain verbal cruelties in such detail I assume they are taken straight from a loop of memory. Ivan, the subway driver, tells a tale of a man who awakens to find he's been transformed into a rat, and must find a way into the sewers beneath the city that he intuitively knows is his new home of pestilence and filth. (When, after his reading, I compliment him on his re-working of Kafka, Ivan looks at me quizzically and says, "I'm sorry. *Kafka*?"). Though Len feels that only the opening paragraph of a proposed "epic horror trilogy" is ready for presentation, it nevertheless goes on forever, a description of night that is a long walk through the thesaurus entry for "dark". And Evelyn promisingly starts her story with a female grad student being screwed by her thesis advisor on the floor of his office while she daydreams about her father teaching her how to skip stones on the lake at the family cottage.

Over the smoke break, those not slipping on their coats get up to stretch. We shuffle around the room without looking at each other or being the first to start up a conversation. All of us steal glances, however. And note where William stands at all times, so we know what corner to avoid.

It's over these awkward minutes of feeling others' eyes on me that I ask myself: How does the rest of the circle see me? Most favourably, how I see myself on the best of days, I suppose: an endearingly rumpled Preppie that Time Forgot. Most unfavourably, how I see myself on the worst of days: a dandruffy channel flipper fast approaching the point of no return. Beyond debate are the wide shoulders that lend the illusion of one-time athleticism. And good teeth. A set of ivory chompers that always impress when encountered in *Say Cheese!* snaps.

Once the smokers return, we get started on the readers who remain.

And this is where things get a little foggy.

I must have read the page I brought with me, as I remember bits of what the other members said afterwards. (Evelyn found the first-person mode "captures your character's sense of being trapped in himself", and Petra could detect a "hidden suffering"). William requested a pass on reading his own work, or I think he did, as I only recall the sound of his voice and not its words. A low grinding, like air forced through wet sand.

But all I really preserve from the second half of the meeting is Angela.

My first thought, as she opens the cracked leather journal on her knees and lifts it slowly, even reluctantly to her eyes, is that she appears younger than I'd guessed the week before. What I took to be the indistinct features of an adult may instead be the unblemished, baby fat smoothness of a girl coming out of her teens.

And yet, even as she reads, this impression of girlish youth turns into something else. Her face is difficult to describe, to remember, to *see*, because it's not a face at all. It is a mask. One that never sharpens into full focus, like an unfinished sculpture in which you can recognize the subject is human, but beyond this, taken at different points of view, it could be a representation of virtually anyone.

These considerations of Angela's appearance come and go within seconds. Soon, all of my attention is on what she reads. We listen without shifting in our seats, without crossing or uncrossing our legs. Even our breathing is calmed to the smallest sips.

It's not the virtuosity of her writing that dazzles us, as her style is simple as a child's. Indeed, the overall effect is that of a strange sort of fairy tale. One that lulls for a time, then breaks its spell with the suggestion of an awaiting threat. It is the voice of youth taking its final turn into the world of adult corruption, of foul, grown-up desire.

I have been playing with the dictaphone in my pocket this meeting as I had at the last, clicking the Record button on and off. Unthinkingly, a nervous tic. Now I press it down and leave it running.

Once she begins her reading I have no other thoughts except for one: I will not attempt to write again. There will be what I do for the newspaper, of course. And I can always force out a page here and there, whatever it takes to bluff my way through the next four sessions. But Angela's story blots out whatever creative light that might have shown itself from within.

It's not envy that makes me so sure of this. It's not the poor sport's refusal to play if he can't win. I know I won't try to write for the circle again because until Angela's journal comes to its end, I am only a reader.

After the meeting, I have a drink with Len at The Fukhouse. That is, I'm the first to nip into the bar below Conrad White's apartment, and Len follows me a moment later. He takes the stool two over from mine, as if we are going to entertain the pretence of not knowing who the other is.

A couple minutes after our facially tattooed bartender delivers our drinks – beer for me, orange juice for Len – the space between us becomes too ridiculous to maintain.

"You enjoying the class so far?" I ask.

"Oh yeah. I think this might turn out to be the best."

"You've done a writing workshop before?"

"Plenty. Like, a *lot*."

"You're an old pro then."

"Never had anything published, though. Not like you."

This takes me by surprise. It does every time someone recognizes me, before I remember that my Prime Time Picks of the Week column on Fridays has a tiny picture of me next to the by-line. A pixillated smirk.

"There's published, and then there's published," I say.

I'm thinking that's about it. Politeness has been maintained, my beer almost guzzled. I'm about to throw my coat on and steel myself for the cold walk home when Len ventures a question of his own.

"That guy's pretty weird, don't you think?"

He could be speaking of Conrad White, or Ivan, or the bartender with a lizard inked into his cheek, or the leader of the free world warning of nerve gas delivered in briefcases on the TV over the bar, but he isn't.

"William's quite a character, alright."

"I bet he's done time. Prison, I mean."

"Looks like the sort."

"He scares me a bit." Len shifts his gaze from his orange juice to me. "What about you?"

"Me?"

"Doesn't he give you the creeps?"

I could admit the truth. And with another man, one I knew better or longer, I would. But Len is a little too openly eager for company to be dealt any favours just yet.

"You should use him as material." I flatten a bill on to the bar sufficient to cover both our drinks. "I thought you *liked* horror stories."

"Definitely. But there's a difference between imagining bad things and doing bad things."

"I hope you're right. Or some of us would be in real trouble," I say, and give Len a comradely pat on the shoulder as I go. The big kid smiles. And damn if I don't feel a smile of my own doing its thing too.

5

Angela's Story
Transcribed from Tape Recording No. 1

There once was a girl who was haunted by a ghost. A terrible man who does terrible things who would visit her in her dreams. The girl had never had a friend, but she knew enough to know this wasn't what he was. No matter how much she prayed or how good she was or how she tried to believe it was true when others would tell her there was no such thing as ghosts, the terrible man would come and prove that all the wishing and prayers in the world could never wish or pray him away. This was why the girl had to keep her ghost to herself.

The only connection, the only intimacy she would allow herself with him was to give him a name.

The Sandman.

* * *

Everyone has parents. Knowing this is like knowing that, one day, all of us will die. Two things common to every person in the world.

But there were times when the girl thought she was the singular exception to this supposedly inescapable rule. Times she felt certain she was the only person who'd ever lived who had neither a mother nor a father. She simply appeared in the middle of her own story, just as the terrible man who does terrible things walked into the middle of her dreams. The girl is real, but only in the way that a character in a story is real. If she *were* a character in a story, it would explain how she had no parents, as characters aren't born but just *are*, brought into being on the whim of their authors.

What troubled the girl almost as much as being haunted by the terrible man who does terrible things was that she had no idea who her author might be. If she knew that, she'd at least know who to blame.

Even characters have a past, though they may not have lived it as the living do. The girl, for instance, was an orphan. People never spoke of where she came from, and the girl never asked, and in this way it was never known. She was a mystery to others as much as to herself. She was a problem that needed solving.

There were books the girl had read where orphans such as herself lived in homes with other orphans. And although these homes were often places of longing and cruelty, the girl wished she could live in one, so that she was not the only one like herself. Instead, she was sent to live in foster homes, which are not like the orphanages in books, but just regular homes with people who are paid to look after someone like the girl. When she was ten, she moved four times. When she was eleven, twice more. When she was twelve, she moved once a month for a year. And all along the Sandman followed her. Showing her the things he would do if he were real, and continued to do in her dreams.

And then, when she was thirteen, she was sent to live in an old farmhouse in the dark forests to the north, further north than most farms were ever meant to be. Her foster parents there were the oldest she'd had yet. Edra was the wife's name, and Jacob the husband's. They had no children of their own, only their hardscrabble farm, which yielded just enough to feed them through the long winters. Perhaps it was their childlessness that made them so happy when the girl came to them. She was still a mystery, still a problem. But Edra and Jacob loved her before they had any reason to, loved her more than if they'd had a child of their own. It was the suffering the girl had seen that prompted their love, for they were farmers of land that fought them over everything they took from it. Edra and Jacob knew suffering, and had some idea of what it could do to a girl, alone.

For a time, the girl was as happy – or as close to happy – as she'd ever been. There was comfort in the kindness her elderly foster parents showed her. She had a home in which she might live for years instead of weeks. There was a school in the town down the road she took the bus to every day, and where there were books for her to read, and fellow students she dreamed of one day making friends of. It was, for a time, what she'd imagined normal might be like.

Her contentment had been so great and without precedent that she'd almost forgotten about the terrible man who does terrible things. It had been a while since her night thoughts had been interrupted by his appearance. So it is with the most awful kind of surprise when she comes home from school one afternoon in late autumn to overhear Edra and Jacob talking about a little girl who'd disappeared from town.

Thirteen years old. The same age as her. Playing outside in the yard one minute, gone the next. The police and volunteer search parties had looked everywhere for her, but for three days the missing girl remained missing. The authorities were forced to presume foul play. They had no suspect in mind. Their only lead was that some in town had lately noticed a stranger walking the cracked sidewalks at night. A tall, sloped-shouldered man, a figure who kept to the shadows. "A man with no face," was how one witness put it. Another said it seemed the man was searching for something, though this was an impression and nothing more. Aside from this, no details were known of him.

But they were known to the girl. For she knew who the dark figure was even though she wasn't there to see him. She knew who had taken a girl in town the same age as her. The Sandman. Except now he'd escaped the constraints of her dream world and entered the real, where he could do all the terrible things he desired to do.

The girl was certain of all this, along with something else. She knew what the Sandman searched for as he walked in the night shadows.

He searched for her.

6

Write What You Know.

This is one of the primary Writers' Rules, though an unnecessary one, as the initial inclination of most is toward autobiography anyway. The imagination comes later, if it comes at all, after all the pages of the family photo album have been turned, love affairs autopsied, coming-of-age revelations and domestic tragedies rehashed on the page. Usually, people find their own lives sufficiently fascinating to never have to confront the problem of making things up. The Kensington Circle is no exception. Evelyn's campus sexcapade, Petra's marital breakdown, Ivan's sewer-rat metamorphosis. I'm jealous of them. It would make writing so much easier if I never tired of seeing the same face in the mirror.

But what if you don't particularly find the life you know all that interesting? *Real*, yes. And marked by its share of loss, redeemed by the love of a son with eyes the colour of his mother's. It's just that I don't see my life as satisfactory material to present as fiction. I find it challenge enough just muddling along as who I am, never mind casting myself as hero.

This is the reasoning I call on when, as now, I try to squeeze out a paragraph to be read at the next circle meeting, and nothing comes. I'm taking lunch at my desk, gnawing on a cafeteria ham-and-cheese, randomly pecking at the keys of my computer. Tim Earheart, who finds my literary aspirations perplexing ("Why do you think anybody would pay to read the shit you're pulling out of your ass?" is how he put it to me, unanswerably, when I told him of my attendance at a fiction-writing circle), comes by to read over my shoulder.

"I'm no judge," he says, "but I'm not sure you're going anywhere with this."

He's right. Over the next hour and a half, only a few sentences remain on the screen.

Here's what good Write What You Know has done for me today:

After my wife died I started hearing voices. Just hers at first. And then others I've never heard before. Strangers. I can't know this for sure but I have the feeling that all of them are dead.

They come to me before I go to sleep. This is what frightens me. Not that they're dead, or that I can hear them. But that I'm awake when I do.

Once this passage of luminous prose has been accomplished, I turn my mind to my Couch Potato column for the weekend edition. This week it's a gloves-off attack on the Canadian franchise of *American MegaStar!*, a talent show that is the top-rated program in this country, as well as the fourteen others it has colonized. An entire, worldwide generation being led to believe they are entitled to be famous. It's toxic. A lie. It's *wrong*. And it's also how my frustration with Writing What I Know opens the gates to Writing How the World Has Gone to Crap, which has never been much of a problem for me.

Even though I know that *Canadian MegaStar!* is owned by the same multinational media behemoth that owns the paper I work for, and even though there have been ominous hints from the section editor to "go easy" on "content" which is produced by said behemoth, I let slip the dogs of war on *MegaStar!* as if it is single-handedly responsible for carrying out a cultural atrocity. In fact, this last phrase makes it into the lede. From this measured opening, the column goes on to be brutal, hyperbolic and libellous, all leading to the kind of hysterical finish where you're actually a little concerned about the mental health of the column's author. It's *personal*.

I stay at work late (Thursdays keep me at the office at least until midnight copyediting the Best on the Box listings) and walk home wondering if today will prove to be my last in my current position. Or, come to think of it, my last in *any* position. It's almost amusing to wonder what else I might be qualified to do. I've always rather liked the idea of running my own business. Something very hands off. Automated, preferably. A laundromat. A spray-it-yourself car wash.

I round the corner on to my street speculating over what kind of pay cut, if any, would be involved in delivering newspapers instead of writing for them, when I notice the yellow police tape around the house across from mine. It is the neighbouring family at 147, and not my own family at 146 that the four police cruisers are parked in front of. But I still run the half-block up Euclid, ring the bell at my front door after twice dropping the keys, and confirm my son is safe with Emmie before going back out to ask the cop turning traffic back toward Queen what's going on.

"Break and enter," he says, chewing the inside of his cheek.

"What'd they take?"

"Didn't touch a thing. The kid was the only one who saw him."

"Joseph. My boy plays with him sometimes."

"Yeah? Well, when Joseph woke up tonight some son of a bitch was standing over his bed."

"Was he able to give a description?"

"All he can say is the guy's a shadow."

"A shadow?"

"Went downstairs to the living room with the kid following behind him. Just stood at the front window, staring out at the street. Then, after a while, he walked out the front door as if he owned the place. Turn it *around*, buddy! Yeah, *you*!"

The cop steps away to have a word with who-ever's behind the wheel of the SUV that refuses to head back to Queen. It gives me a chance to walk up on to the neighbour's patch of lawn and stand with my back to their front window. The same view the shadow would have had, standing behind the glass.

Staring at my place.

Where Sam is now. Standing next to Emmie on the porch, squinting over at me.

I read the nanny's lips – *Wave to Daddy!* – and Sam raises his chubby arm in salute. And as I wave back I wonder if he can see how bad Daddy's shaking.

The next circle meeting is at Petra's house. She had kindly offered to host all of us the week before, though as I step out of my cab at her Rosedale address, I see she was being modest to the point of insult when she described her digs as "Nothing too fancy". The place is a mansion. Copper roof, terraced landscaping that looks expensive even under a couple inches of snow, matching Mercedes coupés (one red, one black) docked in the carport. It makes me wonder how much the husband had *before* the divorce if this is Petra's cut.

Inside the door, my coat is taken by a silver-haired man wearing a better suit than any I have ever owned. A man who serves not only a different class, but a different century. My first honest-to-God butler.

"The group is assembling in the Rose Room," he says, and leads me over marble floors to a sunken lounge of leather chairs, each with their own side table, and a snapping fire in the hearth. At the door, the butler discreetly inquires as to whether I would like a drink. He says it in a way that makes it clear real drinks are included in the offer.

"Scotch?" I say, and he nods, as though my choice had confirmed a suspicion he'd had on first sight.

Most of the other members are already here. Conrad White has chosen a chair near the fire, its orange flickers lending him a devilish air which is only enhanced by the smirk he barely manages to conceal as he notes the room's incoherent collection of Inuit sculptures, garish abstracts and bookshelves lined with leather-bound "classics". In this context of stage-set wealth, the rest of us look like hired help sneaking a break, holding our crystal goblets with both hands so nothing might spill on the rug.

Len in particular seems out of place. Or perhaps this is because he's the only one talking.

"You should come. You *all* should. How about you, Patrick?"

"How about me what?"

"The open mic. There's a launch party for a new litmag, and then afterwards they open the floor to anyone who wants to read."

"I don't know, Len."

"C'mon. You can check out what's *going on* out there."

"They have a bar?"

"Half-price beer if you buy the zine."

"Now you're talking."

All of us are here now except for William and Petra, the latter clipping back and forth to the kitchen on high heels, touchingly anxious about burning the shrimp skewers. When our hostess finally sits, Conrad White decides to go ahead without William. There's a subtle easing in all of our postures at this. I would be surprised if any of us didn't hope that William has moved on to other creative endeavours, if not a different area code altogether.

I'm first, which is something of a relief, as the sooner I can get through the miserable couple of paragraphs I've brought along, the sooner I can get to work on the quadruple single malt Jeeves has poured for me.

Besides, I'm only here for one reason anyway.

Angela.

She doesn't disappoint. I say this even though I'm not really listening. After I click my dictaphone on, I pay less attention to her words than how she speaks them. I have assumed all along that Angela was using a voice distinct from her own in her readings. Now I realize that I have virtually no idea what her "real" voice is like, or whether it would be different from the one I listen to now.

71

She has said so little in the circle (her responses to the other readers little more than a murmured "I liked it a lot") that it may be the at once innocent and debauched little girl tone she uses is the same as her everyday speech.

When she's finished, no one says anything for what may be a minute. The fire hissing like a punctured tire. An ice cube cracks in Len's tumbler of apple juice. And from the moment Angela closes the cover of her journal to the moment Conrad White invites the circle to comment on what we've just heard, she looks at me.

More active than staring. A *taking in*. Every blink marking some new observation. And I do the same. Or try to. To see inside, sort her truth from the make believe. Figure out whether she can spot anything worthwhile in me. Anything she might like.

"Wonderful, Angela. Truly *wonderful*," Conrad White says.

Everyone raises their heads. No one had noticed our silent exchange except for Conrad himself. And Ivan. Both men shifting in their chairs to find relief from an affliction I immediately recognize. A thought that, for the lonely like us, passes more than any other.

Why not me?

After the meeting, we step out into the cold night, none of us knowing which way will lead us out of the enclave's curving streets and cul-de-sacs that discourage entry or exit. I look around for

Angela, but she must have grabbed her coat before us. In any case, there's no sign of her now.

"So, Patrick, we're on for Tuesday?" Len asks. I look at him like I don't have a clue what he's talking about. Which I don't. "The open mic?"

"Right. Yes. Absolutely."

"'Night then," he says, and scuffs off in the opposite direction I would guess to be the way out of here. Leaving just me and Ivan standing there.

"I know the way," Ivan says.

"You're familiar with this neighbourhood?"

"No," he says, exhaling a long, yogic breath. "I can hear the trains."

Ivan tilts his head back, eyes squeezed shut, as though savouring the melody of a violin concerto, when all there is to hear is the clacking of the subway train emerging out of the tunnel somewhere in the ravine below.

"Follow me," Ivan says, and starts out toward the nearest doors to the underworld.

On our walk out of Rosedale's labyrinth of old-money chateaux and new-money castles, enveloped in a cold-hardened March darkness, Ivan tells me he's never hit a jumper. For a subway driver with his years of seniority, this is a rare claim. Not once has one of the bodies standing behind the yellow warning line on the platform made that incongruous leap forward. Yet every time his train bursts out of the tunnel and into the next station lit

73

bright as a surgery theatre, he wonders who it will be to break his good record.

"Every day I see someone who thinks about it," Ivan says as we cross the bridge over the tracks. "The little moves they make. A half step closer to the edge, or putting their briefcase down at their side, or swinging their arms like they're at the end of a diving board. Getting ready. Sometimes you can only read it in their faces. They look at the front of the train – at me behind the glass – and there's this calm that comes over them. How *simple* it would be. But in the next second, they're thinking, 'Why *this* train? If there's another just as good coming along, why not wait? Make sure everything's right.' I can hear them like they're whispering in my ear."

"And then they change their minds."

"Sometimes," Ivan says, spitting over the side of the bridge on to the rails below. "And sometimes the next train *is* the right train."

We walk on toward Yonge Street where it breaks free of the downtown stretch of head shops and souvenir fly-by-nights, and heads endlessly north. Ivan talks without provocation, laying out his thoughts in organized capsules. Even when we come to stand outside the doors to the station he continues on, never looking at me directly, as though he has memorized this speech by heart and cannot allow himself to be distracted. It leaves me to study his head. Hatless and bald. A vulnerable cap of skin turned the blue-veined white of Roquefort.

And what does Ivan tell me? Things I would have already guessed, more or less. Son of Ukrainian immigrants. His father a steel cutter with a temper, his mother an under-the-table seamstress, mending the clothes of the neighbourhood labourers in their flat over what was then a butcher's, now an organic tea shop on Roncesvalles. Never married. Lives alone in a basement apartment, where he writes in the off-hours. Meandering stories that follow the imagined lives of those he shuttles here and there under the city.

"This is the first time I've been with people in a long time," he says. It takes a moment to realize he's talking about the circle. About me.

"It's hard to meet strangers in this town," I say.

"It's not that. It's that I haven't allowed myself to be around others."

"Why not?"

"I was accused of something once," he says. Looks at me straight. "Have you ever been accused of something?"

A rip of freezing wind comes out of nowhere. A furious howl that leaves me with instant headache.

What I took to be Ivan's shyness has dropped away. He reads my face, numbed by the cold so that I have no idea what shape my features have taken. What I do know for sure is that, all at once, the fact that nobody has come in or out of the subway in the time we've been standing here makes me more than a little uncomfortable.

"I suppose I have," I say.

"You suppose you have."

"I mean, I'm not sure what context –"

"The context of being accused of *harming* someone."

Ivan steps away from me. He had meant to have a normal conversation with someone who struck him as normal too, but he'd lost his balance on the home stretch. Yet it's not embarrassment or apology that plays over his face now. It's anger. At me, at himself. At the whole accusing world.

"Better start home," he mumbles, leaning his back into the subway's door. The warmer air from underground moans out through the gap. "I can get you on free if you want."

"No, thanks. I like to walk."

"On a night like this?"

"I'm not too far."

"Yeah? Where?"

"Close enough."

I could tell Ivan where I live, and I almost do. But I just wave vaguely westward instead.

Ivan nods. I can feel him wanting to ask me to keep the last part of our conversation to ourselves. But in the end, he just slips through the door and stands on the descending escalator. His head an empty cartoon thought bubble following him down.

I walk to Bloor and start west, past the funny-money block of Gucci and Chanel and Cartier, then left at the museum. Entering the university

76

campus at Harbord, the traffic is hushed. I'm alone on the street, which invites the return of a habit I've indulged since childhood. Talking to myself. Back then, it was whole conversations carried on with characters from the books I was reading. Now I restrict myself to certain phrases that catch in my mind. Tonight, it's some things from Angela's reading.

Dirty hands.

These two words alone frighten me.

Fear made them see the town, the world, in a way they'd never seen it before.

I try to leave these incantations behind in the dissolving fog of my breath. Work to turn my mind to real concerns. No progress on my writing to speak of. The thinning thread that connects me to my job. Dark feelings that have me wondering: *Is this it?* Is it days like this that start the slide into a hole you can't climb out of?

A smell that soldiers and surgeons would recognize.

Last night Sam awoke from a nightmare. I went to him. Stroked the damp hair back from his forehead. Once I'd settled him down, I asked what his dream was about.

"A man," he said.

"What kind of man?"

"A bad man."

"There's no bad man in here. I wouldn't let anyone bad in this house."

"He's not in *this* house. He's in *that* house."

With his *that*, Sam sat straight and pointed out he window. His finger lined up with the neighbour's house across the street. The window where the shadow had stood a few nights back. Looking out.

"Did you see the bad man who was there?" I asked him, but he heard in my very question the concession that what I'd just assured him didn't exist may in fact be real, and he turned his back to me. What good were a father's empty promises against the bogeyman? He would face any further nightmares on his own.

Blood tattooed on the curtains.

It's on my shortcut through Chinatown that I start to feel less alone. Not because of the few others shuffling homeward on the sidewalks, heads down. It's because I'm being followed.

Past the karaoke bars along Dundas, then the foolish turn south straight through the housing projects between here and Queen. That's when I hear the footsteps echoing my own. There are reports in the City pages of frequent shootings on this very block, yet I'm certain that whatever shadows me isn't interested in my wallet. It wants to see what I will do when I know it is there.

And what do I do?

I run.

A headlong sprint. I'm wearing the wrong shoes for it, so that within the first block my shins send bolts of pain up to the back of my head. Eyes stinging with wind-burned tears. Lungs crackling like a pair of plastic bags in my chest.

Courage is not a matter of will, but of the body.

I take the alley that runs behind the businesses along Queen. The shortest way to my house. But a *dark alley*? What was I thinking? I *wasn't* thinking. I was running. Past walls and fences built against the rats and crackheads. No light to see by. Just the darker outline of the buildings and the square of black that is the alley opening on to the street at the far end.

I don't stop. I don't look back.

Not until I stop and look back.

Standing under the block's lone working streetlight. My house within snowball-throwing distance. The light on in my son's room. Sam up late. Sneak reading. And all I want is to sit on the edge of his bed, close his book, turn off the light. Listen to him breathe.

He is my son.

I love my son.

I would die to protect him.

These conclusions come fast and terse as lightning. Along with one other.

The alley is empty.

7

Angela's Story
Transcribed from Tape Recording No. 2

The girl doesn't tell anyone what she knows of the
Sandman and the terrible thing he's done. In part,
this is because she doesn't actually *know* anything
about the missing girl, not in a way she could ever
prove. Not to mention that a declaration of this kind
might just label her as crazy once and for all. She'd
be taken away from Edra and Jacob and put in a
place far worse than any foster home or orphanage.
Someplace she would never come out of again.

But more frightening than even the consideration
of being taken away is the idea of hurting Edra and
Jacob. Her wellbeing was all they cared about. To
show them that she believed in dark figures born
in her dreams, a monster who had come from the
darkest place to hunt her down, would break both
their hearts. The girl resolved to protect them from
this no matter what.

80

For the next few days, ignoring the fact that something was wrong seemed to work. No more children disappeared. No dark figures were spotted in town. The girl's dreams were the same irrational puzzles that others have, free of any terrible men who do terrible things. It felt like the news of a stranger with no face escaping from the confines of a nightmare was *itself* a nightmare, and no more real than that.

Then the girl sees him.

Not in a dream, but through the window of her classroom at school. She has been sitting at her desk, working through a math quiz. Multiplying fractions. At one equation more difficult than the others, she raises her head to clear her mind of the numbers atop numbers collapsing into a confused pile. She sees him right away. Standing in the shade of the schoolyard's solitary elm. As tall as the lowest limb that, the girl knows from trying, is too high to reach, even when one of the boys offered her a boost. The Sandman's face is obscured by the leaves' latticework of shadow, though the girl has the impression he is staring directly at her. And that he's smiling.

She bends over her quiz again. The fractions have doubled in the time she'd taken her eyes from the page, so that the numbers are now a mocking jumble.

He would still be there if she looked. She doesn't look.

Outside, a lawnmower roars to life. The sound makes the girl gasp. A flare of pain. She feels the lawnmower's blades cutting into her side, halving her. Turning her into a fraction.

Later, sitting in the back row of the schoolbus on the ride home, the girl tries to remember what the Sandman looked like. How could she see him smile without seeing his face? Was this a detail she'd added after the moment had passed? Was she making him up, just as she sometimes thought *she'd* been made up? Was she the author of the terrible man who does terrible things?

As if in answer to all of these questions, the girl looks out the schoolbus window and he is there. Sitting on a swing in the playground. His legs held out straight before him, his boots touching the grass border around the sand. A sloped-shouldered man out of scale on the children's swing set, so that he looks even more enormous.

The girl turns to the other students on the bus, but none of them are looking out their windows. All of them laughing and blowing goobered paper out of straws. For a moment, the girl is knocked breathless by the recognition of how little these other children know. Of what awaits them, watches them. If not the Sandman then some other reshaped darkness.

The bus grinds into gear and lurches forward. Still sitting on the swing, the Sandman turns to watch them go. Even from this distance the girl notices his hands. The fingers swollen and thick as sausages, gripped round the chain. Dirty hands.

Before the bus turns a corner on to the road out of town, the girl squints hard and sees that she was wrong.

It's not dirt that fills the creases and sticks to the hair on the backs of the Sandman's hands. It's blood.

They find the missing girl the next day. Her remains. Down in the trees by the river beyond the graveyard. A place the older kids call the Old Grove, famous for bush parties. Now and forever to be known as the place where a girl, too young for bush parties, was found in pieces, buried in a layer of scattered leaves, as though her murderer had grown bored at the end and cast a handful of deadfall over her just to be done with it.

Because of where they found her, the police turned their suspicions toward the older boys at school who'd gotten in trouble in the past. Perhaps one of them had been in contact with the girl? Had a crush on her, been following her around? But even the most trouble-prone boys at the school had done nothing worse than pocket candy bars or egg windows on Halloween. It was near impossible to imagine any of them had graduated from such crimes to the one in question.

After they found the missing girl, the talk in town shifted from suspicion to fear. It mattered less who had done this terrible thing, and more that a terrible thing not be visited on anyone else. An unofficial curfew was put in place. Lights burned in the houses through the night. Groups of townsmen – doctors and shop owners and tradesmen and drunks, a strange mix that would otherwise be unlikely to associate with each other – patrolled the streets with flashlights and, it was said, shotguns hidden beneath some of their long coats. They had no idea what they might be looking for. Fear made them see the town, the world, in a way they'd never seen it before.

The second girl went missing the same night the first was found. As the men cast their flashlights over lawns and cellar doors and shrub rows, as the lights burned in all the homes, as most stayed up late, unable to sleep, another girl, the same age as the other, was snatched directly out of her bed before dawn. Her ground-floor window left open. Boot prints in the soil by the trampled rose bush. Sheets on the floor. Blood tattooed on the curtains.

They closed the school for the day. Not that the students would be any safer at home. The decision came by way of the instinct to stop whatever had been considered normal, if for no other reason than to match the abnormality of what was happening around them. Edra and Jacob were glad, nevertheless. It was late enough in the season that the crops (however meagre) were already in. There were no church services on Tuesday. And now they'd closed the school. Which meant that the two of them could afford to stay indoors with their adopted daughter, whom they now wanted to protect as much as love.

It was an odd sort of holiday. They baked candied apples. Played cards. Built a fire they didn't really need just to smell the cherry smoke through the house. The girl's thoughts turned to the terrible man who does terrible things only a few times over the course of the entire day. She would sneak long looks at Jacob and Edra, and ventured to think the word *family* as an invisible cord connecting the three of them.

That night she is awakened by the tap of stones against her bedroom window. She hears the first, but only opens her eyes on the second. There is a rule the girl has arrived at through her experience of being haunted. Once could be anything. Two times makes it real.

She's aware that she's making a mistake even as she rises from her bed and goes to the window. What compels her isn't curiosity but duty. She must keep whatever darkness she has brought to this place from touching Edra or Jacob. It isn't their fault that the girl they've shown such kindness to has let her worst dreams free from her head. They mustn't see what she is about to see.

The girl slides her feet over the bare floorboards and the whole house seems to groan a warning at her movement. Her room is small. But the effort it takes to reach the window exhausts her.

Courage, she realizes, is not a matter of will but of the body.

When she reaches the window she has to grip the frame with both hands for balance. There is the sickening stillness that precedes a fainting spell. She makes herself take a breath. As she looks outside, she wonders if her heart has stopped.

The Sandman stands in the yard below. When he sees her, he tosses another stone up at the glass. It is a gesture the girl has seen in old movies. A suitor signalling his arrival for a midnight tryst.

Once he's sure that she's watching, he turns and walks toward the barn. There is a scuffing slowness to his gait that one might mistake for regret. But the girl sees it instead as an expression of his self-certainty, the ease with which he sets about his actions. It's what makes his kind of badness so unpredictable.

He reaches the barn doors and pauses. There's an opening wide enough for him to enter, but he doesn't. He only wants her to see that he's been in there.

The man turns, keeping his back to her. Steps around the side of the barn and is gone.

The girl knows what she must do. That is, what he wants her to do.

She carries her boots down the stairs to quiet her descent. In her haste, she forgets to put her coat on, so that when she steps out the back door

86

and starts into the yard, the cold bites straight through her cotton pajamas. A wind dances dried leaves in figure eights over the dirt. The paper shuffle sound covers her footfall, so that she's able to half-run to the barn.

A step inside the doors and the thicker darkness stops her. She comes into the barn almost every day (it's where she's assigned most of her after-school chores) so she could navigate her way around its stalls and tools hanging on hooks without light. But there is something different about the space she cannot identify at first. It's because it isn't something she can see, but something she can smell.

A trace of the Sandman's scent left hanging in the air. Stronger than the hay and mouldy wood and cow manure, even without him here. It makes her cough. The cough turns into a gag. A smell that soldiers and surgeons would recognize, but that a girl like her would have no reason to have encountered before.

She fights her revulsion and starts toward the stall at the far end. This is where he wants her to go. She knows this as well as if he'd taken her by the hand to lead her there.

As her eyes become used to the dark, faint threads of moonlight find their way in through the slats. When she opens the gate to the stall, she discovers that it's enough light to see by.

The girl in the stall looks like her. He'd likely chosen her because of this. She'd known the second missing girl from her class at school, but had never realized the similar colour of her hair, the round face. For a second, she thinks it may be her own body lying in pieces amongst the spattered clumps of straw. Which would make her a ghost now too.

She sets to digging before there is anything like a plan in her mind. Just beyond the edge of the forest that borders Jacob's unyielding acreage, she goes as deep as the hard earth and time allows her. There's not even the opportunity to be scared. Though more than once she's certain the canvas sack she'd dragged here from the barn jostles with movement from within.

Even as she pushes the seeping bag into the hole and begins to throw spadefuls of soil back in the place it came from, it only vaguely occurs to her that she's doing this to make sure Jacob won't be blamed. Which of course would be the result if they ever found the second girl in his barn. The terrible man who does terrible things forced her into making this decision, which wasn't much of a decision at all. She would rather be an accomplice to the Sandman than allow the man who is as close to a father as she's ever known wrongly go to prison for the rest of his days.

By the time the first pencil line of dawn appears on the horizon, she is patting the mound of the second girl's grave down firm with the back of the spade.

Later, the horror of this night will revisit her in different forms. The girl has enough experience with dreams to know this much.

What she isn't certain of yet is what the Sandman wants from her. He has discovered where she lives. He could take her as easily as he's taken these others any time he felt inclined. But there is a different wish he wishes from her. And though she tries to tell herself that she couldn't possibly imagine what this might be, the truth is she has an idea.

8

Two days after the circle's meeting at Petra's house, the morning paper brings news of another missing person. A man this time. Ronald Pevencey, twenty-four. A hairdresser at one of the avant-garde salons on Queen who hadn't shown up for work all week. When the police were finally alerted, they discovered that the door to his second-floor apartment was left ajar, though no evidence of forced entry or struggle within could be found. This led investigators to a relatively safe assumption. Whoever had come knocking, Ronald had let in.

The reason authorities are announcing suspicions of foul play at all is not only based on Ronald Pevencey's unusual absence from work, but disturbing remarks he'd recently shared with co-workers. His belief he was being followed. Here and there over the past weeks a figure seemed to be watching him. While he didn't say whether he knew who this stalker was, one of his colleagues suspected that Ronald had a theory, and it scared the bejesus out of him. "He wanted to talk about it, but *didn't* want to talk about it," is how his confidante put it.

The rest of the piece, which appears under the by-line of my drinking buddy Tim Earheart, has the police spokesperson bending over backwards to dismiss any speculation that there may be a serial killer at large. First off, there was nothing to indicate that either Carol Ulrich or Ronald Pevencey have been murdered. And while neither had any motive for being a runaway or suicide, there is always the possibility that they just took off for a spontaneous vacation. Postpartum depression. A crystal meth bender. It happened.

It's further pointed out that there is no connection between the two missing persons. A hairdresser. A stay-at-home mom. Different ages, different social circle. Carol had never set foot in the salon where Ronald worked. The only commonality is their residence within six blocks of each other. Within six blocks of us.

If Ronald Pevencey and Carol Ulrich are both dead, odds are they met their ends by different means. Serial killers work in patterns, as the police were at pains to point out. A psychotic glitch in their software makes them seek out versions of the same victim, over and over. In this case, all the two missing persons shared was the city in which they lived.

Yet for all this, I'm certain that whatever hunted these two was the same in both cases. I'm also certain that neither is still alive. Despite what all the forensic psychiatrists and criminologists say, it seems to me that, at least some of the time, unpredictability must be as likely a motivation for murder as any other. A twist. Maybe this is what whoever is doing this likes. Not any one perversity, but the far more unsettling variance afforded by anonymity. If you don't know why a killer does what he does, it makes him more of a threat. It also makes him harder to catch.

But it's not the killer's hypothetical motivation that has me convinced. It's that I believe whatever followed me home the other night is the same shadow that followed Ronald Pevencey and Carol Ulrich. The bad man from my son's nightmares who is now making appearances in my own.

I give Emmie the morning off and walk Sam to daycare myself. Every half-block I turn and scan the street to catch the eyes I feel upon us. Sam doesn't ask why I stop. He just takes my gloved hand in his mitten and holds it, even as he comes within view of his friends in the fenced-in play area, a point at which he would normally run off to join them.

"See you later," he says. And though I intend to say the same thing, an "I love you" slips out instead. But even this is permitted today.

"Ditto," Sam says, with a punch to the elbow before stepping through the daycare's doors.

* * *

92

There's a new box of video cassettes sitting on my chair at the office. More cable freakshows and wife swaps and snuff amateur video compilations with titles like *Falling from Buildings!* and *Animals that Kill!* But it's what I find under the box that is truly disturbing. A post-it note from the Managing Editor. *Come see me. M.* It's the longest piece of correspondence I've ever received from her.

The Managing Editor's office is a glassed-in box in the opposite corner of the newsroom from where I sit. But this is not why I so rarely have any contact with her. She is more a memo drafter, an executive conference attender, an advertiser luncher than a manager of human beings. She has been so successful in this position, it is rumoured that she is currently being headhunted by American TV networks. She is twenty-eight years old.

For now, however, she's still the one who does the hiring and firing at the *National Star*. And I'm fully aware, as I approach her glass cube (bullet-proof, it is said), that she is more inclined toward the firing than the hiring.

"Patrick. Sit," she says when I come in, a canine command that is obeyed. She raises an index finger without looking my way, a gesture that indicates she's in the middle of a thought that could make or break the sentence she's halfway through. I watch her type out the words she finally harnesses – *symbiotic revenue stream* – and tap a button to replace her memo-in-progress with a Tahitian beach screensaver.

"I'm sure you know why you're here," she says, turning to face me. Her eyes do a quick scan of my person. I seem to disappoint her, as expected.

"No, I don't, actually."

"There's been a complaint."

"From a reader?"

The Managing Editor smiles at this. "No, not a reader. A real complaint. Quite real."

"How real are we talking?"

She rolls her eyes ceilingward. A signal that she means an office high up the ladder. So high up, she dare not speak its name.

"We have to look out for our properties. Our brands. And when one of those brands is undermined from within one of our own properties ..." She lets this thought go unfinished, as though where it leads is too unsavoury to even consider.

"You're talking about the *MegaStar!* review."

"It was upsetting. People were upset."

"You don't look upset."

"But I am."

"So this is serious."

"There are certain calls from certain offices I don't like to get."

"Should I be calling my lawyer?"

"You have a lawyer?"

"No."

The Managing Editor pushes a stray hair off her forehead. A brief, but distinctly female motion that, I regret to say, makes me like her a little.

"Are we clear on all this then?"

This question would be funny, given the preceding conversation, if my answer weren't yes. She's made herself perfectly clear.

I stop by Tim Earheart's desk on the way back to my own. I'm not really expecting to find him there. He usually prefers to work in the reeking, greasy bunker that goes by the name of the Smoking Room. Tim doesn't think of himself as a smoker, though he'd eat cigarettes if he couldn't smoke them when he's up against a deadline. Which he must be today, given the talk of a potential killer on the loose. Yet here he is. Throwing the reporter's tools of pen, notepad, dictaphone and digital camera into the knapsack he proudly brought back with him from Afghanistan, complete with bullet hole. A prop he says has got him more "intern action" than he knows what to do with.

"She fire you?" he asks. This is the question first asked of anyone caught walking out of the Managing Editor's office.

"Not yet. Where you off to?"

"Ward's Island. They found one of the missing persons."

"Which one?"

"The Ulrich woman. A dozen or so parts of her, anyway. Spread out over a hundred-foot stretch of beach."

"Oh my God."

"Yessir. It's ugly."

"They know who did it?"

"Right now all they're saying is they're following up on every lead. Which means they don't have a clue."

"He *cut her up*?"

"He. She. They."

"Who would *do* that?"

"Somebody bad."

"It's insane."

"Or not. Just got off the phone with the police profiler guy. He's thinking there's a point to the way the body was on display like that. Some sort of announcement."

"Saying what?"

"How the fuck do I know? 'I'm here,' I guess. 'Come and get me, assholes.'"

Tim slings the knapsack over his shoulders. Even through his aviator sunglasses you can see the excited gleam in his eyes.

"She lived near you, didn't she?" he says.

"Sam recognized her. She had a kid about his age. They went to the same playground."

"Creepy."

"It is."

"I'm going over there now on the ferry. Wanna come?"

"I wouldn't want to spoil it for you."

"Could be great material for your novel."

"It's not that kind of novel," I say, which makes me wonder what kind of novel I *would* write, if I ever could.

* * *

96

By the time I leave work, shortly after five, the day has already taken its wintry turn toward night. The backed-up traffic along King a red line of brake lights as far as the horizon, the only colour against the dusk. The new restaurants that have moved into the former textile warehouses are already full of besuited diners, each of them plunking down the equivalent of my biweekly mortgage payment to taste the dainty constructions of overnight superstar chefs. And what will the Rush boys be eating this evening? One sag paneer, one butter chicken roti, medium spicy, from Gandhi take-out. Sam's favourite.

It's the choice of tonight's menu, however, that leads to my seeing him.

There is the usual clog of people in Gandhi, either eating from styrofoam containers at one of its two tables, or standing close together, waiting to hear our number called and make the last dash home. The air is steamy from the bubbling pans of curry on the stove, the open pot of boiling potatoes, the breath of everyone in here. It makes the windows that look on to Queen cloud and drip with condensation. Through the glass, the bodies of passers-by merge into a single, mutating form.

My number's up. Now that I've side-stepped my way to the front, claustrophobia tickles a mild panic in my chest. One of those momentary near freak-outs I have a couple times a day negotiating my way through the city. A struggle I almost always win by telling myself to hold on. Just do the next thing – *pay for food* – and then the next – *grab the bag, turn, squeeze toward the door* – and everything will be okay.

At the door, I pause to pull my gloves out of my jacket pocket. It allows me to take a last look through the clouded glass.

It is only a darkened outline among other darkened outlines. But I know it's him.

Standing on the far side of the street. Unmoving as the other sidewalkers pass in both directions around him. Taller than any of them.

As I push the door open and the street is brought into sudden focus, William turns his back to me and joins the others heading east.

I don't get a good look at his face. That's not how I know. It's his *presence*. A menacing energy that radiates from him so strongly it knocks me back a few inches, so that I have to lean against the door for balance. Even as he turns the corner at the end of the block and disappears, the density of the space he leaves in his wake holds me where I stand. It's as though the air is turned to black water, taking on a sludgy, unbreathable weight.

Someone pushes against the door and I step aside, murmuring an apology. All around me the inching traffic and striding pedestrians carry on their homeward journeys, oblivious. William had no effect on them. Perhaps this is because *he wasn't there*. A hallucination formed out of the day's gloom, the news of violence, an empty stomach.

But these are only the rationalizations I need to get my feet moving again. Whatever I just saw, just felt, was not a product of the imagination. I'm not sure I even *have* an imagination.

It was William, watching me. Which means it was William, following me.

There is one further possibility, of course.

One day I will look back and recall that to-night, outside Gandhi with a bag of take-out in my hand, was the first step on the road to losing my mind.

Sam and I eat our dinners by candlelight, the good silver and wedding-present wine glasses brought out for the hell of it. Curry on the plate, beer and ginger ale in the crystal. We talk about things. The proto-bullies who terrorize his daycare. A kid who had an allergic reaction at the playground and whose face "got fat and red like a giant zit" before an ambulance took him away.

As for me, I do my best to cushion each of these fears. But even as I do, I wrestle with my own nightmare material. The Managing Editor's warn-ing shot. The picture of Carol Ulrich on the TV, the lady who looks like Tamara. The parts of her found on the beach. Which leads my private thoughts to the larger, geopolitical worries of the day. The fallen towers. Sleeper cells, alternate tar-gets, promises of more trouble to come issued from Afghan caves. How our corner of the world is less and less safe the richer it becomes.

After a while, what Sam is speaking about and what it makes me think of seem like parts of the same observation. *Even here*, we say. *Even here evil can find you.*

Of course I don't tell Sam about seeing William across the street on my way home. What occurs to me now is that it's not just William I'm keeping from him. Since I started going to the meetings at Conrad White's, I have held the Kensington Circle out of his reach. Sam wouldn't be interested. These Tuesday evenings when Emmie stayed late and Daddy went out for some grown-up time were so harmless, so dull, they weren't worth the breath required to explain them.

Yet now I feel the restraint, the mental work required in keeping a certain topic covered over. What goes on in the writing circle has become a secret. And as with most secrets, it is meant to protect as much as conceal.

9

I arrive early the following Tuesday. I'm hoping for a moment to speak with Conrad White on his own. I begin with the irresistible bait of flattery. At least, *I've* always found it irresistible, on the rare occasions it's come my way.

"I'm glad you enjoyed it," the old man says in reply to my praise of *Jarvis and Wellesley*. "It cost me a great deal."

"The controversy."

"That, yes," he says, looking up at me to gauge how much of that I might know. "It would be a lie to say I wasn't inconvenienced by my banishment. But I was thinking more of the cost of writing the thing in the first place."

"It's taxing. The process. I mean, it *must* be taxing."

"It needn't be. That book spilled forth with the ease of a sin in the confessional box. Which turned out to be my mistake. I should have held something back. Saved it for later. The total revelation

101

of our selves in one go does not make for long careers."

Conrad White pushes the room's chairs into their circle formation for the meeting. Even this minor task leaves him winded. I try to help him, but he waves me off the moment I step forward.

"I suppose, in a way, you must be grateful to be out of it," I say, expecting easy agreement. Instead, the old man's knees stiffen, as though preparing to absorb or deliver a blow.

"Out of what?"

"You know. The whole game, the schoolyard politics. Attention/neglect, praise/attack. The so-called rewards of fame."

"You're quite wrong. I would do anything to have it back. Just as you, I suspect, would do anything to have it."

I'm about to object – how could he know what I want? – when he releases a gusting sigh and falls back into his chair.

"Tell me," he says, showing a pair of nicotined incisors to signal a change of subject. "Have you found our meetings edifying?"

"It's been interesting."

"I understand from what you've brought to read that you are a critic by profession."

"I'm paid to watch television."

"So. What do your slumming critical faculties make of your classmates?"

Conrad White's lips part fully into a smile. His question is an amusing parry. But it's also a test.

102

"A mixed bag. As one would expect," I say. "There are a couple of pieces I think show special merit."

"A couple?"

"No. Not a couple."

Conrad White sits forward. The smile drops so quickly I can't be sure it was ever there.

"You never know who might have it," he says.

"Have what?"

"That thing that keeps bringing you to this place week after week, even though you have no faith whatsoever that what I or anyone else might say will assist you. The reason you're sitting here right now."

"What reason is that?"

"You want to know if someone else has been involved in the way you have been involved."

"Sorry. Not following you."

"The only vital currency is story. And yet we spend most of our time blowing flatus about theme or symbol or political context or structural messing about. Why?" The old man's smile returns. "I believe it's because it distracts us from the inadequacies of our own narrative. We avoid speaking of stories *as* stories for the same reason we avoid contemplating the inevitability of death. It can be unpleasant. It can *hurt*."

"I think the story Angela's telling is *about* death."

"Ghost stories usually are."

"How much of it do you think is real?"

"Perhaps the better question is how much of it you have *made* real."

"That's not up to me."

"It's not?"

"It's her story, not mine."

"So you say."

"We're talking about Angela."

"Really? I thought we were talking about you."

I would be lying if I said that Conrad White correctly guessing my involvement (as he called it) in Angela's story didn't catch me a little off guard. I'm not surprised by how intelligent a man he is, but by how much of this intelligence he has applied to me, to us, his raggedy group of bookish refugees. He knows I've been bluffing my way along right from the start, just as he knows that Angela is in possession of a "vital currency". Vital to the people like me and him, anyway. Popcorn crunchers, channel changers, paperback devourers. The hungry audience.

There's a knock at the door. Conrad White gets to his feet. I can hear Len's voice excitedly telling him about a breakthrough in his zombie apocalypse ("I've set it in a prison, because, after the dead rise, prisoners will be the only ones still alive *inside* the walls, and the society that has judged them left *outside*!") followed by Ivan, who slips by them both and takes a seat across from me. I nod at him in welcome, but since our conversation outside the subway station he's pretending he can't see me. It leaves me to measure the hands capped over

104

his knees. Too big for the wrists they're attached to, so that they appear taken from another body altogether, grave-robbed. An impression that reminds me of Ivan telling me what it's like to be accused of harming someone. Those hands could do harm without much effort. They could do it all on their own.

The rest of the circle arrives in a pack. Petra taking the chair next to Len's and politely listening to his how-to remarks on decapitating the undead. Angela slips by Evelyn and Conrad White to sit next to me. We smile hello at each other. It allows me the closest look at her yet. In the room's dimness, a distance of more than a couple feet makes our faces susceptible to distortion, the misreadings of candlelight. Now, however, I can see her more or less as she is. But what strikes me isn't any aspect of her appearance. It's the disarming certainty that *she* is seeing *me* with far greater accuracy than what I can only guess about her. She isn't dreamy or wounded or bashful. She's *working*.

William arrives last. I force myself to take him in at more than a glance, to confirm or dispel my suspicion that it had been him watching me across the street from the Indian take-out. He's the right size, that's for sure. A threat in the very space he occupies, consuming more than his fair share of light, of air. Still, I can't be sure it was him. His beard even thicker now, so that the true shape of his face is impossible to outline. And unlike Angela, a direct look into his eyes reveals nothing.

Where she is busy, William is lifeless. There is no more outward compassion in him than the zombies of Len's stories.

William takes his seat. Each of us slide an inch away from him, and each of us notices it. An instinct of the herd that communicates there is a wolf among us.

It is our second to last meeting, and Conrad White wants to get through as many of our pieces today as possible. We begin with Ivan, who takes his rat character into the tunnels beneath the city, where he watches the humans on the train platforms with the same revulsion that he, as a man, once viewed the vermin skittering around the rails. Evelyn returns her prof-bonking grad student to the family cottage, where she goes for a swim alone at night and symbolically ends up on an island, naked, "baptized by moonlight". Petra's domestic drama leads to her female character making a courageous call to a divorce lawyer. As for me, I nudge along my account of a frustrated TV critic just far enough to satisfy the rules.

Angela is next. Once I've turned on the dictaphone, I *feel* her reading more than anything else. It's as though I am within her, at once distinct and fused as Siamese twins. And this time there's something entirely new, a crackling energy in the inches between us that, for the first time, I interpret in purely physical terms. A literal attraction. I want to be closer to her mouth, look down upon the same scribbled pages she reads from, cheek to cheek. It takes a concerted effort to not let myself drift into her.

When she's finished, it's William's turn. This time, he's actually brought something with him. We soon wish he hadn't.

In his flat voice, he begins his account of "the summer when something broke" in the life of a boy, growing up in "the poorest part of a poor town". Avoiding the house where his father drank and his mother "did what she called her 'day job' in her bedroom", the friendless boy wanders through the dusty streets, bored and furious, like "he was buried under something heavy he couldn't crawl out from under".

One day, the boy picked up the neighbour's cat, took it out to a shed at the far end of an empty lot, and skinned it alive. The animal's cries are "the sound he would make if he could. But he has never cried in his life. It's something that's missing from him. Everything is missing from him." After burying the cat, the boy listens to the woman next door, calling her pet's name in the night, and he sees that "this is something he could do. Something he was good at. He could take things away."

The rest of the story goes on to describe, in the same bland language, the boy's successive gradua-tion from cats to dogs to the horse in the stable at the edge of town, wanting to see if it "was filled with glue, because that's what he'd heard they turned dead horses into".

Eventually, Conrad White breaks his own rule. He interrupts William in the middle of his reading.

"Thank you. I'm sorry, but we have run out of time," the old man lies. A trembling hand smoothing back his remaining wisps of hair. "Perhaps we can return to William's piece at our final meeting".

William folds his papers into a square and returns it to the pocket of his jeans. Looks around at the rest of us, who are now getting up, turning our backs to him. I may be the only one who doesn't move. And while I cannot say I notice anything change in his expression, I sense something that makes me certain it was William who stared at me across the street the other night. The same cruel aura he had then as now. A calmness that speaks not of contentment, but how, as with the boy in his story, everything is missing.

After the meeting, Len reminds me of our plans to check out the litmag launch and open mic at a bar up on College Street. On the way, as he shuffles a few steps ahead of me, anxious to get good seats, Len asks if I've noticed something between Evelyn and Conrad White.

"Something?"

"I don't know. They're always whispering to each other. Making eyes."

"I hadn't noticed."

"Who do you think she's with right now?"

"You mean *with* with?"

"Answer the question."

"Conrad?"

108

"It's kind of *sick*."

"There's got to be forty years between them."

"I told you."

"How do you know?"

"I don't. But what's a writing circle without a little scandal?"

The open mic is on the second floor of a Mexican restaurant, a long, dark-panelled room that smells of sawdust and refried beans. At the door, Len and I buy a copy of the stapled zine on offer, *Brain Pudding*, which entitles us to the beer discount.

"Not much of a turn-out."

"There's a serial killer out there somewhere," Len says. "It can make people stay in and order pizza."

"What are you talking about?"

Len gives me a hopeless, get-with-the-program look.

"The missing hairdresser," he says.

"Ronald Pevencey."

"The police found his body in a dumpster in Chinatown this afternoon. In pieces. Just like that woman on Ward's Island. So now they're thinking the same guy did them both. Two is a series. Thus, serial killer. Which is bad for business."

"We'll just have to do our best to help," I say, ordering a round.

The emcee thanks us for coming. But before he opens the floor to all comers, he has a special announcement. Congratulations for one of *Brain Pudding*'s contributors, Rosalind Canon, a mousy girl sitting with mousy boys in the front. Apparently she learned just this morning that the manuscript for her first novel had been accepted for publication in New York. A bidding war. World rights sold. Film option.

"And as if that wasn't enough," he says, "it's her birthday! Happy twenty-fourth, Rosalind!"

The emcee steps back from the mic, beams down at Rosalind, and starts to clap.

And in the next second, something interesting happens.

A drop in the room's barometric pressure, the sudden hollowness that precedes a thunderstorm. Aside from the emcee's two hands clapping, there is no sound other than our collectively held breath. It leaves each of us exposed. Caught on the coruscated edges of the same desire. Despite our differences of age, of costume, of genre, we are here because we all share the longing to be writers. But in this moment, what we more immediately wish is to be Rosalind. A surge of not-yet-rationalized jealousy powerful enough to alter the composition of the very environment we occupy.

And then, when our limbs finally accept the command given them, we join in the applause. A round of whistles and hearty good wishes you'd never suspect of the effort they required.

"That's great! Wow!" Len says.

"Oh yeah. It's so wow great I could kill her."

I wave my arm barward. From here on, my beers are coupled with bourbon shots. It eases things somewhat. The flatulent sound poetry and same-sex erotica and hate-my-parents short stories that follow pass in a benumbed succession. I even *like* some of it. Or at least, I admire that their authors are here, putting their name in the emcee's hat and, when called upon, ascending the plywood riser and letting it fly. Good or bad, they *made* this stuff. Which is more than I can say for myself.

Some time later, Rosalind Canon's name is called over the PA. She's come to these things before. She even knows the right way to approach the stage: with a slouch, as though her real thoughts are elsewhere, puzzling out some far deeper question than *How do I look?*

As she murmurs on, I resolve that, once she's finished, I will start home. The flush of goodwill that came with the first wave of alcohol is already passing, and I know from experience it will soon leave only regret and self-pity behind. Just one more drink in case the killer out there decides I'm to be next. I'd rather not see it coming. What kind of blade would he have to use to do what he does? Something motorized, perhaps. Or perhaps he is just incredibly strong. What had the monster in Angela's story liked to do? Turn people into fractions.

I'm about to tell Len I'm going to leave when I'm stopped by the realization that half the people in the room have turned in their chairs to look my way.

"Sorry to wake you," Len is saying, his hand on my arm. "But you were snoring."

In my cubicle at the *National Star* the next morning, Tim Earheart stops by to deliver coffee. It will be my fourth of the day, and it's only just turned ten. But I need all the help I can get. The many beers and only slightly fewer Wild Turkeys of the night before have left me fuzzy-headed and furry-mouthed. I take a couple scalding gulps before I'm able to read Tim's lips.

"Let's go down for a smoke," he's saying for the second time, glancing over his shoulder to see if anyone's listening.

"I don't smoke."

"I'll give you one."

"Quit. More or less. Thought you knew –"

Tim raises the back of his hand and for a second I'm sure he's going to slap me. Instead, he bends close to my ear.

"What I've got isn't for general consumption," he whispers, and walks away toward the doors to the main stairwell.

The basement of the *National Star* is the exclusive domain of two species of dinosaur: smokers and historians. It's down here where the pre-electronic database issues of the paper are stored, as well as some archival bric-à-brac including, I have heard, the shrunken head of the newspaper's founder. Aside from a few postgrad researchers the only people who come down here are the last of the nicotine wretches. A dwindling number, even among reporters. The kids coming out of journalism school these days are more likely to carry a yoga mat and an Evian bottle than a flask and a pack of smokes.

It leaves the Smoking Room one of the last places in the building where you can hope to have a private conversation. Sure enough, when I close the door behind me and feel my stomach clench at the carcinogenic stink, it's only Tim Earheart in here with me.

"They're not running it. They're not fucking *running* it," he says, literally fuming, grey exhaust spilling out his nose.

"What aren't they running?"

"The note."

I know that Tim is enough of an obsessive that if he's this excited, he's talking about a story. And his story right now is Carol Ulrich and Ronald Pevencey.

"Left it by her body," he goes on. "A *part* of her body. Her head, as a matter of grotesque fact. Typed out nice and neat for whoever found her."

"You have possession of this note?"

"Sadly, no. One of the cops on the scene told me what it said. He shouldn't have, but he did."

"And you brought it to the suits."

"Expecting it to go A1. Because if this isn't front page, what is? But the police caught wind of it, and they begged us to muzzle it. Ongoing investigation, lives at risk, an eventual arrest could be jeopardized, blah blah blah. Just throw a blanket on it for a few days. So now they're not running it."

"Does it say who wrote it?"

"It's not *signed*. But I think it's pretty damn clear."

Tim finishes his cigarette, grinds the butt under his heel and has another in his mouth in less time than it takes me to speak.

"What did it say?"

"That's the reason I'm telling you. I was hoping you might have some literary insight."

"You're talking about a serial killer's note, not *Finnegans Wake*."

Tim takes a step closer. Smoke rising from his hair.

"It's a *poem*," he says.

The Smoking Room door opens and a lifer from Sports comes in, gives us a distasteful glance and lights up. Tim makes a zipper motion across his lips. I'm about to step outside when he grabs my wrist. Presses something into my palm.

"Call me later about those Leafs tickets," he says. Winks a secret wink.

A business card. Tim Earheart's writing squeezed on to the back. I read it over a few times in my

cubicle, then tear it into confetti and let it fall into
my recycling box.

> *I am the ground beneath your feet*
> *The man in dark alleys you don't want*
>   *to meet*
> *I live in the Kingdom of Not What It Seems*
> *Close your eyes, you will see me – here in*
>   *your dreams.*

Not much, as poems go. Just a pair of rhyming
couplets, a Mother Goose simplicity that gives it
the sing-song of nursery doggerel. Perhaps this is
the point. Given the grisly context in which the
poem was found, the childish tone makes it all the
more threatening. The kind of thing you need only
read once and it, or some part of it, remains
hooked in your mind. A poem meant not to be
admired but remembered.

So what does it say about its author? First,
whoever did this to Carol Ulrich also wrote these
lines. One an act of assembly, the other of dismemberment. Creator and Destroyer in one. *Somebody
bad*, as Tim Earheart had guessed.

Second, he wanted the poem to be read. It
could have been kept to himself, but instead it
was left by the victim's corpse. A killer who –
like all writers – wants an *audience* for their
work. To make us feel something. To invite the
kind of scrutiny I am giving his poem right now.
To be understood.

Third, while it is only a four-line ditty, there are indications of some intelligence. That a poem would occur to him at all puts him at a creative level above the everyday backstreet butcher. And the composition itself offers some indication of talent. It rhymes, for one thing. A rhythm that's not accidental. Good enough that it would likely achieve its macabre effect even if it wasn't deposited next to a corpse.

And then there are the words themselves.

The first line sets out the poem's purpose: the poet seeks to introduce himself. He is the ground beneath our feet. That is, he's everywhere. The next line establishes the character of this presence as menacing, hostile, the "man in dark alleys". Naturally, the mention of alleys rings especially loud for me, as it was only a few days ago that I ran home through one, fearing something that likely wasn't there. But "dark alleys" are universally regarded as places to fear. He wants us to know that he is the one who waits for us there.

The third line introduces a note of dark whimsy. The "Kingdom of Not What It Seems" is where he *lives*, but he is also able to materialize in the ground beneath our feet. At once real and an illusion. A shapeshifter.

All of which is reinforced in the poem's concluding line. If we wish to see him, we must turn not to whatever clues have been left behind, but to our dreams. And these dreams aren't only imagined, but "here", in the real world. We are all part of the same dream whether we like it or not. And it's *his*.

It's not until my walk home that another interpretation occurs to me. "Occurs to me" might not be strong enough. In fact, it almost knocks me over. I have to sit on the curb with my head between my legs to prevent myself from blacking out.

When I'm partly recovered I speak into the dictaphone, still slouched on the curb as cars pass within inches of my feet.

TRANSCRIPT FROM TAPE

March 12, 2003

[Sounds of passing traffic]
I am the ground beneath your feet.
Literally. Whoever first read the poem would have been on Ward's Island. Standing on a beach. On *sand*.
[Aside]
Oh, shit.
[Kid in background]
Look at this pisstank! He's gonna lose ...
[Car horn]
... if he doesn't watch it!
[Background laughter]
Close your eyes, you will see me.
Okay. To know who he is, we have to dream. But who delivers our thoughts while we sleep?
[Singing]
Mr Sandman, bring me a dream ...

117

10

Angela's Story
Transcribed from Tape Recording No. 3

The next week, after the school was re-opened
despite the second missing girl remaining missing
and no leads being discovered as to the perpetrator
of what the town's Chief of Police called "these
heinous crimes" (a word the girl had never heard
before and spelled in her mind as "hayness",
which only reminded her of what she discovered
in the barn), Edra had to go into the hospital a
hundred and sixty miles down the road for
surgery. Her gallbladder. Nothing to worry about,
Jacob assured the girl. Edra would be just fine
without it. Which, if this was true, made the girl
wonder why God gave us gallbladders in the first
place.

Edra is taken to the hospital on a Friday, which
leaves Jacob and the girl alone in the farmhouse
until Edra is brought home, all being well, on

Sunday. The old man and the girl have the week-end to themselves.

As much as the girl is delighted by the idea of exclusive attention from Jacob, part of her dreads their number being reduced from three to two. She wonders if the invisible cord that connected them as a family also acted as a spell, a force field that kept out the terrible man who does terrible things. With Edra gone, a door might be opened. For the sake of her foster parents, the girl would keep a vile secret. She would bury someone in the night and suffer the nightmares that followed. But she isn't sure she could ever close a door to the Sandman once it was opened.

Soon her worry over all of this could be read in every look and gesture the girl makes. No matter how she tries to keep her burden hidden, she wears her trouble like a cloak. Jacob knows her too well not to notice. And when he asks the girl what's wrong, this simple provocation triggers an explosion of tears.

She tells him almost everything. That there's a terrible man who does terrible things who used to live only in her dreams, but has now taken form in the real world. That she believes this man took the two girls from town because they were the same age and general appearance as she.

What she doesn't tell him is what she found in the barn, and what she did with it.

Jacob doesn't speak for a long time after the girl is finished. When he finally finds the words he's looking for, the girl expects him to explain how what she's said could not be possible. But instead he surprises her.

"I have seen him too," the old man says.

The girl can hardly believe it. What was he like? Where did Jacob see him?

"I could not describe him to you any more than I could say what shape the wind takes," the old man answers. "It is something I have *felt*. Moving around the house as though what he seeks is within, but he cannot enter. Not yet."

Perhaps the girl should go to him. If it's only her that the Sandman wants, why risk him doing harm to another girl? Or worse, to Jacob or Edra.

"You mustn't speak like that," Jacob implores her. "Never *ever*. Understand? He will not have you so long as I live. And after I'm gone, you must still resist him. Promise me this."

The girl promises. But what is left for them to do? The girl can't imagine how they might attempt to fight him. How can you kill what may already be dead?

"I cannot say if he is alive or dead. But I believe I can say who he is."

Jacob holds the girl firm by the shoulders as though to prevent her from falling.

"It's your father," he says.

After Jacob failed to pick her up, Edra returned from the hospital in a taxi on Sunday to find the farmhouse empty. The back door left wide open. If someone had come in or gone out by this point of entry there was no way of knowing. Over the last twenty-four hours, the whole county had been buried under three feet of snow. The arrival of winter announced in a November blizzard. Any tracks that might have been left now filled in and sculpted into fin-tailed drifts.

When the police arrive Edra is frantic for them to find the girl. They don't have far to look. Huddled in the corner of the last stall in the barn. Glass-eyed, blue-skinned. Shaking from the hypothermia caused by staying outside all night when the temperature dipped as low as ten below.

They ask her where Jacob is. The girl's only answer is to slip into unconsciousness. For a time, it's judged to be even odds if she will survive or not. Three of her toes are removed, turned black from frostbite. Her brain monitored to determine what parts have died from lack of oxygen while she sleeps.

But the girl doesn't die.

When she comes to the next day, she will not speak to anyone but Edra, and even then, it's not about what happened over the preceding days. Edra buffers the girl from their queries, putting her anxieties regarding her husband second to the girl's need for protection. The police are left to look for Jacob on their own.

After it is determined that Jacob's truck was parked in the farmyard the entire weekend, and there is no sign of a struggle or suicide note inside the house, the forest that borders the end of his fields and carries on for five hundred miles north into the Canadian Shield becomes the prime area of concentration for the police search.

The snowfall from the blizzard, however, makes it difficult. Helicopter fly-overs can spot little more than trees sprouting up from a blanket of white. The dogs they use to track Jacob's scent run a hundred yards into the woods only to sink up to their muzzles, and then must be carried out, whimpering, by their trainers. By the fourth day, the search's urgency is downgraded from a rescue operation to evidence collection. If Jacob is to be found somewhere out in the endless woods, there is no expectation that he will be alive.

It takes another two weeks of mild weather for the snow to melt enough to expose Jacob's body. Four miles from the farm. Lying face down, arms sprawled out at his sides. No injuries aside from cuts to his face and arms that came from branches slashing his skin as he ran. Just socks on his feet, and not wearing any outerwear (his boots and coat were in their usual places in the house). The cause of death determined to be exposure following a collapse from exhaustion. The coroner is amazed that a man of Jacob's age was capable of getting as far as he did. A four-mile run through a blizzard in the night woods. Only someone in a state of mortal panic would be capable of it.

But the questions that followed from this were beyond both the coroner's and forensic investigators' capacity to answer. Was Jacob running *from* or *toward* something? If he had been the one in pursuit, what quarry would have driven him into the forest dressed as he was during the first big snowfall of the year? And if he was the pursued, what would have terrified him enough to run so far he let himself fall and die without anything laying a hand on him?

The police all agreed that if Jacob had been murdered, it was a perfect crime. No suspect. No witness. No tracks left after the snow had filled them in. No weapon to be found aside from the cold.

Only the girl knew – or might know – what happened over the time she and Jacob were alone in the farmhouse. But no matter how many times she was asked, she would not speak of it.

Shock, the doctors said. Extreme emotional trauma. It can cut the tongue out of a child as sure as any blade. She's of no use now, they concluded. You'd have as good a chance asking the trees in Jacob's forest what they saw as this poor girl.

The girl heard everything they said about her, though she acted as though she was deaf. She resolved that there are some things you cannot speak of. But she would record what she knew in a different way from speech. She would write it down. Later, when she was older and on her own, she would tell the truth, if only to herself.

Here, in the pages of this very book.

She even knows how it will begin.

There once was a girl who was haunted by a ghost ...

11

"City in Fear" reads the banner headline of the next day's *National Star*, and for me, at least, it's not overstatement. The accompanying piece is one of those "man on the street", mood-gauging surveys that only retreads what is already known of the two recent victims – unrelated, no known involvements in crime, no indication of sexual assault, nothing of value taken from their persons. Indeed, there is no reason to believe their killer to be the same person. This report is followed by interviews with people in the neighbourhood who admit they're not planning to go out at night until "they catch whatever sick bastard that would do this". I read the article to the end to see if there's any mention of the poem found next to Carol Ulrich's body, but it looks like Tim was right. The editors killed it.

And then, perhaps most troubling of all, there is an account of the various eyewitness statements and anonymous call-in tips received by police.

A well-dressed, bald white man says one. Two black men are cited – one with gold teeth and a Raiders toque, the other grey-haired, nice-looking, a "Denzel Washington look-alike". A pair of curly-haired men who "may be twins". An elderly Portuguese lady in mourning black.

"People are seeing killers in whoever sits next to them on the subway," one policeman points out.

And why not? It *could* be them.

The morning's walk through the City of Fear confirms that the three million hearts pounding their way to work all around me have turned a darker shade of worry. Each cluster of newspaper boxes shows that the *National Star*'s competition have run similarly alarmist pieces, the always hysterical tabloid putting smiling photos of Carol Ulrich and Ronald Pevencey side by side under the headline "Are You Next?" A question that's impossible not to give some thought to. Everyone getting off the streetcars or emerging from the mouths of subway entrances sees these front-page faces and, through them, sees themselves. Not stony-faced mobsters or gangland hoods (the kinds who had it coming), but the faces of those whose primary goal was the avoidance of trouble. That's the security most of us count on: we belong to the majority who never go looking for it. Yet all of us know at the same time that this is an increasingly hollow assurance. Fear is always there, looking for a way to the surface.

No matter how we might keep to ourselves, sometimes the Sandman finds us anyway.

The Quotidian Award, affectionately known as the Dickie, is the nation's second-richest literary prize. The honour was established by Richard "Dickie" Barnham, a Presbyterian minister who, in his retirement, became an enthusiastic memoirist, recounting the mild eccentricities of his quaint Ontario parsonage. He was also, in the year before his death, the purchaser of a $12-million-winning lottery ticket. The Dickie is today awarded to the work of fiction that "best reflects the domestic heritage of Canadian family life", which has led to a series of hushed, defiantly uneventful winners. A rainy-day parade of stolid farmers and fishermen's widows.

It also happens to be one of the gala events of the season. A ticket to the Dickie marks one's membership in the nation's elite, a Who's Who of country club philanthropists, TV talking heads, corporate barons. The *National Star*'s publisher has never missed it. It's in part why, each year, a photo of the winner and a hyperventilating description of the menu and ladies' gowns appear on the front page.

It's the sort of assignment I'm no longer considered for. Even when I was the literary columnist, the paper preferred to send one of the party girls from the Style section who could recognize not only the celebrities in attendance, but the designers who did their outfits. This year, however, the reporter they had in mind called in sick four hours before the event. The Managing Editor was out of town at one of her executive retreats, so the task of choosing a last-minute alternative came down to the News Editor who asked if I could do it for him. I accepted.

The press pass allows me to take a guest. The wise course would be to go alone, write the story they're looking for, and be in bed by midnight. Instead, I call Len.

"You could slip someone your manuscript," I tell him.

"You think?"

"Every editor in town is going to be there."

"Maybe just a couple short stories," he decides after a moment. "Something that could fit under my jacket."

By the time I rent a tux and spin by in a cab to pick up Len (who has also been fitted in black tie, though for someone a foot shorter and thirty pounds lighter than he) we arrive at the Royal York just in time to catch the last half of the cocktail hour.

"Look!" Len whispers on our way into the Imperial Room. "There's Grant Duguay!"

I follow Len's pointing finger and find the emcee of tonight's proceedings. The same waxy catalogue model with a used car salesman grin who acts as host of *Canadian MegaStar!*

"That's him alright."

"And there! That's Rosalind Canon!"

"Who?"

Len looks at me to make sure I'm being serious. "At the *Brain Pudding* launch. The one who got half a million for her first novel."

I get Len to point Rosalind out to me. And there she is, the mousy girl who is now shaking hands with every culturecrat and society wife who make their way to her. Even from across the room I can lip-read the same earnest *Thank you* in reply to the congratulations, over and over. It makes me want to say the same thing to someone. A passing waiter will have to do.

"Thank you," I say, plucking a pair of martinis, one for each hand, from his tray.

We settle at the press table before the other hacks arrive. It allows me to stick one of the two bottles of wine on the table between my feet, just in case the steward is unavailable at a crisis point later on. Then the *MegaStar!* guy is up at the lectern saying something about how reading made him what he is today, which seems reasonably true, given that managing a teleprompter would be tricky for an illiterate. Following this, as the dinner begins to be served, each of the nominated authors take the stage to talk about the genesis of their work. The bottle between my feet is empty before the caribou tartare is cleared.

It's absurd and I know it. It's shallow and unfounded and generally reflects poorly on my character. Because I haven't published a book.

Haven't written a book. I don't have anything in mind to one day turn *into* a book. But in the spirit of full and honest disclosure, I'll tell you what I'm thinking as I sit in the Imperial Room in my itchy tux watching the night's honourees bow into the waves of applause.

Why not me?

Luck. Pulled strings. Marketability. Maybe they have this on their side. Though there is always something else, too. A compelling order to things, a story's *beginning, middle and end*. Me? All I have is all most of us have. The messy garble of a life-in-progress.

To turn my mind from such thoughts, I lean over and share with Len the killer's secret poem. It leaves him goggle-eyed. Encouraged, I go on to outline my interpretation of the poem's meanings, including the unlikely hint at the author's identity.

"You think there's a connection?" he asks, wiping the sweat from his lip.

"I think it's a coincidence."

"Hold on, hold *on*." Len fusses with the cutlery set out in front of him as though it represents the thoughts in his head. "If you're right, then it means whoever's been doing those things is either in our writing circle, or has read Angela's story."

"No, it doesn't. Anyone can call themselves the Sandman. And he doesn't call himself *anything* in the poem. It's just a theory."

"And my theory is it's William."

"Slow down. It's not –"

"Hello! A kid who disembowels cats and horses for fun? He's basically *telling* us what he's capable of."

"It's a *story*, Len."

"Some stories are true."

"If writing fiction about serial killers makes you a murder suspect, there'd be a hundred freaks within ten blocks of here the police would want to talk to."

"Still. *Still*," Len says, chewing his lip. "I wonder what Angela would think if she –"

"You can't tell anyone."

Len is crestfallen. A real horror story dropped in his lap, and he's not allowed to run with it.

"I mean it, Len. I only told you because –"

Why *did* I tell Len? The martinis helped. And I suppose I wanted him to be impressed. I'm a journalist at a real newspaper. I *know* things. But more than this, I think I wanted to *entertain* the big geek.

"Because I believe you can be trusted," I say finally, finishing the sentence Len has been waiting for. And he looks away, visibly touched by the compliment.

After dessert, Mr *MegaStar!* announces the winner. And once I've jotted the name down, I'm out of there.

"I'm off, Len. Got to write this thing up lickety-split."

131

Len eyes my untouched maple syrup cheese-cake. "You going to eat that?"

"All yours."

I squeeze his shoulder as I get up from the table. And although Len smiles in acknowledgment of the gesture, the fact is if I hadn't grabbed him I would have fallen face first into a passing tray of beaver-shaped shortbreads.

After a couple hours punching keys on my lap-top, keeping focused with the help of the Library Bar's Manhattans, I hit Send and start the long stagger home. It's not easy. My legs, lazy rascals, won't do what I tell them. Pretzelling around each other, taking sudden turns toward walls or parking meters. It takes me a half-hour to get two blocks behind me. At least my arms seem to be working. One hugging a lamp-post and the other hailing a cab.

Despite the cold, I roll the window down as the driver rockets us past the Richmond Street nightclubs that, at this late hour, are only now disgorging the sweaty telemarketers, admin assistants and retail slaves who've come down-town to blow half their week's pay on cover, parking and a half-dozen vodka coolers. I hang my elbow out and let the air numb my face. Sleep coils up from the bottoms of my feet.

But it's interrupted by a news reader's voice coming from the speaker behind my head. I roll up the window to hear him tell of a third victim in a murder spree police continue to publicly deny believing is the work of a single killer. Like Carol Ulrich and Ronald Pevencey, the body was found dismembered. A woman again, her name not yet released by investigators. The additionally puzzling twist is that she had only arrived in Toronto the day before from Vancouver. No known relation to the first two victims. Indeed, police have yet to determine if she knew anyone in town at all.

And then, right at the end of the report, come the details that chill me more than if I was being driven home tied to the roof rack.

The victim's body was found in the playground around the corner from us. The one where I take Sam.

And not just anywhere in the playground. The sand box.

"Eight fiddy," the driver says.

"Home. Right. I need to pay you now."

"That's how it works."

I'm stretching out over the back bench, grunting to pull out my wallet when the driver informs me the whole city's gone crazy.

"Kids got guns in the schools. Cops takin' money on the side. And the *drugs*? They sellin' shit that turn people into *robots*. Robots that stick a knife in your gut for pocket change."

"I know it."

"And now this insane motherfucker – 'scuse me – goes round and chops up three people in three weeks. Three *weeks*! What, he don't take no holidays?"

I hand the driver a piece of paper that, in the dark and with my Manhattan-blurred vision, could be either a twenty-dollar bill or a dry-cleaning receipt. It seems to satisfy him, whatever it is.

"I been out here drivin' nights for eight years," he says as I shoulder the door open and spill out into the street. "But I never been scared before."

"Well, you take care then."

The driver looks me up and down. "How 'bout this? How 'bout *you* take care."

I watch the taxi drive up Euclid until its brake lights shrink to nothing. Snow suspended under the streetlights, neither falling nor rising.

In the next moment, there is the certainty that I must not turn around. Not if I want to preserve the illusion that I am alone. So I step off the street, lurch toward my door. Only to see that this is a journey someone has already made.

Boot prints. At least two sizes larger than mine. Leading across the postage-stamp lawn and into the narrow walkway between our house and the house next door.

At least, this is the trail I think I'm following. When I look back, the prints, both mine and the boots', are already obscured by powdery snow.

I am the ground beneath your feet …

I could pull out my keys, unlock the front door, and put this skittishness behind me. Instead, something starts me down the unlit walk between the houses. If there is a danger here, it is my job to face it. No matter how unsteady I am. No matter how frightened.

But it's darker than night in here. A strip of sky running twenty feet over my head and no other way for the light of the city to get in. My heart accelerated to the point it hurts. Hands running over the brick on either side, making sure the walls don't close in on me. It's only thirty feet away, but the space at the far end that is our back yard feels like it's triple that. Uphill.

Along with another impression. This one telling me that someone else was here only moments ago.

The man in dark alleys you don't want to meet.

Once out, I slide my back along the rear wall. The branches of perennials reaching up from the snow like skeletal fingers. The old garden shed I keep meaning to tear down leans against the back fence to remain standing, much as I do using the wall behind me.

I side-step up on to the deck. The sliding glass door is closed. Inside, the living room is illuminated by the TV. An infomercial demonstrating the amazing utility of a slicer-and-dicer gadget. It may be the booze, or the comforting images of advertising, but something holds me here for a moment, peering into my own darkened home. Taking in the mismatched furniture, the frayed rug, the overstuffed bookshelves, as though they are someone else's. As they could well be.

135

Except the room is not empty.

Sam. Asleep with a *Fantastic Four* comic open on his lap, his hands still gripping the cover. Emmie has let him stay up, having retired to the spare room awaiting my return. I look at my son and see the worry in his pose, the evidence of his struggle against sleep. Nightmares. It makes my heart hurt all over again.

I pull my hands from where they were resting against the glass. Step away and search my pockets for the keys to the house. Find them at the same instant I find something else that stops me cold.

A different pair of hand prints above mine on the sliding door. Visible only now I've moved away from the glass and the condensation of my breath has frozen them into silver. Ten fingertips and two smudges of palm that, when I place my own hands on top of them, extend an inch further from every edge.

He was here.

Looking into my home just as I am now, gauging the ease of entering. His eyes studying my sleeping son.

This time, when I push away from the sliding door, my hands smear the glass so that the other's prints are wiped away. Another filled-in boot print, a misguided intuition. A dubious creation of my non-creative mind.

Yet no matter how rational they sound, none of these explanations come close to being believed.

* * *

136

"I'm curious," the Managing Editor says, her face approximating an expression of real curiosity. "What were you thinking when you wrote this?"

It's the next morning. The Managing Editor has the front page of today's *National Star* laid out over her desk. My by-line under the lead story. "Prodigious Pay-Off for Pedantic Prizewinner."

"You mean the headline?" I say. "I've always been a sucker for alliteration."

"I'm speaking of the piece itself."

"I thought it needed some colour, I suppose."

The Managing Editor looks down at the paper. Reads aloud some of the lines she has highlighted.

"'Proceedings interrupted by coughing fits from an audience choking on air thick with hypocrisy.' 'The real prize should have gone to the jury for managing to read the shortlist.' 'There was more irony in listening to the host of an execrable TV show preach the virtues of reading than in the past dozen Dickie winners.' And so on."

The Managing Editor lifts her eyes from the page.

"*Colour*, Patrick?"

I search for a way to apologize. Because I *am* sorry. And I have a handful of excuses to back up my regret. The grief that seems to be turning into something else, something worse. Inoperable writer's block. A ghoul circling my house.

"I haven't been myself lately," I say.

"Oh?"

"It feels like I'm *losing hold* of things. But I can't let myself. I have a son, he's still little, and I'm the only one who –"

"So this," the Managing Editor interrupts, touching a finger to my article, "could be interpreted as a cry for help?"

"Yes. In a way, I think it could."

The Managing Editor reaches for the phone.

"Who are you calling?"

"Security."

"That won't be necessary."

"I know. I just rather *like* the idea of having you escorted out."

"This is it, then?"

"Very much so."

"Would it make any difference if I said I was sorry?"

"None whatsoever." She raises a finger to silence me. "Could you please have Patrick Rush removed from the building? That's right, this is a permanent access denial situation. Thank you."

The Managing Editor hangs up. Gives me a smile that's actually something else. The bared teeth dogs use to show their willingness to rip another's lungs out.

"So, Patrick. How's the family?"

138

12

Even with all my new free time, my final offering to the circle is no better than my previous scraps. Four whole days of wide-open unemployment and I've managed to produce little more than a To Do list stretched into full sentences. Patrick takes a nap. Patrick picks up long-forgotten dry cleaning. Patrick heats a can of soup for his lunch. If I'd set it during a war or the Depression and kept it up for a hundred thousand words, I'd have a shot at the Dickie.

Still, I make my way into Kensington with a fluttery anticipation, the winter showing signs of retreat, an almost clear March afternoon doing its best to lift the temperature past zero. A double espresso along the way has offered a jolt of hope. A caffeinated reminder there are blessings to be counted.

For one, Sam took my dismissal as well as could be expected for a four-year-old. He doesn't understand money. Or mortgages. Or the prospects for unemployed writers. But he seems to think old Dad can pull a few rabbits out of his hat if he puts his mind to it.

The other good news is that I've been doing a half decent job of talking myself out of my Sandman theories. Getting away from the newsroom and Tim Earheart's grisly scoops has downgraded my paranoia to milder levels. My evidence of a connection between Angela's story and the killings of Carol Ulrich, Ronald Pevencey and the unnamed woman from Vancouver amounts to little when considered in the light of day. An over-interpreted four-line poem. Bodies found on a beach and a sand box. Hand prints on glass. That's it. Curious bits and pieces that can be strung together only through the most elastic logic, and even then, outstanding questions remain. Why would someone in the Kensington Circle be inspired to brutally murder complete strangers? Even if there is a Sandman that has walked out of the pages of Angela's journal, what would it want from me?

Tonight is our last meeting. Once we leave Conrad White's drafty apartment we will go our separate ways, to dissolve back into the city and take our places among the other undeclared novelists, secret poets, closeted chroniclers. Whatever peculiarities have animated my dreams since I first heard Angela tell her tale of a haunted little girl will come to an end. And I will be glad when it does. I like a good ghost story as much as anyone. But there comes a time when one must wake up and return to the everyday, to the world in which shadows are only shadows, and dark is nothing more than the absence of light.

We go around the circle one last time, and to my surprise, there has been some improvement from where we started. Ivan's rat, for instance, has become a fully developed character. There's a melancholy that comes out of the writing that I don't remember the first go round. Even Len's horror tales have been revised to be a little less repetitive, their author having learned that not *every* victim of a zombie attack need have their brains scooped out of their skulls for us to understand the undead's motivations.

As we proceed, I pay extra attention to Conrad White, looking for any sign that might confirm his relationship with Evelyn. Yet the old man maintains the same benign gaze on her while she reads as he does for everyone else. Perhaps the attraction only runs the other way. Evelyn doesn't strike me as the sort for him anyway. I'd imagined the "perfect girl" in *Jarvis and Wellesley* as softer, waifish, an innocent (even if this innocence was feigned). Someone who thought less and felt more. Someone like Angela.

If Conrad White shows any special attention to a circle member over the course of the meeting, it's her. I even think I catch him at it at one point, his eyes resting on her in the middle of Len's reading, when her head is turned in profile and she can be observed without detection. His expression isn't lustful. There is something in Angela he has seen before, or at least imagined. It's surprised him. And perhaps it has even frightened him a little too.

In the next second he catches me watching him.

That's when I think I see it. Something I can't be sure of, not in this light. But as his eyes pass over me, I have the idea that his world has been visited by the Sandman as well as mine.

Angela's turn. She apologizes that she brought nothing new with her this week. There is a moan of disappointment from the rest of us, followed by jokey complaints of how now we'll never know how Jacob died, what really happened over the time Edra was in the hospital, who the Sandman was. Conrad White asks if she'd made any changes to her previous draft, and she admits she hadn't found the time. Or this is what she tells us. If I were to guess, I'd say she'd never intended to make any revisions. She hasn't come here for editorial guidance, but to share her story with others. Without an audience, the little girl, Edra and Jacob, and the terrible man who does terrible things are only dead words on the page. Now they live in us.

Following this, we do everything we can – repeat comments we've already made, request a second smoke break – but there is still enough time for William to read. He has been sitting in the chair closest to the door, a few feet back from the others. It has made it almost possible to forget he is here. But now that Conrad White has called on him, he leans forward so that his eyes catch the candlelight, as though emerging from behind a velvet curtain.

His reading is once again brutal, but mercifully short. Another page in the lost summer of a cat-skinning boy. This time, the boy has taken to watching his mother at her "day job" through her bedroom window. He observes "what the men do to her, lying on top with their pants around their ankles, and he sees how they are only animals". The boy doesn't feel shame or disgust, only a clarity, "the discovery of a truth. One that has been hidden by a lie told over and over." If we are all of us animals, the boy concludes, then what difference is there between slicing the throat of a dog and doing the same to one of the men who visit his mother's bedroom? For that matter, what difference would there be in doing such a thing to his mother?

Soon, however, this idle contemplation demands to be tested. The boy feels like "a scientist, an astronaut, a discoverer of something no one had ever seen or thought of before". Proceeding from the assumption that we are all creatures of equal inclinations, it would follow that this makes us worth nothing more than the ants "we step out of our way just to crunch under our shoe". He could prove it. All he had to do was "something he had been taught was very, very wrong". If he was still himself afterward, if nothing changed in the world,

143

then he would be right. The prospect "fills him with an excitement he guesses is the same as the other boys in school have felt kissing girls. But this was not what he had in mind at all."

William leans back in his chair and the light in his eyes is extinguished again. This is as far as his story goes. It's my turn to respond first, and though I'm usually good at coming up with empty comments, in this case I'm stumped.

"This feels very close to the surface to me," I manage finally.

"What does that mean?"

"I suppose it means that it feels real."

"What does real feel like?"

"Like right now."

"What does he do?" a female voice says, and all of us turn to face Angela. She is peering into the dark where William sits. "The boy. Does he carry out his ... experiment?"

That's when William makes a sound all of us immediately regret ever hearing. He laughs.

"I'll show you mine if you show me yours," he says.

After we finish up, Conrad White suggests all of us go out to "whatever ale house may be nearby" to celebrate our accomplishments. We decide on Grossman's Tavern, a blues bar on Spadina I haven't been to since I was an undergrad. Little has changed. The house band working away in the corner, the red streak of streetcars passing the picture window at

144

the front. This is where we push a couple of tables together and order pitchers, all of us a little nervous about speaking of ourselves and not our stories, which despite the similarities in most cases, is still a different matter.

The beer helps. As well as the absence of William, who walked away in the opposite direction outside Conrad White's apartment. It's nearly impossible to imagine how he would act in a social setting, whether he would eat the stale popcorn the waitress brings, how he would bring the little draft glasses to find his lips in his beard. Even more difficult to guess is what he might contribute to the first topic we naturally fall upon. The murders.

I'm giving this some consideration when my thoughts are interrupted by Len shouting at me over a note-for-note T-Bone Walker solo.

"Tell them your theory, Patrick."

"Sorry?"

"The *poem*. Tell them what you told me. About the Sandman."

The circle has turned to look at me. And there is Len, bobbing about in his chair like an ape at feeding time.

"That's a secret, Len."

"It *was*. Didn't you read the paper this morning? I thought you *worked* there."

"Not any more."

"Oh. Wow. That's too bad. I really liked that Couch Potato thing."

"I'm touched."

"That poem? The one they found by the Ulrich woman's body? They published it today."

I haven't looked at the *National Star* since being given the heave-ho, so I hadn't noticed Tim Earheart's triumph. It means two things are quite certain. First, my friend is out there somewhere, getting drunk as a donkey in celebration of his exclusive. Second, the police are no closer to finding the killer than they were when they asked the paper to hold off on running the poem.

"So? What's your Sandman theory?" Petra asks, looking first to me, then Angela, who has been watching me with an unsettling steadiness.

"It's nothing."

"C'mon! It's *good*!" Len says.

I continue to refuse. And then Angela leans forward, places an upturned hand on the table as though inviting me to place mine in hers.

"Please, Patrick," she says. "We'd be very interested."

So I tell her. Tell them.

My Sandman interpretation sounds even more ridiculous when shouted aloud in a bar, the circle leaning forward to hear, an almost comically incongruous bunch who, if you were to walk in right now, you'd wonder what they could possibly have in common. The absurdity makes it easier to make my case, on account of it's an argument that knows it has little chance of being right.

Trouble is, the others take it seriously. I can see I'm convincing them even as I try to laugh it off. What is clear in each of their faces is that they have had similar thoughts these past weeks. They came here believing in the Sandman as much as I do.

Once I'm finished, I excuse myself to call Sam and catch him as Emmie is putting him to bed. (I wish him sweet dreams, and he requests pancakes in the morning.) When I return to our table, the conversation has moved on to domestic complaint (Petra unable to believe how much she had to pay a plumber to replace the faucet on her jacuzzi) and sports (Ivan pleading the case for the Leafs to trade that big Russian kid who can't skate). More pitchers, cigarettes on the sidewalk. Me eventually ordering a round of shots for everyone, and having to down Angela's and Len's when she'd pushed hers aside and he'd reminded me he doesn't drink (I'd remembered, of course, and figured it was an easy way to double up).

Yet even through the increasingly fuzzy proceedings, there are some moments that demand mention.

At one point, there is only myself and Len at one end of the table and Conrad White and Evelyn at the other. The two of them almost cheek to cheek, whispering. Perhaps Len was right after all. Lovers would behave this way after a few drinks, wouldn't they? And yet there is something grave in the secrets they share, a seriousness that doesn't match any form of flirtation I'm familiar with. Not that I'm an expert.

I'm pouring myself another, studying the two of them, when Len leans over with a secret whisper of his own.

"I was followed last night. I think it was You Know Who."

"You *saw* him?"

"More like I felt him. His ... *hunger*. You know what I mean?"

"As a matter of fact, I don't."

"I don't believe you."

"No? Well, let me tell you what I believe. You're taking my read on that poem too seriously. It's bullshit. I was just kidding around."

"No you weren't. And I know what I felt. It was him."

"Him?"

"The bogeyman."

"Look at me, Len. I'm not laughing."

"Whatever it was, it wasn't like you or me."

"I take it that you're talking about William."

"I might have *thought* it was William, but only because it can take different shapes. It's why there haven't been any witnesses. Think about it. Who knows what the bogeyman looks like? Nobody. Because it's whatever scares you the most."

I have to admit this last bit unsettles me enough that I'm not sure I manage to keep it hidden. But it's what Len says next that makes my calm act fall away completely.

"I'm not the only one."

"You told the others what you're telling me?"

"They've told *me*."

"And?"

"Petra saw someone out in her back yard two nights ago," he goes on, sliding even closer, so that now Evelyn and Conrad White are watching. "And last week, Ivan was taking his subway train into the yards at the end of the night, all the stations closed. He's just whizzing through, nobody's supposed to be there. And at one of the stops he sees someone right at the edge of the platform, all alone, like he's going to jump. Except he *can't* be there, right? All the stations are locked up for the night. And this guy, he's not security, he isn't wearing one of those fluorescent maintenance vests. So when Ivan goes by he tries to see his face. And you know what Ivan said? *He didn't have one.*"

"You've got to take a little time away from those *Tales from the Crypt* comics," I say, forcing out a laugh as the others join us from outside. Len wants to say more, but I steal a cigarette from the pack Evelyn left on the table and head outside before he has the chance.

It's only when I'm on the street, trying to light a match with shaking hands, that I allow myself to consider what Len's disclosures might mean. The first possibility is that he's nuts. The other option is he's telling the truth. At best, the Sandman story has got us all jumping at shadows. At worst, he's real.

149

These worries are interrupted by the sense that I'm not alone. It's Petra. Behind me, just around the corner, speaking with some urgency into a cellphone. She went out earlier with the other smokers apparently. A bit odd in itself, as she doesn't smoke, and now she's standing outside in the cold she often complains about. Thinking she's alone.

And then the Lincoln pulls up. One among the city's fleet of black Continentals that prowl the streets, chauffeuring bank tower barons and executive princes between their corner offices, restaurants, mistresses, the opera, and home again. This one, however, has come for Petra.

She snaps her cellphone shut and the back door is pushed open from within. A glimpse of black leather and capped driver behind the wheel. Petra seems to speak to whoever sits in the back seat for a moment. A reluctance that shows itself in her glance back at the doors to Grossman's – then she's spoken to from inside the car again. This time she gets in. The limo speeds away down a Chinatown side street with the assurance of a shark that has swallowed a smaller fish whole.

What stays with me about Petra's departure is how she left without saying goodbye. This, and how she entered the Lincoln as though she had no choice.

The rest of the Kensington Circle's final evening together goes on as one would expect. More drinks, more inevitable celebrity gossip, even some recommendations of good books we'd recently read.

One by one the circle dwindles as someone else announces they have to get up in the morning. I, of course, being recently liberated from professional obligation, stay on. Pitchers keep turning up that I manage single-handedly. I must admit that my farewells become so protracted that, by the end, I'm surprised to find Angela and I the last ones here.

"Looks like we're closing the place," I say, offering her what's left in my pitcher. She passes her hand over her glass in refusal.

"I should be getting home."

"Wait. I wanted to ask you something."

This is out before I know what's coming next. The sudden intimacy of sitting next to Angela has left me thrilled, tongue-tied.

"Your story. It's most ... impressive," I go on. "I mean, I think it's great. Really great."

"That's not a question."

"I'm just stalling for time. My therapist told me that among the first warning signs for alcoholism is drinking alone. That was my last visit to *him*, naturally."

"Can I ask you something, Patrick?"

"Fire away."

"Why do you think you were the only one in the circle not to have a story?"

"Lack of imagination, I guess."

"There's always your own life."

"I know I may *seem* rather fascinating. But, trust me, beneath this mysterious exterior, I'm Mr Boring."

151

"Nobody's boring. Not if they go deep enough."

"Easy for you to say."

"How's that?"

"That journal of yours. Even if only a tenth of it's true, you're still miles ahead of me."

"You make it sound like a competition."

"Well it *is*, isn't it?" I hear the squeak of self-pity in my voice that a cleared throat doesn't make go away. But there's no stopping me now. "Most great writers have had something *happen* to them. Something out of the ordinary. Not me. *Loss*, yes. Bad luck. But nothing *uncommon*. Which would be fine if you're just trying to stay out of trouble. But if you want to be an artist? Not so good."

"Everyone has a secret."

"There are exceptions."

"Not a surprise in you, not a single twist. Is that it?"

"That's it. A hundred per cent What-you-see-is-what-you-get."

It's a staring contest. Angela not just meeting my eyes but measuring the depth of what lies behind them.

"I believe you," she says finally, and drains the last inch of beer in her glass. "So here's hoping something happens to you sometime."

It's late. The band is packing up, the bartender casting impatient glances our way. But there's something in Angela's veiled intensity that holds me here, the suggestion of unseen angles she almost dares me to guess at. It reminds me that there is so

152

much I need to know. Questions I hadn't realized have been rolling around since the Kensington Circle's first meeting. In the end, I manage to voice only one.

"The little girl. In your piece. Is she really you?"

The waitress takes our empty glasses away. Sprays vinegar on the table and wipes it clean. Angela rises to her feet.

"Have you ever had a dream where you're falling?" she says. "Tumbling through space, the ground rushing up at you, but you can't wake up?"

"Yes."

"Is that falling person really you?"

Angela nearly smiles.

She slips her coat on and leaves. Walks by the window without turning to look in. From where I sit, she is visible only from the shoulders up, so that she passes against the backdrop of night like an apparition. A girl with her head down against the wind, someone at once plainly visible and hidden, so that after she's gone, you wouldn't be entirely certain if she was there at all.

PART TWO

The Sandman

13

Victoria Day Weekend

It's the fourth interview of the last five hours and I'm not sure I'm making sense any more. A *New Yorker* staffer doing a 2,000-word profile. A documentary crew from Sweden. *USA Today* wanting a "sneak peek" on what my next book is about.

"I'm retired," I insist, and the reporter smiles, as though to say *Hey, I get it. Us writers like to hold our cards close.*

And now a kid from the *National Star* who I can tell is planning a snark attack from the second he sits across from me and refuses to meet my eyes. A boneless handshake, dewy sweat twinkling over lips and cheeks. I vaguely remember him – a copy-editor who was very touchy about having grown up in Swift Current.

157

"So," he says, clicking the Record button on the dictaphone he has placed on the table. "You've been on the London *Times'* bestseller list since the pub date. Film deal with stars attached. And you've hit six weeks on the *New York Times* list. Was all this your plan from the beginning?"

"Plan?"

"To what extent were you aware of the market factors in advance?"

"I didn't really think about –"

"It's okay. There's no need to be defensive. I believe there should always be a place for pulp fiction."

"That's generous of you."

"I mean, your book – it's not *serious* or anything."

"Of course not. I wouldn't know serious if it kissed me on the lips."

The kid snorts. Flips his notebook closed.

"Do you really think you *deserve* all this? Do you think what you've done –"

He pauses here to toss my book on to the table like a turd he's only now realized he's been holding. "Do you actually think this *thing* is *literature*?"

His lips keep smacking, but no more words come. I watch as the visible effort of searching for the meanest thing he could say squeezes his forehead into red folds. As for me, I squint, making a show of searching through my memory. Click my fingers when it comes to me.

"Swift Current."

"What?"

"I couldn't get the accent at first. But I'm definitely certain now. Swift Current! Must have been such an exciting place to grow up. Exposed to all that *culture*."

I'll give the kid credit. After he storms toward the exit, but is forced to turn back to retrieve the still recording dictaphone that I hold out to him, he has the manners to say thank you.

The thing is, the kid was right to ask if I thought I deserved all this. Because the answer is no. And even as the publicist who's been shuttling me around in a limo from interview to bookstore to TV chat show fills my glass and Sam's with more sparkling water, I feel only the hollowness of the vampire, a man who has achieved immortality but at a monstrous cost.

"Are you nervous, Dad?" Sam asks.

More disgraced than anything. Disgraced and sorry.

"A little," I say.

"But this is your last reading, right?"

"That's right."

"*I'd* be nervous if *I* was you."

The two of us look out at Toronto passing by, at once familiar and new. A North American Everycity. Or Anycity. But this one happens to be home. The limo gliding past the cluster of glass condos and over the railyards toward Harbourfront, where in just a few minutes I, Patrick Rush, am to

159

give a reading from my embarrassingly successful first novel.

It was four years ago that the Kensington Circle gathered for the last time. Then, I was the only aspiring fictioneer among us who was without a story to tell. I never attended another workshop or writing class again. My dream of birthing a novel had been snuffed out once and for all. And I was grateful. Liberated. To be unburdened of an impossible goal is a blessing, believe me, though it admittedly leaves a few scars behind.

Yet here I am. Travel to the foreign nations whose languages my words have been translated into. Dinners and drinks with famous novelists – no, *colleagues* – I have long read and admired from afar. Invitations to write opinion pieces in publications I had previously received only junk mail from. The kind of breakthrough one is obliged to describe as "surreal" in one's *Vanity Fair* write-up, as I did.

And even today, on the occasion of my triumphant homecoming, when nothing I would have dreamed of has been denied me, I know that none of it is real.

"We're almost there, Mr Rush," the publicist says.

She looks concerned. More and more I'm lost in what she likely thinks are pensive moments of creativity, an artist's mulling. Maybe I should tell her. Maybe I should come clean, here in the plush confessional of a limo. And maybe I would, if Sam

160

weren't here. If I did, I'd tell her that my silences aren't caused by the churnings of the imagination. The truth is I'm just trying to hold the shame at bay long enough to get through the next smile, the next thank you, the next signature on the title page of a book that bears my name but isn't really mine.

Backstage I'm given bottled water, a bowl of fruit, a pee break. I'm told it's a full house, asked if I would answer questions from the audience following my reading. People would love to know what it's like to have a first book do what mine has done. I agree, I perfectly understand. I'd love to know the same thing.

Then I'm being guided down the hall into the darkened wings. Whispered voices tell me to watch my step. An opening appears in a velvet curtain and I step through, alone. There's my place in the front row. The publicist is in the seat next to Sam's, waving at me, as though there is some threat I might turn and walk out.

The director of the reading series appears at the lectern. He begins by thanking the corporate sponsors and moneyed donors who make such things possible. Then he starts on his introduction. A funny anecdote involving an exchange between himself and the featured author backstage just moments ago. I laugh along with everyone else, thinking how nice it would be if the charming guest he's just described actually existed. If he could be me.

And then I'm into dangerous territory again. Wishing Tamara were here. A wallop of grief that chokes the breath out of my throat.

"Ladies and gentlemen, without further ado, it gives me great pleasure to present Toronto's own Patrick Rush, reading from his sensational first novel, *The Sandman*!"

Applause. My hands raised against the spotlight in protest at too much love. Along with a private struggle to not be sick all over the front row.

Silence. Clear my throat. Adjust glasses.

Begin.

"There once was a girl who was haunted by a ghost …"

14

A plain envelope bearing a Toronto postmark. Inside, a newspaper clipping. No note attached. A piece from the *Whitley Register*, the local weekly of a northern Ontario town. A pin prick along the rugged, unpeopled spine of Lake Superior.

The story dated Friday, August 24, 2003.

CRASH KILLS TWO ON TRANS-CANADA

Author and Companion in 'Puzzling' Auto Accident

By Carl Luben, Staff Reporter

Whitley, Ont. – An automobile's crash into a stone cliffside on the Trans-Canada twenty minutes outside Whitley has resulted in the death of both its passengers early Tuesday morning.

Conrad White, 69, and Angela Whitmore (age unknown) are believed to have died on impact between the hours of 1 a.m. and 3 a.m. when their car left the highway. At press time, Ms Whitmore's place of residence has yet to be determined, but it is believed that Mr White's current address was in Toronto. It is unknown what purpose had brought them to the Whitley area.

Mr White is the author of the novel *Jarvis and Wellesley*, a controversial work at the time of its publication in 1972. He had been living overseas for the last few decades, and only recently returned to reside in Canada.

So far, the police have yet to contact Angela Whitmore's immediate family, as available identification did not contain next-of-kin information. Readers who are able to provide more information on Ms Whitmore's relations are asked to contact the Ontario Provincial Police, Whitley Detachment.

Police are still at work determining the precise cause of the accident. "It's a little puzzling," commented Constable Dennis Peet at the scene. "There were no other cars involved, and no skid marks, so the chances they went off the road to avoid colliding with an oncoming vehicle or animal crossing seems unlikely."

Investigators have estimated the car's speed on impact in excess of 140 km/hr. This velocity, taken together with the accident occurring along a relatively straight stretch of highway, reduces the possibility of the driver, Ms Whitmore, falling asleep at the wheel.

"Sometimes, with incidents like these, all you know is that you'll never know," Constable Peet concluded.

My first thoughts after learning of the accident weren't for the loss of the two lives involved, but who might have sent me the clipping. I was pretty sure it had to be someone in the circle, as my connection to Angela and Conrad White would have been known to few outside of its members. But, if one of them, why the anonymity? Perhaps whoever sent the envelope wanted to be the bearer of bad tidings and nothing more. Petra, maybe, who would feel obliged to share what she had learned, but didn't want visitors showing up at her door. Or Evelyn, who would be too cool to write a dorky note. And then there was the odds-on favourite: Len. He'd have the time to scour whatever obscure database allowed him to learn of such things, and would appreciate how leaving his name off the envelope would lend the message a mysterious edginess.

Yet these practical explanations inevitably gave way – as all speculations about the circle eventually did – to more fanciful theories. Namely, to William. Once he entered my mind, the secondary questions posed by the article came rushing to the forefront. What were Conrad White and Angela doing travelling together through the bush outside Whitley in the first place? And why did Angela drive off the highway sixty kilometres over the speed limit? By factoring William into these queries, the notion that he was not only the sender of the clipping, but somehow the author of the crash itself, became a leading, if unlikely, hypothesis.

It was only sometime later, sitting on my own in the Crypt, that the fact Conrad and Angela were dead struck me with unexpected force. I lowered the three-month-old *Time* I'd been pretending to read to find my heart drumrolling against my ribs, an instant sweat collaring the back of my neck. Panic. Out-of-nowhere, suffocating. The sort of attack I'd succumbed to on more than a few occasions since Tamara died. But this time it was different. This time, my shock was at the loss of two people I hardly knew.

Hold on. That last bit's not quite true.

It was the thought of Angela alone that stole all the air from the room. The girl with a story I would now never get to the end of.

After the night at Grossman's Tavern, the murderer I'd come to think of as the Sandman stopped killing. The police never arrested anyone for the deaths of Carol Ulrich, Ronald Pevencey and the Vancouver woman eventually identified as Jane Whirter. Though a $50,000 reward was offered for information leading to a conviction and occasional police press releases were issued insisting they were working on the case with unprecedented diligence, the authorities were forced to admit they had no real leads, never mind suspects. It was proposed that the killer had moved on. A drifter with no links to family or friends who would probably continue his work somewhere else down the line.

For a time, though, I couldn't stop feeling that the Pevencey, Ulrich and Whirter deaths were somehow connected to the circle. This is only a side effect of coincidence, of course. It's the ego-centric seduction of coincidence that personalizes larger tragedies, so that we feel what we were doing when the twin towers came down or when JFK was shot or when a serial killer butchered someone in the playground around the corner is, ultimately, *our* story.

I know all this, and yet even after the Sandman was declared to be retired I never believed he was finished. The dark shape I would sometimes catch in my peripheral vision could never simply be nothing, but was always the *something* of coincidence. The lingering trace of fate.

I spotted Ivan on Yonge Street once. Standing on the sidewalk and looking northward, then southward, as though uncertain which way to go. I crossed the street to say hello, and he had turned to look at me, blank-faced. Behind him, the lurid marquee of the Zanzibar strip club blinked and strobed.

"Ivan," I said, touching my hand to his elbow. He looked at me like I was an undercover cop. One he'd been expecting to take him down for some time. "It's Patrick."

"Patrick."

"From the circle. The *writing* circle?"

Ivan glanced over my shoulder. At the doors to the Zanzibar.

"Up for a drink?" he said.

We put the daylight behind us and took a table in the corner. The afternoon girls rehearsing their pole work on the stage. Adjusting their implants in the smoked mirrors. Smearing on the baby oil.

I did the talking. Asked after his writing (he'd been "sitting on" some ideas) and work ("Same tracks, same tunnels"). There was a long silence after that, during which I was waiting for Ivan to ask similar questions of me. But he didn't. At first I assumed this was a symptom of strip-bar shyness. Yet now, looking back on it, I was wrong to think that. It was only the same awkwardness I'd felt the first time I spoke with Ivan, when he'd confessed to having been accused of hurting someone. His loneliness was stealing his voice from him. Driving the underground trains, staring at the walls in his basement flat, paying for a table dance. None of it required speech.

I excused myself to the men's room, and to my discomfort, Ivan followed me. It was only standing side by side at the urinals that he spoke.

Usually, exchanges that take place with another fellow in such a context, dicks in hand, requires strict limits of the subject matter. The barmaid's assets or the game on the big screen are safe bets. But not Ivan's admission that he's been afraid to get close to anyone since he was accused of killing his niece fourteen years ago.

"Her name was Pam. My sister's first born," he started. "Five years old. The father'd left the year

168

before. Scumbag. So my sister, Julie, she's working days, and because I'm driving trains at night, she asks me to stay at her place sometimes to look after Pam. Happy to do it. The kind of kid I'd like to have if I ever had kids. Which I *won't*. Anyways, I was over at Julie's this one time and Pam asks if she can go down to the basement to get some toy of hers. I watched her run off down the hall and start down the stairs and I thought *That's the last time you're ever going to see her alive*. I mean, when you look after kids, you have these thoughts all the time. Yet this time I think *Well, that's it, little Pam is gone*, and it stuck with me a couple seconds longer than usual. Long enough to hear her miss a step. I go to the top of the stairs and turn on the light. And there she is on the floor. Blood. Because she came down on something. A rake somebody'd left on the floor. One of the old kind, y'know? Like a comb except with metal teeth. *Pointing up*. But that's not where it ends. Because Julie thinks I did it. The only family I got. So the police look into it, can't make any conclusions, they're suspicious but they've got to let it slide. But Julie hasn't spoken to me since. I don't even know where she lives any more. That's how a life ends. *Two* lives. It just happens. Except I'm still here."

He shakes. Zips. Leaves without washing his hands.

By the time I made it back to our table, Ivan is ordering another round. I told the waitress one was enough for me.

169

"I'll see you around then," I said to him. But Ivan's eyes remained fixed on the slippery doings onstage.

A few strides on I turned to wave (a gesture I hoped would communicate my need to rush on to some other appointment) but he was still sitting there, looking not, I noticed, at the dancer, but at the ceiling, at nothing at all. His hands hanging cold and white at his sides.

Len, the only one I'd given my home number to, called once. Asked if I wanted to get together to "talk shop", and for some reason I accepted. Perhaps I was lonelier than I thought.

I arranged to meet him at the Starbucks around the corner. As soon as the lumbering kid pushed his way through the doors I knew it was a mistake. Not that things went badly. We spoke of his efforts to give up on horror and "go legit" with his writing. He'd been sending his stories to university journals and magazines, and was heartened by "some pretty good rejection letters".

It was over the same coffee that Len shared the gossip about Petra. Her ex-husband, Leonard Dunn, had been arrested for a whack of fraud schemes, blackmail, and extortion. More than this, reports had suggested that Mr Dunn had close connections to organized crime. Len and I joked about Petra's Rosedale mansion standing on the foundations of laundered money, but I kept to myself my last glimpse of Petra outside

Grossman's, stepping into a black Lincoln she seemed reluctant to enter.

That was about it. Neither of us mentioned William or Angela or any of the others (I had not yet learned of the car accident outside Whitley). Even the apparent end to the Sandman's career was mentioned only in passing. It struck me that Len was as unsure of the police's presumption that we would never hear of him again as I was.

Afterwards, standing outside, Len and I agreed to get together again sometime soon. I think both of us recognized this as a promise best unkept. And as it turned out, it was only some years later, and under circumstances that had nothing to do with fostering a tentative friendship, that we saw each other again.

In interviews, I have repeatedly stated that I only started writing *The Sandman* after my severance pay from the *National Star* had run out, but this is not exactly true. If writing is at least partly a task undertaken in the mind alone, well away from pens or keyboards, then I had started filling in the spaces in Angela's story from the last night I saw her.

Even after the circle and the long, worried days that followed, even as the bank started sending its notices of arrears followed by their lawyers' announcements of foreclosure, some part of my mind was occupied in teasing out possible pasts and futures for the orphan girl, Jacob, Edra, and the terrible man who does terrible things.

It wasn't that these considerations were a comfort. It would be more accurate to say that I returned to Angela's story because I needed it to survive. To be present for my son, I required a fictional tale of horror to visit as an alternative to the real horrors that kept coming at us. I had Sam – but I was *alone*. We'd already lost Tamara. Now here goes the house. Here go Daddy's marbles. And I couldn't tell Sam about any of it.

This is how I thought *The Sandman* could save me. It gave me somewhere to go, something that was mine.

But I was wrong. It was never mine. And it could never save me.

The Sandman had plans of its own. All it needed me for was to set it free.

15

I admit to stealing Angela's story. Even so, it still wasn't a novel. While I used her characters, premise, setting, mimicked her tone, even copied whole pages from her recorded readings, viewed strictly on the basis of a word count, the bulk of *The Sandman* could technically be described as mine.

There was much I needed to add to give it the necessary weight of a book. Whatever it took to roll out what I already had with a minimum of actual *creating*, so that the result had been thinned to cover a couple hundred pages. But what the book still needed was the very thing Angela's story didn't provide. An ending.

After long months of scratching ideas on to index cards and dropping most of them into the recycling box, I managed to wring out a few concluding turns of the screw of my own, though there's little point in going into that here.

Let's just say I decided to make it a ghost story.

* * *

I knew it was plagiarism. There wasn't a moment I thought enough of *The Sandman* was invented that it could be truly considered my own. What relieved me of the crime was that I was only playing around. It was a distraction and nothing else. A kind of therapy during those hours when Sam was asleep, the TV spewed its usual rot, the sentences of my favourite books swam unreadably before my eyes.

Even when it was done, I still had no plans to present it as though I was its sole author. This was partly because I *wasn't*. But there was another reason.

I always saw the writing of the book as a kind of communication, an exchange between Angela and myself. I have read dozens of interviews with real writers who say that, throughout the process, they have in mind an audience of one for their work, an ideal reader who fully understands their intentions. For me, that's who Angela was. The extra set of eyes looking over my shoulder as the words crept down the screen. As I wrote our ghost story, Angela was the one phantom who was with me the whole time.

And then I started wondering if it might not be good. Our book. Angela's and mine. Except Angela was dead now.

What would *someone else* think of what we'd made together?

But even this self-deceiving line of thought wasn't my undoing. My real mistake was printing it out, buying envelopes to slip it into, and telling myself *I'm just curious* as I dropped them in the mail addressed to the biggest literary agents in New York.

That was a mistake.

16

I say now what all those in my position say in response to the most commonly asked question of the after-reading Q&A: *I had always wanted to be a writer*. But in my case, this answer is not precisely true. I had wanted to write, yes, but more primary than this, I had always wanted to be an *author*. Nothing counted unless you were published. I longed to be an embossed name on a spine, to belong to the knighthood of those selected to stand alongside their alphabetical neighbours on bookshop and library shelves. The great and nearly so, the famous and wrongly overlooked. The living and the dead.

But now, all I wanted was to be out of it.

What had seemed so important then now struck me as a contrivance, an invention whose purpose was to complicate that which was, if left alone, cruelly simple. *Life's a bitch and then you die,* as the T-shirts used to say.

I would make do with keeping both hands on the wheel of fatherhood, with weekend barbecues and package beach holidays and rented Westerns and Hitchcock. I would no longer feel the need to *say something*, to stand isolated and furious outside the anesthetized mainstream. Instead I would be among them, my consumer brothers and sisters. The search called off.

There are times I'm walking with Sam, or reading to him, or scrambling an egg for him, and I will be seized mid-step, mid-page-turn, mid-scramble, with paralytic love. For his sake, I try to keep such moments under control. Even at his age he has a keen sensitivity to embarrassment, and me blubbering about what a perfect little fellow he is, how like his mother – well, it's right off the chart. Not that it stops me. Not every time.

It is these pleasures that *The Sandman*'s publication has denied me. All the attention afforded the break-out first novelist – the church basement talks, forty-second syndicated morning radio interviews ("So, Pat, *loved* the book – but, let me ask you, who do you like in the Super Bowl?"), even a few bedroom invitations (politely declined) from book club hostesses and college campus Sylvia Plaths – was poisoned by the fact that I was alone, miles from my son.

"Where *are* you, Dad?" I remember Sam asking over the phone at one of the campaign's low points.

177

"Kansas City."

"Where's that?"

"I'm not sure. Kansas, maybe?"

"*The Wizard of Oz.*"

"That's right. Dorothy. Toto. Over the rainbow."

There was a silence for a time after that.

"Dad?"

"Yes?"

"Remember when Dorothy clicked her heels together three times? *Remember?* Remember what she said?"

That *The Sandman* wasn't my own book didn't help things. Just when a glowing review or snaking bookstore line-up or letter from a high school kid relating how much he thought I was *the shit* came close to making me forget, Angela's recorded voice reading from her journal in Conrad White's apartment would return to me, and any comfort the moment might have brought was instantly stolen away.

There was also the worry I would be found out. Although I hadn't heard from any of them since *The Sandman* was published, it was entirely conceivable that one of the Kensington Circle would come across it, recognize its source material, and go to the press. Perhaps worse, Evelyn or Len would come knocking on my door with my book in their hands, demanding hush money. Worse yet, it would be William. And I would pay no matter who it was. I'd done a wrongful thing. I'm not denying it. But if there was ever a victimless crime, this was it. Now, in order to walk quietly away from my fraudulent, non-starter of a writing career as planned, four people had to keep a secret.

When I finally returned to Toronto, I went through the mail piled on my desk in the Crypt expecting at least one of the envelopes to contain a blackmail letter. But there was only the usual bills.

Life returned to normal, or whatever shape normal was going to take for Sam and me. We watched a lot of movies. Ate out at neighbourhood places, sitting side by side at the bar. For a while, it was like a holiday neither of us had asked for.

And the whole time I waited to walk into someone from the circle. Toronto is a big city, but not so big that you could forever avoid the very people you'd most like to never see again. Eventually, I'd be caught.

I started wearing ballcaps and sunglasses everywhere I went. Took side streets. Avoided eye contact. It was like being followed by the Sandman all over again. Every shadow on the city's pavement a hole in the earth waiting to swallow me down. And what, I couldn't help wondering, would be waiting for me at the bottom?

17

I raise my eyes from the page. Squint into the lights. Dust orbiting like atoms in the white beams. If there are people out there, I can't see them. Perhaps they have learned that I'm not what I've claimed to be, and have left the hall in disgust. Perhaps they are still here, waiting for the police to click the cuffs around my wrists.

But they are only waiting for me. For the words every audience to Angela's story requires to lift the spell that's been cast on them.

"Thank you," I say.

Yellow, flickering movement like the beating of hummingbird wings. Hundreds of hands clapping together.

Sam is there at the side of the stage, smiling at his dad with relief.

I pick him up and kiss him. "It's over," I whisper. And even though there's people watching, he kisses me back.

"We should make our way to the signing table," the publicist says, taking me by the elbow.

I put Sam down to be driven home in the waiting limo and let the publicist guide me through a side door. A brightly lit room with a table at the far end with nothing but a fountain pen, bottle of water and a single rose in a glass vase on its surface. A pair of young men behind a cash register. Copies of *The Sandman* piled around them in teetering stacks. A cover design I've looked at a thousand times and a name I've spelled my whole life, but it still looks unfamiliar, as though I'm confronting both for the first time.

The auditorium doors are already opening as I make my way around the velvet ropes that will organize the autograph seekers into the tidy rows that always make me think of cattle being led to slaughter. In this case, all that will await them at the end is me. My face frozen in a rictus of alarm, or whatever is left of the expression that started out a smile.

And here they come. Not a mob (they are *readers*, after all, the last floral-skirted and corduroyed, canvas bag-clutching defenders of civilization) but a little anxious nevertheless, elbowing to buy their hardcover, have me do my thing, and get out before the parking lot gets too snarled.

What would this labour feel like if the book were wholly mine? Pretty damn pleasant would be my guess. A meeting of increasingly rare birds, writer and reader, acknowledging a mutual engagement in a kind of secret Resistance. There's even little side servings of flirtation, encouragement. Instead, all I'm doing now is defacing private property. More vandal than artist.

I'm really going now. Head down, cutting off any conversation before it has a chance to get started. All I want is to go home. Catch Sam before Emmie puts him to bed. There might even be time for a story.

Another book slides over the table at me. I've got the cover open, pen poised.

"Whatever you do, just don't give me the 'Best Wishes' brush-off."

A female voice. Cheeky and mocking and something else. Or perhaps missing something. The roundness words have when they are intended to cause no harm.

I look up. The book folds shut with a sigh.

Angela. Standing over me with a carnivorous smile on her face. Angela, but a different Angela. A professional suit, hair expensively clipped. Confident, brisk, sexy. Angela's older sister. The one who didn't die in a car crash with a dirty old novelist, and who could never see the big deal about wanting to write novels in the first place.

You're dead, I almost say.

"What, no 'How's the writing coming?'" the living Angela says.

"How's the writing coming?"

"Not as well as yours, by the looks of things."

The publicist makes an almost imperceptible side-step closer to the table. The woman next in line behind Angela shuffles forward. Coughs more loudly than necessary. Taps the toe of a Birkenstock on the floor.

Angela remains smiling, but something changes in her pose. A stiffening at the corners of her mouth.

"Have you –?" she starts, and seems to lose her thought. She bends closer. "Have you *seen* any of them?"

"A couple. Here and there."

Angela ponders this response as though I'd answered in the form of a riddle. The woman behind her takes a full step forward. Her reddening face now just inches from sitting atop Angela's shoulder.

"Perhaps you'd like to speak to Mr Rush *after* the signing?" the publicist says, as pleasantly as an obvious warning could be stated.

"I think –" Angela starts again. I wonder if she is steeling herself to launch some kind of attack. Slap me across the face. Serve a court summons. But it's not that. With her next words she reveals that she isn't angry. She's frightened.

"I think something's … *happening*."

The publicist tries to squeeze between Angela and the table. "May I *help* you?" she asks, reaching toward Angela's arm. But Angela rears back, as though to be touched by another would burn her skin.

183

"Sorry. Oh. I'm *sorry*," she murmurs, nudging the book another inch closer to me. "I suppose I should have this signed."

Now the entire line is getting antsy. The woman behind Angela has come around to stand next to her, an act of rebellion that threatens to create a second line. Fearing the chaos that would result, the publicist pulls back the cover for me, holds the book open to the title page.

"Here we are," she says.

I sign. Just my signature at first. Then, seeing this as too hopelessly impersonal, I scribble a dedication above my name.

> *To the Living,*
> *Patrick Rush*

"Hope you enjoy it," I say, handing the book back to Angela. She takes it, but remains staring at me.

"I'm sure I will," she says. "I'm particularly intrigued by the title."

The Birkenstock woman has heard enough. Drops her copy on to the table from three feet in the air. A single crack on impact that draws gasps from the line.

At the same time, Angela grips the front of the table with her free hand. Whispers something so low I rise out of my chair to hear her.

"I need to *talk* to you," she says. Opens the palm of her hand so that I have to reach into it and take the card she's offered me.

Then all at once she pushes aside the publicist who attempts to usher her toward the exit, makes her way unsteadily around the corner and is gone.

"I liked it," the Birkenstock woman says when my hands steady enough to open her copy. "Didn't totally buy the ending, though."

PART THREE

Story Thieves

18

You wouldn't say climate is Toronto's strong point. Not if you appreciate seasons as they are normally understood as quarters of transition. Instead, the city endures long months of swampy, equatorial heat, and longer months of ear-aching cold, each separated by three pleasant days in a row, one called spring, the other fall.

This morning, for instance, the clock radio woke me with news of the fourth extreme heat alert so far this year, and it is only the first week of June. "Emergency Cool Down Centres" have been established in public buildings, where wanderers can collapse on to chilled marble floors until nightfall. The general citizenry has been advised not to go outside, not to allow the sun to touch its skin, not to move, not to breathe. These are empty warnings, of course, as people still have to work and, worse, *get* to work. After I've dropped Sam off at the daycare, I make my way back along Queen, lines of sweat trickling down my chest, glaring at the passengers on the stalled streetcar, all of them struck in poses of silent suffering.

From here I turn up toward College, past the semi-detached Victorians, each with their own knee-high fencing protecting front lawns so small you could mow them with a pair of tweezers. I stick to the shady reach of trees as best I can. But the heat isn't the only thing that slows my steps: I'm on my way to meet Angela.

The card she'd slipped into my hand at the Harbourfront book signing was blank aside from a scribbled cellphone number, and beneath it, a plaintive *Call Me*. I didn't want to. That is, I was aware that pursuing any further contact with a woman I had actionably wronged and who, if published reports were to be believed, was no longer among the living, could lead to nothing good.

Even now, my legs rubbery from the heat, zigzagging up the sidewalk like some midday boozer, I'm not sure why I called. It must have been the same impulse that had me press the Record button the first time I heard her read. The reason I kept going back to the circle's meetings when it was clear they were of no use. The ancient curse of the curious, the Nosey Parkers, the natural-born readers.

I needed to know.

We decided to meet at Kalendar, a café where we can sit outside. Now, selecting the one remaining table (only half covered by the awning's shade), I wish we'd opted for a cellar somewhere instead. I'm here first, so I take the darker chair. Later, when the sun slides to a new angle that allows it to fire lasers through the side of my head, and the chair across the table from mine is comfortably shielded, I will realize the error of my positioning. But for the time being, I order an intentionally fun-free soda water, believing I am still in control of the events barrelling my way.

At first, when a young woman arrives and, spotting me, comes over with a shy smile below her State Trooper shades, I assume it's a fan. Over the last few months, it has become not entirely uncommon for strangers to approach and offer a word about *The Sandman*. Some will stick around for more than this – the lonely, the tipsy, the crazy. And I'm trying to decide which this one is when she joins me at my table. I'm about to tell her I'm sorry, but I'm waiting for someone, when something in her face changes, a trembling strain at the tops of her cheeks, and I see that it's not a stranger at all.

"I guess we've never seen each other in the light of day," Angela says, studying me. It makes me wish I'd brought sunglasses of my own.

"You're right. We haven't."

"You look different."

"That's just heat stroke."

She looks at my soda water. "Are we having real drinks?"

"We are now."

Once a shot of vodka has been added to my drink and a glass of white wine placed next to Angela's hand, we talk a little about how she's spent the last few years. Following a period of clerical odd-jobbing, she decided she needed something more permanent. She went back to community college and came out with a certificate in legal administration, which landed her a position as an assistant at one of the Bay Street firms. It was this job she was stealing an extra hour away from, having told her boss she had a dental emergency.

"That's why I can afford to have a couple of these," she says, raising the glass of wine to her lips. "Laughing gas."

The waiter arrives to take our order. Angela asks for some kind of salad and I have what she's having (my nerves won't let me eat, only drink, so it doesn't much matter what prop is put in front of me). When he leaves, Angela looks at me. That same measuring gaze I caught her at a couple times in the circle. I don't get up and walk home, or turn my face away, or run to the men's room to hold my wrists under the cold water tap (all things I'd like to do). She knows too much already. My crime, of course. But other things as well. What had she whispered to me when she appeared out of nowhere, risen from the dead?

Something's happening.

Yet for a time the sun, the rare treat of dining outside in the middle of the day, the first edge-numbing blur of alcohol leaves us chatting like a pair on a blind date, one that has so far gone better than expected. In fact, Angela seems almost pleased to be here. It's as though she is a prison escapee who'd never guessed she'd have gotten as far as she has.

Our salads appear. Aggressively healthy-looking nests of radicchio, beets and chickpeas. Normally the sort of thing I'd lay a napkin over to not have to look at, let alone eat. But the illusion of immunity has given me a sudden appetite. I swing my fork down, and it's on its way mouthward as Angela speaks the words I thought we'd decided to leave alone.

"I read your book."

The fork drops. A chickpea makes a run for it.

"Well, yes. Of course you would have. And I suppose you saw that I ... borrowed certain elements."

"You stole my story."

"That's debatable, to a point. I mean, the construction –"

"Patrick."

"– required a good deal of enhancement, not to mention the invention required in –"

"You *stole my story*."

Those sunglasses. They keep me from seeing how serious this is. Whether I am to now endure merely hissed accusations, or whatever wine is left in her glass thrown in my face, or worse. A knife impaling my hand to the table. The naming of lawyers.

"You're right. I stole your story."

I say this. I'm forced to. But I'm not forced to say what I say next. It comes with the unstoppable breakdown, the full impact of facing up to the person you've done injury to, sitting three feet away.

"I just wanted to write a book. But I didn't *have* a book. And then I heard you read at Conrad's and it wouldn't leave me alone. Your journal, novella, whatever – it became an obsession. It had been a while since my wife died – oh *Christ*, here we go – and I needed something. I needed *help*. So I started writing. Then, when I found out about your car accident, I thought … I thought it was more *ours* than just *yours*. But I was wrong. I was wrong about all of it. So now … *now*? Now I'm just sorry. I'm really, really sorry."

By now a few heads have turned our way. Watching me blowing my nose on the napkin I steal from under the next table's cutlery.

"You know something?" she says finally. "I rather enjoyed it."

"*Enjoyed* it?"

"What it said. About you. It made you so much more *interesting* than before."

"What I wrote."

"What you *did*."

My puzzled look nudges Angela further.

"In the circle, you were the only one without a story to tell. Most people at least *think* they have stories. But you assumed all along that there wasn't a character-worthy bone in your body.

194

And then what do you do? You steal mine. Tack on an ending. Publish it. Then regret all of it! That's almost *tragic*."

She takes the first bite of her salad. When the waiter comes to check on us (a look of phony concern for me, the messed-up guy with the already sunburning forehead) Angela orders another round for both of us. There is no talk of retribution, settlements, public humiliation. She just eats her salad and drinks her wine, as though she has said all she needs to say about the matter.

When she's finished her meal she sits back and takes me in anew. My presence seems to remind her of something.

"I guess it's your turn to get an explanation," she says.

"You don't have to tell me anything."

"I don't *have* to. But you probably deserve to know how it is that I'm not dead."

She tells me she heard about Conrad dying with a girl in a car accident, a girl believed to be her. Angela had been seeing him a bit at the time ("He was doing a close reading of my work") and left her purse in his car – which is how the authorities established their identification of the remains. The police didn't look into it much further than this, and had little reason to. The female body had been especially savaged in the crash, so there was no apparent inconsistency between it and the photos on Angela's ID. The accident was circumstantially odd, but there was no evidence of foul play. The presumed victim, Angela Whitmore, was known to have moved around a lot over the preceding years, job to job, coast to coast and back again, so that the authorities weren't surprised they couldn't discover her current address, as she likely didn't have one. Her relationship with Conrad White wasn't looked into either. The old man had a history of enjoying the company of much younger women. It was likely that Conrad and Angela had set out on some cross-country journey together, a sordid, *Lolita*-like odyssey, and hadn't made it through the first night on the winding highway through the Ontario bush.

After she has related all this to me, Angela's posture changes. Shields her face from the street, hiding behind her hair. The playful ease with which she'd introduced and then promptly dismissed the topic of my story-theft has been replaced with a stiffened back.

"So if it wasn't you, who was in the car with him?"

Angela's hands grip the table edges so tight her knuckles are pale buttons.

"Nobody's certain," she says. "But I'm pretty sure it was Evelyn."

"*Evelyn?*"

"They were hanging out together a lot around the time of the circle. And she was coming around to his apartment even after the meetings stopped."

"Were you *following* her?"

"If anything it was *her* following *me*." Angela lifts her wine glass but her shaking hand returns it to the table before taking a sip. "I was there too sometimes. For a while I liked the attention. Then it just got weird. I stopped going. But before I did, Evelyn would come by. I didn't stick around long whenever she showed up. It didn't feel like she was too happy to see me."

"Did you get a sense of why she was seeing him?"

"Not really. It felt like a secret, whatever it was. Like they were working on something together."

"And that's why you think it was her body in the car."

"I looked into it a bit more. After the initial report in the local paper –"

"The clipping you sent to me."

Angela cocks her head. "I didn't send you anything."

"Someone did. In the mail. Unsigned."

"That's how I first found out about it too."

I can't help wanting to know more on this point – if she didn't send the clipping, then who did? – but diverting her any further might shut her down completely. Already she's looking at her watch, wondering how much longer she has.

"Okay, so you followed up," I say.

"Because I thought it was Evelyn, but wasn't sure. And then, in one of the reports, it mentioned that the only distinguishing feature on the female victim's body was a tattoo. A raven tattoo."

"On the back of her wrist. I remember."

"I know I should have come forward. Evelyn probably has family who are still looking for her. They must think she's disappeared."

"So why didn't you?"

"At first, I think I saw it as a chance to just, I don't know, *lose* myself. Be erased. Start over. You know what I mean?"

"It's not too late. You could tell the police now. Straighten it all out."

"I can't do that."

"It's not like you did anything wrong."

"That's not why."

"I don't understand. Someone dies – an acquaintance of yours dies with your name on her toe tag, and you're letting the people who care about her live with the lie that she might still be out there? That Evelyn might be *alive*? I'm not taking any moral high ground here – you know I can't. But what you're doing is hurting others who've got nothing to do with you."

Angela takes off her sunglasses. Pupils darting from one peripheral to the other. Her voice had almost managed to disguise her panic. Now it's her eyes that give her away.

"After the accident, I took on different names," she says. "Changed where I lived, how I looked, my job. It was like I'd disappeared. And I *needed* to disappear."

"Why?"

"Because I was being *hunted*."

The waiter, who has been watching us from the opposite side of the patio for the past few minutes, drifts over to ask if he can bring us coffee or dessert.

"Just the cheque," Angela says, abruptly pulling open her purse.

"Please. This is on me," I say, waving her off, and the enormous understatement of the gesture, under the circumstances, brings a contrite laugh from my throat. But Angela is too agitated to join me in it.

"Listen, Patrick. I don't think I can see you again. So I better say what I came to say."

She blinks her eyes against the sun that is now cast equally on both of us. For a second I wonder if she has forgotten, now that she's come to it, what the point she wanted to deliver actually was. But this isn't what causes her to pause. She is only searching for the simplest way to put it.

"Be careful."

"Of what?"

"He was only watching before. But now ... now it's *different*."

The waiter delivers the bill. Stands there long enough that I have to dig a credit card out of my wallet and drop it on the tray before he reluctantly moves away. In the meantime, Angela has gotten to her feet.

"Wait. Just *wait* a second. Who's 'he'?"

"Do you really think you're the only one?"

"What are you saying?"

"The Sandman," she says, and disappears behind her sunglasses once more. "He's come back."

19

The next morning I refuse to let my thoughts return to my lunch with Angela other than to remind myself that she has no apparent plans to sue me. This is *a good thing*. As for the other stuff – I do my best not to go there.

What's needed are rituals. New habits Sam and I can set about repeating so that they will blaze a trail to follow over the days to come. Starting with food. Instead of the improvised meals we have been surviving on – willy-nilly take-out, tins of corner-store glop, Fruit Loops – I set out with Sam to lay in proper stock.

We drive down to the supermarket by the harbour, where the warehouses and piers are being turned into nightclubs and condominiums. This is where we shop, or used to shop. It's been a while.

Yet here it all is, the pyramids of selected produce, the microwavable entrées, the aisles of sustenance for those who needn't look at price tags. Sam and I drop items in our basket as they glide by. The outrageous bounty of North American choice.

"This is why the rest of the world hates us," I tell Sam. He looks up at me and nods, as though he were having precisely the same thought.

Later, down in the Crypt, our purchases stocked away, I sit at my desk and realize that I have no work to do. No freelance assignment, no novel-in-progress, no review deadline. There's still an hour to kill before lunch, and I click on the computer to indulge in a moment of virtual masturbation: I Google myself.

As always, the entry at the top of the list is my official website. The creation of my publisher's marketing department, www.patrick.rush.com features a Comment section I sometimes visit. The correspondents generally represent one of two extremes: gushing fan or crap-taking critic. The latter favours the sort of spluttering, all-lower-case tirade that soils the screen for a few hours before the Webmaster gets around to striking it from the record. This morning, however, there's something waiting there of an altogether more disturbing nature.

Not an incoherent screed, not a copyedit nit-pick, not a demand for money back. Just a single word of accusation.

Thief.

The correspondent's name is nowhere to be seen. There's only his or her *nom-de-blog*: **therealsandman**.

It could be only coincidence – the specificity of the allegation, the timing of Angela's belief that the Sandman has returned, the identity implied by the name – but I'm certain it's someone who *knows*.

I immediately write back in reply. This requires the creation of a blog identity of my own: **braindead29**.

Why are you afraid to use your real name?

Reading the question over, I see how it's too clear and benign for blogspeak. I make a go at translation.

why r assholes like u 2 afraid to use your reel name?????

Better.

I press Send. Lean back in my chair, confident **therealsandman** will shrink at this direct challenge. But my reply comes within seconds.

You don't know what afraid is yet.

Looking back on it, I wasn't all that surprised when Angela showed up at my book signing table, even though, being deceased, her appearance was an impossibility. Maybe this came from writing about a ghost so much over the preceding years. I've simply gotten used to seeing the dead.

Or maybe not.

This afternoon, while Sam is at his Summer Art Camp in Trinity-Bellwoods fingerpainting or rehearsing a play or writing a poem, I walk up to Bloor Street to buy a book. I may not be able to write any more, but that shouldn't stop me from reading. I'm thinking something non-fictional, a dinner-party talking point (in case I'm ever invited to a dinner party). The melting of the polar ice caps, say, or the emergence of nuclear rogue states. Something light.

I head into Book City with the idea that my earlier efforts at living a normal day may not have been entirely derailed by my encounter with **there-alsandman**. The sheer hopefulness in the stacks of new releases and the customers opening the covers to taste the prose within fills me with a sense of fellowship. It is here, among the anonymous browsers, that I belong. And where I might be allowed to return, once I can slip back into being another bespectacled shuffler, instead of someone, like Angela, who believes they are being hunted.

I'm halfway to convincing myself when I see him.

I have side-stepped my way past New Fiction and headed straight for the Non-Fiction Everyone's Talking About! table at the back. When I pick up my first selection, I hide behind the cover and allow myself a furtive scan of the shop. Right away I notice a man with my book in his hands. In profile, backlit by a sun-bleached Bloor Street through the display windows. *The Sandman* open a hundred pages in, the man's face showing a grimace of disapproval. Conrad White. My writing instructor. Not at all happy with the published results of his worst student.

He turns his head.

An abrupt twist of the neck that allows his hollow eyes to find me instantly. His features shifting, forming deep creases over his ashen skin. A look of reproach so fierce it gives the impression of a snarling animal.

It takes a second to remember he's dead.

That's when my free hand pushes the books to the floor. A pile of travel guides tumbling over the table's edge. A flailing collapse that leaves me sprawled out, trying to push myself up from the slippery paperbacks.

"My God, are you okay?" a clerk asks, rushing out from behind the cash register.

"I'm fine. I just ... sorry about ... I'll pay if there's any ..." I stammer, looking to where Conrad White was standing.

But there's nobody there now. The book he'd been reading left at a crooked angle atop its stack.

Once, having been recognized, I've declined the clerk's invitation to read his own novel-in-progress ("What I *really* need are *connections*, y'know?")

I skulk out of the bookstore into the foul heat. The foreign students and Chardonnay hippies of the Annex pass me by as I stand there, disoriented, trying to figure my east from my west. In my hand, a bag carrying my guilt purchase: the first book I grabbed off the check-out counter, which turned out to be empty and untitled. A journal that the clerk guessed was meant to help with my next book.

"There won't *be* another book," I blurted.

Now, on the walk downtown to pick up Sam, I wonder again if my seeing ghosts is a symptom of a more serious condition. Untended sorrow allowed to turn into a full-blown psychotic break. Acute post-traumatic stress, perhaps (what is the loss of your wife, your career and the defilement of your sole ambition, if not trauma?) Maybe I need help. Maybe it's too late.

Yet the old man had looked so *real*, just fifteen feet away, with none of the foggy edges or spectral floating attributed to most apparitions. It was Conrad White, dead and *looking* dead. But there nevertheless.

Once I've entered the relative cool of the trees in Trinity-Bellwoods, I've decided that if my sanity has to go, it's my job to keep its absence to myself. Sam has already lost one parent. He's got to be better off with a mad father looking over him than none at all.

I come to stand on the other side of the temporary fence the playground has put up around the kids' Art Camp, watching Sam read a book in the

205

pilot's seat of a plane made of scrap wood. He raises his eyes from the page and looks my way. I wave, but he doesn't wave back. I'm sure he's seen me, and for a moment I wonder if I'm confused as to whether that's Sam in there or not. And then I remember: my son is entering the age when your parents are embarrassing. He doesn't want the other kids to see that's his dad over there, waving, clutching a goofy book bag.

But on the walk home he offers an alternative explanation. Sam hadn't waved because there was a strange man staring at him from the other side of the fence.

"That was me."

"Not *you*, Daddy. I saw *you*. The other man. *Behind* you."

"There wasn't anyone behind me."

"Did you look?"

"What do you want for dinner?"

"*Did* you? Did you see –"

"We've got chicken, lasagne, those tacos-in-a-box thingies. C'mon. Name your poison."

"Okay. Burgers. *Take-out* burgers."

"But we bought all those groceries this morning."

"You asked."

After dinner, I check the phone for messages. Three telemarketers, a hang-up, two complete strangers asking if I'd forward their manuscripts to my agent, and Tim Earheart wondering if the "great novelist" wanted to "come out and get shitfaced sometime".

As well as Petra Dunn, the Rosedale divorcée from the circle. Saying she's sorry, she doesn't want to impose, but she thinks it's important we talk.

I take down her number but decide not to call back tonight. A retreat to bed is my best bet. Tuck Sam in, scan a few paragraphs of something and, if precedent holds, I'll be sent off to a dreamless nothing. Trouble is, I didn't end up buying a book to *read* this afternoon, but a book to *write* in.

This may be breaking a promise I've made to myself, but I figure there can't be much harm in just making notes. I take a pen and the journal under the sheets with me and start scribbling. Jotted points covering the events since Angela showed up at my book signing, and then jumping back to the beginning of the circle, my first encounter with the Sandman's story, and here and there over the period of time of the killings four years ago. Not really writing at all, but a compiling of facts, impressions. If I have angered the gods for being a story thief, surely there can be no offence in this, the unadorned chronicling of my own life.

Even in this I'm wrong.

A sound from downstairs.

Something that awakens me from that in-between state of nodding off without being aware that this is what you're doing. A bang. Followed by a millisecond of reverberation, which confirms that whatever it was, it's of sufficient weight to rule out the usual bump-in-the-night suspects, *a creak of the floorboards* or *mice between the walls*. My first thought is it's a bird that's mistaken the clear surface of the sliding back doors for night. And it might have been a bird, if it weren't for the sound that follows. The cry of fingernails scraped over glass.

I slip on the boxers and T-shirt left in a pile next to the bed and check on Sam. Still asleep. I pull his door shut and shuffle to the top of the stairs. Only the usual peeps and sighs of an old house. Miles off, a low rumble of thunder.

Downstairs, there's no sign of disturbance. But why would there be? If someone has forced their way into our home with an intent to do us harm, there'd be little point in overturning a side table or shattering the hall mirror along the way. Still, there's a comfort in seeing Sam's playground sneakers sitting side by side on the mat, the stack of envelopes on the bottom step ready to be tossed in the mailbox in the morning. What evil could possibly be strong enough to pass these talismans?

At the base of the stairs, I move as quietly as I can toward the living room at the rear of the house. From here, I can see a sliver of the sliding glass doors that open on to the deck. The rain has started, slow and dense as oil. A soft drumming on the roof.

Then the rain turns to silver.

The motion-sensor lights I had put in last week activated by something in the yard. Not the rain (they're designed to ignore it), or moving branches (there is no wind). Something large enough to be spotted. Moving from one part of the property to the other. Something I can't see.

I run to the kitchen and pull a pair of scissors from the butcher's block, hold them out in front of me as I dash to the glass doors. The lights flick off before I get there. Just three seconds of brightness. Why had I told the guy who installed them to set the timer for *three seconds*? Not long enough to catch a raccoon's attention, let alone thwart a break-in. But I remember now: I hadn't wanted it to wake up the neighbours. That this is the very point of such devices must have been lost on me at the time.

I unlock the door and slide it open. Thrust the scissors out first, as though to sink the blades into the body of rain.

Once outside, the downpour instantly seals my T-shirt to my skin. I keep moving on to the deck. At its edge, I come into range of the motion sensors and the floodlights come on. The back yard suddenly ablaze, so that everything – the thirsty lawn, weed-ridden flower beds running along the fence, the leaning garden shed in the back corner – is translated from grey outlines to harsh specifics. Nothing else. Nothing out of place.

Three seconds later, the lights are off. The yard expanded by darkness.

Waving my arm over my head, I activate the sensor again. Everything as it was. The curtain of rainfall. The dim shape of neighbouring houses.

I have done my duty. Two a.m. and all's well. Time to go back inside, grab a towel and count sheep.

But I don't.

Absently this time, I lift my arm high, the scissors held skyward. And once more the lights come on.

To show someone standing in the yard.

A man with his back against the far fence, next to the garden shed. His face shielded by the over-hanging branches of the neighbour's willow. Arms loose at his sides. And at the end of those arms, the creased gloves of his hands.

The lights flick off.

There is no way I could swing my arm up again if it weren't for Sam. My son, asleep in his bed upstairs. Counting on me to keep the bogey-man away. It's the thought of Sam that turns the lights on.

But the yard is empty. It's only the same sad square of real estate as before, a neglected garden and shed with cobwebs sprayed over its window. And no one standing by the back fence. If he was here at all, the terrible man who does terrible things is gone.

20

After seeing a ghost reading my book, after my lunch with Angela, after glimpsing a monster in my own back yard, you'd think I'd be packing up and moving me and Sam to a different time zone by now. But the events of the past few days have instead provided the answer to an age-old question: Why do characters in horror movies go back into the haunted house one more time, even when the audience is shouting *Run! Start driving and* keep *driving!* at the screen? It's because you don't know you're *in* a horror movie until it's too late. Even when the rules that separate what is possible from what is not start to give way, you don't believe you're going to end up as just another contribution to the body count, but that you're the hero, the one who's going to figure out the puzzle and survive. Nobody lives their life as though they've only been cast in a grisly cameo.

And besides, in my case it's not the house that's haunted. It's me.

* * *

When I called Petra back she sounded as though she couldn't remember who I was.

"Patrick Rush," I said again. "From the writing circle. *You* called *me*."

"Oh yes. I wonder if you could come around later this afternoon?"

"I wouldn't mind knowing what this is about."

"Say five o'clock?"

"Listen, I'm not sure I —"

"Great! See you then!"

And then she hung up.

I know the sound of someone pretending they're speaking to someone else on the phone (I'm friends with Tim Earheart, after all, surely one of the best multiple-affair managers in contemporary journalism). But what reason would Petra have to conceal my identity from whoever was in the room with her?

Coming out the doors of the Rosedale station I recall my conversation with Ivan in this same place. It makes me wonder if he is still driving trains underground, still writing about his imaginary metamorphosis, still alone. He might well have been behind the controls of the train that brought me here. The thought of it starts a shiver up my back in the hot sunshine. It's not necessarily the idea of Ivan himself that does it, but that if Angela and now Petra have come looking for me, how far behind could Ivan and Len be? And if these two wait for me down the line, why not William too?

"Patrick?"

I turn around to find Petra jogging in place. Brand-new trainers on her feet. Hair tied back under a Yankees cap.

"I should warn you, I'm not in the greatest shape."

"Sorry," she says, and stops hopping. "I usually go for a run around this time, so I figured I'd come meet you here instead of at the house."

"We're not going there?"

"It's best if we don't."

She gives me a pleading look, as though it's possible that I might not only deny her request, but take her forcibly by the arm and drag her home. I've seen versions of the expression on Petra's face before, though not among society divorcées but the bruised faces of women outside the shelters downtown. Women who have been conditioned to be pleading with all men, and to expect the worst anyway.

"Where would you like to go?"

"Down in the ravine. That's where I run," she says. "It's cooler in the shade."

"And more private."

"And more private. Yes."

I gesture for her to lead on, and she starts over the bridge that crosses the tracks. As she goes, she glances over her shoulder every few steps. We are exposed at every angle – to people exiting the station, the traffic on Yonge, as well as the tree-shrouded windows of the mansions that sit along the crest of the ravine. It makes Petra move fast.

213

When she pushes through the brush on the other side of the bridge and rustles down an overgrown trail, I lose her for a couple minutes. But when I break through the patches of wild raspberry at the bottom she's waiting for me.

"I forgot to thank you for coming," she says.

"You made it sound like I had no choice."

"It's not only for my benefit."

Petra walks further along the trail. We carry on like this until the trees become thicker where the ravine opens wide. When we've come along far enough that we can see there's no one for a couple hundred yards in either direction, Petra stops. Turns to me with an agitated expression, as though she hadn't expected to find me following her.

"I don't have a lot of time," she says. "My schedule is pretty much set. And people notice if I make any changes to it."

"People?"

"My personal life," she says vaguely.

Petra puts her hands on her waist and bends over slightly, taking deep breaths as though she's come to the end of her run and not the start of it.

"There's a man who's been watching me," she says finally.

"Do you know who it is?"

"The same person who's been watching all of us."

"Us?"

"The circle. Or some of the circle. Len, Ivan, Angela."

"You've *spoken* with them?"

"Len contacted me. He told me about the others."

The entirety of our conversation to this point has taken less than a minute but it feels much longer than that. It's the effort required in shielding my surprise from her.

"I'm guessing you think it's the Sandman," I say, trying to sound doubtful.

"It's occurred to me, yes."

"This is crazy."

"Are you saying you haven't seen him?"

"I'm saying I have. That's what's crazy."

Petra checks the trail again. I can see her figuring how much longer she has before she should be opening her door and wiping the sweat from her eyes.

"I suppose you've read my book," I say.

"*Your* book?"

"Okay. The book with my name on it."

"I've seen it. Picked it up in the store a couple times. But I don't want it anywhere near me."

Petra looks suddenly lost. It's my turn to say something to keep her here.

"Who was in the limo that picked you up from Grossman's that night?"

"I'm not sure that's any of your business."

"It wasn't. But that was before you told me we're being followed by the same person."

For a second I'm sure Petra is going to walk away. But instead, she comes to some decision in her head. One that brings her a step closer to me.

"My ex-husband's business required his involvement in things that weren't entirely conventional."

"Judging by your house up that hill, it seemed to be working for him."

"Still is."

"So was that him in the limo?"

"It was Roman. Roman Gaborek. My husband's business partner. *Former* business partner."

"A friend of yours."

"My boyfriend. Or something like that. He's who I left my husband for. But my husband doesn't know that. If Leonard knew that I was seeing Roman, it would be bad for everyone."

"Jealous type."

"Leonard *owns* people."

"So maybe he's the one who you've seen around your house."

"It might be. And sometimes it *has* been. But I don't think it's who we're talking about right now."

"Why not?"

"Because this man … he's not *right*."

From somewhere behind us there's the scurrying of something in the underbrush. The sound makes Petra jump back, hands raised in front of her. Even when she realizes there's nobody there, she remains coiled.

"If it is the Sandman, why *now*?" I say. "What brought him back?"

"What do you think?"

"My book."

"Yours. Hers. Whoever's."

Although responding to a signal only she can hear, Petra turns and starts off down the trail, deeper into the humid shade of the ravine. A light, prancing jog at first, then picking up the pace, her arms pumping. By the time she turns a corner and disappears she's running as fast as she can.

The orange sky of a smog-alert dusk has darkened into evening. An hour when most of the suits and skirts are safely locked in their air-conditioned condo boxes, and the others, averse to sunshine, spill out of the dumpster alleys and piss-stained corners. The last four blocks along Queen to my house are predominately populated by the troubled and addicted at the best of times, but tonight there are even more of them milling about. It's because they're *visitors*. Even homeless junkies can be summer tourists, checking to see what the big-city fuss is all about. One toothless beauty who staggers into me takes special offence when I refuse her request for change. "But I'm on *vacation*!" she protests.

That makes two of us. I'm certainly not working any more. After the author tour for *The Sandman* was completed, my plan went no further than a retreat from occupation, from doing. Perhaps this was a mistake. Perhaps the idleness of the past few weeks has left a space open for unwanted elements to enter. How else to explain the return of the Kensington Circle to my life?

Of course I do have a job. A single purpose I committed myself to after Tamara died: to bring up Sam. Be a good father. Share my few good points and try to hide the legion deficiencies.

And yet now, my single responsibility has turned from nurturing my son to protecting him. If there is something wretched that my wretched book has brought into the world, then the vacation is over. My job is now the same as the girl's in Angela's story who tried to keep a threat from the only ones she loved. To make sure that, if it comes for us, it touches only me, not him.

I make the turn on to Euclid and once more there's a sense that something isn't right. No police tape this time, no pursuer making me run for my front door. But there's a lightheaded pause nevertheless, a sudden churning of nausea. A sensation I'm beginning to associate with being close to *him*.

Where's Sam?

He's at home with Emmie. Sam is fine.

So why am I running? Why do I have the keys out of my pocket, the sharp ends poking out between the knuckles of my fist? Why, when my house comes into view, is there the outline of a man standing in the front window?

He sees me coming and stays where he is. Watches me slide the key in and open the door.

The front hallway is dark. He hadn't turned the lights on, hadn't needed to. He knew where he wanted to go.

I round the corner of the dining room where the front window looks on to the street. The room is empty. Nothing to hide behind. From here I step back into the hallway to check the rear of the house. The kitchen drawers closed, nothing unsettled on the counters. And the living room as it was left as well.

I'm about to make my way upstairs when a lick of breeze turns my attention to the sliding doors. Open. What I'd seen at first as glass now revealed as the intruder's means of entry.

But it doesn't mean he left by the same route. It doesn't mean he's not in the house.

"Sam?"

I take the stairs three at a time. Slapping at the wall as my feet skid out on the landing. My shoulder crashing into my son's bedroom door.

"*Sam!*"

Even before I look to see if he's in his bed, I check the window. *Blood tattooed on the curtains.* But it's closed, the curtains untouched. His bed made, just as he'd left it this morning.

Then I remember. He's over at his friend Joseph's across the street. A birthday party. Sam's not here because he's not *supposed* to be here.

I cross the hall and grab the phone. Joseph's mother answers.

"I just … the back door … could you *please* put Sam on?"

Half a minute passes. Something is wrong. All that's left is for Joseph's mother to come back on

219

the line and say, *That's funny. He was here with the other kids the last time I checked.*

"Dad?"

"Sam?"

"What's going on?"

"Are you inside?"

"That's where the phone is."

"Right."

"Where are you?"

"At home. There was ... I forgot to ... Oh, *Jesus* ..."

"Can I go now?"

"I'll come pick you up when the party's over, okay?"

"I'm across the *street*."

"I'll pick you up anyway."

"Sure."

"Bye, then."

"Bye."

Whoever was standing in the window had got the right house this time. But it was the *wrong night*.

Luck. Who'd have thought there'd be any left for me, after all my undeserved laurels, my devil deals? Yet Sam is alive. Eating cake and horsing around in my neighbour's basement.

It's time, however, to get some help. Not of the psychiatric variety (although this seems increasingly inevitable) but the law. There's no more room to wonder if the Sandman is real or not.

There was someone in my *house*. And now it's time to bring in the guys with badges and guns.

But before I can pick up the phone, it starts to ring.

I look up to see that my bedroom curtains are drawn open. Left that way from this morning when I'd pulled them wide to let the light in. But now, at night and with the bedside lamp on, I would be visible to anyone on the street.

The phone keeps ringing.

If I'm about to speak to the terrible man who does terrible things, I can't help wondering what words he wants to share with me.

"Hello?"

"Mr Rush?"

Some sort of accent.

"If this is about your goddamn manuscript, I can't help you. Now if you don't mind stuffing your precious –"

"I've got some bad news for you, Mr Rush."

"Who *is* this? Because I know he's safe, alright? So if you're –"

"I think there's some confusion here –"

"– trying to threaten me, I'll call the police. You hearing me?"

"Mr Rush – *Patrick* – please. This is Detective Ian Ramsay, Toronto Police Services. I'm calling about your friend, Petra Dunn."

A Scottish lilt. The giveaway of an immigrant who's been here for the better part of his life but

221

still hasn't wholly lost the accent of the homeland. It distracts me for a moment, so that when he speaks his next words, I'm still trying to guess whether he'd more likely be from the Edinburgh or Glasgow side of things.

"We believe she's been murdered, Mr Rush," he says.

21

The police, when they arrive, take the form of a single man, a tall plainclothesman with bright green eyes that suggest one needn't take him too seriously. A moustache that seems an afterthought, an obligatory accessory he'd be more comfortable without. I've never been around a real detective before, and I try to prepare myself to be at once cautious and relaxed. And yet his open features, along with finding myself a couple inches wider than he (I'd expected a broad slab of recrimination), instantly make me feel that no real harm can come from this man.

"I'm here about the murder," he says, with practiced regret, as someone in coveralls might arrive at the door to say *I'm here about the cockroaches*.

I extend my arm to invite him in and he brushes past, makes his way directly into the living room. It's the sort of familiar entrance an old friend might make, one comfortable enough to go straight for the bar and not say hello until the first gulp is down.

When I follow him in, however, Detective Ramsay hasn't helped himself to a drink, but is standing in the centre of the room, hands clasped behind his back. He gestures for me to sit – I take the arm of a ratty recliner – while remaining standing himself. Even being half-seated, however, concedes the weight advantage I'd briefly held. For what might be a minute, it seems I'm of little interest to him. He looks around the room as though every magazine and mantelpiece knickknack were communicating directly to him, and he wants to give each of them the chance to speak.

"Are you a married man, Mr Rush?"

"My wife passed away seven years ago."

"Sorry to hear that."

"Yourself?"

He raises his hand to show the gold band around his ring finger. "Twenty years in. I tell my wife a fellow does less time for manslaughter these days."

I try at a smile, but it doesn't seem that he's expecting one.

"Someone told me you're a writer."

"I'm out of it now," I say.

"Going into a new line of work, are you?"

"Not decided on that yet."

"Would've thought the writing life would be close to ideal. No boss, set your own hours. Just making things up. Not work at all, really."

"You make it sound easier than it is."

"What's the hard part?"

"All of it. *Especially* the making things up."

"It's a lot like lying, I imagine."

He steps over to the bookshelf, nodding at the titles but seemingly recognizing none of them.

"I'm a pretty avid reader myself," he says. "Just crime novels, really. Can't be bothered with all that Meaning of Life stuff." Detective Ramsay turns to look at me. His face folds into a disapproving frown. "Can I ask what you find so funny?"

"You're a detective who only reads detective novels."

"So?"

"It's ironic, I guess."

"It is?"

"Perhaps not."

He returns his attention to the shelves until he pulls out my book.

"What is it?" he says.

"I'm sorry?"

"What *kind* of book is it?"

"I'm never quite sure what to say to that."

"Why not?"

"It's tricky to categorize."

Detective Ramsay opens the back cover to look at the author's photo. Me, looking grumpy, contemplative, air-brushed.

"That title's quite a coincidence," he says.

"Yes?"

"The Sandman killings a few years ago. I was the lead investigator on that one."

"Really."

"Small world, isn't it?"

"I suppose, on some level, the title was inspired by those events."

"Inspired?"

"Not that what the murderer did was *inspirational*. I mean it only in the sense that it gave me the idea."

"What idea?"

"The *title*. That's all I was talking about."

His eyes move down and at first I wonder if there's a stain on my shirt. Then I realize he's looking at my hands. I resist the reflex to slip both of them in my pockets.

Ramsay brings his eyes up again. Repeatedly lifting and lowering my book as though judging its merits based on weight alone.

"Mind if I borrow this?"

"Keep it. There's plenty more in the basement."

"Oh? What else have you got down there?"

It's only the laugh he allows himself after a moment that indicates he's joking. In fact, everything he says in his half-submerged brogue could be taken as a dry joke. But now I'm not sure any of it is.

"I need to run through your day with Ms Dunn," he says, putting my book down on a side table and producing a notebook from his jacket pocket.

"It wasn't a *day*. I was with her for twenty minutes at most."

"Your twenty minutes then. Let's start with those."

I tell him how Petra left a message with me the night before, asking to speak in person. The next morning I returned her call, and we arranged to meet at her house at five o'clock. On my way out of the subway she was there, wearing running attire and a Yankees cap. Reluctant to go to her house, she guided me into the ravine. She told me of her concerns about a man who seemed to be following her, someone she'd spotted outside her house at night. She was frightened, and wanted to know if I had noticed a shadow after me as well.

"And have you?" Detective Ramsay says.

There is a point in the telling of every story where the author becomes his own editor. Not *everything* is included in an accounting of events, no record the complete record. Even the adulterer who cannot live with his conscience excludes the smell of his mistress' perfume from his confession. Nations at war provide casualty numbers, but not a tally of missing arms versus legs. Deception, in the active sense of distorting the facts, may not be the cause of these absences. Most of the time it is a matter of providing the gist without inflicting undue pain. It's how one can be truthful and keep secrets at the same time.

This is how I later came to justify my telling Detective Ramsay, No, I haven't been followed, don't know what Petra was talking about in the ravine at all. Even as I take this path I'm aware it may be the wrong one. The police could be the only ones to keep me and Sam safe at this point. But there is something that makes me certain that such disclosure would only make me next. If I am being watched by the Sandman as closely as it feels I am, then I have every intention to play by his rules, not the law's.

Not to mention that I'm starting to get the feeling I may be a suspect in Petra's murder. Trust me on this: one's instinct, in such cases, is to withhold first, and figure out if this was a good idea later.

"So why'd she call you?"

"I suppose it was because of the writing circle we were in together. Years ago. She was trying to draw a connection between us, my book, the concerns she had about a stalker. It was rather vague."

"Vague," he says, pausing to reflect on the word. "Tell me about this circle."

So I do. Give him all the names, the little contact information I have. Again, I decide to leave a couple things out. My meeting with Angela, for instance.

"Just want to confirm the sequence of events with you," he says. "You met with Ms Dunn around five o'clock. Is that right?"

"A couple minutes before five, yes."

"And you left her in the ravine twenty minutes later."

"Give or take."

"You walked home after this?"

"Yes."

"Did you talk to anyone? Stop anywhere?"

"I had a drink in Kensington Market."

"Where, exactly?"

"The Fukhouse. It's a punk bar."

"You don't look the part."

"It happened to be on my way."

"Would anyone recognize you from The Fukhouse?"

"The bartender might. Like you say, I don't look the part."

"When did you arrive home?"

"It was evening. Some time after nine, I guess."

"That's when you called over to the neighbour's to check on your son."

"Yes."

"Did you have any particular reason to be concerned for your son's safety?"

He was standing in my window.

"I'm a widower, Detective. Sam is the only family left to me. I'm never *not* concerned for his safety."

He blinks.

"That's a long walk," he says. "Even with a couple of drinks."

"I like to take my time."

"You might be interested to know that Mrs Dunn disappeared some time between your meeting with her and eight o'clock. Two and a half hours or so."

"Disappeared? I thought you said she was murdered."

229

"I said that's what we *believe*."

How could I have gotten this guy so wrong? The combination of Ramsay's leftover Scots accent and droll demeanour had me thinking that if they really suspected that I could have done whatever was done to Petra, they would have sent over one of their hard cases. But now I see that Ramsay *is* a hard case.

"Do you know of anyone who would have a motive to do this to your friend?" he asks absently. "Aside from her shadow?"

"I'm not her friend. *Wasn't*. I barely knew her."

"'Not friend'," he says, scribbling.

"As for motive, I have no idea. I mean, she mentioned her divorce, and how she was seeing her ex-husband's business partner. It seemed like a delicate situation."

"This is during your twenty minutes in the ravine?"

"It wasn't much more than a name."

"And what name would that be?"

"Roman. The boyfriend. Roman somebody. Petra was concerned that if her relationship with him came to her ex's attention, it would cause her some inconvenience."

"Roman Gaborek."

"That's him."

"Did your friend mention that Mr Gaborek and Mr Dunn are both leaders among the local organized crime community?"

"She alluded to it."

"Alluded. She *alluded* to it."

"That's right."

"It's a funny thing," he says, flipping his note-book closed. "Most of the time, people who hear about something like what you've just heard about ask how it was likely done. But you haven't asked me a thing."

"I don't have much of a stomach for violence."

"It's a good thing you didn't ask me then. Because Ms Dunn, she met with *considerable* violence."

"I thought there was no body."

"But what the body *left behind* – well, it was indicative of certain *techniques*. Reminded me of four years ago. Remember?"

If one were to enter this room right now, one might mistake Detective Ramsay's expression as showing how much he enjoys moments like these. But I can see that it's not pleasure so much as rage. An anger he's managed to disguise, over the years, as something near its opposite.

"Well, that's it," he says. I rise and offer a hand to be shaken, and when he finally takes it, the grip is ruthless.

"Hope I was of some help."

"If you weren't, you might yet be."

Ramsay goes to the door to let himself out and I follow, suddenly desperate to hear the click of the bolt closing behind him.

"One last thing. The cap you say Ms Dunn was wearing when she met you …"

231

"Yes?"

"What team was it again?"

"The Yankees. Why?"

"Nothing. They just never found a cap, Yankees or otherwise."

He opens the door and steps outside. Before he closes it, he shows me a smile. One he's saved right for the end.

The morning brings a funny thought: I'm about to be famous all over again. Whenever they come for me and I make the shackled walk from police cruiser to courtroom, cameras whirring, reporters begging for a quip from the Creep of the Day for the suppertime news.

Then the clock radio clicks on. And I have the same thought all over again.

It's the morning news telling the city that Petra Dunn, forty-five, was abducted yesterday in the Rosedale ravine. Evidence at the scene strongly supports foul play. Police are currently questioning a number of "persons of interest" in connection to the crime.

Person of interest, that's me. Yesterday morning I got out of bed an unemployed pseudo-novelist, and just twenty-four hours later I'm facing a new day as the prime suspect in a probable homicide. But it doesn't stop there. Because if Detective Ian Ramsay thinks I did in poor Petra Dunn, it follows that I did in Carol Ulrich, Ronald Pevencey and Jane Whirter four years ago too.

Angela may have been right. The Sandman's come back. And as far as best guesses go, it's me.

"Dad?"

Sam standing in my bedroom doorway.

"Just had a bad dream," I say.

"But you're *awake*."

He's right. I'm awake.

The first thing I do, once I've showered and shaved, is take Sam to stay with Stacey, Tamara's sister in St Catharines. On the hour's drive there I do my best to explain why a policeman came to talk with me last night, and why it's best if the two of us are separated for a while. I tell him how sometimes people get caught up in things they have nothing to do with, but that they must nevertheless endure questions about.

"Process of elimination," Sam says.

"Kind of, yeah."

"But I thought it was 'innocent until proven guilty'."

"That's only in courtrooms."

"Does this have to do with your book?"

"Indirectly, yes."

"I never liked your book."

Of *course* he's read it. Although forbidden to do so, how was he *not* going to read his father's one and only contribution to the bookshelf? I can't know how much of it he's able to understand – a gifted reader, but still only eight years old – yet it appears he's gathered the main point. The Sandman of *The Sandman* is real.

Once home, I leave a message on Angela's machine, asking her to get back to me as soon as possible.

Waiting for her return call, I consider how many in the circle have already been in contact with each other. After the night at Grossman's, I just assumed all of us went our separate ways. But there may have been relationships formed I had no inkling of at the time. Lovers, rivals, artists and their muses. The sort of passions that have been known to give rise to the most horrific actions.

To kill the time, I check back on the Comment page at www.patrick.rush.com. Once more, it mostly shows the same obsessives debating the finer points of *The Sandman*'s plotlines, unearthing inconsistencies, along with differing personal impressions of the author ("He signed my book and asked if I was a writer too. And I AM! It was like he READ MY MIND!!" vs "actually saw PR on queen street the other day, trying (but failing) to look like a 'normal guy', walking with a bag of groceries(!?) pretentious twat!").

I'm about to log off when the cursor finds the day's most recent entry. Another bulletin from **therealsandman**:

One down.

Angela gets back to me. She has to work late tonight, but can meet me later on. For some reason I insist it be at her place (which she reluctantly agrees to). After she hangs up, I realize I need to see wherever she lives in order to make sure she's real.

I'm set to arrive at Angela's around eight, which gives me time to put in a call to the only number other than hers I have from the circle. Len.

"The police just left," he says, skipping over hello, as though only a day sits between now and our last conversation instead of years. "Did you hear what happened to Petra?"

"I heard. Was the man you spoke to named Ramsay?"

"I was too freaked to really listen. Kind of a funny guy."

"Yeah?"

"Like funny strange and funny ha-ha at the same time."

"That's him."

I would walk to Len's apartment in Parkdale but the heatwave has once again broken the temperature record it set the day before, so I head west along King in the Toyota with the windows down. I turn left toward the lake, into one of the blocks of stately family homes long since cut up into dilapidated rooming houses. Len's building looks even worse than the others. The paint peeling off the porch in long curls.

The front windows obscured by pinned-up flags, tin foil and garbage bags in place of blinds.

Len has the attic flat. The side entrance is open as he said it would be and I climb up the narrow stairs past the suffocating assaults of hash smoke and boiled soup bones and paint thinner seeping out from under the doors.

Rounding the corner to the last flight, I look up to see Len waiting at the top. The big doofus stooped in the doorframe, spongy with sweat but otherwise looking relieved to see me.

"It's you," he says.

"Were you expecting somebody else?"

"The thought had crossed my mind."

Len's apartment is a single room. A small counter, hotplate and bar fridge in one corner, a bare mattress on the floor, and the only natural light coming from two windows the size of hardcover books, one facing the street and the other the yard. The severely sloped ceiling drops on either side from a beam that cuts the space in half, which allows Len to stand straight only when situated in the middle of the room. On the walls, movie posters bubbled with moisture. *The Exorcist*, *Suspiria*, *Night of the Living Dead*. The floor strewn with laundry that smells of a battle between deodorant and old socks.

"Have a seat," Len offers, scooping a pile of paperbacks off a folding chair. It leaves him to sit cross-legged on the floor. An over-heated kid ready for storytime.

"So, how have you been?"

"Okay. Not writing much. I haven't been able to think straight for a while now. It's hard to write spooky stuff when you're living spooky stuff."

Over Len's shoulder, stacked atop makeshift shelves made of milk crates, I notice my book. The cover tattered, the pages within fattened by greasy-fingered rereadings.

"I couldn't sleep for a week the first time I read it," Len says, following my gaze.

"Sorry."

"No need to be. The best parts weren't yours."

"No argument there."

Len glances at the door, as though to make sure it's locked. All at once the haggard, skittish look of him reveals he's been cooking away up here far longer than is healthy.

"When was the last time you went outside?"

"I don't like to go out much any more," he says. "It's like when you have a sense that you're being watched, but when you turn there's nothing there? I have that all the time now."

"Did you tell Ramsay about it?"

"No. It's a secret. A *secret agent* secret. You tell and you're dead."

"I know what you mean."

"He asked about you."

"What did he want to know?"

"If you had any relationship with Petra outside the circle. What I thought of you."

I keep my eyes on Len as he selects what to reveal. He doesn't seem the sort of man who can stand too much pressure, so I do my best to apply some in my stare.

"I told him you were my friend," he says finally.

"That's it?"

"I don't *know* anything else."

"Aside from the source for my book."

"Aside from that."

"And?"

"And I didn't tell him about it."

"Who else have you spoken to?"

"Petra called. Angela, too. She told me about Conrad's accident. Even Ivan came round just the day before yesterday. All of them scared shitless."

"Not William?"

"Are you kidding? The day that guy looks me up it's time to move."

All at once, the stifling heat in the room closes in on me. There isn't half enough air for two sets of lungs to live on, and Len is getting most of it anyway, panting like an overfed retriever.

"Angela told you about Conrad's accident?"

"I told you she did."

"But did she tell you that anyone *else* was in the car when he died?"

"*Was* there someone else?"

"No. No, there wasn't," I say, banging my head on the ceiling when I stand. "Sorry, but I'm late for another meeting."

"Who with?"

"Angela, actually."

"She must be pissed with you."

"Apparently she's decided to let it slide."

Len scratches the islands of beard along his jawline.

"I want to show you something," he says.

Len uncrosses his legs and rolls over the floor to the milk-crate shelves. His thick fingers plow through the piles of comics, digging down into the wreckage of toppled towers of books. By the time he finds what he's looking for his T-shirt is black with perspiration.

He scrambles over on hands and knees to where I'm standing and hands me a book. A literary journal I have heard of, *The Tarragon Review*. One of the dozens of obscure regional publications that print short stories and poems for readerships that number as high as the two figures.

"You in this?" I ask, expecting Len is trying to show off his first appearance in print.

"Check out the table of contents."

I read every title and author on the list. None of it rings a bell.

"Look again," Len urges. "The names."

The second time through I see it. A short story titled "The Subway Driver". Written by one Evelyn Sanderman.

"San-der-man. Sand-man. See?"

"Are you saying Evelyn wrote this?"

"At the back," Len says, excited now. "The Contributors' Notes."

The journal's last pages feature short biographies of the volume's writers, along with a black-and-white photo. At the entry for Evelyn Sanderman the following paragraph:

Evelyn is a traveller who is fascinated by other people's lives. "There is no better research for a writer than to get close to a stranger," she tells us. This is Evelyn's first published story.

Next to this, a photo of Angela.

"When was this published?"

"Last year."

"And why do you have it?"

"I subscribe to *everything*," he says. "I like to follow who's getting published and where. It feeds my jealousy, I guess. Some mornings it's the only thing that gets me out of bed."

Len is kneeling before me now, looking crazed with the heat, the rare visit of human contact. The sharing of a plot twist.

"Can I borrow this?"

"Go ahead. I kind of want it out of here anyway," Len says, eyes ablaze with the narcotic rush of fear.

"The Subway Driver" is good. The critic in me insists on getting this said upfront. A totally different voice from the one who told the story in Angela's journal. This time, the narrative tone is chillingly anesthetized, a man transported through a crowded urban environment, unnoticed and hazy as a phantom. But there are also moments of heartbreaking despair that cut through to the surface. Not Angela's voice at all, or any other strictly fictional creation. It's because the voice belongs to someone real. To Ivan.

As the title partly suggests, "The Subway Driver" is a day in the life of an unnamed man who speeds a train through the underground tunnels during the day, and scratches at chronically unfinished stories at night. What really takes me by surprise, though, the revelation that leaves me shaking in the front seat of the Toyota where I'm parked outside Len's rooming house, isn't this blatant borrowing from the biography Ivan presented to us during the Kensington Circle's meetings, but the private backstory, the tragic secret I assumed he had shared only with me.

At points in the main narrative, the Ivan-character reflects on the accidental (or not) fall of his niece down his sister's basement stairs. The same event he related to me standing at the urinals in the Zanzibar. Even some of the details, the very phrasings (as best as I recall them) make their way into Angela's text.

Her name was Pam ... I watched her run off down the hall and start down the stairs and I thought That's the last time you're ever going to see her alive ... *One of the old kind, y'know? Like a comb except with metal teeth ... That's how a life ends.* Two *lives. It just happens.*

She must have learned Ivan's secret on her own. He *told* her.

And she used it. Used him.

The address Angela gave me included a security code number for her condominium in one of the tall but otherwise nondescript towers of grey metal and glass that have weedishly cropped up around the baseball stadium. I would never have known how to ring her otherwise, as her number isn't listed next to Angela Whitmore, but Pam Turgenov. The name of Ivan's dead niece.

Once she's buzzed me in I take the elevator up, each blinking floor number to the twenty-first ratcheting up the rage within me. Flashpoints bursting into flame.

She is a liar.

A threat to me.

To Sam.

And then:

It wasn't me. It wasn't my book. She has taken my old life away from me.

I've never felt this way before. This angry. Though anger seems to have little to do with what I'm feeling now. It's too soft, a mood among moods. This is *physical*: an electric charge crackling out from my chest. A clean division between a thinking self and an acting self.

Angela left her door open. I know because when I take a running kick at it, the handle crunches into the plaster of the interior wall.

The acting part of me lunges at her.

The thinking part takes note of the cheap furniture, the curtainless picture windows looking west over the lake, the rail lines, the city's sprawl to the horizon. The day's heat hanging over everything.

Angela might have said something before I slammed into her but it made no impression. No words escape her lips now, in any case. It's because I've taken her by the throat. My thumbs pressing down. Beneath her skin, something soft gives way.

Then I'm lifting her up and throwing her on to the sofa. Straddling her hips. Putting all my weight on to my locked arms so that they stop any sound coming from her.

Screaming into her with a voice not my own.

I don't know what you want. I don't know who you are. It doesn't matter. Because if I see whoever you've got tailing me anywhere near my house or my son again, I'll fucking kill you.

Her body spasms.

You getting this? I'll fucking kill you.

I keep my grip on her throat and feel Angela's body yield beneath me. I already *am* killing her. There is a curiosity in seeing how the end will show itself. A final seizure? A stillness?

It's you.

I'm letting her go. That is, I must have let her go, as she appears to be making an attempt to say something.

"I thought you were too … *simple*. But that's the kind of person who does this sort of thing, isn't it? The blank slate."

"It's not *me*."

"You didn't know what you were doing just now. You were a different person. Maybe that person is the one who killed Petra."

Angela struggles to stand. Moves away from me without taking her eyes off my hands.

"*I'm* the one being followed," I say.

"You nearly *strangled* me!"

"Because you're fucking with me. My son."

"Fuck you!"

The exhaustion hits us both at the same time. Our feet dance uncertainly under us, as though we are standing on a ship's deck in a storm.

"Just answer me this. If you're so innocent, why are you hiding behind someone else's name?"

"To stay away from him."

She tells me how she's seen him from time to time. Ever since the Kensington Circle stopped meeting. Someone who would appear across the street from the building where she worked, her different apartments over the years, watching through the window of a restaurant as she ate. Always in shadow. Faceless.

It was the Sandman who forced her into changing her name, her appearance and her job *before* she learned of Conrad White and Evelyn's accident. Afterward, it only let her disappear that much more easily.

"Did disappearing involve sending out stories under pseudonyms?"

"Pseudonyms?"

"Evelyn Sanderman. Pam Turgenov. Who else have you been?"

Angela crosses her arms. " 'The Subway Driver'."

"And very fine it is. Though not entirely yours."

"What you did, you did it to be recognized."

"That's not true."

"No?"

"I did it to have something that was mine."

"Even if it wasn't."

"Yes. Even if it wasn't."

"That's not what interests me."

"What does?"

"People," she says. "*People* are my interest."

It was Angela's belief that no matter how many times she changed her life – or sent her writing out under others' names – he will eventually find her. Most recently, on the same day she had lunch with me, she went to get into her car in an underground parking lot to find a message written on her windshield in lipstick. *Her* lipstick. Taken from where she left it in her bathroom.

"He's been *in* here?"

"And he wants me to know he has. That he can come back whenever he wants."

"What did it say? On your windshield?"

"*You are mine.*"

At first, she thought his surveillance was meant only to threaten her. There was, she supposed, a pleasure he took in knowing her life was shrinking into little more than the exercise of nerves, the fidgety survival instincts of vermin. Now, though, she thinks there is also a logical purpose to his reminders: the traces he leaves may one day work to implicate her. Eventually something of his will stick, and it will be taken as hers. Just as I have begun to think of myself as suspect instead of victim, so has she.

As if to confirm this very thought, I look past Angela's shoulder and notice something on the kitchen counter. Angela turns to look at it too.

"Where'd you get that?" I say.

"It was stuffed in my mailbox this morning."

"It's a Yankees cap."

"Another one of his messages, I guess. Though I can't figure out what it means. Are you okay? You look like you're going to pass out."

I've got both my hands clenched to the back of a chair to hold myself up. The room, the city outside the window, all of it teeter-tottering.

"That cap," I say. "It's the same one Petra was wearing when she disappeared."

Angela looks at me. A wordless expression that proves her innocence more certainly than any denial she might make. Even the greatest actors' performances show signs of artifice at their edges – it's what makes drama dramatic. A little something extra to

246

reach all the way to the cheap seats. But what Angela shows me is so confused, so without the possibility of consideration that it clears any residue of suspicion I held against her.

"It's going to be alright," I say, taking a step closer.

"Who is *doing* this?"

"I don't know."

"Why *us*?"

"I don't know."

Outside, the sky dulls as it begins its fading increments of dusk, and beneath it the city takes on an insistent specificity, the streets and rooftops and signage coming into greater focus. Both of us turn to take it in. And both of us thinking the same thing.

He's out there.

The grid patterns of skulking traffic, the creeping streetcars, the pedestrians who appear to be standing still.

He's one of them.

I wake in the night to the digital billboards along the lakeshore flashing blues and reds and yellows over the ceiling. Money lights.

Sitting up straight against the headboard, I watch Angela sleep, her body curled and still as a child's. I haven't been with another woman since Tamara died, and it's funny – perhaps the funniest of all the funny revelations of this day – that it is Angela whose hair I stroke back from her face as she sleeps.

I watch her for a time. Not as a lover watches his beloved in the night. I look down on her shape as a non-presence, a netherworld witness. A ghost.

But a ghost that needs to go to the bathroom. I fold back the sheet from my legs and slide to the bottom of the bed. Angela's bare feet hang over the side. Pale, blue-veined.

I'm about to lift myself from the mattress when something about these feet holds me still. Three missing toes. The littlest piggy and the two next to it nothing more than healed-over vacancies, an unnatural rounding of the foot that sends a shiver of revulsion down to where my own toes touch the floor.

Angela may go by any number of different names, but the absent digits of her foot tie her to an unmistakable identity. The little girl in her story. The one who lost the same toes to frostbite when she slept overnight in the barn when her foster father disappeared into the woods.

That girl, the one with an unspeakable secret.

This girl, sleeping next to me.

22

This may be hard to believe, to accept as something that a person in a real situation would do (as opposed to what I am unfortunately *not*: a character in a story), but the reason I don't ask Angela, having seen her diminished foot, if she is, in fact, the grown-up version of the little girl in her journal of horrors, is that I don't want her to think I am so unsophisticated a reader. To assume that missing toes prove that whatever happened to the Sandman's girl was autobiography and not fiction – a fiction that, like all fiction, is necessarily made of stitched-together bits of lived as well as invented experience – would reveal me as that most lowly drooler of the true-crime racks, the literal-minded rube who demands the promise of Based on a True Story! from his paperbacks and popcorn flicks: the *unimaginative*.

And why do I care if she held this impression? Pride, for one thing. I may be a charlatan author, but I'm still a *good reader*. Still on the endangered species list of those who know it is only foolish gossip to connect the dots between a writer's life and the lives she writes.

There is this, along with another reason I keep any questions of frostbitten piggies to myself as I step out of her bedroom to find Angela pouring me a cup of coffee: I'm lonely.

"Sleep all right?" she asks, sliding a World-Class Bitch mug over the counter toward me.

"Fine. Bad dreams, though."

"How bad?"

"The usual bad."

"Me too. It's why I'm up. That, and I have to be at work in less than an hour."

I'd forgotten she has a job. I'd forgotten *anyone* has a job. Another of the side effects of the writer's life. You start to think everybody can professionally justify shuffling around the house all day, waiting for the postman, pretending that staring out the window and wondering what to toss in the microwave for lunch is a form of meditation.

"About last night," I start. "I wanted to tell you how much –"

"I think you should talk to some of the others."

"The others?"

"From the circle."

Angela holds her coffee with both hands, warming them against the bracing chill of condo A/C.

"That's funny. I was going to say something about *us*. Something nice."

"I'm not too good at the morning-after thing, I guess."

"So you've had others. Other mornings."

"Yes, Patrick. I've had other mornings."

I take a suave gulp of scalding coffee. Once the burning in my throat has dulled to an excruciating throb, I ask why she wants me to speak to the others.

"To find out what they know. If they've been … involved the same way we have."

I nod at this, and keep nodding. It's the word she's just used. *Involved*. Said in the way Conrad White said it when I asked what he thought of Angela's story. *You want to know if someone else has been involved in the way you have been involved.*

"How did you come to leave your purse in Conrad's car?"

"I told you. We were seeing each other a little at the time."

"Seeing each other? Or *seeing* each other?"

"He was interested in who I was."

And who are you? I nearly ask, but stop it in time with another tonsil-scarring sip of coffee.

"Have you read his work?"

"*Jarvis and Wellesley*? Sure," she says. "Why?"

"I think he saw in you what the character in his book was looking for."

"His dead daughter."

"The perfect girl."

"He told you that?"

"So I'm right."

"You're not wrong."

Angela tells me that Conrad would drive her home sometimes after their get-togethers. At first, their topics were the usual literary matters such as favourite books (*The Trial* for Conrad, *The Magus* for Angela), work habits, writer's block and how it might be overcome. Soon, though, Conrad would focus their discussion on where Angela's story came from. Her childhood, her friends growing up, where her parents were now. Something in the pointedness of his queries put Angela on the defensive, so that her replies became more intentionally vague the more he persevered. It made him angry.

"Like he wasn't just curious, but desperate," Angela says, slipping her cellphone and keys into her purse.

"Was he in love with you?"

"He might have been, in a way. More like a freaky fan than a lover, you know? But that wasn't what made him ask all those questions."

She stops. Not liking where this is taking her.

"I think he was scared," she says.

"Scared of what?"

"The same thing we're scared of."

"And he –"

"He thought it had to do with my story."

I'm following Angela to the door, slipping on watch and socks and shoes as I go.

"Did he have any contact with the Sandman – someone he *thought* was the Sandman? There were those killings back then. Maybe he was making connections in ways none of us had thought of."

"Maybe," Angela says. "Or maybe he was a messed-up shut-in who was driving himself crazy making something out of nothing."

In the elevator down, I ask who from the circle she thinks we should try to look up first.

"We?"

"I thought you said it might be useful to know what the others know."

"But I can't do the asking."

"Why not?"

"Who did he deliver the Yankees cap to?"

The elevator doors open. Outside, the heat bends the air into shimmering vapours.

"Can I call you?" I ask.

"Not for a while."

"Why not?"

"*You are mine.* Remember?" she says, opening the doors to the burning world. "I don't think he'd like it if he thought I was yours."

You wouldn't expect, being caught in a *web of intrigue* (who knew I would ever use this phrase so personally, irreplaceably?) that, in between the recorded scenes of revelation and confrontation, one could still have so much spare time. Unemployment can open yawning chasms in the middle of the most mentally preoccupied days, believe me. There are still the self-maintaining banalities to attend to: the belated meals, the bathroom dashes, the long showers. Still the mail, the erupting laundry hamper, the dental appointment. One can be a murder suspect, a serial killer's prey, and still have time to waste on the last sobbing half-hour of *Dr Phil*.

There are a pair of activities over these melting July days, however, that are returned to with too great a frequency to note each time they occur. The first is my journal. I've graduated from stolen jottings at bedtime to carrying it around wherever I go, recollecting snatches of conversation, the wheres and whens of things. It is, in the rereading, an increasingly unstructured document. What begins as tidy pages of coherent points soon breaks down into messages to Sam, scribbled drawings of Petra, Detective Ramsay (though I don't attempt Angela, can't imagine where the first line would start), even a letter to the Sandman, asking that if he has to take me with him into the Kingdom of Not What It Seems that he leave my son behind. It occurs to me that later, when it's all over, this journal of mine may be the sort of thing that supports the contention that poor old Patrick had lost his way well before the shadow got him. After all, what is sanity other than guarding the border between the fiction and non-fiction sections?

My other habit is to give Sam a ring and see how he's doing. Most of the time he's out in the yard playing with Stacey's kids (they have a pool, an unthinkable suburban luxury for us city mice), or camping overnight (instead of the artsy-craftsy day school I've been sending him to), or one of any other number of healthy summer distractions I have long meant to get around to doing with him, but mostly never have, slipping him books or movie passes instead. In other words, even when I call I don't get to talk to him. But it gives me a chance to thank Stacey yet again for what she's doing, to assure her that I'll collect Sam once I've "cleared the deck of a few things", to ask her to tell him that I called.

There you have it: even a man caught in a web of intrigue still fights against the inevitable with whatever's left to him. To hang on to the shape life used to take before he became trapped, and now can do little but wait for the spider to feel his struggle and decide enough, that's *enough* for this fly. It's time.

Since we parted in her condo's lobby, and despite her asking me not to, I have put in a handful of calls to Angela, and received some cursory excuses in return ("Work is really *crazy* this week", "I don't know, I'm just so *tired*"). I tell her I need to see her. That I miss her.

"I'm not sure I can do that," she says.

"We can just talk."

"What would we talk about?"

"It wouldn't have to be … bad things."

"But that's all there is."

She goes on to tell me how she's gotten a couple more signs from "him". When I ask what these indications are, she goes silent. Her breath clicking in her throat.

"Maybe, if we stay together, we could protect each other," I suggest.

"You don't believe that."

"I said *maybe*."

"I think he wants us apart. For each of us to have our own course."

"And if we don't play along –"

"– he'll separate us. Or worse. We've got to play this the way he wants."

And look how well that's turning out, I want to say. Along with another remark that comes to me too late: *What do we think he wants anyway?* If it is Patrick Rush feeling the profoundest regret for having used his name for the title of a ripped-off novel, then mission accomplished. *Mea culpa*. And if it's just random lives he wants to get back to taking, then I'm certainly not the one standing in his way.

Random lives.

This is the puzzle that fills the next hour. Buried away down here in the Crypt, mapping out the few connections I can make in my journal.

Carol Ulrich.

Ronald Pevencey.

Jane Whirter.

And now Petra Dunn.

Not a thing common between them. But in *his* mind, there must have been. For the Sandman, there was nothing random about them at all. All that's required is to think like a psychopath.

Well, I think. *I'm a retired writer. How hard could it be?*

Even in the four years since the Kensington Circle, the available venues for writers' groups have multiplied. Libraries, bookshops, coffee houses – but also rehab clinics, synagogues, yoga ashrams, Alcoholics Anonymous. There is no limit to the Self-Writing Seminars, (Her)story Workshops, Focus Group Your Novel! round tables one might sign up for. And I sign up for them all. Or as many as I can. Not to learn, to exchange, to discover myself. But to retrace the steps that have delivered me here. The same journey all murderers of passion are obliged to make: a return to the scene of the crime.

With Sam safe at Stacey's, I am free to skip from one circle to another over the sweltering remainder of the week. As I expresswayed and subwayed to the various gatherings uptown, crosstown, and out-of-town, I asked the same question. And a couple of times I got answers.

"Do these names mean anything to you?" I would inquire of my fellow circlers, and offer to them the first names (and surnames if I knew them) of each member of the Kensington Circle. By the end of the week I had confirmed what I'd suspected.

In a basement in Little Italy, I learned that William had been a participant for a time several years ago, and was going to be asked to leave (the boyhood tales of an animal-skinning sociopath too much to take) before he abruptly stopped showing up all on his own. I heard much the same thing in a Coffee Time in Scarborough, a public library in Lawrence Park, a gay bar on Jarvis Street: big scary man with too-real horror story joins writers' club, then disappears.

And that's not all.

There were other names I mentioned in the circles. Names of those I had never met, but were of increasing significance to my situation, nevertheless. Carol Ulrich. Ronald Pevencey. (I left out Jane Whirter, as she had lived in Vancouver for over twenty years prior to her death.) Names that some of the people I asked had heard of before. But not only because Ulrich and Pevencey were among the Sandman's first round of victims. They were remembered because, at one time or another, both of them were participants in some of the city's writing circles.

This is what I have, and what, if newspaper reports are to be believed, the police don't: a connection between the Sandman's "random" victims. They were *writers*. And somehow it got them killed.

23

As I walk home through the city, I take out my cell and pretend to speak to someone at the other end. It's not the first time I've done this. You can be the only pedestrian *not* on the phone for so long before you start to feel yourself disappear. You need to *text*, to *touch base*, to *screen incoming*. We speed-dial, therefore we are.

This time, when I check my messages at home, I'm surprised to hear a voice I recognize. Ivan.

"I've had an ... *encounter*."

A pause so long it's like he's forgotten to hang up. Then he remembers.

Click.

An encounter.

I call the number he gave me as I pass a group of gigglers standing outside the sex-shop window, tapping at the glass ("What *is* that, Brenda?" "I dunno. Must be something you put where the sun don't shine.").

Ivan picks up on the first ring.

"Patrick?"

"You left a message –"

"Museum station. Tomorrow. Southbound platform. Ten a.m."

Click.

Without looking for it, I'm now like everyone else, the millions streaming past on sidewalk and street. I've got plans for the weekend.

Moments after arriving home there's a knock at the door.

"Finished your book. Very interesting," Detective Ramsay says, once again walking past me into the living room as though the place is only nominally mine. Then, even more falsely: "Can't wait to read whatever you're doing next."

"I'm retired."

"Really?"

"Are you actually here to discuss my book?"

"It's an investigation. We have to have *something* to put in the files."

There's a point in every conversation structured around the exchange of accusation and rebuttal – meetings with tax auditors, neighbours disgruntled over the leaves your tree sheds in their yard – where the nasty turn can be either taken or avoided. This is the point Ramsay and I have reached. And I have decided I don't like the man.

"You know something?" I say. "I may have another book in me yet. In fact, you're inspiring a character for me right now."

"Oh? What's this character like?"

"Flawed, naturally. An intrusive investigator who's smart but not as smart as he thinks. The secret about him is that he wants to be a writer. Detective stories – the only thing he reads. He likes to think if he wasn't so busy solving real crimes, he'd be making them up."

To say Ramsay darkens at this would be understatement. His limbs stiffening into the vocabulary of the thug, the backstreet pub brawler. Now I can see the clear answer to my earlier question about him. Definitely more Glasgow than Edinburgh.

"A comic figure," he says.

"I think he is."

"You'd be wrong then."

"You mean he's not funny?"

"I mean you'd be wrong to laugh at him."

He gives me a look that's rather hard to describe. One better grasped in its effects, chief of which is to make me want to make a run for the door.

"What do you say to wish a writer luck?" he says, moving past me. "Break a leg?"

"Usually it's just 'Don't let the bastards get you down.'"

"That applies to my line of work too."

There's the clunk of the door pulled shut. The house waits a full minute before resuming its sighs and ticks.

Later, when I ask myself why I didn't tell Ramsay what I learned about the Sandman's first round of victims all being circle members – not to mention William's appearance at some of the very same meetings – I decide that it wasn't because I don't like the guy, or even that it might put me at greater risk. I didn't tell him because a thought occurred to me at the same moment Ramsay offered a glimpse of his darker self.

It might be him.

This suspicion was born out of nothing more than a flare of intuition, but now that he's gone I'm able to back it up with a reasonable tallying of bits and pieces. The first of these is that he was the lead investigator on the previous Sandman killings. This would have allowed him access not only to the crime scenes and the potential manipulation of evidence, but to his fellow officers, the media. A nice way to clean up any mistakes he may have made (though these would undoubtedly have been few). Then there's his physical aspect: as tall as the Sandman, give or take. And no doubt strong enough to carry out the business of human butchering.

Then again, this may only be my own continued inching toward madness. Suspecting the *detective*?

You don't need to be hunted by a Sandman to see nothing but crime and criminals. All the things you've done, the decisions you made, the possibilities laid out before you – it used to be *your story*. Then the thieves show up to take it. And you're left asking the question that is so compulsive, so bestsellingly popular because it belongs to a universal language. The first utterance of fear. Of failure.

Whodunit?

This isn't the end of my Friday social calls. In fact, I end up going out for drinks with a friend – though this sounds a good deal more normal than it is. Because it's drinks with Len. And because he has asked me to come out in order to share a "totally twisted idea" about Angela.

We decide on The Paddock, an ancient vault south of Queen. When the bartender comes by I order a bourbon sour, and am surprised to hear Len ask for the same.

"I didn't know you started drinking."

"I haven't."

"You could've ordered a juice or something."

"I don't want to call attention to myself," he says, glancing over his shoulder. "And it's important that I talk to you in the kind of place I wouldn't normally go."

"Why?"

"So *she* won't see us."

Once the drinks arrive, he tells me how Angela came to his apartment some days ago. She looked around his attic room, inspecting the bookshelves. *The Sandman* caught her attention, though she made no mention of it. Len couldn't help noticing she was wearing a "nice – you know, *sexy* nice – perfume". And a blouse he felt was missing a couple of buttons.

"When was this exactly?"

"Wednesday. Why?"

"No reason."

Wednesday. Two days after Angela told me we shouldn't see each other again. And then she's calling on *Len* – prematurely balding, cardboard-smelling, man-boy Len. Only a moment's pondering of this and my glass is empty. I knock back Len's too and raise my hand to signal another round.

Len tells me that, at first, she just talked to him like she might have during the circle, if she ever *had* spoken to him during the circle. Writer stuff. Queries about what he's working on, where he'd sent material out to, recent books they'd read.

"Did you ask her about being published under a false name?"

"There wasn't time."

"I thought you were just sitting around talking?"

"We were. But then it got *weird*."

It got weird when she confessed to him, leaning forward to put her hand on his knee, that if she were ever to write a story about him, she knew what title she'd use.

"'The Virgin'," Len says. "So I say 'Why would you call it that?' And she says 'Because you've never been with a girl, have you, Len?' Then she kissed me."

"Kissed you? Where?"

"On the *lips*."

264

"Then what?"

"I don't know. I *resisted*, I guess. Kind of pushed her away."

"Why?"

"Because she wasn't really kissing me. It was more like she was making fun of me."

"How did you know?"

"That's how it *felt*."

I press Len's glass into his hand, urge him to take a sip. And he does. A big one. Followed by a bigger one.

"Welcome to the wonderful world of alcohol therapy," I say.

"It's warm."

"It only gets warmer."

He wipes his eyes with the sleeve of his shirt. I would put a hand on his shoulder to steady him, but the truth is, even now, I don't want to touch him. I offer him time instead. And when he's ready, he says that once Angela was done laughing at him, she said he didn't have to kiss her back. He didn't have to do anything because it was too late. She already knew everything she needed to know.

"About what?"

"About *me*."

"What did she want to know about you?"

"Everything she needed to write her version of me."

"She was writing a story based on you? 'The Virgin'?"

"I think she's writing stories on all of us," Len says, then drifts his face closer. "But I'm next."

"Her subject."

"No. The next to die."

Len is not well. This fact is coming into sharp focus now. He's not just another comic-book-collecting oddball, not one of the half-invisibles, the sort of mouth breather you try to ignore peering over your shoulder at a bank machine. He's *ill*. Yet, now that we're here, in a place where more cocktails are available if things get hairy, I figure there's little harm in nudging him further.

"Then why not me? Why am I not next?"

"You were the only one without a story," Len answers, finishing his drink and unintentionally slamming the glass down on the bar.

"She said that to you?"

"It was kind of obvious."

Len puts his hand on my wrist, pressing it against the bar's varnished surface, and I let him. I also let him come in close once more to whisper into my cheek.

"She isn't what she appears to be," he says.

I try to pull my arm away, but he's got a stronger hold than I thought he was capable of.

"I'm not just saying she's psychotic," Len goes on, suddenly louder. Behind me, there's the chair squeaks and interrupted conversations of other drinkers stopping to hear the agitated guy in the corner. "I'm saying she's not *human*."

"For God's sake, Len."

"In medieval legend, there is a name for a female being that incrementally consumes other beings until their eventual exhaustion or death."

"A succubus."

"Exactly."

"Oh Christ."

"A witch who appears in the form of a temptress."

"Calm down. Here. Take another sip –"

"Usually the succubus' purpose is to steal the semen of sleeping men – their life force. But in this case, it's different. She steals stories."

"Are you saying we need to put a stake through her heart? Shoot her with a silver bullet?"

"I'm serious. And the sooner you get serious about it too, the longer you might live."

Len *is* serious. The whole bar can see it. And it watches him stand, the boldness that had possessed him for these past moments instantly slipping away.

"There are some desires so foul they are never satisfied," he says, and appears to search his mind for something more. But if there was something, it's gone now. *I'm done*, his drooped shoulders and hanging head say as he walks away. *That's all I can manage*.

My Friday winding down to its bourbon-softened end. But even with the assurance that Len's theories are as twisted as initially advertised, the day closes with an unsettling idea. For as the door closes behind him, I can't help thinking I will never see Len again.

24

I start out to my meeting with Ivan early enough, but the sun, already high and merciless by nine, ends up making me late. Twice I have to stop and sit in the shade to get a handle on the dizziness that comes with pushing myself through air not made for walking, or for anything really, other than euthanizing the old and promoting sales of asthma inhalers for the young. By the time I shuffle by the old facade of the Royal Ontario Museum I don't really care if Ivan awaits me underground or not. What I need is to get out of the sun and wait for October to come.

But it's not much better here. Down the stairs the air is almost as warm, the trains growling and screeching below. So what am I doing here, any-way? Why do I want to know what Ivan means by "an encounter"? The smart thing would be to turn back. And not just from my meeting with Ivan, but from everyone. Someone else can tease out the mystery of the Sandman and be rewarded as Carol Ulrich, Petra and the others were rewarded.

But I don't do the smart thing. And it's here, carried down on the sliding escalator stairs, that I figure why: I want to save the day. Dishonoured author, pink-slipped critic, rejected lover – yes to all. Yet there may still be an opportunity for forgiveness, a full pardon that would see me returned from observing the world to the world itself. This is how deep the faulty hopes of fiction have been engrained in me.

It's in the next moment that I notice the man coming up the escalator opposite me.

Both hands gripping the rubber handrails, the hood of his sweatshirt pulled down so that his face is obscured. He would be tall if he were standing straight. But he's not.

He slides past. And I continue down.

It's not the look of him that strikes me, but the smell he leaves in the air once he's passed. A brief taste of compost. The first whiff that meets you upon opening the door of an unplugged fridge.

I have been close enough to that skin to catch its odour before. I have tried to *describe* it before too.

Wood smoke. Sweat. Boiled meat.

William.

He's already disappearing around the corner at the top of the escalator when I turn. The door to the outside squeaking open and vacuuming shut.

I make a hopeless run against the descending steps – one down for every two up – and surrender halfway when a mother with a stroller comes to stand at the top, scowling at me. *Another lunatic*, her organic-only face says. *When is somebody going to clean this town up?*

It's at the ticket kiosk, waiting for the attendant to hand over my change, that I notice the first sign that something worse than a William appearance may be going on down here. The sound of incoherent exclamations – *Don't touch it! Somebody … somebody!* – coming from the platform at the bottom of the stairs. Children bursting into hysterical, echoing cries. A woman's scream.

I push my way through the turnstile at the same time the attendant picks up his phone and starts to wave me back. Ignoring him, I carry on walking backwards to see the woman with the stroller being told she can't enter, and her demanding to know why. The attendant tells her. Whatever it is, it turns her around, her heels tapping out a distress signal on the marble floor.

On the way down to the platform the voices I'd heard earlier have grown in volume. More adult shouts have joined the wailing infants, and there's one or two official order-givers now too – *Stand back! Straight line here, people!* – along with the increasingly panicked *Ohmygod*s of mothers who have brought their children to visit the museum, many of them, by the sounds of it, still disembarking from the train. Shoes sliding against shoes. The grunt and gasp of those jostling for position in shrinking space. Human cattle.

I reach the platform and join them. The only one coming down as everyone else takes their first frenzied steps toward the exits.

Then I see why.

The southbound train has stopped two-thirds of the way into the station. Its doors open, the cars now wholly emptied. Men in fluorescent orange vests push through the crowd to open the door to the control cabin at the front. A moment later the driver emerges, hands trembling at the sides of his face, his lips moving but nothing coming out.

An accident. One that's just happened. Given the way some of the kids break away from their mothers to look over the side of the platform and instantly turn back, it's obvious what sort. A jumper. And that's not all I correctly guess before I push sideways to look over the side for myself. I know who jumped.

One of the most common ways of reckoning individual experience is through the number of times a thing has been seen or done: how many people one has slept with, foreign countries visited, diseases suffered and survived. Along with the dead. How many have you viewed outside of open caskets and TV news? Before today, my count was childishly low: just two. Tamara, of course. And my grandmother, discovered on the floor of her retirement home kitchenette, looking up at me with the same expression of annoyance she'd worn in life.

But I've made up for that now. I peer over the platform's edge and that's it. I'm all caught up on the death front.

What's unforgettable about seeing Ivan's body on the tracks isn't that it's someone I know, nor that parts of him are still webbed over the front of the train, nor that his face, despite the rest of him, is remarkably untouched. It's that he's not dead yet. His jaw's hinging open and half-shut.

Ivan is saying something I can understand. Not that I can hear him. I can tell because he knows it is me standing above him. And that his gulping mouth wants me to know he was pushed.

He stops moving before a uniformed police officer pulls me away from the edge. At first I think I'm being arrested. An exchange takes place in my head so clearly I wait for it to begin with the officer's first words:

– Do you know this man?

– Yes.

– What is your relationship to him?

– We both wanted to be writers. And we were both being hunted.

– Hunted? *Steve! Get over here!* Hunted by who?

– He has a few names, actually. My personal favourite is The Terrible Man Who Does Terrible Things.

But the policeman says nothing but *Please step away, sir*. So I do. Make a tiptoed dash for the stairs.

Joining the other passengers on the ascending escalator, the only ones coming down are more police and a pair of paramedics whose relaxed chatter suggests they've already been told this call is a done deal.

At the exit turnstiles, a pair of plainclothes detectives are asking if anyone saw what happened, and one or two from the shaken crowd stop to give a statement. I keep walking. Up the last staircase to the street, where the blazing heat is almost welcome, an awakening discomfort.

I cut on to the university campus, into the shade of the trees along Philosopher's Walk. Consciously refusing to think of anything but getting home. But before I get there, it will require all I have to simply keep moving.

And I *do* keep moving: from the bourbon to the vodka tonics to the red wine that's meant to rouse an appetite for dinner, but in the end turns out to be dinner itself. A full afternoon of channel surfing and heavy drinking that only partly succeeds in holding the flashes of Ivan's final seconds at bay.

Despite my best efforts, some stark implications of the day's horrors batter through: if Ivan was pushed, and it was William who'd passed me going up the subway escalator, who else could have done the pushing other than him? Even if I'm wrong, and Ivan had jumped, it seems beyond coincidence that William had appeared at the scene at the same time. Then again, *I* had been there. Had Ivan called William to the same meeting he'd called me to? It's possible. Yet the surest bet remains that Ivan had been followed to the Museum station by whoever he wanted to tell me about, but my lateness had allowed his stalker to reach him first. If it was the Sandman, he'd likely noticed me on the escalator. Which means he knows I'm getting closer to him. To who he is.

The evening takes its first truly unfortunate turn, however, when I embark on a tasting tour of the single malts saved for a special occasion. Well, *today* has been special, hasn't it? Seeing Ivan's body on the rails every time I close my eyes, every time I blink. Imagining how it will feel when it's my turn.

What I need is some company. Which leads to my second poor decision: calling Angela. When I get her machine, I call again. A couple hours with the unpronounceable bottles of Scotch laid out over my desk, my free hand speed-dialling Angela and, each time she fails to pick up, me offering new apologies for whatever I'd done, for whatever I am.

After the rain starts to fingertap the basement window, I decide to walk over to her place. Along Front Street and past the convention centre where a twisting line of several hundred kids sit huddled on the sidewalk, camping out overnight in order to be first in line for the morning's *Canadian MegaStar!* auditions. The rain has left them shivering and hairless as chihuahua pups. I shout encouragements as I pass ("Return to your homes! Abandon hope all ye who enter here!") and they

274

moan back at me like injured soldiers, casualties left on the fame battlefield.

Down past Union station, I'm sheltered from the rain as I stumble through the tunnel that runs under the tracks. By the time I make it to the far end, however, the precipitation has turned into something stronger, as though Lake Ontario had been tipped up at the opposite end to drop its contents over the city. It leaves me blind, but I keep going, possibly on the sidewalk, possibly down the middle of the street. All I know is when the downpour finally pauses long enough for me to open my eyes, the first thing I see is the shadow of the Gardiner Expressway overpass ahead. And beneath it, the figure of a man taking shelter from the rain. Staring at me.

At first, when I start my run toward him, he doesn't move. Just watches me come as though curious to see what I have in mind. Or perhaps he *wants* me to come. There is something in his posture – slouching, arms crossed – I hadn't noticed in his previous appearances. His presence, conveying only black threat before, has softened.

At the same time I come into shouting distance, he starts running south toward the lake. His strides longer and surer than mine, but showing a sluggish fatigue that keeps him within view.

"It was you!"

This is me. Screaming. A drunken madman among the other drunken madmen who live under the expressway and watch me pass.

"It was *you*!"

The figure slows. A wheeling of arms that might turn him around to attack, to speak. But he decides against it. Starts away again with fresh speed, his boots smacking against the slick pavement at a pace I couldn't dream of matching.

As I bring myself to a stop, coughing the evidence of a sedentary life on to my shoes, I watch him slip around the corner of a condo tower across from the harbour. Or behind a row of parked cars in the lot across from it. Or perhaps into the churning water itself.

In any case, there's only me here now. Me and the rain.

Once I'm able to breathe and stand up straight at the same time, I carry on to Angela's building only a couple blocks away. I keep my thumb on her condo number until the super comes out and asks me to leave. When I refuse, he executes a nifty bouncer move. The classic, in my experience: grabs the back of my shirt with one fist and the belt of my pants with the other and, kicking the door open, chucks me out on to the patch of manicured lawn like an overstuffed bag of garbage.

It's still raining. I can tell from the way it washes the blood off my hands when I check to see if I've split my lip.

There is no more *doing* tonight. Now is the time to think. To determine the *underlying meaning* of things.

The trouble is, for the second time today, the implications of what I've witnessed seem to slip away, leaving me to walk home teasing out the possibilities aloud. Even the first question gives me problems: was it William who'd run from me? Did I attribute the odour of the man on the subway escalator and posture of the figure under the expressway to him because I actually recalled these aspects, or have I been thinking it's been William all along, and thus any presence I encountered would be seen as him?

Next, an even more dizzying consideration: if it *was* William I saw tonight, was he the same person standing in my living-room window, the murderer of unknown writers, the ghost villain from Angela's journal? Perhaps there is a different monster attached to each of these crimes. Maybe the Sandman is merely one of the names shared by all the agents of the uncanny. The Sandman, the bogeyman, the succubus, the devil.

I tell myself to limit my thoughts to what is known. But what *is* known? Ivan is dead. Petra is missing. Conrad White – and Evelyn, if Angela is to be believed – dead too.

And what connects us is the circle. Or perhaps something more fundamental than that. A shared playing field that, even here in a city of millions, is limited to only a few, the last of the storybook believers. The ones who have not only seen the Sandman standing at the edge of their lives, but invited him in.

* * *

277

The morning is as bad as you'd guess. Complicated not just by a hangover serious enough to share eight of the nine primary symptoms of toxic shock, nor by the afternoon trip to the emergency room to get an intern to pinch and stick and *Oh, damn, I'm sorry* his way to stitching my lip closed, but by the prevailing sense that if what has come before has been worrying, everything from here on in is going to show how justified that worry actually was. I might be paranoid. But there's nothing that says paranoids can't be right sometimes.

On the way back from the hospital, I stop by Angela's building again. Still no answer. An idea strikes me all at once. Whether it was William or someone else, whoever I saw last night had come from calling on Angela too.

I try her work number, and the receptionist informs me she hasn't been in all this week. Len's not answering his phone. These are all the leads I have. Along with the faith that, if Angela were able to, she would have checked in with me by now, if only to tell me to stop bothering her with my sad-sack messages.

She is hiding. She is with him now. She is dead.

No matter which is true, it leaves me to find her on my own.

Later that afternoon I drive out of the city check- ing the rear view to see if I'm being followed. But speeding west along the QEW in a suicidal crush, every car fighting and failing to gain an inch on the competition – there is no way *not* to be followed. Still, there is one vehicle that seems to stick to me more doggedly than the others. A black Lincoln Continental that won't let me steal away whenever a gap opens in the slower lane. Not that this proves anything other than he has the same ideas about getting ahead that I have. And though the slanting light of dusk won't let me get a look at the driver's face, the same could be said for almost every other car jostling for position behind me.

But the Continental is still there forty-five minutes later when the first exit for St Catharines comes up. I wait until the last moment before veering off on to the ramp. At first, it seems the black sedan tries to follow, lurching from the passing to the middle lane. But as the ramp curves into the town's residential streets, I catch sight of the Continental already shrinking down the highway. If I was being followed, the most the driver will know is where I've got off, but not where I'm going.

And where I'm going is to see Sam.

He looks good. Tanned, knee scrapes from roughhousing. Somehow he's aged a year in the past week.

"Am I going back with you?" he asks when we're on our own in the living room, a Disney movie paused on the jumbo screen.

"Afraid not."

"Then when?"

"Another week. Maybe two."

"A *week*?"

"I thought you were having fun here."

"It's okay. It's just – I miss you."

"Any money says I miss you more."

"Then why can't I come home?"

"Because there's something going on that needs to be settled first. And I want you to be safe."

"Are *you* safe?"

"You have to trust me. Can you do that for the next little while?"

Sam nods. Just look at him: he *does* trust me. And though this shouldn't surprise me – I'm his *father* – the weight of it does. It's a gift when another gives you their trust like this. A gift that can be taken back at any time, and easily too. This is what I read as clearly as the banana bruise freckles across my son's cheeks: once it's gone you never get it back. You might think you can. But you can't.

Later that evening when I'm tucking Sam into his bed, I ask if he would like me to read to him from any of the books he'd brought with him. He shakes his head.

"You want me to get you some new stuff? Next time, we can go to the bookstore and go crazy."

"No."

"What's the problem? You too old to be read to?"

"I don't read *any* books any more."

280

There are a thousand declarations a child can make to a parent more painful than this. But there is a seriousness, even a cruelty in what has just been uttered here in the dark of a spare room that smells of another kid's smells.

"Why's that?"

"I don't like them."

"You don't like stories?"

"They're what you've left me here for. Right?"

I deny this. Tell him fiction can inform and influence and provoke, but can't actually hurt anyone. But what we both know, even as I kiss him goodnight and leave the door open an inch, is that he's right. It's the unreal that has stepped off the page to cloud our lives. And until it can be made to go back where it belongs Sam must stay here, awake in the nightlight's glow, preparing to keep his sleep free of all dreams but the one where his father returns to take him home.

After nightfall, I drive back to Toronto. Down here, where the highway hugs the southern shore of the lake, you can look through the gaps between the old motels and fenced-in orchards and catch glimpses of the city's skyline across the water. In the past, I would see it as glamorous, a sexual invitation in the embracing pillars of light. It was the suggestion of possibility, of danger that I liked, and took pride in being associated with, if only by shared address.

Tonight, the sight of the distant towers has a different effect. They are an alien army, moon-glinting beasts rising from a dark sea. Their lights powered by desire alone. Unrequited, insatiable. A terrible wanting that feeds on anything that will submit to being possessed.

I drive on through the winemaking villages, smaller bedroom towns, the conjoined suburbs along the north shore before the final turn into the light. This last framing of the city before you are consumed within it: there was a time I thought it was beautiful, saw in it the beautiful promise of success. And I still do. Though what I know now is that every promise can also be a lie, depending on how it's kept.

25

Tim Earheart rings me again for drinks.

"God, I'm sorry," I tell him, remembering the unanswered emails and phone messages he'd left with me. "Things have been a little messed up the past while. Maybe tomorrow –"

"This isn't exactly a *social* call, Patrick."

"What is it then? Business?"

"Yeah. It's *business*."

We meet at one of the bank tower bars Tim has been favouring since he'd been given a raise following his appointment to Special Investigative Reporter ("What were you before?" "I don't know. But definitely not *special*"), not to mention the income that's been freed up since his second wife "got some other schmuck to pay for all the crap to which she'd become accustomed". This place is the New Tim Earheart, he tells me. He likes all the leather, the halogen pot lights, the sweep of upward mobility evidenced in the twenty-dollar martinis. And then there's the pick-up opportunities.

"Just *being* here signals you as successful," Tim tells me, seductively rolling a bill and dropping it in the coat check girl's jar.

"Successful at what?"

"That's the beauty of it. It doesn't *matter*. The details can be worked out later."

As the first round is consumed, Tim tells me a couple tales of women from these premises with whom he *has* worked it out later. It's vintage Earheart, and it makes me miss him. Companionship. Where had that disappeared to? Nestled in the same basket with a living wife, a job – all of it pushed down the stream and round the bend.

As if to bring this illusion of two friends having a worry-free cocktail to an end, Tim clears his throat at the arrival of the second set of martinis, pulls a piece of paper out of his jacket pocket and slides it over the bar toward me.

"What's this?"

"Read it."

"You wrote this?"

"Just *read* it."

It's a sin, the church says, to do the things
    that I do
But how can I stop until I've done them
    to you?
Later, in hell, is where my bones will be
    burned
'Til then, let it be known: the Sandman's
    returned.

"Where did you get this?"

"It was sent to the paper. To *me*, as a matter of fact."

"You think it's him?"

"What do you think?"

"The style certainly fits."

"Not to mention the name."

Tim watches me. To see how this grim revelation is sinking in. Or to take an accounting of how many years I've aged since he last saw me. I know I don't look *good*. But having my clean-shaven, gym-going friend study me like a coroner studies a corpse – it can't help but make a fellow a little nervous.

"Are you going to run it?" I ask.

"I'd like to."

"But they won't let you."

"It's my decision this time."

"So?"

"So? There's no story."

"'The Sandman Returns.' Sounds like a headline to me."

"He's not claiming any particular homicides. Not much point in terrorizing the public if there's nothing to terrorize them with aside from a shabby limerick."

"It's not a limerick."

"You're the expert."

There *are* victims, of course. Conrad and Evelyn. Ivan an apparent suicide under what the crime hacks call "suspicious circumstances". Not

to mention Petra – and now Angela too – gone missing. But the only thing that connects all of them is the Kensington Circle, and if Tim Earheart hasn't discovered this yet, I'm not about to tell him.

"You know, there *is* a context in which I'd run the poem," Tim says, musing aloud. "It would require a reaction, naturally."

"A reaction?"

"From you. A comment on how an internationally bestselling novelist feels to have inspired copycat psychopaths with a work of fiction. *That* I could I go with."

"Are you kidding me?"

"Just thought it might be fun."

"Me taking credit for spawning a new generation of serial killers? Yes, that's definitely amusing. That would be a *giggle*."

I figure that's about it. Tim had come for a story, not gotten it, and all that's left is for the *National Star* to pick up the tab. We bring things to a close with some banter about the latest newsroom outrages and gossip. It's just killing time. But it makes me nostalgic for the days of journalistic sniping and complaint, when it would have been *me* telling *Tim* about the photo chief's crossdressing weekends.

As it turns out, however, we're not quite done with the business that Tim called me here for.

"Off the record," he says as he raises his finger for the bill, "what do you make of the whole

Sandman thing? Someone using the name of a bad guy in your novel, I mean."

"I don't feel responsible for anything, if that's what you're getting at."

"It isn't."

"Then what *are* you getting at?"

"What do you know?"

"Just what I read in the papers."

"Has he contacted you?"

"Nope."

"I bet you've got a theory."

"You know what, Tim?" I start, slipping off the bar stool and surprised to find myself unsteady on my feet. "Here's the thing: I wrote a book. And I *regret* it. I truly do."

Tim puts his hand out to steady me but I take a step back. What I should do now is leave. But seeing how Tim Earheart, my one-time journalistic equal, looks at me with pity in his eyes, makes me stick around for a few more words.

"I'm just trying to survive. Understand? So if you receive any more third-rate verse from psychos, don't come to me."

"Jesus, Patrick. I'm sorry."

"*Sorry?* No, that's *my* department. Sorry is my *thing*."

My hands are sliding into the arms of my jacket. The coat check girl, God bless her, appears out of nowhere to dress me against the evening's chill. Giving me a commiserating look, smoothing my collar against the back of my neck. A moment that

287

proves there is still comfort in this world, though you may not know where it will come from. I could kiss her for it. Maybe Tim Earheart already has.

I take a cab home but get the driver to drop me off a couple blocks early so I can walk the rest of the way on my own. Continue tipsily homeward feeling my way around a thought: Maybe the shouters and shooters and moon howlers on the streets down here are versions of where all of us are headed. City in Fear. *Yes*. We've been right to be more and more afraid – we've just been afraid of the wrong thing. It won't be a cataclysmic nasty from Out There that will bring us down, not ozone depletion or impacting comet or dirty bomb, but the advance of madness. Why? There isn't enough *room* for sanity any more. Eventually, the asylum doors will be forced open. And it will be us who walk out.

Or maybe it will only be me. Because I am once again of the opinion I am being pursued. Somewhere between the sex shop and the other sex shop I pick up the heavy, thick-soled step of someone behind me.

Past the Prague Deli ("Czech Us Out!") and the used record shops he keeps up without changing the rhythm of his steps. I should start running now. A sudden break for it that might steal the few yards needed to give me a chance. But I'm suddenly too tired.

I round the corner on to the darker stretch of Euclid, straight to the patch of exposed tree roots that is my front yard. When I finally turn it's with the resignation of prey that cannot retreat any further.

"Got some news," Ramsay says, wearing a quarter-grin.

"You couldn't use the phone?"

"People say I'm better in person."

"Better at what?"

He takes a step forward. The streetlight can't reach him where he stands, so that all I can see are flashes of teeth.

"Len Innes has been reported missing."

"Missing? How?"

"That's the point with missing. You don't *know* how."

"Christ."

"When was the last time you spoke with him?"

"I don't know. A while ago."

"And what was the substance of your conversation?"

"Nothing much."

"Just a friendly chat then?"

"You think I killed Len?"

"I thought he was only missing."

"I don't know *anything*."

"Sure you do."

"Is this *fun* for you? This droll, Columbo, cat-and-mouse bullshit?"

"Everyone's a critic."

289

"Not everyone. I'm out of the critic business."

"Idle hands."

"Idle would be *nice*. But you keep coming around accusing me of murdering people. It's the kind of thing that can get in the way of a fellow's retirement plans."

"Here's some news: I don't give a fuck about your retirement plans."

"I don't think you believe I'm a killer, either."

"You might be wrong there."

"So arrest me. Do *something*. If not, get off my property."

Something changes in Detective Ramsay's face. Not in his expression – which remains jaw-clenched, bemused – but in his *face*. The skin pulled taut over the bone, showing the animal-thing beneath. Here is a creature free from the encumbrances of loyalty, of empathy, of seeing the human race as an enterprise that stands a chance over the long haul. All of which likely makes him a more than capable investigator of man's darkest actions. It may also enable him to carry out those actions himself.

"How's Sam?"

"I'm sorry?"

"Your *son*. How is he?"

"Fine."

"Daddy's out pretty late to leave a little guy like that on his own."

"You know he's not inside."

"I do?"

"Sam's safe."

"You sure? Because it's getting less and less safe everywhere you go."

I turn away, expecting him to launch a final remark my way, but I unlock the front door, step inside and close it behind me without another word from him.

Not that he's gone.

I peek out the window without turning on the lights. Ramsay stands under the dark bough of the front yard's maple. Unmoving as a statue and yet somehow undeniably alive, the air around him passing in and out of his lungs as though to be claimed as much as breathed. He belongs to the night world. The widening chasm between what you know is there and what can't be.

Ivan belongs to the night world too. And it is the next night that I see him in the food court of the Eaton Centre, making his way toward the entrance to the Dundas subway. All this is odd, as I hate malls, and hate mall food even more. I'm actually thinking this – *It's odd that I'm here* – when Ivan strolls by my table. Which is odder still, seeing as he's dead.

When I saw Conrad White thumbing through *The Sandman* in a bookstore when he was also among the no-longer-with-us, it gave me a chill. But as I watch Ivan lope through the crowd of tourists and locals like me with nowhere better to go, I'm instantly, paralytically afraid. It's because he's here for a purpose, and it's clear that I'm not going to like it. That's what Ivan tells me in his startling, unphantomly realness, the way he looks back over his shoulder at me, beckoning with hollow drill-holes for eyes. He's here to show me something.

And I follow him. Jumping the queue at the subway ticket booth, pushing through with understandable *fuck you*s fired at my back. Ivan may be dead, but he moves quicker than I ever saw him move in life. Sliding past the others making their way below. Scampering on to the escalator so that I have to take the stairs down two at a time to have a hope of catching him.

Once on the platform, I'm sure I've lost him. That is, I'm sure he wasn't there to begin with. This is what I try to tell myself: you haven't been sleeping, you're under stress, you're *seeing things*.

Ivan steps forward from the crowd at the far end of the platform as the train roars into the station. I start pushing my way toward him even as I expect this moment to play out as his last seconds of life played, with him jumping on to the tracks before the driver has a chance to lock the brakes.

But he doesn't jump. He looks my way.

His eyes find me instantly over the heads and ballcaps and turbans. An expression of the same sort he wore to all the circle meetings, but now somehow intensified. It lets me see what's inside him, what may have been inside him all along. Longing. For someone to talk to. To be forgiven.

The train's doors open. All of us except Ivan step aside to let the passengers off, and they move around the space he takes. It lets him be the first one on. Then the crowd follows him, squeezing in shoulder to shoulder through doors not quite wide enough to accommodate them. By the time I am freed from Ivan's stare I'm left alone on the platform, the doors already closing. I make a dash to get on – a knocking at the glass that earns sneers from within – but I'm too late.

I step back to see if I can spot Ivan inside. And there he is, sitting face out in a window seat, finding me with a jealous glare. Except now he's not alone.

Conrad White sits across from him, knee to knee. Petra behind them. Evelyn a couple seats back. All the Kensington Circle's dead with their noses to the windows. Ovals of malice mixed with the indifferent passengers.

In the next second, as the train releases its brakes and picks up speed, their faces flatten and blur. The car they sit in swallowed into the tunnel's mouth. The faces of the Kensington Circle along with those of the living commuters, good luck awaiters, furious strivers.

If I didn't know who was who, I might say all of them were dead.

26

In the morning, I wake to find William sitting at the end of my bed.

His body shaped in the hunched, head-cocked posture of a concerned friend sitting vigil. Even his face – still densely bearded as an oven brush – could be mistaken for sympathetic, his eyes looking down on me with a still intensity. Yet these are only first impressions. And they are wrong.

William's hands rise from the sheets. Fresh soil dropping off them in clumps. The nails ripped and weeping. Hands reaching for me.

I try to sit up. A weight on my legs prevents them from moving. The only action I'm capable of is watching.

His *hands* are going to kill me. *They* are about to do the most terrible things, not *him*. This is what his cracked lips seem to want to say. He is an instrument of death, but also dead himself.

* * *

I make a note of this – my first fright of the day – in my journal which I have taken to keeping by my bed at night. A chronicle of actual events and dream diary all in one. I should likely have kept separate notebooks for each, but so many passways have opened between my waking and sleeping worlds it doesn't seem to make much difference.

Take the ballcap, for instance.

I'm plodding through my breakfast routine of coffee making and cereal pouring when I first see it. Even then, it takes a few seconds to understand what it means. A Yankees cap. Sitting on the coffee table in the living room.

I pick it up and bring it to my nose – Petra's shampoo, still clinging to the cotton. The sliding glass doors are closed. But unlocked. And the curtains I was sure to have pulled closed the night before stand open.

I can see you.

Once I've closed the curtains and locked the doors, then gone round the basement and main floor to check the other doors and windows, I return to Petra's cap, studying it as though a clue has been stitched into its fabric.

Petra wore it, now she's thought to be dead. It was left with Angela, now she's disappeared. And now it's with me.

It could be you.

Ramsay already thinks (and with some good reason) that I'm involved in Petra's death and perhaps the others from before. If he found out her ballcap was in my possession, it would be more than enough to arrest me. The first piece of hard evidence connecting me to one of the murders. The Sandman wants me to hold it in my hands and know how it feels. To know what can be done to me without ever touching me.

> It's a sin, the church says, to do the things
>   that I do
> But how can I stop until I've done them
>   to you?

The Yankees cap is a promise of things to come, a show of power, a signature. But it's also a *game*.

Tag. I'm it.

The next thing I know I'm being asked to leave the offices of the *National Star*. The lobby, to be precise. It's as far as I get before I'm stopped trying to tiptoe by reception without a pass. When asked my intended business – Patrick Rush, here for a surprise visit to my old friend Tim Earheart – the guy behind the security desk punches my name into his terminal and a flag pops up. Quite a *few* flags, judging by his reddened cheeks and phone at his ear, a digit shy of completing his 911 call.

"Just tell Earheart I'm downstairs," I tell the security guy, whose tortured face shows that while

I'm in no position to be making deals, he might get into some serious trouble if he has to use his flashlight on me.

"Do as he says," a female voice says behind me. I turn to find the Managing Editor smiling one of her death smiles. Except now she's no longer the Managing Editor but the youngest Editor-in-Chief in the paper's history. "Let him say hello and be on his way."

She keeps smiling. If it were real, I'd be halfway to falling in love. But there's absolutely no mistaking the Editor-in-Chief's expression as warmth. As it is I'm backing away with every step she takes closer.

"Always nice to see an ex-employee going out the door," she says.

I'm spinning out into the heat as I glimpse Tim Earheart rushing past the Editor-in-Chief. *It won't happen again* on his lips.

"You can't get fired twice, you know. Or are you trying to get *me* fired?" Tim says as he takes me by the arm and hauls me away from the building. Through the glass doors I can see the Editor-in-Chief still there, her hands on her slim, treadmilled hips.

I follow Tim across Front Street to stand on the narrow edge of grass between the pavement and the fence that keeps pedestrians from the tracks leading in and out of Union station below.

"I'm working," Tim says. "We're not all *novelists* you know."

"I'll make this short."

"The shorter the better."

"Can you get access to government agency databases?"

"Depends which one."

"Children's Aid. Foster care. Whoever does permanent guardianships."

He puts a cigarette in his mouth but makes no move to light it. "Who's asking?"

"I'm looking for someone."

"Someone you know?"

"I know her. Not well, but I know her."

"A kid?"

"She's grown up now."

"So why not give her a call?"

"I don't know where she is."

Tim Earheart reads me closely for the first time, and I sense that what I say next will decide how the rest of this exchange is going to go. I want Tim involved, but not *involved*.

"Are you going to light that thing?"

He pulls the unlit cigarette out of his lips and flicks it over the fence. "What's her name?"

"Angela Whitmore. But that might only be her adoptive parents' surname. Or probably not. I mean, that's the name I know her by, but it may not be real."

"Tracking down an adoption without the kid's name – it's not going to happen."

"I don't think it was a voluntary adoption."

"How's that?"

"She was taken from her natural parents. State intervention. I don't know the specifics. One of those situations where they *had* to."

"That's something."

I tell him whatever other details I have that might be of help, which aren't all that many. Angela's approximate age (late twenties to early thirties), job experience (legal secretary), possible educational background (liberal arts most likely). I end up leaving out more than I give him: her fictional journal and my thieving of its essential contents, our night together and the discovery of missing toes. Maybe later, I tell myself. Maybe, if this all turns out well, I'll fill him in on the whole thing.

"One question," Tim says as I shake his hand in thanks and check both ways along Front Street for a taxi.

"You want to know why I need to find this out."

"No. I want to know what's in it for me."

"Nothing. Aside from a story."

"A newspaper kind of story, or a funny-thing-happened-the-other-day kind of story?"

"Just a girl-trouble kind of story," I tell him, with an embarrassed shake of the head. A gesture I know Tim Earheart will understand without going into the details.

Below us, another train pumps commuters and shoppers and ballgame ticketholders into the city. Tim and I look down and try to pick out individual faces in the windows. But they're a little too far away, moving a little too fast, to see anything but a long row of silhouettes.

"I better get back," Tim says, starting across Front Street.

"Me too," I say in reply, and though the question occurs to both of us – Back to *what*? – he's considerate enough to keep it to himself.

The first email on the Comment board at www.patrick.rush.com is from **therealsandman**.

Hope you liked the gift.

To cheer things up, Detective Ramsay rings with the news that he's discovered Evelyn has not been seen by family or friends for over four years.

"Starting to add up to a lot of missing people from that group of yours," he says. "Does that concern you?"

Is it illegal to hang up on a homicide investigator when he's addressing you directly? If so, Ramsay can add it to the list of charges he's tallying against me.

The phone rings again.

"This is harassment."

"Are you not taking your pills again?"

"Tim. Thought it was someone else."

"More girl trouble?"

"That would be nice. But no."

"Your heart belongs to Angela Whitmore. Is that it?"

In the background, the sound of shuffled papers.

"You've found her," I say.

"Not the person. But an interesting chunk of background. For one thing, turns out you were right about Children's Aid taking her from her birth parents. 'Acute neglect' is how the file puts it. Malnutrition, lack of basic hygiene. 'Indications of physical and emotional abuse.' Something beyond your standard junkie-mom scenario."

"The mother was an addict?"

"Lots of court-ordered rehab. Surprise, surprise: none of it worked."

"You got a name?"

"Mom is Michelle Carruthers. Which makes Whitmore either an assumed name, or maybe the name of her eventual adoptive parents."

"What about Dad?"

"No father on the scene at all, as far as the files show."

"And I'm guessing Michelle Carruthers is six feet under."

"Not as of a year ago. That was when she made an application to have Angela's adoptive parents' identities disclosed to her. They denied her, naturally."

"No kidding."

"Twenty-five years later and she wakes up in a trailer park on Lake Huron and goes, 'Hey, where'd my kid go?'"

"Does your file say where Angela ended up?"

301

"The adoptive parents' records are kept separate from the ones I could get my hands on. They're very particular about it."

"So you don't know."

"I still have a *job*, Patrick."

"Sorry."

"You want me to stay on this? Who knows, if I grease a few more wheels –"

"No, no. This is all I was really curious about anyway. Thanks."

"Listen, I don't usually put my nose into friends' personal stuff, but, given her pedigree, I'd say this Angela of yours might not be an ideal reintroduction to romance."

"Guess I've never known what's good for me."

"Tamara was good for you."

"Yes, she was," I say, the mention of my wife's name forcing something up my throat I don't want him to hear. "I'll let you go now, Tim. And thanks again."

I hang up. But before I pour myself a bourbon in a coffee mug (the glasses all look too small), before I even begin to digest the news of Angela's fatherless past, it strikes me that if Tim Earheart is as worried about me as he sounds, I'm in worse shape than I thought.

Of course I look up Michelle Carruthers. Of course I find her after a few Google searches and process-of-elimination calls – a unit address in Hilly Haven, a "mobile home estate" on Lake

Huron. And of course I make the drive to see her the same day without an idea as to what I want from her, or how it could help even if I did.

Hilly Haven isn't hilly, and what the few spindly poplars and collapsed snow fence around its perimeter might offer haven from would be hard to guess. The whole place has the appearance of an uncorrected accident: a couple dozen mobile homes arranged in rows, some sidled close, others aloof in weedy double lots, all with their backsides facing the lake.

Michelle Carruthers' place is the smallest. A camper trailer of the kind one used to see hitched to station wagons thirty years ago. Now, knocking on its side door and hearing the muffled greeting within ("*Who* the fuck?"), I wonder if Angela's mother can be convinced to step outside. It doesn't seem possible for there to be enough room for both of us inside.

When the door opens, however, I see that the odds of the woman hunched in its frame coming outside are slight. Her papery skin. An oxygen mask attached to her face, a tank on wheels by her side.

"Sorry to disturb you. My name is Patrick Rush," I say, putting out my hand, which her cold fingers weigh more than shake. "I'm looking for Angela."

"Angela?"

"Your daughter, ma'am."

"I know who she goddamn is."

"I was just –"

"Are you her husband or something? She run away on you?"

"I'm a friend. I think she may be in trouble. That's why I'm here. If I can find her, there's a chance I can help her."

After what may be a full minute's consideration, she pushes the trailer door open wide. Pulls the oxygen mask off and lets it necklace her throat.

"You might as well come in out of the sun," she says.

But it's hotter inside than out. And no larger than I'd feared. A stand-up kitchen smelling of canned spaghetti. A living room crowded by a giant TV in one corner and old combination radio-record player in the other. And at the rear, behind a half-drawn curtain, the tousled bunk where she sleeps. The only ventilation a rotating fan sitting atop a stack of LPs, though with all the windows closed, the best it can do is whisper hot air in my face.

"Have a seat," she says, collapsing into her recliner and leaving me to crouch on to a folding chair that, even pushed against the wall, forces my knees to graze hers.

"What I'm interested in learning is any background information that might –"

"Hold on. Just hold *on*," she says, putting her hands behind her head, a manoeuvre which offers me an unfortunate view of her armpits. "How'd you find me?"

"I'm a reporter. *Was* a reporter. We have access to information others don't have."

"They fire you, or you quit?"

"Pardon me?"

"You said you was a reporter. That's the past tense, am I right?"

"They fired me. But it was for the best."

"It's *all* for the best."

"I understand that Angela was put into the foster system when she was a child," I continue.

"You mean was she taken from me? Yes."

"That must have been difficult."

"I can hardly remember it. My life was ... *busy* then."

"Nevertheless, I'm aware that of late you have made some efforts to locate her."

She shows her teeth. A stretching of lips that appears more like the response to a dentist's command than a smile.

"I'm not as old as I look," she says. "But that doesn't mean I've got much time left. So, you start looking back, and thinking, 'Well, nothing I can do about that shit now.'"

"And did you manage to contact her?"

"Nah. I'm out of the picture. Which I *get*, you know?"

She sits forward enough that her face slides into the light of the reading lamp behind her. All premature lines and poison spots.

"What was she like?" I say. "When she was young?"

305

Her hand crawls up her chest to grip the oxygen mask hanging there. "She was innocent."

"Aren't all children?"

"That's what I'm saying. She was just like any other child."

"That's the past tense."

She fits the mask to her face and takes a breath. The mist against the plastic obscures all her features but her eyes. And they blink at me, clouding over.

"She suffered," she says.

"How?"

"Loneliness. She was left *alone*. I sure as hell weren't in any shape to be taking care of her."

"She liked to read."

"She liked to *write*. Diaries. Piles and piles of stuff."

"What were they about?"

"How do I know? I was just glad she had *something*."

She pulls the oxygen mask from her face and I can see that she won't hold up much longer. Just sitting and remembering draws fresh sweat to her cheeks.

"Angela's father," I say, glancing at the door.

"I haven't spoken to that sonofabitch in twenty-seven years."

"Do you know where he is?"

"Look in the penitentiaries. Least that's where I *hope* he is."

"What did he do?"

306

"What *didn't* he do?"

"Was he violent?"

"Something he couldn't control, then didn't *want* to control. You know what I'm sayin'?"

"Tell me."

"What he done ... what he ... with his *own* –" she says, coughing for air it will take the rest of the day to catch. "It's a thing I don't even want to talk about."

"It's important."

"How could *anything* to do with that man ever be important?"

"It might help me find your daughter."

She looks up at me and I can see that there's no strength left in her. But she's still a mother. Even in her, even now, there's the useless wish for everything to have been different.

"Killing," she says, teeth clenched so hard I can hear the chalky scrape of bone against bone. "Little children. *Girls*. He killed little *girls*."

Before I left Michelle Carruthers' trailer and stumbled, sun blind, to my Toyota, she had given me Angela's father's name. Raymond Mull. Which rang a bell the moment she said it, though specifically from where, and specifically for what, it took until I was able to get back to Toronto and start working my computer in the Crypt to discover.

Angela's mother was right. Raymond Mull was a killer of little girls. He was charged for the murders of two of them, in fact, a pair of thirteen-year-olds who went missing almost two decades ago. Roughly the same age that Angela, if she is thirty today, would have been then.

What follows from this? Nothing, perhaps. Or possibly everything.

If Angela was a thirteen-year-old contemporary of the murdered girls, it supports the interpretation (along with her missing toes) that she actually was the narrator of her fictionalized journal. Further, given Raymond Mull's relationship to her, it's probably true that he was the direct inspiration for the Sandman. In her story, she even had Jacob, her foster parent, suspect as much when he stated he believed it was the girl's father who was selecting victims. In the real world, odds are that Raymond Mull was the original terrible man who did terrible things.

What I discover next, however, suggests I wasn't the first member of the Kensington Circle to figure this much out.

A search on the media database I still have a password for left over from my *National Star* days finds dozens of stories on Raymond Mull's trial. There's photos of him too: bearded, eyes set too close together, but otherwise his face absent of expression. He doesn't look like Angela, but they share this. A half-thereness.

Judging from the initial reports covering Raymond Mull's trial, his conviction was viewed as a foregone conclusion. The Crown's evidence included work tools – saws, drills, hunting blades – found in his motel room. And he was identified by witnesses as being in the area over the preceding weeks, following students home from school, standing outside the convenience store where kids stopped for candy. His long list of previous convictions said little of worth about his character.

And yet none of this could prevent the case ending in an acquittal. The tools could render no blood samples from which to make positive DNA matches with the victims. The police argued this was only because Mull had been careful in cleaning them, and that even without blood, there was enough to connect him to the crimes. On this, the court disagreed. Without calling a single witness, the defence filed a motion to dismiss the charges on the grounds that the Crown failed in making a *prima facie* case. All that was left to the prosecution was to nail Mull for previous parole violations, which they did. His sentence was nine months.

Which means that, barring no other subsequent incarceration over the last eighteen years, Raymond Mull is a free man.

But what strikes me even more than this is the location where the murders took place. Whitley, Ontario. The same place where Conrad White and Evelyn drove their car off the highway.

It could just be coincidence. But I don't believe that it was. Evelyn and Conrad White's shared curiosity over Angela's story had led them to

Raymond Mull, to Whitley. That's what they had been up to all the time I'd come to assume them to be having a May-December, teacher-student affair. They were searching.

If I'm right in this, the possibility that Conrad and Evelyn's accident was in fact accidental becomes considerably harder to accept. They drove into a cliff wall. But what made them turn? At that speed, what were they driving *from*? Even the police found the crash "puzzling". One solution would be if it was a double murder. If their killer was Raymond Mull.

Angela's father. The original Sandman.

27

Sam calls me.

I've been sitting in the Crypt all day, intermittently writing in my journal and trying Angela's number over and over, as though persistence is all that's required to bring back the dead. I even try Len, whose answering machine's message is the creepy piano soundtrack from *Halloween*.

All of them gone, or missing. Me too. It's why the ringing of the phone takes me by surprise.

"Dad?"

"What's up?"

"Are you coming to visit today?"

"Not today."

"What are you scared of, Dad?"

"I'm not scared."

"What are you *scared* of?"

"I don't want you to get hurt for something I did," I say finally. "You're *it*. You're all I have. There's nothing more important to me than making sure I don't screw up again."

"What did you do?"

"I stole something."

"Can't you give it back?"

"It's too late."

"Like a ... perishable item."

"That's right. Just like that."

If you take another's past and use it as your own it can't be returned. It's bruised. Perishable. You take someone else's story and chances are even they won't want it back.

That evening, I know something's wrong even before I park the Toyota behind the house. The door to the yard is ajar. The one I'd remembered to padlock over a week ago. It keeps me in the front seat a couple minutes longer, hands on the wheel. A lick of breeze nudges the door open another foot. Even in the dark, I can see the pale cuts in the wood where a crowbar has wrenched it free of the bolt.

It's rage that starts me running two houses down, through the side alley to the street. Unlocking the door and kicking it open with an underwater rush of blood in my ears.

Upstairs. Making my way down the hallway, stepping blind into each room, not bothering to hide my steps or even turn on the lights.

No sign of anything taken or touched. Nothing left behind.

The same goes for downstairs. Every door locked, every window intact. Whoever went to the trouble of ripping the back gate apart was apparently interrupted on his way to the house. That, or the house wasn't his destination in the first place.

I pull back the curtains in the living room and look out the sliding glass doors. The light from a single hanging bulb illuminates the inside of the lopsided garden shed. A surprise. First, because it's been so long since I've been out there at night I didn't even know it had a bulb that still worked. And second, because the light wasn't on when I parked the car no more than four minutes ago.

I go down to the basement. Rummage through the neglected corner of sports equipment and find what I'm looking for at the bottom of the pile. A baseball bat. A Louisville Slugger that feels right in my hands, heavy but capable of decisive speed in the first swing. After that, if it works, I can take my time.

I'm opening the sliding door and shuffling through the uncut grass. The shed's door left open a foot in invitation.

The shed's window is small, maybe two feet square, the glass murky with cobwebs. I try to look in. At the angle I stand at, there are only the shelves and wall hooks that store ignored tools and unopened hardware gifts. A museum of the failed handyman.

I go to the door and bring the bat even with my shoulders.

For a moment, the traffic and air-conditioning thrum of the city is quieted. There is only me. A man standing in his back yard. Holding a baseball bat. Raising his foot to kick in a shed door.

It flies open. Hits the wall. Swings closed again.

Yet there is time enough to peek-a-boo what's inside. The old rotary lawnmower I've yet to take out this year. The 1999 Sunshine Girl calendar Tim Earheart gave me. Red paint dotted over the floor. Petra.

Then: not red paint, but blood.

Not Petra. Petra's body.

What did he use?

This is my first thought upon seeing what remains of Petra on my shed floor. Would a knife do that? A drill? Could you do it on your own?

Did he keep her in a freezer? I think this too. *She looks fresh enough.*

But this is shock talking. This isn't me.

I stare at her. The unfamiliar pinks and coiled blues that normally lie inside a person. I sit on a can of paint and do the same thing I did after finding her Yankees cap once it made its way from Angela's condo to my living-room coffee table. I just *looked* at it. Long enough for the morning to slip into afternoon, for a thunderstorm to come and go. And the whole time I was stuck on the same question as I am now: What do you do with evidence planted in your home that could put you in prison for the rest of your life?

There's going to the police and telling them the whole story, an expensive lawyer by your side, hoping they'll see it your way. Unavailable in my case, however. Not with all the connections that have even me wondering if I did it.

Next there's enlisting help. Calling a friend for advice, a drive across the border. But who would I call? Tim Earheart? Hard to believe he could resist the temptation to print the transcript of my call on tomorrow's front page.

In the end, you might do as I did: put on gardening gloves, wipe the Yankees cap for prints using a wet tea towel, cut the thing into ribbons and stick it in the trash.

Which is the same thing I do with Petra's body.

Yet not right away. Not until after a couple hours of taking deep breaths with my head between my knees. Smoking a cigarette from the emergency pack I keep in the flour jar. A round of dry heaves into the compost bin. It's not easy coming to a decision like that. But that's still nothing. Deciding to do it is a breeze compared with the doing of it.

Not to mention getting *ready* to do it.

Here, finally, is some use for what I learned over the hundreds of hours of prime-time forensic cop TV I studied as the Couch Potato: How to best cover your tracks in the disposal of a body.

I begin by stripping myself naked (later burning the clothes I wore when I entered the shed, just to be sure). After the cutting, I wrap each smaller part in several garbage bags. Dry, air-tight. Place the resulting packages in a larger bag used for yard waste.

Once I'm finished, I cut nails, hair, shave. Shower. Scour every inch of skin with cleansers reserved for kitchen use only. Bleach the bathroom.

315

Then do it all again. And again.

What do I remember now, only minutes after it's done? Bits and pieces. So to speak. The protective walls already going up in my brain. They won't hold, of course. Not forever, and not entirely. But you'd be surprised. You keep the worst of it at bay and you can still pour yourself a drink, look in the mirror and recall your own name.

Let's just say that cutting up a ballcap and doing the same to a woman's body are two different things. The tools required, the time, what it leaves behind. It's just *different*.

And after the mopping, the bleaching, the wiping for toe prints on the concrete floor, I'm still left with six yard-waste bags.

I smoke the rest of the pack.

Today is recycling day. The truck arrives early on my street, usually just after eight. A little over an hour from now. The collectors who work this neighbourhood are used to the sight of me dashing out at their approach, barefoot and in boxer shorts, frantically hauling out the compost I'd forgotten to take to the curb the night before. Every time, they let me apologize for the delay and watch as I insist on swinging the bags into the back myself. Once I'm done, they pull the switch that compacts the load into the truck's hold. Then they're gone.

And today, they'll be taking Petra with them.

28

I suppose it's the guilt over what I did out back in the shed, the ratcheting worry of it being discovered – whatever the reason, I end up staying in all the next day punishing myself. A steady infliction of the most hideous domestic torture: I watch TV.

Not that I don't try reading first. Sniffing at the opening of the latest Philip Roth (too sharp), sampling a random page of Borges (too fanciful), then a re-taste of Patricia Highsmith (too much like real life, or at least *my* real life). It seems likely I will never read again. I feel like the Burgess Meredith bookworm character in that *Twilight Zone* episode who, finding himself the last man alive on earth and prepared to finally savour all the works of literature he'd yet to get around to, sits down on the library steps only to have his specs fall off and shatter into a thousand pieces. That's one nerd's version of hell for you. And here is mine.

Not since I was paid to do so have I settled in for a full day with the early-morning Born Agains, followed by the afternoon Chatty Cathys, the prime-time autopsies, all capped off with the soulless hours of miracle diet pills, phone sex lines, get-rich-quick infomercials. This, I realize now, was likely my true vocation all along. Not the life of one who writes or even writes *about* books, but a malingering low-brow who wrongly thinks he deserves better. No wonder, when his life decides to assume the shape of literature, it isn't a novel of ideas, but a chronicle of murder and suspicion. The kind of thing I always felt I was too good to actually read, but am now being forced to live. A bloody page-turner.

On the positive side, it appears I've gotten away with it. No phone calls from the city's sanitation department inquiring about blue limbs punched out the side of compost bags, no neighbours coming by to complain about my screeching away with a rotary saw in the middle of the night. Petra will turn up some day, she'll have to. But it wasn't yesterday, and it wasn't today. And even when she does show herself, a week, a year, half a lifetime from now, there's no evidence to connect her to me. I likely won't be around for it anyway. If the Sandman's goal is to kill off everyone in the Kensington Circle one by one, he's almost finished. I'd put my money on me being the only one left alive. And he's already made it clear he knows where I live.

So now I wait for him down here in the Crypt, glancing up at any movement outside the basement windows, thinking every skulking cat or fast-food wrapper blown down the walkway are his boots passing by. He is waiting for me to come outside, and if I refuse, he will come for me here. I won't hear him enter. He'll find me in this very chair, the remote clutched in my hand. And he'll do what he'll do.

I wonder if he'll let me see who he is before he does.

All at once there's a collision of noise: the ringing of the doorbell, the sock-hop opening theme of *Happy Days*, the journal I'd been scratching in leaping to the floor. It's morning. A sandy light spills into the basement through the storm-drain windows.

I *must* be awake. Can you smell how bad you smell in your sleep?

The doorbell rings again. I'm tucking in my shirt as I climb the stairs, all the while wondering why I'm bothering to make myself presentable to the Sandman. For *this* is how he's decided to make his entrance. Not at night, but on a listless July morning with the clouds holding the heat over the city like a vast canopy of wool.

There's the shape of a man, tall and long-armed, standing on the other side of the front door's side windows. And I'm going to the door with no further prompting than another musical push of the bell – *Shave and a haircut, five cents!* – clicking the bolt lock open and turning the handle.

Ramsay offers one of his vaguely cruel, ironic smiles. He's in a good mood.

"You want some coffee?"

"I'm trying to cut down," he says. "But you know, I think I will."

I give him his coffee and warn him it's hot. But he wraps his hand around the sides of the mug and takes a thirsty gulp.

"Can't get hot enough for me," he says.

By now Ramsay has walked over to the sliding doors and is looking out at the day. Then, so deliberately I can only assume he wants me to notice, he lowers his eyes from the sky to the shed in the back yard.

"So are you going to put the cuffs on, or do we just walk out of here?" I say, slapping both hands on the counter.

"You think I'm here to arrest you?"

"Yes."

"I thought we were friends."

"What *are* you doing here? Because I've got some important *Beverly Hillbillies* re-runs to get back to."

When he puts his mug down on the counter I see that it's empty, while mine, still steaming, sits next to his.

"I'm here to tell you we found him," he says.

"Found him?"

"Arrested him this morning."

"I'm not following you."

"The Sandman," Ramsay says. "The fellow who killed your writing circle friends. He's *ours*."

By now I'm leaning against the fridge door to remain standing.

"Who is it?"

"You don't know?"

"I've thought it was everyone. Even you."

"In my experience, the first choice is usually the right one."

"William."

"Congratulations."

"And now you have him?"

"He'll be arraigned later this morning. It's why I have to run in a minute. Always like to be there for the reading of the charges."

I suppose I must ask Ramsay other questions after this, because he's telling me things. About the evidence they have on William. His background, criminal record, his aliases. The blood-spotted tools in his rented room. His membership not only in the Kensington Circle, but the ones before, the ones that Carol Ulrich and Ronald Pevencey and Jane Whirter had been a part of. How the police will keep searching for Angela and Petra and Len, and they'll find them too, their remains anyway, because Ramsay hates nothing more than an incomplete file.

"I never *really* thought it was you," Ramsay is saying now. "But you were in that circle. And you were the one with the novel with the same title as the killer's handle. It was *odd*. But the evidence speaks for itself. And besides, you were just using him for material, weren't you? A

321

parasite – if you'll excuse the term. But that's *you*. That's the kind of fellow you *are*."

Ramsay checks his watch. He's still early for court – the kitchen clock has just gone a quarter to nine – but he pretends he's running late. The fun's over at the Rush household.

He strides to the door and I follow him. And though he moves with the self-assurance of a man who has once again been proved right, I realize, with an itchy thrill, that the triumph is actually mine. Nobody's found Petra. Even if they do, they'll attribute my handiwork to William. And Ramsay has done me the favour of catching the Sandman before he had the chance to visit me.

He's halfway down the front walk before he turns.

"You better hope we get a conviction," he says.

I knew it was William. That is, it could *only* have been him. And yet, almost from the very beginning, I had believed that the Sandman wasn't just a killer's pseudonym but an actual being for whom no real name exists. Separate from humanity not just in deed but composition. A monster.

Such was the charm of Angela's story.

As a psychological profile, William's a classic. A kid who lost his parents in swift succession when he was only six – the mother to MS, the father to a stroke – and spent the rest of his youth being traded around from one aunt or uncle to another, from prairie town to prairie town. "Nobody looking out

322

for him," as Ramsay put it. "That, or they were trying to look the other way."

The fact is, little Will was a friendless bully as early as school counsellors started files on him. A teacher beater, window smasher, playground torturer. Followed by the emergence of more explicitly criminal talents. The dismemberment of neighbourhood pets. Thefts, break-and-enters, assaults. A graduation of offences from the petty to the brutal.

Then, a couple years out of high school, William went off the grid. No new charges, no known address. As far as the police could tell, he spent the better part of his twenties rolling between the rougher parts of towns out west, renting rooms in the most forgotten quarters of Winnipeg, Portland, Lethbridge, Spokane. Odd-jobbing for money. Spending his free time on far darker pursuits.

Where William went, missing people followed. A seemingly arbitrary string of men and women with no shared characteristics or backgrounds, all cold cases with little in common other than a tall, bearded man who kept to himself, had spent some time in their towns around the time they disappeared. "Only circumstantial," Ramsay conceded. "But I don't believe it for a second. Not after what we found."

And what had the police found at William's apartment over a bankrupted butcher's shop in the east end? The tools of the trade for a new butcher's shop. Cleavers, saws, meat-cutting wires. Most of it encrusted with human blood. All of it off to the lab for DNA testing. But given some of the other personal items found in William's bathtub, kitchen cabinets, even lying at the end of his bed – Carol Ulrich's purse, Ronald Pevencey's diary – it's certain that the results will prove that his tools were what he used to dispose of them all.

There were also the storybooks. Do-it-yourself editions with cardboard covers. Inside, pages relating the disconnected tales of a shadow that drifted through the night, periodically stopping to carve up complete strangers who caught his eye. Written in William's hand. And the protagonist's name?

"Let me guess," I'd interrupted Ramsay. "The Sandman?"

"Isn't that copyright infringement?"

"Titles can't be owned. Only the contents."

"That's too bad. I thought I might have another charge to lay against our friend."

The police have their man. And their man *is* a man. Nothing supernatural about him, aside from the black magic that enables one to kill for no reason other than pleasure in the doing of it. The Sandman is a creation of fantasy. But the fantastical is not required here, it never is. All that's needed is your off-the-rack dismemberment artist: the unloved child, the world hater, the remorseless sociopath. Check the back pages of any newspaper. There's plenty of them.

I should be relieved. And I am. Sam can come home again. We can start on the business of making new lives.

But there is still the lone survivor's question: Why me? Someone has to tell the story, I suppose.

And this time, it isn't Angela's, it's not stolen. It's mine.

The next day is William's bail hearing, and though I want to go straight down to St Catharines and pick Sam up, I prevent myself with a sobering dose of fear. If the lawyer for the one they call the Sandman somehow manages to loose him on the streets this afternoon, I know where he's most likely to visit first. Sam is safe now. One more day apart is the price for keeping him that way.

Still, the moment seems to call for some kind of celebration.

What I need to do is get out of the house.

A drive in the country.

The sign for Hilly Haven sprouts up from the horizon as a lone interruption of the flat fields. I turn in at the gate and wonder how I'm going to tell Angela's mother that her daughter is likely dead. I suppose I don't have to worry too much about the precise wording. Michelle Carruthers is used to receiving bad news. She'll know before I'm halfway to telling her.

I park on the gravel lane outside her trailer, thankful for the cloud cover that veils some of

Hilly Haven's more dispiriting details. Its unwheeled tricycles, scalped dolls. The stained underwear swinging on the clotheslines.

"Nobody home."

I turn before knocking on the trailer's door to find a woman too old for the pig-tails that reach down to the two chocolate-smeared children at the ends of her hands. None wearing T-shirts of sufficient size to cover the bellies that peek out from over the waists of their sweatpants.

"Will Michelle be back soon?"

"Not soon."

"Is she well?"

"You a friend of hers?"

A cop. That's what I'd look like to her. Hilly Haven must get its share of plainclothes banging on its tin doors.

"My name is Patrick Rush. I was a friend of her daughter's. She's come into some trouble, I'm afraid."

"Trouble?" the woman says, releasing the hands of the chocolatey kids.

"It's a private matter."

"You mean she's dead too?"

"I'm sorry?"

"Michelle. She passed on last week."

"Oh. I see."

"The doctors didn't know exactly what got her. But with her, it could have been *anything*."

There is nothing more to say than this. Yet simply walking past the three of them to the car and driving off without another word doesn't seem possible either. If it weren't for the blackened tongue that the smaller of the two kids sticks out at me, I might not have come up with a question.

"Has there been a funeral already?"

"Two days after she died. A few round here were the only ones who showed up. As well as the son."

"The son?"

"It's who we all figured it was anyway."

"What was his name?"

"Never asked."

"What did he look like?"

"A big guy, I guess. Wasn't the kind who seemed to like you looking at him all that much. Like he wanted to be there, but not have anybody else know it."

I step down off the cement steps at the trailer's door. The midday sun unveils itself from behind a bank of clouds.

"When was the funeral?"

"Last week. I told you."

"Which *day*?"

"Thursday, I think."

Thursday. Two days *before* William's arrest. *A big guy*.

"I better be getting back," I say. But as I try to pass the woman, she stops me with a hand on my arm.

"I suppose someone should look that son of hers up if his sister's passed on."

"I'll let him know."

"So you *know* him? We was right? He was Michelle's boy?"

"You know families," I say vaguely, but the woman seems to understand. She gives me a nod that takes in her own children, Angela's mother's trailer, the blazing sun, all of Hilly Haven.

"Oh yeah," she says. "Full of surprises."

When I get home there's a message from Tim Earheart. He wants to get together, see how I am. But I know even as I return his call and arrange to meet at a bar near his new house in Cabbagetown that he's heard about William's arrest and wants to find out what I know about it. This has been Tim's assignment from the start. And now that the final act is beginning – the public cleansing ritual that is every high-profile criminal proceeding – he wants to milk every advantage he has over the competition.

Tim thinks I know something. And unless something juicier presents itself, he'll keep asking what it is. And yet I still cling to the possibility that I can escape disclosure. It's true that if William does end up going to a full trial, I'll be called as a witness. But if the prosecution ends up not having to probe that far, or, better yet, if William pleads guilty, no one need ever know that the author of *The Sandman* was once in a writing class with the Sandman. I still have a chance. So long as Tim can be discouraged from digging further into the Patrick Rush angle.

"How're you liking the new place?" I ask him as the first round arrives.

"It's an investment. Besides, I'm thinking of settling down pretty soon."

"Stop it. You're killing me."

"I just need to meet someone."

"Haven't you met enough someones?"

"She's out there. Just like your Angela person."

I nod, trying to read Tim to see if he knows something about Angela's disappearance that I don't.

"Must be strange," Tim muses. "Being so close to this William Feld business."

"I wasn't so close to it."

"Your book could have been the guy's biography."

"That's an exaggeration."

"The whole title thing. It's kind of hard to accept as coincidence."

"The police didn't think it was so hard."

"They've talked to you?"

"A detective came round to ask some questions."

"Ramsay."

"I think that's the guy."

"And what did you tell him?"

"What I'm telling you. It's a *novel*. It's all made up. I'm just glad it's over."

Tim chokes on the sip he's taking from his bottle. "Over? Not for me. This is my story. I'm going to be filing on Mr Feld's trial for the next several months. Which could turn out to be a real bitch if I can't come at it through a side door."

He looks at me straight now, hands flat on the bar.

"I wish I could help you," I say, blowing him back an inch with an exhaled belch. "But there's not a goddamn thing I know about William Feld that anybody who read your story in today's paper doesn't know."

I'll never know if Tim believes me or not. But whether out of a sense that what I've said is true, or some last tug of friendship, he lets me go.

"Working on anything new?"

"I was thinking of returning to newspapering. I'd be prepared to try something new. The horoscopes, classifieds, crossword puzzles," I say. "You think the Editor-in-Chief would have me back?"

Oh yes. We both have a good laugh over that one.

In the morning I drive down to St Catharines. I've brought all sorts of presents with me (a plasma screen TV for Stacey and her husband, iPods and a Tolkien collector's set for their kids) but nothing, intentionally, for Sam. Our gift to each other is the reunion itself. It will be up to Sam how he wants to spend the rest of the summer. We will work our way back to what we used to be at our own pace, and with only ourselves to tell us how it is to be done.

On the drive home I make a point of not overdoing how difficult the last weeks have been without him. And for the first hour or so, he offers anecdotes involving his numbskulled cousins, how good a swimmer he's become. He's going easy on me, too.

Then, somewhere around Oakville, flying past the low-rise head offices and steakhouse franchises, Sam decides I'm able to take his coming to the point.

"You have to tell me, Dad."

"I know."

"It doesn't have to be now."

"Okay."

"But sometime."

"I owe you that much."

"It's not about *owing*."

Sam turns in his seat. And there's not an eight-year-old looking back at me but a young man who is surprised at how his father can't appreciate what should be obvious.

"If you don't tell me, you'll be the only one who knows," he says.

August decides to behave, with afternoon breezes off the lake nudging the smog northward to reveal the city it had shrouded in orange for the month before. To honour this change, Sam and I go for long walks. Lunching out in T-shirts and flip-flops, biking along the trails in the Don Valley, sliding our hands over the Henry Moore sculptures at the gallery when the security guards aren't looking. We've even started reading again. Bookish picnics in Trinity-Bellwoods swallowing *Robinson Crusoe* (Sam) and *Atonement* (me) in the shade.

But even these happy days are not free of ghosts.

The first arrives in the form of a voice. A phone call near midnight that sounds like it's coming from a bar.

"Patrick?"

"Who is this?"

"It's *Len*."

"Where are you?"

"The Fukhouse."

"Why?"

"I'm not too sure. I guess it's got some sentimental value."

"This is going to sound stupid, but I have to ask," I say, squeezing my eyes shut against the bedside lamp I click on. "You're not dead, are you?"

"No," Len says after a moment's thought. "I don't think so."

"Where have you been?"

"I just kind of left everything behind and rented places all over town. It was pretty screwed up for a while there."

"It was."

"They got him now though."

"Yeah. They got him."

He sighs into the receiver. A wet-lipped whistle that tells me that until I just confirmed it for him, Len wasn't sure if it was over or not.

"You know what's funny?" he goes on. "I was about to say that maybe I can go home now, but I don't have a clue where that is. My old landlord threw all my books and comics out at my old place."

"You can always start again."

"Start what?"

"Collecting."

"Yeah. Sure."

In the background, someone smashes what sounds like a shot glass against the wall.

"Busy night down there?"

"It's okay," Len says nervously. "Hey, you doing anything right now?"

"I was getting ready for bed, actually."

"Is it that late? I was going to ask if you wanted to come out and meet me. To celebrate."

"Not tonight."

"Another time."

This seems to be it. But Len lingers, the loneliness travelling down the line like an invisible weight.

"I guess we're the only ones left," he says finally.

"What about Angela?"

"You think she could still be alive?"

"No."

"Neither do I."

"Well, here's to us, Len. To the living."

"To the living," Len says, sounding less than certain about who that might be.

* * *

The other phantom of August isn't dead either, but might as well be.

I see him walking back from the corner store one afternoon, Sam gripping my thumb with one hand, and screwing a popsicle into his mouth with the other. A father and son holding hands on a neighbourhood street in summertime. One version of freedom.

We're passing by the punky hair salon on the corner – the place where Ronald Pevencey once cut and coloured – when a black panel van pulls over against the curb twenty feet ahead of us. Although this part of Queen Street has delivery trucks stopping and starting outside throughout the day, something about it draws my attention. Not any detail, but its utter *lack* of detail: no business name painted on the doors, no stickers, no rear licence plate. Even the black paint is of an age that has dulled its finish to an old chalkboard.

I slow our pace as the distance between us and the van shrinks to a couple of strides. Neither driver nor passenger doors have opened, and the angle of the side mirrors doesn't let me see who sits up front. But it's the back of the van that radiates trouble. The two rear windows webbed with dust, along with streaks of something else. Dried smears running from the top of the glass to the bottom. Rain. Or solvent rubbed off of work gloves. Or bare hands split open in an effort to scratch through the glass.

"Why are we stopping, Dad?"

I'm thinking of an answer – *It's such a nice day, I just want to turn around and go home the long way* – when I see him. William's face against the van's back window.

I pull Sam against me. His popsicle drops to the sidewalk.

Nobody sees William but me.

And even *I'm* not seeing William. He's in a solitary confinement cell somewhere, awaiting sentencing. Because there will be no trial. Not now. Not after he pleaded guilty and agreed to sign a written confession just days ago. All that's left to be determined is how many consecutive life sentences he will serve.

So it's not William whose lips are stretched into an oval, his tongue pressed white against the glass in a silent scream. But this doesn't stop me from scuffling backwards to slam my shoulders against the hair salon windows.

This is what terrifies me about the van: not William, but what horrors have taken place within it. The sort of things that would frighten even William. And there's his face to prove it. Never before showing anything but veiled threat – coal-eyed, beard-shrouded – yet now stretched with panic.

The van spews exhaust. When it clears, William isn't there. But the wet circle his tongue cleared on the glass still is. Was there to begin with.

With a lurch, the van re-enters the lane of moving traffic. A half-block on, it makes a turn and is gone.

Sam kicks the melted pool of popsicle goo against the wall. Takes my hand to lead me home. He doesn't ask what I think I saw. He doesn't have to. As with the bad man who lives in the bedroom closet, if you can just hold on to what you know is real, he can't hurt you.

29

The summer ends with a string of identically perfect days, as though in apology for its earlier abuses. A lulling, blue-skied week of becalmed downtown traffic and evenings of clear air flavoured by barbecue smoke. All the uncertainties and worries of what has come before – not just for the especially beleaguered Rushes, but for all who wander, grinning, down the city's streets – are put into more manageable perspectives. Everyone wishing for this to go on forever.

And then, abruptly, it's Labour Day weekend. Overnight, there's an autumnal coolness in the air, the leaves trade half their green for gold. *Now's the time*. The chalky taste of Back to School days tells us this. *If there's something fun you've been meaning to get around to, do it now*.

It's how Sam and I decide to go to the Mustang Drive-in dusk-'til-dawn. The last show of the season at a place Tamara and I used to make the trip to, sneaking in a bottle of white wine under the seat and making out like teenagers. For Sam, the attraction is seeing what he, despite my repeated corrections, calls "My dad's movie".

"North," Sam says, his nose to the glass, as I turn off the concession road and join the line of traffic inching toward the admission booth.

I didn't know my son could tell directions from the stars.

"Look," I tell him, pointing to the back of the screen up the slope. The cowboy riding the bucking bronco atop the marquee, the fields of harvest corn beyond. Sam reads aloud the lettering announcing tonight's feature presentation.

"*The Sandman,*" he says.

I've already seen it. Sam may not be old enough to handle some of the more "mature" subject matter (this is the opinion of the censor board, whose rating fussily warns of "Violence, and Suggestions of Improper Sexual Interest"). But if the guy in the ticket booth is prepared to take my money for two adults, then for tonight, that's what we are.

We park off to the side in front of the concession stand, haul folding chairs out of the Toyota's trunk. Throw a sleeping bag over our knees to guard against the chill.

Although *The Sandman* is based on my novel, my involvement in its being made has been limited to the guilty acceptance of a production-fee cheque. I was invited to the premiere in Los Angeles a couple weeks ago but declined. The studio publicists called to plead their case that my non-attendance might be misconstrued as my having "creative reservations about the project". I assured them I had no creativity with which to hold reservations. In return for my assurance of silence, they sent me champagne and an advance copy of the DVD.

Just the other day I popped it in, uncorked the bubbly, and for the next hour and a half sat myself down in the Crypt and drank straight from the bottle. It wasn't bad. The champagne, I mean. As for the movie, I suppose it possesses a certain propulsiveness, fuelled mainly by chop-chop editing and a techno soundtrack that makes the city in which the film was shot (Toronto, as a matter of fact, though Toronto as intended to look like New York) feel jacked on meth.

What's funny about the movie, what slightly bothers me about it, isn't its quality one way or the other, but how divergent it is from the real thing. From Angela. Her voice. That's what is utterly missing from the Hollywood version, through no fault of its screenwriters and actors and producers. How could they know what it was like to sit in Conrad White's candlelit apartment, the snow scratching at the windows, and listen to Angela reading from the doodle-margined pages of her journal? Even if they *had* been there, would it have changed anything? A movie tells a story, but its world is static. Every set and gesture and image carefully determined, the narrative hermetically sealed. A movie doesn't let you create what you see within yourself. But that's what Angela's voice did. It invited you inside.

"It's starting!" Sam announces as the flood-lights cut out.

The rest you know.

You know from where all this started, deep in the middle of things. The story of the Man Who Lost His Son at the Movies. I say "lost" because that's how the police and newspapers referred to it, as though Sam was a dropped wallet. The media releases are careful to point out that no evidence of foul play was found at the scene. I don't know whether they said this as a matter of general policy or whether they simply didn't accept my account of chasing a shadow through the corn rows.

You already know how this Labour Day turns out for me. But when you start in the middle, there are certain angles that are left out, shades of meaning that wouldn't have made sense the first time around. Consider, for instance, the troubling effect that watching *The Sandman* on a towering screen under the night's stars had on me. How something in the oversized action tried to tell me to *Take your son and leave.* Tried to warn me.

What are you talking about?

The thing that lives under your bed. The eyes in your closet at night, watching you. The dark. Whatever frightens you the most ...

I can only watch the screen for a few seconds at a time. The actors delivering their lines directly to

340

me, their faces looking down with ironic masks of "fear", "determination", "worry". I was wrong about movies being fixed worlds. *These* characters, the action on *this* screen – all of it wants *out*.

"You want anything?" I ask Sam. "Tater tots?"

And he takes my hand. Lets it go only when the cashier takes too long to ring us in.

Then I'm running between the lines of parked cars, trying to tell myself what I know is happening isn't happening. It doesn't work. Because the Sandman is *here*. Not William, who is miles away, sitting in a cell. Not Ramsay. Not Len or Conrad White. Not Raymond Mull.

It's the Sandman who runs into the corn field, letting me catch a glimpse of him so I can follow. This is what he wanted me to do. It gave him the time he needed to disappear, to ensure I was headed in the opposite direction from where Sam was being kept in the trunk of one of the back row cars. Or maybe my son was in the car next to mine the whole time.

I was chasing the Sandman. But he never had Sam to begin with.

By the time I reach the abandoned farmhouse on the far side of the field it's over. I can only stand there, staring back at the Mustang's screen in the distance.

The terrible man who does terrible things isn't William. It isn't even a man. It's a girl. The one whose face is on the drive-in screen, the one who read from her journal in Conrad White's apartment, the one with toes missing from frost-bite. A girl who has grown up to assume different names. Steal different lives.

My mistake was to assume that the villain of my story was the same as the villain in hers. But the monster who has taken the only thing left to me isn't the Sandman. It's the one who created him.

PART FOUR

The Terrible Man
Who Does Terrible Things

30

There is a search. You can imagine. A father loses
his son at the movies, the boy snatched away in the
time it takes to buy hot dogs and onion rings – it's
a summer weekend news editor's dream come true.
In the early morning of that Sunday – before the
dawn of the cancelled dusk-'til-dawn – one of the
networks awakens a "missing person expert" and
tapes an interview in which we are reminded that
"The first twelve hours are crucial in cases of this
kind." Even the police supervisors behind the
microphones at the first news conference of the
day aren't immune to the excitement of a race
against time, especially where there's a kid
involved. It's like something on TV. It is on TV.

Look: there's the Chief of the OPP staring
directly into the cameras and vowing to put all
available resources into locating "little Sam", and
until they do, "I can tell you there won't be sleep
for any of us." There's the shots of local volunteers
marching through the Mustang's neighbouring

345

fields of corn, searching for clues, for body parts. And there's the father, his skin speckled and spongy as oatmeal, robotically pleading for his boy's safe return. *So*, thinks the readership of the Couch Potato, *that's what a novelist looks like*.

He looks suspicious. Even to me. An unconvincing performance of parental concern – not enough panic, the voice emptied, as though he's already made the turn toward grief. I watch a repeated loop of myself on the all-news channel down in the Crypt in disbelief. That's not how I *feel*. That's not even me. Here: this fellow sobbing into his hands, throwing a rock glass against the panelled wall to avoid pouring anything into it, and a minute later cutting his feet on the shards when he gets up to check with the police for the fifth time this hour. I'm your man.

It appears the police might think so too. They're coming around to "go over things" again, and though they once more offer the services of a "family crisis counsellor", I can tell their initial sympathy is already starting to dry up. There are fewer questions about the figure I'd seen at the back of the drive-in's lot, and more about my emotional condition over the last few years. First, there was the loss of my wife to cancer. Then the messy business of the William Feld murders, which, as one investigator puts it, "We had you on the longlist for the whole kaboodle." Plus all the other layers: my son taken at the screening of a movie based on my own book, a book in which a shadowy figure takes the lives of children. "I mean, you can't *write* that kind of stuff," another cop tells me, shaking his head. "But then again, you did."

By Sunday evening, they're suggesting I call a lawyer. When I tell them there's no need, they look at me as though that's just the sort of thing a guilty bastard would say. Out there in the night a search for my son is still under way, but in here, at the father's house on Euclid Street, they've already found the guy they're looking for, and all there's left to do is wait for him to break. In time, the ones like me always do.

With my permission, they're listening in on every phone call. They say it's in case a ransom demand comes in, but I can tell it's more likely evidence collection. A message from an accomplice. A midnight confession.

And I don't blame them. In such cases, the parent is always the prime suspect. Statistically speaking, shadows are merely shadows. Harm tends to come from the ones you know best.

There are always exceptions, however. There's always a Sandman. And when he strikes, don't be surprised when you're the only one who believes it was him.

For the first twenty-four hours, there isn't time to suffer. There's only the same answers to the same questions, showing complete strangers where everything's kept around the house, letting a nice woman straighten your collar and wipe toothpaste from the corner of your mouth before the press conference.

In the end, however, these distractions only make everything worse. In my case this comes on day two, upon awakening from a sleeping-pill nap and collapsing to the bedroom floor – one pant leg on, the other off – under the weight of facts. *Struck by the truth*. I'd never realized how literally this cliché could be taken. It's the truth that leaves me splayed out over the hardwood, blinking at the dust bunnies under the bed, both hands reaching around to the back of my skull to check for blood.

Sam is gone.

They're not going to find him.

I'm the only one who stands a chance of getting him back.

If it weren't for this last thought I'm not at all sure if, an hour later, I would have been able to finish getting dressed. A good thing, seeing as there is the press to be dealt with. Take a peek out the curtains: a pair of TV news vans, their hairsprayed correspondents practicing their serious faces, along with a gaggle of beat writers from the papers, sharing dirty jokes and flicking cigarette butts into my neighbour's garden. If life is to be carried on with – even whatever brittle simulation of a life that might be available to me – they will all have to be satisfied enough to leave me alone at least until their next deadline.

I decide the best way to proceed is to grant an exclusive. It's a reflex that prompts me to choose the *National Star*. And who does the police's media relations person bring in but the kid from Swift Current.

"So you're in hard news now?" I ask him, and despite the wilfully clenched jaw, he allows a grin at my recognizing him.

"No future in arts."

"You're right there."

"Guess they promoted me."

"The Editor-in-Chief knows talent when she sees it."

"This must be a very difficult time," he starts. It's how all of them start. The cops, the counsellors, the wellwishers, the hacks. Thank God for TV.

I follow with some televisual dialogue of my own. About remaining optimistic, asking whoever might know something about my son to come forward. Then the Swift Current kid asks the inevitable follow-up.

"What do you make of the overlap between all this and your novel?"

"I don't make anything of it."

"But isn't it striking how –"

"We're done."

"Sorry?"

I reach over and click off his recorder. "Interview's over. And remind the other vultures outside that you're the only one to get any roadkill today."

It works. Within a couple of hours, the vans have cleared off along with the shivering journos who will be forced to quote from the *National Star*'s piece if they want any comment from Patrick Rush. Even the police have honoured my request for a little privacy. They send over a social worker to sit vigil just in case Sam walks in the door. It allows me to go out.

I head up to Dundas Street and turn east on to the ever-lengthening tentacle of Chinatown. Before I know it was where I was headed I end up outside The Fukhouse. Anarchists. Evelyn told me this is where they met on the night I first saw her. Now it makes me wonder: *Can anarchists hold meetings and still be anarchists?* Then again, if the lawless can't be flexible with the rules, who can?

A light goes on in Conrad White's old apartment. Behind the gauzy curtains a pair of shadows move about in what is likely some domestic chore but, from out here, appears as a ballroom dance. The two figures circling, holding hands for a moment before casting off to the opposite sides of the room.

The bulb flicks off. The room lit for so short a time I doubt the shadows were ever there at all. More ghosts. Evelyn and Conrad glimpsed in an afterlife waltz.

But I'm still alive. My son too. He has to be. There's no point in seeing ghosts any more. They have nothing to tell me other than what has come before. All that remains for the living is to pick up the mystery where the dead left off.

"So this really *is* your local," a voice behind me declares. I turn to find Ramsay grinning at me through The Fukhouse's gloom. "Would have pegged you for something a bit more tweedy."

"The drinks are cheap."

"They ought to be," he says, surveying the room. "Let me buy you one?"

"Buy me two."

Ramsay orders bourbon with beer chasers. We get the former inside us as soon as they arrive.

"Just dropped by your house," he says.

"And I wasn't there."

"Went out for a stroll, did you?"

"You would know. You followed me here."

"I'm a cop," Ramsay shrugs. "Old habits."

We sit looking straight ahead for a time. Our heads floating in the greasy mirror behind the gins, whiskies and rums.

"A terrible thing," Ramsay says finally. "Your boy."

I try to measure the sincerity in his voice, the regretful shake of his head. Seems real to me. Then again, I've gotten Ramsay wrong before. I may have never gotten him right.

"I'm told your best men are on the case," I say.

"Then I'm sure they'll find him."

"I feel like I should be helping them look."

"Why aren't you?"

"They told me to stay at home."

"That's a hard order to follow if you think he's out there."

"I know he is."

"You *know*?"

"Sam is alive. And I'm going to be the one who finds him."

"Sounds like you're on to something."

"If I was, would I tell you?"

"You might. If you wanted to be clear."

"Clear?"

"A show of goodwill. Without it, people can start down wrong paths."

He had me. For a second, I thought now that Ramsay had William in his cell, there was a chance he would actually be sympathetic with a father who'd lost his boy. But suspicion is Ramsay's default position. It's where he lives.

"I would never hurt Sam."

"Nobody says you have."

"Nobody has *said* so, no. So if they're not being honest with me, why should I be honest with them?"

"Like I said. You could make this clear."

"It's clear enough for me."

I start toward the exit. A bit off balance from the bourbon, the rush that comes with the speaking of privately held revelations. But when Ramsay opens his mouth to say something as I go, I'm still able to beat him to it.

"You've found your Sandman," I shout as both palms slap the door wide open. "Now it's my turn."

Ramsay may still be following me, but I don't care. I'm not doing anything wrong. Only walking. And whispering questions out loud. Questions that, over a long night's wander east, lead me out of the fog of shock.

First up is how whoever took Sam knew we were planning to be at the Mustang on that particular night. As far as I can recall, I hadn't spoken of it to anyone. Had Sam? Perhaps. An overheard playground boast ("My dad's taking me to see *his* movie tonight!"), or something let slip to his friend Joseph. Still, these are unlikely scenarios, as Sam doesn't usually gossip with his gang of kids at the park, none of them do, all of them boys of an age where their primary communication is the role play of machine-gunning soldiers or robots with laser beams firing out from their eye sockets.

The far greater probability is that we were followed. A black van. Changing lanes to keep me in view as we headed out of the city.

So why not take this to the police? I've come close to telling them about Angela a couple of times, but held back for reasons both rational and intuitive. On the rational side, I have no proof that it was her. More than this, "Angela" is dead. I've got Petra's disposal to keep hidden. And I'm currently the prime suspect in Sam's disappearance.

Now that I think of it, Angela likely had something on everyone in the circle that they didn't want out in the open. It's how she's kept under the radar all along.

But what really prevents me from mentioning her name is the gut certainty that I'm not *meant* to. If Angela – or whoever it is who has my son – gets the idea that I'm telling the police everything I know, it's over. The only way to Sam is through following the story to the end.

Before I know it the sun is plucking stars from the sky. I've made it all the way out to the Beaches, turned down one of its side streets to the boardwalk. No one out but the few pre-dawn joggers and picnic-table snoozers, the lonely and haunted like me. With shoes off, the sand is cool under my feet. Yet when I step into the first timid waves the water is body temperature, having been simmered over the course of a heatwaved summer. It may never freeze again.

Something touches my hand – a fly, a candy wrapper lifted from the beach on a gust of wind – and I look down expecting Sam to be there. The fact that he is missing is always at the front of my mind, and yet the illusion of his presence comes to me several times every waking hour. He's not here. But he *should* be. Taking my hand and stepping out into the water. Asking if he can go all the way in. Telling me not to be afraid.

The morning brings an ugly specificity to the flatscreen billboards and construction cranes to

354

the west. It turns my eyes back out over the water. But the lake is just as likely an industrial product, its surface wrinkly and thin as aluminum foil.

Here's what I'm thinking as I start back: there is nowhere to go any more that has not been modified, re-invented, enhanced. Places don't *exist* as they once did, simply and convincingly. Virtual reality is the only reality left.

And so what? If I can just have Sam back, the rest of the world can keep its recycled myths, its well-crafted fakery. I don't need anything to be real any more. I just need him.

31

To find Sam, I have to find Angela. But to search for someone who doesn't exist: not the best task for an out-of-work TV critic. So what would Tim Earheart or Ramsay do in my shoes? Start with what's on the table. Not much. There's Angela's name (false), her age (within a decade range), her published work (lifted from others' autobiographical accounts). There's also what I know of her appearance (especially susceptible to the whimsies of shadow and light, so that she was one thing reading from her journal on the opposite side of Conrad White's rug, and another the night she cupped her hands over my ears to muffle the sounds she made in her bed, as though it was me and not her neighbours she needed to save from distraction). For someone who has come to play such a cruelly important role in my life, Angela has done all the taking and in return left next to nothing of herself behind.

One thread I still have of hers takes me to the condo where, eighteen floors above, I had seen

356

and touched parts of her that now, in recollection, fall in favour of the argument that Angela has never been anything but a creation of fantasy. My effort to return my hands to her skin renders only the most generic impression, a softcore going through the motions. The naked Angela comes to me now from too great a distance, implausibly flawless and blue-lit.

If this is the case – if I never was with Angela on what I thought was our only night together – then perhaps Angela isn't to blame. Perhaps *I'm* the psychotic. There *is* no Angela because there never *was* an Angela. Which would mean she isn't the one who has done something terrible to Sam. I am.

Only the building's superintendent throwing me against the wall puts these dark considerations aside.

"You," the man says. The same one who'd given me the heave-ho the last time. Now, however, he's giving me the clinical stare of a physician checking for signs of jaundice. "Tell me. Just between us. Whisper it in my ear if you'd like."

"Yes?"

"What is your *problem*?"

"I'm looking for someone."

"You've found him."

"Not you. A tenant."

"They're not tenants when they own the unit."

"What are they then?"

"They're *unit owners*."

"I'm looking for a unit owner."

"Buzz them."

"They're not here. Or not answering."

"If I'd known it was you down here, I wouldn't have answered either."

His hands have loosened their grip on his belt. It's his calmness that makes it certain he's going to hit me. In my experience, there's always a moment before taking a shot to the face when you see it coming, but don't quite believe it. *Here it comes*, you think. Then *No, he wouldn't*. And then he does.

"She has my son."

The super looks down at me over pockmarked cheeks. "Divorce?"

"Something like that."

"Call your lawyer like everyone else."

"It's not a lawyer kind of thing. If you know what I mean."

Apparently he does. One fist returns to his side, and the other fishes in his pockets for his keys.

"I'll tell you what the building's records show," he says, ushering me through the lobby and into a small office where the Christmas tree is stored. "But I see you in here again and I'll stuff you down the garbage chute."

I tell the super to look up the account under the name Pam Turgenov.

"Thought you said her name was Angela."

"She lies."

"Most of them do."

He pulls up the file on Angela/Pam's financial status with the condominium corporation. The mortgage and purchase agreement solely under Pam Turgenov's name, though the account has recently come under arrears. Unit 1808 hasn't paid its maintenance fee for three months, and the bank has frozen the accounts.

"We're looking for this one," the super says. "But from what I can tell, she hasn't been here for a while. Not since the break-in."

"There was a burglary?"

"Took some crap jewelry, personal stuff. But left the TV."

Personal stuff. Like Petra's Yankees cap. So it could find its way to my house.

"I'm changing the locks this week," the super says.

"It won't matter. She's not coming back."

"All her junk is still up there."

"Trust me."

"But she's got your kid."

"I'll find her."

I must sound convincing. The super gives me a soldierly nod. "When you speak to her," he says as he walks me to the door, "tell her I'm keeping the TV."

From the condo I walk straight up Bay Street toward the gold and silver office towers on the far side of the rail tracks. It takes a while. I'm occupied with working through what shouldn't come as a surprise, but has nevertheless: Angela not only failed to report to the authorities that it was Evelyn behind the wheel of the car she drove into a cliffside with Conrad White, but she likely had a hand in bringing about the crash in the first place. It was Angela who lured them north with breadcrumb clues. More than this, she must have been there. To make sure the job was done. And to replace Evelyn's purse with her own.

This is how Angela managed to live so completely off the grid: she made herself disappear *and* become someone else. And when the debts started to come due under Pam Turgenov's increasingly bad name she was gone again.

There's more support for this suspicion at the offices of the law firm where Angela claimed to work as a legal secretary. This time, I assume a cover – her jilted lover, which I suppose I am, among other things. It buys me enough sympathy with the girl at reception to find out that there was a Pam Turgenov working there for a time, not as a legal secretary but as a temp.

"Never got to really know her," the receptionist says sadly, as though this was her life's main regret. "Always had her nose in a book. Like, *Stay away, I'm* into *this*."

"Do you remember what she was reading?"

The receptionist looks at her nails for an answer. "Actually, now that I think of it, she wasn't reading. She was *writing*."

"How long ago did she leave?"

"A while. Like, *months*. She was probably only here for a couple weeks."

"Do you know where she went after she left? Another firm maybe?"

"It's why they're called temps." The receptionist shrugs. "They come and go."

When I give her the flowers I'd brought with me ("Is Pam here today? I have something for her birthday") I'm rewarded with a blushing thank you.

"If I happen to bump into her, who can I say came calling?" she asks as I start toward the elevators.

"Try Conrad. Or Len. Or Ivan."

It's only as the elevator doors are almost closed that the receptionist raises her narrowing eyes from writing each of these names down.

Dusk. That pinkish light over the city that is the occasionally beautiful by-product of pollution. The chill that comes within seconds of the sun dropping behind the rooftops. I'm headed east for no good reason. Or no better reason than to avoid what I know awaits me at home: messages from the police reporting how they haven't come up with anything yet. Maybe even the kid from the *National Star* camped out in my yard, a copy of *The Sandman* in his knapsack, the pages furry with Post-It notes. Better to keep drifting through the darkening streets than face that.

Yet it's at this time of day, in this kind of light, that you see things. Twilight illusions.

Like the black van that slowly drives past me. A shadow behind the wheel. The outlined head and gloved hands that belong to whatever I chased into the corn rows at the Mustang.

As I start after it – noting again how the model name has been removed from the rear doors, a caking of dried mud obscuring the licence plate – the van picks up speed and chugs around the next corner.

I cross blind against the traffic. A station wagon screeches to a stop. Kisses its grille to my hip. The contact sends me spinning against a panel truck, but my feet continue to slap the pavement, righting my course on the sidewalk. There is honking and *Hey! Hey!*s behind me but I take the same corner the van took and all sound is gulped away. A man my age and in my shape can't run like this more than a hundred yards without his breathing becoming the only thing he can hear. And his heart. His untested heart.

The van is gone. I keep running.

And then he's there.

Up ahead, the shadow slides along the walls. Takes another turn into the grounds of the old Gooderham & Worts distillery. A few clustered blocks of Dickens's London shoehorned between the expressway and condo construction sites. Long, Victorian brick barracks with smokestacks at their ends like exclamation points.

The past slows me down. It's the cobblestone streets that turn anything faster than a walk into a tiptoed dance. During daylight hours, the doors on either side open into galleries and cafés, but they are locked now. No one else in the pedestrian-only lanes but me and the one who's led me here.

And there he is. Slipping into a narrow alley. But slowly. As though waiting for me to catch up.

There are no lights between two of the vacant buildings, so that all I can see of the figure ahead is the rise and fall of its head against the dim brick. And then he stops altogether.

A bit further, the body language of his cocked head says. *You're almost there.*

I come at him in what I intend as a rush, but there is little rush left in me. When I reach the point where he'd been standing I nearly trip over something on the ground. Heavy but with a liquid give. A bag of sand.

It gives him more than enough time. The black van is waiting for him in the parking lot. The extinguished brake lights turning my raised hands from red to pink as it shifts into drive and slides away.

Starting back, I nearly fall over the bag of sand a second time. Except now I have the time to see that it isn't a bag of sand at all.

A body, more or less. No: less.

Propped against the wall like a sleeping drunk. *Legless.* Also armless, noseless, eyeless. A man dissembled into disparate parts laid out over the cobblestones. A human anthology.

It makes me grateful for the dark. Still, I can see enough. And what I can't see my mind fills in with

363

what it remembers from the night in the shed with Petra.

Time to go. Someone else will discover this by morning. There is nothing to be gained by lingering here aside from being seen.

And yet I stay where I am a minute longer. Partly because all the air has been sucked out of the world. Partly because the man scattered at my feet was once a friend.

We were the last ones. This is how I know it's Len even before I use the toe of my shoe to open the wallet next to the body's cupped hand and squint to read his name on the driver's licence inside. If you didn't know what I know, there would be no way of connecting the grinning face in the wallet's ID to his corpse – there is no identity left in him, all of the features that mark someone for who they are cut away. This has likely been Angela's lesson all along: you take a person's story and what remains is nothing more than skin and blood. The body is worthless. What counts is what it does. The lies and truths it tells.

I'm on the news in the morning. Once again they've used my taped statement from the first day of Sam's disappearance. Since then, I have continued to refuse the cameras, as it isn't doing me any favours on the suspicion front. Not to mention that pleading for Sam's safe return isn't going to make any impact on the person I know has him now.

364

A couple of the investigators come by to give me an update on the search efforts, but their eyes now openly betray their doubts. In the name of thoroughness they ask again if I've told them everything. Even after I repeat the same details, they wait for me to go on. *It's alright*, their seen-it-all faces urge me. *Just tell us what you did. We won't judge you.*

I start packing the moment the door closes behind them.

Before I go, I put in a call to Tim Earheart at a payphone around the corner. It strikes me that he's the only person in the world I have to say goodbye to. But I'm denied even this. He's not home, so I'm left to stutter some nonsense into his answering machine. All I remember is attempting a joke ("You know you don't get out enough when you've only got one name on your speed-dial") and asking him to "Look out for Sam if I – if it turns out Sam needs looking out for." The kind of tight-throated message you wish you could erase as soon as you put the receiver down.

I stop off at home one last time after that, trying to think of anything else that needs to be accounted for. I look at the rows of children's books Sam is too old to read any more and think *A father and son used to live here*. But that past tense takes all the life out of it. People used to live in every empty house you've ever stood in, and this makes them no less empty.

32

Whitley, Ontario, is one of the stubborn towns along the two lanes that ride the hump of Lake Superior. Today it is known, to the extent it is known at all, as a stop to fill the tank or, perhaps, find a damp-smelling motel room to sit out a snowstorm. A half-day's drive past the last cottages anyone is willing to drive to, this is the land most can locate only through the abstract – on maps or in the imagination. A door that opens on to one of the last Nothings on the planet.

It's a drive that tortures the Toyota's four cylinders. North of the Soo, the Trans-Canada loses its nerve, coiling into endless aversions to every swamp, hillock and inlet, so that the four hundred miles to Thunder Bay requires an athletic slapping of wheel and stomping of brake. But it's not the wheezing ascents that are so troubling, it's the freefalls that follow, sending the car shuddering helplessly cliffward every five minutes, and each time the turn is made – with a yank at the gearshift and a whispered *Shit, oh shit* – it's a close call.

Not that the driver behind me has the same problems.

Over the afternoon's last hours of light, on the rare straightaways, I glimpse a black sedan in the distance. It could be the Continental I spotted on the way to my visit to Sam in St Catharines. Every time I slow to get a better look, it must slow as well, or pull off to the side altogether – I never catch sight of it unless I'm moving. Later, when the dark forest leans over the road to block out any hint of a slivered moon, it's still there. Winks of headlight.

It was on this road, coming into one of these curves, that Evelyn and Conrad White met their end. And it was probably a car following them like the one following me that forced them into the turn too fast. It may have been the very same Continental. The same driver.

Whoever is behind the wheel doesn't seem to want me dead just yet, in any case. They want to see that I'm going in the right direction. Up here, there are only two choices: forward or back. One of which is no choice at all.

I roll into Whitley some time after midnight. The town itself sits behind a stand of trees, hidden from the highway as though ashamed of itself. A bowling alley. Two "Pre-Owned!" car lots. A tavern with squares of plywood where the windows used to be. Nothing appears to be open. Even the streetlights have been turned off for the night. Or were never turned on.

The TV in the Sportsman Motel's office is working just fine, however. It's how I decide on it over the competition: the sad glow that signals there may be someone else awake in Whitley aside from me. (When was the last time, I wonder, that the manager had to flick on the NO in front of VACANCY on the sign featuring a hunter with a rifle in one hand and a dead goose in the other?)

The guy behind the desk is watching *Canadian MegaStar!* Shaking his head at a girl from Saskatoon mangling a Barry Manilow tune.

"Can you *believe* these people?" he says, handing over the room keys without taking his eyes off the screen. "What are they *thinking*?"

"They want to be famous."

"Oh, this one here's going to be famous, alright. Famous for having a fat ass and a voice like a choked chicken."

He shakes his head at the TV, snorts, folds his arms over his chest, makes his chair squeak. But he doesn't turn the channel.

The room smells of rum and used rubbers. I pour the shampoo from one of the bathroom's little bottles on to the carpet to freshen things up. I'm lathering the floor with my shoes when I think I spot the Continental slide past through the window.

It's already reversing by the time I get the door open. Outside, the cold is a fist to the chest. It holds me there, my breath a grey halo over my head. Not that there would be any point in running after the car, now accelerating back toward the highway.

Whether it was him in the car or not, I know he's here. There is a taste that comes with the Sandman's presence that I'm spitting on to the Sportsman's pavement. He's *here*. Which means that Angela is too.

Aside from what remains of yesterday's donut batch at the Hugga Mugga, the only breakfast in Whitley is to be found at the Lucky Seven Chinese BBQ. The eggs taste of egg rolls, the toast of won ton, but I'm hungry enough to get it down. And when I look up from my plate, Sam is sitting across from me. Looking worried. Not for himself, but for me.

You're not a ghost. This is just me missing you. You're alive.

"More coffee?"

I raise my eyes to the waitress. When I look again, Sam's chair is empty.

On the sidewalk, I peer down Whitley's main street and imagine Angela's father walking its length, searching for her. Just as I am. Raymond Mull is my sole connection to whatever traces she left behind here. What I need is to find the farm where he came to visit her, and to do that, I'll have to find Edra, Angela's foster mother. And if her

369

surname was Stark in her journal, chances are she went by something else in the real world.

I decide to start at the offices of the *Whitley Register*. Although the sign on the door says they open at nine, the place remains locked at a quarter to ten, which forces me to sit on the front steps wishing I'd bought cigarettes at the Lucky Seven. Faces in passing pick-ups openly stare as they pass. I pretend not to notice. Pull the collar up on my overcoat against the stiffening breeze.

Autumn is a month further along up here, so that the trees have already surrendered their colours. A back-to-school litter clogs the storm drains: orange leaves and Red Bull cans. Garbage soon to be buried by snow only to emerge, fermented and soft, in the spring. Just as Jacob Stark's body had shown itself after he'd taken his bootless run into the woods.

When a woman in a plaid hunting jacket pulls up I wonder if she's going to ask me to leave. There is a downturn to her mouth and thickness in her shoulders that suggests expertise at this sort of thing. But when she stands with her hands on her hips and inquires as to what she can do for me, I end up coming right out with it.

"I'm doing some research. Hoping you could help."

"Research? Into what? The history of the Whitley Whippers?"

"Sorry?"

"You're speaking to the *Register*'s sports editor, not the archivist. If we *had* an archivist."

"Maybe there's someone in news I could speak to?"

"I'm news too. And entertainment, business, gardening tips. Some ad sales thrown in when I have the time."

She extends a gloved hand, and I at first shake it, then use it to help pull me to my feet.

"Patrick Rush," I say.

"Jane Tanner. *Acting* Editor-in-Chief. The *real* editor having passed on."

"Sorry to hear that."

"Don't be. It was three years ago. And he was a foul son of a bitch."

Jane Tanner opens the door and lets me in. Offers me coffee from a pot that's been left to stew on its hotplate overnight.

"So what would you be researching in Whitley? I'm thinking mines or crime."

"Why would you say that?"

"That's all we've got up here. A few bad people and some holes in the ground."

"Well you're right, as a matter of fact. I'm looking into the Raymond Mull killings of a few years ago."

Jane Tanner lowers her mug. "Eighteen years."

"I was wondering if I could go through the papers from that time. Your back issues aren't available on-line yet."

"Yet. I like that. *Yet.*"

I'm expecting questions – a stranger shows up asking about the worst thing to ever happen in a neither-here-nor-there town – but Jane Tanner just shows me down into the earth-walled basement where mouldering stacks of *Register*s threaten to bury anyone who gets too close.

"Have fun," she says, and starts back up the stairs.

Eighteen years. I start sorting through the papers at the garden tools and work back toward the broken typewriters. The issues from autumn 1989 are to be found next to the furnace, so that I have to dig out copies while being careful not to burn myself. When I've collected an armload, I clear the rat droppings from an empty milk crate, sit down and start reading.

He was here alright. Over Raymond Mull's child-stealing spree the *Whitley Register* was a weekly memorial issue, with grieving family members and news of the unsuccessful police investigation, along with outraged editorials calling for the return of the death penalty. But it's the smiling school photos of the victims that make what he did unthinkable. Laney Pelle first. Then Tess Warner. And finally Ursula Lyle, the one they never found because, if Angela's journal is to be believed, she did such a good job burying her in the Stark farm's woods.

After they caught him at a roadside motel twenty miles north and discovered – as they'd dis-covered at William's – the pickaxes and hacksaws and gloves, Raymond Mull had nothing to say. The one picture of him in the *Register* shows a man in the grey work pants and matching zip-up jacket of a mechanic, eyes lifeless but with an uncertain grin on his face, as though surprised to find he was the only one to see the dry humour in all this.

I track back over the weeks prior to Mull's arrest, searching for stories of Jacob Stark's mysterious death and his traumatized adopted daughter found nearly frozen to death in the barn, but when I do find mention of the incident, there are notable distinctions from the account in Angela's journal. The name, for one thing. Jacob Stark was actually David Percy. And while his body was found under the unusual circumstances Angela described – buried in the first blizzard of the season, the flesh slashed and torn by a frenzied run into the trees – there is no Angela, no daughter, no girl who refused to share her secret. Along with something else. David Percy was legally blind.

Among the other missing pieces in the *Register* is the specific location of the Percy farm. In fact, it isn't described as a farm at all, only the "Percy residence outside Whitley". No good checking the phone book now, either. Marion (not Edra) Percy would almost certainly be dead now too. There's no way of knowing who currently lives on that property, if anyone.

I drop the last *Register* on to the pile and think *Maybe this is it*. Maybe this is where it ends, in a cobwebbed basement with a man wiping his eyes at his flawed instincts and stupid mistakes.

Sam isn't here. He never was. And in the time I've wasted, she could be anywhere. With him.

This very moment may have been Angela's punchline all along: to make me think that all would be answered in Whitley, only to find that she had never lived here, never buried another girl her age, never been beckoned by the Sandman from her window. It was a story, nothing more.

"Sorry to say so," Jane Tanner says, appearing at the bottom of the stairs, "but seems to me you found what you were looking for."

"As a matter of fact I didn't."

"I can say with some regret that I've lived here all my life. Maybe I can help you."

"David Percy."

"Thought it was Mull you were researching."

"I had an idea they might be connected."

"You wouldn't have been alone in that. At the time, every missing cat and lost car key was being blamed on Raymond Mull."

"Did he have a child? Percy, I mean."

"There was a girl."

"The Percys'?"

"Adopted. Nobody knew her much because she lived outside town and wasn't here long."

"Why didn't you mention her in the paper?"

"To protect her."

"From what?"

"Whatever had come looking for her."

"So they thought it was Mull who'd driven the old man into the woods."

"Who else? Everyone figured it had to be him."

"And that he wanted Percy's daughter."

"She was the right age. And she'd obviously been through something traumatic."

"Hiding from him. In the barn."

Jane Tanner comes to stand directly under one of the basement's hanging bulbs.

"How do you know that?"

"It was just a story I heard."

"You mean just a story you wrote."

"You read my book?"

"Of course. Journalist turns successful novelist. Lucky bastard. You were one of *us*."

She goes on to ask if I'm here to uncover the truth behind the bits and pieces of the Percy case I'd used for *The Sandman*, and I encourage her misunderstanding as best I can. Tell her I'm working on a magazine article. A behind-the-scenes exploration of where fiction comes from.

"Anything else I can help you with?" she offers, though unconvincingly, her body gesturing for me to lead the way up the stairs.

"Probably not. It looks like I can't go much further than this."

"That's the thing about the past. Most of the time, it doesn't *want* to be known."

I'm about to step around her when Jane Tanner surprises me by putting a hand on my arm.

"Sorry about your boy," she says.

"Thank you."

"He's not why you came to Whitley, is he?"

"I told you why I'm here."

"Yes, you did."

She remains standing in the basement even when I make it to the top of the stairs.

"Guess you've already spoken to her?" she calls up at me.

I turn. *This woman knows Angela?*

"She's *here*?"

"Still alive, as far as I know. Up the road a bit. A nursing home called Spruce Lodge."

"I don't understand."

"Marion Percy. She might be able to tell you how wrong or right the story you heard is."

As is often the case with nursing homes, there is little nursing in evidence among the residents of Spruce Lodge. No one checks me in at the front door, and the halls appear empty of all but a couple wheelchairs and their head-slumped passengers, as though paused midway toward a destination they could no longer put a name to.

Things are even more disheartening in the Recreation Lounge. Fluorescent tubes ablaze over a dozen or so jigsaw puzzlers and chin tremblers, nothing on the walls but a taped-up notice on how to perform the Heimlich manoeuvre. The only one who notices my entrance is a fellow standing by the water fountain with his arm down his pants. Spotting me, he releases his grip long enough to take his hand out and offer a welcoming wave.

"You belong to someone here?" a nurse asks after I've been standing in the doorway five minutes or more.

"Marion Percy."

"Family?"

"No."

"Then the church must have sent you."

"Is Mrs Percy here?"

The nurse was just warming up – she looks about as lonely as any other Spruce Lodger – but she can tell I'm not in the mood. She points out a woman sitting on her own next to the room's only window. "That's Maid Marion, right over there."

Who knows how old she is. Marion Percy has reached that post-octogenarian stage of life where any numerical expression of age doesn't do justice to the amazing fact that she is still here, still a blinking, Kleenex-clutching being. A living denial of odds who is at the moment staring out at the tangled woods that surround the rear of Spruce Lodge's lot.

"Mrs Percy?"

I'm not sure she's heard me at first. It's the turning of her head. A twitch that takes a while to become something more intentional.

"You're new," she says.

"I'm a visitor."

"Not a doctor?"

"No."

"Too bad. They could *use* a new doctor."

She might be smiling. I can see her teeth, anyway.

"I know your daughter," I say, watching for whatever effect this announcement has on her, but nothing changes in her face. A waxy stiffness that might be a reaction in itself.

"Oh?" she says finally.

"We were friends."

"But not any more."

"We haven't seen each other in a while."

"Well she isn't here, if that's what you're thinking."

"*Was* she here?"

The smile – if it was a smile – is gone.

"Are you a policeman?" she says.

"Just a friend."

"So you said."

"I don't mean to pry."

"You haven't. But you're about to, would be my guess."

"I'm here to ask about what happened to your husband."

She looks at me like she hasn't heard what I just said. It forces me to speak again, louder this time.

"His accident."

"Accident?" She reaches out to touch my hand. "Would you *accidentally* run four miles half-naked into a snowstorm?"

Her hand returns to her lap. I step between her and the window. She looks through me anyway. Studying the small square of world outside the window she's come to memorize in such detail she needn't look at it to see it.

"Do you believe he was driven into those woods? Mrs Percy? Please?"

"I'm old. Why are you asking me this?"

"I know your daughter, ma'am. I was just interested –"

"But this isn't about her. Is it?"

"No."

"Then what?"

"My son."

"Your son?"

"He's missing."

Maybe it's the sound I make trying to sniff back my show of emotion – a reddening, moistening attack that strikes within seconds – but she sits up straight. Her knuckles white and hard as quartz.

"You're looking for *him*."

"Yes."

She nods. Sucks her bottom lip into her mouth. "What were you asking me?"

"Your husband. Have you thought that perhaps he was pursued into the woods?"

"He wouldn't have left her alone like that. Not unless he thought he was trying to save her."

"Angela."

"Your friend," she says, her eyes clouding over. "Our daughter."

Mrs Percy tells me how in the days before her husband died – and before she went into hospital to have her gallbladder removed – he confessed to hearing voices. David Percy believed someone was coming into the house and tormenting him, nicking him with knife cuts, moving the furniture so that he would trip over it. And a presence he felt, outside but looking in. Waiting. He wondered if he was losing his mind. By the time Marion made it home, her husband was gone. And Angela wasn't talking.

"Do you think it could have been her?"

"Beg pardon?"

"Whatever drove your husband into the woods. Could it have been your daughter?"

The old woman wrinkles her nose. "She was only a child."

"Still, who else could —"

"*Our* child."

Marion Percy may be old, but she is clearly more than able to hold the line. In this case, it's the question of her adopted daughter's involvement in the events of the night that changed everything for her. She has *ideas* of what happened. But that doesn't mean she's about to share them.

"Does she ever come to visit?"

Mrs Percy squints at me through the smudged lenses of her bifocals. "Who *are* you?"

"My name is Patrick Rush."

"And you say you know our girl?"

"Yes, ma'am. I do."

She nods at this, and I'm expecting her to inquire as to Angela's whereabouts, the events of her intervening years, her health. But she only returns to staring out the window.

"What happened to your farm?" I ask. "After you retired?"

"The land took it back. Not that we ever made much of a claim on it. No good for growing more than rocks and trees. Potato mud, David called it."

"Who owns it now?"

"She does."

"Angela?"

"That's the thing about children. Without them, there's no one to say you were ever even here."

33

I start out toward the Percy farm directly from Spruce Lodge, the afternoon light already showing signs of giving up. Although described by Marion Percy as only "a few miles – a dozen, or maybe a baker's dozen – outside town", there are moments when I wonder if the old woman has intentionally led me astray. Her directions are free of road names or numbers, and involve only landmarks ("right at the stone church") and subjective distances ("a bit of a ways", "straight for a good while"). After an hour, I crumple the page of notes I'd made from her telling of the route and toss them into the back seat.

It leaves me to make every turn on instinct. Eventually I'm headed down a private lane with branches scratching to get in on either side. "You won't see a farm, or a house, or anything to make you think anyone ever lived in there," is how Marion Percy described the entrance to her place. Well, *this* certainly qualifies.

It is by now the beginning of that stretched period of a northern autumn day that lingers in *almost darkness*. Almost, *almost* – and then it suddenly is. I turn on the headlights but it makes little difference, the snarled trees ahead flashing orange before clipping off the Toyota's mirror. The lane continues, but does not yield to any sign of habitation. No fence, no gate, no rusting equipment enfolded in the forest's weeds. I'm wrong: this isn't a lane at all, and it doesn't lead to anything. But it's too tight to turn around, and too boggy to risk trying to reverse the whole way. The sole hope is that there is an exit on to some other road at the end.

I turn on the radio. Right away I get the weather forecast: the first storm of the season is coming in. Snow squall warnings overnight for the whole county, with accumulation of up to forty centimetres. Overnight lows of minus twenty. Road closures anticipated. If travel outside the home is not strictly necessary, all are advised to stay indoors for the duration.

Too late for me.

The cold licks in around the windows and brings with it new imaginings of where Sam might be. Inside or out? Tied up, hooded? Have they given him food? Can he see any light? Is he cold?

Is he still alive?

No. I won't allow this one.

My attention must remain on the *doing* of things. Going forward – this alone might bring me to Sam. Or, in my case, going backwards. Because now I'm taking my foot off the gas, slapping the gear shift into reverse, turning around in my seat to see how I might slither out the way I've come –

An opening ahead. There just as I turn my head to start an inching reverse.

I shift back into drive, taking a run at the last branches drooped over the lane. There's a thud as one hits the front windshield, splintering a web of cracks through the glass. I keep my foot down and the car fishtails sideways into the mud. The tires glued a foot into the earth.

Not that it matters now. Because I'm here.

A square, red-brick farmhouse barnacled with leafless vines. A lopsided barn off to the side. Beyond these structures, an open space that was once a cultivated field but would now go by the name of meadow, or whatever one calls land mid-way in its return to chaos.

I step out of the car and take in the farmyard as though a location from my own memory. It is not exactly as I imagined it while listening to Angela read, but this doesn't stop it from being instantly recognizable. The wrought-iron weather vane atop the farmhouse roof, the buckled swing set in the yard, the partial log fence unsuccessful in holding the brush back from a one-time vegetable garden.

I start toward the house. The first flakes falling slow and straight as ash. I hold my arms out in front of me and there is already a thin layer of white over my coat, my shoes. Ghosting me.

* * *

An electric thrum travels up my legs from the earth. Is there an opposite to sacred ground? I suppose certain fields and farmyards in Poland and France store this kind of energy, the memory of horror held within the soil. I know it's only my own apprehensions – however this is going to turn out, it's going to happen here and now – but as I lift my feet up the farmhouse's front steps the history of this place rushes to possess me.

I look skyward. Tongue out, eating snow like a child. But it's to see if anyone stands in the upstairs window to the right. The window where the young Angela once stood, looking down at her father.

The door is open a crack. Something prevents me from touching the handle with bare skin, so that I enter by shouldering it wide enough for me to slip through. The new air rolls dead leaves and vermin droppings over the floor. It's still not enough to hold back the rank odour of the place. Backed-up plumbing. Along with something sweeter, animal.

A smell that soldiers and surgeons would recognize.

"Sam?"

My voice silences the house. It was quiet as I came in, but now some previously unnoticed activity has been stopped. The plaster and floorboards held in the tension of a held breath.

I try to leave the front door open but the angle of the frame eases it almost shut each time.

Although it is not yet dark outside and the curtains that remain are limp ribbons over the glass, the interior holds pockets of shadow in the corners, around every door and down the length of its hall. It is hard to imagine as a building that sunlight ever freely passed through. Bad things happened here because they were always meant to.

The main floor is arranged as rooms that open off a narrow central hallway that leads straight into the kitchen at the rear. A few feet in, the living room opens on the left, the dining room on the right. Both slightly too small for their functions, even now, unpeopled and with most of the furniture missing. In the living room, signs of a stay-over: a trio of wooden chairs, a broken whisky bottle on the floor between them. The fireplace and the brick around it black with soot, charred logs too big for its hearth still teepeed on the grate. I bend to touch them. Cold as the snow collecting on the sill.

The house has darkened further still when I return to the hallway, so that I proceed half-blind down its length, hands sliding over the walls. David Percy must have negotiated this route in much the same way on the last night of his life. Old, his sight gone. Tormented by what he believed to be some demonic intruder.

I turn to see the front door standing open. As the gust from outside loses its force, the door retracts once more. *Only the wind*. But David Percy would have had such thoughts too.

Explanations that didn't quite hold all of his mind together.

The smell is stronger on the way upstairs. Warmer, humid. It makes each step a fight against being sick.

Something happened here.

And not just eighteen years ago.

Something happened here today.

At the landing I see that I'm right.

Blood. A line of dime-sized circles leading to the room at the front of the house. Angela's room.

And a book.

Lying face down on the landing, its spine broken as though to bookmark the page. I know the title before I'm close enough to read the text on the cover. I know what it means before I lift the brittle paper to my eyes and see that it is a paperback from my own bookshelf, a hand-me-down that Sam had chosen for his nightstand pile. *Robinson Crusoe*. The book he brought with him to the Mustang Drive-in the night he disappeared.

"Sam?" I try again, and will his voice to answer. But there's only the squeak of the floor as it makes note of the book dropped from my hands, my shuffled steps toward the front room's partly open door.

My boot kicks the door open wide. It lets the smell out.

A single bed with Beatrix Potter rabbits painted on the headboard. A wooden school desk. Animal stickers – a smirking skunk, a giggling giraffe – on the cracked dresser mirror. And blood on all of it. Thin lines crosshatched over the room, as though squeezed from a condiment bottle. Not so much that it is evidence of a butchering, but of a struggle. Something half-done and then interrupted. Or half-done to be finished elsewhere.

And then I notice the chains laid out on the mattress. Four links attached to each of the bedposts with metal loops at the end. Shackles.

I'm not sure what I do in these next moments. They may not be moments at all. All I know is that I'm tracing the lines of blood and looping a finger through a rusted link of chain. Everything still. Everything falling away.

That's when I hear it.

Faint but unmistakable in the distance. From somewhere within the woods beyond the fields.

A voice calling for me.

The snow has gained weight over the last hour. The wind throwing it into my eyes. Dusk a black umbrella opened against the sky. My legs seem to know where to go. Out of the farmhouse yard and into the frozen ruts of the abandoned field.

Sam doesn't call out for me again as I make my way toward the woods. It doesn't stop me from hearing him.

Daddy!

Daddy, not Dad. His name for me when he was little, the second syllable dropped a couple years ago in favour of the more grown-up short form.

The reversion only happens now when he's been hurt. Or when he's scared.

The trees close in. Nightfall arrives at the same time as the bare limbs overhead deny what little moonlight there might be. The relatively even earth allows me greater speed here than over the furrows, but there is also more to hold me back. Interlocked branches. Stumps rising out of the gathering snow to crack my shins. Buried stones.

A hand swiped across my eyes comes away wet. Cut.

The weather forecast was right. Not just about the squall, but the cold. The temperature has dropped to whatever level it is that freezes your nostrils closed. Tightens the skin over your cheeks until it feels like the bone could rip through.

I stop and try to tell myself I'm determining which course to take, that it's not the cold and the panic that has freeze-dried all oxygen out of the air. Which way is north? If Sam is out here, this is where he'd be. And only Sam would know how to get out again. He could read the stars. Through momentary pauses of the snowfall I can make out some of the brightest constellations, but I didn't listen when Sam tried to explain how they could show you the way. The thought that I may never have the chance to let my son teach me this doubles me over. Puking a stain into a creamy drift.

Sam's shouted name is lost in the blizzard. A new inch of snow on the ground with every count to twenty in my head. In the creek beds it's already up past my knees.

The struggle now isn't against the cold but my desire to lean against the nearest pine and go to sleep. Forty winks. It would be a nap of the forever kind, I know. But it's how David Percy exited the world. Who's to say I have any greater reason to live than he had? A pair of fools who thought good intentions alone might find them a way through.

I'm bending down to curl into a nice spot when I see him. A human form against a tree in a clearing ahead.

"Sam."

A whisper this time. Louder than any of my shouts.

But as I get closer I see that the figure is too large to be Sam. And that whoever it is, he has long since frozen. Not that freezing was how he died. Iced blood pooled in his lap. Stiff hands plugging the wounds. Lashed to the trunk with wire that has sliced deep through his last struggles to free himself.

The man's chin slumped against his chest. I lift his head so that his lifeless eyes, still open, look up.

It's strange to see Ramsay's face showing anything but his wry cockiness. There is nothing of the kind about it now. A mask of terror waxed over the self-certainty he maintained over all the preceding years of his life.

Whatever was done to him in Angela's room took some time. And then he was brought out here. Aware of what was coming, but clinging to the possibility of escape nevertheless. Isn't that what the detectives in his detective novels did? Wait for a last-minute opportunity just when things looked their worst?

I regain my feet. Ramsay already halfway to buried. In half an hour, you would never know he's here.

There isn't a reason I keep walking but I do. Sam isn't out here, if he ever was. It's more probable that what I heard came from within my own head, or was Ramsay himself, instructed to find the right pitch with the assistance of the wire around his throat. It doesn't matter. The point is what it's always been: the determination of beginnings, middles and ends. Stories like symmetry, and my fate is to act out David Percy's concluding moments. I carry on now only to see the place they'll find me whenever they do.

Maybe it will be here. Out in the open of the Percys' field. An unintended circling back to where I started.

A single light appears through the snow. The bulb over the farmhouse porch.

Someone's home.

I fall to my knees. Across the field, a looming shadow takes its time coming to me. A darkness on its way to swallow me whole. Behind it, emerging from the house, what may be a smaller figure looking on.

Something about the two of them suggests they have always been here. Not just today, but forever. They have all the time in the world.

34

Do shadows cast shadows?

Firelight over a cracked plaster ceiling. Gradations of darkness nudging each other aside. Peeling paint lent a sinister animation. Hooked fingers reaching down for me.

Random connections, mini-hallucinations. I'm aware that this is all they are. Hospital room thoughts.

Except I'm not in a hospital.

No, don't ask. Just leave it alone – watch the shadows make shadows. Don't *ask*.

Where am I?

Now I've done it. You can't deny a query like that once it's out. It's the first information we insist upon when we wake.

Which means I am awake.

Which means I'm here.

* * *

Out and in again.

There was a gap, anyway, that only blacking out can explain. While away, the timid fire in the hearth has been stoked. The blizzard quieted to the suspended feathers that follow a pillow fight. And though it was unthinkably cold before, just beyond the range of the fire's heat – where my blue left hand rests, as opposed to the pinkish right – it has dropped a few more degrees.

For a moment or two I entertain the possibility that this could be another abandoned farmhouse altogether, another empty living room with windows that look out into a night dark and confining as a mine shaft. But there's the broken whisky bottle at my feet. And the chair I'm seated in feels like the one I noticed when I looked into the Percys' living room. Splintery but solid, its legs firmly planted.

And me firmly planted in it.

Chains looped around my wrists, holding both arms flat to the armrests. Tying ankle to ankle. A bruising yoke around my neck. I can't see what fixes the chair to the floor but given how it won't move no matter how I shift my weight, it must be screwed in.

I'm clothed but coatless. Only socks on my feet. I suppose this was done to get a good fit around my chest and legs, but the side effect is an even greater vulnerability to the cold. Without the fire I won't last long. Even with it, I can feel the sweat turning to frost on my upper lip. The hard air stinging my eyes.

My strength is gone. I never had much to begin with. And there are the tingly black dots of unconsciousness dancing around my peripheral vision, waiting for the chance to bury me.

But I have to try. There's nothing else to do but try.

I figure the best way to test the chains is to pull on each limb one at a time, seeing if there's some give anywhere. The concentration required in this – turn *this* wrist, lift *that* foot, now *that* foot – proves that my mind has weakened as much as the rest of me. And while I'm able to twist some parts an inch or two, there is no indication that anything might be slid out if teased a bit more. If I'm to get out of this chair, it won't be gently.

So I try the hard way.

A crazed spasm. Lunging forward and back, trying to topple the chair. Kicks and punches that don't go anywhere.

When I'm done I'm still here. Except now I've left the door open to the black dots. A nauseous sleep rolling in like fog.

My eyes won't open. That, or I'm blind. But there is movement somewhere within the house. The sense of vibrations more than the sounds themselves. Hearing as the deaf hear.

A heavy footfall along the upstairs hallway. And something lighter, metallic. A clattering of pots and cutlery in the kitchen.

I try to stand again. It doesn't work. And this time it hurts.

"Who's there?" I shout, or attempt to shout, but it's nothing more than a dry ripple of air. The turning of a newspaper page.

Yet there's a pause in the sounds. Was I heard? The black dots gathering round again.

Where's my son?

This finds a way out. A broken cry that carries through the bones of the house.

A minute passes after the echo of it has faded. Nothing other than knuckles of wind against the glass.

And then it resumes. Boots clumping through the floorboards above, the noise of cooking. But no voices in reply. No recognition that there is a man freezing to death in the front room. A father whose only wish is to know if his son is here and could hear him if he could find the breath to speak his name.

A figure beyond the doorframe. Standing in the hallway holding a candle in a teacup. A frantic play of the dim light. Glimpses of fur-topped boots, a knitted toque, the ridged tendons down a white neck.

She doesn't come forward. Holds the candle to the side so that it won't illuminate her face directly. A pose struck by the subject of a gothic portrait.

Don't hurt him.

When my tongue refuses to form the words I try to send this to her through the silence. But she has been pleaded to before. She knows the things people ask for at the end.

Don't.

A fight for air. And by the time I find it, the hallway is empty.

She is there again when I next wake.

In the room with me, standing in the corner. Still huddled in the deeper darkness, as though shy. But it's not that. She simply prefers to watch than be watched.

I jump toward her – but the chains restrain the motion to a hiccup jolt.

A small fire flickering its last sparks in the hearth. Outside there is the black clarity that comes with the deepest dives below zero.

"Where is he?" My voice a dry crinkle. The peeling of an onion. "Where's Sam?"

"Not here."

"Bring him to me."

"He's not *here*."

"Is he alive?"

The question passes through her.

I make another attempt to rise from the chair. A snake wriggle. It makes the bindings even tighter than before.

"Let me go."

"You *know* you're never getting out of here."

"I wish I'd fucked you in the ass."

"This is out of character."

"I'm not a character."

"Depends on the perspective."

"Ask my perspective. You? You're an empty, talentless bitch. You're *nothing*."

"That won't do you any good either."

"Am I hurting your feelings?"

"It's going to be a long night. Anger takes up so much energy."

"Then how are you still standing?"

"Me?" she says. "*I'm* not angry."

Angela steps toward me. The floor groaning as if accommodating the weight of a giant. As she passes, the disturbance of the air creates a feathering breeze against my face.

"They're going to find you," I say.

"Really?"

"The police. They'll come after me. After Ramsay. They know where we went."

She has bent to the fire. Placing fresh logs, nothing more than thick branches really, atop one another. The flames hiss at the ice under the bark.

"No one is coming here," she says.

The only part of her exposed from here is the back of her neck. Hair up, with just the downy strands beneath curling against the collar of her parka. I stare at this one point and will it closer. If she allowed herself just one incautious approach, I could rip through her spine from back to front with my teeth.

What is required first is for her not to leave.

"That's how David Percy died, wasn't it? You did to him what you did to me."

398

"What did I do?"

"Had him believe that you were out there. A blind man who thought he'd lost his child. He wasn't chased by a ghost, or a Sandman. He ran into the woods to look for *you*."

"Maybe that's how you should have ended your novel."

"But it's what happened."

"You're blinder than that old man ever was."

"What part am I wrong about?"

"It's not the killing. Not for *me*, anyway."

"Tell me."

Angela puts down the crowbar she was using to arrange the fire. Stands facing me.

"It's getting into someone else's head, right at the point when everything is laid bare," she says.

"You think this is *research*?"

"It's more than that. It's material. You and I have more in common than you'd guess. Trouble making things up out of nothing, for one thing."

"I don't understand."

"We both wanted to write *books*. And this is mine. The life I'm living. The lives I'm taking. It's all going into my novel. A novel that's not *really* a novel, because, in a way, it's all true."

"An autobiography."

"Not exactly. The point-of-view won't be mine. I'm not sure whose yet. I need to find the right voice."

"So you're stealing your book as much as I did."

"I'm not stealing. I'm assembling."

"You have a title?"

"*The Killing Circle*. Like it?"

"Can't say I do. But I suppose I'm biased. Given that you're going to kill me just so you can end a chapter. Just like you killed the others."

Angela comes at me with surprising speed. Instead of meeting her with whatever fury is left in me, I reflexively rear back. She grabs my hair. The fused seams of the chains audibly tearing the skin.

"*I* never killed *anyone*," she says.

Another waking. Another recognition that my believing myself bound to a chair in a haunted house isn't a dream.

She has Sam.

I will die after the fire goes out.

I cannot leave this place.

The hope that I will be released because I am the teller of this tale, and the teller never dies in his own tale: another falsehood.

I close my eyes. Try to let sleep return. But whatever it is that comes to smother my next breath isn't sleep at all.

She is sitting in a chair ten feet away. It may be further. There being nothing else to look at, no furniture or picture on the wall within range of the diminishing firelight, she looms where she might otherwise shrink. I've never thought of her as large. But she is. She's all there is.

400

She looks out the window. Taps her heels against the floor. A schoolgirl growing impatient at the bus stop.

"No wonder you're so fucked up. Having someone like Raymond Mull for your father."

Angela turns her eyes to me. A dull sheen of interest over the black pupils.

"What do you know about him?"

"That he hurt you. How did that make you feel?"

"How did that make you feel?"

"It would explain a lot."

"How I was such a bad girl at such a young age? How I drove a blind old man to the point he ran into the woods in a snowstorm?"

"Why you have no self."

"I have plenty of selves."

She stands. Peers out at a particular point on the night's horizon.

"You know something? I almost feel sorry for you."

"Artists enjoy certain privileges," she says. "They also endure certain sacrifices."

"Sounds like something Conrad White would say."

"I think he *did* say it."

"Was this while he was telling you how you were his perfect girl? His dead daughter returned?"

"People see in me what they wish to see."

"A mirror."

"Sometimes. Or sometimes it's someone else. A twin. A lover. Someone they lost. Or would like to be."

"What did I see?"

"You? That's easy. You saw your muse."

Angela goes to the fire. Places a pair of spindly branches on to the flames.

"Not much of a wood pile," I say.

"It's enough."

"Not staying long?"

She ignores this.

"How did you do it on your own?" I try again.

"Do what?"

"What was done to some of the bodies – that's some heavy lifting."

"You'd know."

I work to push aside the images of Petra in the shed as best I can. "You were watching me?"

"I was always watching. But *that* – that was unexpected."

"Was it William? Did you convince him to help you?"

"I urged him to study his fellow man."

"But he didn't kill the people from the circle. Or Carol Ulrich, Pevencey. The earlier ones."

"You forgot Jane Whirter."

"Yes. Why did she come to Toronto?"

"I invited her. She had suspicions. So I told her I did as well."

My chin falls against my chest. It awakens me with a gasp.

"You put the bloody tools in his apartment," I say. "William's."

"The police needed to catch a monster. Now they have one."

"Not the right one."

"Do you hear him protesting his innocence?"

"Why isn't he?"

"I convinced him otherwise."

Angela backs away from the fire and walks to the far side of the room. Her shoulders folded in, her hair greasy from a few days without water. The girl has been busy. And she *is* a girl again. Through her fatigue, the years that had been added since she first opened her journal in Conrad White's apartment have fallen away to reveal someone a little lost, uncertain of where she is and what has brought her here. It's an illusion, of course. Another mistake that leads to more mistakes. This is what she is as much as anything else: a collection of misreadings.

"Why Ramsay?" I say, and she half turns.

"What I do – it requires improvisation."

"They'll come looking for him."

"They won't."

"Why?"

"I spoke to him. And he – he *assured* me that he came here on his own time. No one knew where he was headed, because he was tracking you."

"You don't think he was bullshitting you?"

"He was in a position where lying would be unlikely."

"You're not clever, you know," I find myself coughing as she drifts toward the hallway. "You might *think* you're some kind of artist. But you're not. You're shit."

Angela stops. Out of the range of firelight, so that she's a shadow that surprises with its ability to speak.

"You're a *plagiarist*, Patrick," she says. "At least what I do is original."

I flinch awake at what I think at first is a sound, but it isn't. It's light. Two white pins pushing through the darkness outside. Growing brighter, surrounded by a widening penumbra of snow.

Angela is here with me. Standing by the window, rolling back on her heels.

"Who's that?"

"A harder question to answer than you'd guess," she says.

"The Sandman."

"But he could be anyone."

"Not anyone. He killed Petra and Len. The one who drove Conrad and Evelyn off the road. The hands that pushed Ivan on to the tracks."

"That's not really a guess."

She turns from the window. Outside, the headlights swing around and point away, exposing the side of the vehicle. A black van. The one I'd seen on Queen Street. The one that drove off from where I'd found Len's body.

"I suppose I'll be meeting him soon enough," I say.

"You'd *like* to?"

"I'd enjoy nothing more than to meet the man of your dreams."

Angela giggles in fake embarrassment. "It's not like that."

The child's sound of her voice reminds me that, whatever she is now, happened when she was young. It's why her age is so hard to guess, how even in her bed she was play-acting at being an adult. Part of her belongs to the past because part of her died there.

"Whatever your father is making you do, it's not your fault."

"Thank you. My burden has been lifted."

"If you let me go, I could help you."

"Help me?"

"Show me where Sam is, and we could all go away together. Or go our separate ways. But I'd make it so that your father couldn't touch us ever again. We'd be safe."

"I am safe."

"Angela, please. You don't have to keep doing this. Not for him."

"I could be with you instead? Your replacement bride? Your co-author?"

The van door swings shut. A workman's vehicle's screech of neglect. After a moment, there's the heavy footsteps coming up on to the porch.

I am the ground beneath your feet ...

The door opens. Snow being stomped off his boots. Then the few steps along the hallway it takes to stand in the archway, looking in.

A giant's shadow. The same one I'd seen coming for me before collapsing in the field outside. But somehow familiar now that it is indoors. The shape of a man I've seen before.

"I'd like you to meet my brother," she says.

The figure steps forward to the edge of the firelight. Tentative, gloved hands crossed over his stomach. Grinning in a trembly, rubber-lipped way that suggests he's trying not to, but can't help himself.

"Len?"

"That's how you knew him," Angela says, sliding close to him but carefully. Without touching. "Virgin Len. But he, like me, has gone by a number of different names over the years. Different *incarnations*."

"But I *saw* you. In the alley."

"You saw what you thought you saw," Len says, his grin widening. "We counted on that. We've *always* counted on that."

"Oh Christ."

"You alright?"

"Oh *Christ*."

The room is swimming. No, not the room – *I'm* swimming. Fits of motion through the nearly solid air. A fish finning through a tank.

"I'm going to take a look around upstairs," Angela says to him.

406

Len nods. When she moves past him into the hallway she brushes against his nylon jacket and the sound is like a knife rendering tin foil.

"That was you," I say. "At Michelle Carruthers' funeral. Mull was your father too."

"As far as we know."

"And you were taken into foster care just like your sister."

"Shared experience can bind people in powerful ways."

"So you decided to take other people's lives to replace your own."

"Too simple. *Way* too simple."

Len spits on the floor. The white foam of it on the hardwood holds his attention, and in his stare I can see the emptiness in him, the sterile indifference.

"You're a good actor."

"I'm not Len," he says, taking a predatory step into the room. "If that's what you mean."

"Len was somebody. It was a performance, but there was a personality there. You, on the other hand, are nobody."

"Are you trying to insult me?"

"It wouldn't work if I was. There's nothing in you to hurt. Just like your sister."

"Angela is an artist."

"And you're the king of the Kingdom of Not What It Seems."

"No."

"The Sandman."

"No."

"Who is?"

"Whoever scares you most."

Len takes his gloves off, stuffs them in his pocket. His big hands creased with black lines.

Dirty hands.

"Where's my son?"

"That's a secret."

"You're going to hurt him, aren't you? You already have."

"Now, now. You'll only upset yourself."

"He's just a child. Doesn't that make a difference to you?"

"We were *all* children once."

I cough back a surge of sick. My throat burning from the inside out.

"It was you," I say. "You took those girls in Whitley."

"Before my time."

"Then who?"

"That was *him*."

"Mull? You sure it wasn't you shadowing your little sister? It wasn't you who wanted her?"

"I *protected* her."

"How?"

"By making Daddy go away."

"You killed him?"

"We needed to make a new world," he says, showing the ground stumps of his teeth. "And he couldn't be in it."

Len watches the eyes roll back in my head.

"I don't feel so great," I say.

"It's the dehydration."

"Can I have some water?"

"That's good. That's *funny*."

He steps over to the fire. Picks up a branch and considers adding it to the flames. After a moment, he puts the branch back on the pile he got it from.

Upstairs, Angela is opening doors, closing them, putting things into a bag. If I'm counting the bedrooms right, she's almost done.

"Who was it?" I ask. There's the idea I'm about to throw up but there is little time left now. "The body I thought was you."

Len comes to stand directly in front of me. He unclasps his hands so that they swing against his hips.

"The *National Star* should have a job opening pretty soon," he says.

And then I do throw up. A painful choking that summons a half-cup of bile on to the floor.

Angela appears in the hallway holding a duffel bag. Black stains seeping through the canvas. She shares a look with Len.

"I think it's time," she says.

She starts away, then stops. Comes to me and slips her hand into my pocket. Pulls out the dicta-phone.

"I made other tapes," I say.

"We have them all now."

"There's copies."

"No, there aren't. And we have your journals too. Right up to you arriving here. You left that one in your car's glove box."

Angela asks Len if he's checked the kitchen, and he lowers his head slightly when he admits he hasn't. She looks at her watch. Gives him two minutes.

He does as he's told. Leaving Angela leaning against the archway, looking past me out the window. Like I'm not even here. Already dead.

"You got me wrong," I say, and the unexpected laugh that comes after spills warm spit down my chin.

"Oh?"

"You don't have my whole story."

"The voice of desperation."

"It's the truth."

"I know everything I need to know about you."

"No, you don't. There's a secret I've kept so long that even I don't remember it half the time. Something that changes everything."

"This is *sad*," she says. But she's watching me now.

"I'm the last character in the circle. And without this, something will be missing. Your book will have a hole in it. Because Mr Boring is not who you think he is. He has a twist."

In the kitchen, Len pulls a cutlery drawer out too far and it falls to the floor. The clatter of knives and forks. A barked profanity as he bends to pick them up.

Angela comes closer.

"Go on then," she says.

"Promise me. I'll tell you if you promise Sam will be safe."

"I told you. I wouldn't –"

"I *know* it's not you. Killing isn't your department. It's *his*."

"Maybe it's already been done."

"Maybe it has. And if it hasn't, he's going to. To keep Sam quiet, or to punish me, or just because it's what he does."

"You think your little secret might stop him?"

"No. I think you might."

"Why should I do anything for a dead man's lie?"

"Because it isn't a lie."

"How would I know?"

"You'll know as soon as you hear it."

Down the hall, Len slides the drawer back into its slot. Claps his hands together for warmth.

"Fine," she says, unable to entirely hide her interest. "I'm listening."

So I tell her. In a rushed whisper of run-on sentences and bullet points, clipped and unadorned. It's not what I say that proves it's true. It's the voice. Breaking as soon as I begin, a thin note that thins even more over the telling.

What I tell Angela is how I killed Tamara. My wife. How what I did makes both of us murderers.

It wasn't an assisted suicide either, not the carrying out of a consensual plan. It was my idea alone. I must be clear on this. Yet even though she was asleep when I pressed the needle into her arm, I believe that when Tamara wakened and saw what I was doing she was thankful, that she understood it was for love. Because it *was*. It may have been wrong according to certain laws or gods, it may have stolen restful sleep and guiltless dreams from me for the rest of my life, it may be where the out-of-nowhere tears have been coming from these past years – it may have been done *too early* – but I wanted only to take her pain away, to prevent the worse pain to come. To show as much courage as she showed, working up a white-lipped smile whenever Sam was around. Cancer did most of the killing on its own. It was the villain who stole into her room without turning on the light, not me.

These are the kind of thoughts that made what I did no easier. What I now share with another for the first time. With Angela, who watches the words drift out of me in grey puffs of steam.

Len returns to the doorway. Takes a breath as though savouring a scent in the air.

"Ready," he says.

Angela turns to him. There is nothing in her expression – nothing at all – that would suggest she has just heard something surprising. She is good at hiding things. Or maybe it is only that there is nothing for her to hide, as she's decided that what she has heard is little more than an overplayed bluff. The hollow glance she gives me

412

as she follows Len to the door makes it impossible to tell.

I hear her step outside. A pause as Len takes a last look down the hall. When he leaves, he pulls the door only partway closed. The wind moaning through the house, grieving. Sorry to see them go.

35

It's been some hours since there's been any feeling in my legs. I was hoping this was one of the benefits of dying from exposure – at least it kept the pain to a minimum. Now it seems I was wrong about that. The body doesn't let go of feeling easily, even if the only sensation left to it is setting itself on fire. Frostbite? Sounds *chilly*, doesn't it? Try gripping an ice cube tight in your palm. It's only cold at first. Then it burns.

The screaming helps. My voice pushing back against the darkness that draws closer as the flames diminish in the hearth. And even now there is an idea that someone might hear me. Perhaps Angela has arranged for a *deus ex machina* – a kindly neighbour? a local cop? – to walk in the door and give me a lift to the Sportsman for a hot shower and a stiff drink. And I will be reformed by my experiences, the one she'd chosen as the recipient of her tough love. Wasn't *The Magus* her favourite book, after all?

But this isn't a book.

I'm taking in a breath to let out another howl when I hear the radio.

It must have been on for the whole time of this most recent wakening, but it doesn't have a firm grasp on the frequency, so that the signal drops out from time to time. Now, abruptly, it has found itself again. The last fading bars of "Raindrops Keep Falling on My Head", crackling out of the dark.

An old transistor unit on the floor by my feet. The antenna fully extended, wavering in the drafty crosscurrents. A dim blue light from the tuning dial that turns the floor around it into a shallow pool.

The announcer comes on to inform me that it's Whitley's easy listening station ("The smoothest sounds north of Superior"). Coming up: Perry Como, Streisand, The Carpenters. "And pull your sweetheart a little closer," the DJ says with an audible wink, "because next we've got a real blast from the past – with Paul Anka!"

It makes me wonder: did Angela leave the radio with me for comfort, or further punishment? *Easy listening?* Maybe that was the only station she could get. Or maybe there's a message in its selection. Milquetoast music to send off the man with no imagination.

And they call it puppy love. But I guess they'll never know …

The fire nothing more than a stack of hissing embers. Red stars twinkling against the black bricks. Soon it will be cold and dead. Ditto the slumped man turning into a shadow.

I told her.

This comes with a stab to the chest. Followed by a shuddering fight to pull a whole breath in. A blown nose leaves a spray of blood over my pant legs.

I told her the story. It wasn't a dream. I told her.

Two bits of discouraging news from the radio between the Jefferson Airship retrospective and "Careless Whisper": it's 3.42 a.m. and minus nineteen outside. I'd been nurturing some hope that I might make it to the morning, if only to see the patterns of frost over the glass, the stark line of trees beyond. But it seems these small consolations are to be denied me.

Engelbert Humperdinck next. Always loved that name.

Please release me. Let me go …

The news comes on. The second item (after the day's Middle Eastern death count) is a breaking story. One I only focus on halfway through the reception's broken account.

"The son of author … street corner in Dryden, Ontario … taken to the local hospital to be checked over for any possible … unknown at this time … appeared unharmed, though a statement has not yet been released regarding information on his kidnappers' identity … also apparently missing, and therefore not available for … unconfirmed initial reports that the boy has offered

416

information which may lead to his father's whereabouts ... repeated their policy of not answering questions until they have followed ... In sports, Leafs lose another close one ..."

There's to be a follow-up report a half-hour later. It gives me something to keep breathing for. Fighting sleep that isn't sleep. Humming along to crackly patches of "Everybody Plays the Fool" and "Someday We'll Be Together".

Then the news again. This time around, the reception is good enough to get the facts down.

Sam Rush, son of the bestselling author, was discovered wandering alone on a residential street in Dryden, the next town along the Trans-Canada from Whitley. Early reports indicate that he appeared in good health, and has made a statement to authorities that may assist them in locating the boy's father, who has also been recently designated a Missing Person. Police are now working to locate a farmhouse where the boy was kept, and are using geographic parameters he has provided regarding its location in relation to the stars. There are currently no leads as to the identity of the boy's abductors as he was unable or unwilling to provide detailed physical descriptions. Parents are urged to monitor their children more closely than usual over the coming days, though they can be assured that the Rush investigation is now a top priority. The police spokesperson went out of his way to emphasize that, despite the boy's statements, there is no evidence to support the contention that

Sam Rush's abduction and his father's missing status are related.

There's no mention of Ramsay. Nothing about Tim Earheart either, though the police have surely made a positive identification by this point. Soon, they'll start pulling some of the connections together. But they'll never find Angela and Len. I'm sure of this. They're gone and won't come back. With different names and faces they will slip across borders, shedding themselves as they go. Somewhere else, eventually, they will join another circle. And someone will start believing in the Sandman again.

The radio's reception starts to fade. The batteries mostly used up to start with. She wanted me to hear the news, to let me know. But once I had, she wanted the silence to return.

And now, with a last rustle of static, it has.

Outside, the wind stills to nothing. The snow drifted up against the walls like breaking waves. Even the house holds its breath.

Sam is alive.

It's this fact, this pain-killing knowledge, that allows me to let go.

I've been fighting harder than I knew. To be here for him. Just in case he found his way out of the storm. Instead, he is far away, in the care of others. I wish it were my arms that held him, my comfort that will send him off to sleep. No matter. We've had our bedtime stories. There will be my voice for him to hold on to.

418

Goodnight, son. Sweet dreams.

They may find me, of course. And maybe even before my breath has turned to crystal in my chest. The radio said they were looking for me, following the directions Sam gave them, the Norths and Wests and Easts he read from the stars. Odds are it will be too late to make any difference. And yet, even as I resign myself to the inevitable, there is a renewed struggle to stay here, in this moment, a thinking, remembering thing. Fighting for another minute, for the possibility of dawn. Of seeing Sam again.

There is even the time to dream of revenge. A plan to sell the house on Euclid, leave the city altogether and disappear with Sam, make ourselves safe. Then, a thousand miles away, I will set myself to work. To take something from Angela, the only thing that might matter to her. *The Killing Circle.* If I make it out of here, maybe I'll write it myself. Stick a knife in her heart. Steal back the book she's been assembling from the stories of the dead.

But these are only lullabye thoughts. The drifting weightlessness before the crash. For the first time in what feels like forever, I'm not striving for anything, not searching. No envy, unrequited admirations, the hollow yearning to be noticed. Not afraid.

Last thoughts?

There's the notion I might have some kicking around, perhaps a lesson or two of the kind you find at the end of novels. Something affirming and buoyant. I'm sure I could come up with something

419

if I had the time, but I don't. Because here it comes: a wool blanket being pulled up over my shoulders, my head. Darkness. Blocking the light from the inside out. But before it takes me I surprise myself by laughing. A terrible, shaking, coughing mirth that echoes through the empty rooms of the farmhouse. A ghost sound. The laughter of a man without a story who sees that what has brought him here might have made a good one, if there was only someone else, one Dear Reader to tell it to.

Acknowledgments

My thanks to those who have helped this book – and helped me to write it – whether as listeners, questioners, editors or friends: Maya Mavjee, Julia Wisdom, John Parsley, Peter Joseph, Anne O'Brien, Anne McDermid, Martha Magor, Vanessa Matthews, Sally Riley, Lesley Thorne, Brent Sherman and Sean Kane.

FIFTH EDITION General and Systematic

Pathology

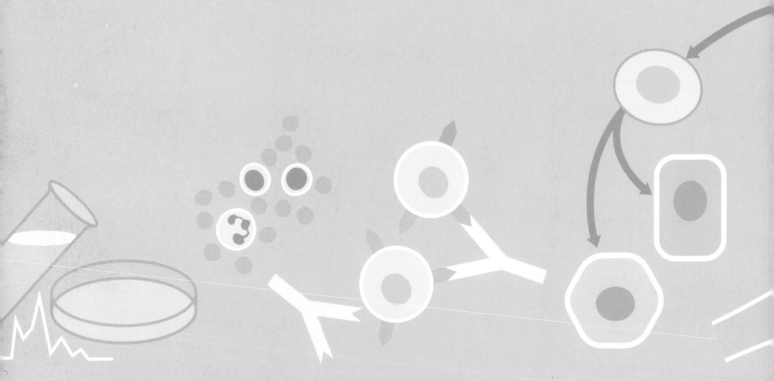

Commissioning Editor: Timothy Horne
Development Editor: Clive Hewat
Project Manager: Jane Dingwall
Cover Design: Charles Gray
Text Design: Erik Bigland
Illustration Manager: Bruce Hogarth

FIFTH EDITION
General and Systematic
Pathology

EDITED BY

J. C. E. Underwood MD FRCPath FRCP FMedSci

Emeritus Professor of Pathology, University of Sheffield, Sheffield, UK

S. S. Cross MD FRCPath

Reader and Honorary Consultant, Academic Unit of Pathology, School of Medicine and Biomedical Sciences, University of Sheffield, Sheffield, UK

Illustrations and chapter icons by Robert Britton

CHURCHILL LIVINGSTONE

ELSEVIER

EDINBURGH LONDON NEW YORK OXFORD PHILADELPHIA ST LOUIS SYDNEY TORONTO 2009

CHURCHILL LIVINGSTONE
An imprint of Elsevier Limited

First published © Churchill Livingstone 1992
Second edition © Churchill Livingstone 1996
Third edition © Churchill Livingstone 2000
Fourth edition © Elsevier Limited 2004
Fifth edition © Elsevier Limited. All rights reserved

ISBN 9780443068881
International ISBN 9780443068898

British Library Cataloguing in Publication Data
A catalogue record for this book is available from the British
Library

Library of Congress Cataloging in Publication Data
A catalog record for this book is available from the Library of
Congress

Notice
Knowledge and best practice in this field are constantly changing.
As new research and experience broaden our knowledge, changes
in practice, treatment and drug therapy may become necessary
or appropriate. Readers are advised to check the most current
information provided (i) on procedures featured or (ii) by the
manufacturer of each product to be administered, to verify the
recommended dose or formula, the method and duration of
administration, and contraindications. It is the responsibility of
the practitioner, relying on their own experience and knowledge of
the patient, to make diagnoses, to determine dosages and the best
treatment for each individual patient, and to take all appropriate
safety precautions. To the fullest extent of the law, neither the
Publisher nor the Editors assume any liability for any injury and/
or damage to persons or property arising out of or related to any
use of the material contained in this book.
The Publisher

PREFACE

General and Systematic Pathology has been written, designed and produced primarily for students of medicine and for those studying related health science subjects. The causes and mechanisms of disease and the pathology of specific conditions are presented in the contexts of modern cellular and molecular biology and of contemporary clinical practice.

Emphasis on problem-based and self-directed learning in medicine continues to grow, often with a concomitant reduction in didactic teaching and practical pathology experience. Therefore, the student's need for a well-illustrated comprehensive source of reliable knowledge about disease has never been greater. *General and Systematic Pathology* fulfils that need.

Part 1 (Basic Pathology) introduces the student to key general principles of pathology, both as a medical science and as a clinical activity with a vital role in patient care. Part 2 (Disease Mechanisms) provides fundamental knowledge about the cellular and molecular processes involved in diseases, invariably providing the rationale for their treatment. Part 3 (Systematic Pathology) deals in detail with specific diseases, with emphasis on the clinically important aspects.

Innovative features in this fifth edition are intended to increase further the book's utility in problem-based learning. For example, in Part 3, each chapter begins with a body diagram annotated with common or important clinical features and the relevant diseases. There is also a new problem-based index listing signs and symptoms; this directs the user to main pages featuring the pathological conditions causing them. We must emphasise that the body diagrams and problem-based index are for educational purposes rather than for use as a diagnostic aid. Supplementary material is available on the book's website.

General and Systematic Pathology has been praised for its relevance, content and clarity. Maintaining this high standard involves much activity between editions, often in response to feedback from students and their teachers. We continue to welcome comments and suggestions for further improvements.

JCEU
SSC

Sheffield
2009

ACKNOWLEDGEMENTS

The international popularity of *General and Systematic Pathology* is a tribute to the work of many individuals. We are particularly indebted to our team of contributors who have thoroughly reviewed, revised and updated their chapters. The demands on our colleagues' time are ever increasing, and our gratitude is correspondingly greater.

As always, the preparation of a new edition of *General and Systematic Pathology* is guided by comments from our panel of International Advisers, which has been enlarged for this edition by the recruitment of Professor Wolter Mooi (The Netherlands), Professor Shahid Pervez (Pakistan) and Professor Irene Ng (Hong Kong). We have also greatly valued the many comments and suggestions received from students and their teachers worldwide. In this regard, special thanks are due to two medical students – Gwinyai Masukume (University of Zimbabwe) and Arpan Mehta (University of Oxford) – who independently have drawn our attention to some errors and ambiguities in the previous edition. We also acknowledge the suggestions received from Dr Venkatesh Shashidhar (James Cook University, Australia).

We thank Friyana Dastur-Mackenzie for her assistance in compiling the problem-based index for the book.

We thank the publishing team at Elsevier for continuing the highly professional standard of this book's production. Robert Britton, who has been involved with *General and Systematic Pathology* since its inception, has revised some illustrations and produced others that are new; the clarity of the illustrations is a credit to his graphic skills and knowledge.

Being editor of a major textbook becomes an obsession that reaches a crescendo as the next edition looms. It diverts our attention away from professional and domestic duties that others may regard as having higher priority. Therefore, as editors we (JCEU and SSC, respectively) acknowledge the support and understanding from our partners, Alice and Frances, to whom we are deeply indebted.

JCEU
SSC

Sheffield
2009

INTERNATIONAL ADVISERS

The following individuals have made a valuable contribution to the development of the fifth edition of this textbook. In utilising their extensive knowledge of their countries' medical curricula and the teaching of pathology, it is hoped that this textbook will prove a valuable learning resource internationally. Their contribution is gratefully recognised.

Professor Y. Collan
Department of Pathology
University of Turku
Turku
Finland

Dr J. P. Cruse
King Fahad National Guard Hospital
Riyadh
Saudi Arabia

Dr I. Damjanov
Department of Pathology
University of Kansas
Kansas City
United States of America

Dr H. Goldman
Harvard Medical School
Boston
United States of America

Professor Lai-Meng Looi
Department of Pathology
University of Malaya
Kuala Lumpur
Malaysia

Professor T. L. Miko
Department of Histopathology
Szent-Györgyi University Medical School
Szeged
Hungary

Professor W. J. Mooi
Department of Pathology
VU University Medical Centre
Amsterdam
The Netherlands

Professor S. Mori
Institute of Medical Sciences
University of Tokyo
Tokyo
Japan

Professor H. K. Muller
Department of Pathology
University of Tasmania
Hobart
Australia

Professor I. O. L. Ng
Department of Pathology
University of Hong Kong
Hong Kong

Professor S. Pervez
Department of Pathology and Microbiology
Aga Khan University Hospital
Karachi
Pakistan

Professor K. Ramnarayan
Department of Pathology
Melaka Manipal Medical College
Manipal
India

Dr K. Ramesh Rao
Department of Pathology
Sri Ramachandran Medical College
Chennai
India

Professor R. H. Riddell
Department of Pathology and Laboratory Medicine
University of Toronto
Toronto
Canada

CONTRIBUTORS

Jonathan P. Bury BMedSci MBChB MPhil
School of Medicine and Biomedical Sciences, University of Sheffield, Sheffield, UK

Dominic J. Culligan BSc MD FRCP FRCPath
Consultant Haematologist and Honorary Senior Lecturer, Aberdeen Royal Infirmary, Aberdeen, UK

Michael F. Dixon MD FRCPath
Emeritus Professor of Gastrointestinal Pathology; Visiting Professor, Leeds Institute of Molecular Medicine, Pathology and Tumour Biology, University of Leeds, Leeds, UK

P. J. Gallagher MD PhD FRCPath
Reader in Pathology, University of Southampton; Honorary Consultant Pathologist, Southampton University Hospital, Southampton, UK

J. R. Goepel MBChB FRCPath
Consultant Histopathologist, Sheffield Teaching Hospitals NHS Foundation Trust, Sheffield; Honorary Clinical Senior Lecturer, University of Sheffield, Sheffield, UK

Mansel R. Haeney MSc MBBCh FRCP FRCPath
Consultant Immunologist, Department of Immunology, Salford Royal Hospitals NHS Trust, Salford; Honorary Lecturer, University of Manchester, Manchester, UK

David E. Hughes BMedSci MBChB PhD FRCPath
Consultant Histopathologist, Sheffield Teaching Hospitals NHS Foundation Trust, Sheffield; Honorary Senior Lecturer, University of Birmingham, Birmingham, UK

James W. Ironside CBE BMSc MBChB FRCPath FRCPEdin FMedSci
Professor of Clinical Neuropathology, National CJD Surveillance Unit, Western General Hospital, Edinburgh, UK

K. A. MacLennan DM FRCPath
Professor of Tumour Pathology, University of Leeds; Consultant Histopathologist, St James's University Hospital, Leeds, UK

J. R. Shortland BSc MBChB PhD FRCPath
Formerly Consultant Histopathologist, Northern General Hospital, Sheffield, and Honorary Clinical Senior Lecturer, University of Sheffield, Sheffield, UK

David N. Slater MBChB BMedSci FRCPath
Consultant Dermatopathologist, Royal Hallamshire Hospital, Sheffield; Honorary Clinical Senior Lecturer, University of Sheffield, Sheffield, UK

T. J. Stephenson MBChB MA MBA MD FRCPath
Consultant Histopathologist, Sheffield Teaching Hospitals NHS Foundation Trust; Honorary Professor in Histopathology, Sheffield Hallam University, Sheffield, UK

Allard C. van der Wal MD PHD
Consultant Pathologist and Lecturer, Academic Medical Centre, University of Amsterdam, Amsterdam, The Netherlands

Rosemary A. Walker MD FRCPath
Professor of Pathology, Department of Cancer Studies and Molecular Medicine, University of Leicester, Leicester Royal Infirmary, Leicester, UK

William A. H. Wallace BSc MBChB PhD FRCPEdin FRCPath
Consultant Pathologist, Royal Infirmary of Edinburgh, and Honorary Senior Lecturer in Pathology, College of Medicine and Veterinary Medicine, University of Edinburgh, Edinburgh, UK

Henry G. Watson MBChB MD FRCPEdin FRCPath
Consultant Haematologist, Aberdeen Royal Infirmary, Aberdeen, UK

M. Wells BSc MD FRCPath
Professor of Gynaecological Pathology, University of Sheffield; Honorary Consultant, Sheffield Teaching Hospitals NHS Foundation Trust, Sheffield, UK

CONTENTS

ix

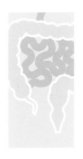

xi

BASIC PATHOLOGY

1

Introduction
to pathology

3

Of all the clinical disciplines, pathology is the one that most directly reflects the demystification of the human body that has made medicine so effective and so humane. It expresses the truth underpinning scientific medicine, the inhuman truth of the human body, and disperses the mist of evasion that characterizes folk medicine and everyday thinking about sickness and health.

From: *Hippocratic Oaths* by Raymond Tallis

Pathology is the *scientific study of disease*. Pathology constitutes a large body of scientific knowledge and investigative methods essential for understanding disease and for effective medical practice.

Pathology embraces the *functional* and *structural* changes in disease, from the molecular level to the effects on the individual.

Pathology is continually subject to change, revision and expansion as new scientific research illuminates our knowledge of disease.

The ultimate goal of pathology is the identification of the causes of disease, a fundamental objective leading to successful therapy and to disease prevention.

HISTORY OF PATHOLOGY

The evolution of concepts about the causes and nature of human disease reflects the prevailing ideas about the explanation for all worldly events and the techniques available for their investigation (Table 1.1). Thus, the early dominance of animism, in the philosophies of Plato (424–348 BC) and Pythagoras (c. 580–c. 500 BC), resulted in the belief that disease was due to the adverse effects of immaterial or supernatural forces, often as punishment for wrongdoing. Treatment was often brutal and ineffective.

Even when the clinical significance of many abnormal physical signs and postmortem findings was established early in the long history of medicine, the underlying disease was

thought to be due to an imbalance ('isonomia') of the various humours—phlegm, black bile, and so on—as proposed by Empedocles (490–430 BC) and Hippocrates (c. 460–370 BC). These concepts are now firmly and irrevocably consigned to medical antiquity.

Galen (129–c. 200) built on Hippocrates' naturalistic ideas about disease by giving it an anatomical and physiological basis. However, it was probably Ibn Sina (980–1037)—commonly known as Avicenna — who, by his *Canon of Medicine*, had the greatest influence on advancing medicine through scientific discovery.

Morbid anatomy

Some of the greatest advances in the scientific study of disease came from the thorough internal examination of the body after death. *Autopsies* (necropsies or postmortem examinations) have been performed scientifically from about 300 BC and have revealed much information that has helped to clarify the nature of many diseases. As these examinations were confined initially to the gross (rather than microscopic) examination of the organs, this period is regarded as the era of *morbid anatomy*. During the 18th and 19th centuries in Europe, medical science was advanced by Baillie, Rokitansky and Aschoff, who meticulously performed and documented many thousands of autopsies and correlated their findings with the clinical signs and symptoms of the patients and with the natural history of a wide variety of diseases.

Microscopic and cellular pathology

Pathology, and indeed medicine as a whole, was revolutionised by the application of *microscopy* to the study of diseased tissues from about 1800. Before this, it was postulated that tissue alterations in disease resulted from a process of *spontaneous generation*; that is, by metamorphosis independent of any external cause or other influence. This notion seems ridiculous to us today, but 200 years ago nothing was known of

Table 1.1 Historical relationship between the hypothetical causes of disease and the dependence on techniques for their elucidation

Hypothetical cause of disease	Techniques supporting causal hypothesis	Period
Animism	None	Primitive, though the ideas persist in some cultures
Magic	None	Primitive, though the ideas persist in some cultures
Humours (excess or deficiency)	Early autopsies and clinical observations	c. 500 BC to c. AD 1500
Spontaneous generation (abiogenesis)	Analogies with decomposing matter	Prior to AD 1800
Environmental	Modern autopsy Cellular pathology (e.g. microscopy) Toxicology Microbiology Epidemiology	1850 to present
Genetic	Molecular pathology (e.g. DNA analysis) and clinical observations on inherited defects	20th century to present

bacteria, viruses, ionising radiation, carcinogenic chemicals, and so on. So Louis Pasteur's (1822–1895) demonstration that micro-organisms in the environment could contaminate and impair the quality of wine was a major advance in our perception of the environment and our understanding that pathogens within it cause disease.

Rudolf Virchow (1821–1902), a German pathologist and ardent advocate of the microscope, recognised that the cell was the smallest viable constituent unit of the body and he contrived a new and lasting set of ideas about disease—*cellular pathology*. The light microscope enabled him to see changes in diseased tissues at a cellular level and his observations, extended further by electron microscopy, have had a profound influence. That does not mean to say that Virchow's cell pathology theory is immutable. Indeed, advances in biochemistry have revolutionised our understanding of many diseases at a molecular level.

Molecular pathology

The impact of *molecular pathology* is exemplified by advances in our knowledge of the biochemical basis of congenital disorders and cancer. Techniques with relatively simple principles (less easy in practice) reveal the change of a single nucleotide in genomic DNA resulting in the synthesis of the defective gene product that is the fundamental lesion in a particular disease (Ch. 3).

Cellular and molecular alterations in disease

As a result of the application of modern scientific methods, we now have a clearer understanding of the ways in which diseases can be attributed to disturbances of normal cellular and molecular mechanisms (Table 1.2).

SCOPE OF PATHOLOGY

Pathology is the foundation of medical practice. Without pathology, the practice of medicine would still rely on myths and folklore.

Clinical and experimental pathology

Scientific knowledge about human diseases is derived from observations on patients or, by analogy, from experimental studies on animals and cell cultures. The greatest contribution comes from the detailed study of tissue and body fluids from patients. Pathology has a key role in translational research by facilitating the transfer of knowledge derived from laboratory investigations into clinical practice.

Clinical pathology

Clinical medicine is based on a longitudinal approach to a patient's illness—the patient's history, the examination and investigation, the diagnosis, and the treatment. Clinical pathology is more concerned with a cross-sectional analysis at the level of the disease itself, studied in depth—the cause and mechanisms of the disease, and the effects of the disease upon the various organs and systems of the body. These two perspectives are complementary and inseparable: clinical medicine cannot be practised without an understanding of pathology; pathology is meaningless if it is bereft of clinical implications.

In the UK, it is estimated that c. 70% of clinical diagnoses rely on pathology investigations. In the USA, c. 90% of the objective data in electronic patient records are derived from pathology laboratories.

Subdivisions of clinical pathology

Pathology is a vast subject with many ramifications. In practice, however, it has major subdivisions:

- *histopathology:* the investigation and diagnosis of disease from the examination of tissues
- *cytopathology:* the investigation and diagnosis of disease from the examination of isolated cells
- *haematology:* the study of disorders of the cellular and coagulable components of blood
- *microbiology:* the study of infectious diseases and the organisms responsible for them
- *immunology:* the study of the specific defence mechanisms of the body
- *chemical pathology:* the study and diagnosis of disease from the chemical changes in tissues and fluids
- *genetics:* the study of abnormal chromosomes and genes
- *toxicology:* the study of the effects of known or suspected poisons
- *forensic pathology:* the application of pathology to legal purposes (e.g. investigation of death in suspicious circumstances).

These subdivisions are more important professionally (because each requires its own team of expert specialists) than educationally at the undergraduate level. The subject must be taught and learnt in an integrated manner, for the body and its diseases make no distinction between these professional subdivisions.

This book, therefore, adopts a multidisciplinary approach to pathology. In the systematic section (Part 3), the normal structure and function of each organ is summarised, the pathological basis for clinical signs and symptoms is described, and the clinical implications of each disease are emphasised.

Experimental pathology

Experimental pathology is the observation of the effects of manipulations on experimental systems such as animal models of disease or cell cultures. Although advances in cell culture technology have reduced the usage of laboratory animals in medical research and experimental pathology, it is extremely difficult to mimic in cell cultures the physiological milieu that prevails in the intact human body.

TECHNIQUES OF PATHOLOGY

Our knowledge of the nature and causation of disease has been disclosed by the continuing application of technology to its study.

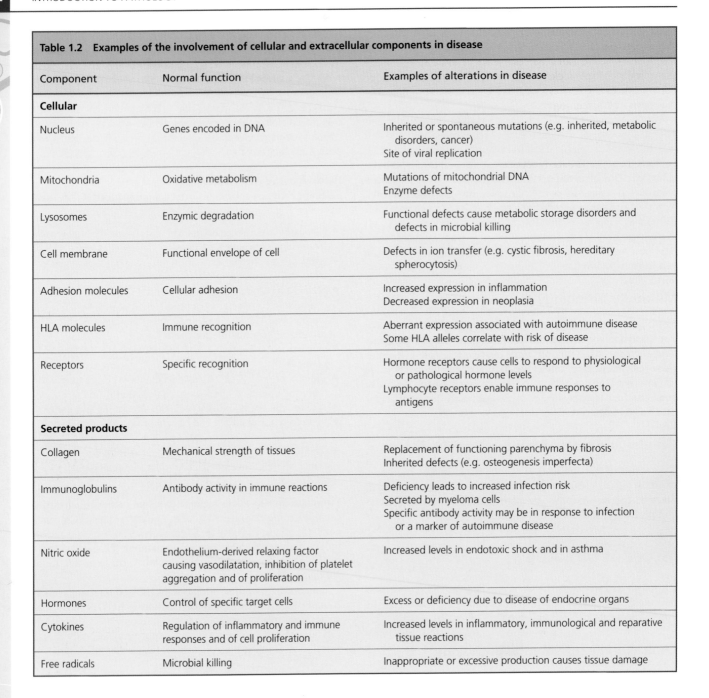

Table 1.2   Examples of the involvement of cellular and extracellular components in disease

Component	Normal function	Examples of alterations in disease
Cellular		
Nucleus	Genes encoded in DNA	Inherited or spontaneous mutations (e.g. inherited, metabolic disorders, cancer) Site of viral replication
Mitochondria	Oxidative metabolism	Mutations of mitochondrial DNA Enzyme defects
Lysosomes	Enzymic degradation	Functional defects cause metabolic storage disorders and defects in microbial killing
Cell membrane	Functional envelope of cell	Defects in ion transfer (e.g. cystic fibrosis, hereditary spherocytosis)
Adhesion molecules	Cellular adhesion	Increased expression in inflammation Decreased expression in neoplasia
HLA molecules	Immune recognition	Aberrant expression associated with autoimmune disease Some HLA alleles correlate with risk of disease
Receptors	Specific recognition	Hormone receptors cause cells to respond to physiological or pathological hormone levels Lymphocyte receptors enable immune responses to antigens
Secreted products		
Collagen	Mechanical strength of tissues	Replacement of functioning parenchyma by fibrosis Inherited defects (e.g. osteogenesis imperfecta)
Immunoglobulins	Antibody activity in immune reactions	Deficiency leads to increased infection risk Secreted by myeloma cells Specific antibody activity may be in response to infection or a marker of autoimmune disease
Nitric oxide	Endothelium-derived relaxing factor causing vasodilatation, inhibition of platelet aggregation and of proliferation	Increased levels in endotoxic shock and in asthma
Hormones	Control of specific target cells	Excess or deficiency due to disease of endocrine organs
Cytokines	Regulation of inflammatory and immune responses and of cell proliferation	Increased levels in inflammatory, immunological and reparative tissue reactions
Free radicals	Microbial killing	Inappropriate or excessive production causes tissue damage

Gross pathology

Before microscopy was applied to medical problems (c. 1800), observations were confined to those made with the unaided eye, and thus was accumulated much of our knowledge of the *morbid anatomy* of disease. Gross or macroscopic pathology is the modern nomenclature for this approach to the study of disease and, especially in the autopsy, it is still an important investigative method. The gross pathology of many diseases is so characteristic that, when interpreted by an experienced pathologist, a fairly confident diagnosis can often be given before further investigation by, for example, light microscopy.

Light microscopy

Advances in optics have yielded a wealth of new information about the structure of tissues and cells in health and disease.

If solid tissues are to be examined by light microscopy, the sample must first be thinly sectioned to permit the transmission of light and to minimise the superimposition of tissue components. These sections are routinely cut from tissue hardened by permeation with and embedding in wax or, less often, transparent plastic. For some purposes (e.g. histochemistry, very urgent diagnosis) sections have to be cut from tissue that has been hardened rapidly by freezing. The sections are stained to help distinguish between different components of the tissue (e.g. nuclei, cytoplasm, collagen).

The microscope can also be used to examine cells from cysts, body cavities, sucked from solid lesions or scraped from body surfaces. This is *cytology* and is used widely in cancer diagnosis and screening.

Histochemistry

Histochemistry is the study of the chemistry of tissues, usually by microscopy of tissue sections after they have been treated with specific reagents so that the features of individual cells can be visualised.

Immunohistochemistry and immunofluorescence

Immunohistochemistry and immunofluorescence employ antibodies (immunoglobulins with antigen specificity) to visualise substances in tissue sections or cell preparations; these techniques use antibodies linked chemically to enzymes or fluorescent dyes, respectively. Immunofluorescence requires a microscope specially modified for ultraviolet illumination and the preparations are often not permanent (they fade). For these reasons, immunohistochemistry has become more popular; in this technique, the end product is a deposit of opaque or coloured material that can be seen with a conventional light microscope and does not deteriorate. The repertoire of substances detectable by these techniques has been greatly enlarged by the development of monoclonal antibodies.

Electron microscopy

Electron microscopy has extended the range of pathology to the study of disorders at an organelle level, and to the demonstration of viruses in tissue samples from some diseases. The most common diagnostic use is for the interpretation of renal biopsies.

Biochemical techniques

Biochemical techniques applied to the body's tissues and fluids in health and disease are now one of the dominant influences on our growing knowledge of pathological processes. The clinical role of biochemistry is exemplified by the importance of monitoring fluid and electrolyte homeostasis in many disorders. Serum enzyme assays are used to assess the integrity and vitality of various tissues; for example, raised blood levels of cardiac enzymes and troponin indicate damage to cardiac myocytes.

Haematological techniques

Haematological techniques are used in the diagnosis and study of blood disorders. These techniques range from relatively simple cell counting, which can be performed electronically, to assays of blood coagulation factors.

Cell cultures

Cell cultures are widely used in research and diagnosis. They are an attractive medium for research because of the ease with which the cellular environment can be modified and the responses to it monitored. Diagnostically, cell cultures are used to prepare chromosome spreads for *cytogenetic analysis*.

Medical microbiology

Medical microbiology is the study of diseases caused by organisms such as bacteria, fungi, viruses and parasites. Techniques used include direct microscopy of appropriately stained material (e.g. pus), cultures to isolate and grow the organism, and methods to identify correctly the cause of the infection. In the case of bacterial infections, the most appropriate antibiotic can be selected by determining the sensitivity of the organism to a variety of agents.

Molecular pathology

Molecular pathology reveals defects in the chemical structure of molecules arising from errors in the genome, the sequence of bases that directs amino acid synthesis. Using *in situ hybridisation* it is possible to visualise specific genes or their messenger RNA in tissue sections or cell preparations. Minute quantities of nucleic acids can be amplified by the use of the *polymerase chain reaction* using oligonucleotide primers specific for the genes being studied.

DNA microarrays can be used to determine patterns of gene expression (mRNA). This powerful technique can reveal novel diagnostic and prognostic categories, indistinguishable by other methods.

Molecular pathology is manifested in various conditions, for example: abnormal haemoglobin molecules, such as in sickle cell disease (Ch. 23); abnormal collagen molecules in osteogenesis imperfecta (Chs 7, 25); and alterations in the genome governing the control of cell and tissue growth, playing a pivotal role in the development of tumours (Ch. 11).

LEARNING PATHOLOGY

Pathology is best learnt in two stages:

- *general pathology*: the mechanisms and characteristics of the principal types of disease process(e.g. inflammation, tumours, degenerations)
- *systematic pathology*: the descriptions of specific diseases as they affect individual organs or organ systems (e.g. appendicitis, lung cancer, atheroma).

General pathology

General pathology is our current understanding of the causation, mechanisms and characteristics of the major categories of disease.

These processes are covered in Part 2 of this textbook and many specific diseases are mentioned by way of illustration. The principles of general pathology must be understood before an attempt is made to study systematic pathology. General pathology is the foundation of knowledge that has to be acquired before studying the systematic pathology of specific diseases.

Systematic pathology

Systematic pathology is our current knowledge of specific diseases as they affect individual organs or systems. ('Systematic' should not be confused with 'systemic'. Systemic pathology would be characteristic of a disease that pervaded *all* body systems!) Each specific disease can usually be attributed to the operation of one or more categories of causation and mechanism featuring in general pathology. Thus, acute appendicitis is acute inflammation affecting the appendix; carcinoma of the lung is the result of carcinogenesis acting upon cells in the lung, and the behaviour of the cancerous cells thus formed follows the pattern established for malignant tumours; and so on.

Systematic pathology comprises Part 3 of this textbook.

Building knowledge and understanding

There are two apparent difficulties facing the new student of pathology: *language* and *process*. Pathology, like most branches of science and medicine, has its own vocabulary of special terms. These need to be learnt and understood not just because they are the language of pathology: they are also a major part of the language of clinical medicine. The student must not confuse the learning of the language with the learning of the mechanisms of disease and their effects on individual organs and patients. In this book, each important term will be clearly defined in the main text or the glossary, or both.

A logical and orderly way of thinking about diseases and their characteristics must be cultivated. For each disease entity the student should be able to list the chief characteristics:

- epidemiology
- aetiology
- pathogenesis
- pathological and clinical features
- complications and sequelae
- prognosis
- treatment.

Our knowledge about many diseases is still incomplete, but at least such a list will prompt the memory and enable students to organise their knowledge.

Pathology is learnt through a variety of media. Even the bedside, operating theatre and outpatient clinic provide ample opportunities for further experience of pathology; hearing a diastolic cardiac murmur through a stethoscope should prompt the listening student to consider the pathological features of the narrowed mitral valve orifice (mitral stenosis) responsible for the murmur, and the effects of this stenosis on the lungs and the rest of the cardiovascular system.

Pathology in the problem-oriented integrated medical curriculum

Although medicine, surgery, pathology and other disciplines are still taught as separate subjects in some curricula, students must develop an integrated understanding of disease.

To encourage this integration, in this textbook the pathological basis of common clinical signs is frequently emphasised so that students can relate their everyday clinical experiences to their knowledge of pathology.

In general, the development of a clinicopathological understanding of disease can be gained by two equally legitimate and complementary approaches:

- problem-oriented
- disease-oriented.

In learning pathology, the disease-oriented approach is more relevant because medical practitioners require knowledge of diseases (e.g. pneumonia, cancer, ischaemic heart disease) so that correct diagnoses can be made and the most appropriate treatment given.

The problem-oriented approach

The problem-oriented approach is the first step in the clinical diagnosis of a disease. In many illnesses, symptoms alone suffice for diagnosis. In other illnesses, the diagnosis has to be supported by clinical signs (e.g. abnormal heart sounds). In some instances, the diagnosis can be made conclusively only by special investigations (e.g. laboratory analysis of blood or tissue samples, imaging techniques).

The links between *diseases* and the *problems* they produce are emphasised in the systematic chapters (Part 3) and are exemplified here (Table 1.3).

Justifications for the problem-oriented approach are:

- Patients present with 'problems' rather than 'diagnoses'.
- Some clinical problems have an uncertain pathological basis (this is true particularly of psychiatric conditions such as depressive illness).
- Clinical treatment is often directed towards relieving the patient's problems rather than curing their disease (which may either remit spontaneously or be incurable).

The disease-oriented approach

The disease-oriented approach is the most appropriate way of presenting pathological knowledge. It would be possible to produce a textbook of pathology in which the chapters were entitled, for example, 'Cough', 'Weight loss', 'Headaches' and 'Pain' (these being problems), but the reader would be unlikely to come away with a clear understanding of the diseases. This is because one disease may cause a variety of problems—for example, cough, weight loss, headaches and pain—and may therefore crop up in several chapters. Consequently, this textbook, like most textbooks of pathology (and, indeed, of medicine), adopts a disease-oriented approach.

MAKING DIAGNOSES

Diagnosis is the act of naming a disease in an individual patient. The diagnosis is important because it enables the patient to benefit from treatment that is known, or is at least likely, to be effective from having observed its effects on other patients with the same disease.

The process of making diagnoses involves:

- taking a clinical history to document *symptoms*
- examining the patient for clinical *signs*

Table 1.3   The problem-oriented approach: examples of combinations of clinical problems and their pathological basis

Problems	Pathological basis (diagnosis)	Comment
Weight loss and haemoptysis	Lung cancer or tuberculosis	Can be distinguished by finding either cancer cells or mycobacteria in sputum
Dyspnoea and ankle swelling	Heart failure	Due to, for example, valvular disease
Chest pain and hypotension	Myocardial infarction	Should be confirmed by ECG and serum assay of cardiac enzymes
Vomiting and diarrhoea	Gastroenteritis	Specific microbial cause can be determined
Headache, impaired vision and microscopic haematuria	Hypertension	May be due to various causes or, more commonly, without evident cause
Headache, vomiting and photophobia	Subarachnoid haemorrhage or meningitis	Can be distinguished by other clinical features and examination of cerebrospinal fluid

- if necessary, performing *investigations* guided by the provisional diagnosis based on signs and symptoms.

Although experienced clinicians can diagnose many patients' diseases quite rapidly (and usually reliably), the student will find that it is helpful to adopt a formal strategy based on a series of logical steps leading to the gradual exclusion of various possibilities and the emergence of a single diagnosis. For example:

- First decide which organ or body system seems to be affected by the disease.
- From the signs and symptoms, decide which general category of disease (inflammation, neoplasia, etc.) is likely to be present.
- Then, using other factors (age, gender, previous medical history, etc.), infer a diagnosis or a small number of possibilities for investigation.
- Investigations should be performed only if the outcome of each one can be expected to resolve the diagnosis, or influence management if the diagnosis is already known.

This strategy can be refined and presented in the form of decision trees or diagnostic algorithms, but these details are outside the scope of this book.

Diagnostic pathology

In living patients we often investigate and diagnose their illness by applying pathological methods to the examination of *tissue biopsies* and *body fluids*. If there are clinical indications

to do so, it may be possible to obtain a series of samples from which the course of the disease can be monitored.

The applications of pathology in clinical diagnosis and patient management are described in Chapter 4.

Autopsies

Autopsy (necropsy and postmortem examination are synonymous) means to 'see for oneself'. In other words, rather than relying on clinical signs and symptoms and the results of diagnostic investigations during life, here is an opportunity for direct inspection and analysis of the organs.

Autopsies are useful for:

- determining the *cause of death*
- *audit* of the accuracy of clinical diagnosis
- *education* of undergraduates and postgraduates
- *research* into the causes and mechanisms of disease
- gathering accurate *statistics* about disease incidence.

The clinical use of information from autopsies is described in Chapter 4.

For the medical undergraduate and postgraduate, the autopsy is an important medium for the learning of pathology. It is an unrivalled opportunity to correlate clinical signs with their underlying pathological explanation.

PATHOLOGY AND POPULATIONS

Although pathology, as practised professionally, is a laboratory-based clinical discipline focused on the care of individual patients and the advancement of medical knowledge, our ideas about the causes of disease, disability and death have wide implications for society.

Causes and agents of disease

There is socially (and politically) relevant controversy about what actually constitutes the *cause* of a disease. Critics argue that the science of pathology leads to the identification of merely the *agents* of some diseases rather than their underlying causes. For example, the bacterium *Mycobacterium tuberculosis* is the infective agent resulting in tuberculosis but, because many people exposed to the bacterium alone do not develop the disease, social deprivation and malnutrition (both of which are epidemiologically associated with the risk of tuberculosis) might be regarded by some as the actual causes. Without doubt, the marked fall in the incidence of many serious infectious diseases during the 20th century was achieved at least as much through improvements in housing, hygiene, nutrition and sewage treatment as by specific immunisation and antibiotic treatment directed at the causative organisms. This distinction between agents and causes is developed further in Chapter 3.

The health of a nation

Because the methods used in pathology enable reliable diagnoses to be made, either during life by, for example, biopsy or after death by autopsy, the discipline has an important

role in documenting the incidence of disease in a population. Cancer registration data are most reliable when based on histologically proven diagnoses; this happens in most cases. Epidemiological data derived from death certificates are notoriously unreliable unless verified by autopsy. The information thus obtained can be used to determine the true incidence of a disease in a population and the resources for its prevention and treatment can be deployed where they will achieve the greatest benefit.

Preventing disability and premature death

Laboratory methods are used increasingly for the detection of early disease by population screening. The prospects of cure are invariably better the earlier a disease is detected.

For example, the incidence of death from cancer of the cervix is lowered by screening programmes; in many countries, women have their cervix scraped at regular intervals and the exfoliated cells are examined microscopically to detect the earliest changes associated with development of cancer. Screening for breast cancer is primarily by mammography (X-ray imaging of the breast); any abnormalities are further investigated either by examining cells aspirated from the suspicious area or by histological examination of the tissue itself.

FURTHER READING

Porter R 1997 The greatest benefit to mankind: a medical history of humanity from antiquity to the present. HarperCollins, London

Rosai J 1997 Pathology: a historical opportunity. American Journal of Pathology 151: 3–7

Tallis R 2004 Hippocratic oaths. Atlantic Books, London

2

Characteristics, classification and incidence of disease

WHAT IS DISEASE?

A disease is a condition in which the presence of an abnormality of the body causes a loss of normal health (dis-ease). The mere presence of an abnormality is insufficient to imply the presence of disease unless it is accompanied by ill health, although it may denote an early stage in the development of a disease. The word disease is, therefore, synonymous with ill health and illness.

Each separately named disease is characterised by a distinct set of features (cause, signs and symptoms, morphological and functional changes, etc.). Many diseases share common features and thereby are grouped together in disease classification systems.

The abnormalities causing diseases may be structural or functional, or both. In many instances the abnormalities are obvious and well characterised (e.g. a tumour); in other instances the patient may be profoundly unwell but the nature of the abnormality is less well defined (e.g. depressive illness).

Limits of normality

Normal is impossible to define as a single discrete state for any biological characteristic. In addition to differences between individuals, the human body changes naturally during fetal development, childhood, puberty, pregnancy (gender permitting), ageing, etc. Therefore, 'normal' means the most frequent state in a population defined by age distribution, gender, etc.

Most quantifiable biological characteristics are normally distributed, in statistical terms, about an average value. There are no constant numbers that can be used to define a normal height, weight, serum sodium concentration, etc. Normality, when quantifiable, is expressed as a normal range, usually encompassed by two standard deviations (for a 'normally' distributed feature) either side of the mean (Ch. 4). The probability that a measurable characteristic is abnormal increases the nearer it is to the limits of the normal range, but a value lying outside the normal range is not necessarily indicative of abnormality—it is just very probably abnormal.

A distinction must also be drawn between what is usual and what is normal. It is usual to find atheroma (Ch. 13) in an elderly individual—but is it normal? In contrast, atheroma in a teenager is so unusual that it would be regarded as abnormal and worthy of further investigation.

Responses to the environment

The natural environment of any species contains potentially injurious agents to which the individual or species must either adapt or succumb.

Adaptation

Adaptation of the individual to an adverse environment is well illustrated by the following examples. Healthy mountaineers ascending rapidly to the rarefied atmosphere at high altitudes often develop 'mountain sickness'; they recover by a process of adaptation (increased haemoglobin, etc.), but failure to do so can result in death from heart failure.

Fair-skinned people get sunburnt from excessive exposure to ultraviolet light from the sun; some adapt by developing a protective tan, but untanned individuals run a higher risk of skin cancer if they persist in unprotected exposure to the sun for long periods. Environmental micro-organisms are a common cause of disease; those individuals who develop specific defences against them (e.g. antibodies) can resist the infection, but those who fail to adapt may succumb.

Disease: failure of adaptation

Susceptibility of a species to injurious environmental factors results in either its extinction or, over a long period, the favoured selection of a new strain of the species better adapted to withstand such factors. However, this holds true only if the injury manifests itself in the early years of life, thus thwarting propagation of the disease susceptibility by reproduction. If the injury manifests only in later life, or if a lifetime of exposure to the injurious agent is necessary to produce the pathological changes, then the agent produces no evolutionary pressure for change.

An arguable interpretation of disease is that it represents a set of abnormal bodily responses to agents for which, as yet, the human species has little or no tolerance.

Darwinian medicine

The relatively new science of Darwinian medicine is based on the belief that diseases not only have *proximate* causes and mechanisms (e.g. viruses, bacteria, mutations) but also have *evolutionary* causes. Darwinian medicine focuses on the latter aspect and, while it may not yield cures for many serious diseases, it can help us to understand their current prevalence. Darwinian medicine is also rooted in the belief that natural selection favours reproductive success rather than health or life-span.

In *Why we get sick: the new science of Darwinian medicine*, Randolph Nesse, an evolutionary biologist, and George Williams, a psychiatrist, explain the application of evolutionary ideas to medicine with these examples:

- Pyrexia and malaise in patients with infections, while unpleasant, have evolved as a way of compromising the metabolism of pathogenic organisms. Thus, antipyretic treatments (e.g. paracetamol) that make the patient more comfortable can prolong the illness.
- Microbes evolve more rapidly than humans, thus explaining the perpetual struggle against infection and its worsening by the inappropriate use of antibiotics to which resistance soon develops.
- Some modern health problems are due to the evolutionary legacy of thrifty 'stone age' bodies living in a plentiful modern environment, thus explaining the rising prevalence of obesity.
- Allergic reactions are due to an immune system that is biased towards hypersensitivity to innocent agents rather than insufficient reactivity to genuine threats.

Ageing and adaptation

One of the main features of ageing is progressive inability of the individual to deal with new or worsening environmental threats (Ch. 12). This is exemplified by the gradual impairment of immune responses, resulting in:

- re-emergence of dormant infections such as tuberculosis and herpes zoster
- failure to mount an effective immune response to newly encountered pathogens.

Disease predisposition as an adaptive advantage

Paradoxically, a disease or disease predisposition can have beneficial effects on the individual. A few diseases or susceptibilities to diseases, in addition to their deleterious effects, confer adaptive protection against specific environmental pathogens. This advantage may explain the high prevalence of a disease in areas where the specific pathogen for another disease is endemic.

The best examples are:

- the sickle cell gene (HbS) and the glucose-6-phosphate dehydrogenase (G6PD) deficiency gene which confer protection against malaria by creating a hostile environment for the plasmodium parasite within red cells
- heterozygosity for the most common mutation (deletion of phenylalanine at position 508) in the cystic fibrosis conductance regulator which renders the individual less susceptible to *Salmonella typhi* infection.

CHARACTERISTICS OF DISEASE

- ▶ *Aetiology:* the cause of a disease
- ▶ *Pathogenesis:* the mechanism causing the disease
- ▶ *Pathological and clinical manifestations:* the structural and functional features of the disease
- ▶ *Complications and sequelae:* the secondary, systemic or remote consequences of a disease
- ▶ *Prognosis:* the anticipated course of the disease in terms of cure, remission, or fate of the patient
- ▶ *Epidemiology:* the incidence, prevalence and population distribution of a disease

All diseases have a set of characteristic features enabling them to be better understood, categorised and diagnosed. For many diseases, however, our knowledge is still incomplete or subject to controversy. The characteristics of any disease are (Fig. 2.1):

- aetiology (or cause)
- pathogenesis (or mechanism)
- morphological, functional and clinical changes (or manifestations)
- complications and sequelae (or secondary effects)
- prognosis (or outcome)
- epidemiology (or incidence).

The aetiology and pathogenesis of a disease may be combined as *aetiopathogenesis.*

Aetiology

The aetiology of a disease is its *cause:* the initiator of the subsequent events resulting in the patient's illness. Diseases are caused by a variable interaction between host (e.g. genetic) and *environmental* factors. Environmental causes of diseases are called *pathogens,* although this term is used commonly only when referring to microbes; bacteria capable of causing disease are pathogenic bacteria and those that are harmless are non-pathogenic.

General categories of aetiological agents include:

- genetic abnormalities
- infective agents, e.g. bacteria, viruses, fungi, parasites
- chemicals
- radiation
- mechanical trauma.

Some diseases are due to a combination of causes, such as genetic factors and infective agents, and are said to have a *multifactorial aetiology.*

Sometimes the aetiology of a disease is unknown, but the disease is observed to occur more commonly in people with certain constitutional traits, occupations, habits or habitats; these are regarded as *risk factors.* These factors may provide a clue to an as yet unidentified aetiological agent. Other risk factors may simply have a permissive effect, facilitating the development of a disease in that individual; examples include malnutrition, which favours infections.

Some agents can cause more than one disease depending on the circumstances; for example, ionising radiation can cause rapid deterioration leading to death, scarring of tissues, or tumours.

Identification of the causes of disease

In terms of causation, diseases may be:

- entirely genetic
- multifactorial (genetic and environmental interplay)
- entirely environmental.

Most common diseases have an entirely environmental cause, but genetic influences in disease susceptibility are being increasingly discovered, and many diseases with no previously known cause are being shown to be due to genetic abnormalities (Ch. 3). This is the reward of applying the principles of clinical genetics and the new techniques of molecular biology to the study of human disease. The extent to which a disease is due to genetic or environmental causes can often be deduced from some of its main features or its association with host factors.

Features pointing to a significant genetic contribution to the occurrence of a disease include a high incidence in particular families or races, or an association with an inherited characteristic (e.g. gender, blood groups, histocompatibility alleles). Diseases associated with particular occupations or geographic regions tend to have an environmental basis; the most abundant environmental causes of disease are microbes (bacteria, viruses, fungi, etc.).

Probability of disease

The relationship between the quantity of causal agent and the probability that disease will result is not always simply linear (Fig. 2.2). For example, many infections occur only on exposure to a sufficient dose of micro-organisms; the body's defence mechanisms have to be overcome before disease

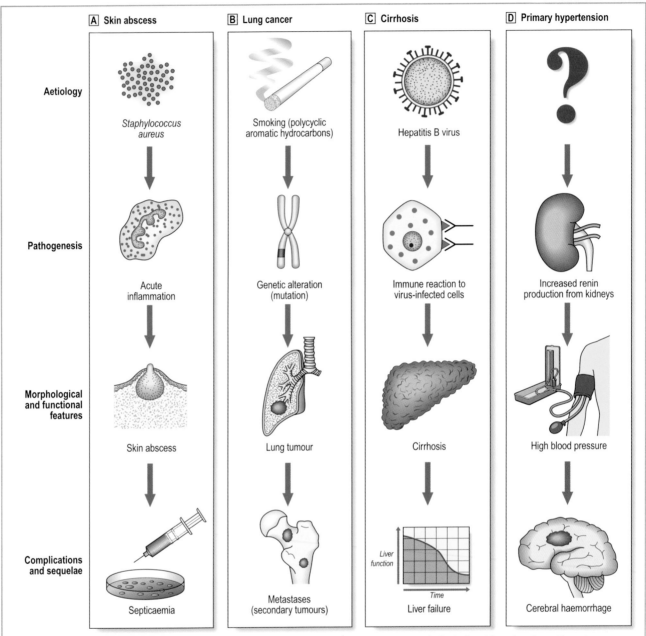

Fig. 2.1 Characteristics of disease. The relationship between aetiology, pathogenesis, morphological and functional manifestations, and complications and sequelae is exemplified by four diseases. [A] Skin abscess. [B] Lung cancer. [C] Cirrhosis. [D] Primary hypertension.

results. Some agents capable of causing disease, such as alcohol, are actually beneficial in small doses; those who abstain from alcohol have a slightly higher risk of premature death from ischaemic heart disease.

Host predisposition to disease

Many diseases are the *predictable* consequence of exposure to the initiating cause; host factors make relatively little contribution. This is particularly true of physical injury: the immediate results of mechanical trauma or radiation injury are dose-related; the outcome can be predicted from the strength of the injurious agent.

Other diseases are the *probable* consequence of exposure to causative factors, but they are not inevitable. This is exemplified by infections with potentially harmful bacteria: the outcome can be influenced by various host factors such as nutritional status, genetic influences and pre-existing immunity.

Some diseases occur more commonly in individuals with a congenital predisposition. For example, ankylosing spondylitis (Ch. 25), a disabling inflammatory disease of the spinal joints of unknown aetiology, occurs more commonly in individuals with the HLA-B27 allele.

Some diseases predispose patients to the risk of developing other diseases. Diseases associated with an increased risk

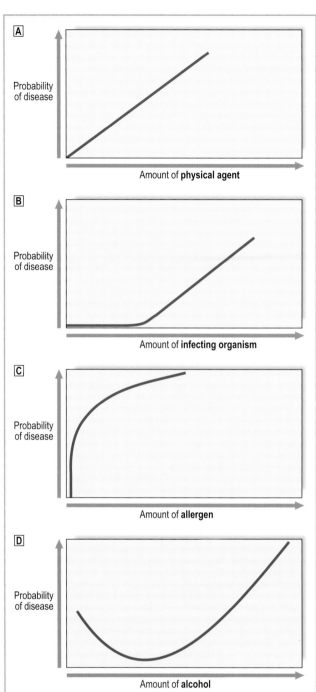

Fig. 2.2 Relationships between the amount of a causal agent and the probability of disease. A Physical agents. For example, the risk of traumatic injury to a pedestrian increases in proportion to the kinetic energy of the motor vehicle. **B Infectious agents.** Many infectious diseases result only if sufficient numbers of the micro-organism (e.g. bacterium, virus) are transmitted; smaller numbers are capable of being eliminated by the non-immune and immune defences. **C Allergens.** In sensitised (i.e. allergic) individuals, minute amounts of an allergen will provoke a severe anaphylactic reaction. **D J-shaped curve.** Best exemplified by alcohol, of which small doses (c. 1–2 units per day) reduce the risk of premature death from ischaemic heart disease, but larger doses progressively increase the risk of cirrhosis.

of cancer are designated *premalignant conditions;* for example, hepatic cirrhosis predisposes to hepatocellular carcinoma, and ulcerative colitis predisposes to carcinoma of the large intestine. The histologically identifiable antecedent lesion from which the cancers directly develop is designated the *premalignant lesion.*

Some diseases predispose to others because they have a permissive effect, allowing environmental agents that are not normally pathogenic to cause disease. This is exemplified by *opportunistic infections* in patients with impaired defence mechanisms resulting in infection by organisms not normally harmful (i.e. non-pathogenic) to humans (Ch. 9). Patients with leukaemia or the acquired immune deficiency syndrome (AIDS), organ transplant recipients, or other patients treated with cytotoxic drugs or steroids, are susceptible to infections such as pneumonia due to *Aspergillus* fungi, cytomegalovirus or *Pneumocystis jiroveci.*

Causes and agents of disease

It is argued that a distinction should be made between the *cause* and the *agent* of a disease. For example, tuberculosis is caused, arguably, not by the tubercle bacillus (*Mycobacterium tuberculosis*) but by poverty, social deprivation and malnutrition—the tubercle bacillus is 'merely' the agent of the disease; the underlying cause is adverse socio-economic factors. There is, in fact, incontrovertible evidence that the decline in incidence of many serious infectious diseases is attributable substantially to improvements in hygiene, sanitation and general nutrition rather than to immunisation programmes or specific anti-microbial therapy. Such arguments are of relevance here only to emphasise that the socio-economic status of a country or individual may influence the prevalence of the environmental factor or the host susceptibility to it. In practice, causes and agents are conveniently embraced by the term *aetiology.*

Causal associations

A causal association is a marker for the risk of developing a disease, but it is not necessarily the actual cause of the disease. The stronger the causal association, the more likely it is to be the aetiology of the disease. Causal associations become more powerful if:

- they are *plausible,* supported by experimental evidence
- the presence of the disease is associated with *prior exposure* to the putative cause
- the risk of the disease is *proportional* to the level of exposure to the putative cause
- *removal* of the putative cause lessens the risk of the disease.

The utility of these statements is exemplified by reference to the association between lung cancer and cigarette smoking. Lung cancer is more common in smokers than in non-smokers; tobacco yields carcinogenic chemicals; the risk of lung cancer is proportional to cigarette consumption; population groups that have reduced their cigarette consumption (e.g. doctors) show a commensurate reduction in their risk of lung cancer.

Causal associations may be neither exclusive nor absolute. For example, because some heavy cigarette smokers never develop lung cancer, smoking cannot alone be regarded as a *sufficient* cause; other factors are required. Conversely, because some non-smokers develop lung cancer, smoking cannot be regarded as a *necessary* cause; other causative factors must exist.

Causal associations tend to be strongest with infections. For example syphilis, a venereal disease, is always due to infection by the spirochaete *Treponema pallidum*; there is no other possible cause for syphilis; syphilis is the only disease caused by *Treponema pallidum*.

Koch's postulates

An infective (e.g. bacterial, viral) cause for a disease is not usually regarded as proven until it satisfies the criteria enunciated by Robert Koch (1843–1910), a German bacteriologist and Nobel prizewinner in 1905:

- The organism must be sufficiently abundant in every case to account for the disease.
- The organism associated with the disease can be cultivated artificially in pure culture.
- The cultivated organism produces the disease upon inoculation into another member of the same species.
- Antibodies to the organism appear during the course of the disease.

The last was added subsequently to Koch's list. Although Koch's postulates have lost their novelty, their relevance is undiminished. However, each postulate merits further comment because there are notable exceptions:

- In some diseases the causative organism is very sparse. A good example is tuberculosis, where the destructive lung lesions contain very few mycobacteria; in this instance, the destruction is caused by an immunological reaction triggered by the presence of the organism.
- Cultivation of some organisms is remarkably difficult, yet their role in the aetiology of disease is undisputed.
- Ethics prohibit wilful transmission of a disease from one person to another, but animals have been used successfully as surrogates for human transmission.
- Immunosuppression may lessen the antibody response and also render the host extremely susceptible to the disease. In addition, if an antibody is detected it should be further classified to confirm that it is an *IgM* class antibody, denoting recent infection, rather than an *IgG* antibody, denoting long-lasting immunity due to previous exposure to the organism.

Pathogenesis

The pathogenesis of a disease is the *mechanism* through which the aetiology (cause) operates to produce the pathological and clinical manifestations. Groups of aetiological agents often cause disease by acting through the same common pathway of events.

Examples of pathogeneses of disease include:

- inflammation: a response to many micro-organisms and other harmful agents causing tissue injury
- degeneration: a deterioration of cells or tissues in response to, or failure of adaptation to, a variety of agents

- carcinogenesis: the mechanism by which cancer-causing agents result in the development of tumours
- immune reactions: undesirable effects of the body's immune system.

These pathways of disease development constitute our knowledge of general pathology, and their description forms Part 2 of this textbook.

Latent intervals and incubation periods

Few aetiological agents cause signs and symptoms immediately after exposure. Usually, some time elapses. In the context of carcinogenesis, this time period is referred to as the *latent interval*; it is often two or three decades. In infectious disorders (due to bacteria, viruses, etc.), the period between exposure and the development of disease is called the *incubation period*; it is often measured in days or weeks, and each infectious agent is usually associated with a characteristic incubation period.

The reason for discussing these time intervals here is that it is during these periods that the pathogenesis of the disease is being enacted, culminating in the development of symptomatic pathological and clinical manifestations that cause the patient to seek medical help.

Structural and functional manifestations

The aetiological agent (cause) acts through a pathogenetic pathway (mechanism) to produce the *manifestations* of disease, giving rise to clinical signs and symptoms (e.g. weight loss, shortness of breath) and the abnormal features or *lesions* (e.g. carcinoma of the lung) to which the clinical signs and symptoms can be attributed. The pathological manifestations may require biochemical methods for their detection and, therefore, should not be thought of as only those visible to the unaided eye or by microscopy. The biochemical changes in the tissues and the blood are, in some instances, more important than the structural changes, many of which may appear relatively late in the course of the disease.

Although each separately named disease has its own distinctive and diagnostic features, it is possible to generalise about the range of structural and functional abnormalities, alone or combined, resulting in ill health.

Structural abnormalities

Common structural abnormalities causing ill health are:

- space-occupying lesions (e.g. tumours) destroying, displacing or compressing adjacent healthy tissues
- deposition of an excessive or abnormal material in an organ (e.g. amyloid)
- abnormally sited tissue (e.g. tumours, heterotopias) as a result of invasion, metastasis or developmental abnormality
- loss of healthy tissue from a surface (e.g. ulceration) or from within a solid organ (e.g. infarction)
- obstruction to normal flow within a tube (e.g. asthma, vascular occlusion)
- distension or rupture of a hollow structure (e.g. aneurysm, intestinal perforation).

Other structural abnormalities, visible only by light or electron microscopy, are very common and, even though they do not directly cause clinical signs or symptoms, they are nevertheless diagnostically useful and often specific manifestations of disease. For this reason, the morphological examination of diseased tissues is very rewarding for patient management and for clinical research. At an ultrastructural level (electron microscopy), one might see alien particles such as viruses in the affected tissue; there could be abnormalities in the number, shape, internal structure or size of tissue components such as intracellular organelles or extracellular material. By light microscopy, abnormalities in cellular morphology or tissue architecture can be discerned. Immunohistochemistry (Ch. 4) can be used to make visible otherwise invisible, but important, alterations in cells and tissues. With the unaided eye, changes in the size, shape or texture of whole organs can be discerned either by direct inspection or by indirect means such as radiology.

Functional abnormalities

Examples of functional abnormalities causing ill health include:

- excessive secretion of a cell product (e.g. nasal mucus in the common cold, hormones having remote effects)
- insufficient secretion of a cell product (e.g. insulin lack in diabetes mellitus)
- impaired nerve conduction
- impaired contractility of a muscular structure.

What makes patients feel ill?

The 'feeling' of illness is usually due to one or a combination of common symptoms:

- pain
- fever
- nausea
- malaise.

Each of these common symptoms has a pathological basis and, in those conditions that remit spontaneously, all that is required for treatment is symptomatic relief.

In addition to the general symptoms of disease, there are other specific expressions of illness that help to focus attention, diagnostically and therapeutically, on a particular organ or body system. Examples include:

- altered bowel habit (diarrhoea or constipation)
- abnormal swellings
- shortness of breath
- skin rash (which may or may not itch).

The symptoms of disease (the patient's presenting complaints) invariably have an identifiable scientific basis. This is important to know because often nothing more than symptomatic treatment is required because either the disease will remit spontaneously (e.g. the common cold) or there is no prospect of recovery (e.g. disseminated cancer). Examples of known mediators of symptoms are listed in Table 2.1.

Lesions

A lesion is the structural or functional abnormality responsible for ill health. Thus, in a patient with myocardial infarction, the infarct or patch of dead heart muscle is the lesion; this lesion is in turn a consequence of another lesion—occlusion of the supplying coronary artery by a thrombus (coronary artery thrombosis). A lesion may be purely biochemical, such as a defect in haemoglobin synthesis in a patient with a haemoglobinopathy.

Of course, not all diseases have overtly visible lesions associated with them, despite profound consequences for the patient; for example, schizophrenia and depressive illness yield nothing visibly abnormal in the brain if examined using conventional methods.

Pathognomonic abnormalities

Pathognomonic features are restricted to a single disease, or disease category, and without them the diagnosis is impossible or uncertain. For example, Reed–Sternberg cells are said to be pathognomonic of Hodgkin's disease; they are exceptionally rare in any other condition. Similarly, the presence of *Mycobacterium tuberculosis*, in the appropriate context, is pathognomonic of tuberculosis.

Pathognomonic abnormalities are extremely useful clinically, because they are absolutely diagnostic. Their presence leaves no doubt about the diagnosis. Unfortunately, some diseases are characterised only by a combination of abnormalities, none of which on its own is absolutely diagnostic; it is the particular combination that is diagnostic. Some diseases characterised by multiple abnormalities are called *syndromes* (p. 20).

Complications and sequelae

Diseases may have *prolonged*, *secondary* or *distant* effects. Examples include the spread of an infective organism from the original site of infection, where it had provoked an inflammatory reaction, to another part of the body, where a similar reaction to it will occur. Similarly, malignant tumours arise initially in one organ as primary tumours, but tumour cells eventually permeate lymphatics and blood vessels and thereby spread to other organs to produce secondary tumours or metastases. The course of a disease may be prolonged and complicated if the body's capacity for defence, repair or regeneration is deficient.

Prognosis

The prognosis forecasts the known or likely *course of the disease* and, therefore, the fate of the patient. When we say that the 5-year survival prospects for carcinoma of the lung are about 5%, this is the prognosis for that condition. Sometimes we can be very specific because the information available about an individual patient and their disease may enable an accurate forecast; for example, a patient who presents with a carcinoma of the lung that has already spread to the liver, bones and the brain very probably (and unfortunately) has a 6-month survival prospect of nil.

Table 2.1 Examples of the known mediators of the symptoms of disease		
Symptom	Mediators	Comment
Pain	Free nerve endings stimulated by mechanical, thermal or chemical agents (e.g. bradykinin, 5-HT, histamine; prostaglandins enhance sensitivity)	May signify irritation of a surface (e.g. peritoneum), distension of a viscus (e.g. bladder), ischaemia (e.g. angina), erosion of a tissue (e.g. by tumour) or inflammation
Swelling	Increased cell number or size, or abnormal accumulation of fluid or gas	Common manifestation of inflammation and of tumours
Shortness of breath (dyspnoea)	Increased blood CO_2 or, to a lesser extent, decreased blood O_2 concentration	Usually due to lung disease, heart failure or severe anaemia
Fever (pyrexia)	Interleukin-1 (IL-1) released by leukocytes acts on thermoregulatory centre in hypothalamus, mediated by prostaglandins (PG)	IL-1 release frequently induced by bacterial endotoxins Aspirin reduces fever by blocking PG synthesis
Weight loss	Inadequate food intake or catabolic state mediated by humoral factors from tumours	Common manifestation of cancer, not necessarily of the alimentary tract or disseminated
Bleeding	Weakness or rupture of blood vessel wall or coagulation defect	Coagulation defects lead to spontaneous bruising or prolonged bleeding after injury
Diarrhoea	Malabsorption of food results in osmotic retention of water in stools Decreased transit time, possibly due to humoral effects Damage to mucosa impairing absorption and exuding fluid	Most commonly due to infective causes not requiring specific treatment other than fluid replacement
Itching (pruritus)	Mast cell degranulation and release of histamine	Manifestation of, for example, allergy
Cough	Neuropeptide release in response, usually, to irritation of respiratory mucosa	Common manifestation of respiratory tract disease
Vomiting	Stimulation of vomiting centre in medulla, usually by afferent vagal impulses	Usually denotes upper gastrointestinal disease (e.g. gastroenteritis), but may be due to CNS lesions
Cyanosis	Reduced oxygen content of arterial haemoglobin	Due to respiratory disease, cardiac failure or congenital shunting

The prognosis for any disease is of course subject to influence by medical or surgical intervention. So one must distinguish between the prognosis for a disease that is allowed to follow its natural course and the prognosis for the same disease in a group of patients receiving appropriate therapy.

In assessing the long-term prognosis for a chronic disease, it is important to compare the survival of a group of patients with actuarial data for comparable populations without the disease. The survival data for the group with the disease should be corrected to allow for deaths that are likely to occur from other diseases.

Remission and relapse

Not all chronic diseases pursue a relentless course. Some are punctuated by periods of quiescence when the patient enjoys relatively good health. *Remission* is the process of conversion from active disease to quiescence. Later, the signs and symptoms may reappear; this is the process of *relapse*. Some diseases may oscillate through several cycles of remission and relapse before the patient is cured of or succumbs to the disease. Diseases characterised by a tendency to remit and relapse include chronic inflammatory bowel disease (Crohn's disease and ulcerative colitis) and treated acute leukaemia (particularly in childhood).

The tendency of some diseases to go through cycles of remission and relapse can make it difficult to be certain about prognosis in an individual case.

Morbidity and mortality

The *morbidity* of a disease is the sum of the effects upon the patient. The morbidity of a disease may or may not result in *disability* of the patient. For example, a non-fatal myocardial infarct (heart attack) leaves an area of scarring of the myocardium, impairing its contractility and predisposing to heart failure: this is the morbidity of the disease in that particular patient. The heart failure manifests itself with breathlessness, restricting the patient's activities: this is the patient's disability.

The *mortality* of a disease is the probability that death will be the end result. Mortality is expressed usually as a percentage of all those patients presenting with the disease. For example, the mortality rate of myocardial infarction could be stated as 50% under defined circumstances.

Disability and disease

Many diseases result in only transient disability; for example, influenza or a bad cold may necessitate time off work for an employed person. Some diseases, however, are associated with a significant risk of permanent disability; in such cases, treatment is intended to minimise the risk of disability. Some investigations and treatments carry a small risk of harm, often permanent, and the risk of disability must be outweighed by the potential benefit to the patient.

As a general rule, the earlier a disease is diagnosed, the smaller the risk of disability either from the disease itself or from necessary treatment. This is one of the main objectives of screening programmes for various conditions (e.g. for cancers of the cervix and breast). The objective assessment, preferably measurement, of disability is important in the evaluation of the impact of a disease or the adverse effects of its treatment. There is, for example, a balance between the longevity of survival from a disease and the quality of life during the period of survival after diagnosis: a treatment that prolongs life may be unacceptable because it prolongs suffering; treatment that makes a patient more comfortable, but does not prolong life and may actually shorten it, may be more acceptable. The measure that takes account of the duration and quality of survival is QALYs (*quality-adjusted life years*), and enables scientifically based judgements about the impact of diseases, treatments and preventive measures.

NOMENCLATURE OF DISEASE

▶ Uniform nomenclature helps communication and enables accurate epidemiological studies
▶ Many standard rules are used to derive names of diseases
▶ Eponymous names commemorate, for example, the discoverer or signify ignorance of cause or mechanism
▶ Syndromes are defined by the aggregate of signs and symptoms

Before proceeding to a detailed discussion of disease it is important to clarify the meaning of some of the common terms, prefixes and suffixes used in the nomenclature of diseases and their pathological features. Until the 19th century, many diseases and causes of death were recorded in a narrative form, often based on symptoms. The early medical statisticians, William Farr (1807–1883) and Jacques Bertillon (1851–1922), pioneered a systematic and uniform approach to disease classification, thereby laying the foundations of modern disease nomenclature.

Primary and secondary

The words *primary* and *secondary* are used in two different ways in the nomenclature of disease:

1. They may be used to describe the *causation* of a disease. Primary in this context means that the disease is without evident antecedent cause. Other words that have the same meaning in this context are *essential, idiopathic, spontaneous* and *cryptogenic*. Thus, primary hypertension is defined as abnormally high blood pressure without apparent cause. The precise cause awaits discovery.

   Secondary means that the disease represents a complication or manifestation of some underlying lesion. Thus, secondary hypertension is defined as abnormally high blood pressure as a consequence of some other lesion (e.g. renal artery stenosis).
2. The words primary and secondary may be used to distinguish between the initial and subsequent *stages* of a disease, most commonly in cancer. The primary tumour is the initial tumour from which cancer cells disseminate to cause secondary tumours elsewhere in the body.

Acute and chronic

Acute and chronic are terms used to describe the *dynamics* of a disease. Acute conditions have a rapid onset, often but not always followed by a rapid resolution. Chronic conditions may follow an acute initial episode, but often are of insidious onset, and have a prolonged course lasting months or years. Subacute, a term not often used now, is intermediate between acute and chronic. These terms are most often used to qualify the nature of an inflammatory process. However, they can be used to describe the dynamics of any disease. The words may be used differently by patients to describe some symptoms, such as an 'acute' pain being sharp or severe.

Benign and malignant

Benign and malignant are emotive terms used to classify certain diseases according to their likely *outcome*. Thus, benign tumours remain localised to the tissue of origin and are very rarely fatal unless they compress some vital structure (e.g. brain), whereas malignant tumours invade and spread from their origin and are commonly fatal. Benign hypertension is relatively mild elevation of blood pressure that develops gradually and causes insidious injury to the organs of the body. This situation contrasts with malignant hypertension, in which the blood pressure rises rapidly and causes severe symptoms and tissue injury (e.g. headaches, blindness, renal failure, cerebral haemorrhage).

Prefixes

Commonly used prefixes and their usual meanings are:

- *ana-*, meaning absence (e.g. anaphylaxis)
- *dys-*, meaning disordered (e.g. dysplasia)
- *hyper-*, meaning an excess over normal (e.g. hyperthyroidism)
- *hypo-*, meaning a deficiency below normal (e.g. hypothyroidism)
- *meta-*, meaning a change from one state to another (e.g. metaplasia)
- *neo-*, meaning new (e.g. neoplasia).

Suffixes

Commonly used suffixes and their usual meanings are:

- *-itis*, meaning an inflammatory process (e.g. appendicitis)
- *-oma*, meaning a tumour (e.g. carcinoma)
- *-osis*, meaning state or condition, not necessarily pathological (e.g. osteoarthrosis)
- *-oid*, meaning bearing a resemblance to (e.g. rheumatoid disease)
- *-penia*, meaning lack of (e.g. thrombocytopenia)
- *-cytosis*, meaning increased number of cells, usually in blood (e.g. leukocytosis)
- *-ectasis*, meaning dilatation (e.g. bronchiectasis)
- *-plasia*, meaning a disorder of growth (e.g. hyperplasia)
- *-opathy*, meaning an abnormal state lacking specific characteristics (e.g. lymphadenopathy).

Eponymous names

An eponymous disease or lesion is named after a person or place associated with it. Eponymous names are used commonly either when the nature or cause of the disease or lesion is unknown, or when long-term usage has resulted in the name entering the language of medicine, or to commemorate the person who first described the condition. Examples include:

- Graves' disease: primary thyrotoxicosis
- Paget's disease of the nipple: infiltration of the skin of the nipple by cells from a cancer in the underlying breast tissue
- Crohn's disease: a chronic inflammatory disease of the gut affecting most commonly the terminal ileum and causing narrowing of the lumen
- Hodgkin's disease: a neoplasm of lymph nodes characterised by the presence of Reed–Sternberg cells
- Reed–Sternberg cells: large cells with bilobed nuclei and prominent nucleoli which are virtually diagnostic of Hodgkin's disease.

Syndromes

A syndrome is an aggregate of signs and symptoms or a combination of lesions without which the disease cannot be recognised or diagnosed. Syndromes often have eponymous titles. Examples include:

- Cushing's syndrome: hyperactivity of the adrenal cortex resulting in obesity, hirsutism, hypertension, etc. (Cushing's *disease* is this syndrome resulting specifically from a pituitary tumour secreting ACTH)
- nephrotic syndrome: albuminuria, hypoalbuminaemia and oedema; this syndrome can result from a variety of glomerular and other renal disorders.

Numerical coding systems

Standard numerical codes, rather than names, are often used for disease registration and in epidemiological studies. Each disease or disease group is designated a specific number. The most widely used systems are ICD (International Classification of Diseases, a World Health Organization System) and SNOMED (Systematized Nomenclature of Medicine).

PRINCIPLES OF DISEASE CLASSIFICATION

- ▶ Classifications aid diagnosis and learning
- ▶ May change with advances in medical knowledge
- ▶ Diseases may be classified by a variety of complementary methods

Diseases do not occur to conform to any classification. Disease classifications are creations of medical science and are justified only by their utility. Classifications are useful in diagnosis to enable a name (disease or disease category) to be assigned to a particular illness.

Disease classification at a relatively coarse level of categorisation is unlikely to change quickly. However, the more detailed the level of classification, the more likely it is to change as medical science progresses. The general classification of disease into categories such as inflammatory and neoplastic (see below) is long established.

General classification of disease

The most widely used general classification of disease is that based on pathogenesis or disease mechanisms (Fig. 2.3). Most diseases can be assigned a place in the following classification:

- congenital
  - genetic (inherited or sporadic mutations)
  - non-genetic
- acquired
  - inflammatory
  - haemodynamic
  - growth disorders
  - injury and disordered repair
  - disordered immunity
  - metabolic and degenerative disorders.

Two important points must be made here. First, the above classification is not the only possible classification of disease. Second, many diseases share characteristics of more than one of the above categories.

Patients might prefer the following disease classification:

- recovery likely
  - with residual disability
  - without residual disability
- recovery unlikely
  - with pain
  - without pain.

This classification is perfectly legitimate and may be foremost in the patient's mind, but it is not particularly useful either as a diagnostic aid or for categorisation according to the underlying pathology.

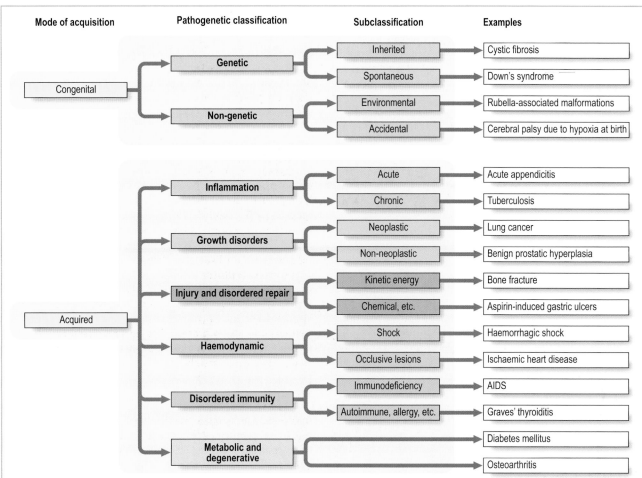

Fig. 2.3 A general classification of disease. The most widely used general classification of disease is based on the mode of acquisition of the disease (i.e. congenital or acquired) and the principal disease mechanism (e.g. genetic, vascular). The main pathogenetic classes are divided into two or more subclasses. There is, however, significant overlap and many acquired diseases are more common in those with a genetic predisposition.

Congenital diseases

Congenital abnormalities (genetic/chromosome disorders and malformations) occur in approximately 5% of births in the UK. They comprise:

- malformations in 3.5%
- single gene defects in 1%
- chromosome aberrations in 0.5%.

Common malformations include congenital heart defects, spina bifida and limb deformities. Single gene defects include conditions such as phenylketonuria and cystic fibrosis. Chromosomal aberrations are exemplified by Turner's syndrome (XO sex chromosomes) and Down's syndrome (trisomy 21—three copies of chromosome 21). The risk of chromosomal abnormalities increases with maternal age: for example, the risk of a child being born with Down's syndrome, the commonest chromosome abnormality, is estimated at 1 in 1500 for a 25-year-old mother, rising to 1 in 30 at the age of 45 years.

Congenital diseases are initiated before or during birth, but some may not cause clinical signs and symptoms until adult life. Congenital diseases may be due to genetic defects, either inherited from the parents or genetic mutations before birth, or to external interference with normal embryonic and fetal development. An example of a genetic defect is cystic fibrosis, which is a disorder of cell membrane transport inherited as an autosomal recessive abnormality. Examples of non-genetic defects include congenital diseases such as deafness and cardiac abnormalities resulting from fetal infection by maternal rubella (German measles) during pregnancy.

A common natural consequence of an abnormal pregnancy is a miscarriage or spontaneous abortion. However, some abnormal pregnancies escape natural elimination and may survive to full-term gestation unless there is medical intervention.

Fetal origins of adult disease

Some diseases occurring in late adult life, such as ischaemic heart disease, are more common in individuals who had a low weight at birth. This is postulated to be due to subtle abnormalities of morphogenesis associated with nutritional deprivation in utero (the 'Barker hypothesis').

Acquired diseases

Acquired diseases are due to environmental causes. Most diseases in adults are acquired.

Acquired diseases can be further classified according to their pathogenesis.

Inflammatory diseases

Inflammation (Ch. 10) is a physiological response of living tissues to injury. Diseases in which an inflammatory reaction is a major component are classified accordingly. They are usually named from the organ affected followed by the suffix '-itis'. Thus the following are all examples of inflammatory diseases:

- encephalitis (brain)
- appendicitis (appendix)
- dermatitis (skin)
- arthritis (joints).

There are, however, potentially confusing exceptions to the nomenclature. For example, tuberculosis, leprosy and syphilis are infections characterised by an inflammatory reaction. Pneumonia and pleurisy refer to inflammation of the lung and pleura respectively.

Each separate inflammatory disease has special features determined by:

- cause (microbial, chemical, etc.)
- precise character of the body's response (suppurative, granulomatous, etc.)
- organ affected (lungs, liver, etc.).

Vascular disorders

Vascular disorders (Chs 8 and 13) are those resulting from abnormal blood flow to, from or within an organ. Blood vessels are vital conduits. Any reduction in flow through a vessel leads to *ischaemia* of the tissue it supplies. If the ischaemia is sustained, then death of the tissue or *infarction* results. Vascular disorders have become major health problems in developed countries. Examples include:

- myocardial infarction ('heart attack')
- cerebral infarction or haemorrhage ('stroke')
- limb gangrene
- shock and circulatory failure.

Growth disorders

Diseases characterised by abnormal growth include adaptation to changing circumstances. For example, the heart enlarges (by hypertrophy) in patients with high blood pressure, and the adrenal glands shrink (by atrophy) if a disease of the pituitary gland causes loss of ACTH production. The most serious group of diseases characterised by disordered growth is neoplasia or new growth formation, leading to the formation of solid tumours (Ch. 11) and leukaemias (Ch. 23).

The suffix '-oma' usually signifies that the abnormality is a solid tumour. Exceptions include 'granuloma', 'haematoma' and 'atheroma'; these are not tumours.

Injury and repair

Mechanical injury or trauma leads directly to disease, the precise characteristics of which depend upon the nature and extent of the injury. The progress of disease is influenced by the body's reaction to it. In particular, repair mechanisms may be defective due to old age, malnutrition, excessive mobility, presence of foreign bodies, and infection. This subject is discussed in detail in Chapter 6.

Metabolic and degenerative disorders

Metabolic and degenerative disorders are numerous and heterogeneous. Some metabolic disorders are congenital (inborn errors of metabolism) and due to defective parental genes. Other metabolic disorders are mainly acquired (e.g. diabetes mellitus, gout), although there may be a degree of genetic predisposition, and some are abnormalities secondary to disease (e.g. hypercalcaemia due to hyperparathyroidism). Degenerative disorders are characterised by a loss of the specialised structure and function of a tissue; as such, this category could include almost every disease, but the designation is reserved for those conditions in which degeneration appears to be the primary or dominant feature and the cause poorly understood. These disorders are discussed in detail in Chapter 7.

Iatrogenic diseases

The broad meaning of iatrogenic disease is any ill health induced by a medical practitioner's words or actions. Currently, iatrogenic diseases are regarded as those attributable to practitioners' actions. However, the suggestion that words could induce harm is not as fanciful as it seems. For example, a patient with a relatively trivial respiratory complaint is likely to be alarmed when asked by a doctor, who mistakenly suspects lung cancer, 'How much weight have you lost?' and 'Have you coughed up any blood?' The disturbing suggestions implicit in the line of questioning cause iatrogenic 'dis-ease' in the patient. (While it is perfectly reasonable to consider the possibility of lung cancer, such questions are better asked in the neutral form of 'What's been happening to your weight recently?' and 'Have you noticed anything about your sputum?')

All medical intervention is associated with some risk to the patient. Ethically, the probability that harm might result must be outweighed by the probability that the patient will benefit. If harm results, litigation may follow. However, there is a considerable difference in principle between harm resulting from culpable negligence and that resulting from appropriate intervention justified by the clinical circumstances.

The scope of iatrogenic diseases is very wide (Table 2.2). It includes harm resulting from investigations and treatment, from drugs and surgery. It is said, with justification, that in the 20th century surgery became safer while medicine became more dangerous. Adverse drug reactions constitute a major category of iatrogenic disease and surveillance arrangements are in force in many countries, for example the 'yellow card' system of reporting to the Commission on Human Medicines in the UK.

Table 2.2 Examples of iatrogenic diseases

Causative agent	Resulting disease or abnormality
Radiation (therapeutic)	Skin erythema Fibrosis Neoplasia
Radiation (diagnostic)	Neoplasia Fetal malformations
Blood transfusion and blood products (e.g. clotting factor concentrates)	Hepatitis (due to viruses) Haemolysis (if mismatched blood) AIDS (due to HIV)
Penicillin	Allergy
Aspirin and other non-steroidal anti-inflammatory drugs	Gastritis and gastric erosions
Aminoglycoside antibiotics	Deafness
Chlorpromazine	Cholestatic jaundice
Steroid therapy	Cushing's syndrome

Adverse drug reactions

Adverse drug reactions can be categorised as follows:

- dose-dependent or predictable (type A)
- unpredictable (type B).

Dose-dependent drug reactions occur predictably in any person taking a sufficient dose of the drug. For example, paracetamol always produces hepatic necrosis if, unwisely, a sufficiently large dose is taken. Similarly, steroids can cause Cushing's syndrome (obesity, hirsutism, osteoporosis, etc.) in any patient receiving doses in excess of the usual bodily requirements. Often, the adverse effects disappear when the dosage is reduced, and mortality tends to be low.

Unpredictable adverse drug reactions are due to:

- idiosyncrasy or allergy
- permissive effects.

One of the commonest idiosyncratic drug reactions is due to allergy to penicillin. Another common example is cholestatic jaundice induced by chlorpromazine. Idiosyncratic reactions are due to unexpected metabolic or immunological responses to the drug. This type of drug reaction merits withdrawal of the drug and substitution of alternative therapy. The mortality rate is higher than that associated with predictable reactions.

In unpredictable adverse drug reactions where the effect is *permissive*, the drug itself produces no harm, but it predisposes the patient to other diseases. For example, some antibiotic therapy may be complicated by pseudomembranous colitis (Ch. 15) because it permits overgrowth of *Clostridium difficile* in the colon. Steroids and other immunosuppressive agents predispose to infections by organisms that would not normally be harmful (e.g. *Pneumocystis jiroveci* pneumonia, cytomegalovirus pneumonia).

EPIDEMIOLOGY

- Epidemiology is the pathology of populations
- Scope includes the incidence, prevalence, remission and mortality rates of a disease
- Variations may provide clues to aetiology and guide optimal use of health care resources

Epidemiology is the study of disease in populations. It also concerns the identification of the causes and modes of acquisition of disease. Epidemiology involves recording and analysing data about disease in groups of people rather than in the individual patient.

Knowledge about the population characteristics of a disease is important for:

- providing aetiological clues
- planning preventive measures
- provision of adequate medical facilities
- population screening for early diagnosis.

Epidemiological clues to the causes of disease

Epidemiology, sometimes referred to as the 'pathology of populations', often provides important clues to the causes of a disease. If, for example, in a particular geographical region or group of individuals the actual incidence of a disease exceeds the expected incidence, this suggests that the disease may be due to:

- a genetic predisposition more prevalent in that population, or
- an environmental cause more prevalent in that geographical region or group of individuals, or
- a combination of genetic and environmental factors.

The analysis of epidemiological data can be very arduous. Humans live in a complex and changing environment, often modified by their own action. Populations vary in their ethnic origins, their age distribution, their occupational histories and their lifestyles. These variations and the concomitant variations in disease incidence provide fertile opportunities for epidemiological study.

Epidemiologically derived clues about the causes of a disease invariably require direct confirmation by laboratory testing.

Disease incidence, prevalence, remission and mortality rates

Incidence, prevalence, remission and mortality rates are numerical data about the impact of a disease on a population:

- the *incidence rate* is the number of new cases of the disease occurring in a population of defined size during a defined period

- the *prevalence rate* is the number of cases of the disease to be found in a defined population at a stated time
- the *remission rate* is the proportion of cases of the disease that recover
- the *mortality rate* is the number or percentage of deaths from a disease in a defined population.

From these four measures one can deduce much about the behaviour of a disease (Fig. 2.4). Chronic (long-lasting) diseases have a high prevalence: although the incidence of new cases might be low, the total number of cases in the population accumulates. Diseases with relatively acute manifestations may have a high incidence but a low prevalence, because cases have either high remission rates (e.g. chickenpox) or high mortality rates (e.g. lung cancer).

In comparing the occurrence of a disease in different populations, epidemiologists have to standardise the data to eliminate any bias due to the average age of the population and its life expectancy. Diseases that are more common in the elderly may be relatively rare in some populations, simply because most of the people do not live long enough to develop them.

Migrant populations are especially useful to epidemiologists, enabling them to separate the effects of genetic (racial) factors and the environment (e.g. diet) (Ch. 3).

The net effect of disease and nutritional deprivation on a population can be illustrated as *age pyramids*, the profiles often revealing striking contrasts between countries (Fig. 2.5).

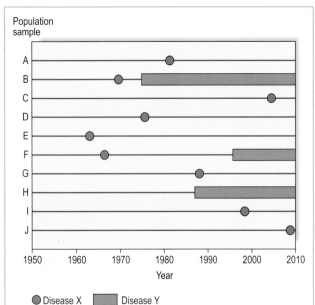

Fig. 2.4 Disease incidence and prevalence. A population sample of 10 individuals (A to J), all born in 1950, is followed for 60 years to determine the relative incidence and prevalence of two diseases. Disease X is an acute illness with no long-term effects; it has a very high incidence (affecting 90% in this sample), but a low prevalence because at any one time the number of cases to be found is very low. Disease Y is a chronic illness; it has a lower incidence (affecting only 30% in this sample) but a relatively high prevalence (from 1990 onwards in this sample) because of the accumulation of cases in the population.

Data capture

Data on the frequency of diseases are often more likely to be in the form of mortality statistics rather than actual disease incidence. The reason is that, unless legislation requires cases of the disease under study to be formally notified to some

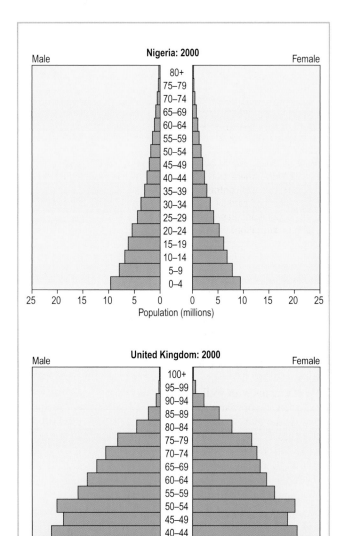

Fig. 2.5 National health revealed by age pyramids. In Nigeria, among other African countries, disease and nutritional problems severely curtail life expectancy. In the United Kingdom, among other 'developed countries', a high proportion of the population survives into old age, albeit often accompanied by chronic ill health. (Data from US Census Bureau, International Data Base)

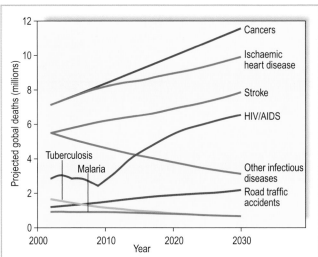

Fig. 2.6 Projected global causes of death, 2002–2030. Other than HIV/AIDS, there is an anticipated decline in mortality from infectious diseases contrasting with the steady increase in deaths from cancer and cardiovascular conditions due to ageing of the global population. (Based on World Health Statistics 2007, World Health Organization)

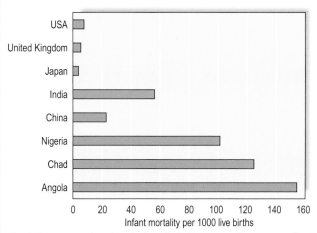

Fig. 2.7 International variations in infant mortality rates. Infant (age less than 1 year) mortality rates are important and sensitive indicators of a nation's health and health service provision. Common causes of infant death in countries with high infant mortality rates are diarrhoeal diseases and pneumonia. (Data derived from World Health Statistics 2007, World Health Organization)

register, the most reliable data are likely to be derived from official death certificates. This means that, if a disease does not often have a fatal outcome, mortality data will severely underestimate its incidence. The only common exceptions to this are certain infectious diseases, designated as notifiable in the UK, and cancers, for which many developed countries have registries.

In countries with well-developed health care systems, the epidemiology of many serious diseases should be relatively easy to determine from statistical data already held on databases (e.g. cancer registries); retrospective studies are usually possible. In countries with relatively poor systems, however, it may be necessary to search actively for the disease in order to determine its true incidence and the distribution in the general population; most studies have to be done prospectively.

Geographic variations

Although many diseases occur worldwide, there are many geographic variations, even within one country. There are considerable differences between so-called developed and developing countries; for example, cardiovascular disorders, psychiatric illness and some cancers predominate in countries such as the USA and the UK, but these conditions are less common in most of Africa and Asia. In developing countries, the major health problems are due to infections and malnutrition.

Historical changes in disease incidence and mortality

Changes in disease incidence with time (Fig. 2.6) reflect variation in the degree of exposure to the cause, or preventive

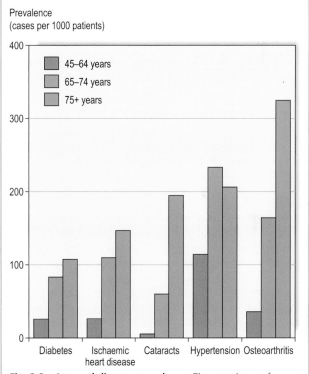

Fig. 2.8 Age and disease prevalence. The prevalence of many diseases increases with age. Thus, elderly individuals are more likely to have one or more diseases in addition to the immediate problem for which they seek medical attention. (Data from Nijmegen Continuous Morbidity Registration, 1991–95)

measures such as immunisation. Changes in mortality additionally reflect the success of treatment.

The reduced incidence or elimination of serious infections (e.g. typhoid, cholera, tuberculosis, smallpox) is the result of improved sanitation and, in some instances, the

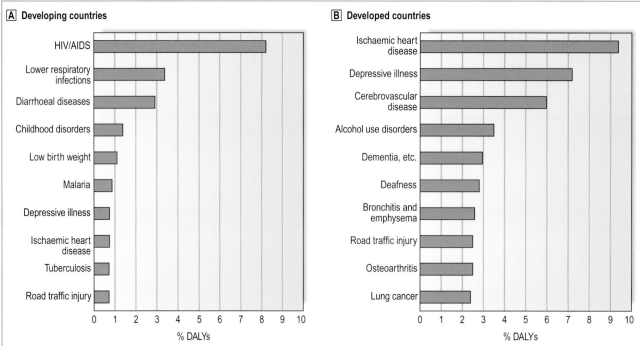

Fig. 2.9 The top ten major burdens of disease in 'developing' and 'developed' countries (2000). Based on the *The World Health Report 2002* (World Health Organization), the burden of disease is estimated in disability-adjusted life years (DALYs). **A** In developing countries, infections such as HIV/AIDS account for much ill health and death. **B** In contrast, in developed countries, cardiovascular conditions are among the leading causes.

effectiveness of immunisation programmes. Indeed, it is likely that sanitation, particularly sewerage and the provision of fresh water supplies, has had a much greater impact on the incidence of these diseases than have advances in medical science. Mortality from bacterial infections is also much reduced due to the advent of antibiotic therapy. Many viral infections elude specific treatment, but mass immunisation has led to a considerable reduction in their incidence.

During the 19th and 20th centuries, the declining incidence in many serious infections was accompanied by an increasing incidence of other conditions, notably cardiovascular disorders (e.g. hypertension, atherosclerosis) and their complications (e.g. ischaemic heart disease, strokes). The apparent increase is partly due to the fact that the average age of the population in most developed countries is increasing; cardiovascular disorders are more common with increasing age, unlike infections which afflict all ages. Nevertheless, irrespective of this age-related trend, there is a genuine increased incidence of these disorders. This increase is due to changes in diet (e.g. fat content) and lifestyle (e.g. smoking, lack of exercise) and the consequent obesity. Intervention by reducing dietary and behavioural risk factors has begun to yield a beneficial reduction in the risk of developing the complications of cardiovascular disorders.

Historical changes in the incidence of neoplastic diseases (i.e. tumours) can provide vital clues to their aetiology. For example, a dramatic increase in the incidence of a formerly uncommon tumour may be the result of exposure to a new environmental hazard. Historical changes led to the discovery of the association between ionising radiation and many types of cancer, and between smoking and lung cancer.

Socio-economic factors

Socio-economic factors undoubtedly influence the incidence of certain diseases and the host response to them. Overcrowding encourages the spread of infections, leading to the rapid development of epidemics. Economic hardship is commonly accompanied by malnutrition (Ch. 7), a condition causing ill health directly and also predisposing to infections.

A particularly sensitive and widely used indicator of the socio-economically related health of a population is the *infant mortality rate*. This rate varies considerably between countries, but in general the rate is lower in countries regarded as being developed (Fig. 2.7).

Within a developed country, such as the UK, less affluent individuals have a higher incidence of cervical cancer, ischaemic heart disease and respiratory infections, among many other conditions.

Occupational factors

The association of a disease with a particular occupation can reveal the specific cause. Well-documented, but now less common, associations include:

- coal-worker's pneumoconiosis due to coal dust inhalation
- asbestosis due to asbestos dust inhalation

- skin cancer due to lubricating oils
- nasal sinus cancer due to hardwood dust
- bladder cancer due to aniline dye manufacture.

It is important to identify occupational hazards so that they can be minimised. Furthermore, in many countries, patients disabled by occupational diseases may be entitled to compensation.

Hospital and community contrasts

Medical students often develop a biased impression of the true incidence of diseases because most of their training takes place in a hospital environment. The patients and diseases they see are selected rather than representative; only those cases requiring hospital investigation or treatment are sent there. For most diseases, even in countries with well-developed health services, patients remain in the community. For example, patients seen by a community medical practitioner are most likely to have psychiatric illness, upper respiratory tract infections and musculoskeletal problems. The general hospital cases are more likely to be patients with cardiovascular diseases, proven or suspected cancer, drug overdoses, severe trauma, etc.

Age and disease

Many diseases become more prevalent with increasing age (Fig. 2.8). Indeed, the occurrence of these diseases is a key feature of elderly populations and an important determinant of health care planning.

Common causes of mortality and morbidity

Death is inevitable. In many people surviving into their seventies and eighties, death may be preceded by a variable period of senility, during which there is cumulative deterioration of the structure and function of many organs and body systems (Ch. 12). Unless an acute episode of serious illness supervenes, the accumulated deterioration of the body reduces its viability until it reaches the point where death supervenes. In almost every case, however, there is a final event that tips the balance and is registered as the immediate cause of death. In younger individuals dying prematurely, death is usually more clearly attributable to a single fatal condition in an otherwise reasonably healthy individual.

In developed countries, such as the USA and in Europe, diseases of the cardiovascular system account for much ill health (Fig. 2.9). It is estimated that a newborn infant in these countries has a 1 in 3 chance of ultimately dying in adult life from ischaemic heart disease, and a 1 in 5 chance of ultimately dying from cancer. In some famine-ridden countries, newborn infants have similar probabilities of dying from diarrhoeal diseases and malnutrition in childhood.

FURTHER READING

Coggon D, Rose G, Barker D J P 2003 Epidemiology for the uninitiated. BMJ Publishing, London

Donaldson R J, Donaldson L J 2000 Essential public health, 2nd edn. Librapharm, Newbury

Harris E E, Malyango A A 2005 Evolutionary explanations in medical and health profession courses: are you answering your students' 'why' questions? BMC Medical Education 5: 16–23

Lazarou J, Pomeranz B H 1998 Incidence of adverse drug reactions in hospitalized patients. JAMA 279: 1200–1205

Nesse RM, Williams G C 2004 Why we get sick: the new science of Darwinian medicine. Vintage, New York

Stearns S C, Koella J C 2007 Evolution in health and disease. Oxford University Press, Oxford

Webb P, Bain C, Pirozzo S 2005 Essential epidemiology: an introduction for students and health professionals. Cambridge University Press, Cambridge

World Health Organization. World Health Statistics 2007. WHO, Geneva

US Census Bureau: International Data Base. http:// www.census.gov/ipc/www/idb/index.html

World Health Organization website. http://www.who.int

3

Genetic, environmental and infectious causes of disease

CAUSES OF DISEASE

▶ Diseases are due to genetic, environmental or multifactorial causes
▶ Role of genetic and environmental factors can be distinguished by epidemiological observations, family studies or laboratory investigations
▶ Some diseases with a genetic basis may not appear until adult life
▶ Some diseases with environmental causes may have their effects during embryogenesis

In terms of causation, diseases may be:

- entirely *genetic*—either inherited or prenatally acquired defects of genes
- *multifactorial*—interaction of genetic and environmental factors
- entirely *environmental*—no genetic component to risk of disease.

Features pointing to a significant genetic contribution to the cause of a disease include a high incidence in particular families or races, or an association with a known inherited feature (e.g. gender, blood groups, histocompatibility haplotypes). Environmental factors are suggested by disease associations with occupations or geography. Ultimately, however, only laboratory investigation can provide irrefutable identification of the cause of a disease. The extent to which a disease is due to genetic or environmental causes can often be deduced from some of its main features (Table 3.1).

Infectious agents (e.g. viruses, bacteria) are the most common and important environmental agents of disease.

Predisposing factors and precursors of disease

Many diseases are the *predictable* consequence of exposure to the initiating cause; host (i.e. genetic) factors make relatively little contribution to the outcome. This is particularly true of physical injury: the results of mechanical trauma and radiation injury are largely dose-related; the effect is directly proportional to the physical force.

Other diseases are the *probable* consequence of exposure to causative factors, but they are not absolutely inevitable. For example, infectious diseases result from exposure to potentially harmful environmental agents (e.g. bacteria, viruses), but the outcome is often influenced by various host factors such as age, nutritional status and genetic variables.

Some diseases *predispose* to others; for example, ulcerative colitis predisposes to carcinoma of the colon, and hepatic cirrhosis predisposes to hepatocellular carcinoma. Diseases predisposing to tumours are called *pre-neoplastic conditions;* lesions from which tumours can develop are called *pre-neoplastic lesions.* Some diseases occur most commonly in those individuals with a congenital predisposition. For example, ankylosing spondylitis, a disabling inflammatory disease of the spinal joints of unknown aetiology, is much more common in people with the HLA-B27 haplotype (Ch. 25).

Some diseases predispose to others because they have a *permissive effect* allowing environmental agents that are not normally pathogenic to cause disease. For example, *opportunistic infections* occur in those patients with impaired defence mechanisms, allowing infection by normally non-pathogenic organisms (Ch. 9).

Prenatal factors

Prenatal factors, other than genetic abnormalities, contributing to disease risk are:

- transplacental transmission of environmental agents
- nutritional deprivation.

Diseases due to transplacental transfer of environmental agents from the mother to the fetus include fetal alcohol syndrome, congenital malformations due to maternal rubella infection, and vaginal adenocarcinoma due to administration of diethylstilbestrol (DES). Fetal alcohol syndrome is still a serious problem, but malformations due to rubella are much less common now that immunisation is widespread. DES is no longer used during pregnancy.

The notion that disease risk in adult life could be due to fetal nutritional deprivation has gained support from the work of David Barker. The *Barker hypothesis* is that an adult's risk of, for example, ischaemic heart disease and hypertension is programmed partly by nutritional deprivation in utero. This is plausible; nutritional deprivation could have profound effects during critical periods of fetal morphogenesis.

Table 3.1 Clues to a disease being caused by either genetic or environmental factors		
Disease characteristic	**Genetic cause**	**Environmental cause**
Age of onset	Usually early (often in childhood)	Any age
Familial incidence	Common	Unusual (unless family exposed to same environmental agent)
Remission	No (except by gene therapy)	Often (when environmental cause can be eliminated)
Incidence	Relatively uncommon	Common
Clustering	In families	Temporal or spatial or both
Linkage to inherited factors	Common	Relatively rare

Aetiology and age of disease onset

Do not assume that all diseases manifest at birth have an inherited or genetic basis; as noted previously (Ch. 2), diseases present at birth are classified into those with a genetic basis (further sub-divided into those in which the genetic abnormality is inherited and those in which the genetic abnormality is acquired during gestation) and those without a genetic basis. Conversely, although most adult diseases have an entirely environmental cause, genetic influences to disease susceptibility and vulnerability to environmental agents are being increasingly discovered.

The incidence of many diseases rises with age because:

- Probability of contact with an environmental cause increases with duration of exposure risk.
- The disease may depend on the cumulative effects of one or more environmental agents.
- Impaired immunity with ageing increases susceptibility to some infections.
- The latent interval between the exposure to cause and the appearance of symptoms may be decades long.

Multifactorial aetiology of disease

Many diseases with no previously known cause are being shown to be due to an interplay of environmental factors and genetic susceptibility (Fig. 3.1). These discoveries are the rewards of detailed family studies and, in particular, application of the new techniques of molecular genetics. Diseases of adults in which there appears to be a significant genetic component include:

- breast cancer
- Alzheimer's disease
- diabetes mellitus
- osteoporosis
- coronary atherosclerosis.

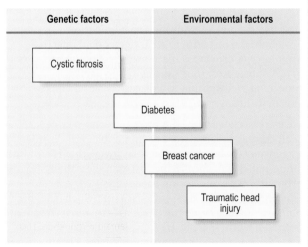

Fig. 3.1 Proportionate risk of disease due to genetic or environmental factors. Some conditions are due solely to genetic (e.g. cystic fibrosis) or environmental (e.g. traumatic head injury) factors. An increasing number of other diseases (e.g. diabetes, breast cancer) are being shown to have a genetic component to their risk, particularly in cases diagnosed at a relatively young age.

One of the reasons why there may be only slow progress in characterising the genetic component of the diseases listed above and others is that two or more genes, as well as environmental factors, may be involved. Pursuing the genetic basis of these *polygenic disorders* requires complex analyses.

Evidence for genetic and environmental factors

Genetic contributions to disease incidence are exposed when any putative environmental factors are either widely prevalent (most individuals are exposed) or non-existent (no known environmental agents). The epidemiologist Geoffrey Rose exemplified this by suggesting that, if every individual smoked 40 cigarettes a day, we would never discover that smoking was responsible for the high incidence of lung cancer; however, any individual (especially familial) variation in susceptibility to lung cancer would have to be attributed to genetic differences. An environmental cause, such as smoking, is easier to identify when there are significant individual variations in exposure which can be correlated with disease incidence; indeed, this enabled Doll and Hill in the 1950s to demonstrate a strong aetiological link to lung cancer risk.

Family studies

Strong evidence for the genetic cause of a disease, with little or no environmental contribution, comes from observations of its higher than expected incidence in families, particularly if they are affected by a disease that is otherwise very rare in the general population. Such diseases are said to 'run in families'.

Having identified the abnormality in a family, it is then important to provide *genetic counselling* so that parents can make informed decisions about future pregnancies. The precise mode of inheritance (p. 36) will determine the proportion of family members (i.e. children) likely to be affected. Because inherited genetic disorders are either sex-linked or autosomally dominant or recessive, not all individuals in one family may be affected even if the disease has no environmental component.

Studies on twins
Observations on the incidence of disease in monozygotic (identical) twins are particularly useful in disentangling the relative influences of 'nature and nurture'; of greatest value in this respect are identical twins who, through unfortunate family circumstances, are reared in separate environments. Uncommon diseases occurring in both twins are more likely to have a genetic component to their aetiology, especially if the twins have been brought up and lived in different environments.

Studies on migrants

The unusually high incidence of a particular disease in a country or region could be due either to the higher prevalence of a genetic predisposition in the racial or ethnic group(s) in that country or to some environmental factor such as diet or climatic conditions. Compelling evidence of the relative contributions of genetic and environmental factors in the aetiology and pathogenesis of a disease can be yielded by observations on disease incidence in migrant populations (Fig. 3.2). For example, if a racial group with a low incidence of a particular disease migrates to another country in which the disease is significantly more common, there are two possible outcomes leading to different conclusions:

1. If the incidence of the disease in the migrant racial group rises, it is likely that environmental factors (e.g. diet) are responsible for the high incidence in the indigenous population.
2. If the incidence of the disease in the migrant racial group remains low, it is more likely that the higher incidence in the indigenous population is due to genetic factors.

Most observations on disease incidence in migrant populations have been made on neoplastic disorders (cancer). This is because cancer is a major illness, likely to be reliably diagnosed by biopsy, and, in many countries, documented in cancer registries.

Association with gene polymorphisms

Within the population there are many normal genetic variations or polymorphisms. The effect of some of these polymorphisms is obvious: examples are skin, hair and eye colour, body habitus, etc. When possessed by large groups of people of common ancestry, a cluster of polymorphic variants constitutes racial characteristics. In other instances

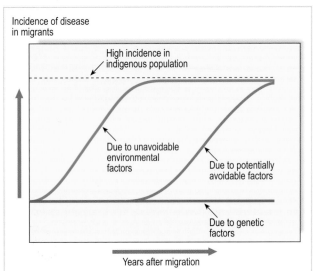

Fig. 3.2 Clues to genetic and environmental causes from disease incidence in migrants. When people with a low incidence of a disease migrate to a country in which the indigenous population has a high incidence, any change in the incidence of the disease in the migrants provides important clues to the role of genetic and environmental factors in causing the disease. A rapid rise in incidence would attribute the disease to unavoidable environmental factors such as climate or widely prevalent micro-organisms. A more gradual rise would be due to factors such as diet, over which there may be some initial cultural resistance to change. No change in disease incidence attributes the high incidence to genetic factors in the indigenous population. The distinctions are rarely as clear-cut as in this graphic example.

the polymorphism has no visible effects: examples are blood groups and HLA types (see below); these are evident only by laboratory testing.

The polymorphisms of greatest relevance to disease susceptibility are:

- HLA types
- blood groups
- cytokine genes.

HLA types

Clinical and experimental observations on the fate of organ transplants led to the discovery of genes known as the major histocompatibility complex (MHC). In humans, the MHC genes reside on chromosome 6 and are designated *HLA genes* (human leukocyte antigen genes). HLA genes are expressed on cell surfaces as substances referred to as 'antigens', not because they normally behave as antigens in the host that bears them, but because of their involvement in graft rejection (Ch. 9). The body does not normally react to these substances, because it is immunologically tolerant of them and they are recognised as 'self' antigens.

HLA types are grouped into classes, principally:

- Class I are expressed on the surface of all nucleated cells. In all diploid cells there are pairs of allelic genes at each of three loci: these genes are known as A, B and C. The normal role of class I types is to enable cytotoxic T-lymphocytes to recognise and eliminate virus-infected cells.
- Class II are expressed on the surface of those cells that interact with T-lymphocytes by physical contact, such as antigen-presenting cells (e.g. Langerhans' cells). The pairs of allelic genes at each of three loci are known as DP, DQ and DR. The normal role of class II types is the initiation of immune responses.

Diseases may be associated with HLA types because:

- some infective micro-organisms bear antigens similar to those of the patient's HLA substances and thereby escape immune recognition and elimination
- the immune response to an antigen on an infective micro-organism cross-reacts with one of the patient's HLA substances, thus causing tissue damage
- the gene predisposing to a disease is closely linked (genetic linkage; p. 39) to a particular HLA gene.

Diseases associated with HLA types are listed in Table 3.2. They are all chronic inflammatory or immunological disorders. In some instances the association is so strong that HLA testing is important diagnostically: the best example is the association of HLA-B27 with ankylosing spondylitis (Ch. 25).

Autoimmune diseases (diseases in which the body's immunity destroys its own cells) are most frequently associated with specific HLA types. The combination of HLA-DR3 and HLA-B8 is particularly strong in this regard, but it must be emphasised that it is present in only a minority of patients with autoimmune disease. Autoimmune diseases also illustrate a separate feature of the association between HLA types and disease. Normally, class II types are not expressed on epithelial cells. However, in organs affected by autoimmune disease, the target cells for immune

Table 3.2 Examples of disease associated with HLA types

Disease	HLA type(s)	Comments
Allergic disorders (e.g. eczema, asthma)	A23	Requires environmental allergen
Ankylosing spondylitis	B27	Associated in c. 90% of cases
Coeliac disease	DR3, B8	Gluten sensitivity
Graves' disease (primary thyrotoxicosis)	DR3, B8	Due to thyroid-stimulating immunoglobulin
Hashimoto's thyroiditis	DR5	Aberrant HLA class II expression on thyroid epithelium
Insulin-dependent (juvenile onset) **diabetes mellitus**	DR3, DR4, B8	Immune injury to beta-cells in pancreatic islets
Rheumatoid disease	DR4	Autoimmune disease

destruction are often found to express class II types. This expression enables their immune recognition and facilitates their destruction.

Blood groups

Blood group expression is directly involved in the pathogenesis of a disease only rarely; the best example is haemolytic disease of the newborn due to rhesus antibodies (Ch. 23). A few diseases show a weaker and indirect association with blood groups. This association may be due to genetic linkage; the blood group determinant gene may lie close to the gene directly involved in the pathogenesis of the disease.

Examples of blood group-associated diseases include:

- duodenal ulceration and group O
- gastric carcinoma and group A.

Cytokine genes

There is evidence linking the incidence or severity of chronic inflammatory diseases to polymorphisms within or adjacent to cytokine genes. Cytokines are important mediators and regulators of inflammatory and immunological reactions. It is logical, therefore, to explore the possibility that enhanced or abnormal expression of cytokine genes may be relevant.

Associations have been found between a tumour necrosis factor (TNF) gene polymorphism and Graves' disease of the thyroid (Ch. 17) and systemic lupus erythematosus (Ch. 25). The TNF gene resides on chromosome 6 between the HLA classes I and II loci, linkage with which may explain an indirect association between TNF gene polymorphism and disease. There are also associations between interleukin-1 gene cluster (chromosome 2) polymorphisms and chronic inflammatory diseases. The associations seem to be stronger with disease severity than with susceptibility.

Gender and disease

Gender, like any other genetic feature of an individual, may be directly or indirectly associated with disease. An example of a direct association, other than the absurdly simple (e.g. carcinoma of the uterus and being female), is haemophilia.

Haemophilia is an inherited X-linked recessive disorder of blood coagulation. It is transmitted by females to their male children. Haemophilia is rare in females because they have two X chromosomes, only one of which is likely to be defective. Males always inherit their single X chromosome from their mother; if the mother is a haemophilia carrier, half of her male children are likely to have inherited the disease.

Some diseases show a predilection for one of the sexes. For example, autoimmune diseases (e.g. rheumatoid disease, systemic lupus erythematosus) are generally more common in females than in males; the reason for this is unclear. Atheroma and its consequences (e.g. ischaemic heart disease) tend to affect males earlier than females, but after the menopause the female incidence approaches that in males. Females are more prone to osteoporosis, a common cause of bone weakening, particularly after the menopause.

In some instances the sex differences in disease incidence are due to social or behavioural factors. The higher incidence of carcinoma of the lung in males is due to the fact that they smoke more cigarettes than do women.

Racial differences

Racial differences in disease incidence may be genetically determined or attributable to behavioural or environmental factors. Racial differences may also reflect adaptational responses to the threat of disease. A good example is provided by malignant melanoma (Ch. 24). Very strong evidence implicates ultraviolet light in the causation of malignant melanoma of the skin; the highest incidence is in Caucasians living in parts of the world with high ambient levels of sunlight, such as Australia. The tumour is, however, relatively uncommon in Africa, despite its high sunlight levels, because the indigenous population has evolved with an abundance of melanin in the skin; they are classified racially as blacks and benefit from the protective effect of the melanin in the skin.

Some abnormal genes are more prevalent in certain races. For example, the cystic fibrosis gene is carried by 1 in 20 Caucasians, whereas this gene is rare in blacks and Asians. Conversely, the gene causing sickle cell anaemia is more common in blacks than in any other race. These associations may be explained by a *heterozygote advantage* conferring protection against an environmental pathogen (Table 3.3).

Other diseases in different races may be due to socio-economic factors. Perinatal mortality rates are often used as an indicator of the socio-economic welfare of a population. Regrettably, the perinatal mortality rate is much higher in certain racial groups, but this outcome is due almost entirely to their social circumstances and is, therefore, theoretically capable of improvement.

Parasitic infestations are more common in tropical climates, not because the races predominantly dwelling there are more susceptible, but often because the parasites cannot complete their life-cycles without other hosts that live only in the prevailing environmental conditions.

GENETIC ABNORMALITIES IN DISEASE

▶ Genetic abnormalities may be inherited, acquired during conception or embryogenesis, or acquired during post-natal life
▶ Genetic abnormalities inherited or prenatally acquired are often associated with congenital metabolic abnormalities or structural defects
▶ Polygenic disorders result from interaction of two or more abnormal genes
▶ Neoplasms (tumours) are the most important consequences of post-natally acquired genetic abnormalities

Advances in genetics and molecular biology have revolutionised our understanding of the aetiology and pathogenesis of many diseases and, with the advent of gene therapy, may lead to their amelioration in affected individuals (Table 3.4).

Defective genes in the germline (affecting all cells) and present at birth, because of either inherited or acquired abnormalities, cause a wide variety of conditions, such as:

Table 3.3 Associations between disease and race

Disease	Racial association	Explanation
Cystic fibrosis	Caucasians	Hypothesised that defective gene increases resistance to intestinal infection by *Salmonella* bacteria
Sickle cell anaemia (HbS gene)	Blacks	Sickle cells resist malarial parasitisation
		HbS gene more common in blacks in areas of endemic malaria
Haemochromatosis	Caucasians	Mutant HFE protein may have conferred protection against European plagues caused by *Yersinia* bacteria

Table 3.4 Landmarks in genetics and molecular biology

Date	Discovery
1940s	Genes encoded by combinations of only four nucleotides in nuclear DNA
1950s	Complementary double-stranded helical structure of DNA 46 chromosomes in humans DNA polymerase enzyme
1960s	Plasmids—providing a mechanism for transfer of genes to bacteria Lyon hypothesis Restriction endonucleases
1970s	Recombinant DNA technology Chromosome banding Hybridisation techniques Southern blotting
1980s	Gene polymorphisms Polymerase chain reaction Transgenic mice
1990s	Gene therapy
Early 21st century	Human genome project completed RNA-mediated interference (RNAi)

● *metabolic defects* (e.g. cystic fibrosis, phenylketonuria)
● *structural abnormalities* (e.g. Down's syndrome)
● *predisposition to tumours* (e.g. familial adenomatous polyposis, retinoblastoma, multiple endocrine neoplasia syndromes).

Most well-characterised inherited abnormalities are attributable to a single defective gene (i.e. they are *monogenic*). However, some inherited abnormalities or disease predispositions are determined by multiple genes at different loci; such conditions are said to be *polygenic*.

Genetic damage after birth, for example due to ionising radiation, is not present in the germline and causes neither obvious metabolic defects affecting the entire individual, because the defect is concealed by the invariably larger number of cells with normal metabolism, nor structural abnormalities, because morphogenesis has ceased. The main consequence of genetic damage after birth is, therefore, tumour formation (Ch. 11). There is, however, increasing evidence to suggest that cumulative damage to mitochondrial genes contributes to ageing (Ch. 12).

Gene structure and function

Nuclear DNA

Each of the 23 paired human chromosomes contains, on average, approximately 10^7 base (nucleotide) pairs arranged on the double helix of DNA; genes are encoded in a relatively small proportion of this DNA. To accommodate this length of DNA within the relatively small nucleus, the DNA is tightly folded. The first level of compaction involves wrapping the double helix around a series of *histone* proteins; the bead-like structures thus formed are *nucleosomes*. At the second level of compaction, the DNA strands are coiled to form a *chromatin* fibre and then tightly looped. During metaphase, when the duplicated chromosomes separate before forming the nuclei of two daughter cells, the DNA is even more tightly compacted.

During DNA synthesis (S phase) the bases are copied by complementary nucleotide pairing. Any copying errors are at risk of being inherited by the daughter cells and may result in disease. Copying during DNA synthesis starts in a co-ordinated way at approximately 1000 places along an average chromosome.

Nuclear genes

Genes are encoded by combinations of four nucleotides (adenine, cytosine, guanine, thymine) within DNA. Nuclear DNA is double-stranded with complementary specific bonding between nucleotides on the *sense* and *anti-sense* strands—adenine to thymine, guanine to cytosine—the anti-sense strand thereby serving as a template for synthesis of the sense strand. Most of the DNA in eukaryotic (nucleated, e.g. mammalian) cells is within nuclei; a relatively smaller amount resides in mitochondria.

The nuclear DNA in human cells is distributed between 23 pairs of chromosomes: 22 are called *autosomes*; 1 pair are *sex chromosomes* (XX in females, XY in males). Only approximately 10% of nuclear DNA encodes functional genes; the remainder comprises a large quantity of anonymous variable and repetitive sequences distributed between genes and between segments of genes. These non-coding sequences include *satellite DNA* which is highly repetitive, located at specific sites along the chromosomes and probably important for maintaining chromosome structure. A crucial site of repetitive non-coding DNA is the *telomere* at the ends of each chromosome. Its integrity is essential for chromosomal replication. In cells lacking *telomerase* (i.e. most somatic cells) the telomeres shorten with each mitotic division, until eventually the cells are incapable of further replication.

The segments of genes encoding for the final product are known as *exons*; the segments of anonymous DNA between exons are called *introns* (Fig. 3.3). The exons comprise sequences of codons, triplets of nucleotides each encoding for an amino acid via messenger RNA (mRNA). In addition, there are start and stop codons defining the limits of each gene. Some genes are regulated by upstream promoters. During mRNA synthesis from the DNA template, the introns are spliced out and the exons may be rearranged.

Gene linkage and recombination

Linkage and recombination are important processes enabling tracing of genes associated with disease. During meiosis there is exchange of chromosomal material between maternally and paternally derived chromosomes. Adjacent genes on the same chromosome are unlikely to be separated by this process and are said to show a high degree of *linkage*. When exchange of chromosomal material does occur, the result is called *recombination*. The distance between genes can be expressed in *centimorgans* (after a geneticist called T H Morgan); one centimorgan is the distance between two gene loci showing recombination in 1 in 100 gametes.

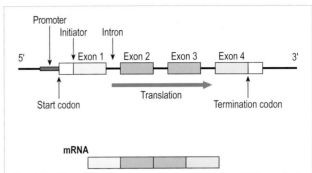

Fig. 3.3 Simplified structure of a gene and its mRNA product. Upstream of the gene is a promoter DNA sequence through which, by specific binding with regulating proteins, the translation of the gene is controlled. Start and termination codons mark the limits of the gene, bounded by untranslated sequences. The encoding portion of the gene is divided into exons, four in this example, interspersed with introns which do not appear in the mRNA product.

These processes of linkage and recombination are not only responsible for the balance between familial characteristics and individual diversity but are also important phenomena enabling defective genes to be identified, even when their precise function or sequence is unknown, by tracking the inheritance of neighbouring DNA in affected individuals and families.

Gene transcription and translation

The normal flow of biochemically encoded information is that a messenger RNA transcript is made corresponding to the nucleotide sequence of the gene encoded in the DNA (in RNA, uracil replaces thymine). The RNA transcript comprises nucleotide sequences encoding only the exons of the gene. The RNA is then translated into a sequence of amino acids specified by the code and the protein is assembled.

Under some circumstances, however, the flow of genetic information is reversed. In the presence of *reverse transcriptase*, an enzyme present in some RNA viruses, a DNA copy can be made from the RNA (Fig. 3.4).

Recently, *RNA-mediated interference* (RNAi) has been discovered as a potentially important mechanism of target gene inhibition. This may have novel therapeutic uses.

Homeobox genes

Homeobox (HOX) genes contain a highly conserved 183 base-pair sequence. They are clustered on chromosomes as a

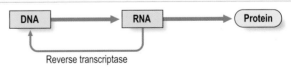

Fig. 3.4 Reverse transcription of DNA from RNA. Normally, the genetic information encoded in DNA is transcribed to RNA and translated into amino acids from which the protein is synthesised. However, some RNA viruses contain reverse transcriptase, an enzyme that produces a DNA transcript of the RNA; this may then be incorporated into the genome of the cell, possibly altering permanently its behaviour and potentially leading to tumour formation (Ch. 11).

homeotic sequence. Their expression during embryogenesis follows the order in which they are arranged, thereby sequentially directing body axis formation.

HOX genes can be subject to endocrine regulation, for example in the endometrium through the menstrual cycle and pregnancy. They can also be modulated by vitamin A (or its analogues such as retinoic acid), thus accounting for the malformations induced by excess or deficiency.

Mitochondrial genes

Most inherited disorders are carried on abnormal genes within nuclear DNA. There are, however, a small but significant number of genetic abnormalities inherited through mitochondrial DNA. Mitochondrial DNA differs from nuclear DNA in several important respects; it is characterised by:

- circular double-stranded conformation
- high rate of spontaneous mutation
- few introns
- maternal inheritance.

The structure of mitochondrial DNA resembles that of bacterial DNA. Consequently, it is postulated that eukaryotic cells acquired mitochondria as a result of an evolutionary advantageous symbiotic relationship with bacteria.

Because the head of the fertilising spermatozoon consists almost entirely of its nucleus, the mitochondria of an individual are derived from the cytoplasm of the mother's ovum. Thus, mitochondrial disorders are transmitted by females, but may be expressed in males and females.

The genes in mitochondrial DNA encode mainly for enzymes involved in oxidative phosphorylation. Therefore, defects of these enzymes resulting from abnormal mitochondrial genes tend to be associated with clinicopathological effects in tissues with high energy requirements, notably neurones and muscle cells. Examples of disorders due to inheritance of defective mitochondrial genes include *familial mitochondrial encephalopathy* and *Kearns–Sayre syndrome*.

Mitochondria and ageing

Because mitochondria play a key role in intracellular oxygen metabolism, it is hypothesised that defects of mitochondrial genes and the enzymes encoded by them could lead to the accumulation of free oxygen radical-mediated injury. Such injury could include damage to nuclear DNA, thus explaining not only the phenomenon of ageing (Ch. 12) but also the higher incidence of neoplasia in the elderly (Ch. 11).

Gene therapy

Currently, significant advances are anticipated in the specific treatment of genetic disorders (such as inherited metabolic disorders and cancer). This is the relatively new clinical science of gene therapy.

There are two approaches. First, it may be possible to replace a defective gene with a normal version in the affected tissues. This would be an ideal solution to the problem of inherited disorders such as cystic fibrosis and Duchenne muscular dystrophy. Indeed, attempts are being made to correct the respiratory tract problems in cystic fibrosis by local gene therapy

applied by inhalation to the airways. Second, the function of an abnormal gene may be abrogated by administering anti-sense RNA or by RNA-mediated interference, as is being explored for Huntington's disease.

Techniques for studying genetic disorders

Genetic disorders can be studied at various complementary levels:

- population
- family
- individual
- cell
- chromosomes
- genes.

At the population level, one is seeking variations in disease that cannot be explained by environmental factors; the study of migrant populations is particularly useful in disentangling the relative contributions made by genetic and environmental factors to the incidence of a disease (p. 31). In families and individuals, one is seeking evidence of the mode of inheritance—whether it is sex-linked or autosomal, whether it is dominant or recessive (Fig. 3.5); in diseases in which the abnormality is poorly characterised, studies of linkage with neighbouring genes (positional genetics) can lead to elucidation of the structure and function of defective and normal proteins. In cells, expression of the protein can be studied. It is, however, chromosomes and genes that have yielded the greatest advances in recent years.

Modes of inheritance in families

> ▶ May be inherited as autosomal or sex-linked genes
> ▶ Genes coding for abnormalities may be dominant or recessive
> ▶ Abnormal genes may be detected either directly from the presence of the gene itself or the defective product, or indirectly by virtue of its linkage with a detectable polymorphism

Although some inborn errors are attributable to genetic mutations, most are inherited through parental genes. Genes located on autosomes (chromosomes other than the sex chromosomes) are *autosomal;* genes on the sex chromosomes are *sex-linked.* By studying the pattern of inheritance in an affected family (Fig. 3.5), the mode of transmission can be classified as either:

- *dominant*—only one abnormal copy of the paired gene (allele) is necessary for expression of the disease
- *recessive*—both copies of the paired gene are required to be abnormal for expression of the disease.

Single gene defects inherited as an autosomal dominant are almost twice as common as autosomal recessive disorders. A minority of single gene defects are sex-linked. Most inborn errors of *metabolism* are autosomal recessive disorders, whereas inherited disorders resulting in *structural* defects are autosomal dominant disorders; there are, however, exceptions to these

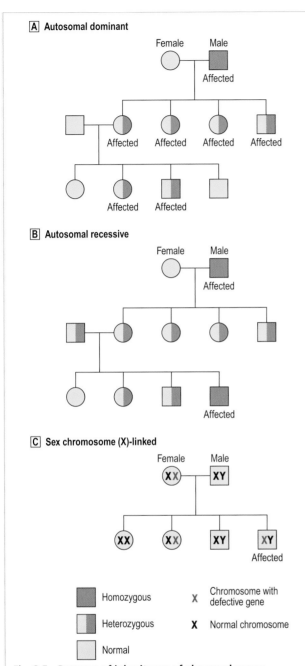

Fig. 3.5 Patterns of inheritance of abnormal genes.
A **Autosomal dominant.** Only one abnormal copy of the gene needs to be inherited for the disease to be expressed; thus, both homozygous and heterozygous individuals are affected.
B **Autosomal recessive.** Both copies of the gene must be abnormal for the disease to be expressed; thus, homozygous individuals are affected and heterozygous individuals are asymptomatic carriers. **C** **Sex chromosome-linked.** In this example, a defective gene (e.g. for haemophilia) is located on the X chromosome. In females, the other normal X chromosome corrects the abnormality, but females can be asymptomatic carriers. In males, the disease is expressed because there is no normal X chromosome to correct the abnormality.

general tendencies. A few inherited disorders are sex-linked; haemophilia (Ch. 23) is a notable example.

Homozygous and heterozygous states
The two genes at an identical place (locus) on a pair of chromosomes are known as *alleles*. Individuals with identical alleles at a particular locus are said to be *homozygous*. If the alleles are not identical, the term used is *heterozygous*. Dominant genes are expressed in heterozygous individuals because only one abnormal copy of the gene is required. However, by definition, recessive genes are expressed only in homozygous individuals because both copies of the gene must be abnormal. The importance of this situation is that a parent carrying only one copy of a recessive abnormal gene (who is, therefore, heterozygous for this gene) appears to be normal. If the other parent is also heterozygous for this abnormal gene, then the disease will be inherited and expressed, on average, by 25% of their children. There is a higher incidence of homologous autosomal recessive heterozygosity in related individuals and, for that reason, there is a greater risk of inherited abnormalities in the children of closely related parents (e.g. cousins). Marriage between close relatives is, therefore, prohibited by law or discouraged by tradition in many communities.

One problem in tracing genetic disorders through families is that the gene may show variable expression or *penetrance*. Although an abnormal gene is present, it may not necessarily always manifest itself and, when it does, the abnormality may be only slight.

Chromosomal analysis

The chromosomal constitution of a cell or individual is known as the *karyotype*. The 46 chromosomes in human nuclei can be seen more clearly during mitosis, especially in metaphase, when they separate. To obtain a sufficient number of cells in metaphase, colchicine can be added to the culture medium in which they are growing; this inhibits polymerisation of tubulin, preventing formation of the mitotic spindle along which the chromosomes migrate and thus blocking cell division in metaphase. The chromosomes can be:

- counted
- banded by staining
- grouped according to size, banding pattern, etc.
- probed for specific DNA sequences.

Counting reveals disorders associated with abnormal numbers of chromosomes (e.g. trisomy in, for example, Down's syndrome). Banding is a technique revealing, at a fairly gross level, the structure of a chromosome (Fig. 3.6). The most widely used technique is *G-banding*; the chromosomes are first partially digested with trypsin and then treated with Giemsa stain. This reveals alternating light and dark bands characteristic to each chromosome; the light bands comprise *euchromatin* (gene-rich DNA); the dark bands comprise *heterochromatin* (rich in repetitive sequences).

The size, characteristic banding, and position of the centromere enable each pair of chromosomes to be identified according to a scheme in which they are numbered from 1 to 22 (the sex chromosomes, X or Y, are not identified by number).

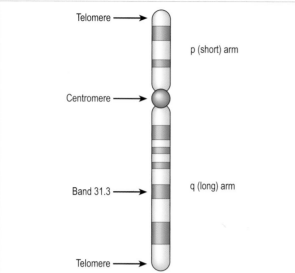

Fig. 3.6 Structure of a chromatid after banding. The centromere is a constriction at which the chromatids are joined. The short arm is designated 'p' (petit) and the long arm is 'q'. The arms terminate in telomeres rich in repetitive sequences. The dark bands are numbered in order from the centromere to the tip of each arm; sub-bands are preceded by a decimal point (for example, the cystic fibrosis gene locus is on chromosome 7 and designated 7q31.3).

Probing for specific DNA sequences (either genes or repetitive sequences) can be done by incubating either chromosome spreads or interphase nuclei with complementary DNA sequences labelled with a reporter molecule such as a fluorescent dye (revealed by ultraviolet microscopy). This powerful technique enables individual genes to be mapped to chromosomes.

Molecular analysis of genetic disorders

With the techniques of molecular biology the genetic abnormality in many disorders can be identified precisely. Formerly, this identification could be done only at the level of the gene product (e.g. the defective protein); now it is possible to locate which part of which chromosome is defective and to determine the gene sequence.

The motivation to study these conditions at the genetic level of detail is twofold:

- to identify accurately the abnormality so that its detection can be used in prenatal diagnosis and in parental counselling
- to improve our understanding of the expression of defective and normal genes and of the function of their products.

This approach is yielding important advances, but many inherited disorders are not yet completely characterised at the genetic level.

Prenatal detection can be achieved by the molecular analysis of *chorionic villus biopsies* in cases known to be at risk.

Functional and positional genetics

There are two possible strategies for the elucidation of the genetic abnormality in genetic diseases—functional and positional (Fig. 3.7). Which strategy is used depends on the nature of the genetic disorder and, in particular, whether the key biochemical abnormality is known.

If the biochemical abnormality resulting from the genetic defect is known, then the chromosomes or DNA from them can be probed with a complementary DNA sequence corresponding to the gene being investigated. The sequence can be deduced from the amino acid sequence of the known gene product. This is the strategy of functional genetics.

If the biochemical abnormality is not known, it can be determined by an alternative strategy of positional genetics (also called *reverse genetics*). 'Positional' in this context refers to the position of the abnormal gene in relation to well-characterised neighbouring genes with which it is linked on the same chromosome. The neighbouring genes will probably be inherited along with the defective gene, so that by studying the affected

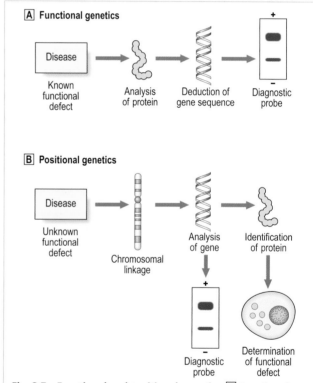

Fig. 3.7 Functional and positional genetics. A **Functional genetics** is the strategy employed to investigate a genetic disorder in which the biochemical defect is known. This enables determination of the amino acid sequence of the abnormal protein and deduction of the DNA sequence. A complementary DNA probe can then be synthesised and used, for example in diagnostic testing for the abnormality. B **Positional genetics** is employed when the biochemical defect associated with the genetic disorder is unknown. However, the abnormal gene can be located by studying its linkage with neighbouring genes in affected individuals. The gene can then be analysed and the protein encoded by it deduced from the DNA sequence. Complementary DNA can be used as a diagnostic probe and the function of the defective protein can be determined.

and unaffected individuals it may be possible to determine the DNA sequence of the defective gene and deduce the amino acid sequence of the gene product.

Genetic linkages

Immediately prior to meiosis leading to the production of haploid germ cells (ova and spermatozoa) from their diploid precursors, there is a random interchange of DNA segments between the homologous paternally or maternally derived chromosomes to form new, recombinant chromosomes. The process of interchange occurs over such short lengths of DNA that only those genes lying adjacent on chromosomes are likely to remain together and be inherited through successive generations. This phenomenon is useful in positional genetics only if the genes and their products are polymorphic; *polymorphic genes* show natural (and normal) variations in their base sequences and protein products—HLA types are good examples. This polymorphism enables the gene and its immediate neighbours to be mapped through a family and to the chromosomal level (Fig. 3.8).

DNA polymorphisms

Although polymorphic genes are useful for the mapping of abnormalities, it must be remembered that most of the DNA in chromosomes is redundant or anonymous; it does not encode any genes and has no phenotypic manifestations. However, because it lacks any function, this anonymous DNA tolerates a higher frequency of polymorphic variation than the DNA in which genes are encoded. In human nuclear DNA, these random polymorphic variations occur in approximately 1 in 200 base pairs. These variations are inherited and can be used to map the inheritance of neighbouring linked genes, even though the neighbouring genes may not have been fully characterised.

These polymorphisms comprise:

- RFLP (restriction fragment length polymorphisms)
- VNTR (variable number tandem repeats)
- satellites—mini- and micro-.

Polymorphic variations arise as a result of:

- substitution of a single base on the DNA strand
- presence of variable numbers of tandem repeats of base sequences.

Variations in anonymous DNA are detected, not by using its polymorphic products (it has none), but by determining the variations in size of the smaller DNA fragments produced by incubation with restriction enzymes. These enzymes, derived from bacteria, break DNA strands at specific points by virtue of the ability of the enzymes to recognise specific sequences of bases. By electrophoretic separation of the broken DNA strands according to their size, it is possible to detect polymorphic differences between individuals (Fig. 3.9).

Some gene variants of clinical significance are *single nucleotide polymorphisms* (SNPs or 'snips') resulting from substitution of a single nucleotide. Arbitrarily, such variations must occur in at least 1% of the population to qualify as an SNP. SNPs can predispose to disease; for example, the E4 allelic variant of apolipoprotein E is associated with an increased risk of Alzheimer's disease (Ch. 26).

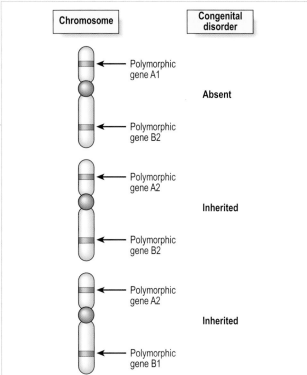

Fig. 3.8 Identification of the chromosome locus for an inherited disease by genetic linkage. Prior to meiosis there is interchange of segments of DNA between homologous chromosomes, but adjacent genes are unlikely to be separated by this process. Polymorphic (variant) DNA sequences for normal genes (e.g. for blood groups) or restriction fragment length polymorphisms in 'anonymous' DNA may be used as markers for the inheritance of a congenital disease, if the abnormal gene for the disease is on the same part of the same chromosome as the polymorphic marker. In this simplified example showing homologous chromosomes from three different individuals, two of whom are affected by the disease, the evidence favours the abnormal gene being very close to the polymorphic gene A2.

Polymerase chain reaction

The polymerase chain reaction (PCR) technique is being used increasingly for the prenatal identification of genetic polymorphisms associated with congenital diseases when the precise base sequence of the polymorphic gene is known (e.g. in cystic fibrosis). The technique is especially applicable to prenatal diagnosis because it enables the abnormal gene to be amplified biochemically from only minute starting samples, even a single cell.

The PCR technique has wide applications in molecular medicine. It is a method of specifically amplifying predetermined segments of DNA from a small sample. The specificity is determined by *primers*, short DNA sequences complementary to the known flanking regions of the DNA segment being sought. The amplification is achieved by using a type of *DNA polymerase* enzyme that can withstand the cyclical heating of the reaction mixture necessary to separate the DNA strands and then cooling to permit DNA synthesis. The reaction mixture must also contain free *nucleotides* for incorporation into

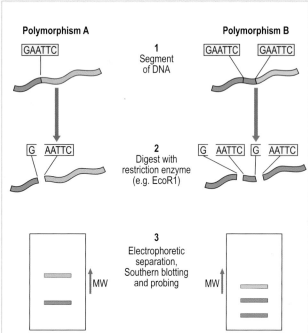

Polymorphism A

GAATTC

1
Segment
of DNA

Polymorphism B

GAATTC   GAATTC

2
Digest with
restriction enzyme
(e.g. EcoR1)

G   AATTC

G   AATTC   G   AATTC

3
Electrophoretic
separation,
Southern blotting
and probing

MW

MW

Fig. 3.9   Restriction fragment length polymorphism.
Homologous regions of anonymous DNA from two individuals are
shown. The polymorphic variations can be detected as follows:
Step 1. The DNA is isolated. *Step 2.* The DNA is incubated with
a restriction enzyme (EcoR1 in this example) that specifically
recognises and splits DNA at sites only where there is a GAATTC
base sequence. One such site exists in polymorphism A; an additional site is present in polymorphism B. *Step 3.* The enzymatically
digested DNA fragments are loaded on to a gel and separated in
an electric field according to their molecular size. After absorption on to a sheet of nitrocellulose filter paper (Southern blot),
the location of the fragments of the polymorphous region can
be visualised by probing with a radioactive complementary DNA
strand. (MW, molecular weight.)

the newly synthesised DNA segments. Within a few hours
the specific DNA segment, if present in the starting sample,
will have been amplified about 1 million-fold. It can then be
analysed in a variety of ways including determination of the
full DNA sequence.

The PCR technique can be used also to study RNA, first
employing reverse transcriptase to produce an amplifiable
DNA transcript.

Diseases due to genetic defects

The important role of genetic abnormalities in carcinogenesis
and tumour pathology is covered in Chapter 11. Here we deal
with non-neoplastic disorders associated with:

- abnormalities of chromosome numbers
- fragile chromosomes
- single gene defects.

Abnormal chromosome numbers

Abnormal chromosome numbers are usually obvious in
karyotypic analyses and are frequently associated with grossly

evident morphological abnormalities (Table 3.5). If three
copies, rather than the normal pair, of a particular chromosome are present, the abnormality is referred to as *trisomy*.
If only one of the normally paired chromosomes is present,
this is *monosomy*. A complete triploid karyotype resulting
from fertilisation of the ovum by two haploid sets of paternal
chromosomes is often associated with formation of a partial
hydatidiform mole (Ch. 19).

Autosomes

The commonest numerical autosomal abnormality is Down's
syndrome; the features are listed in Table 3.5. The risk of
a child being affected by Down's syndrome increases dramatically with maternal age (Fig. 3.10). In most cases, the
abnormality is trisomy 21. Some of the consequences may be
attributable to an increased level of gene products encoded
on chromosome 21; for example, patients with Down's
syndrome develop changes in their brains similar to those
seen in Alzheimer's disease, characterised by deposition
of an amyloid glycoprotein, the gene for which resides on
chromosome 21 (Ch. 26).

Sex chromosomes

Numerical aberrations of sex chromosomes may be characterised by absence of one of the usual pair, as in Turner's
syndrome (X), or extra sex chromosomes, as in Klinefelter's
syndrome (XXY). These relatively uncommon conditions are
usually associated with abnormalities of sexual development
and, therefore, may not be obvious until puberty.

Fragile sites and chromosomal translocations

Some individuals have an inherited predisposition to
chromosomal translocations (Table 3.5); that is, there
is a tendency for chromosomal material to be exchanged
between one chromosome and another. These translocations depend on the presence of 'fragile sites' at specific
locations on the affected chromosomes. Translocations
are often involved in the molecular pathogenesis of cancer
(Ch. 11); it is, therefore, not surprising that individuals
with these rare conditions associated with an increased
risk of translocations have a significantly increased risk of
developing tumours.

Although they are rare, study of these conditions enables a
better understanding of the functional role of the genes involved
in translocations and in the tumours and other abnormalities
resulting from them.

Single gene defects

Single gene defects usually cause discrete biochemical or
structural abnormalities. For example, most of the inherited
metabolic disorders (inborn errors of metabolism) are due to
single gene defects (Ch. 7).

As a rule (there are exceptions) single gene abnormalities resulting in structural manifestations (e.g. tumours)
in adult life are inherited in a dominant manner; those
resulting in biochemical abnormalities (e.g. enzyme deficiencies) in childhood are inherited in a recessive manner
(Table 3.5).

Table 3.5 Examples of genetic diseases

Disease	Genetic defect	Frequency per 1000 births	Features
AUTOSOMAL SINGLE GENE ABNORMALITIES			
Autosomal dominant			
Neurofibromatosis	Defective neurofibromin gene on chromosome 17	0.25	Multiple nerve sheath tumours Skin pigmentation (*café au lait* spots)
Familial adenomatous polyposis	Mutated *APC* gene on chromosome 5	0.1	Numerous benign colorectal polyps with increased risk of colorectal carcinoma
Huntington's disease	Excess tandem CAG repeats in the *huntingtin* gene on chromosome 4	0.2	Adult onset Unco-ordinated movement (chorea) Dementia
Autosomal recessive			
Phenylketonuria	Phenylalanine hydroxylase deficiency	0.2–0.5	Neurological abnormalities
Cystic fibrosis	Cell membrane transport defect	0.5–0.6	Chest infections Pancreatitis
Albinism	Tyrosinase deficiency	0.025	Absence of melanin pigmentation Increased risk of skin cancer from UV light exposure
ABNORMAL CHROMOSOME NUMBERS			
Sex chromosomes			
Turner's syndrome	45X	0.1	Female gender Webbed neck Broad chest Increased elbow angle Undeveloped ovaries
Klinefelter's syndrome	47XXY	1.3	Male gender with female habitus
Autosomes			
Down's syndrome	47, trisomy 21 (in c. 95% cases)	1.4	Upward slanting eyes Flat nasal bridge Single palmar crease Mental subnormality Congenital heart defects
Patau's syndrome	47, trisomy 13	0.1	Microcephaly Small eyes Cleft palate Low-set ears
FRAGILE CHROMOSOMES			
Ataxia telangiectasia	High frequency of non-random translocations	*	Vascular dilatations on skin Ataxia (unco-ordinated movement) Predisposition to tumours
Bloom syndrome	High frequency of non-random translocations	*	Vascular dilatations on skin Immune deficiency Predisposition to tumours
Fragile X syndrome	Fragile site on Xq27.3	0.5	High forehead Prominent jaw Mental retardation More severe in males
X-LINKED DISORDERS			
Duchenne muscular dystrophy	Dystrophin deficiency	0.3[a]	Progressive muscular weakness
Haemophilia	Factor 8 deficiency	0.1[a]	Tendency to bleed
Glucose 6-phosphate dehydrogenase (G6PD) deficiency	G6PD deficiency	[b]	Haemolysis Resistance to malaria

*Reliable frequency data not available; [a]frequency in males; [b]considerable inter-racial variation

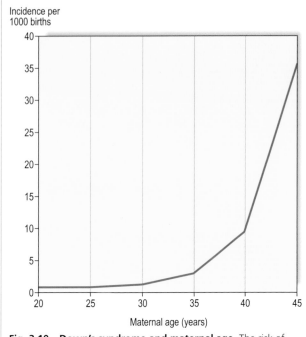

Fig. 3.10 Down's syndrome and maternal age. The risk of a child being born with Down's syndrome increases dramatically with maternal age.

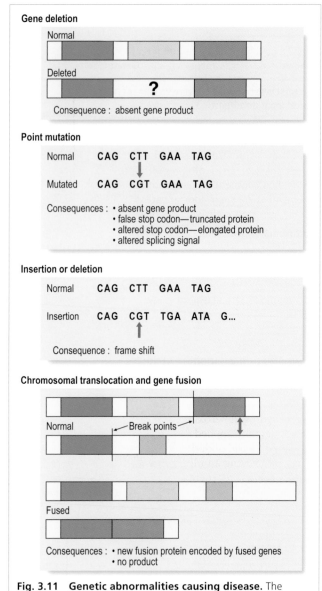

Fig. 3.11 Genetic abnormalities causing disease. The molecular consequence of a genetic abnormality depends on whether the resulting nucleotide sequence corresponds either to a codon for an alternative amino acid (*mis-sense* mutations) or to a premature stop or non-coding codon (*non-sense* mutations).

Single gene defects may result from (Fig. 3.11):

- deletion of the gene
- point mutation (substitution of a nucleotide)
- insertion or deletion (addition or removal of one or more nucleotides resulting in a shift of the reading sequence)
- fusion of a gene with another (by chromosomal translocation).

The effect of the genetic alteration may be:

- *loss of function*, as in mutation of the dystrophin gene in Duchenne muscular dystrophy
- *gain of function*, as results from trinucleotide repeat expansion in the *huntingtin* gene in Huntington's disease
- *lethal*, because the structural or functional consequences are not survivable.

X-linked single gene disorders

In addition to conditions due to abnormal numbers of sex chromosomes (Table 3.5), there are disorders due to defective genes carried on the sex chromosomes. However, because females carry two X chromosomes they only rarely develop disorders due to abnormal X chromosome genes; both X chromosomes would have to carry the same defective gene for the abnormality to appear, and that is relatively improbable. In most instances, the normal X chromosome compensates for the genetic defect on its unhealthy partner.

One of the paired X chromosomes is randomly inactivated in early embryogenesis; this is the *Lyon hypothesis* (after the geneticist Mary Lyon). Thus, approximately half of the cells of a female express genes on the maternally derived X chromosome, and the other cells express genes on the paternally derived partner. Females inheriting a defective gene on one X chromosome are therefore cellular mosaics: some cells are normal, others are defective.

ENVIRONMENTAL FACTORS

Most diseases are due to environmental causes, rather than to genetic abnormalities. This section deals with non-infectious environmental causes of disease.

Chemical agents causing disease

▶ Chemical agents causing disease may be environmental pollutants, industrial and domestic materials, drugs (used therapeutically or recreationally), etc.
▶ Effects include tissue corrosion, interference with metabolic pathways, injury to cell membranes, allergic reactions and neoplastic transformation
▶ Smoking and alcohol are major causes of disease

The study of environmental chemicals causing disease is *toxicology*. The range of possible harmful chemical agents in the environment is enormous and considerable effort is expended in their identification and safe handling. All new drugs, food additives, pesticides, etc. must be exhaustively tested for safety before they can be introduced for public use.

Mechanisms of chemical injury

The cellular mechanisms of chemical injury are described in Chapter 6.

Corrosive effects
Strong acids (e.g. sulphuric acid) and alkalis (e.g. sodium hydroxide) have a direct corrosive effect on tissues. They cause digestion or denaturation of proteins, and thus damage the structural integrity of the tissue. Powerful oxidising agents, such as hydrogen peroxide, have a similar effect.

If accidentally applied to the skin, corrosive agents cause the epidermis and underlying tissues to become necrotic and slough off, leaving an ulcer with a raw base that eventually heals by cellular regeneration.

Metabolic effects
The metabolic effects of chemicals causing disease are usually attributable to interaction with a specific metabolic pathway. However, the harmful metabolic effects of some chemicals affect many organs. Alcohol (ethanol) is a good example: it causes drowsiness and impaired judgement, liver damage, pancreatitis, cardiomyopathy, etc.

The widespread effects of some chemicals are due either to the ubiquity of a particular metabolic pathway or to the multiple effects of a single agent on different pathways.

Some chemicals are directly toxic. Others are relatively harmless until they have been converted into an active metabolite within the body.

Membrane effects
If cells had an Achilles heel, it would be the membrane that invests them. The cell membrane is not merely a bag to prevent spillage of the cytoplasm; it has numerous specific functions. In particular, it bears many receptors and channels for the selective binding and transport of natural substances. These structures are vulnerable to injurious chemicals and their damage can severely disrupt the function of the cell.

Mutagenic effects
Chemical agents or their metabolites that bind to or alter DNA can result in genetic alterations (e.g. base substitutions) called mutations. Chemicals acting in this way are classified as *mutagens*. Mutagens have two serious consequences:

● They can affect embryogenesis, leading to congenital malformations (Ch. 5). Agents acting in this way are said to be *teratogenic*.
● They may be *carcinogenic*, leading to the development of tumours (Ch. 11).

Allergic reactions
Large molecules (e.g. peptides and proteins) may induce immune responses if the body's immune system recognises them as foreign substances. Very small molecules are unlikely to be antigenic, but they may act as *haptens*; that is, they are too small to constitute antigens on their own, but do so by binding to a larger molecule such as a protein. The allergic reaction to chemicals may be mediated by antibodies or by cells, such as lymphocytes (Ch. 9), causing tissue damage.

Important chemical agents

There is insufficient space comprehensively to list all chemicals known to be harmful, but major examples are summarised here.

Smoking
Tobacco smoking is, without doubt, a major cause of illness and premature death. In 1604, it was condemned by King James I of England as *'loathsome to the eye, hateful to the nose, harmful to the brain, dangerous to the lungs, and in the black stinking fume thereof, nearest resembling the horrible Stygian smoke of the pit that is bottomless'*! Epidemiological studies during the latter half of the 20th century provide irrefutable evidence of the causal relationship between smoking and a range of neoplastic and non-neoplastic disorders including:

● carcinoma of the lung
● carcinoma of the larynx
● carcinoma of the bladder
● carcinoma of the cervix
● ischaemic heart disease
● gastric ulcers
● chronic bronchitis and emphysema.

Paradoxically, the addictive component of tobacco smoke (nicotine) is probably the least harmful constituent. Carcinogens within the polycyclic aromatic hydrocarbon fraction of the smoke are responsible for the increased incidence of tumours of the respiratory tract and other sites in smokers. The carbon monoxide in the inhaled smoke is probably responsible for endothelial hypoxia accelerating the development of atheroma.

Alcohol
Alcohol (ethyl alcohol) in moderation appears to have beneficial effects on health. Some epidemiological studies suggest that regular consumption of one or two units per day can slightly reduce the risk of premature death from ischaemic heart disease. This apparent relationship between mortality and alcohol consumption is referred to as the J-shaped curve (the line plotted to show the relationship graphically is roughly J-shaped). However, on balance, alcohol consumption

exceeding this modest allowance is probably responsible for more harm than good.

Alcohol is incriminated in the aetiology of diseases including:

- hepatic cirrhosis
- gastritis
- cardiomyopathy
- chronic pancreatitis
- fetal alcohol syndrome (due to maternal consumption)
- neurological disease (e.g. Wernicke–Korsakoff disease, neuropathy).

Alcohol is also a factor in many road traffic accidents and in physical injury by assault.

Dusts

Not all dusts cause harm by reacting chemically with cells and body tissues. Some evoke a reaction simply because they are 'foreign' particles and elicit a granulomatous response (Ch. 10). Most illness resulting from dusts is due to their inhalation; this may cause:

- asthma
- pneumoconiosis
- extrinsic allergic alveolitis
- lung and pleural tumours (due to asbestos dust).

Drugs

Many of the drugs used in therapy have a risk of adverse effects. Some of these drugs and others are also used (abused) for 'recreational' purposes.

Adverse effects of drugs are a major problem in modern medicine. Many of the drugs and other treatments (e.g. surgery, radiotherapy) commonly used have adverse as well as beneficial effects. The mechanism of the adverse effect varies according to the chemistry of the drug, its metabolism, and the condition of the patient (Ch. 2).

Drug abuse is a major social and medical problem in developed countries. The medical harm that results may be due directly to the abused drug or to coincidental problems. For example, intravenous drug abusers are harmed not only by the effects of the self-administered drugs but also by viruses transmitted by sharing equipment with infected addicts. Human immunodeficiency virus (HIV, causing AIDS) and hepatitis C virus (HCV, causing chronic liver disease) are particularly common.

Physical agents causing disease

> ▶ Agents include kinetic force, excessive heat loss or gain, and radiant energy
> ▶ Mechanical trauma due to kinetic force depends on tissue integrity, more likely to be impaired in the elderly
> ▶ Thermal effects may be localised (e.g. frostbite, burns) or affect the whole body (e.g. hypothermia, heatstroke)
> ▶ Effects of radiant energy range from provoking inflammation (e.g. sunburn) to neoplasia (e.g. skin cancer)

Tissue damage by mechanical injury is obvious and direct. The mediation of thermal or radiation injury is more complex.

Mechanical injury

Mechanical injury to tissues is called *trauma* (although by common usage this word has acquired a wider meaning, e.g. 'psychological trauma'). Cells and tissues are disrupted by trauma, causing cell and tissue loss. Depending on the tissue, regeneration may be possible. The reaction of different tissues to trauma is described in Chapter 6.

Thermal injury

The body is more tolerant of reductions in body temperature than of increases. Indeed, cooling of tissues and organs is commonly used for their short-term preservation prior to transplantation. For major cardiac surgery the body is often cooled to reduce the metabolic requirements of vital organs, such as the brain, when the circulation is temporarily arrested. Accidental *hypothermia* is a common medical emergency in the elderly during winter in countries such as the UK; however, recovery is usually possible unless the body temperature has fallen below 28°C.

Increased body temperature is known as *pyrexia*. In infections, it is usually mediated by the action of interleukins on the hypothalamus. Body temperatures above 40°C are associated with increasing mortality. Enzyme systems are severely disturbed, with severe metabolic consequences.

Local heating of the skin causes increasing local damage. Heat coagulates proteins and thereby disrupts the structure and function of cells. As the temperature rises, burns occur in the following ascending order of severity:

- first degree: skin erythema (redness) only
- second degree: epidermal necrosis and blistering of the skin
- third degree: epidermal and dermal necrosis.

Thermal injury is commonly used in surgery to coagulate tissues and arrest bleeding; this is the technique of *diathermy*.

Radiation injury

Potentially harmful radiant energy is a source of considerable alarm because it is invisible and there is no immediate sensation of its presence.

The effects depend upon the type of radiation, the dose and the type of tissue. Cell and tissue injury from radiation is described in detail in Chapter 6.

Ionising radiation

The harmful effects of ionising radiation are:

- at high doses, rapid clinical effects due to tissue damage from the production of free radicals
- injury to rapidly dividing cell populations (e.g. haemopoietic cells)
- inflammatory reactions leading to scarring of tissues due to induction of fibrosis (e.g. radiation stricture of the bowel)
- neoplasia (solid tumours and leukaemias).

The injury to rapidly dividing cells is immediate and becomes evident clinically within a few days or weeks (anaemia, bleeding, etc.). Fibrosis takes longer to appear—usually months or even years. Neoplasia occurs only decades after irradiation; leukaemias tend to occur earlier than solid tumours.

Despite these serious adverse effects of radiation, carefully controlled doses are used widely in medicine for diagnostic imaging of tissues (e.g. chest X-ray, radionuclide scanning) and for therapy (e.g. irradiation of tumours).

Non-ionising radiation

Ultraviolet (UV) light, particularly UVB, is harmful to the skin. It would also harm deeper tissues if it were not for the skin acting as a screen. UV light causes:

- skin tumours (e.g. melanoma; Ch. 24)
- dermal elastosis (Ch. 12).

INFECTIVE AGENTS

▶ Infective agents include: bacteria, viruses, yeasts and fungi, parasites, and prions
▶ Major cause of disease in all age groups and all countries
▶ Transmission may be vertical (mother to child), horizontal or from animals (zoonoses)
▶ Specific disease characteristics determined by the properties of infective agents and the body's response

The main classes of infective agent are:

- bacteria
- viruses
- yeasts and fungi
- parasites
- prions.

Infective agents often demonstrate tissue specificity. Some organisms selectively infect particular organs or body systems. For example, the hepatitis viruses usually infect and harm only the liver and no other organ; they are said to be hepatotropic viruses. In contrast, *Staphylococcus aureus* is capable of producing injury in almost any tissue. Tissue specificity is attributable to:

- specific attachment of agent to cell surfaces (Table 3.6) mediated by the binding of microbial adhesins to tissue receptors
- specific vulnerability of cells to products of the agent (Table 3.7).

The mode of transmission often reflects the tissue environmental preferences of the micro-organisms. For example, *venereal infections* are acquired through intimate foreplay or sexual intercourse and are caused by a relatively small group of organisms that thrive in the warm, moist micro-environment prevailing in the genital regions. *Anaerobic bacteria,* such as clostridia and bacteroides, have a preference for the hypoxic environment of tissue with an impaired blood supply. Infections due to agents acquired from non-human animals are called *zoonoses.*

Another aspect of the mode of transmission is whether it is *vertical* (i.e. from mother to infant) or, more commonly, *horizontal* (i.e. between unconnected individuals) (Fig. 3.12).

Bacteria

▶ Most are classified according to Gram staining (positive or negative), shape (cocci or bacilli) and cultural characteristics (e.g. aerobic or anaerobic)
▶ Many bacteria are harmless except in patients with impaired defences (opportunistic infections)
▶ Pathogenic (harmful) bacteria cause disease often by toxins and enzymes that damage host tissues
▶ Most pathogenic bacteria provoke acute or chronic inflammatory reactions

Not all bacterial infections are of immediate environmental origin; they all come from the environment but may have colonised the body harmlessly long before they cause disease in that particular individual. Soon after birth the surface of the skin, gut and vagina become colonised by a range of bacteria that are beneficial to the host; these normally present bacteria are *commensals*. However, if the body's resistance is impaired, these commensal bacteria can enter the tissues, causing disease. Other bacteria causing disease are not normally present in the body.

Not all bacteria are capable of causing disease. Those that are capable are called *pathogenic bacteria* and their ability to do so is related to their *virulence*.

Bacteria usually cause disease through the production of enzymes and toxins that injure host tissues. They may also cause tissue damage indirectly by prompting a defensive reaction in excess of that justified by their innate capacity to injure.

Table 3.6	Examples of mediators of specific attachments of micro-organisms to host cells		
Disease	**Micro-organism**	**Microbial adhesin**	**Target cell and surface receptor**
Influenza	Influenza virus	Viral haemagglutinin	Neuraminic (sialic) acid on respiratory epithelium
Common cold	Rhinovirus	Viral capsid protein	ICAM-1 on respiratory epithelium
Measles	Measles virus	Viral haemagglutinin	CD46 on many cells
AIDS	HIV	Viral gp120 protein	CD4 and chemokine receptors on CD4+ T-cells
Typhoid	*Salmonella typhimurium*	Types I and II fimbriae	EGF receptor on intestinal epithelium
Malaria	*Plasmodium vivax*	Merozoite surface proteins	Duffy antigen on erythrocytes
	P. falciparum	Merozoite surface proteins	Glycophorin A, B on erythrocytes

Table 3.7   Examples of specific effects of microbial products on vulnerable cells

Disease	Micro-organism	Microbial product	Effect and vulnerable cells
Cholera	*Vibrio cholerae*	Cholera exotoxin	cAMP activation in intestinal epithelium
Diphtheria	*Corynebacterium diphtheriae*	Diphtheria exotoxin	Inhibition of protein synthesis in myocardium and nerves
Tetanus	*Clostridium tetani*	Tetanospasmin	Spastic paralysis of skeletal muscle
Whooping cough	*Bordetella pertussis*	Pertussis toxin	Cell death in tracheal epithelium

For example, most of the tissue destruction seen in tuberculosis is due to the body's reaction to the causative bacterium rather than to any bacterial enzymes or toxins.

Bacterial lesions are often localised within a particular tissue. However, if bacteria are found within the blood, the patient is said to have *bacteraemia*. If the bacteria within the blood are proliferating and producing a systemic illness, then the patient is said to have *septicaemia*; this is a very serious condition with a high mortality.

Bacteria constitute a very large group of organisms subdivided according to their characteristics (Table 3.8) and causing a wide variety of diseases. The correct classification of a bacterium causing a clinical infection is important so that the most appropriate antibiotic can be administered without delay and so that the epidemiology of the infection can be monitored. The major classification of bacteria is according to shape—e.g. *bacilli* (rods) and *cocci* (spheres)—and staining characteristics—e.g. *Gram-negative* and *Gram-positive*; thus there are Gram-negative bacilli and cocci and there are Gram-positive bacilli and cocci. In addition, there are other major categories, such as spirochaetes and mycobacteria. Some bacteria are capable of surviving hostile conditions by forming *endospores* (often referred to as just spores).

Although bacteria are widely prevalent, the prevention and therapy of bacterial infections have been great triumphs of modern medicine. Successful preventive measures have included general improvements in sanitation (drinking water, drainage, etc.) as well as the development of specific vaccines and a range of antibiotics. Coincident with the major advances in medical microbiology, immunisation and antimicrobial chemotherapy, there has been an increased incidence of troublesome endemic hospital-acquired (*nosocomial*) infections. The organisms causing these infections (e.g. meticillin-resistant *Staphylococcus aureus*) are often resistant to a wide range of antibiotics and are particularly difficult to eradicate.

The harmful effects (pathogenicity) of bacteria are mediated by (Fig. 3.13):

● pili and adhesins
● toxin
● aggressins
● undesirable consequences of immune responses.

Bacterial pili and adhesins

Pili, or *fimbriae*, are slender processes on the surface of some bacteria. They are coated with recognition molecules called *adhesins*. Pili and their adhesin coats serve two functions:

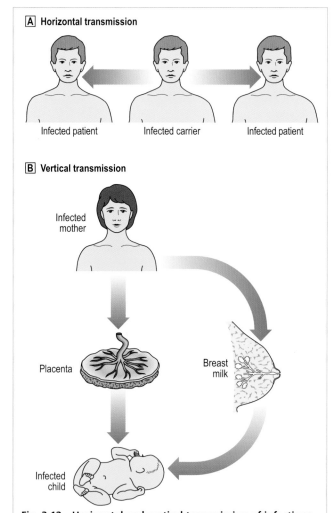

Fig. 3.12   Horizontal and vertical transmission of infections.
A Horizontal transmission. The micro-organism is spread between individuals through droplet infection (i.e. coughing, sneezing), venereal transmission, faecal–oral transmission, etc.
B Vertical transmission. The micro-organism is spread from the mother to her child, either in utero through transplacental infection, or by contact with her body fluids (e.g. breast milk).

Table 3.8 Examples of bacteria causing diseases

Bacterium	Classification	Diseases
Staphylococci *S. aureus*	Gram-positive cocci	
		Boils, carbuncles, impetigo of skin; abscesses in other organs following septicaemia
		Staphylococcal toxin causes scalded skin syndrome, food poisoning and toxic shock syndrome
S. epidermidis		Skin commensal causing disease only in immunosuppressed hosts
Streptococci *S. pyogenes*	Gram-positive cocci Beta-haemolytic	Cellulitis, otitis media, pharyngitis
		Streptococcal toxin causes scarlet fever
		Immune complex glomerulonephritis
S. pneumoniae (pneumococcus)	Alpha-haemolytic	Pneumonia, otitis media
S. viridans	Alpha-haemolytic	Mouth commensal causing bacterial endocarditis on previously damaged valves
Neisseria *N. gonorrhoeae*	Gram-negative cocci	Venereally transmitted genital tract infection
N. meningitidis		Meningitis
Corynebacteria *C. diphtheriae*	Gram-positive bacilli	Pharyngitis with toxin production causing myocarditis and paralysis
Clostridia *C. tetani*	Anaerobic Gram-positive bacilli	Wound infection producing an exotoxin causing muscular spasm (tetanus)
C. perfringens (welchii)		Gas and toxin-producing infection of ischaemic wounds (gas gangrene)
C. difficile		Toxin causes pseudomembranous colitis
Bacteroides	Anaerobic Gram-negative bacilli	Wound infections
Enterobacteria *Shigella* (e.g. *S. sonnei*)	Gram-negative bacilli	Colitis with diarrhoea
Salmonella (e.g. *S. typhi*)		Enteritis with diarrhoea sometimes complicated by septicaemia
Parvobacteria *Haemophilus influenzae*	Gram-negative bacilli	Pneumonia, bronchitis, meningitis, otitis media
Bordetella pertussis		Bronchitis (whooping cough)
Pseudomonas *P. aeruginosa*	Gram-negative bacilli	Pneumonia, wound infections, and septicaemia in immunosuppressed hosts
Vibrios *V. cholerae*	Gram-negative bacilli	Severe diarrhoea due to exotoxin activating cAMP (cholera)
Mycobacteria *M. leprae*	Acid/alcohol-fast bacilli	Chronic inflammation, the precise character and outcome determined by the host immune response (leprosy)
M. tuberculosis		Chronic inflammation, the precise character and outcome determined by the host immune response (tuberculosis)

(Continued)

Table 3.8   Examples of bacteria causing diseases—cont'd

Bacterium	Classification	Diseases
Spirochaetes *Treponema pallidum*	Spiral bacteria	Venereally transmitted genital tract infection, leading to secondary and tertiary lesions in other organs (syphilis)
Borrelia burgdorferi		Lyme disease
Leptospira interrogans (serotype *icterohaemorrhagiae*)		Weil's disease
Helicobacter *H. pylori*	Spiral flagellate bacteria	Gastritis, peptic ulcers and gastric lymphoma
Campylobacter *C. jejuni*	Spiral flagellate bacteria	Enteritis with diarrhoea
Actinomyces *A. israelii*	Gram-positive filamentous bacteria	Mouth commensal causing chronic inflammatory lesions of face, neck or lungs
Chlamydiae *C. psittaci*	Obligate intracellular bacteria	Causes psittacosis, from infected birds; pneumonia
C. trachomatis		Various subtypes causing trachoma (keratoconjunctivitis), urethritis, salpingitis, Reiter's syndrome and lymphogranuloma venereum
Rickettsiae *Coxiella burnetii*	Obligate intracellular bacteria	Causes Q ('query') fever, from infected animals; pneumonia, endocarditis
Mycoplasma *M. pneumoniae*	Bacteria without cell wall	Pneumonia, often described as atypical
cAMP, cyclic adenosine monophosphate		

- sexual interaction between bacteria: sex pili
- adhesion to body surfaces: adhesion pili.

Adhesion pili are the means by which bacteria stick to body surfaces. These processes enable them to become fixed and thereby infect that site. Pili are a feature predominantly of Gram-negative bacteria (e.g. enterobacteria causing gastro-intestinal infections, neisseriae causing meningitis and genital infections). A few Gram-positive bacteria also possess pili, notably beta-haemolytic streptococci, enabling them to adhere to the pharyngeal mucosa.

Host factors rendering some individuals more susceptible to certain types of infection include polymorphisms of the glycoproteins on cell surfaces to which the adhesin-coated pili stick. These include blood group substances.

Bacterial toxins

There are two categories of bacterial toxin:

- exotoxins
- endotoxins.

These toxins are responsible for many of the local and remote effects of bacteria. The toxins can be neutralised by specific antibodies.

Exotoxins

These are enzymes secreted by bacteria and have local or remote effects. Their effects tend to be more specific than those of endotoxins. Examples of exotoxin-mediated effects of bacteria include:

- pseudomembranous colitis due to *Clostridium difficile*
- neuropathy and cardiomyopathy due to *Corynebacterium diphtheriae*
- tetanus due to tetanospasmin produced by *Clostridium tetani*
- scalded skin syndrome due to *Staphylococcus aureus*
- diarrhoea due to activation of cyclic AMP by *Vibrio cholerae*.

The genes directing the synthesis of exotoxins are usually an intrinsic part of the bacterial genome. In a few instances, however, bacteria acquire the gene in the form of a *plasmid*, a loop of DNA that can convey genetic information from one bacterium to another; this is also a mechanism by which bacteria can acquire resistance to an antibiotic. Genes encoding for exotoxins can also be transmitted by *phages*: these are viruses that affect bacteria. The toxin produced by *Corynebacterium diphtheriae* is encoded on a gene conveyed to the bacterium by a phage; strains of this and other organisms synthesising exotoxins are known as *toxigenic*.

Occasionally, disease results from the ingestion of pre-formed exotoxin; this is the mechanism in some cases of

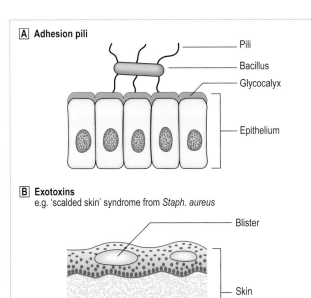

A Adhesion pili

- Pili
- Bacillus
- Glycocalyx
- Epithelium

B Exotoxins
e.g. 'scalded skin' syndrome from *Staph. aureus*

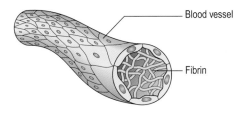

- Blister
- Skin

C Endotoxins
e.g. disseminated intravascular coagulation from Gram-negative bacilli

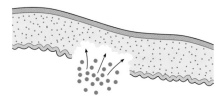

- Blood vessel
- Fibrin

D Aggressins
Erosion of tissues by, e.g., hyaluronidase from *Staph. aureus*

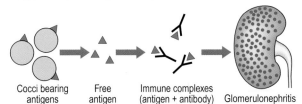

E Immune damage
e.g. post-streptococcal glomerulonephritis

Cocci bearing antigens | Free antigen | Immune complexes (antigen + antibody) | Glomerulonephritis

Fig. 3.13 Pathogenesis of diseases caused by bacteria.
Various factors may be responsible for the local and remote effects of a bacterial infection. Not all factors are relevant to every bacterial infection. **A** Adhesion pili. **B** Exotoxins. **C** Endotoxins. **D** Aggressins. **E** Immune damage.

food poisoning. A typical, but fortunately rare, example is botulism due to contamination of food with a neurotoxin from *Clostridium botulinum*. Toxins acting upon the gut are often referred to as *enterotoxins*.

Endotoxins

These are lipopolysaccharides from the cell walls of Gram-negative bacteria (e.g. *Escherichia coli*). They are released on death of the bacterium. The most potent is lipid A, a powerful activator of:

- the complement cascade—causing inflammatory damage
- the coagulation cascade—causing disseminated intravascular coagulation
- interleukin-1 (IL-1) release from leukocytes—causing fever.

When these effects are severe, as in an overwhelming infection, the patient is said to suffer from *endotoxic shock*. The patient is feverish and hypotensive; cardiac and renal failure may ensue. Disseminated intravascular coagulation may be evinced by bruising and prolonged bleeding from venepuncture sites, as well as more serious internal manifestations. Bilateral adrenal haemorrhage, particularly associated with overwhelming meningococcal infection (Waterhouse–Friderichsen syndrome, Ch. 17), is a dramatic consequence of endotoxic shock.

Aggressins

These are bacterial enzymes with predominantly local effects, altering the tissue environment in a way that favours the growth or spread of the organism. Thus, aggressins inhibit or counteract host resistance. Examples include:

- *coagulase* from *Staphylococcus aureus*—inducing coagulation of fibrinogen to create a barrier between the focus of infection and the inflammatory reaction
- *streptokinase* from *Streptococcus pyogenes*—digesting fibrin to enable the organism to spread within the tissue
- *collagenase* and *hyaluronidase*—digesting connective tissue substances, thus facilitating the invasion of the organism into the host tissues.

Some bacterial enzymes have brought great benefit to medicine through therapeutic uses. For example, streptokinase is used to dissolve thrombi in patients with blood vessel thrombosis.

Undesirable consequences of immune responses

Bacteria can indirectly cause tissue injury by inducing an immune response that harms the host. Fortunately, this mechanism is rare and most immune responses to bacteria are helpful to the host.

Immune responses can harm host tissues by three possible mechanisms:

- *Immune complex formation*. Soluble antigens from the bacteria combine with host antibody to form insoluble immune complexes in the patient's blood. These complexes can usually be removed by phagocytic cells lining the vascular sinusoids of the liver and spleen, causing no further harm. However, under certain conditions the complexes can become entrapped in the walls of blood vessels, notably the glomeruli of the kidney (causing glomerulonephritis), and capillaries in the skin (causing cutaneous vasculitis). Post-streptococcal glomerulonephritis (Ch. 21) is a good example of this phenomenon.

- *Immune cross-reactions.* The host tissues of some individuals have antigenic similarities to some bacteria. The defensive antibody response to some bacteria can, therefore, cross-react with normal tissue antigens; rheumatic fever (Ch. 13) is a good example.
- *Cell-mediated immunity.* The degree of tissue destruction seen in tuberculosis is not attributable to the organism itself but to the host's immune reaction to the organisms. Without much host immunity, *Mycobacterium tuberculosis* induces the formation of small granulomas teeming with bacteria that can become widely disseminated and thus be fatal. In the presence of host immunity, if the organism gains a foothold, it induces a severely destructive tissue reaction in which the organisms are relatively sparse.

Viruses

- ▶ Structure comprises nucleic acid core (DNA or RNA) and protein coat
- ▶ RNA retroviruses possess reverse transcriptase enabling synthesis of DNA versions of viral genes
- ▶ Require living cells for their replication
- ▶ Infection may become latent and then re-activated
- ▶ Harmful effects include cell death, acute and chronic inflammatory reactions, triggering of autoimmune disease, and neoplastic transformation

Viruses are submicroscopic infectious particles consisting of a nucleic acid core and a protein coat. They can be broadly divided into RNA and DNA viruses according to the type of nucleic acid core, but there are many further subdivisions (Table 3.9).

Table 3.9 Examples of diseases caused by viruses

Disease	Virus classification	Features
AIDS (acquired immune deficiency syndrome)	HIV (human immunodeficiency virus) (RNA retrovirus)	Infects CD4 T-helper lymphocytes causing lymph node enlargement, immune suppression and opportunistic infections
Acute viral nasopharyngitis (common cold)	Rhinovirus (RNA)	Inflammation of nasal mucosa
Genital herpes	Herpes simplex type 2 virus (DNA)	Sexually transmitted infection causing inflammation of genitalia
Herpetic stomatitis	Herpes simplex type 1 virus (DNA)	Latent infection in nerve ganglia re-activated to cause vesicles in skin around mouth
Infectious mononucleosis (glandular fever)	Epstein–Barr (EB) virus (herpes group; DNA)	Fever, pharyngitis, generalised lymph node enlargement EB virus also associated with Burkitt's lymphoma (with malaria as co-factor) and nasopharyngeal carcinoma
Measles	Paramyxovirus (RNA)	Fever, skin rash, respiratory tract inflammation Can be fatal in association with malnutrition
Mumps	Paramyxovirus (RNA)	Fever, salivary gland inflammation and, occasionally, pancreatitis and orchitis
Poliomyelitis	Enterovirus (RNA)	Enteric infection initially, then viraemia, from which anterior horn cells become infected, causing paralysis
Rabies	Rhabdovirus (RNA)	Acute encephalomyelitis
Rotavirus diarrhoea	Reovirus (RNA)	Fever, vomiting and diarrhoea
Rubella (German measles)	Togavirus (RNA)	Fever, lymph node enlargement, skin rash, rhinitis; usually mild Maternal rubella associated with high risk of fetal malformations
SARS (severe acute respiratory syndrome)	Coronavirus (RNA)	Fever, severe respiratory infection; significant mortality
Squamous epithelial tumours (e.g. warts, carcinoma of cervix)	Human papillomavirus (DNA)	Transformation of cells causing their uncontrolled growth
Varicella (chickenpox)	Herpes group (DNA)	Fever, vesicular skin rash Latent infection of dorsal nerve root ganglia; can be re-activated later causing herpes zoster (shingles)

Viruses can survive outside cells, but they always require the biochemical machinery of cells for their multiplication. Viruses show more evidence of tissue specificity than do bacteria. The ability to infect a cell type depends upon the virus binding to a substance on the cell surface; for example, human immunodeficiency virus (HIV)—the AIDS virus—selectively infects a subpopulation of T-lymphocytes expressing the CD4 (CD = cluster of differentiation) substance on their surface because viral gp120 specifically binds to it.

Some viruses circulate in the blood to reach other organs from their portal of entry; this process is called *viraemia*. For example, the polio virus enters the body through the gastrointestinal tract, eventually causing a viraemia to reach spinal motor neurones, resulting in their destruction and the patient's paralysis.

The possible effects of viruses are:

- acute tissue damage exciting an immediate inflammatory response
- slow virus infections causing chronic tissue damage
- the triggering of autoimmune tissue injury
- transformation of cells to form tumours.

The clinical manifestations of viral infections are, therefore, protean. Slow virus infections are a known or postulated cause of several neurodegenerative disorders (Ch. 26). The ability of some viruses to transform normal cells into cells capable of forming tumours is covered in Chapter 11. For many diseases where the cause is still unknown, a viral aetiology is inevitably being considered.

DNA and RNA viruses

The properties and behaviour of viruses differ according to their nucleic acid content. Unlike cells (e.g. bacteria, plant and animal cells), viruses contain either DNA or RNA, never both; the viral nucleic acid can be either single- or double-stranded.

Viruses with a DNA core are capable of surviving in the nucleus of the cell they infect, utilising the biochemical machinery there to maintain the DNA of the host cell. The DNA of some viruses can become integrated into the DNA of the host cell. These properties enable DNA virus infections to become latent, re-activated under certain circumstances, and possibly result in neoplastic transformation of the cell (Ch. 11).

RNA viruses have high mutation rates because their RNA polymerase, which copies the viral genome, is incapable of detecting and repairing replication errors. These mutations lead to changes in antigenicity, enabling RNA viruses often to evade host immunity. Some RNA viruses, called *retroviruses*, contain reverse transcriptase (p. 35); this enzyme produces a DNA transcript of the virus which can then become integrated in the genome of the host cell and transform its behaviour.

Tissue specificity

Unlike bacteria, viruses are incapable of replication outside cells. Therefore, a key factor in determining whether an individual becomes infected is the ability of the virus to enter the cells of the body after it has become specifically attached to their surface. There are two alternative mechanisms:

- entry by endocytotic vesicle (e.g. influenza virus)
- fusion directly with the cell membrane (e.g. HIV).

Many viruses show a high degree of tissue specificity, infecting a limited range of organs or cell types. This is known as *tropism*, and invariably results from the fact that the virus must bind first to a specific receptor present on a limited range of cells. Some receptors are, however, widely distributed and enable a virus to infect a wide variety of cell types.

Examples of receptor-mediated virus infection include:

- CD4 receptors on T-helper lymphocytes which bind HIV
- complement receptors which bind Epstein–Barr virus
- cell adhesion molecule ICAM-1 which binds rhinovirus
- neuraminic (sialic) acid receptors which bind influenza virus.

Pathogenesis of cell injury

Viruses can produce tissue injury by a variety of mechanisms (Fig. 3.14):

- *Direct cytopathic effect.* Cells harbouring viruses may be damaged by their presence. This effect can often be demonstrated in cell cultures where, after incubation with the virus, a cytopathic effect is observed: the cells swell and die. This

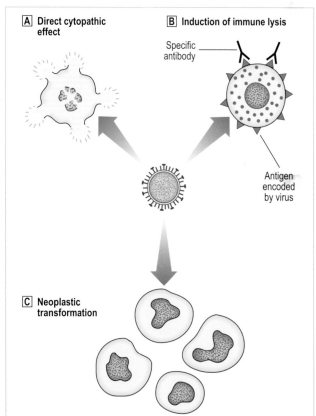

Fig. 3.14 Pathogenesis of diseases caused by viruses.
A Directly cytopathic viruses, injuring or killing cells infected by them. **B** Immune destruction of virus-infected cells. However, in the absence of an effective immune response, the cell may tolerate the virus infection. **C** Incorporation of viral genes into host cell genome. This incorporation may transform the cell into a neoplastic state.

effect is mediated by injury to the cell membranes, causing fatal ionic equilibration with respect to the extracellular electrolyte concentrations, or by depriving the cell of its nucleotides and amino acids. An example of a directly cytopathic virus is hepatitis A virus (Ch. 16).

- *Induction of immune response.* Some viruses do not harm cells directly but cause new antigens to appear on the cell surface. These new virus-associated antigens are recognised as foreign by the host's immune system and the virus-infected cells are destroyed. A consequence of this phenomenon is that, if the immune response is weak or non-existent, the virus-infected cells are not harmed. This situation may benefit the patient because their infected cells are not destroyed, but on the other hand the patient becomes an asymptomatic and apparently healthy carrier of the virus, capable of infecting other people. This is exemplified by hepatitis B virus (Ch. 16).
- *Incorporation of viral genes into the host genome.* This phenomenon underlies the ability of some viruses to induce tumours (Ch. 11). Genes of DNA viruses can become directly incorporated into the host genome, but the genes of RNA viruses require the action of reverse transcriptase enzymes to produce a DNA transcript that can be inserted. RNA viruses with reverse transcriptase activity are called *retroviruses*.

Effective therapeutic remedies against many viral infections are emerging from intensive research. There are vaccines for immunisation against particularly serious or common viral infections. One of the body's own antiviral mechanisms—*interferon production*—can be used in some instances. Interferons are produced by virus-infected cells and, in vitro, can be shown to interfere with or inhibit viral replication. Interferons can now be produced in large amounts and are being used in the treatment of potentially serious viral infections.

Yeasts and fungi

Yeasts and fungi constitute a relatively heterogeneous collection of micro-organisms causing disease (Table 3.10). The diseases caused by yeasts and fungi are known as *mycoses*.

Fungal infections are less common than bacterial or viral infections. However, they assume a special importance in patients with impaired immunity; in these patients, otherwise harmless fungi take advantage of the opportunity to infect a defenceless host. This situation is known as *opportunistic infection* and is shared by a few viruses and bacteria.

The usual tissue reaction to yeasts and fungi is inflammation, often characterised by the presence of granulomas and sometimes also eosinophils.

Mycotoxins

Mycotoxins are toxins produced by fungi. The mycotoxins of greatest medical relevance are the *aflatoxins* produced by *Aspergillus flavus*. Food stored in warm humid conditions can become infected with this fungus, thus contaminating the food with aflatoxins. Animals ingesting sufficiently high doses will develop acute hepatic damage. In humans the greatest problem is the increased risk of hepatocellular carcinoma from ingestion of relatively small doses.

Parasites

Parasites differ from other infectious agents in that they are nucleated unicellular or multicellular living organisms deriving sustenance from their hosts. Some parasites are situated on the skin (e.g. lice) and are designated *ectoparasites*, but most are internal residents (e.g. intestinal worms) and are referred to as *endoparasites*.

Parasites are the most heterogeneous group of infectious agents (Tables 3.11–3.14). Due to their requirement for

Table 3.10 Examples of yeasts and fungi causing diseases		
Organism	Classification	Disease
Aspergillus species	Fungus	Common environmental fungus causing: 1. Allergic asthma 2. Colonisation of lung cavity (mycetoma) 3. Invasive aspergillosis, e.g. pneumonia (in immunosuppressed patients) 4. Hepatocellular carcinoma (due to aflatoxins from *Aspergillus flavus*)
Candida albicans	Yeast	Oral and vaginal commensal causing local disease (thrush) or systemic disease (septicaemia) in immunosuppressed hosts, diabetics, and when local bacterial flora are altered by antibiotics
Cryptococcus neoformans	Fungus (yeast-like)	From bird droppings Causes systemic infection (cryptococcosis) in immunosuppressed hosts
Histoplasma capsulatum	Fungus (yeast-like)	From bird and bat droppings Causes acute or chronic lung infections; systemic infection in immunosuppressed hosts
Pneumocystis jiroveci	Fungus (yeast-like)	Often present in normal lungs Causes pneumonia in immunosuppressed hosts, notably in AIDS cases

Table 3.11 Protozoal causes of disease

Disease	Parasite	Vector/route	Comment
Amoebiasis	*Entamoeba histolytica*	Faecal–oral spread of amoebic cysts	Causes amoebic dysentery and 'amoebomas'
Cryptosporidiosis	*Cryptosporidium*	Faecal–oral	Intestinal infection causing diarrhoea and weight loss; common in AIDS
Giardiasis	*Giardia lamblia (intestinalis)*	Faecal–oral	Intestinal infection causing diarrhoea and weight loss
Leishmaniasis	*Leishmania* sp.	Sandfly	Cutaneous and visceral leishmaniasis (kala-azar) caused by different species
Malaria	*Plasmodium* sp.	Female anopheline mosquito	Acute fever; *P. falciparum* often fatal
Toxoplasmosis	*Toxoplasma gondii*	Cats are definitive hosts	Humans are inadvertent hosts; infection from animal faeces or contaminated meat; lesions in various organs
Trichomoniasis	*Trichomonas vaginalis*	Venereal transmission between humans	Venereal disease
Trypanosomiasis African	*Trypanosoma gambiense* and *rhodesiense*	Tsetse fly	'Sleeping sickness'
American	*Trypanosoma cruzi*	Reduviid bug	Chagas' disease

Table 3.12 Diseases due to trematodes (flukes)

Disease	Trematode	Vector/source	Life-cycle
Clonorchiasis	*Clonorchis sinensis*	Water snails then fish	Eggs from faeces ingested by snail and hatch releasing miracidia which then develop into cercariae; cercariae penetrate fish skin and then encyst to be ingested by humans; metacercariae enter bile ducts where they mature
Fascioliasis	*Fasciola hepatica*	Water snails then fish	As for clonorchiasis
Schistosomiasis (bilharzia)	*Schistosoma haematobium* *S. japonicum* *S. mansoni*	Water snails	Eggs from faeces or urine hatch in water releasing miracidia which penetrate skin of snail; snail releases cercariae which penetrate human skin; schistosomules travel in blood to mature in portal vein (*S. mansoni/japonicum*) or bladder veins (*S. haematobium*) where they lay eggs; these cause granulomas and fibrosis

particular environmental conditions and, in some instances, other hosts for their life-cycle, parasitic infections are generally more common in particular regions or countries.

Parasites are subdivided structurally into:

- *protozoa*: unicellular organisms
- *helminths*: worms (cestodes or tapeworms, nematodes or roundworms, and trematodes or flukes)
- *arthropods*: exoskeleton and jointed limbs (e.g. ticks, mites).

Parasites, particularly helminths, have complex and exotic life-cycles requiring more than one host (Fig. 3.15). Furthermore, within one host there may be successive involvement of more than one organ. Humans may be either *definitive hosts* or *inadvertent intermediate hosts*.

The tissue reactions to parasites are extremely variable (Fig. 3.16). If an inflammatory reaction is prompted, it is often characterised by the presence of eosinophils and granulomas. Some parasites are associated with an increased risk of tumours: *Schistosoma haematobium* is associated with bladder cancer, and *Clonorchis sinensis* is associated with bile duct cancer.

Prions

Prions (proteinaceous infective particles) are recently discovered causes of transmissible spongiform encephalopathies, the most topical of which are Creutzfeldt–Jakob disease (including the variant form) and bovine spongiform encephalopathy ('mad cow' disease). Susceptible individuals

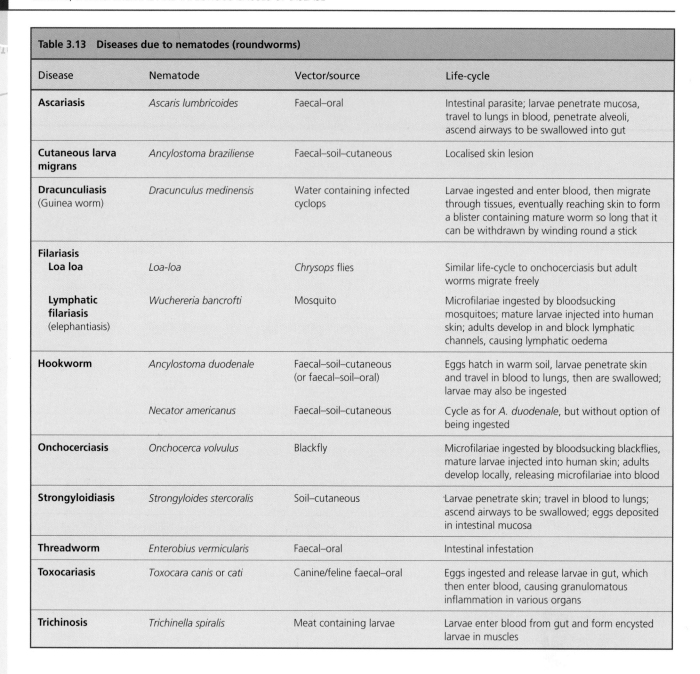

Table 3.13   Diseases due to nematodes (roundworms)

Disease	Nematode	Vector/source	Life-cycle
Ascariasis	*Ascaris lumbricoides*	Faecal–oral	Intestinal parasite; larvae penetrate mucosa, travel to lungs in blood, penetrate alveoli, ascend airways to be swallowed into gut
Cutaneous larva migrans	*Ancylostoma braziliense*	Faecal–soil–cutaneous	Localised skin lesion
Dracunculiasis (Guinea worm)	*Dracunculus medinensis*	Water containing infected cyclops	Larvae ingested and enter blood, then migrate through tissues, eventually reaching skin to form a blister containing mature worm so long that it can be withdrawn by winding round a stick
Filariasis **Loa loa**	*Loa-loa*	*Chrysops* flies	Similar life-cycle to onchocerciasis but adult worms migrate freely
Lymphatic filariasis (elephantiasis)	*Wuchereria bancrofti*	Mosquito	Microfilariae ingested by bloodsucking mosquitoes; mature larvae injected into human skin; adults develop in and block lymphatic channels, causing lymphatic oedema
Hookworm	*Ancylostoma duodenale*	Faecal–soil–cutaneous (or faecal–soil–oral)	Eggs hatch in warm soil, larvae penetrate skin and travel in blood to lungs, then are swallowed; larvae may also be ingested
	Necator americanus	Faecal–soil–cutaneous	Cycle as for *A. duodenale*, but without option of being ingested
Onchocerciasis	*Onchocerca volvulus*	Blackfly	Microfilariae ingested by bloodsucking blackflies, mature larvae injected into human skin; adults develop locally, releasing microfilariae into blood
Strongyloidiasis	*Strongyloides stercoralis*	Soil–cutaneous	Larvae penetrate skin; travel in blood to lungs; ascend airways to be swallowed; eggs deposited in intestinal mucosa
Threadworm	*Enterobius vermicularis*	Faecal–oral	Intestinal infestation
Toxocariasis	*Toxocara canis* or *cati*	Canine/feline faecal–oral	Eggs ingested and release larvae in gut, which then enter blood, causing granulomatous inflammation in various organs
Trichinosis	*Trichinella spiralis*	Meat containing larvae	Larvae enter blood from gut and form encysted larvae in muscles

Table 3.14   Diseases due to cestodes (tapeworms)

Disease	Cestode	Vector/source	Life-cycle
Cysticercosis	*Taenia solium* *Taenia saginata*	Infected pork Infected beef	Usually asymptomatic intestinal parasites but *T. solium* may form cysticerci (encysted larvae) in humans in muscle and brain
Vitamin B$_{12}$ deficiency	*Diphyllobothrium latum*	Fish	Humans infected by ingesting fish infected by feeding upon water fleas carrying cestode eggs
Hydatid disease	*Echinococcus granulosus*	Dog	Cattle, pigs and sheep are usual intermediate hosts; humans infected by ingesting parasite eggs which release onchosphere, eventually forming hydatid cyst in liver, lung, etc.

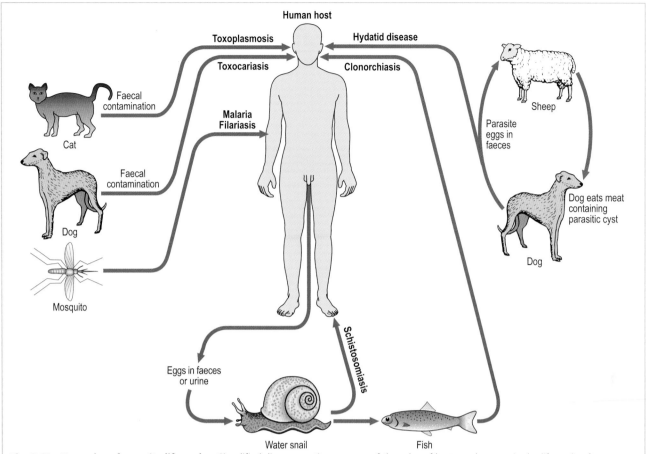

Fig. 3.15 Examples of parasite life-cycles. Simplified diagrammatic summary of the roles of hosts and vectors in the life-cycle of some parasitic diseases.

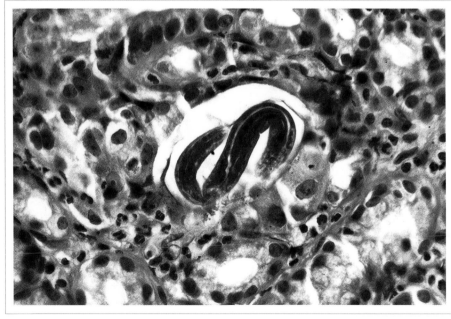

Fig. 3.16 Strongyloidiasis. Intestinal mucosa containing a larva of *Strongyloides stercoralis* that has hatched from ova laid by an adult female worm in the intestine. In immunosuppressed patients, numerous larvae are present. This is hyperinfection and can be life-threatening.

have an endogenous homologous protein which accumulates in excessive quantities in the brain when the exogenous prion is ingested, although other factors are involved in determining whether disease results.

FURTHER READING

Baxter P J, Adams P H, Aw T-C et al 2000 Hunter's diseases of the occupations, 9th edn. Arnold, London

Connor M, Ferguson-Smith M 1997 Essential medical genetics. Blackwell Science, Oxford

Cowman A F, Crabb B S 2006 Invasion of red blood cells by malaria parasites. Cell 124: 755–760

Daftary G S, Taylor H S 2006 Endocrine regulation of HOX genes. Endocrine Reviews 27: 331–355

Greenwood D, Slack R C B, Peutherer J F 2007 Medical microbiology: a guide to microbial infections. Churchill Livingstone, Edinburgh

Khaw K T 1994 Genetics and environment: Geoffrey Rose revisited. Lancet 343: 838–839

Mims C A, Dimmock N J, Nash A, Stephen J 1995 Mims' pathogenesis of infectious disease. Academic Press, London

Mueller R F, Young I D 2001 Emery's elements of medical genetics. Churchill Livingstone, Edinburgh

Peter W, Gilles H M 1989 A colour atlas of tropical medicine and parasitology, 3rd edn. Wolfe Medical, London

Prusiner S B (ed) 2004 Prion biology and diseases, 2nd edn. CSHL Press, New York

Scott J R, Zähner D 2006 Pili with strong attachments: Gram-positive bacteria do it differently. Molecular Microbiology 62: 320–330

Shi Y 2003 Mammalian RNAi for the masses. Trends in Genetics 19: 9–12

Trent RJ 2005 Molecular medicine: an introductory text, 3rd edn. Academic Press, London

Human Genome Project: http://www.sanger.ac.uk/HGP/

Online Mendelian Inheritance in Man: http://www.ncbi.nlm.nih.gov/sites/entrez?db=omim

4

Diagnostic pathology in clinical practice

Laboratory techniques play an important part in the diagnosis and treatment of disease in patients. Many of the tests performed in pathology laboratories are diagnostic, quantitative measurements or prognostic, but these are complemented by expert advice on the interpretation of the results. Microbiologists are also involved in formulating policies designed to prevent spread of infection in hospitals; haematologists have clinical responsibilities for treating patients with haematological malignancies and other disorders.

In this chapter the general principles of diagnostic tests, quantitative measurements and prognostic tests are given and these are then related to the specific roles of clinical chemistry, cytogenetics, cytopathology, haematology, histopathology, immunology, microbiology and autopsies.

TYPES OF LABORATORY TESTS

▶ Diagnostic tests assign patients to diagnostic categories
▶ Quantitative tests may assist in diagnosis, prognosis or management
▶ Effectiveness of diagnostic tests can be expressed as accuracy (the proportion of cases correctly diagnosed) and sensitivity (the proportion of cases of the disease detected by the test)
▶ 'Normal ranges' for quantitative tests assume normal (Gaussian) distribution of values; 5% of normal individuals have results lying outside this range

Diagnostic tests

Diagnostic tests are those that are made on a sample from a patient, the result allocating the case to a diagnostic grouping; an example would be a needle core biopsy of a lesion of the breast which is sent for histopathological examination and classified into a benign or malignant (i.e. cancer) category. Quantitative measurements, such as haemoglobin concentration or arterial blood oxygen tension, may be used in the clinician's diagnostic process but they do not by themselves assign a patient to a particular diagnostic category. A diagnostic test may be based on:

● *quantitative measurement*, such as the level of beta-human chorionic gonadotrophin in the diagnosis of trophoblastic disease
● *subjective assessment*, based on past experience such as a histopathologist's assessment of a needle core biopsy or fine needle aspirate of the breast.

The ideal diagnostic test would produce complete separation between two diagnostic categories; usually, however, there is some overlap. This problem can be illustrated by taking as an example a screening test for colorectal carcinoma which makes measurements on a sample of faeces (many attempts have been made to devise such a test using measurements of blood contained in the faeces and other parameters). An ideal diagnostic test would produce complete separation of patients with and without colorectal carcinoma (Fig. 4.1). The majority of real diagnostic tests do not provide complete separation between diagnostic categories and there is overlap (Fig. 4.2).

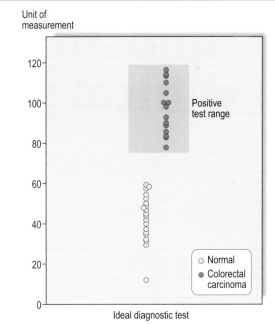

Fig. 4.1 Distribution graph for an ideal diagnostic test. There is complete separation of the population into those with colorectal carcinoma (shaded area) and those without. In this example a measurement of above 70 units would indicate that the subject had colorectal carcinoma and a measurement below 60 units would indicate that the subject did not have colorectal carcinoma.

The effectiveness of a diagnostic test can be expressed using a number of different parameters:

● A *true positive* result (TP) is a positive result from the test under consideration which is confirmed by the real outcome of the situation (e.g. a needle core biopsy of the breast (NCB) which is reported as malignant and the subsequently excised breast tissue contains invasive carcinoma; Table 4.1).
● A *true negative* result (TN) is a negative test result confirmed by a negative real outcome.
● A *false positive* result (FP) is a positive test result that has a negative real outcome (e.g. an NCB that is reported as malignant but the subsequently excised breast tissue shows no evidence of malignancy).
● A *false negative* result (FN) is the reverse of this.

These can be combined into the following measures:

$$\text{Accuracy} = \frac{(\text{TN} + \text{TP})}{(\text{TN} + \text{TP} + \text{FN} + \text{FP})} \times 100$$

$$\text{Sensitivity} = \frac{(\text{TP})}{(\text{TP} + \text{FN})} \times 100$$

$$\text{Specificity} = \frac{(\text{TN})}{(\text{TN} + \text{FP})} \times 100$$

$$\text{Predictive value of positive result} = \frac{(\text{TP})}{(\text{TP} + \text{FP})} \times 100$$

$$\text{Predictive value of negative result} = \frac{(\text{TN})}{(\text{TN}) + (\text{FN})} \times 100$$

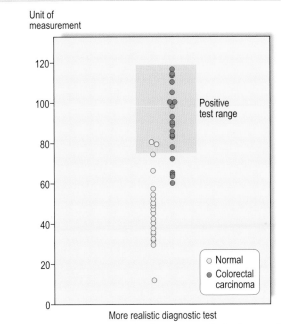

Fig. 4.2 Distribution graph of a more realistic diagnostic test. In this example there is a range of values between 60 and 80 units where there are subjects with and without colorectal carcinoma.

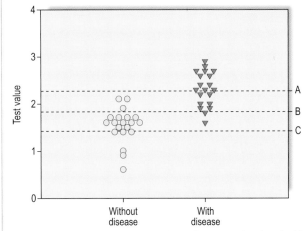

Fig. 4.3 A graph showing the effect of moving the threshold value for a test on its sensitivity and specificity. If the threshold is set at A then there are no false positives so the specificity is 100% but the sensitivity is low at about 60%. If the threshold is moved down to C there are no false negatives so the sensitivity is 100% but the rise in false positives has led to a reduction in the specificity to about 30%. At threshold B the test gives the greatest overall accuracy with three false positives and two false negatives.

Actual outcome	Test result from NCB	
	Benign	Malignant
Benign	True negative	False positive
Malignant	False negative	True positive

Table 4.1 True and false test results in needle core biopsy of the breast (NCB)

The desired values of these for a particular test will vary according to the action taken on the result. A malignant NCB result can result in a surgeon excising the breast (mastectomy), so the specificity and predictive value of a positive result must be as close to 100% as possible. In contrast, if a disease has a relatively safe, non-toxic treatment (such as a course of antibiotics) but the consequences of not detecting the disease can be fatal (e.g. bacterial meningitis), the sensitivity and predictive value of a negative result should be as high as possible. In most situations there is a direct 'trade-off' between sensitivity and specificity and a suitable threshold has to be set that will give the best overall performance (Fig. 4.3).

In many medical situations a continuous biological spectrum is arbitrarily divided into a number of discrete categories which will always lead to some apparent misclassification but is necessary to give information on which clinicians can base their management decisions (e.g. division of intra-epithelial neoplasia of the uterine cervix into three categories, see Ch.19).

A laboratory's performance in diagnostic tests should be monitored by a formal *audit process* and by use of appropriate positive and negative controls in tests.

Quantitative measurements

Many tests in pathology do not categorise results into discrete groups but give a quantitative result which is interpreted in relation to a 'normal' range of values. Examples of such tests include measurement of haemoglobin concentration, electrolyte concentrations, and blood oxygen and carbon dioxide levels.

The measures of performance for such tests differ from diagnostic grouping tests. In quantitative tests the *accuracy* of the measurement (how close the measured value is to the 'true' value determined by a more accurate or absolute method) and the *reproducibility* of the measurement (what variation there is when measuring the same sample many times) are important parameters. These can be assessed by using reference samples with 'known' values and putting these through the measurement system at regular intervals; most laboratories will have their own reference samples which are used frequently (internal quality assurance), and graphs of single measurement and running mean values will be used to ensure that the test is performing within expected limits and not showing 'drift' away from the central expected value (Fig. 4.4). Many countries also have *external quality assurance schemes* where reference samples are sent to all participating laboratories to ensure acceptable analytical performance.

When a laboratory gives a quantitative result for a parameter that is under physiological control, a reference range is often given to facilitate interpretation of the result. If a parameter shows normal (Gaussian) distribution in the local population, the 'normal' range is often given as two standard deviations below the mean to two standard deviations above the mean. If a value lies outside this range then it lies outside 95% of the results for that population (Fig. 4.5) and may be regarded as abnormal, but 2.5% of the healthy population will have values lying outside the range at either end. Thus, all the

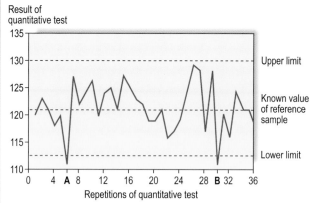

Fig. 4.4 Internal quality assurance graph for a quantitative pathological test. A reference sample is used for each test; tests A and B lie outside the acceptable range and the process of the test would have to be investigated for sources of error (e.g. out of date reagents, contamination, etc.).

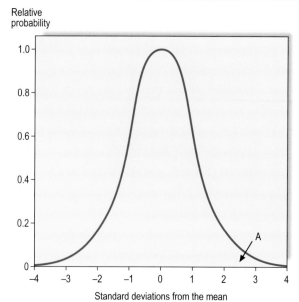

Fig. 4.5 Quantitative measurement with a normal (Gaussian) distribution in the population. The result at A lies more than two standard deviations away from the mean and so may be regarded as abnormal, but 2.5% of the normal population will have values in this area.

details of the individual case must be considered, including other measurements, as a number of results at the top end of the 'normal' range could be more significant than a single result just above the 'normal' range. If the distribution is not Gaussian it may require normalisation by transformation, or non-parametric methods must be used.

Prognostic tests

In many tumours, assignment to a diagnostic category (e.g. adenoma or carcinoma) gives an indication of the prognosis for the individual patient, but within such groupings (e.g. colorectal carcinoma) there may be wide variation in the biological behaviour of the tumour. In order to plan appropriate treatment and to be able to give useful information and counselling to individual patients, many prognostic pathological tests have been developed.

In tumour pathology one of the most predictive prognostic tests is *staging* of the tumour (extent of spread), which is always assessed in the histopathological examination of specimens. One of the best examples of this is Dukes' staging of colorectal carcinoma (Ch. 11 and Ch. 15). *The histological type* of tumour has important prognostic implications, particularly in some organs; subjects with papillary thyroid carcinoma have a life expectancy that is the same as for the rest of the general population without the tumour, whereas subjects with anaplastic thyroid carcinoma have a median survival of a few months. The *grade* of the tumour, an assessment of its degree of differentiation and proliferative activity, also has predictive value; well-differentiated tumours (closely resembling parent tissue) with few mitoses have a better prognosis.

In tumours that produce substances that enter the blood or urine (e.g. alpha-fetoprotein produced by testicular teratomas, see Ch. 20), measurement of the levels of these at the time of diagnosis may be predictive of prognosis (and can be used in follow-up). As more becomes known of the molecular abnormalities of tumours, the possibilities for specific molecular tests that will have prognostic value increase, but the translation of an apparently significant research result into a routinely used prognostic test is not straightforward. When evaluating any new prognostic test the significance for the individual patient has to be considered; a test that shows a statistically significant difference between two large groups of patients may not assign individual cases to a prognostic category with a sufficient degree of certainty to be useful in management decisions or patient information. One recently developed test that has found usage is the detection of expression of the transmembrane receptor tyrosine kinase KIT, which is defined by the CD117 antigen and is the product of the *c-kit* proto-oncogene in stromal tumours of the gastrointestinal tract. This can be detected by immunohistochemistry (Fig. 4.6), which, if positive, predicts that the patient's tumour will respond to treatment with a specific tyrosine kinase inhibitor, imatinib mesylate.

SPECIALISED TESTS

- ▶ Clinical chemistry: measurement and interpretation of substances in blood, other body fluids and tissues
- ▶ Cytogenetics: analysis of chromosomal and genetic abnormalities
- ▶ Cytopathology: diagnostic interpretation of the morphology and other characteristics of cells; commonly used in cancer screening and diagnosis
- ▶ Haematology: diagnosis of diseases of the bone marrow and blood; blood transfusion
- ▶ Histopathology: diagnostic interpretation of tissue samples
- ▶ Immunology: investigation of immunological responses
- ▶ Microbiology: detection and identification of viruses, bacteria, fungi and parasites

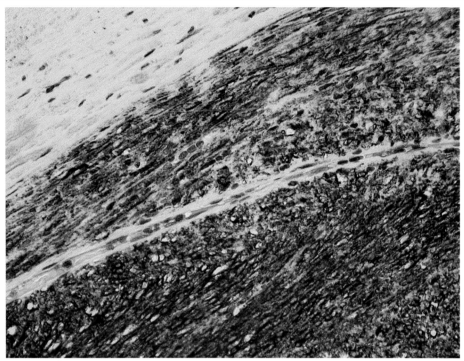

Fig. 4.6 Molecular markers. A gastrointestinal stromal tumour showing expression of the transmembrane receptor tyrosine kinase KIT, which is visualised as the brown staining in this immunohistochemical preparation.

Clinical chemistry

Methods in clinical chemistry detect and measure subcellular substances—usually in the blood but also in other bodily fluids and tissue:

- blood
  — serum
  — plasma
  — red blood cells
- urine
- faeces
- gastric contents/aspirate
- effusions (e.g. pleural, pericardial).

The range of molecules measured is constantly expanding, ranging through electrolytes (such as sodium and potassium), larger inorganic molecules (urea), proteins (including many enzymes) and exogenous molecules (such as carbon monoxide and drugs):

- *blood gases*: e.g. oxygen, carbon dioxide
- *electrolytes*: e.g. sodium, potassium
- *smaller organic molecules*: e.g. urea, creatinine
- *hormones*: e.g. thyroid stimulating hormone, prolactin
- *non-enzymatic proteins*: e.g. albumin, lipoproteins
- *enzymes*: e.g. aspartate transaminase, amylase
- *drugs*: e.g. lithium, digoxin.

Since many of the tests in clinical chemistry are quantitative, the laboratories have extensive programmes of internal and external quality control, and laboratory reports quote reference ranges. For many tests, ranges appropriate for the age and sex of the patient may be quoted.

As with all pathological tests the clinician with direct responsibility for the patient must decide whether a particular test is an appropriate investigation and what sample is most appropriate for that test. These considerations are especially important in clinical chemistry where large automated machines can measure a wide range of substances on a single sample and, if not used selectively, may generate non-essential data which may be difficult to interpret and lead to unnecessary further investigations.

The type of sample and the circumstances in which it is taken are also important. It is outside the scope of this chapter to give specific recommendations for individual tests but examples of inappropriate samples would be blood taken for glucose analysis shortly after a large carbohydrate-rich meal, blood taken for electrolyte analysis from a vein in an arm receiving an intravenous infusion, and blood taken for a digoxin level immediately after a dose of the drug.

The interpretation of results also requires knowledge about the substances being assayed, and the advice of a specialist clinical chemist is often useful. An example of this is the use of cardiac enzymes measured to determine whether a myocardial infarct has occurred. The enzymes lactate dehydrogenase, aspartate transaminase and creatine phosphokinase normally reside intracellularly in muscle cells; if muscle is damaged, the enzymes gain entry to the blood and elevated levels may be detected. The interpretation of these assays requires knowledge about the time course of the enzyme release and the possible sites of enzyme release. The enzymes are not released immediately when the myocytes become hypoxic because the cell membranes take some time to break down; Figure 4.7 shows typical curves of the enzymes in blood after a myocardial infarct;

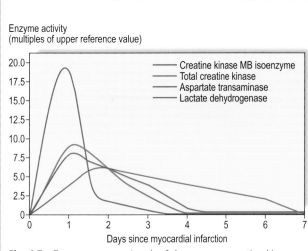

Enzyme activity
(multiples of upper reference value)

— Creatine kinase MB isoenzyme
— Total creatine kinase
— Aspartate transaminase
— Lactate dehydrogenase

Days since myocardial infarction

Fig. 4.7 Enzyme assays. Levels of the enzymes creatine kinase (total and MB isoenzyme), aspartate transaminase and lactate dehydrogenase at time intervals after a myocardial infarct.

it can also be seen from this graph that total creatine kinase and aspartate transaminase reach their peaks earlier than lactate dehydrogenase. The interpretation of the enzyme results will thus require knowledge of these properties and an estimate of when the ischaemic myocardial event is likely to have occurred in the patient. Cardiac muscle is not the only tissue to contain these enzymes; they are also present in skeletal muscle, but different forms of the enzymes (isoenzymes) are present in the different sites. If an assay is used that measures the total amount of these enzymes, damage to skeletal muscle would produce elevations. Thus, if a patient had been found collapsed at home and had been lying on the floor, measurement of the isoenzymes, such as creatine kinase MB, or muscle proteins would be required to ascertain whether an ischaemic myocardial event had precipitated the collapse. Similar interpretative considerations apply to all tests in clinical chemistry.

Cytogenetics and molecular pathology

Cytogenetics and molecular pathology are playing an increasingly important role in clinical pathology (Ch. 3) with more discrete genetic abnormalities being identified in specific tumours (Ch. 11). Laboratory techniques may look at the number and form of chromosomes, the karyotype, or at more specific areas of DNA within chromosomes. The techniques for investigating individual genetic abnormalities are described in Chapter 3.

The karyotype can be examined using a sample of peripheral blood. Phytohaemagglutinin is added to the blood, which stimulates the T-lymphocytes to divide; colchicine is then added to arrest the dividing cells in metaphase when the chromosomes will be most easily visible. The chromosomes may be stained by several methods but the most common is the Giemsa method which produces alternate light and dark bands when the preparation is viewed by light microscopy (G-banding); the patterns of banding allow identification of each chromosome and visualisation of missing or additional material of about 4000 kilobases or more. Abnormalities may be divided into:

- numerical abnormalities
  — aneuploidy
  — polyploidy
- structural abnormalities
  — translocation
  — deletion and ring chromosome
  — duplication
  — inversion
  — isochromosome
  — centric fragment.

The number of chromosomal abnormalities associated with specific tumours is growing rapidly; currently there are over 30 human tumour types associated with non-random chromosomal abnormalities. One of the chromosomal abnormalities with the strongest association with a malignancy is the Philadelphia chromosome in chronic myeloid leukaemia. This abnormality is a reciprocal translocation between chromosomes 9 and 22 resulting in the translocation of the *abl* oncogene to a breakpoint cluster region, which results in a hybrid gene producing a novel protein that may be responsible for the neoplastic transformation (Ch. 23). Another chromosomal abnormality strongly associated with a specific tumour is the 13q14 microdeletion seen in retinoblastoma.

The karyotyping of chromosomes is a relatively coarse method of detecting genetic abnormalities. A more specific technique is fluorescent in situ hybridisation (FISH) which is used to detect and localise the presence or absence of specific DNA sequences on chromosomes. The technique uses fluorescent probes that bind to only those parts of the chromosome with which they show a high degree of sequence similarity. Fluorescence microscopy can then be used to localise the fluorescent probe in relation to the tissue being examined. A common use of FISH is to detect amplification of the *HER2* gene in breast cancers, which then indicates that trastuzumab (Herceptin) therapy will be effective against that tumour.

As more of these abnormalities are found it becomes increasingly important to send tumour samples for cytogenetic analysis as a diagnostic/prognostic procedure. Cytogenetic analysis requires fresh tissue that has been placed in an appropriate transport medium and that must be transported rapidly to the cytogenetics laboratory. It is important to send appropriate samples, which might include 'normal' background tissue as well as tumour; the most appropriate staff to do this might be the histopathologists if they receive the specimen fresh before immersion in a fixative solution.

Cytopathology

Cytopathology specimens consist of single cells or clumps of cells that are dissociated from their surrounding tissues (Fig. 4.8). The technique is used mainly for the investigation and diagnosis of malignancy. The cells are distributed on glass slides, either by the person who takes the sample smearing them directly onto the slide at the time the sample is taken or by centrifugation methods in the laboratory. The slides are stained by an appropriate method, which is most often the

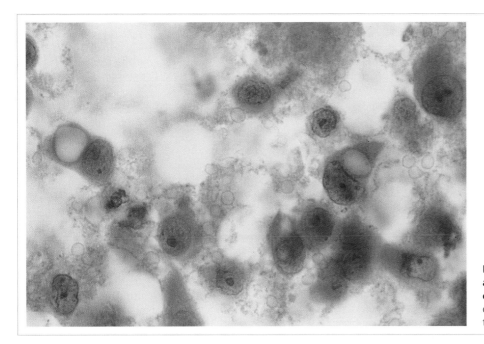

Fig. 4.8 Cytological preparation of a fine needle aspirate of a breast carcinoma. The specimen consists of dissociated cells with no surrounding tissue.

Papanicolaou technique, and examined by light microscopy. Since the cells are dissociated from their surrounding tissue, some features that are used in histopathological diagnosis, such as invasion and other architectural abnormalities, are not available for assessment. The main features used in cytopathological diagnosis are:

- variation in size of nuclei (nuclear pleomorphism)
- increased staining of DNA in the nucleus (nuclear hyperchromatism)
- ratio of nuclear area to cytoplasmic area (by subjective assessment).

Cells may be collected for cytological examination from epithelium shed or scraped from a body surface (*exfoliative cytology*) or by aspirating cells through a fine-bore needle into a syringe (*aspiration cytology*). Many cytopathological specimens are taken to assess dysplasia or malignancy in tissues but infective pathologies may also be diagnosed by this method; for example, *Pneumocystis jiroveci* pneumonia in immunosuppressed patients may be detected by cytological examination of alveolar washings.

Cancer screening

Cervix

One of the most frequent uses of cytopathological techniques is in the detection and assessment of dysplasia and neoplasia in the uterine cervix (Ch. 19). The surface of the cervix is relatively accessible by speculum examination and cells are scraped from the surface at the junction between the squamous and glandular epithelium (the transformation zone) using a spatula. The cells are either spread directly onto a glass slide and fixed or put into a liquid transport medium and sent to the laboratory where the cells can be centrifuged onto a slide (liquid-based cytology which gives specimens that are easier to interpret). The cells are stained using the Papanicolaou technique. Cells from areas of dysplasia or neoplasia are recognised by their abnormal nuclear (*dyskaryotic*) features and the degree of abnormality is graded in a range from mild to severe. Mild abnormalities represent early dysplastic or reactive changes in the cervical epithelium, which may regress, so the usual management for those women is surveillance by further smears. More severe changes (Fig. 4.9) represent marked dysplasia or carcinoma; women whose smears show such changes are referred to gynaecologists for further assessment and probable surgical treatment. In many countries cervical cytology is performed as a screening programme; the aim is to take samples at regular intervals from all women who are at risk of developing cervical cancer (which is most women with a uterus who have had sexual intercourse) and to detect early abnormalities which can be treated before invasive carcinoma has developed. The method of cytopathological examination of cells from the uterine cervix is effective in detecting the abnormalities but most cervical screening programmes have not been totally effective because a significant proportion of women have failed to attend for screening.

Haematology

Haematology covers diseases of the blood; the pathology of these is described in Chapter 23. The work of haematologists is usually divided into three areas:

- diagnosis of haematological disorders
- management of haematological disorders
- blood transfusion.

The diagnosis of haematological disorders is based on clinical history and examination, measurement of parameters

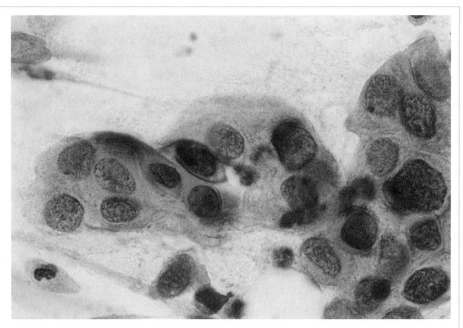

Fig. 4.9   Smear of cervical epithelial cells. There is nuclear hyperchromatism and pleomorphism consistent with a severe degree of dysplasia or actual carcinoma.

in the blood, microscopic examination of blood films and often microscopic examination of bone marrow aspirates and trephine samples.

Automated machines measure many parameters in a sample of blood; the most common are:

- haemoglobin concentration
- red cell count
- packed cell volume (haematocrit)
- mean cell volume
- mean cell haemoglobin
- mean cell haemoglobin concentration
- white cell count and differential count
- platelet count
- coagulation times
  — prothrombin time
  — activated partial thromboplastin time
  — thrombin time
- fibrinogen concentration.

Such machines can produce a plethora of data and the same problems of interpretation may occur as described in the section on clinical chemistry above, but in haematology many of the parameters (e.g. haemoglobin, red cell count and mean cell volume) are linked and need to be examined together when making a diagnosis. Other measurements, such as of serum ferritin or cyanocobalamin (vitamin B_{12}), may need to be made to confirm the diagnosis.

Examination of the blood film can reveal abnormalities of red blood cell shape and size (e.g. anisocytosis, poikilocytosis, macrocytosis—see Ch. 23) and abnormal white blood cells such as blast cells in leukaemia. Some features, such as rouleaux formation by red blood cells, may suggest abnormalities in the non-cellular components of blood (in this case possible overproduction of antibodies or immunoglobulin).

Bone marrow examination

Samples of the bone marrow may be taken by insertion of a relatively large-bore needle into a site, such as the iliac bone, and aspiration by a syringe. At the same time a tissue sample of marrow can be sampled with a trephine needle. A smear of aspirated cells, stained by the Giemsa method, allows identification of cells, and their relative proportions may be quantified. This is an integral part of the diagnosis of leukaemia and assessment of its response to treatment (Ch. 23). Trephine samples of bone marrow retain the architecture of the tissue and allow assessment of the overall cellularity, amount of reticulin and site of different cell types; such samples are essential in diseases that produce fibrosis of the bone marrow, such as myelofibrosis or metastatic prostatic carcinoma, as aspirates will usually produce a very low cellular yield.

Blood transfusion

The primary purpose of blood transfusion is the supply of a product for the treatment of patients. The blood products that can be supplied include:

- red cell concentrates, for rapid correction of anaemia
- fresh frozen plasma, to replace coagulation factors
- platelets, for treatment of thrombocytopenia
- plasma fractions
  — albumin, to correct hypoalbuminaemia
  — immunoglobulin, for passive immunisation
  — factors VIII and IX, to treat or prevent bleeding in haemophilia A or B.

Primary concerns in the operation of a blood transfusion laboratory will include an error-free system of cross-matching (as a mismatched transfusion may prove fatal), safeguards against transmission of microbiological agents (such as human immunodeficiency virus (HIV), hepatitis B and C) by transfusion, and balancing supply and demand of the products.

Histopathology

Histopathology involves the macroscopic examination of tissue with selection of tissue samples for light microscopic examination. Histopathology is usually the primary mode of diagnosis for tumours and also gives prognostic information by grading and staging of surgical resection specimens. Diagnosis of infective and inflammatory conditions can also be made as, for instance, in the detection of *Helicobacter pylori* in gastric biopsies or the diagnosis of inflammatory conditions of the skin.

Most diagnostic histopathology is performed on haematoxylin and eosin (H&E)-stained sections of paraffin wax-embedded tissue. The tissue removed by surgical excision or biopsy is placed in a solution of fixative (most commonly formaldehyde) and transported to the histopathology laboratory. On receipt it is examined by the laboratory staff; a macroscopic description is given and tissue is selected for light microscopic examination. Larger specimens, where most of the tissue will not be examined by light microscopy, are assessed and sampled by medically trained staff who are familiar with a wide range of macroscopic appearances and have a detailed knowledge of anatomy. The samples taken will vary but in a resection specimen would include samples of:

- tumour (for histogenetic pattern of differentiation and grading)
- resection margins
- lymph nodes
- background tissue.

The samples of tissue are processed by machine into paraffin wax, a process involving progressive dehydration through increasingly pure solutions of alcohol that is usually carried out overnight. The wax-embedded tissue samples are then mounted on a microtome and sections 5–7 μm in thickness are cut, mounted on glass slides and stained. These slides are interpreted by expert pathologists and reports are issued to the clinicians who sent the specimens. The reports are tailored to the type of specimen and the clinical details given on the request form. If a tumour is being examined the report will include the type of tumour, its grade (well, moderately or poorly differentiated), its stage (how far it has spread locally, whether any vascular invasion is detected and whether any sampled lymph nodes contain tumour) and comments on the surrounding tissue (e.g. whether there is dysplasia in background epithelium).

Although H&E is the most commonly used stain, there are other stains that may be used to investigate specific features of the tissue. Many of these are standard tinctorial procedures (Table 4.2).

Immunohistochemistry

An increasingly commonly used technique is *immunohistochemistry*. In this method antibodies are used that have been raised artificially to specific substances of interest (e.g. low

Table 4.2 Commonly used stains in histopathology	
Stain	Use
Haematoxylin and eosin (H&E)	Routine stain for histological sections
Masson's trichrome	Fibrous tissue
Perls'	Haemosiderin
Masson–Fontana	Melanin
Modified Giemsa	*Helicobacter*
Ziehl–Neelsen	Acid-fast bacilli
Gram	Bacteria
Periodic acid–Schiff (PAS)	Glycogen, fungi
Grocott's silver stain	Fungi
Alcian blue	Acidic mucin
Periodic acid–Schiff with diastase	Neutral mucin

molecular weight cytokeratins in a suspected epithelial tumour) and these bind to the specific substances if they are present in the tissue section. The bound antibody is then visualised using one of a variety of methods, such as antibodies against the initial antibody and a dye complex such as diamino benzidine. Immunohistochemistry is useful in:

- typing tumours that are poorly differentiated and so are difficult to categorise from appearances on H&E staining
- typing of lymphomas
- classification of glomerulonephritis.

In situ hybridisation (ISH)

DNA probes can be constructed that will bind to specific DNA or messenger RNA (mRNA) in tissue sections. The DNA probes are single-stranded sequences of DNA from tens to thousands of kilobases long and are labelled with radioisotopes, or now more commonly biotin or digoxigenin, to visualise the site of hybridisation using a colorimetric or fluorescent agent (the same method as used in cytogenetics). The DNA in the tissue section is made into a single-stranded form, by conditions such as strong alkalis, and the probe will bind to complementary sequences in the target DNA or mRNA. This technique is useful for detecting infectious agents in tissue sections, such as cytomegalovirus or Epstein–Barr virus. It can also be used to detect production (rather than simply storage) of proteins in cells by detection of the mRNA for the specific protein.

An excellent example of how all these histopathology techniques are integral to patient management is the current treatment of breast cancer. Breast cancer may be detected by mammographic screening, or a woman may present with a self-discovered lump, but the diagnosis is made by histological

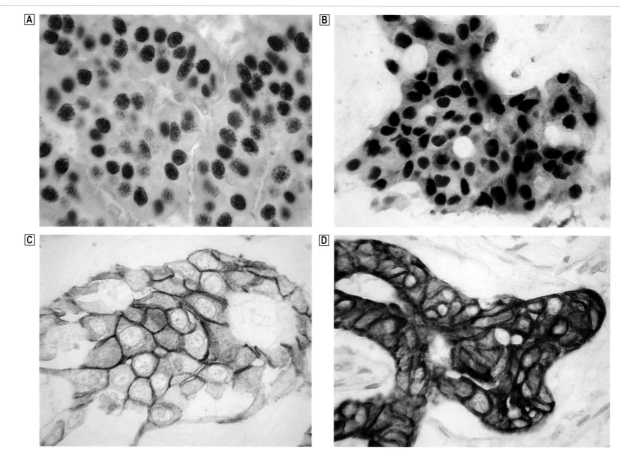

Fig. 4.10   Immunohistochemical staining of breast cancers for specific proteins. [A] A breast cancer showing strong nuclear positivity for oestrogen receptor (dark brown staining nuclei). [B] A breast cancer showing strong nuclear positivity for progesterone receptor (dark brown staining nuclei). [C] A breast cancer showing strong membranous staining for the HER2 protein which indicates amplification of the *HER2* gene. [D] A breast cancer showing strong staining for an antibody directed against a basal cytokeratin suggesting that this tumour is showing a basal phenotype.

examination of a sample of the lesion—most commonly by needle core biopsy. The most usual treatment of breast cancer is primary surgical excision, with sampling of the axillary lymph nodes to detect metastases. These specimens are sent to the histopathology laboratory where examination produces a large amount of information that is vital for further management. Examination of H&E-stained sections will give the histological type of the breast cancer, its histological grade, the size of the cancer and whether the axillary lymph nodes contain metastases. This information makes a reasonably reliable prediction of the biological behaviour of the breast cancer. A small, low-grade tumour with no lymph nodes metastases is unlikely to have metastasised at the time of surgical resection and the side-effects of adjuvant systemic chemotherapy will probably outweigh the possible benefits (i.e. the ablation of metastases that have not yet been detected). A large, high-grade tumour that has already metastasised to the axillary lymph nodes has a high risk of spread to other parts of the body, and the benefits of adjuvant systemic chemotherapy in eradicating or reducing the size and number of these is likely to be greater than the side-effects of this treatment.

There are now a range of immunohistochemical tests that are performed on breast cancers and are useful in planning therapy for individual patients (Fig. 4.10). If the tumour expresses oestrogen and progesterone receptors then anti-oestrogen drugs, such as tamoxifen, will reduce the risk of recurrence or metastases. If the tumour has amplification of the human epidermal growth factor receptor-2 (*HER2*) gene (seen by overexpression of the Her2 protein on immunohistochemistry or by FISH for the *HER2* DNA sequence), then adjuvant trastuzumab (Herceptin) therapy will markedly reduce the risk of death. A basal phenotype of breast cancer has recently been defined by its expression of basal cytokeratins (and absence of oestrogen receptor expression and lack of *HER2* amplification) that has a poor prognosis but does respond to a specific chemotherapy regimen. It is likely that more of these markers will be developed for a wider range of tumours, heralding an era of individualised therapy for cancer patients.

Electron microscopy

Electron microscopy may be used to visualise subcellular detail in tissue samples. In the past this technique was used for detecting features of differentiation in tumours (such as melanosomes in malignant melanomas) but immunohistochemistry has largely replaced this function. Electron microscopy is still used in the classification of glomerulonephritis, where the site and nature of immune complexes in the glomerular basement membrane may be visualised (Ch. 21).

Immunology

Immunology is concerned with the immune response, both antibody and cell mediated, in health and disease. The range of antibodies and cellular features that can be detected and measured has increased so much in recent years that many centres have a separate immunology department to deal with these. The various tests may be divided into those measuring antibodies and those measuring cells.

Immunoglobulins and antibodies

The overall levels of antibodies of certain classes can be measured but this is of little diagnostic use except in generalised immunodeficiencies such as hypogammaglobulinaemia. Detection or measurement of antibodies directed against specific antigens is important in the diagnosis and assessment of *autoimmune diseases*. Samples of a patient's serum are placed on tissue sections and any bound antibody can be visualised by applying further antibodies against human immunoglobulin (or a specific subclass) to which is attached an immunofluorescent dye. Auto-antibodies detected in this way include antinuclear antibodies found in systemic lupus erythematosus. To detect auto-antibodies bound to the patient's own tissues a sample of tissue is taken from the patient (this might be skin or a renal biopsy), antibodies against human immunoglobulins are applied to the biopsy and any bound antibody is visualised by immunofluorescent or other techniques. This technique is used in the assessment of glomerulonephritis (Ch. 21) and bullous skin disorders (pemphigus, pemphigoid, dermatitis herpetiformis, etc., see Ch. 24).

Lymphocytes

There are now antibodies to the specific antigens of most subsets of lymphocytes, such as T-cells or B-cells, T-suppressor cells, T-helper cells, etc., and in conjunction with other techniques (such as fluorescence-activated cell sorting—FACS) the number of lymphocytes in each subclass can be measured. These measurements can give important information about a patient's immune status. In acquired immune deficiency syndrome (AIDS) there is selective destruction of T-helper cells by HIV so that a reduction in the T-helper cell : T-suppressor cell ratio in HIV-positive subjects can indicate the onset of AIDS (Ch. 9). In organ transplantation the detection of acute cellular rejection is important if appropriate immunosuppressive therapy is to be given in time to prevent loss of the graft. Rejection is primarily detected by histological examination of a biopsy of the graft (e.g. kidney) but measurement of the T-cell helper : suppressor ratio provides useful additional information and, with more specific subtyping of lymphocytes, such tests may eventually replace graft biopsy.

Microbiology

Microbiology involves the detection and identification of micro-organisms, including viruses, bacteria, fungi, protozoa and helminths. These may be detected by direct examination of a sample from a patient or by culture of such a sample to increase the number of organisms before using a detection method. Evidence of infection can also be inferred from serological tests for an antibody response to the organism. The susceptibility of cultured organisms to therapeutic agents, such as antibiotics, will also be assessed and microbiologists have wider responsibilities for general control of infection in hospitals and the community.

Direct detection methods in microbiology include:

- direct microscopy (by light or electron microscopy)
- specific antibody detection methods (visualised by enzyme-linked immunosorbent assay (ELISA), radio-immunoassay or immunofluorescence)
- nucleic acid hybridisation technology with labelled probes or the polymerase chain reaction (PCR).

These methods give rapid results, which can be very useful to clinicians. Examples of direct detection include the identification of *Pneumocystis jiroveci* in bronchoalveolar washings from immunosuppressed patients (such as those with AIDS), immunofluorescent detection of *Cryptosporidium* in faeces, and immunofluorescent detection of respiratory syncytial virus in nasopharyngeal aspirates.

Viruses

Viruses are obligate intracellular parasites and so can be grown only in a cellular culture, such as 'immortal' cells derived from tumours or cultures with a finite life-span derived from embryonic tissues. The presence of a virus may be detected by the presence of a cytopathic effect, by haemadsorption/ haemagglutination or by the direct methods described above. The identity of the virus is confirmed by neutralisation of the cytopathic effect or haemadsorption/haemagglutination by antibodies raised against specific viruses. Serological tests are often used to diagnose viral infection: such tests involve the measurement of antibodies against specific viruses using a detection system such as ELISA, radio-immunoassay, immunofluorescence or complement fixation tests. A detectable level of virus-specific IgM or a four-fold rise in the titre of other classes of virus-specific antibody is an indication of recent infection with that virus.

Bacteria

Bacteria may be cultivated in cell-free media. For most purposes the medium used is solid rather than liquid ('broth'). Most solid culture media are based on agar, to which blood or other nutrients are added. Where it is wished to identify a specific pathogen existing in the presence of other bacteria, substances may be incorporated that will inhibit the growth of these other bacteria while not affecting the specific pathogen being sought ('selective media'). For any given type of specimen a range of media is chosen that will support the growth of all pathogens relevant to the clinical condition.

Cultures are then incubated at appropriate temperatures and atmospheric conditions (i.e. aerobic and anaerobic). Most bacteria will grow within a few days and can then be identified by:

- the specific conditions in which they have grown
- morphology of their colonies on the culture plate
- *Gram staining* of samples from the cultured colonies
- biochemical tests (such as the breakdown of carbohydrates)
- enzyme production (e.g. coagulase production by *Staphylococcus aureus*)
- serological tests of antigenic structure.

Some bacteria require specialised media and prolonged incubation in order to produce detectable colonies (for example *Mycobacterium tuberculosis* may need up to 8 weeks' incubation on Löwenstein–Jensen medium). The susceptibility of bacteria to antibiotics may be determined by various methods, most commonly by observing inhibition of bacterial growth around antibiotic-impregnated filter-paper discs placed on culture plates prior to incubation (Fig. 4.11). Microbiologists should provide advice on the empirical choice of antibiotics in cases where treatment may need to begin before the results of susceptibility tests are available.

Fungi

Fungi are grown on simple media (such as glucose peptone agar or blood agar with antibiotics to inhibit bacterial overgrowth) in aerobic conditions. Cultured fungi are identified by the method of spore production (asexual and sexual), morphology of the colony, morphology of vegetative and aerial hyphae, biochemical reactions and antigenic structure.

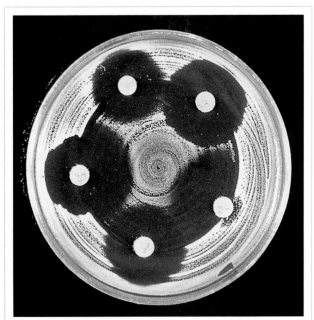

Fig. 4.11 Antibiotic sensitivities. A culture plate with antibiotic-impregnated discs showing inhibition of growth of bacteria around the discs and thus sensitivity to those antibiotics.

Parasites

Diseases caused by parasites are major problems in many countries, particularly those with tropical climates in which the vectors (e.g. insects) thrive. Parasites may be identified in, for example, tissue samples or faeces by their often distinctive morphology.

Precautions

When requesting microbiological tests it is especially important to send suitable specimens. Such samples should come from the likely site of infection, should not contain contaminants, should not contain substances likely to inhibit growth (such as antibiotics), should be put into a suitable container (which may contain a transport medium) and should be transported rapidly to the microbiology laboratory. If septicaemia is suspected but no focus of infection has been identified, multiple samples, including blood and urine, should be sent before systemic antibiotic therapy is started. The risk to staff looking after patients with microbiological infections, or handling specimens from them, is roughly classified according to the degree of hazard (Table 4.3). Most infective agents are included in category 2 (according to the scheme used in the UK). If a patient potentially has a category 3 pathogen then all samples should be marked as such because laboratories receiving these samples will have to take special precautions in handling them (this includes samples sent for non-microbiological investigations).

Hospital-acquired infections

Hospitals contain many patients with microbiological infections and there is considerable potential for spread to other patients. All hospitals should have agreed procedures for preventing the spread of infection, including adequate sterilisation and disinfection, and isolation or barrier nursing when required. Such policies will have been formulated in consultation with the microbiologists of the hospital. The microbiological laboratory will be in a position to detect outbreaks of particular infections if there is suitable monitoring of laboratory results. An increasing problem in hospitals is the emergence of bacteria that are resistant to antibiotics, and this can be limited by the development of protocols for antibiotic usage.

AUTOPSIES

- ▶ May be performed for legal or medical purposes
- ▶ Information from autopsies is useful for clinical audit, education, medical research and allocation of resources
- ▶ Diagnostic discrepancies are revealed by autopsies in approximately 30% of cases

In most countries autopsies fall into two main categories:

1. those performed under the instruction of a legal authority
2. those performed with permission from the deceased's relatives for gathering further information about the nature and extent of the deceased's disease.

Table 4.3 Categories of risk (in the UK) for infectious organisms*

Category	Risk	Examples
1	An organism that is most unlikely to cause human disease	Algae
2	An organism that may cause human disease and may be a hazard to those handling it, but is unlikely to spread to the community and effective prophylaxis or treatment is usually available	*Staphylococcus aureus, Escherichia coli*
3	An organism that may cause severe human disease and present a serious hazard to those handling it. It may present a risk of spread to the community but there is usually effective prophylaxis available	Hepatitis B virus, *Mycobacterium tuberculosis, Salmonella typhi*
4	An organism that causes severe human disease and is a serious hazard to those handling it. It may present a high risk of spread to the community and there is usually no effective prophylaxis or treatment	Lassa fever virus, Marburg virus

*Adapted from: Categorisation of pathogens according to hazard and categories of containment 1990, 2nd edn. ACDP, HMSO

Medicolegal autopsies

Medicolegal autopsies are performed to determine the cause of death and to collect evidence that may be used in the prosecution of those alleged to be responsible for the death. In many cases of murder the cause of death (e.g. bullet wounds or stab wounds) is obvious and most of the work of the pathologist is the collection of evidence, such as trace evidence confirming contact between the deceased and the person accused of the murder (e.g. blood stains, tissue beneath the deceased's fingernails, semen in body orifices) or evidence to link a specific weapon with the deceased's wounds (e.g. retrieval of bullets from wounds).

Clinical autopsies

Non-medicolegal (clinical) autopsies performed on patients who die in hospital may appear to be diagnostic tests that have been performed too late, but much useful information can be gathered from these procedures. Many studies have shown that the certified cause of death given by the clinicians with primary responsibility for the patient shows a discrepancy with the cause identified at autopsy, to the extent of being in a different organ system in about 30% of cases. The hospital autopsy is therefore very useful in providing more accurate data about the cause of death; this is important for *clinical audit*, for *education* of clinicians, and for national *allocation of health resources* if the cause of death is used as an index of the prevalence of disease (which it is in many countries, including the UK). The hospital autopsy is also useful in defining the extent of disease and response to treatment. If a patient has had a malignant tumour, such as malignant melanoma, that has spread to other sites in the body and that patient has then received systemic treatment, it is important to have the most accurate data available about the organs to which the tumour had spread and whether the therapy had any apparent effect on the tumour. Modern methods of in vivo imaging, such as computed tomography and magnetic resonance imaging, may provide some of these data but, if the patient dies, an autopsy is a simple and cost-effective method of gathering accurate data.

The rate of autopsies on patients dying in hospital has shown a decline in most countries over the past decade; this will inevitably lead to loss of much useful information about human disease.

Autopsy techniques

Performing an autopsy is a relatively cheap, low technology procedure that has not changed much since the pioneering work of Virchow in the 19th century. A midline incision from the neck to the symphysis pubis is made and the thoracic and abdominal organs are removed. The scalp is reflected from the skull and the cranium is opened to remove the brain. All the organs are dissected in detail by a medically trained pathologist and the macroscopic appearances and weights are recorded; samples may be taken for microscopic examination, clinical chemistry analysis or microbiological culture. Return of the organs to the body cavities and reconstruction of the body produces an acceptable cosmetic result so that relatives can view the body after autopsy. More limited examination of the body can still generate useful information and so the examination may be limited (by the deceased's relatives' wishes) to certain areas of the body. This may allow an autopsy examination to be performed where permission would otherwise be refused (e.g. exclusion of examination of the cranial cavity in a patient who had received chemotherapy and had no hair, making any scalp incision clearly visible). The ultimate limited autopsy is the *needle autopsy* where percutaneous samples of organs are taken for histological examination using a needle core biopsy needle or fine needle aspiration techniques; such a technique is useful to assess liver disease in cases of hepatitis B or C where risk of infection may preclude a full autopsy.

FURTHER READING

Generic aspects of pathology in clinical practice
Plebani M 2007 Errors in laboratory medicine and patient safety: the road ahead. Clinical Chemistry and Laboratory Medicine 45: 700–707

Clinical chemistry
Marshall W J, Bangert S K 2004 Clinical chemistry, 5th edn. Mosby, Oxford

Cytogenetics and molecular pathology
Shaffer L G, Bejjani B A 2006 Medical applications of array CGH and the transformation of clinical cytogenetics. Cytogenetic and Genome Research 115: 303–309
Sreekantaiah C 2007 FISH panels for hematologic malignancies. Cytogenetic and Genome Research 118: 284–296

Cytopathology
Jenkins D 2007 Histopathology and cytopathology of cervical cancer. Disease Markers 23: 199–212

Haematology
Hoffbrand A V, Pettit J, Moss P 2006 Essential haematology, 5th edn. Blackwell Publishing, Oxford

Histopathology
Bao T, Prowell T, Stearns V 2006 Chemoprevention of breast cancer: tamoxifen, raloxifene, and beyond. American Journal of Therapeutics 13: 337–348
Boughey J C, Buzdar A U, Hunt K K 2008 Recent advances in the hormonal treatment of breast cancer. Current Problems in Surgery 45: 13–55
Gusterson B A, Ross D T, Heath V J, Stein T 2005 Basal cytokeratins and their relationship to the cellular origin and functional classification of breast cancer. Breast Cancer Research 7: 143–148
Hudis C A 2007 Trastuzumab—mechanism of action and use in clinical practice. New England Journal of Medicine 357: 39–51

Immunology
Delves P J, Martin S, Burton D, Roitt I 2006 Roitt's essential immunology, 11th edn. Blackwell Publishing, Oxford

Microbiology
Goering R, Dockrell H, Zuckerman M, Wakelin D, Roitt I 2007 Mims' medical microbiology, 4th edn. Mosby, Oxford

Autopsies
Burton J L, Rutty G N 2001 The hospital autopsy, 2nd edn. Oxford University Press, Oxford

PART 2

DISEASE MECHANISMS

5

Disorders of growth, differentiation and morphogenesis

Growth, differentiation and morphogenesis are the processes by which a single cell, the fertilised ovum, develops into a large complex multicellular organism, with co-ordinated organ systems containing a variety of cell types, each with individual specialised functions. Growth and differentiation continue throughout adult life, as many cells of the body undergo a constant cycle of death, replacement and growth in response to normal (physiological) or abnormal (pathological) stimuli.

There are many stages in human embryological development at which anomalies of growth and/or differentiation may occur, leading to major or minor abnormalities of form or function, or even death of the fetus. In post-natal and adult life, some alterations in growth or differentiation may be beneficial, as in the development of increased muscle mass in the limbs of workers engaged in heavy manual tasks. Other changes may be detrimental to health, as in cancer, where the outcome may be fatal.

This chapter explores the wide range of abnormalities of growth, differentiation and morphogenesis that may be encountered in clinical practice, relating them where possible to specific deviations from normal cellular functions or control mechanisms.

DEFINITIONS

Growth

Growth is the process of increase in size resulting from the synthesis of specific tissue components. The term may be applied to populations, individuals, organs, cells, or even subcellular organelles such as mitochondria.

Types of growth in a tissue (Fig. 5.1A) are:

- *Multiplicative*, involving an increase in numbers of cells (or nuclei and associated cytoplasm in syncytia) by mitotic cell divisions. This type of growth is present in all tissues during embryogenesis.
- *Auxetic*, resulting from increased size of individual cells, as seen in growing skeletal muscle.
- *Accretionary*, an increase in intercellular tissue components, as in bone and cartilage.
- *Combined patterns* of multiplicative, auxetic and accretionary growth as seen in embryological development, where there are differing directions and rates of growth at different sites of the developing embryo, in association with changing patterns of cellular differentiation.

Differentiation

Differentiation is the process whereby a cell develops an overt specialised function or morphology that distinguishes it from its parent cell. There are many different cell types in the human body, but all somatic cells in an individual have identical genomes. Differentiation is the process by which genes are expressed selectively and gene products act to produce a cell with a specialised function (Fig. 5.1B). After fertilisation of the human ovum, and up to the eight-cell stage of development, all of the embryonic cells are

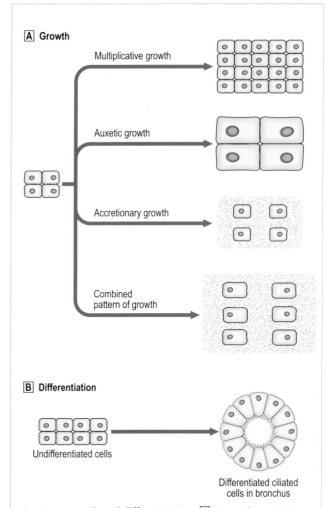

Fig. 5.1 Growth and differentiation. [A] Types of growth in a tissue. [B] Differentiation of undifferentiated cells into ciliated cells in bronchus.

apparently identical. Thereafter, cells undergo several stages of differentiation in their passage to fully differentiated cells, such as, for example, the ciliated epithelial cells lining the respiratory passages of the nose and trachea. Although the changes at each stage of differentiation may be minor, differentiation can be said to have occurred only if there has been overt change in cell morphology (e.g. development of a skin epithelial cell from an ectodermal cell), or an alteration in the specialised function of a cell (e.g. the synthesis of a hormone).

Morphogenesis

- ▶ Complex process of embryological development
- ▶ Responsible for formation of shape and organisation of body organs
- ▶ Involves cell growth and differentiation, and relative movement of cell groups
- ▶ Programmed cell death (apoptosis) removes unwanted features

Morphogenesis is the highly complex process of development of structural shape and form of organs, limbs, facial features, etc. from primitive cell masses during embryogenesis. For morphogenesis to occur, primitive cell masses must undergo co-ordinated growth and differentiation, with movement of some cell groups relative to others, and focal programmed cell death (apoptosis) to remove unwanted features.

NORMAL AND ABNORMAL GROWTH IN SINGLE TISSUES

Within an individual organ or tissue, increased or decreased growth takes place in a range of physiological and pathological circumstances as part of the adaptive response of cells to changing requirements for growth. In both fetal and adult life, tissue growth depends upon the balance between the increase in cell numbers, due to cell proliferation, and the decrease in cell numbers, due to cell death. Non-proliferative cells are termed 'quiescent'; such cells differentiate and adopt specific phenotypes capable of carrying out their specific function (Fig. 5.2).

In fetal life, growth is rapid and all cell types proliferate, but even in the fetus there is constant cell death, some of which is an essential (and genetically programmed) component of morphogenesis. In post-natal and adult life, however, the cells of many tissues lose their capacity for proliferation at the high rate of the fetus, and cellular replication rates are variably reduced. Some cells continue to divide rapidly and continuously, some divide only when stimulated by the need to replace cells lost by injury or disease, and others are unable to divide whatever the stimulus.

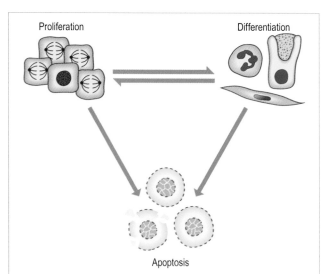

Fig. 5.2 Cell proliferation and death. Individual cells have three potential fates: proliferation, differentiation or apoptosis. After division, individual daughter cells may differentiate, and under some circumstances some differentiated cells may re-enter the cell cycle. The growth rate of a tissue is determined by the net balance between proliferation, differentiation and apoptosis.

Regeneration

▶ Process of replacing injured or dead cells
▶ Cell types vary in regenerative ability
▶ *Labile cells:* very high regenerative ability and rate of turnover (e.g. intestinal epithelium)
▶ *Stable cells:* good regenerative ability but low rate of turnover (e.g. hepatocytes)
▶ *Permanent cells:* no regenerative ability (e.g. neurones)

Regeneration enables cells or tissues destroyed by injury or disease to be replaced by functionally identical cells. These replaced 'daughter' cells are usually derived from a tissue reservoir of 'parent' stem cells (discussed below, p. 92). The presence of tissue stem cells, with their ability to proliferate, governs the regenerative potential of a specific cell type. Mammalian tissues fall into three classes according to their regenerative ability:

- labile
- stable
- permanent.

Labile cells proliferate continuously in post-natal life; they have a short life-span and a rapid 'turnover' time. Their high regenerative potential means that lost cells are rapidly replaced by division of stem cells. However, the high cell turnover renders these cells highly susceptible to the toxic effects of radiation or drugs (such as anti-cancer drugs) that interfere with cell division. Examples of labile cells include:

- haemopoietic cells of the bone marrow, and lymphoid cells
- epithelial cells of the skin, mouth, pharynx, oesophagus, the gut, exocrine gland ducts, the cervix and vagina (squamous epithelium), endometrium, urinary tract (transitional epithelium), etc.

The high regenerative potential of the skin is exploited in the treatment of patients with skin loss due to severe burns. The surgeon removes a layer of skin which includes the dividing basal cells from an unburned donor site, and fixes it firmly to the burned graft site where the epithelium has been lost (Ch. 6). Dividing basal cells in the graft and the donor site ensure regeneration of squamous epithelium at both sites, enabling rapid healing in a large burned area where regeneration of new epithelium from the edge of the burn would otherwise be prolonged.

Stable cells (sometimes called 'conditional renewal cells') divide very infrequently under normal conditions, but their stem cells are stimulated to divide rapidly when such cells are lost. This group includes cells of the liver, endocrine glands, bone, fibrous tissue and the renal tubules.

Permanent cells normally divide only during fetal life, but their active stem cells do not persist long into post-natal life, and they cannot be replaced when lost. Cells in this category include neurones, retinal photoreceptors and neurones in the eye, cardiac muscle cells and skeletal muscle (although skeletal muscle cells do have a very limited capacity for regeneration).

The cell cycle

Successive phases of progression of a cell through its cycle of replication are defined with reference to DNA synthesis and cellular division. Unlike the synthesis of most cellular constituents, which occurs throughout the interphase period between cell divisions, DNA synthesis occurs only during a limited period of the interphase; this is the *S phase* of the cell cycle. A further distinct phase of the cycle is the cell-division stage or *M phase* (Fig. 5.3) comprising nuclear division (mitosis) and cytoplasmic division (cytokinesis). Following the M phase, the cell enters the *first gap (G_1) phase* and, via the S phase, the *second gap (G_2) phase* before entering the M phase again. Although initially regarded as periods of inactivity, it is now recognised that these 'gap' phases represent periods when critical processes occur, preparing the cells for DNA synthesis and mitosis.

After cell division (mitosis), individual daughter cells may re-enter G_1 to undergo further division if appropriate stimuli are present. Alternatively, they may leave the cycle and become quiescent or 'resting' cells—a state often labelled as G_0. Entry to G_0 may be associated with a process of *terminal differentiation*, with loss of potential for further division and death at the end of the lifetime of the cell; this occurs in permanent cells, such as neurones. Other quiescent cells retain some ability to proliferate by re-entering G_1 if appropriate stimuli are present.

Molecular events in the cell cycle

Cell division is a highly complex process and cells possess elaborate molecular machinery to ensure its successful completion. A number of internal 'checkpoints' exist to ensure that one phase is complete before the next commences (Fig. 5.3). This is vital to ensure, for example, that DNA replication

has been performed accurately and that cells do not divide before DNA replication is complete. The various proteins and enzymes that carry out DNA replication, mitotic spindle formation, etc. are typically only present and active during the appropriate phases of the cycle. The timely production and activation of these proteins is regulated by the activity of a family of evolutionarily conserved proteins called *cyclin dependent kinases* (CDKs), which activate their target proteins by phosphorylation. The activity of CDKs is, in turn, regulated by a second family of proteins, the *cyclins*. Transitions from one phase of the cycle to the next are initiated by rises in the levels of specific cyclins. The transition from G_0 to G_1 at the initiation of the cell cycle, for example, is triggered by external signals such as growth factors leading to rises in the levels of *cyclin D*. Problems during cell division, such as faulty DNA replication, result in rises in the levels of a third family of proteins, the *CDK inhibitors (CDKIs)*, which can prevent CDKs from triggering the next phase of cell division until the issue is resolved. In the face of major failures, cells will typically initiate apoptosis rather than permit the generation of improperly formed progeny. Damage to the genes that encode proteins involved in the regulation of cell-cycle progression is seen in many cancers (Ch. 11).

Duration of the cell cycle

In mammals, different cell types divide at very different rates, with observed cell cycle times (also called generation times) ranging from as little as 8 hours, in the case of gut epithelial cells, to 100 days or more, exemplified by hepatocytes in the normal adult liver. However, the duration of the individual phases of the cycle is remarkably constant and independent of the rate of cell division. The principal difference between rapidly dividing cells and those that divide slowly is the time spent temporarily in G_0 between divisions; some cells remain in the G_0 phase for days or even years between divisions, whilst others rapidly re-enter G_1 after mitosis.

Therapeutic interruption of the cell cycle

Many of the drugs used in the treatment of cancer affect particular stages within the cell cycle (Fig. 5.4). These drugs inhibit the rapid division of cancer cells, although there is often inhibition of other rapidly dividing cells, such as the cells of the bone marrow and lymphoid tissues. Thus, anaemia, a bleeding tendency and suppression of immunity may be clinically important side-effects of cancer chemotherapy.

Cell death in growth and morphogenesis

It seems illogical to think of cell death as a component of normal growth and morphogenesis, although we recognise that the loss of a tadpole's tail, which is mediated by the genetically programmed death of specific cells, is part of the metamorphosis of a frog. It is now clear that such cell death has an important role in human development and in the regulation of tissue size throughout life. Alterations in the rate at which cell death occurs are important in situations such as hormonal growth regulation, immunity and neoplasia.

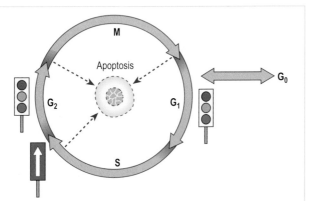

Fig. 5.3 The four stages of the cell cycle. G_1 represents preparation for DNA synthesis (S phase), and G_2 represents preparation for mitosis (M phase). After mitosis individual daughter cells may each re-enter the cycle at G_1 if appropriate stimuli are present. Alternatively, they may permanently or temporarily enter G_0 and differentiate. Progress around the cell cycle is one-way. 'Checkpoints' ensure one phase does not commence until the previous phase is completed. Failure of a phase to complete satisfactorily results in cell cycle arrest, or—if the problem is irretrievable—apoptosis.

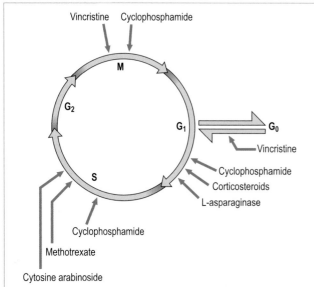

Fig. 5.4 Pharmacological interruption of the cell cycle. The sites of action in the cell cycle of drugs that may be used in the treatment of cancer.

Apoptosis

The term *apoptosis* is used to denote a physiological cellular process in which a defined and programmed sequence of intracellular events leads to the death of a cell without the release of products harmful to surrounding cells. It is a biochemically specific mode of cell death characterised by activation of non-lysosomal endogenous endonuclease which digests nuclear DNA into smaller DNA fragments. Morphologically, apoptosis is recognised as death of scattered single cells which form rounded, membrane-bound bodies; these are eventually phagocytosed (ingested) and broken down by adjacent unaffected cells.

The co-existence of apoptosis alongside mitosis within a cell population ensures a continuous renewal of cells, rendering a tissue more adaptable to environmental demands than one in which the cell population is static.

Apoptosis can be triggered by factors outside the cell or it can be an autonomous event ('programmed cell death'). In embryological development, there are three categories of autonomous apoptosis:

- morphogenetic
- histogenic
- phylogenetic.

Morphogenetic apoptosis is involved in alteration of tissue form. Examples include:

- interdigital cell death responsible for separating the fingers (Fig. 5.5)
- cell death leading to the removal of redundant epithelium following fusion of the palatine processes during development of the roof of the mouth
- cell death in the dorsal part of the neural tube during closure, required to achieve continuity of the epithelium, the two sides of the neural tube and the associated mesoderm

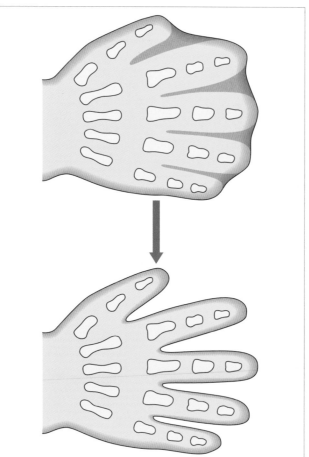

Fig. 5.5 Morphogenesis by apoptosis. Genetically programmed apoptosis (individual cell death) causing separation of the fingers during embryogenesis.

- cell death in the involuting urachus, required to remove redundant tissue between the bladder and umbilicus.

Failure of morphogenetic apoptosis in these four sites is a factor in the development of *syndactyly* (webbed fingers), *cleft palate*, *spina bifida*, and *bladder diverticulum* (pouch) or *fistula* (open connection) from the bladder to the umbilical skin, respectively.

Histogenic apoptosis occurs in the differentiation of tissues and organs, as seen, for example, in the hormonally controlled differentiation of the accessory reproductive structures from the Müllerian and Wolffian ducts. In the male, for instance, anti-Müllerian hormone produced by the Sertoli cells of the fetal testis causes regression of the Müllerian ducts (which in females form the fallopian tubes, uterus and upper vagina) by the process of apoptosis.

Phylogenetic apoptosis is involved in removing vestigial structures from the embryo; structures such as the pronephros, a remnant from a much lower evolutionary level, are removed by the process of apoptosis.

Regulation of apoptosis

Apoptosis may be triggered by external signals, such as detachment from the extracellular matrix, the withdrawal of growth factors, or specific signals from other cells. This mode of

activation of apoptosis is called the extrinsic pathway. By contrast, the intrinsic pathway is activated by intracellular signals, such as DNA damage or failure to conduct cell division correctly. Although apoptosis can be induced by diverse signals in a variety of cell types, a few genes appear to regulate a final common pathway. The most important of these are the members of the *bcl*-2 family (*bcl*-2 was originally identified at the t(14;18) chromosomal breakpoint in follicular B-cell lymphoma, and it can inhibit many factors that induce apoptosis). The bax protein (also in the *bcl*-2 family) forms bax–bax dimers which enhance apoptotic stimuli. The ratio of bcl-2 to bax determines the cell's susceptibility to apoptotic stimuli, and constitutes a 'molecular switch' which determines whether a cell will survive, leading to tissue expansion, or undergo apoptosis.

The study of factors regulating apoptosis is of considerable importance in finding therapeutic agents to enhance cell death in malignant neoplasms.

Increased growth: hypertrophy and hyperplasia

> ▸ Hyperplasia and hypertrophy are common tissue responses
> ▸ May be physiological (e.g. breast enlargement in pregnancy) or pathological (e.g. prostatic enlargement in elderly men)
> ▸ Hypertrophy: increase in cell size without cell division
> ▸ Hyperplasia: increase in cell number by mitosis

The response of an individual cell to increased functional demand is to increase tissue or organ size (Fig. 5.6) by:

- increasing its size without cell replication (hypertrophy)
- increasing its numbers by cell division (hyperplasia)
- a combination of these.

The stimuli for hypertrophy and hyperplasia are very similar, and in many cases identical; indeed, hypertrophy and hyperplasia commonly co-exist. In permanent cells hypertrophy is the only adaptive option available under stimulatory conditions. In some circumstances, however, permanent cells may increase their DNA content (ploidy) in

hypertrophy, although the cells arrest in the G_2 phase of the cell cycle without undergoing mitosis; such a circumstance is present in severely hypertrophied hearts, where a large proportion of cells may be polyploid.

An important component of hyperplasia, which is often over-looked, is a *decrease* in cell loss by apoptosis; the mechanisms of control of this decreased apoptosis are unclear, although they are related to the factors causing increased cell production (Fig. 5.7).

Physiological hypertrophy and hyperplasia

Examples of physiologically increased growth of tissues include:

- *Muscle hypertrophy* in athletes, both in the skeletal muscle of the limbs (as a response to increased muscle activity) and in the left ventricle of the heart (as a response to sustained outflow resistance).
- *Hyperplasia of bone marrow cells* producing red blood cells in individuals living at high altitude. This is stimulated by increased production of the growth factor erythropoietin.

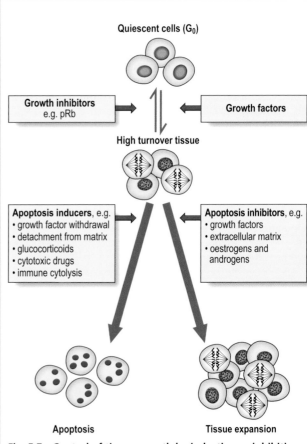

Fig. 5.7 Control of tissue growth by induction or inhibition of apoptosis. Quiescent (mitotically inactive) cells in G_0 are recruited into a high turnover (mitotically active) state by growth factors. Their subsequent fate depends on the presence or absence of apoptosis inducers or inhibitors. The inducers and inhibitors are mediated by the bax and bcl-2 proteins respectively, among others.

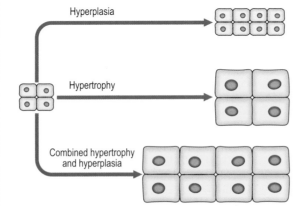

Fig. 5.6 Hyperplasia and hypertrophy. In hypertrophy, cell size is increased. In hyperplasia, cell number is increased. Hypertrophy and hyperplasia may co-exist.

- *Hyperplasia of breast tissue* at puberty, and in pregnancy and lactation, under the influence of several hormones, including oestrogens, progesterone, prolactin, growth hormone and human placental lactogen.
- *Hypertrophy and hyperplasia of uterine smooth muscle* at puberty and in pregnancy, stimulated by oestrogens.
- *Thyroid hyperplasia* as a consequence of the increased metabolic demands of puberty and pregnancy.

In addition to such physiologically increased tissue growth, hypertrophy and hyperplasia are also seen in tissues in a wide range of *pathological* conditions.

Pathological hypertrophy and hyperplasia

Many pathological conditions are characterised by hypertrophy or hyperplasia of cells. In some instances, this is the principal feature of the condition from which the disease is named. The more common examples are summarised in Table 5.1. For more detail, consult the relevant chapters.

Apparently autonomous hyperplasias
In some apparently hyperplastic conditions, cells appear autonomous, and continue to proliferate rapidly despite the lack of a demonstrable stimulus or control mechanism. The question then arises as to whether these should be considered to be hyperplasias at all, or whether they are autonomous

and hence neoplastic. If the cells can be demonstrated to be monoclonal (derived as a single clone from one cell), then this suggests that the lesion may indeed be neoplastic, but clonality is often difficult to establish.

Three examples are:

- *psoriasis*, characterised by marked epidermal hyperplasia (Ch. 24)
- *Paget's disease of bone*, in which there is hyperplasia of osteoblasts and osteoclasts resulting in thick but weak bone (Ch. 25)
- *fibromatoses*, which are apparently autonomous proliferations of myofibroblasts, occasionally forming tumour-like masses, exemplified by palmar fibromatosis (Dupuytren's contracture), desmoid tumour, retroperitoneal fibromatosis and Peyronie's disease of the penis.

Hyperplasia in tissue repair

The proliferation of vascular (capillary) endothelial cells and myofibroblasts in scar tissue, and the regeneration of specialised cells within a tissue, are the important components of the response to tissue damage.

Angiogenesis is the process whereby new blood vessels grow into damaged, ischaemic or necrotic tissues in order to supply oxygen and nutrients for cells involved in regeneration and repair (the term 'vasculogenesis' should be reserved

Table 5.1 Examples of non-regenerative hypertrophy and hyperplasia

Organ/tissue	Condition	Comment
Myocardium	Right ventricular hypertrophy	Response to pulmonary valve stenosis, pulmonary hypertension or ventricular septal defect (Ch. 13)
	Left ventricular hypertrophy	Response to aortic valve stenosis or systemic hypertension (Ch. 13)
Arterial smooth muscle	Hypertrophy of arterial walls	Occurs in hypertension (Ch. 13)
Capillary vessels	Proliferative retinopathy	Complication of diabetes mellitus (Ch. 26)
Bone marrow	Erythrocyte precursor hyperplasia	Response to increased erythropoietin production (e.g. due to hypoxia) (Ch. 23)
Cytotoxic T-lymphocytes	Hyperplastic expansion of T-cell populations	Involved in cell-mediated immune responses (Ch. 9)
Breast	Juvenile hypertrophy (females)	Exaggerated pubertal enlargement (Ch. 18)
	Gynaecomastia (males)	Due to high oestrogen levels (e.g. in cirrhosis, iatrogenic, endocrine tumours) (Ch. 18)
Prostate	Epithelial and connective tissue hyperplasia	Relative excess of oestrogens stimulates oestrogen-sensitive central zone (Ch. 20)
Thyroid	Follicular epithelial hyperplasia	Most commonly due to a thyroid-stimulating antibody (Graves' disease) (Ch. 17)
Adrenal cortex	Cortical hyperplasia	Response to increased ACTH production (e.g. from a pituitary tumour or, inappropriately, from a lung carcinoma) (Ch. 17)
Myointimal cells	Myointimal cell hyperplasia in atheromatous plaques	Myointimal cells in plaques proliferate in response to platelet-derived growth factor (Ch. 13)

specifically for the blood vessel proliferation that occurs in the developing embryo and fetus). In response to local tissue damage, vascular endothelial cells within pre-existing capillaries are activated by angiogenic growth factors such as vascular endothelial growth factor (VEGF), released by hypoxic cells or macrophages. These activated endothelial cells then migrate towards the angiogenic stimulus to form a 'sprout'. Cell migration is facilitated by the secretion of enzymes including the matrix metalloproteinases, which selectively degrade extracellular matrix proteins. Adjacent sprouts connect to form vascular loops, which canalise and establish a blood flow. Later, mesenchymal cells—including pericytes and smooth muscle cells—are recruited to stabilise the vascular architecture, and the extracellular matrix is remodelled.

Two other initiating mechanisms exist in addition to the above 'sprouting' form of angiogenesis: existing vascular channels may be bisected by an extracellular matrix 'pillar' (intussusception), with the two channels subsequently being extended towards the angiogenic stimulus. The final mechanism involves circulating primordial stem cells which are recruited at sites of hypoxia and differentiate into activated vascular endothelial cells. Note that a similar process of angiogenesis occurs in response to tumour cells, as an essential component of the development of the blood supply of enlarging neoplasms. Such angiogenesis is a potential therapeutic target in the treatment of malignant neoplasms,

although theoretically such drugs might impair angiogenesis and therefore delay healing of wounds.

Myofibroblasts often follow new blood vessels into damaged tissues, where they proliferate and produce matrix proteins such as fibronectin and collagen to strengthen the scar. Myofibroblasts eventually contract and differentiate into fibroblasts. The resulting contraction of the scar may cause important complications, such as:

- deformity and reduced movements of limbs affected by extensive scarring following skin burns around joints
- bowel stenosis and obstruction caused by annular scarring
- detachment of the retina due to traction caused by contraction of fibrovascular adhesions between the retina and the ciliary body following intra-ocular inflammation.

Thus vascular endothelial cell and myofibroblast hyperplasia are important components of repair and regeneration at various sites in the body, as described below.

Skin

The healing of a skin wound is a complex process involving the removal of necrotic debris from the wound and repair of the defect by hyperplasia of capillaries, myofibroblasts and epithelial cells. Figure 5.8 illustrates some of the key events, most of which are mediated by growth factors.

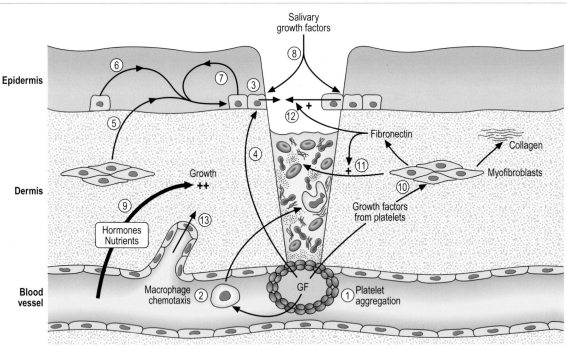

Fig. 5.8 Factors mediating wound healing. A wound is shown penetrating the skin and entering a blood vessel. **(1)** Blood coagulation and platelet degranulation, releasing growth factors (GF). **(2)** These are chemotactic for macrophages, which migrate into the wound to phagocytose bacteria and necrotic debris **(3)**. Epidermal basal epithelial cells are activated by released growth factors from the platelets **(4)** and dermal myofibroblasts **(5)**; from epidermal cells by paracrine **(6)** and autocrine **(7)** mechanisms; and from saliva **(8)** (if the wound is licked). Nutrients and oxygen **(9)** and circulating hormones and growth factors diffusing from blood vessels all contribute to epidermal growth. Growth factors from the platelets stimulate cell division in myofibroblasts **(10)**, which produce collagen and fibronectin. Fibronectin stimulates migration of dermal myofibroblasts **(11)** and epidermal epithelial cells **(12)** into and over the wound. Angiogenic growth factors (not shown) stimulate the proliferation and migration of new blood vessels into the area of the wound **(13)**.

When tissue injury occurs there is haemorrhage into the defect from damaged blood vessels; this is controlled by normal haemostatic mechanisms, during which platelets aggregate and thrombus forms to plug the defect in the vessel wall. Because of interactions between the coagulation and complement systems, inflammatory cells are attracted to the site of injury by chemotactic complement fractions. In addition, platelets release two potent growth factors, platelet-derived growth factor (PDGF) and transforming growth factor-beta (TGF-beta), which are powerfully chemotactic for inflammatory cells, including macrophages; these migrate into the wound to remove necrotic tissue and fibrin.

In the *epidermis*, PDGF acts synergistically with epidermal growth factor (EGF), derived from epidermal cells, and the somatomedins, insulin-like growth factor 1 (IGF-1) and insulin-like growth factor 2 (IGF-2), to promote proliferation of basal epithelial cells. EGF is also present in high concentrations in saliva and may reach wounds when they are licked. In the *dermis*, myofibroblasts proliferate in response to PDGF (and TGF-beta); collagen and fibronectin secretion is stimulated by TGF-beta, and fibronectin then aids migration of epithelial and dermal cells. Capillary budding and proliferation are stimulated by angiogenic factors such as VEGF. The capillaries ease the access of inflammatory cells and fibroblasts, particularly into large areas of necrotic tissue.

Hormones (e.g. insulin and thyroid hormones) and nutrients (e.g. glucose and amino acids) are also required. Lack of nutrients or vitamins, the presence of inhibitory factors such as corticosteroids or infection, or a locally poor circulation with low tissue oxygen concentrations, may all materially delay wound healing; these factors are very important in clinical practice.

Liver

In severe chronic hepatitis (Ch. 16) extensive hepatocyte loss is followed by scarring, as is the case in the skin or other damaged tissues. Like epidermal cells in the skin, hepatocytes have massive regenerative potential and surviving hepatocytes may proliferate to form nodules. Hyperplasia of hepatocytes and fibroblasts is presumably mediated by a combination of hormones and growth factors, although the mechanisms are far from clear. Regenerative nodules of hepatocytes and scar tissue are the components of cirrhosis of the liver.

Heart

Myocardial cells are permanent cells (i.e. they remain permanently in G_0 and cannot enter G_1), and so cannot divide in a regenerative response to tissue injury. In myocardial infarction, a segment of muscle dies and, if the patient survives, it is replaced by scar tissue. As the remainder of the myocardium must work harder for a given cardiac output, it undergoes compensatory hypertrophy (without cell division) (Fig. 5.9). Occasionally, there may be right ventricular hypertrophy as a result of left ventricular failure and consequent pulmonary hypertension.

Decreased growth: atrophy

> ▶ Atrophy: decrease in size of an organ or cell
> ▶ Organ atrophy may be due to reduction in cell size or number, or both

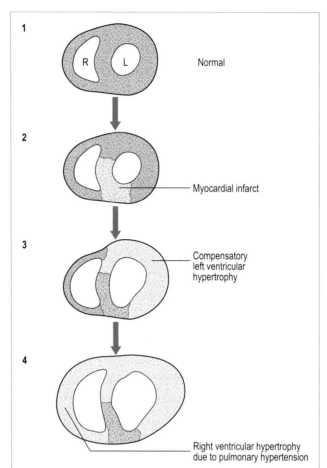

Fig. 5.9 Cardiac hypertrophy. A horizontal slice through the myocardium of the left (L) and right (R) ventricles. **(1)** Normal. **(2)** Area of anteroseptal left ventricular infarct. **(3)** Compensatory hypertrophy of the surviving left ventricle. **(4)** Right ventricular hypertrophy secondary to left ventricular failure and pulmonary hypertension.

> ▶ May be mediated by apoptosis
> ▶ Atrophy may be physiological (e.g. post-menopausal atrophy of uterus)
> ▶ Pathological atrophy may be due to decreased function (e.g. an immobilised limb), loss of innervation, reduced blood or oxygen supply, nutritional impairment or hormonal insufficiency

Atrophy is the decrease in size of an organ or cell by reduction in cell size and/or reduction in cell numbers, often by a mechanism involving apoptosis. Tissues or cells affected by atrophy are said to be atrophic or atrophied. Atrophy is an important adaptive response to a decreased requirement of the body for the function of a particular cell or organ. It is important to appreciate that for atrophy to occur there must be not only a cessation of growth but also an active reduction in cell size and/or a decrease in cell numbers, mediated by apoptosis.

Atrophy occurs in both physiological and pathological conditions.

Physiological atrophy and involution

Physiological atrophy occurs at times from very early embryological life, as part of the process of morphogenesis. The process of atrophy (mediated by apoptosis of cells) contributes to the physiological involution of organs such as the thymus gland in early adult life, and late old age is accompanied by atrophy of various tissues (Table 5.2).

Pathological atrophy

There are several categories of pathological condition in which atrophy may occur.

Decreased function

As a result of decreased function as, for example, in a limb immobilised as a consequence of a fracture, there may be marked muscle atrophy (due to decrease in muscle fibre size). Extensive physiotherapy may be required to restore the muscle to its former bulk, or to prevent the atrophy.

In extreme cases of 'disuse' atrophy of a limb, bone atrophy may lead to osteoporosis and bone weakening; this is also a feature of conditions of prolonged weightlessness, such as occurs in astronauts.

Loss of innervation

Loss of innervation of muscle causes muscle atrophy, as is seen in nerve transection or in poliomyelitis, where there is loss of anterior horn cells of the spinal cord. In paraplegics, loss of innervation to whole limbs may also precipitate 'disuse' atrophy of bone, which becomes osteoporotic.

Loss of blood supply

This may cause atrophy as a result of tissue hypoxia, which may also be a result of a sluggish circulation. Epidermal atrophy is seen, for example, in the skin of the lower legs in patients with circulatory stagnation related to varicose veins or with atheromatous narrowing of arteries.

'Pressure' atrophy

This occurs when tissues are compressed, by either exogenous agents (atrophy of skin and soft tissues overlying the sacrum in bedridden patients producing 'bed sores') or endogenous factors (atrophy of a blood vessel wall compressed by a tumour). In both of these circumstances a major factor is actually local tissue hypoxia.

Lack of nutrition

Lack of nutrition may cause atrophy of adipose tissue, the gut and pancreas and, in extreme circumstances, muscle. An extreme form of systemic atrophy similar to that seen in severe starvation is termed 'cachexia'; this may be seen in patients in the late stages of severe illnesses such as cancer. In some wasting conditions, such as cancer, cytokines such as tumour necrosis factor (TNF) are postulated to influence the development of cachexia.

Loss of endocrine stimulation

Atrophy of the 'target' organ of a hormone may occur if endocrine stimulation is inadequate. For example, the adrenal gland atrophies as a consequence of decreased ACTH secretion by

Table 5.2 Tissues involved in physiological atrophy and involution	
Embryo and fetus	**Early adult**
Branchial clefts	Thymus
Notochord	
Thyroglossal duct	**Late adult and old age**
Müllerian duct (males)	Uterus, endometrium (females)
Wolffian duct (females)	Testes (males)
	Bone (particularly females)
Neonate	Gums
Umbilical vessels	Mandible (particularly edentulous)
Ductus arteriosus	Cerebrum
Fetal layer adrenal cortex	Lymphoid tissue

the anterior pituitary; this may be caused by destruction of the anterior pituitary (by a tumour or infarction), or as a result of the therapeutic use of high concentrations of corticosteroids (in, for example, the treatment of cancer), with consequent 'feedback' reduction of circulating ACTH levels.

Hormone-induced atrophy

This form of atrophy may be seen in the skin, as a result of the growth-inhibiting actions of corticosteroids. When corticosteroids are applied topically in high concentrations to the skin, they may cause dermal and epidermal atrophy which may be disfiguring. All steroids, when applied topically, may also be absorbed through the skin to produce systemic side-effects, e.g. adrenal atrophy when corticosteroids are used.

Decreased growth: hypoplasia

▶ Hypoplasia: failure of development of an organ
▶ Process is related to atrophy
▶ Failure of morphogenesis

Although the terms 'hypoplasia' and 'atrophy' are often used interchangeably, the former is better reserved to denote the failure in attainment of the normal size or shape of an organ as a consequence of a developmental failure. Hypoplasia is, therefore, a failure in morphogenesis, although it is closely related to atrophy in terms of its pathogenesis. An example of hypoplasia is the failure in development of the legs in adult patients with severe spina bifida and neurological deficit in the lower limbs.

Metaplasia

▶ An acquired form of altered differentiation
▶ Transformation of one mature differentiated cell type into another
▶ Response to altered cellular environment
▶ Affects epithelial or mesenchymal cells
▶ Often associated with an increased risk of malignancy (e.g. squamous cell carcinoma associated with squamous metaplasia in bronchi)

Metaplasia is the transformation of one type of differentiated cell into another fully differentiated cell type. It occurs in the context of alterations in the cellular environment, particularly if associated with chronic cellular injury and repair. Metaplasia may be due to the inappropriate activation or repression of groups of genes involved in the maintenance of cellular differentiation, or by mutations in such genes. The metaplastic 'daughter' cells replace the original cells, giving rise to a tissue type that may in some circumstances be better able to withstand the adverse environmental changes.

Examples of metaplasia in *epithelial* tissues include a change to squamous epithelium (squamous metaplasia) in a variety of tissues, including:

- ciliated respiratory epithelium of the trachea and bronchi in smokers (Fig. 5.10)
- ducts of the salivary glands and pancreas, and bile ducts in the presence of stones
- transitional bladder epithelium in the presence of stones, and in the presence of ova of the trematode *Schistosoma haematobium*
- transitional and columnar nasal epithelium in vitamin A deficiency.

Another example is the replacement of normal squamous epithelium of the oesophagus by columnar glandular epithelium (glandular metaplasia), sometimes showing overt intestinal differentiation. This condition, known as Barrett's oesophagus, is caused by the chronic reflux of gastro-duodenal contents, including acid and bile, into the oesophagus.

Examples of metaplasia in *mesenchymal* tissues are bone formation (osseous metaplasia):

- following calcium deposition in atheromatous arterial walls
- in bronchial cartilage
- following longstanding disease of the uveal tract of the eye.

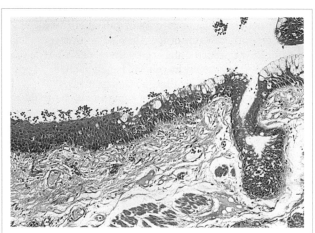

Fig. 5.10 Squamous metaplasia in the bronchus of a smoker.
On the right is the mature ciliated pseudostratified columnar epithelium. On the left, the epithelium has undergone metaplasia to a thicker, mature, stratified squamous epithelium.

Metaplasia is frequently associated with the subsequent development of malignancy within the metaplastic tissue. This is presumably because the environmental changes that initially caused the metaplasia may also induce dysplasia, which, if it is persistent, may progress to tumour formation.

Metaplasia is sometimes said to occur in tumours as, for example, in squamous or glandular 'metaplasia', which may occur in transitional carcinomas of the bladder. These examples of disordered cellular differentiation certainly do occur in tumours, but the term 'metaplasia' is best reserved for changes in non-neoplastic tissues.

Dysplasia

> ▸ Dysplasia is characterised by increased cell proliferation (e.g. more mitoses visible than normal), presence of atypical morphology (e.g. abnormally large nuclei), and decreased differentiation (e.g. cellular immaturity)
> ▸ May be caused by chronic physical or chemical injury
> ▸ May be reversible only in early stages
> ▸ Dysplastic lesions are often pre-neoplastic

Dysplasia is a *premalignant* condition characterised by increased cell proliferation, the presence of cellular atypia, and decreased differentiation. It may be caused by longstanding irritation and injury of a tissue with chronic inflammation, or by exposure to carcinogenic substances. Whilst early mild forms of dysplasia may be reversible if the initial stimulus is removed, severe dysplasia is a reflection of underlying DNA damage and such lesions may progress to frank malignancy without appropriate treatment.

In affected tissues, dysplasia may be recognised by:

- evidence of increased growth, such as increased tissue bulk (e.g. increased epithelial thickness), and increased numbers of mitoses
- presence of cellular atypia, with pleomorphism (variation in the size and shape of cells and their nuclei), a high nuclear/cytoplasmic ratio and increased nuclear DNA content (recognised by hyperchromasia, i.e. more darkly stained nuclei)
- decreased differentiation, as the cells often appear more primitive than normal. For example, dysplastic squamous epithelium may not show the normal differentiation from basal cells to flattened surface cells of the skin; this appearance is described as showing 'loss of epithelial polarity'.

Dysplasia may occur in tissue that has coincident metaplasia (e.g. dysplasia developing in metaplastic squamous epithelium from the bronchus of smokers). Dysplasia may also develop without co-existing metaplasia, for example in squamous epithelium of the uterine cervix, glandular epithelium of the stomach, or the liver.

Dysplasia may be present for many years before a malignant neoplasm develops. This is the rationale for screening programmes, such as the cervical cancer screening programme, in which early dysplastic changes can be identified and appropriate treatment given before the condition progresses to malignancy.

The term 'dysplasia' is sometimes used misleadingly to denote the failure of differentiation of an organ which may retain primitive embryological structures. To avoid confusion, it is better to substitute the terms 'maldifferentiation' or 'dysgenesis' for this condition.

Polyps

The term 'polyp' is used to describe the macroscopic ('naked eye') appearance of a smooth mass of tissue that projects outwards from the surface of an organ. Polyps are described as 'sessile' when they are flat and 'pedunculated' when they have a stalk.

The term 'polyposis' is used to describe a condition or syndrome where there are multiple polyps in an organ (e.g. polyposis coli, affecting the colon) or an organ system (e.g. hamartomatous polyposis of the gastrointestinal tract in Peutz–Jeghers syndrome).

The term 'polyp', when used alone and without further qualification, is purely descriptive of the shape of a lesion and does not signify any specific underlying pathological process (such as hyperplasia, metaplasia, dysplasia or neoplasia). A polyp results from focal tissue expansion at a site at (or near) the organ surface, when the enlarging mass takes the line of least mechanical resistance as it expands outwards, rather than into the underlying tissue. The pathological process that causes both the focal tissue expansion and polyp formation may be either non-neoplastic (e.g. inflammation, hyperplasia, metaplasia, dysplasia) or neoplastic (e.g. neoplasms of epithelial, mesenchymal, lymphoid or other cellular origin). Non-neoplastic polyps and most neoplastic polyps are common and benign, but a small proportion of malignant neoplasms can have a polypoid appearance (e.g. lymphomatous polyposis of the gastrointestinal tract; polypoid adenocarcinoma of the large bowel).

Neoplasia

> ▸ Neoplasia is characterised by abnormal, unco-ordinated and excessive cell proliferation
> ▸ Persists after initiating stimulus has been withdrawn
> ▸ Associated with genetic alterations
> ▸ Neoplastic cells influence behaviour of normal cells by the production of hormones and growth factors

The word 'neoplasia' literally means 'new growth', and the lesion so produced is termed a neoplasm. A neoplasm is an abnormal tissue mass, the excessive growth of which is unco-ordinated with that of normal tissues, and which persists after the removal of the neoplasm-inducing stimulus. The term tumour is often used to denote a neoplasm. Numerous factors have been implicated in the development of human tumours, and these are discussed in detail in Chapter 11.

Cell proliferation is essential in development and in adult life. Carefully regulated cell proliferation permits the growth, maintenance and repair of tissues and organs, and allows the body to respond flexibly to various environmental stimuli.

Neoplasia results from acquired damage to critical genes that encode the proteins responsible for regulating the proliferation of individual cells, and manifests as excessive and purposeless growth. There are multiple steps in the development of neoplasms, and many of these involve subversion of the normally controlled mechanisms of growth and cellular differentiation, e.g. hormones, growth factors and growth factor-simulating proteins such as some of the oncoproteins. The growth of neoplasms continues in an autonomous manner, in the absence of normal physiological stimuli and without normal negative feedback mechanisms to arrest the cellular proliferation. Finally, it is worth noting that in continually renewing tissues, such as skin or gut epithelium, the only cells that are likely to persist for sufficient time to acquire the number of genetic changes needed for development of such neoplasms are the stem cells (p. 92); cancers in these tissues can therefore be viewed as disorders of the relevant stem cells.

SYSTEMIC GROWTH DISORDERS

The most rapid normal growth occurs during fetal life, when the embryo undergoes the equivalent of some 42 cell divisions in progressing from a fertilised ovum to term (at 40 weeks), with only five more cell divisions needed to achieve adult size. In the first 2 months of embryological life, differing rates of growth, death and migration of cells are responsible for morphogenesis (development of form) within the developing fetus. Maximal growth velocity, however, does not occur until about 20 weeks (for body length) and 34 weeks (for body weight) of gestation; growth velocity then slows until term.

Despite apparently precise genetic programming of growth, marked variations in birth size can occur due to either normal physiological processes or disease. The most obvious manifestation of growth is an increase in height, which is largely a function of longitudinal skeletal growth. In infancy and childhood there may be variations in height between individuals of the same sex, but the most important normal variations are those between the heights of the two sexes. In childhood, girls are typically shorter than boys, but they become temporarily taller than boys as a result of their pre-pubertal growth spurt (9 cm/year), which starts at around 10.5 years of age. The boys' growth spurt starts at about 12.5 years, but the higher growth velocity (10.3 cm/year) results in their overtaking the girls in height at about 14 years, and accounts for the final height advantage in boys.

Within an individual, different parts of the body do not follow the same pattern as longitudinal growth. Children have relatively larger heads compared with the trunk and legs than do adults. The reproductive organs grow little before puberty, but then increase rapidly in size. Lymphoid organs grow maximally before puberty, and their growth velocity decreases before skeletal growth velocity.

Growth is controlled by and susceptible to variations in:

- hormones and growth factors
- genetic factors
- nutrition
- environmental factors
- disease.

Endocrinological growth control and its disorders

Cells may be stimulated into growth by the action of hormones and growth factors (Fig. 5.11). *Hormones* are synthesised and stored in specific tissues (glands) and released into the blood to exert their effect on distant target cells; this is the *endocrine* mechanism. Individual *growth factors* are synthesised in many different cell types throughout the body. They often act on the cell in which they are synthesised (an *autocrine* mechanism), or on nearby cells in the same tissue (a *paracrine* mechanism), but they may have additional endocrine actions on distant cells via the blood stream.

Individual hormones and growth factors require highly specific cellular receptors to mediate their actions on target cells. Steroid hormone receptors are intracellular, but receptors for peptide hormones and growth factors are located on the cell membrane. A high concentration of a receptor renders a cell highly susceptible to the actions of a hormone or growth factor; conversely, the absence of a receptor leads to hormone or growth factor insensitivity.

Post-natal growth

In post-natal life, growth is controlled by an endocrine pathway that regulates total body size (Fig. 5.12). Growth hormone (GH) is central to the endocrine control of post-natal growth.

The release of GH from the pituitary is regulated by the opposing actions of hypothalamic growth hormone releasing factor (GRF) and the inhibitory hormone somatostatin. Growth hormone acts via intermediary hormones—the somatomedins, IGF-1 and IGF-2; these are predominantly (but not exclusively) synthesised in the liver. Somatomedins may also be released from the liver under the influence of insulin, sex-steroid hormones, thyroid hormone and nutritional factors. Growth hormone may have a minor direct anabolic effect on non-skeletal tissues, but here too IGF-1 and IGF-2 are quantitatively more important.

Again, it is important to appreciate that each of the above hormone actions is mediated via individual specific cellular

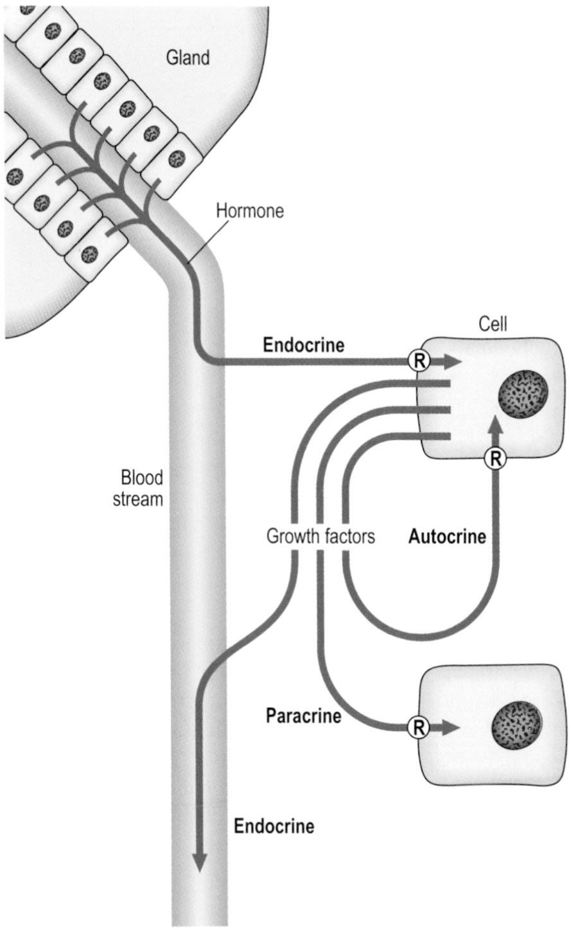

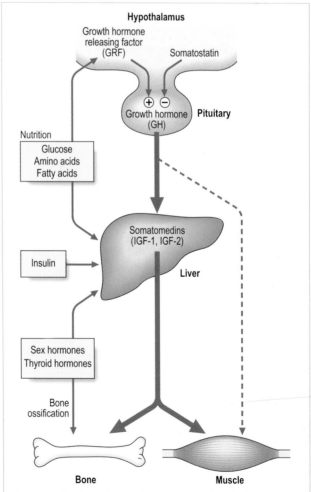

Fig. 5.11 Endocrine, paracrine and autocrine mechanisms of hormones and growth factors. In each case, the hormone and growth factors have their effects through specific receptors **(R)**.

Fig. 5.12 Post-natal growth. The hormonal control of post-natal growth is mediated by hypothalamic and pituitary hormones, and liver somatomedins—the insulin-like growth factors 1 and 2 (IGF-1 and IGF-2).

receptor proteins, the concentration of which principally determines the sensitivity of the target cell to the hormone.

Reduced growth

Reduced GH production due to hypopituitarism (of whatever pathological cause) in childhood leads to dwarfism, which can be corrected by regular GH injections given before puberty arrests skeletal growth by epiphyseal fusion. Dwarfism due to GH deficiency is characterised by normal body proportions, in contrast to the effects of reduced thyroid hormones (see below).

Reduced GH receptors are a feature of the rare Laron dwarfism. Although circulating GH concentrations are high, the liver is insensitive to GH, and circulating somatomedins are greatly reduced. Treatment with GH will not increase growth rate.

Reduced thyroid hormone secretion causes a reduction in hepatic IGF-1 secretion. In the resultant dwarfism, the head is of normal size but the limbs are stunted because bone ossification is reduced. Treatment with GH has no effect, but thyroxine is corrective if given before puberty.

Block between GH and IGF-1 release may occur in malnutrition or emotionally based growth retardation, although the metabolite-mobilising actions of GH are maintained. IGF-1 levels correlate positively with the protein content of the diet and nitrogen balance.

Inhibition of growth by corticosteroids may occur with endogenous corticosteroids, e.g. Cushing's disease, or with exogenous corticosteroids used, for example, in the treatment of asthma or leukaemia.

Increased growth

Increased GH secretion from a normal pituitary or a pituitary tumour results in increased IGF-1 and increased growth. Before puberty this causes *gigantism;* after puberty, longitudinal skeletal growth cannot occur (due to maturation and ossification with resulting epiphyseal fusion), but the hands, feet and head increase in size to produce *acromegaly*.

Increased sex-steroid hormone secretion in childhood may lead to precocious puberty, with an initial increase in height resulting from a premature rise in pubertal IGF-1 levels. However, epiphyseal fusion in long bones is accelerated, and the final height may be *below* normal.

Embryo and fetal growth

The control of growth later in fetal life is very different from that in the post-natal child. The fetus is a self-contained unit with respect to growth, as maternal peptide and thyroid hormones do not cross the placenta in physiologically significant concentrations and, although sex-steroid hormones and other steroids do cross the placenta, they are generally metabolised into inactive forms.

The fetus produces its own GH, but this is not used to promote growth as the GH receptor is greatly reduced in the fetus (particularly in the liver). Indeed, fetal growth does not require any pituitary hormonal influence, and anencephalic human fetuses often attain normal weights for gestational age.

The most important growth-regulating hormone in the fetus is, without doubt, insulin (Fig. 5.13). As in the adult, blood insulin concentrations in the fetus are controlled by

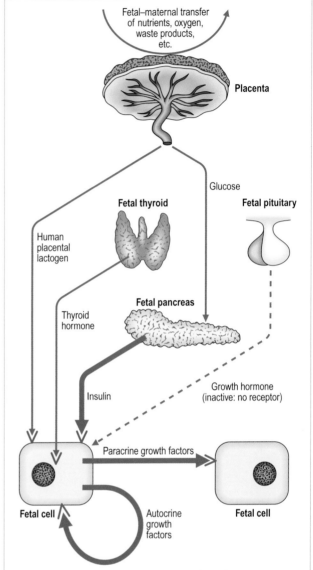

Fig. 5.13 Fetal growth regulation. Insulin is the major hormone stimulating growth in the fetus; its action is mediated by growth factors. Growth hormone receptors are not present during most of fetal life. Placental and thyroid hormones are also important.

glucose concentrations, and both insulin and glucose are required for normal metabolic functions of the fetus and the placenta. In addition, however, insulin directly stimulates the production of growth factors (in particular the somatomedin IGF-2) in cells, and these act on the IGF-2-synthesising cells and adjacent cells, by autocrine and paracrine mechanisms respectively, to stimulate growth. Additional, but relatively less important, effects on growth factor synthesis are stimulated by human placental lactogen (HPL)—a hormone that has marked structural similarity to GH, and is synthesised by the placenta—and fetal thyroid hormones. Although fetal growth is not GH-mediated, somatomedins (particularly IGF-2 in the fetus) are important, although they are not yet under GH control. Other growth factors, such as EGF, PDGF,

TGF-beta and nerve growth factor (NGF), are probably also involved.

Birth weight

Many factors may affect fetal growth rate and ultimate size (Table 5.3). Although insulin levels are crucial, the most common causes of low birth weight are premature delivery (before 40 weeks' gestation) and genetically controlled small size (a small baby born to small parents). It is therefore important to relate the birth weight first to gestational age and then to allow for parental size.

Reduced growth

Reduced fetal insulin production may lead to a low birth weight, e.g. 1.2–2 kg (normal mean 3 kg). The causes are uncommon, and include:

- fetal diabetes mellitus.
- pancreatic agenesis (failure of development).

Reduced fetal insulin receptors, with resultant insensitivity to circulating insulin, cause a similar growth reduction (the rare Leprechaun syndrome).

Increased growth

Increased growth occurs due to increased circulating insulin levels in the fetus (hyperinsulinaemia).

Diabetic mothers may have heavy infants, although birth lengths are not usually increased. Increased glucose diffuses passively into the fetus from the mother, stimulating fetal insulin secretion. The increased weight is due mainly to excess fat.

Infants with hyperinsulinaemia associated with the rare condition *nesidioblastosis* (an uncontrolled proliferation of pancreatic endocrine cells) or Beckwith–Weidemann syndrome (see below) are more obviously overgrown, e.g. birth weight 4.5–5.5 kg (normal mean 3 kg).

Table 5.3 Factors affecting fetal growth rate and size	
Factors	**Examples**
Decreased growth	
Genetic	Small parents Racial origin (e.g. pygmies)
Endocrine	Reduced fetal insulin or insulin receptor levels (rare)
Nutrition	Maternal intake <1500 kcal/day
Intra-uterine environment	Placental disease Decreased oxygen (high altitude) Maternal smoking Maternal alcohol consumption Maternal drug abuse Infection
Increased growth	
Endocrine	Fetal hyperinsulinaemia (e.g. in maternal diabetes mellitus)

Genetic factors in growth control

The most important genetic factors that regulate the height of an individual are:

- parental height, probably mediated by multifactorial genetically controlled endocrinological factors
- the sex of the individual, mediated by sex-steroid hormones (as discussed above).

As such a large number of hormones, growth factors, receptors, enzymes and other proteins play a co-ordinated role in normal growth, it is not surprising that a wide range of chromosomal abnormalities can interfere with normal growth. Some of these conditions are inherited; others are the result of sporadic gene mutation or chromosomal aberration. Some conditions are incompatible with life; others are compatible with a normal life modified only by reduced stature.

Primary genetically mediated growth abnormalities are classified into two broad groups, according to whether growth of the limbs and/or trunk with respect to the head is *proportionate* or *disproportionate*.

Proportionate alterations of skeletal growth

Autosomal chromosomes
Proportionate alterations of skeletal growth may result from abnormalities of autosomal chromosomes including:

- *pygmies*: genetically mediated inability to make the somatomedin IGF-1 (chromosome 12), or defects in IGF receptor function
- *Down's syndrome*: short stature associated with trisomy 21 (extra 21 chromosome)
- *Beckwith–Weidemann syndrome*: increased growth due to a rare duplication of the short arm of chromosome 11 (carrying the genes for insulin and the somatomedin IGF-2).

Sex chromosomes (X and Y)
Sex chromosome abnormalities leading to proportional abnormalities of skeletal growth include:

- *Turner's syndrome*: females have an XO rather than XX genotype. In its most extreme form, girls have no ovaries, and lack of oestrogen prevents a normal pubertal growth spurt.
- *pseudohypoparathyroidism*: a very rare X-linked dominant condition characterised by tissue insensitivity to parathyroid hormone (PTH), probably due to reduced or absent PTH receptors.

Disproportionate alterations of skeletal growth

Disproportionate shortness of stature at birth is often the result of the genetically mediated *osteochondrodysplasias* (specific disorders of growth of bone and/or cartilage). These can be classified into two groups, depending upon whether the disproportionate shortness of limbs is, or is not, accompanied by a significantly shortened spine. Examples of these conditions include the following.

Achondroplasia

Achondroplasia, the most common of the osteochondrodysplasias, is an autosomal dominant condition (although there are many sporadic cases). The genetically mediated defect is considered to be a primary disturbance of endochondral ossification which occurs in early life and is well established by birth (although severely affected fetuses may die towards the end of pregnancy). Patients with achondroplasia, if they survive the neonatal period, usually reach adult life but with reduced stature. They have severe shortening of the limbs (hypomelia or micromelia), with long bones as little as half the normal length. Epiphyses are greatly enlarged, and the shafts of long bones widen to surround the enlarged epiphyses at the ends of long bones. Accompanying changes in the base of the skull may cause narrowing of the foramen magnum, with spinal cord compression. The spine itself is not shortened.

Rare osteochondrodysplasias

Many (but not all) of these rare conditions have an autosomal recessive mode of inheritance. They include severe conditions such as achondrogenesis, which is incompatible with life, and conditions such as pseudoachondroplasia, where the spine is shortened in addition to the limbs.

Nutritional factors in growth control

Maternal nutrition, surprisingly, has a very small influence on human fetal size, and even severe food deprivation results in little more than a 200–300 g reduction in birth weight. In the Dutch winter famine of 1944, birth weight declined only when maternal nutritional input was less than 1500 kcal per day, and then by no more than 500 g.

The fetus is, however, highly susceptible to placental disorders such as infection or to partial detachment, both of which reduce the fetal intake of nutrients and impair gas exchange; the result, if not fatal, may be a severe reduction in birth weight. Small local defects, such as small haemangiomas, do not affect placental function, and hence do not affect growth.

In *post-natal life*, growth may be severely affected by low or poorly balanced nutritional intake. Starvation, in the form of kwashiorkor (protein deprivation) or marasmus (protein and total calorie deprivation; see Ch. 7), severely disturbs growth endocrinology, producing a negative nitrogen balance as part of a catabolic state.

Environmental factors in growth control

Fetal growth can be affected by several physiological and pathological environmental factors:

- *Uterine size.* The size of the uterus is an important constraining influence on fetal size, as shown in classic experiments by Walton and Hammond in 1938 in which reciprocal hybrids of the huge Shire horse and the tiny Shetland pony grew much larger in the uterus of the Shire horse than the Shetland pony. Clinical observations of humans suggest that the uterine effect on fetal growth occurs late in gestation, and does not affect the fetus during early pregnancy.

- *Altitude.* Infants born at an altitude of 15 000 feet (4570 m) have a birth weight 16% less than infants born at 500 feet (150 m); this is due to decreased intra-uterine oxygen availability.

- *Maternal smoking.* The effect of smoking 20 cigarettes per day is to reduce birth weight by about 200 g (about 7%), probably by reducing uterine blood flow.

- *Maternal alcohol abuse.* This retards fetal growth, and catch-up growth does not occur. Fetuses may be microcephalic, with hypotonia and mental retardation. Cardiac atrial septal defects are common, and there may be altered facies (facial features). This is the 'fetal alcohol syndrome'.

- *Maternal drug abuse.* About half of the fetuses exposed to heroin have a low birth weight. The mechanism is uncertain, but it may involve co-existent socio-economic factors rather than a direct effect of heroin. The newborn infants often develop withdrawal symptoms.

Post-natal environmental growth effects can be seen in children suffering from emotional deprivation or physical abuse, who may have a reduced rate of growth. Catch-up growth occurs following hospitalisation, without medication.

Effect of intercurrent disease on growth

The commonest growth alterations in childhood are those that are caused indirectly by a wide range of diseases, that decrease growth for the duration of the illness and are followed by a period of 'catch-up' growth. These diseases include common bacterial and viral illnesses experienced by many children. Some are relatively short-lived and the decreased growth may not be noticed. However, with increasing severity and chronicity of the illness, it is more likely that the growth disturbance will be noticeable and clinically significant. Thus, severe growth disturbance may be present in chronic cardiovascular or respiratory disease, renal disease, hepatic cirrhosis, chronic gastrointestinal disease (e.g. coeliac disease, Crohn's disease), and chronic infections such as AIDS, malaria or tuberculosis.

The effect of intercurrent diseases may compound growth disturbances due to the nutritional or environmental factors discussed above, and/or primary endocrinological or genetic growth disorders.

DIFFERENTIATION AND MORPHOGENESIS IN HUMAN DEVELOPMENT

Differentiation is the process whereby a cell develops an overt specialised function that was not present in the parent cell. It is an important component of morphogenesis; this is the means by which limbs or organs are formed from primitive groups of cells. Thus, abnormalities of differentiation often lead to abnormal morphogenesis and fetal abnormality. It must be remembered, however, that growth also plays an important role in morphogenesis; cells that vary in their differentiation may have very different growth characteristics. Variations in differentiation may also affect the ability of some cells to migrate with respect to others. Thus, normal embryological development requires highly co-ordinated processes of differentiation, growth and cell migration which together comprise morphogenesis.

Control of normal differentiation

> ▶ Embryonic differentiation of cells is controlled by genes, systemic hormones, position within the fetus, local growth factors and matrix proteins
> ▶ Maintenance of the differentiated state is dependent upon persistence of some of these factors
> ▶ Differentiation and morphogenesis may be disturbed by environmental factors (e.g. teratogens)

A fertilised ovum may develop into a male or female, a human or a blue whale; the outcome depends on the structure of the genome. There are many similarities between the corresponding cell types in different species. Individual cell types are distinct only because, in addition to the many universal proteins required by all cell types for 'housekeeping' functions such as cellular metabolism, each cell produces a characteristic set of specialised proteins which define that particular cell type.

Most differentiated cells contain the same genome as in the fertilised ovum. This has been demonstrated elegantly by injecting the nucleus of a differentiated tadpole gut epithelial cell into an unfertilised frog ovum, the nucleus of which was destroyed using ultraviolet light; the result was a normal frog with the normal variety of differentiated cell types (Fig. 5.14). More recently a variety of mammalian species—most notably a sheep—have been cloned from a single ovarian cell.

There are very few exceptions to the rule that differentiated cells contain an identical genome to that of the fertilised ovum. In humans, for example, they include B- and T-lymphocytes which have antigen receptor genes rearranged to endow them with a large repertoire of possible receptors (Ch. 9).

Transcriptional control

As most differentiated cells have an identical genome, differences between them cannot be due to amplification or deletion of genes. The cells of the body differ not in the range of genes present in each cell, but in how those genes are expressed, i.e. transcribed and translated into proteins. Genes are selectively switched on or off to control the synthesis of gene products.

The synthesis of a gene product can in theory be controlled at several levels:

- *transcription*: controlling the formation of mRNA
- *transport*: controlling the export of mRNA from the nucleus to the ribosomes in the cytoplasm
- *translation*: controlling the formation of gene product within the ribosomes.

In practice, the modulation of transcription is the main mechanism by which gene expression is regulated in many of the important 'decision' stages of differentiation in embryogenesis.

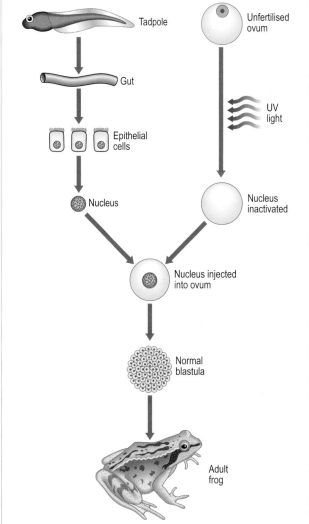

Fig. 5.14 Potential of the genome of somatic cells.
Differentiated cells from the gut of a tadpole have the complete genome and potential for control of production of the whole frog. (After J B Gurdon.)

For a cell to differentiate in a particular way, multiple genes must be switched on whilst many others must be switched off. There is now ample evidence that the regulation of transcription of entire groups of genes is mediated by the gene products of a small number of 'control' genes (or *transcription factors*), which may themselves be regulated by the product of a single 'master' gene (Fig. 5.15).

Positional control in early embryogenesis

Some insight into possible control mechanisms in human differentiation and morphogenesis has been gained from observations of the fruit fly, *Drosophila*. Disturbances of single 'master' genes in *Drosophila* have been shown to result in major malformations, such as the development of legs on the head in place of antennae, mediated by the response of many controlled genes to the alteration in 'master' gene product. Such a *homeotic* mutation (the transformation of one body

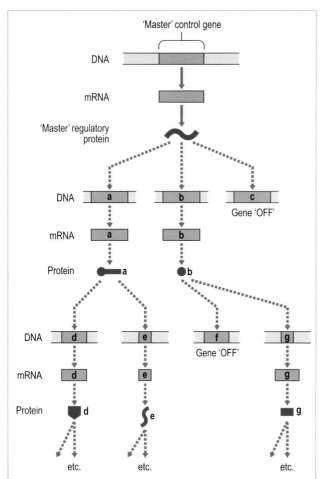

Fig. 5.15 Interaction of genes. A single 'master' gene produces a regulatory protein that switches genes **a** and **b** on and gene **c** off; these in turn switch on or off a cascade of other genes.

part into another part that is usually found on a different body segment) highlights the importance of another factor in the control of differentiation and morphogenesis, namely the three-dimensional spatial co-ordinates (position) of a cell within an embryo at a given time.

In *Drosophila*, a group of genes, which individually cause a range of homeotic mutations, have been found to share a 60-amino-acid sequence domain which is common to genes controlling normal larval segmentation. This sequence, named the *homeobox*, has also been demonstrated in vertebrates, including humans (Ch. 3). Homeobox-containing genes (also known as homeobox genes) are transcriptional regulators influencing morphogenesis. Parts of human anatomy appear to be constructed on a segmental basis, for example rows of somites, teeth and limb segments, and here it is probable that homeobox genes have an important morphogenetic role.

Cell determination

The homebox genes, and other genes that regulate embryogenesis, act on the embryo at a very early stage, before structures such as limbs have begun to form. Nonetheless, by observing the effects of selective marking or obliteration of

cells, a 'fate map' of the future development of cells in even primitive embryos can be constructed. Thus, some of the cells of somites become specialised at a very early stage as precursors of muscle cells, and migrate to their positions in primitive limbs. These muscle-cell precursors resemble many other cells of the limb rudiment, and it is only after several days that they differentiate and manufacture specialised muscle proteins. Thus, long before they differentiate, the developmental path of these cells is planned; such a cell which has made a developmental choice before differentiating is said to be *determined*. A determined cell must:

- have differences that are heritable from one cell generation to another
- be committed and commit its progeny to specialised development
- change its internal character, not merely its environment.

Determination therefore differs from differentiation, in which there must be *demonstrable* tissue specialisation.

Some cells which are determined, but not differentiated, may remain so for adult life; good examples are the *stem cells*, such as bone marrow haemopoietic cells or basal cells of the skin, which proliferate continuously and produce cells committed to a particular form of differentiation. Hypoplastic and aplastic anaemia, which result in anaemia, neutropenia and thrombocytopenia, are thought to be due to a failure or suppression of bone marrow haemopoietic stem cells (Ch. 23).

Cell position and inductive phenomena

As the fields of cells over which spatial chemical signals act are generally small, large-scale changes to the whole individual are the result of factors operating very early in embryonic development, whilst more specific minor features of differentiation within small areas of an organ or limb are specified later and depend on the position of the cell within the structure. Simple changes may occur in response to a diffusible substance (such as vitamin A in the developing limb bud), and serve to control local cell growth and/or differentiation according to the distance from the source. Additional differentiation changes may, however, occur as a result of more complex cellular interactions.

Many organs eventually contain multiple distinct populations of cells that originate separately but later interact. The pattern of differentiation in one cell type may be controlled by another, a phenomenon known as *induction*. Examples of induction include:

- the action of mesoderm on ectoderm at different sites to form the various parts of the neural tube
- the action of mesoderm on the skin at different sites to form epithelium of differing thickness and accessory gland content
- the action of mesoderm on developing epithelial cells to form branching tubular glands
- the action of the ureteric bud (from the mesonephric duct) to induce the metanephric blastema in kidney formation.

Inductive phenomena also occur in cell migrations, sometimes along pathways that are very long, controlled by generally uncertain mechanisms (although it is known, for example, that migrating cells from the neural crest migrate along pathways that are defined by the host connective tissue). Inductive phenomena control the differentiation of the migrating cell when it arrives at its destination—neural crest cells differentiate into a range of cell types, including sympathetic and parasympathetic ganglion cells, and some cells of the neuroendocrine (APUD) system.

Maintenance and modulation of an attained differentiated state

Once a differentiated state has been attained by a cell, it must be maintained. This is achieved by a combination of factors:

- 'cell memory' inherent in the genome, with inherited transcriptional changes
- interactions with adjacent cells, through secreted paracrine factors
- secreted factors (autocrine factors) including growth factors and extracellular matrix.

Even in the adult, minor changes to the differentiated state may occur if the local environment changes. These alterations to the differentiated state are rarely great, and most can be termed *modulations*, i.e. reversible interconversions between closely related cell phenotypes. An example of a modulation is the alteration in synthesis of certain liver

enzymes in response to circulating corticosteroids. More substantial changes in cell phenotype represent metaplasia (see p. 82).

In the neonatal stage of development, cell *maturation* may involve modulations of the differentiated state. Examples are:

- the production of surfactant by type II pneumonocytes under the influence of corticosteroids
- the synthesis of vitamin K-dependent blood-clotting factors by the hepatocyte
- gut maturation affected by EGF in milk.

Normal differentiation and morphogenesis: summary

Differentiation

During development of an embryo, determination and differentiation occur in a cell by transcriptional modifications to the expression of the genome, without an increase or decrease in number of genes present. The factors involved are summarised in Figure 5.16. Expression of individual genes within the genome is *modified* during development by:

- positional information carried by a small number of 'control' gene products, causing local alterations in growth and differentiation

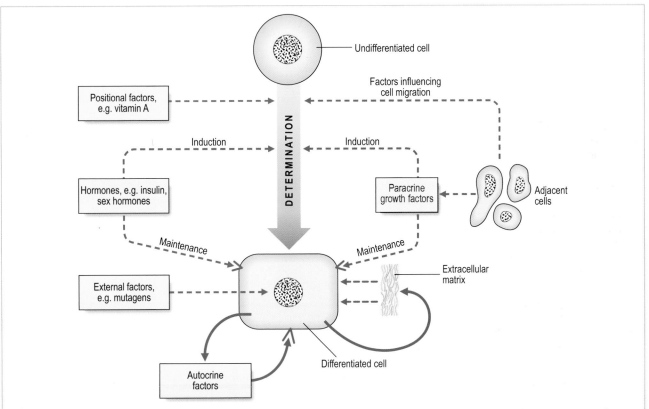

Fig. 5.16 Differentiation. Factors affecting determination, differentiation, maintenance and modulation of the differentiated state of a cell during embryogenesis include positional factors, hormones, paracrine growth factors and external factors such as teratogens. With the exception of positional factors, all of these are important in influencing the differentiated state of cells in post-natal and adult life.

- migrations of cells and modifications mediated by adjacent cells (paracrine factors) or endocrine factors.

Once attained, the differentiated state is *maintained* or *modulated* by:

- paracrine factors (interactions with adjacent cells)
- autocrine factors, such as growth factors and the extracellular matrix secreted by the cell.

External factors may cause alterations to the differentiated state of the cell, either during development or at any stage of adult life.

Morphogenesis

The main features of morphogenesis are summarised in Figure 5.17.

Stem cells and transdifferentiation

Stem cells are 'parent' cells that retain replicative potential, and whose progeny may differentiate into many different types of 'daughter' cell, although different stem cell types have varying potential for this:

- The fertilized human ovum (zygote) and cells from its first two divisions are *totipotent*—able to form all of the cells of the embryo and placenta.
- Embryonic stem cells derived from the early blastocyst and aborted fetuses are *pluripotent*—producing almost all cells derived from the endoderm, mesoderm and ectoderm (but not cells from the placenta or its supporting tissues).
- In normal circumstances, most individual tissues have either *multipotent* or *unipotent* stem cells, capable of generating only small numbers of cell types, or only one cell type respectively.

The presence or absence of tissue stem cells within a single tissue is related to the ability of the cells of that tissue to regenerate after physiological or pathological cell loss or destruction. Thus haemopoietic stem cells in bone marrow replace the different blood cell types after haemorrhage (blood cells are 'labile' cells), while brain neurones ('permanent' cells) cannot be replaced, because there are no functioning neuronal stem cells in the adult brain.

When organs (such as the kidneys) or cells (such as brain neurones) fail because of ageing or disease, a patient may die or suffer increasing disability. Organ transplantation may be possible, although there are insufficient organ donors, and the transplanted organ may be rejected. In 1998, human embryonic stem (ES) cells were successfully extracted from blastocysts and aborted fetuses and grown in vitro. This raises the possibility that these ES cells could be induced to differentiate into organs or cells for transplantation. While some biotechnology companies can produce cells for simple bone or joint repairs from mesenchymal stem cells, creation of more complicated tissues or organs (such as the kidney) will be much more difficult. Because of the ethical issues associated with the use of embryonic stem cells, more recent research has focused on the possibility of inducing stem cells from one organ system, such as

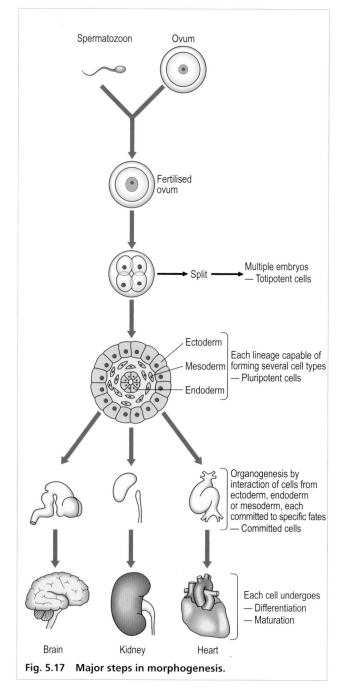

Fig. 5.17   Major steps in morphogenesis.

haemopoietic stem cells (bone marrow cells differentiating into red and white blood cells and platelets) to develop into cells of other organ systems (e.g. kidney, liver or brain) by a process of 'transdifferentiation' (Fig. 5.18). Through such 'adult stem cell plasticity', it is possible that in the future an adult patient's own bone marrow stem cells could be induced artificially to transdifferentiate, and replace cells or organs (such as the kidney) that have been damaged by disease. This would also avoid the risk of immunological rejection of transplanted organs.

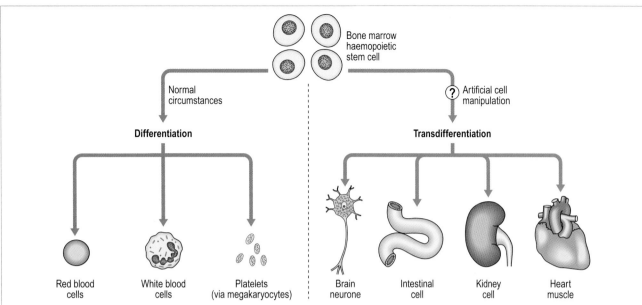

Figure 5.18   Stem cell differentiation and transdifferentiation. Under normal conditions, adult bone marrow haemopoietic stem cells differentiate into red blood cells (erythrocytes), white blood cells (neutrophils) and megakaryocytes to produce platelets. However, artificial manipulation of these cells in vitro may induce them to transdifferentiate into cells of other organs. This ability to make substantial changes of cell type is termed 'plasticity' of the stem cells. (Modified from Bonnet D 2002 Haemopoietic stem cells. Journal of Pathology 197: 430–440, Figure 2.)

Congenital disorders of differentiation and morphogenesis

A congenital disorder is defined as one present at birth. The term thus embraces chromosomal disorders, hereditary and spontaneous genetic diseases, non-genetically determined failures of differentiation and morphogenesis, and other conditions that have detrimental effects on the growth, development and well-being of the fetus.

The processes involved in human conception and development are so complex that it is perhaps remarkable that any normal fetuses are produced; the fact that they are produced is a result of the tight controls of growth and morphogenesis which are involved at all stages of development. The usual outcome of human conception is abortion; 70–80% of all human conceptions are lost, largely as a consequence of chromosomal abnormalities (Fig. 5.19). The majority of these abortions occur spontaneously in the first 6–8 weeks of pregnancy, and in most cases the menstrual cycle might appear normal, or the slight delay in menstruation causes little concern. Chromosomal abnormalities are present in 3–5% of live-born infants, and a further 2% have serious malformations that are not associated with chromosomal aberrations. The most common conditions in these two categories are illustrated in Table 5.4.

Chromosomal abnormalities affecting whole chromosomes

Autosomal chromosomes
The three most common autosomal chromosome defects involve the presence of additional whole chromosomes (trisomy). The incidence of trisomies increases with maternal

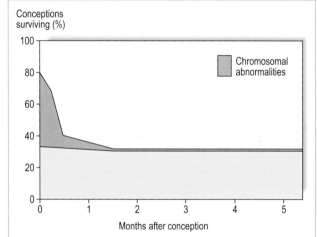

Fig. 5.19   Fate of human conceptions. Between 70% and 80% of human conceptions are lost by spontaneous abortion in the first 6–8 weeks of pregnancy, most as a consequence of chromosomal abnormality. Chromosomal abnormalities are present in 3–5% of live-born infants.

age, and to a lesser extent paternal age. Most trisomies are incompatible with life and result in early abortion. As the genome of every cell in the body has an increased number of genes, gene product expression is greatly altered and multiple abnormalities result during morphogenesis. Those trisomies that are compatible with life have more serious manifestations the larger the chromosome involved, presumably since a greater number of individual genes are involved.

Table 5.4 Incidence of some congenital abnormalities	
Chromosomal abnormality	Incidence per 1000 live births
Down's syndrome (47, +21)	1.4
Klinefelter's syndrome (47XXY)	1.3
Double Y male (47XYY)	<1
Multiple X female (47XXX)	<1
Major malformations	Incidence per 1000 stillbirths + live births
Congenital heart defects	6
Pyloric stenosis	3
Spina bifida	2.5
Anencephaly	2
Cleft lip (± cleft palate)	1
Congenital dislocation of the hip	1

Trisomy 21 (Down's syndrome) affects approximately 1 in 1000 births; it is associated with mental retardation, a flattened facial profile and prominent epicanthic folds. The hands are short, with a transverse palmar crease. There are also abnormalities of the ears, trunk, pelvis and phalanges.

Trisomy 18 (Edwards' syndrome) affects 1 in 5000 births. It is associated with ear and jaw, cardiac, renal, intestinal and skeletal abnormalities.

Trisomy 13 (Patau's syndrome) affects 1 in 6000 births, with microcephaly and microphthalmia, hare lip and cleft palate, polydactyly, abnormal ears, 'rocker-bottom' feet, and cardiac and visceral defects. As with Edwards' syndrome, most affected infants die in the first year of life.

Sex chromosomes

Chromosomal disorders affecting the sex chromosomes (X and Y) are relatively common, and usually induce abnormalities of sexual development and fertility. In general, variations in X chromosome numbers cause greater mental retardation.

Klinefelter's syndrome (47XXY) affects 1 in 850 male births. There is testicular atrophy and absent spermatogenesis, eunuchoid bodily habitus, gynaecomastia, female distribution of body hair and mental retardation. Variants of Klinefelter's syndrome (48XXXY, 49XXXXY, 48XXYY) are rare, and affected individuals have cryptorchidism and hypospadias, in addition to more severe mental retardation and radio-ulnar synostosis.

Double Y males (47XYY) form 1 in 1000 male births; they are phenotypically normal, although most are over 6 feet (1.8 m) tall. The condition is said to be associated with aggressive or criminal behaviour, although this may be a manifestation of lower intelligence.

Turner's syndrome (gonadal dysgenesis; 45X) occurs in 1 in 3000 female births. About one-half are mosaics (45X/46XX) and some have 46 chromosomes and two X chromosomes, one of which is defective. Turner's syndrome females may have short stature, primary amenorrhoea and infertility, webbing of the neck, broad chest and widely spaced nipples, cubitus valgus, low posterior hairline and coarctation of the aorta.

Multiple X females (47XXX, 48XXXX) comprise 1 in 1200 female births. They may be mentally retarded, and have menstrual disturbances, although many are normal and fertile.

True hermaphrodites (most 46XX, some 46XX/47XXY mosaics) have both testicular and ovarian tissue, with varying genital tract abnormalities.

Parts of chromosomes

The loss (or addition) of even a small part of a chromosome may have severe effects, especially if 'controlling' or 'master' genes are involved, as these affect many other genes. An example of a congenital disease in this group is *cri-du-chat syndrome* (46XX, 5p− or 46XY, 5p−). This rare condition (1 in 50 000 births) is associated with deletion of the short arm of chromosome 5 (5p−), and was so named because infants have a characteristic cry like the miaow of a cat. There is microcephaly and severe mental retardation; the face is round, there is gross hypertelorism (increased distance between the eyes) and epicanthic folds.

Single gene alterations

All of the inherited disorders of single genes are transmitted by autosomal dominant, autosomal recessive or X-linked modes of inheritance (Ch. 3). There are more than 2700 known Mendelian disorders; 80–85% of these are familial, the remainder are the result of new mutations. Sometimes the expression of the altered gene product has important effects on growth and morphogenesis, although in other cases a specific single abnormality in a particular biochemical pathway results.

Single gene disorders fall into three categories, discussed below.

Enzyme defects

An altered gene may result in decreased enzyme synthesis, or the synthesis of a defective enzyme (Ch. 7). A failure to synthesise the end products of a reaction catalysed by an enzyme may block normal cellular function. This occurs, for example, in albinism, caused by absent melanin production due to tyrosinase deficiency. Another effect may be the accumulation of the enzyme substrate, for example:

- accumulation of galactose and consequent tissue damage in galactose-1-phosphate uridyl transferase deficiency
- accumulation of phenylalanine, causing mental abnormality, in phenylalanine hydroxylase deficiency
- accumulation of glycogen, mucopolysaccharides, etc. in lysosomes in the enzyme deficiency states of the lysosomal storage disorders.

Defects in receptors or cellular transport

The lack of a specific cellular receptor causes insensitivity of a cell to substances such as hormones. In one form of male pseudohermaphroditism, for example, insensitivity of tissues to androgens, caused by lack of androgen receptor, prevents the development of male characteristics during fetal development.

Table 5.5 Teratogens and their effects

Teratogen	Teratogenic effect
Irradiation	Microcephaly
Drugs	
Thalidomide	Amelia/phocomelia (absent/rudimentary limbs), heart, kidney, gastrointestinal and facial abnormalities
Folic acid antagonists, e.g. 4-amino PGA	Anencephaly, hydrocephalus, cleft lip/palate, skull defects
Anticonvulsants	Cleft lip/palate, heart defects, minor skeletal defects
Warfarin	Nasal/facial abnormalities
Testosterone and synthetic progestagens	Virilisation of female fetus, atypical genitalia
Alcohol	Microcephaly, abnormal facies, oblique palpebral fissures, growth disturbance
Infections	
Rubella	Cataracts, microphthalmia, microcephaly, heart defects
Cytomegalovirus	Microcephaly
Herpes simplex	Microcephaly, microphthalmia
Toxoplasmosis	Microcephaly

Cellular transport deficiencies may lead to disorders such as cystic fibrosis (Ch. 7), a condition in which there is a defective cell membrane transport system across exocrine secretory cells.

Non-enzyme protein defects

Failure of production of important proteins, or production of abnormalities in proteins, has widespread effects. Thus, sickle cell anaemia is caused by the production of abnormal haemoglobin, and Marfan's syndrome and Ehlers–Danlos syndrome are the result of defective collagen production.

Anomalies of fetal development

Abnormalities can occur at almost any stage of embryonic or fetal development; the mechanisms by which the anomaly occurs are sometimes unknown. Genetic factors may play a role in some conditions, but in many cases no simple genetic defect is identifiable. Anomalies of normal development caused by extrinsic physical forces (such as uterine constraint or amniotic bands) are termed *deformations* or *disruptions*. Intrinsic failures of morphogenesis, differentiation or growth are termed *malformations*.

The term *syndrome* refers to a collection of specific anomalies typically seen together but without an obvious single initiating localised defect. The term 'sequence' similarly refers to a condition with a constellation of typical individual features, but in which these features are secondary to an identified single localised primary anomaly which then leads to secondary effects elsewhere in the developing fetus. In the Potter sequence, for example, various primary causes of a decreased volume of amniotic fluid (oligohydramnios) all lead to fetal compression, with resultant deformations of the hands, feet, hips and facies. The sequential causal relationship between oligohydramnios, fetal compression and the observed resultant deformations distinguishes this condition as a syndrome rather than a sequence.

Embryo division abnormalities

Monozygotic twins result from the separation of groups of cells in the early embryo, well before the formation of the primitive streak. On occasion, there is a defect of embryo division, resulting in:

- *Siamese twins*: the result of incomplete separation of the embryo, with fusion of considerable portions of the body (or minor fusions that are easily separated).
- *Fetus in feto*: one of the fused twins develops imperfectly and grows on the other, either externally or within the abdominal cavity. It is possible that some extragonadal 'teratomas' in neonates belong to this group.

Teratogen exposure

Physical, chemical or infective agents can interfere with growth and differentiation, resulting in fetal abnormalities; such agents are known as *teratogens*. The extent and severity of fetal abnormality depend on the nature of the teratogen and the developmental stage of the embryo when exposed to the teratogen. Thus, if exposure occurs at the stage of early organogenesis (4–5 weeks of gestation), the effects on developing organs or limbs are severe.

Clinical examples of teratogenesis include the severe and extensive malformations associated with use of the drug thalidomide (absent/rudimentary limbs, defects of the heart, kidney, gastrointestinal tract, etc.), and the effects of rubella (German measles) on the fetus (cataracts, microcephaly, heart defects, etc.). Some other teratogens are listed in Table 5.5.

Failure of cell and organ migration

Failure of migration of cells may occur during embryogenesis.

Kartagener's syndrome. In this rare condition there is a defect in ciliary motility, due to absent or abnormal dynein arms, the structures on the outer doublets of cilia that are responsible for ciliary movement. This affects cell motility during embryogenesis, which often results in situs inversus (congenital lateral inversion of the position of body organs resulting in, for example, left-sided liver and right-sided spleen). Complications in later life include bronchiectasis, and infertility due to sperm immobility.

Hirschsprung's disease is a condition leading to marked dilatation of the colon and failure of colonic motility in the neonatal period, due to absence of Meissner's and Auerbach's nerve plexuses. It results from a selective failure of craniocaudal migration of neuroblasts in weeks 5–12 of gestation. It is, interestingly, 10 times more frequent in children with trisomy 21 (Down's syndrome), and is often associated with other congenital anomalies.

Undescended testis (cryptorchidism) is the result of failure of the testis to migrate to its normal position in the scrotum. Although this may be associated with severe forms of Klinefelter's syndrome (e.g. 48XXXY), it is often an isolated anomaly in an otherwise normal male. There is an increased risk of neoplasia in undescended testes.

Anomalies of organogenesis

> ▸ *Agenesis (aplasia):* failure of development of an organ or structure within it
> ▸ *Atresia:* failure of the development of a lumen in a normally tubular structure
> ▸ *Hypoplasia:* failure of an organ to attain its normal size
> ▸ *Maldifferentiation (dysgenesis):* failure of normal organ differentiation or persistence of primitive embryological structures
> ▸ *Ectopia (heterotopia):* development of mature tissue in an inappropriate site

Agenesis (aplasia)

The failure of development of an organ or structure is known as agenesis (aplasia). Obviously, agenesis of some structures (such as the heart) is incompatible with life, but agenesis of many individual organs is recorded. These include:

- *Renal agenesis.* This may be unilateral or bilateral (in which case the affected infant may survive only a few days after birth). It results from a failure of the mesonephric duct to give rise to the ureteric bud, and consequent failure of metanephric blastema induction.
- *Thymic agenesis* is seen in DiGeorge syndrome, where there is failure of development of T-lymphocytes, and consequent severe deficiency of cell-mediated immunity. Recent evidence suggests that there is failure of processing of stem cells to T-cells as a result of a defect in the thymus anlage.
- *Anencephaly* is a severe neural tube defect in which the cerebrum, and often the cerebellum, are absent (Ch. 26). The condition is lethal.

Atresia

Atresia is the failure of development of a lumen in a normally tubular epithelial structure. Examples include:

- *oesophageal atresia*, which may be seen in association with tracheo-oesophageal fistulae, as a result of anomalies of development of the two structures from the primitive foregut
- *biliary atresia*, which is an uncommon cause of obstructive jaundice in early childhood
- *urethral atresia*, a very rare anomaly, which may be associated with recto-urethral or urachal fistula, or congenital absence of the anterior abdominal wall muscles ('prune belly' syndrome).

Hypoplasia

A failure in development of the normal size of an organ is termed hypoplasia. It may affect only part of an organ, e.g. segmental hypoplasia of the kidney. A relatively common example of hypoplasia affects the osseous nuclei of the acetabulum causing congenital dislocation of the hip, due to a flattened roof to the acetabulum.

Maldifferentiation (dysgenesis, dysplasia)

Maldifferentiation, as its name implies, is the failure of normal differentiation of an organ, which often retains primitive embryological structures. This disorder is often termed 'dysplasia', although this is a potential cause of confusion, as the more common usage of the term dysplasia implies the presence of a pre-neoplastic state (p. 83).

The best examples of maldifferentiation are seen in the kidney ('renal dysplasia') as a result of anomalous metanephric differentiation. Here, primitive tubular structures may be admixed with cellular mesenchyme and, occasionally, smooth muscle.

Ectopia, heterotopia and choristomas

Ectopic and heterotopic tissues are usually small areas of mature tissue from one organ (e.g. the gastric mucosa) that are present within another tissue (e.g. Meckel's diverticulum) as a result of a developmental anomaly. Another clinically important example is endometriosis, in which endometrial tissue is found around the peritoneum in some women, causing abdominal pain at the time of menstruation.

A choristoma is a related form of heterotopia, where one or more mature differentiated tissues aggregate as a tumour-like mass at an inappropriate site. A good example of this is a complex choristoma of the conjunctiva (eye), which has varying proportions of cartilage, adipose tissue, smooth muscle, and lacrimal gland ascini. A conjunctival choristoma consisting of lacrimal gland elements alone could also be considered to be an ectopic (heterotopic) lacrimal gland.

Complex disorders of growth and morphogenesis

Three examples of complex multifactorial defects of growth and morphogenesis will be discussed: neural tube defects, disorders of sexual differentiation, and cleft palate and related disorders.

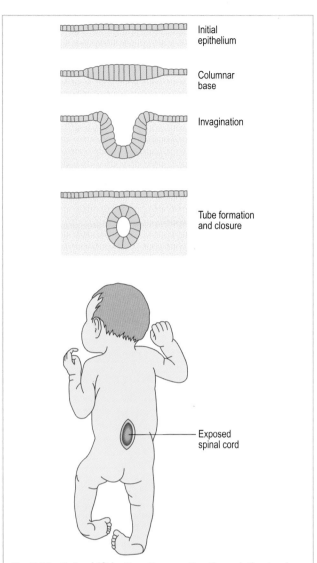

- Initial epithelium
- Columnar base
- Invagination
- Tube formation and closure
- Exposed spinal cord

Fig. 5.20 Spina bifida. Top: Cross-section through the developing embryo. During the 4th week of development the neural tube is formed by invagination of the dorsal ectoderm. Failure of the neural tube to invaginate fully or of the overlying ectoderm to close afterwards results in neural tube defects such as spina bifida, in which the spinal cord is exposed (bottom). Deformity and hypoplasia of the legs results from the associated neurological deficit.

Neural tube defects

The development of the brain, spinal cord and spine from the primitive neural tube is highly complex and, not surprisingly, so too are the developmental disorders of the system (Fig. 5.20).

Neural tube malformations are relatively common in the UK and are found in about 1.3% of aborted fetuses, and 0.1% of live births. There are regional differences in incidence, and social differences, the condition being more common in social class V than in classes I or II. The pathogenesis of these conditions—anencephaly, hydrocephalus and spina bifida—is uncertain and probably multifactorial (Ch. 26), although dietary deficiency of folate (vitamin B₉) during the early stages of embryogenesis is one established factor.

Disorders of sexual differentiation

Disorders of sexual differentiation are undoubtedly complex, and involve a range of individual chromosomal, enzyme and hormone receptor defects. The defects may be obvious and severe at birth, or they may be subtle, presenting with infertility in adult life.

Chromosomal abnormalities causing ambiguous or abnormal sexual differentiation have already been discussed (p. 94).

Female pseudohermaphroditism, in which the genetic sex is always female (XX), may be due to exposure of the developing fetus to the masculinising effects of excess testosterone or progestagens, causing abnormal differentiation of the external genitalia. The causes include:

- an enzyme defect in the fetal adrenal gland, leading to excessive androgen production at the expense of cortisol synthesis (with consequent adrenal hyperplasia due to feedback mechanisms which increases ACTH secretion)
- exogenous androgenic steroids from a maternal androgen-secreting tumour, or administration of androgens (or progestagens) during pregnancy.

Male pseudohermaphroditism, in which the genetic sex is male (XY), may be the result of several rare defects:

- testicular unresponsiveness to human chorionic gonadotrophin (hCG) or luteinising hormone (LH), by virtue of reduction in receptors to these hormones; this causes failure of testosterone secretion
- errors of testosterone biosynthesis in the fetus, due to enzyme defects (may be associated with cortisol deficiency and congenital adrenal hyperplasia)
- tissue insensitivity to androgens (androgen receptor deficiency)
- abnormality in testosterone metabolism by peripheral tissues, in 5-alpha reductase deficiency
- defects in synthesis, secretion and response to Müllerian duct inhibitory factor
- maternal ingestion of oestrogens and progestins.

These defects result in the presence of a testis that is small and atrophic, and a female phenotype.

Cleft palate and related disorders

Cleft palate, and the related cleft (or hare) lip, are relatively common (about 1 per 1000 births). Approximately 20% of children with these disorders have associated major malformations. The important stages of development of the lips, palate, nose and jaws occur in the first 9 weeks of embryonic life. From about 5 weeks of gestational age the maxillary processes grow anteriorly and medially, and fuse with the developing fronto-nasal process at two points just below the nostrils, forming the upper lip. Meanwhile, the palate develops from the palatal processes of the maxillary processes, which grow medially to fuse with the nasal septum in the midline at about 9 weeks.

Failure of these complicated processes may occur at any stage, producing small clefts or severe facial deficits (Fig. 5.21). A cleft lip is commonly unilateral but may be bilateral; it may involve the lip alone, or extend into the nostril

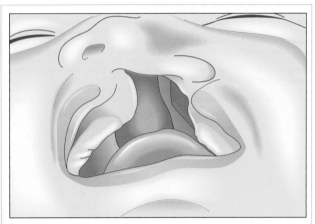

Fig. 5.21 **Cleft palate.** Diagram demonstrating a large defect involving the upper lip, the upper jaw and the palate.

or involve the bone of the maxilla and the teeth. The mildest palatal clefting may involve the uvula or soft palate alone, but can lead to absence of the roof of the mouth. Cleft lip and palate occur singly or in combination, and severe combined malformations of the lips, maxilla and palate can be very difficult to manage surgically.

Recently, lip and palate malformations have been extensively studied as a model of normal and abnormal states of morphogenesis in a complicated developmental system. It appears from the relatively high incidence of these malformations that the control of palatal morphogenesis is particularly sensitive to both genetic and environmental disturbances:

- genetic: e.g. Patau's syndrome (trisomy 13) is associated with severe clefting of the lip and palate
- environmental: e.g. the effects of specific teratogens such as folic acid antagonists or anticonvulsants, causing cleft lip and/or palate

Recent experimental evidence has suggested that several cellular factors are involved in the fusion of the fronto-nasal and maxillary processes. The differentiation of epithelial cells of the palatal processes is of paramount importance in fusion of the processes. It is thought that the most important mechanism is mediated by mesenchymal cells of the palatal processes; these induce differentiation of the epithelial cells, to form either ciliated nasal epithelial cells or squamous buccal epithelial cells, or to undergo programmed cell death by apoptosis to allow fusion of underlying mesothelial cells. Positional information of a genetic and chemical (paracrine) nature is important in this differentiation, and is mediated via mesenchymal cells (and possibly epithelial cells). In addition, the events may be modified by the actions of EGF and other growth factors through autocrine or paracrine mechanisms, and by the endocrine actions of glucocorticoids and their intercellular receptors.

As yet, the precise way in which all of these factors interact in normal palatal development or cleft palate is unclear. In the mouse, it is known that physiological concentrations of glucocorticoids, their receptors and EGF are required for normal development, but that altered concentrations may precipitate cleft palate.

Commonly confused conditions and entities relating to growth, differentiation and morphogenesis	
Commonly confused	Distinction and explanation
Hyperplasia and *hypertrophy*	Both result in organ enlargement, in *hyperplasia* by cellular proliferation and in *hypertrophy* by cellular enlargement. Generally, the innate replicative capacity (i.e. permanent, stable or labile) of the organ's cells determines whether it responds by hyperplasia or hypertrophy.
Agenesis, aplasia, atresia, achalasia and *atrophy*	*Agenesis* and *aplasia* imply a failure of formation of an organ or cell lineage; if the structure has a lumen, then *atresia* is often used (e.g. biliary atresia). *Achalasia* is failure of a sphincter to relax, causing proximal dilatation; it is not a disorder of growth. *Atrophy* is shrinkage of an organ; when it occurs naturally during maturation and ageing, the process is often called 'involution'.
Dysplasia and *dystrophy*	*Dysplasia* means disordered growth or differentiation and, in epithelia, is often considered to be a precursor of neoplasia. *Dystrophy* means either abnormal development (e.g. muscular dystrophy) or, less commonly, a degenerative change (e.g. dystrophic calcification).
Congenital and *genetic*	*Congenital* refers to a condition present at birth, and often is used specifically to denote a condition with a visible morphological manifestation. *Genetic* conditions are those caused by abnormalities in genes or chromosomes, although the influence of these abnormalities may be modulated by environmental factors.

FURTHER READING

Alberts B, Johnson A, Lewis J, Raff M, Roberts K, Walter O 2002 Molecular biology of the cell, 4th edn. Academic Press, New York

Alison M R, Poulsom R, Wright N A (eds) 2002 Stem cells. Journal of Pathology 197: 417–565

Alison M R, Lovell M, Direckze N, Poulsom R 2005 Adult stem cells and transdifferentiation. In: Recent advances in histopathology, vol 21. RSM Press, London

Berry C L 1996 Paediatric pathology, 3rd edn. Springer, London

Drury P L, Howlett T A 2002 Endocrinology. In: Kumar P, Clark M (eds) Clinical medicine, 5th edn. WB Saunders, Edinburgh

Eckfeldt C E, Mendenhall E M, Verfaillie C M 2005 The molecular repertoire of the 'almighty' stem cell. Nature Reviews. Molecular Cell Biology 6: 726–737

Gilbert S F, Singer S R 2001 Developmental biology, 8th edn. Sinauer, Sunderland, MA.

Hall P A 1992 Differentiation, stem cells and tumour histogenesis. In: Anthony P P, MacSween R N M (eds) Recent advances in histopathology, vol 15. Churchill Livingstone, Edinburgh, pp 1–15

Iles R K, Kumar P J 2002 Cell and molecular biology and genetic disorders. In: Kumar P, Clark M (eds) Clinical medicine, 5th edn. WB Saunders, Edinburgh

Lawrence P A 1992 The making of a fly. The genetics of animal design. Blackwell Scientific Publications, Oxford

Lodish H, Berk A, Kaiser C A, Krieger M 2008 Molecular cell biology, 6th edn. WH Freeman, Basingstoke

Michalides R J A M 1999 Cell cycle regulators: mechanisms and their role in aetiology, prognosis, and treatment of cancer. Journal of Clinical Pathology 52: 555–568

Sadler T W 2006 Langman's medical embryology, 10th edn. Lippincott Williams & Wilkins, Baltimore

Thompson C B 1995 Apoptosis in the pathogenesis and treatment of disease. Science 267: 1456–1462

Tosk D, Slack J M W 2002 How cells change their phenotype. Nature Reviews. Molecular Cell Biology 3: 187–194

Wilmut I, Schnieke A E, McWhir J, Kind A J, Campbell K H S 1997 Viable offspring derived from fetal and adult mammalian cells. Nature 385: 810–813

Wyllie A H 1997 Apoptosis: an overview. British Medical Bulletin 53: 451–465

Browder L 1998 Dynamic development: http://www.ucalgary.ca/UofC/ eduweb/virtualembryo/dev_biol.html

Gilbert S F 1997: http://zygote.swarthmore.edu/index.html

Hill M A (2007) Embryology; University of New South Wales: http:// embryology.med.unsw.edu.au/

Online Mendelian Inheritance in Man (OMIM Home Page): http://www. ncbi.nlm.nih.gov/omim

6

Responses to cellular injury

CELLULAR INJURY

> ▶ Numerous causes: physical and chemical agents including products of micro-organisms
> ▶ Various mechanisms: disruption, membrane failure, metabolic interference (respiration, protein synthesis, DNA), free radicals
> ▶ May be reversible, or end in cell death

Cell survival depends upon several factors: a constant supply of energy, intact plasma membrane, biologically safe and effective function of generic and specific cellular activities, genomic integrity, controlled cell division, and internal homeostatic mechanisms. Cell death may result from significant disturbance of these factors. However, cell replication proceeds in a human body at a rate of c. 10 000 new cells per second; so, although eventually some will be lost to the environment via the skin or gut surfaces, many will inevitably need to be deleted. Thus, cell death is a normal physiological process as well as a reaction to injury. Similarly, failure or poor regulation of death processes may underlie some diseases.

Causative agents and processes

A wide range of possible agents or circumstances result in cellular injury (Fig. 6.1). These could be categorised according to the nature of the injurious agent, the cellular target, the pattern of cellular reaction or mode of cell death. The sequence of agent, target and mode will be uniform, but some injurious agents have variable effects depending on concentration, duration or other contributory influences such as co-existent disease. Some examples are given in Table 6.1. Major types of cellular injury include:

- trauma
- thermal injury, hot or cold
- poisons
- drugs
- infectious organisms
- ischaemia and reperfusion
- plasma membrane failure
- DNA damage
- loss of growth factors
- ionising radiation.

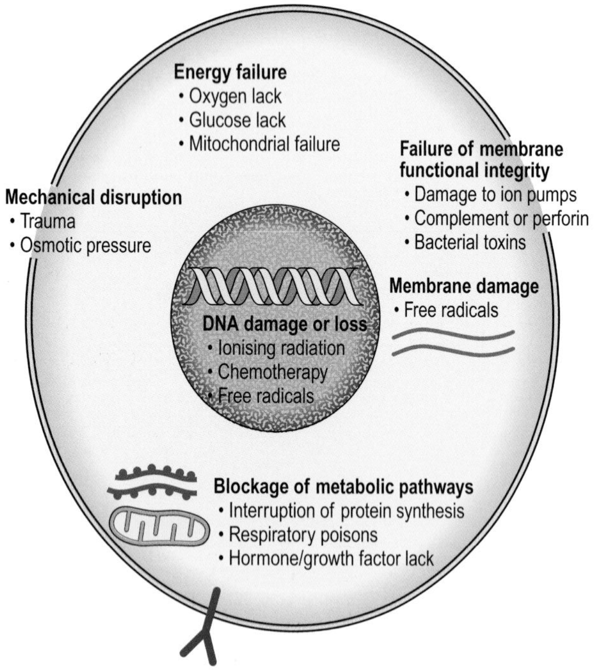

Physical agents

Most physical agents cause passive cell destruction by gross membrane disruption or catastrophic functional impairment. Trauma and thermal injury cause cell death by disrupting cells and denaturing proteins, and also cause local vascular thrombosis with consequent tissue ischaemia or infarction (Ch. 8). Freezing damages cells mechanically because their membranes are perforated by ice crystals. Missile injury combines the effects of trauma and heat; much energy is dissipated into tissues around the track. Blast injuries are the result of shearing forces, where structures of differing density and mobility are moved with respect to one another; traumatic amputation is a gross example. Microwaves (wavelengths in the range from 1 mm to 1 m) cause thermal injury. Laser light falls into two broad categories: relatively low energy produces tissue heating, with coagulation for example; higher energy light breaks intramolecular bonds by a photochemical reaction, and effectively vaporises tissue. Ionising radiation is considered on p. 115.

Chemical and biological agents

Cells may be injured by contact with drugs and other chemicals; the latter may include enzymes and toxins secreted by micro-organisms. This category of agents can give rise to the full range of modes of death.

Fig. 6.1 Mechanisms of cellular injury. Different agents can injure the various structural and functional components of the cell. Some cells with specific function are selectively prone to certain types of injury.

Table 6.1 Examples of causes of cellular injury and their mode of action	
Example agent	Mode of action
Trauma (e.g. road traffic accident)	Mechanical disruption of tissue
Carbon monoxide inhalation	Prevents oxygen transport
Contact with strong acid	Coagulates tissue proteins
Paracetamol overdose	Metabolites bind to liver cell proteins and lipoproteins
Bacterial infections	Toxins and enzymes
Ionising radiation (e.g. X-rays)	Damage to DNA

Drugs and poisons

Many naturally occurring and synthetic chemicals cause cellular injury; the effect is usually dose-related, but in a few instances the effect is exacerbated by constitutional factors.

Some are highly toxic systemic metabolic poisons, while others exert their damage locally; the latter includes caustic liquids applied to skin or mucous membranes, or gases that injure the lung. Furthermore, some substances produce one effect locally and another systemically. For example, some drugs are potentially caustic, and care needs to be taken to avoid extravasation into soft tissues when giving them by intravenous injection.

Caustic agents cause rapid local cell death due to their extreme alkalinity or acidity, in addition to having a corrosive effect on the tissue by digesting proteins.

Infectious organisms

The mechanisms of tissue damage produced by infectious organisms are varied, but with many bacteria it is their metabolic products or secretions that are harmful (Ch. 3). Thus, the host cells receive a chemical insult that may be toxic to their metabolism or membrane integrity. The mode of cell death generally induces an acute inflammatory response, which may be damaging to adjacent cells; organisms that do this are called pyogenic. In contrast, bacterial endotoxin (lipopolysaccharide) induces apoptosis with different pathological consequences. Intracellular agents such as viruses often result in the physical rupture of infected cells, but with some viruses such as hepatitis B (Ch. 16) local tissue damage may result from host immune reactions. Therefore, the cellular response to injury caused by infections will depend on a combination of the damage inflicted directly by the agent and indirectly as a result of the host response to the agent.

Blockage of metabolic pathways

Cell injury may result from specific interference with intracellular metabolism, effected usually by relative or total blockage of one or more pathways.

Cellular respiration

Prevention of oxygen utilisation results in the death of many cells due to loss of their principal energy source. Cyanide ions act in this way by binding to cytochrome oxidase and thus interrupting oxygen utilisation. Cells with higher metabolic requirements for oxygen (e.g. cardiac myocytes) are most vulnerable.

Glucose deprivation

Glucose is another important metabolite and source of energy. Some cells, cerebral neurones for example, are highly dependent. In diabetes mellitus there is inadequate utilisation of glucose due to an absolute or relative lack of insulin.

Protein synthesis

Cell function and viability will also be compromised if protein synthesis is blocked at the translational level because there is a constant requirement to replace enzymes and structural proteins. Ricin, a potent toxin from the castor oil plant, acts in this manner at the ribosomal level. Many antibiotics, such as streptomycin, chloramphenicol and tetracycline, act by interfering with protein synthesis, although toxic effects by this mechanism are fortunately rare.

Loss of growth factor or hormonal influence

Many cells rely on growth factors for their survival. Typically, these bind to growth factor receptors spanning the plasma membrane, triggering an intracellular cascade, often via a tyrosine kinase. This pathway can fail or be blocked at many points including growth factor deficit, receptor loss or blockade, or tyrosine kinase inhibitor (e.g. imatinib) (Ch. 4); affected cells may undergo apoptosis. Similar consequences can follow hormone withdrawal, as either a physiological response or part of a disease process. If widespread in an organ, it will shrink (*atrophy*).

Ischaemia and reperfusion injury

Impaired blood flow (Ch. 8) causes inadequate oxygen delivery to cells. Mitochondrial production of ATP will cease, and anaerobic glycolysis will result in acidosis due to the accumulation of lactate. The acidosis promotes calcium influx. Cells in different organs vary widely in their vulnerability to oxygen deprivation; those with high metabolic activity such as cortical neurones and cardiac myocytes will be most affected.

When the blood supply is restored, the oxygen results in a burst of mitochondrial activity and excessive release of reactive oxygen species (free radicals).

Free radicals

Free radicals are atoms or groups of atoms with an unpaired electron (symbolised by a superscript dot); they avidly form chemical bonds. They are highly reactive, chemically unstable, generally present only at low concentrations, and tend to participate in or initiate chain reactions.

Free radicals can be generated by two principal mechanisms:

- Deposition of energy, e.g. ionisation of water by radiation. An electron is displaced, resulting in free radicals. This is discussed further under the mode of action of ionising radiation (p. 117).
- Interaction between oxygen, or other substances, and a free electron in relation to oxidation–reduction reactions. In this instance the superoxide radical ($O_2^{\bullet -}$) could be generated. Mitochondria are the main source, and in pathological circumstances can produce toxic quantities of reactive oxygen species.

The consequences of free radical formation include the following:

- A chain reaction may be initiated in which other free radicals are also formed. Common final events are damage to polyunsaturated fatty acids, which are an essential component of cell membranes, or damage to DNA.
- The free radical may be scavenged by endogenous or exogenous anti-oxidants, e.g. sulphydryl compounds such as cysteine.
- Superoxide radicals may be inactivated by the copper-containing enzyme, superoxide dismutase, which generates hydrogen peroxide; catalase then converts this to water.

The clinicopathological events involving free radicals include:

- toxicity of some poisons (e.g. carbon tetrachloride)
- oxygen toxicity
- tissue damage in inflammation
- intracellular killing of bacteria.

Cells irreversibly damaged by free radicals are deleted, generally by apoptosis.

Failure of membrane integrity

Cell membrane damage is an important mode of cellular injury for which there are several possible mechanisms:

- complement-mediated cytolysis
- perforin-mediated cytolysis
- specific blockage of ion channels
- failure of membrane ion pumps
- free radical attack.

Cell membrane damage is one of the consequences of *complement activation* (Ch. 9); some of the end products of the complement cascade have cytolytic activity. Another effector of cytolysis is *perforin*, a mediator of lymphocyte cytotoxicity that causes damage to the cell membrane of the target cells such as those infected by viruses. Incidental membrane tears or perforations can be repaired very quickly, so do not necessarily result in cell death.

Intramembrane channels permit the controlled entry and exit of specific ions. Blockage of these channels is sometimes used therapeutically. For example, verapamil is a calcium channel blocker used in the treatment of hypertension and ischaemic heart disease. Used in inappropriate circumstances or at high dosage, however, the calcium channel blockage may have toxic effects.

Membrane ion pumps that are responsible for maintaining intracellular homeostasis, for example calcium, potassium and sodium concentrations within cells, are dependent on an adequate supply of ATP. Any chemical agents that deplete ATP, either by interfering with mitochondrial oxidative phosphorylation or by consuming ATP in their metabolism, will compromise the integrity of the membrane pumps and expose the cell to the risk of lysis. The Na/K ATPase in cell membranes can be directly inhibited by ouabain. Failure of membrane ion pumps frequently results in *cell swelling*, also called *oncosis* or *hydropic change* (see below), which may progress to cell death.

Just as disastrous for the cell is biochemical alteration of the lipoprotein bilayer forming the cell membrane. This can result from reactions with either the phospholipid or protein moieties. Membrane phospholipids may be altered through peroxidation by reactive oxygen species and by phospholipases. If the membrane damage results in lysosome permeability, release of its contents precipitates further cell damage or death. Membrane proteins may be altered by cross-linking induced by free radicals.

DNA damage or loss

Damage to DNA results primarily from reactive oxygen species attack, for example following ionising radiation (p. 117).

Damage may not be evident immediately; dividing cells are more susceptible. Cell populations that are constantly dividing (i.e. labile cells such as intestinal epithelium and haemopoietic cells) are soon affected by a dose of radiation sufficient to alter their DNA. Other cell populations may require a growth or metabolic stimulus before the DNA damage is revealed. Since non-lethal DNA damage may be inherited by daughter cells, a clone of transformed cells with abnormal growth characteristics may be formed; this is the process of neoplastic transformation that results in tumours (Ch. 11).

Normal erythrocytes are particularly sensitive to injury because they lack a nucleus and, therefore, the means for inducing repair mechanisms. This will also be the fate of any cell in which the nucleus is severely damaged, or when mitosis is attempted but its completion is blocked. The latter is the result of DNA strand breaks or cross-linkages; ionising radiation and some cytotoxic drugs used in cancer therapy have this effect. Damaged cells are deleted, usually by apoptosis.

Cellular appearances following injury

The agents and mechanisms mentioned above cause a variety of histological abnormalities, although very few are specific for each agent. Two patterns of sublethal cellular alteration seen fairly commonly are hydropic change and fatty change.

Hydropic change (oncosis)

In hydropic change the cytoplasm becomes pale and swollen due to accumulation of fluid. Hydropic change generally results from disturbances of metabolism such as hypoxia or chemical poisoning. These changes are reversible, although they may herald irreversible damage if the causal injury is persistent.

Fatty change (steatosis)

Vacuolation of cells is due often to the accumulation of lipid droplets as a result of a disturbance to ribosomal function and uncoupling of lipid from protein metabolism. The liver is commonly affected in this way by several causes, such as hypoxia, alcohol or diabetes. Moderate degrees of fatty change are reversible, but severe fatty change may not be.

Mechanisms of cell death

There are two distinct mechanisms by which cells die: necrosis and apoptosis. However, there are also other cellular deaths combining features of both these processes. Discussion of cell death is further complicated by a lack of uniform nomenclature; some authors use the term necrosis to denote cell death by any cellular mechanism, but more often it is used to describe a specific mechanism. Although there are usually particular triggers for one process or another, there are some situations where apoptosis follows a lower dose or shorter duration of insult while necrosis occurs above that threshold. Mechanisms of cell death involve defined metabolic pathways. Consequently, cell death processes may be amenable to therapeutic interventions.

Necrosis

▶ Necrosis is death of tissues following bioenergetic failure and loss of plasma membrane integrity
▶ Induces inflammation and repair
▶ Causes include ischaemia, metabolic, trauma
▶ Coagulative necrosis in most tissues; firm pale area, with ghost outlines on microscopy
▶ Colliquative necrosis is seen in the brain; the dead area is liquefied
▶ Caseous necrosis is seen in tuberculosis; there is pale yellow semi-solid material
▶ Gangrene is necrosis with putrefaction: it follows vascular occlusion or certain infections and is black
▶ Fibrinoid necrosis is a microscopic feature in arterioles in malignant hypertension
▶ Fat necrosis may follow trauma and cause a mass, or may follow pancreatitis visible as multiple white spots

Necrosis is characterised by bioenergetic failure and loss of plasma membrane integrity. The ischaemia–reperfusion model has been the focus of much research. Failure of ATP production renders plasma membrane ion pumps ineffective with resulting loss of homeostasis, influx of water, oncosis, lysis and cell death, but in many circumstances this sequence may be an oversimplification.

Anaerobic conditions result in acidosis, thus promoting calcium inflow. Calcium uptake by mitochondria eventually exceeds their storage capacity, and contributes to disruption of the inner membrane (mitochondrial permeability transition); ATP production ceases and contents leak into the cytosol. This mitochondrial sequence is particularly exacerbated, if not initiated, by reperfusion causing a burst of reactive oxygen species production.

DNA damage, for example by free radicals or alkylating agents, initiates repair sequences including activation of the nuclear enzyme poly (ADP-ribose) polymerase (PARP). In proliferating cells, as they are dependent on glycolysis, this leads to NAD depletion and thus ATP depletion and consequently necrosis.

Falling ATP levels can open plasma membrane channel-mediated calcium uptake (death channels); large rises in cytosol calcium activate calcium-dependent proteases or lead on to mitochondrial permeability transition. In contrast, free radical damage to endoplasmic reticulum allows calcium stores to leak into the cytosol; smaller rises in calcium tend to cause apoptosis rather than necrosis.

Free radical damage to lysosomal membranes releases proteases, such as cathepsins which damage other membranes and can cause cell death. By a similar mechanism, binding of tumour necrosis factor to its cell surface receptor stimulates excessive mitochondrial reactive oxygen species with the results noted above and hence necrosis.

All these pathways eventually lead to rupture of the plasma membrane and spillage of cell contents, but this is not the end of the sequence. Some of the contents released are immunostimulatory, for example heat shock proteins and purine metabolites. These provoke the inflammatory response (Ch. 10), which paves the way for repair.

Several distinct morphological types of necrosis are recognised:

- coagulative
- colliquative
- caseous
- gangrene
- fibrinoid
- fat necrosis.

The type of tissue and nature of the causative agent determine the type of necrosis.

Necrosis must be distinguished from apoptosis, in which cell death results from a different mechanism. The cell membrane remains intact and there is no inflammatory reaction.

Coagulative necrosis

Coagulative necrosis is the commonest form of necrosis and can occur in most organs. Following devitalisation, the cells retain their outline as their proteins coagulate and metabolic activity ceases. The gross appearance will depend partly on the cause of cell death, and in particular on any vascular alteration such as dilatation or cessation of flow. Initially, the tissue texture will be normal or firm, but later it may become soft as a result of digestion by macrophages. This can have disastrous consequences in necrosis of the myocardium following infarction, as there is a risk of ventricular rupture (Ch. 13).

Microscopic examination of an area of necrosis shows a variable appearance depending on the duration. In the first few hours, there will be no discernable abnormality. Subsequently, there will be progressive loss of nuclear staining until it ceases to be haematoxyphilic; this is accompanied by loss of cytoplasmic detail (Fig. 6.2). The collagenous stroma is more resistant to dissolution. The result is that, histologically, the tissue retains a faint outline of its structure until such time as the damaged area is removed by phagocytosis (or sloughed off a surface), and is then repaired or regenerated. The presence of necrotic tissue usually evokes an inflammatory response; this is independent of the initiating cause of the necrosis.

Colliquative necrosis

Colliquative necrosis occurs in the brain because of its lack of any substantial supporting stroma; thus, necrotic neural tissue may totally liquefy. There will be a glial reaction around the periphery, and the site of necrosis will be marked eventually by a cyst.

Caseous necrosis

Tuberculosis is characterised by caseous necrosis, a pattern of necrosis in which the dead tissue is structureless. Histological examination shows an amorphous eosinophilic area stippled by haematoxyphilic nuclear debris. Although not confined to tuberculosis, nor invariably present, caseation in a biopsy should always raise the possibility of tuberculosis.

Gangrene

Gangrene is necrosis with putrefaction of the tissues, sometimes as a result of the action of certain bacteria, notably clostridia. The affected tissues appear black because of the deposition of

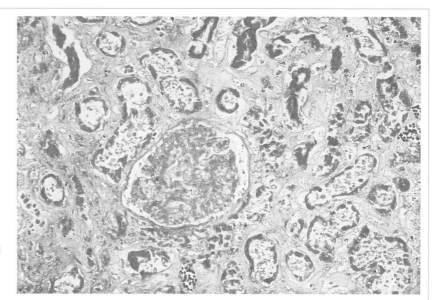

Fig. 6.2 Necrosis. Histology of part of a kidney deprived of its blood supply by an arterial embolus (Ch. 8). This is an example of coagulative necrosis. Cellular and nuclear detail has been lost. The ghost outline of a glomerulus can be seen in the centre, with remnants of tubules elsewhere.

iron sulphide from degraded haemoglobin. Thus, ischaemic necrosis of the distal part of a limb may proceed to gangrene if complicated by an appropriate infection. As clostridia are very common in the bowel, intestinal necrosis is particularly liable to proceed to gangrene; it can occur as a complication of appendicitis, or incarceration of a hernia if the blood supply is impeded. These are examples of 'wet' gangrene. In contrast, 'dry' gangrene is usually seen in the toes, as a result of gradual arterial or small vessel obstruction in atherosclerosis or diabetes mellitus, respectively. In time, a line of demarcation develops between the gangrenous and adjacent viable tissues.

In contrast to the above, primary infection with certain bacteria or combinations of bacteria may result in similar putrefactive necrosis. Gas gangrene is the result of infection by *Clostridium perfringens,* while synergistic gangrene follows infection by combinations of organisms, such as *Bacteroides* and *Borrelia vincenti.*

Fibrinoid necrosis

In the context of malignant hypertension (Ch. 13), arterioles are under such pressure that there is necrosis of the smooth muscle wall. This allows seepage of plasma into the media with consequent deposition of fibrin. The appearance is termed fibrinoid necrosis. With haematoxylin and eosin staining, the vessel wall is a homogeneous bright red. Fibrinoid necrosis is sometimes a misnomer because the element of necrosis is inconspicuous or absent. Nevertheless, the histological appearance is distinctive and its close resemblance to necrotic tissue perpetuates the name of this lesion.

Fat necrosis

Fat necrosis may be due to:

- direct trauma to adipose tissue and extracellular liberation of fat
- enzymatic lysis of fat due to release of lipases.

Following trauma to adipose tissue, the release of intracellular fat elicits a brisk inflammatory response, with polymorphs and macrophages phagocytosing the fat, proceeding eventually to fibrosis. The result may be a palpable mass, particularly at a superficial site such as the breast.

In acute pancreatitis, there is release of pancreatic lipase (Ch. 16). As a result, fat cells have their stored fat split into fatty acids, which then combine with calcium to precipitate out as white soaps. In severe cases, hypocalcaemia can ensue.

Apoptosis

- ▶ Individual cell deletion in physiological growth control and in disease
- ▶ Activated or prevented by a variety of stimuli
- ▶ Reduced apoptosis contributes to cell accumulation, e.g. neoplasia
- ▶ Increased apoptosis results in excessive cell loss, e.g. atrophy

Apoptosis is quite different from necrosis (Table 6.2); indeed, it includes suppression of necrosis. It is an energy-dependent process for deletion of unwanted individual cells. Apoptosis is involved in morphogenesis (Ch. 5), and is the mechanism for controlling organ size. Unwanted or defective cells also undergo apoptosis; thus, lymphocyte proliferation in germinal centres and the thymus is followed by apoptosis of unwanted cells. Factors controlling apoptosis include substances outside the cell and internal metabolic pathways:

- *Inhibitors* include growth factors, cell matrix, sex steroids, some viral proteins.
- *Inducers* include growth factor withdrawal, loss of matrix attachment, glucocorticoids, some viruses, free radicals, ionising radiation, DNA damage, Fas ligand.

Exposure to inducers or withdrawal of inhibitors acts via the bcl-2 protein family, which then inhibit or activate the death pathway, resulting in activation of initiator and executioner

Table 6.2	Comparison of cell death by apoptosis and necrosis	
Feature	Apoptosis	Necrosis
Induction	May be induced by physiological or pathological stimuli	Invariably due to pathological injury
Extent	Single cells	Cell groups
Biochemical events	Energy-dependent fragmentation of DNA by endogenous endonucleases	Energy failure
		Impairment or cessation of ion homeostasis
	Lysosomes intact	Lysosomes leak lytic enzymes
Cell membrane integrity	Maintained	Lost
Morphology	Cell shrinkage and fragmentation to form apoptotic bodies with dense chromatin	Cell swelling and lysis
Inflammatory response	None	Usual
Fate of dead cells	Ingested (phagocytosed) by neighbouring cells	Ingested (phagocytosed) by neutrophil polymorphs and macrophages
Outcome	Cell elimination	Defence, and preparation for repair

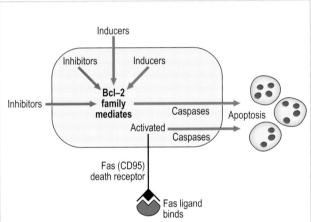

Fig. 6.3 Mechanisms of apoptosis. Apoptosis results from activation of caspases triggered either by the bcl-2 family or by the binding of Fas ligand to its receptor.

caspases. Alternatively, activation of the plasma membrane receptor Fas (CD95) by its ligand bypasses bcl-2 to activate other caspases (Fig. 6.3). These result in degradation of the cytoskeletal framework, fragmentation of DNA and loss of mitochondrial function. The nucleus shrinks (pyknosis) and fragments (karyorrhexis). The cell shrinks, retaining an intact plasma membrane (Fig. 6.4), but alteration of this membrane rapidly induces phagocytosis. Dead cells not phagocytosed fragment into smaller membrane-bound *apoptotic bodies.* There is no inflammatory reaction to apoptotic cells, probably because the cell membrane is intact. Various diseases are associated with reduced or increased apoptosis.

Reduced apoptosis

The product of the *p53* gene checks the integrity of the genome before mitosis; defective cells are switched to apoptosis instead. In contrast, bcl-2 protein inhibits apoptosis. Therefore,

loss of p53 function or excess bcl-2 expression may result in failure of initiation of apoptosis with resulting cell accumulation; both these defects are important in neoplasia (Ch. 11). Autoimmune disease (Ch. 9) might reflect failure of induction of apoptosis in lymphoid cells directed against host antigens; in systemic lupus erythematosus, alterations are reported in the Fas lymphocyte receptor. Some viruses enhance their survival by inhibiting apoptosis of cells they infect, and latent infection by Epstein–Barr virus upregulates bcl-2.

Increased apoptosis

Diseases in which increased apoptosis is probably important include acquired immune deficiency syndrome (AIDS), neurodegenerative disorders and anaemia of chronic disorders (Ch. 23). In AIDS, human immunodeficiency virus proteins may activate CD4 on uninfected T-helper lymphocytes, inducing apoptosis with resulting immunodepletion. Apoptosis is the usual mode of cell death in exposure to ionising radiation (p. 117).

Autophagy

Autophagy is another cellular response to stress, such as deficiency of nutrients or growth factor-mediated effects, or organelle damage. Cell components are isolated into intracellular vacuoles and then processed through to lysosomes. Although generally a means of staving off cell death, it may progress to cell death if the stimulus is more severe, or the cell metabolic pathways may switch to apoptosis.

Patterns of cell death in systematic pathology

The clinical value of knowing the metabolic pathways to cell death lies in the potential to modify them by increasing or decreasing cell survival as appropriate by targeting cell death or cell survival pathways. Thus, exposure to minor degrees of

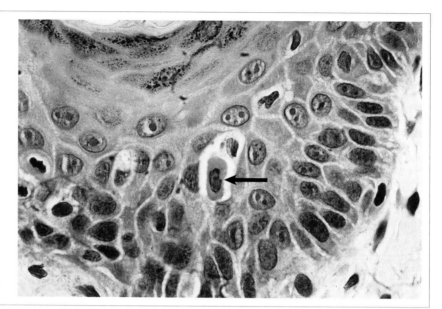

Fig. 6.4 Apoptosis. Histology of skin from a case of graft-versus-host disease (Ch. 9) in which there is individual cell death (arrowed) in the epidermis as a result of immune injury.

hypoxia has a protective effect in subsequent severe hypoxia; this is called preconditioning. Diseases such as myocardial infarction and stroke are major causes of morbidity, so any intervention improving cell survival could have major benefits. Solid organ transplantation includes an episode of graft ischaemia and reperfusion, so reduction in harm to the graft may be achievable. In contrast, increasing cell kill in cancer treatment is beneficial. In recognition of the complexity of pathways in necrosis, the phrase 'programmed cell necrosis' has been suggested as a balance to the established phrase 'programmed cell death' (apoptosis).

The outline of necrosis and apoptosis above treats these as particular events in particular circumstances; the reality of disease is often more complex. For example, myocardial ischaemia and reperfusion is characterised by necrosis, but probably has an element of apoptosis in marginally affected tissues. Acute lung injury (adult respiratory distress syndrome) results in widespread alveolar damage following a wide range of circumstances (Ch. 14); thus the precise pathway to cell death varies between Gram-positive sepsis, Gram-negative sepsis, trauma, oxygen toxicity and so on, and includes combinations of necrosis, oncosis, apoptosis and caspase-independent cell death. Treatment strategies will presumably need to be tailored to the precise circumstances; at present generic approaches, such as blocking pro-inflammatory cytokines like tumour necrosis factor, give limited success.

REPAIR AND REGENERATION

▸ Cells can be divided into labile, stable or permanent populations; only labile and stable cells can be replaced if lost
▸ Complex tissue architecture may not be reconstructed
▸ Healing is restitution with no, or minimal, residual defect, e.g. superficial skin abrasion, incised wound healing by first intention
▸ Repair is necessary when there is tissue loss: healing by second intention

The ultimate consequences of injury depends on many factors. Most important is the capability of cells to replicate, replacing those that are lost, coupled with the ability to rebuild complex architectural structures.

Structures such as intestinal villi depending largely on the epithelium for their shape can be rebuilt. However, complex structures such as the renal glomeruli cannot be reconstructed if destroyed.

Cell renewal

Cells in adult individuals are classified according to their potential for renewal (Ch. 5):

- *Labile cells* have a good capacity to regenerate. Surface epithelial cells are typical of this group; they are constantly being lost from the surface and replaced from deeper layers.
- *Stable cell populations* divide at a very slow rate normally, but still retain the capacity to divide when necessary. Hepatocytes and renal tubular cells are good examples.
- Nerve cells and striated muscle cells are regarded as *permanent* because they have no effective regeneration.

Stem cells

Cells lost through injury or normal senescence are replaced from the *stem cell pool* present in many labile and stable populations. When stem cells undergo mitotic division, one of the daughter cells progresses along a differentiation pathway according to the needs and functional state of the tissue; the other daughter cell retains the stem cell characteristics. Stem cells are a minority population in many tissues and are often located in discrete compartments: in the epidermis, stem cells are in the basal layer immediately adjacent to the basement membrane, in the hair follicles and sebaceous glands; in intestinal mucosa, the stem cells are near the bottom of the crypts. The liver has an equivalent population of progenitor cells, lying between hepatocytes and bile ducts.

There also seems to be a separate pool of stem cells available in the bone marrow; these haemopoietic stem cells are able to seed into other organs and differentiate locally into the appropriate tissue.

The ability of a tissue to regenerate may be dependent on the integrity of the stem cell population. Stem cells are particularly vulnerable to radiation injury; this can result either in their loss, thus impairing the regenerative ability of the tissue, or in mutations propagated to daughter cells with the risk of neoplastic transformation.

Complete restitution

Loss of part of a labile cell population can be completely restored. For example, consider the result of a minor skin abrasion (Fig. 6.5). The epidermis is lost over a limited area, but at the margins of the lesion there remain cells that can multiply to cover the defect. In addition, the base of the lesion probably transects the neck of sweat glands and hair follicles; cells from here can also proliferate and contribute to healing. At first, cells proliferate and spread out as a thin sheet until the defect is covered. When they form a confluent layer, the stimulus to proliferate is switched off; this is referred to as *contact inhibition*, and controls both growth and movement. Once in place, the epidermis is rebuilt from the base upwards until it is indistinguishable from normal. This whole process is called *healing*.

Contact inhibition of growth and of movement are important control mechanisms in normal cells. In neoplasia (Ch. 11) these control mechanisms are lost, allowing the continued proliferation of tumour cells.

The contribution of adnexal gland cells to regeneration is made use of in plastic surgery when using split skin grafts. The whole of the epidermis is removed and positioned as the donor graft, but the necks of adnexa are left in place to generate a replacement at the donor site.

Organisation

▶ The repair of specialised tissues by the formation of a fibrous scar
▶ Occurs by the production of granulation tissue and removal of dead tissue by phagocytosis

Organisation is the process whereby specialised tissues are repaired by the formation of mature fibrovascular connective tissue. Granulation tissue is formed in the early stages, often on a scaffold of fibrin, and any dead tissue is removed by phagocytes such as neutrophil polymorphs and macrophages. The granulation tissue contracts and gradually accumulates collagen to form the scar, which then undergoes remodelling.

Organisation is a common consequence of pneumonia (Ch. 14). The alveolar exudate becomes organised. Organisation also occurs when tissue dies as a result of cessation of its blood supply (an infarct). In all instances, the organised area is firmer than normal, and often shrunken or puckered.

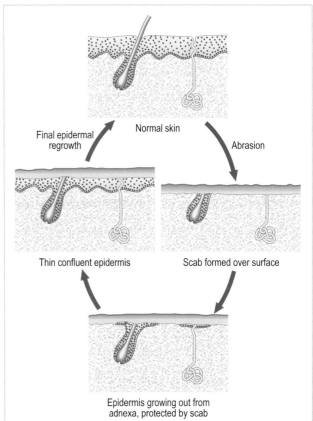

Final epidermal regrowth — Normal skin — Abrasion

Thin confluent epidermis — Scab formed over surface

Epidermis growing out from adnexa, protected by scab

Fig. 6.5 Healing of a minor skin abrasion. The scab, a layer of fibrin, protects the epidermis as it grows to cover the defect. The scab is then shed and the skin is restored to normal.

Granulation tissue

▶ A repair phenomenon
▶ Loops of capillaries, supported by myofibroblasts
▶ Inflammatory cells may be present
▶ Actively contracts to reduce wound size; this may result in a stricture later

When specialised or complex tissue is destroyed, it cannot be reconstructed. A stereotyped response then follows—a process known as *repair*. Capillary endothelial cells proliferate and grow into the area to be repaired; initially they are solid buds but soon they open into vascular channels. The vessels are arranged as a series of loops arching into the damaged area. Simultaneously, fibroblasts are stimulated to divide and to secrete collagen and other matrix components. They also acquire bundles of muscle filaments and attachments to adjacent cells. These modified cells are called *myofibroblasts* and display features and functions of both fibroblasts and smooth muscle cells. As well as secreting a collagen framework, they play a fundamental role in wound contraction. This combination of capillary loops and myofibroblasts is known as *granulation tissue*. (The name derives from the appearance of the base of a skin ulcer. When the repair process is observed, the capillary loops are just visible and impart a granular texture.) Excessive granulation tissue protruding from a surface is called *proud flesh*. Granulation tissue must not be confused with a granuloma (an aggregate of epithelioid histiocytes).

Wound contraction and scarring

Wound contraction is important for reducing the volume of tissue for repair; the tissue defect may be reduced by 80%. It results from the contraction of myofibroblasts in the granulation tissue. These are attached to each other and to the adjacent matrix components, so that granulation tissue as a whole contracts and indraws the surrounding tissues. Collagen is secreted and forms a scar, replacing the lost specialised tissues. Infection and associated inflammation are liable to increase scarring.

Although wound contraction serves a very useful function, it can also lead to problems. If the tissue damage is circumferential around the lumen of a tube such as the gut, subsequent contraction may cause stenosis (narrowing) or obstruction due to a *stricture*. Similar tissue distortion resulting in permanent shortening of a muscle is called a *contracture*. Similarly, burns to the skin can be followed by considerable contraction, with resulting cosmetic damage and often impaired mobility.

Outcome of injuries in different tissues

Having considered the general principles of healing and repair, the particular outcome of injuries to a variety of tissues will be considered.

Skin

The process of healing of a skin wound depends on the size of the defect.

Incised wound: healing by first intention
An incision, such as that made by a surgical scalpel, causes very little damage to tissues on either side of the cut. If the two sides of the wound are brought together accurately, then healing can proceed with the minimum of delay or difficulty (Fig. 6.6). Obviously, some small blood vessels will have been cut, but these will be occluded by thrombosis, and close

apposition of wound edges will help. Fibrin deposited locally will then bind the two sides. Coagulated blood on the surface forms the scab and helps to keep the wound clean. This join is very weak, but is formed rapidly and is a framework for the next stage. It is important that it is not disrupted; sutures, sticking plaster or other means of mechanical support are invaluable aids. Over the next few days, capillaries proliferate sufficiently to bridge the tiny gap, and fibroblasts secrete collagen as they migrate into the fibrin network. If the sides of the wound are very close, then such migration is minimal, as would be the amount of collagen and vascular proliferation required. By about 10 days, the strength of the repair is sufficient to enable removal of sutures. The only residual defect will be the failure to reconstruct the elastic network in the dermis.

While these changes are proceeding in the dermis, the basal epidermal cells proliferate to spread over any gap. If the edges of the wound are gaping, then the epidermal cells will creep down the sides. Eventually, when the wound is healed, these cells will usually stop growing and be resorbed, but occasionally they will remain and grow to form a keratin-filled cyst (implantation dermoid).

Tissue loss: healing by second intention
When there is tissue loss or some other reason why the wound margins are not apposed, then another mechanism is necessary for repair. For example, if there is haemorrhage (persistent bleeding) locally, this will keep the sides apart and prevent healing by first intention; infection similarly compromises healing. The response will be characterised by:

- phagocytosis to remove any debris
- granulation tissue to fill in defects and repair specialised tissues lost
- epithelial regeneration to cover the surface (Fig. 6.7).

The timescale depends on the size of the defect, as this determines the amount of granulation tissue to be generated and the area to cover with epithelium. Quite large expanses of tissue can be removed if necessary, and the defect left to heal by second intention. The final cosmetic result depends on how much tissue loss there has been, as this affects the amount of scarring.

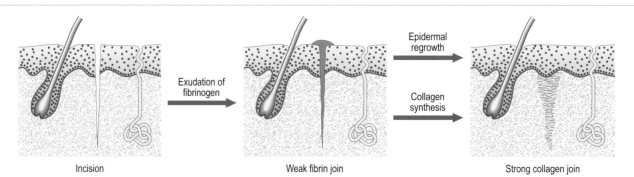

Incision   Exudation of fibrinogen   Weak fibrin join   Epidermal regrowth   Collagen synthesis   Strong collagen join

Fig. 6.6   Skin incision healed by first intention. As little or no tissue has been lost, the apposed edges of the incision are joined by a thin layer of fibrin, which is ultimately replaced by collagen covered by surface epidermis.

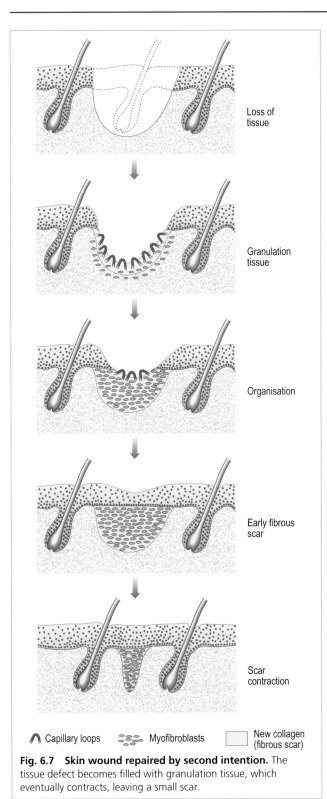

Loss of tissue

Granulation tissue

Organisation

Early fibrous scar

Scar contraction

∧ Capillary loops   Myofibroblasts   New collagen (fibrous scar)

Fig. 6.7 Skin wound repaired by second intention. The tissue defect becomes filled with granulation tissue, which eventually contracts, leaving a small scar.

Keloid nodules

Dermal injury is sometimes followed by excessive fibroblast proliferation and collagen production. This phenomenon is genetically determined, and is particularly prevalent among blacks. A mass several centimetres across may follow surgery or injury, particularly burns.

Mechanism of skin healing and repair

Healing and repair involve a complex interplay of cytokines (Ch. 5). There is considerable complexity and redundancy in this system, with the same cell producing many cytokines, and most cytokines having many functions. The initiating signals are probably hypoxia together with the release of growth factors from platelet degranulation. These trigger the production of numerous cytokines such as epidermal growth factors (EGFs) and keratinocyte growth factor (KGF) from platelets, macrophages and dermal fibroblasts, to stimulate keratinocyte proliferation and mobility. Keratinocytes and macrophages produce vascular endothelial growth factor (VEGF), inducing new blood vessel formation (angiogenesis). Platelet-derived growth factor (PDGF) from platelets, macrophages and keratinocytes facilitates the local accumulation and activation of macrophages, proliferation of fibroblasts and matrix production. Control of myofibroblasts and collagen formation is partly influenced by transforming growth factor-beta (TGF-beta); abnormalities can result in hypertrophic scars or keloid.

Failure to regenerate structures such as skin adnexal glands and hair is a post-natal problem. Formation of these complex cellular configurations is controlled by a small number of homeotic (patterning) genes which then control the necessary growth and differentiation genes. Damage to fetal skin is healed completely, but in the adult the homeotic genes are not activated, necessitating an imperfect repair. Adult epidermis is capable of responding to produce hairs and so forth, but the wounded dermis fails to produce the required signals.

Peritoneum

The healing of a peritoneal defect may follow two distinct alternative patterns. If it is sutured or contaminated with fibrin or foreign material such as glove powder, then local ischaemia or platelet granules initiate the cytokine networks seen in skin healing (and elsewhere) with resulting angiogenesis. Contact with another surface, such as serosa of the intestine, can then result in adhesion. In time a band of collagen is laid down which may subsequently cause bowel obstruction.

However, a peritoneal defect that is simply cleaned and left unsutured will heal by a different mechanism. Perivascular connective tissue cells in the base of the defect proliferate to fill it, while any debris is removed by macrophages. When this is complete, the surface cells differentiate into new mesothelial lining cells, rather than awaiting migration over the surface from the surviving mesothelial cells at the margin (Fig. 6.8). Healing is thus rapid and complete, irrespective of the size of the defect, with very little risk of forming adhesions.

Gastrointestinal tract

The fate of an intestinal injury depends upon its depth.

Mucosal erosions

An erosion is defined as loss of part of the thickness of the mucosa. Viable epithelial cells are immediately adjacent to the defect and proliferate rapidly to regenerate the mucosa.

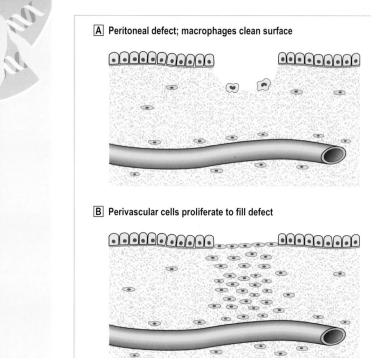

A   Peritoneal defect; macrophages clean surface

B   Perivascular cells proliferate to fill defect

C   Surface cells differentiate to mesothelial lining cells

Fig. 6.8   Healing of an unsutured peritoneal defect.

Such an erosion can be re-covered in a matter of hours, provided that the cause has been removed. Notwithstanding this remarkable speed of recovery, it is possible for a patient to lose much blood from multiple gastric erosions before they heal. If endoscopy to identify the cause of haematemesis is delayed, the erosions may no longer be present, and thus escape detection.

Mucosal ulceration

Ulceration is loss of the full thickness of the mucosa, and often the defect goes much deeper to penetrate the muscularis propria; further complications are discussed in Chapter 15. The principles of repair have been outlined above. Destroyed muscle cannot be regenerated, and the mucosa must be replaced from the margins. The outcome of mucosal ulceration is discussed below with reference to a gastric ulcer, but colonic ulcers show similar features. Damaged blood vessels will have bled and the surface will become covered by a layer of fibrin. Macrophages then remove any dead tissue by phagocytosis. Meanwhile, granulation tissue is produced in the ulcer base,

as capillaries and myofibroblasts proliferate. Also, the mucosa will begin to regenerate at the margins and spread out on to the floor of the ulcer.

If the cause persists, the ulcer becomes chronic and there is oscillation between further ulceration and repair, possibly resulting in considerable destruction of the gastric wall. If healing ever proceeds far enough, the fibrous scar tissue that has replaced muscle will contract, with distortion of the stomach and possible obstruction. Any larger arteries that lie in the path of the advancing ulceration are at risk of rupture, with resulting haemorrhage. However, there may be a zone of inflammation around the ulceration, and if this abuts the vessel it results in a reactive proliferation of the vascular intima. This feature is referred to as *endarteritis obliterans* because of the obliteration of the lumen (it has nothing to do with end arteries).

Bone

> ▶ Haematoma organised and dead bone removed
> ▶ Callus formed, then replaced by trabecular bone
> ▶ Finally remodelled
> ▶ Fracture healing delayed if bone ends are mobile, infected, very badly misaligned or avascular

Fracture healing

Immediately after the fracture there will be haemorrhage within the bone from ruptured vessels in the marrow cavity, and also around the bone in relation to the periosteum. A *haematoma* at the fracture site facilitates repair by providing a foundation for the growth of cells (Fig. 6.9). There will also be devitalised fragments of bone, and probable soft tissue damage nearby. Thus, the initial phases of repair involve removal of necrotic tissue and organisation of the haematoma. In the latter, the capillaries will be accompanied by fibroblasts and osteoblasts. These deposit bone in an irregularly woven pattern. The mass of new bone, sometimes with islands of cartilage, is called *callus;* that within the medullary cavity is internal callus, while that at the periosteum is external callus. The latter is helpful as a splint, although it will need to be resorbed eventually. Woven bone is subsequently replaced by more orderly, lamellar bone; this in turn is gradually remodelled according to the direction of mechanical stress.

Problems with fracture healing

Several factors can delay, or even arrest, the repair of a fracture:

- movement
- interposed soft tissues
- gross misalignment
- infection
- pre-existing bone disease.

Movement between the two ends, apart from causing pain, also results in excessive callus and prevents or slows down tissue union. Persistent movement prevents bone formation, and collagen is laid down instead to give fibrous union; this results in a false joint at the fracture site. Movement of a

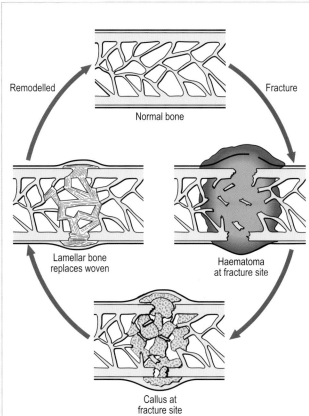

Fig. 6.9 Healing of a bone fracture. The haematoma at the fracture site gives a framework for healing. It is replaced by a fracture callus, which is subsequently replaced by lamellar bone, which is then remodelled to restore the normal trabecular pattern of the bone.

Labels on figure: Remodelled / Normal bone / Fracture / Lamellar bone replaces woven / Haematoma at fracture site / Callus at fracture site

lesser degree leads to excessive callus which takes longer to be resorbed and may impinge on adjacent structures.

Interposed soft tissues between the broken ends delay healing at least until they are removed, and there is an increased risk of non-union.

Gross misalignment also slows the rate of healing and will prevent a good functional result, leading to increased risk of degenerative disease (osteoarthrosis) in adjacent joints.

Infection at the fracture site will delay healing and there is the additional risk of chronic osteomyelitis. Infection is more likely if the skin over the fracture is broken; this is referred to as a *compound fracture*.

If the bone broken was weakened by disease, the break is called a *pathological fracture*. Pathological fracture may be the result of a primary disorder of bone, or the secondary involvement of bone by some other condition, such as metastatic carcinoma. In most instances, a pathological fracture will heal satisfactorily, but sometimes treatment of the underlying cause will be required first.

Liver

Hepatocytes, a stable cell population, have excellent regenerative capacity. In some circumstances, hepatic regeneration comes from liver progenitor cells rather than hepatocytes;

bone marrow-derived stem cells are a third option. The hepatic architecture, however, cannot be satisfactorily reconstructed if severely damaged. Consequently, conditions that result only in hepatocyte loss may be followed by complete restitution, whereas damage destroying both the hepatocytes and architecture may not. In the latter situation, the imbalance between hepatocyte regeneration and failure to reconstruct the architecture may proceed to cirrhosis (Fig. 6.10).

Kidney

The kidney is similar to the liver with respect to tissue injury, in that it has an epithelium that can be regenerated but an architecture that cannot. Loss of tubular epithelium following an ischaemic episode or exposure to toxins may result in renal failure, but in general there is sufficient surviving epithelium to repopulate the tubules and enable normal renal function to return. Inflammatory or other damage resulting in destruction of the glomerulus is likely to be permanent or result in glomerular scarring, with loss of filtration capacity. Similarly, interstitial inflammation is liable to proceed to fibrosis and, thus, impaired reabsorption from tubules.

Muscle

Cardiac muscle fibres and smooth muscle cells are permanent cells; vascular smooth muscle may be different, in that new vessels can be formed. This means that damaged muscle is replaced by scar tissue. However, if the contractile proteins only are lost, then it is possible to synthesise new ones within the old endomysium. Voluntary muscle has a limited capacity for regeneration from satellite cells.

Neural tissue

- ▶ Central nervous system does not repair effectively
- ▶ Peripheral nerves show Wallerian degeneration (Ch. 26) distal to trauma; variable recovery depending on alignment and continuity
- ▶ May produce amputation neuroma

Even though recent evidence suggests that adult nerve cells may have a low replicative capacity, there is no effective regeneration of neurones in the central nervous system. Glial cells, however, may proliferate in response to injury, a process referred to as *gliosis*.

Peripheral nerve damage affects axons and their supporting structures, such as Schwann cells. If there is transection of the nerve, axons degenerate proximally for a distance of about one or two nodes; distally, there is Wallerian degeneration followed by proliferation of Schwann cells in anticipation of axonal regrowth. If there is good realignment of the cut ends, the axons may regrow down their previous channels (now occupied by proliferated Schwann cells); however, full functional recovery is unusual. When there is poor alignment or amputation of the nerve, the cut ends of the axons still proliferate, but in a disordered manner, to produce a tangled

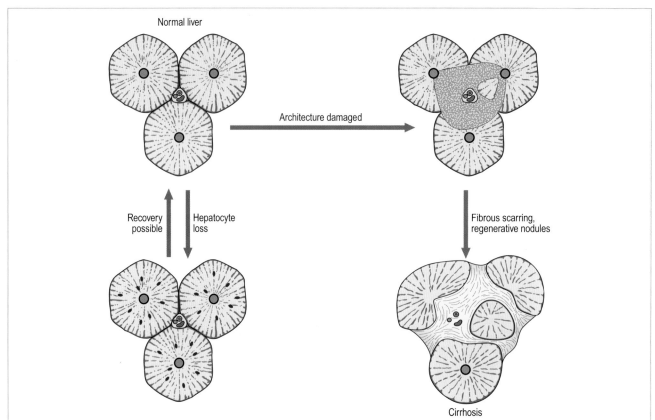

Fig. 6.10   Consequences of liver injury depending on extent of tissue damage. Loss of only scattered liver cells, or even small groups, can be restored without architectural disturbance. However, if there is confluent loss of liver cells and architectural damage, the liver heals by scarring and nodular regeneration of liver cells, resulting in cirrhosis.

mass of axons and stroma called an *amputation neuroma*. Sometimes, these are painful and require removal.

Modifying influences

▸ Damage to fetus or infant may affect subsequent development
▸ In general, children heal rapidly
▸ In old age, reserve capacity is reduced and there may be co-existent disease, such as ischaemia
▸ Vitamin C deficiency impairs collagen synthesis
▸ Malnutrition impairs healing and resistance to disease
▸ Excess steroids, advanced malignancy and local ischaemia impair healing
▸ Denervation increases tissue vulnerability

The description of tissue injury and repair given above applies to an otherwise healthy adult. However, various factors can impair healing and repair:

● age, both very young and elderly
● disorders of nutrition
● neoplastic disorders
● Cushing's syndrome and steroid therapy
● diabetes mellitus and immunosuppression
● vascular disturbance
● denervation.

Age

Early in life, cellular injury is likely to impair or prevent the normal growth and development of an organ. Organogenesis is at risk if there is impaired function, differentiation or migration of the precursor cells. For example, rubella infection or thalidomide administration in early pregnancy can cause congenital abnormalities; therapeutic doses of radiation are associated with microcephaly and mental retardation.

Similar considerations apply to childhood, in that there may be growth disturbance following tissue damage. For example, the distal pulmonary airways may be permanently damaged by severe infection or mechanical stress, as in whooping cough. High doses of radiation will result in loss of replicating cells and in local failure to grow; the affected area will then be smaller in proportion to the rest of the body. On the other hand, wound healing proceeds rapidly in healthy children, and fractures unite more quickly than in adults.

The physiology of ageing is complex (Ch. 12); one characteristic is a reduced ability to repair damaged tissues. Connective tissues become less elastic, renal function diminishes, bones weaken and cerebral neurones are lost. Consequently, a more substantial effect from the same insult occurs when compared with that in a younger adult. Wound healing is often delayed in old age because of ischaemia or other significant disease.

Disorders of nutrition

Wound healing is profoundly influenced by the ability to synthesise protein and collagen. The latter is dependent on vitamin C for the hydroxylation of proline as a step in collagen synthesis. Scurvy (vitamin C deficiency) leads to wound healing of greatly reduced strength; capillaries are also fragile and thus haemorrhages occur.

Protein malnutrition, whether due to dietary deficiency or the consequence of protein loss, also impairs wound healing. In addition, severe malnutrition impairs the response to infection which may then proceed to a fatal outcome. For example, measles is generally a transient problem in well-nourished children, but is frequently fatal in the malnourished.

Neoplastic disorders

In advanced malignant neoplastic disease with widely disseminated tumours, or gastrointestinal symptoms such as dysphagia, the patient is malnourished. However, a catabolic state with profound weight loss may be an early feature of some cancers. Such patients have impaired healing, and this may compromise the recovery from attempted surgical removal of the lesion.

There may also be evidence of impaired healing in the vicinity of the tumour. Skin stretched over a superficial tumour will often break down and ulcerate, and it is necessary to treat the tumour to promote healing of the ulcer. A pathological fracture of bone through a metastatic tumour may not heal unless the tumour is dealt with first.

Cushing's syndrome and steroid therapy

Excessive circulating corticosteroids, whether they result from tumour or from therapeutic administration, have two effects on tissue injury.

- Due to their immunosuppressive actions, the consequences of injury or infection may be more severe.
- Steroids impair healing by interfering with the formation of granulation tissue and, thus, wound contraction.

Diabetes mellitus and immunosuppression

Both diabetes mellitus (Ch. 7) and immunosuppression (Ch. 9) increase susceptibility to infection by low-virulence organisms, and increase the risk of tissue damage. Normal healing responses are possible, although they may be impaired by continuing infection. Diabetes may affect polymorph function, and may also result in occlusion of small blood vessels and cause neuropathy. There also seems to be a direct effect on keratinocytes, reducing their motility, and also that of myofibroblasts, both of which delay healing.

Vascular disturbance

An adequate vascular supply is essential for normal cellular function. An impaired supply can result in ischaemia or infarction (Ch. 8). Note that an adequate supply for resting tissue may prove inadequate if the demand increases. For example, in coronary artery disease, the blood flow may be sufficient for the resting state, but not for exertion when the cardiac output increases. The deficit of oxygen may then result in tissue damage.

Another effect of a reduced vascular supply is impaired healing. This occurs because hypoxia and reduced local nutrition result in poorer tissue regrowth or repair.

Denervation

An intact nerve supply supports the structural and functional integrity of many tissues. In addition, nerves have a role in mediating the inflammatory response as part of the host mechanism for limiting the effects of injury. Denervated tissues may become severely damaged, probably through a combination of unresponsiveness to repeated minor trauma, and lack of pain of intercurrent infection or inflammation. Thus, patients with conditions such as peripheral neuropathy or leprosy may develop foot ulcers (neuropathic ulcers). A neuropathic joint (Charcot's joint) may be damaged unwittingly and progressively beyond repair.

INJURY DUE TO IONISING RADIATION

- ▶ Electromagnetic and particulate: background, accidental, occupational and medical exposure
- ▶ Indirect effect of oxygen radicals and hydroxyl ions on DNA
- ▶ Rapidly dividing cell populations show early susceptibility
- ▶ Late effects: fibrosis and increased tumour risk
- ▶ Tumour induction roughly proportional to dose received

Radiation is generally perceived by the public as harmful. In the European Union it is now mandatory that medical practitioners using radiation for investigating or treating patients know about radiation protection. This section deals with certain aspects of this, particularly in relation to:

- nature of ionising radiation and its interaction with tissue
- genetic and somatic effects of ionising radiation.

Definition and sources

Radiation of medical importance is largely restricted to that which causes the formation of ions on interaction with matter (ionising radiation). The exception to this is some ultraviolet light. Ionising radiation includes:

- electromagnetic radiation: X-rays and gamma rays
- particulate radiation: alpha particles, beta particles (electrons), neutrons.

Electromagnetic radiation

Only part of the electromagnetic spectrum produces ionising events. The production of ions requires a photon of high energy and thus of short wavelength, in practice shorter than that of ultraviolet light. If the photon is emitted by a machine,

the radiation is called an X-ray. If it is emitted as a result of the disintegration of an unstable atom, it is referred to as a gamma ray. It follows that X-rays can be switched on and off, while gamma ray emission is continuous so protection requires a physical barrier.

Particulate radiation

As well as photons, certain subatomic particles may also produce ionisation. These include alpha particles (helium nuclei), beta particles (electrons) and neutrons. The distinction between beta particles and electrons is the same as that between gamma rays and X-rays: beta particles are produced through the process of radioactive decay, whereas electrons are a structural component of atoms that may be artificially projected as a beam.

Units of dose

Various units have been used for measuring radiation. The current unit of *absorbed dose* is the gray (Gy)—1 joule of radiation energy deposited in 1 kg of matter—and is the usual measure of therapeutic radiation when a uniform type of radiation is administered to a specified tissue.

However, different forms of radiation vary in the distribution of energy deposited in tissues, hence the biological effect. Alpha particles, having a high linear energy transfer (LET), deposit a large amount of energy over a short distance, so are about 20 times more damaging than beta particles or X-rays, which have low LET. Tissues also differ in their sensitivity (Table 6.3). Therefore, when subjects are exposed to a mixture of different forms of radiation to several tissues, it is useful to make mathematical corrections for comparative purposes, and express the result as the *effective dose equivalent*, measured in sieverts (Sv) (Fig. 6.11).

Another relevant unit is a measure of the rate of disintegration of unstable atoms; 1 becquerel (Bq) is one emission per second. The becquerel is not itself a measure of dose, because it expresses only a rate of disintegration irrespective of the nature or energy of the products of disintegration. However, for any particular atom the latter is known, so the dose can be calculated.

Background radiation

Everyone is exposed to background radiation from their environment. In the UK the average annual dose is 2.7 mSv, which comes from:

- natural sources (84%)
- artificial sources (16%).

Over 90% of the artificial component is from medical usage, such as diagnostic X-rays and nuclear medicine. The amount has increased recently, reflecting greater use of CT scans. (Note that magnetic resonance imaging does not use ionising radiation.) The natural component is made up from cosmic, terrestrial, airborne and food sources. The most locally variable among these is airborne radiation, which derives mainly from radon and radon daughters; these diffuse out of the ground and are commoner in certain types of rock, such as

Table 6.3 Relative sensitivities of different tissues to harmful effects of ionising radiation	
Tissue	Factor
Gonads	0.25
Breasts	0.15
Haemopoietic tissue	0.12
Lungs	0.12
Liver	0.06
Thyroid	0.03
Bone	0.03
Other organs (total)	0.24
Total for body = 1.00	

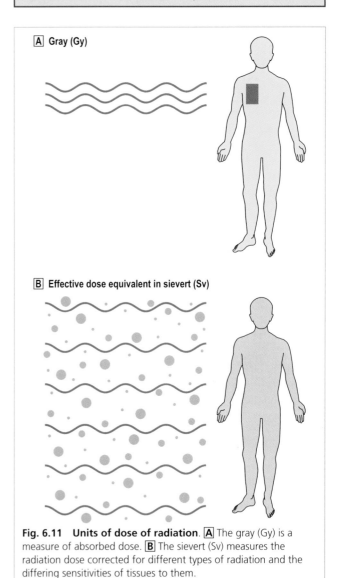

Fig. 6.11 Units of dose of radiation. **A** The gray (Gy) is a measure of absorbed dose. **B** The sievert (Sv) measures the radiation dose corrected for different types of radiation and the differing sensitivities of tissues to them.

granite. In the UK, there are 100-fold differences from one place to another. Some draught-proofed homes in areas of high natural airborne radiation accumulate radon to concentrations exceeding acceptable industrial limits, thereby placing occupants at risk of lung disease from irradiation.

Mode of action

When radiation passes through tissue, any collisions within it will be randomly distributed amongst its components. However, it seems that direct damage as a result of ionisation of proteins or membranes does not make a major contribution to the biological end result. Water is the most prevalent molecule, and following ionisation several types of short-lived but highly reactive radicals are formed such as $H^{\bullet}$ and hydroxyl radical $OH^{\bullet}$. In a well-oxygenated cell, oxygen radicals will also be formed, e.g. hydroperoxyl radical, $HO_2^{\bullet}$ and superoxide radical $O_2^{\bullet -}$.

These radicals then interact with macromolecules, of which the most significant are membrane lipids and DNA.

DNA damage

The types of radiation-induced DNA damage include:

- strand breaks
- base alterations
- cross-linking.

Breakage of the DNA strand (Fig. 6.12) is a common result of radiation. When only one strand is broken, repair can generally be accomplished accurately. Double-strand breaks may be irreparable because there is no template. Also, multiple double-strand breaks may rejoin incorrectly, resulting in chromosome translocation or inversion.

Base alterations are also frequent, such that the DNA strand no longer transcribes correctly (mutation). The result may be unreadable (nonsense mutation) or may read incorrectly (missense mutation).

DNA strand cross-linking occurs when radiation-induced reactive oxygen species cause linkage between the complementary strands, resulting in an inability to separate and thus to make a new copy. DNA replication is therefore blocked. DNA damage of these types is not caused solely by radiation; it is also the mechanism of action of some chemotherapy. For example, alkylating agents cause cross-linkage and platinum-based drugs cause strand breaks.

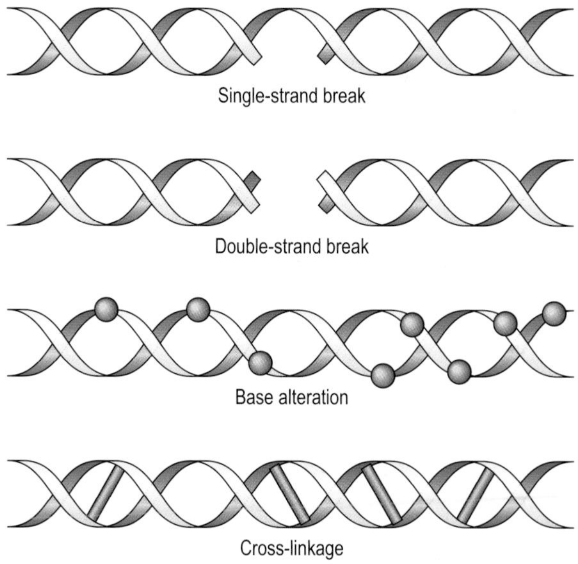

The consequences of DNA damage depend on its nature and extent, and on the results of any attempts at repair. The mean lethal dose per cell is in the range 0.5–2 Gy. Most double-strand breaks are repaired promptly, but some result in misrepair or failure to repair. Cells affected in this way are described as having 'reproductive death'; the combination of genetic instability and lethal mutations results in cell death after two or three mitotic cycles. A much smaller proportion of cells die immediately by apoptosis or necrosis.

There are several DNA repair enzyme systems, sufficient for incidental strand breaks. Some people have defective DNA repair, so are more susceptible to ionising radiation or ultraviolet light. Loss of function mutations of the *ATM* gene impair excision repair of double-strand breaks, and explain the enhanced radiation sensitivity of patients with ataxia telangiectasia. Similarly, the mutated *ERCC6* gene is the defect in xeroderma pigmentosum, in which there is extreme skin sensitivity to sunlight, causing tumours.

Effects on tissues

Despite knowledge of the molecular events following irradiation, there is continuing debate about how these are translated into the observed tissue responses. The immediate physicochemical events and consequent biomolecular damage are over in a few milliseconds; the varied outcomes are manifest in hours to years.

DNA damage may have three possible consequences:

- cell death, either immediately or at the next attempted mitosis
- repair and no further consequence
- a permanent change in genotype.

The dose given will influence this outcome, as will the radiosensitivity of the cell. Tissue and organ changes will reflect the overall reactions in the component parts. Tissue consequences are usually divided into early tissue reactions or deterministic effects, which are predictable according to the dose received, and later stochastic effects, where only the probability is related to the dose. Thus, cataract and skin erythema (tissue reactions) will not occur below a certain threshold dose, while in contrast there is no dose threshold below which there is no probability of cancer (a stochastic effect).

Early effects

Early effects of radiation are generally the result of cell killing and the interruption of successful mitotic activity. Hierarchical cell organisations, such as the bone marrow or gut epithelium, which have a dividing stem cell population and daughter cells of finite life expectancy, will show the most pronounced effects. In essence, the supply of functioning differentiated cells is cut off or suspended. In addition,

Fig. 6.12 DNA damage by radiation. Single-strand breaks can be reconstituted by DNA repair enzymes, because the complementary strand forms a template. The other injuries are less easily remedied. Cross-linkage causes reproductive death.

Single-strand break

Double-strand break

Base alteration

Cross-linkage

there is vascular endothelial damage, resulting in fluid and protein leakage rather like that of the inflammatory response (Ch. 10).

Late effects

Late effects of radiation are the result of several factors, and the contribution of each is contentious. Vascular endothelial cell loss will result in exposure of the underlying collagen. This will prompt platelet adherence and thrombosis, which is subsequently incorporated into the vessel wall and is associated with the intimal proliferation of endarteritis obliterans. A possible result of this is long-term vascular insufficiency with consequent atrophy and fibrosis.

However, the observed atrophy may simply be a function of continuing cell loss over a long period of time, reflecting an inherently slow rate of proliferation of cells in the tissue concerned. If this is the case, the vascular alterations are part of the late effects of radiation, but not the cause of the atrophy.

The cellular alterations induced by radiation are permanent. The limits of tissue tolerance cannot be exceeded even if many years have elapsed. In addition to the effects mentioned above, radiation-induced mutation of the genome causes an increased risk of neoplastic transformation (see below).

Bone marrow

Haemopoietic marrow is a hierarchical tissue that maintains the blood concentration of functional cells of limited life-span by a constant high rate of mitotic activity. The effect of radiation is to suspend renewal of all cell lines. Subsequent blood counts will fall at a rate corresponding to the physiological survival of cells; granulocytes will diminish after a few days but erythrocytes survive much longer.

The ultimate outcome will depend on the dose received, and will vary from complete recovery to death from marrow failure (unless a marrow transplant is successful). In the long-term survivor, there is a risk of leukaemia. Localised heavy radiation will not alter the blood count, but it will result in local loss of haemopoiesis and fibrosis of the marrow cavity.

Intestine

The surface epithelial lining of the small intestine is renewed every 24–48 hours. A significant dose of radiation will therefore result in loss of protective and absorptive functions over a similar timescale; diarrhoea and the risk of infection then follow. If a high dose is given to a localised region, the mucosa will regrow, although often with a less specialised cell type, and with the probability of mutations in the remaining cells. The muscle coat will also have been damaged, and there is the risk of granulation tissue causing a stricture later.

Skin

The changes in the skin reflect its composition from epithelium, connective tissue and blood vessels. Epidermis will suffer the consequences of cessation of mitosis, with desquamation and hair loss. Provided enough stem cells survive, hair will regrow, and any defects in epidermal coverage can be re-epithelialised. The regenerated epidermis will lack rete ridges and adnexa. Damage to keratinocytes and melanocytes results in melanin deposition in the dermis where it is picked up by phagocytic cells; these tend to remain in the skin and result in local hyperpigmentation (post-inflammatory pigmentation). Some fibroblasts in the dermis will be killed, while others are at risk of an inability to divide, or to function correctly. As a consequence, the dermis is thinned, and histology shows bizarre, enlarged fibroblast nuclei.

The vessels show various changes depending on their size. Endothelial cell loss or damage is the probable underlying factor. Small and thin-walled vessels will leak fluid and proteins, and mimic the inflammatory response; in the long term, they can be permanently dilated and tortuous (telangiectatic). Larger vessels develop intimal proliferation and may permanently impair blood flow.

In summary, the skin is at first reddened with desquamation, and subsequently shows pigmentation. Later, it is thinned with telangiectasia; if damage is too severe, it will break down and ulcerate (radionecrosis).

Gonads

Germ cells are very radiosensitive, and permanent sterility can follow relatively low doses. Also of great significance is the possibility of mutation in germ cells, which could result in passing on defects to the next generation; this is a teratogenic effect. However, although this has been demonstrated experimentally in mice, no studies of radiated populations have proven a teratogenic effect in humans.

Lung

Ionising radiation is one of several agents that can damage alveoli, culminating in fibrosis (Ch. 14). Inhaled radioactive materials induce pulmonary tumours.

Kidney

Renal irradiation results in gradual loss of parenchyma and impaired renal function. Systemic effects include the development of hypertension.

Whole body irradiation

Whole body irradiation can be the result of accidental or therapeutic exposure. The consequences can mostly be predicted (Fig. 6.13). At very high doses, death occurs rapidly with convulsions due to cerebral injury. At lower doses, the clinical picture is dominated in the first few days by gastro-intestinal problems, and later by bone marrow suppression; either may prove fatal. In the long term, there is the risk of neoplasia.

Therapeutic usage of total body irradiation is mainly for the deliberate ablation of the bone marrow prior to transplantation of marrow, using either stored marrow from the patient or marrow from another donor.

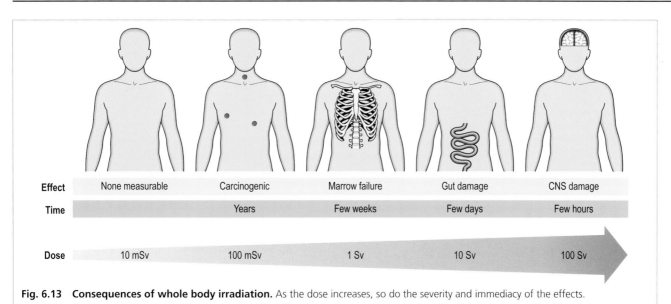

Effect	None measurable	Carcinogenic	Marrow failure	Gut damage	CNS damage
Time		Years	Few weeks	Few days	Few hours
Dose	10 mSv	100 mSv	1 Sv	10 Sv	100 Sv

Fig. 6.13   Consequences of whole body irradiation. As the dose increases, so do the severity and immediacy of the effects.

Ionising radiation and tumours

There is no doubt that ionising radiation causes tumours (Ch. 11). This is now firmly established for relatively high doses, but with low-dose radiation some uncertainty remains.

There is a roughly linear relationship between the dose received and the incidence of tumours. The mechanism is incompletely understood, but the fundamental event is mutation of the host cell DNA; it is unlikely that a single point mutation is sufficient and more probably many will be present. As the radiation dose increases, so a greater number of cells will be lethally irradiated, thus reducing the number surviving and at risk of neoplastic transformation.

The dose–response information comes from several sources, including animal experiments and observations on patients or populations exposed to radiation. Thus, children who received radiation of the thyroid gland show an incidence of tumours corresponding to the dose received. Occupational exposure to radon gas in mines also shows a correlation with the risk of lung tumours. For a given dose, the risk of neoplasia varies between tissues (Table 6.4).

Common to all these observations is a time delay between exposure to radiation and development of the tumour. Studies of Japanese survivors of the atomic bombs show significant numbers of cases of leukaemia by about 6 years, with a mean delay of 12.5 years and thereafter a decreasing incidence. For solid cancers, however, the mean delay was 25 years with a continuing increased incidence in these people four decades later; in total, there have now been many more solid cancers than leukaemias (Fig. 6.14).

Regarding low doses (less than 100 mSv), it is more difficult to be sure if the radiation is carcinogenic because the anticipated number of tumours would be so small compared with the overall number of tumours in the exposed population. However, more recent studies of a cohort of 100 000 Japanese atomic bomb survivors exposed to low doses suggest that linear extrapolation with no minimum threshold gives a reasonable

Table 6.4 Relative lifetime risk of fatal cancer from a standard dose of ionising radiation	
Tissue	**Risk factor (Sv^{-1})**
Lung	1 in 80
Female breast	1 in 90
Haemopoietic tissue	1 in 360
Bone	1 in 2000
Thyroid	1 in 4000
Other organs (total)	1 in 43
Total for body = 1 in 20	

fit with observed cancers. By way of illustration, a single CT scan of the abdomen can result in a dose of about 15 mSv to the digestive tract which, for a 40 year old, may result in a lifetime risk of 0.02% of death from digestive tract cancer. However, estimates of the risk of cancer in this dose range may be two or three times too high or too low. Children may be at a greater risk than adults for any given dose, an effect compounded by their projected longer survival at risk.

Ultraviolet light

Ultraviolet light has three wavelength classes:

- UVA 315–400 nm
- UVB 280–315 nm
- UVC 100–280 nm.

UVB is associated with sunburn and can also cause skin tumours; although not ionising, it damages DNA by inducing pyrimidine dimers and strand linkage. UVB is also immunosuppressive. UVA probably induces non-dimer damage, and also inhibits DNA repair processes. The tumours produced are basal cell and squamous cell carcinomas, and malignant melanomas. Melanin pigmentation, itself induced by ultraviolet light, is protective against these effects.

UVC is very toxic and is used in germicide lamps. However, solar radiation in this range is filtered out by the ozone layer.

Principles of radiation protection

In view of the risk of harm from ionising radiation, it is important that it is used safely and only when there are no suitable alternatives. The International Commission on Radiological Protection (ICRP) has published recommendations with three central requirements:

- No practice shall be adopted unless its introduction produces a net benefit.
- All exposures shall be kept as low as reasonably achievable, economic and social factors being taken into account.

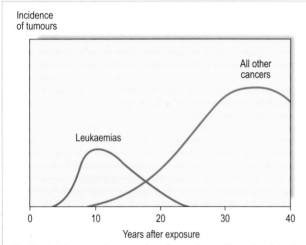

Fig. 6.14 **Tumours in atom bomb survivors.** There is a latent interval between exposure to radiation and detection of the tumours. This is relatively short for leukaemias, but up to several decades for solid tumours.

- The dose equivalent to individuals shall not exceed the limits recommended for the appropriate circumstances by the Commission.

In view of the risk of harm from ionising radiation, it must be used in a discriminating manner that takes alternatives into account. In the European Union, the Ionising Radiation (Medical Exposure) Regulations (IRMER) require the doctor to consider whether a procedure, or an investigation, involving radiation is justifiable in each and every circumstance.

The second requirement is sometimes referred to as the ALARA principle. This emphasises that doses should be 'as low as reasonably achievable, not simply kept below dose limits'.

Therapeutic radiation: radiotherapy

▸ Fractionation enables higher dose to be given
▸ Typical tumours treated: basal cell carcinoma of skin, squamous carcinoma of larynx, malignant lymphoma, seminoma of testis
▸ Effects and complications are delineated by the fields given

Like most effective treatments in medicine, radiotherapy carries certain risks of undesirable or unpredictable side-effects. This means that it tends to be reserved for serious or life-threatening conditions, or palliation of incurable diseases. The most common effect required from radiation is the ability to kill cells; this is used in the treatment of tumours. Sometimes, the object is to induce fibrosis or vascular occlusion, as in the treatment of vascular malformations.

Radiation may be given with the intention of cure, generally for a tumour. Usually, the aim is to give as high a dose as possible to the tumour, while producing the least possible damage to adjacent normal tissues. Some tumours are relatively radiosensitive, so that the therapeutic margin between

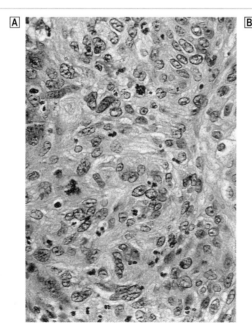
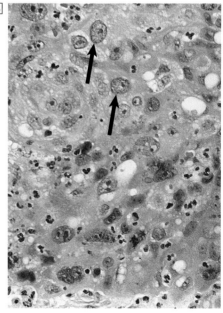

Fig. 6.15 **Effect of radiation on carcinoma of the cervix.** A Before irradiation. B One week after high-dose irradiation, showing injury to the tumour cells (note bloating of arrowed nuclei) and the induced inflammatory reaction.

tumour cell kill and tissue damage is wide; but in others the normal tissue tolerance is the limiting factor.

Basal cell carcinoma of the skin is very common and often managed by radiotherapy, although local excision is also effective. Squamous carcinoma of the larynx is usually irradiated in the first instance, because this preserves voice production. Squamous carcinoma of the uterine cervix is a tumour that may be managed by primary surgery or radiotherapy (Fig. 6.15). Localised malignant lymphoma is often irradiated, whereas generalised lymphoma is treated by chemotherapy. Metastatic seminoma of testis in para-aortic lymph nodes is usually irradiated, illustrating that radical treatment is possible even when metastases are present. Seminoma is an example of a very radiosensitive tumour. Carcinoma of the breast is usually treated by surgery, but as local recurrence is a risk patients often proceed to post-operative radical radiotherapy.

Even when there is no hope of cure, there is much that can be done to relieve symptoms. Palliative radiotherapy is often given to treat metastatic tumour deposits, such as painful bone metastases.

Fractionation

A higher dose of radiation may be given without increasing side-effects if it is divided into a number of fractions and given on different days. In practice, it is common to treat on only 5 days a week, so that a dose divided into 25 fractions would be given over 5 weeks. Each treatment fraction induces tissue damage, but is followed by attempts at repair. Normal cells included in the treated tissue volume are better able to repair effectively than are neoplastic cells. Consequently, there is a differential cell killing of more tumour cells than normal cells. Modern radiotherapy equipment and planning techniques allow a high degree of conformation of the radiated volume to the tumour itself, with less normal tissue included in the field. Palliative treatment is often a lower dose given as fewer larger fractions, in order to get a more rapid response.

Response modifiers

In addition to the benefits of fractionating treatment, there has been considerable interest in modifying the tissue response to radiation. There are often conflicting interests, in that an increased sensitivity is required in the tumour and increased resistance in the normal tissue.

The most common reason for reduced sensitivity in a tumour is a low oxygen tension. The probable explanation is the central role of oxygen radicals in mediating the biological impact of ionising radiation; a lower oxygen concentration means, quite simply, that fewer oxygen radicals are generated. Many tumours have a poorly developed vascular network, resulting in hypoxic areas; patients are also often anaemic, which increases the problem. Blood transfusion can correct anaemia.

Radiosensitisers are drugs that diffuse into tissues and, by mimicking the effect of oxygen, enhance the response.

Fig. 6.16 Skin erythema due to therapeutic irradiation. Skin erythema is an immediate tissue reaction to radiation.

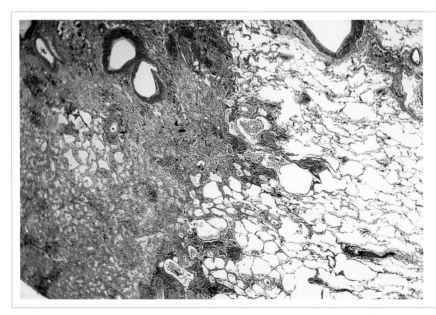

Fig. 6.17 Histology of lung fibrosis due to therapeutic irradiation. Note the abrupt demarcation between the solid scarred lung (left) and the adjacent normally aerated lung (right); this is due to the sharp cut-off at the edge of the irradiated field, to minimise the extent of damage to adjacent structures.

Commonly confused conditions and entities relating to cellular injury	
Commonly confused	**Distinction and explanation**
Apoptosis and *necrosis*	Both are modes of cell death. *Apoptosis* is an active process involving single-cell death occurring in normal (e.g. embryogenesis) and abnormal situations; the cell membrane is intact and no inflammatory reaction is elicited. *Necrosis* is a response to injury, almost always pathological and involving groups of cells; cell membrane integrity is lost and an inflammatory and repair response is common.
Coagulative and *colliquative* necrosis	In *coagulative* necrosis the cells are dead but the tissue architecture is often preserved in the early stages; the tissue then softens and eventually heals by fibrosis and scarring. *Colliquative* (or liquefactive) necrosis occurs characteristically in the brain; the tissue liquefies and heals by cyst formation.
Granuloma and *granulation tissue*	A *granuloma* is an aggregate of epithelioid histiocytes and a feature of some specific chronic inflammatory disorders. *Granulation tissue* is an important component of healing and comprises small blood vessels in a connective tissue matrix with myofibroblasts.
Stenosis and *stricture*	*Stenosis* most often refers to narrowing of an orifice (e.g. pylorus), aperture or valve, whereas a *stricture* is usually used to describe a narrowed tube (e.g. intestine).
First and *second intention* healing	Healing by *first intention* occurs when there has been no significant loss of tissue (e.g. a clean surgical incision). When there has been a significant loss of tissue (e.g. by trauma) the defect is filled initially by granulation tissue before further healing; this is *second intention*.
X-rays and *gamma rays*	Both have similar physical properties, but *X-rays* are produced by a machine and their production can be controlled by a switch, whereas *gamma rays* are produced by radioactive decay and protection from them can be achieved only by a barrier.

Although they are under investigation, none is in current use. The nearest equivalent is the use of psoralens to enhance the efficacy of ultraviolet light in the management of psoriasis (Ch. 24). Hyperbaric oxygen and hyperthermia have both been used, but neither has passed into routine practice. Regarding reducing the harmful effects of radiation, research has been conducted into compounds that inhibit apoptosis, or reduce a damaging inflammatory response following irradiation.

Complications of radiotherapy

Irrespective of the part of the body treated, nausea and vomiting are very common side-effects of radiotherapy. The mechanism is not understood, but it is more likely to occur when large volumes of tissue are treated.

Major and minor salivary glands are liable to undergo permanent atrophy after irradiation. If treatment has been given from both sides of the body then this can result in a troublesome dry mouth.

Depending on the type of radiation, the skin will receive a proportion of any dose given to any internal target. Certain techniques result in skin-sparing, and radionecrosis is unlikely unless the skin itself is the target of irradiation. However, skin reactions are very common and range from the expected acute inflammatory phases to residual pigmentation. All these phenomena will be strictly delineated by the margins of the treatment field with its straight edges (Fig. 6.16). They can thus be distinguished from other diseases.

Fibrosis is a late manifestation in irradiated tissue and will also be restricted to the treated field (Fig. 6.17). Most treatment techniques take care to avoid clinical consequences from such fibrosis, but occasionally an individual patient will show an excessive reaction, such as a stricture of the bowel. Sometimes,

fibrosis is the desired objective of therapy, as in the treatment of intracerebral vascular malformations by inducing scarring.

FURTHER READING

Bomford C K, Kunkler I H 2002 Walter and Miller's textbook of radiotherapy, 6th edn. Churchill Livingstone, Edinburgh

Brenner D J, Hall E J 2007 Computed tomography—an increasing source of radiation exposure. New England Journal of Medicine 357: 2277–2284

Fajardo L P, Berthrong M, Anderson R E 2001 Radiation pathology. Oxford University Press, Oxford, Ch 1

Foley-Comer A J, Herrick S E, Al Mishlab T et al 2002 Evidence for incorporation of free-floating mesothelial cells as a mechanism of serosal healing. Journal of Cell Science 115: 1383–1389

Fuchs E 2008 Skin stem cells: rising to the surface. Journal of Cell Biology 180: 273–284

Gabbiani G 2003 The myofibroblast in wound healing and fibrocontractive diseases. Journal of Pathology 200: 500–503

Letai A G 2008 Diagnosing and exploiting cancer's addiction to blocks in apoptosis. Nature Reviews. Cancer 8: 121–132

Maiuri M C, Zalckvar E, Kimchi A, Kroemer G 2007 Self-eating and self-killing: crosstalk between autophagy and apoptosis. Nature Reviews. Molecular Cell Biology 8: 741–752

Metz C N 2003 Fibrocytes: a unique cell population implicated in wound healing. Cellular and Molecular Life Sciences 60: 1342–1350

Price P, Sikora K 2002 Treatment of cancer, 4th edn. Chapman and Hall, London

Taylor R C, Cullen S P, Martin S J 2008 Apoptosis: controlled demolition at the cellular level. Nature Reviews. Molecular Cell Biology 9: 231–241

Zong W X, Thompson C B 2006 Necrotic death as a cell fate. Genes and Development 20: 1–15

Health Protection Agency, radiation division (National Radiological Protection Board): http://www.hpa.org.uk/radiation

Health Risks from Exposure to Low Levels of Ionizing Radiation: BEIR VII Phase 2 (Free Executive Summary): http://www.nap.edu/catalog/11340.html

7

Disorders of metabolism and homeostasis

Some *metabolic disorders,* congenital or acquired, are specific abnormalities of metabolic pathways, often having considerable clinical effects. Congenital metabolic disorders usually result from inherited enzyme deficiencies.

Other metabolic disorders are characterised by perturbations of the body's homeostatic mechanisms maintaining the integrity of fluids and tissues. These conditions are almost always acquired and their effects can be diverse.

INBORN ERRORS OF METABOLISM

▶ Single-gene defects due to inherited or spontaneous mutations
▶ Usually manifested in infancy or childhood
▶ May result in: defective carbohydrate or amino acid metabolism; pathological effects of an intermediate metabolite; impaired membrane transport; synthesis of a defective protein

The concept of inborn errors of metabolism was formulated by Sir Archibald Garrod in 1908 as a result of his studies on a condition called alkaptonuria, a rare inherited deficiency of homogentisic acid oxidase.

Inborn (usually inherited) errors of metabolism are important causes of illness presenting in infancy. Some require prompt treatment to avoid serious complications. Others defy treatment. All deserve accurate diagnosis so that parents can be counselled about the inherited risk to further pregnancies. Inborn metabolic errors are potentially chronic problems, because the primary abnormality is innate rather than due to any external cause that could be eliminated by treatment.

Inborn errors of metabolism are *single-gene defects* resulting in the absence or deficiency of an enzyme or the synthesis of a defective protein. Single-gene defects occur in about 1% of all births, but the diseases caused by them show geographic variations in incidence; this is exemplified by the high incidence of thalassaemias—due to defects in haemoglobin synthesis (Ch. 23)—in Mediterranean regions. These variations reflect the prevalence of specific abnormal genes in different populations.

Inborn errors of metabolism have four possible consequences:

● accumulation of an intermediate metabolite (e.g. homogentisic acid in alkaptonuria)
● deficiency of the ultimate product of metabolism (e.g. melanin in albinos)
● synthesis of an abnormal and less effective end product (e.g. haemoglobin S in sickle cell anaemia)
● failure of transport of the abnormal synthesised product (e.g. alpha-1 antitrypsin deficiency).

Accumulation of an intermediate metabolite may have toxic or hormonal effects. However, in some conditions the intermediate metabolite accumulates within the cells in which it has been synthesised, causing them to enlarge and compromising their function or that of neighbouring cells; these conditions are referred to as *storage disorders* (e.g. Gaucher's disease). Other inborn metabolic errors lead to the production of a protein with defective function; for example, the substitution of just a single amino acid in a large protein can have considerable adverse effects (e.g. haemoglobinopathies).

The genetic basis of the inheritance of these disorders is discussed in Chapter 3.

Inherited metabolic disorders may be classified according to the principal biochemical defect (e.g. amino acid disorder) or the consequence (e.g. storage disorder).

Disorders of carbohydrate metabolism

The commonest disorder of carbohydrate metabolism with an inherited component in its aetiology is diabetes mellitus (see p. 128). Much less common, but with an autosomal recessive pattern of inheritance and often presenting at an early age, are:

● *glycogen storage disease,* in which the principal effects are due to the intracellular accumulation of glycogen
● *fructose intolerance,* in which liver damage results due to a deficiency of fructose-1-phosphate aldolase, particularly if dietary fructose is taken before 6 months of age
● *galactosaemia,* in which damage to the liver occurs due to a deficiency of galactose-1-phosphate uridyl transferase
● *tyrosinaemia,* in which liver damage and, in chronic cases, liver cell carcinoma results from a deficiency of fumarylacetoacetate hydrolase.

Disorders of amino acid metabolism

Several inherited disorders of amino acid metabolism involve defects of enzymes in the phenylalanine/tyrosine pathway (Fig. 7.1).

Phenylketonuria

This autosomal recessive disorder affects approximately 1 in 10 000 infants. It is due to a deficiency of *phenylalanine hydroxylase,* an enzyme responsible for the conversion of phenylalanine to tyrosine (Fig. 7.1).

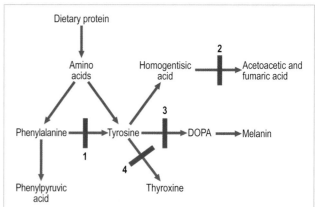

Fig. 7.1 Inborn errors of metabolism in the phenylalanine/ tyrosine pathway. 1. Phenylketonuria. Lack of phenylalanine hydroxylase blocks conversion of phenylalanine to tyrosine; phenylalanine and phenylpyruvic acid appear in the urine. **2. Alkaptonuria.** Lack of homogentisic acid oxidase causes accumulation of homogentisic acid. **3. Albinism.** Lack of the enzyme tyrosinase prevents conversion of tyrosine via DOPA to melanin. **4. Familial hypothyroidism.** Deficiency of any one of several enzymes impairs iodination of tyrosine in the formation of thyroid hormone.

In the UK and many other countries the clinical effects of phenylketonuria are now seen only very rarely, because it is detected by screening all newborn infants and treated promptly. Testing is done by analysing a drop of blood, dried on to filter paper, for phenylalanine (Guthrie test). If phenyl-ketonuria is not tested for in this way and the affected infant's diet contains usual amounts of phenylalanine, then the disorder manifests itself with skin and hair depigmentation, fits and mental retardation. Treatment involves a low phenylalanine diet until the child is at least 8 years old. When affected females themselves become pregnant, the special diet must be resumed to avoid the toxic metabolites damaging the developing fetus.

Alkaptonuria

This rare autosomal recessive deficiency of *homogentisic acid oxidase* (Fig. 7.1) is a good example of an inborn metabolic error that does not produce serious effects until adult life. The condition is sometimes recognised from the observation that the patient's urine darkens on standing; the sweat may also be black! Homogentisic acid accumulates in connective tissues, principally cartilage, where the darkening is called *ochronosis*. This accumulation causes joint damage. The underlying condition cannot be cured; treatment is symptomatic only.

Homocystinuria

Like most inherited disorders of metabolism, homocystinuria is an autosomal recessive disorder. There is a deficiency of *cystathionine synthase*, an enzyme required for the conversion of homocystine via homocysteine to cystathionine. Homocysteine and methionine, its precursor, accumulate in the blood. Homocystine also accumulates, interfering with the cross-linking of collagen and elastic fibres. The ultimate effect resembles Marfan's syndrome (see p. 128), but also with mental retardation and fits.

Homocysteine and atherosclerosis

Several studies have shown a correlation between high blood levels of homocysteine and premature development of atherosclerosis, augmenting the risks from hypertension and hyperlipidaemia.

Storage disorders

Inborn metabolic defects result in storage disorders if a deficiency of an enzyme, usually lysosomal, prevents the normal conversion of a macromolecule (e.g. glycogen or gangliosides) into its smaller subunits (e.g. glucose or fatty acids). The macromolecule accumulates within the cells that normally harbour it, swelling their cytoplasm (Fig. 7.2) and causing organ enlargement and deformities. This situation is harmful to the patient because the swelling of cells often impairs their function, or that of their immediate neighbours due to pressure effects, and because of conditions resulting from deficiency of the smaller subunits (e.g. hypoglycaemia in the case of glycogen storage disorders).

Major categories of these autosomal recessive disorders (Table 7.1) are:

- glycogenoses
- mucopolysaccharidoses
- sphingolipidoses.

Disorders of cell membrane transport

Inborn metabolic errors can lead to impairment of the specific transport of substances across cell membranes. Examples include:

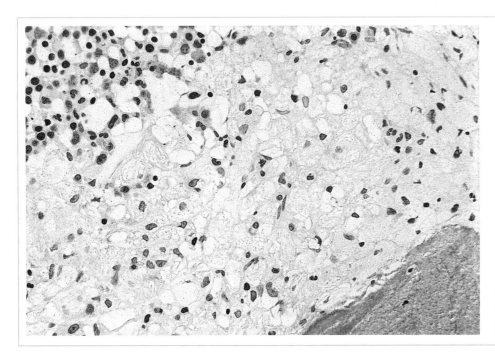

Fig. 7.2   Bone marrow biopsy revealing Gaucher's disease. Pale foamy macrophages distended with gangliosides have displaced much of the haemopoietic tissue (top left), thereby causing anaemia.

Table 7.1 Examples of inborn errors of metabolism resulting in storage disorders		
Type of disease/examples	Deficiency	Consequences
Glycogenoses	Debranching enzyme	Hepatomegaly Hypoglycaemia Cardiac failure Muscle cramps
McCardle's syndrome	Muscle phosphorylase	
von Gierke's disease	Glucose-6-phosphate dehydrogenase	
Pompe's disease	Acid maltase	
Mucopolysaccharidoses	Lysosomal hydrolase	Hepatosplenomegaly Skeletal deformity Mental deterioration
Hurler's syndrome	Alpha-L-iduronidase	
Hunter's syndrome	Iduronate sulphate sulphatase	
Sphingolipidoses	Lysosomal enzyme	Variable hepatosplenomegaly Neurological problems
Gaucher's disease	Glucocerebrosidase	
Niemann–Pick disease	Sphingomyelinase	
Tay–Sachs disease	Hexosaminidase A	

- *cystic fibrosis*—a channelopathy (see below) affecting exocrine secretions
- *cystinuria*—affecting renal tubules and resulting in renal stones
- *disaccharidase deficiency*—preventing absorption of lactose, maltose and sucrose from the gut
- *nephrogenic diabetes insipidus*—due to insensitivity of renal tubules to antidiuretic hormone (ADH).

Channelopathies

A channelopathy is a disease caused by the dysfunction of a specific ion channel in cell membranes. The ion channel dysfunction may result from:

- mutations, usually inherited, in the genes encoding proteins involved in transmembrane ionic flow (e.g. cystic fibrosis)
- autoimmune injury to ion channels in cell membranes (e.g. myasthenia gravis).

Cystic fibrosis

Cystic fibrosis, a channelopathy, is the commonest serious inherited metabolic disorder in the UK; it is much commoner in Caucasians than in other races. The autosomal recessive abnormal gene is carried by approximately 1 in 20 Caucasians and the condition affects approximately 1 in 2000 births. The defective gene, in which numerous mutations have been identified, is on chromosome 7 and ultimately results in abnormal water and electrolyte transport across cell membranes.

Cystic fibrosis transmembrane conductance regulator (CFTR)

The commonest abnormality (ΔF508) in the *CFTR* gene is a deletion resulting in a missing phenylalanine molecule. The defective CFTR is unresponsive to cyclic AMP control, so transport of chloride ions and water across epithelial cell membranes becomes impaired (Fig. 7.3).

Clinicopathological features

Cystic fibrosis is characterised by mucous secretions of abnormally high viscosity. The abnormal mucus plugs exocrine ducts, causing parenchymal damage to the affected organs. The clinical manifestations are:

- meconium ileus in neonates
- failure to thrive in infancy
- recurrent bronchopulmonary infections, particularly with *Pseudomonas aeruginosa*
- bronchiectasis
- chronic pancreatitis, sometimes accompanied by diabetes mellitus due to islet damage
- malabsorption due to defective pancreatic secretions
- infertility in males.

Diagnosis

The diagnosis can be confirmed by measuring the sodium concentration in the sweat; in affected children it is usually greater than 70 mmol/l. Pregnancies at risk can be screened by prenatal testing of chorionic villus biopsy tissue for the defective *CFTR* gene.

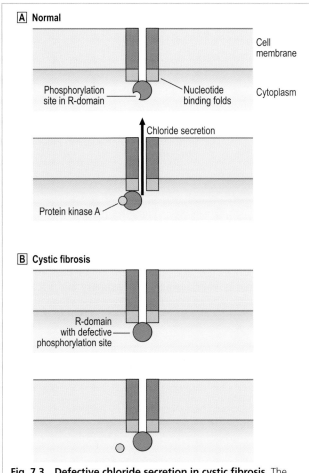

Fig. 7.3 Defective chloride secretion in cystic fibrosis. The normal CFTR is a transmembrane molecule with intracytoplasmic nucleotide binding folds and a phosphorylation site on the R-domain. **A** In normal cells, interaction of the R-domain with protein kinase A results in opening of the channel and chloride secretion. **B** In cystic fibrosis, a common defect prevents phosphorylation of the R-domain with the result that chloride secretion is impaired.

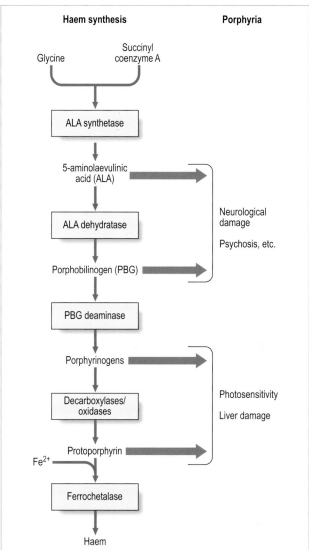

Fig. 7.4 Porphyrias. Enzyme deficiencies in the pathway of synthesis of haem from glycine and succinyl coenzyme A through 5-aminolaevulinic acid result in the accumulation of toxic intermediate metabolites. Removal of product inhibition due to deficient synthesis of haem enhances the formation of intermediate metabolites. Accumulation of 5-aminolaevulinic acid or porphobilinogen tends to be associated with neurological damage and psychiatric symptoms. Accumulation of porphyrinogens, of which there are several types (uro-, copro-, proto-), tends to be associated with photosensitivity.

Treatment

Treatment includes vigorous physiotherapy to drain the abnormal secretions from the respiratory passages, and oral replacement of pancreatic enzymes.

Porphyrias

The porphyrias, transmitted as autosomal dominant disorders, are due to defective synthesis of haem, an iron–porphyrin complex, the oxygen-carrying moiety of haemoglobin. Haem is synthesised from 5-aminolaevulinic acid. The different types of porphyrin accumulate due to inherited defects in this synthetic pathway (Fig. 7.4).

Clinicopathological features

Accumulation of porphyrins can cause clinical syndromes characterised by:

- acute abdominal pain
- acute psychiatric disturbance
- peripheral neuropathy
- photosensitivity (in some porphyrias only)
- hepatic damage (in some porphyrias only).

The pain and psychiatric disturbances are episodic. During the acute attacks, the patient's urine contains excess 5-aminolaevulinic acid and porphobilinogen. Consequently, the urine may gradually become dark red, brown or even purple ('porphyria' is derived from the Greek word 'porphura' meaning purple pigment) on exposure to sunlight.

Acute attacks of porphyria can be precipitated by some drugs, alcohol and hormonal changes (e.g. during the menstrual

cycle). The most frequently incriminated drugs include barbiturates, sulphonamides, oral contraceptives and anticonvulsants; these should therefore be avoided.

The skin lesions are characterised by severe blistering, exacerbated by light exposure, and subsequent scarring. This photosensitivity is a distressing feature, but it has led to the beneficial use of injected porphyrins in the treatment of tumours by phototherapy with laser light.

Disorders of connective tissue metabolism

Most inherited disorders of connective tissue metabolism affect collagen or elastic tissue. Examples include:

- osteogenesis imperfecta
- Marfan's syndrome
- Ehlers–Danlos syndrome
- pseudoxanthoma elasticum
- cutis laxa.

Osteogenesis imperfecta

Osteogenesis imperfecta is a group of disorders in which there is an inborn error of type I collagen synthesis (Ch. 25). Type I collagen is most abundant in bone, so the principal manifestation is skeletal weakness resulting in deformities and a susceptibility to fractures; the other names for this condition are 'fragilitas ossium' and 'brittle bone disease'. The teeth are also affected and the sclerae of the eyes are abnormally thin, causing them to appear blue. It occurs in dominantly and recessively inherited forms with varying degrees of severity.

Marfan's syndrome

Marfan's syndrome is a combination of unusually tall stature, long arm span, dislocation of the lenses of the eyes, aortic and mitral valve incompetence, and weakness of the aortic media predisposing to dissecting aneurysms (Ch. 13). The condition results from a defect in the *FBN1* gene encoding for *fibrillin*, a glycoprotein essential for the formation and integrity of elastic fibres.

ACQUIRED METABOLIC DISORDERS

Many diseases result in secondary metabolic abnormalities. In others the metabolic disturbance is the primary event. For example, renal diseases almost always result in metabolic changes that reflect the kidneys' importance in water and electrolyte homeostasis. In contrast, a disease like gout is often due to a primary metabolic disorder that may secondarily damage the kidneys. This section deals with metabolic abnormalities as both consequences and causes of disease. Acquired metabolic disorders frequently cause systemic problems affecting many organs: for example, diabetes mellitus is associated with microvascular damage in the retinas, nerves, kidneys and other organs; electrolyte imbalance compromises the function of cells in all tissues.

Two of the disorders discussed in this section—diabetes mellitus and gout—are categorised as 'acquired' largely because they occur most commonly in adults, but both have a significant genetic component in their aetiology.

Diabetes mellitus

- ▶ Multifactorial aetiology: genetic and environmental factors
- ▶ Relative or absolute insufficiency of insulin, causing hyperglycaemia
- ▶ Insulin-dependent and non-insulin-dependent groups
- ▶ Long-term complications include atheroma, renal damage, microangiopathy, neuropathy

Diabetes mellitus is a group of diseases characterised by impaired glucose homeostasis resulting from a relative or absolute insufficiency of insulin. Insulin insufficiency causes hyperglycaemia and glycosuria. Diabetes is covered in Chapter 17, but a brief account is relevant here.

The aetiology is multifactorial; although the disorder is acquired, there is a significant genetic predisposition. Diabetes mellitus is subclassified into primary and secondary types. Primary diabetes is much more common than diabetes secondary to other diseases.

Primary diabetes mellitus

Primary diabetes mellitus (DM) is subdivided into:

- insulin-dependent (IDDM) or type 1
- non-insulin-dependent (NIDDM) or type 2
- maturity-onset diabetes of the young (MODY).

Juvenile-onset diabetes, usually appearing before the age of 20 years, is almost always of IDDM type. There is an inherited predisposition associated with human leukocyte antigens (HLA) DR3 and DR4. The initiating event may be a viral infection of the insulin-producing beta-cells of the islets of Langerhans, precipitating their immune destruction.

Diabetes mellitus developing in adults (over 25 years of age) is most likely to be NIDDM type. It is associated with an acquired resistance to insulin. There is no HLA association, but there is a familial tendency to develop the disease. The affected patients are often, but not always, obese.

Secondary diabetes mellitus

Diabetes may be secondary to:

- chronic pancreatitis (Ch. 16)
- haemochromatosis (Ch. 16)
- acromegaly (Ch. 17)
- Cushing's syndrome (Ch. 17).

Complications of diabetes mellitus

Good control of blood sugar levels reduces the risk of complications. Nevertheless, many diabetics develop complications of their disease. These are covered in more detail in the relevant chapters, but a summary is given here:

- accelerated development of atheroma
- glomerular damage leading to nephrotic syndrome and renal failure

- microangiopathy, causing nerve damage and retinal damage
- increased susceptibility to infections
- cataracts
- diabetic ketoacidosis
- hyperosmolar diabetic coma.

To this list should be added hypoglycaemia, which is a frequent and troublesome complication of insulin therapy in IDDM.

There are two possible biochemical explanations for the tissue damage that results from long-term diabetes mellitus:

- *Glycosylation.* The high blood sugar encourages binding of glucose to many proteins; this can be irreversible. This glycosylation often impairs the function of the proteins. The level of glycated haemoglobin (HbA1c) is commonly used as a way of monitoring blood sugar control.
- *Polyol pathway.* Tissues containing aldose reductase (e.g. nerves, kidneys and the lenses of the eyes) are able to metabolise the high glucose levels into sorbitol and fructose. The products of this polyol pathway accumulate in the affected tissues, causing osmotic swelling and cell damage.

Gout

> ▶ Multifactorial disorder characterised by high blood uric acid levels
> ▶ Urate crystal deposition causes skin nodules (tophi), joint damage, renal damage and stones

Gout is a common disorder resulting from high blood uric acid levels. Uric acid is a breakdown product of the body's purine (nucleic acid) metabolism (Fig. 7.5), but a small proportion comes from the diet. Most uric acid is excreted by the kidneys. In the blood, most uric acid is in the form of monosodium urate. In patients with gout, the monosodium urate concentration may be very high, forming a supersaturated solution, thus risking urate crystal deposition in tissues causing:

- tophi (subcutaneous nodular deposits of urate crystals)
- synovitis and arthritis (Ch. 25)
- renal disease and calculi (Ch. 21).

Gout occurs more commonly in men than in women, and is rare before puberty. A rare form of gout in children—Lesch–Nyhan syndrome—is due to absence of the enzyme HGPRT (hypoxanthine guanine phosphoribosyl transferase) (Fig. 7.5) and is associated with mental deficiency and a bizarre tendency to self-mutilation.

Aetiology

Like diabetes mellitus, the aetiology of gout is multifactorial. There is a genetic component, but the role of other factors justifies the inclusion of gout under the heading of acquired disorders. Aetiological factors include:

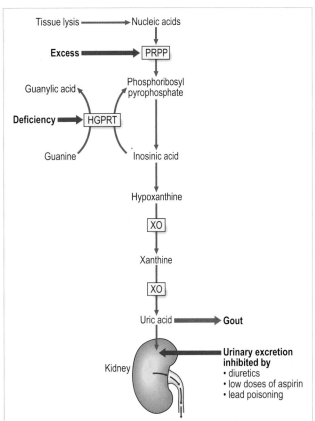

Fig. 7.5 Pathogenesis of gout. The metabolic pathway shows the synthesis of uric acid from nucleic acids. Primary gout can arise from an inherited (X-linked) deficiency of hypoxanthine guanine phosphoribosyl transferase (HGPRT) or excessive activity of 5-phosphoribosyl-1-pyrophosphate (PRPP). Secondary gout results either from increased tissue lysis (e.g. due to tumour chemotherapy) liberating excess nucleic acids or from inhibition of the urinary excretion of uric acid. Xanthine oxidase (XO) is inhibited by allopurinol, an effective long-term remedy for gout.

- gender (male > female)
- family history
- diet (meat, alcohol)
- socio-economic status (high > low)
- body size (large > small).

Some of these factors may, of course, be interdependent. Accordingly, gout can be subdivided into *primary gout,* due to some genetic abnormality of purine metabolism, or *secondary gout,* due to increased liberation of nucleic acids from necrotic tissue or decreased urinary excretion of uric acid.

Clinicopathological features

The clinical features of gout are due to urate crystal deposition in various tissues (Fig. 7.6). In joints, a painful acute arthritis results from phagocytosis of the crystals by neutrophil polymorphs, in turn causing release of lysosomal enzymes along with the indigestible crystals, thus accelerating and

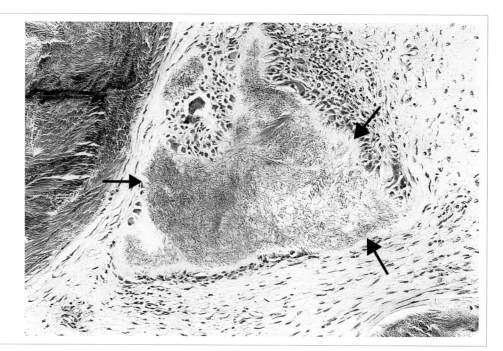

Fig. 7.6   Histology of urate crystal deposition in gout. Aggregates of needle-shaped crystals (arrowed) have provoked an inflammatory and fibrous reaction.

perpetuating a cyclical inflammatory reaction. The first metatarsophalangeal joint is typically affected.

Water homeostasis

> ▶ Abnormal water homeostasis may result in excess, depletion or redistribution
> ▶ Excess may be due to overload, oedema or inappropriate renal tubular reabsorption
> ▶ Dehydration is most commonly due to gastrointestinal loss (e.g. gastroenteritis)
> ▶ Oedema results from redistribution of water into the extravascular compartment

Water and electrolyte homeostasis is tightly controlled by various hormones, including antidiuretic hormone (ADH), aldosterone and atrial natriuretic peptide, acting upon selective reabsorption in the renal tubules (Ch. 21). The process is influenced by the dietary intake of water and electrolytes (in food or drinking in response to thirst or social purposes) and the adjustments necessary to cope with disease or adverse environmental conditions.

Many diseases result in problems of water and electrolyte homeostasis. Disturbances can also occur in post-operative patients receiving fluids and nutrition parenterally. Fortunately, any changes are fairly easy to monitor and control by making adjustments to the fluid and electrolyte intake.

Water is constantly lost from the body—in urine, in faeces, in exhaled gas from the lungs, and from the skin. The replenishment of body water is controlled by a combination of the satisfaction of the sensation of thirst and the regulation of the renal tubular reabsorption of water mediated by ADH.

Water excess

Excessive body water may occur in patients with extensive oedema or if there is inappropriate production of ADH (e.g. as occurs with small-cell lung carcinoma) or if the body sodium concentration increases due to excessive tubular reabsorption (for example, due to an aldosterone-secreting tumour of the adrenal cortex). Water overload can be caused iatrogenically by excessive parenteral infusion of fluids in patients with impaired renal function; this should be avoided by carefully monitoring fluid input and output.

Dehydration

Dehydration results from either excessive water loss or inadequate intake or a combination of both. Inadequate water intake is a common problem in regions of the world affected by drought and famine.

Excessive water loss can be due to:

- vomiting and diarrhoea
- extensive burns
- excessive sweating (fever, exercise, hot climates)
- diabetes insipidus (failure to produce ADH)
- nephrogenic diabetes insipidus (renal tubular insensitivity to ADH)
- diuresis (e.g. osmotic loss accompanying the glycosuria of diabetes mellitus).

Dehydration is recognised clinically by a dry mouth, inelastic skin and, in extreme cases, sunken eyes. The blood haematocrit (proportion of the blood volume occupied by cells) will be elevated, causing an increase in whole blood viscosity. This results in a sluggish circulation and consequent impairment of the function of many organs.

The plasma sodium and urea concentrations are typically elevated, reflecting haemoconcentration and impaired renal function.

Oedema and serous effusions

> ▶ Oedema is excess water in tissues
> ▶ Oedema and serous effusions have similar pathogeneses
> ▶ May be due to increased vascular permeability, venous or lymphatic obstruction, or reduced plasma oncotic pressure

Oedema is an excess of fluid in the intercellular compartment of a tissue. A serous effusion is an excess of fluid in a serous or coelomic cavity (e.g. peritoneal cavity, pleural cavity). The main ingredient of the fluid is always *water*. Oedema and serous effusions share common mechanisms.

Oedema is recognised clinically by diffuse swelling of the affected tissue. If the oedema is subcutaneous, the affected area shows pitting; i.e. if the skin is indented firmly with the fingers, an impression of the fingers is left transiently on the surface. There is, therefore, usually little difficulty in diagnosing subcutaneous oedema. Oedema of internal tissues may be evident during surgery because they are swollen and, when incised, clear or slightly opalescent fluid oozes from the cut surfaces. Pulmonary oedema gives a characteristic appearance of increased radio-opacity on a plain chest X-ray and can be heard, through a stethoscope, as crepitations on inspiration.

Oedema, irrespective of its cause, has serious consequences in certain organs. For example, *pulmonary oedema* fluid fills the alveoli and reduces the effective lung volume available for respiration; the patient becomes breathless (dyspnoeic) and, if the oedema is severe, cyanosed. *Cerebral oedema* is an ominous development because it occurs within the rigid confines of the cranial cavity; compression of the brain against the falx cerebri, the tentorial membranes or the base of the skull leads to herniation of brain tissue, possibly causing irreversible and fatal damage. Cerebral oedema can be diagnosed clinically by finding *papilloedema* (oedema of the optic disc) on ophthalmoscopy.

Oedema and serous effusions are due to:

- excessive leakage of fluid from blood vessels into the extravascular spaces
- impaired reabsorption of fluid from tissues or serous cavities.

Oedema is classified into four pathogenetic categories (Fig. 7.7):

- inflammatory: due to increased vascular permeability
- venous: due to increased intravenous pressure
- lymphatic: due to obstruction of lymphatic drainage
- hypoalbuminaemic: due to reduced plasma oncotic pressure.

Serous effusions can be attributable to any of the above causes, but in addition there is another important diagnostic category: neoplastic effusions due to primary or secondary neoplasms (tumours) involving serous cavities (Ch. 11).

Inflammatory oedema

Oedema is a feature of acute inflammation (Ch. 10). In acutely inflamed tissues there is increased vascular (mainly venular) permeability due to the separation of endothelial cells under the influence of chemical mediators. Fluid with a high protein content leaks out of the permeable vessels into the inflamed tissue causing it to swell. This is beneficial, because the proteins in the oedema fluid assist in defeating the cause of the inflammation. For example:

- albumin increases the oncotic pressure of the extravascular fluid, causing water to be imbibed, thus diluting any toxins
- fibrinogen polymerises to form a fibrin mesh which helps to contain the damage
- immunoglobulins and complement specifically destroy bacteria or neutralise toxins.

In addition to the fluid component, the extravasate contains numerous neutrophil polymorphs.

Tissues affected by inflammatory oedema also have the other features of acute inflammation, such as pain and redness.

Venous oedema

Oedema results from increased intravenous pressure because this pressure opposes the plasma oncotic pressure, largely due to the presence of albumin, that draws fluid back into the circulation at the venous end of capillary beds. Increased intravenous pressure results from either *heart failure* or impairment of blood flow due to *venous obstruction* by a thrombus or extrinsic compression. The affected tissues are often intensely congested due to engorgement by venous blood under increased pressure. In heart failure, there is also *pulmonary congestion with oedema* and so-called *passive venous congestion of the liver.*

Venous oedema is seen most commonly in dependent parts of the body, notably the legs; indeed, it is not unusual for mild degrees of venous oedema to occur at the ankles and feet of normal people who have sat in aircraft on long flights—immobilisation impairs venous return. The fluid in venous oedema has a low protein content.

Oedema of just one leg is almost always due to venous obstruction by a thrombus. This is a common complication of immobilisation following major surgery or trauma. Bilateral leg oedema, if due to venous causes (there may be other explanations, see below), is more likely to be due to heart failure than venous thrombotic obstruction. In either case it is a serious manifestation prompting immediate attention to the underlying condition.

Lymphatic oedema

Some fluid normally leaves capillary beds and drains into adjacent lymphatic channels to return eventually to the circulation through the thoracic duct. If the lymphatic channels are obstructed, the fluid remains trapped in the tissues and oedema results.

Causes of lymphatic oedema include blockage of lymphatic flow by filarial parasites (Ch. 3) or by tumour metastases (Ch. 11), or as a complication of surgical removal of lymph

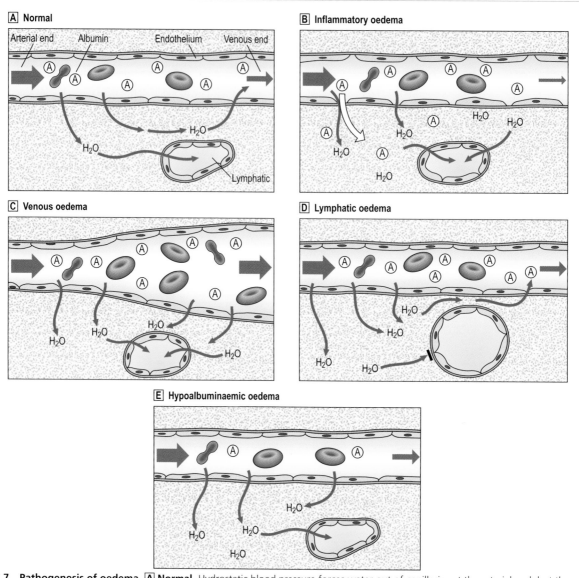

Fig. 7.7 Pathogenesis of oedema. A **Normal.** Hydrostatic blood pressure forces water out of capillaries at the arterial end, but the plasma oncotic pressure attributable to albumin sucks water back into capillary beds at the venous end. A small amount of water drains from the tissues through lymphatic channels. B **Inflammatory oedema.** Gaps between endothelial cells (mostly at venular level) allow water and albumin (and other plasma constituents) to escape. There is increased lymphatic drainage, but this cannot cope with all the water released into the tissues and oedema results. C **Venous oedema.** Increased venous pressure (e.g. from heart failure, venous obstruction due to thrombus) causes passive dilatation and congestion of the capillary bed. Increased venous pressure exceeds that of plasma oncotic pressure and so water remains in the tissues. D **Lymphatic oedema.** Lymphatic obstruction (e.g. by tumour deposits, filarial parasites) prevents drainage of water from tissues. E **Hypoalbuminaemic oedema.** Low plasma albumin concentration reduces the plasma oncotic pressure so that water cannot be sucked back into the capillary bed at the venous end.

nodes. Blockage of inguinal lymphatics by filarial parasites frequently causes gross oedema of the legs and, in males, the scrotum; the resulting deformity is called *elephantiasis*. Blockage of lymphatic drainage from the small intestine, usually because of tumour involvement, causes *malabsorption* of fats and fat-soluble substances. Blockage of lymphatic drainage at the level of the thoracic duct, or at least close to it, causes *chylous effusions* in the pleural and peritoneal cavities; the fluid is densely opalescent due to the presence of numerous tiny fat globules (chyle).

Fortunately, oedema due to surgical removal of lymph nodes is now a rare event. It used to be a complication of radical mastectomy for breast cancer, but surgical treatment for this tumour now tends to be more conservative.

Hypoalbuminaemic oedema
A low plasma albumin concentration results in oedema because of the reduction in plasma oncotic pressure; thus, fluid cannot be drawn back into the venous end of capillary beds and it remains in the tissues. Causes of hypo-albuminaemia are:

- protein malnutrition (as in kwashiorkor)
- liver failure (reduced albumin synthesis)
- nephrotic syndrome (excessive albumin loss in urine)
- protein-losing enteropathy (a variety of diseases are responsible).

Hypoalbuminaemia as the cause of oedema can be verified easily by measuring the albumin concentration in serum. The underlying cause is then investigated and, if possible, treated. Infusions of albumin will have a beneficial, but temporary, effect.

Ascites and pleural effusions

Ascites is an excess of fluid in the peritoneal cavity. It is one of the five general causes of a distended abdomen: the complete alliterative list is—fluid, fat, faeces (constipation or obstruction), fetus, flatus (gas in the bowel).

Ascites and pleural effusions may be due to any of the above causes of oedema. However, the increased vascular permeability causing inflammatory oedema and effusions may also be induced by tumours. Thus, tumour cells growing within the cavities or on their serous linings cause excessive leakage of fluid. Serous effusions may be a presenting feature of cancer or they may complicate a previously diagnosed case. The fluid has a high protein content, and cytological examination to look for abnormal cells is often diagnostic.

Serous effusions may be divided into *transudates* and *exudates* by their protein content. Transudates have a protein concentration of less than 2 g/100 ml, whereas the concentration in exudates is higher. Involvement by tumour is the most important cause of an exudate.

Electrolyte homeostasis

Of all the electrolytes in plasma, sodium and potassium are among the most abundant and the most likely to be affected by pathological processes (Table 7.2).

Sodium and potassium homeostasis

- Sodium may be retained excessively by the body due to inappropriately high levels of mineralocorticoid hormones acting on renal tubular reabsorption
- Sodium may be lost excessively in urine, due to impaired renal tubular reabsorption, or in sweat
- Potassium may accumulate excessively in the body if there is extensive tissue necrosis or renal failure
- High serum potassium level is a medical emergency because of risk of cardiac arrest
- Potassium may be lost excessively in severe vomiting and diarrhoea

Hypernatraemia

Hypernatraemia (high serum sodium) may occur in conditions in which there is excessive mineralocorticoid (such as aldosterone) production acting on renal tubular reabsorption; Conn's syndrome, due to an adrenal adenoma of the zona glomerulosa cells, is a typical example. The increased total body sodium content may be concealed by a commensurate increase in body water content in an attempt to sustain a normal plasma osmolarity; the serum sodium concentration may therefore underestimate the increase in total body sodium.

Hyponatraemia

Hyponatraemia (low serum sodium) is a logical consequence of impaired renal tubular reabsorption of sodium. This occurs in Addison's disease of the adrenal glands due to loss of the aldosterone-producing zona glomerulosa cortical cells. Sodium is the electrolyte most likely to be lost selectively in severe sweating in hot climates or during physical exertion such as marathon running; the syndrome of 'heat exhaustion' is due mainly to a combination of dehydration and hyponatraemia. Falsely low serum sodium concentrations may be found in hyperlipidaemic states; the sodium concentration in the

Table 7.2 Common abnormalities of serum electrolytes

Abnormality	Causes	Consequences
Hypernatraemia (i.e. high sodium)	Renal failure Cushing's syndrome Conn's syndrome	Compensatory increased blood volume Oedema
Hyponatraemia (i.e. low sodium)	Addison's disease Excessive diuretic therapy	Reduced blood volume Hypotension
Hyperkalaemia (i.e. high potassium)	Renal failure Acidosis Extensive tissue necrosis	Risk of cardiac arrest
Hypokalaemia (i.e. low potassium)	Vomiting Diarrhoea Diuretic therapy Alkalosis Cushing's syndrome Conn's syndrome	Weakness Cardiac dysrhythmias Metabolic alkalosis

The abnormalities listed often do not occur in isolation and may be associated with other electrolyte changes.

aqueous phase of the serum is actually normal but the lipid contributes to the total volume of serum assayed.

Hyperkalaemia

Potassium is more abundant within cells than in extracellular fluids, so relatively small changes in plasma concentration can underestimate possibly larger changes in intracellular concentrations. Furthermore, extensive tissue necrosis can liberate large quantities of potassium into the plasma, causing the concentration to reach dangerously high levels. The commonest cause is renal failure causing decreased urinary potassium excretion. Severe hyperkalaemia (>c. 6.5 mmol/l) is a serious medical emergency demanding prompt treatment because of the risk of cardiac arrest. Moderate hyperkalaemia is relatively asymptomatic, emphasising the importance of regular biochemical monitoring to avoid sudden fatal complications.

Hypokalaemia

Hypokalaemia (low serum potassium) has many causes (Table 7.2). It is often accompanied by a metabolic alkalosis due to hydrogen ion shift into the intracellular compartment. Clinically, it presents with muscular weakness and cardiac dysrhythmias.

Vomiting and diarrhoea result in combined loss of water, sodium and potassium. Superimposed on this may be alkalosis from vomiting due to loss of hydrogen ions, or acidosis from diarrhoea due to loss of alkaline intestinal secretions.

Calcium homeostasis

> ▶ Serum calcium levels are controlled by vitamin D and parathyroid hormone and their effects on intestinal absorption, renal tubular reabsorption and osteoclastic activity
> ▶ Persistent hypercalcaemia can cause 'metastatic' calcification of tissues
> ▶ Clinical effects of hypocalcaemia (i.e. tetany) can result from fall in total serum calcium or from respiratory alkalosis reducing the ionised serum calcium

Serum calcium levels are regulated by the vitamin D metabolite—1,25-dihydroxyvitamin D—and by parathyroid hormone (PTH). The precise role of calcitonin in humans is uncertain, but it has a serum calcium-lowering effect when administered to patients with hypercalcaemia; however, patients with the calcitonin-producing medullary carcinoma of the thyroid (Ch. 17) do not present with hypocalcaemia.

Hypercalcaemia

Acute hypercalcaemia causes fits, vomiting and polyuria. Persistent hypercalcaemia additionally results in 'metastatic' calcification (see p. 141) of tissues and urinary calculi. Causes of hypercalcaemia include:

- primary hyperparathyroidism (Ch. 17)
- hypervitaminosis D
- extensive skeletal metastases
- PTH-like secretion from tumours.

Primary hyperparathyroidism is most commonly due to an adenoma of the parathyroid glands. The excessive and uncontrolled PTH secretion enhances the absorption of calcium and the osteoclastic erosion of bone, thus releasing calcium.

Hypercalcaemia due to neoplasms of other organs is seen most commonly with breast cancer. In the absence of extensive skeletal metastases, this is attributed to a PTH-like hormone secreted by the tumour cells.

Hypocalcaemia

Hypocalcaemia causes neuromuscular hypersensitivity manifested by *tetany*. This condition can be corrected rapidly by giving calcium gluconate intravenously. The commonest cause of acute hypocalcaemia is accidental damage to or removal of parathyroid glands during thyroid surgery. Low serum calcium levels resulting from renal disease or intestinal malabsorption are rapidly corrected, in a patient with intact parathyroid glands, by stimulation of PTH secretion. This eventually causes hyperplasia of the parathyroid glands (secondary hyperparathyroidism) and weakening of the skeleton due to excessive osteoclastic resorption under the influence of PTH.

Tetany also results from respiratory alkalosis, often in patients with hysterical hyperventilation who excessively eliminate carbon dioxide, due to a reduction in the ionised calcium concentration as the pH rises.

Acid–base homeostasis

> ▶ Body has innate tendency to acidification
> ▶ Buffers (bicarbonate/carbonic acid, proteins) have limited capacity
> ▶ Acidosis or alkalosis may be due to respiratory or metabolic causes
> ▶ Body attempts to restore pH by varying rate of respiration or by adjusting renal tubular function

Metabolic pathways are intolerant of pH deviations. The extracellular pH is tightly controlled at an approximate value of 7.4, but the intracellular pH is marginally lower and varies within an even narrower range. Acidic deviation outside the normal plasma pH range is sensed by chemoreceptors at the carotid bifurcations (carotid bodies), in the aortic arch and in the medulla of the brain.

The body has an innate tendency towards acidification due to production of:

- carbon dioxide from aerobic respiration
- lactic acid from glycolysis
- fatty acids from lipolysis.

This acidic tendency is counteracted by basic (alkaline) buffers (bicarbonate, proteins) in the first instance, but these have limited capacity. Acid–base balance in the plasma is ultimately regulated by:

- elimination of carbon dioxide by exhalation
- renal excretion of hydrogen ions
- metabolism of fatty and lactic acids
- replenishment of bicarbonate ions.

Acidosis and alkalosis

Deviations outside the normal pH range are called acidosis (low pH) and alkalosis (high pH). Either deviation may be

further classified as *respiratory* (due to insufficient or excessive elimination of carbon dioxide from the lungs) or *metabolic* (due to non-respiratory causes). Thus there are four possible combinations:

- respiratory acidosis
- metabolic acidosis
- respiratory alkalosis
- metabolic alkalosis.

The causes of these abnormalities of acid–base balance are shown in Table 7.3. The role of normal respiration and respiratory tract diseases in influencing acid–base balance is discussed in Chapter 14.

Respiratory acidosis
Respiratory acidosis can be corrected by increased renal tubular reabsorption of bicarbonate ions (which are alkaline) or by increased urinary loss of hydrogen ions (which are acidic). By either mechanism, the pH is not corrected as promptly as it can be in metabolic acidosis by immediate stimulation of hyperventilation.

Metabolic acidosis
Metabolic acidosis stimulates hyperventilation, often with deep sighing respiratory excursions (Kussmaul respiration), in order to blow off carbon dioxide and thereby maintain the equilibrium of the bicarbonate/carbonic acid ratio, restoring the pH to neutrality.

Respiratory alkalosis
Respiratory alkalosis is always due to hyperventilation, causing excessive elimination of carbon dioxide (which is acid in solution as carbonic acid). There is limited scope for correction by increasing the urinary loss of bicarbonate ions.

Metabolic alkalosis
Metabolic alkalosis is more difficult to correct naturally because the vitally important hypoxic drive to respiration overrides the extent to which carbon dioxide can be conserved by hypoventilation.

METABOLIC CONSEQUENCES OF MALNUTRITION

Malnutrition, a serious medical and socio-economic problem, may be a consequence or a cause of disease. Diseases and conditions commonly complicated by malnutrition include:

- anorexia nervosa
- carcinoma of the oesophagus or stomach
- post-operative states
- dementia.

This section concentrates on the clinicopathological consequences of malnutrition. Malnutrition may be:

Table 7.3 Features of respiratory and metabolic acidosis and alkalosis

Abnormality	Condition	pH	Pa_{CO_2}	HCO_3	Consequences
Acidosis					
Acute respiratory	Asthma Pneumonia Respiratory impairment	↓	↑	N	CO_2 is retained
Chronic respiratory	Emphysema	N	↑	↑↑	Renal retention of HCO_3 normalises plasma pH
Acute metabolic	Diabetic ketoacidosis Cardiac arrest	↓	N	↓	H^+ ions retained
Chronic metabolic	Renal failure	N	↓	↓	Hyperventilation normalises plasma pH by accelerating loss of CO_2
Alkalosis					
Acute respiratory	Hysterical hyperventilation	↑	↓	N	Accelerated loss of CO_2 Reduced ionised Ca^{2+} causes tetany
Chronic respiratory	Diffuse pulmonary fibrosis	N	↓	↓↓	pH normalised by increased renal HCO_3 excretion
Acute metabolic	Excess bicarbonate administration	↑	N	↑	Direct effect of HCO_3
Chronic metabolic	Persistent vomiting	↑	N	↑↑	Ineffective attempts to normalise pH by increased urinary loss of HCO_3 and respiratory retention of CO_2 by hypoventilation

In chronic cases, the consequences reflect the body's attempts to normalise plasma pH.
Pa_{CO_2}, partial arterial pressure of carbon dioxide; HCO_3, bicarbonate; CO_2, carbon dioxide; H^+, hydrogen ions; Ca^{2+}, calcium ions; N, normal.

- protein–energy malnutrition
- vitamin deficiencies
- a combination of both.

Protein–energy malnutrition

▸ Kwashiorkor: severe wasting is concealed by oedema
▸ Marasmus: severe wasting
▸ Both may be complicated by infections, parasitic infestations and vitamin deficiencies
▸ Cachexia: profound wasting often occurring terminally in cancer patients

Protein–energy malnutrition results from the frequent combination of insufficient protein, carbohydrate and fat in the diet. Carbohydrate and fat together account for approximately 90% of the energy content of a typical healthy diet. Protein alone cannot replace the necessary energy yield from fats and carbohydrates.

Protein–energy malnutrition frequently co-exists with infections. The infections may exacerbate the deficiency, thus exposing the malnourished state, or they may complicate the deficiency because of impaired body defence mechanisms. In children prolonged malnutrition leads to stunted development due to retardation of linear growth. A shorter period of malnutrition produces body wasting.

Malnutrition in children

Severe malnutrition in children results in two clinical conditions (Fig. 7.8):

- kwashiorkor
- marasmus.

The factors determining which condition will develop in a malnourished child remain uncertain; some cases show features of both conditions. These conditions often co-exist with infections, parasitic infestations and vitamin deficiencies.

Kwashiorkor
Kwashiorkor is characterised by oedema, which may be very extensive and so belie the extreme wasting of the underlying tissues. The skin is scaly and the hair loses its natural colour. The condition often develops when a child is weaned off breast milk, but without the compensation of adequate dietary protein.

The serum albumin is low and this accounts for the oedema due to reduced plasma oncotic pressure. Hypokalaemia and hyponatraemia are common. The liver is enlarged due to severe fatty change; this occurs because the lack of protein thwarts the production of lipoprotein and, therefore, transport of fat from the liver.

Marasmus
Marasmus is characterised by severe emaciation rather than oedema. The skin is wrinkled and head hair is lost. The serum albumin is usually within the normal range, but hypokalaemia and hyponatraemia are common.

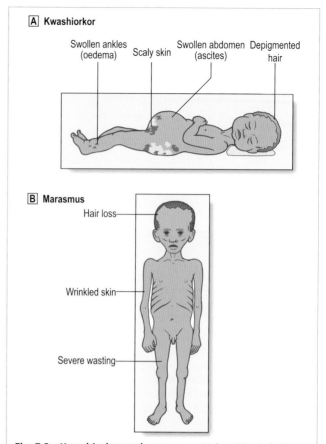

Fig. 7.8 Kwashiorkor and marasmus. Malnutrition in both cases leads to severe wasting. **A** Wasting is concealed to some extent in kwashiorkor by the oedema and ascites. **B** Wasting is obvious in marasmus.

Cachexia

Cachexia is a state of severe debilitation associated with profound weight loss. It is seen in malnutrition (marasmus is akin to cachexia), but is most widely associated with the profound weight loss suffered by patients with cancer. When the tumour involves the gastrointestinal tract, the explanation for the cachexia is often obvious. However, weight loss can be a very early manifestation of any cancer and is a particularly common feature of carcinoma of the lung; in this instance, it may be due to factors causing increased protein catabolism as the patient's food intake may be still within normal limits. Among several factors postulated to be responsible for the increased catabolic state in cachexia is *tumour necrosis factor*, a peptide secreted by tumour tissue.

Vitamin deficiencies

▸ Multiple vitamin deficiencies may occur in severe malnutrition
▸ Each vitamin deficiency is associated with specific consequences

Deficiencies of vitamins—so named by Casimir Funk (1884–1967) because he believed (mistakenly) that they were all

vital amines—produce more specific abnormalities (Table 7.4) than those encountered in protein–energy malnutrition. This is because of their involvement in specific metabolic pathways. Some vitamin deficiencies merit comment here, because either they are relatively frequent or the consequences are profound.

Thiamine (B₁) deficiency

Thiamine deficiency impairs glycolytic metabolism and affects the nervous system and the heart. The classic deficiency state is called beri-beri (from the Sinhalese word 'beri' meaning weakness). This state is characterised by peripheral neuropathy and, in some cases, cardiac failure.

Alcoholism is a common predisposing cause in countries such as the UK, where it is often associated with an inadequate diet. Alcoholics with thiamine deficiency can develop two central nervous system syndromes:

- *Korsakoff's psychosis*—characterised by confusion, confabulation and amnesia
- *Wernicke's encephalopathy*—characterised by confusion, nystagmus and aphasia.

Folate and vitamin B₁₂ deficiency

Folate and vitamin B₁₂ (cobalamin) are essential for DNA synthesis. Deficiency of either impairs cellular regeneration; the effects are seen most severely in haemopoietic tissues, resulting in megaloblastic changes and macrocytic anaemia (Ch. 23). In addition, vitamin B₁₂ deficiency also causes subacute combined degeneration of the spinal cord (Ch. 26).

Folate deficiency may result from:

- dietary insufficiency (principal source is fresh vegetables)
- intestinal malabsorption (e.g. coeliac disease—Ch. 15)
- increased utilisation (e.g. pregnancy, tumour growth)
- anti-folate drugs (e.g. methotrexate).

Vitamin B₁₂ deficiency may result from:

- autoimmune gastritis resulting in loss of intrinsic factor, thus causing pernicious anaemia
- surgical removal of the stomach (e.g. gastric cancer)
- disease of the terminal ileum, the site of absorption (e.g. Crohn's disease—Ch. 15)
- blind loops of bowel in which there is bacterial overgrowth
- infestation with *Diphyllobothrium latum*, a parasitic worm.

Vitamin C deficiency

Vitamin C deficiency is now most common in elderly people and in chronic alcoholics, whose diet is often lacking in fresh fruit and vegetables. The vitamin (ascorbic acid) is essential principally for collagen synthesis: it is necessary for the production of chondroitin sulphate and hydroxyproline from proline. Minor degrees of deficiency may be responsible for lassitude and an unusual susceptibility to bruising. Severe deficiency causes *scurvy*, a condition characterised by swollen, bleeding gums, hyperkeratosis of hair follicles, and petechial skin haemorrhages.

Table 7.4 Vitamin deficiency states		
Vitamin	**Dietary sources**	**Consequence of deficiency**
A	Beta-carotene in carrots, etc. Vitamin A in fish, eggs, liver, margarine	Night blindness, xerophthalmia, mucosal infections
B₁ (thiamine)	Cereals, milk, eggs, fruit, yeast extract	Beri-beri, neuropathy, cardiac failure, Korsakoff's psychosis, Wernicke's encephalopathy
B₂ (riboflavine)	Cereals, milk, eggs, fruit, liver	Mucosal fissuring
B₆ (pyridoxine)	Cereals, meat, fish, milk	Confusion, glossitis, neuropathy, sideroblastic anaemia
B₁₂ (cobalamin)	Meat, fish, eggs, cheese	Megaloblastic anaemia, subacute combined degeneration of the spinal cord
Niacin (nicotinic acid)	Meat, milk, eggs, peas, beans, yeast extract	Pellagra, dermatitis, diarrhoea, dementia
Folate	Green vegetables, fruit	Megaloblastic anaemia, mouth ulcers, villous atrophy of small gut
C (ascorbic acid)	Citrus fruits, green vegetables	Scurvy, lassitude, swollen bleeding gums, bruising and bleeding
D	Milk, fish, eggs, liver	Rickets (in childhood), osteomalacia (in adults)
E	Cereals, eggs, vegetable oils	Neuropathy, anaemia
K	Vegetables, liver	Blood coagulation defects

Vitamin D deficiency

Vitamin D is derived either from the diet (milk, fish, etc.) as ergocalciferol (D_2) or from the action of ultraviolet light on 7-dehydrocholesterol (D_3) to form cholecalciferol in the skin. The intermediate precursors are activated by hydroxylation sequentially in the liver and kidneys to give 1,25-dihydroxy-cholecalciferol, a steroid hormone. Hydroxylation in the kidney is stimulated by parathyroid hormone and hypocalcaemia. An apparent deficiency can therefore result from:

- lack of dietary vitamin D with inadequate sunlight
- intestinal malabsorption of fat (vitamin D is fat-soluble)
- impaired hydroxylation due to hepatic or renal disease.

People of races with deeply pigmented skin rely more heavily on dietary vitamin D when they migrate to countries with less sunlight than in their native lands.

Vitamin D is vital for normal calcium homeostasis. Its action resembles that of parathyroid hormone, ultimately causing elevation of the serum calcium concentration. It does so by:

- promotion of the absorption of calcium (and phosphate to a lesser extent) from the gut
- increased osteoclastic resorption of bone and mobilisation of calcium.

In children, lack of vitamin D impairs mineralisation of the growing skeleton, thus causing *rickets*. In adults, vitamin D deficiency results in *osteomalacia* (Ch. 25). However, the pathogenesis of rickets and osteomalacia is identical; the two conditions are different clinical manifestations of vitamin D deficiency occurring at different stages of skeletal development.

Vitamin K deficiency

Vitamin K is essential for the synthesis of blood-clotting factors. It is involved in the carboxylation of glutamic acid residues on factors II, VII, IX and X. The principal dietary sources are vegetables, leguminous plants and liver. Deficiency may result from:

- lack of dietary vitamin K
- intestinal malabsorption of fat (vitamin K is fat-soluble).

The commonest situation leading to dietary insufficiency is found in neonates on breast milk deficient in vitamin K.

Bruising and an abnormal bleeding tendency are the clinical manifestations of vitamin K deficiency. This occurs not only in the circumstances outlined above, but also in patients with liver failure in whom there is impaired hepatic synthesis of the vitamin K-dependent clotting factors; this can be corrected by giving large doses of vitamin K. It is essential to check the prothrombin time before performing a liver biopsy or any surgery on a patient with suspected liver disease.

OBESITY

Obesity is defined as a *body mass index* equal to or greater than 30. The body mass index is calculated by dividing the individual's body weight in kilograms by the square of their height in metres (kg/m^2). The cause of obesity is now cosidered to be multifactorial, resulting from an interaction between genetic and environmental factors, and is not regarded in all cases as being simply due to overeating. In a few cases, mutations of the *leptin* gene or the leptin receptor have been discovered.

Obesity significantly reduces life expectancy by increasing the risk of many serious pathological disorders, including:

- ischaemic heart disease
- diabetes mellitus (mainly type 2)
- hypertension
- osteoarthritis
- carcinomas of breast, endometrium and large bowel.

For conditions treated surgically, there is also a substantially increased risk of serious post-operative complications, such as deep leg vein thrombosis and wound infections.

The prevalence of obesity is increasing rapidly, particularly in the USA and Europe, where it has been described as an 'epidemic' (Fig. 7.9). This has considerable implications for the health of the population and for the future demands on the health care system.

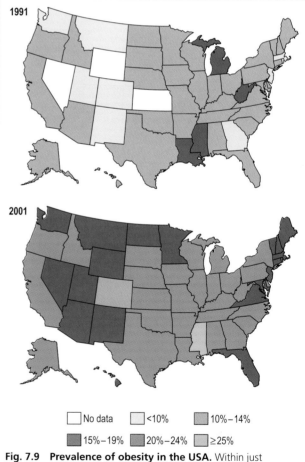

Fig. 7.9 Prevalence of obesity in the USA. Within just 10 years there was a massive increase in the prevalence of obesity (body mass index >30) in the USA. This predisposes affected individuals to an increased risk of serious disorders and a reduced life expectancy. (Data from Mokdad AH, Bowman BA, Ford ES et al 2001 The continuing epidemics of obesity and diabetes in the United States. JAMA 286: 1195–1200.)

Metabolic syndrome

Although the metabolic syndrome (also called syndrome X and insulin resistance syndrome) was first recognised in the early 1900s, marked rises in obesity and type 2 diabetes—common features of the syndrome—have greatly increased its prevalence and importance. In the USA, for example, over 40% of those >60 years of age are affected.

The diagnostic criteria for the metabolic syndrome are still debated, but commonly cited features are:

- central obesity
- impaired glucose tolerance (e.g. type 2 diabetes)
- dyslipidaemia
- hypertension.

This cluster of features of the metabolic syndrome has been called the 'deadly quartet'.

The metabolic syndrome is associated with an increased risk of cardiovascular disease, principally atheroma and its complications, and of type 2 diabetes (in those who have not already developed it as one of the diagnostic criteria for the syndrome). However, it should be noted that several features of the syndrome also independently increase the risk and severity of atheroma, so the precise extent of the morbidity and mortality due to the syndrome itself is difficult to quantify.

TRACE ELEMENTS AND DISEASE

Trace elements are those present at an arbitrarily defined low concentration in a given situation. Some trace elements in humans are of vital importance, despite the meagre quantities found in the human body. Trace elements cause disease when the body levels are higher or lower than normal, depending on the specific biological effects of the element.

Many elements, such as iron, cannot be regarded as trace elements because of their abundance in the body; nevertheless, diseases can result from either a deficiency or an excess (anaemia and haemosiderosis respectively in the case of iron).

Diseases associated with trace element abnormalities are summarised in Table 7.5. Some examples of well-documented associations of disease and trace elements will be summarised.

Aluminium

Aluminium is one of the most abundant elements in the Earth's crust, but only traces are found in the normal human body. Toxic quantities can enter the body in a variety of ways. Aluminium is present in variable concentrations in water supplies and it is used therapeutically in the form of aluminium hydroxide as an antacid. Aluminium is also used in some cooking utensils, from which it can be leached under acid conditions. Aluminium powder has also been used for the treatment of pneumoconiosis, a chronic lung disorder resulting from the inhalation of toxic or allergenic dusts (Ch. 14).

Aluminium has been incriminated in the development of skeletal abnormalities and encephalopathy in patients on regular haemodialysis for chronic renal failure. In such cases,

Table 7.5 Trace elements and disease

Element	Abnormality	Consequences
Aluminium	Excess	Bone changes Encephalopathy
Cobalt	Excess	Cardiomyopathy
Copper	Excess	Hepatic damage Basal ganglia damage (i.e. Wilson's disease)
Iodine	Deficiency	Goitre
Lead	Excess	Neuropathy Anaemia
Mercury	Excess	Neuropathy
Selenium	Deficiency	Cardiac failure Hepatic necrosis
Zinc	Deficiency	Impaired wound healing Acrodermatitis enteropathica

aluminium has been found deposited on mineralisation fronts in the skeleton, where it may interfere with bone turnover. Dialysis encephalopathy, first reported in 1972, is characterised by progressive dementia, epileptic fits and tremors. In 1976, dialysis encephalopathy was shown to be associated with an abnormally high aluminium concentration in brain tissue obtained from autopsies on affected patients. This finding then led to discovery of a link between aluminium and dialysis bone disease.

Aluminium is often detectable in the brain lesions in Alzheimer's disease, a relatively common neurodegenerative disorder, but evidence that it is an aetiological factor is very weak.

Copper

Copper is essential for the function of several enzymes (e.g. superoxide dismutase). Copper deficiency appears to be rare. Some people with arthritis claim to derive benefit, undoubtedly psychological, from wearing copper bracelets, although the only observable change is a green discoloration of the underlying skin.

Wilson's disease is the most important disorder of copper metabolism. This is inherited as an autosomal recessive condition in which copper accumulates in the liver (Fig. 7.10), basal ganglia of the brain, kidneys and eyes. The brown ring of copper deposition around the corneal limbus—the Kayser–Fleischer ring—is absolutely diagnostic. Serum caeruloplasmin levels are usually low. In the liver, the copper accumulation is associated with chronic hepatitis, frequently culminating in cirrhosis (Ch. 16). The neurological changes are seriously disabling. Although Wilson's disease is rare, it is absolutely vital to consider the diagnosis in any patient presenting with chronic liver disease and neurological signs. D-Penicillamine, a chelating agent, has revolutionised the treatment of Wilson's

139

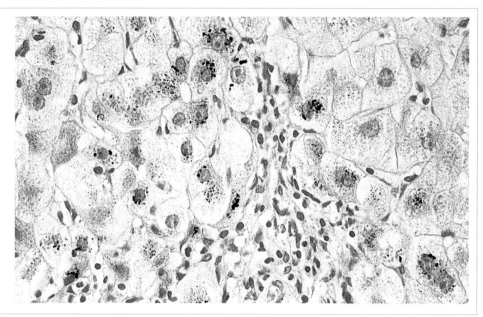

Fig. 7.10   Copper in liver. Liver biopsy, stained for copper (dark granules), showing excessive copper in periportal liver cells. No stainable copper would be present in a normal liver. Copper accumulates in the liver in Wilson's disease and in patients with chronic obstructive jaundice (e.g. primary biliary cirrhosis).

disease, but it is to little avail if the liver and brain have already been irreversibly damaged.

Iodine

The human body contains only 15–20 mg of iodine, most of which is in the thyroid gland. Iodine is almost unique among elements in having just one known role in the human body: it is essential for the synthesis of thyroxine.

Ingestion of modestly excessive quantities of iodine (as potassium iodide, for example) has no serious adverse consequences. Indeed, large stocks of potassium iodide tablets are kept in the vicinity of nuclear power stations for use in the event of accidental release of radioactive iodine, a cause of thyroid cancer. The potassium iodide competes with the smaller amounts of radioactive iodine for uptake by the thyroid gland.

Iodine deficiency results in goitre (enlargement of the thyroid gland, Ch. 17). Goitre was prevalent in regions where the water and solid food lacked an adequate iodine content, usually in mountainous regions (hence, for example, 'Derbyshire neck'). Maternal iodine deficiency during pregnancy causes cretinism in neonates, characterised by mental retardation and stunted growth. These problems have been eliminated in many countries by the addition of iodides and iodates to table salt.

Lead

Much effort is being made in many countries to reduce environmental contamination by lead. The human body contains approximately 120 mg of lead and the daily intake should not exceed 500 µg. Excessive ingestion or inhalation can result from contaminated food, water or air; the main sources in the UK appear to be old lead piping in water supplies, and tetra-ethyl and tetra-methyl lead added to petrol as anti-knocking agents. Old plumbing is gradually being replaced and the use of unleaded petrol now common.

Toxic effects of lead include central and peripheral nervous system damage, renal damage and sideroblastic anaemia (Ch. 23). It has been alleged that lead exposure may be responsible for mental retardation in children, but it has been difficult to dissociate this from the other consequences of socio-economic deprivation prevalent in the urban environments contaminated with lead.

Mercury

The average human body contains only 13 mg of mercury. The safe daily intake is <50 µg.

Mercury has been used in dental amalgams for filling tooth cavities since 1818. Although doubts have been expressed about its safety, metallic mercury and mercury-containing dental amalgams are insoluble in saliva and are, therefore, not absorbed to an appreciable extent. Dentists must, of course, use mercury cautiously to minimise the risk of cumulative occupational exposure.

Mercury is neurotoxic. Chronic poisoning also results in a characteristic blue line on the gums. Perhaps the best-known (but fictitious) case is that of the Mad Hatter in *Alice in Wonderland*; hatmakers used mercuric nitrate for making felt out of animal fur! In the 1950s at Minamata, Japan, there was serious water pollution with methyl mercury, causing at least 50 deaths and many more cases of permanent neurological disability.

Despite its known toxicity, mercury has been used therapeutically, though not to any great effect. It was a popular, though ineffectual, remedy for syphilis; this gave rise to the heavenly adage 'A night with Venus; a lifetime on Mercury'! More recently, pharmaceutical preparations containing mercury were advocated for treating childhood ailments such as measles, teething and diarrhoea. One such preparation containing calomel (mercurous chloride) was sold as a teething powder. Many years later this was suggested—and eventually proven—to be the cause of 'pink disease', a distressing condition affecting infants and young children, formerly of unknown aetiology.

TISSUE DEPOSITIONS

Tissues can become altered as a result of deposition of excessive quantities of substances present normally in only small amounts. These include haemosiderin, as in haemochromatosis (Ch. 16), lysosomal storage disorders (see p. 125), and lipofuscin, which accumulates particularly in the liver with ageing (Ch. 12). Pathological calcification and amyloid deposition are detailed below.

Calcification

▶ Dystrophic calcification in previously damaged tissues
▶ 'Metastatic' calcification due to hypercalcaemia
▶ Pathological calcification may be radiologically evident and diagnostically useful
▶ Resulting hardening of tissues may lead to malfunction

Although calcium ions are vital for the normal function of all cells, precipitates of calcium salts are normally found only in bones, otoliths and teeth. In disease states, however, tissues can become hardened by deposits of calcium salts; this process is called calcification. Calcification may be:

● dystrophic
● 'metastatic'.

'Metastatic' calcification must not be confused with the process of metastasis of tumours. It is an entirely separate condition. In the context of calcification, 'metastatic' only means widespread.

Dystrophic calcification

Calcification is said to be dystrophic if it occurs in tissue already affected by disease. In these cases the serum calcium is normal. The calcification is due to local precipitation of insoluble calcium salts. Common examples are:

● atheromatous plaques
● congenitally bicuspid aortic valves
● calcification of mitral valve ring
● old tuberculous lesions
● fat necrosis
● breast lesions
● calcinosis cutis.

The calcified lesions will often be detectable on a plain X-ray as opacities or, if detected at surgery, will feel extremely hard. Dystrophic calcification does not usually have any special consequences for the patient, with the notable exception of calcification of a congenitally bicuspid aortic valve. A bicuspid aortic valve can function quite normally, but when it becomes calcified, a common event in the elderly, the valve cusps become thick and rigid; this causes stenosis, incompetence and, ultimately, cardiac failure (Ch. 13). The biochemical basis of dystrophic calcification is uncertain except in the instance of fat necrosis, a common result of trauma to adipose tissue

or of acute pancreatitis (Ch. 16); the liberated fatty acids bind calcium to form insoluble calcium soaps, sometimes causing hypocalcaemia and tetany.

The presence of dystrophic calcification in breast lesions, particularly some carcinomas, is one of the abnormalities looked for by radiologists in the interpretation of mammograms (X-rays of the breasts) when screening for breast cancer.

A few tumours contain minute concentric lamellated calcified bodies. These are called *psammoma bodies* ('psammos' is Greek for sand) and are most commonly found in:

● meningiomas (Ch. 26)
● papillary carcinomas of thyroid (Ch. 17)
● papillary ovarian carcinomas (Ch. 19).

Psammoma bodies assist the histopathologist in correctly identifying the type of tumour, but their pathogenesis is unknown.

'Metastatic' calcification

Metastatic calcification is much less common than dystrophic calcification and occurs as a result of hypercalcaemia. Calcification may be widespread and occurs in otherwise normal tissues. Frequent causes are:

● hyperparathyroidism
● hypercalcaemia of malignancy.

In hyperparathyroidism, an adenoma or, less often, a diffuse hyperplasia of the parathyroid glands secretes excess quantities of parathyroid hormone; this liberates calcium from the bone, resulting in hypercalcaemia. In some patients with malignant neoplasms, hypercalcaemia results from either the secretion of a parathyroid hormone-like substance or extensive bone erosion due to skeletal metastases.

In this condition the calcium salts are precipitated on to connective tissue fibres (e.g. collagen, elastin; Fig. 7.11).

Amyloid

▶ Extracellular beta-pleated sheet material
▶ Composed of immunoglobulin light chains, serum amyloid protein A, peptide hormones, prealbumin, etc.
▶ Systemic amyloidosis may be due to a plasma cell neoplasm (e.g. myeloma) or to a chronic inflammatory disorder
▶ Localised amyloid deposits occur in some peptide hormone-producing tumours
▶ Amyloid often impairs the function of the organ in which it is deposited
▶ Heart failure and nephrotic syndrome are common complications

Amyloid (meaning starch-like from the Greek 'amylon') is the name given to a group of proteins or glycoproteins that, when deposited in tissues, share the following properties:

● beta-pleated sheet molecular configuration with an affinity for certain dyes (e.g. Congo or Sirius red; Fig. 7.12)
● fibrillar ultrastructure (Fig. 7.13)
● presence of a glycoprotein of the pentraxin family (amyloid P protein)

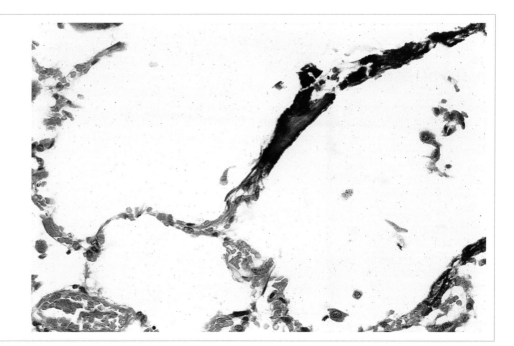

Fig. 7.11 Calcification of alveolar walls. The purple-staining material deposited on alveolar walls is calcification in a patient with hypercalcaemia.

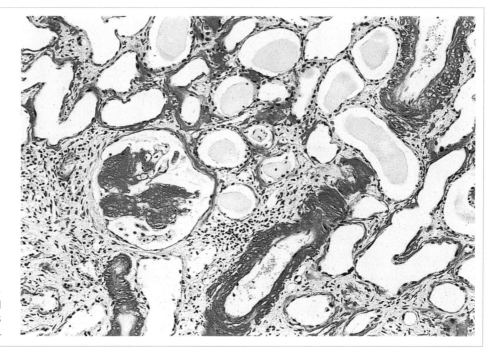

Fig. 7.12 Renal amyloidosis. Renal biopsy stained to show amyloid (red). The amyloid is deposited in the glomeruli, blood vessel walls and tubular basement membranes.

- extracellular location, often on basement membranes
- resistance to removal by natural processes
- a tendency to cause the affected tissue to become hardened and waxy.

Small asymptomatic deposits of amyloid are not uncommon in the spleen, brain, heart and joints of elderly people.

The beta-pleated molecular configuration is an important feature because the body has no enzymes capable of digesting large molecules in this form, so they remain permanently in the tissues.

Classification

Amyloid can be classified according to:

- chemical composition—the substance in the amyloid material
- tissue distribution—whether localised or systemic
- aetiology—the nature of the underlying cause, if known.

These are all equally legitimate and complementary methods of classification. The chemical composition often correlates

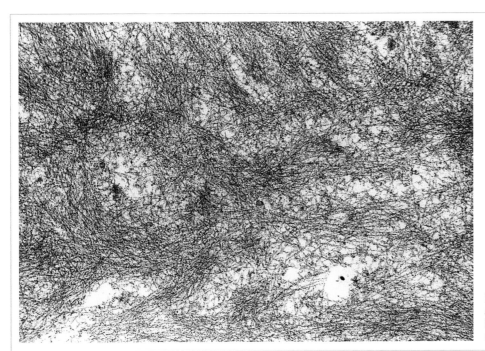

Fig. 7.13 Amyloid ultrastructure. Amyloid substances are characterised by a fibrillar appearance on electron microscopy.

Table 7.6 Classification of amyloid substances	
Condition	Amyloid substance
Myeloma-associated (primary)	AL (immunoglobulin light chains or fragments)
Reactive (secondary)	AA (serum amyloid protein A, an acute-phase reactant)
Alzheimer's disease	A-beta (derived from amyloid precursor protein)
Haemodialysis-associated	A-beta-2M (beta-2 microglobulin)
Hereditary and familial Familial neuropathic	ATTR (transthyretin)
Familial Mediterranean fever	AA
Finnish amyloidosis	AGel (gelsolin)
Medullary carcinoma of thyroid	AMCT (calcitonin)

In addition to those amyloid substances listed, all amyloid deposits also contain amyloid P glycoprotein as a common constituent.

with the clinical classification (Table 7.6); it can, therefore, be helpful diagnostically and lead to the discovery of the aetiology in an individual case.

Clinically, however, amyloidosis presents with organ involvement which is either:

- systemic (Fig. 7.14)
- localised.

Systemic amyloidosis

In systemic amyloidosis the material is deposited in a wide variety of organs; virtually no organ is exempt. Clinical features suggesting amyloidosis include generalised diffuse organ enlargement (e.g. hepatomegaly, splenomegaly, macroglossia) and evidence of organ dysfunction (e.g. heart failure, proteinuria).

Systemic amyloidosis is further classified according to its aetiology:

- myeloma-associated (primary)
- reactive (secondary)
- senile
- haemodialysis-associated
- hereditary.

Myeloma-associated amyloidosis

The amyloid substance in myeloma-associated amyloidosis is *AL amyloid*—immunoglobulin light chains.

A *myeloma* is a plasma cell tumour, often multiple, arising in bone marrow and causing extensive bone erosion. It produces excessive quantities of immunoglobulin of a single class (e.g. IgG) with a uniform light chain (e.g. kappa). The light chain forms the amyloid material. The amyloid is deposited in many organs—heart, liver, kidneys, spleen, etc.—but shows a predilection for the connective tissues within these organs.

In some cases, myeloma-associated amyloidosis is called *primary amyloidosis* because of the absence of any clinically obvious myeloma. However, invariably there is a clinically occult plasma cell tumour, with little bone erosion to declare itself, but with a monoclonal immunoglobulin band on serum electrophoresis; this is referred to as a benign *monoclonal gammopathy*.

Amyloidosis is a serious complication of myeloma, exacerbating the ill health of the patient.

143

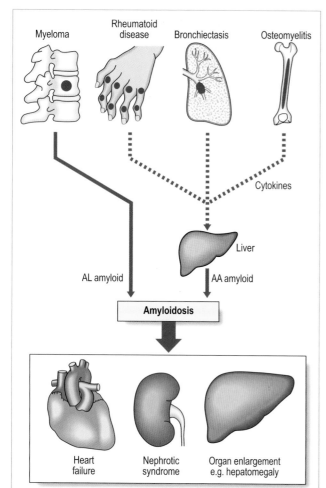

Fig. 7.14   Common causes and consequences of systemic amyloidosis. In primary or myeloma-associated amyloidosis the AL amyloid comprises light chains secreted by neoplastic plasma cells. In reactive or secondary amyloidosis the production of AA amyloid by the liver is stimulated by cytokines secreted by chronic inflammatory cells.

Reactive (secondary) amyloidosis

The amyloid substance in reactive or secondary amyloidosis is *AA amyloid,* derived from serum amyloid protein A.

Serum amyloid protein A, synthesised in the liver, is an acute phase reactant protein, one of several so called because the serum concentrations rise in response to the presence of a variety of diseases.

Reactive amyloidosis, by definition, always has a predisposing cause; this is invariably a chronic inflammatory disorder. Chronic inflammatory disorders frequently predisposing to secondary amyloidosis are:

- rheumatoid disease
- bronchiectasis
- osteomyelitis.

The amyloid in reactive amyloidosis shows the same tendency to widespread deposition as in myeloma-associated amyloidosis, but it has a predilection for the liver, spleen and kidneys (Fig. 7.14).

Senile amyloidosis

Minute deposits of amyloid, usually derived from serum pre-albumin, may be found in the heart and in the walls of blood vessels in many organs of elderly people. However, only in a few cases do they result in significant signs or symptoms.

Haemodialysis-associated amyloidosis

The association of amyloidosis with long-term haemodialysis for chronic renal failure has been recognised only recently. The clinical manifestations include arthropathy and carpal tunnel syndrome. In a few cases there is much more extensive involvement of other organs. The amyloid material deposited in the affected tissues appears to be beta-2 microglobulin.

Hereditary amyloidosis

Hereditary and familial forms of amyloid deposition are rare and include:

- familial Mediterranean fever
- Portuguese neuropathy
- Finnish amyloidosis.

Localised amyloidosis

Amyloid material is often found in the stroma of tumours producing peptide hormones. It is particularly characteristic of medullary carcinoma of the thyroid, a tumour of the calcitonin-producing interfollicular C-cells. In this instance, the amyloid contains calcitonin molecules arranged in a beta-pleated sheet configuration.

Localised deposits of amyloid may be found, without any obvious predisposing cause, in virtually any organ; this is, however, a rare occurrence. The skin, lungs and urinary tract seem to be the most frequent sites.

Cerebral amyloid is found in Alzheimer's disease (see Ch. 26) and in the brains of elderly people in:

- neuritic (senile) plaques
- the walls of small arteries (amyloid angiopathy).

The amyloid in plaques in Alzheimer's disease comprises A-beta protein complexed with apolipoprotein E (apoE). The latter occurs in several allelic variants, of which apoE4 is a risk factor for Alzheimer's disease.

Clinical effects and diagnosis

The clinical manifestations of amyloidosis are:

- nephrotic syndrome, eventually renal failure
- hepatosplenomegaly
- cardiac failure due to restricted myocardial movement
- macroglossia
- purpura
- carpal tunnel syndrome
- coagulation factor X deficiency (in AL amyloid).

Amyloidosis may be suspected on clinical examination because of enlargement of various organs, especially the liver and spleen. As the kidneys are often involved and the amyloid is deposited in glomerular basement membranes, altering their filtration properties, the patients often have proteinuria; in

Commonly confused conditions and entities relating to disorders of metabolism and homeostasis	
Commonly confused	**Distinction and explanation**
Cystine, cysteine, homocysteine and *homocystinuria*	Both cystine and cysteine are sulphur-containing amino acids: one molecule of *cystine* can be reduced to two molecules of *cysteine*. *Homocysteine* is an intermediate in the synthesis of cysteine; high blood levels are found in *homocystinuria*.
Tetany and *tetanus*	*Tetany* is muscular spasm induced by hypocalcaemia, either an absolute reduction in serum calcium or, as in respiratory alkalosis (e.g. hysterical hyperventilation), a reduction in the amount of ionised calcium. *Tetanus* is the disease resulting from infection by *Clostridium tetani* which produces a toxin causing muscular spasm.
Kwashiorkor and *marasmus*	*Marasmus* is severe wasting due to protein–energy malnutrition. In *kwashiorkor* the wasting is somewhat concealed by oedema of the tissues.
Dystrophic and *'metastatic'* calcification	Calcification of diseased tissues (e.g. atheromatous plaques, old tuberculous lesions) is called *dystrophic*. Calcification of previously normal tissues in a patient with hypercalcaemia is often said to be *'metastatic'*, but this should not be confused with the process of tumour metastasis.
Primary and *secondary* amyloidosis	In *primary amyloidosis* the amyloid deposits contain immunoglobulin light chains; although there may be no underlying cause (hence 'primary'), the light chains probably originate from a neoplastic clonal proliferation of plasma cells. In *secondary amyloidosis* the amyloid comprises serum amyloid protein A produced by the liver in response to cytokines from chronically inflamed tissues.

severe cases the proteinuria can result in nephrotic syndrome (Ch. 21). The diagnosis is best confirmed by biopsy of the rectal mucosa, commonly involved in cases of systemic amyloidosis; this procedure is relatively safe and painless. The amyloid in the biopsy can be stained histologically using Congo red or Sirius red dyes, or immunohistochemically using specific antibodies. When examined using one fixed and one rotating polarising filter in the light path on either side of the section, the red colour changes to green (dichroism); this simple optical test is quite specific for amyloid. Using special techniques it may be possible to characterise the amyloid substance more precisely to determine its origin and to identify thereby the underlying cause.

Localised amyloid in a tumour is of no clinical consequence other than serving to assist the histopathologist in correctly identifying the tumour as, for example, a medullary carcinoma of the thyroid.

A solitary amyloid deposit is of clinical significance either because it mimics a tumour (e.g. on a plain chest X-ray) or because it compresses a vital structure (e.g. a ureter).

FURTHER READING

Daneman D 2006 Type 1 diabetes. Lancet 367: 847–858

Eckel R H, Grundy S M, Zimmet P Z 2005 The metabolic syndrome. Lancet 365: 1415–1428

Kass R S 2005 The channelopathies: novel insights into molecular and genetic mechanisms of human disease. Journal of Clinical Investigation 115: 1986–1989

Kellum J A 2000 Determinants of blood pH in health and disease. Critical Care 4: 6–14

Kraut J A, Madias N E 2001 Approach to patients with acid–base disorders. Respiratory Care 46: 392–403

Labib M 2003 The investigation and management of obesity. Journal of Clinical Pathology 56: 17–25

Lenihan J 1988 The crumbs of creation: trace elements in history, medicine, industry, crime and folklore. Adam Hilger, Bristol

Marshall W J 2000 Clinical chemistry. Mosby, Edinburgh

Nyhan W L, Barshop B A, Ozand P T 2005 Atlas of metabolic diseases. Oxford University Press, Oxford

Pepys M B 2006 Amyloidosis. Annual Review of Medicine 57: 223–241

Ratjen F, Doring G 2003 Cystic fibrosis. Lancet 361: 681–689

Scriver's Online Metabolic & Molecular Bases of Inherited Disease. http://www.ommbid.com/

Wong L L, Verbalis J G 2002 Systemic diseases associated with disorders of water homeostasis. Endocrinology and Metabolism Clinics of North America 31: 121–140

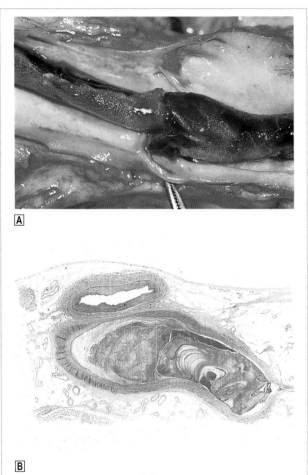

A

B

Fig. 8.3 Venous thrombus. **A** Femoral vein opened at autopsy to reveal a thrombus. **B** Histological section showing the characteristic laminated or coralline structure of a thrombus.

Clinical effects

The effects of thrombosis are apparent only if the thrombus is sufficiently large to affect the flow of blood significantly. Arterial thrombosis results in loss of pulses distal to the thrombus and all the signs of impaired blood supply: the area becomes cold, pale and painful, and eventually the tissue dies and gangrene results. In venous thromboses, 95% of which occur in leg veins, the area becomes tender, swollen and reddened, as blood is still carried to the site by the arteries but cannot be drained away by the veins. The tenderness is due to developing ischaemia in the vein wall initially, but there is also general ischaemic pain as the circulation worsens. The more specific clinical effects of thrombosis depend on the tissue that is affected.

Myocardial infarction is often associated with thrombus formation in coronary arteries and is responsible for numerous sudden deaths (Ch. 13).

Strokes may be due to the formation of thrombus in a cerebral vessel, although they may be also the result of haemorrhage or embolism (Ch. 26).

Thrombophlebitis migrans occurs in previously healthy veins in any area of the body. The thromboses appear and disappear,

changing site all the time, and the condition may persist for months or even years. It is extremely ominous and usually indicates the presence of visceral cancer, commonly of the pancreas. The mechanism remains obscure.

Fate of thrombi

Various fates await the newly formed thrombus (Fig. 8.4). In the best scenario it may resolve; the various degradative processes available to the body may dissolve it and clear it away completely. It is not known what proportion of thrombi follow this course, but the total number is likely to be large. A second possibility is that the thrombus may become *organised* into a scar by the invasion of macrophages, which clear away the thrombus, and fibroblasts, which replace it with collagen, occasionally leaving a mural nodule or web that narrows the vessel lumen. A third possibility is that the intimal cells of the vessel in which the thrombus lies may proliferate, and small sprouts of capillaries may grow into the thrombus and later fuse to form larger vessels. In this way the original occlusion may become *recanalised* and the vessel patent again. Another common result is that the thrombus affects some vital centre and causes death before either the body or the clinicians can make an effective response; this event is very common. Finally, fragments of the thrombus may break off into the circulation, a process known as *embolism*.

Embolism

> ▸ An embolus is a mass of material in the vascular system able to become lodged within a vessel and block its lumen
> ▸ Most emboli are derived from thrombi
> ▸ Other types of embolic material include: atheromatous plaque material; vegetations on heart valves (infective endocarditis); fragments of tumour (causing metastases); amniotic fluid; gas and fat
> ▸ The most common occurrence is pulmonary embolism from deep leg vein thrombosis

An embolus is a mass of material in the vascular system able to lodge in a vessel and block its lumen. The material may have arisen within the body or have been introduced from outside. The material may be solid, liquid or gaseous. The end results of embolism are more dependent upon the final resting place of the embolic material than on its nature. Emboli travel in the circulation, passing through the vascular tree until they reach a vessel whose diameter is small enough to prevent their further passage. The clinical effects will therefore depend upon the territory supplied by that vessel and the presence or absence of an alternative (collateral) circulation to that area. The most frequent source of embolic material is a thrombus formed in any area of the circulatory system, but other sources of embolic material should not be disregarded. Over 90% of major emboli are derived from thrombi, so we shall first consider the principal clinical syndromes associated with this situation and then briefly mention other forms of embolism.

Pulmonary embolism

Around 95% of venous thrombosis occurs in leg veins; the majority of the rest occur in pelvic veins, and a very few occur in the

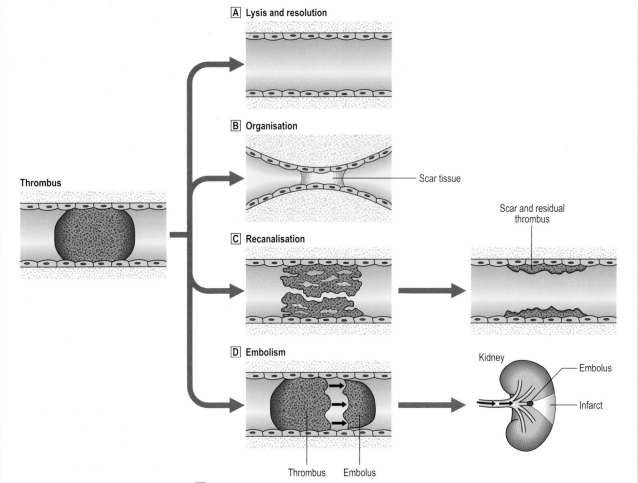

Fig. 8.4 Consequences of thrombosis. **A** Lysis of the thrombus and complete restitution of normal structure usually can occur only when the thrombus is relatively small and is dependent upon fibrinolytic activity (e.g. plasmin). **B** The thrombus may be replaced by scar tissue which contracts and obliterates the lumen; the blood bypasses the occluded vessel through collateral channels. **C** Recanalisation occurs by the ingrowth of new vessels which eventually join up to restore blood flow, at least partially. **D** Embolism caused by fragmentation of the thrombus and resulting in infarction at a distant site.

intracranial venous sinuses. Therefore, most emboli from such thrombi will arrive in the pulmonary circulation—*pulmonary embolism*. The only possibility for such emboli to arrive in the arterial side of the circulation is if there is an arterial–venous communication, such as a perforated septum in the heart (paradoxical embolus), but this event is exceptionally rare.

The effects of pulmonary emboli depend upon their size. Small emboli may occur unnoticed and be lysed within the lung or they may become organised and cause some permanent, though small, respiratory deficiency. Such a respiratory deficiency may only come to light with the eventual accumulation of damage from many such tiny embolic events. The accumulation of such damage over a long period may be the cause of so-called 'idiopathic' *pulmonary hypertension* (Ch. 14).

A second class of pulmonary emboli may be large enough to cause *acute respiratory and cardiac problems* that may resolve slowly with or without treatment. The main symptoms are chest pain and shortness of breath due to the effective loss of the area of lung supplied by the occluded vessel; the area may even become infarcted. This occlusion puts some strain on

the heart, which is evident on the ECG as right heart strain with deep S waves in lead 1 and the presence of Q waves and inverted T waves in lead 3 (S1, Q3, T3). This ECG pattern is one of the few that a pathologist will look for in the case notes before performing an autopsy on a patient suspected of having had a pulmonary embolus in life; without these findings the embolus is unlikely to have caused death. Although many patients recover from such episodes, their lung function is impaired and, of course, they are at risk from further emboli from the same source. Consequently, they require symptomatic therapy for the embolus as well as treatment for the causative thrombus.

The third class of pulmonary emboli are massive and result in *sudden death*. These are usually long thrombi derived from leg veins and have the shape of the vessels in which they arose, rather than that of the vessels in which they are found at postmortem examination. They are often impacted across the bifurcation of one of the major pulmonary arteries as a 'saddle embolus', a descriptive term for their appearance. As with all thrombi, even if they have undergone embolisation they retain the appearance of a thrombus, with lines of Zahn and a granular, friable consistency. This consistency is distinct from the elastic, 'chicken fat and redcurrant jelly' appearance of postmortem clots.

Systemic embolism

Systemic emboli arise in the arterial system and again their effects are due to their size and to the vessel in which they finally lodge. The thrombi from which they come generally form in the heart or on atheromatous plaque (Fig. 8.5). In the heart, thrombi may form on areas of cardiac muscle that has died as a result of myocardial infarction, as these areas will have lost their normal endothelial lining and will expose the underlying collagen to the circulating platelets. These areas of dead myocardium will also be adynamic and will disrupt the normal blood flow within the heart, creating turbulence and predisposing to thrombus formation at that site.

Another common cause of thrombosis within the heart is the presence of atrial fibrillation. This ineffectual movement of the atria causes blood to stagnate in the atrial appendages and thrombosis to occur. When the normal heart rhythm is re-established the atrial thrombus may be fragmented and emboli broken off.

Emboli from the heart are usually derived from thrombi on the left side of the circulation. These emboli may travel to the brain, causing cerebrovascular incidents such as transient ischaemic attacks or strokes, or they may travel to any of the viscera, or to the limbs.

Large emboli may lodge at the bifurcation of the aorta as a saddle embolus cutting off the blood supply to the lower limbs, a situation that requires rapid diagnosis if the embolus is to be removed before the changes in the limbs become irreversible. Smaller emboli may lodge in smaller vessels nearer the periphery and cause gangrene of the digits. Small emboli may travel into the kidneys or spleen and be relatively asymptomatic, even when they cause the death of the area of tissue distal to their site of impaction; ischaemic scars are not uncommon findings at autopsy with no clinical history to lead one to suspect that such events had been occurring.

More dramatic consequences develop as a result of emboli travelling to the intestine, often passing down the superior mesenteric artery; this impaction can cause death of whole sections of small bowel, which, unlike kidneys or spleen, depends upon the whole organ to be intact in order to function. The death of even a small area of bowel means perforation and peritonitis, whereas the death of a small area of kidney or spleen means only a small scar.

Vegetations on the heart valves are an important source of emboli. Most seriously, in *infective endocarditis* the vegetations consist of micro-organisms, usually bacteria, and are extremely friable. Marantic vegetations, consisting of platelets and

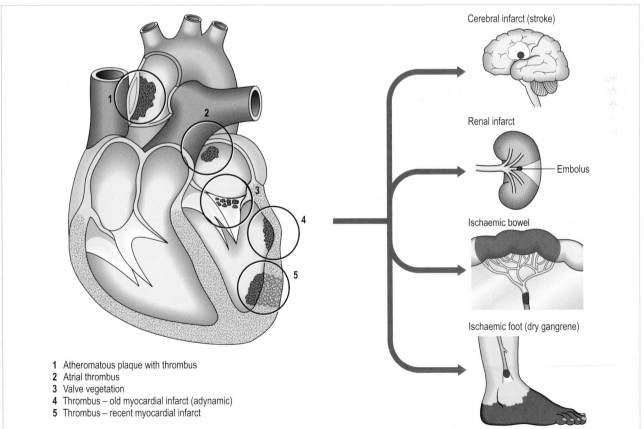

1 Atheromatous plaque with thrombus
2 Atrial thrombus
3 Valve vegetation
4 Thrombus – old myocardial infarct (adynamic)
5 Thrombus – recent myocardial infarct

Cerebral infarct (stroke)

Renal infarct

Embolus

Ischaemic bowel

Ischaemic foot (dry gangrene)

Fig. 8.5 Origins and effects of systemic arterial emboli. Systemic arterial emboli almost invariably originate from the left side of the heart or from major arteries. Infarction or gangrene is the usual consequence.

fibrin, occur on the heart valves of patients who are severely debilitated, for example by cancer; these vegetations are often firmly adherent and are less likely to embolise.

Embolic atheroma

Fragments of atheromatous plaque may embolise and these are frequently seen in the lower limbs of arteriopathic patients. The precise cause of such ischaemic toes is rarely investigated thoroughly enough to be diagnosed. The embolic fragments may be recognised in histological preparations by the cigar-shaped clefts left behind when the cholesterol crystals dissolve out during histological processing.

Platelet emboli

Since the early stages of atheroma involve mainly platelet deposition, emboli from early lesions may be composed solely of platelets. In general these are very tiny emboli and do not present with severe clinical signs. The exception is in the brain, where even small emboli manifest with striking clinical symptoms and signs. A stroke that lasts for less than 24 hours and that is associated with complete clinical recovery is termed a *transient ischaemic attack* (TIA); although these show complete resolution, they are risk markers for subsequent major strokes. While many TIAs are thought to be due to platelet emboli, there is some evidence that in some cases they may also be caused by arterial spasm.

Infective emboli

Infected lesions within the blood stream, in particular the vegetations on diseased heart valves (Ch. 13), may break off and lodge in small vessels in the usual way. But here, the usual effects of emboli are compounded by the infective agent present and this agent may weaken the wall of the vessel, causing the development of a 'mycotic' aneurysm. (Mycotic is a misnomer because the infective agent is usually bacterial, not fungal.)

Fat embolism

Fat embolism usually arises following some severe trauma with fracture to long bones. Fat from the bone marrow is released into the circulation and comes to lodge in various organs. A similar situation arises in severe burns and in extensive soft tissue injury. Much of the circulating fat enters the lungs and this indicates that it must travel by way of the venous system. However, fat globules are fluid and so small that they may cross the pulmonary vascular bed and, therefore, many also enter the systemic arterial circulation, causing confusion or coma, renal impairment and skin petechiae. It has also been suggested that systemic effects of trauma, particularly burns, can cause changes in the stability of fat held in micellar suspension, resulting in free fat appearing in the circulation. This fat could then travel in the circulation in exactly the same way as a true fat embolism. Some degree of fat embolism probably occurs in most cases of long bone injury but it is generally asymptomatic.

Gas embolism

There are various causes of embolic events involving gas; several are iatrogenic. The classic form is *caisson disease*, experienced by divers when they are transferred too rapidly from high to low pressure environments. At high pressure, increased volumes of gas dissolve in the blood and during rapid decompression these come out as bubbles. In the case of air, the oxygen and carbon dioxide redissolve but the nitrogen bubbles remain and enter bones and joints, causing the pains of the 'bends', or they lodge in the lungs, causing the respiratory problems of the 'chokes'.

The other causes of gas embolism are mainly surgical when some vessel is opened to the air. This also occurs in suicide attempts when the neck veins are cut, or accidentally when patients are disconnected from intravenous lines and air enters. The 'secret murders' by air injection so favoured by thriller writers are rare, as the volume of air needed to cause death in this fashion is around 100 ml.

The pathological signs of this condition at autopsy include visible bubbles in the vessels, such as those of the meninges, and sometimes a frothy ball of fibrin and air in the right side of the heart, occluding one of the valves.

Amniotic embolism

With the vastly increased pressures in the uterus during labour, amniotic fluid may be forced into the maternal uterine veins. These amniotic fluid emboli travel in the circulation and lodge in the lungs, causing respiratory distress like other pulmonary emboli. They can be recognised histologically because they contain the shed skin cells of the infant.

Tumour embolism

Tumour emboli are mainly small and break off as tumours that penetrate vessels (Ch. 11). They do not usually cause immediate physical problems in the way that other emboli do, but this mechanism is a major route of dissemination of malignancies through the body (metastasis).

Embolism of foreign matter

Particles of foreign matter may contaminate fluids injected intravenously. This is rare when such fluids are injected for medical reasons, but talc, etc. is a common contaminant of fluids injected by intravenous drug abusers. The foreign particles elicit a granulomatous reaction in the organs in which they lodge.

INFARCTION

- ▶ Ischaemic death (necrosis) of tissue
- ▶ Infarcts elicit an inflammatory reaction
- ▶ Gangrene is infarction of mixed tissues in bulk (e.g. gut wall, part of a limb)
- ▶ In some tissues, ischaemic necrosis may result from impaired vascular flow short of total cessation

Infarction is ischaemic death of tissue within the living body. This means that death of tissue from other causes, such as toxins or trauma, is not infarction but is simply necrosis, which is the general term for death of tissue within the living organism. Only death of tissue due to restricted blood supply is infarction. The word infarction means 'stuffed full' and reflects the fact that the first types of infarction that were recognised were those in which the blockage was venous and the arterial supply continued to pump blood into the organ when the outlet was blocked. A similar effect may be seen in those cases where a second blood supply is present and, although the arterial inflow is blocked, blood still enters the organ from this second supply; a good example of this is the lung, which has both pulmonary and bronchial arterial supplies. In the past, pathologists classically divided infarcts into grey and red infarcts, but these merely represent stages in the same process; not all infarcts in the same organ go through these stages, so the division is pointless.

Reperfusion injury

Many of the tissue effects of ischaemic injury paradoxically seem to occur not during the ischaemic episode but when perfusion is re-established. This is not as illogical as it may seem because much of this damage is oxygen dependent and the only way for oxygen to get to the site is by blood flow. When the blood flow returns to an area of tissue that has been ischaemic, it encounters tissue where transport mechanisms across the cell membrane have been disrupted to a variable extent and, in particular, where calcium transport out of the cell and from organelles such as mitochondria is impaired. This appears to be the trigger for the activation of oxygen-dependent free radical systems that begin the clearing away of dead cells which we recognise as a part of reperfusion injury. At the same time polymorphs and macrophages enter the area and begin to clear away debris and themselves import their own intrinsic oxygen free radicals into the area.

Experimental studies reveal that cell death in reperfusion injury and, in some instances, in pure ischaemia involves the intracellular mechanisms of apoptotic cell death. This may result from disruption of the cell–matrix interactions on which cells depend for survival.

Experimentally, reperfusion injury can be prevented with anti-oxidants but this has only a small effect on the ultimate amount of tissue loss. What we see here is another example of an adaptive process (clearing up of dead and damaged cells) that produces deleterious effects (scarring) and that can be marginally modified pharmacologically.

Morphology of infarcts

Infarcted areas vary in appearance depending on the time that has elapsed between the infarct occurring and the lesion coming to the attention of the pathologist (Fig. 8.6). If the tissue is examined within 24 hours of the infarct there will be no direct evidence of the event. Between 24 and 48 hours the dead tissue is beginning to evoke a response from the surrounding living tissues and inflammatory cells can be seen moving into the infarcted area. In routine histological sections stained with haematoxylin and eosin the cytoplasm contains proteins, which stain pink, and RNA, which stains blue. In normal tissue, the cytoplasm therefore has a slightly purple tinge and in areas that have been dead a few hours the RNA is broken down and the cytoplasm becomes bright pink. It should be borne in mind that all histological sections of tissue are 'dead' and that what we are looking at is the consequence of the time that has elapsed between the infarcted tissue dying and the rest of the tissue being killed by being dropped into formalin or some other fixative.

If the infarcted tissue has stayed in the living patient for some days before being removed (by biopsy, surgery or autopsy), the degradative processes of the body in the form of macrophages and polymorphs will have begun to clear away the dead tissue, which will consequently have an amorphous, acellular appearance apart from the numerous inflammatory cells. At this stage, the tissue is at its weakest; subjects with myocardial infarction who have survived the acute episode 10 days previously may suddenly die with rupture of the healing infarct and consequent haemopericardium and cardiac tamponade (Ch. 13). The gross appearance of the tissue at this time is very variable; if small blood vessels in the vicinity

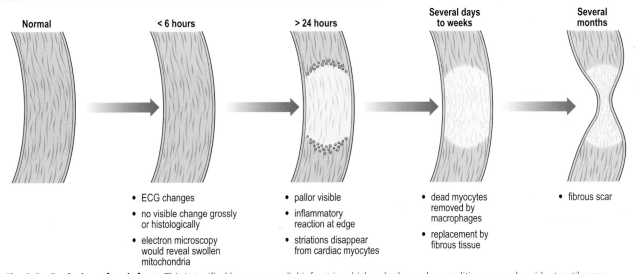

| Normal | < 6 hours | > 24 hours | Several days to weeks | Several months |

- ECG changes
- no visible change grossly or histologically
- electron microscopy would reveal swollen mitochondria

- pallor visible
- inflammatory reaction at edge
- striations disappear from cardiac myocytes

- dead myocytes removed by macrophages
- replacement by fibrous tissue

- fibrous scar

Fig. 8.6 Evolution of an infarct. This is typified by a myocardial infarct in which naked-eye abnormalities are rarely evident until many hours have elapsed. The dead tissue elicits an inflammatory reaction, characteristically neutrophil polymorphs and, later, macrophages. Unless complications intervene, the infarct heals by fibrosis.

have also become ischaemic they may die and blood will escape into the infarct, giving it a patchy or confluent red appearance. On the other hand, there may be no bleeding into the area, in which case it remains pale with a red hyperaemic rim, and grows progressively paler as healing takes place.

If the patients survive this danger period the damaged tissue either regenerates or repairs itself with the formation of a scar (Ch. 6). Such a scar is apparent as a grey, contracted area consisting of collagenous fibrous tissue. A scar solves the tissue deficit in the sense that the organ is intact and the hole is mended, but the scarred area is no longer functional; a healed myocardial infarct is adynamic and can be the site of further problems for the patient. In the heart, this may take the form of an aneurysm as the scar is subjected to cyclic pressure loads and becomes stretched without any ability to contract again.

The overall shape of infarcts depends upon the territory of perfusion of the occluded blood supply; some classic appearances are the wedge-shaped infarcts seen in the lung and the triangular infarcts (conical in three dimensions) seen in the kidneys at autopsy. Other scarred infarcts, such as those in the spleen (Fig. 8.7), are less predictable because the blood supply is less regular and marked overlaps of vascular territories occur, and because the soft tissue distorts as the scar contracts. In the brain the dead tissue is cleared away so efficiently that a fluid-filled cyst is often all that remains (Ch. 26).

Gangrene

When whole areas of a limb or a region of the gut have their arterial supply cut off and large areas of mixed tissues die in bulk, such a process is termed gangrene. Two types of gangrene are recognised:

- Dry gangrene—where the tissue dies and becomes mummified and healing occurs above it, so that eventually the dead area drops off. This is a sterile process, and is the common fate of gangrenous toes as a complication of diabetes.
- Wet gangrene—where bacterial infection supervenes as a secondary complication; in this case the gangrene spreads proximally and the patient dies from overwhelming sepsis.

Another mechanism that results in gangrene is torsion: the gut may twist on a lax mesentery, or an ovary or testis may twist on its pedicle, occluding the venous return. The organ swells and the oedema further compresses the drainage. The arteries continue to pump blood into the organ, but ischaemia supervenes and infarction develops.

Gas gangrene results from infection of ischaemic tissue by gas-producing anaerobic bacteria such as *Clostridium perfringens*.

Capillary ischaemia

In frostbite, the capillaries are damaged in exposed areas and contract so severely that the area they normally supply becomes ischaemic and dies. Exposure to cold without freezing causes capillary contraction followed by a fixed dilatation; this is the mechanism of damage in 'trench foot' and related conditions.

Capillaries may also be blocked by parasites, by abnormal cells in sickle cell disease or by abnormal proteins that precipitate in the cold (cryoglobulinaemia) and these phenomena also lead to local ischaemia and infarction.

The balance of thrombotic and thrombolytic mechanisms is delicate; this balance may be secondarily disturbed by several different disease processes and, unfortunately, by some therapeutic interventions. In such cases, thrombosis may become activated without effective counterbalance, with the result that minute thrombi may form throughout the body and, consequently, bleeding may occur at multiple sites due to consumption of clotting factors; this phenomenon is called *disseminated intravascular coagulation* or *DIC* (Fig. 8.8). It occurs as a complication of many disease states such as cancer or infection (Ch. 23).

Susceptibility to ischaemia

Different tissues show differing susceptibility to ischaemia for a variety of reasons. Some tissues have only one arterial supply and if this is blocked there is no possibility of collateral supplies taking over; one such 'end artery' situation is the

Fig. 8.7   Splenic infarcts. Note the pallor of the infarcts.

1cm

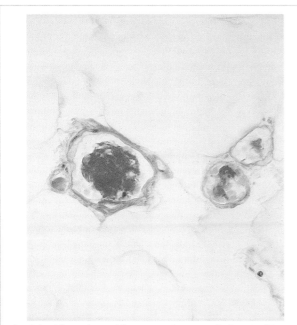

Fig. 8.8   Disseminated intravascular coagulation. In this condition, small vessels are occluded by minute thrombi (stained red in this histological section), causing scattered ischaemic lesions in many organs.

retinal artery and thrombosis of this artery leads inevitably to blindness. Tissues also vary in the degree of ischaemia that they can tolerate, commonly as a function of differing metabolic needs; even within a tissue, different areas have different susceptibilities. Within the heart the sub-endocardial zone is at a watershed between the coronary supply from the outside and the diffusion zone from blood within the chambers. If the coronary arteries are narrowed by the presence of atheroma, these patients are at great risk of developing sub-endocardial infarctions if their systemic blood pressure drops for any reason. Consequently, such patients may develop the complications of sub-endocardial infarction following trauma, surgery or toxic shock from infections.

Low-flow infarction

In some tissues, infarction may be due to impaired blood flow (or oxygenation) rather than an absolute cessation of flow. Tissues that are especially vulnerable to low-flow infarction include:

- 'watershed' areas
- tissues perfused by a portal vasculature
- tissues distal to pathological arterial stenoses
- metabolically active tissues.

'Watershed' areas

Tissue at the interface between the adjacent territories of two arteries is prone to infarction if there is an impairment of blood or oxygen supply. The tissue is normally situated precariously on the fringes of the territories perfused by the arteries, with no collateral circulation to provide blood from alternative vessels.

Examples include:

- the splenic flexure of the colon; this is situated at the interface between the territories of the superior and inferior mesenteric arteries
- regions of the cerebral hemispheres at the interface between the territories of the major cerebral arteries
- the myocardium between the sub-endocardial myocardium (oxygenated directly from blood in the ventricles) and that which is perfused by the coronary arteries.

Patients who are severely shocked and hypotensive may develop ischaemic lesions in these sites.

Portal vasculature

Some tissues are perfused by blood that has already passed through one set of capillaries; this vascular arrangement is described as portal. Therefore, there is normally a drop in intravascular pressure across the first set of capillaries and a reduction in oxygen saturation, rendering the tissue perfused by the second set of capillaries vulnerable to ischaemic injury.

Examples include:

- the anterior pituitary, which is perfused by blood that has already perfused the median eminence of the hypothalamus
- the renal tubular epithelium, which is perfused by blood issuing from the glomerular capillaries
- some parts of the exocrine pancreas, which are perfused by blood that has already perfused islets of Langerhans in the vicinity.

These patterns of vascular microanatomy account for the pituitary infarction, renal tubular necrosis and acute pancreatitis that may occur in severely shocked patients.

Arterial stenoses

Atheromatous narrowing or stenosis of arteries may be of insufficient severity to cause infarction distally in normotensive individuals. However, if the blood pressure and, therefore, blood flow falls, the tissue distal to the arterial stenosis may become infarcted. Thus, patients who become severely shocked may develop ischaemic changes in various organs without there being any sign of *total* vascular occlusion.

Transient arterial spasm can also cause infarction in vulnerable tissues such as the brain and heart.

Infarction and metabolic activity

Cells with large metabolic requirements are exceptionally vulnerable to ischaemic damage and infarction. Cerebral neurones are the most at risk; irreversible damage occurs within a few minutes of cessation of blood flow and oxygenation. Cardiac myocytes also have a considerable requirement for oxygen and other nutrients; they may be irreversibly damaged if the coronary arteries, which may be narrowed by atheroma, cannot supply these requirements during tachycardia associated with exertion.

Low flow without infarction (erectile impotence)

Male sexual function (and arousal in both sexes) depends upon effective vascular responsiveness of the sexual apparatus to produce penile erection. This may be impaired in many clinical situations (diabetes, drug treatment of systemic hypertension, surgery, etc.). Recently a new drug (sildenafil, Viagra) has been developed which specifically targets this vascular bed with consequent improvement in erectile responsiveness.

SHOCK

> ▶ Profound circulatory failure causing hypoperfusion of vital organs
> ▶ Classified as cardiogenic or hypovolaemic
> ▶ Many tissues vulnerable to ischaemic injury
> ▶ Shock due to bacterial toxaemia may be accompanied by disseminated intravascular coagulation

The word 'shock' has different meanings in different contexts. In the emotional context, which almost all of us experience to varying degrees, it means a severe psychological reaction to an event for which we were unprepared. Another meaning is the unpleasant and often painful sensation experienced when high voltage electricity flows through the body. These meanings of the word 'shock' are not relevant here, but they can be a source of great confusion when talking to patients.

Shock as a pathological process is characterised by profound circulatory failure resulting in life-threatening hypoperfusion of vital organs. Compensatory mechanisms maintain blood pressure until they too are defeated, resulting in hypotension. Shock may be classified as:

- cardiogenic—commonly due to myocardial infarction
- hypovolaemic—due to reduction in the *effective* circulating blood volume.

In the early stages the arterial networks in many vital organs can compensate to some extent. For example, by a process of autoregulation, the cerebral arteries dilate when blood pressure is reduced, so that the cerebral vascular resistance falls and a normal rate of flow is maintained. In other tissues, with less vital functions, there is compensatory vasoconstriction in order to increase peripheral vascular resistance and thus maintain the effective blood pressure supplying vital organs; this increased vascular tone is mediated by adrenergic mechanisms and by the effects of angiotensin.

If the compensatory mechanisms fail and hypotension ensues, various tissues will be vulnerable to ischaemic injury (Fig. 8.9). This is an extremely serious clinical problem which, depending on the primary cause, is frequently fatal. The clinicopathological consequences include:

- irreversible neuronal injury
- renal failure due to acute tubular necrosis
- acute pancreatitis

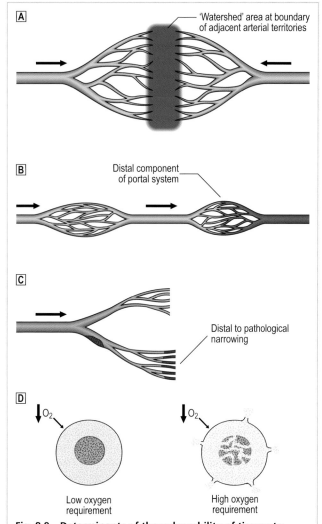

Fig. 8.9 Determinants of the vulnerability of tissues to ischaemic damage in hypotensive shock. [A] Ischaemic damage may occur at the boundary ('watershed' area) between adjacent arterial territories (e.g. splenic flexure of the colon between superior and inferior mesenteric arterial supplies, and regions of the brain at the border of cerebral arterial territories). [B] Tissues supplied by the distal components of portal vascular systems (e.g. anterior pituitary, renal tubules, some pancreatic acini) may suffer ischaemia due to critical fall in perfusion pressure across the proximal capillary bed. [C] Hypotension may precipitate ischaemic damage distal to a region of arterial narrowing (e.g. by atheroma). [D] Cells with high oxygen requirements (e.g. cerebral neurones) may die from hypoxia, whereas neighbouring cells with lower oxygen demands survive.

- risk of cerebral infarction in 'watershed' areas between the adjacent territories of cerebral arteries
- infarction distal to any pathological arterial narrowing, usually atheromatous.

Cardiogenic shock

The commonest cause of cardiogenic shock is acute myocardial infarction. Death of part of the left ventricular myocardium reduces the heart's functional capacity and, even at rest, the left ventricular stroke volume is reduced. If shock proceeds to the hypotensive phase, it should be corrected only with extreme caution; by artificially increasing the blood pressure, additional strain will be placed on the myocardium, with the risk of catastrophic failure.

Hypovolaemic shock

Hypovolaemic shock is characterised by loss of effective circulating blood volume. This may be due to:

- haemorrhage, internally or externally
- generalised increased vascular permeability and/or dilatation.

The pathogenesis of shock resulting from haemorrhage is logical. Internal or external bleeding, for example due to traumatic rupture of an internal organ or accidental severing of a major vessel, causes a reduction in the normal blood volume. Blood pressure is initially maintained by compensatory mechanisms, some of which enable the condition to be suspected clinically; symptoms and signs include a cold, clammy skin and a high pulse rate.

Shock due to generalised increased vascular permeability and/or dilatation can occur as a result of:

- neurogenic mechanisms (e.g. spinal cord injury)
- anaphylactic reactions
- extensive burns
- bacterial toxaemia.

In these situations there are varying degrees of vasodilatation and increased vascular permeability. Blood pools in the dilated vessels and, if there is endothelial damage (for example in

severe burns or bacterial toxaemia), fluid leaks from the vessels into the extravascular compartment, causing a profound reduction in the effective circulating blood volume. Examples mediated by bacterial toxins include (Ch. 3):

- the *toxic shock syndrome*, first described as a serious consequence of prolonged retention of a tampon which then became infected with staphylococci
- *Gram-negative septicaemia*, due to serious infection with endotoxin-producing bacteria.

Other vascular effects of bacterial toxaemia

The bacterial toxins not only have a hypotensive effect but also activate the complement and blood coagulation cascades. The latter may lead to *disseminated intravascular coagulation (DIC)* (Ch. 23). In this condition, which may also be precipitated by the release of tissue thromboplastins from necrotic tissue, fibrin is deposited on endothelial surfaces of blood vessels, thus interfering with trans-endothelial flow of nutrients. The fibrin may also form a mesh across the lumen of small blood vessels resulting in:

- haemolysis due to mechanical injury to circulating erythrocytes
- microinfarcts
- thrombocytopenia due to fibrin-induced platelet aggregation.

The fibrinolytic activity of endothelial cells can cope with small amounts of fibrin deposition; DIC results when the rate of fibrin deposition exceeds the rate of fibrinolysis. DIC is diagnosed by its multisystem clinical features, by the frequent accompaniments of haemolysis and thrombocytopenia, by the haemorrhagic tendency due to consumption of coagulation factors (consumption coagulopathy), and by finding fibrin degradation products.

Commonly confused conditions and entities relating to ischaemia, infarction and shock	
Commonly confused	Distinction and explanation
Clot and *thrombus*	Both are blood solidified by coagulation, but a *clot* is formed in non-flowing blood whereas a *thrombus* is formed in flowing blood and, therefore, often has a laminated structure.
Phlebothrombosis and *thrombophlebitis*	*Phlebothrombosis* is thrombosis in a vein (Greek: phlebos). *Thrombophlebitis* is an inflammatory reaction to phlebothrombosis.
Necrosis and *infarction*	*Necrosis* means abnormal death of sheets of cells or tissue (normal single cell death is usually by apoptosis). *Infarction* is necrosis due to deprivation of blood supply.
Infarction and *gangrene*	*Gangrene* is *infarction* of mixed tissues in bulk (e.g. all layers of bowel wall, part of limb from skin to bone).

FURTHER READING

Gowda R M, Fox J T, Khan I A 2008 Cardiogenic shock: basics and clinical considerations. International Journal of Cardiology 123: 221–228

Hovens M M, Snoep J D, Tamsma J T, Huisman M V 2006 Aspirin in the prevention and treatment of venous thromboembolism. Journal of Thrombosis and Haemostasis 4: 1470–1475

Kuipers S, Schreijer A J, Cannegieter S C, Büller H R, Rosendaal F R, Middeldorp S 2007 Travel and venous thrombosis: a systematic review. Journal of Internal Medicine 262: 615–634

Levi M 2007 Disseminated intravascular coagulation. Critical Care Medicine 35: 2191–2195

Munford R S 2006 Severe sepsis and septic shock: the role of Gram-negative bacteremia. Annual Review of Pathology 1: 467–496

Prandoni P 2006 Acquired risk factors of venous thromboembolism in medical patients. Pathophysiology of Haemostasis and Thrombosis 35: 128–132

Stafford I, Sheffield J 2007 Amniotic fluid embolism. Obstetrics and Gynecology Clinics of North America 34: 545–553

Taviloglu K, Yanar H 2007 Fat embolism syndrome. Surgery Today 37: 5–8

Tissier R, Berdeaux A, Ghaleb B, et al 2008 Making the heart resistant to infarction: how can we further decrease infarct size? Frontiers in Bioscience 13: 284–301

9

Immunology and immunopathology

DEFENCE AGAINST INFECTION

▶ Non-specific mechanisms include the skin barrier, lysozyme in some secretions, ciliary motion in the respiratory tract, and colonisation by harmless bacteria
▶ Innate mechanisms lack memory
▶ Specific immunity is characterised by specificity and memory

The immune system evolved as a defence against infectious diseases. Individuals with deficient immune responses, if untreated, succumb to infections in early life. There is, therefore, a selective evolutionary pressure for an efficient immune system. *Specific immunity* is called into play only when micro-organisms bypass *non-specific* or *innate* mechanisms.

Non-specific defences

Many non-specific mechanisms prevent invasion of the body by micro-organisms:

- *Mechanical barriers* (Fig. 9.1) are highly effective and their failure often results in infection: for instance, defects in the mucociliary lining of the respiratory tract, as in cystic fibrosis, are associated with recurrent lung infection.
- *Secretory factors* (Fig. 9.1) present formidable chemical barriers to many organisms. If the acid pH of the stomach is compromised, as in atrophic gastritis with achlorhydria, bacterial overgrowth may occur in the intestine.

Innate immunity

The innate immune system is activated by *pattern recognition receptors* on dendritic cells recognising conserved polysaccharide molecular patterns on microbes. Key components include:

- *Toll-like receptors (TLRs)*—evolutionarily conserved proteins found on macrophages, dendritic cells and neutrophils. More than 10 different TLRs are found in humans, each recognising a range of conserved motifs on pathogens. On binding to their ligands, TLRs induce signal transduction, sequential cellular events and the induction of pro-inflammatory cytokines.
- *Cellular factors*—include polymorphonuclear leukocytes, natural killer cells and macrophages which phagocytose and kill micro-organisms.
- *Complement*—a complex series of interacting plasma proteins that forms a major effector mechanism for antibody-mediated immune reactions but can also be activated directly by some bacteria.

Specific immunity

The immune system has four essential features:

- specificity
- diversity
- memory
- recruitment of other defence mechanisms.

A specific or adaptive immune response consists of two parts: a *specific response* to the particular antigen and a *non-specific augmentation* of the effect of that response. For the specific response there is a quicker and larger response the second time that a particular antigen is encountered; memory of the initial specific immune response provides the efficiency.

The immune system has to recognise all pathogens, past and future, and must have considerable diversity of response. This diversity is partly genetic (germline encoded) and partly generated by somatic mutation during maturation of the immune system.

Immune responses, both innate and adaptive, have two phases: first the *recognition phase*, involving antigen-presenting cells and T-lymphocytes (see Key molecules), in which the antigen is recognised as foreign; and second the *effector phase*, in which antibodies and effector T-lymphocytes eliminate the antigen, often by recruiting innate mechanisms such as complement or macrophage activation.

KEY MOLECULES

▶ Antigens are substances able to provoke an immune response and react with the products of that response
▶ Antibodies are immunoglobulin molecules produced by plasma cells. Antigen-binding properties reside in the Fab fragments, while effector functions lie in the Fc fragment
▶ T-cells recognise antigens through their T-cell receptors associated with the CD3 molecule
▶ Major histocompatibility complex (MHC) antigens are of two main types—class I and class II. They play a fundamental role in the normal immune response by presenting antigenic peptides to T-cells
▶ Helper T-cells recognise antigen in association with MHC class II molecules, while cytotoxic T-cells recognise antigen associated with MHC class I
▶ T-cell receptors will recognise antigen only as part of a complex of antigenic peptide and the MHC molecule—a process termed MHC restriction
▶ Adhesion and accessory molecules play a key role in the migration of leukocytes into sites of inflammation and in the interactions between antigen-presenting cells and T-lymphocytes
▶ Cytokines are soluble mediators that act as stimulatory or inhibitory signals between cells. Cytokines that act between cells of the immune system are called interleukins while those that induce chemotaxis of leukocytes are called chemokines

Antigens

Antigens are substances able to provoke an immune response and react with the immune products. They react both with the T-cell recognition receptor and with antibody. An antigenic molecule may have several antigenic determinants (epitopes); each *epitope* can bind with an individual antibody, and a single antigenic molecule can therefore provoke many antibody molecules with different binding sites. Some low molecular weight molecules, called *haptens*, are unable to provoke an

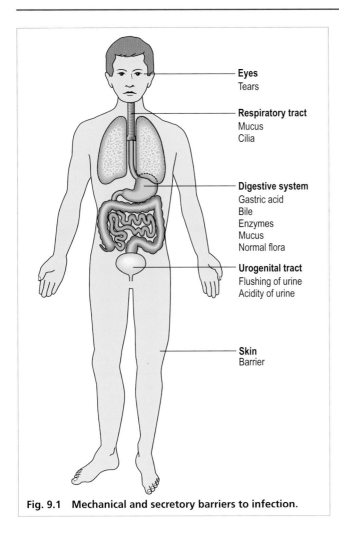

Fig. 9.1 Mechanical and secretory barriers to infection.

Eyes
Tears

Respiratory tract
Mucus
Cilia

Digestive system
Gastric acid
Bile
Enzymes
Mucus
Normal flora

Urogenital tract
Flushing of urine
Acidity of urine

Skin
Barrier

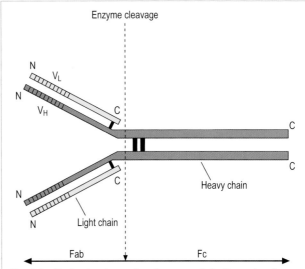

Enzyme cleavage

V_L

V_H

Heavy chain

Light chain

Fab   Fc

Fig. 9.2   Basic structure of an immunoglobulin molecule.
The two identical light chains and two identical heavy chains
are held together by disulphide bonds. (Fab, fragment antigen
binding; Fc, fragment crystallisable; V_L, variable domain of a light
chain; V_H, variable domain of a heavy chain.)

immune response themselves, although they can react with
existing antibodies. Such substances need to be coupled to
a carrier molecule in order to have sufficient epitopes to be
antigenic. For some chemicals, such as drugs, the carrier
may be a host protein—called an auto-antigen. The tertiary
structure, as well as the amino acid sequence, is important
in determining antigenicity.

Antigens are conventionally divided into thymus-dependent
and thymus-independent antigens. *Thymus-dependent antigens*
require T-cell participation to provoke the production of
antibodies; most proteins are examples. *Thymus-independent
antigens* require no T-cell co-operation for antibody production; they directly stimulate specific B-lymphocytes by cross-
linking antigen receptors on the B-cell surface but provoke
poor immunological memory. Such antigens include bacterial
cell wall polysaccharides.

Factors other than the intrinsic properties of the antigen
also influence the quality of the immune response. These
include:

- nature of molecule
- dose
- route of entry
- addition of substances with synergistic effects
- genetic background of recipient.

Substances that improve a host's immune response to a separate antigen are called *adjuvants;* these are routinely used in
immunisation programmes in childhood.

Superantigen is the term given to foreign proteins that
simultaneously activate large numbers of T-lymphocytes
carrying a particular T-cell receptor V-beta gene (see T-cell
receptors). Widespread T-cell activation results in florid
cytokine release, as exemplified by toxic shock syndrome
induced by certain streptococcal toxins.

Antibody

Humoral immunity is dependent on the production of
antibodies and their actions. All antibodies belong to the
immunoglobulin class of proteins and are produced by
plasma cells, themselves derived from B-lymphocytes. The
basic structure of an immunoglobulin molecule is shown in
Figure 9.2. It has a four-chain structure: two identical heavy
(H) chains (molecular weight 50 kD) and two identical light
(L) chains (mol wt 25 kD). There are two alternative types
of light chain, known as kappa and lambda; an antibody
molecule has either two kappa or two lambda light chains,
never one of each. In contrast, there are five types of heavy
chain, each with important functional differences (Table
9.1). The heavy chains determine the class (isotype) of the
antibody and the physiological function of the antibody
molecule. Once the antigen-binding site has reacted with
its antigen, the molecule undergoes a change in the conformation of its heavy chains in order to take part in effector
functions (Table 9.1).

The amino (N) terminal regions of the heavy and light chains
include the *antigen-binding sites*. The amino acid sequences of
these N- terminal domains vary between different antibody
molecules of the same isotype and are known as variable (V)
regions. Most of these differences reside in three hypervariable

Table 9.1 Immunoglobulin classes and their functions

Ig class	Structure	Heavy chain	Serum concentrations (g/l)	Molecular weight	Antigen-binding sites	Complement activation	Antibody activity and properties
IgG		Gamma	5–15	150 000	2	Yes	Can cross placenta. Characteristic of secondary immune response
IgA		Alpha	1.5–5	380 000 (dimer in secretions)	4	No	Secreted locally in tears, saliva, mucus. Two molecules (dimer) of Ig joined by a J chain. Transported by a secretory component
IgM		Mu	0.5–1.5	900 000 (pentamer)	10	Yes	Characteristic of primary immune response
IgE	Mast call	Epsilon	$2–4.5 \times 10^{-7}$	200 000	2	No	Largely bound to mast cells and to basophils. Anaphylactic hypersensitivity and immune responses to parasites
IgD	B-lymphocyte	Delta	0–0.5	185 000	2	No	Lymphocyte membrane receptor

areas of the molecule, each only 6–10 amino acid residues long. In the folded molecules, these *hypervariable regions* in each chain come together, with their counterparts on the other pair of heavy and light chains, to form the antigen-binding site. The structure of this part of the antibody molecule is unique to that molecule and is known as the *idiotypic deter-minant*. In any individual, about 10^6–10^7 different antibody molecules could be made up by 10^3 different heavy chain variable regions associating with 10^3 different light chain variable regions. Somatic mutation during multiple divisions of B-lymphocytes generates further diversity of around 10^{14} antibody specificities.

IgM is the oldest class of immunoglobulin in evolutionary terms. It is a large molecule consisting of five basic units held together by a joining (J) chain; it penetrates poorly into tissues on account of its large size (Table 9.1). The major physiologi-cal role of IgM is intravascular neutralisation of organisms (especially viruses) aided by its 10 antigen-binding sites. IgM also has multiple complement-binding sites; this results in excellent complement activation and lysis of the organism or removal of the antigen–antibody–complement complexes by complement receptors on phagocytic cells. It is the first class of antibody to be formed in response to an initial encounter with an antigen *(primary immune response)*.

IgG is a smaller immunoglobulin which penetrates tissues easily. It is the most abundant immunoglobulin in the plasma and extracellular fluid. It is the only immunoglobulin that crosses the placenta to provide immune protection to the neonate; this is an active process involving specific placental receptors for the Fc portion of the IgG molecule. Polymorphs and macrophages also have surface receptors for the Fc frag-ment of IgG; thus binding of IgG to particulate antigen pro-motes adhesion of these cells and subsequent phagocytosis of the antigen.

There are four subclasses of IgG: IgG_1 and IgG_3 activate complement efficiently and are responsible for clearing most protein antigens; IgG_2 and IgG_4 react predominantly with carbohydrate antigens (in adults).

IgA is sometimes referred to as 'mucosal antiseptic paint'. It is secreted locally by plasma cells in the intestinal and respiratory mucosa and is an important constituent of breast milk. It consists of two basic units (a dimer) linked by a 'joining' or J chain. The addition of a 'secretory component' prevents digestion of the immunoglobulin molecule by enzymes present in intestinal or bronchial secretions. Secretory component is a fragment of the polymeric immunoglobulin receptor synthesised by epithelial cells and transports secretory IgA from the mucosa into the lumen of the gut or bronchi.

There is little free IgD or IgE in serum or normal body fluids. These two classes mainly act as cell receptors. *IgD* is synthesised by antigen-sensitive B-lymphocytes and acts as a cell surface receptor for antigen. *IgE* is produced by plasma cells but taken up by specific IgE receptors on mast cells and basophils. IgE probably evolved as a way of expelling intestinal parasites via mast cell degranulation.

T-cell receptors

Like B-cells, each T-cell is committed to a given antigen, which it recognises by one of two types of T-cell receptor (TCR). T-cells have either alpha/beta TCR (a heterodimer of alpha and beta chains) or gamma/delta TCR (a heterodimer of gamma and delta chains). Alpha/beta TCRs predominate in adults, although 10% of T-cells in epithelial structures are of the gamma/delta TCR type. Each type of TCR is associated with several transmembrane proteins which make up the cluster differentiation 3 (CD3) molecule (Fig. 9.3) to form the CD3–TCR complex responsible for taking the antigen recognition signal inside the cell (transduction). The CD3 antigen is widely used as a marker of mature T-cells in diagnostic and investigative pathology.

The TCR complex recognises small processed antigen peptides in the context of major histocompatibility complex (MHC) class I and II antigens (see below), depending on the type of T-cell. Helper T-cells recognise MHC class II molecules in association with foreign antigen and use the CD4 molecule to enhance binding and intracellular signalling. Cytotoxic T-cells recognise antigen associated with MHC class I molecules and use CD8 molecules for increased binding and signalling. However, recognition of processed antigen alone is not enough to activate T-cells. Additional signals through soluble interleukins are needed; some of these are generated during 'antigen processing'.

Major histocompatibility complex antigens

Histocompatibility antigens were so named because of the vigorous reactions they provoked during mismatched organ transplantation. However, these antigens play a fundamental role in the normal immune response by presenting antigenic peptides to T-cells. Human *major histocompatibility complex* (MHC) antigens are also known as *human leukocyte antigens* (HLAs). MHC antigens are cell surface glycoproteins of two basic types: class I and class II (Fig. 9.4). They exhibit extensive genetic polymorphism with multiple alleles at each locus. As a result, genetic variability between individuals is very great and most unrelated individuals possess different HLA molecules. This means that it is very difficult to obtain perfect HLA matches between unrelated persons for transplantation.

The antigen-specific receptor of an individual T-cell (TCR) will only recognise antigen as part of a complex of antigenic peptide and that individual's MHC. This process of dual recognition of peptide and MHC molecule is known as MHC restriction because the MHC molecule restricts the ability of the T-cell to recognise antigen. T-cells from one person will not co-operate with antigen-presenting cells from a person of different HLA type.

MHC class I antigens are subdivided into three groups: A, B and C. Each group is controlled by a different gene locus within the major histocompatibility complex on chromosome 6 (Fig. 9.4). The products of the genes at all three loci are chemically similar. MHC class I antigens (Fig. 9.5) are made up of a heavy chain (alpha) controlled by a gene in the relevant MHC locus, associated with a smaller chain called beta-2-microglobulin, controlled by a gene on chromosome 15. The differences between individual MHC class I antigens are due to variations in the alpha chains; the beta-2-microglobulin component is constant. The detailed structure of class I antigens was determined by X-ray crystallography. This shows that small antigenic peptides are tightly bound to a groove in the surface alpha chains.

MHC class II antigens have a folded structure similar to class I antigens with the peptide-binding groove found between the alpha and beta chains (Fig. 9.5). Whereas class I molecules are expressed by most nucleated cells, expression of class II molecules is restricted to dendritic cells, B-lymphocytes, activated T-cells, macrophages, inflamed vascular endothelium and some epithelial cells. However, other cells (e.g. thyroid, pancreas, gut epithelium) can be induced to express class II molecules under the influence of interferon-gamma released

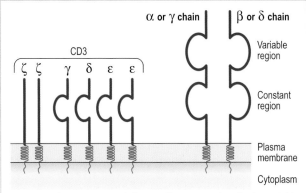

Fig. 9.3 The structure of the T-cell receptor (TCR). The variable regions of the alpha (α) and beta (β) chains make up the T idiotype. The TCR is closely associated on the cell surface with the CD3 molecule.

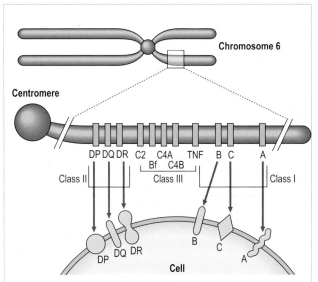

Fig. 9.4 The major histocompatibility complex on chromosome 6 and MHC class I and II antigens.

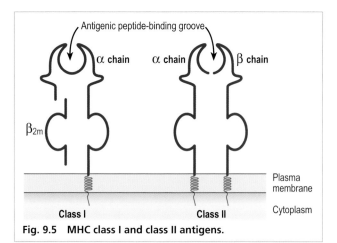

Fig. 9.5 MHC class I and class II antigens.

during inflammation. In humans, there are three groups of class II antigen: the loci are known as HLA-DP, HLA-DQ and HLA-DR.

MHC class III antigens (Fig. 9.4) constitute early complement proteins C4 and C2. Other inflammatory proteins, e.g. tumour necrosis factor (TNF), are encoded in adjacent areas.

Accessory and co-stimulatory molecules

T-cell activation needs more than just binding between the T-cell receptor and the MHC class II molecule and processed antigen complex on the antigen-presenting cell.

Accessory and co-stimulatory molecules are needed for efficient binding and signalling (Fig. 9.6). Each accessory molecule has a corresponding protein, or ligand, to which it binds. The interaction between antigen-presenting cells and

T-cells is strongly influenced by accessory molecules which function as co-stimulators; for example, CD80 and CD86 on the activated dendritic cell engage with their counter-receptors CD28 and CTLA-4 (CD152) on the T-cell surface (Fig. 9.6). A functional co-stimulatory pathway is essential for T-cell activation. In the absence of a co-stimulatory signal, interaction between the dendritic cell and T-cell leads to T-cell unresponsiveness (a state called *anergy*).

Adhesion molecules mediate cell-to-cell adhesion as well as adhesion between leukocytes and endothelial cells, and are grouped into two main families: *integrins* and *selectins*.

The migration of leukocytes to sites of inflammation depends on three key sequential steps mediated by adhesion molecules:

1. Rolling of leukocytes along activated vascular endothelium is selectin-dependent.
2. Tight adhesion of leukocytes is integrin-dependent.
3. Transendothelial migration occurs under the influence of chemokines.

Integrins are subdivided into five families (beta-1 to beta-5 integrins) which mediate binding of lymphocytes and monocytes to the endothelial adhesion receptor called vascular cell adhesion molecule (VCAM-1). Defective expression of certain integrins is associated with a severe immunodeficiency characterised by marked neutrophil leukocytosis because neutrophils are unable to migrate from blood vessels into sites of infection.

The selectin family comprises three glycoproteins designated by the prefixes E- (endothelial), L- (leukocyte) or P- (platelet) to denote the cells on which they were first described. Selectins bind strongly to carbohydrate molecules on leukocytes and endothelial cells, and regulate the homing of these cells to sites of inflammation.

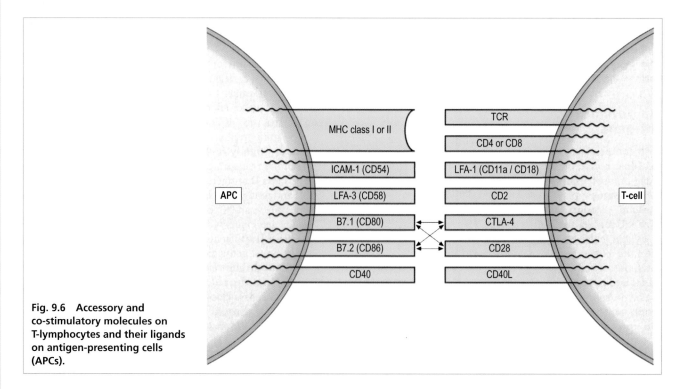

Fig. 9.6 Accessory and co-stimulatory molecules on T-lymphocytes and their ligands on antigen-presenting cells (APCs).

Cytokines

Cytokines are soluble mediators secreted by lymphocytes (*lymphokines*) or by macrophages/monocytes (*monokines*). They act as stimulatory or inhibitory signals between cells.

Cytokines that act between cells of the immune system are called *interleukins;* those that induce chemotaxis of leukocytes are called *chemokines.* All cytokines share common features:

- short half-lives
- rapid degradation
- local action within the microenvironment of cells
- may act on cytokine receptors on the surface of the cell of production to promote further activation and differentiation
- may affect multiple organs in the body
- exhibit overlapping functions.

Among the array of cytokines produced by macrophages and T-cells, interleukin-1 (IL-1) and interleukin-2 (IL-2) have a pivotal role in amplifying immune responses. IL-1 acts on a wide range of targets, including T- and B-cells (Table 9.2). In contrast, the effects of IL-2 are restricted largely to lymphocytes: it has a trophic effect on T-cells, IL-2 receptor-bearing B-cells and natural killer (NK) cells. The considerable overlap between individual cytokines and interleukins is summarised in Table 9.3.

STRUCTURAL ORGANISATION OF THE IMMUNE SYSTEM

▶ All lymphoid cells originate in the bone marrow
▶ Lymphoid precursors destined to become T-lymphocytes mature in the thymus (hence T-cells)
▶ Development of B-lymphocytes occurs entirely in the bone marrow (hence B-cells)
▶ The thymus and bone marrow are primary lymphoid organs
▶ Lymph nodes, spleen and mucosa-associated lymphoid tissue are secondary lymphoid organs
▶ Peripheral blood T- and B-lymphocytes circulate in a defined pattern through secondary lymphoid organs. Circulation is strongly influenced by adhesion molecules and chemokine receptors
▶ Lymph node architecture is well adapted to its function

T- and B-lymphocyte development

All lymphoid cells originate in the bone marrow although the nature of the uncommitted lymphoid stem cell remains unclear (Fig. 9.7). An understanding of the developmental pathway is important, not only to clarify the physiology of the normal immune response but also because some leukaemias and immunodeficiency states reflect maturation arrest of cells in their early stages of development. Lymphoid progenitors destined to become T-lymphocytes migrate from the bone marrow into the cortex of the thymus where further differentiation into mature T-cells occurs. Passage of T-cells from the thymic cortex to the medulla is associated with the acquisition of characteristic surface glycoprotein molecules so that medullary thymocytes

Table 9.2 Actions of interleukin-1

Target cell	Effect
T-lymphocytes	Proliferation Differentiation Lymphokine production Induction of IL-2 receptors
B-lymphocytes	Proliferation Differentiation
Neutrophils	Release from bone marrow Chemoattraction
Macrophages Fibroblasts Osteoblasts Epithelial cells	Proliferation/activation
Osteoclasts	Reabsorption of bone
Hepatocytes	Acute-phase protein synthesis
Hypothalamus	Prostaglandin-induced fever
Muscle	Prostaglandin-induced proteolysis

resemble mature peripheral blood T-cells. T-cell development in the thymus is characterised by a process of *positive selection* whereby T-cells that recognise and bind with low affinity to fragments of self-antigen in association with self-MHC molecules proceed to full maturation. In contrast, T-cells that do not recognise self-MHC or that recognise and bind with high affinity to self-antigen are selected out—*negative selection*—and do not develop further. Negatively selected T-cells kill themselves by apoptosis, i.e. programmed cell death. This process is an important mechanism in preventing autoimmune disease. In summary, the thymus selects out the useful, neglects the useless and destroys the harmful, i.e. autoreactive T-cells.

In contrast, B-cell development occurs in the bone marrow and depends on the secretion of cytokines by stromal cells.

Primary and secondary lymphoid organs

The thymus and the bone marrow are *primary lymphoid organs.* They contain cells undergoing a process of maturation from stem cells to antigen-sensitive but antigen-restricted cells. This process of maturation is independent of antigenic stimulation. In contrast, *secondary lymphoid organs* are those that contain antigen-reactive cells in the process of re-circulating through the body. They include the lymph nodes, spleen and mucosa-associated lymphoid tissues. Antigenic stimulation changes the relative proportions of mature cell types in secondary tissues.

Peripheral T- and B-cells circulate in a characteristic pattern through the secondary lymphoid organs. Most of the recirculating cells are T-cells and the complete cycle takes about 24 hours; some B-cells, including long-lived memory B-cells, also recirculate. Lymphocyte circulation is strongly influenced by chemokine receptors on lymphocyte surfaces which act as homing agents. Adhesion molecules direct cells to their respective ligands on high endothelial venules of lymph nodes.

Table 9.3	Cytokines and their actions	
Cytokine	Source	Action
IL-2	T-cells	Proliferation and maturation of T-cells, induction of IL-2 receptors and activation of NK cells
IL-4 **IL-5**	T-cells, basophils/mast cells T-cells, mast cells	Induction of MHC class II, FcR and IL-2R on B- and T-cells; induction of isotype switching in B-cells; facilitate IgE production (mainly IL-4)
IL-6	Macrophages, fibroblasts, T-cells, mast cells	Growth and differentiation of T-, B- and haemopoietic cells; acute phase response
IL-8	Monocytes/macrophages, T-cells, fibroblasts, keratinocytes, endothelial cells, NK cells	Chemotaxis of neutrophils
IL-10	T-cells, monocytes, keratinocytes	Inhibitory cytokine production
IL-12	B-cells, monocytes/macrophages	Synergism with IL-2; regulates IFN-gamma production
IL-13	T-cells	Actions overlap with IL-4
GM-CSF	T-cells, macrophages, endothelial cells	Stimulates growth of polymorphs and mononuclear progenitors
IFN-gamma	T-cells, NK cells	Activation of macrophages, endothelial cells and NK cells; increases expression of MHC class I and II; inhibits IgE production
TNF	Macrophages, T-cells, B-cells	Promotion of inflammation; interferes with catabolism in muscle and fat

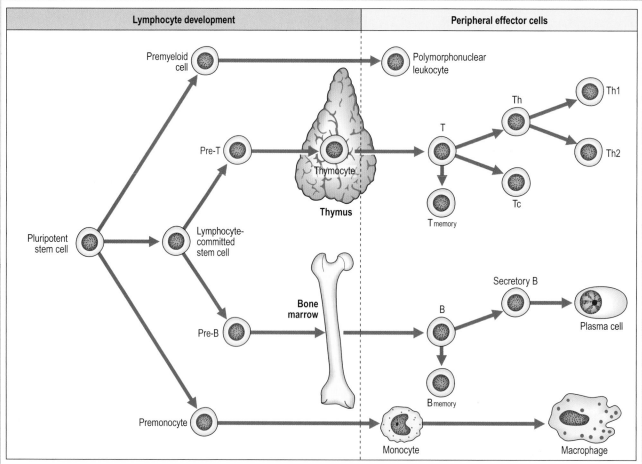

Fig. 9.7   Development of lymphocytes from a pluripotential stem cell in the bone marrow.

Lymph node architecture is well adapted to its function (Fig. 9.8). Lymphatic vessels draining the tissues penetrate the lymph node capsule and drain into the marginal sinus from which a branching network of sinuses passes through the cortex to the medulla and into the efferent lymphatic. This network provides a filtration system for antigens entering the node from peripheral tissue.

The cortex contains *primary follicles* of B-lymphocytes, surrounded by T-cells in the '*paracortex*' (Figs 9.9–9.11). There is a meshwork of dendritic cells that express MHC class II antigen throughout the lymph node, and these cells filter and present antigen to lymphoid cells. On antigen challenge, the 'primary' follicles of the lymph node develop into 'secondary' follicles which contain *germinal centres*. These comprise mainly B-cells with a few helper T-cells and a mantle zone of the original primary follicle B-cells. B-cells in a secondary follicle are antigen-activated and more mature; most have IgG on their surfaces, whereas those in the primary follicle and mantle zone bear both IgD and IgM. Activated B-cells migrate from the follicle to the medulla, where they develop into plasma cells (Fig. 9.12) in the medullary cords before releasing antibody into the efferent lymph.

The majority of naive T-cells entering the lymph node will leave again immediately via efferent lymphatics. Naive T-cells that recognise specific antigen differentiate into effector T-cells before re-entering the circulation.

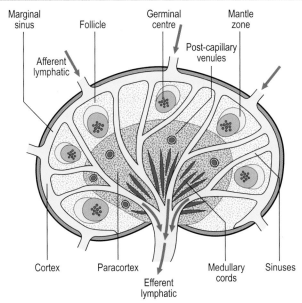

Fig. 9.8   Structure of a normal lymph node. The locations of T- and B-lymphocytes are shown in Figs 9.10–9.12.

FUNCTIONAL ORGANISATION OF THE IMMUNE RESPONSE

▶ Processing and presentation of antigen to lymphocytes is performed by specialised antigen-presenting cells (APCs). The most efficient APCs are dendritic cells in lymph nodes
▶ Each B-lymphocyte is committed to the production of an antibody with a unique antigen-binding site—the idiotype
▶ The speed, vigour and efficiency of secondary antibody responses are the result of clonal expansion
▶ Antibody production usually requires a second signal provided by helper T-lymphocytes
▶ Helper T-lymphocytes (Th) fall into two subgroups—Th1 and Th2 cells—which produce different cytokines
▶ T-lymphocytes can directly kill virus-infected cells or release cytokines which contribute to inflammation

Antigen presentation

The first stage of an immune response to any antigen is the processing and presentation of that antigen to lymphocytes by specialised *antigen-presenting cells* (APCs). T-cells cannot recognise antigen without it. The interaction between APCs

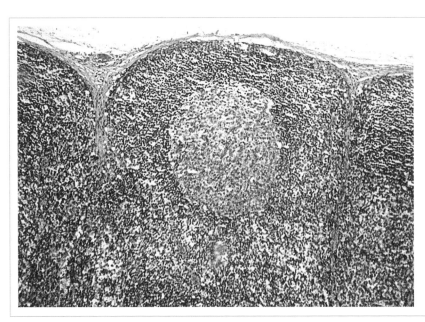

Fig. 9.9   Lymphoid follicle in a lymph node, surrounded by paracortex.

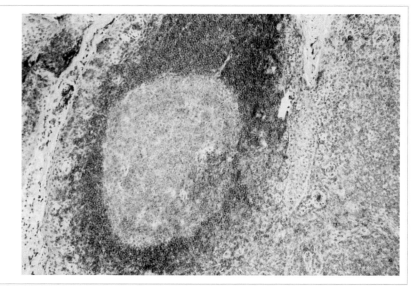

Fig. 9.10   A lymphoid follicle stained with a monoclonal antibody (anti-CD20) that reacts with B-cells. (Positive cells stain brown.)

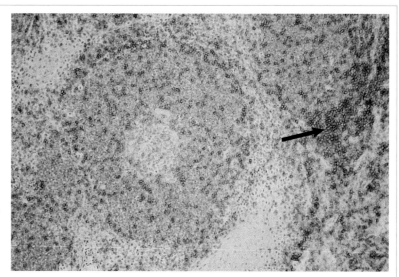

Fig. 9.11   Immunohistochemical identification of T-cells. This section, adjacent to that in Fig. 9.10, is stained with a monoclonal antibody that reacts with T-cells (anti-CD3). Cells of the paracortex are stained (arrow) and there are few T-cells in the follicle.

and T-cells is strongly influenced by a group of cell-surface molecules that act as *co-stimulators*. Thus, CD80 and CD86 on the APC engage with their counter-receptors CD28 and CTLA-4 (cytotoxic T-lymphocyte antigen 4; CD152) on the T-cell surface (Fig. 9.6). Normal functioning of the co-stimulatory pathway is vital for T-cell activation. In the absence of a co-stimulatory signal, interaction between the APC and T-cell leads to T-cell unresponsiveness, or anergy. Antagonists to co-stimulatory molecules disrupt immune responses, an observation of potential therapeutic importance; for instance, antagonists to CTLA-4 are being used experimentally to treat severe autoimmune diseases and to prevent graft rejection.

Processed antigen is presented to T-cells alongside MHC class II antigens on the APC surface because T-cells do not recognise processed antigen alone. The most efficient APCs are the interdigitating dendritic cells found in the T-cell regions of a lymph node. Such cells have high concentrations of MHC class I and II molecules, co-stimulatory molecules (CD80, CD86) and adhesion molecules on their surfaces but limited enzymatic powers, so enabling effective processing and presentation of antigen without complete digestion.

Antibody production

Antibody production involves at least three types of cell: antigen-presenting cells, B-lymphocytes and helper T-cells.

Antibodies are synthesised by B-cells and their mature progeny, called *plasma cells* (Fig. 9.12). B-cells are readily recognised because they express immunoglobulin on their surfaces. During development, B-cells first show intra-cellular mu chains and then surface IgM. These cells are able

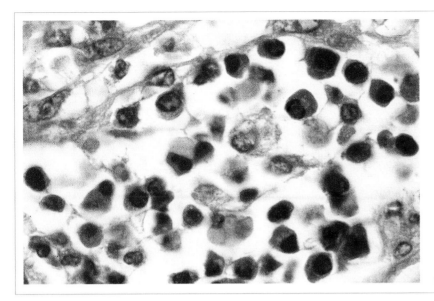

Fig. 9.12   Plasma cells. Note the eccentrically placed nuclei.

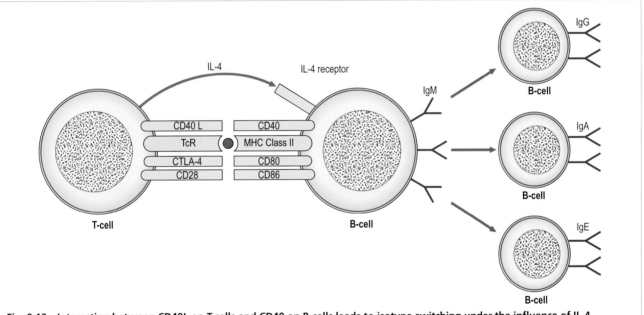

Fig. 9.13   Interaction between CD40L on T-cells and CD40 on B-cells leads to isotype switching under the influence of IL-4.
(TcR, T-cell receptor.)

to switch from production of IgM to IgG, IgA or IgE as they mature, a process known as *isotype switching* (Fig. 9.13). This maturation sequence fits with the kinetics of an antibody response: the primary response is mainly IgM and the secondary response predominantly IgG (Fig. 9.14).

Isotype switching is mediated by the interaction of two important proteins: CD40 expressed on the B-cell surface engages with its ligand, CD40L (CD154), on activated T-cells (under the influence of IL-4) to induce B-cells to switch immunoglobulin production from IgM to IgG, IgA or IgE (Fig. 9.13). Deficiency of either CD40 or CD40L in humans leads to a severe immunodeficiency characterised by inability to switch from IgM to IgG antibody production.

Each B-cell is committed to the production of an antibody that has a unique V_H–V_L combination, the idiotype, and the surface immunoglobulin and secreted immunoglobulin are identical. Contact with antigen and factors released by helper T-cells (IL-4, -5, -6) stimulate the B-cell to divide and differentiate, generating more antibody-producing cells, all of which make the same antibody with the same idiotype. Simultaneously, a population of *memory cells* is produced which express the same surface immunoglobulin receptor. The result of these cell divisions is that a greater number of antigen-specific B-cells becomes available when the animal is exposed to the same antigen at a later date. This process, known as *clonal expansion*, helps to account for the amplified

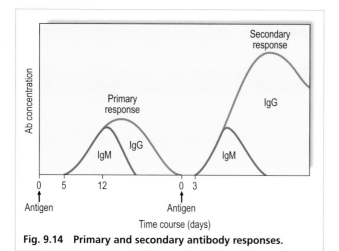

Fig. 9.14   Primary and secondary antibody responses.

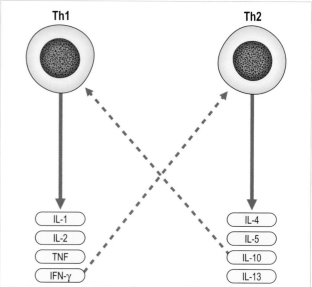

Fig. 9.15   Th1 and Th2 cells secrete different cytokines. Some cytokines provide inhibitory feedback (- - - -) on subsets of Th cells.

secondary response. As well as being quicker and more vigorous (Fig. 9.14), secondary responses are more efficient because the antibodies bind more effectively to the antigen, i.e. with higher affinity.

A minority of B-cells will respond directly to antigens called T-independent antigens, which have repeating, identical, antigenic determinants and provoke predominantly IgM antibody responses. B-cells, however, will not usually respond directly to antigen, even when presented by appropriate accessory cells. A second signal is needed to trigger the B-cell; this signal is normally provided by CD4+ helper T-cells.

T-cell help is antigen-specific. Only helper T-cells that have responded to antigen presented by macrophages can subsequently help B-cells already committed to that antigen. Helper T-cells recognise both antigen and MHC class II antigens as a complex on the presenting cells. They then recognise the same combination of antigen and class II molecule on the corresponding B-cell but co-stimulation is also required (Fig. 9.13). When helper T-cells meet an antigen for the first time, the limited number reacting with that antigen are activated to provide help for B-cells. They undergo blast transformation and proliferation, i.e. *clonal expansion*, so the immune response on second and subsequent exposures is quicker and more vigorous.

Other mechanisms help to improve this efficiency. Memory cells (which bear the surface marker CD45RO) have increased numbers of adhesion molecules (LFA-1, CD2, LFA-3, ICAM-1) plus a higher proportion of high-affinity receptors for the relevant antigen. Memory cells are therefore easily activated and produce high concentrations of IL-2 to recruit more helper T-cells. Thus T-cell memory is a combination of a quantitative increase of T-cells and a qualitative change in the efficiency of those T-cells.

Helper T-cells are further grouped into two distinct subsets depending on their cytokine profile. Th1 cells secrete TNF and interferon-gamma and mediate cellular immunity. In contrast, Th2 cells predominantly secrete IL-4, IL-5, IL-10 and IL-13 (Fig. 9.15) and are responsible for stimulating vigorous antibody production by B-cells. T-cells expressing cytokine profiles common to both Th1 and Th2 cells are designated Th0.

A Th1 cytokine profile provides protection against intracellular pathogens, while a Th2 profile is found in those diseases associated with overproduction of antibodies, especially IgE.

The effects of helper T-cells are balanced by those of functional suppressor T-cells that express the characteristic surface glycoprotein CD8.

Cell-mediated responses

Antigen-specific cell-mediated responses are carried out by T-lymphocytes. T-cells can lyse cells expressing specific antigens *(cytotoxicity)*, release cytokines that trigger inflammation *(delayed hypersensitivity)*, or regulate immune responses. These T-cell responses are mediated by distinct T-cell subpopulations: cytotoxicity is the role of cytotoxic T-cells and delayed hypersensitivity that of Th1 cells. These cells are responsible for fighting intracellular pathogens (all viruses, parasites and certain bacteria) which are inaccessible to antibodies.

Cytotoxic T-cells kill cells infected with virus (and possibly those tumour cells expressing recognisable tumour antigens). Such cytotoxicity is virus specific—only cells expressing the relevant viral proteins on their surfaces are killed. Since infected cells express surface viral proteins prior to the assembly of new virus particles and viral budding, cytotoxic T-cells are important in the recovery phase of an infection, destroying the infected cells before new virus particles are generated.

Cytotoxic T-cells recognise viral antigens together with MHC class I molecules. They show exquisite specificity for self-MHC antigens, in that they can only lyse cells expressing the same MHC class I molecules, i.e. express MHC restriction.

Regulatory T-cells are a subset of CD4+ T-cells with a distinct phenotype (CD4+, CD25+) under the control of a gene called

FoxP3. These cells dampen down activation and expansion of self-reactive T-cells. Mutations in *FoxP3* result in severe autoimmune disease and allergy.

NON-SPECIFIC EFFECTOR MECHANISMS

▶ Complement is a complex series of proteins acting as an enzymatic cascade
▶ Complement can be activated by antibody (the classical pathway), by bacterial cell walls (the alternative pathway) or by mannose-binding lectin (the lectin pathway)
▶ Complement activation results in increased vascular permeability, chemoattraction of leukocytes, enhanced phagocytosis and cell lysis
▶ Monocytes and macrophages comprise the mononuclear phagocyte system
▶ Natural killer (NK) cells are important in the response to viral infection

Complement

Complement is a complex series of interacting plasma proteins which form a major effector system for antibody-mediated immune reactions. Many complement components exist as inactive precursors; once activated, the component may behave as an enzyme which cleaves several molecules of the next component in the sequence. Each precursor is cleaved into two or more fragments. The major fragment (usually designated 'b') has two biologically active sites: one for binding to cell membranes or the triggering complex, and the other for enzymatic cleavage of the next complement component. Minor cleavage fragments (designated 'a') have

important biological properties in the fluid phase. Control of complement activation involves spontaneous decay of any exposed attachment sites and inactivation by specific inhibitors. The major purpose of the complement pathway is to remove or destroy antigen, either by direct lysis or by opsonisation.

Complement activation

Complement activation occurs in two sequential phases:

● activation of the C3 component
● activation of the 'attack' or lytic pathway.

The critical step (Fig. 9.16) is cleavage of C3 by complement-derived enzymes called C3 convertases. The major fragment of activated C3—called C3b—mediates a number of vital biological activities, particularly opsonisation.

The cleavage of C3 is achieved via three main routes, the classical, alternative and lectin pathways, all of which generate C3 convertases but in response to different stimuli (Fig. 9.16).

Classical pathway activation
The classical pathway is activated when binding of IgM or IgG to antigen causes a conformational change in the Fc region of the antibody to reveal a binding site for the first component in the classical pathway, C1.

C1 is a macromolecular complex of three subcomponents—C1q, C1r and C1s. C1q is a collagen-like protein composed of six subunits. C1q reacts with Fc regions via its globular heads but attachment by two critically spaced binding sites is needed for activation. IgM is more efficient than IgG in activating C1q. IgA, IgD and IgE do not activate the classical pathway.

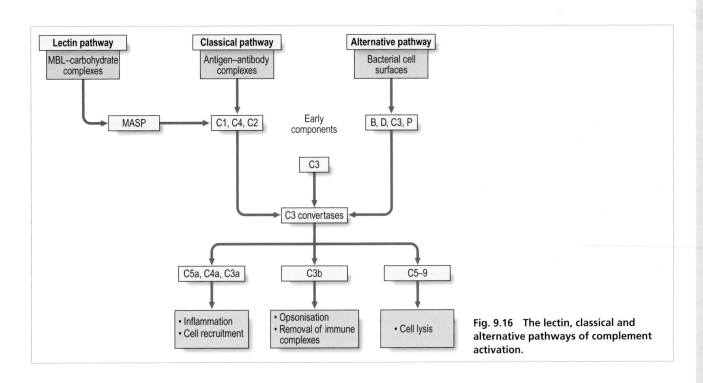

Fig. 9.16 The lectin, classical and alternative pathways of complement activation.

Once C1q is activated, C1r and C1s are sequentially bound to generate enzyme activity (C1 esterase) for C4 and C2, splitting both molecules into a and b fragments. The complex C4b2b is the *classical pathway C3 convertase*. C4b2b cleaves C3 into two fragments, one (C3a) possessing anaphylatoxic and chemotactic activity (see below) and one that binds to the initiating complex and promotes many of the biological properties of complement. The C4b2b3b complex so generated is an enzyme, C5 convertase, which initiates the final lytic pathway (the 'attack' sequence).

Alternative pathway activation

The central reaction in this pathway, as in the classical one, is the activation of C3. The alternative pathway, however, generates a C3 convertase without the need for antibody, C1, C4 or C2. Instead, the most important activators are bacterial cell walls and endotoxin (Fig. 9.16). Thus, the alternative pathway is responsible for innate defence against invading organisms, as it functions in the absence of preformed specific antibody.

The initial cleavage of C3 in the alternative pathway happens continuously and spontaneously (Fig. 9.16), generating a low level of C3b. C3b is then able to use factors D and B of the alternative pathway to produce the active enzyme 'C3bBb' which can break down more C3, providing still more C3b. In the absence of any regulation, this positive feedback loop would continue to cleave C3 until the supply was exhausted.

Regulation is provided by the control proteins, factors H and I. H competes with factor B for binding to C3b, and I then cleaves and inactivates the displaced C3b. Microbial agents that activate the alternative pathway circumvent the effects of factor H and I, and allow the pre-existing low-grade turnover to be amplified. This self-destructive property seems to depend on the carbohydrate composition of the bacterial cell wall.

Lectin pathway activation

The lectin pathway is initiated by mannose-binding lectin (MBL), a circulating protein that binds avidly to carbohydrate on the surface of certain micro-organisms. MBL is structurally related to C1q and activates complement through MASP (MBL-associated serine proteinase) which is similar to C1r and C1s of the classical pathway. The lectin pathway also contributes to innate immunity.

The membrane attack complex

There are two ways of producing the C5 splitting enzyme—the C5 convertase: in the classical pathway it is made up of C3b, C4b and C2b; in the alternative pathway it is composed of C3b, Bb and properdin (Fig. 9.16). Thereafter, the final lytic pathway of complement is the same, involving the sequential attachment of the components C5, C6, C7, C8 and C9, and resulting in lysis of the target cell. This target may be an invading organism or a virally infected cell. The lytic pathway complex binds to the cell membrane and a transmembrane channel is formed which leads to osmotic lysis of the cell.

Biological effects of complement

Complement-mediated *lysis* of antigen is dramatic but is not the most important role (Fig. 9.16). Instead, complement-dependent *phagocytosis* is crucial in defence. Micro-organisms coated (i.e. opsonised) with C3b can be bound by cells that possess receptors—called complement receptors type 1 (CR1)—for this ligand. CR1 receptors are present on phagocytic cells. Complement activation results in the release of the *pro-inflammatory mediators* C5a, C4a and C3a. These act as anaphylatoxins to increase vascular permeability, release vasoactive amines and induce smooth muscle spasm. C5a is a potent chemoattractant and stimulates neutrophils and macrophages to synthesise cytokines, undergo oxidative metabolism and release degradative enzymes.

Control of the complement pathway

This occurs by three mechanisms:

- Many activated complement components are inherently unstable and decay rapidly if the next protein in the pathway is not immediately available.
- There are several specific inhibitors, e.g. C1 esterase inhibitor, factor I and factor H.
- There are cell membrane proteins that accelerate the breakdown of activated complement components.

These mechanisms ensure that the potentially harmful effects of the complement cascade are confined to the initiating microbial antigen without damaging host cells.

Macrophages

Macrophages are the tissue equivalent of monocytes and together represent the *mononuclear phagocytic system*. Lymphocytes and macrophages are derived from closely related stem cells in the bone marrow but each cell lineage has different colony-stimulating factors. *Monocytes* circulate for only a few hours before entering the tissues where they may differentiate and live for weeks or months as mature macrophages. Tissue macrophages are heterogeneous in appearance, in metabolism and probably also in function; they include freely mobile alveolar and peritoneal macrophages, fixed Kupffer cells in the liver and those lining the sinusoids of the spleen. When found in other tissues, they are called *histiocytes*.

A major function of the mononuclear phagocyte system is the phagocytosis of invading organisms and other antigens. Macrophages have prominent lysosomal granules containing acid hydrolases and other degradative enzymes with which to destroy phagocytosed material. The material may be an engulfed viable organism, a dead cell, debris, an antigen or an immune complex. In order to carry out their functions effectively, macrophages must be 'activated'; in this state they show increased phagocytic and killing activity. Stimuli include cytokines (see above), substances that bind to Fc receptors of IgG or soluble inflammatory mediators such as C5a. Toll-like receptors (TLRs) are pattern recognition receptors on macrophages and other cells that contribute to innate immunity. They recognise combinations of sugars, proteins and lipids on pathogens—such as Gram-negative bacterial lipopolysaccharide—and trigger inflammatory responses by up-regulating pro-inflammatory cytokines such as TNF or IL-1. Macrophages are also important for the presentation of antigen to other cells of the immune system, as described earlier.

Neutrophil polymorphonuclear leukocytes

Neutrophils play a major role in the body's defence against acute infection. They synthesise and express adhesion receptors so that they can adhere to, and migrate out of, blood vessels into tissues. They do this in response to chemotactic agents produced at the site of inflammation; such substances include the chemokine CXCL8 (also called IL-8), complement-derived factors (such as C3a and C5a), lymphokines released by Th1 cells and chemokines produced by mast cells.

Neutrophils are phagocytic cells. Morphologically, the process of phagocytosis is similar in both neutrophils and mononuclear phagocytes. Neutrophils are also able to kill and degrade the substances they take in. This requires a considerable amount of energy and is associated with a 'respiratory burst' of oxygen consumption, increased hexose monophosphate shunt activity and superoxide production.

Antibody-dependent cell-mediated cytotoxicity (ADCC)

ADCC is a mechanism by which antibody-coated target cells are destroyed by cells bearing low-affinity receptors for the Fc fragment of IgG (FcγRIII)—natural killer cells, monocytes, neutrophils—with no involvement of the major histocompatibility complex. The mechanism of target cell destruction is not fully understood but includes the discharge of granules containing perforin and granzymes.

Natural killer cells

Natural killer (NK) cells look like large granular lymphocytes. They can kill target cells even in the absence of any antibody or antigenic stimulation. They do not need prior activation but already have the relevant recognition molecules on their surfaces. They are further activated non-specifically by mitogens, interferon and IL-12. NK cells are not immune cells in the strictest sense because, like macrophages, they are not clonally restricted; they show minimal specificity and have no memory. The range of their potential targets is broad. Animals and rare patients with deficient NK cell function have an increased incidence of certain tumours and viral infections. NK cells are therefore thought to be important in the early host response to viral infection and in 'immune' surveillance against tumours.

OUTCOMES OF IMMUNE RESPONSES

- ▶ Antibody, especially IgM, can neutralise viruses and toxins
- ▶ Opsonisation of bacteria with IgG antibodies makes phagocytosis more efficient
- ▶ C3b generated by complement activation is also an efficient opsonin
- ▶ Target cells may be killed specifically by cytotoxic T-cells or non-specifically by macrophages or natural killer cells
- ▶ Many components of the immune response contribute to inflammation

Once the immune response is initiated, the end result depends on the nature and localisation of the antigen, on whether the predominant response has been humoral or cell mediated, on the type of antibody provoked, and whether non-specific effector mechanisms have been involved.

Direct effects of antibody

Neutralisation is one direct effect of antibody, and IgM is particularly good at this. A number of antigens, including diphtheria toxin, tetanus toxin and many viruses, can be neutralised by antibody. Once neutralised, these substances are no longer able to bind to receptors in the tissues; the resulting antigen–antibody complexes are usually removed from the circulation and destroyed by macrophages.

Indirect effects of antibody

Opsonisation is the process by which an antigen becomes coated with substances (such as antibodies or complement) that make it more easily engulfed by phagocytic cells. The coating of soluble or particulate antigens with IgG antibodies renders them more susceptible to cells that have surface receptors for the Fc portions of IgG (FcγRIII). Neutrophils and macrophages have Fc receptors and can phagocytose IgG-coated antigens; however, this process is relatively inefficient if only Fc receptors are involved. The activation of complement by antibody (via the classical pathway) or by bacterial cell walls (via the alternative or lectin pathways) generates C3b on the surface of micro-organisms and makes them susceptible to binding by C3b receptors (CR1) on macrophages and neutrophils; C3 receptors are very efficient in triggering phagocytosis.

Killing of target cells

Target cells killed as a result of an immune response include organisms and cells bearing virally altered or tumour-specific antigens on their surfaces. They may be killed directly by antigen-specific mechanisms such as antibody and complement, antibody-dependent cell-mediated cytotoxicity or cytotoxic T-cells. Cytokine production results in activation of NK cells and macrophages.

Inflammation

Inflammation is defined as increased vascular permeability accompanied by infiltration of 'inflammatory' cells, initially neutrophil polymorphonuclear leukocytes and later macrophages, lymphocytes and plasma cells. Vascular permeability may be increased by complement fragments such as C3a or C5a. Some fragments (C3a, C5a and C567) also attract neutrophils and mobilise them from the bone marrow; cytokines generated by activated dendritic cells, T-cells and macrophages have similar properties. The triggering of mast cells via IgE also causes inflammation due to release of histamine and leukotrienes. Inflammation is covered in detail in Chapter 10.

IMMUNODEFICIENCY

▶ Immunodeficiency presents as serious, persistent, unusual or recurrent infections—'SPUR'
▶ Secondary causes of immunodeficiency are much more common than primary disorders
▶ Patients with antibody deficiency present with recurrent bacterial infections of the respiratory tract
▶ Patients with defects in cellular immunity present with invasive and disseminated viral, fungal and opportunistic bacterial infections involving any organ
▶ Infants with severe combined immunodeficiency (SCID) will die before the age of 2 years unless bone marrow transplantation is performed
▶ Clinical presentations of defects in phagocytes and complement function show the dependence of humoral immunity on non-specific effector mechanisms
▶ In some primary immunodeficiencies, the gene responsible has been identified and somatic gene therapy is possible
▶ Secondary immunodeficiency occurs when synthesis of key immune components is suppressed (e.g. bone marrow infiltration or infection with an immunosuppressive virus) or their loss is accelerated (e.g. nephrotic syndrome or protein-losing enteropathy)
▶ Acquired immune deficiency syndrome (AIDS) is the result of infection with human immunodeficiency virus (HIV)
▶ The dominant clinical features of AIDS are opportunistic infections and tumours

Because the immune system evolved as a defence against infectious organisms, the most dramatic examples of its importance are provided by those disorders where one or more vital components of the immune system are missing or fail to function. Defects in immunity can be classified as primary, due to an intrinsic defect in the immune system, or secondary to an underlying condition (Fig. 9.17). These defects may involve specific or non-specific (innate) immune mechanisms. Underlying immunodeficiency should be suspected in every patient who has recurrent, persistent, severe or unusual infections, irrespective of age.

Primary antibody deficiencies

Defects in antibody synthesis can involve all immunoglobulin classes (panhypogammaglobulinaemia) or only one class or subclass of immunoglobulin (selective deficiency). Antibody deficiency can occur in children or adults although the underlying physiological defects may differ.

In congenital forms of antibody deficiency, recurrent infections usually begin between 4 months and 2 years of age, because maternally transferred IgG affords passive protection for the first 3–4 months of life (Fig. 9.18). Some forms of primary antibody deficiency are inherited as X-linked or autosomal recessive traits; a history of affected relatives, especially boys, is therefore of diagnostic value. However, the average size of a family in developed countries is now so small that a negative family history does not exclude an inherited condition.

Recurrent infections of the upper and lower respiratory tracts occur in almost all antibody-deficient patients (Fig. 9.19). Many patients also present with skin sepsis (boils, abscesses or cellulitis), gut infection, meningitis, arthritis, splenomegaly or purpura. The commonest infecting organisms in antibody deficiency states are pyogenic bacteria such as staphylococci, *Haemophilus influenzae* and *Streptococcus pneumoniae* (Fig. 9.20). In general, these patients are not unduly susceptible to viral or fungal infections because cell-mediated immunity is preserved, but exceptions do occur.

There are rarely any diagnostic physical signs of antibody deficiency, although examination often shows failure to thrive in children and the consequences of previous sepsis such as ruptured tympanic membranes or bronchiectasis. Measurement of serum immunoglobulin levels will reveal any gross quantitative abnormality but the ability of a patient to make antibody is a better guide to susceptibility to infection than total immunoglobulin levels. Some individuals fail to make specific antibody after test immunisation despite normal serum immunoglobulin levels. Measurements of IgG subclasses are of little clinical value unless backed up by test immunisation and detection of specific antibody responses.

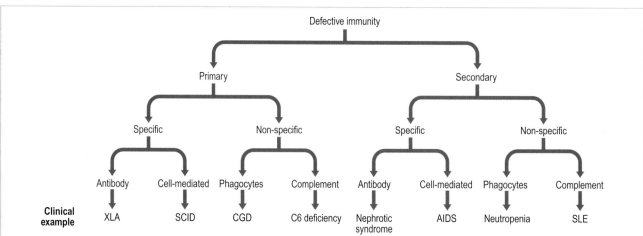

Fig. 9.17 Classification of immunodeficiency. (AIDS, acquired immune deficiency syndrome; CGD, chronic granulomatous disease; SCID, severe combined immunodeficiency; SLE, systemic lupus erythematosus; XLA, X-linked agammaglobulinaemia.)

Transient hypogammaglobulinaemia of infancy

Maternal IgG is actively transported across the placenta to the fetal circulation from the fourth month of gestational life, although maximum transfer takes place during the final 2 months. At birth, the infant has a serum IgG at least equal to that of the mother (Fig. 9.18); at first, catabolism of maternal IgG is only partly compensated by IgG synthesised by the newborn child. The period between 3 and 6 months of age represents a phase of 'physiological hypogammaglobulinaemia'. The normal infant is not unduly susceptible to infection because functioning antibody is present despite the low

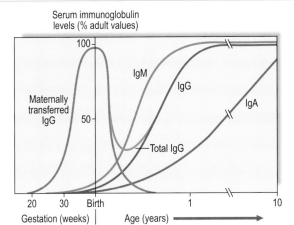

Fig. 9.18 Serum immunoglobulin levels in relation to age. Maternally transferred IgG has mostly been catabolised by 6 months. As the neonate synthesises IgG the level rises slowly but a physiological trough of IgG is seen between 3 and 6 months.

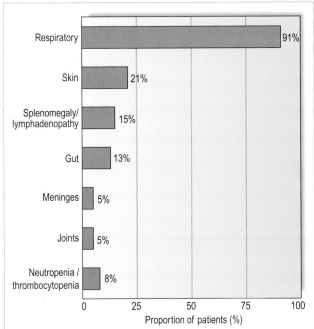

Fig. 9.19 Presenting infections/clinical signs in patients with primary antibody deficiency, irrespective of age.

IgG level, and T-cell function is intact. However, the trough in IgG is more severe and the risk of sepsis much greater if the gift of IgG acquired from the mother is severely reduced, as in extremely premature infants born around 28 weeks' gestation or earlier.

X-linked agammaglobulinaemia (XLA)—Bruton's disease

Boys with this condition usually present with recurrent pyogenic infections between the ages of 4 months and 2 years. The sites of infection and the organisms involved are similar to other types of antibody deficiency (Figs 9.19 and 9.20), although these patients are susceptible to enteroviruses. In almost all patients, circulating mature B-cells are absent but T-cells are normal and even increased. No plasma cells are found in the bone marrow, lymph nodes or gastrointestinal tract. The clinical diagnosis rests on the very low serum levels of all classes of immunoglobulin and the absence of circulating mature B-lymphocytes.

The gene responsible for XLA is found on the long arm of the X chromosome. Its product is a cytoplasmic enzyme known as *Bruton's tyrosine kinase*, or Btk. In its absence pre-B-cells are unable to differentiate into B-cells. The identification of a mutation in the *Btk* gene confirms the diagnosis and enables asymptomatic female carriers to be identified and counselled. Management consists of replacement immunoglobulin for the affected boy.

Hyper-IgM syndrome

Some children with antibody deficiency have normal or high serum IgM levels. An X-linked form is due to a failure of CD40 ligand expression on CD4+ T-lymphocytes (Fig. 9.13). As a result, T-cells fail to trigger the switch from IgM to IgG or IgA production in antigen-stimulated B-cells with poor organisation of germinal centres in lymph nodes.

As well as bacterial infections, affected boys are susceptible to *Pneumocystis jiroveci* pneumonia because macrophage and dendritic cell function are also impaired. Replacement immunoglobulin therapy and co-trimoxazole prophylaxis (to prevent *Pneumocystis* infection) are required in the long term, and bone marrow transplantation is now considered to be the treatment of choice.

Selective IgA deficiency

This is the commonest primary defect of specific immunity with a prevalence of 1:700 in the UK. It is characterised by undetectable serum IgA levels with normal concentrations of IgG and IgA. Most IgA-deficient individuals are asymptomatic but selective IgA deficiency predisposes the individual to a variety of disorders (Fig. 9.21). About 20% of individuals make antibodies to IgA and some may develop adverse reactions following transfusions of blood or plasma.

Common variable immunodeficiency (CVID)

CVID embraces a group of disorders presenting as antibody deficiency in late childhood or adult life. Patients experience the same range of bacterial infections as other patients with

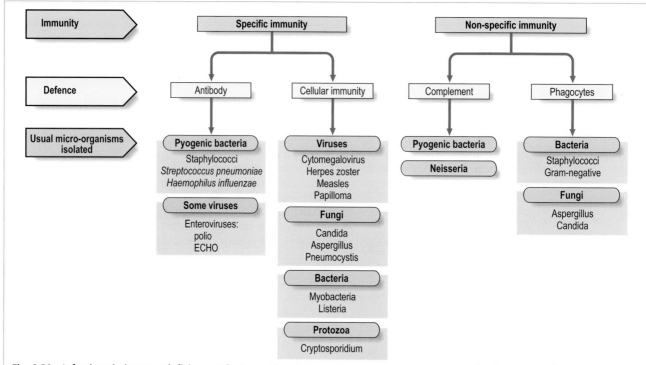

Fig. 9.20 Infections in immunodeficiency. Infections with certain micro-organisms are characteristic of various forms of immunodeficiency.

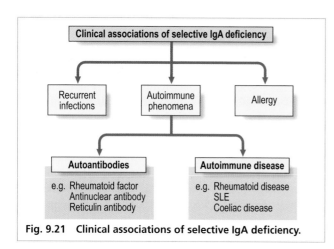

Fig. 9.21 Clinical associations of selective IgA deficiency.

antibody deficiency (Figs 9.19 and 9.20). CVID is much more common than XLA. About 20% of patients have affected relatives with CVID or selective IgA deficiency and several contributory genetic mutations have been identified. CVID patients also have a 40-fold increase in incidence of lymphoma.

Primary defects in cell-mediated immunity

Impairment of T-cell function is usually accompanied by variable degrees of B-cell dysfunction, reflecting the T–B-cell co-operation needed for efficient antibody production. Most defects are therefore *combined* immunodeficiencies and this is reflected in the wide range of infections experienced by such patients. Some examples are illustrated below.

Severe combined immunodeficiency

Infants in whom there is major failure of both T- and B-lymphocyte function have severe combined immunodeficiency (SCID). There are several genetic variants but all affected children present in the first few weeks or months of life with failure to thrive, chronic diarrhoea ('gastroenteritis') and respiratory infections. Usually, there is lymphopenia, which is often overlooked.

Immunisation with live vaccines and conventional blood transfusions must be avoided in patients with proven or suspected defects in cell-mediated immunity: live vaccines can lead to disseminated infection, and blood transfusion may result in *graft-versus-host disease*.

Infants with SCID die before they are 2 years old unless haemopoietic stem cell transplantation is undertaken. Some types of SCID caused by a specific genetic defect are prototypes for somatic gene therapy.

DiGeorge syndrome ('Catch 22' anomaly)

In this condition, severely affected neonates present with cardiovascular defects, hypocalcaemia, abnormal facies and thymic dysfunction. Most deaths are due to the heart lesions and not to the immunodeficiency, which is usually mild. The genetic defect (chromosome 22q11 deletion) results in impaired intrauterine development of the third and fourth pharyngeal pouches.

Primary defects in phagocyte function

Humoral immunity depends not only upon antibody synthesis but also upon effector mechanisms which eliminate antigen bound to antibody. Micro-organisms coated (i.e. opsonised) with IgG antibodies are readily bound and ingested by phagocytic cells. Thus, specific immunity requires non-specific effector mechanisms for its efficient operation; this partly explains similarities between the infectious complications experienced by patients with defects of antibody synthesis and those with neutrophil dysfunction (Fig. 9.20).

The major role of the neutrophil is to ingest, kill and digest invading micro-organisms, particularly bacteria and fungi. Failure to fulfil this role leads to infection. Defects in neutrophil function can be quantitative *(neutropenia)* or qualitative *(neutrophil dysfunction)*. However, irrespective of the basic cause, the clinical features of infections are similar and certain generalisations are possible:

- Infections are recurrent and prolonged.
- Clinical features may be minimal despite severe infection.
- Infections are poorly responsive to antibiotics.
- They are commonly staphylococcal.
- They involve skin and mucous membranes.
- They are complicated by suppurative lymphadenopathy.

Chronic granulomatous disease

Chronic granulomatous disease (CGD) is a group of disorders resulting from a failure to produce high concentrations of toxic oxygen radicals during the 'respiratory burst' that accompanies activation of phagocytes. The classic type is inherited as an X-linked recessive disorder, and typically presents in the first 3 months of life as severe skin sepsis caused by *Staphylococcus aureus* or fungal infections with *Candida albicans* or *Aspergillus fumigatus* (Fig. 9.22). The resulting complications include regional lymphadenopathy, hepatosplenomegaly, hepatic abscesses and osteomyelitis. Affected organs show multiple abscesses and non-caseating giant-cell granulomas.

Primary complement deficiency

Inherited deficiencies of complement components are associated with characteristic clinical syndromes (Fig. 9.23). Many patients with C1, C4 or C2 deficiency present with a syndrome of malar flush, arthralgia, glomerulonephritis, fever or chronic vasculitis.

Patients with C3 deficiency occurring as a primary defect or secondary to deficiencies of factor H or factor I (see Fig. 9.16) have an increased susceptibility to life-threatening bacterial infections such as pneumonia, septicaemia and meningitis, illustrating the important role of C3 in defence against infection.

There is a striking association between deficiencies of C5, C6, C7, C8 or properdin and recurrent neisserial infection. Most patients present with recurrent meningococcal meningitis, less commonly with gonococcal septicaemia and arthritis. However, many patients experience only one episode of meningitis, or many years may elapse between attacks.

Hereditary angioedema is caused by deficiency of the inhibitor of the first component of complement (C1 inhibitor). Patients experience recurrent attacks of cutaneous, intestinal or laryngeal oedema which can be fatal if the airway is occluded.

Secondary immunodeficiency

Secondary causes of immunodeficiency are far more common than primary causes. Since levels of immune components represent the net balance of synthesis versus catabolism (or loss), low levels reflect either depressed production or accelerated catabolism or loss (Fig. 9.24). Protein loss severe enough to cause hypogammaglobulinaemia occurs mainly via the kidney *(nephrotic syndrome)* or through the gut *(protein-losing enteropathy)* in a variety of active inflammatory diseases such as Crohn's disease or ulcerative colitis. In intestinal lymphangiectasia, the dilated lymphatics leak lymphocytes as well as protein.

Impaired synthesis is exemplified by *protein–energy malnutrition*. Malnourished individuals show impaired specific antibody production following immunisation, and even

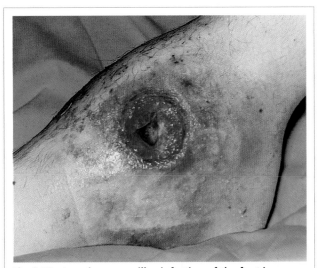

Fig. 9.22 Invasive aspergillus infection of the foot in a young man with chronic granulomatous disease.

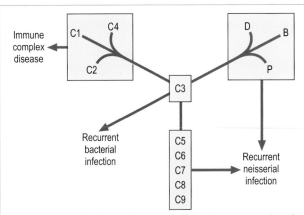

Fig. 9.23 Inherited complement deficiencies are associated with characteristic clinical syndromes.

more striking defects in cell-mediated immunity, phagocyte function and complement activity. Many of these defects reverse after adequate protein and calorie supplementation of the diet.

Patients with *lymphoproliferative diseases* are very prone to infection. The infection risk in patients with multiple myeloma is 5–10 times higher than in age-matched controls, while untreated chronic lymphocytic leukaemia is commonly associated with hypogammaglobulinaemia and recurrent chest infections, which tend to become more severe as the disease progresses. Non-Hodgkin's lymphoma may be associated with defects of both humoral and cell-mediated immunity.

Immunosuppressive drugs affect many aspects of cell function. Lymphocyte and polymorph activity are often impaired, although severe hypogammaglobulinaemia is unusual. Patients taking drugs to prevent organ transplant rejection can develop unusual opportunistic infections.

Another iatrogenic form of secondary immune deficiency is that associated with *splenectomy*. Death occurs from sudden, overwhelming infection due to *Streptococcus pneumoniae*. The risk of death from infection following splenectomy is 1–2% over 15 years. All patients should receive immunisation with pneumococcal conjugate vaccine as well as penicillin prophylaxis.

In a number of *infections*, the micro-organism paradoxically suppresses rather than stimulates the immune system. Severe, though transient, impairment of cell-mediated immunity has been noted in many viral illnesses, particularly cytomegalovirus, measles, rubella, infectious mononucleosis and viral hepatitis; however, the most florid example is infection with the human immunodeficiency virus (HIV).

Acquired immune deficiency syndrome (AIDS)

AIDS is a worldwide (pandemic) form of immunodeficiency first recognised in 1981 and caused by the retroviruses human immunodeficiency virus (HIV) types 1 and 2 (Fig. 9.25). At the end of 2007, the number of people living with HIV worldwide was estimated to be 33 million, 2.5 million of whom had become newly infected during 2007, with 1.7 million of these living in Sub-Saharan Africa. About half of new HIV infections occur in women and 40% in young people aged from 15 to 24 years. Almost all new childhood infections are due to mother to child (vertical) transmission, before or during childbirth or through breastfeeding.

Transmission of HIV

HIV is transmitted through sexual intercourse, both heterosexual and homosexual, and through the sharing of contaminated needles and syringes by intravenous drug abusers or via therapeutic procedures in areas of the world where reuse of contaminated equipment occurs. Other methods of transmission are through the receipt of infected blood or blood products, donated organs or semen. Cases of seroconversion and death among health care workers after needlestick injuries or blood splashes have also been reported (0.3% seroconvert).

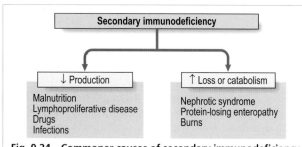

Fig. 9.24 **Commoner causes of secondary immunodeficiency.**

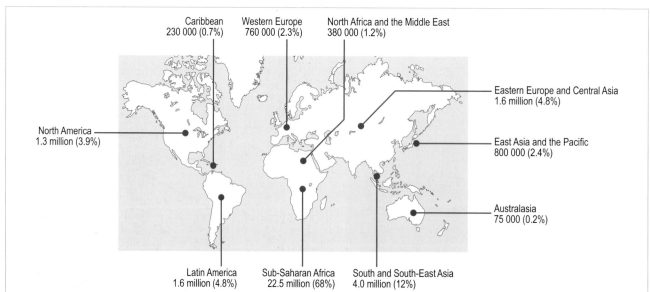

Fig. 9.25 **People living with HIV/AIDS.** Estimated number and distribution of people living with HIV/AIDS by December 2007 (estimated total over 33 million). (Source: UNAIDS/WHO.)

Clinical spectrum of HIV infection

HIV produces a spectrum of disorders (Fig. 9.26) which are classified by the Centers for Disease Control in the USA. A transient, acute *glandular fever-like illness* (CDC I) may occur in 10–20% of patients within a few weeks of initial HIV infection and precedes seroconversion (i.e. production of antibodies to HIV). Peripheral blood shows many atypical lymphocytes and an increased number of CD8+ T-cells at this time. Most seropositive individuals then remain symptom-free (CDC II) for 2–10 years or more. Development of AIDS depends on the contribution of many co-factors, such as genetic background, repeated immune stimulation (multiple co-infections speed the rate of progression) and pregnancy.

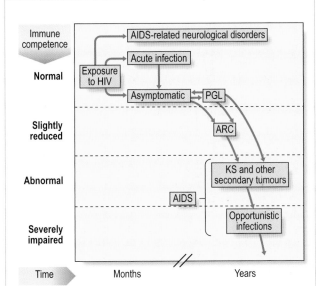

Fig. 9.26 The spectrum of HIV infection and its progression towards AIDS.

The most important prognostic factor for progression to AIDS is the concentration of HIV RNA in the blood—the viral load—at diagnosis.

After this latent period, some individuals develop asymptomatic *persistent generalised lymphadenopathy* (PGL; CDC III), defined as enlarged nodes in two or more extra-inguinal sites persisting for at least 3 months in the absence of any illness associated with lymphadenopathy. Some seropositive people show constitutional and clinical features such as unexplained lymphadenopathy, diarrhoea, night sweats, oral candidiasis and weight loss—the *AIDS-related complex* (ARC; CDC IV A).

HIV is *neurotropic*: acute aseptic meningitis, encephalopathy, myelopathy and neuropathy have been reported around the time of seroconversion, whereas chronic meningitis, cerebral lymphoma, encephalopathy and dementia (CDC IV B) may occur later (Ch. 26). Up to 70% of AIDS patients suffer from HIV-related dementia which is probably a direct neurotropic effect of HIV.

The dominant clinical manifestations of AIDS are *opportunistic infections* and *tumours* (CDC IV C and D). Typical infections include *Pneumocystis jiroveci* pneumonia (Fig. 9.27), cytomegalovirus or herpes simplex infections (Fig. 9.28), cerebral toxoplasmosis, atypical mycobacterial infections, systemic fungal infection and parasitic infestations of the gastrointestinal tract. The presentation in African patients may be characterised by a diarrhoea–wasting syndrome, called 'slim' disease, and opportunistic infection with tubercle bacillus, cryptococcus or cryptosporidium.

Common tumours are the consequences of the activities of oncogenic viruses operating in an immunocompromised host: Kaposi's sarcoma (KS) (Fig. 9.29) is caused by human herpes virus type 8 and non-Hodgkin's lymphoma by Epstein–Barr virus.

Immunopathogenesis of HIV infection

HIV enters susceptible cells through binding of viral envelope glycoprotein (gp120) to specific receptors on the cell surface, mainly the CD4 molecule itself, although other cell surface

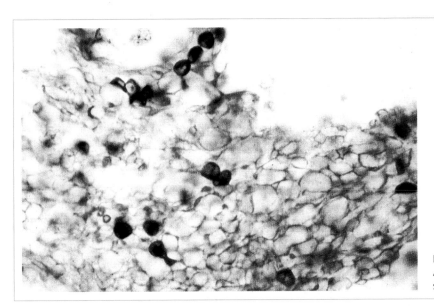

Fig. 9.27 *Pneumocystis jiroveci* pneumonia.
A foamy exudate fills the alveoli. The methenamine silver stain shows the organism as black spheres.

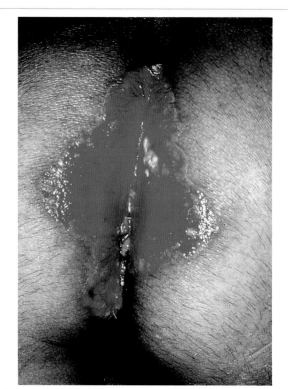

Fig. 9.28 Anorectal herpes simplex infection in a homosexual man with AIDS.

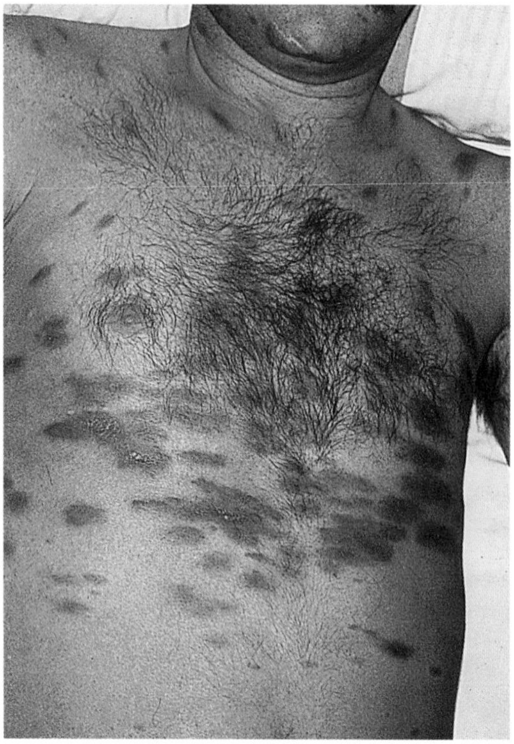

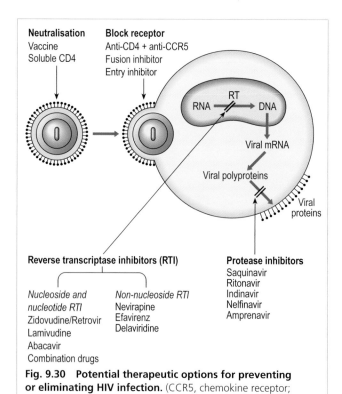

Fig. 9.29 Kaposi's sarcoma. A disseminated tumour caused by human herpes virus type 8 in an immunocompromised host.

molecules—the chemokine receptors CXCR4 and CCR5—are also involved. Any cell bearing the CD4 antigen can be infected by HIV; typically these are helper T-cells but macrophages, glial cells of the central nervous system and epithelial cells of the gut can be infected via CCR5 or other HIV receptors.

The most striking effects of HIV are on T-lymphocyte-mediated responses. HIV replicates at a rate of 10^9–10^{10} new virions per day, resulting in up to 10^8 new mutants per day, so the immune system has an enormous task to limit HIV spread. The hallmark of disease progression is the inexorable fall in the absolute number of CD4+ T-cells, the result of the destructive, cytopathic effects of HIV. While HIV infection may be latent clinically for many years, the destruction of CD4+ cells takes place continuously within lymph nodes and other lymphoid organs, particularly gut-associated lymphoid tissue, until the virus can no longer be contained and reappears in the blood stream—*HIV antigenaemia*.

Therapeutic options

Knowledge of the way in which HIV gains access into CD4+ cells and its method of replication has led to exploration of potential therapies (Fig. 9.30).

Binding of virus to the CD4 antigen in the cell membrane might be blocked by antibody to the viral envelope or to CD4 or to the chemokine receptor CCR5. Traditional vaccines, using killed or attenuated organisms, are unlikely to be of value. The fragile nature of the HIV envelope makes it a poor immunogen, while its high mutation rate poses a problem in selecting a stable common epitope able to provoke a protective immune response. Safety is a major concern because a mutation of an

Fig. 9.30 Potential therapeutic options for preventing or eliminating HIV infection. (CCR5, chemokine receptor; RT, reverse transcriptase.)

attenuated HIV back to its virulent state would be catastrophic. The search for a candidate 'AIDS vaccine' continues.

However, an entry inhibitor drug blocks HIV from entering the host cell by binding CCR5 while fusion inhibitors block HIV from fusing with a cell's membrane to enter and infect that cell.

Inhibition of viral replication can be achieved by inhibiting activity of reverse transcriptase (RT) as this is a unique retroviral enzyme with no mammalian equivalent. Such inhibitors fall into two groups: nucleoside and nucleotide RT inhibitors and non-nucleoside RT inhibitors. Protease inhibitors also prevent the assembly of new infectious virions. Current management uses combinations of drugs from different therapeutic groups—called highly active antiretroviral therapy, or HAART—to control viral replication and limit progression of immune deficiency.

HYPERSENSITIVITY REACTIONS

▶ These are damaging immunological reactions to extrinsic antigens
▶ Immediate hypersensitivity (type I) reactions result from the binding of antigen by IgE on mast cells or basophils
▶ Antibody to cell-bound antigen (type II) causes cell destruction by activating complement or promoting phagocytosis
▶ Type III reactions result from deposition or formation of immune complexes in tissues, particularly the skin, joints and kidneys. Chronic immune complex nephritis accounts for most cases of glomerulonephritis in humans
▶ Type I, II and III reactions are caused by antibodies: type IV reactions are caused by T-lymphocytes
▶ Delayed-type hypersensitivity (type IV) reactions are mediated by interleukin-2, interferon-gamma and other cytokines released by T-lymphocytes
▶ Complex hypersensitivity reactions cannot be explained solely on the basis of one type of reaction

Unfortunately, the recognition of foreign antigen by the immune system can cause incidental tissue damage as well as the intended destruction of the antigen. Such reactions are called 'hypersensitivity' reactions; Gell and Coombs defined four main types:

Type I: immediate hypersensitivity, or 'allergy,' due to activation of IgE antibody on mast cells or basophils
Type II: antibody to cell-bound antigen
Type III: immune complex reactions
Type IV: delayed hypersensitivity mediated by T-cells.

Immediate hypersensitivity (type I)

Immediate hypersensitivity (type I) reactions are those in which antigen interacts with IgE bound to tissue mast cells or basophils (Fig. 9.31).

IgE is embedded in the membranes of mast cells, exposing the antigen-binding sites of the molecule to the microenvironment of the cell. Exposure to specific antigen bridges two adjacent IgE molecules and this bridging effect triggers the mast cell to release its mediators. There are two groups of mediators: those that are preformed and those that are newly synthesised (Fig. 9.31).

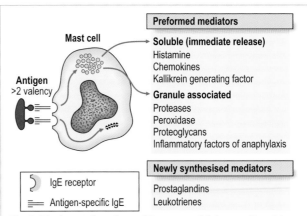

Fig. 9.31 Immediate (type I) hypersensitivity mediated by IgE antibody bound to mast cells.

The *preformed mediators* include histamine, lysosomal enzymes, chemokines and heparin. Because they are preformed, immediate (type I) hypersensitivity reactions are rapid: clinically the effects begin within 5–10 minutes and peak around 30 minutes. This is well illustrated by skin prick tests: if the antigen is pricked or scratched into the skin of an allergic individual a 'wheal and flare' reaction rapidly appears (Fig. 9.32). IgE responses are usually directed against antigens that enter at epithelial surfaces, i.e. inhaled or ingested antigens.

Allergic diseases are common: about 15–20% of the population has some form of allergy. Such patients are frequently *atopic*: atopy defines an inherited tendency for overproduction of IgE antibodies to common environmental antigens. Several genes predispose to this familial tendency but environmental factors must be involved because there is only 50% concordance in monozygotic twins. Typical atopic disorders include seasonal allergic rhinitis ('hay fever'), asthma and atopic eczema. However, life-threatening reactions can occur if the antigen enters the systemic circulation or if the patient has very high levels of circulating IgE antibodies. Generalised degranulation of IgE-sensitised mast cells and basophils leads to sudden hypotension, severe bronchoconstriction and collapse, a condition called *anaphylaxis*. Common allergens are bee and wasp venom, antibiotics (e.g. penicillin), peanuts and latex. Similar reactions that are not mediated by IgE antibodies are called *anaphylactoid*: the same mast cell mediators are responsible but the stimulus for their release differs. Substances inducing anaphylactoid reactions act directly on mast cells; they include anaesthetic induction agents and radiological contrast media.

Complex 'allergic' conditions such as asthma or eczema cannot be explained solely on the basis of IgE-mediated release of mediators. T-lymphocytes play a major role in the activation and/or recruitment of IgE antibody-producing B-cells, mast cells and eosinophils, the cellular triad involved in allergic inflammation. Two major subsets of helper T-cells (Th) have been identified by their profile of cytokine secretion. Sensitised T-cells found in bronchial biopsies and bronchoalveolar lavage fluid from allergic individuals are of the Th2 subset, and cytokines IL-4 and IL-13 produced by these cells stimulate IgE production (Fig. 9.33). When an atopic subject is exposed

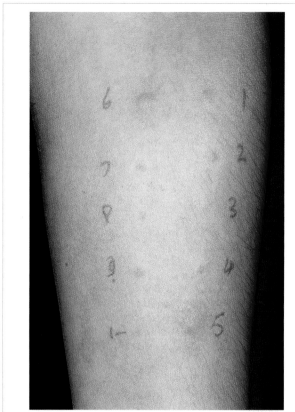

Fig. 9.32   **Positive skin prick tests showing 'wheal and flare' responses to house dust mite (number 5) and dog dander (number 6) in a patient with allergic rhinitis.**

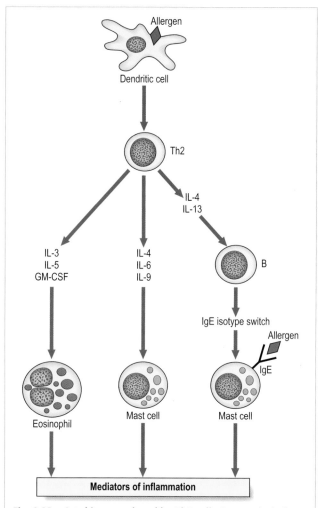

Fig. 9.33   **Cytokines produced by Th2 cells.** Immunological recognition can occur via the T-cell receptor or via IgE on mast cells.

to the relevant antigen, immunological recognition can occur both via the T-cell receptor and via IgE bound to mast cells.

Once the lining of the airways becomes inflamed it is susceptible to any irritant, such as airways cooling, tobacco smoke, diesel particles or sulphur dioxide. Thus, bronchial *hyper-responsiveness* is the hallmark of asthma. Much of the inflammatory damage is induced by eosinophils which contain major basic protein (MBP) capable of damaging epithelial cells of the airways. Damage to the epithelium by MBP, cytokines and mediators also exposes sensory nerve endings in the basement membrane and further increases irritability through neural triggering.

Antibody to cell-bound antigen (type II)

Type II hypersensitivity reactions are triggered by antibodies reacting with antigenic determinants which form part of the cell membrane. The consequences of the reaction depend on whether or not complement or accessory cells are involved and whether the metabolism of the cell is affected. IgM or IgG antibodies are typically implicated (Fig. 9.34).

Many examples of type II hypersensitivity involve drugs or their metabolites which have bound to the surface of red blood cells or platelets to form highly immunogenic epitopes. Antibodies formed against the drug or its metabolite inadvertently destroy the cell as well—'bystander lysis'—resulting in

haemolytic anaemia or thrombocytopenic purpura. The same mechanism is responsible for certain autoimmune disorders where the target antigen is intrinsic (i.e. self) antigen rather than extrinsic (Fig. 9.34). Under these circumstances, auto-antibodies can also cause disease by binding to the functional sites of self-antigens, such as receptors for hormones or neurotransmitters, so mimicking or blocking the action of the hormone without causing inflammation or tissue damage. Some textbooks regard stimulation of cell function by antibody as a separate category of hypersensitivity—type V: an example is Graves' disease where antibodies against the thyroid stimulating hormone receptor drive overproduction of thyroid hormones by the cell.

Immune complex hypersensitivity (type III)

Type III reactions result from the deposition or formation of immune complexes in the tissues. Localisation of immune complexes depends on their size, their electrostatic charge, and the nature of the antigen. If they accumulate in the tissues in large quantities, they may activate complement and accessory cells and produce extensive tissue damage (Fig. 9.35).

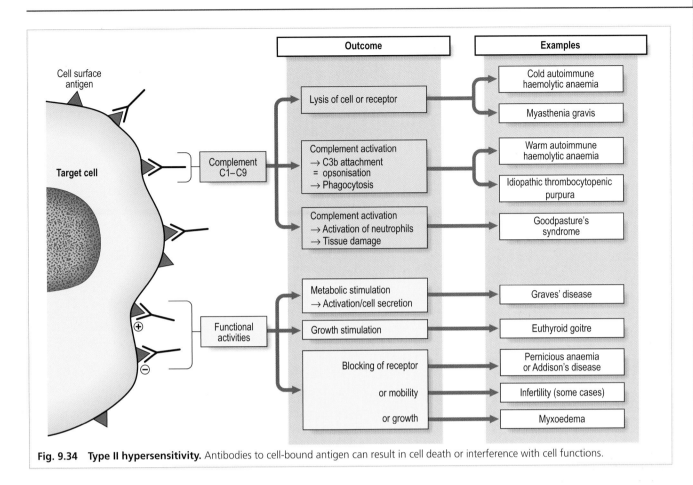

Fig. 9.34   Type II hypersensitivity. Antibodies to cell-bound antigen can result in cell death or interference with cell functions.

A classic example is the *Arthus reaction,* an experimental model where an antigen is injected into the skin of an animal that has been previously sensitised (Fig. 9.36). The reaction of preformed antibody with this antigen results in high concentrations of local immune complexes; these cause complement activation and neutrophil attraction and result in local inflammation 6–24 hours after the injection.

Acute 'one-shot' serum sickness is another example; in this condition, urticaria, arthralgia and glomerulonephritis occur about 10 days after initial exposure to the antigen. This is the time when IgG antibody, produced in response to antigen stimulation, reacts with remaining antigen to form circulating, soluble immune complexes (Fig. 9.37). As these damaging complexes are formed, the antigen concentration is rapidly lowered; the process continues only as long as circulating antigen persists and is usually self-limiting.

Such reactions were common when antisera raised in animals were injected repeatedly into humans to neutralise bacterial toxins, e.g. tetanus antitoxin. The animal serum immunoglobulins were highly immunogenic and resulted in an IgG antibody response to the foreign serum, hence *'serum sickness'.* This reaction is now rare because animal serum is no longer used in this way.

Acute post-streptococcal glomerulonephritis (Ch. 21) is caused by a similar mechanism. It occurs 10–12 days after a streptococcal infection of the throat or skin and results in deposition of immune complexes of IgG and C3 in the glomerular basement membrane. Streptococcal antigens are rarely found in

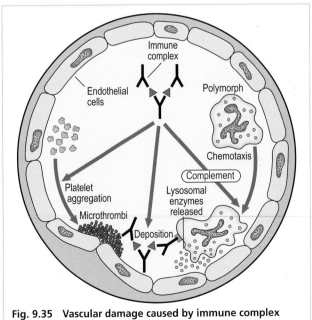

Fig. 9.35   Vascular damage caused by immune complex deposition.

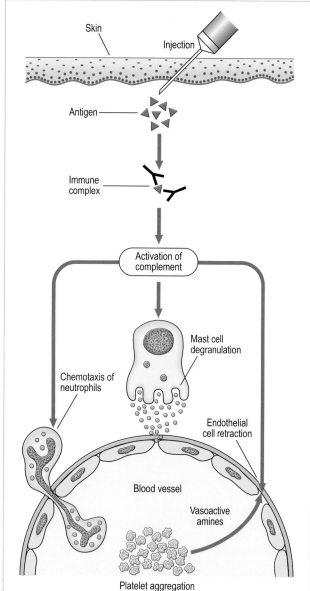

Fig. 9.36 The Arthus reaction. Intradermal injection of antigen results in local immune complex formation with complement activation.

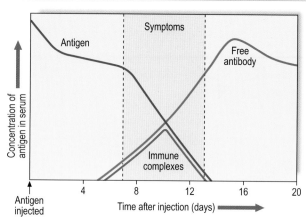

Fig. 9.37 Acute 'one-shot' serum sickness and the time of deposition of immune complexes.

the complexes but antigenic fragments from certain 'nephritogenic' strains of streptococci bind to the glomerular basement membrane, so localising antibody to this site.

Chronic immune complex nephritis accounts for most cases of chronic glomerulonephritis in humans. When compared with the 'one-shot' model, chronic immune complex formation and deposition will occur if:

- antigen exposure is persistent
- the host makes an abnormal immune response
- local factors, such as defective complement function, promote deposition of complexes.

Persistent antigen exposure is most likely to occur if the antigen is a micro-organism capable of replication

despite a host response, a medically prescribed drug, or an auto-antigen.

Delayed-type hypersensitivity (type IV)

Type IV reactions are mediated by T-lymphocytes which react with antigen and release interleukin-2, interferon-gamma and other Th1 cytokines. Once T-cells have been sensitised by primary exposure, secondary challenge is followed by a delayed-type hypersensitivity reaction (DTH), a local inflammatory response which takes 2–3 days to develop clinically. Histologically, these reactions consist of infiltrating T-lymphocytes, macrophages and occasional eosinophils. Experimentally, DTH can be transferred by T-lymphocytes but not by serum, i.e. antibodies are not involved.

A classic example of DTH is the *tuberculin reaction*. If a small amount of purified protein derivative (PPD) of tubercle bacilli is injected intradermally (Mantoux or Heaf test) into non-immune individuals, there is no effect. However, in individuals with cell-mediated immunity to tubercle bacilli, as a result of previous tuberculous infection or immunisation with BCG (bacille Calmette–Guérin, a live but non-virulent strain of *Mycobacterium bovis*), an area of reddening and induration develops after 24–48 hours (Fig. 9.38). The dermis of the reaction site becomes infiltrated by lymphocytes and macrophages around small blood vessels, with oedema and vascular dilatation.

DTH may result from the normal cell-mediated immune response to infection with viruses, fungi and certain bacteria, notably *Mycobacterium tuberculosis* and *Mycobacterium leprae*. If macrophages are unable to destroy ingested organisms, they may undergo differentiation into epithelioid cells or multinucleate giant cells. A collection of these cells forms a *granuloma* (Fig. 9.39). Local tissue damage is an unwanted side-effect of this otherwise protective immune response. If the DTH response is absent or impaired, however, T-lymphocytes are unable to localise the invading micro-organism and patients develop invasive, aggressive disseminated disease, such as acute miliary tuberculosis (Fig. 9.40) or lepromatous leprosy.

Contact dermatitis (Ch. 24) to occupational and other antigens is also a type IV reaction. Agents that do this are of relatively

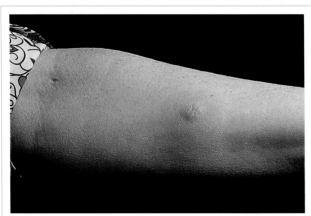

Fig. 9.38 A positive Mantoux test in a person previously immunised with BCG.

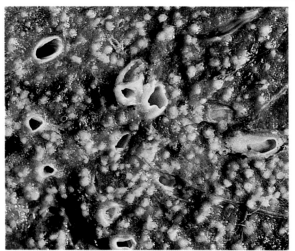

Fig. 9.40 Miliary tuberculosis of the lung showing multiple granuloma formation.

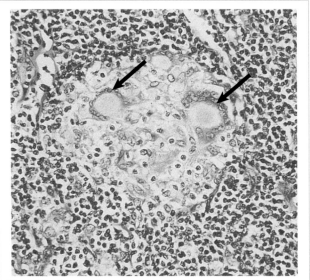

Fig. 9.39 A granuloma in a tuberculous lymph node, containing multinucleate giant cells (arrowed).

is inspected after 2 and 4 days. In a positive response, there is inflammation and induration at the test site.

Delayed-type hypersensitivity is also a key mechanism underpinning the rejection of transplanted tissues and organs (p. 193).

AUTOIMMUNITY AND AUTOIMMUNE DISEASE

▶ Autoimmunity is an immune response against a self-antigen
▶ Autoimmune disease is tissue damage or disturbed function resulting from an autoimmune response
▶ Disease may be restricted to a single organ (organ-specific), usually an endocrine gland, or involve auto-antigens widely distributed throughout the body (non-organ-specific)
▶ Most, but not all, autoimmune diseases are much commoner in females
▶ The immune system is normally specifically unreactive (tolerant) to self-antigens: autoimmune disease occurs when tolerance breaks down

Autoimmunity is an immune response against a self (auto) antigen or antigens. *Autoimmune disease* is tissue damage or disturbed physiological function resulting from an auto-immune response. This distinction is important as auto-immune responses can occur without resulting disease. Proof that autoimmunity causes a particular disease requires a number of criteria to be met, similar to Koch's postulates for micro-organisms in infectious diseases:

● Demonstrate immunological reactivity to a self-antigen.
● Characterise or isolate the inciting auto-antigen.
● Induce immunological reactivity against the same antigen by immunisation of experimental animals.
● Show pathological changes (similar or identical to those found in human disease) in the appropriate organs/tissues of an actively sensitised animal.

low molecular weight (<1 kD) and not immunogenic in their own right; instead, they are highly reactive molecules that bind covalently to skin or tissue proteins. The sensitising chemical is known as a hapten and the host protein as the carrier. The range of potential sensitising antigens is wide. Two phases of pathogenesis are recognised: the induction phase and the elicitation phase. In the *induction phase*, antigen-presenting cells in the skin—Langerhans' cells—bind the hapten–carrier protein complex and present it to T-lymphocytes in associa-tion with MHC class II antigen. Induction of T-cells usually occurs after months of exposure to small amounts of antigen. Re-exposure to the relevant antigen triggers the *elicitation phase* where effector T-cells migrate to the skin to meet the protein complex presented by Langerhans' cells in the epidermis with consequent cytokine release and skin inflammation.

The diagnosis of the offending agent is made by *patch testing*. A suspected contact sensitiser is applied to normal skin on the patient's back and covered for 48 hours. The reaction site

Patterns of autoimmune disease

Autoimmune diseases can affect any organ in the body although certain systems, such as endocrine glands, seem particularly susceptible. They are conventionally classified into organ-specific and non-organ-specific disorders.

Organ-specific autoimmune diseases

These affect a single organ; one or another endocrine gland is commonly involved. The antigen targets may be molecules expressed on the surface of living cells (particularly hormone receptors) or intracellular molecules, particularly intracellular enzymes (Table 9.4).

Non-organ-specific autoimmune diseases

Non-organ-specific disorders affect multiple organs and are usually associated with autoimmune responses against self-molecules which are widely distributed through the body, particularly intracellular molecules involved in transcription and translation of the genetic code.

Epidemiology of autoimmune disease

Around 3% of the population has an autoimmune disease. Many chronic disabling diseases are considered to have an autoimmune basis, including multiple sclerosis, rheumatoid arthritis and insulin-dependent diabetes mellitus. Auto-immune diseases show clustering within families but are rare in childhood; the peak years of onset are from 15 to 65 years, the major exception being the childhood-onset form of diabetes mellitus.

There are striking sex differences in the risk of developing an autoimmune disease. Almost all are more common in women, and for some autoimmune diseases the risk may be eight times greater. A notable exception is ankylosing spondylitis, which is much commoner in young men.

Immunological tolerance

Autoimmune responses are similar to immune responses to non-self-antigens. Both are driven by antigen, involve the same immune cell types and produce tissue damage by the same effector mechanisms. The key point is to understand what regulatory mechanisms prevent autoimmune responses occurring in everyone.

The immune system can generate a vast diversity of different T-cell antigen receptors and immunoglobulin molecules by differential genetic recombination. This process produces many antigen-specific receptors capable of binding to self-molecules. To avoid autoimmune disease, the T- and B-cells bearing these self-reactive molecules must be either eliminated or down-regulated so that the immune system is made specifically unreactive—*tolerant*—to self-antigens. Because T-cells (in particular CD4+ T-cells) have a central role in controlling nearly all immune responses, the process of T-cell tolerance is of greater importance in avoidance of autoimmunity than B-cell tolerance, since most self-reacting B-cells will not be able to produce auto-antibodies unless they receive appropriate T-cell help.

Those processes that induce specific tolerance arise inside the thymus (thymic tolerance) or outside (peripheral tolerance).

Thymic tolerance

T-cell development in the thymus plays a major role in eliminating T-cells capable of recognising peptides from self-proteins. The principles of positive and negative selection are explained above (p. 167).

Table 9.4   Some examples of self-antigens and associated autoimmune diseases

Self-antigen	Disease
Hormone receptors	
TSH receptor	Hyper- or hypothyroidism
Insulin receptor	Hyper- or hypoglycaemia
Neurotransmitter receptor	
Acetylcholine receptor	Myasthenia gravis
Cell adhesion molecules	
Epidermal cell adhesion molecules	Blistering skin diseases
Plasma proteins	
Factor VIII	Acquired haemophilia
Beta-2 glycoprotein I and other anticoagulant proteins	Antiphospholipid syndrome
Other cell surface antigens	
Red blood cells (multiple antigens)	Haemolytic anaemia
Platelets	Thrombocytopenic purpura
Intracellular enzymes	
Thyroid peroxidase	Thyroiditis, probable hypothyroidism
Steroid 21-hydroxylase (adrenal cortex)	Adrenocortical failure (Addison's disease)
Glutamate decarboxylase (beta-cells of pancreatic islets)	Autoimmune diabetes
Lysosomal enzymes (phagocytic cells)	Systemic vasculitis
Mitochondrial enzymes (particularly pyruvate dehydrogenase)	Primary biliary cirrhosis
Intracellular molecules involved in transcription and translation	
Double-stranded DNA	Systemic lupus erythematosus (SLE)
Histones	SLE
Topoisomerase I	Diffuse scleroderma
Amino-acyl t-RNA synthases	Polymyositis
Centromere proteins	Limited scleroderma

Auto-antibodies to some self-antigens are involved in disease pathogenesis (e.g. acetylcholine receptor antibodies); others are useful diagnostic markers but not pathogenic (e.g. anti-mitochondrial enzyme antibodies).

This process of thymic education is only partially successful. Thymic tolerance can fail if self-peptides are not expressed at a sufficient level in the thymus to induce negative selection. Most peptides found bound to MHC molecules in the thymus are from either ubiquitous intracellular or membrane-bound proteins present in the extracellular fluid. Thymic tolerance is induced to some but not all tissue-specific proteins (such as might be found in the brain, muscle, joints, islets of Langerhans, etc.) and it is not surprising that autoreactive T-cells can be detected in healthy people.

Peripheral tolerance

A second level of control over potentially autoreactive cells is termed peripheral tolerance. Several mechanisms are involved.

Immunological ignorance

Some self-antigens are effectively invisible to the immune system—immunological ignorance. This occurs because the antigen is sequestered in an avascular organ such as the vitreous humour of the eye. Immunological ignorance also occurs because CD4+ T-cells will only recognise antigens presented in association with MHC class II molecules. The very limited distribution of these molecules, confined to professional antigen-presenting cells, means that most organ-specific molecules will not be presented at levels high enough to induce T-cell activation. To prevent large amounts of self-antigen from gaining access to antigen-presenting cells, debris from self-tissue breakdown must be cleared rapidly and destroyed. This is achieved by cell death through apoptosis, so preventing widespread spilling of cell contents, together with a variety of scavenger mechanisms that mop up cell debris.

Self-antigens and lymphocytes are also kept separate by the restricted routes of lymphocyte circulation which limit naive lymphocytes to secondary lymphoid tissue and the blood.

Anergy

Naive CD4+ T-cells need two signals to become activated and initiate an immune response: an antigen-specific signal through the T-cell antigen receptor and a second, non-specific co-stimulatory signal, usually signalled by CD28 (on the T-cell) binding to CD80 or CD86 on the stimulator (see Fig. 9.6). If the T-cell receives both signals, then it will become activated and proliferate and produce cytokines. If no co-stimulatory molecules are engaged, then stimulation through the T-cell receptor alone leads to apoptosis or a state of longstanding unresponsiveness called anergy. Expression of these co-stimulatory molecules is tightly controlled and confined to specialised antigen-presenting cells such as dendritic cells. Given their distributions, interaction between CD4+ cells and dendritic cells is only likely to occur in secondary lymphoid tissues such as lymph nodes. The restricted expression of co-stimulatory molecules means that even if a T-cell recognises a tissue-specific peptide–MHC molecule complex (e.g. an antigen derived from a pancreatic islet cell), then anergy rather than activation is likely to follow, as no antigen-presenting cell will be available in healthy tissue to provide the co-stimulatory signal. T-cells also express cell surface molecules similar in structure to co-stimulatory molecules but which exert a negative effect on T-cell activation (see Fig. 9.6). CTLA-4 (CD152), which has a similar structure to CD28 and binds to the same ligands (CD80 or CD86), induces anergy or apoptosis and may be important in terminating an immune response to self-antigens.

Regulation and suppression

Self-reactive T-cells may be actively suppressed by inhibitory populations of T-cells that recognise the same antigen—so-called *regulatory* or *suppressor T-cells* with a distinctive CD4+ CD25+ phenotype. The best defined mechanism involves cytokines produced by antigen stimulation which either inhibit or alter the activation of nearby T-cells. For example, a Th2 response may specifically inhibit a Th1 response through IL-10 production (see Fig. 9.15).

B-cell tolerance

B-cell tolerance operates at a peripheral rather than a central level and is less complete than T-cell tolerance. The production of self-reactive antibodies is limited mainly by the lack of T-cell help for self-antigens, despite the fact that new B-cells are being produced continuously from bone marrow precursors and many of these are autoreactive.

Breakdown of tolerance

For autoimmune responses to occur, the key mechanisms of immunological tolerance outlined above must be broken down.

Overcoming peripheral tolerance

This can result from inappropriate access of self-antigens to antigen-presenting cells, inappropriate or increased local expression of co-stimulatory molecules, or alterations in the ways in which self-molecules are presented to the immune system (Fig. 9.41). All of these are more likely to happen when inflammation or tissue damage is present. The increased activity of proteolytic enzymes in inflammatory sites can cause both intra- and extracellular proteins to be broken down, leading to high concentrations of peptides being presented to responsive T-cells. These novel peptides are known as *cryptic epitopes*. The structures of self-peptides may also be altered by viruses, free radicals or ionising radiation, thus bypassing previously established tolerance. For antigens that are sequestered from the immune system (e.g. in the eye), sufficient antigen may be released by tissue damage to initiate an immune response.

Molecular mimicry

Structural similarity between self-proteins and microbial antigens may trigger an autoimmune response. In systemic infection, this cross-reactivity will cause expansion of the responsive T-cell population recognising the self-peptide if local conditions allow. The process is known as *molecular mimicry* (Table 9.5).

Once tolerance has broken down, the resulting process of inflammation may allow presentation of further peptides. The immune response broadens and local tissue damage accelerates. This domino-like process is known as *epitope spreading*. This is best demonstrated in experimental models, where immunisation with a single peptide from a protein found in myelinated nerve sheaths (known as myelin basic protein or MBP) can lead to widespread inflammation in the central nervous system with an immune response against many peptides found in both MBP and other CNS proteins. This implies that, once the barrier of tolerance is broken down, autoimmune responses may be easier to sustain.

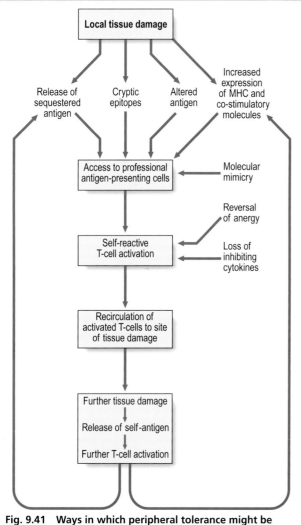

Fig. 9.41   Ways in which peripheral tolerance might be overcome to produce autoimmune responses.

Aetiology of autoimmune disease

In autoimmune diseases, interactions between genetic and environmental factors are critically important (Fig. 9.42).

Genetic factors

Twin and family studies have confirmed a genetic contribution in all autoimmune diseases studied. Multiple autoimmune diseases may cluster within the same family, and subclinical autoimmunity is common among family members. The genetic contribution to autoimmune disease usually involves multiple genes but some single-gene defects involve defects in apoptosis.

The strongest and best characterised associations involve alleles of the major histocompatibility complex (MHC), as might be expected from the central role of the products of many of these genes in T-cell function, and the involvement of other MHC genes in control of immunity and inflammation (Table 9.6).

Environmental factors

Environmental triggers in autoimmunity include:

- hormones
- infection
- drugs
- UV radiation.

Hormones
Females are far more likely than males to develop most autoimmune diseases and hormonal factors must play a major role in this gender difference. Most autoimmune diseases have their peak age of onset within the reproductive years and evidence implicates oestrogens as triggering factors. Removal of the ovaries inhibits the onset of spontaneous autoimmunity in animal models of systemic lupus erythematosus (SLE), while administration of oestrogen accelerates the onset of disease.

Infection
The relationship between infection and autoimmunity is clearest in the situation of molecular mimicry but infection of an organ may also cause upregulation of co-stimulatory molecules and altered patterns of antigen breakdown and presentation. Autoimmune diseases tend to be less common in parts of the world that carry a high burden of parasitic diseases and

Table 9.5 Molecular mimicry		
Microbial antigen	Self-antigen with similar structure	Disease in which consequent molecular mimicry may play a role
Group A streptococcal M protein	Antigen found in cardiac muscle	Rheumatic fever
Bacterial heat shock proteins	Self heat shock proteins	Links suggested with several autoimmune diseases but none proven
Coxsackie B4 nuclear protein	Pancreatic islet cell glutamate decarboxylase	Insulin-dependent diabetes mellitus
Campylobacter jejuni glycoproteins	Myelin-associated gangliosides and glycolipids	Guillain–Barré syndrome

there is a one-in-four chance that siblings will possess identical pairs of haplotypes (Fig. 9.45).

Kidney transplantation

Kidney transplantation is the treatment of choice for most patients with end-stage renal failure and illustrates the principles underpinning solid organ allografts.

Selection of recipient and donor

In kidney transplantation, organs can come from cadavers or living related donors. Because humans have two kidneys (unlike most other solid organs), a relative may choose to donate one to the recipient. Relatives must be screened clinically and psychologically, and ABO and HLA typed so that the most suitable donor can be chosen.

The selection of a donor kidney is rigorous (Table 9.7). Knowing the ABO blood group and HLA type of a *cadaver kidney*, national and international registers of potential recipients can be searched by computer to find an ABO-compatible patient who matches the donor at as many loci as possible. Once the recipient has been selected, the recipient's serum is then cross-matched against the donor's lymphocytes. If the patient has cytotoxic antibodies to donor MHC class I antigens (positive T-cell cross-match), then the kidney is unsuitable for that recipient.

Once the donor kidney has been removed, it is perfused with cold physiological fluids. Provided cooling begins within 30 minutes of cutting the renal blood supply (warm ischaemia time), the kidney has an excellent chance of functioning in the recipient. The duration of the perfusion (cold ischaemia time) should be less than 48 hours.

The post-transplantation period

The transplanted kidney is usually sited in the iliac fossa. Great care is taken with the vascular anastomosis and implantation of the ureter. Once the vascular anastomoses are complete, the graft often starts to function immediately.

Renal function may deteriorate immediately after surgery for several reasons. Acute tubular necrosis can occur due to low blood pressure in either the recipient or the donor. If this happens, the recipient can be dialysed until renal function recovers. Alternatively, poor renal function may indicate hyperacute rejection (see below) or urinary obstruction, which must be relieved surgically.

It is crucial to distinguish rejection from infection, as the treatment differs. Rejection can be detected by percutaneous fine-needle aspiration of the transplant. Immunosuppressive therapy is vital to prevent graft rejection.

Clinical rejection

Rejection of the organ graft may be:

- hyperacute
- acute
- chronic.

Table 9.7 Selection of donor and recipient in kidney transplantation

Recipient selection
- ABO compatible
- Negative serum cross-match with donor's T-lymphocytes
- HLA match—as near as possible, especially at D loci

Kidney selection
Cadaver donor
- Good renal function
- No infection (sepsis, HIV, etc.)
- No malignancy or systemic disease (diabetes, hypertension)
- Short warm ischaemia time

Living donor
- Two functioning kidneys
- No transmissible disease
- No anomalous blood vessels
- Psychologically suitable
- Excellent health

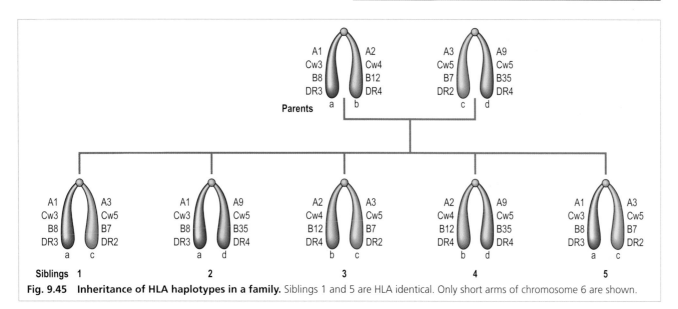

Fig. 9.45 Inheritance of HLA haplotypes in a family. Siblings 1 and 5 are HLA identical. Only short arms of chromosome 6 are shown.

Hyperacute rejection occurs minutes to hours following revascularisation of the graft. It is due to preformed circulating cytotoxic antibody which reacts with MHC class I antigens in the donor kidney. Activation of complement results in an influx of polymorphonuclear leukocytes, platelet aggregation, obstruction of the blood vessels, and ischaemia. Histologically, the microvasculature becomes plugged with leukocytes and platelets, resulting in infarction. The kidney swells dramatically and is tender. Renal function declines; oliguria or anuria follows. There is no successful therapy and the kidney must be removed.

Acute rejection occurs a few weeks or months following transplantation. Early diagnosis is important because prompt treatment with intravenous methylprednisolone and/or anti-CD3 antibody reverses renal damage. Histologically, there is a mononuclear infiltrate in the renal cortex, and necrosis of arterial walls; after successful treatment, the inflammatory infiltrate clears. Acute rejection is associated with increased expression of MHC class I and class II antigens in inflamed grafts, and with early infiltration of CD8+ T-lymphocytes.

Chronic rejection is seen after months or years of good renal function. There is slowly progressive renal failure and hypertension. Dominant histological findings are thickening of the glomerular basement membrane, hyalinisation of the glomeruli, interstitial fibrosis, and proliferation of endothelial cells. This picture of chronic allograft nephropathy must be distinguished from recurrence of the original glomerular disease.

Immunopathology of graft rejection

CD4+ T-lymphocytes play a central role in rejection.

The rejection process has two parts (Fig. 9.46):

- an afferent phase (initiation or sensitising component)
- an efferent phase (effector component).

In the *afferent phase*, donor MHC molecules found on 'passenger leukocytes' (dendritic cells) within the graft are recognised by the recipient's CD4+ T-cells, a process called *allorecognition*, which takes place either in the graft itself or in the lymphoid tissue of the recipient.

The *effector phase* of rejection is orchestrated by CD4+ T-cells which enter the graft parenchyma and recruit effector cells responsible for the tissue damage of rejection, namely macrophages, CD8+ T-cells, natural killer cells and B-lymphocytes. The most important cytokines in graft rejection are interleukin-2 and interferon-gamma.

Not all parts of the graft need to be attacked for rejection to occur. The critical targets are the endothelium of the microvasculature and the specialised parenchymal cells of the organ, such as renal tubules, pancreatic islets of Langerhans or cardiac myocytes.

Immunosuppression

Immunosuppressive drugs are used to prevent graft rejection. *Azathioprine* is inactive until metabolised by the liver but then affects all dividing cells, including lymphocytes, by inhibiting DNA synthesis. *Corticosteroids* have their main immunosuppressive effects on macrophage activity but are ineffective alone in preventing the early phase of rejection.

Graft rejection has been reduced dramatically by the discovery of *ciclosporin A, tacrolimus* and comparable agents. Ciclosporin is a powerful drug on its own or in combination with azathioprine and prednisolone.

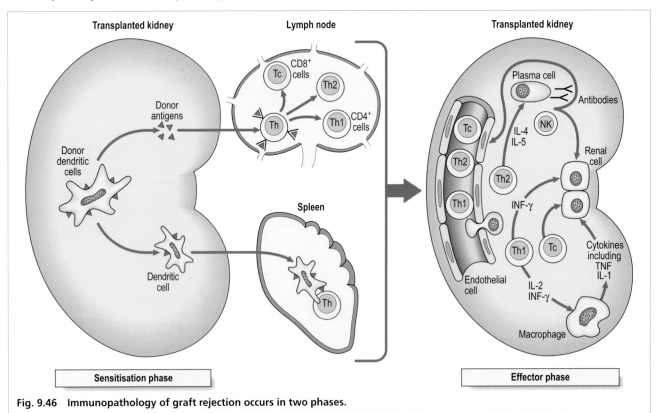

Fig. 9.46   Immunopathology of graft rejection occurs in two phases.

Monoclonal antibodies that destroy T-lymphocytes in the graft recipient can also be used as immunosuppressive agents.

Graft survival

Long-term graft survival is closely correlated with the degree of HLA matching, particularly at the class II locus. About 50% of fully matched cadaveric grafts survive 17 years but mismatched grafts survive for only 8 years.

Complications

Patients have an increased susceptibility to *infection* after transplant. Major causes of infection in the first month after transplantation are those related to surgical wounds, indwelling cannulae, or post-operative lung infections. The effects of such infections, however, are often considerable in the immuno-compromised host. After 1–4 months of immunosuppression, cytomegalovirus dominates a picture that includes various fungal, viral and protozoal infections. Infections occurring beyond 4 months fall into three main groups:

- chronic viral infections
- occasional opportunistic infections, such as cryptococcus
- infections normally present in the community.

A late complication of organ transplantation is *recurrence of the original disease*. This should always be considered in patients in whom there is functional deterioration following long periods of stable graft function. The incidence of *malignancy*, particularly lymphoma, in transplant recipients is 40 times greater than in the general population. Both lymphoma and Kaposi's sarcoma are more common when profound immune suppression is used, and are related to persistent viral stimulation with Epstein–Barr virus or human herpes virus 8 respectively.

Transplanted patients also have an increased risk of *acute myocardial infarction*. This may be linked to hypertension, hypertriglyceridaemia or insulin-resistant diabetes, as these conditions are often present before transplantation and are aggravated by steroids.

Transplantation of other organs

Liver transplantation

The results of human liver transplantation have improved dramatically in the last 15 years. Hepatic surgery poses unique problems; these include the bleeding tendency of a recipient with liver failure and the technically difficult surgery required to revascularise a grafted liver. However, compared with transplants of other organs, rejection episodes are milder and require less immunosuppression. Hepatitis C is the commonest indication for transplantation; other indications include biliary atresia, hepatocellular carcinoma, primary biliary cirrhosis and alcoholic cirrhosis (Ch. 16).

Heart transplantation

Unlike renal transplantation, there is no satisfactory long-term support available if the donated heart is rejected. Consequently, early diagnosis of rejection is crucial. Electrocardiographic changes are closely monitored and serial endomyocardial biopsies show lymphocytic infiltration with increased MHC class I expression by myocardial cells.

A major post-operative problem is accelerated atherosclerosis in the graft coronary arteries. This is the major cause of death in patients who survive more than 1 year.

Pancreatic transplantation

Improvements in surgical technique and better immunosuppression have resulted in 90% survival at 1 year of transplanted vascularised pancreatic grafts but longer-term results are disappointing.

Skin grafting

Allogeneic skin grafting in humans is useful in providing skin cover in severely burned patients. HLA typing is not required because the endogenous immunosuppressive effect of severe burns allows prolonged survival of unmatched skin. Although the graft is finally rejected, the short-term protective barrier afforded by covering burns during this time is vital to the patient in resisting infection.

Corneal grafting

Corneas are obtained from cadaveric donors. There is no need to HLA type or systemically immunosuppress the recipient because corneal rejection does not occur unless the graft becomes vascularised. In grafts that do become vascularised following chemical burns or chronic viral infection, HLA matching significantly improves survival.

Bone marrow transplantation

The transplantation of haemopoietic stem cells (HSCT) from bone marrow offers the only chance of cure for many patients with a wide range of disorders:

- aplastic anaemia
- leukaemia
- immunodeficiency disorders
- inborn errors of metabolism.

Graft rejection is common, but HSCT has the unique and often fatal complication of graft-versus-host disease (GVHD), in which the grafted immunocompetent cells recognise the host as foreign and mount an immunological attack.

Selection and preparation of patients
Theoretically, any abnormality of bone marrow stem cells is correctable by transplantation.

Preparation for transplantation begins 10 days before grafting. Measures to reduce infection risk include strict reverse-barrier nursing, decontamination of the skin and gut, the use of appropriate antibiotics and antimycotics, and immunoglobulin replacement if necessary.

The *grafting procedure* is straightforward; small amounts of marrow are taken from multiple sites under general anaesthetic. Bone spicules are removed by filtration through graded sieves.

Commonly confused conditions and entities relating to immunology and immunopathology	
Commonly confused	Distinction and explanation
Interleukins, cytokines, lymphokines and chemokines	Cytokines are soluble mediators of stimulatory or inhibitory signalling between cells; those produced by lymphocytes are called lymphokines. Cytokines acting between cells of the immune system (although some also have effects on other cells) are called interleukins. Cytokines inducing leukocyte chemotaxis are called chemokines.
Atopy, allergy and anaphylaxis	All three terms apply to type I (immediate) hypersensitivity or allergy. Atopy is an inherited tendency to produce IgE antibodies to environmental allergens. Exposure of the individual to an allergen may result in allergy as a result of mast cell degranulation. A severe, systemic, life-threatening allergic reaction is termed anaphylaxis.
Monocytes, macrophages and histiocytes	Monocytes are the newly-formed cells of the mononuclear phagocyte system. After a few hours in the blood, they enter tissues and undergo further differentiation into macrophages. Some macrophages in tissues have specific features and names (e.g. Kupffer cells); others are referred to as histiocytes.
Graft rejection and graft-versus-host disease	Graft rejection is an immunologically mediated reaction against a transplanted tissue or organ. Graft-versus-host disease occurs when immunologically active cells in the donor tissue (e.g. bone marrow transplant) damage the recipient's tissues.

Cells can then be given either without fractionation or after removal of immunocompetent T-lymphocytes responsible for graft-versus-host disease (see below). Cells are then transplanted by intravenous infusion.

A successful graft is indicated by a rise in the peripheral white cell count and the appearance of haemopoietic precursors in the marrow 10–20 days after transplantation.

Complications

Three major problems dominate the post-transplant period:

- failure of engraftment
- infection
- graft-versus-host disease (GVHD).

Failure of engraftment can be due to using insufficient haemopoietic stem cells or rejection of the grafted cells by the host. Patients with some residual immunity (e.g. as in leukaemia

in remission or partial immune deficiencies) require immune suppression— or *conditioning*—prior to grafting to ensure that rejection does not occur. Patients with no immune function (e.g. severe combined immune deficiency) do not, in theory, require conditioning as they are unable to reject the graft.

Serious bacterial, fungal and viral *infections* occur despite the elaborate measures aimed at reducing their incidence and severity. Infection with cytomegalovirus (CMV) is a common cause of death; evidence of CMV reactivation is seen in 75% of patients who are CMV positive before transplant.

Graft-versus-host disease (GVHD) occurs in most patients who receive allogeneic bone marrow transplants. About 7–14 days later, a skin rash, fever, hepatosplenomegaly, bloody diarrhoea and breathlessness develop. Skin biopsy shows lymphocytic infiltration with vascular cuffing and basal cell degeneration. The mortality of GVHD is considerable; over 70% of those with severe GVHD and about one-third with mild GVHD will die. Treatment requires an increase in immunosuppression but, once established, GVHD is very difficult to eradicate.

Prevention of GVHD involves ways to eliminate or reduce the numbers of immunocompetent T-cells in the engrafted bone marrow. T-cell-specific monoclonal antibodies can help deplete the T-cell load.

Peripheral blood stem cell transplantation

Because pluripotent stem cells can be mobilised from peripheral blood using colony-stimulating factors, stem cell transplants can theoretically be used as an alternative to bone marrow. There is interest in using umbilical cord blood as a source of stem cells in view of its ready availability. Allogeneic or autologous stem cell transplantation is under investigation for the management of autoimmune diseases such as rheumatoid arthritis and multiple sclerosis, for solid tumours such as breast cancer and neuroblastoma, and for haematological malignancies.

ACKNOWLEDGEMENT

The following figures are reproduced and modified, with permission, from *Essentials of Clinical Immunology* (5th edn), Blackwell Science, Oxford: 9.1, 9.2, 9.3, 9.4, 9.5, 9.6, 9.7, 9.13, 9.14, 9.15, 9.18, 9.20, 9.23, 9.24, 9.31, 9.33, 9.34, 9.37, 9.41, 9.44 and 9.46.

FURTHER READING

Albiger B, Dahlberg S, Henriques-Normark B, Normark S 2007 Role of the innate immune system in host defence against bacterial infections: focus on the Toll-like receptors. Journal of Internal Medicine 261: 511–528

Andrews P A 2002 Renal transplantation. British Medical Journal 324: 530–534

Belkaid Y 2007 Regulatory T cells and infection: a dangerous necessity. Nature Reviews. Immunology 7: 875–888

Carter R H 2006 B cells in health and disease. Mayo Clinic Proceedings 81: 377–384

Changanti R K 2006 Complement deficiencies. http://www.emedicine.com/med/topic419.htm

Chapel H M, Haeney M R, Misbah S A, Snowden H N 2006 Essentials of clinical immunology, 5th edn. Blackwell Science, Oxford. http://www.immunologyclinic.com

Copelan E A 2006 Medical progress: haematopoietic stem-cell transplantation. New England Journal of Medicine 354: 1813–1826

Davidson A, Diamond B 2001 Autoimmune diseases. New England Journal of Medicine 345: 340–350

Delves P J, Roitt I M 2000 The immune system. New England Journal of Medicine 343: 37–49,108–117

Jiang H, Chess L 2006 Mechanisms of disease: regulation of immune responses by T cells. New England Journal of Medicine 354: 1166–1176

Kay A B 2001 Allergy and allergic diseases. New England Journal of Medicine 344: 30–37, 109–113

Klein J, Sato A 2000 The HLA system. New England Journal of Medicine 343: 702–709, 782–786

Letvin N L 2006 Progress and obstacles in the development of an AIDS vaccine. Nature Reviews. Immunology 6: 930–939

Ley K, Laudanna L, Cybulsky M I, Nourshaugh S 2007 Getting to the site of inflammation: the leukocute adhesion cascade update. Nature Reviews. Immunology 7: 678–689

Marodi L, Notarangelo L D 2007 Immunological and genetic bases of new primary immunodeficiencies. Nature Reviews. Immunology 7: 851–861

Medzhitov R 2007 Recognition of microorganisms and activation of the immune response. Nature 449: 819–826

Miller S D, Turley D M, Podojil J R 2007 Antigen-specific tolerance strategies for the prevention and treatment of autoimmune disease. Nature Reviews. Immunology 7: 665–677

National Cancer Institute 2006 Understanding Cancer Series: The Immune System. www.cancer.gov/cancertopics/understandingcancer/immune system

Newburger P E 2006 Disorders of neutrophil number and function. Hematology. American Society of Hematology. Education Program: 104–110

Uniting the world against AIDS (UNAIDS): http://www.unaids.org

10

Inflammation

Inflammation is the local physiological response to tissue injury. It is not, in itself, a disease, but is usually a manifestation of disease. Inflammation may have beneficial effects, such as the destruction of invading micro-organisms and the walling-off of an abscess cavity, thus preventing spread of infection. Equally, it may produce disease; for example, an abscess in the brain would act as a space-occupying lesion compressing vital surrounding structures, or fibrosis resulting from chronic inflammation may distort the tissues and permanently alter their function.

Inflammation is usually classified according to its time course as:

- *acute inflammation*—the initial and often transient series of tissue reactions to injury
- *chronic inflammation*—the subsequent and often prolonged tissue reactions following the initial response.

The two main types of inflammation are also characterised by differences in the cell types taking part in the inflammatory response.

ACUTE INFLAMMATION

- ▶ Initial reaction of tissue to injury
- ▶ Vascular component: dilatation of vessels
- ▶ Exudative component: vascular leakage of protein-rich fluid
- ▶ Neutrophil polymorph is the characteristic cell recruited to the tissue
- ▶ Outcome may be resolution, suppuration (e.g. abscess), organisation, or progression to chronic inflammation

Acute inflammation is the initial tissue reaction to a wide range of injurious agents; it may last from a few hours to a few days. The process is usually described by the suffix '-itis', preceded by the name of the organ or tissues involved. Thus, acute inflammation of the meninges is called meningitis. The acute inflammatory response is similar whatever the causative agent.

Causes of acute inflammation

The principal causes of acute inflammation are:

- microbial infections, e.g. pyogenic bacteria, viruses
- hypersensitivity reactions, e.g. parasites, tubercle bacilli
- physical agents, e.g. trauma, ionising radiation, heat, cold
- chemicals, e.g. corrosives, acids, alkalis, reducing agents, bacterial toxins
- tissue necrosis, e.g. ischaemic infarction.

Microbial infections

One of the commonest causes of inflammation is microbial infection. Viruses lead to death of individual cells by intracellular multiplication. Bacteria release specific exotoxins—chemicals synthesised by them that specifically initiate inflammation—or endotoxins, which are associated with their cell walls. Additionally, some organisms cause immunologically mediated inflammation through hypersensitivity reactions (Ch. 9). Parasitic infections and tuberculous inflammation are instances where hypersensitivity is important.

Hypersensitivity reactions

A hypersensitivity reaction occurs when an altered state of immunological responsiveness causes an inappropriate or excessive immune reaction that damages the tissues. The types of reaction are classified in Chapter 9 but all have cellular or chemical mediators similar to those involved in inflammation.

Physical agents

Tissue damage leading to inflammation may occur through physical trauma, ultraviolet or other ionising radiation, burns or excessive cooling ('frostbite').

Irritant and corrosive chemicals

Corrosive chemicals (acids, alkalis, oxidising agents) provoke inflammation through gross tissue damage. However, infecting agents may release specific chemical irritants that lead directly to inflammation.

Tissue necrosis

Death of tissues from lack of oxygen or nutrients resulting from inadequate blood flow (infarction; Ch. 8) is a potent inflammatory stimulus. The edge of a recent infarct often shows an acute inflammatory response, presumably in response to peptides released from the dead tissue.

Essential macroscopic appearances of acute inflammation

The essential physical characteristics of acute inflammation were formulated by Celsus (30 BC–AD 38) using the Latin words rubor, calor, tumor and dolor. Loss of function is also characteristic.

Redness (rubor)
An acutely inflamed tissue appears red, for example skin affected by sunburn, cellulitis due to bacterial infection or acute conjunctivitis. This is due to dilatation of small blood vessels within the damaged area (Fig. 10.1).

Heat (calor)
Increase in temperature is seen only in peripheral parts of the body, such as the skin. It is due to increased blood flow (hyperaemia) through the region, resulting in vascular dilatation and the delivery of warm blood to the area. Systemic fever, which results from some of the chemical mediators of inflammation, also contributes to the local temperature.

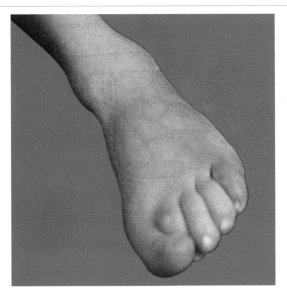

Fig. 10.1 Cellulitis. The skin over the lateral part of the foot is red (erythema) due to vascular dilatation associated with acute inflammation.

Swelling (tumor)

Swelling results from oedema—the accumulation of fluid in the extravascular space as part of the fluid exudate—and, to a much lesser extent, from the physical mass of the inflammatory cells migrating into the area (Fig. 10.2). As the inflammation response progresses, formation of new connective tissue contributes to the swelling.

Pain (dolor)

For the patient, pain is one of the best-known features of acute inflammation. It results partly from the stretching and distortion of tissues due to inflammatory oedema and, in particular, from pus under pressure in an abscess cavity. Some of the chemical mediators of acute inflammation, including bradykinin, the prostaglandins and serotonin, are known to induce pain.

Loss of function

Loss of function, a well-known consequence of inflammation, was added by Virchow (1821–1902) to the list of features drawn up by Celsus. Movement of an inflamed area is consciously and reflexly inhibited by pain, while severe swelling may physically immobilise the tissues.

Early stages of acute inflammation

In the early stages, oedema fluid, fibrin and neutrophil polymorphs accumulate in the extracellular spaces of the damaged tissue. The presence of the cellular component, the *neutrophil polymorph*, is essential for a histological diagnosis of acute inflammation. The acute inflammatory response involves three processes:

- changes in vessel calibre and, consequently, flow
- increased vascular permeability and formation of the fluid exudate
- formation of the cellular exudate—emigration of the neutrophil polymorphs into the extravascular space.

Changes in vessel calibre

The microcirculation consists of the network of small capillaries lying between arterioles, which have a thick muscular wall, and thin-walled venules. Capillaries have no smooth muscle in their walls to control their calibre, and are so narrow that red blood cells must past through them in single file. The smooth muscle of arteriolar walls forms precapillary sphincters which regulate blood flow through the capillary bed. Flow through the capillaries is intermittent, and some form preferential channels for flow while others are usually shut down (Fig. 10.3).

In blood vessels larger than capillaries, blood cells flow mainly in the centre of the lumen (axial flow), while the area near the vessel wall carries only plasma (plasmatic zone). This feature of normal blood flow keeps blood cells away from the vessel wall.

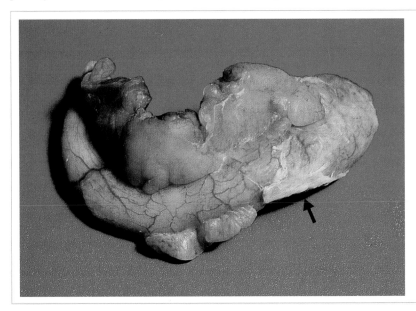

Fig. 10.2 Early acute appendicitis. The appendix is swollen due to oedema, the surface is covered by fibrinous exudate (arrowed), and the blood vessels are prominent because they are dilated.

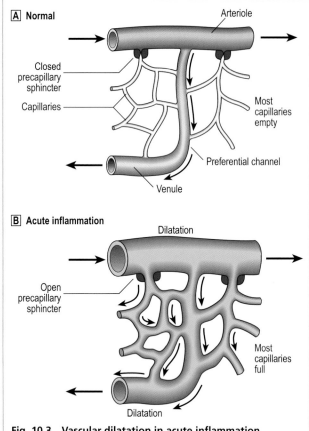

A Normal

Arteriole

Closed precapillary sphincter

Capillaries

Most capillaries empty

Preferential channel

Venule

B Acute inflammation

Dilatation

Open precapillary sphincter

Most capillaries full

Dilatation

Fig. 10.3   Vascular dilatation in acute inflammation.
A Normally, most of the capillary bed is closed down by precapillary sphincters. **B** In acute inflammation, the sphincters open, causing blood to flow through all capillaries.

Changes in the microcirculation occur as a physiological response; for example, there is hyperaemia in exercising muscle and active endocrine glands. The changes following injury that make up the vascular component of the acute inflammatory reaction were described by Lewis in 1927 as 'the triple response to injury': a flush, a flare and a wheal. If a blunt instrument is drawn firmly across the skin, the following sequential changes take place:

- A momentary white line follows the stroke. This is due to arteriolar vasoconstriction, the smooth muscle of arterioles contracting as a direct response to injury.
- *The flush*: a dull red line follows due to capillary dilatation enabled by relaxation of precapillary sphincters.
- *The flare*: a red, irregular, surrounding zone then develops, due to arteriolar dilatation. Both nervous and chemical factors are involved in these vascular changes.
- *The wheal*: a zone of oedema develops due to fluid exudation into the extravascular space.

The initial phase of arteriolar constriction is transient, and probably of little importance in acute inflammation. The subsequent phase of vasodilatation (active hyperaemia, in contrast to passive hyperaemia due to vascular distension from abnormally high venous pressure) may last from 15 minutes

to several hours, depending upon the severity of the injury. There is experimental evidence that blood flow to the injured area may increase up to 10-fold.

As blood flow begins to slow again, blood cells begin to flow nearer to the vessel wall, in the plasmatic zone rather than the axial stream. This allows 'pavementing' of leukocytes (their adhesion to the vascular epithelium) to occur, which is the first step in leukocyte emigration into the extravascular space.

The slowing of blood flow that follows the phase of hyperaemia is due to increased vascular permeability, allowing plasma to escape into the tissues while blood cells are retained within the vessels. The blood viscosity is therefore increased.

Increased vascular permeability

Small blood vessels are lined by a single layer of endothelial cells. In some tissues, these form a complete layer of uniform thickness around the vessel wall, while in other tissues there are areas of endothelial cell thinning, known as fenestrations. The walls of small blood vessels act as a microfilter, allowing the passage of water and solutes but blocking that of large molecules and cells. Oxygen, carbon dioxide and some nutrients transfer across the wall by diffusion, but the main transfer of fluid and solutes is by ultrafiltration, as described by Starling. The high colloid osmotic pressure inside the vessel, due to plasma proteins, favours fluid return to the vascular compartment. Under normal circumstances, high hydrostatic pressure at the arteriolar end of capillaries forces fluid out into the extravascular space, but this fluid returns into the capillaries at their venous end, where hydrostatic pressure is low (Fig. 10.4). In acute inflammation, however, not only is capillary hydrostatic pressure increased, but there is also escape of plasma proteins into the extravascular space, increasing the colloid osmotic pressure there. Consequently, much more fluid leaves the vessels than is returned to them. The net escape of protein-rich fluid is called *exudation*; hence, the fluid is called the *fluid exudate*.

Features of the fluid exudate

The increased vascular permeability means that large molecules, such as proteins, can escape from vessels. Hence, the exudate fluid has a high protein content of up to 50 g/l. The proteins present include immunoglobulins, which may be important in the destruction of invading micro-organisms, and coagulation factors, including fibrinogen, which result in fibrin deposition on contact with the extravascular tissues. Hence, acutely inflamed organ surfaces are commonly covered by fibrin: the *fibrinous exudate*. There is a considerable turnover of the inflammatory exudate; it is constantly drained away by local lymphatic channels to be replaced by new exudate.

Ultrastructural basis of increased vascular permeability

The ultrastructural basis of increased vascular permeability was originally determined using an experimental model in which histamine, one of the chemical mediators of increased vascular permeability, was injected under the skin. This caused

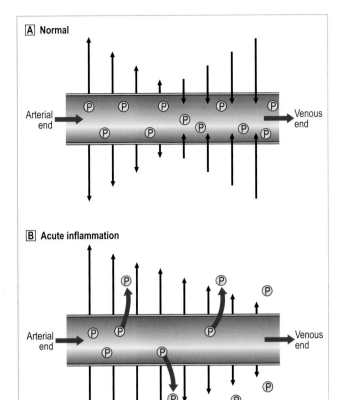

A Normal

Arterial end → Venous end

B Acute inflammation

Arterial end → Venous end

Fig. 10.4 Ultrafiltration of fluid across the small blood vessel wall. **A** Normally, fluid leaving and entering the vessel is in equilibrium. **B** In acute inflammation, there is a net loss of fluid together with plasma protein molecules (P) into the extracellular space, resulting in oedema.

Table 10.1 Causes of increased vascular permeability	
Time course	Mechanisms
Immediate transient	Chemical mediators, e.g. histamine, bradykinin, nitric oxide, C5a, leukotriene B4, platelet activating factor
Immediate sustained	Severe direct vascular injury, e.g. trauma
Delayed prolonged	Endothelial cell injury, e.g. X-rays, bacterial toxins

Tissue sensitivity to chemical mediators
The relative importance of chemical mediators and of direct vascular injury in causing increased vascular permeability varies according to the type of tissue. For example, vessels in the central nervous system are relatively insensitive to the chemical mediators, while those in the skin, conjunctiva and bronchial mucosa are exquisitely sensitive to agents such as histamine.

Formation of the cellular exudate

The accumulation of *neutrophil polymorphs* within the extracellular space is the diagnostic histological feature of acute inflammation. The stages whereby leukocytes reach the tissues are shown in Figure 10.5.

Margination of neutrophils
In the normal circulation, cells are confined to the central (axial) stream in blood vessels, and do not flow in the peripheral (plasmatic) zone near to the endothelium. However, loss of intravascular fluid and increase in plasma viscosity with slowing of flow at the site of acute inflammation allow neutrophils to flow in this plasmatic zone.

Adhesion of neutrophils
The adhesion of neutrophils to the vascular endothelium that occurs at sites of acute inflammation is termed 'pavementing' of neutrophils. Neutrophils randomly contact the endothelium in normal tissues, but do not adhere to it. However, at sites of injury, pavementing occurs early in the acute inflammatory response and appears to be a specific process occurring independently of the eventual slowing of blood flow. The phenomenon is seen only in venules.

Increased leukocyte adhesion results from interaction between paired *adhesion molecules* on leukocyte and endothelial surfaces. There are several classes of such adhesion molecules: some of them act as lectins which bind to carbohydrates on the partner cell. Leukocyte surface adhesion molecule expression is increased by:

- complement component C5a
- leukotriene B4
- tumour necrosis factor.

transient leakage of plasma proteins into the extravascular space. Electron microscopic examination of venules and small veins during this period showed that gaps of 0.1–0.4 μm in diameter had appeared between endothelial cells. These gaps allowed the leakage of injected particles, such as carbon, into the tissues. The endothelial cells are not damaged during this process. They contain contractile proteins such as actin, which, when stimulated by the chemical mediators of acute inflammation, cause contraction of the endothelial cells, pulling open the transient pores. The leakage induced by chemical mediators, such as histamine, is confined to venules and small veins. Although fluid is lost by ultrafiltration from capillaries, there is no evidence that they too become more permeable in acute inflammation.

Other causes of increased vascular permeability
In addition to the transient vascular leakage caused by some inflammatory stimuli, certain other stimuli, e.g. heat, cold, ultraviolet light and X-rays, bacterial toxins and corrosive chemicals, cause delayed prolonged leakage. In these circumstances, there is direct injury to endothelial cells in several types of vessel within the damaged area (Table 10.1).

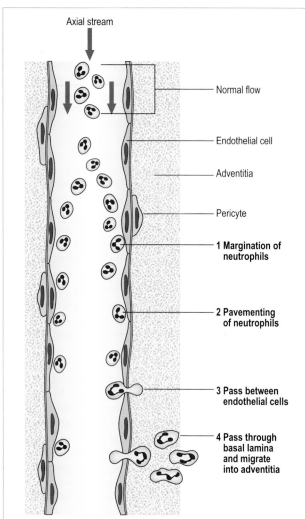

Axial stream

Normal flow

Endothelial cell

Adventitia

Pericyte

1 Margination of neutrophils

2 Pavementing of neutrophils

3 Pass between endothelial cells

4 Pass through basal lamina and migrate into adventitia

Fig. 10.5 Steps in neutrophil polymorph emigration.
Neutrophils (1) marginate into the plasmatic zone; (2) adhere to endothelial cells; (3) pass between endothelial cells; and (4) pass through the basal lamina and migrate into the adventitia.

Endothelial cell expression of *selectins*, such as endothelial–leukocyte adhesion molecule-1 (ELAM-1), which establishes the first loose contact between leukocytes and endothelium (resulting in 'rolling'), integrins, and intercellular adhesion molecule-1 (ICAM-1), to which the leukocytes' surface adhesion molecules bond, is increased by:

- interleukin-1
- endotoxins
- tumour necrosis factor.

In this way, a variety of chemical inflammatory mediators promote leukocyte–endothelial adhesion as a prelude to leukocyte emigration.

Neutrophil emigration
Leukocytes migrate by active amoeboid movement through the walls of venules and small veins, but do not commonly exit from capillaries. Electron microscopy shows that neutrophil and eosinophil polymorphs and macrophages can insert pseudopodia between endothelial cells, migrate through the gap so created between the endothelial cells, and then on through the basal lamina into the vessel wall. The defect appears to be self-sealing, and the endothelial cells are not damaged by this process.

Diapedesis
Red cells may also escape from vessels, but in this case the process is passive and depends on hydrostatic pressure forcing the red cells out. The process is called diapedesis, and the presence of large numbers of red cells in the extravascular space implies severe vascular injury, such as a tear in the vessel wall.

Later stages of acute inflammation

Chemotaxis of neutrophils

It has long been known from in vitro experiments that neutrophil polymorphs are attracted towards certain chemical substances in solution—a process called chemotaxis. Time-lapse cine photography shows apparently purposeful migration of neutrophils along a concentration gradient. Compounds that appear chemotactic for neutrophils in vitro include certain complement components, cytokines and products produced by neutrophils themselves. It is not known whether chemotaxis is important in vivo. Neutrophils may possibly arrive at sites of injury by random movement, and then be trapped there by immobilising factors (a process analogous to the trapping of macrophages at sites of delayed-type hypersensitivity by migration inhibitory factor; Ch. 9).

Chemical mediators of acute inflammation

The spread of the acute inflammatory response following injury to a small area of tissue suggests that chemical substances are released from injured tissues, spreading outwards into uninjured areas. Early in the response, histamine and thrombin released by the original inflammatory stimulus cause upregulation of P-selectin and platelet-activating factor (PAF) on the endothelial cells lining the venules. Adhesion molecules, stored in intracellular vesicles, appear rapidly on the cell surface. Neutrophil polymorphs begin to roll along the endothelial wall due to engagement of the lectin-like domain on the P-selectin molecule with sialyl Lewis^x carbohydrate ligands on the neutrophil polymorph surface mucins. This also helps platelet-activating factor to dock with its corresponding receptor which, in turn, increases expression of the integrins' lymphocyte function-associated molecule 1 (LFA-1) and membrane attack complex 1 (MAC-1). The overall effect of all these molecules is very firm neutrophil adhesion to the endothelial surface. These chemicals, called *endogenous chemical mediators*, cause:

- vasodilatation
- emigration of neutrophils
- chemotaxis
- increased vascular permeability
- itching and pain.

Chemical mediators released from cells

Histamine. This is the best-known chemical mediator in acute inflammation. It causes vascular dilatation and the immediate transient phase of increased vascular permeability. The immediate effect is assisted by its storage as preformed granules. In humans, mast cells are the most important source of histamine, but it is also present in basophil and eosinophil leukocytes, and platelets. Histamine release from these sites (for example, mast cell degranulation) is stimulated by complement components C3a and C5a, and by lysosomal proteins released from neutrophils.

Lysosomal compounds. These are released from neutrophils and include cationic proteins, which may increase vascular permeability, and neutral proteases, which may activate complement.

Prostaglandins. These are a group of long-chain fatty acids derived from arachidonic acid and synthesised by many cell types. Some prostaglandins potentiate the increase in vascular permeability caused by other compounds. Others include platelet aggregation (prostaglandin I_2 is inhibitory while prostaglandin A_2 is stimulatory). Part of the anti-inflammatory activity of drugs such as aspirin and the non-steroidal anti-inflammatory drugs is attributable to inhibition of one of the enzymes involved in prostaglandin synthesis.

Leukotrienes. These are also synthesised from arachidonic acid, especially in neutrophils, and appear to have vasoactive properties. SRS-A (slow-reacting substance of anaphylaxis), involved in type I hypersensitivity (Ch. 9), is a mixture of leukotrienes.

5-Hydroxytryptamine (serotonin). This is present in high concentration in platelets. It is a potent vasoconstrictor.

Chemokines. This large family of 8–10-kD proteins selectively attracts various types of leukocytes to the site of inflammation. Some chemokines such as IL-8 are mainly specific for neutrophil polymorphs and to a lesser extent lymphocytes, whereas other types of chemokine are chemotactic for monocytes, natural killer (NK) cells, basophils and eosinophils. The various chemokines bind to extracellular matrix components such as heparin and heparan sulphate glycosaminoglycans, setting up a gradient of chemotactic molecules fixed to the extracellular matrix.

Plasma factors

The plasma contains four enzymatic cascade systems—complement, the kinins, the coagulation factors and the fibrinolytic system—which are inter-related and produce various inflammatory mediators.

- It is safer to have inactive precursors rather than active mediators.
- Each step results in amplification of the response.
- A larger number of possible regulators can modulate the response.
- Each step results in end products with possibly different activities.

Coagulation system. The coagulation system (Ch. 23) is responsible for the conversion of soluble fibrinogen into fibrin, a major component of the acute inflammatory exudate.

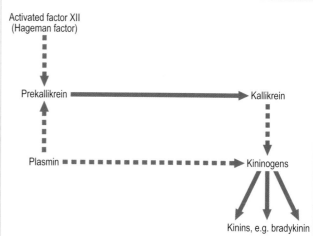

Fig. 10.6 Interactions between the systems of chemical mediators. Coagulation factor XII activates the kinin, fibrinolytic and coagulation systems. The complement system is in turn activated.

Coagulation factor XII (the Hageman factor), once activated by contact with extracellular materials such as basal lamina, and various proteolytic enzymes of bacterial origin, can activate the coagulation, kinin and fibrinolytic systems. The inter-relationships of these systems are shown in Figure 10.6.

Kinin system. The kinins are peptides of 9–11 amino acids; the most important is bradykinin. The kinin system is activated by coagulation factor XII (Fig. 10.7). Bradykinin is also a chemical mediator of the pain that is a cardinal feature of acute inflammation.

Fibrinolytic system. Plasmin is responsible for the lysis of fibrin into fibrin split products, which may have local effects on vascular permeability.

Complement system. The complement system is a cascade system of enzymatic proteins (Ch. 9). It can be activated during the acute inflammatory reaction in various ways:

- In tissue necrosis, enzymes capable of activating complement are released from dying cells.
- During infection, the formation of antigen–antibody complexes can activate complement via the *classical pathway*, while the endotoxins of Gram-negative bacteria activate complement via the *alternative pathway* (Ch. 9).
- Products of the kinin and fibrinolytic systems can activate complement.

The products of complement activation most important in acute inflammation include:

- C5a: chemotactic for neutrophils; increases vascular permeability; releases histamine from mast cells
- C3a: similar properties to those of C5a, but less active
- C567: chemotactic for neutrophils
- C56789: cytolytic activity (the 'membrane attack complex')
- C4b, 2a, 3b: opsonisation of bacteria (facilitates phagocytosis by macrophages).

Table 10.2 summarises the chemical mediators involved in the three main stages of acute inflammation.

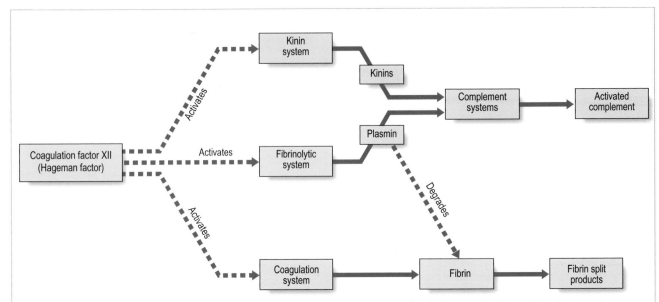

Fig. 10.7 The kinin system. Activated factor XII and plasmin activate the conversion of prekallikrein to kallikrein. This stimulates the conversion of kininogens to kinins, such as bradykinin. Prekallikrein can also be activated by leukocyte proteases (e.g. trypsin).

Role of tissue macrophages

These secrete numerous chemical mediators when stimulated by local infection or injury. Most important are the cytokines interleukin-1 (IL-1) and tumour necrosis factor-alpha (TNF-alpha), whose stimulatory effect on endothelial cells occurs after that of histamine and thrombin. Other late products include E-selectin, an adhesion molecule that binds and activates neutrophils, and the chemokines IL-8 and epithelium-derived neutrophil attractant 78, which are potent chemotaxins for neutrophil polymorphs. Additionally, IL-1 and TNF-alpha cause endothelial

cells, fibroblasts and epithelial cells to secrete MCP-1, another powerful chemotactic protein for neutrophil polymorphs.

Role of the lymphatics

Terminal lymphatics are blind-ended, endothelium-lined tubes present in most tissues in similar numbers to capillaries. The terminal lymphatics drain into collecting lymphatics, which have valves and so propel lymph passively, aided by contraction of neighbouring muscles, to the lymph nodes. The basal lamina of lymphatic endothelium is incomplete, and the junctions between the cells are simpler and less robust than those between capillary endothelial cells. Hence, gaps tend to open up passively between the lymphatic endothelial cells, allowing large protein molecules to enter.

In acute inflammation, the lymphatic channels become dilated as they drain away the oedema fluid of the inflammatory exudate. This drainage tends to limit the extent of oedema in the tissues. The ability of the lymphatics to carry large molecules and some particulate matter is important in the immune response to infecting agents; antigens are carried to the regional lymph nodes for recognition by lymphocytes (Ch. 9).

Role of the neutrophil polymorph

The neutrophil polymorph is the characteristic cell of the acute inflammatory infiltrate (Fig. 10.8). The actions of this cell will now be considered.

Movement
Contraction of cytoplasmic microtubules and gel/sol changes in cytoplasmic fluidity bring about amoeboid movement. These active mechanisms are dependent upon calcium ions and are controlled by intracellular concentrations of cyclic nucleotides. The movement shows a directional response (chemotaxis) to the various chemicals of acute inflammation.

Table 10.2 Endogenous chemical mediators of the acute inflammatory response	
Status of acute inflammatory response	**Chemical mediators**
Vascular dilatation	Histamine Prostaglandins PGE_2/I_2 VIP Nitric oxide PAF
Increased vascular permeability	Transient phase—histamine Prolonged phase—mediators such as bradykinin, nitric oxide, C5a, leukotriene B4 and PAF, potentiated by prostaglandins
Adhesion of leukocytes to endothelium	Up-regulation of adhesion molecules on endothelium, principally by IL-8, C5a, leukotriene B4, PAF, IL-1 and TNF-alpha
Neutrophil polymorph chemotaxis	Leukotriene B4, IL-8 and others

Adhesion to micro-organisms

Micro-organisms are *opsonised* (from the Greek word meaning 'to prepare for the table'), or rendered more amenable to phagocytosis, either by immunoglobulins or by complement components. Bacterial lipopolysaccharides activate complement via the alternative pathway (Ch. 9), generating component C3b which has opsonising properties. In addition, if antibody binds to bacterial antigens, this can activate complement via the classical pathway, also generating C3b. In the immune individual, the binding of immunoglobulins to micro-organisms by their Fab components leaves the Fc component (Ch. 9) exposed. Neutrophils have surface receptors for the Fc fragment of immunoglobulins, and consequently bind to the micro-organisms prior to ingestion.

Phagocytosis

The process whereby cells (such as neutrophil polymorphs and macrophages) ingest solid particles is termed phagocytosis. The first step in phagocytosis is adhesion of the particle to be phagocytosed to the cell surface. This is facilitated by opsonisation. The phagocyte then ingests the attached particle by sending out pseudopodia around it. These meet and fuse so that the particle lies in a phagocytic vacuole (also called a phagosome) bounded by cell membrane. Lysosomes, membrane-bound packets containing the toxic compounds described below, then fuse with phagosomes to form phagolysosomes. It is within these that intracellular killing of micro-organisms occurs.

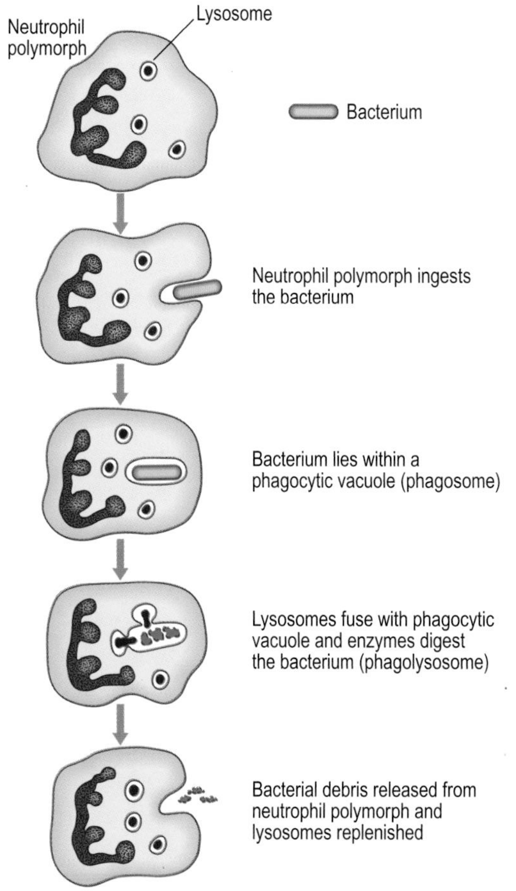
Neutrophil polymorph
Lysosome
Bacterium
Neutrophil polymorph ingests the bacterium
Bacterium lies within a phagocytic vacuole (phagosome)
Lysosomes fuse with phagocytic vacuole and enzymes digest the bacterium (phagolysosome)
Bacterial debris released from neutrophil polymorph and lysosomes replenished

Fig. 10.8 Diagram of a neutrophil polymorph. The nucleus is polylobate and the cytoplasm shows dense granules which contain myeloperoxidase and other enzymes. Some of these enzymes are contained within lysosomes. These fuse with a phagocytic vacuole containing a phagocytosed bacterium, forming a phagolysosome in which the bacterium is digested by the enzymes.

Intracellular killing of micro-organisms

Neutrophil polymorphs are highly specialised cells, containing noxious microbicidal agents, some of which are similar to household bleach. The microbicidal agents may be classified as:

- those that are oxygen-dependent
- those that are oxygen-independent.

Oxygen-dependent mechanisms. The neutrophils produce hydrogen peroxide which reacts with myeloperoxidase in the cytoplasmic granules (Fig. 10.8) in the presence of halide, such as Cl^-, to produce a potent microbicidal agent. Other products of oxygen reduction also contribute to the killing, such as peroxide anions (O_2^-), hydroxyl radicals ($\bullet OH$) and singlet oxygen ($^1O_2$).

Oxygen-independent mechanisms. These include lysozyme (muramidase), lactoferrin, which chelates iron required for bacterial growth, cationic proteins, and the low pH inside phagocytic vacuoles.

Release of lysosomal products

Release of lysosomal products from the cell damages local tissues by proteolysis by enzymes such as elastase and collagenase, activates coagulation factor XII, and attracts other leukocytes into the area. Some of the compounds released increase vascular permeability, while others are pyrogens, producing systemic fever by acting on the hypothalamus.

The role of mast cells

Mast cells have an important role in acute inflammation. On stimulation by the C3a/C5a complement components they release preformed inflammatory mediators stored in their granules and metabolise arachidonic acid into newly synthesised inflammatory mediators such as leukotrienes, prostaglandins and thromboxanes.

Special macroscopic appearances of acute inflammation

The cardinal signs of acute inflammation are modified according to the tissue involved and the type of agent provoking the inflammation. Several descriptive terms are used for the appearances.

Serous inflammation

In serous inflammation, there is abundant protein-rich fluid exudate with a relatively low cellular content. Examples include inflammation of the serous cavities, such as peritonitis, and inflammation of a synovial joint, acute synovitis. Vascular dilatation may be apparent to the naked eye, the serous surfaces appearing injected (Fig. 10.2), i.e. having dilated, blood-laden vessels on the surface (like the appearance of the conjunctiva in 'blood-shot' eyes).

Catarrhal inflammation

When mucus hypersecretion accompanies acute inflammation of a mucous membrane, the appearance is described as catarrhal. The common cold is a good example.

Fibrinous inflammation

When the inflammatory exudate contains plentiful fibrinogen, this polymerises into a thick fibrin coating. This is often seen in acute pericarditis and gives the parietal and visceral pericardium a 'bread and butter' appearance.

Haemorrhagic inflammation

Haemorrhagic inflammation indicates severe vascular injury or depletion of coagulation factors. This occurs in acute pancreatitis due to proteolytic destruction of vascular walls, and in meningococcal septicaemia due to disseminated intravascular coagulation (see Ch. 23).

Suppurative (purulent) inflammation

The terms 'suppurative' and 'purulent' denote the production of pus, which consists of dying and degenerate neutrophils, infecting organisms and liquefied tissues. The pus may become walled-off by granulation tissue or fibrous tissue to produce an *abscess* (a localised collection of pus in a tissue). If a hollow viscus fills with pus, this is called an *empyema*, for example empyema of the gallbladder (Fig. 10.9) or of the appendix (Fig. 10.10).

Membranous inflammation

In acute membranous inflammation, an epithelium becomes coated by fibrin, desquamated epithelial cells and inflammatory cells. An example is the grey membrane seen in pharyngitis or laryngitis due to *Corynebacterium diphtheriae*.

Pseudomembranous inflammation

The term 'pseudomembranous' describes superficial mucosal ulceration with an overlying slough of disrupted mucosa, fibrin, mucus and inflammatory cells. This is seen in

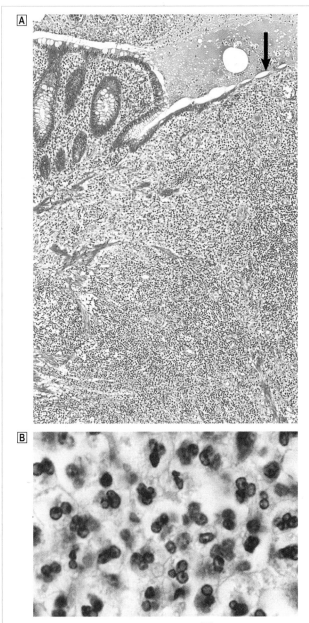

Fig. 10.10 Empyema of the appendix. Ⓐ The appendix lumen is filled with pus, there is focal mucosal ulceration (arrow) and the appendicular wall and mesoappendix (bottom) are thickened due to an acute inflammatory exudate. Ⓑ Pus in the lumen of the appendix. Pus consists of living and degenerate neutrophil polymorphs together with liquefied tissue debris.

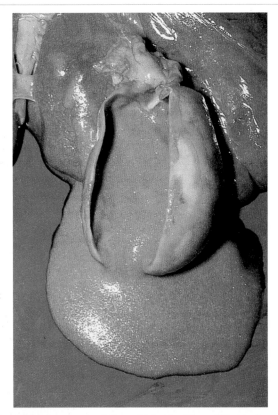

Fig. 10.9 Empyema of the gallbladder. The gallbladder lumen is filled with pus.

pseudomembranous colitis due to *Clostridium difficile* colonisation of the bowel, usually following broad-spectrum antibiotic treatment (Ch. 15).

Necrotising (gangrenous) inflammation
High tissue pressure due to oedema may lead to vascular occlusion and thrombosis, which may result in widespread septic necrosis of the organ. The combination of necrosis and bacterial putrefaction is *gangrene*. Gangrenous appendicitis is a good example.

Effects of acute inflammation

Acute inflammation has local and systemic effects, both of which may be harmful or beneficial. The local effects are usually clearly beneficial, for example the destruction of invading micro-organisms, but at other times they appear to serve no obvious function, or may even be positively harmful.

Beneficial effects

Both the fluid and cellular exudates may have useful effects. Beneficial effects of the fluid exudate are:

- *Dilution of toxins*, such as those produced by bacteria, allows them to be carried away in lymphatics.
- *Entry of antibodies*, due to increased vascular permeability into the extravascular space, where they may lead either to lysis of micro-organisms, through the participation of complement, or to their phagocytosis by opsonisation. Antibodies are also important in neutralisation of toxins.
- *Transport of drugs* such as antibiotics to the site where bacteria are multiplying.
- *Fibrin formation* (Fig. 10.11) from exuded fibrinogen may impede the movement of micro-organisms, trapping them and so facilitating phagocytosis, and serves as a matrix for the formation of granulation tissue.
- *Delivery of nutrients and oxygen,* essential for cells such as neutrophils that have high metabolic activity, is aided by increased fluid flow through the area.
- *Stimulation of immune response* by drainage of this fluid exudate into the lymphatics allows particulate and soluble antigens to reach the local lymph nodes, where they may stimulate the immune response.

The role of neutrophils in the cellular exudate has already been discussed. They have a life-span of only 1–3 days and must be constantly replaced. Most die locally, but some leave the site via the lymphatics. Some are actively removed by apoptosis. It is probable that apoptosis and its regulation play a major role in determining the outcome of episodes of inflammation. Blood *monocytes* also arrive at the site and, on leaving the blood vessels, transform into *macrophages*, becoming more metabolically active, motile and phagocytic. Phagocytosis of micro-organisms is enhanced by *opsonisation* by antibodies or by complement. In most acute inflammatory reactions, macrophages play a lesser role in phagocytosis compared with that of neutrophil polymorphs. Macrophages start to appear within a few hours of the commencement of inflammation, but do not predominate until the later stages when the neutrophils have diminished in number and the

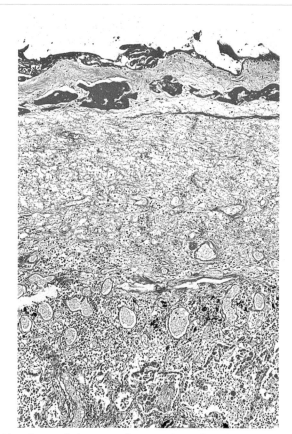

Fig. 10.11 Fibrinous exudate. Histology of the fibrinous exudate (dark-stained material) adherent to the pleura in acute lobar pneumonia.

macrophage population has enlarged by local proliferation. They are responsible for clearing away tissue debris and damaged cells.

Both neutrophils and macrophages may discharge their lysosomal enzymes into the extracellular fluid by exocytosis, or the entire cell contents may be released when the cells die. Release of these enzymes assists in the *digestion of the inflammatory exudate*.

Harmful effects

The release of lysosomal enzymes by inflammatory cells may also have harmful effects:

- *Digestion of normal tissues*. Enzymes such as collagenases and proteases may digest normal tissues, resulting in their destruction. This may result particularly in vascular damage, for example in type III hypersensitivity reactions (Ch. 9), in some types of glomerulonephritis (Ch. 21), and in abscess cavities.
- *Swelling*. The swelling of acutely inflamed tissues may be harmful: for example, in children the swelling of the epiglottis in acute epiglottitis due to *Haemophilus influenzae* infection may obstruct the airway, resulting in death. Inflammatory swelling is especially serious when it

occurs in an enclosed space such as the cranial cavity. Thus, acute meningitis or a cerebral abscess may *raise intracranial pressure* to the point where blood flow into the brain is impaired, resulting in ischaemic damage, or may force the cerebral hemispheres against the tentorial orifice and the cerebellum into the foramen magnum (pressure coning; Ch. 26).

- *Inappropriate inflammatory response.* Sometimes, acute inflammatory responses appear inappropriate, such as those that occur in type I hypersensitivity reactions (e.g. hay fever; Ch. 9) where the provoking environmental antigen (e.g. pollen) otherwise poses no threat to the individual. Such allergic inflammatory responses may be life-threatening, for example extrinsic asthma.

Sequelae of acute inflammation

The sequelae of acute inflammation depend upon the type of tissue involved and the amount of tissue destruction, which depend in turn upon the nature of the injurious agent. The possible outcomes of acute inflammation are shown in Figure 10.12.

Resolution

The term resolution means the complete restoration of the tissues to normal after an episode of acute inflammation. The conditions that favour resolution are:

- minimal cell death and tissue damage
- occurrence in an organ or tissue that has regenerative capacity (e.g. the liver) rather than in one that cannot regenerate (e.g. the central nervous system)

- rapid destruction of the causal agent (e.g. phagocytosis of bacteria)
- rapid removal of fluid and debris by good local vascular drainage.

A good example of an acute inflammatory condition that usually resolves completely is acute lobar pneumonia (Ch. 14). The alveoli become filled with acute inflammatory exudate containing fibrin, bacteria and neutrophil polymorphs. The alveolar walls are thin and have many capillaries (for gas exchange) and lymphatic channels. The sequence of events leading to resolution is usually:

- phagocytosis of bacteria (e.g. pneumococci) by neutrophils and intracellular killing
- fibrinolysis
- phagocytosis of debris, especially by macrophages, and carriage through lymphatics to the hilar lymph nodes
- disappearance of vascular dilatation.

Following this, the lung parenchyma would appear histologically normal.

Suppuration

Suppuration is the formation of pus, a mixture of living, dying and dead neutrophils and bacteria, cellular debris and sometimes globules of lipid. The causative stimulus must be fairly persistent and is virtually always an infective agent, usually pyogenic bacteria (e.g. *Staphylococcus aureus, Streptococcus pyogenes, Neisseria* species or coliform organisms). Once pus begins to accumulate in a tissue, it becomes surrounded by a 'pyogenic membrane' consisting of sprouting capillaries, neutrophils and occasional fibroblasts; this is a manifestation

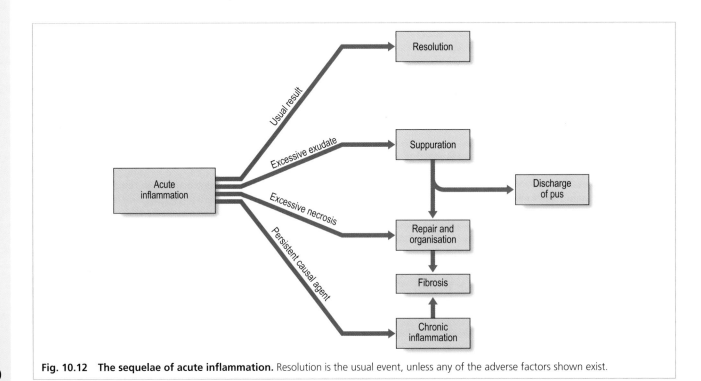

Fig. 10.12 The sequelae of acute inflammation. Resolution is the usual event, unless any of the adverse factors shown exist.

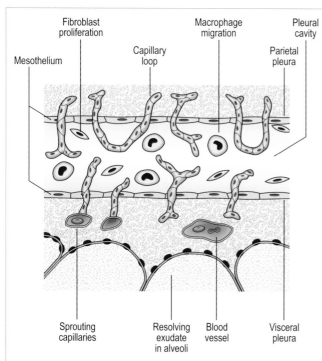

Fig. 10.13 Organisation of the fibrinous pleural exudate.
Capillary loops are growing into the exudate, accompanied by fibroblasts and capillaries.

The fibrous walls of longstanding abscesses may become complicated by *dystrophic calcification* (Ch. 7).

Organisation

Organisation of tissues is their replacement by granulation tissue as part of the process of repair. The circumstances favouring this outcome are when:

- large amounts of fibrin are formed, which cannot be removed completely by fibrinolytic enzymes from the plasma or from neutrophil polymorphs
- substantial volumes of tissue become necrotic or if the dead tissue (e.g. fibrous tissue) is not easily digested
- exudate and debris cannot be removed or discharged.

During organisation, new capillaries grow into the inert material (inflammatory exudate), macrophages migrate into the zone and fibroblasts proliferate under the influence of TGF-beta, resulting in *fibrosis* and, possibly, scar formation. A good example of this is seen in the pleural space following acute lobar pneumonia. Resolution usually occurs in the lung parenchyma, but very extensive fibrinous exudate fills the pleural cavity (Fig. 10.11). The fibrin is not easily removed and consequently capillaries grow into the fibrin, accompanied by macrophages and fibroblasts (the exudate becomes 'organised'). Eventually, fibrous adhesion occurs between the parietal and visceral pleura (Fig. 10.13). Fibrous adhesions also occur commonly in the peritoneal cavity after surgery or an episode of peritonitis; these can hamper further surgery and can also lead to intestinal obstruction.

Progression to chronic inflammation

If the agent causing acute inflammation is not removed, the acute inflammation may progress to the chronic stage. In addition to organisation of the tissue just described, the character of the cellular exudate changes, with lymphocytes, plasma cells and macrophages (sometimes including multinucleate giant cells) replacing the neutrophil polymorphs (Fig. 10.14). Often, however, chronic inflammation occurs as a primary event, there being no preceding period of acute inflammation.

Systemic effects of inflammation

Apart from the local features of acute and chronic inflammation described above, an inflammatory focus produces systemic effects.

Pyrexia
Polymorphs and macrophages produce compounds known as *endogenous pyrogens* which act on the hypothalamus to set the thermoregulatory mechanisms at a higher temperature. Interleukin-2 probably has the greatest effect. Release of endogenous pyrogen is stimulated by phagocytosis, endotoxins and immune complexes.

Constitutional symptoms
Constitutional symptoms include malaise, anorexia and nausea.

of healing, eventually resulting in granulation tissue and scarring. Such a collection of pus is called an abscess, and bacteria within the abscess cavity are relatively inaccessible to antibodies and to antibiotic drugs (thus, for example, acute osteomyelitis, an abscess in the bone marrow cavity, is notoriously difficult to treat).

Abscess
An abscess (for example, a boil) usually 'points', then bursts; the abscess cavity collapses and is obliterated by organisation and fibrosis, leaving a small scar. Sometimes, surgical incision and drainage is necessary to eliminate the abscess.

If pus accumulates inside a hollow viscus (e.g. the gallbladder) the mucosal layers of the outflow tract of the viscus may become fused together by fibrin, resulting in an empyema (Fig. 10.9).

Such deep-seated abscesses sometimes discharge their pus along a *sinus tract* (an abnormal connection, lined by granulation tissue, between the abscess and the skin or a mucosal surface). If this results in an abnormal passage connecting two mucosal surfaces or one mucosal surface to the skin surface, it is referred to as a *fistula*. Sinuses occur particularly when foreign body materials are present, which are indigestible by macrophages and which favour continuing suppuration. The only treatment for this type of condition is surgical elimination of the foreign body material.

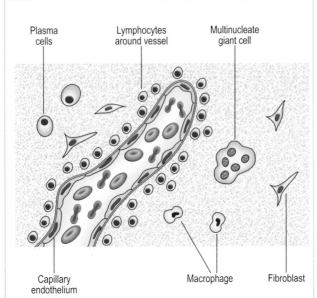

Plasma cells
Lymphocytes around vessel
Multinucleate giant cell
Capillary endothelium
Macrophage
Fibroblast

Fig. 10.14   The cells involved in chronic inflammation.
Neutrophil polymorphs have disappeared from the site, and mononuclear cells such as lymphocytes and macrophages are prominent. Some specialised lymphocytes called plasma cells are present; these produce immunoglobulins. Some of the macrophages may become multinucleate giant cells. Fibroblasts migrate into the area and lay down collagen.

Weight loss
Weight loss, due to negative nitrogen balance, is common when there is extensive chronic inflammation. For this reason, tuberculosis used to be called 'consumption'.

Reactive hyperplasia of the reticulo-endothelial system
Local or systemic lymph node enlargement commonly accompanies inflammation, while splenomegaly is found in certain specific infections (e.g. malaria, infectious mononucleosis).

Haematological changes
Increased erythrocyte sedimentation rate. An increased erythrocyte sedimentation rate is a non-specific finding in many types of inflammation and is due to alterations in plasma proteins resulting in increased rouleaux formation of red cells.
Leukocytosis. Neutrophilia occurs in pyogenic infections and tissue destruction; eosinophilia in allergic disorders and parasitic infection; lymphocytosis in chronic infection (e.g. tuberculosis), many viral infections and in whooping cough; and monocytosis occurs in infectious mononucleosis and certain bacterial infections (e.g. tuberculosis, typhoid).
Anaemia. This may result from blood loss in the inflammatory exudate (e.g. in ulcerative colitis), haemolysis (due to bacterial toxins), and 'the anaemia of chronic disorders' due to toxic depression of the bone marrow.

Amyloidosis
Longstanding chronic inflammation (for example, in rheumatoid arthritis, tuberculosis and bronchiectasis), by elevating serum amyloid A protein (SAA), may cause amyloid to be deposited in various tissues, resulting in secondary (reactive) amyloidosis (Ch. 7).

CHRONIC INFLAMMATION

▶ Lymphocytes, plasma cells and macrophages predominate
▶ Usually primary, but may follow recurrent acute inflammation
▶ Granulomatous inflammation is a specific type of chronic inflammation
▶ A granuloma is an aggregate of epithelioid histiocytes
▶ May be complicated by secondary (reactive) amyloidosis

The word 'chronic' applied to any process implies that the process has extended over a long period of time. This is usually the case in chronic inflammation, but here the term 'chronic' takes on a much more specific meaning, in that the type of cellular reaction differs from that seen in acute inflammation. Chronic inflammation may be defined as an inflammatory process in which lymphocytes, plasma cells and macrophages predominate. As in acute inflammation, granulation and scar tissue are also formed, but in chronic inflammation they are usually more abundant. Chronic inflammation is usually primary, sometimes called chronic inflammation *ab initio*, but does occasionally follow acute inflammation.

Causes of chronic inflammation

Primary chronic inflammation

In most cases of chronic inflammation, the inflammatory response has all the histological features of chronic inflammation from the onset, and there is no initial phase of acute

Table 10.3   Some examples of primary chronic inflammation

Cause of inflammation	Examples
Resistance of infective agent to phagocytosis and intracellular killing	Tuberculosis, leprosy, brucellosis, viral infections
Endogenous materials	Necrotic adipose tissue, bone, uric acid crystals
Exogenous materials	Silica, asbestos fibres, suture materials, implanted prostheses
Some autoimmune diseases	Organ-specific disease, e.g. Hashimoto's thyroiditis, chronic gastritis of pernicious anaemia Non-organ-specific autoimmune disease, e.g. rheumatoid arthritis Contact hypersensitivity reactions, e.g. self-antigens altered by nickel
Specific diseases of unknown aetiology	Chronic inflammatory bowel disease, e.g. ulcerative colitis
Primary granulomatous diseases	Crohn's disease, sarcoidosis

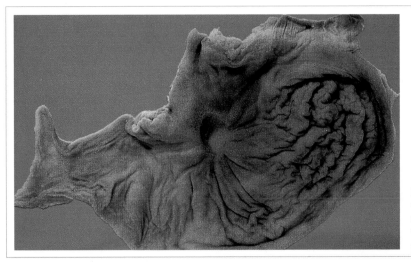

Fig. 10.15 Chronic peptic ulcer of the stomach. Continuing tissue destruction and repair cause replacement of the gastric wall muscle layers by fibrous tissue. As the fibrous tissue contracts, permanent distortion of the gastric shape may result.

inflammation. Some examples of primary chronic inflammation are listed in Table 10.3.

Transplant rejection
Cellular rejection of, for example, renal transplants involves chronic inflammatory cell infiltration.

Progression from acute inflammation

Most cases of acute inflammation do not develop into the chronic form, but resolve completely. The commonest variety of acute inflammation to progress to chronic inflammation is the suppurative type. If the pus forms an abscess cavity that is deep-seated, and drainage is delayed or inadequate, then by the time that drainage occurs the abscess will have developed thick walls composed of granulation and fibrous tissues. The rigid walls of the abscess cavity therefore fail to come together after drainage, and the stagnating pus within the cavity becomes organised by the ingrowth of granulation tissue, eventually to be replaced by a fibrous scar.

Good examples of such chronic abscesses include: an abscess in the bone marrow cavity (osteomyelitis), which is notoriously difficult to eradicate; and empyema thoracis that has been inadequately drained.

Another feature that favours progression to chronic inflammation is the presence of indigestible material. This may be keratin from a ruptured epidermal cyst, or fragments of necrotic bone as in the sequestrum of chronic osteomyelitis (Ch. 25). These materials are relatively inert, and are resistant to the action of lysosomal enzymes. The most indigestible forms of material are inert foreign body materials, for example some types of surgical suture, wood, metal or glass implanted into a wound, or deliberately implanted prostheses such as artificial joints. It is not known why the presence of foreign body materials gives rise to chronic suppuration, but it is a well-established fact that suppuration will not cease without surgical removal of the material.

Foreign bodies have in common the tendency to provoke a special type of chronic inflammation called 'granulomatous inflammation' (p. 216), and to cause macrophages to form multinucleate giant cells called 'foreign body giant cells'.

Recurrent episodes of acute inflammation

Recurring cycles of acute inflammation and healing eventually result in the clinicopathological entity of chronic inflammation. The best example of this is chronic cholecystitis, normally due to the presence of gallstones (Ch. 16); multiple recurrent episodes of acute inflammation lead to replacement of the gallbladder wall muscle by fibrous tissue and the predominant cell type becomes the lymphocyte rather than the neutrophil polymorph.

Macroscopic appearances of chronic inflammation

The commonest appearances of chronic inflammation are:
- *Chronic ulcer*, such as a chronic peptic ulcer of the stomach with breach of the mucosa, a base lined by granulation tissue and with fibrous tissue extending through the muscle layers of the wall (Fig. 10.15).
- *Chronic abscess cavity*, for example osteomyelitis, empyema thoracis.
- *Thickening of the wall of a hollow viscus* by fibrous tissue in the presence of a chronic inflammatory cell infiltrate, for example Crohn's disease, chronic cholecystitis (Fig. 10.16).
- *Granulomatous inflammation*, perhaps with caseous necrosis as in chronic fibrocaseous tuberculosis of the lung.
- *Fibrosis*, which may become the most prominent feature of the chronic inflammatory reaction when most of the chronic inflammatory cell infiltrate has subsided. This is commonly seen in chronic cholecystitis, 'hour-glass contracture' of the stomach, where fibrosis distorts the gastric wall and may even lead to acquired pyloric stenosis, and in the strictures that characterise Crohn's disease (Ch. 15).

Microscopic features of chronic inflammation

The cellular infiltrate consists characteristically of lymphocytes, plasma cells and macrophages. A few eosinophil polymorphs may be present, but neutrophil polymorphs are scarce. Some of the macrophages may form multinucleate giant cells. Exudation of fluid is not a prominent feature, but there may

Fig. 10.16   Gallbladder showing chronic cholecystitis. The wall is greatly thickened by fibrous tissue. One of the gallstones was impacted in Hartmann's pouch, a saccular dilatation at the gallbladder neck.

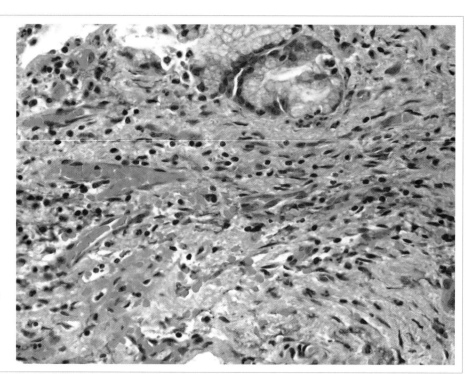

Fig. 10.17   Chronic inflammation in the wall of a gallbladder that has experienced previous episodes of acute cholecystitis. Aggregates of lymphocytes are appearing and there are ingrowing fibroblasts.

be production of new fibrous tissue from granulation tissue (Figs 10.15–10.17). There may be evidence of continuing destruction of tissue at the same time as tissue regeneration and repair. Tissue necrosis may be a prominent feature, especially in granulomatous conditions such as tuberculosis. It is not usually possible to predict the causative factor from the histological appearances in chronic inflammation.

Paracrine stimulation of connective tissue proliferation

Healing involves regeneration and migration of specialised cells, while the predominant features in repair are angiogenesis

followed by fibroblast proliferation and collagen synthesis resulting in granulation tissue. These processes are regulated by low molecular weight proteins called *growth factors* which bind to specific receptors on cell membranes and trigger a series of events culminating in cell proliferation (Table 10.4).

Cellular co-operation in chronic inflammation

The lymphocytic tissue infiltrate contains two main types of lymphocyte (described more fully in Ch. 9). B-lymphocytes, on contact with antigen, become progressively transformed into plasma cells, which are cells specially adapted for the production of antibodies. The other main type of lymphocyte, the T-lymphocyte, is responsible for cell-mediated immunity. On contact with antigen, T-lymphocytes produce a range of soluble factors called cytokines, which have a number of important activities.

- *Recruitment of macrophages into the area.* It is thought that macrophages are recruited into the area mainly via factors such as migration inhibition factor (MIF) which trap macrophages in the tissue. Macrophage activation factors (MAFs) stimulate macrophage phagocytosis and killing of bacteria.
- *Production of inflammatory mediators.* T-lymphocytes produce a number of inflammatory mediators, including cytokines, chemotactic factors for neutrophils, and factors that increase vascular permeability.
- *Recruitment of other lymphocytes.* Interleukins stimulate other lymphocytes to divide and confer on other lymphocytes the ability to mount cell-mediated immune responses to a variety of antigens. T-lymphocytes also co-operate with B-lymphocytes, assisting them in recognising antigens.
- *Destruction of target cells.* Factors, such as perforins (Ch. 6), are produced that destroy other cells by damaging their cell membranes.
- *Interferon production.* Interferon-gamma, produced by activated T-cells, has antiviral properties and, in turn, activates macrophages. Interferon-alpha and -beta, produced by macrophages and fibroblasts, have antiviral properties and activate natural killer (NK) cells and macrophages.

These pathways of cellular co-operation are summarised in Figure 10.18.

Table 10.4 Growth factors involved in healing and repair associated with inflammation

Growth factor	Abbreviation	Main function
Epidermal growth factor	EGF	Regeneration of epithelial cells
Transforming growth factor-alpha	TGF-alpha	Regeneration of epithelial cells
Transforming growth factor-beta	TGF-beta	Stimulates fibroblast proliferation and collagen synthesis Controls epithelial regeneration
Platelet-derived growth factor	PDGF	Mitogenic and chemotactic for fibroblasts and smooth muscle cells
Fibroblast growth factor	FGF	Stimulates fibroblast proliferation, angiogenesis and epithelial cell regeneration
Insulin-like growth factor-1	IGF-1	Synergistic effect with other growth factors
Tumour necrosis factor	TNF	Stimulates angiogenesis

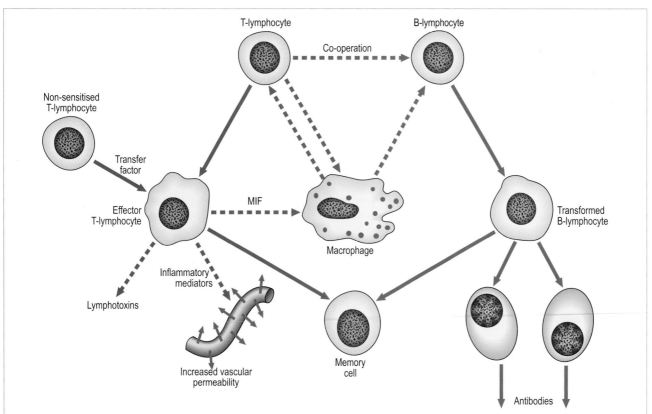

Fig. 10.18 Cellular co-operation in chronic inflammation. Solid arrows show pathways of cellular differentiation. Dotted arrows show intercellular communication. (MIF, migration inhibition factors.)

Macrophages in chronic inflammation

Macrophages are relatively large cells, up to 30 μm in diameter, that move by amoeboid motion through the tissues. They respond to certain chemotactic stimuli (possibly cytokines and antigen–antibody complexes) and have considerable phagocytic capabilities for the ingestion of micro-organisms and cell debris. When neutrophil polymorphs ingest micro-organisms, they usually bring about their own destruction and thus have a limited life-span of up to about 3 days. Macrophages can ingest a wider range of materials than can polymorphs and, being long-lived, they can harbour viable organisms if they are not able to kill them by their lysosomal enzymes. Examples of organisms that can survive inside macrophages include mycobacteria, such as *Mycobacterium tuberculosis* and *M. leprae*, and organisms such as *Histoplasma capsulatum*. When macrophages participate in the delayed-type hypersensitivity response (Ch. 9) to these types of organism, they often die in the process, contributing to the large areas of necrosis by release of their lysosomal enzymes.

Macrophages in inflamed tissues are derived from blood monocytes that have migrated out of vessels and have become transformed in the tissues. They are thus part of the mononuclear phagocyte system (Fig. 10.19), also known as the reticulo-endothelial system.

The mononuclear phagocyte system, shown in Figure 10.19, is now known to include macrophages, fixed tissue histiocytes in many organs and, probably, the osteoclasts of bone. All are derived from monocytes, which in turn are derived from a haemopoietic stem cell in the bone marrow.

The 'activation' of macrophages as they migrate into an area of inflammation involves an increase in size, protein synthesis, mobility, phagocytic activity and content of lysosomal enzymes. Electron microscopy reveals that the cells have a roughened cell membrane bearing lamellipodia, while the cytoplasm contains numerous dense bodies—phagolysosomes (formed by the fusion of lysosomes with phagocytic vacuoles).

Macrophages produce a range of important cytokines, including interferon-alpha and -beta, interleukin-1, -6 and -8, and tumour necrosis factor-alpha (TNF) (see Ch. 9).

Specialised forms of macrophages and granulomatous inflammation

A *granuloma* is an aggregate of epithelioid histiocytes (Fig. 10.20). It may also contain other cell types such as lymphocytes and histiocytic giant cells. Granulomatous diseases comprise some of the most widespread and serious diseases in the world, such as tuberculosis and leprosy.

Epithelioid histiocytes

Named for their vague histological resemblance to epithelial cells, epithelioid histiocytes have large vesicular nuclei, plentiful eosinophilic cytoplasm and are often rather elongated. They tend to be arranged in clusters. They have little phagocytic activity, but appear to be adapted to a secretory function. The full range, or purpose, of their secretory products is not known, although one product is *angiotensin converting enzyme*. Measurement of the activity of this enzyme in the blood can act as a marker for systemic granulomatous disease, such as sarcoidosis.

The appearance of granulomas may be augmented by the presence of caseous necrosis (as in tuberculosis) or by the conversion of some of the histiocytes into multinucleate giant cells. The association of granulomas with eosinophils often indicates a parasitic infection (e.g. worms). A common feature of many of the stimuli that induce granulomatous inflammation is indigestibility of particulate matter by macrophages. In other conditions, such as the systemic granulomatous disease *sarcoidosis*, there appear to be far-reaching derangements in immune responsiveness favouring granulomatous inflammation. In other instances, small traces of elements such as beryllium induce granuloma formation, but the way in which they

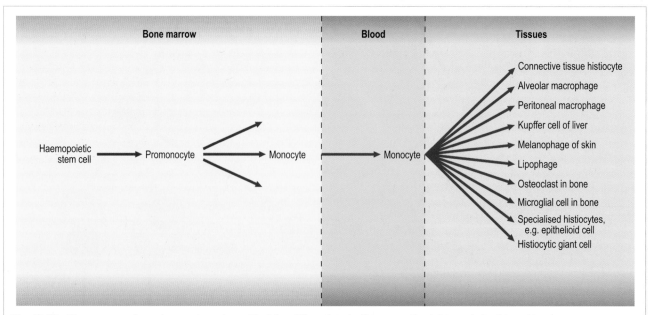

Fig. 10.19   The mononuclear phagocyte system. All of the differentiated cell types on the right are derived from blood monocytes.

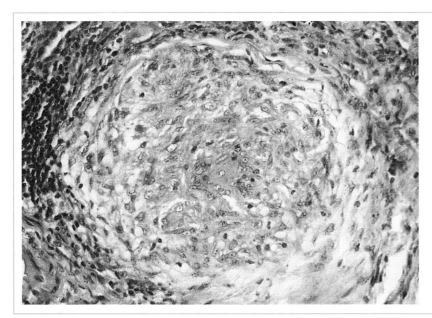

Fig. 10.20   A granuloma: a collection of epithelioid histiocytes. This example is from a case of sarcoidosis involving the liver.

Table 10.5 Causes of granulomatous disease	
Cause	**Example**
Specific infections	Mycobacteria, e.g. tuberculosis, leprosy, atypical mycobacteria Many types of fungi Parasites, larvae, eggs and worms Syphilis
Materials that resist digestion	Endogenous, e.g. keratin, necrotic bone, cholesterol crystals, sodium urate Exogenous, e.g. talc, silica, suture materials, oils, silicone
Specific chemicals	Beryllium
Drugs	Hepatic granulomas due to allopurinol, phenylbutazone, sulphonamides
Unknown	Crohn's disease Sarcoidosis Wegener's granulomatosis

induce the inflammation is unknown. Some of the commoner granulomatous conditions are shown in Table 10.5.

Histiocytic giant cells

Histiocytic giant cells tend to form where particulate matter that is indigestible by macrophages accumulates, for example inert minerals such as silica, or bacteria such as tubercle bacilli, which have cell walls containing mycolic acids and waxes that resist enzymatic digestion. Histiocytic giant cells form particularly when foreign particles are too large to be ingested by just one macrophage. The multinucleate giant cells, which may contain over 100 nuclei, are thought to develop 'by accident' when two or more macrophages attempt simultaneously to engulf the same particle; their cell membranes fuse and the cells unite. The multinucleate giant cells resulting have little phagocytic activity and no known function. They are given specific names according to their microscopic appearance.

Langhans' giant cells
Langhans' giant cells have a horseshoe arrangement of peripheral nuclei at one pole of the cell and are characteristically seen in tuberculosis, although they may be seen in other granulomatous conditions. (They must not be confused with Langerhans' cells, the dendritic antigen-presenting cells of the epidermis; Ch. 9.)

Foreign body giant cells
So-called 'foreign body giant cells' are large cells with nuclei randomly scattered throughout their cytoplasm. They are characteristically seen in relation to particulate foreign body material.

Touton giant cells
Touton giant cells have a central ring of nuclei; the peripheral cytoplasm is clear due to accumulated lipid. They are seen at sites of adipose tissue breakdown and in xanthomas (tumour-like aggregates of lipid-laden macrophages).

Although giant cells are commonly seen in granulomas, they do not constitute a defining feature. Solitary giant cells in the absence of epithelioid histiocytes do not constitute a granuloma.

Role of inflammation in systemic and organ-specific diseases

Acute inflammation is involved in the cardiovascular system in the response to acute myocardial infarction (Ch. 13) and the generation of some complications of myocardial infarction such as cardiac rupture. It is also involved in infective endocarditis, pericarditis and myocarditis, and in some vasculitic syndromes. One mechanism of vasculitis is that immune complexes deposit in the vessel wall, activate complement, and thus excite an inflammatory response.

Commonly confused conditions and entities relating to inflammation	
Commonly confused	**Distinction and explanation**
Acute and *chronic*	In inflammation, acute and chronic denote both the dynamics and character of the process. *Acute* inflammation has a relatively rapid onset and, usually, resolution, and neutrophil polymorphs are the most abundant cells. *Chronic* inflammation has a relatively insidious onset, prolonged course and slow resolution, and lymphocytes, plasma cells and macrophages (sometimes with granuloma formation) are the most abundant cells.
Exudate and *transudate*	*Exudates* have a high protein content because they result from increased vascular permeability. *Transudates* have a low protein content because the vessels have normal permeability characteristics.
Granuloma and *granulation tissue*	A *granuloma* is an aggregate of epithelioid histiocytes and a feature of some specific chronic inflammatory disorders. *Granulation tissue* is an important component of healing and comprises small blood vessels in a connective tissue matrix with myofibroblasts.
Monocytes, macrophages and *histiocytes*	*Monocytes* are the newly formed cells of the mononuclear phagocyte system. After a few hours in the blood, they enter tissues and undergo further differentiation into *macrophages*. Some macrophages in tissues have specific features and names (e.g. Kupffer cells); others are referred to as *histiocytes*.
Fibrin and *fibrous*	*Fibrin* is deposited in blood vessels and tissues or on surfaces (e.g. in acute inflammation) as a result of the action of thrombin on fibrinogen. *Fibrous* describes the texture of a non-mineralised tissue of which the principal component is collagen (e.g. scar tissue).

Chronic inflammation is involved in myocardial fibrosis after myocardial infarction.

Inflammation makes an important contribution to development of atheroma (Ch. 13). Macrophages adhere to endothelium, migrate into the arterial intima and, with T-lymphocytes, express cell adhesion molecules which recruit other cells into the area. The macrophages are involved in processing the lipids that accumulate in atheromatous plaques.

Inflammation also features in the tissue injury associated with neurodegenerative disorders of the central nervous system. Multiple sclerosis is a relatively common chronic demyelinating neurodegenerative disorder in which chronic inflammation plays an important role. Perivascular cuffing by plasma cells and T lymphocytes is seen in zones of white matter where macrophages break down myelin.

FURTHER READING

Badolato R, Oppenheim J J 1996 Role of cytokines, acute-phase proteins, and chemokines in the progression of rheumatoid arthritis. Seminars in Arthritis and Rheumatism 26: 526–538

Balkwill F 1997 Cytokine amplification and inhibition of immune and inflammatory responses. Journal of Viral Hepatitis 4 (Suppl 2): 6–15

Ballou S P, Kushner I 1997 Chronic inflammation in older people: recognition, consequences, and potential intervention. Clinics in Geriatric Medicine 13: 653–669

Baumert P W Jr 1995 Acute inflammation after injury. Quick control speeds rehabilitation. Postgraduate Medicine 97: 35–36

Borregard N, Sørensen O E, Theilgaard-Mönch K 2007 Neutrophil granules: a library of innate immunity proteins. Trends in Immunology 28: 340–345

Brewer D P 1972 Activities of the neutrophil polymorph. British Medical Journal 5810: 396–400

Burger D, Dayer J M 1995 Inhibitory cytokines and cytokine inhibitors. Neurology 45 (Suppl 6): S39–S43

Cohen M S 1994 Molecular events in the activation of human neutrophils for microbial killing. Clinical Infectious Diseases 18 (Suppl 2): 170–179

Collins T 2001 Leukocyte recruitment, endothelial cell adhesion molecules, and transcriptional control. Insights for drug discovery. Kluwer, London

Di Perry G, Bonora S, Allegranzi B, Concia E 1999 Granulomatous inflammation and transmission of infectious disease. Immunology Today 20: 337–338

Edwards S W 1994 Biochemistry and physiology of the neutrophil. Cambridge University Press, Cambridge

Epstein W L, Fukuyama K 1989 Mechanisms of granulomatous inflammation. Immunology Series 46: 687–721

Faurschou M, Borregaard N 2003 Neutrophil granules and secretory vesicles in inflammation. Microbes and Infection 5: 1317–1327

Formela L J, Galloway S W, Kingsnorth A N 1995 Inflammatory mediators in acute pancreatitis. British Journal of Surgery 82: 6–13

Furie M B, Randolph G J 1995 Chemokines and tissue injury. American Journal of Pathology 146: 1287–1301

Galli S J 1997 The Paul Kallos Memorial Lecture. The mast cell: a versatile effector cell for a challenging world. International Archives of Allergy and Immunology 113: 14–22

Goldblatt D, Thrasher A J 2000 Chronic granulomatous disease. Clinical and Experimental Immunology 122: 1–9

Gordon S 1998 The role of the macrophage in immune regulation. Research in Immunology 149: 685–688

Kasama T, Miwa Y, Isozaki T, Odai T, Adachi M, Kunkel S L 2005 Neutrophil-derived cytokines: potential therapeutic targets in inflammation. Current Drug Targets 4: 273–279

Kobayashi S D, Voyich J M, DeLeo F R 2003 Regulation of neutrophil-mediated inflammatory response to infection. Microbes and Infection 5: 1337–1344

Kornfeld H, Mancino G, Colizzi V 1999 The role of macrophage in cell death and tuberculosis. Cell Death and Differentiation 6: 71–78

Lakhani S R, Dilly S A, Finlayson C J, Dogan A 2003 Basic pathology, 3rd edn. Hodder Arnold, London

Lawrence T, Gilroy D W 2007 Chronic inflammation: a failure of resolution. International Journal of Experimental Pathology 88: 85–94

Lee W Y, Chin A C, Voss S, Parkos C A 2006 In vitro neutrophil transepithelial migration. Methods in Molecular Biology 341: 205–215

Leung D Y 1997 Immunologic basis of chronic allergic diseases: clinical messages from the laboratory bench. Pediatric Research 42: 559–568

Levin N W, Ronco C 2002 Chronic inflammation: an overview. Contributions to Nephrology 137: 364–370

Levy J H 1996 The human inflammatory response. Journal of Cardiovascular Pharmacology 27 (Suppl 1): S31–S37

Ley K 2001 Physiology of inflammation. Oxford University Press, Oxford

Lue H, Kleemann R, Calandra T, Roger T, Bernhagen J 2002 Macrophage migration inhibitory factor (MIF): mechanisms of action and role in disease. Microbes and Infection 4: 449–460

Mahmoudi M, Curzen N, Gallagher P J 2007 Atherogenesis: the role of inflammation and infection. Histopathology 50: 535–546

Majno G 1998 Chronic inflammation: links with angiogenesis and wound healing. American Journal of Surgical Pathology 153: 1045–1049

Mannaioni P F, Di Bello MG, Masini E 1997 Platelets and inflammation: role of platelet-derived growth factor, adhesion molecules and histamine. Inflammation Research 46: 4–18

Sartor R B 1997 Pathogenesis and immune mechanisms of chronic inflammatory bowel diseases. American Journal of Gastroenterology 92 (Suppl): 5S–11S

Savill J 1997 Apoptosis in resolution of inflammation. Journal of Leukocyte Biology 61: 375–380

Schultz D R, Tozman E C 1995 Antineutrophil cytoplasmic antibodies: major autoantigens, pathophysiology, and disease associations. Seminars in Arthritis and Rheumatism 25: 143–159

Serhan C N, Brain S D, Buckley C D et al 2007 Resolution of inflammation: state of the art, definitions and terms. FASEB Journal 21: 325–332

Thomson A W, Lotze M T 2003 The cytokine handbook, 4th edn. Academic Press, London

Tremblay G M, Janelle M F, Bourbonnais Y 2000 Anti-inflammatory activity of neutrophil elastase inhibitors. Current Opinion in Investigational Drugs 4: 556–565

Vallance P, Collier J, Bhagat K 1997 Infection, inflammation, and infarction: does acute endothelial dysfunction provide a link? Lancet 349: 1391–1392

Walker A, Ward C, Taylor E L et al 2005 Regulation of neutrophil apoptosis and removal of apoptotic cells. Current Drug Targets 4: 447–454

11

Carcinogenesis and neoplasia

GENERAL CHARACTERISTICS OF NEOPLASMS (TUMOURS)

▶ Tumours result from genetic alterations (e.g. mutations) in cells, resulting in abnormal (neoplastic) growth persisting in the absence of the initiating causes
▶ Malignant (invasive) tumours develop in approximately 25% of individuals
▶ Incidence increases with age
▶ Structure comprises neoplastic cells and connective tissue stroma of which the vascular supply is essential for growth

Definitions

The word *tumour* means literally an abnormal swelling. However, in modern medicine, the word has a much more specific meaning. *A tumour (neoplasm) is a lesion resulting from the autonomous or relatively autonomous abnormal growth of cells that persists after the initiating stimulus has been removed.*

Tumours result from the *neoplastic transformation* of any nucleated cell in the body; the transformed cells are called *neoplastic cells.* By transformation involving a series of *genetic alterations* (e.g. mutations), cells escape permanently from normal growth regulatory mechanisms. The neoplastic cells in tumours designated *malignant* possess additional potentially lethal abnormal characteristics enabling them to *invade* and to *metastasise,* or spread, to other tissues.

Neoplastic cells grow to form abnormal swellings (except for leukaemias), but note that swellings or organ enlargement can also result from inflammation, cysts, hypertrophy or hyperplasia.

The term *neoplasm* (new growth) is synonymous with the medical meaning of the word tumour and is often used in preference because it is less ambiguous and not quite so alarming when overheard by patients. *Cancer* is a word used more in the public arena than in medicine; it has emotive connotations and generally refers to a *malignant* neoplasm.

Incidence of tumours

Malignant neoplasms—those that invade and spread and are therefore of greater clinical importance—develop in approximately 25% of the human population. The risk increases with age, but tumours can occur even in infancy (Fig. 11.1). The mortality rate is high, despite modern therapy, so that cancer accounts for about one-fifth of all deaths in developed countries. However, the mortality rate varies considerably between specific tumour types.

The relative incidence by diagnosis of various common types of cancer is shown in Fig. 11.2. Lung cancer is the most frequent malignant neoplasm in the UK and USA, and its importance is compounded by the extremely poor prognosis. In other countries other cancers are more common, and these differences often provide important aetiological clues.

For various reasons most epidemiological data on cancer incidence probably underestimate the true incidence. Not all tumours become clinically evident and, unless a thorough

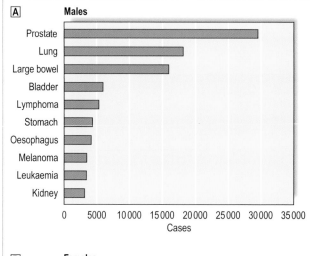

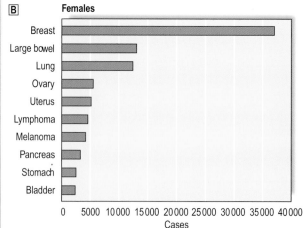

Fig. 11.2 Incidence of the ten most frequent cancers in the UK (2004). [A] Top ten cancers in males. [B] Top ten cancers in females. The data exclude non-melanoma skin cancers (e.g. basal cell carcinoma) because, although common, they are so rarely fatal. (Data published by Cancer Research UK, 2007)

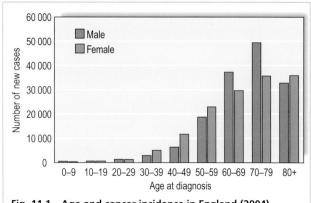

Fig. 11.1 Age and cancer incidence in England (2004). Cancer occurs at all ages but is most common over the age of 50 years. (Based on data from the Office for National Statistics)

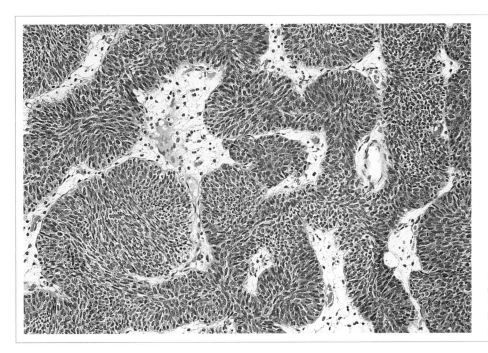

Fig. 11.3 Tumour cells and stroma. Histology of an epithelial neoplasm showing the darkly staining tumour cells embedded in a paler connective tissue stroma.

autopsy is performed, may never be detected. For example, autopsy surveys have revealed a higher than expected incidence of occult carcinoma of the prostate in elderly men, although these often minute lesions are probably of little clinical consequence. Cancer incidence may also be underestimated due to a failure of detection or diagnosis in countries and communities with poor health care.

Structure of tumours

Solid tumours consist of *neoplastic cells* and *stroma* (see below and Fig. 11.3). The neoplastic cells reproduce to a variable extent the growth pattern and synthetic activity of the parent cell of origin. Depending on their functional resemblance to the parent tissue, they continue to synthesise and secrete cell products such as collagen, mucin or keratin; these often accumulate within the tumour where they are recognisable histologically. Other cell products may be secreted into the blood where they can be used clinically to monitor tumour growth and the effects of therapy (p. 234).

Stroma

The neoplastic cells are embedded in and supported by a connective tissue framework called the stroma (from the Greek word meaning a mattress), which provides mechanical support and nutrition to the neoplastic cells. The process of stroma formation, called a *desmoplastic reaction* when it is particularly fibrous, is due to induction of connective tissue proliferation by growth factors in the immediate tumour environment.

The stroma always contains blood vessels which perfuse the tumour (Fig. 11.4). The growth of a tumour is dependent upon its ability to induce blood vessels to perfuse it, for unless it becomes permeated by a vascular supply its growth will be limited by the ability of nutrients to diffuse into it, and the tumour cells will cease growing when the nodule has attained

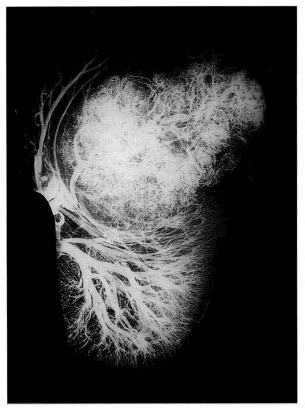

Fig. 11.4 Vascular stroma. Increased vascularity of a malignant tumour in a kidney, revealed by radiology after intra-arterial injection of X-ray contrast fluid.

a diameter of no more than 1–2mm (Fig. 11.5). Angiogenesis in tumours is induced by factors such as *vascular endothelial growth factor* (VEGF). This action is opposed by factors such as *angiostatin* and *endostatin* which have potential in cancer therapy.

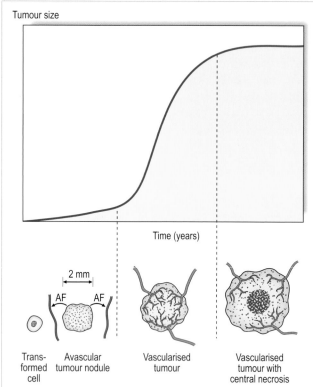

Fig. 11.5 **Tumour angiogenesis.** Neoplastic transformation of a single cell results in the growth of a tumour nodule, limited by the ability of nutrients to diffuse into it, to a diameter of 1–2 mm. Production of angiogenic factors (AF) stimulates the proliferation and ingrowth of blood vessels, enabling tumour growth to be supported by perfusion. Eventually, the tumour outgrows its blood supply, and areas of necrosis appear, resulting in slower growth.

Labels in figure: Tumour size; Time (years); 2 mm; AF; AF; Transformed cell; Avascular tumour nodule; Vascularised tumour; Vascularised tumour with central necrosis

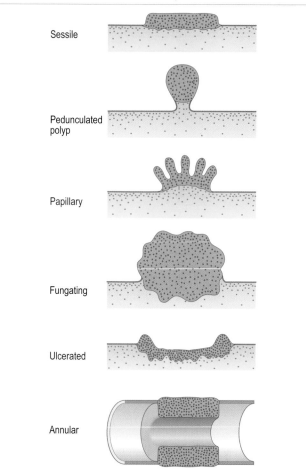

Fig. 11.6 **Tumour shapes.** Sessile, polypoid and papillary tumours are usually benign. Fungating, ulcerated or annular tumours are more likely to be malignant. Annular tumours encircling a tubular structure (e.g. intestine) are common in the large bowel, where they often cause intestinal obstruction.

Labels in figure: Sessile; Pedunculated polyp; Papillary; Fungating; Ulcerated; Annular

Fibroblasts and the matrix they secrete give some mechanical support to the tumour cells and may in addition have nutritive properties. Stromal myofibroblasts are often abundant, particularly in carcinomas of the breast; their contractility is responsible for the puckering and retraction of adjacent structures.

The stroma often contains a lymphocytic infiltrate of variable density. This may reflect a host immune reaction to the tumour (Ch. 9), a hypothesis supported by the observation that patients whose tumours are densely infiltrated by lymphocytes tend to have a better prognosis.

Tumour shape and correlation with behaviour

The gross appearance of a tumour on a surface (e.g. gastrointestinal mucosa) may be described as sessile, polypoid, papillary, fungating, ulcerated or annular (Fig. 11.6). The behaviour of a tumour (i.e. whether it is benign or malignant) can often be deduced from its gross appearance: polypoid tumours are generally benign, i.e. unlikely to spread beyond the tissue of origin (Fig. 11.7); ulceration is more commonly associated with aggressive behaviour because invasion is the defining feature of malignancy (Fig. 11.8).

Ulcerated tumours can often be distinguished from nonneoplastic ulcers, such as peptic ulcers in the stomach, because the former tend to have heaped-up or rolled edges.

The shape of connective tissue neoplasms can be misleading. Although circumscription by a clearly defined border is one of the characteristics of benign epithelial tumours, some malignant connective tissue tumours are also well circumscribed.

Tumours are usually firmer than the surrounding tissue, causing a palpable lump in accessible sites such as the breasts. Extremely hard tumours are often referred to as 'scirrhous'. Softer lesions are sometimes called 'medullary'; they occur in the thyroid and breast.

The cut surfaces of malignant tumours are often variegated due to areas of necrosis and degeneration, but some, such as lymphomas and seminomas, appear uniformly bland.

Tumour histology

Neoplasms differ histologically from their corresponding normal tissue by various features; these are useful in diagnosis and include:

- loss of differentiation
- loss of cellular cohesion

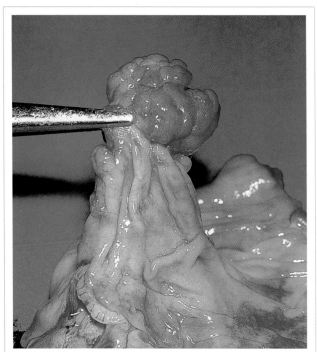

Fig. 11.7 Adenomatous polyp of the colon. This common lesion has a clearly visible stalk. Although benign, these lesions are precursors of adenocarcinoma of the large bowel. When seen endoscopically, adenomatous polyps can be removed by snaring the stalk.

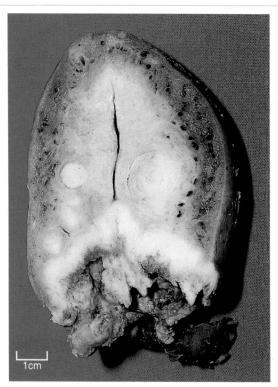

Fig. 11.8 Squamous cell carcinoma of the cervix. This uterus is invaded by a carcinoma arising in and destroying the cervix. The small round tumours in the myometrium are benign leiomyomas ('fibroids').

- nuclear enlargement
- increased mitotic activity.

These features are often seen to their greatest degree in malignant neoplasms (Fig. 11.9).

CLASSIFICATION OF TUMOURS

▶ Behavioural classification: benign or malignant
▶ Histogenetic classification: cell of origin
▶ Precise classification of individual tumours is important for planning effective treatment

Tumours are classified according to their *behaviour* and *histogenesis* (cell of origin).

Behavioural classification

The behavioural classification divides tumours into:

- benign
- malignant.

The principal pathological criteria for classifying a tumour as benign or malignant are summarised in Table 11.1. Some tumours, such as some ovarian tumours, defy precise behavioural classification, because their histology is intermediate between that associated with benign and malignant tumours; these are often referred to as 'borderline' tumours.

Benign tumours

▶ Non-invasive and remain localised
▶ Slow growth rate
▶ Close histological resemblance to parent tissue

Benign tumours remain localised. They are slowly growing lesions that do not invade the surrounding tissues or spread to other sites in the body. They are often enveloped by a thin layer of compressed connective tissue (i.e. encapsulated).

When a benign tumour arises in an epithelial or mucosal surface, the tumour grows away from the surface, because it cannot invade, often forming a *polyp* which may be either pedunculated (stalked) or sessile; this non-invasive outward direction of growth creates an *exophytic* lesion (Fig. 11.10). Histologically, benign tumours closely resemble the parent cell or tissue.

Although benign tumours are, by definition, confined to their site of origin, they may cause clinical problems due to:

- pressure on adjacent tissues (e.g. benign meningeal tumour causing epilepsy)
- obstruction to the flow of fluid (e.g. benign epithelial tumour blocking a duct)

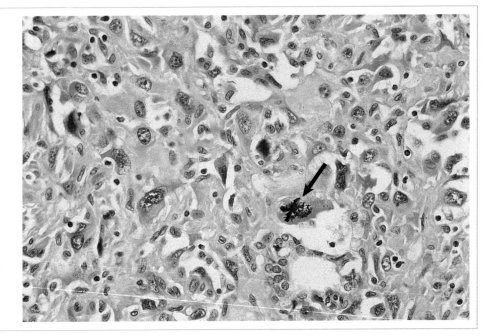

Fig. 11.9 Histological features of neoplasia. A malignant neoplasm showing no immediately recognisable differentiated features, loss of cellular cohesion, and increased nuclear size and mitotic activity. Abnormal mitoses are present (arrowed).

- production of a hormone (e.g. benign thyroid tumour causing thyrotoxicosis)
- transformation into a malignant neoplasm (e.g. adenomatous polyp progressing to an adenocarcinoma)
- anxiety (because the patient fears that the lesion may be something more sinister).

Malignant tumours

▶ Invasive and thus capable of spreading directly or by metastasis
▶ Relatively rapid growth rate
▶ Variable histological resemblance to the parent tissue

Malignant tumours are, by definition, invasive. They are typically rapidly growing and poorly circumscribed. Histologically, they resemble the parent cell or tissue to a lesser extent than do benign tumours. Malignant tumours encroach on and destroy the adjacent tissues (Fig. 11.10), enabling the neoplastic cells to penetrate the walls of blood vessels and lymphatic channels and thereby disseminate to other sites. This important process is called *metastasis* and the resulting secondary tumours are called *metastases*. Patients with widespread metastases are often said to have *carcinomatosis*.

Not all tumours categorised as malignant exhibit metastatic behaviour. For example, basal cell carcinoma of the skin (rodent ulcer) rarely forms metastases, yet is regarded as malignant because it is highly invasive and destructive.

Malignant tumours on epithelial or mucosal surfaces may form a protrusion in the early stages, but eventually invade the underlying tissue; this invasive inward direction of growth gives rise to an *endophytic* tumour. Ulceration is common.

Malignant tumours in solid organs tend to be poorly circumscribed, often with strands of neoplastic tissue penetrating adjacent normal structures. The resemblance of the cut surface of these lesions to a crab (Latin: *cancer*) gives the disease its popular name. Malignant tumours often show *central necrosis* because of inadequate vascular perfusion.

Table 11.1 Principal characteristics of benign and malignant tumours

Feature	Benign	Malignant
Growth rate	Slow	Relatively rapid
Mitoses	Infrequent	Frequent and often atypical
Histological resemblance to normal tissue	Good	Variable, often poor
Nuclear morphology	Often normal	Usually hyperchromatic, irregular outline, multiple nucleoli and pleomorphic
Invasion	No	Yes
Metastases	Never	Frequent
Border	Often circumscribed or encapsulated	Often poorly defined or irregular
Necrosis	Rare	Common
Ulceration	Rare	Common on skin or mucosal surfaces
Direction of growth on skin or mucosal surfaces	Often exophytic	Often endophytic

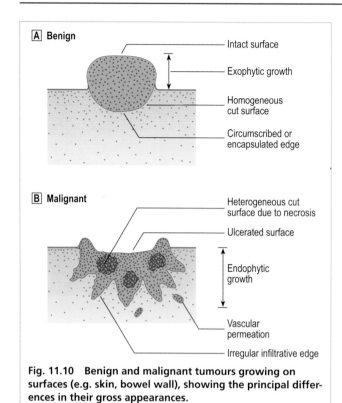

Fig. 11.10   Benign and malignant tumours growing on surfaces (e.g. skin, bowel wall), showing the principal differences in their gross appearances.

Table 11.2 Principal characteristics of carcinomas and sarcomas		
Feature	Carcinoma	Sarcoma
Origin	Epithelium	Connective tissues
Behaviour	Malignant	Malignant
Frequency	Common	Relatively rare
Preferred route of metastasis	Lymph	Blood
In situ phase	Yes	No
Age group	Usually over 50 years	Usually below 50 years

The considerable morbidity and mortality associated with malignant tumours may be due to:

- pressure on and destruction of adjacent tissue
- formation of secondary tumours (metastases)
- blood loss from ulcerated surfaces
- obstruction of flow (e.g. malignant tumour of the colon causing intestinal obstruction)
- production of a hormone (e.g. ACTH and ADH from some lung tumours)
- other paraneoplastic effects causing weight loss and debility
- anxiety and pain.

Histogenetic classification

- ▶ Classification by cell of origin
- ▶ Histologically determined
- ▶ Degree of histological resemblance to parent tissue allows tumours to be graded
- ▶ Histological grade correlates with clinical behaviour

Histogenesis—the specific cell of origin of an individual tumour—is determined by histopathological examination and specifies the tumour *type*. This is then incorporated in the name given to the tumour (e.g. squamous cell carcinoma).

Histogenetic classification includes numerous subdivisions, but the major categories of origin are:

- from epithelial cells
- from connective tissues
- from lymphoid and haemopoietic organs.

Although some general differences exist between the main groups of malignant tumours (Table 11.2), individual lesions have to be categorised more precisely both in clinical practice and for epidemiological purposes. It is inadequate to label the patient's tumour as merely having an epithelial or connective tissue origin; efforts must be made to determine the precise cell type. The classification of individual tumours is vitally important. Thorough histological examination of the tumour, sometimes using special techniques like genetic analysis and immunocytochemistry, detects subtle features that betray its provenance.

Histological grade (degree of differentiation)

The extent to which the tumour resembles histologically its cell or tissue of origin determines the tumour *grade* (Fig. 11.11) or degree of differentiation. Benign tumours are not usually further classified in this way because they nearly always closely resemble their parent tissue and grading the degree of differentiation offers no further clinical benefit in terms of choosing the most appropriate treatment. However, the degree of differentiation of malignant tumours is clinically useful both because it correlates strongly with patient survival (prognosis), and because it often indicates the most appropriate treatment. Thus, malignant tumours are usually graded either as well, moderately or poorly differentiated, or numerically, often by strict criteria, as grade 1, grade 2 or grade 3.

A well-differentiated tumour more closely resembles the parent tissue than does a poorly differentiated tumour, while moderately differentiated tumours are intermediate between these two extremes. Poorly differentiated tumours are more aggressive than well-differentiated tumours.

A few tumours are so poorly differentiated that they lack easily recognisable histogenetic features. There may even be great difficulty in deciding whether they are carcinomas or lymphomas, for example, although immunocytochemistry and genetic analysis often enable a distinction to be made. Tumours defying precise histogenetic classification are often referred to as 'anaplastic', or by some purely descriptive term such as 'spindle cell' or 'small round cell' tumour. Fortunately, advances

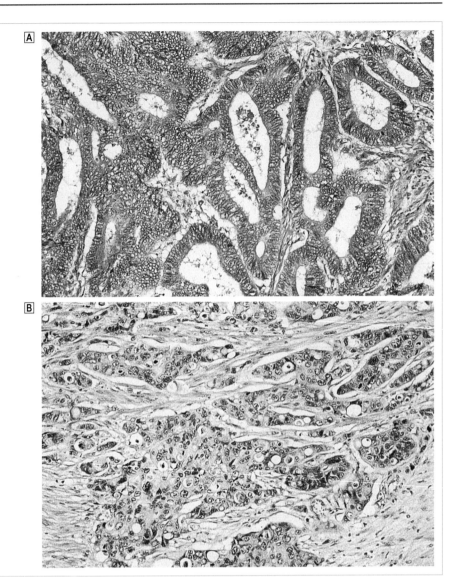

Fig. 11.11 Histological grading of differentiation. A Well-differentiated adenocarcinoma of the colon characterised by glandular structures similar to those in normal mucosa. B Poorly differentiated adenocarcinoma of the colon characterised by a more solid growth pattern with little evidence of gland formation.

in diagnostic histopathology have resulted in considerably fewer unclassifiable tumours and these descriptive terms are rapidly becoming obsolete.

NOMENCLATURE OF TUMOURS

▶ All have the suffix '-oma'
▶ Benign epithelial tumours are either papillomas or adenomas
▶ Benign connective tissue tumours have a prefix denoting the cell of origin
▶ Malignant epithelial tumours are carcinomas
▶ Malignant connective tissue tumours are sarcomas

Tumours justify separate names because, although they are all manifestations of the same disease process, each separately named tumour has its own characteristics in terms of cause, appearance and behaviour. Accurate diagnosis and naming of tumours is essential so that patients can be optimally treated. A tumour that defies accurate classification is designated *anaplastic;* such tumours are always malignant.

The specific name of an individual tumour invariably ends in the suffix '-oma'. However, relics of this suffix's former wider usage remain, as in 'granuloma' (an inflammatory aggregate of epithelioid macrophages), 'tuberculoma' (the large fibrocaseating lesion of tuberculosis), 'atheroma' (lipid-rich intimal deposits in arteries), and 'mycetoma' (a fungal mass populating a lung cavity) and 'haematoma' (mass of coagulated blood); these are *not* neoplasms.

There are exceptions to the rules of nomenclature that follow and these are a potential source of misunderstanding. For example, the words 'melanoma' and 'lymphoma' are both commonly used to refer to malignant tumours of melanocytes and lymphoid cells respectively, even though, from the rules of tumour nomenclature, these terms can be mistakenly interpreted as meaning benign lesions. To avoid confusion, which could be clinically disastrous, their names are often preceded by the word 'malignant'. Similarly, a 'myeloma' is a malignant neoplasm of plasma cells.

The suffix for neoplastic disorders of blood cells is '-aemia', as in leukaemia; but again, exceptions exist. For example, anaemia is not a neoplastic disorder.

Detailed descriptions of individual tumours are, in most instances, included in the relevant systematic chapters. Examples of tumour nomenclature are given below and, for reference, in Table 11.3.

Epithelial tumours

Epithelial tumours are named histogenetically according to their specific epithelial type and behaviourally as benign or malignant.

Benign epithelial tumours

Benign epithelial tumours are either:

- papillomas
- adenomas.

A *papilloma* is a benign tumour of non-glandular or non-secretory epithelium, such as transitional or stratified squamous epithelium (Fig. 11.12). An *adenoma* is a benign tumour of glandular or secretory epithelium (Fig. 11.13). The name of a papilloma or adenoma is incomplete unless prefixed by the name of the specific epithelial cell type or glandular origin; examples include squamous cell papilloma, transitional cell papilloma, colonic adenoma and thyroid adenoma.

Malignant epithelial tumours

Malignant tumours of epithelium are always called *carcinomas*. Carcinomas of non-glandular epithelium are always prefixed by the name of the epithelial cell type; examples include squamous cell carcinoma and transitional cell carcinoma. Malignant tumours of glandular epithelium are always designated *adenocarcinomas*, coupled with the name of the tissue of origin; examples include adenocarcinoma of the breast, adenocarcinoma of the prostate and adenocarcinoma of the stomach.

Carcinomas should be further categorised according to their degree of differentiation: their resemblance to the tissue of origin.

Carcinoma in situ

The term *carcinoma in situ* refers to an epithelial neoplasm exhibiting all the cellular features associated with malignancy, but which has not yet invaded through the epithelial basement membrane separating it from potential routes of metastasis—blood vessels and lymphatics (Fig. 11.14). Complete excision at this very early stage will guarantee a cure. Detection of carcinomas at the in situ stage, or of their precursor lesions, is the aim of population screening programmes for cervical, breast and some other carcinomas.

Table 11.3	Examples of tumour nomenclature	
Type	**Benign**	**Malignant**
Epithelial		
Squamous cell	Squamous cell papilloma	Squamous cell carcinoma
Transitional	Transitional cell papilloma	Transitional cell carcinoma
Basal cell	Basal cell papilloma	Basal cell carcinoma
Glandular	Adenoma (e.g. thyroid adenoma)	Adenocarcinoma (e.g. adenocarcinoma of breast)
Mesenchymal		
Smooth muscle	Leiomyoma	Leiomyosarcoma
Striated muscle	Rhabdomyoma	Rhabdomyosarcoma
Adipose tissue	Lipoma	Liposarcoma
Blood vessels	Angioma	Angiosarcoma
Bone	Osteoma	Osteosarcoma
Cartilage	Chondroma	Chondrosarcoma
Mesothelium	Benign mesothelioma	Malignant mesothelioma
Synovium	Synovioma	Synovial sarcoma

Fig. 11.12 Histology of a benign tumour of non-secretory epithelium: squamous cell papilloma. The tumour is non-invasive and grows outwards from the skin surface (i.e. it is exophytic). The tumour cells closely resemble those of the normal epidermis. This benign tumour is commonly caused by a human papillomavirus.

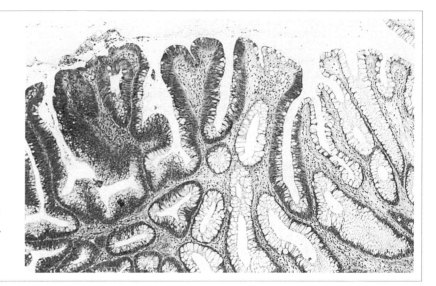

Fig. 11.13 Histology of a benign tumour of secretory epithelium: adenoma of the colon. The tumour cells closely resemble those of the normal colonic epithelium and contain mucin within their cytoplasm.

The phase of in situ growth may last for several years before invasion commences.

Carcinoma in situ may be preceded by a phase of *dysplasia*, in which the epithelium shows disordered maturation short of frank neoplasia. Some dysplastic lesions are almost certainly reversible. As there are other applications of the word 'dysplasia', as well as some difficulty in reliably distinguishing between carcinoma in situ and dysplasia in biopsies, the term is now less favoured. The term '*intra-epithelial neoplasia*', as in cervical intra-epithelial neoplasia (CIN), is used increasingly to encompass both carcinoma in situ and the precursor lesions formerly known as dysplasia.

Connective tissue and other mesenchymal tumours

Tumours of connective and other mesenchymal tissues are, like epithelial tumours, named according to their cell of origin and their behavioural classification.

Benign connective tissue and mesenchymal tumours

Benign mesenchymal tumours are named after the cell or tissue of origin suffixed by '-oma', as follows:

- *lipoma:* benign tumour of the lipocytes of adipose tissue
- *rhabdomyoma:* benign tumour of striated muscle
- *leiomyoma:* benign tumour of smooth muscle cells
- *chondroma:* benign tumour of cartilage
- *osteoma:* benign tumour of bone
- *angioma:* benign vascular tumour.

Malignant connective tissue and mesenchymal tumours

Malignant tumours of mesenchyme are always designated *sarcomas*, prefixed by the name that describes the cell or tissue of origin. Examples include:

- *liposarcoma:* malignant tumour of lipocytes
- *rhabdomyosarcoma:* malignant tumour of striated muscle
- *leiomyosarcoma:* malignant tumour of smooth muscle
- *chondrosarcoma:* malignant tumour of cartilage
- *osteosarcoma:* malignant tumour of bone
- *angiosarcoma:* malignant vascular tumour.

As with carcinomas, sarcomas can be further categorised according to their grade or degree of differentiation (Fig. 11.15).

Eponymously named tumours

Some tumours have inherited the name of the person who first recognised or described the lesion. Examples include:

- *Burkitt's lymphoma:* a B-cell lymphoma associated with the Epstein–Barr virus and malaria and endemic in certain parts of Africa
- *Ewing's sarcoma:* a malignant tumour of bone of uncertain histogenesis
- *Hodgkin's lymphoma:* a malignant lymphoma characterised by the presence of Reed–Sternberg cells
- *Kaposi's sarcoma:* a malignant neoplasm derived from vascular endothelium, now commonly associated with venereal AIDS and human herpes virus-8 infection.

Miscellaneous tumours

Most tumours can be categorised according to the scheme of nomenclature already described. There are, however, important exceptions.

Teratomas

A teratoma is a neoplasm formed of cells representing all three germ cell layers: ectoderm, mesoderm and endoderm. In their benign form, these cellular types are often easily

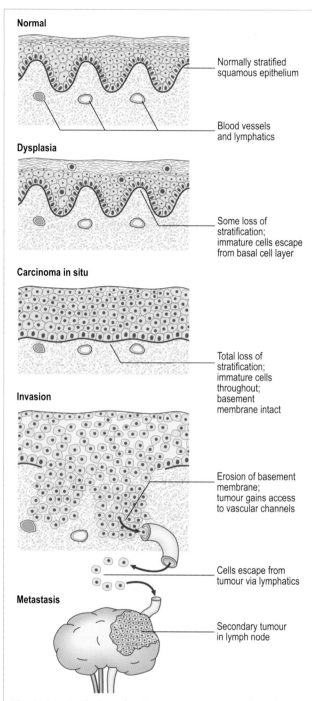

Normal

Normally stratified squamous epithelium

Blood vessels and lymphatics

Dysplasia

Some loss of stratification; immature cells escape from basal cell layer

Carcinoma in situ

Total loss of stratification; immature cells throughout; basement membrane intact

Invasion

Erosion of basement membrane; tumour gains access to vascular channels

Cells escape from tumour via lymphatics

Metastasis

Secondary tumour in lymph node

Fig. 11.14 Evolution of an invasive squamous cell carcinoma from the precursor lesions of dysplasia and carcinoma in situ (usually grouped together as intra-epithelial neoplasia). Note that the tumour cells cannot reach routes of metastasis such as blood vessels and lymphatics until the basement membrane has been breached.

Teratomas are of germ cell origin. They occur most often in the gonads, where germ cells are abundant. Although all cells in the body contain the same genetic information, arguably in germ cells this information is in the least repressed state and is therefore capable of programming such divergent lines of differentiation. Supporting evidence for a germ cell origin for teratomas comes from karyotypic analysis of their sex chromosome content. Teratomas in the female are always XX, whereas only 50% of those in the male are XX and the remainder XY; this correlates with the sex chromosome distribution in the germ cells of the two sexes.

Ovarian teratomas are almost always benign and cystic; in the testis, they are almost always malignant and relatively solid. As germ cells in the embryo originate at a site remote from the developing gonads, teratomas arise occasionally elsewhere in the body, usually in the midline, possibly from germ cells that have been arrested in their migration. These extragonadal sites for teratomas include the mediastinum and sacro-coccygeal region.

Embryonal tumours: the 'blastomas'

Some types of tumour occur almost exclusively in the very young, usually in those below 5 years of age, and bear a histological resemblance to the embryonic form of the organ in which they arise. Examples include:

- *retinoblastoma*, which arises in the eye and for which there is an inherited predisposition
- *nephroblastoma* or *Wilms' tumour*, which arises in the kidney
- *neuroblastoma*, which arises in the adrenal medulla or nerve ganglia and occasionally 'matures' into a harmless benign ganglioneuroma
- *hepatoblastoma*, which arises in the liver.

Mixed tumours

Mixed tumours show a characteristic combination of cell types. The best example is the mixed parotid tumour (pleomorphic salivary adenoma); this consists of glands embedded in a cartilaginous or mucinous matrix derived from the myoepithelial cells of the gland. Another common mixed tumour is the fibroadenoma of the breast, a lobular tumour consisting of epithelium-lined glands or clefts in a loose fibrous tissue matrix.

The occurrence of mixed tumours in an individual organ can sometimes be predicted from its embryology. This is illustrated by the Müllerian tract tumours that occur in the female genital tract; these often contain a mixture of carcinomatous and sarcomatous elements reflecting the intrinsic capacity of the tissue for divergent differentiation.

A tumour may also have a mixed appearance because of metaplasia within it. For example, transitional cell carcinomas of the bladder sometimes have foci of glandular or squamous differentiation.

Carcinosarcomas combine the appearances of carcinoma and sarcoma in one tumour, as a result of either collision of adjacent carcinoma and sarcoma or divergent carcinomatous and sarcomatous differentiation from one original transformed cell.

recognised; the tumour may contain teeth and hair, and, on histology, respiratory epithelium, cartilage, muscle, neural tissue, etc. In their malignant form, these representatives of ectoderm, mesoderm and endoderm will be less easily identifiable.

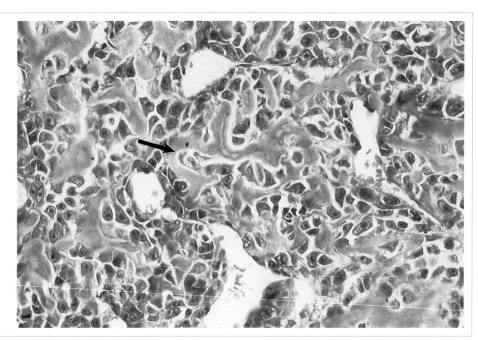

Fig. 11.15 Osteosarcoma. Histology showing pleomorphic tumour cells sufficiently differentiated to produce the amorphous pink-stained osteoid (arrow) lying between them.

Neuroendocrine tumours

Neuroendocrine tumours are derived from peptide hormone-secreting cells scattered diffusely in various epithelial tissues. These cells are sometimes referred to as APUD cells; this acronym signifies their biochemical properties (amine content and/or precursor uptake and decarboxylation). (For this reason, the tumours have been called 'apudomas'.)

The name of those neuroendocrine tumours producing a specific peptide hormone is usually derived from the name of the hormone, together with the suffix '-oma'. For example, the insulin-producing tumour originating from the beta-cells of the islets of Langerhans is called an insulinoma. There are exceptions: for example, the calcitonin-producing tumour of the thyroid gland is called a 'medullary carcinoma of the thyroid gland' because it was described as a specific entity before calcitonin had been discovered.

Neuroendocrine tumours of the gut and respiratory tract that do not produce any known peptide hormone are called *carcinoid tumours*. The appendix is the commonest site, but, here, these tumours are usually an incidental finding of little clinical significance. Carcinoids arising elsewhere (the small bowel is the next commonest site) often metastasise to mesenteric lymph nodes and the liver. Extensive metastases lead to the carcinoid syndrome (tachycardia, sweating, skin flushing, anxiety and diarrhoea) due to excessive production of 5-hydroxytryptamine and prostaglandins.

Many neuroendocrine tumours are functionally active, and clinical syndromes often result from excessive secretion of their products (Table 11.4).

These neoplasms often pursue an indolent course, growing relatively slowly and metastasising late. Their behaviour cannot always be predicted from their histological features.

Table 11.4 Some neuroendocrine tumours and their associated clinical syndromes

Tumour	Clinical syndrome
Insulinoma	Episodes of hypoglycaemia
Gastrinoma	Extensive peptic ulceration of the upper gut (Zollinger–Ellison syndrome)
Phaeochromocytoma	Paroxysmal hypertension
Carcinoid	If metastases are present, flushing, palpitations and pulmonary valve stenosis

Some individuals inherit a familial predisposition to develop neuroendocrine tumours; they have a multiple endocrine neoplasia (MEN) syndrome (Ch. 17).

Hamartomas

A hamartoma is a tumour-like lesion, the growth of which is co-ordinated with the individual; it lacks the autonomy of a true neoplasm. Hamartomas are always benign and usually consist of two or more mature cell types normally found in the organ in which the lesion arises. A common example occurs in the lung, where a hamartoma typically consists of a mixture of cartilage and bronchial-type epithelium (the so-called 'adenochondroma'; Ch. 14). Pigmented naevi or 'moles' (Ch. 24) may also be considered as hamartomatous lesions. Their clinical importance is:

- hamartomas may be mistaken for malignant neoplasms, on a chest X-ray for example
- hamartomas are sometimes associated with clinical syndromes, as, for example, in tuberous sclerosis (Ch. 26).

Cysts

A cyst is a fluid-filled space lined by epithelium. Cysts are not necessarily tumours or neoplasms but, because they may have local effects similar to those produced by true tumours and some tumours are typically cystic, it is pertinent to consider them here. Common types of cyst are:

- *congenital* (e.g. branchial and thyroglossal cysts) due to embryological defects
- *neoplastic* (e.g. cystadenoma, cystadenocarcinoma, cystic teratoma)
- *parasitic* (e.g. hydatid cysts due to *Echinococcus granulosus*)
- *retention* (e.g. epidermoid and pilar cysts of the skin)
- *implantation* (e.g. as a result of surgical or accidental implantation of epidermis).

The only type of cyst whose aetiology merits its inclusion within this chapter is the neoplastic cyst. This is seen most commonly in the ovary, where it may be either a benign cystic teratoma, filled with sebaceous material, or a cystadenoma or cystadenocarcinoma, each of which may be filled with either serous fluid or mucus depending on the secretory properties of the lining epithelium.

BIOLOGY OF TUMOUR CELLS

▶ No single biological feature is unique to neoplastic cells
▶ Neoplastic cells are relatively or absolutely autonomous, unresponsive to extracellular growth control
▶ Neoplastic cells frequently have quantitative and qualitative abnormalities of DNA
▶ Tumour products include fetal substances and unexpected hormones

Contrary to past claims and an enduring hope, there is no therapeutically exploitable feature unique to neoplastic cells other than the general property of relative or absolute growth autonomy. Many of the other features have normal counterparts: mitotic activity is a feature also of regenerating cells; placental trophoblast is invasive; and the nucleated cells of the blood and lymph wander freely around the body, settling in other sites.

The autonomy of neoplastic cells is often relative rather than absolute. For example, approximately two-thirds of breast carcinomas contain oestrogen receptors; these tumours are better differentiated than receptor-negative breast carcinomas and they have a better prognosis. Furthermore, if women with oestrogen receptor-positive breast carcinomas are given tamoxifen (a drug that blocks the receptor) they survive longer than women with receptor-positive tumours who have not been treated in this way.

One of the many difficulties in studying tumours is their genetic instability, leading to the formation of many clones with divergent properties within one tumour. This is often reflected in the histology which may show a heterogeneous growth pattern, some areas appearing better differentiated than others. Clinically, this instability and consequent cellular

heterogeneity is important because thereby some tumours resist chemotherapy; consequently, many chemotherapy regimes involve a combination of agents administered simultaneously or sequentially.

Cellular immortalisation

Cells that have undergone neoplastic transformation appear immortal, especially when studied in cell cultures. Whereas normal untransformed cells have a limited life-span, neoplastic cells have a prolonged or indefinite life-span. This is enabled by:

- *autocrine growth stimulation* due to abnormal expression of genes (i.e. oncogenes) encoding for growth factors, receptors or intracellular signals
- *reduced apoptosis* due to abnormal expression of apoptosis-inhibiting genes (e.g. *bcl*-2)
- *telomerase*, an enzyme not normally present in most untransformed cells, but which prevents the telomeric shortening with each cell cycle that would eventually restrict the number of cell replication cycles (Ch. 12).

DNA of tumour cells

Tumour cells have abnormal nuclear DNA. The total amount of DNA per cell commonly exceeds that of the normal diploid (2N) population. This is evident in histological sections as *nuclear hyperchromasia*. The amount of DNA may increase in exact multiples of the diploid state (polyploidy) such as tetraploid (4N) and octaploid (8N); alternatively there may be aneuploidy—the presence of inexact multiples of DNA per cell.

Aneuploidy and *polyploidy* are associated with increased tumour aggressiveness and are recognisable in histological sections as variations in nuclear size and staining (*pleomorphism*).

At a chromosomal level these abnormalities of DNA are associated with the presence of additional chromosomes and often with chromosomal translocations. Some of these *karyotypic abnormalities* have a regular association with specific tumours; the best known and one of the most consistent is the association of the Philadelphia chromosome with chronic myeloid leukaemia.

Genetic abnormalities are being discovered with increasing frequency in tumours. Some of these may be relatively late events, epiphenomena with no central role in the cancer process. However, others are of fundamental importance, appearing at an early stage in the development of the tumour. Abnormalities of *oncogenes* and *tumour suppressor genes* are of considerable interest in this regard because of their central involvement in carcinogenesis (p. 246).

Mitotic and apoptotic activity

Malignant tumours frequently exhibit more mitotic activity than the corresponding normal cell population. In histological sections, mitoses are abundant, and mitotic figures are often grossly abnormal, showing tripolar and other bizarre arrangements. Cellular proliferation can be estimated by mitosis counting, DNA measurements and determination of the frequency of expression of cell cycle-associated proteins (e.g. Ki-67 antigen). Prognostic information can be derived from these estimations: higher frequencies of cellular proliferation are associated with a worse prognosis.

However, assessment of the growth characteristics of a tumour must involve also an appraisal of the rate of cell loss, through either ischaemic necrosis or apoptotic cell death. Although tumours often contain abundant apoptotic bodies, a common biological defect of neoplastic cells is abrogation of the cell death mechanisms. In some lymphomas, for example, this is mediated by abnormal expression of *bcl*-2, an apoptosis-inhibiting gene.

Metabolic abnormalities

Although tumour cells show a tendency towards *anaerobic glycolysis,* there are no metabolic abnormalities entirely specific to the neoplastic process. The known metabolic abnormalities of tumour cells are simply discordant with the normal physiological state of the tissue or host.

The surface of tumour cells is abnormal. Tumour cells are less cohesive. In many neoplasms, poor cellular cohesion is due to a reduction in specialised intercellular junctions such as desmosomes. This loss of adhesiveness enables malignant tumour cells to spread through tissues and detach themselves to populate distant organs.

Tumour cells may retain the capacity to synthesise and secrete products characteristic of the normal cell type from which they are derived, often doing so in an excessive and uncontrolled manner. In addition, tumours often show evidence of *gene derepression*. All somatic cells contain the same genetic information, but only a small proportion of the genome is transcribed into RNA and translated into protein in any normal cell. Most genes are repressed, and only those required for the function of the particular cell are selectively expressed. However, in many tumour cells, some genes become *derepressed*, resulting in the inappropriate synthesis of unexpected substances.

Tumour products

The major types of tumour product are:

- substances appropriate to their cell of origin (e.g. keratin from a squamous cell carcinoma, steroid hormones from an adrenocortical adenoma)
- substances inappropriate or unexpected for their cell of origin (e.g. ACTH and ADH from small cell carcinomas of the lung)
- fetal reversion substances (e.g. carcinoembryonic antigen from adenocarcinomas of the gastrointestinal tract, alpha-fetoprotein from liver cell carcinomas and testicular teratomas)
- substances required for growth and invasion (e.g. autocrine growth factors, angiogenic factors, collagenases).

Some tumour products are useful as markers for diagnosis or follow-up (Table 11.5). They can be detected in histological sections or their concentrations measured in the blood. Rising blood levels suggest the presence of tumour; falling levels indicate a sustained response to therapy (Fig. 11.16).

CARCINOGENESIS

Carcinogenesis is the process that results in the transformation of normal cells to neoplastic cells by causing permanent genetic alterations.

Neoplasms arise from single cells that have become transformed by cumulative mutational events. Because of this presumed single-cell origin, neoplasms are said to be *clonal* proliferations; this distinguishes them from non-neoplastic masses which are typically *polyclonal*. Spontaneous mutations during normal DNA replication are probably common, but many are rectified by repair mechanisms. The probability of neoplastic transformation increases with the number of cell divisions experienced by a cell; this may explain why the incidence of cancer increases with age. Exposure to carcinogens increases the probability of specific mutational events.

A *carcinogen* is an environmental agent participating in the causation of tumours. Such agents are said to be *carcinogenic* (cancer causing) or *oncogenic* (tumour causing). The ultimate site of action of all carcinogens is the DNA in which genes are encoded. Carcinogens are therefore also mutagenic. Very often more than one carcinogen is necessary for the complete neoplastic transformation of a cell, and there is good evidence that the process occurs in several discrete steps; this is the *multistep hypothesis.*

Once established, neoplastic behaviour does not require the continued presence of the carcinogen. It is rather a 'hit-and-run' situation and evidence of the specific causative agent(s) is not usually found in the eventual tumours. Exceptions include some suspected carcinogenic viruses, genetic material of which persists in the resulting tumours, and some insoluble substances, such as asbestos, which cannot be eliminated from the tissues. The 'hit-and-run' character of carcinogenesis is one of several reasons why carcinogens have proved so elusive.

Recent research has considerably improved our knowledge and understanding of the molecular basis of carcinogenesis. Genetic alterations are absolutely fundamental to the carcinogenic process. The central role of these genetic abnormalities will be considered in detail after the different classes of carcinogen have been described.

Identification of carcinogens

- ▶ Most cancers are attributed to environmental causes
- ▶ Laboratory testing can identify some carcinogens
- ▶ Some carcinogens can be suspected from epidemiological studies
- ▶ Many carcinogens require co-factors
- ▶ Long latent interval between exposure and detection of the consequent tumour hampers identification

Most tumours are thought to result from an environmental cause, although there is increasing evidence, in some tumours, of an inherited risk. It has been estimated that approximately 85% of the cancer risk is due to environmental agents.

Ethics prohibit the testing of suspected carcinogens in humans, so much of our knowledge of carcinogenesis in humans is derived from indirect or circumstantial evidence.

Table 11.5 Tumours secreting markers used in diagnosis or follow-up

Tumour	Marker	Comment
Myeloma	Monoclonal immunoglobulin Bence Jones protein	In blood Immunoglobulin light chain (kappa or lambda) in urine
Hepatocellular carcinoma	Alpha-fetoprotein (AFP)	Also associated with testicular teratoma
Gastrointestinal adenocarcinomas	Carcinoembryonic antigen (CEA)	False positives occur in some non-neoplastic conditions
Neuroendocrine tumours	Peptide hormones (e.g. insulin, gastrin)	Excessive hormone production may have clinical effects
Phaeochromocytoma	Vanillyl mandelic acid (VMA)	Metabolite of catecholamines in urine
Carcinoid	5-Hydroxyindole-acetic acid (5-HIAA)	Metabolite of 5-hydroxytryptamine (5-HT) in urine
Choriocarcinoma	Human chorionic gonadotrophin (hCG)	In blood or urine
Malignant teratoma	AFP hCG	In blood In blood or urine

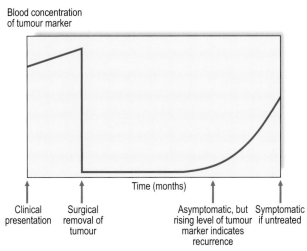

Fig. 11.16 Use of tumour markers to monitor clinical progress. Abnormally high levels of the marker can be used to detect tumours before they become symptomatic, either by screening a population at risk or, as in the example shown here, by regular monitoring to detect early recurrences. The events shown here could take place over a total period of 12 months.

Identification is hampered both by the complexity of the human environment, which makes it difficult to isolate a single causative factor from the many possible candidates, and by the very long time interval between exposure to a carcinogen and the appearance of signs and symptoms leading to the diagnosis of the tumour; this *latent interval* may be two or three decades.

Carcinogens may be identified from:

- epidemiological studies
- assessment of occupational risks
- direct accidental exposure
- carcinogenic effects in laboratory animals
- transforming effects on cell cultures
- mutagenicity testing in bacteria.

Epidemiological evidence

Some types of cancer are more common in certain countries, regions or communities within them (Fig. 11.17). Epidemiology has proved to be a fruitful source of information about the causes of tumours. Tumour incidence is more important than mortality data in this regard, because only a proportion of tumours prove fatal and the precise causes of death may not be well documented. It is thus essential to survey populations thoroughly for tumour incidence; in countries with well-developed health services, investigators can usually rely on diagnostic records and cancer registries, but elsewhere it may be necessary to visit and examine the population under study. Variations in tumour incidence may genuinely be due to environmental factors, but the data must first be standardised to eliminate the effect of, for example, any differences in the age distribution. The long latency between exposure to a carcinogen and the appearance of the tumour makes it necessary to consider also the effect of population movement. This effect can be used to distinguish between racial (hereditary) and environmental factors in determining cancer incidence in migrants.

Having found a high tumour incidence in a population, comparisons of lifestyle, diet and occupational risks with those of a low tumour-incidence control population often leads to specific causative associations being identified.

The following examples illustrate how carcinogens can be identified in this way.

Hepatocellular carcinoma

In countries such as the UK and the USA, hepatocellular carcinoma is a relatively uncommon tumour and, when it does occur, it usually arises in a cirrhotic liver. However, the worldwide incidence of hepatocellular carcinoma is high, and in some countries it is the most common tumour (Ch. 16). Epidemiology reveals two factors that may be involved in the high prevalence in endemic areas: *mycotoxins* and *hepatitis viruses B and C*.

The incidence of hepatocellular carcinoma in different regions of Uganda is associated with the frequency with which food samples in those regions were found to be contaminated

235

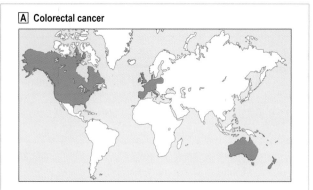

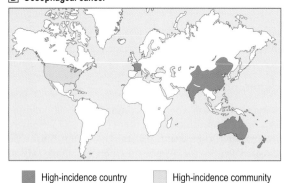

High-incidence country   High-incidence community

Fig. 11.17   World map showing countries in which there is a relatively high incidence of specific types of cancer.
A Colorectal cancer. B Oesophageal cancer. Low-incidence countries may conceal high-incidence regions or communities; for example, oesophageal carcinoma is more common among blacks in the USA (lighter shaded area). Note that colorectal cancer is much commoner in countries whose inhabitants eat a more refined diet. Dietary associations with oesophageal cancer are less well defined.

with aflatoxins. Aflatoxins are mycotoxins produced by the fungus *Aspergillus flavus*, and are a highly carcinogenic group of compounds. The fungus grows on food stored in humid conditions in the high-incidence areas. However, the situation is not clear-cut, because of the prevalence of hepatitis B virus in the area. There is a high incidence of point mutations of specific codons in *p53*, a tumour suppressor gene, in hepatocellular carcinomas associated epidemiologically with aflatoxins.

There is a strong correlation between the incidence of hepatitis B and C virus infection and hepatocellular carcinoma in many countries. Suspicion that hepatitis B virus may be oncogenic (tumour-causing) is reinforced by the discovery, in such cases, of a copy of the viral genome incorporated within the genome of the liver cancer cells.

Oesophageal carcinoma
The very high incidence of oesophageal carcinoma in China and in the Caspian littoral region of Iran has been intensively studied by epidemiologists. Several factors have been implicated, including the dyes used in carpet making, nitrates in the soil, abrasives in the diet, and opium dross, but no single aetiological factor has yet emerged from these studies.

One of the most informative natural experiments on the causation of oesophageal carcinoma took place in China when a reservoir was built in the Linhsien area. People living in this district were known to have a very high incidence of oesophageal carcinoma as, remarkably, did their domestic chickens. A dietary factor was suspected because the chickens were usually fed with their owners' waste food. The reservoir displaced these people to Fanhsien, where they continued to have a high incidence of oesophageal carcinoma. They left their chickens behind and re-stocked with a local strain in which oesophageal carcinoma was uncommon. However, fed with the table-scraps and waste food from their new owners, the local strain subsequently developed a high incidence of oesophageal carcinoma. A dietary factor was clearly implicated.

Occupational and behavioural risks

Certain types of cancer are, or have been, more common in people engaged in specific activities. The discovery in a given community of a link between a higher risk of developing a cancer and the person's occupation helps to separate general environmental causes of carcinogenesis from those that are probably specific to an individual person or group in the community.

Scrotal carcinoma
Percival Pott is credited with the first observation, in 1777, linking a particular tumour with a specific occupation. He noticed a high incidence of carcinoma of the scrotal skin in men who were or had been chimney sweeps, and postulated that the soot was responsible. It was not until 150 years later that the specific carcinogen, a polycyclic aromatic hydrocarbon, was identified.

Lung carcinoma
Lung carcinoma is a major public health problem in many countries. In the UK, more then 30 000 deaths are attributed to this cause annually; the actual incidence is only marginally higher because this form of cancer has an extremely poor prognosis. The unarguable association with cigarette smoking was established by meticulous epidemiological research. The problem, a common one for epidemiologists, was that people who smoke are commonly exposed to many other possible risks: they tend to live in cities, inhale atmospheric pollutants from motor vehicles, domestic fires and industry, be fond of alcoholic drinks, etc. However, careful analysis of environmental factors showed that cigarette smoking correlated most strongly with the incidence of lung carcinoma. There is an almost linear dose–response relationship between the number of cigarettes smoked daily and the risk of developing lung cancer (Fig. 11.18). Furthermore, the incidence of lung carcinoma declined in those groups of people, such as British male doctors, whose tobacco consumption fell substantially.

Carcinoma of the cervix
The observation that carcinoma of the cervix is commonest amongst prostitutes and an extreme rarity in celibate nuns suggested that the disease may be due to a venereally transmitted agent. The risk of carcinoma of the cervix is strongly associated with sexual intercourse, in particular

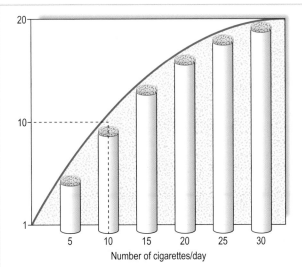

Fig. 11.18   Approximate dose–response relationship between cigarette consumption and the relative risk of developing lung cancer. Smoking at the rate of 10 cigarettes per day increases the risk of developing lung cancer 10-fold. (1 = non-smoker.)

with the number of partners and thus the risk of exposure to a possible carcinogenic agent conveyed by the male. Specific genotypes of human papillomavirus (HPV) are now proven to cause cancer of the cervix. Indeed, the evidence is so compelling that HPV immunisation is being introduced with the specific aim of reducing the incidence of this disease. HPV is an essential causative agent for squamous carcinoma of the cervix. Smoking is an aetiological co-factor.

Bladder carcinoma
In the 1890s, epidemiologists noted a higher than expected incidence of bladder cancer among men employed in the aniline dye and rubber industries. Further analysis led to the identification of beta-naphthylamine as the causative agent. Although stringent precautions are now taken to minimise the risk, people working in these industries are regularly screened for bladder cancer by cytological examination of their urine and, if bladder cancer occurs, the patient is entitled to compensation on the assumption that the disease has been acquired occupationally.

Direct evidence

It is fortunately a rare event for someone to be knowingly exposed to a single agent that causes cancer. Sadly, such happenings are often the adverse result of diagnostic or therapeutic medical intervention, but we must not overlook the opportunity to learn much from them.

Thorotrast
Thorotrast was a colloidal suspension of thorium dioxide widely used in many countries during 1930–1950 as a contrast medium in diagnostic radiology. When it was first introduced for medical use, two potentially hazardous properties of Thorotrast were known: thorium dioxide is naturally radioactive, emitting alpha-radiation and possessing an extremely

long half-life of 1.39×10^{10} years; the colloidal suspension is rapidly and irreversibly taken up by the body's phagocytic cells, such as those lining the vascular sinusoids in the liver and the spleen. Despite these potential hazards, Thorotrast proved such a good contrast medium, particularly for angiography, that its popularity was assured. However, in 1947 the first report was published of a patient who developed angiosarcoma of the liver after Thorotrast administration. As other cases were recognised, Thorotrast was withdrawn from use. Nevertheless, this unfortunate episode has given us an opportunity to learn about and confirm the carcinogenic effects of alpha-radiation.

Thyroid carcinoma and radiation in children
The thyroid gland is vulnerable to the carcinogenic effects of external irradiation and of the radioactive isotopes of iodine (the latter are concentrated by the thyroid gland in the synthesis of thyroid hormone). For example, in April 1986 a nuclear reactor exploded at Chernobyl in Ukraine, releasing a large quantity of radioactive material into the atmosphere. The material released included radioactive iodine. After a 4-year latent interval, there has been a dramatic increase in the local incidence of thyroid carcinoma in children (Fig. 11.19). To minimise this risk, non-radioactive iodine is usually given to people immediately after any accidental exposure to radioactive iodine to compete with the latter for uptake by the thyroid gland.

Experimental testing

Carcinogens are not united by any common physical or chemical properties; it is therefore considered necessary to screen all new drugs, food additives and potential environmental pollutants in non-human systems before they are introduced for human use. Three types of test system for carcinogenic or mutagenic activity are employed:

- laboratory animals in which the incidence of tumours is monitored
- cell and tissue cultures in which growth-transforming effects are sought
- bacterial cultures for mutagenicity testing (Ames test).

None of these is perfect; animals and isolated cell cultures often metabolise the agent being tested in a way that differs from normal human metabolic pathways, and mutagenicity in bacterial DNA may not correspond to carcinogenicity. In addition, the dynamics of these test systems are very different from that of clinical cancer; cancer in humans is a chronic process often lasting decades, whereas tests for carcinogenic activity in experimental systems usually seek more immediate effects. Nevertheless, despite these limitations, it is still appropriate to investigate possible carcinogens in this way.

Known or suspected carcinogens

The main classes of carcinogenic agent are:

- chemicals
- viruses
- ionising and non-ionising radiation

237

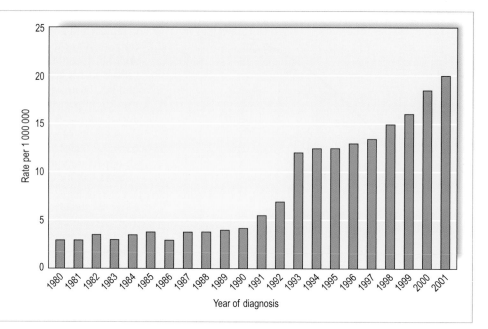

Fig. 11.19 Rising incidence of thyroid carcinoma in children (0–14 years) in Belarus. Thyroid carcinoma in children is relatively uncommon, but since the nuclear reactor explosion in 1986 at Chernobyl there has been a significantly increased local incidence. (Based on data in Mahoney MC, Lawvere S, Falkner KL et al 2004 Thyroid cancer incidence trends in Belarus. International Journal of Epidemiology 33: 1025–1033.)

- exogenous hormones
- bacteria, fungi and parasites
- miscellaneous agents.

As a result of direct testing for mutagenicity, or from accidental exposures or epidemiological evidence, many known or strongly suspected carcinogens have been identified (Fig. 11.20). In many countries, legislation prohibits or restricts the use of proven carcinogens.

Chemical carcinogens

▸ No common structural features
▸ Most require metabolic conversion into active carcinogens
▸ Major classes include polycyclic aromatic hydrocarbons, aromatic amines, nitrosamines, azo dyes, alkylating agents

Many chemical carcinogens have now been identified. The main categories are shown in Table 11.6.

The carcinogenic risk cannot be predicted from the structural formula alone; even apparently closely related compounds can have different effects.

Some agents act directly, requiring no metabolic conversion. Others (*procarcinogens*) require metabolic conversion into active carcinogens (*ultimate carcinogens*) (Fig. 11.21). If the enzyme required for conversion is ubiquitous within tissues, tumours will occur at the site of contact or entry; for example, polycyclic aromatic hydrocarbons induce skin tumours if painted on to the skin, or lung cancer if inhaled in tobacco smoke. Other agents require metabolic conversion by enzymes confined to certain organs, and thus often induce tumours remote from the site of entry; for example, aromatic amines require hydroxylation in the liver before expressing their carcinogenic effects. In a few instances the carcinogen is synthesised in the body from ingredients in the diet; thus,

carcinogenic nitrosamines are synthesised by gut bacteria utilising dietary nitrates and nitrites.

Polycyclic aromatic hydrocarbons

Polycyclic aromatic hydrocarbons were the first chemical carcinogens to be intensively studied. In 1917, Yamagiwa and Itchikawa in Japan showed that skin tumours could be induced in rabbits by painting their skin with tar. Tar was a suspected carcinogen because of the high incidence of skin cancer among tar-workers, particularly on the hands, which were frequently in contact with it. In the 1930s in London, Cook and Kennaway fractionated tar and attributed the carcinogenic effect to the polycyclic aromatic hydrocarbons. Like many chemicals implicated in the development of cancer, these are procarcinogens, requiring metabolic conversion by hydroxylation to form ultimate carcinogens. In this case, the carcinogenic effect is invariably at the site of contact because the hydroxylating enzymes (e.g. aryl carbohydrate hydroxylase) are ubiquitous in human tissues and readily induced in susceptible individuals. However, if the substance is absorbed into the body, this may lead to a risk of cancer at sites remote from the point of initial contact; there is, for example, an increased incidence of bladder cancer in tobacco smokers.

The tumour most commonly associated with exposure to polycyclic aromatic hydrocarbons is carcinoma of the lung. This tumour is much more common in smokers than in non-smokers and the risk to an individual or group parallels the quantity of tobacco consumed. Tobacco smoke contains many candidates for carcinogenic activity; the most important is probably 3,4-benzpyrene. Tobacco is also chewed in some countries, and there it is associated with a risk of carcinoma of the mouth.

Aromatic amines

The high incidence of bladder carcinoma in workers in the dye and rubber industries has now been attributed to beta-naphthylamine. Unlike the polycyclic aromatic hydrocarbons, this substance has no local carcinogenic effect. It requires

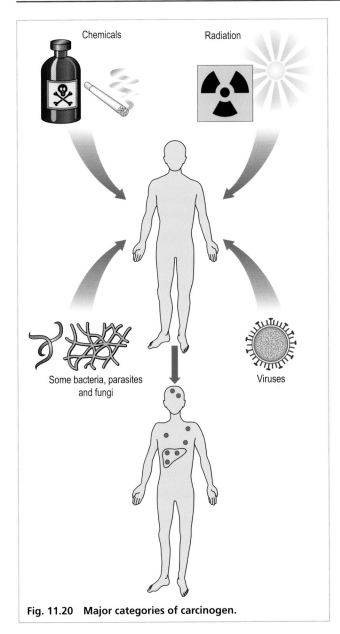

Fig. 11.20 Major categories of carcinogen.

conversion by hydroxylation in the liver into the active carcinogenic metabolite, 1-hydroxy-2-naphthylamine. However, the carcinogenic effect is masked immediately by conjugation with glucuronic acid in the liver. Bladder cancer results because the conjugated metabolite is excreted in the urine and deconjugated in the urinary tract by the enzyme glucuronidase, thus exposing the urothelium to the active carcinogen.

Nitrosamines

While ultimate proof of a causal relationship with human cancers is lacking, there is epidemiological evidence linking carcinomas of the gastrointestinal tract to the ingestion of nitrosamines and to dietary nitrates and nitrites. Nitrates are used widely as fertilisers, and are eventually washed by the rain into rivers and underground water tables where they can contaminate drinking water. In addition, both nitrates and nitrites have been used as food additives. Although these radicals are not in themselves carcinogenic, they are readily metabolised by commensal bacteria within the gut and converted to carcinogenic nitrosamines by combination with secondary amines and amides. Direct proof of a major role in carcinogenesis in humans is still awaited, but these substances are potent carcinogens in laboratory animals and it is unlikely that humans would be exempt from this effect.

Azo dyes

The carcinogenic potential of azo dyes, derivatives of aromatic amines, was recognised at an early stage and their use has thus been severely restricted. In laboratory animals, dimethylaminoazobenzene—otherwise known as 'butter yellow' because it was once used to impart an appetising yellow colour to margarine—causes liver cancer.

Alkylating agents

Many categories of chemical carcinogen, including polycyclic hydrocarbons, have alkylation as the ultimate common pathway, so it is not surprising that alkylating agents themselves can be carcinogenic. Alkylating agents bind directly to DNA, the ultimate site of action of all carcinogens. Nitrogen mustard is a well-known example, but these agents are not otherwise widely implicated as a major cause of human cancer.

Table 11.6 Examples of proven or suspected chemical carcinogens and the tumours with which they are associated

Chemical	Tumour	Comments
Polyciclic aromatic hydrocarbons (e.g. 3,4-benzpyrene)	Lung cancer Skin cancer	Strong link with smoking Following repeated exposure to mineral oils
Aromatic amines (e.g. beta-naphthylamine)	Bladder cancer	In rubber and dye workers
Nitrosamines	Gut cancers	Proven in animals
Azo dyes (e.g. 2-acetylaminofluorene)	Bladder and liver cancer	Proven in animals
Alkylating agents (e.g. cyclophosphamide)	Leukaemia	Small risk in humans
Other organic chemicals (e.g. vinyl chloride)	Liver angiosarcoma	Used in PVC manufacture

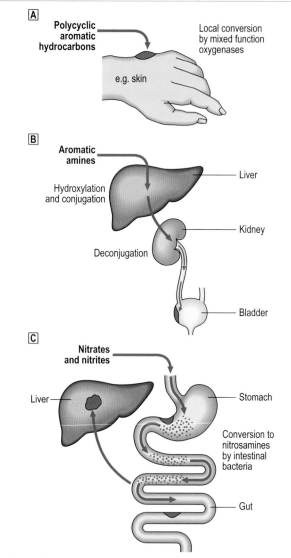

Fig. 11.21 Summary of some metabolic pathways for conversion of chemical procarcinogens into the active ultimate carcinogens. [A] Polycyclic aromatic hydrocarbons. [B] Aromatic amines. [C] Nitrates and nitrites. (See text for details.)

Oncogenic viruses

▶ Clusters of cancer cases in space and time suggest a viral aetiology
▶ Tumours associated with viruses tend to be more common in youth
▶ Immunosuppression favours viral oncogenesis
▶ Viruses implicated in human carcinogenesis include Epstein–Barr virus (Burkitt's lymphoma) and human papillomavirus (cancer of the cervix)
▶ Oncogenic DNA viral genome is directly incorporated into host cell DNA
▶ Oncogenic RNA viral genome is transcribed into DNA by reverse transcriptase prior to incorporation (oncogenic retrovirus)

Viruses were first implicated as carcinogenic agents through the experiments of Rous (in 1911) and Shope (in 1932), who studied fowl sarcomas and rabbit skin tumours, respectively. They showed that it was possible to transmit the tumours from one animal to another, in the manner of an infectious disease; tumours could be induced by injecting a cell-free filtrate of each tumour. The only possible transmissible agent was considered to be a virus, because the pores of the filter were too fine to permit the passage of bacteria or whole tumour cells. The study of oncogenic retroviruses in laboratory animals has had a seminal effect on our understanding of the molecular basis of tumour development and has led to the discovery of *oncogenes* (Fig. 11.22 and Table 11.12, p. 251).

Many human tumours are now known to be associated with viruses (Table 11.7).

Human tumours for which a viral aetiology has been proposed or proven include:

- carcinoma of the cervix (human papillomavirus)
- Burkitt's lymphoma (Epstein–Barr virus)
- nasopharyngeal carcinoma (Epstein–Barr virus)
- hepatocellular carcinoma (hepatitis B and C viruses)
- T-cell leukaemia/lymphoma in Japan and the Caribbean (RNA retrovirus).

Human papillomavirus

Human papillomavirus (HPV), of which there are many subtypes, causes the common wart (squamous cell papilloma). This lesion occurs most commonly on the hand, a frequent site of physical contact enabling transmission between individuals, and the virus is abundant within the abnormal cells of the lesion. Anogenital warts are also due to HPV, raising the possibility that other genital epithelial neoplasms may also be attributable to this cause. Evidence is also accumulating to suggest involvement of HPV in squamous neoplasia of the upper respiratory and digestive tracts.

Epidemiological and laboratory evidence reveals HPV as an essential cause of cancer of the cervix; this is discussed in more detail in Chapter 19.

Epstein–Barr virus

The Epstein–Barr (EB) virus was discovered first in cell cultures from Burkitt's lymphoma, a B-cell lymphoma endemic in certain regions of Africa and occurring only sporadically elsewhere. Early hopes that EB virus was the sole cause of Burkitt's lymphoma were dashed when it was discovered, following the accidental infection of a laboratory worker, that infection by the virus on its own causes infectious mononucleosis, a common, benign lymphoproliferative disorder which remits spontaneously in most cases. Clearly a co-factor is involved in the pathogenesis of Burkitt's lymphoma; epidemiological evidence suggests that this is malaria.

EB virus is also implicated in the causation of nasopharyngeal carcinoma in the Far East, where there is a relatively high incidence of this tumour.

Radiant energy

▶ Ultraviolet light is a major cause of skin cancer
▶ Exposure to ionising radiation is associated with an increased risk of cancer of many sites, including leukaemia

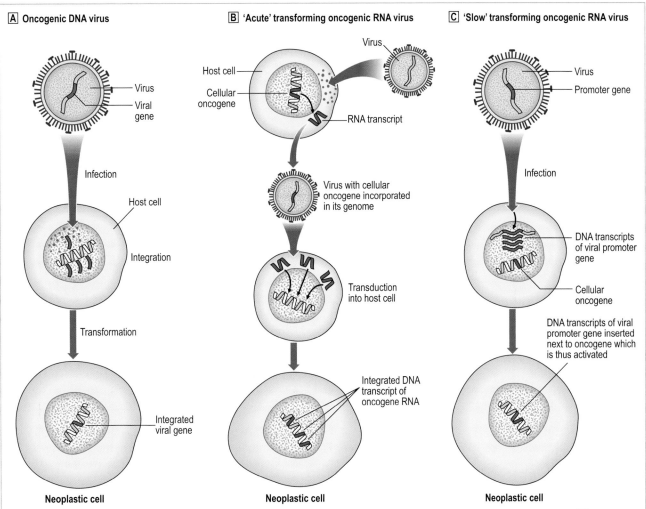

A Oncogenic DNA virus

Virus
Viral gene
Infection
Host cell
Integration
Transformation
Integrated viral gene
Neoplastic cell

B 'Acute' transforming oncogenic RNA virus

Virus
Host cell
Cellular oncogene
RNA transcript
Virus with cellular oncogene incorporated in its genome
Transduction into host cell
Integrated DNA transcript of oncogene RNA
Neoplastic cell

C 'Slow' transforming oncogenic RNA virus

Virus
Promoter gene
Infection
DNA transcripts of viral promoter gene
Cellular oncogene
DNA transcripts of viral promoter gene inserted next to oncogene which is thus activated
Neoplastic cell

Fig. 11.22   Simplified mechanisms of integration of oncogenic viral genes, or DNA transcripts, into the host cell DNA. **A** Oncogenic DNA virus: the viral genome is integrated into host cell DNA; neoplastic transformation is a postulated consequence. **B** 'Acute' transforming oncogenic RNA virus: transduction into the host cell of an RNA transcript of a cellular oncogene picked up from another cell. **C** 'Slow' transforming oncogenic RNA virus: insertion of a viral promoter gene next to a cellular oncogene. In both **B** and **C**, DNA transcripts are made from the RNA conveyed by the virus using the enzyme reverse transcriptase and, in contrast to cellular oncogenes, they lack introns.

Ultraviolet light

Skin cancer is more common on parts of the body regularly exposed to sunlight, and ultraviolet light (UVL) is now considered to be a major causal factor, UVB more so than UVA. Skin cancer is less common in people with naturally pigmented skin, as the melanin has a protective effect; it is more common in fair-skinned people, particularly those who get sunburnt easily, living in sunny climates (e.g. Australia).

Most types of skin cancer are associated with UVL exposure, but the risk is particularly high for malignant melanoma and basal cell carcinoma ('rodent ulcer'). This risk is greatly increased in patients with *xeroderma pigmentosum*, a rare congenital deficiency of DNA repair enzymes, in whom numerous skin cancers occur due to unrepaired damage to the DNA of the skin cells induced by UVL.

Ionising radiation

The carcinogenic effects of radiation are long-term and must be distinguished from the more immediate, dose-related,

acute effects such as skin erythema and, more seriously, bone marrow aplasia (Ch. 6).

Evidence that relatively high doses of ionising radiation are carcinogenic is indisputable. The carcinogenic effect of low levels of radiation continues to be a matter of great public concern because of the debate over the safety of nuclear power sources. Exposure to some ionising radiation from cosmic and other natural sources (background radiation) is inescapable; however, linear extrapolation of the low-dose risk from the quantifiable carcinogenic risk from higher levels of radiation is generally conceded to exaggerate the problem.

An increased incidence of cancer following exposure to ionising radiation has been witnessed since the earliest work with radioactive materials. Before protective measures were introduced there was a well-recognised increased incidence of leukaemia in radiology workers, and of skin cancer in those who regularly placed their hands in X-ray beams. The therapeutic use of radiation, often without adequate justification (e.g. radiation of the thymus gland in children with miscellaneous

Table 11.7 Viruses implicated in human tumours		
Virus	Tumour	Comments
Human papillomavirus	Common wart (squamous cell papilloma) Cervical carcinoma	Benign, spontaneously regressing lesion Strong association with HPV types 16 and 18
Epstein–Barr virus	Burkitt's lymphoma Nasopharyngeal cancer	Requires a co-factor, probably malaria In Far East and Africa
Hepatitis B and C viruses	Hepatocellular carcinoma	Strong association
Human herpes virus-8	Kaposi's sarcoma Pleural effusion lymphoma	Explains association between venereally acquired AIDS and Kaposi's sarcoma
Human T-cell lymphotropic virus-1	Adult T-cell leukaemia/lymphoma	Endemic in Southern Japan and Caribbean basin

ailments; Ch. 6), has resulted in cancers. Radiation from military sources, such as in Hiroshima and Nagasaki in 1945, resulted in a high incidence of certain tumours in survivors. Industrial exposure to radiation includes the risk of carcinoma of the lung associated with the mining of radioactive uranium. There has been a dramatic increase in the incidence of thyroid cancer in children near Chernobyl in Ukraine, the site of a nuclear accident in 1986 (p. 237).

Some tissues are more vulnerable than others to the carcinogenic effects of ionising radiation, and specific risks are associated with particular radioactive elements if they are concentrated in specific tissues, for example radioactive iodine concentrated in the thyroid gland. Tissues that appear particularly sensitive to the carcinogenic effects of ionising radiation include thyroid, breast, bone and haemopoietic tissue.

Hormones

It is somewhat surprising that substances occurring naturally in the body and indispensable for normal bodily functions should be implicated as at least co-factors in carcinogenesis. For example, exogenous oestrogens can be shown experimentally to promote the formation of mammary and endometrial carcinomas; the association between breast carcinoma and oral contraceptives containing oestrogens is weak. Androgenic and anabolic steroids are known to induce hepatocellular tumours in humans, and oestrogenic steroids may make pre-existing lesions (e.g. adenomas and focal nodular hyperplasia) abnormally vascular, thus causing otherwise asymptomatic lesions to present clinically.

Bacteria, fungi and parasites

Cancer may also result from infection with other living organisms (e.g. bacteria, parasites) or from the ingestion of food contaminated with the metabolic products of other organisms (e.g. mycotoxins).

Bacteria
Helicobacter pylori, a major cause of gastritis and peptic ulceration, is now strongly implicated in the pathogenesis of gastric lymphomas. Initially, the lesions are dependent on the continuing presence of *H. pylori* (the lymphoma regresses

if the bacteria are eradicated), but eventually the lymphoma becomes fully autonomous.

Fungi
Mycotoxins are toxic substances produced by fungi. Those having the greatest relevance in human carcinogenesis are the aflatoxins produced by *Aspergillus flavus.* Aflatoxins, particularly aflatoxin B_1, are among the most potent carcinogens and have been specifically linked to the high incidence of hepatocellular carcinoma in certain parts of Africa (Ch. 16).

Parasites
There is good evidence, both epidemiological and direct, to implicate *Schistosoma haematobium, Opisthorchis viverrini* and *Clonorchis sinensis* in the causation of human cancer. In such cases, there is a high incidence of the tumour in infested areas, and the parasites can often be found actually within or in the immediate vicinity of the tumour.

Schistosoma haematobium is strongly implicated in the high incidence of bladder carcinoma, usually of squamous cell type, in areas where infestation with the parasite is rife, such as Egypt. The ova of the parasite can often be found in or close to the tumour.

The liver flukes *Clonorchis sinensis* and *Opisthorchis viverrini* dwell in the bile ducts, where they induce an inflammatory reaction, epithelial hyperplasia and sometimes eventually adenocarcinoma of the bile ducts (cholangiocarcinoma). There is a high incidence of this tumour in parts of the Far East and other fluke-infested areas.

Miscellaneous carcinogens

In contrast to radiation, chemicals and viruses, which ultimately damage or bind to DNA, there are some miscellaneous carcinogens whose mechanism of action is not well understood, despite their proven association with cancer.

Asbestos
Inhalation of asbestos fibres results in various lesions: asbestosis, pleural plaques, mesothelioma and carcinoma of the lung (Fig. 11.23). Of the two neoplastic consequences, the association with mesothelioma is the more specific because this tumour is exceptionally rare in the absence of asbestos

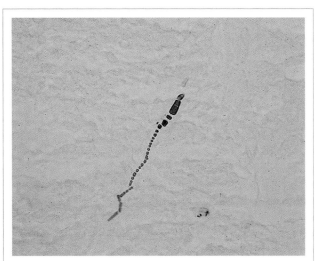

Fig. 11.23 Asbestos body in lung cancer. Seen in a histological section of a carcinoma of the lung associated with industrial exposure, the asbestos body consists of an asbestos fibre encrusted with beads of haemosiderin.

exposure. The pleura is the most frequent site for mesothelioma, but the association with asbestos is just as strong for peritoneal mesothelioma. There is also an association with carcinoma of the lung, which is enhanced by cigarette smoking.

Metals
Some metals are associated with a cancer risk, particularly in industrial situations. For example, exposure to compounds containing nickel leads to a risk of carcinoma of the mucosa lining the nasal cavities and of the lung.

Host factors in carcinogenesis

In addition to the extrinsic or environmental factors in carcinogenesis, there are also several important host factors that influence the cancer risk. These are:

- race
- diet
- constitutional factors (gender, inherited risks, etc.)
- premalignant lesions and conditions
- transplacental exposure.

Race

The precise role of race in determining an individual's risk of developing specific types of cancer is complicated by the fact that racial differences often coincide with differences in place of residence, diet and habit. While in some instances the link is obvious—for example, skin cancer is uncommon in blacks because the melanin in their skin protects them from the carcinogenic effects of ultraviolet sunlight—apparent racial differences are often explicable in terms of habit or cultural practices. Thus, oral cancer is relatively common in India and South-East Asia; but this is not associated directly with race, rather with tobacco or betel chewing and the remarkable habit of 'reverse smoking' in which the burning end of the cigarette is habitually placed in the mouth!

The relative contributions of race and environment to the incidence of cancer can be deduced from comparing the incidence in racial groups that have migrated to other countries. For example, cancer of the stomach is relatively uncommon in Africa, but the incidence in North American blacks of African descent approximates to the higher risk in the white population.

Diet

Dietary factors may be linked to cancer risk because:

- the diet may contain procarcinogens or carcinogens
- the diet may lack protective factors
- intestinal transit time may alter exposure of gut mucosa to carcinogens in the diet.

There is a positive correlation between high dietary fat and the risk of breast and colorectal cancer; alcohol appears to be a risk factor for breast and oesophageal cancer; and there is experimental evidence to suggest that a low protein diet has a protective effect against certain chemical carcinogens by reducing the levels of mixed-function oxygenases in the liver. Dietary fibre appears to be protective for colorectal cancer by promoting more rapid intestinal transit; any carcinogens in the bowel contents therefore remain in contact with the mucosa for a shorter time.

Constitutional factors

Inherited predisposition
Some individuals inherit an increased risk of developing certain tumours (Table 11.8). There is, for example, an inherited predisposition to breast cancer; a woman whose mother and one sister have developed breast cancer has a c. 50% probability of developing it herself. Genes responsible for this inherited risk (*BRCA1* on chromosome 17 and *BRCA2* on chromosome 13) have been identified. Sometimes the inherited risk is well defined, as in the condition xeroderma pigmentosum, a deficiency of DNA repair enzymes. Polyposis coli is an autosomal dominant inherited predisposition to develop multiple adenomatous polyps of the large bowel; consequently there is an increased risk of carcinoma of the colon and rectum arising in these polyps. Retinoblastoma, a malignant tumour of the eye in children, is familial and often bilateral in approximately one-third of cases; in these patients there is usually an abnormality of the *RB1* gene on chromosome 13.

Age
The incidence of cancer increases with age. There are several possible explanations: the cumulative risk of exposure to carcinogens with increasing age; the long latent interval between exposure to the initiating carcinogenic agent and the clinical appearance of the resulting tumour means that there is inevitably a tendency for most tumours to begin to appear only after a few decades of life have elapsed; accumulating genetic lesions (mutations) may render the ageing cell more sensitive to carcinogenic effects. Finally, it may be that incipient tumours developing in young individuals are recognised and eliminated by some innate defence system,

Table 11.8 Examples of inherited cancer risks

Inherited disorder	Tumour(s)	Comment
Multiple endocrine neoplasia (MEN) syndromes	Endocrine tumours, e.g. phaeochromocytoma, medullary carcinoma of the thyroid, parathyroid adenoma	Several types (MEN I, II, etc.) attributed to *RET* gene on chromosome 10 and others on chromosome 11
Xeroderma pigmentosum	Skin cancers, e.g. basal cell carcinoma, melanoma	Deficiency of DNA repair enzymes
Familial polyposis coli	Colorectal carcinoma	Preceded by numerous adenomatous polyps; autosomal dominant *APC* gene on chromosome 5
Hereditary non-polyposis colorectal cancer	Colorectal carcinoma	Mutated genes (*MLH1*, *MSH2*) involved in DNA repair
von Hippel–Lindau syndrome	Cerebellar haemangioblastoma, phaeochromocytoma, hypernephroma	Autosomal dominant inheritance associated with *VHL* gene on chromosome 3
Li–Fraumeni syndrome	Breast carcinoma, soft-tissue sarcomas	Autosomal dominant inheritance associated with abnormalities on chromosomes 13 (*RB1* gene), 11 and 17 (*p53* gene)
Retinoblastoma	Retinoblastoma (frequently bilateral)	Inherited allelic loss of one inhibitory *RB1* gene on chromosome 13
Familial breast carcinoma	Breast carcinoma Ovarian carcinoma (Prostatic carcinoma in male family members)	Attributed to mutated *BRCA1* gene on chromosome 17

such as natural killer cells, and that this protective effect is lost with age.

Gender

Breast cancer is at least 200 times commoner in women than in men. This is probably due to the greater mammary epithelial volume and to the promoting effects of oestrogens in females. It is more common in women who are nulliparous or who have not breast-fed their children, and those who have experienced an early menarche and/or late menopause. Endocrine factors are undoubtedly important.

Associations with gender occur in other cancers, but these are more often due to, for example, smoking habits than to hormonal factors.

Premalignant lesions and conditions

A *premalignant lesion* is an identifiable local abnormality associated with an increased risk of a malignant tumour developing at that site. Examples include adenomatous polyps of the colon and rectum, and epithelial dysplasias in various sites, notably the cervix. Studies of these lesions reinforce the multistep theory of carcinogenesis (Fig. 11.24); it may be that these lesions represent the growth of partially transformed cells which have not yet achieved full neoplastic status.

A *premalignant condition* is one that is associated with an increased risk of malignant tumours. In chronic ulcerative colitis, for example, there is an increased risk of colorectal cancer and this can be predicted by seeking the premalignant lesion (in this case dysplasia) in rectal biopsies. Sometimes congenital abnormalities predispose to cancer; the undescended testis is, for example, more prone to neoplasms than the normally located organ.

If patients are found to have premalignant lesions and conditions they can be followed up carefully, and tumours detected at an early stage when they are more amenable to potentially curative treatment (Table 11.9). This is the principle of the population screening programmes for carcinoma of the cervix.

Transplacental carcinogenesis

In the 1940s some pregnant women with threatened miscarriages were treated with diethylstilbestrol, a synthetic oestrogenic compound, in an attempt to avert the fetus from being aborted. The female progeny of those pregnancies that went successfully to full term were later discovered to have a high incidence of vaginal adenocarcinoma, an otherwise rare tumour, in early adult life. This is an example of transplacental carcinogenesis; the carcinogen, presumably diethylstilbestrol, was administered to the mother, but the carcinogenic effect was exhibited only in the child resulting from the pregnancy, when she reached young adulthood.

CELLULAR AND MOLECULAR EVENTS IN CARCINOGENESIS

▶ Multistep process
▶ May require initiating and promoting agents
▶ Growth persists in the absence of the causative agents
▶ Genetic alterations of oncogenes and tumour suppressor genes

Having considered the various types of carcinogen, we can now turn our attention to the way in which these agents actually transform normal cells into neoplastic cells, capable of autonomous growth and, in malignant neoplasms, of invasion and metastasis.

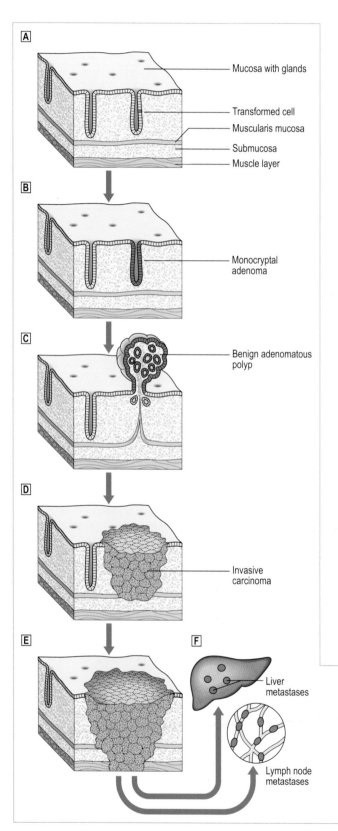

Mucosa with glands

Transformed cell
Muscularis mucosa
Submucosa
Muscle layer

Monocryptal adenoma

Benign adenomatous polyp

Invasive carcinoma

Liver metastases

Lymph node metastases

Fig. 11.24 Carcinoma of the large bowel as a model of tumour progression. [A] A single epithelial cell within a mucosal gland becomes transformed into a tumour cell by carcinogenic events. [B] The abnormal cell proliferates to produce a clone of cells populating one gland. [C] Further proliferation results in the formation of a benign, non-invasive polyp (adenoma) protruding from the mucosal surface. [D] The transformed cells become invasive as a result of further genetic changes; the lesion is now regarded as malignant (carcinoma). [E] The malignant cells invade blood vessels and lymphatics, and are carried to the liver and lymph nodes, respectively, to form secondary tumours (metastases) [F].

Experimental observations

Evidence for a *multistep theory* of carcinogenesis is derived from observations on the experimental induction of tumours in laboratory animals and from the sequential genetic alterations in the development of human tumours.

Latency

Part of the reason for the long latent interval between exposure to a carcinogen and clinical recognition of the tumour is the fact that tumours result from the clonal proliferation of single cells; it takes an appreciable time for this transformed single cell to grow into a nodule of cells large enough to cause signs and symptoms. However, another important factor is that, with the possible exceptions of ionising radiation and of some fast-transforming oncogenic retroviruses, the change from a normal cell into a growing and potentially fatal neoplasm is thought to entail more than one genetic event.

Initiation, promotion and progression

Experimental carcinogenesis has revealed two major steps— initiation and promotion—in the transformation of cells from normal to neoplastic and a further step—progression— resulting in the malignant phenotype.

* *Initiation* is the event that induces the genetic alteration that gives the transformed cell its neoplastic potential.
* *Promotion* is the event stimulating clonal proliferation of the initiated transformed cell.
* *Progression* is the process culminating in malignant behaviour characterised by invasion and its consequences.

A frequently cited example of this sequence is the effect of successive applications of methylcholanthrene and croton oil on mouse skin. A single application of methylcholanthrene results in a visible tumour only if it is followed by repeated painting of the site with non-carcinogenic croton oil. Methylcholanthrene is the initiator inducing lesions in the DNA of the target cell, and croton oil promotes the growth of the initiated cell; further mutational events then cause the lesion to progress to malignancy (Fig. 11.25).

Such experiments cannot, of course, be performed in humans, but there are many malignant tumours that develop from observable precursor lesions such as epithelial dysplasia or benign adenomas; for example, the adenoma–carcinoma sequence is well characterised in the large bowel.

Table 11.9 Examples of premalignant lesions and conditions

Lesion/condition	Cancer risk
Premalignant lesion	
Adenomatous polyp of colorectum	Colorectal adenocarcinoma
Cervical epithelial dysplasia	Carcinoma of the cervix
Mammary ductal epithelial hyperplasia	Carcinoma of the breast
Premalignant condition	
Hepatic cirrhosis	Hepatocellular carcinoma
Xeroderma pigmentosum	Skin cancer
Ulcerative colitis	Colorectal adenocarcinoma Bile duct carcinoma

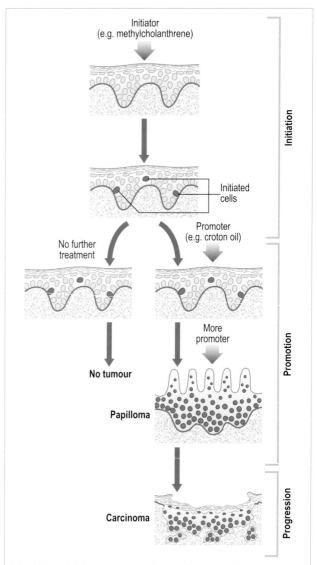

Fig. 11.25 Initiation, promotion and progression, as illustrated by the multiple steps involved in experimental chemical carcinogenesis in the epidermis. Latency is represented by the time interval between exposure to the initiating agent and the growth of a detectable neoplasm. (See text for details.)

This sequential development of neoplasms is associated with genetic abnormalities which drive the uncontrolled proliferation of tumour cells and, in malignant tumours, their progression to invasive behaviour.

Genetic abnormalities in tumours

▶ Chromosomal abnormalities, sometimes consistent (e.g. Philadelphia chromosome), are common
▶ Oncogenes, genes directing cell growth and differentiation, are abnormally expressed in many tumours
▶ Inactivation or inherited or mutational loss of tumour suppressor genes permits tumour development
▶ Oncogene expression results in autocrine growth stimulation

Chromosomal abnormalities

The simplest technique for examining the genome of cells is chromosomal (karyotypic) analysis. This involves culturing the cells in the presence of colchicine, which blocks formation of the mitotic spindle and arrests mitosis in metaphase. On exposure to a hypotonic medium, the osmotic shock causes the cells to explode and spill their chromosomes onto the surface of a glass slide where they can be stained, counted and examined in detail. Unfortunately, at this relatively crude level of analysis in molecular terms, very few recurring patterns of chromosomal abnormality have been found in tumours. Abnormalities such as additional chromosomes and translocation of part of one chromosome to another are very common, but few are constant even among a single tumour type (Table 11.10). A notable exception is the Philadelphia chromosome; this 9;11 translocation resulting in the *bcr–abl* fusion gene is one of the most consistent chromosomal abnormalities yet discovered, and is commonly found in chronic myeloid (granulocytic) leukaemia. More recently, however, chromosomes have been studied by in situ hybridisation, a technique that enables determination of the number and location of specific DNA sequences (Fig. 11.26).

Genetic mechanisms in carcinogenesis

Genetic alterations are the root cause of neoplastic cellular behaviour. Research has revealed that a minimum of three genetic alterations are needed to transform a normal cell into a neoplastic cell (Fig. 11.27):

● expression of *telomerase*, to avoid replication senescence resulting from telomeric shortening with each cell division
● loss or inactivation of recessive *tumour suppressor gene* function, to remove the inhibitory control of cellular replication
● enhanced or abnormal expression of dominant *oncogenes*, to self-stimulate cellular replication.

Telomerase expression confers immortalisation on the cells. Cells lacking telomerase (most cells in the body) have only

Table 11.10   Examples of non-random chromosomal abnormalities in neoplastic diseases

Neoplasm	Chromosomal abnormality	Comment
Burkitt's lymphoma	Translocation of **c**-*myc* oncogene from chromosome 8 to an immunoglobulin gene locus on chromosome 14	Results in expression of **c**-*myc* gene
Chronic myeloid leukaemia	Translocation involving chromosomes 9 and 22 (Philadelphia chromosome)	Results in fusion of **c**-*abl* and *bcr* genes; bcr-abl protein has tyrosine kinase activity
Follicle centre cell lymphoma	Translocation involving chromosomes 14 and 18	Results in expression of *bcl*-2 gene inhibiting apoptosis
Ewing's tumour Peripheral neuroectodermal tumour	Translocation involving chromosomes 11 and 22	Distinguishes these tumours from neuroblastoma, which they may resemble histologically

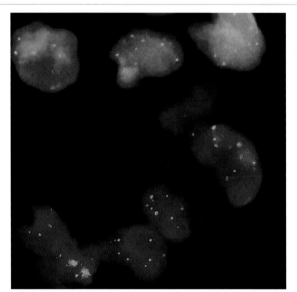

Fig. 11.26   Fluorescent in situ hybridisation (FISH) of nuclei from an adult germ cell tumour of testis. This reveals, as green dots, extra copies of the short arm of chromosome 12 (12p). The fewer red dots mark the normally represented long arm of chromosome 12 (12q). The extra copies of 12p are in the form of isochromosomes (i(12p)), a useful diagnostic marker of adult germ cell tumours. (Courtesy of Jill Elliott, Sheffield Regional Cytogenetics Service, Sheffield Children's Hospital.)

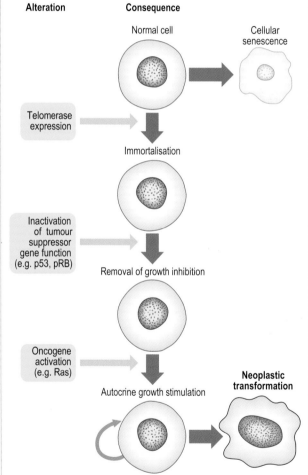

Fig. 11.27   Essential steps in neoplastic transformation. Three key genetic events are the minimum needed to convert a normal human cell into a neoplastic cell. *Telomerase expression* prevents telomeric shortening with each cell division and thus thwarts cellular senescence. *Inactivation of tumour suppressor gene function* in the immortalised cells removes inhibition of growth control. *Oncogene activation* sets up autocrine growth stimulation; the cell now produces a growth factor for which it already has a receptor or expresses a receptor for a growth factor it normally produces. The cell is now fully transformed. (Based on observations by Hahn WC, Counter CM, Lundberg AS et al 1999 Creation of human tumor cells with defined genetic elements. Nature 400: 464–468)

a limited replicative ability. Our chromosomal telomeres shorten as we age. Eventually the telomeres become so short with each cell division that replication cannot start, and cellular senescence and death ensues.

Tumour suppressor gene inactivation and abnormal oncogene expression work in concert (Fig. 11.28) to drive cells from their normal state of regulated growth to the dysregulated and uncontrolled growth that characterises neoplastic cells.

Genomic instability

Maintenance of genomic integrity involves genes and their products (e.g. p53) involved in sensing and repairing DNA damage. Failure of these processes causes genomic instability, an important general mechanism enabling the specific genetic alterations associated with neoplastic transformation. Cells that have lost these mechanisms for preserving genomic integrity are said to have a *mutator phenotype*.

Genomic instability increases naturally with age and is itself postulated to be involved in the ageing process. However, there are also inherited conditions characterised by genomic instability that indicate two major levels at which preservation of DNA integrity may fail:

- *chromosomal instability* (e.g. Fanconi anaemia) causing chromosome breaks
- *microsatellite instability* (e.g. hereditary non-polyposis colon cancer) due to defective DNA mismatch repair.

Tumour suppressor genes

Clues to the existence of inhibitory genes came from observations on the behaviour of transformed cells that were fused with untransformed cells; the resulting hybrid cells behaved like untransformed cells until specific chromosomes bearing the inhibitory genes were lost, causing the cells to revert to their transformed state.

The existence of these inhibitory genes was also postulated by Alfred Knudson in 1971. Using a statistical approach to familial cancer incidence he formulated a *two-hit hypothesis*. The first 'hit' is the inheritance of a defective (mutant) allele of a tumour suppressor gene, the other allele being normal (wild) and expressing sufficient suppressive effect. The

second 'hit' is the mutational loss of function of the normal allele, thus now fully depriving the cell of the suppressive effect of that tumour suppressor gene.

'Caretakers' and 'gatekeepers'

Tumour suppressor genes are categorised further according to their mechanism of action:

- *caretaker* genes maintain the integrity of the genome by repairing DNA damage
- *gatekeeper* genes inhibit the proliferation or promote the death of cells with damaged DNA.

Examples and the tumour susceptibilities with which inherited abnormalities of these genes are associated are given in Table 11.11.

The *RB* gene was the first inhibitory gene to have been well characterised, and is associated with retinoblastomas. Retinoblastomas are malignant tumours derived from the retina; they occur almost exclusively in children. In some cases they are hereditary, occurring bilaterally and also in some of the patient's siblings. In other cases they are sporadic, occurring unilaterally and without any familial associations. Individuals with hereditary retinoblastomas show a germline deletion on chromosome 13, corresponding to the known site of the *RB1* gene. Therefore, only one further mutational loss of the paired gene in the target retinal cell is required for the tumour to develop. Sporadic retinoblastoma cases have a normal chromosome 13 and therefore require two mutational losses before the tumour can develop (Fig. 11.29).

The tumour suppressor gene *p53*, situated on the short arm of chromosome 17, is the gene most frequently mutated and extensively studied in human cancer. The normal functions of p53 are to enable:

- repair of damaged DNA before S-phase in the cell cycle by arresting the cell cycle in G_1 until the damage is repaired
- apoptotic cell death if there is extensive DNA damage.

The p53 levels rise in cells that have sustained DNA damage, until either the damage is repaired or the cell undergoes apoptosis. This prevents propagation of possibly mutated

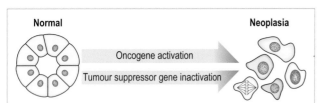

Fig. 11.28   Oncogenes and tumour suppressor genes.
Abnormal expression of oncogenes drives normal cells towards the neoplastic state. Loss of tumour suppressor gene function enables neoplastic transformation by permitting mutations.

Table 11.11	Tumour suppressor genes: functional categories and tumour associations			
Category	Gene	Function	Tumour susceptibility if germline mutation	Comment
Gatekeepers	*p53*	Transcription factor	Li–Fraumeni syndrome	Also mutated in c. 50% of human cancers
	RB1	Transcriptional regulator	Familial retinoblastoma	Often mutated in other human cancers
	APC	Regulates beta-catenin function	Familial adenomatous polyposis	Often mutated in sporadic colorectal cancers
Caretakers	*BRCA1*	DNA repair	Breast and ovarian cancer	Rarely mutated in sporadic breast cancers
	BRCA2	DNA repair	Breast, prostate and pancreatic cancer	Homozygous mutation associated with Fanconi anaemia
	MSH2 *MLH1*	DNA mismatch repair	Hereditary non-polyposis colorectal cancer	Mutation permits further mutations ('mutator phenotype')

genes. This important function of p53 results in it being called 'the guardian of the genome'. p53 can lose its normal function by a variety of mechanisms:

- *mutations* that either render the gene unreadable (nonsense mutations) or encode for a defective protein (missense mutations)
- *complexes* of normal p53 and mutant p53 (in heterozygous individuals or cells) inactivating the function of the normal allele
- binding of normal p53 protein to proteins encoded by *oncogenic DNA viruses* (e.g. human papillomavirus, polyomaviruses).

These events have major implications. Cells with damaged DNA, possibly with mutated oncogenes, undergo mitotic replication rather than apoptotic death (Fig. 11.30). Also,

cytotoxic chemotherapy against the tumour may be less effective if the cells fail to respond by apoptosis.

Inherited germline (present in all cells) mutations of *p53* occur in the rare *Li–Fraumeni syndrome*. Affected individuals have an inherited predisposition to a wide range of tumours. At birth they are heterozygous for the defective gene (only very rarely are the maternal and paternal alleles both defective). Eventually, the normal allele is itself lost or mutated *(loss of heterozygosity)* in a variety of cells, thus enabling their neoplastic transformation.

Oncogenes

Oncogenes are genes driving the neoplastic behaviour of cells. Originally proposed as a hypothesis, oncogenes were discovered as a result of studies of oncogenic RNA retroviruses. These are RNA viruses that have the ability to transfer their genome, or parts of it, to the genome of the cells they infect. Normally the transfer of genomic information is in the opposite direction: DNA sequences are transcribed into RNA, which then determines the amino acid sequence of a peptide or protein. However, retroviruses contain an enzyme, *reverse*

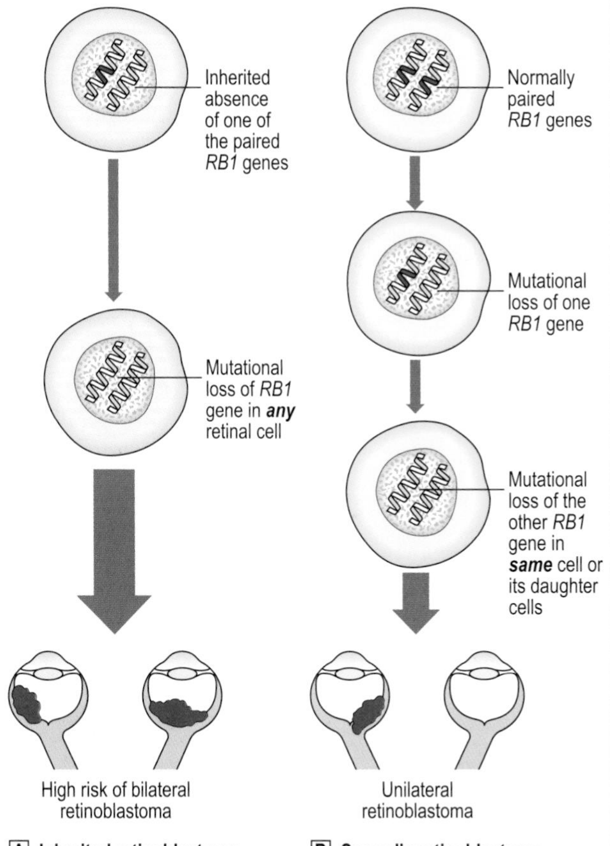

Fig. 11.29 Loss of tumour suppressor gene function and inherited retinoblastoma. Loss of functional tumour suppressor genes permits tumour development. **A** Individuals with an inherited risk of retinoblastoma are born with a predisposing germline mutation in one of the paired alleles of the *RB1* suppressor gene; mutational loss of the remaining *RB1* allele is required for retinoblastomas to develop. **B** Normal individuals without an inherited germline mutation of the *RB1* gene have a low incidence of retinoblastoma because acquired mutations in *both* alleles have to occur in the *same* cell or its daughters; sporadic retinoblastoma is, therefore, a rare event.

[A] Inherited retinoblastoma — Inherited absence of one of the paired *RB1* genes; Mutational loss of *RB1* gene in *any* retinal cell; High risk of bilateral retinoblastoma

[B] Sporadic retinoblastoma — Normally paired *RB1* genes; Mutational loss of one *RB1* gene; Mutational loss of the other *RB1* gene in *same* cell or its daughter cells; Unilateral retinoblastoma

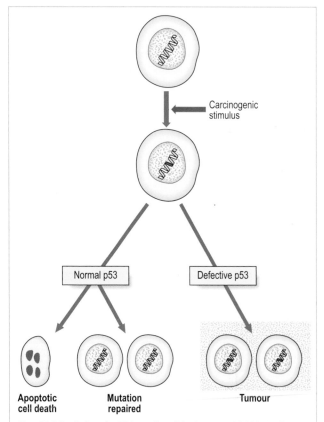

Fig. 11.30 Role of p53 in cells with damaged DNA. In the presence of normal p53, cells with a mutation resulting from a potentially carcinogenic stimulus are arrested in G_1 of the cell cycle until either the mutation is repaired or, if the damage is severe, apoptosis occurs. If the p53 is defective, as a result of mutation or binding, the cells proceed to S phase and the mutation is propagated to daughter cells, possibly eventually leading to a tumour.

Carcinogenic stimulus

Normal p53 — Defective p53

Apoptotic cell death — Mutation repaired — Tumour

transcriptase, that enables the viral RNA to be transcribed into complementary DNA which is then incorporated into the infected cell's genome. In the case of oncogenic retroviruses, these genes were called *oncogenes.*

The next major discovery was of the presence of DNA sequences almost identical to viral oncogenes (*v*-oncogenes) in the genome of normal cells (cellular or proto-oncogenes). Numerous oncogenes have now been identified. However, in normal cells these oncogenes are present at the frequency of only one copy per haploid genome, and their transcription is tightly controlled as required for cell growth and differentiation.

They are present in the genome of even the most primitive protozoa and metazoa; this high degree of evolutionary conservation implies a function indispensable to normal life. The result of much research now leads us to conclude that these cellular oncogenes are essential for normal cell and tissue growth and differentiation, particularly during embryogenesis and healing. But when they are aberrant or inappropriately expressed they result in the growth of a tumour.

Normal or partially transformed cell cultures can be fully transformed by the addition of DNA bearing oncogenes, a process known as *transfection.* Alternatively, oncogenic (or carcinogenic) retroviruses can transform cells by transferring oncogenes from another cell, a process known as *transduction.*

Oncogenes can be classified into five groups according to the function of the gene product (oncoprotein):

- *nuclear-binding oncoproteins* involved in the regulation of cellular proliferation (e.g. myc)
- *tyrosine kinase activity* (e.g. src)
- *growth factors* (e.g. sis coding for platelet-derived growth factor)
- *receptors for growth factors* (e.g. *erb*B coding for epidermal growth factor receptor)
- *cyclic nucleotide binding activity* (e.g. ras and GTP) disrupting intracellular signalling.

Abnormalities of oncogene expression are crucial for the growth and behaviour of tumour cells.

Abnormalities of oncogene expression in tumours

Oncogenes can have tumour-promoting effects by either:

- *mutation* resulting in an oncoprotein molecule altered in such a way that it is excessively active
- *excessive production of a normal oncoprotein* because of gene amplification or enhanced transcription.

Increased expression of oncogenes has been found in most tumours. The mechanisms are summarised in Figure 11.31. Increased expression may be detected by:

- the presence of more of the oncogene product (*oncoprotein*) within or on the cells
- increased production of mRNA transcripts of the oncogene
- increased numbers of copies of the oncogene in the genome.

Increased numbers of oncogene copies may result from infection by a retrovirus which causes reverse transcription of its RNA and insertion of *multiple copies* of the resulting

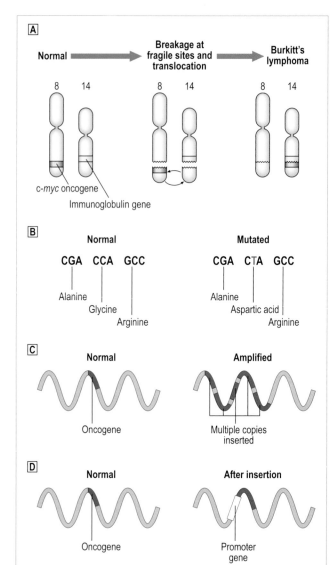

Fig. 11.31 Mechanisms of oncogene activation. **A** Translocation of an oncogene from an untranscribed site to a position adjacent to an actively transcribed gene; e.g. simplified chromosomal translocation in Burkitt's lymphoma, in which the c-*myc* oncogene is often translocated from chromosome 8, its normal location, to chromosome 14, where it is placed adjacent to one of the immunoglobulin genes and is thus inappropriately transcribed. **B** Point mutation (in this case in codon 12 of the *ras* oncogene), in which the substitution of a single base in the oncogene is translated into an amino acid substitution in the oncoprotein causing it to be hyperactive. **C** Amplification by the insertion of multiple copies of the oncogene (in this case, c-*myc* in neuroblastoma), resulting in cellular proliferation stimulated by excessive quantities of the oncoprotein. **D** Increased oncogene expression by gene insertion (*insertional mutagenesis*) resulting in proximity of an oncogene to a promoter or enhancing gene; this is one mechanism of retroviral carcinogenesis.

DNA into the DNA of the host cell genome. A more common occurrence in human tumours is *gene amplification* resulting in multiple copies, such as in the *myc* family of oncogenes in neuroblastoma; this can be recognised in chromosome preparations from tumour cells by the presence of *homogeneously staining regions and double minute chromosomes*.

Increased transcription can occur if a normally silent (i.e. not transcribed) oncogene is moved to another part of the genome where active transcription is occurring. This is often evident from the karyotype; part of one chromosome which is known to bear an oncogene may be translocated to another chromosome where a gene known to be actively transcribed is situated. Specific examples include:

- translocation of the c-*abl* gene from chromosome 9 to chromosome 22, an event that results in the formation of the Philadelphia chromosome and expression of a *bcr–abl* fusion gene product in chronic myeloid leukaemia
- translocation of the c-*myc* oncogene from chromosome 8 to chromosome 14, where its expression is assured by juxtaposition with one of the immunoglobulin genes which will be actively transcribed in the B-cell that is the origin of Burkitt's lymphoma.

Alternatively, the cellular oncogene may undergo a *point mutation* resulting in a gene product, such as a protein kinase, with increased or inappropriate activity.

Autocrine stimulation of neoplastic cell growth

Oncogene products play an important role in cellular growth and behaviour (Table 11.12). By their expression in inappropriate circumstances a cell can become autonomous, proliferating without the usual requirement for external signals (Fig. 11.32). For example, an oncogene product may be a receptor for a growth factor (Ch. 5) already normally produced by that cell; the cell then responds to stimulation by its own growth factor. Alternatively, the oncogene product may be a growth factor for which the cell already normally bears a specific receptor. In both cases the result is *autocrine stimulation of growth*.

Other oncogene products act directly within the nucleus to stimulate mitosis or on intracytoplasmic second messengers, such as cyclic nucleotides, thus modulating *intracellular signalling*.

Interaction of carcinogens with oncogenes and tumour suppressor genes

The neoplastic behaviour of tumour cells persists after withdrawal of carcinogenic stimuli and this behaviour is passed on to subsequent cellular generations through mitotic divisions; it is therefore concluded that the lesion responsible for neoplastic behaviour is within the genome. This has led to a search for the final common pathway through which the very diverse range of known carcinogens acts—a search for the molecular lesion within the genome that is the end result of carcinogenesis.

Ultimately, the metabolism of chemical carcinogens results in the formation of DNA adducts, but the mere presence of adducts is insufficient for tumours to develop. Further molecular alterations, such as mutations, during DNA replication, and clonal expansion of the mutated cells are required before a tumour results. The formation of adducts can be reversed by virtue of their innate instability, or by DNA repair enzymes; their effect may also be minimised by dilution with new DNA through normal replication.

Table 11.12	Examples of oncogenes and the function of their products	
Oncogene	Function of oncoprotein	Abbreviated from
abl	Protein-tyrosine kinase activity	Abelson mouse leukaemia
myc	Binds to DNA, directly stimulating synthesis	Myelocytomatosis
sis	Growth factor (platelet-derived growth factor)	Simian sarcoma
erbB	Receptor for epidermal growth factor	Avian erythroblastosis (also *erbA*)
ras	Acts on intracellular signalling (cyclic nucleotides)	Rat sarcoma

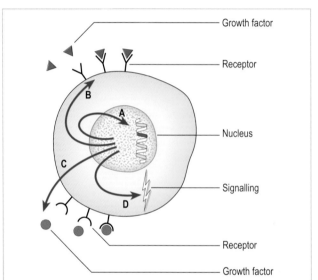

Fig. 11.32 Self-stimulation of neoplastic cell proliferation mediated by oncoproteins. (A) Direct stimulation of DNA synthesis by an oncoprotein that binds to DNA, **(B)** Synthesis of receptors (Υ) for a growth factor (red triangles) already present in the extracellular environment. **(C)** Synthesis of a growth factor (green circles), receptors for which (Υ) are normally present on the cell. **(D)** Interference with intracellular signalling between the cell membrane and the nucleus.

The selectivity of a carcinogenic metabolite for a particular nucleotide is thought to explain the site-specific mutations induced in oncogenes that can result in their abnormal expression. For example, several chemical carcinogens have been shown experimentally to result in single base substitutions in codons 12 and 61 of the *ras* oncogene, leading to the synthesis of a hyperactive mutant protein. Site-specific mutations of *p53* are present in hepatocellular carcinomas associated with aflatoxin exposure.

The mutational effects of ionising radiation are probably random throughout the genome, but when they occur in oncogenes or tumour suppressor genes the cells harbouring the mutant genes have a selective growth advantage, eventually resulting in tumours.

The role of viruses in tumour induction can be attributed directly to the genetic material within them and its incorporation within the host cell.

Epigenetic control of tumour growth

Current evidence emphasises the *genetic theory* of carcinogenesis, that tumours result only from induced or congenital genetic abnormalities that dictate the aberrant behaviour of the cells. Experimental evidence favouring the *epigenetic theory*—that the behaviour of tumour cells results from the expression of deregulated or abnormally controlled *nonmutated genes*—does not necessarily imply that the primary carcinogenic event is epigenetic; it simply shows that, in some instances, the neoplastic behaviour of tumour cells can be influenced by epigenetic factors. Possible mechanisms include:

- gene silencing by hypermethylation of promoter sequences
- interference with gene transcription by microRNA (short sequences of inhibitory RNA).

In some neoplasms at least, an epigenetic influence can be demonstrated. If the cells of a malignant teratoma are injected into an early mouse embryo, the neoplastic cells differentiate normally and no tumour develops. In other words, the otherwise autonomous growth and incompletely differentiated state of this particular malignant neoplasm can be corrected by an epigenetic influence.

BEHAVIOUR OF TUMOURS

The clinical effects of tumours are determined by the biological behaviour of the neoplastic cells within them. The most important property of malignant tumours is the ability to invade and metastasise.

Invasion and metastasis

- ▶ Invasion is the most important sole criterion for malignancy
- ▶ Invasion is due to abnormal cell motility, reduced cellular cohesion, and production of proteolytic enzymes
- ▶ Metastasis is the process of formation of distant secondary tumours
- ▶ Common routes of metastasis include lymphatic channels, blood vessels, and through body cavities

Invasion and metastasis are responsible for most of the fatal consequences of tumours. They also dictate the most appropriate treatment. There is no point in simply removing the tumour itself. In most instances the tumour should be removed in continuity with a wide margin of apparently normal tissue, to ensure that the plane of resection is clear of the often ill-defined invasive edge of the tumour; the regional lymph nodes may also be resected. Incomplete local removal of a tumour may result in a local recurrence because the original plane of resection transected the invasive edge of the lesion.

Tumours should be manipulated with care during clinical examination or surgical removal, to minimise the risk of pumping tumour cells into blood and lymphatic channels. A ligature is therefore often tied around the vascular pedicle at an early stage in the surgical removal of a tumour.

In epithelial neoplasms, invasion and metastasis require the acquisition of motile and migratory properties normally associated with cells of mesenchymal lineage. This shift in behaviour is often referred to as *epithelial–mesenchymal transition*.

Invasion

The invasiveness of malignant neoplasms is determined by the properties of the neoplastic cells within them. Factors influencing tumour invasion are:

- abnormal or increased cellular motility
- secretion of proteolytic enzymes
- decreased cellular adhesion.

Cellular motility is abnormal in that the cells are not only more motile than their normal counterparts (which may not move at all), but also show loss of the normal mechanism that arrests or reverses normal cellular migration: contact inhibition of migration.

Proteinases and inhibitors

Matrix metalloproteinases are among the most important proteinases in neoplastic invasion. These enzymes are secreted by malignant neoplastic cells, enabling them to digest the surrounding connective tissue. There are three families:

- *interstitial collagenases*—degrade types I, II and III collagen
- *gelatinases*—degrade type IV collagen and gelatin
- *stromelysins*—degrade type IV collagen and proteoglycans.

These enzymes are counteracted by *tissue inhibitors of metalloproteinases* (TIMPs). The net effect is determined by the balance between metalloproteinases and their inhibitors. It may be possible to limit the invasiveness of tumour cells by artificially increasing the level of inhibitory activity.

Invasion often occurs along tissue planes offering less resistance to tumour growth, such as perineural spaces and, of course, vascular lumina. Other tissues are extremely resistant to neoplastic invasion, such as cartilage and the fibrocartilage of intervertebral discs.

Clinicopathological significance

Invasion is the single most important criterion of malignancy. Metastases are a consequence of invasion and, when detected clinically, are unequivocal markers of malignancy. In epithelial tumours, invasion is relatively easy to recognise because the basement membrane serves as a clear line of demarcation between the tissue boundaries (Fig. 11.14). In connective tissue tumours, invasion is less easy to recognise unless there is clear evidence of vascular or lymphatic permeation; other histological features, such as mitotic activity, are usually assessed for prognostic purposes.

Invasion within epithelium is known as *pagetoid infiltration*; it is named after Paget's disease of the nipple, which is due to

infiltration of the epidermis of the nipple by tumour cells from a ductal carcinoma in the underlying breast. This pattern of invasion can also occur with a few other epithelial malignancies.

Metastasis

Metastasis is the process whereby malignant tumours spread from their site of origin (the *primary tumour*) to form other tumours (*secondary tumours*) at distant sites. The total tumour burden resulting from this process can be very great indeed, and the total mass of the secondary tumours invariably exceeds that of the primary lesion; it is not uncommon at autopsy to find a liver weighing several kilograms more than normal, laden with metastases. The word *carcinomatosis* is used to denote extensive metastatic disease.

Sometimes, metastases can be the presenting clinical feature. Bone pain or fractures due to skeletal metastases can be the first manifestation of a clinically occult internal malignancy. Palpable lymph nodes, due to metastatic involvement, may appear before the signs and symptoms of the primary tumour.

The metastatic cascade

Neoplastic cells must successfully complete a cascade of events before forming a metastatic tumour (Fig. 11.33). Only a proportion of the neoplastic cells in a malignant tumour may have the full repertoire of properties necessary for completion of the cascade. Many tumours studied experimentally in animals consist of metastatic and non-metastatic clones, and metastatic tumours in humans often appear histologically less well differentiated than the primary lesion, suggesting that there is clonal evolution of the metastatic phenotype. There is experimental evidence for the inactivation of 'anti-metastatic' genes ('metastogenes'), such as *nm23*, in neoplastic cells capable of metastasis, but their precise role in the metastatic cascade in human tumours is uncertain.

The sequential steps involved in the metastatic cascade are:

1. *detachment* of tumour cells from their neighbours
2. *invasion* of the surrounding connective tissue to reach conduits for metastasis (blood and lymphatic vessels)
3. *intravasation* into the lumen of vessels
4. *evasion* of host defence mechanisms, such as natural killer cells in the blood
5. *adherence* to endothelium at a remote location
6. *extravasation* of the cells from the vessel lumen into the surrounding tissue.

On reaching the site of metastasis there is a recapitulation of the events that were required for primary tumour growth. The tumour cells must proliferate and, if they are to grow to form a nodule larger than a few millimetres in diameter, the ingrowth of blood vessels must be elicited by angiogenic factors.

Alterations in cell adhesion molecules are important at several points in the metastatic cascade; these affect cell–cell and cell–substrate adhesion. Studies on experimental and human tumours show that reduced expression of *cadherins*, which are involved in adhesion between epithelial cells, correlates positively with invasive and metastatic behaviour. Increased expression of *integrins* appears to be important for the invasive migration of neoplastic cells into connective tissues.

Routes of metastasis

The routes of metastasis are (Fig. 11.34):

- *haematogenous*, by the blood stream, to form secondary tumours in organs perfused by blood that has drained from a tumour
- *lymphatic*, to form secondary tumours in the regional lymph nodes
- *transcoelomic*, in pleural, pericardial and peritoneal cavities where this invariably results in a neoplastic effusion
- *implantation*, for example by accidental spillage of tumour cells during the course of surgery.

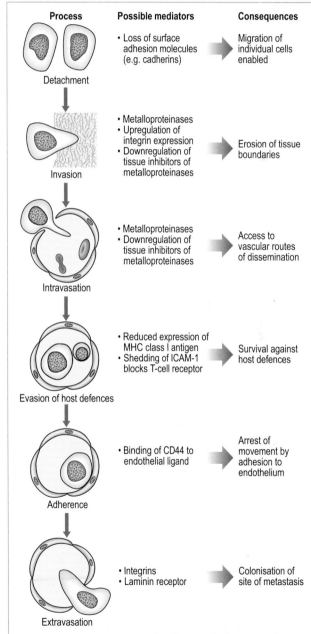

Fig. 11.33 Metastatic cascade. The spread of tumour cells from the site of origin, the primary tumour, to form secondary tumours in other locations requires completion of a logical sequence of events mediated by tumour–host interactions.

Carcinomas tend to prefer lymphatic spread, at least initially, while sarcomas prefer haematogenous spread. However, exceptions to these tendencies are common, and carcinomas often generate blood-borne metastases.

Haematogenous metastasis

Bone is a site favoured by haematogenous metastases from five carcinomas—lung, breast, kidney, thyroid and prostate. Other organs commonly involved by haematogenous metastases are lung, liver and brain (Fig. 11.35). The metastases are frequently multiple, whereas primary tumours arising in the affected organs are usually solitary. Curiously, tumours rarely metastasise to skeletal muscle or to the spleen, despite their lavish blood supply.

Lymphatic metastasis

Tumour cells reach the lymph node through the afferent lymphatic channel. The tumour cells settle and grow in the periphery of the node, gradually extending to replace it (Fig. 11.36). Lymph nodes involved by metastatic tumours are usually firmer and larger than normal. Groups of involved lymph nodes may be matted together by both tumour tissue and the connective tissue reaction to it. Lymph node metastases often interrupt lymphatic flow, thus causing oedema in the territory that they drain.

Clinically, it is necessary to be cautious in interpreting the significance of enlarged lymph nodes draining tumours because the enlargement could simply be due to reactive changes.

Transcoelomic metastasis

The peritoneal, pleural and pericardial cavities are common sites of transcoelomic metastasis, which results in an effusion of fluid into the cavity. The fluid is rich in protein (i.e. it is an exudate) and may contain fibrin. The fluid also contains the neoplastic cells causing the effusion, and cytological examination of the aspirated fluid is very important in diagnosing the cause of effusions into body cavities. The tumour cells often grow as nodules on the mesothelial surface of the cavity.

Peritoneal effusions (ascites) may be due to involvement by any abdominal tumour, but primaries within the ovaries are particularly common. Pleural and pericardial effusions are common consequences of carcinomas of the breast and lung.

Clinical effects of tumours

> ▶ Local effects due to compression, invasion, ulceration or destruction of adjacent structures
> ▶ Metabolic effects due to appropriate or unexpected neoplastic cell products
> ▶ Effects due to metastases if tumour is malignant

The clinical effects of tumours are attributable to their location, their cell of origin and their behaviour. The effects may be local, or occur at some distance from the tumour.

Local effects

Tumours exert local effects through *compression* and *displacement* of adjacent tissues and, if malignant, through their *destruction* by actual invasion. These effects can be clinically inconsequential if the organ is large relative to the size of the tumour or if no vital structure is threatened. However, even benign tumours can have life-threatening effects on neighbouring structures; for example, a functionally inactive adenoma of the pituitary gland may obliterate the adjacent functioning pituitary tissue, such is the confined space in which the gland sits, resulting in hypopituitarism.

Malignant neoplasms obviously have more serious local effects because they *invade* and destroy local structures. This may be

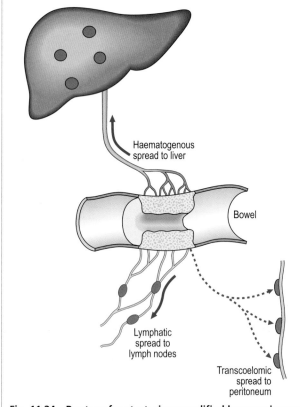

Fig. 11.34   Routes of metastasis exemplified by a carcinoma of the bowel.

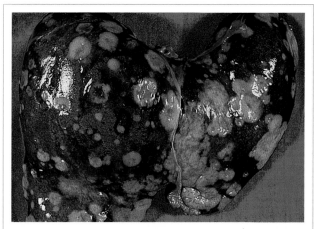

Fig. 11.35   Liver metastases. Liver from an autopsy on a patient who died from carcinomatosis due to carcinoma of the breast.

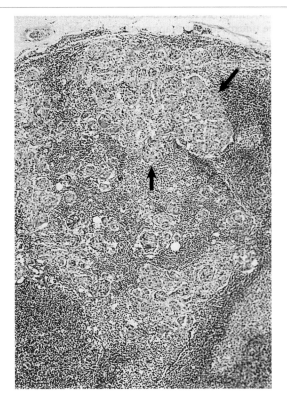

Fig. 11.36 Lymph node metastasis. The lymph node is partly replaced by a deposit of metastatic adenocarcinoma (arrowed) from a primary in the stomach.

Sometimes the metabolic consequences of a tumour are unexpected or inappropriate, at least in the light of our current knowledge; for example, small-cell carcinomas of the lung commonly secrete ACTH and ADH, although this rarely gives rise to clinically significant consequences.

Other specific tumour-associated phenomena have no metabolic consequences but are nevertheless probably mediated by humoral factors. The most common example is finger-clubbing and hypertrophic osteoarthropathy in patients with carcinoma of the lung.

Non-specific metabolic effects

Disseminated malignant tumours are commonly associated with profound weight loss despite apparently adequate nutrition. The catabolic clinical state of a cancer patient with severe weight loss and debility is known as cachexia and is thought to be mediated by tumour-derived humoral factors that interfere with protein metabolism. Cachexia can also occur quite early in the course of the disease, notably in patients with carcinoma of the lung. Weight loss can, of course, also be due to interference with nutrition because of, for example, oesophageal obstruction, severe pain or depressive illness.

Neuropathies and *myopathies* are associated with the presence of malignant neoplasms, particularly with carcinoma of the lung. A tendency to *venous thrombosis* is associated with mucus-producing adenocarcinomas, notably of the pancreas. *Glomerular injury* can result from deposition of immune complexes in which one of the ingredients is tumour antigen (Ch. 9).

Prognosis

Malignant tumours have a variable prognosis (Table 11.13). This is determined partly by the innate characteristics of the tumour cells (e.g. growth rate, invasiveness), and partly by the effectiveness of modern cancer therapy for individual types of tumour.

Prognostic indices

One of the major efforts in histopathology continues to be the search for features that more accurately predict the likely behaviour of individual tumours. It is insufficient merely to diagnose a tumour as malignant and to identify its origin. The patient's treatment is guided by the most accurate determination of:

- tumour type (e.g. melanoma, squamous cell carcinoma, leiomyosarcoma)
- grade or degree of differentiation
- stage or extent of spread.

It is also important to determine whether the presenting lesion is a primary tumour or a metastasis. This can be difficult. There may be little point in performing radical surgery to remove a tumour if it is a metastasis, and the primary tumour and perhaps other metastases remain in the patient.

Tumour type

The tumour type is usually determined from the growth pattern of the tumour and its relationship to the surrounding

rapidly fatal if a vital structure is eroded, for example a pulmonary artery by a carcinoma of the lung. In the case of basal cell carcinoma of the skin ('rodent ulcer'), its local effects are sufficient to justify the label 'carcinoma' because, although the tumour rarely metastasises, its invasiveness can be very disfiguring.

Malignant tumours on mucosal surfaces are often ulcerated. Blood can ooze from these lesions; this blood loss can be occult in the case of gastrointestinal tumours and this is a very important cause of *anaemia*. Ulcerated surfaces also expose the patient to the risk of infection.

Metabolic effects

The metabolic effects of tumours can be subdivided into those specific to individual tumours and those common to many tumours.

Tumour-type specific effects

Well-differentiated endocrine tumours often retain the functional properties of the parent tissue. Since such tumours are relatively autonomous and because the total number of functioning cells often greatly exceeds that in the normal organ, clinical effects are common. For example:

- thyrotoxicosis may result from a thyroid adenoma
- Cushing's syndrome may result from an adrenocortical adenoma
- hyperparathyroidism may result from a parathyroid adenoma.

Table 11.13 Prognosis of some different types of solid malignant tumour, based on experience of responses to treatment in the UK			
Prognostic category			
Good	**Intermediate**	**Poor**
Seminoma of testis Teratoma of testis Choriocarcinoma Malignant melanoma Basal cell carcinoma of skin	Carcinomas of breast, colon, rectum, larynx, uterus, bladder and kidney Osteosarcoma	Carcinomas of lung, pancreas, stomach, oesophagus and liver Mesothelioma

A good prognosis implies a greater than 80% 5-year survival; poor prognosis implies a less than 20% 5-year survival. Prognosis in individual cases is, of course, influenced by tumour grade and stage at presentation.

structures from which a direct origin may be evident. Thus, a gland-forming neoplasm in the breast is most likely to be a primary adenocarcinoma of the breast, particularly if carcinoma cells are also present within the breast ducts near the tumour (ductal carcinoma in situ). A squamous cell carcinoma is often recognisable from the production of keratin, and it may be in continuity with adjacent squamous epithelium that may show carcinoma in situ.

Some types of tumour need to be subclassified because variants with differing behaviour exist. Malignant lymphomas, for example, are subclassified into Hodgkin's and non-Hodgkin's lymphoma, each of which is then further subclassified by detailed appraisal of the histology (Ch. 22).

Genetic analysis or immunohistology may be necessary to type tumours that do not have obvious differentiated features detectable on routine light microscopy.

Tumour grade

The grade of a tumour is an assessment of its degree of malignancy or aggressiveness. This can be inferred from its histology. The most important features contributing to the assessment of tumour grade are:

- mitotic activity
- nuclear size and pleomorphism
- degree of resemblance to the normal tissue (i.e. differentiation).

Grading systems have been devised for many types of tumour, and most involve an assessment of the above features. Tumours are often heterogeneous, and the grading should be performed on what appears to be the least differentiated area as this is likely to contain the most aggressive clone or clones of tumour cells.

Tumour stage

The stage of a tumour is the extent of spread. This is determined by histopathological examination of the resected tumour and by clinical assessment of the patient, often involving imaging techniques. Perhaps the best-known staging system is that devised in the 1930s by Cuthbert Dukes for colorectal carcinomas (Ch. 15):

- Dukes' A: invasion into, but not through, the bowel wall
- Dukes' B: invasion through the bowel wall but without lymph node metastases
- Dukes' C: involvement of the local lymph nodes
- Dukes' D (a stage added later): hepatic metastases present.

The most generally applicable staging system is the TNM system (Fig. 11.37):

- 'T' refers to the primary tumour and is suffixed by a number that denotes tumour size or local anatomical extent. The number varies according to the organ harbouring the tumour.
- 'N' refers to lymph node status and is suffixed by a number denoting the number of lymph nodes or groups of lymph nodes containing metastases.
- 'M' refers to the anatomical extent of distant metastases.

For example, a T1 breast carcinoma is equal to, or less than, 20 mm in diameter; large numbers denote large tumours. N0 denotes no nodal metastases, N1 one or few nodal metastases, and N2 many nodal metastases. M0 denotes an absence of metastases, and M1 and greater denotes increasing extent of distant metastases.

For many tumours, the TNM status is used to derive a stage score. Typically, a stage 1 tumour is confined to the organ of origin and a stage 4 tumour has disseminated widely.

Tumour dormancy

After surgical removal, radiotherapy and/or chemotherapy there may be no clinically detectable tumour remaining in a patient. This does not necessarily mean that the tumour has been completely eradicated: minute deposits can evade detection by even the most sophisticated imaging techniques. These occult tumour foci can remain clinically dormant for perhaps several years before their regrowth causes signs and symptoms. For this reason, it is virtually impossible to speak of a cancer patient as being 'cured', and prognosis can be given only in terms of the probability of survival or the length of the disease-free interval. The prognostic information derived from

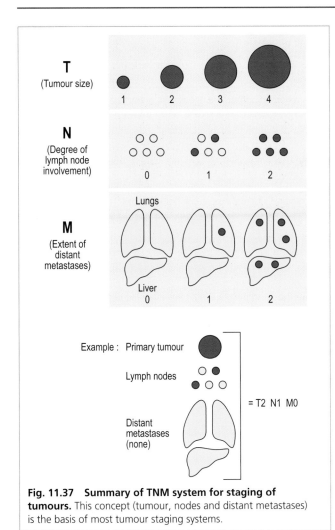

Fig. 11.37 Summary of TNM system for staging of tumours. This concept (tumour, nodes and distant metastases) is the basis of most tumour staging systems.

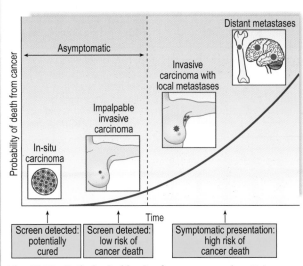

Fig. 11.38 Pathological basis of cancer screening. Using breast cancer as the example, detection at the pre-invasive stage of ductal carcinoma in situ confers a potential cure because there is no risk of metastases. Once the tumour has invaded and gained access to blood vessels and lymphatics, the prospect of cure progressively diminishes.

tumour type, grade and stage is used to predict the patient's chances of surviving, say, 5 years.

EARLY DETECTION OF CANCER BY SCREENING

Because of the dynamics of neoplastic progression and spread, early diagnosis is just as important as treatment in determining the outcome of the disease. The success of early diagnosis relies upon finding tumours at a curable stage before they have had a chance to spread from their site of origin. This is best achieved by screening asymptomatic people, concentrating on those at greatest risk, in the hope of detecting very early lesions (Fig. 11.38). In many countries there are active screening programmes for cervical and breast cancer; screening for colorectal cancer is also being introduced.

Cervical intra-epithelial neoplasia (CIN) can be detected by exfoliative cytology of the cervix. Cells are scraped from the cervix, deposited on to glass slides, stained, and then examined by an expert cytologist trained to detect subtle abnormalities. Breast cancer can be detected at an early stage by regular screening by mammography (X-ray imaging of the breast), followed by diagnosis of any abnormalities by fine-needle aspiration cytology or biopsy.

While early cancer detection is of proven benefit in individual cases, the overall population benefit may be less than anticipated. This is partly because some people are reluctant to be screened; those that do volunteer may not be from the socio-economic groups most at risk, particularly in the case of cancer of the cervix. Furthermore, early detection may not significantly affect the overall mortality from the screened cancer, but merely cause individuals premature anxiety about a disease that would not have become symptomatic for a few more years. Finally, it is not certain that all of the early abnormalities detected by screening would have progressed to more serious lesions within the otherwise natural lifetime of the individual concerned. Thus, the biases that must be allowed for in measuring the benefits of screening are:

- *lead time bias*—earlier detection does not affect the inevitable fatal outcome, but prolongs the apparent survival time
- *length bias*—preferential detection of indolent tumours with intrinsically better prognosis
- *over-diagnosis bias*—diagnosis of lesions that, although histologically malignant, are clinically relatively harmless
- *selection bias*—volunteers for screening are more at risk of good prognosis tumours.

However, despite these possible reasons for an exaggerated benefit, screening for early cancers and precursor lesions is yielding genuine reductions in cancer mortality.

Commonly confused conditions and entities relating to carcinogenesis and neoplasia	
Commonly confused	**Distinction and explanation**
Proto-oncogenes, cellular oncogenes and *oncogenes*	*Proto-oncogenes* and *cellular oncogenes* are normal unmutated genes with important functions in morphogenesis and in the growth and differentiation of normal cells. When these genes become mutated or abnormally expressed as part of the neoplastic process, they are referred to as *oncogenes*.
Gatekeepers and *caretakers*	These are two categories of tumour suppressor gene. *Gatekeeper* genes stop cells with mutated or damaged DNA from proceeding through the cell cycle and replicating the error. *Caretaker* genes repair damaged DNA.
Grade and *stage*	The *grade* of a tumour is its degree of histological resemblance to the parent tissue. The *stage* of a tumour is its anatomical extent of spread.
Histogenesis and *differentiation*	*Histogenesis* indicates the cell type from which a neoplasm has arisen; this can be often deduced from the morphological features of the neoplastic cells. *Differentiation* is the extent to which the neoplastic cells resemble the normal cell lineage from which they are assumed to have arisen.
Sarcoma and *carcinoma*	Both are malignant neoplasms. A *sarcoma* is of connective tissue (mesenchymal) origin. A *carcinoma* is of epithelial origin.
In situ carcinoma and *intra-epithelial neoplasia*	An *in situ carcinoma* has all the cytological features of a malignant epithelial neoplasm, but has not yet invaded through the basement membrane and, therefore, cannot have metastasised. Because epithelial dysplasia (disordered differentiation) may progress to in situ carcinoma and histopathologists may be unable reliably to distinguish the entities, they are merged together as *intra-epithelial neoplasia* and, for example, in the cervix categorised according to the severity of the abnormality (CIN1, CIN2 or CIN3).

FURTHER READING

Alizadeh A A, Ross D T, Perou C M, van de Rijn M 2001 Towards a novel classification of human malignancies based on gene expression patterns. Journal of Pathology 195: 41–52

Baak J P A, Hermsen M A J A, Meijer G, et al 2003 Genomics and proteomics in cancer. European Journal of Cancer 39: 1199–1215

Bicknell R, Lewis C E, Ferrara N 1997 Tumour angiogenesis. Oxford University Press, Oxford

Butel J S 2000 Viral carcinogenesis: revelation of molecular mechanisms and etiology of human disease. Carcinogenesis 21: 405–426

De Wever O, Mareel M 2003 Role of tissue stroma in cancer cell invasion. Journal of Pathology 200: 429–447

Eccles S A, Welch D R 2007 Metastasis: recent discoveries and novel treatment strategies. Lancet 369: 1742–1757

Fearon E R 1997 Human cancer syndromes: clues to the origin and nature of cancer. Science 278: 1043–1050

Finkel T, Serrano M, Blasco M A 2007 The common biology of cancer and ageing. Nature 448: 767–774

Fletcher C D M (ed) 2007 Diagnostic histopathology of tumours, 3rd edn. Churchill Livingstone, Edinburgh

Haber D A, Fearon E R 1998 The promise of cancer genetics. Lancet 351: (SII) 1–8

Hanahan D, Weinberg R A 2000 The hallmarks of cancer. Cell 100: 57–70

Jass J R 2000 Familial colorectal cancer: pathology and molecular characteristics. Lancet Oncology 1: 220–226

Kastan M B, Bartek J 2004 Cell-cycle checkpoints and cancer. Nature 432: 316–323

Keith W N, Evans T R, Glasspool R M 2001 Telomerase and cancer: time to move from a promising target to a clinical reality. Journal of Pathology 195: 404–414

Kinzler K W, Vogelstein B 1997 Gatekeepers and caretakers. Nature 386: 761–763

Loeb L A 2001 A mutator phenotype in cancer. Cancer Research 61: 3230–3239

Murphy G 2007 Matrix metalloproteinases in neoplastic progression: where are we now? Recent Advances in Histopathology 22: 81–92

Rabbitts T H 1994 Chromosomal translocations in human cancer. Nature 372: 143–149

Stiewe T 2007 The p53 family in differentiation and tumorigenesis. Nature Reviews. Cancer 7: 165–8

Thompson E W, Newgreen D F 2005 Carcinoma invasion and metastasis: a role for epithelial–mesenchymal transition. Cancer Research 65: 5991–5999

Weitzman J B, Yaniv M 1999 Rebuilding the road to cancer. Nature 400: 401–402

Yokota J 2000 Tumor progression and metastasis. Carcinogenesis 21: 497–503

Cancer Research UK website (a good source of key facts about different cancers, with statistical data): http://www.cancerresearchuk.org

12

Ageing and death

Ageing and death are linked: as people age their death becomes more likely until, in extreme old age, we may be surprised more by continued life than by the event of death. In general we believe that the older an object is the more likely it is that some disaster will occur; old cars break down, old buildings fall down, many old trees succumb to storms. But this is not a universal phenomenon; in a sense, unicellular animals that reproduce by asexual division live for ever. Every amoeba alive today is in direct line of cytoplasmic and nuclear descent from the very first amoeba that ever lived. The single cells of multicellular animals do not behave like this. Some, such as neurones or heart muscle cells, stop dividing at around the time of birth and, if one cell dies, it is usually not replaced. Even those cells that can reproduce in the human body do so less efficiently with the passage of time (Fig. 12.1); thus, elderly individuals experience slower wound healing. If cells from young animals are cultured they seem to be capable of about 50 cell divisions, but cells from older individuals are capable of progressively fewer cell divisions.

AGEING

Let us consider some of the clinical features of old age. It is often said that we are as old as our arteries, suggesting that arterial disease, which certainly increases with old age, is the cause of all the clinical signs of old age. Arterial degeneration, particularly arteriosclerosis (most frequently due to atheroma), is the commonest cause of debility and death in developed countries (Ch. 2). It would seem logical to think that many diseases might also have their roots in a progressively diminishing supply of oxygen and nutrients. However, in autopsies it is not uncommon to see people who have apparently died from 'old age' without significant arterial disease; this shows that at least some cases of ageing are not

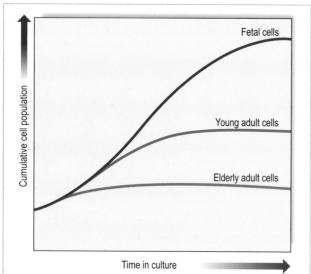

Fig. 12.1 Ageing and the replicative capacity of cells. In cell cultures, the number of mitotic divisions of which cells are capable is inversely proportional to the age of the individual from which the cells were obtained. Thus, fetal cells have considerable growth potential, whereas those from an elderly person are capable of only a few divisions. This is the 'Hayflick limit'.

due to arterial problems even though this is commonly associated with ageing. In many developing societies the elderly population is not particularly afflicted by atherosclerosis and yet such individuals show all of the classic bodily features of old age. There is also a significant difference between the diseases that patients die *with* and the diseases that they die *from*, but this difference is often very difficult to establish scientifically.

THEORIES OF AGEING

▸ Hypotheses include inbuilt genetic mechanisms (clonal senescence) and 'wear and tear' (replication senescence)
▸ Ageing is influenced by genetic and environmental factors
▸ Replicative life-span of untransformed cells is limited (Hayflick limit)
▸ Cumulative free radical-mediated intracellular injury may be important

Basically there are two main groups of ageing theories: *inbuilt genetic* mechanisms and environmental *'wear and tear'* mechanisms. There is evidence to support both theories but like the nature/nurture arguments in other areas of biology, such as the development of intelligence or of sexual orientation, the two possibilities are not mutually exclusive.

Inbuilt genetic mechanisms (clonal senescence)

Common experience supports the idea that there is an inbuilt 'allotted life-span' for humans and other animals. For instance, each animal species seems to have a characteristic *natural life expectancy* ranging from one day for a mayfly to well over 100 years for some amphibia; not all individuals reach this—under natural conditions prevailing in the wild it may be that no individual reaches this natural limit because of the effects of predators, accidents and disease, or the younger individuals may actively drive out or kill aged members of the group or more passively neglect them when they are no longer useful or economically viable. If animals are kept under ideal conditions it does appear that they age and die at around the same time; barring accidents, there is a characteristic life-span. Most human societies reflect this in their belief that there is a natural life expectancy and that there are natural phases in life: infancy, adolescence, adulthood and ageing.

Evidence for genetic factors

From a scientific point of view, few would deny that the processes of embryogenesis, infancy, adolescence and maturity are genetically programmed, although the individual experience of these stages in life may be very highly modified by environmental conditions; the current estimate is that the more complex and variable features such as behaviour are about 60% genetic and 40% environmental. The process of ageing seems to have a genetic component: members of the same family tend to live to a similar age and they age at a similar rate, leaving aside accident and disease.

The actual inherited mechanism(s) responsible for the genetic component of ageing is still unclear but it is worth noting that longevity appears to be inherited through the female line and that all mammalian mitochondria come from the egg and none is transmitted via the sperm. Cell culture experiments suggest that some gene(s) affecting human ageing are carried on chromosome 1, but, again, the way in which they influence ageing is unclear. There are also some remarkable 'natural experiments' in which some human subjects with rare genetic conditions (progerias) such as Werner's syndrome show premature ageing and die from old-age diseases such as advanced atheroma while still chronologically in their teens or early adulthood. Similarly, Down's syndrome patients generally age more rapidly; their fibroblasts are capable of fewer cell divisions in culture than those from age-matched controls.

Two related theories of ageing—the *disposable soma* and *antagonistic pleiotropy*—are related in that they reflect the priority given to reproduction in natural selection. The optimal deployment of genetic and metabolic resources gives primacy to reproduction rather than to ensuring longevity. Consequently, ageing is the passive result of a lack of genetic drive to optimise or prolong life-span. Indeed, some genes involved in enhancing reproduction are hypothesised to have later deleterious effects.

These observations reveal that at least some features of ageing are genetically based.

Interaction with environmental factors

Social correlations with ageing and death are more difficult to interpret. Many diseases are more common in people from lower socio-economic groups; these individuals exhibit ageing changes and die earlier than age- and sex-matched people from higher socio-economic groups. The most immediate interpretation of these phenomena is that people in these groups are disadvantaged in terms of diet, housing and social welfare generally.

Wear and tear (replication senescence)

The 'wear and tear' theories suggest that the normal loss of cells due to the vicissitudes of daily life and the accumulation of sublethal damage in cells lead eventually to system failure of sufficient magnitude that the whole organism succumbs. This theory provides a good explanation of why it is that cardiac and central nervous system failure are such common causes of death, as the functionally important cells in these crucial tissues have very limited ability to regenerate. This theory ultimately depends upon a statistical view of ageing, suggesting that we are all exposed to roughly the same amount of wear and tear and therefore have a narrow range of life expectancy that appears to give us a characteristic life-span.

The various cellular and subcellular mechanisms that have been suggested to cause cumulative damage include:

- protein cross-linking
- DNA cross-linking
- true mutations in DNA making essential genes unavailable or functionally altered

- damage to mitochondria
- other defects in oxygen and nutrient utilisation.

Role of free radicals

The common pathway resulting in cellular deterioration is currently thought to be the generation of highly reactive molecular species called 'free radicals' (Ch. 6). Free radicals are created in neutrophils and macrophages, under carefully controlled conditions, to kill ingested infective organisms; if they are generated accidentally elsewhere there are numerous enzymatic and quenching processes in cells to dispose of them before they can do harm. However, the greater the exposure to free radical inducers (such as toxins in the diet, ionising radiation, etc.), the greater the chance that some damage will occur; these insults will accumulate until they become evident as the ageing process.

Defective repair

Natural experiments lend support to the wear and tear model. There are mechanisms in the cell that deal with damage, particularly DNA damage. These DNA repair mechanisms are numerous but very few deficiency states are well known; the best characterised of these is *xeroderma pigmentosum*. In this condition young children who are exposed to sunlight develop skin atrophy and numerous skin tumours that are more characteristic of elderly subjects with a long history of chronic sun exposure. This condition suggests that there are at least some mechanisms that hold many of the manifestations of ageing at bay; it is certainly possible that these mechanisms themselves could be susceptible to wear and tear, thus paving the way for more general decline.

Living systems are distinguished from most mechanical systems by their ability to regenerate. If the gastric mucosa is damaged, as it is every day by the simple process of eating, then unspecialised reserve cells at the base of the crypts divide and one of the progeny differentiates to become a new crypt cell; this mechanism is common to most tissues. However, the *Hayflick phenomenon* suggests that most cells have the capacity for only a limited number of divisions (unlike cancer cells which seem to be immortal) and that this is under genetic control. Therefore, in the final analysis, *replicative senescence* seems to be dependent upon some form of *clonal senescence*, and the modifications to the cell during its lifetime act upon an intrinsic life-span programme (Fig. 12.2).

Telomeric shortening

At the tip of each chromosome, there is a non-coding tandemly repetitive DNA sequence; this is the *telomere*. These telomeric sequences are not fully copied during DNA synthesis prior to mitosis. As a result, a single-stranded tail of DNA is left at the tip of each chromosome; this is excised and, with each cell division, the telomeres are shortened. Eventually the telomeres are so short that DNA polymerase is unable to engage in the subtelomeric start positions for transcription and the cell is then incapable of further replication. In human cells, it is only in germ cells and in embryos that telomeres are replicated by

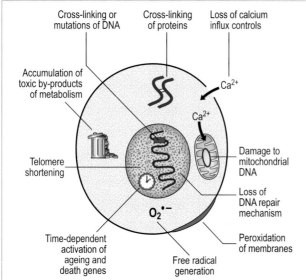

Fig. 12.2 Suggested cellular mechanisms of ageing and death. There is direct or circumstantial evidence supporting each of the mechanisms illustrated. Some mechanisms interact with others; for example, free radicals may be responsible for DNA mutations.

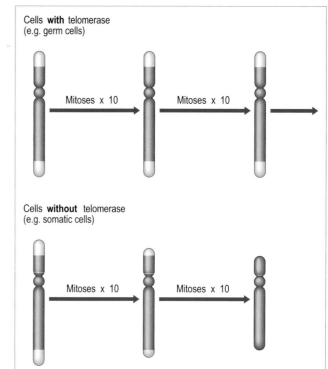

Fig. 12.3 Telomeres, telomerase and replicative capacity. Telomeres are essential for chromosomal copying during the S phase of the cell cycle. However, most somatic cells lack telomerase (the enzyme that regenerates telomeres), so the telomeres shorten with each cell division until chromosomal copying becomes impossible. Germ cells and some neoplastic cells express telomerase and thereby have extended replicative capacity.

the enzyme telomerase. We might also expect telomerase to be active in cancer cells as these are immortal; recent studies have shown that this is true of many, but not all, cancers.

Telomeric shortening could explain the replication ('Hayflick') limit of cells. This is supported by the finding that telomeric length decreases with the age of the individual from which the chromosomes are obtained (Fig. 12.3). In progeria, there is premature telomeric shortening. Furthermore, short telomeres permit chromosomal fusion, and this correlates with the higher incidence of karyotypic aberrations in cells from elderly individuals and in senescent cells in culture.

CLINOPATHOLOGICAL FEATURES OF AGEING

▶ Some features associated with ageing are merely accompaniments; others are directly involved in the ageing process
▶ Every organ changes with age, often with progressive functional impairment
▶ Multiple pathology and comorbidity are common in the elderly

The chronological age of a human subject can often be estimated to within a decade or so on the basis of physical appearances alone. This is true at all ages and is certainly true in the elderly. The processes of development merge into the processes of ageing, interrupted only by a period of maximum biological capacity commonly referred to as maturity. In most mammals maturity is the period of maximum reproductive capacity and is also the period of greatest prowess in the various 'pecking orders' and other social hierarchies that permit the transmission of an individual's genetic characteristics. As old age supervenes, this complex biological peak or prime begins to deteriorate and the chances

of transmitting various genetic combinations decrease. The situation is a little complicated in the human in that the accumulation of wealth in males and the manipulation of fertility in females can modify this decline, but these exceptions are rare and do not affect the general rule.

One of the consequences of a cessation of reproductive capacity in the elderly is that diseases with a genetic component, whose expression in a young adult might result in negative selection pressure, have no such effect; such diseases therefore become preponderant in the elderly. For instance, a disease with a genetic component that proves lethal before or during the reproductive phase would impair the reproductive potential of that individual and the trait would eventually die out apart from new mutations; this obviously does not affect those diseases that become manifest only in old age as these individuals will already have reproduced and passed on the defective gene(s). In any case, there is a direct limit placed on the reproductive ability of the female by the post-menopausal involution of much of the generative system.

There are also other situations in which diseases may be associated with old age but are not related to the causes of old age. Any individual who has lived for 60 years has had more opportunities for accidents than an individual who has lived for only 10 years so far. But this does not mean that accidents are part of the ageing process, although elderly individuals may be more prone to accidents because of failing eyesight and decreased agility. So we should attempt to distinguish

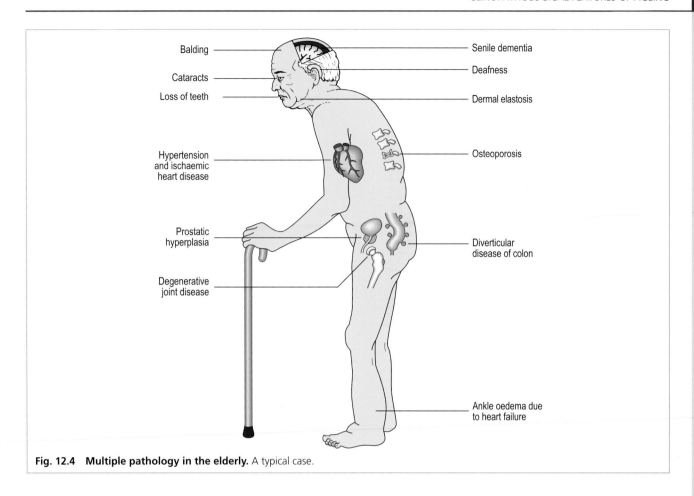

Fig. 12.4 Multiple pathology in the elderly. A typical case.

between the *process* of ageing and *accompaniments* of ageing, and this proves very difficult to do (Fig. 12.4).

Ageing of skin

At a fairly gross level the elderly are identifiable from their wrinkled skin, loss of hair and sagging facial muscles, even if mental acuity is unimpaired (Fig. 12.5). Often the skin is also fragile, loses its youthful elastic recoil and is prone to bruising. Histologically the skin contains less collagen and less elastin, and what is still present is abnormal (Fig. 12.6), as judged by its biochemical properties. Both of these proteins are produced by fibroblasts so it is tempting to wonder whether fibroblasts alter with ageing. Research carried out on fibroblasts in culture has shown that cells from young individuals are capable of more cell divisions (about 50 in total) than are cells from elderly individuals.

However, it is not enough to concentrate on the obvious; as in all clinical assessments we must consider the whole patient. A full assessment of the skin reveals that the wrinkling that we took to be a cardinal sign of ageing is most pronounced on the sun-exposed areas of the skin; those areas that have remained covered for most of the patient's life look decades 'younger' by this criterion. So, what are we to conclude? Is ageing an environmental phenomenon induced by sunlight? This seems unlikely as it is hard to believe that the diffuse, multi-organ phenomena that we

associate with ageing could all be produced by exposing the skin to ultraviolet light.

Osteoarticular ageing

Elderly individuals are often stooped and susceptible to fractures, particularly of the femoral neck. Many post-menopausal women and elderly men have some degree of osteopenia or bone loss. In most cases this is due to *osteoporosis* (Ch. 25), in which the bone matrix is mineralised as normal but the trabeculae in particular are thinned; this results in fractures from relatively minor trauma and even in spontaneous fractures, commonly of the vertebral bodies leading to a stooped posture (so-called 'dowager's hump'). This would appear to be a clear indication that spontaneous deterioration in hormonal function (ovarian function in the case of post-menopausal women) leads to a classic ageing phenomenon; this is often treated with hormone replacement therapy (HRT). However, it is now becoming clear that the development of osteoporosis in old age is much more common in those who were inactive or who had diets low in calcium or vitamin D in youth. Epidemiological evidence is accumulating that many classic features of old age are determined by things that happen during the youth of the individual; an example that has been known for many years is the development of valvular heart disease in the elderly due to rheumatic fever in youth (Ch. 13).

Fig. 12.5 Bertrand Russell in old age. The processes of ageing do not run synchronously. Bertrand Russell (1872–1970), an eminent philosopher, was very active intellectually into his tenth decade. (Painting by Barry Fantoni)

Impaired immunity

The relative immune paresis of old age can result in the recurrence of infections that were contracted many years before and that have never been cleared from the body but have lain dormant. Tuberculosis may erupt again in the elderly, particularly if they become immunosuppressed due to the development of cancer or due to the therapy for cancer, both of which may be immunosuppressive. If *Mycobacterium tuberculosis* organisms are present, tuberculosis can also arise as a spontaneous expression of progressive decline in the immune system which has been constraining the organism, often for many years. Similarly, the chickenpox (varicella) virus can emerge from its hiding place in nerve ganglia and appear as shingles (herpes zoster) whenever the immune system is suppressed, whether by disease, chemotherapy or just old age.

The ageing of the immune system results in a partial loss of the ability to resist new infections and to continue to control old ones, but there is a paradoxical increase in autoimmune diseases with advancing age. Several possible explanations might be advanced for this: perhaps the processes that maintain immune self-tolerance age quicker than the immune system; autoimmune diseases often follow damage to the tissue concerned and the elderly have had more time to accumulate damage; autoimmune diseases often follow infections and we know that the elderly are more prone to infection. The mechanisms are discussed in Chapter 9.

Brown atrophy

Many body organs in the elderly are reduced in size (atrophy, Ch. 5) and are abnormally brown; this condition is 'brown atrophy'. The heart and liver are affected commonly. The

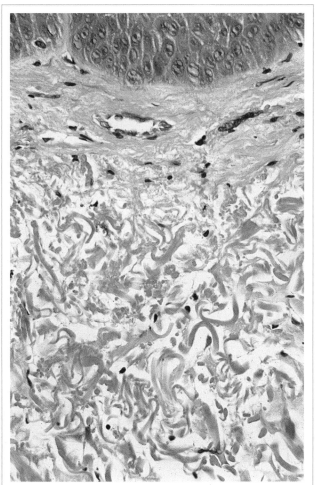

Fig. 12.6 Elastosis in skin. Skin biopsy from the face of an elderly man showing masses of thick homogeneous fibres in the dermis resulting from chronic damage to the dermal collagen by sunlight. This causes the skin to appear wrinkled.

atrophy is due to senile involution. The brown appearance is caused by excessive amounts of *lipofuscin*, a granular brown intracellular pigment, often referred to as 'wear-and-tear' pigment because of its supposed association with excessive usage of an organ. The mere presence of excess lipofuscin does not appear to interfere with the function of the affected organ.

Cardiovascular changes

In the developed world the major cause of death in adults is the various deteriorations in the cardiovascular system, particularly heart attacks and strokes (Ch. 13). So common is this that we begin to believe that this is the final common pathway of ageing and death. In the developing world, however, these diseases are rare, although they are becoming more common as affluent lifestyles spread; although a smaller percentage of the population survives into old age, those that do still show the classical features of senescence. Interestingly, those who do survive into old age tend to die at the same age as their more affluent counterparts; it is just that considerably fewer actually survive the dangers of infancy and adulthood. Postmortem observations show that in affluent societies most people die with the features of cardiovascular disease, but otherwise identical people in both the developed and developing world die without these features and with no obvious causes for death other than that they are old.

A very common concomitant of ageing is a progressive increase in blood pressure—*idiopathic hypertension*. This is an interesting condition because the initial pathological event appears to be a sustained increase in small vessel resistance; the hypertension is a 'physiological' attempt to overcome this and to maintain the essential perfusion pressure to peripheral tissues. Unfortunately, the increased blood pressure has detrimental effects in larger vessels, such as increased atheroma with increased damage to cardiovascular function—this produces the age-associated major causes of death in affluent societies. A significant clinical dilemma arises from this situation: it is tempting to treat hypertension because of its known association with disease. However, elderly patients need at least part of their hypertension to maintain effective perfusion; pharmacologically lowering their blood pressure to that of a healthy young adult is likely to produce disastrous effects on the end organs that one is trying to protect. The treatment of idiopathic hypertension is a delicate balance of short-term and long-term clinical advantages and disadvantages.

Atheroma itself is a disease we associate with increasing age, but autopsies on young adult males often reveal fatty streaks in the aorta. This again provides evidence that the diseases of old age have unexpected roots in youth and young adulthood.

Fate of permanent cells

Neurological function often declines with age; although a part of this can be attributed to decreased cardiovascular function, many subjects show specific deteriorations and accumulations peculiar to the brain (Ch. 26). Nerve cells, like myocardial cells, are normally incapable of replication. There are no reserve cells and so damage to both brain and heart tissue is permanent. The advantage of this is that nerve cells and cardiomyocytes rarely give rise to tumours in the adult; brain tumours in the adult are derived from the various connective tissue cells of the brain or are secondary deposits from cancers elsewhere in the body. It seems strange that such cells cannot replicate, especially as this inability results in so much clinical damage, but both organs rely upon highly ordered complex electrical activity and it may be that replicating cells within such a system would create more problems than they could solve.

Neoplastic diseases

Most neoplasms are commoner in old age but some, such as neuroblastoma and retinoblastoma, occur only in children. Other tumours may have a biphasic distribution, such as osteosarcoma in which there is a peak incidence in adolescence and a second peak in old age (Ch. 25); the tumours arising in adolescents appear spontaneous whereas those arising in old age almost always occur on the basis of longstanding disease

(such as osteomyelitis, malunion of a fracture or Paget's disease) and it seems probable that these are two different tumours that are just impossible to separate morphologically. A similar situation applies with malignant melanoma of the skin; the peak incidence of melanoma on the legs of women and the backs of men (the commonest sites for melanoma) occurs around the third decade, but another type of malignant melanoma occurs on the face of the elderly (lentigo maligna melanoma). This curious age distribution appears to be related to episodic and severe sun exposure in the younger group, but to chronic long-term exposure in the elderly.

DEATH

▶ Modes of death differ according to the ultimate cause
▶ Causes of death are categorised as natural (due to disease) or unnatural (due to accident, homicide, etc.)
▶ Sudden infant death syndrome requires thorough investigation to exclude specific causes

Most definitions of death are, in general, rather unsatisfactory; death could be defined as the permanent disappearance of all signs of life, but this presupposes that we have a useful and clear definition of life, which is far from being the case. One of the prime characteristics of living systems is that they are able to maintain homeostasis in the presence of quite extreme fluctuations in the environment; our core body temperature, the concentration of ions in cells, the circulation of the blood and the level of oxygenation of tissues are all kept constant within a tight range that we recognise as physiological. Other factors within the body may vary but we can see these as attempts to bring the body back into a normal range; shivering generates heat in cold situations, sweating causes heat to be lost in hot situations—the end effect is to return the individual to the normal physiological state. Sometimes these mechanisms are overwhelmed, as in hypothermia or in heat-stroke, but we immediately recognise these situations as pathological. If the body cannot return these functions to normal then vital homeostatic control has been permanently lost and death supervenes. This is true at the level of the whole organism (death of the individual) and at the cellular level (cell death, apoptosis). In some cases death of a large group of cells (such as heart cells or brain cells) may result in death of the individual, but death of a single cell by apoptosis cannot, by itself, result in death of the whole organism.

Even though many genetically controlled factors seem to contribute to ageing and death, they do not seem to be synchronous; one individual may be physically very fit and yet develop pre-senile dementia, while another may continue to dominate some intellectual field despite being physically severely incapacitated by old age. Others may be crippled by osteoarthritic disease (an age-associated condition) and yet show no deterioration in any other system. It seems that, although ageing occurs (at least potentially) in all tissues, the final collapse and dissolution is due not to *orchestrated* deterioration but to the effects of one of the systems reaching a critical and catastrophic point; this then becomes the cause of death (Table 12.1).

Table 12.1   Common modes of death

Mode of death	Common causes	Clinical manifestations
Cardiac arrest or dysrhythmia	Ischaemic heart disease	Sudden and often unexpected death
	Pulmonary embolism	Sudden death after period of immobilisation causing deep vein thrombosis
Shock	Haemorrhage	Profound hypotension and tachycardia
	Toxaemia due to infection	Hypotension, tachycardia and pyrexia
Respiratory failure	Emphysema, pneumonia, asthma	Cyanosis, tachypnoea
Stroke	Raised intracranial pressure (e.g. tumour, bleeding)	Localised neurological defects, coma
	Cerebral infarction	
Renal failure	Chronic renal disease	Low renal output, high blood urea and creatinine
Liver failure	Acute hepatitis, decompensated cirrhosis, paracetamol poisoning	Jaundice, coma, bleeding

DYING AND DEATH

Dying and death must be carefully distinguished. This is not just an interesting academic point—it also concerns many patients. People will often make the distinction by saying that they are not afraid of death, but they are afraid of dying because this may be painful, undignified or distressing to their relatives. Also the relationship between dying and death is by no means automatic: someone killed in a road traffic accident was not necessarily dying immediately beforehand; someone with a ruptured aortic aneurysm is certainly dying but in some instances may be saved and not die.

CLINICAL FEATURES OF DEATH

The collapsed elderly patient with no clinical history poses a significant problem. There are no obvious signs of life and preliminary resuscitation attempts have not altered the patient's state. The ECG shows no complexes. There is no rigor mortis (postmortem muscular spasm) and there is no obvious wound of sufficient severity to suggest a cause of death. Is the patient dead? In practical terms there is a sequence of tests that most doctors will use because any one test is fallible. These are the so-called 'vital' signs:

- respiration (both by observation and aided by the stethoscope)
- pulses (at the wrist, in the neck, in the groins)
- responses to progressively greater pain stimuli
- stagnation in the circulation in the form of 'beading' of blood in the arteries, visible in retinal arteries.

In the absence of all such vital signs, the possibility of hypothermia and deep drug comas should be considered as well as more obscure conditions. If there is doubt early on and if there are no contraindications (such as obvious advanced cancer) then more active resuscitation techniques may be tried involving direct electrical stimulation of the heart or intravenous drugs for the same purpose. If none of these manoeuvres is effective then most doctors will be satisfied and willing to declare the subject dead. Can they still be wrong? Unfortunately in very rare cases the answer is 'yes'.

The practical importance of accurately establishing the presence of death (or absence of life) is brought into sharp focus by the needs of organ retrieval for transplant surgery; there are strict criteria for deeming a patient to be dead (or *brain dead*) under these circumstances:

1. The pupils are fixed in diameter and do not respond to sudden changes in the intensity of incident light.
2. There is no corneal reflex.
3. The vestibulo-ocular reflexes are absent.
4. No motor responses within the cranial nerve distribution can be elicited by adequate stimulation of any somatic area.
5. There is no gag reflex or reflex response to bronchial stimulation by a suction catheter passed down the trachea.
6. No respiratory movements occur when the patient is disconnected from the mechanical ventilator for long enough to ensure that the arterial CO_2 level rises above the threshold for stimulation of respiration.

It is important to recognise that factors such as body temperature and the presence of drugs in the body can modify these circumstances. For practical purposes the application of these tests is restricted to doctors with a suitable level of expertise, in the presence of another, independent, doctor who must not be part of the transplant team.

All this serves to underline the difficulty in defining death and in satisfactorily demonstrating it. The definition of death that describes it as the 'permanent loss of all signs of life' is doubtless true, but it depends upon the term 'permanent'—in clinical situations this is often the crucial central issue. It is obviously very unpleasant for all concerned to make a mistake over this issue and it is clinically unacceptable to allow someone to progress from a deep but reversible hypothermic coma to the permanence of death. The problem has been brought into even sharper focus by organ retrieval for transplants where the interests of establishing death, or its imminent inevitability, with certainty and the need to retrieve the tissues in as viable a condition as possible may come into conflict.

BIOLOGICAL MECHANISMS OF DEATH

Sometimes death is sudden and results from damage that exceeds the body's ability to restore homeostasis. Such situations are common in severe trauma or in cases of system failure of great severity such as total coronary artery occlusion or massive cerebral haemorrhage. In many other cases the immediately pre-terminal state is either coma or shock (Ch. 8). In the case of *shock* many of the measured features are aberrant biochemical states, such as ketoacidosis, that are themselves the pathological event that, if uncorrected, may go on to cause death. Many other features are bodily mechanisms that have been activated in an attempt to limit or reverse the damage; these include the adrenergic surge leading to vasoconstriction, increased heart rate and redirection of blood flow away from non-essential sites, together within incidental effects, such as sweating, that characterise shock, exemplified by the typical cold, sweaty, 'shut down' patient with a rapid pulse. If these adjustments prove inadequate and effective medical intervention is not available, then the patient will progress to death. Under such circumstances it is important to work with the bodily processes that are attempting to restore a normal physiological state and not to try to correct them just because they appear 'abnormal'.

Blood loss is a particular variant of hypovolaemic shock; here the main thrust of therapy is to identify and treat the cause while returning the circulating volume to normal. Hypovolaemic shock may also be due to infection by bacteria producing toxins that damage vascular endothelium, resulting in vascular dilatation and increased permeability and fluid loss.

Cardiogenic shock produces relative hypovolaemia by failure of the heart to pump an adequate volume into the vessels; simply increasing the circulating volume would convert the signs of acute cardiac failure into those of chronic cardiac failure. In anaphylactic shock the basis of treatment is to withdraw the precipitating cause and to give therapy aimed at reducing the symptoms. Neurogenic shock is often induced by partial abortion where some products of conception are stuck in the uterine os; treatment consists of removing these as rapidly as possible. The salient point is that treatment should be directed at the specific type and cause of shock in order to prevent its progression to death.

CAUSES OF DEATH

Natural causes

The accurate recording of the causes of death is crucial to our understanding of disease in society (Ch. 2), but what exactly caused death in a particular situation is not always easy to determine. Although many people die with widespread cancer and their deaths are quite validly recorded as being due to that cancer, it is by no means always clear what it was about the cancer that killed them. For instance, if someone is said to have died from bronchial carcinoma it is always possible to find a case in which another patient died at a much later stage with a far greater load of cancer, so the volume of disease per se cannot explain why it can kill some people and not

others. In such cases we commonly fall back on rather diffuse explanations involving one person's 'resistance' or 'strength' compared to another, but the differences can be huge. Cancers produce various substances that have body-wide effects, such as cachexin (tumour necrosis factor-alpha), and there are many other interleukins that may play a role in the disturbed metabolism of many cancer patients. Tumours may also produce various hormones, resulting in paraneoplastic syndromes (Ch. 11). Thus it is entirely possible that many cancer deaths are metabolic deaths. Careful examination of the heart in advanced cancer cases reveals a surprising number of occult deposits of metastatic tumours, and terminal dysrhythmias probably account for a significant number of cancer deaths.

Unnatural causes

Death due to disease and old age is generally regarded as 'death from natural causes', but a wide variety of deaths cannot be considered 'natural'; some deaths involve a synergistic combination of natural and unnatural causes. Obvious unnatural causes include *suicide, murder* and *accidents;* less clear are suicides by the mentally ill and accidents caused by natural disease, such as a car crash resulting from a heart attack. From the point of view of the law and the issuing of death certificates, a death is natural if caused by natural disease or old age and is accidental if the accident would not have occurred in the absence of the disease. These decisions are for the medico-legal authorities, as is the decision of whether a death is suicide or murder.

All deaths in which there is an element of doubt must be referred to the appropriate legal officer (for example, the Coroner in England and Wales or the Procurator Fiscal in Scotland). The doctor's role in these cases is to offer a medical opinion as to the ultimate cause of death. The motivation is a matter for the legal agencies; a doctor may decide that death was due to hanging or paracetamol overdose, but cannot say whether this was accident, suicide or murder.

Within the category of unnatural death we still need to be careful in our interpretation of what caused death. Pressure on the neck can cause death and it may appear to be clear from the circumstances that death was due to hanging or to strangulation. However, pressure on the neck can kill in a variety of ways: mild pressure may be enough to occlude venous return and the subject will die with a congested appearance, swollen protruding tongue and petechial haemorrhages in the eyes; firmer pressure may occlude arterial supply to the brain and the congested features will be much less marked, although the death will still be due to cerebral ischaemia; yet stronger pressure may occlude the trachea, usually breaking the hyoid bone, and death will be due to asphyxia; sudden pressure on the neck may result in instant death by vaso-vagal inhibition with no physical features of congestion at all.

Sudden infant death syndrome

The cause of deaths attributed to 'sudden infant death syndrome' remains obscure. The event occurs in very young children in all social classes and no overwhelming common factor has been detected. It may be a collection of disparate and as yet unrecognised disease states, possibly related to the infant's social condition, or it is still possible that it has a genetic basis. The term 'sudden infant death syndrome' is used only when an exhaustive postmortem examination, including histology, fails to reveal an identifiable cause of death. Postmortems under these circumstances are often difficult to contemplate but the results of such examinations are often viewed as a great consolation by bereaved parents as they demonstrate that they were not negligent or culpable in any other way.

TERMINAL EVENTS

In many cases of terminal states that have been studied it seems that perturbations of the central nervous system are the final common pathway leading to irreversibility. Curiously, similar changes are found in elderly patients who are otherwise fit; a sudden decrease in intellectual ability often precedes spontaneous natural death, a situation referred to as the 'terminal drop'. Perhaps it is not so surprising that a highly complex organism such as the human body should be so crucially dependent upon its co-ordinating and control system that we should come to use this system to determine death and to find that its disruption so closely precedes the end of life.

Pathology of bed rest

Terminally ill patients are often confined to bed. However, prolonged bed rest is not without complications; some are serious. Most complications can be prevented by careful nursing and active physiotherapy.

Decubitus ulcers (bed sores)

Decubitus ulcers occur over pressure points, such as the sacrum and heels in a patient lying supine. They are due to ischaemic necrosis of the skin caused by compression of the vascular supply. Emaciated patients are especially liable to develop decubitus ulcers because there is less subcutaneous fat to diffuse the pressure over bony prominences.

The skin first appears discoloured and becomes gangrenous and then sloughs to expose a raw base of connective tissue. The resulting ulcer frequently becomes infected and may lead to septicaemia.

Decubitus ulcers can be prevented by regularly turning the patient and by using special mattresses. Comatose or severely debilitated patients require highly skilled nursing care to prevent this complication.

Venous thrombosis

Venous return of blood from the legs results from the movement of the surrounding muscles combined with the effect of valves. Immobilised patients commonly develop deep leg vein thrombosis because of venous stasis; this has two consequences:

- venous oedema of the leg
- risk of pulmonary embolism.

The latter is an ominous event causing either pulmonary infarction or even sudden death (Ch. 8).

Leg vein thrombosis can be prevented by anticoagulation or compression stockings in cases at risk and by physiotherapy.

Osteoporosis and muscle wasting

Osteoporosis is a condition in which there is a reduction in bone mass (Ch. 25). Patients confined to bed for prolonged periods inevitably lose some bone mass. It also occurs in astronauts in the weightless environment of space. Osteoporosis not only weakens the skeleton, but also liberates much calcium, leading to hypercalciuria and a risk of renal stone formation.

Skeletal muscle mass reduces in immobilised or bed-ridden patients. This mass can be restored when the patient recovers, but physiotherapy may be necessary to accelerate the process.

Hypostatic pneumonia

Patients lying supine in bed have a reduced respiratory excursion and, if severely ill, may have reduced cough reflexes. Furthermore, the posterior regions of the lungs become congested with blood and alveolar oedema can occur. These events combine to predispose the patient to develop a form of bronchopneumonia (Ch. 14) known as hypostatic pneumonia. Hypostatic pneumonia is a serious complication requiring vigorous physiotherapy and antibiotics, but these measures may be unjustified if the patient has some otherwise incurable disease.

FURTHER READING

Balaban R S, Nemoto S, Finkel T 2005 Mitochondria, oxidants and aging. Cell 120: 483–495

Cawthon R M, Smith K R, O'Brien E, Sivatchenko A, Kerber R A 2003 Association between telomere length in blood and mortality in people aged 60 years or older. Lancet 361: 393–395

Cotton D W K 1995 Death: the cell. Progress in Pathology 2: 1–11

Cottrell D A, Blakely E L, Johnson M A et al 2001 Mitochondrial DNA mutations in disease and ageing. In: Ageing vulnerability: causes and interventions. Wiley, Chichester

Crews D E 2007 Senescence, aging and disease. Journal of Physiological Anthropology 26: 365–372

Fossel M 2002 Cell senescence in human aging and disease. Annals of the New York Academy of Sciences 959: 14–23

Gonzalez-Crussi F 1987 Three forms of sudden death. Picador, London

Goyns M H 2002 Genes, telomeres and mammalian ageing. Mechanisms of Ageing and Development 123: 791–799

Hayflick L 1996 How and why we age. Ballantine, New York

Holliday R 1995 Understanding ageing. Cambridge University Press, Cambridge

Kirkwood T B 2002 Molecular gerontology. Journal of Inherited Metabolic Disease 25: 189–196

Kirkwood T 2002 Time of our lives: the science of human aging. Oxford University Press, Oxford

Lynch T 1998 The undertaking: life studies from the dismal trade. Penguin, London

Nuland S B 1993 How we die: reflections of life's final chapter. Chatto & Windus, London

Rose M R 1991 Evolutionary biology of ageing. Oxford University Press, Oxford

Steel M 1995 Telomerase that shapes our ends. Lancet 354: 935–936

PART 3

SYSTEMATIC PATHOLOGY

13

Cardiovascular system

COMMON CLINICAL PROBLEMS FROM CARDIOVASCULAR DISEASE

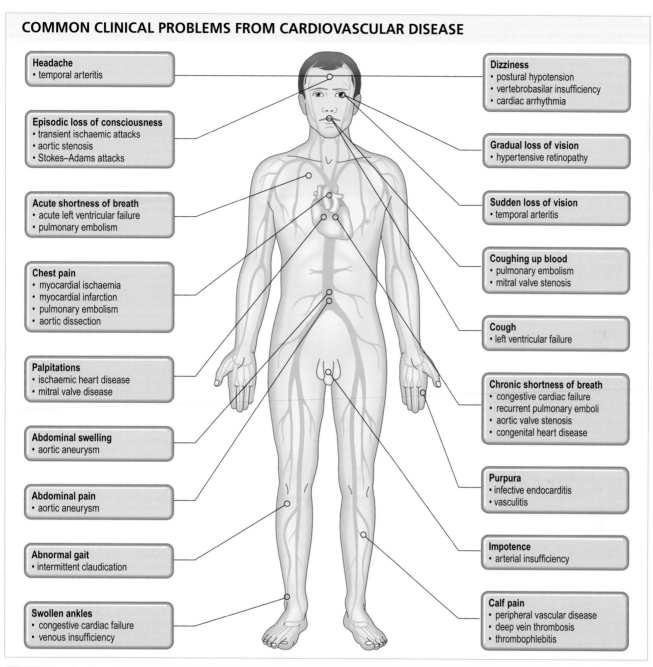

Headache
• temporal arteritis

Episodic loss of consciousness
• transient ischaemic attacks
• aortic stenosis
• Stokes–Adams attacks

Acute shortness of breath
• acute left ventricular failure
• pulmonary embolism

Chest pain
• myocardial ischaemia
• myocardial infarction
• pulmonary embolism
• aortic dissection

Palpitations
• ischaemic heart disease
• mitral valve disease

Abdominal swelling
• aortic aneurysm

Abdominal pain
• aortic aneurysm

Abnormal gait
• intermittent claudication

Swollen ankles
• congestive cardiac failure
• venous insufficiency

Dizziness
• postural hypotension
• vertebrobasilar insufficiency
• cardiac arrhythmia

Gradual loss of vision
• hypertensive retinopathy

Sudden loss of vision
• temporal arteritis

Coughing up blood
• pulmonary embolism
• mitral valve stenosis

Cough
• left ventricular failure

Chronic shortness of breath
• congestive cardiac failure
• recurrent pulmonary emboli
• aortic valve stenosis
• congenital heart disease

Purpura
• infective endocarditis
• vasculitis

Impotence
• arterial insufficiency

Calf pain
• peripheral vascular disease
• deep vein thrombosis
• thrombophlebitis

Pathological basis of cardiovascular signs and symptoms			
Sign or symptom	Pathological basis	Sign or symptom	Pathological basis
Angina	Myocardial ischaemia due to spasm, atheroma or thrombosis of coronary arteries	**Abnormal heart sounds**	
Abnormal blood pressure		• Murmurs	Turbulence of blood flow through stenotic or incompetent valves
• Hypertension	Either 'essential' (primary, idiopathic) due to as yet undefined genetic and environmental factors, or secondary to a disease resulting in increased levels of hormones with hypertensive effects	• Friction rub	Pericarditis
		• Indistinct sounds	Pericardial effusion
• Hypotension	Reduction of actual or effective circulating blood volume		

(Continued)

Pathological basis of cardiovascular signs and symptoms—cont'd			
Sign or symptom	Pathological basis	Sign or symptom	Pathological basis
Abnormal ECG • Altered waveform	Disturbed myocardial depolarisation/repolarisation commonly due to ischaemia or infarction	**Raised serum troponin or creatinine phosphokinase**	Release of cardiac enzymes into blood due to myocardial infarction
• Altered rhythm	Disturbed conduction of electrical activity due to, for example, disease affecting conducting tissue or causing appearance of foci of ectopic electrical activity	**Joint pains**	Synovial inflammation in rheumatic fever
Abnormal pulse	Disordered heart rhythm or arterial flow	**Skin lesions** • Leg ulcers	Impaired arterial or venous flow
		• Gangrene	Interruption of arterial supply
Raised jugular venous pressure	Increased central venous pressure due to right or congestive cardiac failure	• Splinter haemorrhages (under nails)	Microemboli from infective endocarditis
Oedema	If due to vascular disease, attributable to raised venous pressure (e.g. in cardiac failure or venous thrombosis) exceeding plasma oncotic pressure	• Purpuric rash	Microhaemorrhages in skin due to vasculitis
		Hemiplegia	Cerebral haemorrhage or cerebral artery occlusion by thrombus or embolus
Dyspnoea	Pulmonary oedema due to left ventricular failure or mitral stenosis	**Visual impairment**	Cranial (giant cell) arteritis Hypertensive retinopathy
Cyanosis	Partial bypass of pulmonary circulation or acquired impairment of circulation or oxygenation	**Sudden collapse**	Vaso-vagal syncope Severe dysrhythmia (e.g. ventricular fibrillation) due to myocardial infarction

DISEASES OF THE ARTERIES AND OTHER VESSELS

Cardiovascular disorders are now the leading cause of death in most Western societies (Ch. 2). In England and Wales ischaemic heart disease currently accounts for 27%, and cerebral vascular disorders for 13%, of all deaths. Atherosclerosis is the commonest and most important vascular disease, but many other vascular disorders are recognised.

Normal arterial structure

In all parts of the arterial system, three anatomical layers can be distinguished. The innermost, the *intima*, is composed of a single layer of endothelium with a thin supporting framework of connective tissue. The internal elastic lamina separates the intima from the middle layer, the *media* (Fig. 13.1). The aortic media is particularly rich in elastic tissue, but in most medium-sized arteries, such as the coronary arteries, smooth muscle predominates. The outermost layer, the *adventitia*, is fibrous connective tissue. Small blood vessels, the vasa vasorum, enter from the adventitial aspect and supply much of the media. The intima and innermost media receive nutrients by direct diffusion from the vascular lumen.

AGE-RELATED VASCULAR CHANGES

A variety of ageing changes occur in the aorta, arteries and arterioles. Although there is considerable individual variation, changes are usually inconsequential before 40 and most common after 70 years of age. The most important changes are:

- progressive fibrous thickening of the intima
- fibrosis and scarring of the muscular or elastic media
- the accumulation of mucopolysaccharide-rich ground substance
- fragmentation of the elastic laminae.

The net effect of these changes is to reduce both the strength and the elasticity of the vessel wall. Progressive dilatation is a common ageing phenomenon in both the aorta and the coronary arteries. In the ascending aorta this can lead to stretching of the aortic valve ring and aortic incompetence. Dilatation of the arch and thoracic aorta produces the characteristic 'unfolding' seen in chest X-rays (Fig. 13.2).

The age-related changes that occur in muscular arteries are usually termed *arteriosclerosis*. Even arterioles can be affected. Characteristic alterations include smooth muscle hypertrophy and the apparent reduplication of the internal elastic laminae by extra layers of collagen. There is often marked intimal fibrosis and this further reduces the diameter of the vessel. Arteriosclerosis contributes to the high frequency of cardiac, cerebral, colonic and renal ischaemia in the elderly population. The clinical effects become most apparent when the cardiovascular system is further stressed by haemorrhage, major surgery, infection or shock.

ATHEROSCLEROSIS

▶ Affects large and medium-sized arteries
▶ Lesions comprise fatty streaks, fibrolipid plaques and complicated lesions

▶ Risk factors include increasing age, male gender, hypertension, smoking and diabetes
▶ Associated with increased levels of low-density lipoprotein (LDL) cholesterol, Lp(a), fibrinogen and factor VII, and reduced levels of high-density lipoprotein (HDL) cholesterol
▶ Major cause of organ ischaemia (e.g. myocardial infarction)

Atherosclerosis is a disease characterised by formation of focal elevated lesions in the intima of large (aorta) and medium-sized arteries (such as coronary arteries)—termed atherosclerotic plaques. Plaques alone are usually benign asymptomatic lesions, even when they are present in large numbers throughout the arterial tree, but life-threatening ischaemic damage of vital organs may occur when an occlusive thrombosis forms on a spontaneously disrupted plaque (atherothrombosis). Such acute obstructions can occur in many different arteries, resulting in a wide range of clinical disorders (Fig. 13.3). The frequency of atherothrombotic complications has increased drastically during the past 50 years, and the condition is now also common in parts of the Middle and Far East, particularly in those countries where a 'Western style' of living has been adopted. Coronary atherothrombosis—'coronary heart disease'—is one of the commonest causes of death in many societies.

Atherosclerotic lesions

The formation of lesions starts in young children, especially in societies with a high dietary fat intake. The earliest significant lesion is called a fatty streak. It is a yellow linear elevation of the intimal lining and is composed of masses of lipid-laden macrophages. These fatty streaks have no clinical significance. They may disappear from the arterial intima, but in patients at risk they progress to atherosclerotic plaques (Fig. 13.4). The fully developed plaque is a lesion with a central lipid core

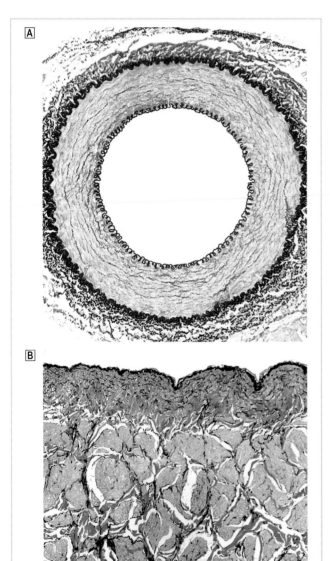

Fig. 13.1 Structure of blood vessels. **A** Muscular artery from a young child. The intima is extremely thin. **B** Renal vein from a 72-year-old man. Elastic lamellae are indistinct and there is some intimal fibrosis (red coloration). The underlying muscle bundles (pale yellow) are not arranged as regularly as in arteries.

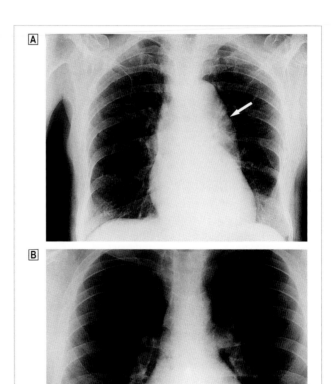

Fig. 13.2 Unfolding of the aorta. **A** There is a prominent bulge (arrow) caused by dilatation of the arch and descending aorta. If the dilatation involves the aortic valve ring, aortic incompetence may result. **B** Normal X-ray for comparison.

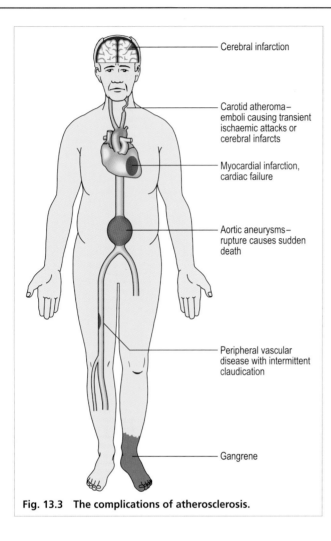

Cerebral infarction

Carotid atheroma–
emboli causing transient
ischaemic attacks or
cerebral infarcts

Myocardial infarction,
cardiac failure

Aortic aneurysms–
rupture causes sudden
death

Peripheral vascular
disease with intermittent
claudication

Gangrene

Fig. 13.3   The complications of atherosclerosis.

What causes atherosclerosis?

Hypercholesterolaemia is by far the most important risk factor for atherosclerosis. It can cause plaque formation and growth in the absence of other known risk factors. It has been suggested that if plasma cholesterol levels in a population were below 2.5 mmol/l (such as in the traditional Chinese culture), symptomatic atherosclerotic disease would be almost nonexistent. The most compelling evidence for the importance of LDL cholesterol comes from studies of patients and animals that have a genetically determined lack of cell membrane receptors for LDL (Fig. 13.6). About 1 in 500 Caucasians is heterozygous for this type of mutation, and has reduced numbers of functional receptors on their cell surfaces and elevated plasma LDL-cholesterol levels (over 8 mmol/l). Such individuals often develop coronary heart disease in their forties or fifties. The rare patients who are homozygous for one of these mutations (approximately 1 per million) have much higher cholesterol levels and usually die from coronary atheroma in infancy or the teens.

The importance of other risk factors beyond hypercholesterolaemia is illustrated by the huge variation in expression of severity of disease among groups of patients with the same cholesterol levels. Major risk factors are *smoking, hypertension, diabetes, male gender* and *increasing age*. They appear to accelerate the process of plaque formation driven by lipids. Less strong risk factors include *obesity*, a *sedentary lifestyle, low socio-economic status* and *low birth weight*. At present there is also increasing interest in the role of micro-organisms in the evolution of atherosclerotic disease. The cumulative effect of several, often innocent or subclinical, infections with common bacteria such as *Chlamydia pneumoniae*, cytomegalovirus, influenza and dental pathogens are thought to increase the risk of atherosclerosis by switching on evolutionarily conserved pathways of inflammation. There is also recent evidence that high-fat diets and obesity may promote translocation of commensal-derived endotoxin from the gut into the general circulation and there induce inflammation, insulin resistance and atherosclerosis.

How do lesions develop?

Generally, the development of atherosclerosis is a two-step process. The first step is injury to the endothelium of the arterial wall and the second is a tissue response of the vascular wall to the injurious agents. Chronic or episodic exposure of the arterial wall to these processes leads over many years to formation of plaques. This concept, initially introduced by Ross and Glomset in 1972, is now convincingly supported by carefully designed postmortem studies of patients of different ages and racial origin and from studies in animals that develop atherosclerosis either spontaneously or following high-fat or cholesterol-supplemented diets.

Injured endothelial cells at sites of lesion formation undergo profound functional alterations which include an enhanced expression of cell adhesion molecules, including ICAM-1 and E-selectin, a high permeability for macromolecules such as LDL, and increased thrombogenicity. This allows inflammatory cells and lipids to enter the intimal layer and form plaques. In more advanced stages of

with a cap of fibrous tissue covered by the arterial endothelium (Fig. 13.5). Connective tissues in the cap, mainly collagens, provide the structural strength of the plaque and are produced by smooth muscle cells (SMCs). Inflammatory cells, including macrophages, T-lymphocytes and mast cells, reside in the fibrous cap. They are recruited from the arterial endothelium or, in advanced plaques only, from newly formed microvessels present at the base of, or around, the atheroma.

The atheroma is rich in cellular lipids and cellular debris derived from macrophages that have died inside the plaque. It is soft (semi-fluid), highly thrombogenic and often bordered by a rim of so-called foam cells. The foam cell results from uptake of oxidised lipoproteins via a specialised membrane-bound scavenger receptor. This is one of the most distinctive pathological processes in plaque formation. Dystrophic calcification of the plaque can be extensive and occurs late in the process of plaque development. It may serve as a marker for atherosclerotic vessel disease in angiograms or in CT images. Plaques have a tendency to form at arterial branching points and bifurcations. This illustrates the important role of turbulent blood flow in the pathogenesis of atherosclerosis. In the late stages many individual lesions may become confluent and cover large parts of arteries (Fig. 13.4B).

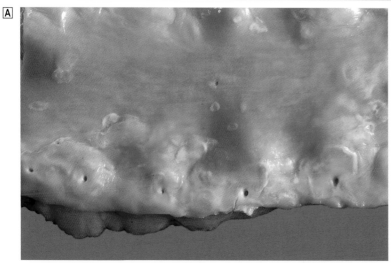

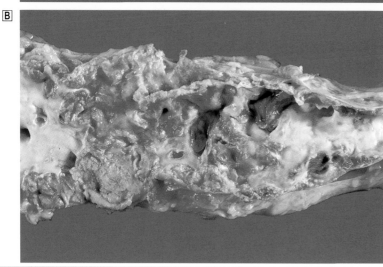

Fig. 13.4 Lesions of atherosclerosis. **A** Early aortic atherosclerosis. Note the many small fatty streaks. Some larger dot-like lesions are also present. These are common lesions in all racial groups and both genders. **B** Advanced complicated atherosclerosis in the abdominal aorta. Many of the lesions have ruptured and become thrombosed.

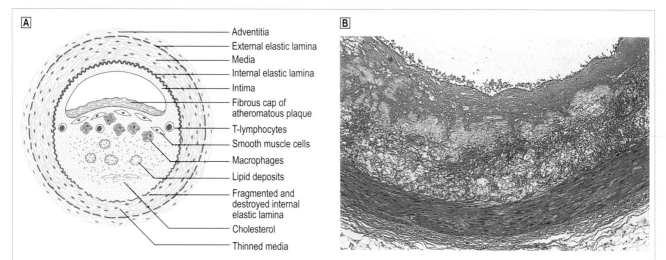

Fig. 13.5 Atheromatous plaque. **A** Diagram of an atheromatous plaque. Some of the features can be seen in the photomicrograph **B** from the coronary artery of a 72-year-old.

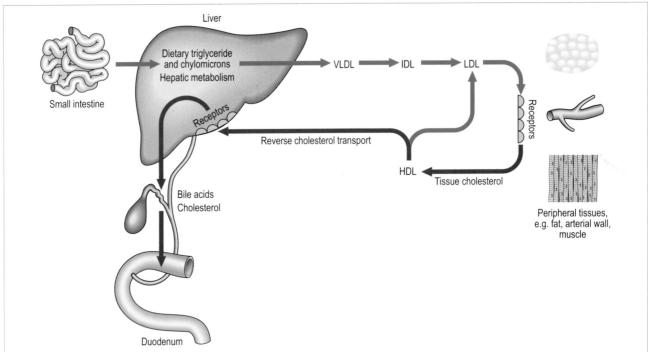

Fig. 13.6 Major pathways of lipoprotein metabolism. This is a much simplified outline of lipid metabolism. Note that LDL uptake in peripheral tissues is receptor-mediated. HDL apoprotein accepts cholesterol from tissues. This can then be absorbed by specific receptors in the liver (reverse cholesterol transport) or recycled into LDL. (HDL, high-density lipoprotein; IDL, intermediate-density lipoprotein; LDL, low-density lipoprotein; VLDL, very-low-density lipoprotein.)

plaque formation large amounts of macrophages and T-cells accumulate in the plaque tissue. Lipid-laden macrophages (foam cells) die through apoptosis, spilling their lipid into an ever-enlarging lipid core. In this respect the response to injury in atherosclerosis has all the features of a chronic inflammatory process.

As in all chronic inflammatory diseases the inflammatory reaction is followed by a process of tissue repair. Growth factors, particularly platelet-derived growth factor (PDGF), stimulate the proliferation of intimal smooth muscle cells (myointimal cells) and the subsequent synthesis of collagen, elastin and mucopolysaccharide by smooth muscle cells. A fibrous cap encloses the lipid-rich core (Fig. 13.5). Growth factors are secreted by platelets, injured endothelium, macrophages and smooth muscle cells themselves.

Another important mechanism of plaque growth is initiated by small areas of endothelial loss, especially in fully developed plaques. Microthrombi are formed at the denuded areas of the plaque surface. These become organised by the same repair process of smooth muscle cell invasion and collagen deposition. Repeated cycles of this process gradually increase the plaque volume.

Clinical manifestations of atherosclerosis

Over a lifetime many plaques may develop in a given patient, the great majority of which will remain clinically unnoticed. Clinical disease is usually provoked by only one out of many plaques, and ranges in severity from relatively benign

symptoms to life-threatening diseases. The more serious conditions often follow acute changes in the plaques.

1. *Progressive lumen narrowing due to high-grade plaque stenosis.* Stenosis of more than 50–75% of the vessel lumen leads to critical reduction of blood flow in the distal arterial bed. Consequently, reversible tissue ischaemia develops, especially during effort. Examples are stable angina pectoris (stenosed coronary artery) or intermittent claudication (iliac, femoral or popliteal artery stenosis). When the stenosis is severe, ischaemic pain may also occur at rest. Moreover, longstanding tissue ischaemia may also lead to atrophy of an affected organ, for example renal atrophy in cases of atherosclerotic renal artery stenosis.

2. *Acute atherothrombotic occlusion.* Major complications of atherosclerosis are acute events that are initiated by rupture of an atherosclerotic plaque. Plaque rupture exposes highly thrombogenic plaque components (collagen, lipid debris) to the blood stream which leads to activation of the coagulation cascade and thrombotic occlusion of the vessel lumen in a (very) short period of time. Total occlusion leads to irreversible ischaemia causing necrosis (infarction) of the tissues supplied by the obstructed artery. Examples are myocardial infarction (coronary arteries), stroke (carotid or cerebral arteries) and lower limb gangrene (iliac, femoral or popliteal arteries).

3. *Embolisation of the distal arterial bed.* Another complication that may arise from atherothrombosis is detachment of small thrombus fragments. These then embolise the arterial bed distal to the ruptured plaque. Embolic occlusion

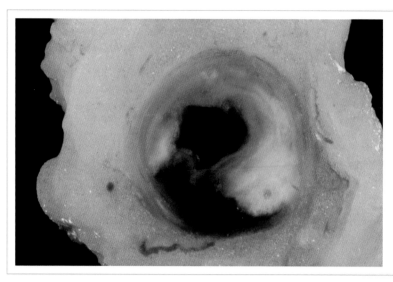

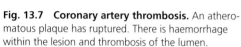
Fig. 13.7 Coronary artery thrombosis. An atheromatous plaque has ruptured. There is haemorrhage within the lesion and thrombosis of the lumen.

of small vessels may cause small infarctions in organs. In the heart this can be dangerous, since small foci of necrosis can also serve as a substrate for dangerous arrhythmias. In cases of large ulcerating plaques of the aorta, small soft (lipid-rich) parts of plaques can lodge in small distal vessels of kidney, leg or skin (cholesterol emboli). Embolisation of carotid arterial atheromatous debris is a common cause of stroke.

4. *Ruptured abdominal atherosclerotic aneurysm.* The media beneath atherosclerotic plaques gradually weaken, probably due to the lipid-related inflammatory activity in the plaque. This causes gradual dilatation of the vessel. This is a slow but progressive process, and hence a disease of the elderly. This process is often asymptomatic. Sudden rupture causes massive retroperitoneal haemorrhage with a high mortality. Aneurysms of more than 5 cm in diameter have a high risk of rupture. In addition, thrombus detached from the inner surface of aneurysms is a source of embolisation in the legs.

Plaque morphology and the vulnerable plaque concept

Autopsy studies on large series of patients who died from myocardial infarction have shown that the atherosclerotic plaques that develop a plaque rupture and subsequent thrombus have distinct morphological features. This has led to the recognition of so-called vulnerable plaques: plaques with a high risk of developing thrombotic complications (Fig. 13.7). Typically vulnerable plaques have a thin fibrous cap, a large lipid core and prominent inflammation. It is thought that pronounced inflammatory activity contributes to degradation and weakening of the plaque that increases the risk of rupture. Secretion of proteolytic enzymes, cytokines and reactive oxygen species by the plaque inflammatory cells orchestrates this process. On the other hand, the plaques that gradually progress to highly stenotic lesions (as, for example, in stable angina pectoris) often have a large fibrocalcific component with little inflammatory activity.

Preventive and therapeutic approaches to atherosclerosis and atherothrombosis

Smoking cessation, control of blood pressure, weight reduction, regular exercise and dietary modifications are all of benefit and are now widely promoted. In Mediterranean communities, a much lower proportion of energy is obtained from saturated fat, and coronary heart disease death rates are much lower. Diets rich in polyunsaturated fat are associated with low coronary heart disease rates. This is the logic behind the advice that we should all eat five portions of fruit or vegetables each day. Fatty acids found in fish have cardioprotective effects. The American Heart Association now recommends at least two servings of fish, especially oily fish, per week.

Secondary prevention of atherosclerotic complications

There is good evidence from many different trials that treatment with cholesterol-lowering drugs reduces cardiac events both in patients with a history of coronary heart disease and in asymptomatic subjects with hypercholesterolaemia. At present 'statins' are the most widely used compounds. They act as specific inhibitors of HMG CoA reductase, an enzyme that has a rate-limiting action in hepatic cholesterol synthesis. Besides their cholesterol-lowering effect, they probably reduce inflammation within atheromatous lesions and promote plaque stability (conversion of a lipid-rich inflamed plaque into a fibrous plaque).

Another approach is to minimise the risk of thrombus formation on established atheromatous lesions. The earliest changes in thrombus formation include platelet activation following interaction with thrombogenic plaque components. Low doses of aspirin, which inhibits aggregation of platelets, are given to many patients with clinical evidence of atheromatous disease and have undoubted beneficial effects. The United Kingdom National Service Framework for Coronary Heart Disease also recommends that patients with established coronary heart disease should receive beta-blockers and angiotensin converting enzyme inhibitors or angiotensin receptor antagonists.

Surgical and percutaneous interventions

Several invasive techniques have been developed to reduce the size of lesions, to remove a thrombus or to bypass a severely narrowed or occluded artery. Endarterectomy is a technique by which the atheromatous intima is 'cored out' from the underlying media. Embolism of atheromatous debris from the carotid bifurcation is a common cause of transient ischaemic attacks and completed strokes. Controlled trials have shown that carotid endarterectomy reduces the risk of further neurological events. Percutaneous angioplasty is used to 'crack open' atheromatous plaques with an inflatable balloon. A metallic expandable stent is usually inserted to maintain the patency of the vessel. These techniques are used in both coronary and lower limb arteries. Surgical bypass procedures use segments of saphenous vein or fabric grafts to divert blood past obstructed segments of lower limb arteries. An atheromatous aneurysm of the distal aorta may be replaced with a Y-shaped fabric graft. Coronary artery stenoses are bypassed with segments of saphenous veins sewn into the proximal aorta or by dissecting the internal mammary artery from the chest wall and anastomosing its distal end to an artery on the anterior surface of the heart, usually the anterior descending branch of the left coronary artery.

ANEURYSMS

- ▶ Localised, permanent, abnormal dilatation of a blood vessel
- ▶ *Atherosclerotic.* Usually occur in the abdominal aorta; rupture causes retroperitoneal haemorrhage
- ▶ *Dissecting.* Usually occur in the thoracic aorta; dissection along the media causes vascular occlusion and haemopericardium
- ▶ *Berry.* Occur in the circle of Willis; rupture causes subarachnoid haemorrhage
- ▶ *Capillary micro-aneurysms.* May be intracerebral (in hypertension), causing cerebral haemorrhage, or retinal (in diabetes), causing diabetic retinopathy
- ▶ *Syphilitic.* Usually occur in the thoracic area
- ▶ *Mycotic.* Rather rare; commonest in the cerebral arteries

An aneurysm is a localised permanent dilatation of part of the vascular tree. Permanent dilatation implies that the vessel wall has been weakened. In contrast, a false aneurysm is a blood-filled space that forms around a blood vessel, usually after traumatic rupture or a perforating injury. A haematoma forms and is contained by the adventitial fibrous tissue. A common cause of false aneurysm formation is femoral artery puncture during arteriography or percutaneous angioplasty. The clinical and pathological features of aneurysms are summarised in Table 13.1.

Atherosclerotic aortic aneurysms

Atherosclerotic abdominal aortic aneurysms commonly develop in elderly patients (Fig. 13.8). They can be detected by ultrasound examination and the value of screening for

these aneurysms is under study. They may impair blood flow to the lower limbs and contribute to the development of peripheral vascular disease. Most importantly, they may rupture into the retroperitoneal space. Elective repair of these aneurysms is comparatively safe but repair after rupture has a high mortality. Some are now managed by percutaneous insertion of supportive stents and this form of treatment may become more common in the future. Aneurysms of the proximal and thoracic aorta are much less common. As with abdominal aneurysms, atherosclerosis is the commonest cause. In atherosclerotic aneurysms there is usually a pronounced loss of elastic tissue and fibrosis of the media. This is due to ischaemia of the aortic media, and release of macrophage enzymes causing fragmentation of elastic fibres. There is evidence that some aortic aneurysms are familial, and inherited defects in collagen have been postulated as the underlying cause.

Aortic dissection (dissecting aneurysms)

In aortic dissection, blood is forced through a tear in the aortic intima to create a blood-filled space in the aortic media (Fig. 13.9). This can track back into the pericardial cavity, causing a fatal *haemopericardium*, or can rupture through the aortic adventitia. In occasional cases the track re-enters the main lumen to create a 'double-barrelled' aorta. The intimal tear and the anatomical features of the aorta can be demonstrated in life by CT or MRI scanning. The underlying pathology is poorly understood. In some, but by no means all, cases there is pronounced degeneration of the aortic media. This is the so-called *cystic medial necrosis* and is characterised by mucoid degeneration and elastic fibre fragmentation. An exaggerated form of this change is seen in *Marfan's syndrome*, a congenital disorder of the expression of a glycoprotein, *fibrillin*, closely associated with elastin fibres. The strongest risk factor for dissecting aneurysm is systemic hypertension. In some cases the intimal 'entry' tears are around atheromatous plaques, but in most cases they involve disease-free parts of the aorta. Without treatment, the mortality from dissecting aneurysm is at least 50% at 48 hours, and 90% within 1 week. The immediate aim of treatment is to contain the propagating haematoma by reducing arterial pressure. Surgical repair is feasible in some patients, especially if the process affects the proximal aorta.

'Berry' aneurysms

In the so-called 'berry' aneurysms in the circle of Willis, the normal muscular arterial wall is replaced by fibrous tissue. The lesions arise at points of branching on the circle of Willis, and are more common in young hypertensive patients. The most important complication is *subarachnoid haemorrhage* (Ch. 26).

Capillary micro-aneurysms

Capillary micro-aneurysms (Charcot–Bouchard aneurysms) are associated with both hypertension and diabetic vascular disease (p. 284). In hypertension, they are common in branches of the middle cerebral artery, particularly the lenticulo-striate. They are thought to be the precursors of primary hypertensive

Table 13.1   Clinical effects of aneurysms

Type of aneurysm	Site	Clinical effects
Atherosclerotic	Lower abdominal aorta and iliac arteries	Pulsatile abdominal mass Lower limb ischaemia Rupture, with massive retroperitoneal haemorrhage
Aortic dissection	Aorta and major branches	Loss of peripheral pulses (e.g. radials) Haemopericardium External rupture (retroperitoneal haemorrhage) Re-entry from dissected media to lumen causing 'double-barrelled' aorta
Berry	Circle of Willis	Subarachnoid haemorrhage
Micro-aneurysms (Charcot–Bouchard)	Intracerebral capillaries	Intracerebral haemorrhage, associated with hypertension
Syphilitic	Ascending and arch of aorta	Aortic incompetence
Mycotic (infective)	Root of aorta (direct extension from aortic valve endocarditis) Any vessel	Thrombosis or rupture, causing cerebral infarction or haemorrhage

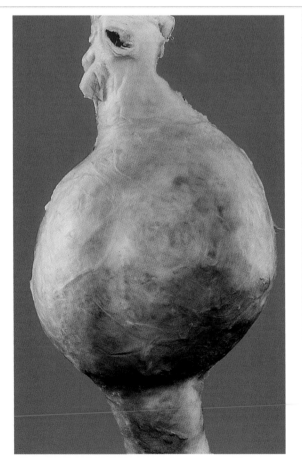

Fig. 13.8   Atherosclerotic abdominal aortic aneurysm. This large aneurysm was an incidental finding at postmortem. Screening by ultrasound may detect these aneurysms in life.

intracerebral haemorrhage, which characteristically occurs in the basal ganglia, cerebellum or brainstem.

Syphilitic aneurysms

Tertiary syphilis is now rare in the developed world but was previously a common cause of proximal aortic aneurysms. They rarely rupture but frequently produce aortic incompetence. The aneurysm is due to ischaemic damage to the media, causing fibrosis and loss of elasticity, secondary to inflammation and narrowing of the vasa vasorum.

Mycotic aneurysms

Mycotic aneurysms are the result of weakening of the arterial wall, secondary to bacterial or fungal infection. The organisms are thought to reach the arterial wall via the blood stream and enter the media via the vasa vasorum. Lesions are commonest in the cerebral arteries (Fig. 13.10) but almost any area can be affected. Bacterial endocarditis is the commonest underlying infection.

HYPERTENSION

▶ Classified aetiologically into essential (primary) hypertension, in which there is no evident cause, and secondary hypertension
▶ Secondary hypertension may be due to renal disease, adrenal cortical and medullary tumours, aortic coarctation or steroid therapy
▶ Further classified dynamically into benign hypertension, in which there is gradual organ damage, and malignant hypertension, in which there is severe and often acute renal, retinal and cerebral damage

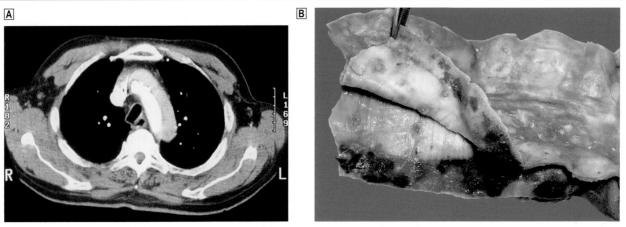

Fig. 13.9   Aortic dissection. [A] A CT scan of a patient with an acute dissection of the ascending aorta. There are two patterns of contrast enhancement in the aorta. The whiter is the main lumen and the greyer the false lumen. [B] The innermost portion of the aortic wall has been peeled away to reveal the underlying haemorrhagic tract.

Fig. 13.10   Mycotic aneurysm in brain. This patient had infective endocarditis. A mycotic aneurysm (arrow) has ruptured. There is haemorrhage into the basal ganglia, which has extended into the subarachnoid space.

Definition

Hypertension is the commonest cause of cardiac failure in many societies and a major risk factor for atherosclerosis. Furthermore, it is a major risk factor for cerebral haemorrhage, another leading cause of death worldwide. There is no universally agreed definition of hypertension, but most authorities would accept that a sustained resting blood pressure of more than 160/95 mmHg is definite hypertension. Furthermore, this would be categorised as:

- *mild* when the diastolic pressure is between 95 and 104 mmHg
- *moderate* at 105–114 mmHg
- *severe* at pressure above 115 mmHg.

Borderline hypertension encompasses the range 140/90 to 160/95 mmHg. In the past, less emphasis was placed on high systolic pressure readings if the diastolic pressure was normal or nearly normal. This is now known to be incorrect practice. Guidelines for the diagnosis and treatment of hypertension are altering as new information becomes available. In the future, treatment is likely to be started at lower blood pressure levels, especially in diabetics.

The diagnosis of an individual patient as hypertensive can be fraught with difficulties. Single blood pressure readings are often spuriously high and many patients have 'ambulatory' blood pressure monitoring over a 24-hour period. Care must be taken to ensure that the blood pressure is accurately recorded with an inflatable cuff of appropriate size and shape.

Epidemiology

Hypertension is a serious cause of morbidity and mortality. The incidence of hypertension varies markedly in different countries. In most, but not all, communities, blood pressure tends to rise with age. There is good evidence that high blood pressure is heritable. The precise genetic pattern is not known, but the pattern is polygenic. Blood pressures of parents and their natural children are correlated, whereas those of parents and adopted children are not. The correlation of blood pressures in monozygotic twins is higher than in dizygotic twins. Many black communities, both in western Africa and North America, have a high incidence of hypertension, whereas values tend to be lower on the Indian subcontinent. In certain parts of Africa and the South Pacific, average blood pressures are unusually low. Many epidemiological studies have confirmed a positive correlation between body weight and both systolic and diastolic blood pressure. This association is strongest in the young and middle-aged, but is less predictable in the elderly. Hypertensive patients who lose weight can reduce their blood pressure.

Aetiological classification

Hypertension can be classified aetiologically according to whether the cause is unknown—essential (primary or idiopathic) hypertension—or is known—secondary hypertension. Most cases of hypertension are classified as 'essential', but the possibility of an underlying cause should always be considered.

Essential hypertension

Up to 90% of patients who present with elevated blood pressure will have no obvious cause for their hypertension and are therefore said to have essential or primary hypertension (Table 13.2).

- Detailed clinical and physiological investigations in patients with essential hypertension indicate that it is not a single entity, and that several different mechanisms may be responsible. The key feature in all patients with established hypertension is an increase in total peripheral vascular resistance.

Ultimately it is the kidneys that are responsible for the control of blood volume and blood pressure, largely through the handling of sodium in the renal tubules. Factors that influence this include:

- the activity of the sympathetic nervous system and the renin–angiotensin–aldosterone system
- genetic factors that control vascular tone and influence the reabsorption of sodium in the kidney
- the absolute numbers of functional nephrons
- low-grade renal damage due to hypertension or inflammation
- the rate of renal medullary blood flow
- dietary intakes of sodium and potassium.

Table 13.2 Pathogenesis of systemic hypertension

Aetiological classification	Causes
Essential (primary) hypertension	Unknown, but probably multifactorial involving: • Genetic susceptibility • Excessive sympathetic nervous system activity • Abnormalities of Na/K membrane transport • High salt intake • Abnormalities in renin–angiotensin–aldosterone system
Secondary hypertension	Renal disease • Chronic renal failure • Renal artery stenosis • Glomerulonephritis Endocrine causes • Adrenal tumours (cortical or medullary) • Cushing's syndrome Coarctation of aorta Drugs, e.g. corticosteroids, oral contraceptives

The sympathetic nervous system

Blood pressure is a function of total peripheral resistance and cardiac output; both of these are, to some extent, under the control of the sympathetic nervous system. When compared with controls, patients with essential hypertension have higher blood pressures at any given level of circulating plasma catecholamines, suggesting an underlying hypersensitivity to these agents. The circulating levels of catecholamines are highly variable and can be influenced by age, sodium intake, posture, stress and exercise. Nevertheless, young hypertensives tend to have higher resting plasma noradrenaline levels than age-matched, normotensive controls.

The renin–angiotensin–aldosterone system

Renin is released from the juxtaglomerular apparatus of the kidney, diffusing into the blood via the efferent arterioles (Ch. 17). It then acts on a plasma globulin, variously called 'renin substrate' or angiotensinogen, to release angiotensin I. This is in turn converted to angiotensin II by angiotensin converting enzyme (ACE). Angiotensin II is a powerful vasoconstrictor and is therefore capable of inducing hypertension. However, only a small proportion of patients with essential hypertension have raised plasma renin levels, and there is no simple correlation between plasma renin activity and the pathogenesis of hypertension. There is some evidence that angiotensin can stimulate the sympathetic nervous system centrally, and many patients with essential hypertension respond to treatment with ACE inhibitors.

Several therapeutic trials have shown that ACE inhibitors given soon after an acute myocardial infarction decrease mortality, perhaps by preventing myocardial dilatation. Recently, variations or mutations in the genes coding for

angiotensinogen, ACE and some of the receptors for angiotensin II have been linked with hypertension.

Dietary sodium and potassium

The role of dietary factors in hypertension is controversial. Hypertension is almost unknown in populations with dietary intakes of sodium of less than 50 mmol/day. In most Western societies daily sodium intakes are above 100 mmol daily, but there is no predictable relationship between intake and blood pressure. Studies in hypertensive patients have shown that a 50-mmol/day reduction in sodium intake reduces systolic blood pressure by 4 mmHg. Human kidneys are efficient at conserving sodium and excreting potassium. This was ideal in prehistoric populations where diets were high in potassium and low in sodium—the converse of the modern Western diets. Fruit and vegetables are rich in potassium as well as polyunsaturated fats.

Secondary hypertension

Hypertension may result from several underlying conditions:

- renal hypertension
- endocrine causes
- coarctation of the aorta
- drug therapy.

Renal hypertension

Some forms of acute, and all forms of chronic, renal disease can be associated with hypertension. The two chief mechanisms involved are:

- renin-dependent hypertension
- salt and water overload.

The possibility of renal disease should be considered in all patients with hypertension. In a few cases, a focal stenosis of one renal artery, as a result of atheroma or fibromuscular dysplasia of the renal artery, is responsible for unilateral renal ischaemia and hyper-reninism. Surgical treatment can be curative in selected patients. Patients in terminal renal failure are extremely sensitive to changes in salt and water balance. Hypertension in these patients can often be managed by restriction of salt and water intake and by careful dialysis.

Endocrine causes

The hypersecretion of corticosteroids in Cushing's syndrome is associated with systemic hypertension. Similarly, adrenal tumours that secrete aldosterone (Conn's syndrome) or catecholamines (phaeochromocytoma) can cause hypertension. However, these are found in less than 1% of all hypertensive patients.

Coarctation of the aorta

Systemic hypertension is one of the commonest features in coarctation. Raised blood pressure will be detected in either arm, but not in the legs. The femoral pulse is often delayed relative to the radial. Death usually results from cardiac failure, hypertensive cerebral haemorrhage or dissecting aneurysm (see Fig. 13.43).

Drug therapy

Corticosteroids, some types of contraceptive pill and some nonsteroidal anti-inflammatory drugs can induce hypertension.

Pathological classification

Hypertension is classified also according to the clinicopathological consequences of the blood pressure elevation. *Benign* or *essential* hypertension is often asymptomatic and discovered only during a routine medical examination. *Malignant* hypertension is a serious condition necessitating prompt treatment to minimise organ damage or the risk of sudden death from cerebral haemorrhage.

Benign (essential) hypertension

The increased peripheral vascular resistance and cardiac workload associated with hypertension produce left ventricular hypertrophy. During life this can be detected electrocardiographically, and at postmortem there is often substantial concentric thickening of the left ventricle. With the development of congestive cardiac failure, the hypertrophy can be obscured by left ventricular dilatation. Some patients with hypertension also have coronary arterial atherosclerosis and evidence of consequent ischaemic heart disease.

Longstanding hypertension produces generalised disease of arterioles and small arteries, in addition to enhancing the development of atherosclerosis. The changes are most easily appreciated in the retina during life, and in the kidneys at autopsy. Medium-sized renal arteries and renal arterioles show marked *intimal proliferation* and *hyalinisation of the muscular media*. This produces focal areas of ischaemia with scarring, loss of tubules and periglomerular fibrosis. The cortical surfaces are finely granular.

Malignant hypertension

Malignant hypertension is a clinical and pathological syndrome. The characteristic features are a markedly raised diastolic blood pressure, usually over 130–140 mmHg, and progressive renal disease. Renal vascular changes are prominent, and there is usually evidence of acute haemorrhage and papilloedema (Fig. 13.11). Malignant hypertension can occur in previously fit individuals, often black males in their third or fourth decade. However, most cases occur in patients with evidence of previous benign hypertension; this is sometimes termed *accelerated hypertension*.

The consequences of malignant hypertension are:

- cardiac failure with left ventricular hypertrophy and dilatation
- blurred vision due to papilloedema and retinal haemorrhages
- haematuria and renal failure due to fibrinoid necrosis of glomeruli
- severe headache and cerebral haemorrhage.

The characteristic histological lesion of malignant hypertension is *fibrinoid necrosis* of small arteries and arterioles (Fig. 13.12). The kidney is frequently affected and some degree of renal dysfunction is inevitable. Occasionally there is massive

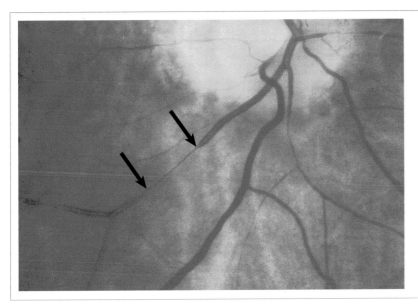

Fig.13.11   Hypertensive fundus. Ocular fundus from a patient with hypertension. The outline of the blood vessels is caused by the reflection of light from the column of blood (the light reflex). Because the wall of the arteriole is thickened in hypertension, the lumen of the vessel is narrowed and the light reflex is reduced (between the arrows).

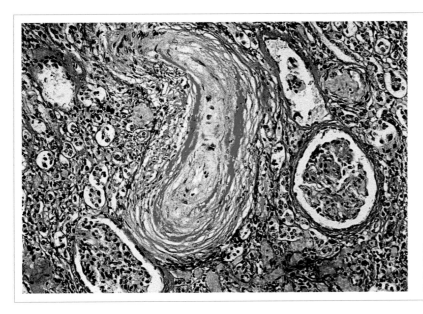

Fig. 13.12   Malignant hypertension. There is fibrinoid necrosis (red) in the wall of a medium-sized renal artery. Glomeruli are below and to the right of this artery.

proteinuria, and renal failure develops. Acute left ventricular failure can occur.

Pulmonary hypertension

The pathophysiological mechanisms associated with pulmonary hypertension are summarised in Table 13.3.

When pulmonary hypertension develops rapidly (following acute left ventricular failure, for example), there is massive transudation of fluid from the pulmonary capillaries into the pulmonary interstitial space and alveoli. This causes the characteristic clinical picture of acute and distressing shortness of breath and expectoration of lightly bloodstained, watery fluid. In chronic pulmonary hypertension, the pulmonary arteries develop a progressive series of reactive changes. These include muscular hypertrophy, intimal fibrosis and dilatation.

There are repeated episodes of haemorrhage into the alveolar spaces, which contain haemosiderin (iron pigment)-laden macrophages.

Vascular and systemic effects

Vascular changes

Hypertension accelerates atherosclerosis, but the lesions have the same histological appearances and distribution as in normotensive subjects. However, hypertension also causes thickening of the media of muscular arteries. This is the result of hyperplasia of smooth muscle cells and collagen deposition close to the internal elastic laminae. In contrast to atherosclerosis, which affects larger arteries, it is the smaller arteries and arterioles that are especially affected in hypertension (Fig. 13.11).

Table 13.3 Pathological causes and physiological changes in pulmonary hypertension	
Cause	**Pathophysiology**
Acute or chronic left ventricular failure	Raised left ventricular pressure → raised venous pressure
Mitral stenosis	Raised left atrial pressure → raised pulmonary venous pressure
Chronic bronchitis and emphysema	Hypoxia → pulmonary vasoconstriction → raised pulmonary venous pressure
Emphysema	Loss of pulmonary tissue → reduced vascular bed
Recurrent pulmonary emboli	Reduction in pulmonary vascular bed available for perfusion
Primary pulmonary hypertension	Cause of raised pulmonary pressure unknown

Hypertension increases the normal flow of protein into the vessel wall and the amount of high molecular weight protein, such as fibrinogen, that passes through the junctions between endothelial cells, resulting in protein deposition. These deposits are called *hyaline* in benign and *fibrinoid* in malignant hypertension. Hyaline change is a common degenerative feature of many ageing arteries, and refers to the homogeneous appearance of the vessel wall, due to the insudation of plasma proteins. Fibrinoid change is a combination of fibrin with necrosis of the vessel wall. There is no evidence that an immunological reaction is involved in hypertensive vascular disease.

Heart
Hypertension accelerates atherosclerosis, thus *ischaemic heart disease* is a frequent complication. A large, ongoing longitudinal population study in Framingham, Massachusetts, has shown hypertension to be a major cause of cardiac failure in previously fit subjects. The left ventricle undergoes hypertrophy and may 'outgrow' its blood supply, particularly if there is associated coronary atherosclerosis. Patients with hypertensive *left ventricular hypertrophy* are more liable to spontaneous arrhythmias than normal subjects. The decreased prevalence of systemic hypertension and left ventricular hypertrophy in Western populations has been attributed to the increasing use of antihypertensive medications.

Nervous system
Intracerebral haemorrhage is a frequent cause of death in hypertension. There is good evidence that effective control of blood pressure reduces the risk of hypertensive cerebral haemorrhage.

Kidneys
The degree of renal damage due to glomerular sclerosis or necrosis varies considerably from patient to patient. *Proteinuria* may be a complication of benign hypertension, while *renal failure* is a characteristic of the malignant phase.

DIABETIC VASCULAR DISEASE

- ▶ Lesions include premature atherosclerosis, and microangiopathy causing damage to kidneys, nerves and retina
- ▶ Complications include gangrene, renal failure and blindness
- ▶ Effective control of diabetes reduces the incidence of renal and retinal disease

Patients with diabetes, particularly juvenile-onset insulin-dependent diabetes, may develop three forms of vascular disease.

Atherosclerosis. Both males and females develop premature, and sometimes severe, atherosclerosis. Even diabetic pre-menopausal females can develop substantial atheroma.

Hypertensive vascular disease. This is a frequent complication, especially when there is diabetic renal disease (Ch. 21).

Capillary microangiopathy. This is the most important and characteristic change in diabetes. The alterations are found throughout the systemic circulation and can be viewed directly in the retina (Fig. 13.13). Small arterioles and capillaries are affected and the principal clinical effects are diabetic retinopathy, diabetic glomerulosclerosis and peripheral neuropathy. The biochemical changes are complex and include abnormal glycosylation of proteins within the vessel wall. Although thickened, the basement membranes are unusually permeable, and there is increased passive transudation of protein. Small vessels dilate, forming capillary micro-aneurysms. In the eye, protein leakage stimulates a fibrous and vascular response, which damages the complex neural network of the retina. Capillary thrombosis causes retinal ischaemia. This is a stimulus to the ingrowth of new capillaries, which causes further retinal damage. Some degree of diabetic retinal disease is inevitable in longstanding diabetes, but only a minority of patients become blind. Intimal thickening of renal arterioles and micro-aneurysm formation in the glomerular capillaries are the underlying causes of diabetic renal disease. The excretion of small amounts of protein in the urine (micro-albuminuria) is the first evidence of this. Peripheral neuropathy results from disease of small vessels supplying nerves. Multicentre trials have shown that the rate of progression of major complications such as diabetic retinopathy and nephropathy can be reduced by careful control of blood sugar levels and prompt treatment of hypertension.

VASCULITIS

- ▶ Multisystem disorders but with a predilection for highly vascular tissues such as skin, renal glomerulus, upper respiratory and gastrointestinal tract
- ▶ Now classified according to the size of vessel affected, i.e. small, medium and large vessel vasculitis
- ▶ Exact mechanisms uncertain but include disordered immunity with complement activation and in some cases immune complex deposition. Auto-antibodies may be present

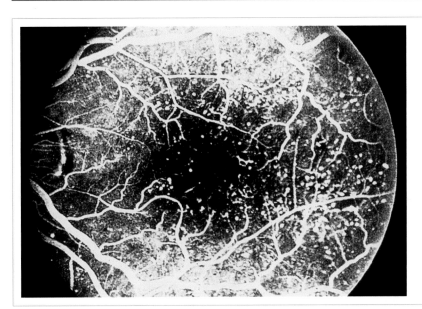

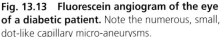

Fig. 13.13   Fluorescein angiogram of the eye of a diabetic patient. Note the numerous, small, dot-like capillary micro-aneurysms.

Pathogenesis

Vasculitis is the name given to inflammatory diseases of blood vessels. The cause of most forms of vasculitis is unknown but clinical and experimental studies suggest that in some cases the underlying pathology is a deposition of complexes of antigen and antibody in the vessel wall. Immune complexes are not inherently harmful, but if they lodge in tissues and activate complement they incite an acute inflammatory re-action and trigger the coagulation system. Repeated minor trauma may be the reason that the lesions of some vascular disorders develop on the extensor surfaces of the arms and on the buttocks (Fig. 13.14). Venous stasis may account for the fact that some examples of vasculitis are particularly prominent in the lower leg.

Clinicopathological features

In most forms of vasculitis the pathological changes in the vessels are broadly similar. A dense infiltrate of acute and chronic inflammatory cells is usually present and in some instances immunological techniques may demonstrate ab-normal deposits of immunoglobulin and complement in the intima and media. The patterns of disease in vasculitis are largely a result of the organ and the size of the vessel affected. Because of this, systemic vasculitis can present with a wide variety of different signs and symptoms. Pathologists prefer to classify vasculitis according to the type and size of vessel that is chiefly involved. The major clinical and pathological features of some common immunological vascular disorders are summarised in Table 13.4.

A skin rash is one of the commonest presenting features of *acute vasculitis*, and is sometimes closely related to treat-ment with a particular drug. In these circumstances the foreign substance probably acts as a hapten in the induction of an immunological reaction. Many forms of vasculitis are self-limiting, but their clinical course can sometimes be shortened by anti-inflammatory drugs. When the disease affects several different organs and systems the term *systemic*

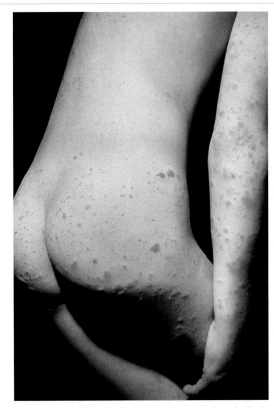

Fig. 13.14   Henoch–Schönlein purpura. Note that the lesions in this 20-year-old man are most prominent on the buttocks and elbows, sites of everyday trauma. In this condition IgA is usually demonstrated in the walls of affected vessels.

vasculitis is used. Examples include polyarteritis nodosa (Fig. 13.15), rheumatoid vasculitis and Wegener's granu-lomatosis. Without treatment the prognosis in systemic vasculitis is poor. The possibility of systemic vasculitis must

Table 13.4 Clinical and pathological features of some types of vasculitis

Disease	Clinical features	Vessels involved	Antigenic stimulus	Auto-antibodies
Polyarteritis nodosa	Microinfarcts and haemorrhages from aneurysms	Muscular arteries	HbsAg in some cases	None consistently
Rheumatoid vasculitis	Arthritis Cutaneous vasculitis	Aorta, arteries and arterioles	DNA in some cases	Anti-DNA Rheumatoid factor
Wegener's granulomatosis	Destructive nasal lesions Lung and renal lesions	Arteries, arterioles and venules	Not known	Anti-neutrophil cytoplasmic antibody (ANCA)
Systemic lupus erythematosus	Skin rash Renal disease	Arterioles and capillaries	DNA and RNA in some cases	Anti-DNA
Henoch–Schönlein purpura	Characteristic skin rash	Capillaries and venules	Not known but IgA deposited	None

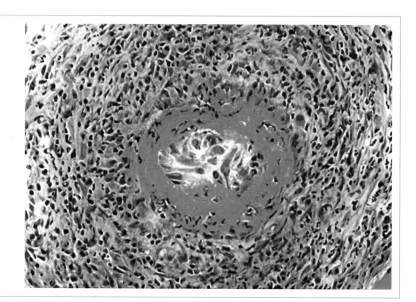

Fig. 13.15 Polyarteritis nodosa. Fibrinoid necrosis and heavy inflammatory cell infiltration in a medium-sized artery in a patient with polyarteritis nodosa.

be considered in any patient with a multisystem pattern of illness, especially if the respiratory tract is involved. Anti-inflammatory and cytotoxic drugs, such as steroids and cyclophosphamide, may induce clinical remissions in 75% of patients.

Complications

Complications of vasculitis include thrombosis with resulting ischaemia or infarction. Multiple sites are usually involved simultaneously. Tissues with a high blood flow, such as the skin and the glomeruli, are preferentially affected.

In many patients with these disorders there are increased levels of circulating immune complexes, and the complement concentrations may be low, particularly when the disease is active. Auto-antibodies are present in some patients (Table 13.4). Some are directed against components of vascular endothelial cells (anti-neutrophil cytoplasmic antibodies—ANCA) and are useful in supporting a clinical diagnosis.

VASCULAR DISEASES WITH SPECIFIC CLINICAL FEATURES

Some vascular disorders have characteristic clinical and histological features. Very little is known about their cause but, as some show prominent inflammation, they are classified as forms of vasculitis.

Scleroderma (systemic sclerosis)

The vascular changes of scleroderma (systemic sclerosis) are similar to those of benign or malignant hypertension, but only 25% of the patients are hypertensive. Muscular arteries and arterioles are narrowed by newly formed layers of collagen and mucopolysaccharide (Ch. 25). The cause of this curious disorder is unknown. There may be an underlying abnormality of collagen synthesis which affects not only arteries but also the subcutaneous tissues of the extremities and gastrointestinal tract. The most characteristic clinical feature is progressive subcutaneous fibrosis, which leads to marked tightening of the skin of the arms and hands. There is no effective treatment.

Cranial (giant cell) arteritis

Cranial (giant cell) arteritis was first recognised by Sir Jonathan Hutchinson, who in 1890 described an 80-year-old retired hospital porter who was prevented from wearing his hat by tender and inflamed temporal arteries. The arteries of the head and neck, including the aorta, are most frequently involved. If the disease affects the ophthalmic or posterior ciliary arteries, blindness can result. It is the most common form of large vessel vasculitis.

In florid clinical cases the superficial temporal artery is hard, tender and pulseless, and the patient complains of a severe headache. The ESR is usually high, generally above 50 mm/h. Microscopically there is marked intimal thickening and oedema, and a dense, sometimes granulomatous, chronic inflammatory and giant cell reaction with phagocytosis of fragmented elastic fibres (Fig. 13.16). The clinical diagnosis can often be confirmed by biopsy, but this is not always positive; focal involvement of the superficial temporal artery is the probable reason for these negative biopsies.

The cause of cranial arteritis is unknown. There is little evidence that it is immunological in origin. In up to 50% of cases it is associated with a polymyalgia rheumatica-like illness. Almost all cases of cranial arteritis respond well to steroid therapy and, in severe cases, prompt treatment can prevent blindness.

Pulseless (Takayasu's) disease

Pulseless, or Takayasu's, disease is a rare inflammatory disorder of the aorta and its proximal branches. Most patients are young or middle-aged females, who present with hypertension or ischaemic symptoms in the arms. Renal arterial involvement can cause hypertension. Characteristically, there is a severe necrotising inflammation with some similarities to cranial arteritis. Unfortunately, only a proportion of these patients respond to treatment, with either steroids or other agents, and the outlook is much worse than in cranial arteritis. Few patients make a complete recovery, and the associated hypertension may be difficult to control.

Buerger's disease

Buerger's disease (thrombo-angiitis obliterans) is a rare disease more strongly associated with smoking than any other vascular disorder. Most patients are male, and Jews are affected twice as commonly as non-Jews. The clinical picture is very distinctive. Peripheral gangrene develops in the fingers and toes, but the changes are progressive and serial amputations are often required (Fig. 13.17).

Pathological alterations are less specific. Small arteries in the arms and lower leg are mainly involved and show marked intimal fibrosis, thrombus formation with evidence of recanalisation, and peri-arteritis with adventitial tissue changes affecting adjacent veins and nerves. Apart from the striking association with heavy smoking, little is known of its cause.

RADIATION VASCULAR DISEASE

Some pathological change is almost inevitable in any tissue that has been irradiated. The most prominent chronic reactions in vascular tissue are intimal thickening of arteries and

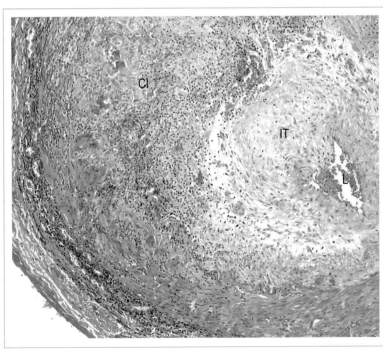

Fig. 13.16 Cranial arteritis. This biopsy of a superficial temporal artery shows marked intimal thickening (IT) and a dense mononuclear and giant cell infiltrate (CI). The lumen is restricted to a tiny slit (L).

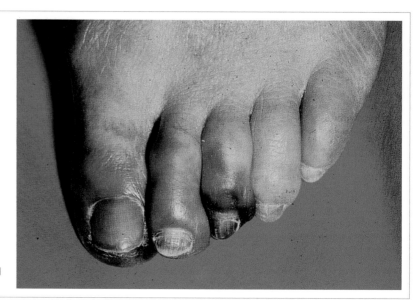

Fig. 13.17   **Buerger's disease.** The toes are gangrenous. After 9 months this patient required a below-knee amputation.

arterioles, and dilatation of capillaries and venules. Following radiation there is a substantial reduction of the capillary vascular bed, and this inevitably produces ischaemia and subsequent fibrosis. Strictures in the large and small intestines sometimes follow radiotherapy for carcinoma of the cervix. Patients with lymphoma or other tumours who receive mediastinal radiotherapy frequently develop pericarditis, but damage to small myocardial vessels may produce patchy interstitial fibrosis, and proximal coronary arteries occasionally develop premature atherosclerosis.

DISEASES OF VEINS

Normal venous structure

Like arteries, veins have an intima, media and adventitia (Fig. 13.1B). There is no definite internal elastic lamina and, as in arteries, the thickness of the intima increases with age (phlebosclerosis). Small veins have only a thin muscular wall but in larger channels, such as the saphenous vein and the inferior vena cava, there are coarse bundles of irregular muscle, partially organised into longitudinal and circular layers.

Venous thrombosis

Any condition that impedes normal venous return predisposes to thrombosis (Ch. 8). Common predisposing causes include:

- immobility (e.g. in severe cardiac failure, post-operative phase, bed rest, leg fractures, long haul flights)
- in patients with cancer
- pregnancy and childbirth
- oestrogen therapy (e.g. oral contraceptives, therapy for carcinoma of the prostate)
- haematological disorders (e.g. polycythaemia and other dyshaemopoietic syndromes, factor V Leiden

and antithrombin III deficiency, dehydration producing increased blood viscosity)
- intravenous cannulae.

The veins of the lower abdomen, pelvis and legs are most frequently affected. Thrombi often form in the deep veins of the leg when patients are immobilised in bed, for example after a fracture or surgical operation (where the risk is exacerbated by a rise in coagulation factors and platelets) or during a serious illness. There is evidence that anticoagulant drugs reduce the incidence of post-operative deep venous thrombosis, but their beneficial effects must be weighed against the increased danger of post-operative haemorrhage.

In haematological disorders, such as polycythaemia, and in some patients with malignant tumours, the blood is hypercoagulable and venous thrombosis is common. In the distinctive clinical syndrome of *thrombophlebitis migrans*, superficial venous thrombi form and resolve in different subcutaneous sites.

Inherited disorders enhancing coagulation are of increasing clinical interest (Ch. 23). The most important of these is a specific point mutation in the gene coding for coagulation factor V (factor V Leiden). This abnormal form of factor V is resistant to degradation by activated protein C. In Europe about 5% of subjects are heterozygous for this mutation and have at least a three-fold increased risk of venous thrombosis and pulmonary embolism.

Varicosities

Tortuous and distended ('varicose') veins or *varices* are a common clinical problem. There is often associated ulceration, usually on the medial aspect of the ankle and lower leg (Fig. 13.18). There are both superficial and deep venous plexuses in the lower limb, connected by perforating veins. The return of blood from the deep veins is aided by the normal contraction of the calf and thigh muscles. If the valves in the perforating veins become incompetent, blood can be forced from the deep to the superficial venous plexuses; this is a major factor in the development of varicosities. The exact cause of varicose

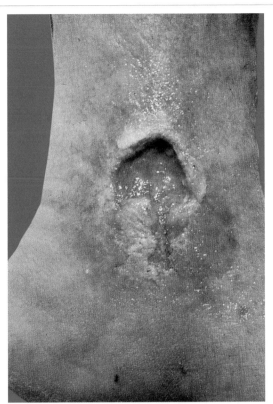

Fig. 13.18   Venous ulceration of the ankle. These ulcers are the result of poor venous drainage from the lower leg. Immobility, previous deep vein thrombosis and varicose veins all contribute to their development.

ulceration is uncertain, but impaired venous return with resulting stasis, lower limb oedema and fibrin deposition around small capillaries and veins has been implicated. In many cases, there has been a previous deep leg vein thrombosis. Some ulcers heal after surgical treatment of varicose veins.

Varices frequently develop close to the oesophagogastric junction in portal hypertension due to, for example, hepatic cirrhosis (Ch. 16).

COMPLICATIONS IN VESSELS USED AS ARTERIAL BYPASSES

Surgical operations in which atheromatous coronary or lower limb arteries are bypassed with the internal mammary artery or a length of saphenous vein are now common. Although these procedures are often successful in restoring distal blood flow, complications can occur. The two most important are:

- *Thrombosis of the graft.* This usually occurs within days or weeks of the operative procedure and is often related to technical complications. If the graft is either too long or too short, blood flow is not optimal and this predisposes to thrombosis. Thrombus can also form at the surgical anastomosis. If the distal part is grafted on to a narrowed segment of artery, the blood flow, or 'run-off', is impeded, and this predisposes to thrombosis.

- *Atherosclerotic lesions.* Veins subjected to arterial pressure develop intimal thickening and this progresses in time to produce lesions indistinguishable from atherosclerosis. This process is particularly marked in veins used as coronary bypass grafts. This may lead to recurrent ischaemic heart disease, even necessitating replacement of the original graft.

Prosthetic vessels made of various types of cloth can be used to repair lower abdominal aortic aneurysms or to bypass iliac or femoral arteries. Although these grafts do not develop true atherosclerosis, a fibrous pseudo-intima develops. Thrombosis may also occur.

DISEASES OF LYMPHATICS

Normal lymphatic structure

The largest lymphatic vessels, such as the thoracic duct, resemble veins. They are lined by endothelium and have a well-defined muscular wall. In contrast, the most peripheral lymphatics begin as closed sacs, lined by a single layer of endothelium and supported by thin strands of collagen. They have valves that give them a beaded appearance.

Lymphatic involvement in disease

Frequently lymphatics provide the channels by which malignant tumours can spread from the primary site to the regional lymph nodes (Ch. 11). In acute inflammation the flow of lymph is markedly increased and, occasionally, lymphatic vessels draining such an area become secondarily inflamed. In infestations with filarial parasites, lymphatic channels are obstructed and marked swelling results; the skin becomes thickened and boggy ('elephantiasis').

TUMOURS OF BLOOD VESSELS

Benign tumours

Haemangiomas are common benign tumours of small capillaries (Fig. 13.19). They are particularly common on the face and scalp area of infants, and frequently regress. In adults they can occur on almost any part of the skin. On the lips and fingers they are frequently inflamed and are usually known as *pyogenic granulomas*; they are probably reactive lesions rather than true neoplasms.

A *glomus tumour* is a distinctive, benign, but sometimes exquisitely painful, blood vessel neoplasm that generally arises in the finger or nail bed. It may develop from some component of the arteriovenous anastomosis that is particularly common in these sites.

Arteriovenous malformations are not strictly true tumours. They are most common in the cerebral and cerebellar hemispheres and in the lungs. The possibility of an arteriovenous malformation should be considered in any young person who presents with cerebral haemorrhage.

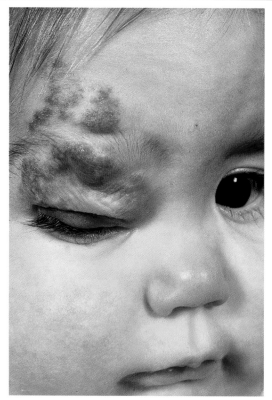

Fig. 13.19 Haemangioma in a child. Although these lesions in this 18-month-old child are unsightly, they are benign and often regress.

Malignant tumours

Angiosarcoma is rare, but has a notoriously aggressive behaviour. The lesion is composed of masses of interconnecting vascular channels lined by a pleomorphic endothelium. Lesions most commonly develop in the soft tissues of the lower limbs, and the head and neck of elderly individuals.

Kaposi's sarcoma, originally described by a Hungarian dermatologist, is a common malignant tumour in black Africans. Its precise cell of origin is uncertain but may well be lymphatic endothelium. In both blacks and whites, Kaposi's sarcoma is one of the tumours that develops in patients with acquired immune deficiency following HIV infection.

CARDIAC DISEASE

NORMAL STRUCTURE AND FUNCTION OF THE HEART

The heart is a muscular pump divided on each side into two chambers—an *atrium* and a *ventricle*—each separated by a *valve*, tricuspid on the right, mitral on the left. The embryogenesis of these chambers and valves is covered in the section on congenital cardiovascular disease, where it is of immediate relevance. The inner wall of the cardiac chambers and the surface of the valve cusps are lined by a layer of endothelial cells—the *endocardium*. The bulk of the chamber wall—the *myocardium*—comprises a network of striated muscle cells, each separated by an intercalated disc. The heart is invested by patches of adipose tissue and a layer of mesothelium—the *epicardium*. This layer of mesothelium forms the visceral aspect of the *pericardial sac* which normally contains a small volume of clear fluid to lubricate the surfaces during cardiac contraction.

Venous blood from the systemic circulation drains into the right atrium, which contracts during *diastole* to force the blood through the *tricuspid valve* into the right ventricle. During *systole* the right ventricle contracts, expelling the blood through the *pulmonary valve* and into the pulmonary circulation. A synchronous sequence of events takes place on the left side: the pulmonary veins drain oxygenated blood into the *left atrium*; in diastole the blood is forced through the *mitral valve*; in systole the left ventricle contracts to expel blood through the *aortic valve* into the aorta. The atria on each side are of similar dimensions, but the myocardium of the left ventricle is much thicker than that of the right ventricle; this is commensurate with the relative systolic blood pressure in the aorta and pulmonary artery trunk.

The regular and co-ordinated contraction of the myocardium is determined by the pacemaker cells in the *sino-atrial (SA)* and *atrio-ventricular (AV) nodes*; the action potentials propagate through the *bundle of His* and *Purkinje network*. The electrical activity of the heart can be monitored on the skin surface by electrocardiography (ECG); the P wave corresponds to atrial contraction; the QRS complex reflects propagation of the action potential into the ventricles and their subsequent contraction; and the T wave is due to repolarisation of the myocardium.

Myocardial cell contraction and relaxation is brought about by changes in the concentration of cytosolic calcium. The cyclical contraction of the heart is initiated by the spontaneous depolarisation of the pacemaker cells in the SA node during diastole. The contraction rate, however, is modulated by the autonomic nervous system: beta-adrenergic receptors permit the heart rate to be accelerated by sympathetic stimulation; the vagus nerve through its parasympathetic effects, mediated by acetylcholine, slows the heart rate.

The myocardium is supplied by the *coronary arteries* originating from the root of the aorta just above the aortic valve cusps. The right coronary artery usually supplies the right ventricle, the posterior part of the interventricular septum, and part of the posterior wall of the left ventricle. The left coronary artery, via its principal branches—the anterior descending and the circumflex arteries—supplies the anterior part of the interventricular septum and most of the left ventricular myocardium. It is not unusual, however, to find that one artery is dominant, supplying a larger territory than usual. Blood flow through the coronary arteries is maximal during diastole when the ventricular myocardium is relaxed.

In life, cardiac structure can be assessed by a variety of invasive and non-invasive techniques. Chest X-rays provide a general guide to cardiac and aortic size. Echocardiography, coupled with Doppler techniques, gives a detailed view of individual chambers and in particular the contractile function of the ventricular cavities, the appearances of the individual valves and the direction of blood flow through them. More

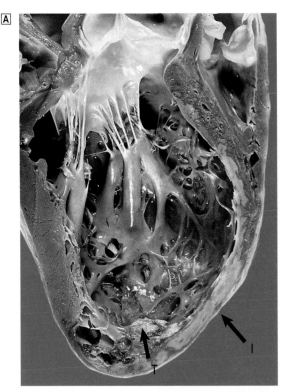

Fig. 13.23 Myocardial infarction. $\boxed{A}$ Note the pale and focally haemorrhagic appearance of the infarcted muscle (I). There is adherent mural thrombus (T). $\boxed{B}$ This patient died 3 days after an acute anteroseptal infarct. Note the extensive haemorrhage into the infarct.

coronary plaques, acute coronary thrombosis and acute myocardial infarction. The ECG gives a good guide as to which coronary artery is narrowed and the extent of myocardial damage. Acute infarcts are now classified according to the presence or absence of ST-segment elevation. Infarcts with ST elevation on the initial ECG (STEMIs) require emergency treatment to reopen the obstructed coronary artery. This may be achieved with drugs that activate the plasminogen system. Increasingly these patients are treated with emergency angioplasty to reopen the obstructed artery physically. Patients with chest pain but no evidence of ST-segment elevation require emergency estimation of troponin, a cardiac muscle protein that is released into the circulation after cardiac muscle cell death. Significantly increased levels indicate a so-called non-STEMI infarct. In these patients it is thought that the infarct is limited largely to the subendocardial zone of the myocardium. However, detailed clinicopathological studies linking the precise pattern of infarction with ECG changes are difficult to complete in the era of declining autopsy rates. Patients with severe chest pain but no ECG or biochemical evidence of infarction are said to have unstable angina. The underlying pathological change is thought to be rupture or erosion of a plaque of coronary artery atheroma.

Morphology

The location and size of the infarct depend on:

- the site of the coronary artery occlusion
- the anatomical pattern of blood supply
- the presence or absence of an anastomotic circulation within the coronary arterial tree.

In clinical practice the ECG changes give a good guide to the area of myocardium that is infarcted (Fig. 13.24).

When coronary angiography is performed in patients with typical symptoms and signs of acute myocardial infarction, a complete obstruction of a major coronary artery can be demonstrated in up to 90% of cases. The immediate objectives of treatment are to relieve pain with opiate analgesia and to restore blood flow in the occluded artery. Activation of the plasminogen system with recombinant forms of human plasminogen activator will partially lyse thrombi and improve blood flow in the occluded artery in at least 50% of patients. Emergency coronary angioplasty is also effective at breaking down thrombi and restoring blood flow. It is used as a primary treatment for coronary thrombosis in most centres worldwide.

The macroscopic and microscopic changes of myocardial infarcts follow a predictable sequence (Table 13.5). The chief features are necrosis, inflammatory cell infiltration and, as cardiac muscle cannot regenerate, repair by fibrous tissue. The extensive necrosis of cardiac muscle is associated with the release of cardiac enzymes and proteins into the circulation. A rapid bedside test for the diagnosis of acute infarction would allow more rational use of thrombolytic drugs or emergency angioplasty. Assays for the blood level of the cardiac muscle protein troponin are the most reliable early biochemical indicator of acute myocardial infarction but may not be increased for some hours after the onset of pain. Raised serum levels of creatine kinase also suggest acute myocardial infarction. Neither of these markers is

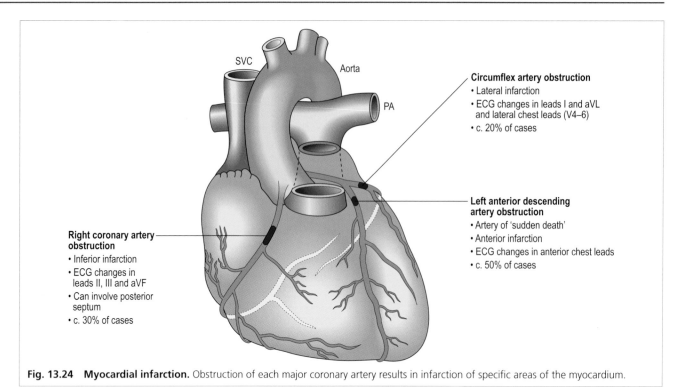

Circumflex artery obstruction
- Lateral infarction
- ECG changes in leads I and aVL and lateral chest leads (V4–6)
- c. 20% of cases

Left anterior descending artery obstruction
- Artery of 'sudden death'
- Anterior infarction
- ECG changes in anterior chest leads
- c. 50% of cases

Right coronary artery obstruction
- Inferior infarction
- ECG changes in leads II, III and aVF
- Can involve posterior septum
- c. 30% of cases

SVC   Aorta   PA

Fig. 13.24   Myocardial infarction. Obstruction of each major coronary artery results in infarction of specific areas of the myocardium.

Table 13.5   Macroscopic and microscopic features of myocardial infarcts

Time after onset of clinical symptoms	Macroscopic changes	Microscopic changes
Up to 18 hours	None	None
24–48 hours	Pale oedematous muscle	Oedema, acute inflammaory cell infiltration, necrosis of myocytes
3–4 days	Yellow rubbery centre with haemorrhagic border	Obvious necrosis and inflammation; early granulation tissue
1–3 weeks	Infarcted area paler and thinner than unaffected ventricle	Granulation tissue, then progressive fibrosis
3–6 weeks	Silvery scar becoming tough and white	Dense fibrosis

entirely specific for myocardial infarction. Most patients show a transient leukocytosis in the first 1–3 days, but the value rarely exceeds $15 \times 10^9/l$. In clinical practice this is of limited value, largely because of the many other causes of a transient leucocytosis.

Complications

The complications of myocardial infarction are listed in Table 13.6, and see Figures 13.25 and 13.26.

Early detection and prompt treatment of complications are important in the management of patients with myocardial infarction. Cardiac arrhythmias, sometimes leading to ventricular fibrillation and sudden death, are frequent in the first 24–48 hours after the initial infarct. Cardiac rupture produces electromechanical dissociation (pulseless electrical activity) and rapid death (Fig. 13.27). The incidence of this important complication has been reduced by thrombolytic therapy. Pericarditis, mitral incompetence and cardiac failure are the important complications in the first week after infarction. Later complications include embolism from mural thrombus formation, and the development of ventricular aneurysms.

As with all patients who are immobilised, there is a substantial risk of deep venous thrombosis and the possibility of subsequent pulmonary embolism. Prolonged bed rest is not essential for cases of uncomplicated myocardial infarction, and early mobilisation has done much to reduce the incidence of post-infarction pulmonary embolism.

Table 13.6 Complications of myocardial infarcts		
Complication	Interval	Mechanism
Sudden death	Usually within hours	Often ventricular fibrillation
Arrhythmias	First few days	
Persistent pain	12 hours–few days	Progressive myocardial necrosis (extension of infarct)
Angina	Immediate or delayed (weeks)	Ischaemia of non-infarcted cardiac muscle
Cardiac failure	Variable	Ventricular dysfunction following muscle necrosis Arrhythmias
Mitral incompetence	First few days	Papillary muscle dysfunction, necrosis or rupture
Pericarditis	2–4 days	Transmural infarct with inflammation of pericardium
Cardiac rupture (ventricular wall, septum or papillary muscle)	3–5 days	Weakening of wall following muscle necrosis and acute inflammation
Mural thrombosis	1 week or more	Abnormal endothelial surface following infarction
Ventricular aneurysm	4 weeks or more	Stretching of newly formed collagenous scar tissue
Dressler's syndrome (chest pain, fever, effusions)	Weeks–few months	Autoimmune
Pulmonary emboli	1 week or more	Deep venous thrombosis in lower limbs

Chronic ischaemic heart disease

Clinical features

Angina is one of the commonest clinical features of patients with a long history of ischaemic heart disease. A history of chest pain, induced by exercise and relieved by rest, should be sought in any patient in whom ischaemic heart disease is suspected. Impaired left ventricular function, following one or more previous episodes of myocardial infarction, may result in left ventricular and, ultimately, congestive cardiac failure. Some patients present with severe or rapidly progressive anginal chest pain. This is termed *unstable* or *crescendo* angina. It may progress to myocardial infarction and requires emergency management.

Morphology

Most patients with a definite clinical history of angina have extensive coronary arterial atheroma. Typically, two or three of the major coronary arteries have patches of stenosis in which the lumen is reduced to less than 75% of its normal cross-sectional area (Fig. 13.28). Careful postmortem studies in patients who have died after episodes of unstable angina have demonstrated recent rupture of the fibrous cap of large, often eccentric and lipid-rich atheromatous plaques. Paradoxically some patients with a typical clinical history of angina have relatively normal coronary angiograms. It may be that the recurrent episodes

of coronary spasm are responsible for pain in these patients; this is sometimes called 'variant angina'.

Postmortem examinations on patients with a long history of ischaemic heart disease frequently demonstrate areas of healed myocardial infarction, dilatation of the left ventricle, and other changes related to chronic heart failure such as peripheral oedema, pleural and peritoneal effusions, and pulmonary oedema and congestion.

SUDDEN CARDIAC DEATH

The sudden, unexpected death of a previously fit person is an all too common tragedy in the community. General practitioners, junior hospital doctors and the police are commonly involved, and a medicolegal autopsy may be ordered. In the majority of cases, the cause is directly or indirectly related to the cardiovascular system. Epidemiological studies have demonstrated that there are at least 80 sudden unexpected deaths per 100 000 patients per year in the UK.

Aetiology

Acute cardiac failure as a result of ischaemic heart disease is one of the commonest diagnoses made by pathologists in cases of sudden unexpected death. In many cases, significant narrowing of one or more coronary arteries is identified. When detailed

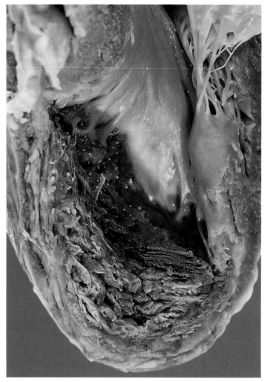

Fig. 13.25 Mural thrombus. Many layers of thrombus have formed on the infarcted myocardium. This can fragment and embolise.

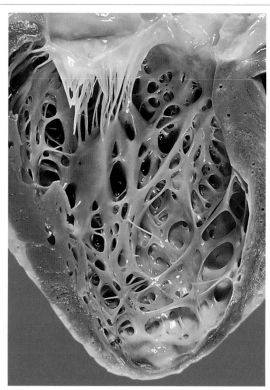

Fig. 13.26 Healed myocardial infarction. Note that the ventricular wall is very thin at the apex of the heart where there is a white fibrous scar.

radiological and histological studies are made in patients dying within 6 hours of the onset of ischaemic symptoms, a coronary thrombosis can be found in approximately 55% of cases. At this stage, however, there will be no associated macroscopic or histological evidence of recent myocardial infarction. In the remainder of cases due to ischaemic heart disease there is severe narrowing of one or more coronary arteries, with or without evidence of previous healed myocardial infarction. It is assumed that these patients have died from a ventricular arrhythmia. Pathologists rely on the police evidence that there are no suspicious circumstances. About 50% of patients with established cardiac failure die suddenly, while the remainder deteriorate gradually. Sudden death is also a feature of patients with all forms of cardiomyopathy.

Other common causes of sudden death include ruptured atherosclerotic aneurysms of the abdominal aorta, dissecting aortic aneurysms and pulmonary emboli. Aortic stenosis is a cause of Stokes–Adams ('drop') attacks and can also lead to sudden death; acute coronary insufficiency is the probable mechanism (Fig. 13.29). Rupture of a berry aneurysm in the circle of Willis or massive intracerebral haemorrhage from a capillary micro-aneurysm may lead rapidly to death. Despite careful postmortem examination and toxicology, the cause of sudden unexpected death is sometimes not determined. This is increasingly recognised and is sometimes termed sudden adult (or arrhythmic) death syndrome (SADS). In a proportion of these cases biochemical abnormalities in sodium or

potassium channels in cardiac muscle have been demonstrated, some of which are due to heritable mutations. It is therefore essential that relatives of sudden cardiac death victims are screened for cardiac abnormalities.

Prevention

Ventricular fibrillation is often the immediate cause of death in patients with acute ischaemic heart disease. Many ambulance crews now carry a defibrillator and administer DC shock to appropriate patients en route to hospital. Defibrillators are also installed in public areas such as football grounds and railway stations and are carried in some aircraft. There is good evidence from community studies that prompt cardiopulmonary resuscitation can prevent death in such circumstances. Patients with a history of ventricular arrhythmias can be treated with an implantable defibrillator that senses ventricular fibrillation and automatically delivers a defibrillating shock. Guidelines for the insertion of these devices have been developed and implantation rates are increasing. In some cases cardiac electrophysiologists can 'map' the pattern of electrical activity within the ventricle and, using a radiofrequency electrode, ablate the segment of myocardium that is responsible for abnormal electrical impulses.

Pulmonary embolism causes many tragic deaths, sometimes in previously fit patients in the post-operative period. Early mobilisation helps to minimise the risk of deep venous

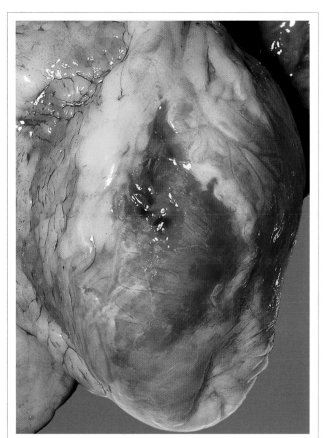

Fig. 13.27 **Sudden death following rupture of an acute anterior myocardial infarct.** There was a large haemopericardium and the patient died from cardiac tamponade.

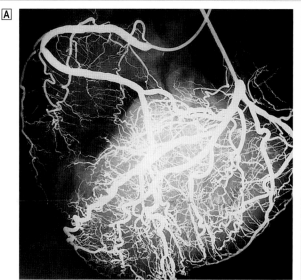

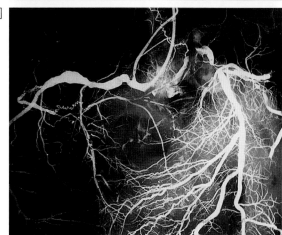

Fig. 13.28 **Postmortem coronary angiograms.** [A] Normal; note the widely patent right coronary artery, upper left. [B] The contours of the right coronary are irregular and there is a complete obstruction of the circumflex branch. Coronary angiograms made in life do not demonstrate all the small vessels shown above.

thrombosis. Anticoagulant therapy reduces the incidence of venous thrombosis and subsequent embolism, and patients at high risk of developing venous thrombi are sometimes treated prophylactically.

VALVULAR HEART DISEASE

At least 10% of cases of heart failure are caused by disease of the cardiac valves. The normal function of cardiac valves is to prevent retrograde flow of blood between the atria and ventricles, and between the ventricles and the aorta or pulmonary artery. Valves open noiselessly but heart sounds are produced by the vibration of blood as valves close. The first heart sound is the result of the closure of the mitral valve and, to a lesser extent, the tricuspid valve, early in systole. In the same way, the second heart sound results from aortic and pulmonary valve closure. In many healthy children and adults, the aortic valve closes shortly before the pulmonary valve, leading to a double or 'split' second sound. In life the movement of valve leaflets can be studied by echocardiography. Additional heart sounds occur during the filling of an abnormal ventricle. The third heart sound occurs in early diastole because of vibrations produced when blood impacts against an abnormal ventricular wall, for example an immobile

area of fibrosis due to ischaemic heart disease. A fourth heart sound is heard later in diastole, just before the first heart sound, and is the result of late diastolic filling of the ventricle in a failing heart.

Pathological problems result from:

- *valvular stenosis*, in which valves become thickened or calcified and obstruct the normal flow of blood into a chamber or vessel (Figs 13.29 and 13.30)
- *valvular incompetence* (also called regurgitation or insufficiency), in which valves lose their normal function as valves and fail to prevent the reflux of blood after contraction of an individual cardiac chamber (Fig. 13.31)
- *vegetations*, in which the valve leaflets develop either infective or thrombotic nodules that impair normal valve mobility and can fragment and embolise.

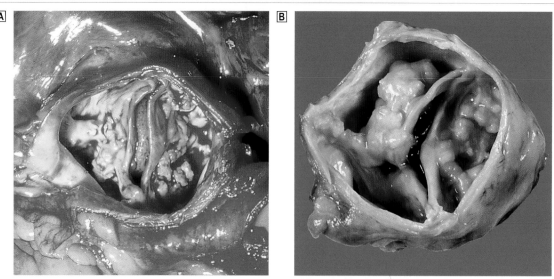

Fig. 13.29   Aortic stenosis. A This 58-year-old male died suddenly. Note that the valve is bicuspid and nodular due to heavy calcification. B This is the more typical pattern of aortic stenosis in a tricuspid aortic valve. Again there are heavy nodular areas of calcification.

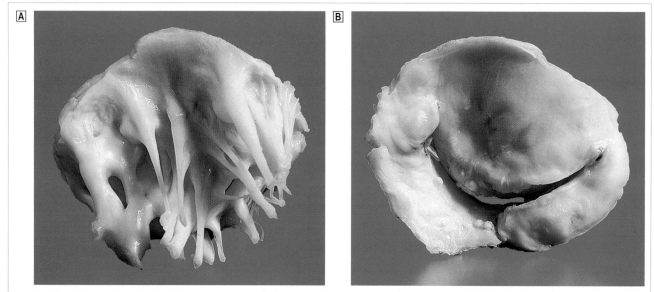

Fig. 13.30   Rheumatic valvular disease. This patient had longstanding mitral stenosis, and a successful mitral valve replacement was performed. A Thickening of chordae tendineae. B The atrial aspect shows how narrow the mitral orifice was.

Clinicopathological features

The most important clinicopathological features of mitral and aortic valve lesions are summarised in Table 13.7. The main pathological causes of diseases in these valves are:

- dilatation of the ventricles, increasing the cross-sectional area of valve orifices
- ischaemic fibrosis of the left ventricle, with impairment of normal papillary muscle function
- calcific degeneration of the aortic valve
- age-related degenerative changes in valve leaflets, particularly the mitral valve

- scarring and calcification of valve cusps as a late consequence of rheumatic fever.

Mitral incompetence

Mitral incompetence is one of the commonest valvular lesions and is sometimes referred to as mitral insufficiency or regurgitation. The commonest cause of mitral incompetence is ischaemic heart disease. Fibrous scarring impairs the normal mobility of the papillary muscle, which leads to tethering of the valve leaflets. Ventricular dilatation may be associated with dilatation of the mitral valve annulus and this in turn worsens mitral incompetence (Fig. 13.32).

Fig. 13.31   Mitral incompetence. Ⓐ Acute mitral incompetence. The mitral valve has become acutely incompetent due to infarction and rupture of the capillary muscle. Ⓑ Mitral valve prolapse (mucoid degeneration of the mitral valve). Note the marked billowing of the cusps in this postmortem specimen.

Table 13.7   Pathological causes and clinical features of mitral and aortic valvular lesions

Valvular lesion	Pathological cause	Clinical features
Mitral stenosis	Rheumatic fever	Pulmonary hypertension, left atrial and right ventricular hypertrophy Opening snap and diastolic murmur
Mitral incompetence	Rheumatic fever Dilatation of mitral valve annulus Papillary muscle fibrosis and dysfunction Mucoid degeneration of valve cusps (mitral valve prolapse)	Variable haemodynamic effects Pansystolic murmur Mid-systolic click and late systolic murmur in mitral prolapse
Aortic stenosis	Calcific degeneration Rheumatic fever	Ejection systolic murmur Left ventricular hypertrophy Angina, syncope, left ventricular failure or sudden death
Aortic incompetence	Rheumatic fever Dilatation of aortic root (age-related or syphilitic) Some rheumatological disorders, e.g. rheumatoid arthritis, ankylosing spondylitis	Diastolic murmur Wide pulse pressure, collapsing pulse, angina, left ventricular failure

Left atrial pressure is considerably lower than that of the aorta, so blood regurgitates through the mitral valve immediately after the start of ventricular contraction. By the time the aortic valve has opened, as much as a quarter of the stroke volume may already have entered the left atrium. This causes a murmur that begins immediately after the first heart sound and may last throughout systole ('pansystolic murmur'). Acute mitral incompetence is usually the result of papillary muscle rupture in myocardial infarction (Fig. 13.31A). Most patients go into cardiogenic shock and will die within 48 hours. Surgical replacement of the valve can be life-saving, but the associated mortality is inevitably high.

Mucoid degeneration of the mitral valve is a common finding at postmortem and is seen in at least 15% of patients over the age of 70. The valves have a floppy or billowed appearance

(Fig. 13.31B) and prolapse towards the left atrium during ventricular contraction; this is easily seen on echocardiography. Classic clinical signs are a mid-systolic click and a late systolic murmur. In severe disease abnormal stresses on the mitral valve predispose to rupture of chordae tendineae. Excellent results can be obtained by excising segments of the abnormal valve or, if the process is extensive, by mitral valve replacement.

Mitral stenosis

The primary abnormality in mitral stenosis is mechanical obstruction to emptying of the left atrium. The normal cross-sectional area of the mitral valve annulus is about 5 cm², and signs and symptoms of mitral stenosis result when this is reduced to 1 cm² or less. In the vast majority of cases mitral

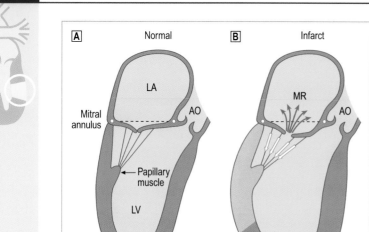

Fig. 13.32 Ischaemic mitral regurgitation. This is now the commonest and most important form of mitral regurgitation (MR). **A** The papillary muscle complex controls the normal closure of the mitral valve during ventricular systole. **B** A dilated ischaemic left ventricle (LV) with an area of fibrous scarring following previous myocardial infarction (grey colour). The movement of the papillary muscle is impaired and this effectively tethers the mitral valve leaflets away from the mitral valve ring (shown as arrows on the chordae tendinae). In addition, dilatation of the left ventricle increases the diameter of the mitral valve. (AO, aorta; LA, left atrium.)

stenosis is a long-term result of rheumatic fever. Although this is now a rare disease in the West, a small number of new cases of mitral stenosis present each year. However, in many parts of Africa and the Middle and Far East rheumatic fever is common and there are many cases of rheumatic valve disease. Typically, rheumatic fever develops 2–3 weeks after a streptococcal upper respiratory tract infection. Recurrent attacks are typical, usually in children between 5 and 15 years of age. Although an arthritis and a skin rash (erythema marginatum) are often the presenting signs, involvement of the heart is the most important feature. There may be inflammation in all layers with pericarditis, myocarditis and endocarditis ('pancarditis'). Heart murmurs are usually heard and heart failure may develop.

Little is known about the exact pathogenesis of rheumatic fever. Bacterial cultures of the heart, joints and other tissues are sterile, but there is serological evidence of a streptococcal infection. Antibodies to streptococcal polysaccharides are substantially elevated (antistreptolysin O titre, ASOT). The chief pathological features are oedema and fibrinoid necrosis of collagen, small aggregates of lymphocytes and macrophages (Aschoff bodies) and fibrosis.

It is even more difficult to explain why some patients go on to develop rheumatic valvular disease. Although rheumatic fever is more common in boys, it is young women who typically present with mitral stenosis, sometimes precipitated by the haemodynamic changes of pregnancy. Pathologically there is scarring of the valve cusps and shortening and thickening of chordae tendineae. Cardiac surgical centres in the East have vast experience of rheumatic valve disease and are especially skilled in its treatment.

Mitral stenosis causes poor emptying of the left atrium, increased pulmonary venous pressure, pulmonary hypertension and right ventricular hypertrophy, dilatation and failure. *Atrial fibrillation* often complicates mitral stenosis due to rheumatic valvulitis. Other causes of atrial fibrillation include ischaemic heart disease, thyrotoxicosis, hypertension, alcohol abuse and cardiac surgery. Ineffective atrial contraction leads to stasis and thrombus formation within the atrial appendages; these are a potential source of systemic thrombo-emboli.

Aortic stenosis

Calcific aortic valve disease is increasing in importance as the incidence of rheumatic heart disease declines, at least in Western countries. Severe calcific disease produces rigid cusps and results in aortic stenosis. This causes progressive and substantial left ventricular hypertrophy. Coronary blood flow may become inadequate, particularly if there is associated coronary atheroma. Most elderly patients with calcific aortic valve disease have pure aortic stenosis, whereas in rheumatic heart disease there is sometimes aortic incompetence and the mitral valve is also usually involved. The pathological processes responsible for calcification of the aortic valve, largely a disorder of the elderly, are unknown. Approximately 1% of the population have a bicuspid, rather than a tricuspid, aortic valve; these valves are particularly liable to calcification, sometimes at a relatively young age (Fig. 13.29). Unsuspected aortic stenosis is a frequent postmortem finding. The lesion can be present for many years and produce few, if any, clinical symptoms. The major features of aortic stenosis are syncope (abrupt episodes of faintness), angina and left ventricular failure. The systolic murmur typical of aortic stenosis begins well after the first heart sound, and ends before the second. It reaches a peak of intensity in mid or late systole. Older patients should be carefully screened for aortic stenosis. Aortic valve replacement is a successful surgical procedure, even in the very elderly.

Aortic incompetence

In aortic incompetence, blood flows back from the aorta into the left ventricle, producing an increased end diastolic volume. This causes an increased stroke volume, systolic hypertension and a wide pulse pressure, producing the typical 'collapsing' or 'water-hammer' pulse. A diastolic murmur is characteristic, but systolic ejection murmurs can result from the large stroke volume, and mitral diastolic murmurs from impairment of normal mitral opening by the regurgitant aortic stream. Left ventricular failure is a feature of severe aortic incompetence. Mild aortic incompetence is sometimes detected in healthy subjects, some of whom have bicuspid valves, and in some rheumatological disorders (Ch. 25).

Tricuspid and pulmonary valve disease

Disorders of the aortic and mitral valves produce far more substantial symptoms than do disorders affecting the valves of the right side of the heart.

Many patients with cardiac failure develop tricuspid incompetence, but this may not produce clinical symptoms. The absence of an effective tricuspid valve alters the pattern

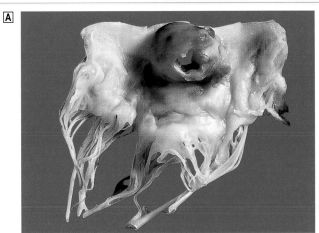
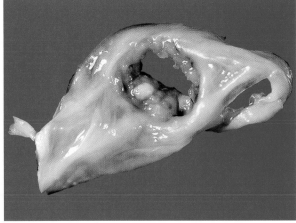

Fig. 13.33 Infective endocarditis. A A surgical resection specimen of a mitral valve. Note the large vegetation, which has perforated. **B** Another surgical resection specimen. This aortic valve cusp has also perforated.

of the jugular venous pulse during systole. The pulmonary valve is seldom affected by acquired disease, but pulmonary stenosis can occur as an isolated congenital lesion or as part of a complex of malformations such as Fallot's tetralogy. Pulmonary stenosis can be treated surgically or by percutaneous dilatation with a balloon catheter.

Infective endocarditis

Infective endocarditis is a serious disease resulting from infection of a focal area of the endocardium. The incidence has recently been estimated as between 2 and 6 per 100 000 population per year, and if anything is increasing. The incidence increases with age, and males are affected twice as commonly as females. The median in-hospital mortality rate is 16% (range 11–26%).

A heart valve is usually involved, but the process may affect the mural endocardium of the atrium or ventricle, or a congenital defect such as a patent ductus arteriosus or coarctation of the aorta.

General risk factors for infective endocarditis include poor dental hygiene, systemic sepsis, diabetes mellitus, long-term haemodialysis, immunosuppression and recent surgery or non-surgical invasive procedures. In the past, rheumatic valvular disease was the usual underlying lesion but this has now been replaced by degenerative processes such as aortic valve calcification or mucoid degeneration of the mitral valve. Intravenous drug misuse, previous valve replacement and vascular procedures, such as pacemaker implantation, are now of increasing importance. Infective endocarditis acquired in hospital (noscomial infection) accounts for about 20% of cases. Intravenous and urinary catheters, and recent surgery are particular risk factors. The heart is structurally normal in up to 50% of these cases.

Aetiology

Many different organisms can cause endocarditis. Most of these originate from the normal flora of the body surfaces, liberated into the blood stream in a variety of different ways. In order to survive in the blood stream, they must be resistant to the killing action of antibody and complement. For this reason Gram-positive bacteria, which have a thick layer of rigid mucopeptide protecting the cell membrane, are the usual causes of endocarditis. The proportion of cases caused by staphylococci is increasing. These infections often progress rapidly and may be difficult to treat. Streptococci, especially *Streptococcus viridans*, form a major part of the normal microbial flora of the oropharynx. Dental procedures, including descaling of teeth and minor fillings, instrumentation of the upper respiratory tract or even aggressive chewing, release small showers of organisms into the blood stream. Various staphylococci and yeasts such as *Candida* are normally present on skin surfaces. These can be introduced into the blood stream by insertion of cannulae or simple venepuncture. Sometimes, they are directly implanted from the surgeon's skin if a glove is punctured during an operation. *Str. faecalis* is normally present in the large intestine and can cause urinary tract infections. During cystoscopy or prostatectomy, organisms may be disseminated into the blood stream and initiate endocarditis (sometimes called enterococcal endocarditis).

Morphology

The characteristic lesion of infective endocarditis is the vegetation. This can vary in size from a small nodule to a large friable mass that can all but occlude the valve orifice (Fig. 13.33). Almost all vegetations occur on valve leaflets or chordae tendineae. Occasionally, congenital defects such as patent ductus arteriosus, coarctation or an arteriovenous fistula can be involved. Surprisingly, vegetations never occur on atheromatous plaques in the aorta; the marked surface irregularities of the latter should make these ideal sites for a vegetation to develop, and why this does not occur is a mystery. Experimental work suggests that vegetations form in areas where there is flow across a high pressure gradient, as in an incompetent valve.

In the course of septicaemia, virulent bacteria, such as *Staphylococcus aureus*, are thought to invade normal endocardial

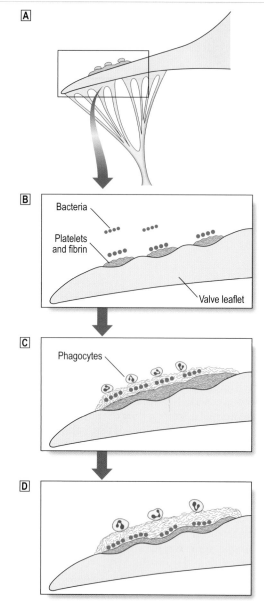

Fig. 13.34   Formation of vegetation on a valve leaflet in infective endocarditis. [A] A focal area of abnormality on the endocardium of a valve leaflet is covered with tiny deposits of platelets and fibrin; this is in effect the beginnings of a thrombus. [B] Circulating micro-organisms (released into the blood stream under any of the circumstances described in the text) colonise the platelet thrombus. [C] and [D] When sufficient bacteria have settled, further blankets of platelets and fibrin are laid down. The bacteria proliferate slowly to form colonies occupying a relatively superficial position in the vegetation. They are separated from the blood stream by a thin layer of fibrinous material. This layer prevents the phagocytes reaching the bacteria, but is not a significant barrier to the diffusion of nutrients from the blood stream.

Important diseases that predispose to endocarditis include:

- degenerative valve disease
- congenital heart disease
- prosthetic heart valves (see below)
- immunosuppression and haemodialysis
- intravenous drug abuse
- invasive procedures performed in hospital.

The probable sequence of events in the formation of a vegetation is shown in Figure 13.34.

Endocarditis in unusual hosts

Patients with prosthetic heart valves

Up to 2–3% of patients with artificial heart valves develop endocarditis (Fig. 13.35). Staphylococci account for at least 50% of cases. Many of these are coagulase-negative.

The commonest initial presenting symptom is post-operative fever. When residual wound sepsis and pulmonary or urinary tract infections have been excluded, prosthetic valve endocarditis should be seriously considered. Typically the process develops about 2 months after valve replacement. Echocardiography and repeated blood cultures are essential for diagnosis. Despite medical and surgical treatment, the mortality rate can be as high as 70%. In some patients, prosthetic valve endocarditis develops many months or years after the operation, and this possibility should always be considered in a pyrexial patient who has had a previous valve replacement.

The elderly

Endocarditis is increasing in incidence in elderly patients. Calcific valve disease is the most frequent pathology. Predisposing factors include genito-urinary infection, diabetes, tooth extraction, pressure sores and surgical procedures. It appears that virulent organisms such as *Staph. aureus* may be more frequent as the infecting organism in elderly patients. Complications also appear to be more common than in younger patients. Presenting signs and symptoms are often atypical because of other co-existing disease processes, such as respiratory tract infection and cardiac failure.

Drug addicts

Infective endocarditis in drug addicts has increased in all Western societies. The skin is the most common source of micro-organisms; most cases are due to *Staph. aureus* or *Staph. epidermidis*, and fungi such as *Candida*. The bacteraemia has various causes:

- The drug preparation, and the water used to dilute it, can contain virulent micro-organisms that enter the circulation by direct inoculation.
- Bacterial cellulitis may occur at the sites of injection. If drugs are then injected through the inflamed skin, bacteraemia will result.
- If the cellulitis is extensive, thrombophlebitis will develop and this in itself can lead directly to bacteraemia.

Very few intravenous drug abusers presenting with their first episode of endocarditis have previously damaged heart

tissue. However, less virulent organisms, such as some streptococci, can infect the endocardium only at the sites of pre-existing damage. Binding to endothelial surfaces is facilitated by adhesive processes termed 'pili'.

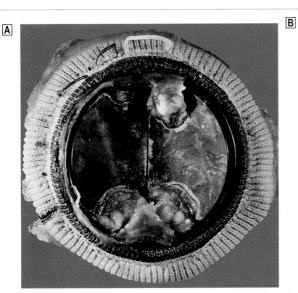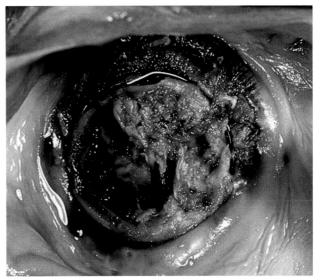

Fig. 13.35 Prosthetic valve endocarditis. **A** This patient had a mitral valve replacement 5 months previously but developed prosthetic valve endocarditis. Note the large vegetations forming at the margins of the tilting discs. Fortunately this patient recovered. **B** This patient underwent mitral valve replacement 7 months before death. Vegetations have virtually obscured the underlying prosthetic valve.

valves. Perhaps the repeated intravenous injection of 'foreign' material damages the endocardial surfaces, producing abnormal (roughened) areas. These become sites of platelet aggregation and therefore the development of vegetations. This may account for the high incidence of tricuspid valvular involvement in drug addicts, as this valve is closest to the injection site.

Vegetations in drug addicts are often large, particularly in fungal endocarditis. As infection primarily involves the right side of the heart, vegetations can embolise to the lungs. Endocarditis must be suspected in any drug addict presenting with signs or symptoms of pneumonia, pulmonary embolism or infarction.

Complications

The complications of endocarditis are summarised in Figure 13.36.

Local effects
All but the smallest vegetations have some effect on valvular function, and many cause *valvular incompetence*. A heart murmur is one of the most important physical signs of infective endocarditis. As the vegetations enlarge, valve cusps can perforate or chordae tendineae rupture. This is one cause of death in endocarditis and is now one of the indications for valvular replacement. *Myocarditis* is an important complication of endocarditis; the inflammation probably spreads directly from the valve leaflet to involve the annulus and adjacent myocardium. Vegetations can embolise to coronary arteries but this is extremely uncommon.

Systemic effects
Fever, weight loss, malaise and splenomegaly are the classical findings in infective endocarditis and can be attributed to the persistent bacteraemia. Parts of the vegetations may

break away from the heart valves and lodge in many different sites; the spleen, kidney and brain are those most frequently involved. Small *emboli* produce tiny haemorrhagic lesions, essentially small infarcts, in the skin, mucous membranes and retina. Linear haemorrhages beneath the tips of the nails (splinter haemorrhages, Fig. 13.37A) are frequent in infective endocarditis, but equally can follow everyday trauma. *Clubbing* (Fig. 13.37B, C) is another clinical feature; its cause is unknown. It is also known as Schamroth's sign after the physician who described the changes in his own fingers while suffering from endocarditis.

A focal segmental *glomerulonephritis* can be seen in infective endocarditis. This is almost certainly the result of immune complex deposition in glomeruli (Ch. 21). The antigen is probably derived from the micro-organism and the antibody produced by the host in response to it. Some other manifestations of infective endocarditis, such as Osler's nodes in the fingers, may be the result of an *immune complex arteritis* in the soft tissues.

Diagnosis, treatment and prevention

Investigations
Once a diagnosis of infective endocarditis has been considered, two lines of investigation are essential. The heart valves must be imaged by trans-thoracic or trans-oesophageal echocardiography, and the organism must be cultured from the blood stream. Delay in either of these may have serious consequences and their importance cannot be overemphasised. Echocardiography is valuable in identifying vegetations at initial presentation, for following how their size changes with treatment and for selecting cases for surgical treatment (Fig. 13.38).

It is important to isolate the causative organism from the blood stream. This not only establishes the diagnosis

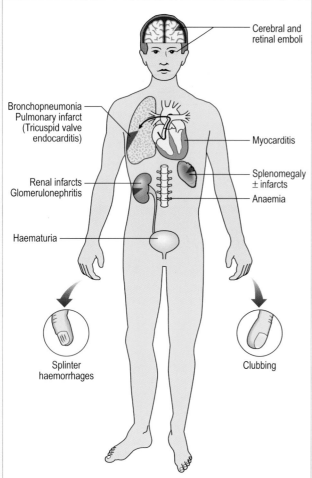

Fig. 13.36   **The complications of infective endocarditis.** The full range of complications are now rarely encountered in the Western world; for example, clubbing and splenomegaly may not be present in the early stages of the disease. (See text for detail.)

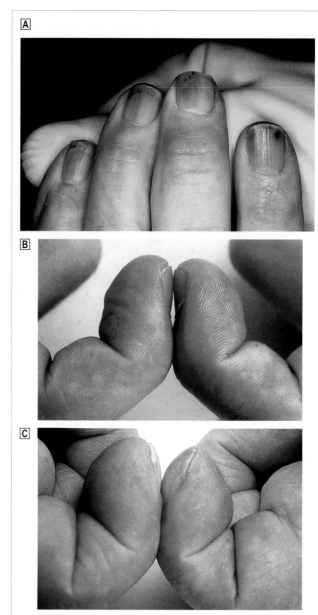

Fig. 13.37   **Changes in the hands and nails in infective endocarditis.** A Prominent splinter haemorrhages. B Normal nail beds. C Clubbing in infective endocarditis. This is sometimes known as Schamroth's sign. There are of course many other causes of clubbing, including pulmonary carcinoma, intrathoracic infections and congenital heart disease.

but indicates which antibiotic or combination of drugs is needed to destroy the infecting organism. In taking blood cultures, it is essential to prevent skin and airborne bacteria contaminating the blood sample. Particular care should be taken to sterilise the skin overlying the vein, using a strong antiseptic such as chlorhexidine in 70% ethanol. Up to one-quarter of blood cultures grow skin bacteria, and this can lead to erroneous diagnoses and inappropriate treatment. Release of bacteria from vegetations is probably episodic and the numbers released may be small. Multiple blood cultures should be taken each day, perhaps for two or even three days. In practice, patients are often so ill that treatment must be started as soon as the diagnosis is suspected clinically, and certainly before the results of blood culture are available. In around 5% of patients with good clinical evidence of endo-carditis blood cultures are negative. Failure to recover the causative organism can be due to:

- 'walling off' of bacteria within the fibrinous masses of the vegetation

- antibiotic treatment before blood cultures were taken; where there is serious clinical doubt it may be justified to stop treatment temporarily and then take blood cultures
- infection with slow-growing or difficult-to-culture organisms; these include *Coxiella, Legionella,* the HACEK group (*Haemophilus* species, *Actinobacillus, Cardiobacterium hominis, Eikenella corrodens* and *Kingella kingae*), *Chlamydia, Bartonella,* and fungi including *Candida.*

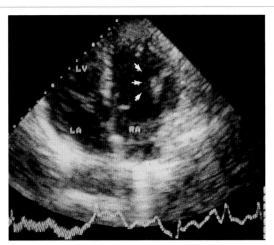

Fig. 13.38 Echocardiographic appearance of valve vegetations. In this case the vegetations are on the tricuspid valve (arrowed). The patient was an intravenous drug abuser.

Treatment

Ideally patients should be treated in a cardiac unit with ready access to cardiac surgery. Without adequate antibiotic treatment endocarditis is uniformly fatal. The avascular structure of the vegetation prevents the invasion of large numbers of phagocytes, and because of this it is essential to sterilise the heart valve with antibiotics. The antibiotics chosen must kill the bacteria, not just inhibit their growth. Cardiologists and microbiologists work closely together to select the most appropriate combination and dosages of antibiotics. Serial echocardiography is used to assess the change in size of vegetations. Surgical replacement of valves is increasingly used, especially if vegetations do not reduce in size with antibiotic treatment.

Prevention

Any patient with valvular heart disease is at risk of developing endocarditis as a result of bacteraemia associated with even the most minor surgical or dental procedure. It is therefore essential that the blood contains a high concentration of bactericidal antibiotics immediately before and during these procedures. The aim is to kill bacteria in the blood stream before they settle on the heart valve. Endocarditis still has an appreciable mortality, and the importance of these prophylactic measures cannot be overemphasised. Tragically, cases of endocarditis still occur in previously fit individuals not given appropriate antibiotic cover during minor procedures.

Non-infective endocarditis

Small thrombotic vegetations can occur on the closure lines of valve cusps in debilitated patients, especially those with cancer. These are called *marantic vegetations*. Thrombotic vegetations develop in some cases of systemic lupus erythematosus (Libman–Sacks endocarditis). In both conditions the thrombotic material can fragment and embolise.

Table 13.8 Clinical causes and pathological forms of pericarditis	
Clinical causes	Pathology
Acute non-specific or acute viral pericarditis	Acute fibrinous pericarditis
Myocardial infarction	Initially acute fibrinous, and later fibrous, pericardial adhesions
Uraemia	Acute fibrinous reaction
Carcinomatous pericarditis	Secondary neoplastic deposits (often from bronchus) Serous or haemorrhagic effusion
Connective tissue disease (e.g. rheumatic fever or rheumatoid arthritis)	Fibrinous pericarditis
Bacterial pericarditis	Acute purulent or fibrinopurulent reaction
Tuberculosis	Fibrous or calcific pericarditis, sometimes causing constrictive pericarditis
Post-cardiac surgery	Acute fibrinous reaction
Post-myocardial infarction (Dressler's syndrome)	Autoimmune infarction

PERICARDITIS AND MYOCARDITIS

Pericarditis

In pericarditis, there is an inflammatory reaction involving the visceral and/or parietal pericardial layers. There are many causes (Table 13.8) but the commonest are acute, non-specific (viral) pericarditis, myocardial infarction and uraemia.

Acute pericarditis

In acute pericarditis there is invariably a fibrinous exudate on the pericardial surfaces, with associated acute inflammation (Fig. 13.39). In many cases, there is an exudate of serous fluid (pericardial effusion) and this may become haemorrhagic. Common viral causes include coxsackievirus A and B, herpes simplex and influenza. Bacterial pericarditis results either from direct spread from an intrathoracic focus or from a blood stream infection.

Chronic pericarditis

Chronic pericarditis may have no obvious cause but is a feature of connective tissue diseases such as rheumatoid arthritis, and of tuberculosis. In many cases an effusion develops and there is marked fibrous thickening of the pericardial layers. Many patients with a previous history of myocardial infarction

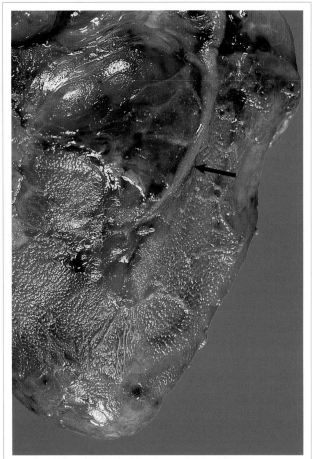

Fig. 13.39 Acute pericarditis. Acute fibrinous pericarditis. Note the granular masses of fibrin on the visceral pericardial surface. Common causes of pericarditis include acute myocardial infarction, uraemia, viral infections and recent cardiac surgery. This patient had a cardiac bypass procedure 7 days before his death. The vein graft is arrowed.

have areas of old pericardial fibrosis, the result of healing of previous acute pericarditis.

Clinicopathological features

Typically, patients with pericarditis complain of chest pain, which may be either sharp or dull and aching. Young patients who present with acute non-specific or viral pericarditis often have severe chest pain which can be confused with acute myocardial infarction. Severe pain is uncommon in other forms of pericarditis. A pericardial friction rub is a characteristic feature of acute fibrinous pericarditis, but it may be transient and variable in its intensity. Pericardial effusions of less than 50 ml are usually undetectable clinically. With large effusions, the area of cardiac dullness to percussion is increased and the heart sound may be diminished. Echocardiography is essential for correct diagnosis. Large effusions may interfere with diastolic filling of the heart and produce cardiac tamponade. The jugular venous pressure is raised,

and there is an exaggerated variation in pulse pressure during inspiration and expiration (pulsus paradoxus). Characteristic pressure tracings may be obtained during cardiac catheterisation. Constrictive pericarditis may seriously impair cardiac function, and surgical excision of the pericardium may improve cardiac output. In many cases there is associated calcification of the pericardium, which may be seen on chest X-rays, particularly lateral views.

Myocarditis

Pathogenesis

The chief causes of inflammation of the myocardium are:

- viral infections, e.g. Coxsackie groups A and B, influenza, echovirus, Epstein–Barr virus (infectious mononucleosis), HIV
- bacterial infections, e.g. diphtheria, leptospirosis, meningococcus
- parasitic infections, e.g. trypanosomiasis (sleeping sickness), Chagas' disease
- ionising radiation
- drugs, e.g. doxorubicin.

Coxsackie B virus is the commonest *known* infectious cause of pericarditis and myocarditis in western Europe and North America. The diagnosis is suggested by rising titres of specific antibodies in the serum. Many other viruses have been implicated. Diphtheria has not been eradicated from developing countries and cardiac failure is a frequent cause of death; an exotoxin inhibits protein synthesis in cardiac muscle. Myocarditis can complicate infective endocarditis and in some cases myocardial abscesses form around valve rings.

Clinicopathological features

In most patients myocarditis is a self-limiting condition with only mild pleuritic chest pain. Fatalities are relatively uncommon (Fig. 13.40). In some patients cardiac failure develops and coronary angiography may be performed to exclude coronary artery disease. An endomyocardial biopsy may be performed at the same time and may show lymphocytic infiltration and myocyte necrosis. However, even in the most typical clinical cases the proportion of positive biopsies is small. Viral or molecular studies may identify an underlying causative agent. Anti-inflammatory drugs may be used in severe myocarditis but there is no definite evidence that they are effective.

CONGENITAL CARDIOVASCULAR DISEASE

- ▶ Relatively common and the usual cause of heart failure in children
- ▶ Haemodynamic consequences vary according to the location and nature of anomaly
- ▶ Multiple anomalies occur (e.g. Fallot's tetralogy)
- ▶ Many patients can be treated or palliated surgically

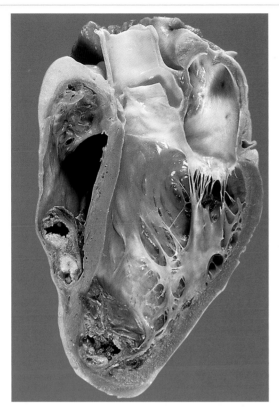

Fig. 13.40 Coxsackievirus myocarditis. This heart is from a 19-year-old female who was fit 6 months before her death. Note the marked thinning of the right ventricular wall and the areas of adherent mural thrombus.

Aetiology

Congenital cardiovascular disease is the result of a structural or functional abnormality of the cardiovascular system at birth. In the vast majority of cases, the structural defects can be attributed to a specific disturbance of normal embryological development.

The incidence of congenital heart disease (CHD) is around 8 per 1000 live births and is much higher if bicuspid aortic valves are included. In about one-third of cases critical illness develops early in life. Associated extracardiac abnormalities occur in about a quarter of infants with CHD. In Down's syndrome, for example, there is a high incidence of atrial or ventricular septal defect, or a patent ductus arteriosus.

In at least 80% of cases the cause of congenital heart disease is unknown. Environmental factors, such as maternal viral infections (especially rubella), chronic maternal alcohol abuse and drugs such as thalidomide, are all clearly related to CHD. These factors are of greatest importance between the fourth and ninth weeks after conception. During this period, the common atrial and ventricular chambers are divided by septa, the cardiac valves develop and the primitive truncus arteriosus divides into the aorta and pulmonary artery. The incidence of CHD is somewhat increased in the children of mothers with insulin-dependent diabetes or phenylketonuria.

There is a weak but definite family incidence of congenital cardiovascular disorders and the genetic basis of these defects is under investigation. Some congenital heart defects are associated with extracardiac abnormalities and in a small number of these specific chromosomal abnormalities have been detected. The risk of a congenital heart lesion in the siblings of affected individuals varies with the nature of the defect, for example from 2% for coarctation of the aorta to over 4% for ventricular septal defects. When two or more members of a family are affected, the risk appears to be substantially higher and, in these instances, clinical geneticists may be able to provide advice to parents.

Clinicopathological features

Some of the most prominent clinical and pathological features of CHD are:

- poor feeding, failure to thrive and impaired growth
- respiratory disease or tachypnoea
- cyanosis
- clubbing
- polycythaemia
- cardiac failure
- pulmonary hypertension
- infective endocarditis.

Most children under 1 year of age who present with cardiac failure have a structural abnormality of the cardiovascular system. The severity of cardiac failure and the presence or absence of additional signs, such as cyanosis, depend on the precise structural abnormalities. Echocardiography and cardiac catheterisation now permit a detailed understanding of disordered anatomy before cardiac surgery.

Individual cardiac disorders

Atrial septal defects (ASD)

Between the fourth and seventh weeks of fetal life two distinct flaps of tissue develop to divide the common cavity into the left and right atria. The first, the *septum primum*, has two defects but these are normally covered when the second partition, the *septum secundum*, grows upwards from the atrioventricular ring. The higher of these defects, the *ostium secundum*, is covered by a flap of the septum secundum. In fetal life this acts as a flap valve, allowing blood entering the right atrium from the systemic veins to bypass the lungs by flowing into the left atrium. When the pulmonary circulation is established, it closes, and in most cases the two layers of the flap fuse together. In many children and some adults a probe can be passed between the layers, the so-called *'probe patent' foramen ovale*. A defect in this area is the usual form of atrial septal defect (ASD). Less common types of ASD are related to defects low in the interatrial septum, close to the atrioventricular ring. There may be associated abnormalities in the mitral valve, and surgical repair is more complex. Other uncommon types of ASD are associated with defects in the development of the pulmonary veins or the coronary sinus.

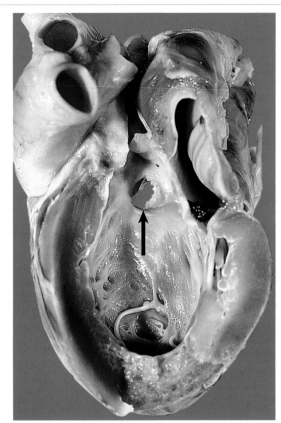

Fig. 13.41   Ventricular septal defect. This child was 4 years old at the time of his death. He had marked left ventricular hypertrophy. This is the heart of a child who died in Africa in the 1970s. Ideally lesions such as these should be treated surgically within the first year of life.

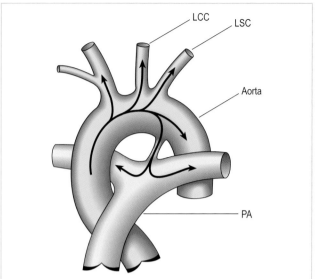

Fig. 13.42   Circulation in patent ductus arteriosus. The duct should normally close very soon after birth. (LCC, left common carotid artery; LSC, left subclavian artery; PA, pulmonary artery.)

Atrial septal defects make up approximately 10% of all congenital abnormalities of the heart. Although they are often asymptomatic, in the past many untreated patients developed signs of right heart failure in the third and fourth decades. A diastolic rumbling murmur, due to increased flow across the tricuspid valve, may be heard and, because of delayed closure of the pulmonary valve, there is often wide splitting of the second heart sound. The right ventricle is compliant and easily dilates to accommodate the increased pulmonary blood flow, but right ventricular hypertrophy and pulmonary hypertension inevitably develop. Closure is therefore indicated.

Ventricular septal defects

Ventricular septal defects account for approximately 25% of all cases of congenital heart disease in infancy. A variety of anatomical forms are recognised and their size and position can be estimated by echocardiography. Small defects in the muscular wall may close spontaneously as the heart grows. Surgical closure is indicated for larger muscular defects and those involving the membranous (fibrous) portion of the septum, close to the atrioventricular ring (Fig. 13.41). As the left ventricular pressure is substantially greater than that in the right, there is always some shunting of blood through the defect. The size and site of the ventricular defect determine the extent of this shunt. In some cases, defects in the membranous septum are also associated with valvular abnormalities, particularly aortic incompetence, and this influences the clinical presentation.

The most prominent physical sign of ventricular septal defect is a loud pansystolic murmur, often with an associated thrill. The most important complication is cardiac failure but there is also a risk of infective endocarditis.

Patent ductus arteriosus

In fetal life, the pulmonary vascular resistance is high and the right heart pressure exceeds that of the left. Consequently there is a flow from the right to the left atrium through the foramen ovale, and from the pulmonary artery to the aorta via the ductus arteriosus. At birth, the pulmonary vascular resistance declines dramatically, and the ductus arteriosus closes within the first few days of life. If the ductus remains open (patent), there is an abnormal shunt of blood from the *aorta to the pulmonary artery*. This increases both pulmonary arterial and left heart blood flow, but the right atrium and ventricle are virtually unaffected (Fig. 13.42).

As in ventricular septal defects the symptoms are proportional to the size of the left-to-right shunt. A continuous 'machinery' murmur is characteristic, and is loudest at the time of the second heart sound. If the shunt is large, a left ventricular impulse ('heave') is usually present. If a patent ductus does not close spontaneously, surgical treatment is indicated. In all forms of aortic surgery pre-operative echocardiographic and angiographic investigations are used to define the precise anatomy of the aortic arch and its branches.

Coarctation of the aorta

A congenital localised constriction in the diameter of the aorta is known as a 'coarctation'. This defect accounts for up

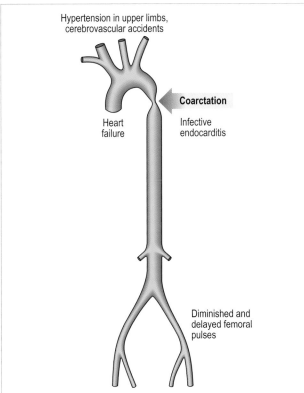

Fig. 13.43 Coarctation of the aorta: clinical features. Echocardiography now detects most cases early in life. The diagnosis should be considered in any child who fails to thrive.

to 5% of all forms of congenital cardiovascular disease and is substantially more common in males. In the usual form of coarctation the narrowing occurs just distal to the ductus arteriosus, which is usually closed. In a proportion of cases there are associated aortic valve abnormalities, usually a congenitally bicuspid valve.

The signs and symptoms are largely dependent on the degree of constriction (Figs 13.43 and 13.44). If this is severe, symptoms develop soon after birth. If the coarctation is undetected or untreated, a collateral circulation develops to increase blood flow to the lower part of the body. This process involves branches of the intercostal arteries, which become dilated and tortuous. In time, the enlarged vessels may erode portions of the rib, producing 'notching' on chest X-ray. The most characteristic clinical finding is hypertension in the upper limbs, with a much lower pressure in vessels distal to the coarctation. The intensity of the femoral pulse is often much reduced. The abnormal blood flow through the coarcted segment may produce a systolic murmur, best heard in the posterior chest.

Some patients with coarctation are asymptomatic but most die prematurely, usually as a result of:

- *congestive heart failure* following prolonged hypertension
- *intracerebral haemorrhage*
- *bacterial endocarditis*, either at the site of aortic constriction or, less commonly, in association with a bicuspid aortic valve

- *rupture of a dissecting aneurysm*; this is substantially more common in patients with both hypertension and bicuspid aortic valves.

In view of these complications, and the shortened life-span of many patients, surgical treatment is usually indicated.

Complex congenital heart disease

These are rare disorders in which individual cardiac chambers are imperfectly developed or incorrectly connected. An exact diagnosis is made by defining the anatomical features using cardiac ultrasonography or other radiological techniques. These disorders usually present soon after birth and a wide range of corrective or palliative surgical techniques have been developed.

The commonest of the complex abnormalities is *Fallot's tetralogy*, first described in Marseilles in the 19th century. The four components are:

- ventricular septal defect
- an enlarged aorta that 'overrides' the defect and receives blood from both the right and left ventricles
- stenosis of the pulmonary valve
- associated right ventricular hypertrophy.

The clinical features are often characteristic. As the aorta receives both oxygenated blood from the left ventricle and deoxygenated blood from the right, cyanosis develops. Pulmonary stenosis restricts blood flow from the right ventricle into the lungs and, if this is severe, survival is only possible if the ductus arteriosus remains open. The systolic murmurs result from either the ventricular septal defect, or, if severe, the pulmonary stenosis. As in all hypoxic patients, the haemoglobin concentration is increased. Right heart failure is inevitable and bacterial endocarditis can ensue. Dyspnoeic children with Fallot's sometimes adopt a characteristic squatting posture, with both the knee and hip joint sharply bent, or sit in a 'knee–chest' position. This may be an attempt to increase venous return from the lower limbs or, more speculatively, to reduce peripheral arterial perfusion, thereby increasing the flow across the ductus arteriosus or ventricular septal defect to the right side of the circulation. Before the advent of surgical treatment (Fig. 13.45), most patients died well before adult life.

Another important complex abnormality is *transposition of the great arteries*. This presents early in life and requires prompt surgery. There are several different forms but in the most important the aorta drains the right ventricle and the pulmonary artery the left. This creates two closed circulations. Post-natal life is only possible if these mix via an atrial or ventricular septal defect or a patent ductus arteriosus. A complete surgical correction is often possible, usually by 'switching' the pulmonary artery and aorta at their origin from the heart and re-implanting the coronary arterial ostia. In the best surgical centres excellent results are now obtained, with mortality rates well below 10%.

Congenital valvular abnormalities

The only common congenital abnormality is a bicuspid aortic valve. The vast majority of these are asymptomatic, and the

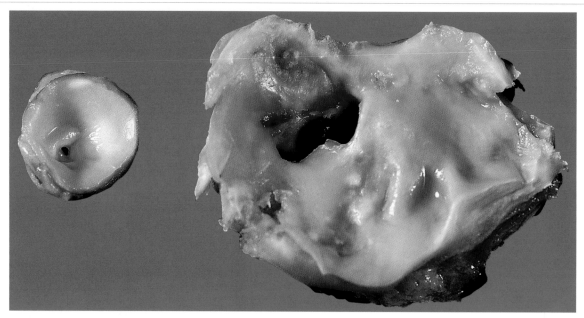

Fig. 13.44 Coarctation of the aorta. Left: A section of an aorta from a 3-day-old child. Note that the lumen of the aorta is less than 2 mm in diameter. Right: A specimen from a 24-year-old male who was found to be hypertensive. The aortic lumen is approximately 5 mm in diameter. Note that atherosclerosis has formed proximal to the coarctation because of turbulent blood flow.

valve is neither incompetent nor stenotic. However, the risk of aortic stenosis in adult life is substantially increased (Fig. 13.29A) and there is a strong association with dissection of the aorta. Small defects (fenestrations) are frequently observed at autopsy, usually in aortic valves, but have no functional significance.

Occasional cases of congenital aortic or pulmonary stenosis do occur. Most tricuspid and mitral abnormalities are part of complex abnormalities rather than isolated lesions.

Coronary arterial abnormalities

There is considerable variation in the normal anatomy of the major coronary vessels and this is usually of no clinical importance. For example, the circumflex branch of the left coronary artery is sometimes small and there is a corresponding increase in the length and distribution of the terminal parts of the right artery. Similarly, the coronary arterial ostia are occasionally malpositioned, but these cause no obvious clinical effects. Many different anomalies have been described. Some are of no clinical importance, while others are associated with an increased risk of sudden death or cardiac disease. For example, one of the coronary arteries may arise from the pulmonary artery, and the myocardium is therefore perfused with deoxygenated blood.

UNUSUAL CARDIAC DISEASES

Most cases of cardiac failure can be attributed to ischaemic heart disease, hypertension, valvular disorders, congenital defects or lung disease. Only when these have been excluded

are unusual causes considered. The term *cardiomyopathy* is often loosely applied to these disorders, but strictly speaking this term should be restricted to disorders of completely unknown cause or clinical association, i.e. *idiopathic* or *primary cardiomyopathy*. In practice, expressions such as alcoholic cardiomyopathy, amyloid cardiomyopathy and occasionally ischaemic cardiomyopathy are used to describe cardiac disease in patients with a known systemic disorder that affects the heart.

Unusual disorders of known cause or association

Multisystem diseases

Cardiac changes are often present in association with multisystem disease. In *sarcoidosis* and *rheumatoid disease*, for example, granulomatous lesions can develop in the heart, and, if they involve the conduction pathways, arrhythmias or heart block can develop. In some forms of *amyloidosis* (Ch. 7), the heart is involved. At autopsy, the cardiac muscle has a characteristic glassy brown appearance and, if deposits are extensive, cardiac failure develops. Massive cardiac hypertrophy is a feature of *acromegaly*, and cardiac failure is the usual cause of death in these patients.

Major cardiac abnormalities are well recognised in both thyrotoxicosis and myxoedema. In severe *thyrotoxicosis*, the increase in the metabolic rate necessitates an increased cardiac output and peripheral blood flow. Occasionally, this may in itself precipitate 'high output' cardiac failure. More frequently, thyrotoxicosis unmasks subclinical coronary or hypertensive heart disease. Atrial fibrillation is particularly common in elderly patients with thyrotoxicosis.

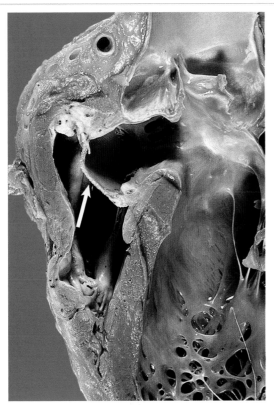

Fig. 13.45   Fallot's tetralogy. The full features in a classical case are right ventricular hypertrophy, ventricular septal defect, pulmonary hypertension and an overriding aorta. This patient underwent surgical correction as a teenager when pulmonary hypertension was well established. Note the thicknesses of the right and left ventricles are almost equal. An arrow shows a patch that was used to close the ventricular septal defect. This is an old specimen. Nowadays lesions such as these would be corrected within the first year of life.

Most patients with *myxoedema* have an enlarged cardiac outline on chest X-ray. This may be due to left ventricular dilatation or pericardial effusion; these can be distinguished by echocardiography. Characteristically, there is a bradycardia, low voltage ECG and decreased cardiac output. There are usually no specific pathological findings either macroscopically or microscopically. The response to thyroid hormone therapy is often excellent, but angina, and even myocardial infarction, can be precipitated with anything but the smallest doses.

Alcoholism

Cardiac failure is not uncommon in chronic alcoholism. In some cases it can be attributed to common disorders such as coronary artery disease or hypertension. However, in a proportion of patients, no specific cause is determined and 'alcoholic cardiomyopathy' is diagnosed. In these patients the macroscopic and microscopic findings are identical to those of other forms of idiopathic cardiomyopathy, and there is some debate as to the exact role of heavy alcohol consumption.

Alcohol abuse is associated with an increased risk of sudden death.

Pregnancy

Substantial circulatory changes occur in pregnancy, most notably an increase in circulating blood volume. Cardiac failure may become apparent for the first time during pregnancy, especially in patients with valvular disorders, such as mitral stenosis. Hypertension is one of the cardinal signs of pre-eclampsia but, while cardiac failure and pulmonary oedema can develop in the full syndrome, the disorder is not primarily cardiac in origin (Ch. 19). A characteristic form of cardiomyopathy (discussed below) occasionally develops in the post-partum period.

Iatrogenic disease

Iatrogenic ('doctor-induced') cardiac disease is now of some importance because of the increasing use of cytotoxic drugs and of radiotherapy in the treatment of mediastinal tumours. Radiotherapy causes patchy areas of interstitial fibrosis in the myocardium (probably as a result of direct damage to small capillaries) and pericarditis. Some degree of cardiac muscle cell necrosis is a frequent result of treatment with cytotoxic drugs, such as doxorubicin, that interfere with DNA and RNA replication and protein synthesis. This can produce acute cardiac toxicity but may also be associated with an increased long-term incidence of cardiac failure. An increased incidence of heart failure has recently been reported in patients receiving the erb-2 antagonist trastuzumab (Herceptin). It is therefore possible that this agent has a direct cardiotoxic effect.

Cardiomyopathies

A cardiomyopathy is a heart muscle disease of uncertain cause. Consequently the diagnosis of cardiomyopathy should be made only when all other causes of cardiac failure, such as hypertension, ischaemic heart disease, valvular and congenital heart disease, have been excluded. Most patients have either a 'dilated' or 'hypertrophic' pattern of disease. However, it is now clear that many cases of both forms of cardiomyopathy have a genetic basis. In the future it is likely that individual cases will be classified according to the nature of the underlying mutation in cardiac muscle.

Dilated (congestive) cardiomyopathy (DSCM)

The incidence of this disorder in Europe and North America is about 35 cases per 100 000 per year. The median age at presentation is about 50 years but young adults may be affected. Typically, the coronary arteries are free of significant atheroma but the ventricles are dilated and hypertrophied (Fig. 13.46). There may be adherent mural thrombi and histological evidence of interstitial fibrosis and hypertrophy of muscle fibres. There is clinical evidence of cardiac disease in the relatives of at least 20% of patients. Current studies are demonstrating an increasing range of mutations. The pattern of inheritance can be autosomal dominant or recessive, X-linked or mitochondrial. These

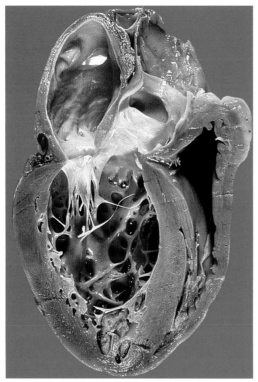

Fig. 13.46   Dilated (congestive) cardiomyopathy. There is marked hypertrophy of both the left and right ventricles. Note the adherent mural thrombus at the apex of the left ventricle. No underlying cause was determined in this patient.

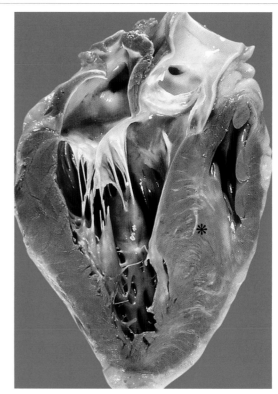

Fig. 13.47   Hypertrophic cardiomyopathy. The patient was a 24-year-old male who died suddenly. Note the marked and asymmetrical enlargement of the interventricular septum (asterisk).

mutations involve genes that code for both cytoskeletal and sarcomeric proteins. A variety of other genetic abnormalities have been detected in young patients with cardiomyopathy. Some relate to fatty acid oxidation, mitochondrial oxidative phosphorylation or the cardiac-specific expression of the *dystrophin* gene.

Some cases of viral myocarditis appear to progress to dilated cardiomyopathy but there is no firm evidence of viral infection in the majority of cases. The pathological features of chronic alcoholic heart disease and dilated cardiomyopathy are similar. The outlook in dilated cardiomyopathy is poor and only 50–60% of patients survive 2 years. It is essential to investigate these patients in the hope of identifying a treatable disorder such as coronary artery or aortic valve disease. Young patients with dilated cardiomyopathy are often considered for cardiac transplantation.

Hypertrophic (obstructive) cardiomyopathy (HOCM)

This is a common autosomal dominant disorder that is thought to affect 1 in 500 of the population. The clinical, echocardiographic and pathological features in hypertrophic cardiomyopathy are often characteristic (Fig. 13.47). The chief feature is massive left ventricular hypertrophy, usually most marked in the interventricular septum close to the aortic outflow tract. In most cases the disease becomes apparent after the pubertal growth phase or in early adult life. Patients present with a variety of signs or symptoms but atrial

fibrillation, ventricular arrhythmias and sudden death are the most important complications. Histological sections of the left ventricle show fibre hypertrophy, interstitial fibrosis and a characteristic disordered arrangement of muscle fibres termed disarray.

Many cases are familial and chromosomal abnormalities can be identified in up to 50% of patients. Mutations have been described in many different cardiac muscle proteins, and in some the exact nature of the amino acid substitution influences the course of the disease. The products of the genes implicated in hypertrophic cardiomyopathy include the structural proteins troponin T and alpha-tropomyosin and cardiac myosin-binding proteins.

Arrhythmogenic right ventricular cardiomyopathy (ARVC)

Although less common than dilated or hypertrophic cardio-myopathy, this is an important disorder with a strong familial tendency. The exact incidence of this disorder is not known, but after hypertrophic cardiomyopathy it is the commonest cause of unexpected cardiac death in a previously fit young person. The characteristic change is progressive loss of right ventricular myocytes with associated fibrosis, inflammation and adipose tissue replacement. In some cases there is clear evidence of septal or left ventricular disease. A small number of gene mutations have been identified, including proteins involved in cell to cell adhesion, such as desmoplakin. Some

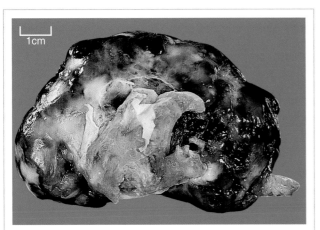

Fig. 13.48 Atrial myxoma. This tumour measured more than 80 mm in diameter and obstructed the mitral valve orifice. The brown tissue in the centre is its point of attachment to the left atrium.

patients have unusually curled or woolly hair, and peripheral hyperkeratosis.

In the future it is likely that many forms of cardiomyopathy will be classified and treated on the basis of the exact underlying genetic abnormality.

Other cardiomyopathies

Many other forms of cardiomyopathy have been described, usually in specific clinical settings.

Puerperal cardiomyopathy occurs in the last months of pregnancy, or within 6 months of delivery. There is no history of pre-existing cardiac disease and the clinical outcome is variable. In some cases cardiac failure resolves completely, although recurrence in subsequent pregnancies is likely.

In *restrictive cardiomyopathy* there is restrictive filling and decreased diastolic volume of one or both ventricles. This is caused by myocardial or endocardial disease that stiffens the heart by infiltration or fibrosis. In some cases there is no obvious cause and the disease is termed primary restrictive cardiomyopathy.

Endomyocardial fibrosis is a curious form of myocardial disease found in the tropics, chiefly in Uganda and the Sudan. The cause is unknown, but there is marked fibrosis of the inner parts of the myocardium, and mural thrombi are common. In some patients with severe cardiac failure, there is a prominent persistent peripheral blood eosinophilia and evidence of multiple systemic emboli (Löffler's endocarditis). This occurs in both tropical Africa and, sporadically, in the West and is usually fatal. The cause is uncertain.

The most important cause of secondary restrictive cardiomyopathy is infiltration of the myocardium by amyloidosis, of either light chain (AL) or transthyretin-related (ATTR) type. Familial forms of cardiac amyloidosis are caused by mutated *TTR*.

Newly described forms of cardiac disease

Studies of young patients presenting with cardiac arrhythmias or sudden death have defined a number of important cardiac disorders that have little or no associated cardiac pathology. As discussed in the section on sudden cardiac death (p. 297), a significant number of sudden deaths in young patients are unexplained. Electrophysiological and genetic studies have shown that a proportion of these cases have mutations in myocardial sodium or potassium channels or receptor molecules. These disorders are now termed channelopathies, and some have characteristic alterations in the QT interval. In some patients arrhythmias may be provoked by sudden noise or during swimming. It is likely that many cases of drowning in young subjects were the result of sudden fatal cardiac arrhythmias rather than accidental deaths.

The Brugada syndrome is another potentially fatal disorder with characteristic ECG changes and a normal cardiac structure. Families of these patients require careful assessment in a specialised centre and often contact patient support organisations.

TUMOURS OF THE HEART AND PERICARDIUM

Primary tumours of the heart and pericardium are extremely rare; only a few cases are seen annually in each regional cardiothoracic centre in the UK. The myxoma is the most frequent primary tumour (25%) and usually arises from the endocardium as a polypoid or pedunculated tumour mass (Fig. 13.48). Three-quarters of myxomas occur in the left atrium, and in almost one-half of all cases there are signs and symptoms of mitral valve disease. The tumours are often friable and can fragment and embolise. Myxomas can be present at almost any age, but are most common in adults. The tumours have a characteristic histological appearance and probably arise from undifferentiated connective tissue cells in the sub-endocardial layers of the heart wall. Other primary tumours include *lipomas*, which are usually found in the interatrial septum. *Rhabdomyomas* arise from cardiac muscle and are often multiple. Many occur in newborn infants and cause stillbirth, or death within the first days of life. Primary malignant tumours of the myocardium include *angiosarcoma* and other sarcomas such as leiomyosarcomas.

Inevitably, the heart and pericardium are often involved by local extension of primary intrathoracic tumours. Bronchial carcinoma is by far the commonest cause of this and can lead to clinically important pericardial effusions. Malignant mesothelioma, a pleural tumour associated with asbestos exposure, often infiltrates the pericardium. Pericardial effusions may be the result of secondary tumour deposits and require aspiration or drainage. Lung and breast are the commonest primary sites.

Commonly confused conditions and entities relating to cardiovascular pathology	
Commonly confused	**Distinction and explanation**
Atherosclerosis and *arteriosclerosis*	*Atherosclerosis* implies hardening (sclerosis) or loss of elasticity of arteries due specifically to atheroma. *Arteriosclerosis* is hardening or loss of elasticity of arteries from any cause.
Angiitis, arteritis and *vasculitis*	*Angiitis* is inflammation of any vessel (even a lymphatic, as in lymphangitis). *Arteritis* is inflammation of an artery or arteriole. *Vasculitis* is inflammation of any blood vessel (arterial, capillary or venous).
Cardiomyopathy and *myocarditis*	*Cardiomyopathy* should strictly be reserved for any myocardial disorder of unknown aetiology (once the aetiology is known, the entity is given a more specific name). *Myocarditis* is inflammation of the myocardium. Both can result in cardiac failure.
Phlebothrombosis and *thrombophlebitis*	*Phlebothrombosis* is thrombosis in a vein (Greek: phlebos). *Thrombophlebitis* is an inflammatory reaction to phlebothrombosis.
Rheumatic fever and *rheumatoid disease*	*Rheumatic fever* is an immunologically mediated post-streptococcal illness affecting the heart and joints. *Rheumatoid disease* is an autoimmune disorder causing arthritis, completely unrelated to rheumatic fever.

FURTHER READING

Adrogué H J, Madias N E 2007 Sodium and potassium in the pathogenesis of hypertension. New England Journal of Medicine 356: 1966–1978

Andreotti F, Marchese N 2008 Women and coronary disease. Heart 94: 108–116

Braunwald E 2008 Biomarkers in heart failure. New England Journal of Medicine 358: 2148–2159

Erridge C 2008 The roles of pathogen-associated molecular patterns in atherosclerosis. Trends in Cardiovascular Medicine 18: 52–56

Hansson G K 2005 Inflammation, atherosclerosis and coronary heart disease. New England Journal of Medicine 352: 1685–1695

Hughes S E, McKenna W J 2005 New insights into the pathology of inherited cardiomyopathy. Heart 91: 257–264

Prendergast B D 2006 The changing face of infective endocarditis. Heart 92: 879–885

Roden D M 2008 Long QT syndrome. New England Journal of Medicine 358: 167–176

Shinebourne E A, Babu-Narayan S V, Caravalho J S 2006 Tetralogy of Fallot; from fetus to adult. Heart 92: 1353–1359

Van der Wal A C 2007 Coronary artery pathology. Heart 93: 1484–1489

Zipes D P, Libby P, Bonow R O, Braunwald E (eds) 2005 Braunwald's heart disease. A textbook of cardiovascular medicine, 7th edn. Saunders, Philadelphia

ACKNOWLEDGEMENT

The photographs were prepared and edited by the Learning Media Department, Southampton University Hospitals.

14

Respiratory tract

COMMON CLINICAL PROBLEMS FROM RESPIRATORY TRACT DISEASE

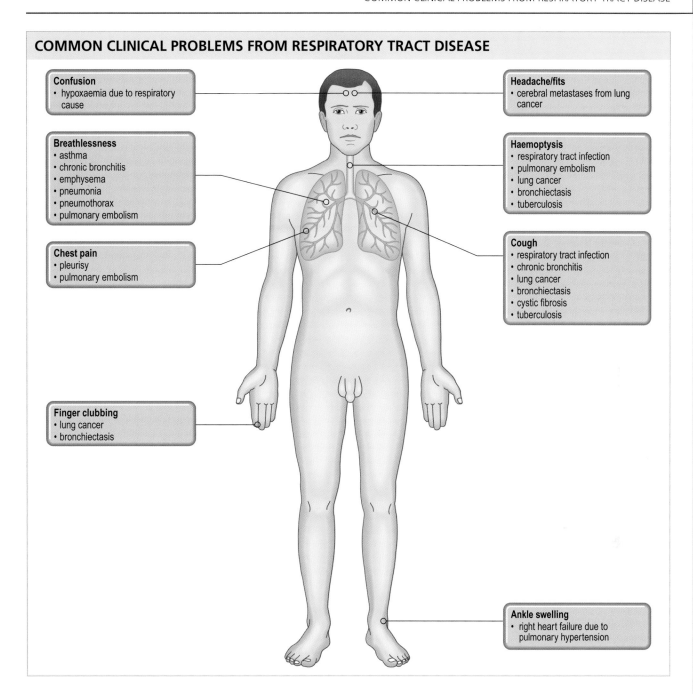

Confusion
• hypoxaemia due to respiratory cause

Breathlessness
• asthma
• chronic bronchitis
• emphysema
• pneumonia
• pneumothorax
• pulmonary embolism

Chest pain
• pleurisy
• pulmonary embolism

Finger clubbing
• lung cancer
• bronchiectasis

Headache/fits
• cerebral metastases from lung cancer

Haemoptysis
• respiratory tract infection
• pulmonary embolism
• lung cancer
• bronchiectasis
• tuberculosis

Cough
• respiratory tract infection
• chronic bronchitis
• lung cancer
• bronchiectasis
• cystic fibrosis
• tuberculosis

Ankle swelling
• right heart failure due to pulmonary hypertension

Pathological basis of respiratory signs and symptoms	
Sign or symptom	Pathological basis
Sputum	
• Clear or mucoid	Excess secretion from bronchial mucous glands in, for example, asthma and chronic bronchitis
• Purulent	Inflammatory exudate from respiratory tract infection
• With blood	Extravasation of red cells due to cardiac failure, pulmonary infarction or ulceration of respiratory mucosa (e.g. by tumour)
Cough	Physiological reflex response to presence of mucus, exudate, tumour or foreign material

(Continued)

Pathological basis of respiratory signs and symptoms—cont'd	
Sign or symptom	Pathological basis
Wheezing • On inspiration • On expiration	Narrowing of larynx, trachea or proximal bronchi (e.g. by tumour) Distal bronchial narrowing (e.g. asthma)
Dyspnoea	Decreased oxygen in the blood from impaired alveolar gas exchange, left heart failure or anaemia
Cyanosis	Increased non-oxygenated haemoglobin, e.g. circulatory bypassing of lungs in congenital heart diseases or impaired alveolar gas exchange
Pleuritic pain	Irritation of the pleura due to pulmonary inflammation, infarction or tumour
Pleural effusion • Transudate (low protein) • Exudate (high protein)	Cardiac failure. Hypoalbuminaemia (e.g. cirrhosis, nephrotic syndrome) Pleural inflammation Tumour
Clubbing	Often accompanies carcinoma of lung and pulmonary fibrosis, as well as, less commonly, cirrhosis and chronic inflammatory bowel disease
Weight loss	Protein catabolic state induced by chronic inflammatory disease (e.g. tuberculosis) or tumours
Auscultation signs • Crackles • Wheezes • Pleural rub	Sudden inspirational opening of small airways resisted by fluid or fibrosis Generalised or localised airway narrowing Pleural surface roughened by exudate
Percussion signs • Dullness • Hyper-resonance	Solidification of lung by exudate (pneumonia) or fibrosis Pleural effusion Increased gas content of thorax due to pneumothorax or emphysema

Globally respiratory diseases, particularly lung infections, together with gastrointestinal infection, account for most deaths in the developing world. Respiratory disease is also a common cause of death in the industrialised nations, accounting for about 14% of deaths in each sex. Out of a global total of 55.69 million deaths in 2000, 3.86 million were due to acute lower respiratory tract infections, 1.66 million to tuberculosis, 2.94 million to HIV/AIDS, 1.21 million to lung cancer and 3.54 million to a variety of other respiratory diseases, mainly chronic obstructive pulmonary disease (2.52 million). There is also considerable morbidity due to respiratory diseases: it is estimated that, in the UK, about 40% of absence from work is the result of such diseases, approximately 85% of which are transient infections of the upper respiratory tract (Table 14.1).

NORMAL STRUCTURE AND FUNCTION

The respiratory system extends from the nasal orifices to the periphery of the lung and the surrounding pleural cavity. From the nose to the distal bronchi, the mucosa is lined by mainly pseudostratified ciliated columnar epithelium with mucus-secreting goblet cells; this is *respiratory mucosa* (Fig. 14.1). A portion of the larynx is covered with stratified squamous epithelium.

Nasal passages and sinuses

These constitute the upper respiratory tract. The nasal passages and sinuses are in continuity and are lined with respiratory mucosa. The hairs in the nose trap large particles of foreign material, thereby filtering the air. The air is also warmed and humidified as it passes through the nasal cavity. The middle ear, also lined with respiratory epithelium, connects with the nasal cavity via the Eustachian tube.

Larynx

The larynx connects the trachea to the pharynx. Consisting of a complicated system of cartilages and muscles, it allows air into the trachea, with the epiglottis preventing the passage of food into the lungs, and also produces sound for speaking. Part of the larynx, including the vocal cords and epiglottis, is covered with non-keratinising squamous epithelium similar to that lining the oral cavity, pharynx and oesophagus.

Lungs

The *lower respiratory tract* consists of the trachea, bronchi, bronchioles, alveolar ducts and alveoli (Fig. 14.2). The structure of each portion differs (Table 14.2).

The lungs develop from an outpouching of the anterior wall of the primitive foregut at about the fifth week of development. From this tube, two lateral outgrowths appear which eventually form the right and left lungs. These outgrowths are surrounded by mesenchyme from which forms the connective tissue of the respiratory tree. Thus the lungs, like the gastro-intestinal tract, develop from endoderm, and developmental abnormalities such as cysts can therefore be lined by either respiratory or gastrointestinal mucosa.

Table 14.1 Major aetiological factors in respiratory disease	
Aetiological factor	**Disease**
Genetic	Cystic fibrosis
	Alpha-1 antitrypsin deficiency
	Some asthma
Environmental	
Smoking	Lung cancer
	Chronic bronchitis and
	emphysema
	Susceptibility to infection
Air pollution	Chronic bronchitis
	Susceptibility to infection
Occupation	Pneumoconiosis
	Asbestosis, mesothelioma and
	lung cancer
Infection	Influenza
	Measles
	Bacterial pneumonias
	Tuberculosis

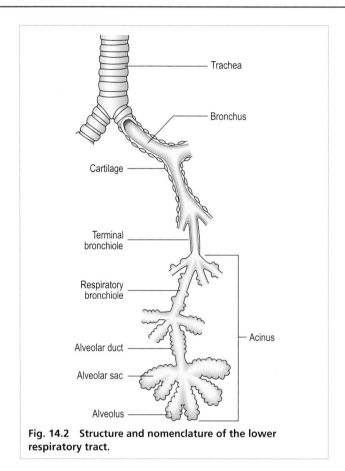

Fig. 14.2 Structure and nomenclature of the lower respiratory tract.

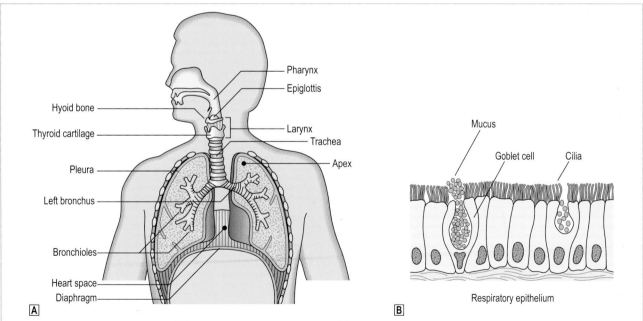

Fig. 14.1 The respiratory system. [A] Anatomy of the respiratory tract. [B] Histology of respiratory epithelium. With the exception of the pharynx, epiglottis and vocal cords, the respiratory tract is lined by specialised epithelium compring ciliated columnar epithelia cells with admixed mucus-secreting goblet cells and scattered neuroendocrine cells.

Table 14.2 Structure of the respiratory tree	
Part of respiratory tract	**Structure**
Trachea	Anterior C-shaped plates of cartilage with posterior smooth muscle. Mucous glands
Bronchi	Discontinuous foci of cartilage with smooth muscle. Mucous glands
Bronchioles	No cartilage or submucosal mucous glands. Clara cells secreting proteinaceous fluid. Ciliated epithelium
Alveolar duct	Flat epithelium. No glands. No cilia
Alveoli	Type I and II pneumocytes

The lungs are divided into *lobes:* the right lung has three lobes (upper, middle, lower); the left lung has only two lobes (upper and lower). Each lung is formed of 10 anatomically defined bronchopulmonary segments. Each segment is supplied by a segmental branches of the pulmonary artery and bronchus (the bronchovascular bundle). The veins draining adjacent segments often anastomose before they reach the hilum and run principally in the fibrous septae of the lungs.

The *respiratory* tree is designed to transport clean, humidified air into distal airways and alveoli, where the waste product of metabolism (CO_2) is exchanged for O_2.

Bronchioles branch until they form terminal bronchioles less than 2 mm in diameter. The respiratory system distal to the terminal bronchiole is called the *acinus* or *terminal respiratory unit,* where gas exchange occurs. Small airways, defined as having an internal diameter of less than 2 mm, consist of terminal and respiratory bronchioles. Respiratory bronchioles are involved with gas exchange, having alveoli in their walls. A group of three to five respiratory acini is called a *lobule.*

The *alveoli* are lined by flattened type I pneumocytes with occasional type II pneumocytes; the latter are rounded cells with surface microvilli and are believed to be the stem cell population for the alveolus. Type II cells secrete surfactant, and replicate quickly after injury to alveolar walls. Beneath the alveolar cells lie a basement membrane which is shared by the alveolar capillary epithelial cells and some interstitial matrix, including elastin fibres. The structure of the alveolar–capillary membrane permits rapid and efficient diffusion of oxygen and carbon dioxide.

The lung is encased by the visceral *pleura* which is a thin layer of fibroconnective tissue and elastin with overlying mesothelial cells. The lungs sit within the chest cavity surrounded by the parietal pleura, by the diaphragm, ribs and intercostal muscles, vertebral column and sternum.

Blood supply and lymphatic drainage

The lungs are perfused by a *dual arterial blood supply.* The trunk of the *pulmonary artery* arises from the right ventricle, splits into main right and left pulmonary arteries and thence follows the airways, forming the bronchovascular bundles. The *bronchial arteries* arise from the descending thoracic aorta and supply oxygenated blood to lung parenchyma around the hilum. Pulmonary veins take all the blood from the lungs back to the left atrium.

Pulmonary *veins* course along the interlobular septa with *lymphatics.* These lymphatic channels and those in the pleura drain into the thoracic duct.

Control of respiration

Respiration is controlled by the *respiratory centre* in the medulla oblongata, and the carotid bodies situated at the carotid bifurcations. The medullary centre senses any change in CO_2 concentration in the cerebrospinal fluid, and modifies respiration by nervous stimulation of respiratory muscles and the diaphragm. The partial pressure of O_2 in the blood is monitored by the *carotid bodies,* which can then stimulate the respiratory centre through the glossopharyngeal nerves. Carotid bodies can become hyperplastic in response to chronic arterial hypoxaemia, such as occurs in:

- high–altitude dwellers
- pulmonary emphysema
- diffuse pulmonary fibrosis
- kyphoscoliosis with chronic hypoventilation
- Pickwickian syndrome (gross obesity with chronic hypoxaemia).

Gas exchange

Air is drawn into the lungs by contraction of the diaphragm and intercostal muscles, creating a negative intrapleural pressure. On relaxation of these muscles, air is expelled as the lungs contract under the action of gravity and the elasticity in the lung connective tissue. The stiffness of the lungs, or *compliance,* is a measure of change in volume per unit change in pressure, and is therefore a measure of compressibility; for example, in pulmonary fibrosis the lungs cannot be easily compressed and therefore the compliance is decreased.

Clearly, gas exchange occurs only in alveoli that are both perfused and ventilated. Ventilation of non-perfused alveoli increases the 'dead space', that proportion of inspired air not involved with gas exchange. Perfusion of non-ventilated alveoli leads to physiological right-to-left shunting of non-oxygenated blood as it passes through the pulmonary circulation.

Acid–base balance

Normal acid–base balance in blood is dependent on both efficient alveolar ventilation and perfusion, with consequent successful gas exchange. This leads to the normal partial pressures of O_2 and CO_2 in arterial blood (Pa_{O_2} and Pa_{CO_2}), and a normal blood pH. Various metabolic disease states lead to disturbances in acid–base balance (Fig. 14.3). If the disease becomes chronic, compensatory mechanisms by both the lungs and kidneys operate in an attempt to restore blood pH.

PULMONARY FUNCTION TESTS

In normal quiet respiration only a relatively small proportion of the *total lung* capacity (TLC) is inhaled and exhaled; this is the *tidal volume* (TV). TLC is made up of the amount of air totally exhaled after maximum inspiration (the *vital capacity* or VC) and the *residual volume* (RV). TLC, RV, TV and VC are all easily measured in the laboratory using helium dilution techniques.

In addition to calculating volume parameters, some techniques also assess actual pulmonary function. *Spirometry* measures the amount of exhaled air per second. The maximum volume of air blown from the lungs within the first second after a previous maximum inspiration is called the *forced expiratory volume* (FEV_1). This figure, highly reproducible in each individual, is a measure of small airway resistance. It is also dependent on the patient's age, sex and size; for example, the small lungs of a child obviously cannot expel as much air as those of an adult. The ratio FEV_1:VC compensates to a degree for the variability of lung size. It is possible to inhale more rapidly than exhale because, during inspiration, forces on the airways tend to open them further; during expiration, opposite forces tend to close the airways and thus restrict airflow. For a given lung volume, the *expiratory flow rate* reaches a peak (PEFR), which is again a measure of airways resistance.

An assessment of the ability of the lungs to exchange gas efficiently can be made by measuring the *transfer factor* for carbon monoxide (T_{CO}). Air containing a known concentration of carbon monoxide is inhaled; the breath is held for 15 seconds and then exhaled. The amount of carbon monoxide absorbed is a measure of pulmonary gas exchange. T_{CO} is dependent on the concentration of blood haemoglobin, which has a strong affinity for carbon monoxide. Diseases that diffusely affect the alveolar–capillary membrane (such as diffuse pulmonary fibrosis or emphysema where there is loss of alveolar surface area) will result in a low T_{CO}.

Recently the level of nitric oxide (NO) in exhaled air has been added as a useful test; increased levels have been associated with asthma and other causes of bronchial irritation, while decreased levels have been found in cigarette smokers, patients with pulmonary hypertension and during treatment with corticosteroids.

Obstructive and restrictive defects

There are two major patterns of abnormal pulmonary function tests: *obstructive defects* (e.g. asthma) and *restrictive defects* (e.g. pulmonary fibrosis) (Table 14.3).

In obstructive airways disease, RV and TLC are mildly increased due to hyperinflation of the lung while FEV_1, FVC and the FEV_1: VC ratio is decreased. Clearly, in conditions such as asthma, the results of pulmonary function tests will depend on the clinical state of the patient, whether in an acute attack of asthma or in remission. Restrictive diseases are those that restrict normal lung movement during respiration and are associated with reduced RV and TLC. The FEV_1 and VC may be reduced but their ratio remains normal.

These tests are of most value in the follow-up of patients. They can also give an indication as to the possible benefits of treatment; for example, observing the improved FEV_1:VC and PEFR after treatment with a bronchodilator would be a measure of the reversibility of the airways obstruction.

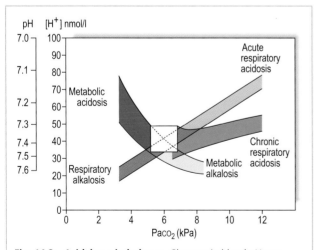

Fig. 14.3 Acid–base imbalance. Changes in blood pH can occur as a result of alterations in hydrogen ion and carbon dioxide concentrations. These lead to different states of acidosis and alkalosis.

Table 14.3 Respiratory function tests and their diagnostic significance

Test	Diagnostic significance
Peak expiratory flow rate (PEFR)	Reduced with obstructed airways or muscle weakness
Forced expiratory volume in 1 second (FEV_1)	Reduced with obstructed airways, pulmonary fibrosis or oedema, or muscle weakness
Vital capacity (VC)	Reduced with reduction in effective lung volume (fibrosis or oedema), chest wall deformity (kyphoscoliosis), or muscle weakness Increased in emphysema
Forced expiratory ratio (FEV_1:VC)	Low in obstructive defects Normal or high in restrictive defects
Carbon monoxide transfer (T_{CO})	Reduced in pulmonary fibrosis, emphysema, oedema, embolism and anaemia
Exhaled nitric oxide (NO)	Increased in asthma, bronchiectasis and infections Decreased in pulmonary hypertension, cigarette smokers and after treatment with corticosteroids

RESPIRATORY FAILURE

Respiratory failure can occur as a result of:

- ventilation defects
  — nervous, e.g. due to narcotics, encephalitis, a cerebral space-occupying lesion, poliomyelitis, motor neurone disease, etc.
  — mechanical, e.g. airway obstruction, trauma, kypho-scoliosis, muscle disease, pleural effusion, gross obesity (Pickwickian syndrome)
- perfusion defects, if diffuse or extensive, e.g. cardiac failure or multiple pulmonary emboli
- gas exchange defects, if diffuse and severe, e.g. emphysema or diffuse pulmonary fibrosis.

The effects of respiratory failure include impaired clearance of CO_2 from the lungs, resulting in hypercapnia, and impaired absorption of O_2 from the air, resulting in hypoxaemia. The patient is typically dyspnoeic, cyanosed and lapsing into coma. Hypercapnia (high blood CO_2 concentration) is associated with a bounding pulse and warm, moist extremities.

DISEASES OF INFANCY AND CHILDHOOD

Respiratory diseases of infancy and childhood are predominantly infectious; such diseases, together with diarrhoea, are the primary cause of death in childhood in the developing world. Rarely disease may arise as a result of either developmental abnormalities or immaturity.

Developmental abnormalities

Developmental abnormalities include:

- tracheo-oesophageal fistula
- congenital diaphragmatic hernia with pulmonary hypoplasia
- congenital cystic adenomatoid malformations
- bronchogenic/foregut cysts
- pulmonary sequestration
- congenital lobar emphysema.

Tracheo-oesophageal fistula
Embryologically, the oesophagus and the trachea begin as a single tube; the trachea then buds off to form the pulmonary tree. In a tracheo-oesophageal fistula, the oesophagus ends in a blind pouch; the trachea then usually connects to the stomach via a fistula. On ingestion of food, the upper pouch quickly fills and overflows into the pulmonary tree, with choking and coughing, leading to aspiration pneumonia. Treatment is by surgery, usually after a period of feeding via gastrostomy.

Congenital diaphragmatic hernia with pulmonary hypoplasia
This presents as neonatal respiratory distress due to herniation of the stomach and loops of bowel into the thorax; usually the left diaphragm is defective. Surgical correction to restore normal thoracic and abdominal anatomy is essential at the earliest possible opportunity. However, even after this there is still a considerable mortality from the associated severe pulmonary hypoplasia, usually of the left lung.

Congenital cystic adenomatoid malformations
These are characterised by abnormalities in the development of small airways and the alveolar tissue of the lung. This results in the development of cysts within the lung which may be of varying size and can be localised to one lobe or be extensive and bilateral. The prognosis depends on the pattern of abnormality present and any other associated abnormalities. Localised areas are cured by surgical excision of the affected lobe.

Bronchogenic/foregut cysts
These occur in the lung or mediastinum and may be lined either by bronchial elements such as cartilage, smooth muscle and ciliated respiratory epithelium (bronchogenic cysts), or by squamous or even gastric or pancreatic type epithelium (foregut cysts). Usually, such cysts are asymptomatic, although complications may occur.

Pulmonary sequestration
A sequestered piece of lung is a mass of abnormal lung that does not communicate anatomically with the tracheo-bronchial tree; it is supplied by an anomalous artery, usually from the aorta. Sequestered segments of lung are found most often within the left lower lobe. Histology shows a multilobulated cystic mass with fibrosis and variable inflammation. An endogenous lipid pneumonia may result.

Congenital lobar emphysema
This condition is characterised by overdistension of a lobe due to intermittent bronchial obstruction. Symptoms arise due to pressure effects caused by the massively distended lobe. Usually, the left upper lobe is affected. The pathogenesis is thought to be abnormal bronchial cartilage allowing inspiration of air but not expiration. Extrabronchial compression by enlarged lymph nodes may produce a similar clinical picture. Treatment is surgical removal of the diseased lobe.

Immaturity

Diseases due to immaturity include:

- hyaline membrane disease or idiopathic respiratory distress syndrome
- bronchopulmonary dysplasia.

Hyaline membrane disease or idiopathic respiratory distress syndrome

- ▶ Complication of prematurity (less than 36 weeks' gestation)
- ▶ Due to deficiency of pulmonary surfactant
- ▶ Tachypnoea, dyspnoea, expiratory grunting, cyanosis
- ▶ Diffuse alveolar damage with hyaline membranes
- ▶ Associated with maternal diabetes, multiple pregnancy, caesarean section, amniotic fluid aspiration
- ▶ Many similarities to adult respiratory distress syndrome (ARDS)

Hyaline membrane disease (HMD) is almost always seen in premature infants of birth weight less than 2.5 kg. Infants are usually of less than 36 weeks' gestation, and the incidence of HMD rises as the gestational age decreases. The risk of developing HMD may be decreased by giving mothers oral corticosteroids prior to delivery of the baby as this appears to stimulate surfactant production in the lungs.

Clinical features

After a few hours of relatively normal respiration, symptoms of tachypnoea and dyspnoea with expiratory grunting appear. Cyanosis quickly follows, with worsening respiratory distress. Hypoxaemia refractory to high concentration of inhaled oxygen is one hallmark of the disease, a finding also characteristic of adult respiratory distress syndrome (ARDS).

Pathogenesis

The pathogenesis is thought to be due to a deficiency of surfactant. This is secreted by type II pneumocytes, and normally lines distal airways; it reduces surface tension, thereby allowing airway opening during inspiration. Without normal quantities of surfactant, airways need greater effort to open, leading to respiratory distress.

Morphology

At autopsy the lungs are heavy, purple and solid, and sink in water. Histology shows collapsed alveoli with hyaline membranes lining alveolar ducts. Pulmonary lymphatics are dilated. As in ARDS, if the infant survives, resolution follows within the next few days, although pulmonary fibrosis may occur. Treatment is with oxygen and artificial ventilation.

Bronchopulmonary dysplasia

Bronchopulmonary dysplasia is the term used to describe the picture of lung organisation after HMD. Often, infants have been previously treated with high levels of oxygen, and it is not clear whether bronchopulmonary dysplasia is a separate disorder, solely related to oxygen toxicity, or merely a result of organisation after HMD. Certainly, the features are almost identical to those seen with organisation of ARDS; there is interstitial fibrosis, peribronchial fibrosis, and features of pulmonary hypertension. The airways may show extensive squamous metaplasia.

NASAL PASSAGES, MIDDLE EAR AND SINUSES

▶ Inflammatory diseases, e.g. rhinitis, are very common
▶ Nasal polyps are either inflammatory or allergic
▶ Malignant tumours are rare

INFLAMMATORY DISORDERS

Rhinitis (the common cold) is caused by many different viruses, especially rhinoviruses, although respiratory syncytial virus (RSV), para-influenza viruses, coronaviruses, coxsackieviruses, echoviruses and bacteria, such as *Haemophilus influenzae*, may also be implicated. Rhinitis may also be caused by inhaled allergens as in 'hay fever' where the inflammatory reaction is mediated via type I and type III hypersensitivity reactions (Chs 9 and 10).

Nasal polyps may result from either chronic infective inflammation or chronic allergic inflammation. They consist of polypoid oedematous masses of mucosal tissue infiltrated with chronic inflammatory cells, especially plasma cells; eosinophils may be numerous if allergy is the cause.

Sinusitis is inflammation of the paranasal sinuses; it may be acute or chronic. If the drainage orifice is blocked by inflamed swollen mucosa, an abscess may follow. Cranial osteomyelitis, meningitis or cerebral abscess may then result from sinusitis by direct extension.

Wegener's granulomatosis, a granulomatous form of vasculitis may involve the nose and upper respiratory tract and present with septal perforation or collapse of the nasal cartilages.

Otitis media is infection of the middle ear, often associated with generalised upper respiratory tract infection (URTI). The Eustachian tube may become swollen and blocked, leading to trapping of exudate in the middle ear. Eardrum perforation may ensue, followed by drainage of the effusion. More serious complications include mastoiditis, meningitis and brain abscess.

TUMOURS

Tumours of the nasal passages and sinuses are uncommon. They may be:

● benign: haemangioma, squamous papilloma, juvenile angiofibroma
● malignant: squamous cell carcinoma, adenocarcinoma, melanoma, lymphoma, plasmacytoma.

Haemangioma and squamous papilloma are benign lesions, the former often presenting with troublesome epistaxis (nosebleeds). Some squamous papillomas may be caused by human papillomavirus.

Juvenile angiofibromas are rare and occur exclusively in males, usually during adolescence. They are extremely vascular, and surgical removal can be difficult. These tumours contain androgen receptors, explaining the male preponderance.

Squamous cell carcinoma may be well differentiated, producing keratin, or very poorly differentiated. The latter may contain many lymphocytes and have been misnamed 'lymphoepitheliomas'. Such tumours are most common in South-East Asia and account for 18% of all cancers in China; evidence suggests the Epstein–Barr virus is involved in the aetiology and pathogenesis of squamous cell carcinoma.

Adenocarcinoma of the nasal passages and sinuses occurs more frequently in people who have worked in woodwork and furniture industries. These tumours may present clinically up to 40 years after initial exposure.

Primary mucosal melanomas of the nose and sinuses are rare but have a very poor prognosis.

Primary extranodal lymphomas are almost always of non-Hodgkin's type.

Plasmacytomas are tumours composed of plasma cells. They can occur as part of multiple myeloma or as isolated lesions without systemic disease.

LARYNX

▶ Laryngitis may be infective, allergic or irritative
▶ Polyps and papillomas are benign lesions
▶ Squamous cell carcinoma, typically in male smokers

INFLAMMATORY DISORDERS

Laryngitis may occur in association with viral or bacterial inflammation of trachea and bronchi; this is laryngotracheobronchitis. *Diphtheria* was once a common, and serious, bacterial cause of laryngitis, leading to the formation of a fibrinopurulent membrane that could cause airway obstruction. Now, partly as a result of immunisation in infancy with diphtheria toxoid, the disease is rare.

Epiglottitis is caused by capsulated forms of *Haemophilus influenzae* type B. The epiglottis becomes inflamed and greatly swollen, leading to airway obstruction (Fig. 14.4). Treatment is by intubation, although, rarely, tracheostomy may be necessary; antibiotics are also given to treat the infection.

Allergic laryngitis occurs after inhalation of an allergen. There may be gross oedema leading to airway obstruction. Irritative laryngitis may be due to cigarette smoke or mechanical factors, e.g. endotracheal intubation.

Laryngeal polyps often develop in singers and are thus sometimes referred to as 'singer's nodes'. Even when only a few millimetres in diameter they can alter the character of the voice. They consist of oedematous myxoid connective tissue covered with squamous mucosa with amyloid-like material in the stroma.

TUMOURS

Laryngeal tumours may be:

● benign: papilloma
● malignant: squamous cell carcinoma.

Papilloma may be caused by types of human papillomavirus. Papillomas consist of squamous epithelium covering fibrovascular cores of stroma. They may be multiple and recurrent, especially in children, but are usually single in adults. Such papillomas can extend into the trachea and bronchi.

Squamous cell carcinoma of the larynx typically affects males over 40 years of age and is associated with cigarette smoking. There may also be an increased risk in asbestos workers. As in squamous epithelium of the cervix, neoplasia is thought to be preceded by a phase of dysplasia. The dysplasia, especially if low grade, may be reversible on withdrawal of causative factors.

Most laryngeal carcinomas arise on the vocal cords (Fig. 14.5), although they may arise above, in the pyriform fossa, or below, as upper tracheal carcinomas. The lesions ulcerate, fungate and invade locally, later causing metastases in regional lymph nodes in the neck and beyond. Symptoms are hoarseness of voice and, later, pain, haemoptysis and dysphagia. Treatment is by chemo-radiotherapy and/or resection. These patients often have widespread mucosal abnormalities throughout the respiratory tract and are at high risk of developing further cancers, especially if they continue to smoke.

THE LUNGS

RESPIRATORY INFECTIONS

The lungs have an internal surface area of approximately 500 m² which is exposed to the external environment and potentially subjected to inhaled microbes with every breath. It is therefore not surprising that respiratory infections are relatively common, with the World Health Organization projecting such infections to continue as one of the global leading causes of death and disability. Countering the threat of pathogens are the defence mechanisms, any abnormality in which will predispose to infection. Such abnormalities include:

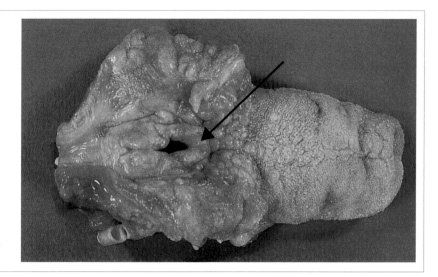

Fig. 14.4 Acute epiglottitis. Gross swelling of the epiglottis (arrowed) leading to respiratory obstruction in a child.

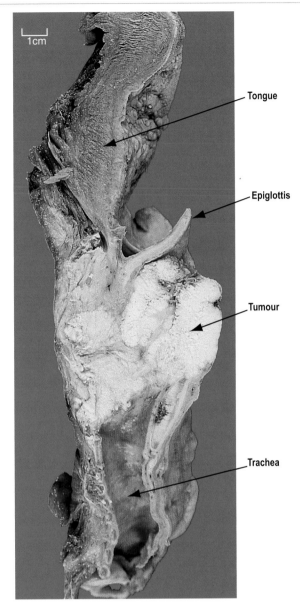

1cm

→ Tongue

→ Epiglottis

→ Tumour

→ Trachea

Fig. 14.5 Laryngeal carcinoma. The tumour is protruding into the larynx and invading the underlying tissues.

- loss or suppression of the cough reflex, e.g. in coma, anaesthesia, neuromuscular disorders, or after surgery
- ciliary defects, e.g. in immotile cilia syndromes, or loss of ciliated cells with squamous metaplasia
- mucus disorders, e.g. excessive viscosity as in cystic fibrosis or chronic bronchitis
- acquired or congenital hypogammaglobulinaemia, e.g. with decreased IgA in the mucus
- immunosuppression, e.g. with loss of B- and/or T-lymphocytes
- macrophage function inhibition, e.g. in people who smoke or are hypoxic
- pulmonary oedema with flooding of the alveoli.

Infections can be classified as *primary,* with no underlying predisposing condition in a healthy individual, or *secondary,*

when local or systemic defences are weakened. The latter are by far the most common types of respiratory infection in developed countries, and are becoming yet more important with the spread of AIDS.

Bronchitis

> ▶ Characterised by cough, dyspnoea, tachypnoea, sputum
> ▶ Usually viral

In acute bronchitis, the trachea and larynx are involved as well as the lungs, and the disease is then known as *acute laryngotracheobronchitis* (or 'croup'). The disease is most severe in children, with symptoms of cough, dyspnoea and tachypnoea. Viruses are usually the cause, especially respiratory syncytial virus (RSV), although *Haemophilus influenzae* and *Streptococcus pneumoniae* are frequent bacterial causes. Episodes of acute bronchitis are common in chronic obstructive airways disease, and cause a sudden deterioration in pulmonary function with cough and the production of purulent sputum. Acute bronchitis may be caused by direct chemical injury from air pollutants, such as smoke, sulphur dioxide and chlorine.

Chronic bronchitis is a clinical term defined as cough and sputum for 3 months in 2 consecutive years; it is discussed below under diffuse obstructive airways disease (p. 338).

Bronchiolitis

> ▶ Usually a primary viral infection in infants (respiratory syncytial virus)
> ▶ May be secondary to other inhaled irritants or part of a systemic disease process
> ▶ Causes dyspnoea and tachypnoea

Primary bronchiolitis is an uncommon respiratory infection caused by viruses, especially RSV, in infants. Symptoms are of acute respiratory distress with dyspnoea and tachypnoea. Most cases resolve within a few days, although a minority may develop secondary pneumonia.

Follicular bronchiolitis with lymphoid aggregates and germinal centres, compressing the airway, can occur in rheumatoid disease.

Bronchiolitis obliterans is characterised by concentric fibrosis of the submucosa of small bronchioles resulting in obliteration of the lumen. It may occur in viral infections, especially RSV, after inhalation of toxic fumes, in lung transplant rejection, after aspiration, and with collagen vascular diseases.

Pneumonia

> ▶ Alveolar inflammation
> ▶ Protein-rich exudate
> ▶ Polymorphs and later lymphocytes and macrophages
> ▶ Lobar or bronchopneumonia

Pneumonia is usually due to infection affecting distal airways and alveoli, with the formation of an inflammatory exudate. It may be classified according to several criteria (Table 14.4, Fig. 14.6).

Table 14.4	Classifications of pneumonia	
Criterion	Type	Example/comment
Clinical circumstances	Primary	In an otherwise healthy person
	Secondary	With local or systemic defects in defence
Aetiological agent	Bacterial	*Streptococcus pneumoniae, Staphylococcus aureus, Mycobacterium tuberculosis*, etc.
	Viral	Influenza, measles, etc.
	Fungal	*Cryptococcus, Candida, Aspergillus*, etc.
	Other	*Pneumocystis jiroveci, Mycoplasma*, aspiration, lipid, eosinophilic
Host reaction	Fibrinous Suppurative	According to dominant component of exudate
Anatomical pattern	Bronchopneumonia Lobar pneumonia	Most widely used classification before identifying aetiological agent

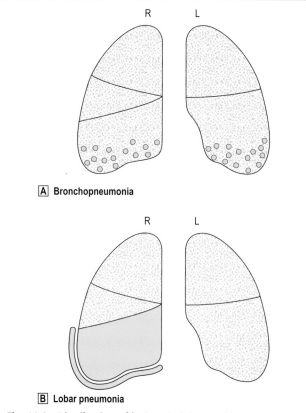

Fig. 14.6 Distribution of lesions in lobar and broncho-pneumonia. A Bronchopneumonia is characterised by focal inflammation centred on the airways; it is often bilateral. B Lobar pneumonia is characterised by diffuse inflammation affecting the entire lobe. Pleural exudate is common.

Bronchopneumonia

- ▶ Patchy consolidation—often several lobes or billateral
- ▶ Centred on bronchioles or bronchi
- ▶ Usually in infancy or old age
- ▶ Usually secondary to pre-existing disease

Bronchopneumonia has a characteristic patchy distribution, centred on inflamed bronchioles and bronchi with subsequent spread to surrounding alveoli (Fig. 14.6). It occurs most commonly in old age, in infancy and in patients with debilitating diseases, such as cancer, cardiac failure, chronic renal failure or cerebrovascular accidents. Bronchopneumonia may also occur in patients with acute bronchitis, chronic obstructive airways disease or cystic fibrosis. Failure to clear respiratory secretions, such as is common in the post-operative period, also predisposes to the development of bronchopneumonia.

Typical organisms include staphylococci, streptococci and *Haemophilus influenzae*. Patients often become septicaemic and toxic, with fever and reduced consciousness.

Affected areas of the lung tend to be basal and bilateral, and appear focally grey or grey–red at postmortem (Fig. 14.7). The inflamed lung parenchyma can be demonstrated by gently pressing on an affected area; normal lung recoils like a sponge, whereas pneumonic lung offers little resistance. Histology shows typical acute inflammation with exudation. With antibiotics and physiotherapy, the areas of inflammation most commonly resolve but may heal by organisation with scarring.

Lobar pneumonia

- ▶ Affects anatomically delineated segment(s) or the entirety, of a lobe
- ▶ Relatively uncommon in infancy and old age
- ▶ Affects males more than females
- ▶ 90% due to *Streptococcus pneumoniae* (pneumococcus)
- ▶ Cough and fever with purulent or 'rusty' sputum

Pneumococcal pneumonia typically affects otherwise healthy adults between 20 and 50 years of age; however, lobar pneumonia caused by *Klebsiella* typically affects the elderly, diabetics or alcoholics. Symptoms include a cough, fever and production of sputum. The sputum appears purulent and may contain flecks of blood, so-called 'rusty' sputum. Fever can be very high (over 40°C), with rigors. Acute pleuritic chest pain on deep inspiration reflects involvement of the pleura. As the lung becomes consolidated (Fig. 14.8), the chest signs are dullness to percussion with bronchial breathing. The dullness recedes with resolution of the exudate.

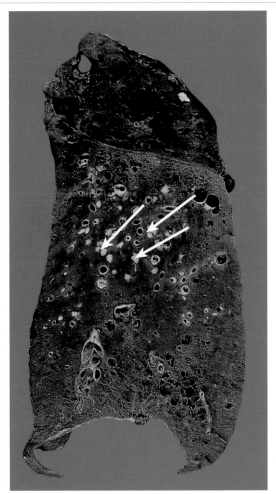

Fig. 14.7 Bronchopneumonia. Note the patchy areas of consolidation and pus-filled bronchi (arrowed) in this lung which also shows upper lobe emphysema.

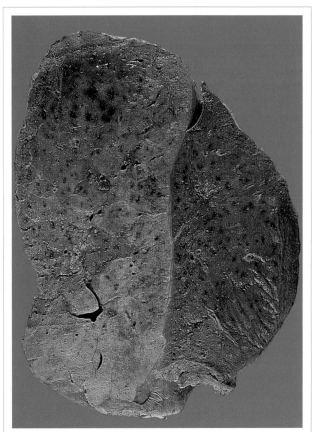

Fig. 14.8 Lobar pneumonia. An entire lobe, paler than the other, has become consolidated due to accumulation of acute inflammatory exudate within the alveoli. Note the abrupt demarcation at the interlobar fissure.

The pathology of lobar pneumonia is a classic example of acute inflammation, involving four stages:

1. *Congestion*. This first stage lasts for about 24 hours and represents the outpouring of a protein-rich exudate into alveolar spaces, with venous congestion. The lung is heavy, oedematous and red.
2. *Red hepatisation*. In this second stage, which lasts for a few days, there is massive accumulation in the alveolar spaces of polymorphs, together with some lymphocytes and macrophages. Many red cells are also extravasated from the distended capillaries. The overlying pleura bears a fibrinous exudate. The lung is red, solid and airless, with a consistency resembling fresh liver.
3. *Grey hepatisation*. This third stage also lasts a few days and represents further accumulation of fibrin, with destruction of white cells and red cells. The lung is now grey–brown and solid.
4. *Resolution*. This fourth stage occurs at about 8–10 days in untreated cases, and represents the resorption of exudate and enzymatic digestion of inflammatory debris, with preservation of the underlying alveolar wall architecture. Most cases of acute lobar pneumonia resolve in this way.

Special pneumonias

Special pneumonias may be sub-classified into those occurring in non-immunosuppressed hosts and those occurring in immunosuppressed hosts.

In non-immunosuppressed hosts

Pneumonia may be due to:

- viruses, e.g. influenza, RSV and adenovirus
- mycoplasma
- legionnaires' disease.

Viral and mycoplasma pneumonia
The clinical course is varied depending on the extent and severity of the disease. In fatal cases, the lungs appear heavy, red and consolidated, as in adult respiratory distress syndrome (ARDS). Histology shows interstitial inflammation consisting of lymphocytes, macrophages and plasma cells. Hyaline membranes of fibrinous exudate are prominent. The alveoli may be relatively free of cellular exudate. Secondary bacterial infection is, however, common and may be severe, for example staphylococcal pneumonia complicating flu.

Mycoplasma pneumonia tends to cause a more low-grade pneumonia, with interstitial inflammation and less exudation.

Legionnaires' disease

Since the first well-described outbreak in 1976, in a group of American Legion conventioneers, this disease has become increasingly recognised; 201 cases were reported in 1996 in the United Kingdom. It is caused by a bacillus, *Legionella pneumophila*, transmitted in water droplets from contaminated air humidifiers and water cisterns. Patients may be previously well, although a proportion have an underlying chronic illness, such as heart failure or carcinoma. Symptoms include cough, dyspnoea and chest pain, together with more systemic features, such as myalgia, headache, confusion, nausea, vomiting and diarrhoea. About 5–20% of cases are fatal depending on the age of the population affected. At autopsy the lungs are very heavy and consolidated.

In immunosuppressed hosts

Immunosuppression may be relative, as occurs in patients at the extremes of age, diabetics or those who are malnourished, or severe, as in those on high-dose steroid therapy, undergoing chemotherapy for malignancy, immunosuppression for transplantation or those with HIV/AIDS infection.

Most lung infections in these patients are with organisms similar to those seen in the general population. In addition, however, patients with severe immunosuppression are prone to infection with unusual organisms that are usually non-pathogenic in non-immunosuppressed individuals; these are known as 'opportunistic' infections. In any immunosuppressed patient, the onset of fever, shortness of breath and cough, together with pulmonary infiltrates, is an ominous event.

Common offending 'opportunistic' agents include:

- *Pneumocystis jiroveci*
- fungi, e.g. *Candida, Aspergillus*
- viruses, e.g. cytomegalovirus, herpes simplex virus, varicella zoster.

Pneumocystis jiroveci

Alveoli are filled with a bubbly pink exudate. Round or crescent-shaped organisms are seen using a silver impregnation stain. There may also be diffuse alveolar damage.

Fungi

Both *Candida* and *Aspergillus* species can cause widespread areas of necrosis (Fig. 14.9). Micro-abscesses contain the characteristic fungal filaments (hyphae).

Viruses

Viral infection may produce diffuse alveolar damage and areas of lung necrosis. Characteristic intranuclear inclusions are seen with infections by cytomegalovirus (CMV) and herpes viruses.

HIV lung disease

Pulmonary disease accounts for up to 70% of AIDS-defining illnesses and is the cause of death in at least a third of all AIDS patients.

The lung is frequently involved with infections, the commonest globally being tuberculosis, although combinations of common bacteria, *Pneumocystis jiroveci,* viruses and even fungi are commonly seen in AIDS patients in Western society.

Non-infective pneumonias

Cryptogenic organising pneumonia

Cryptogenic organising pneumonia is described in the Chronic interstitial diseases section (p. 341).

Fig. 14.9 Aspergillus pneumonia.
Lung at autopsy showing focal yellow areas of consolidation.

Aspiration pneumonia

Aspiration pneumonia occurs when fluid or food is aspirated into the lung, resulting in secondary inflammation and consolidation. Clinical situations where patients are at risk include sedation, operations, coma, stupor, laryngeal and oesophageal carcinoma, and severe debility. The parts of the lung affected vary according to the patient's posture: lying on the back, the affected area is the apical segment of the lower lobe; lying on the right side, the posterior segment of the upper lobe is affected. Often, such areas of aspiration pneumonia contain anaerobic organisms, and a lung abscess containing foul material may ensue.

Lipid pneumonia

Lipid pneumonia may be endogenous, associated with airway obstruction causing distal collections of foamy macrophages and giant cells. This is often seen distal to bronchial carcinoma or an inhaled foreign body. Alternatively, lipid pneumonia may be exogenous, due to aspiration of material containing a high concentration of lipid. Such materials include liquid paraffin or oily nose drops. Vacuoles of lipid are ingested by foreign-body giant cells; there may be some interstitial fibrosis.

Eosinophilic pneumonia

Acute eosinophilic pneumonia is usually idiopathic and associated with a blood eosinophilia (Löffler's syndrome); it is characterised by numerous eosinophils in the interstitium and alveoli. There is usually a swift response to steroid therapy.

Chronic eosinophilic pneumonia is less frequently associated with a peripheral eosinophilia. The lung shows extensive infiltration with eosinophils and the presence of organising exudates which may go on to give rise to fibrosis. The aetiology is often unclear but can be the result of allergic type reaction to drugs or other environmental agents.

Pulmonary tuberculosis

▶ Lung is commonest site for tuberculosis
▶ Chronic alcoholism, diabetes mellitus, immunosuppression (especially HIV/AIDS), etc. are predisposing conditions
▶ Often reactivation of primary or secondary lesion
▶ A major cause of death in developing countries

Pulmonary tuberculosis (TB) is the leading cause of death globally from a single infectious agent; it has been estimated that a third of the world's population has been infected with the organism. Most cases of pulmonary TB are the result of infection with *M. tuberculosis* although other so-called 'atypical mycobacteria' may be encountered (e.g. *M. avian intracellulare*, *M. kansasii*, etc.). The number with active disease is approximately 22 million, and about 1.66 million people die annually from TB.

Disease, however, occurs in only about 10% of cases of infection, when the balance between host resistance and the pathogenicity of the bacteria tips in favour of the latter. TB is therefore the principal cause of HIV-related death in Africa

and the Far East, with 33% of people living with HIV/AIDS being co-infected with TB. In 1990, 4.2% of TB cases were attributed to HIV infection; this rose to 11% by the year 2000. Before the advent of antituberculous treatment, therapy was aimed at improving host resistance using special diets and bed rest together with a change in socio-economic factors such as improved living conditions. Now therapy is aimed at killing the organism using combination antibacterial chemotherapy, and immunisation against infection using BCG (bacille Calmette–Guérin).

Clinicopathological features

Clinical and pathological features of pulmonary tuberculosis are extremely variable, and depend on the extent, stage and activity of the disease (Fig. 14.10). Symptoms may vary from insidious weight loss with night sweats and a mild chronic cough, to rampant bronchopneumonia with fever, dyspnoea and respiratory distress ('galloping consumption'). Most early cases of primary tuberculosis are clinically silent.

Primary tuberculosis

The lungs are usually the initial site of contact between tubercle bacilli and humans. The focus of primary infection, which is usually asymptomatic, is called a Ghon complex. The pulmonary lesion is usually about 10 mm in diameter, and consists of a central zone of caseous necrosis surrounded by palisaded epithelioid histiocytes, the occasional Langhans' giant cell and lymphocytes. Similar granulomas are seen in lymph nodes that drain the affected portion of the lung.

In almost all cases, a primary lesion will organise, leaving a fibrocalcific nodule in the lung, and there will be no clinical sequelae. However, tubercle bacilli may still be present within such scarred foci and may persist as viable organisms for years. In a few cases the infection may progress with systemic spread.

Secondary tuberculosis

As indicated above, most secondary TB represents reactivation of old primary infection. These lesions are nearly always located in the lung apices, sometimes bilaterally (Fig. 14.11). Histologically, typical granulomas are seen, most having central zones of caseous necrosis. Progression of the disease depends on the balance between host sensitivity and organism virulence. Most lesions are converted to fibrocalcific scars, a frequent finding in the lungs of elderly people at autopsy. However, as in primary TB, many complications can ensue.

Miliary tuberculosis

Miliary TB may be a consequence of either primary or secondary TB in which there is severe impairment of host resistance. The disease becomes widely disseminated, resulting in numerous small granulomas in many organs. Lesions are commonly found in the lungs, meninges, kidneys, bone marrow and liver, but no organ is exempt. The granulomas often contain numerous mycobacteria, and the Mantoux test is frequently negative (see below). This is an acute medical emergency necessitating prompt treatment with antituberculous chemotherapy if a fatal outcome is to be averted.

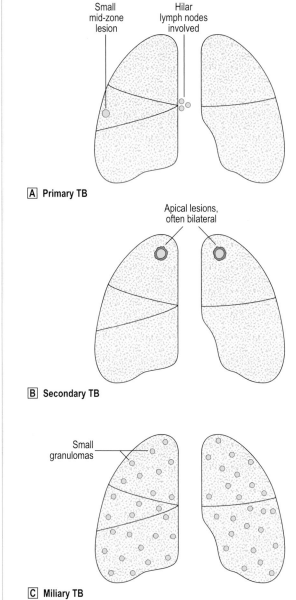

Fig. 14.10 **Types of pulmonary tuberculosis.** [A] Primary TB produces a small mid-zone lesion with involvement of hilar lymph nodes. [B] In secondary TB, the lesions are usually apical and often bilateral. [C] In miliary TB, the lungs and many other organs contain numerous small granulomas.

Fig. 14.11 **Secondary pulmonary tuberculosis.** Lung at autopsy showing cavitation and scarring at the apex of the right upper lobe.

Host resistance to tuberculosis and the tuberculin (Mantoux or Heaf) test

A delicate balance exists between the properties of the tubercle bacillus and host (human) resistance. Tuberculosis is the classical infective example of the type IV delayed hypersensitivity reaction (Ch. 9). Killing is mediated by T-lymphocyte recruitment and activation of macrophages by cytokines, such as interferon-gamma. This process takes time; sensitivity to tubercle bacilli becomes detectable only about 2–4 weeks after inoculation. Antigenicity and virulence are probably related to the lipid properties of the bacillus cell wall; hence hypersensitivity can usually be induced by immunisation with BCG, a vaccine made from non-virulent tubercle bacilli.

It follows that, in a primary infection, there is no specific hypersensitivity to tubercle bacilli and the inflammatory reaction is relatively mild with little caseous necrosis. In secondary tuberculosis, sensitised T-cells recognise the organism and recruit macrophages which form large granulomas; caseous tissue necrosis is extensive. The disease may disseminate when resistance becomes lowered (Fig. 14.12). Nevertheless, even when host resistance is strong, tubercle bacilli remain extremely difficult to eradicate, and may survive and replicate within the same macrophages recruited as their executioners.

Bronchiectasis

Bronchiectasis is characterised by permanent dilatation of bronchi and bronchioles (Fig. 14.13).

▶ Results from pulmonary inflammation and scarring due to infection, bronchial obstruction or lung fibrosis (e.g. following radiotherapy)

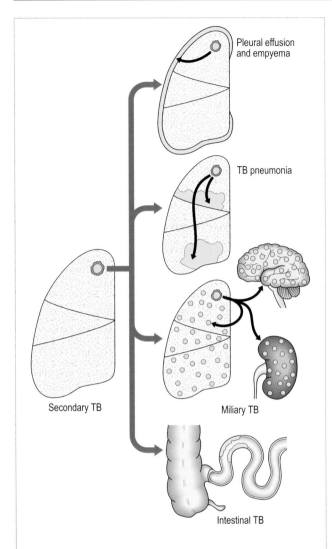

Fig. 14.12 Complications of pulmonary tuberculosis. The most frequent complications are intrapulmonary or pleural spread. Miliary dissemination and intestinal disease are less common.

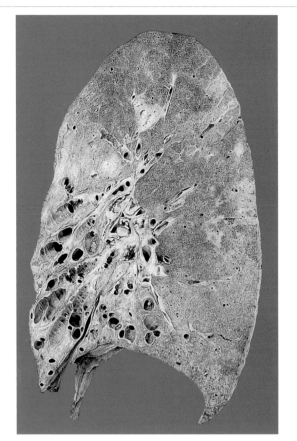

Fig. 14.13 Bronchiectasis. Permanent dilatation of bronchi.

- genetic conditions, e.g. cystic fibrosis, Kartagener's syndrome (immotile cilia)
- childhood infection, e.g. whooping cough
- chronic lung infections, e.g. tuberculosis
- radiotherapy given for lung cancer or breast cancer
- distal to a bronchial obstruction
- chronic aspiration pneumonia
- immunodeficiency, e.g. hypogammaglobulinaemia
- bronchopulmonary aspergillosis (see asthma below).

Clinical features
Usually, the lower lobes are affected, leading to pooling of bronchial secretions with further infection. Symptoms are usually a chronic cough with expectoration of large quantities of foul-smelling sputum, sometimes flecked with blood. Patients may have finger-clubbing. Recurrent respiratory tract infections result from the inability of the patient to clear pooled secretions. Infective processes may remain localised to the bronchi, or spread.

Morphology
There is dilatation of bronchi and bronchioles, with inflammatory infiltration, especially polymorphs, during acute exacerbations. The inflammation and associated fibrosis extend into the adjacent lung tissue. The dilated bronchi and bronchioles can appear cylindrical, saccular or fusiform; these terms are purely descriptive of the variable morphology and are of no aetiological or prognostic significance.

▶ Airways then dilate, as surrounding scar tissue (fibrosis) contracts
▶ Secondary inflammatory changes lead to further destruction of airways
▶ Symptoms are a chronic cough with dyspnoea and production of copious amounts of foul-smelling sputum
▶ Complications include pneumonia, lung abscess, emphysema, remote abscesses, amyloid, pulmonary fibrosis and cor pulmonale

Aetiology
Bronchiectasis arises as a result of chronic inflammation that damages the alveolated lung around the airways and the airway walls. The resulting scarring causes airway distortion and dilatation with further inflammatory process in the wall of the damaged airway due to secondary infection. Bronchiectasis can arise from a wide range of lung insults:

333

Lung abscess

Lung abscesses may arise as a result of:

- pneumonias from a wide range of pathogens but particularly with virulent organisms such as *Staphylococcus aureus*, coliforms and anaerobes
- aspiration
- bronchial obstruction, e.g. by tumour or foreign body proximal to the abscess
- infection in a pulmonary infarct
- embolisation of septic material from other sites (metastatic abscesses), e.g. from a focus of osteomyelitis.

Lung abscesses are essentially identical to those found at other sites. They comprise a thick fibrous wall containing mixed inflammatory cells with acute inflammatory debris in the centre. Radiologically the appearances are of a cavitating mass and the differential diagnosis is that of tumour. These patients will, however, usually be clinically septic. Treatment is with antibiotics including cover for anaerobic organisms. The lesion will usually shrink with time to leave an area of fibrous scarring.

Aspergilloma

An aspergilloma is a fungal ball of *Aspergillus* organisms that grows in a saprophytic manner, usually in a pre-existing cavity. It most commonly complicates old tuberculous cavities but can also complicate cavitated infarcts, abscess cavities or areas of cystic bronchiectasis. The wall of the cavity is fibrotic and inflamed, and there is commonly ulceration of the lining mucosa; this can result in haemoptysis which may be severe. Aspergillomas may remain static for years or increase in size. Treatment with antifungal drugs may be helpful but some cases require surgical excision.

VASCULAR DISEASE OF THE LUNGS

Vascular disease of the lungs may be caused by:

- damage to vessel walls, e.g. arteritis
- obstruction, e.g. emboli
- variations in intravascular pressure, e.g. pulmonary arterial or venous hypertension.

Damage to vessel walls

> ▸ Arteritis, e.g. Wegener's granulomatosis, Churg–Strauss syndrome
> ▸ Goodpasture's syndrome with anti-glomerular basement membrane antibody

Diseases of the lungs due to vessel wall damage are uncommon; most are thought to be immunologically mediated. *Wegener's granulomatosis* is a necrotising vasculitis affecting the lungs, upper respiratory tract and kidneys (Ch. 21). The aetiology is unknown. Pulmonary involvement is characterised by large areas of necrosis associated with a granulomatous vasculitis affecting veins and arterioles. *Churg–Strauss syndrome* (allergic angiitis and granulomatosis)

may lead to similar necrotising granulomas in the lungs. There is often a history of bronchial asthma. The kidneys and upper respiratory tract are not involved. *Goodpasture's syndrome* is associated with the development of circulating antibodies which bind to antigens on the basement membranes of the alveoli and the glomerulus (Ch. 21). In the lung this is associated with the development of extensive lung haemorrhage.

Obstruction

> ▸ Most commonly due to emboli of thrombus, air, fat, cancer cells, amniotic fluid
> ▸ Occlusion may lead to a pulmonary infarct
> ▸ Multiple emboli can cause pulmonary arterial hypertension
> ▸ Risk factors for thrombo-embolism include immobilisation, pregnancy, oral contraceptives, malignancy (especially pancreatic), cardiac failure, and the post-operative recovery phase

Thrombo-embolism

Thrombo-embolism is the commonest pulmonary vascular lesion. Most emboli are thrombotic, originating in veins (Ch. 8); typical sites are the deep pelvic veins or the deep veins of the calf (Fig. 14.14).

Depending on the size, emboli may lodge in various sites in the pulmonary arterial tree. Symptoms will be related to the volume of lung tissue deprived of blood:

- A saddle embolus at the bifurcation of the left and right pulmonary arteries usually causes sudden death or severe chest pain with dyspnoea and shock. Most patients die acutely.
- Occlusion of one main pulmonary artery (Fig. 14.15) also frequently leads to death. Alternatively, there may be severe chest pain and shock, mimicking myocardial infarction.
- Occlusion of a lobar or segmental artery causes chest pain and may lead to distal lung infarction, especially in the presence of raised pulmonary venous pressure, as in left ventricular failure or mitral stenosis.
- Multiple small emboli occluding arterioles result in gradual occlusion of the pulmonary arterial bed; this leads to pulmonary arterial hypertension. The effects are discussed below.

Clearly, prevention of deep vein thrombosis is of major importance. Encouragement of improved venous flow in deep leg veins is effected by early ambulation of patients after operations, the use of tight elastic stockings, and leg exercises. Prophylactic anticoagulation is also used in some high-risk patients. Treatment of a major pulmonary embolus includes fibrinolytic agents and even surgical embolectomy. Such heroic measures must be tempered by the fact that patients with a pulmonary embolus have about a 30% chance of developing further emboli. Some patients experiencing repeated pulmonary embolism have an inherited thrombotic tendency (Ch. 23) or may be harbouring an occult malignancy.

Fat emboli

Fat emboli may occlude pulmonary arterioles, leading to breathlessness and sudden death. Such emboli result from fractures of bones containing fatty marrow, or from massive injury to subcutaneous fat. Globules of lipid enter the torn veins and thereby lead to embolism (Fig. 14.16). Marrow tissue may also be seen within pulmonary vessels following trauma but is also frequently seen in autopsy histology in cases of failed CPR.

Air emboli

Air emboli occur occasionally during childbirth or with abortion. Bubbles in the circulation can also occur when dissolved nitrogen comes out of solution, for example in divers during rapid decompression (Caisson disease or 'the bends'). These micro-emboli can cause tiny infarcts in several organs, including muscle, bone, brain and lung.

Amniotic fluid emboli

Amniotic fluid emboli may occur during delivery or abortion. Flakes of keratin and vernix from fetal skin are seen in pulmonary arterioles.

Tumour emboli

Tumour emboli are, of course, very common; this is an important mechanism in the development of metastases (Ch. 11).

Variations in intravascular pressure

Several disorders are associated with changes in intravascular pressure:

- venous congestion and pulmonary oedema
- pulmonary hypertension and 'cor pulmonale'
- pulmonary veno-occlusive disease
- pulmonary arterial hypertension with a right-to-left shunt.

Venous congestion and pulmonary oedema

Pulmonary oedema can result from:

- increased venous hydrostatic pressure
- injury to the alveolar–capillary wall
- lowered plasma oncotic pressure (a rare cause of pulmonary oedema)
- blockage of lymphatic drainage.

An initial increase in venous hydrostatic pressure leads to pulmonary venous congestion. Common causes are:

- left ventricular failure
- mitral stenosis
- mitral incompetence.

Secondary pulmonary venous hypertension follows, with congestion of alveolar wall capillaries. Fluid is then forced out of the venous circulation into the alveoli to form pulmonary oedema.

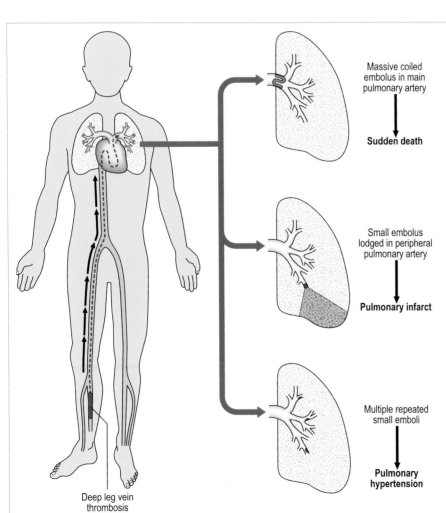

Massive coiled embolus in main pulmonary artery

Sudden death

Small embolus lodged in peripheral pulmonary artery

Pulmonary infarct

Multiple repeated small emboli

Pulmonary hypertension

Deep leg vein thrombosis

Fig. 14.14 Pathogenesis of pulmonary thrombo-embolism. The thrombus usually originates from the deep leg veins and, after detachment, becomes lodged in the pulmonary artery vasculature, causing sudden death (if massive), pulmonary infarction (if small), or pulmonary hypertension (if small and multiple).

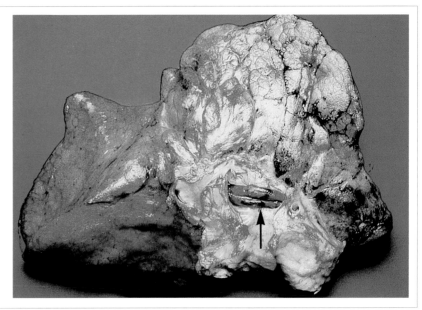

Fig. 14.15　Pulmonary embolism. A massive fatal embolus (arrowed) lodged in a major branch of the pulmonary artery.

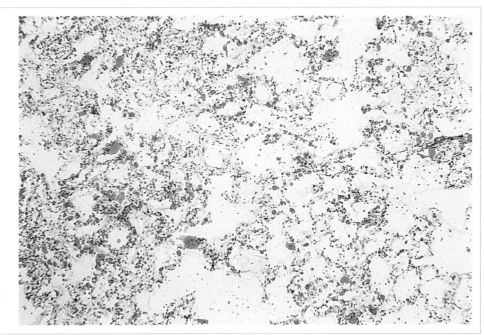

Fig. 14.16　Fat embolism. Lung histology stained to show numerous fat globules (stained orange) in alveolar capillaries from a patient with multiple bone fractures.

The lungs are heavy, congested and contain bubbly fluid. In chronic congestion, recurrent alveolar haemorrhages lead to the accumulation of haemosiderin-laden macrophages (heart-failure cells) with some interstitial fibrosis, so-called 'brown induration of the lung'.

Clinically, there is dyspnoea with a cough, producing bubbly fluid. Auscultation reveals fine crackles in the chest due to air bubbling through numerous fluid-soaked airways. There is respiratory impairment with hypoxaemia. The boggy lungs are prone to secondary infection.

Pulmonary hypertension and 'cor pulmonale'

Pulmonary hypertension may be:

- pre-capillary, e.g. pulmonary emboli, left-to-right shunts, primary pulmonary hypertension
- capillary, e.g. emphysema
- post-capillary, e.g. left ventricular failure, mitral stenosis
- chronic hypoxaemia, e.g. Pickwickian syndrome, kyphoscoliosis, poliomyelitis, chronic lung disease such as COPD.

All the above mechanisms may lead to 'cor pulmonale' or heart failure caused primarily by respiratory disease, which is manifested by pulmonary hypertension and right ventricular hypertrophy.

Pre-capillary pulmonary hypertension may be:

- due to multiple *pulmonary emboli:* numerous tiny emboli block arterioles leading to eventual obliteration of the vascular bed
- due to *left-to-right shunts,* such as cardiac septal defect: blood shunts from the high-pressure left heart to the right heart, causing an increase in its volume and pressure on the pulmonary arterial tree
- primary or of *unknown cause:* this disease tends to affect young women and may be familial. The cause of primary pulmonary hypertension is uncertain and requires other causes such as ingestion of drugs and toxins (the appetite suppressant, Aminorex, and plant alkaloid, *Crotalaria spectabilis,* are known to cause pulmonary hypertension or 'occult' showers of tiny pulmonary emboli) to be excluded. In familial cases there is recognised to be a high incidence of mutation in the gene coding for the signalling peptide bone morphogenic protein 2 (BMP2) receptor. Exhaled nitric oxide (NO) levels are lower in patients with pulmonary hypertension than in normal controls; giving NO by inhalation to such patients leads to pulmonary vasodilatation. Other vasodilators that may give some success include prostacyclins, calcium channel blockers, adenosine and endothelin receptor antagonists. Patients with severe disease refractory to medical management should be considered for lung transplantation.

Capillary pulmonary hypertension is due to disease in the pulmonary vascular bed. Severe chronic obstructive airways disease may also cause pulmonary hypertension and 'cor pulmonale'.

Post-capillary pulmonary hypertension is due to high pressure in the pulmonary venous system causing secondary back pressure into the arterial tree. Examples include mitral stenosis, left ventricular failure from any cause, and the rare pulmonary veno-occlusive disease.

Any cause of *chronic* hypoxaemia may lead to pulmonary hypertension, including living at high altitude. The Pickwickian syndrome is characterised by chronic hypoxaemia and pulmonary hypertension caused by poor respiration associated with gross obesity.

Obviously, the gross and microscopic pathology in each instance is determined by the underlying cause. There are also relatively constant changes seen in the pulmonary arterial tree, including muscular hypertrophy, intimal proliferation, capillary dilatation and, in severe cases, necrotising arteritis.

Pulmonary veno-occlusive disease

Pulmonary veno-occlusive disease is rare; it leads to chronic venous congestion with interstitial fibrosis and many haemosiderin-laden macrophages in alveolar spaces. The left heart is normal, and disease is caused by internal thickening and occlusion of pulmonary veins in the septa. The aetiology is largely unknown, although some cases have been reported in association with drugs and connective tissue disorders. Symptoms are of progressive dyspnoea and 'cor pulmonale'.

Pulmonary arterial hypertension with right-to-left shunt

In patients with a congenital atrial septal defect (Ch. 13), often asymptomatic, who subsequently develop pulmonary hypertension, the raised right intra-atrial blood pressure causes blood to flow through the defect into the left atrium (right-to-left shunt). Right-to-left shunts may also occur in patients with longstanding left-to-right shunts (i.e. the shunt reverses), for example in ventricular septal defects following the development of secondary pulmonary hypertension (Eisenmenger's syndrome).

This has two important consequences:

- *Paradoxical embolism.* Venous emboli usually impact in the pulmonary arteries. If there is a right-to-left shunt there is a risk of venous emboli bypassing the pulmonary arteries and entering the systemic arterial circulation, thus causing infarcts in the brain, kidneys, spleen, etc.
- *Impaired oxygenation.* Diversion of venous blood through the atrial septal defect from right to left causes dilution of the blood in the left atrium with blood that has not been oxygenated by passage through the lungs. This exacerbates the impaired oxygenation that already exists in patients with lung disorders associated with pulmonary hypertension.

OBSTRUCTIVE AIRWAYS DISEASE

Obstructive airways disease falls into two major groups:

- localised
- diffuse.

Localised obstructive airways disease

- ▶ Obstruction by tumour or foreign body
- ▶ Causes distal collapse or overexpansion
- ▶ May be complicated by distal obstructive or infective pneumonia
- ▶ Usually normal pulmonary function tests

Localised obstructive airways disease is caused by mechanical factors, for example a foreign body or tumour obstructing an airway. The area involved is limited and may be associated with little respiratory embarrassment, unless the patient has underlying lung disease.

When a bronchus or bronchiole becomes obstructed, the distal lung usually collapses. Numerous lipid-laden macrophages may fill the alveolar spaces distal to the obstruction, with possible secondary infection leading to bronchopneumonia (Fig. 14.17). Bronchiectasis may result if the obstruction is not relieved. Occasionally, the lung distal to an obstruction may become over-expanded, perhaps due to a valve effect caused by the obstruction.

Clinical symptoms are related to the underlying pathology and to secondary obstructive events. A localised expiratory wheeze may be heard over the affected lobe. Bronchoscopy usually identifies a proximal cause. Partial obstruction of the trachea (or larynx) may be associated with stridor

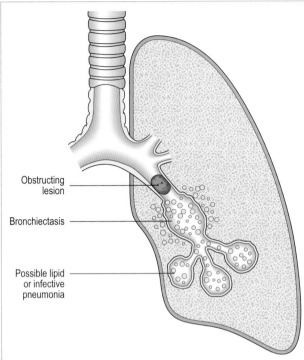

Obstructing
lesion

Bronchiectasis

Possible lipid
or infective
pneumonia

Fig. 14.17 Bronchial obstruction. The obstructing lesion causes a lipid or infective pneumonia in the distal lung and, if unrelieved, distal bronchiectasis.

(inspiratory 'wheeze') with severe respiratory distress and requires urgent intervention to prevent possible complete respiratory tract obstruction.

Diffuse obstructive airways disease

> ▶ Reversible and intermittent, or irreversible and persistent
> ▶ Centred on small bronchi and bronchioles
> ▶ 'Obstructive' pulmonary function tests
> ▶ Usually many airways involved, therefore a diffuse disease

Diffuse obstructive airways disease is due to reversible or irreversible abnormalities in numerous small bronchi and/or bronchioles as these are the main 'resistance vessels' for air movement in the lungs. There is, therefore, significant respiratory impairment causing chronic airflow limitation and a characteristic obstructive pattern of pulmonary function tests:

- reduced FEV_1 and VC
- reduced FEV_1:VC ratio (i.e. the FEV_1 is more reduced than the VC)
- reduced peak expiratory flow rate (PEFR).

The major diseases are:

- chronic obstructive pulmonary disease (COPD)
- chronic bronchitis
- emphysema
- asthma
- obliterative bronchiolitis.

Chronic obstructive pulmonary disease (COPD)

COPD is a clinical syndrome that pathologically is associated with two patterns of disease in the lung—chronic bronchitis and emphysema. Although pathologically these are two distinct processes, they almost always co-exist to some degree. Together they rank fifth in the global burden of disease: in the UK COPD affects approximately 6% of men and 4% of women over the age of 45, and in the USA it is the fourth leading cause of death, claiming ~120 000 lives annually. COPD is closely linked with cigarette smoking and is associated with progressive loss of lung function: increasing breathlessness, hypoxia and respiratory failure with cor pulmonale.

Clinical features

The clinical features of COPD are essentially cough that is productive of sputum, breathlessness and, in some patients, respiratory failure and cor pulmonale. The clinical features are the result of the presence in most patients of both chronic bronchitis and emphysema, although on occasion one pattern of disease may predominate. Chronic bronchitis is defined clinically as chronic cough and sputum for at least 3 months each year for 2 consecutive years. Emphysema can be demonstrated and assessed on CT scans and by measuring gas transfer (Tco). Breathlessness is contributed to by the small airways obstruction induced by chronic bronchitis and the loss of alveolar walls seen in emphysema. It is important to note that patients with COPD who develop respiratory failure may become hypocapnic (type 1 respiratory failure) while others hypoventilate and become hypercapnic (type 2 respiratory failure). This latter group are especially at risk of developing respiratory pulmonary hypertension and right heart failure (cor pulmonale). Patients with COPD have an increased risk of spontaneous pneumothorax due to rupture of bullae on the surface of the lung and, due to their smoking history, lung cancer.

Clinical exacerbations are associated with recurrent bronchial infections caused by bacteria such as *Haemophilus influenzae* and *Streptococcus pneumoniae*, or viruses such as respiratory syncytial virus and adenovirus. Treatment is with physiotherapy, controlled oxygen therapy and, sometimes, short-term use of antibiotics. During such exacerbations there may also be a reversible element to the airways obstruction due to local bronchial irritation causing bronchoconstriction; bronchodilators, such as salbutamol, are therefore also used in the treatment of an attack of chronic bronchitis. Although disease progression and prognosis are improved significantly in patients who stop smoking, it is important to recognise that in patients who develop respiratory failure the 3-year survival rate is less than 50%.

Chronic bronchitis

> ▶ Defined clinically as cough and sputum for 3 months in 2 consecutive years
> ▶ Mucus hypersecretion with bronchial mucous gland hypertrophy
> ▶ Respiratory bronchiolitis
> ▶ Most cases caused by smoking

Aetiology

There is no doubt that chronic bronchitis is almost always entirely due to cigarette smoking. In the United Kingdom, before the Clean Air Act of 1956, urban air pollution was a significant factor. However, the incidence of chronic bronchitis over the last 15 years has remained steady in spite of ever-reducing air pollution; the only change has been a small reduction in male chronic bronchitis, undoubtedly resulting from less cigarette smoking in males.

Morphology

Histologically, chronic bronchitis is characterised by a rather non-specific chronic inflammatory infiltrate within the walls of bronchi of all sizes and bronchioles. This may be associated with the development of bronchial associated lymphoid tissue (BALT) with identifiable lymphoid aggregates and germinal centres. There is often marked hyperplasia of the submucosal glands in the larger airways and goblet cell metaplasia of the surface epithelium in smaller airways. The walls of these smaller airways show evidence of scarring. Hypersecretion of mucus may lead to mucous plugging of airways resulting in yet further airways obstruction. During exacerbations there may be evidence of more florid inflammation including neutrophils and even bronchopneumonia. Squamous metaplasia is also a common finding in these patients as a result of their smoking but this is not specifically associated with chronic bronchitis.

Emphysema

> ▶ Defined anatomically as abnormal enlargement of alveolar airspaces
> ▶ Usually seen in smokers in association with chronic bronchitis

There are various patterns of emphysema (Fig. 14.18). Although each category has a precise anatomical definition, it must be emphasised that in advanced cases there is usually a *mixed* picture, and an accurate classification in an individual patient is therefore not possible. Suffice to say that all forms of pulmonary emphysema show loss of distal lung parenchyma with resultant airspace enlargement (Fig. 14.19). The pathogenesis is poorly understood but may result from an imbalance of tissue remodelling favouring removal of connective tissue as a result of smoking-induced inflammation. The fact that there are different patterns present may, however, suggest that different pathogenetic process occur.

Centrilobular emphysema

Centrilobular (or centriacinar) emphysema involves airspaces in the centre of lobules. This lesion is commonest in men, and is closely associated with cigarette smoking, although centrilobular emphysema may also be seen in patients exposed to coal dust. In Britain coal mine dust is accepted to be a cause of centrilobular emphysema in the absence of coal-worker's pneumoconiosis in miners who have worked underground for 20 years or more. In centrilobular emphysema the lesions are most common in the upper lobes. As noted above, a respiratory bronchiolitis with scarring is also frequently present, together with some large airways disease such as is seen in chronic bronchitis.

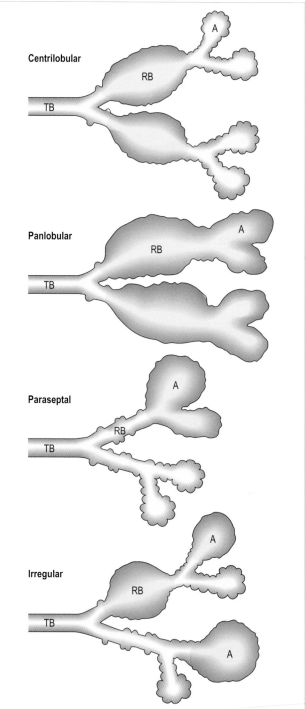

Fig. 14.18 Classification of emphysema. Emphysema is classified according to the pattern of distribution of lesions. These can, to some extent, be correlated with specific aetiological factors, e.g. centrilobular emphysema and cigarette smoke. A, alveolus; RB, respiratory bronchiole; TB, terminal bronchiole.

Panlobular emphysema

Panlobular (panacinar) emphysema involves all airspaces distal to the terminal bronchioles. Usually, lower lobes are affected, the bases being most severely involved, although

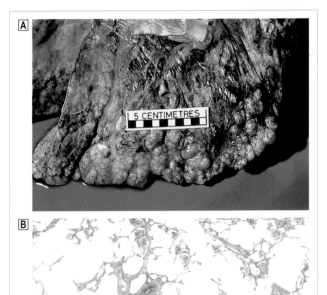

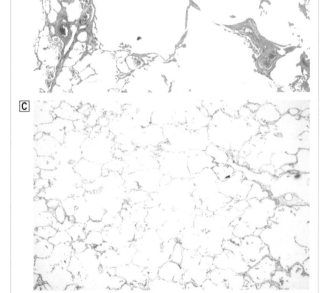

Fig. 14.19 Emphysema. [A] This is severe emphysematous change characterised by large bullae at the pleural surface. [B] Histology shows the presence of enlarged alveolar spaces characteristic of emphysema in comparison with that in a normal lung [C].

Alpha-1 antitrypsin is an acute phase serum protein which inhibits the actions of collagenase, elastase and other proteases, including trypsin. One action of alpha-1 antitrypsin is to inhibit enzymes released from dying neutrophils and macrophages. Any stimulus, such as smoking, that leads to increased numbers of inflammatory cells in the lung will lead to alveolar wall destruction (emphysema) in patients with alpha-1 antitrypsin deficiency. The enzyme deficiency is inherited as an autosomal dominant trait, and the homozygous deficiency state is said to affect 1 in 3630 Caucasians; the defect is even rarer in black people.

Paraseptal emphysema

Paraseptal (distal acinar) emphysema involves airspaces at the periphery of the lobules, typically adjacent to pleura. There is often adjacent scarring and fibrosis. The dilated airspaces can become large and, if over 10 mm in diameter, are termed bullous. Upper lobes are more frequently involved.

Irregular emphysema

Irregular emphysema irregularly involves the respiratory acinus. This type is almost always associated with scarring and there is almost certainly an overlap with paraseptal emphysema. The pathogenesis is thought to be air trapping caused by fibrosis; this irregular pattern of emphysema is therefore commonly present around old healed tuberculous scars at lung apices.

Other pathological types

In addition to the four anatomical types of pulmonary emphysema discussed above, some other categories exist.

Bullous emphysema. This is not a separate category of emphysema but refers merely to the presence of balloon-like foci of emphysema over 10 mm in diameter. Cases of emphysema with bullae should, where possible, be classified into one of the four anatomical types discussed above. Bullae are prone to rupture, causing *spontaneous pneumothorax*. They are typically subpleural and apical.

Interstitial emphysema. This refers to inflation of the interstitium of the lung by air, and is most commonly due to traumatic rupture of an airway or spontaneous rupture of an emphysematous bulla. Interstitial emphysema may spread to the mediastinum or subcutis, giving the characteristic spongy crepitus on palpation.

Senile emphysema. This is also a misnomer, as there is no destruction of alveolar walls. Alveolar surface area decreases, and alveolar ductular size increases, progressively after the age of 30 years, leading to the overdistended, apparently voluminous lungs seen at autopsy in aged patients. This process is one of normal senile involution and is not a disease.

Asthma

▶ Reversible small airways obstruction characterised by bronchospasm, inflammation and oedema
▶ Paroxysmal attacks
▶ Overdistended lungs
▶ Mucous plugs in bronchi
▶ Enlarged bronchial mucous glands

the distribution can be patchy. Grossly, the lungs appear overdistended and voluminous. In cases where this is seen predominantly in the upper lobes, it is likely to represent severe centrilobular emphysema that has extended to involve the whole lobule. This pattern of emphysema is, however, seen in 70–80% of patients with homozygous alpha-1-antitrypsin deficiency. These patients often develop severe emphysema, usually before the age of about 50 years, especially if they smoke. These patients also have an increased risk of developing cirrhosis.

Asthma is defined as hyper-reactivity of the bronchial tree with paroxysmal narrowing of the small airways (Fig. 14.20), which may reverse spontaneously or after treatment. Asthma is increasingly common in many countries, but it is a relatively rare cause of death.

There are five major clinical categories of asthma:

- atopic
- non-atopic
- aspirin-induced
- occupational
- allergic bronchopulmonary aspergillosis.

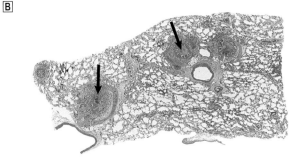

Fig. 14.20 Asthma. A Tracheal mucous plug (arrowed) in death from status asthmaticus. B Histological section of lung at autopsy showing occlusion of airways by oedema and mucous plugs (arrowed) accompanied by alveolar distension with entrapped gas.

Each type has different predisposing factors, and is mediated in different ways. However, the resulting clinical symptoms and pathology are similar to those seen in atopic asthma. Any important differences are outlined below.

Atopic asthma

Atopic asthma is triggered by a variety of environmental agents, including dust, pollens, foods and animal danders, e.g. faecal pellets from housedust mites. There is often a family history of asthma, hay fever or atopic eczema. Patients with atopic asthma may also suffer from atopic disorders such as hay fever or eczema. Increased levels of endogenous nitric oxide (NO) produced by a variety of cells in the respiratory tract have been found in exhaled air from asthmatics when compared with normal controls; whether NO is merely a marker of airway irritation or has a more fundamental role in the pathogenesis of asthma is not known. Recently the gene labelled *ADAM33* (a disintegrin and metalloproteinase) has been identified that may underlie the variation in bronchial hypersensitivity between individuals.

Bronchoconstriction is mediated by a type I hypersensitivity reaction (Ch. 9); bronchoconstriction leads to the clinical effects of wheezing, tachypnoea and dyspnoea (Fig. 14.21). Rarely, symptoms persist for days (status asthmaticus), leading to respiratory failure and even death. Release of histamine and slow-reacting substance of anaphylaxis (SRS-A) leads to bronchoconstriction, increased vascular permeability and mucus hypersecretion. Eosinophil chemotactic factor of anaphylaxis (ECF-A) attracts numerous eosinophils to the bronchial walls.

Platelet activating factor (PAF) leads to the aggregation of platelets with the release of further histamine and 5-hydroxytryptamine (5-HT) from their granules. The hypersensitivity reaction results in acute and chronic changes, with the former being identifiable during an acute episode and the latter being the result of airway remodelling following repeated attacks:

- Acute
  - bronchial obstruction with distal overinflation or atelectasis (collapse)
  - mucous plugging of bronchi
  - bronchial inflammation with prominent numbers of eosinophils, lymphocytes and plasma cells
  - bronchial epithelial shedding and subsequent regeneration
  - Curschmann's spirals: whorls of shed epithelium within mucous plugs
  - Charcot–Leyden crystals: crystals within aggregates of eosinophils
- Chronic
  - mucous gland hypertrophy
  - development of mucosa–associated lymphoid tissue
  - bronchial wall smooth muscle hypertrophy
  - thickening of bronchial basement membrane.

Non-atopic asthma

Non-atopic asthma is frequently characterised by episodes of bronchospasm, often associated with respiratory tract infections. Testing for allergens by skin patching is negative. Bronchoconstriction may be due to local irritation in patients with unusually reactive airways.

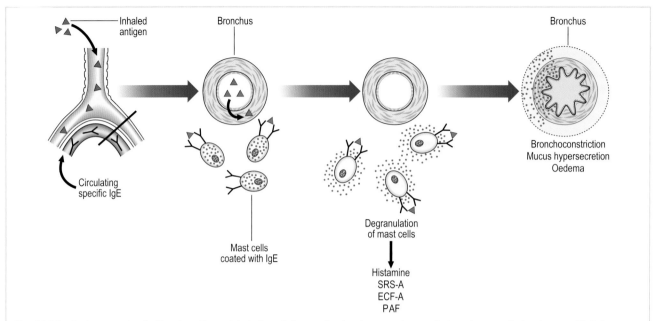

Fig. 14.21 Pathogenesis of allergic asthma. Inhalation of allergen (antigen) causes degranulation of mast cells bearing specific IgE molecules. Release of vasoactive substances from the mast cells causes bronchial constriction, oedema and mucus hypersecretion.

Aspirin-induced asthma
Patients with this form of asthma may also have recurrent rhinitis with nasal polyps, and skin urticaria. The mechanism of induction of asthma by aspirin is unknown but may involve locally decreased prostaglandins or increased leukotrienes leading to airway hyper-reactivity.

Occupational asthma
Occupational asthma is induced by hypersensitivity to an agent inhaled at work. Inhaled agents may act as non-specific irritants precipitating bronchospasm in those with hyper-reactive airways, or they may act as agents capable of inducing asthma and airway hyper-reactivity. There are many different occupationally inhaled agents that can cause asthma. The diagnosis is often difficult and relies on demonstrating variation in lung function and symptoms during time at work and away from work. The mechanism of airway reaction is thought to be a combination of type I and type III hypersensitivity (Ch. 9).

In the United Kingdom, if asthma can be proved to be the result of an agent inhaled at work, the patient is entitled to statutory compensation.

Allergic bronchopulmonary aspergillosis
Allergic bronchopulmonary aspergillosis is a type of proximal bronchiectasis seen in patients with asthma and is due to inhalation of spores of the fungus *Aspergillus fumigatus*, inducing an immediate type I and delayed immune complex type III hypersensitivity reaction. Mucous plugs in bronchi contain the hyphae of aspergilli.

Pathogenesis of asthma
As noted above, some forms of asthma are mediated by type I and type III hypersensitivity reactions, yet in others the mechanisms are unknown. One hypothesis that would

explain all types of asthma is that patients have bronchial beta-receptors relatively insensitive to catecholamines; thus, bronchi are partially constricted in the non-challenged resting state, and do not dilate well to beta-agonists, such as adrenaline (epinephrine). In addition to reacting to specific agents, these hyper-reactive airways also react to non-specific factors, such as cold, exercise and emotional stress. Why this should happen remains a mystery.

Obliterative bronchiolitis
This is a rare condition where the lumina of small bronchioles become progressively obliterated by fibrous tissue. It may follow episodes of acute airway injury following inhalation of gases (e.g. chlorine or ammonia), smoke or following severe viral bronchiolitis in children. It may also occur in patients with connective tissue disorders or inflammatory bowel disease. The most frequent setting in which this pattern of lung disease is observed is, however, in transplantation. Obliterative bronchiolitis is seen as a feature of chronic lung allograft rejection and is the commonest cause of ultimate graft failure. It also seen as part of the spectrum of graft-versus-host disease that may occur following bone marrow transplantation.

INTERSTITIAL DISEASES OF THE LUNG

The interstitial lung diseases (ILDs) or diffuse parenchymal lung diseases (DPLDs) are a heterogeneous group of conditions that present with a history of increasing breathlessness, hypoxia, restrictive lung function tests and bilateral shadowing in the lungs on chest X-ray and CT scans. These conditions primarily involve the alveoli of the lung. Diseases may be grouped into acute and chronic categories on the basis of clinical history and histological findings, with each disorder showing a basic pattern of either acute alveolar injury or chronic pulmonary fibrosis. In some instances they may display characteristic features, allowing the specific aetiology to be identified, but in many instances the trigger is unclear (idiopathic). It is also important to recognise that different aetiologies may result in a clinically and pathologically identical pattern in the lung.

> ▶ Inflammatory infiltrates and/or increased fibrous tissue in the lung causing increased stiffness and decreased compliance
> ▶ Alveolar–capillary wall is the site of the lesion
> ▶ Acute or chronic clinical picture
> ▶ Numerous different causes giving similar ultimate pathology
> ▶ Restrictive lung defect
> – reduced T_{CO}
> – reduced VC
> – reduced FEV_1
> – relatively normal FEV_1:VC ratio

Acute interstitial diseases

Acute interstitial diseases are characterised by a short history of dyspnoea, tachypnoea and respiratory distress. There is diffuse alveolar damage with alveolar exudation, formation of hyaline membranes and type II pneumocyte hyperplasia. Pathologically this is termed acute interstitial pneumonitis or diffuse alveolar damage syndrome, and clinically is seen most frequently in the context of adult respiratory distress syndrome (ARDS). This syndrome came to prominence during the Vietnam War when it was found that many soldiers were dying from respiratory failure during the first few days of recovery from severe wounds; most had suffered shock from blood loss, but this had been successfully treated at the battleground. Clinically, there was respiratory distress with tachypnoea, dyspnoea and hypoxaemia refractory to oxygen therapy.

Aetiology
Severe acute interstitial pneumonitis or ARDS can arise as a result of direct or indirect lung injury:

- shock, e.g. haemorrhagic, cardiogenic, septic, anaphylactic, endotoxic
- trauma, e.g. direct pulmonary trauma, or multisystem trauma
- local infections, e.g. viral or bacterial pneumonia
- systemic infection, e.g. septicaemia, peritonitis
- cytotoxic drugs, e.g. methotrexate
- gas inhalation, e.g. NO_2, SO_2, smoke, Cl_2
- narcotic abuse, e.g. heroin, methadone
- ionising radiation
- gastric aspiration
- disseminated intravascular coagulation
- oxygen toxicity
- paraquat poisoning.

Pathogenesis
All the clinical situations listed above deliver a massive insult to alveolar–capillary walls, leading to diffuse alveolar damage. In many cases, the exact pathogenesis is unknown. Polymorphs

are thought to be important in the pathogenesis, with release of enzymes, activation of complement and massive cytokine release. In the acute stages the lungs are heavy, oedematous and congested with areas of haemorrhage. Exudation of protein-rich fluid results in the formation of hyaline membranes lining alveolar ducts and alveoli, together with pulmonary oedema and extravasation of red cells. In most cases this exudate progresses to give rise to a fibro-proliferative phase and, if the patient survives long enough, extensive alveolar fibrosis. Resolution may occur via resorption of the oedema, and ingestion of red cells and hyaline membranes by alveolar macrophages; there is then regeneration of type II pneumocytes, which later differentiate to type I flattened pneumocytes.

Prognosis
About 40% of patients with severe acute lung injury (ARDS) die within the first few days despite intensive therapy. Most of the survivors progress to full recovery with resolution of the inflammation and restoration of the normal alveolar architecture; however, some survivors heal by organisation, leading to pulmonary fibrosis.

Radiation pneumonitis

The clinical effects of radiation toxicity to the lungs are highly dependent on the dose given (Ch. 6), the volume of lung irradiated and the length of treatment. If heavily exposed, a picture of diffuse alveolar damage may be seen as described above. If exposure is less severe and occurs over a longer period, progressive pulmonary fibrosis is seen with the typical restrictive defect of pulmonary function.

Diffuse intrapulmonary haemorrhage

Goodpasture's syndrome is characterised by haemoptysis, haematuria, anaemia and pulmonary infiltrates. Most cases have circulating anti-glomerular basement membrane antibody in their blood. This antibody causes glomerulonephritis, and also acts on alveolar membranes leading to pulmonary haemorrhage.

Idiopathic pulmonary haemosiderosis is a rare condition presenting most often in children. Clinically, patients may present with recurrent episodes of intra-alveolar haemorrhage associated with haemoptysis, cough and dyspnoea; alternatively, they may present with insidious pulmonary fibrosis. The more acute form shows evidence of diffuse alveolar damage, with type II pneumocyte hyperplasia.

Chronic interstitial diseases

Chronic interstitial lung diseases give a clinical history lasting months or years with slowly increasing respiratory insufficiency, hypoxia and bilateral changes on chest X-ray. These conditions are essentially inflammatory/fibrotic in nature although other processes such as pulmonary oedema and lymphangitic carcinomatosis can occasionally mimic these ILDs. Examples include:

- idiopathic pulmonary fibrosis
- pneumoconiosis

- extrinsic allergic alveolitis (EAA) or hypersensitivity pneumonitis
- sarcoidosis
- cryptogenic organising pneumonia
- Langerhans' cell histiocytosis (histiocytosis X)
- alveolar lipoproteinosis
- connective tissue disorders, e.g. rheumatoid disease, scleroderma.

Idiopathic pulmonary fibrosis (IPF)

IPF is a progressive chronic pulmonary fibrosis of unknown aetiology, although approximately 20% of patients give a history of occupational exposure to metals and wood dusts. Most patients are aged over 60 years and present with increasing dyspnoea and a dry cough. Men are affected twice as often as women. The disease progresses to respiratory failure, with or without cor pulmonale, within about 5 years. Fatigue and considerable weight loss may occur, raising the clinical suspicion of malignancy. Examination often shows finger- and toe-clubbing; auscultation of the chest reveals dry crackles, reflecting the opening and closing of fibrotic airspaces. Signs of right ventricular strain or failure may be present. These patients also have an excess risk of carcinoma of the lung and ischaemic heart disease.

Pathogenesis
The pathogenesis of IPF is unknown. It is important to realise, however, that a very similar if not identical pattern of disease may be seen in association with connective tissue disorders and with asbestosis. Pulmonary function tests show the characteristic restrictive pattern.

Morphology
The majority of patients with IPF show a pattern of lung disease described as *usual interstitial pneumonitis* (UIP). This pattern of disease is characteristically patchy with the subpleural regions of the lower lobes predominantly affected. There is a variable interstitial inflammatory infiltrate in the affected areas of the lung with collapse of the lung architecture and the development of cystically dilated spaces within the fibrotic areas of the lung (honeycombing). A characteristic feature is the presence of areas of immature fibrous tissue or 'fibroblastic foci' in the less severely affected areas.

More recently it has been recognised that a group of patients with clinical IPF has a different pattern of lung fibrosis called *non-specific interstitial pneumonitis* (NSIP). This is characterised by a more even and diffuse pattern of alveolar wall inflammation and fibrosis with none of the 'fibroblastic foci' or honeycomb fibrosis typical of UIP. There is a suggestion that this pattern of disease may have a better prognosis than the more typical pattern of UIP.

Pneumoconioses

Exposure to inhaled materials may have several potential consequences depending on the nature of the dust and the degree of exposure:

- inert, e.g. simple coal-worker's pneumoconiosis
- fibrous, e.g. progressive massive fibrosis, asbestosis, silicosis
- allergic, e.g. extrinsic allergic alveolitis (see below)
- neoplastic, e.g. mesothelioma, lung carcinoma (see below).

These conditions are often all regarded as 'occupational' or 'industrial' lung disease although it is important to remember that exposure can occur outwith the workplace. Pneumoconiosis is, however, defined as lung fibrosis secondary to inhaled inorganic dust (e.g. coal dust, silica, metals, etc.). In many industrial settings patients may be exposed to a wide variety of different dusts and identifying which dust might be responsible for lung disease may be difficult.

The distribution of lung disease depends on the physical properties of each separate type of dust, which determine where the particles settle in the lung. Only very small particles reach distal alveoli, as larger particles are trapped in the nose or excreted by mucociliary clearance from the larger airways.

Dust particles are phagocytosed by alveolar macrophages, which then collect and drain into peribronchiolar lymphatics and thence to hilar lymph nodes. Not surprisingly, dusts causing disease in the lungs are also often present in the sinuses of hilar lymph nodes.

Coal-worker's pneumoconiosis
In coal-worker's pneumoconiosis (CWP), coal dust is phagocytosed by alveolar macrophages (dust cells), which then aggregate around bronchioles; the degree of black pigment in the lung (*anthracosis*) is related to the amount of inhaled carbon. Anthracosis is also commonly seen in smokers and those living in urban environments. The consequences of coal-dust inhalation are variable, ranging from trivial to fatal.

Simple CWP is associated with minimal scarring and no significant disability. The predominant pattern is of dust macules consisting of focal aggregates of dust-laden macrophages in and around the walls of respiratory bronchioles, pulmonary arterioles and pulmonary veins. Similar cells are seen in lymphatics and hilar lymph nodes. There may be some associated airspace enlargement consistent with emphysema. To qualify as pneumoconiosis there must, however, be evidence of fibrosis and this is characterised by the development of fibrous nodules. This is usually regarded as a progression from the macular stage. In simple CWP nodules less than 10 mm in diameter are seen in a background of macular CWP.

Complicated CWP or *progressive massive fibrosis* (PMF) is characterised by large, irregular nodules with scarring (Fig. 14.22); they are greater than 10 mm in diameter and can be very large. These fibrotic black nodules may show central liquefaction and, when cut at autopsy, exude viscid jet-black liquid. They may contract, leading to adjacent irregular emphysema. Large nodules are usually mid-zonal or in upper lobes, and may be bilateral. The associated emphysema is always severe, often with the formation of bullae. Progression of the disease leads to further scarring and lung destruction with respiratory failure, or cor pulmonale.

It is recognised that in a group of miners working at the same pit for the same length of time, some will develop

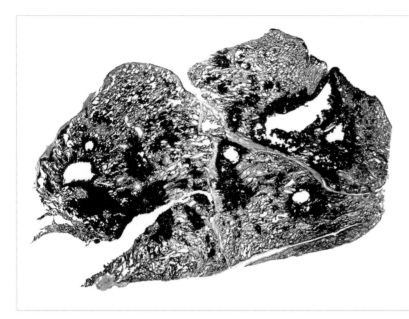

Fig. 14.22 Coal-worker's pneumoconiosis. This transilluminated thin slice of lung shows several large black fibrotic nodules. which measure more than 10 mm, consistent with complicated coal-worker's pneumoconiosis (progressive massive fibrosis). In some cases these may cavitate as shown in this example.

PMF and die, while others develop little respiratory impairment. The reasons why only some miners develop PMF are unknown and some investigators believe that the determining factor is merely the amount of coal dust inhaled. It is clear, however, that PMF is seen more commonly in some coal fields compared with others, which may suggest that exposure to other dusts such as silica in the rocks may play a role. Whatever the cause, the progression of CWP to PMF is an ominous event.

Caplan's syndrome is characterised by the presence of large pigmented necrobiotic nodules in patients with CWP. This occurs in the presence of seropositive rheumatoid disease, although lung nodules may precede the development of systemic features. The nodules may regress.

Silicosis

Silicates are inorganic minerals abundant in stone and sand. Consequently, individuals working in a wide range of occupations involving the cutting, drilling, grinding or mining of stone or sand will be at risk from silicosis. Small particles of silica reach the distal lung where they are ingested by alveolar macrophages. However, in contrast to pure coal dust, silicates are toxic to macrophages, leading to their death with release of proteolytic enzymes and the undigested silica particles. The enzymes cause local inflammation, tissue destruction and subsequent fibrosis; the silica particles are ingested by other macrophages and the cycle repeats itself.

Nodules tend to form in the lungs after many years of exposure. With progressive fibrosis and increasing numbers of nodules, respiratory impairment increases. Pulmonary function tests show a restrictive defect like any other chronic interstitial lung disease. There is a recognised increased risk of reactivation of tuberculosis and, more controversially, a possible excess risk of the development of lung cancer.

The lungs show scattered nodules of hard, fibrous tissue with surrounding irregular emphysema. Similar changes may be apparent in hilar and mediastinal lymph nodes. Advanced cases show extensive diffuse pulmonary fibrosis, together with numerous large silicotic nodules.

Asbestosis

The name 'asbestos' is derived from a Greek word meaning 'inconsumable', and, indeed, asbestos has been used for its fire-resistant qualities for many centuries. Asbestos is used for insulation and the manufacture of brake linings and other friction materials. There are several types of asbestos: amphiboles are the fibres that cause pulmonary disease in humans, and of these crocidolite (blue asbestos) is probably the most dangerous.

Inhaled asbestos fibres collect in alveoli at the lung bases. Many become coated in acid mucopolysaccharide and encrusted with haemosiderin to form 'asbestos bodies' or 'ferruginous bodies', appearing as characteristic beaded structures. The majority of fibres are, however, detectable only by electron microscopy.

Asbestosis is characterised by the development of a pattern of lung fibrosis that is essentially similar to UIP described above with destructive subpleural honeycomb changes (Fig. 14.23). It is usually seen only in patients with relatively heavy asbestos exposure and is therefore most common in those who have worked extensively with insulation materials, for example in shipyards or power stations. Disease progression is much slower and the prognosis in most cases considerably better than for IPF. Differentiation of asbestosis from IPF may be important in terms of compensation but can be difficult. Quantification of the number of asbestos fibres may be helpful in this regard but clearly the finding of fibres by itself only proves previous exposure, not causation of the disease present.

Extrinsic allergic alveolitis (hypersensitivity pneumonitis)

Interstitial lung disease caused by inhalation of organic dusts results from the individual being sensitised (hypersensitive) to the inhaled antigen (see also occupational

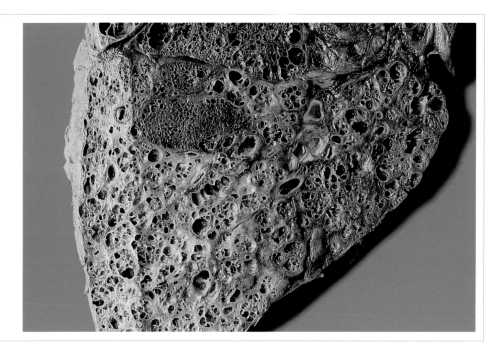

Fig. 14.23 Asbestosis.
The fibrous reaction to inhaled asbestos has resulted in a 'honeycomb' lung.

asthma). Many antigens have been described as causing an allergic interstitial lung disease known as extrinsic allergic alveolitis or hypersensitivity pneumonitis. These include: cotton fibres, causing byssinosis; sugar cane fibres, causing bagassosis; and bird faeces, causing bird fancier's lung. Whilst many of these may be associated with occupational exposure and thus can be regarded as an 'occupational lung disease', exposure to antigens in the domestic environment and even drugs can give an identical pattern of disease in the lung.

The best known and most typical example of an occupational extrinsic allergic alveolitis is *farmer's lung*. In this disorder, a fungus present in poorly stored, mouldy hay is inhaled by whoever disturbs the hay. If the individual is already sensitised to the organism, a type III immune complex hypersensitivity reaction follows. One of the earliest features is a bronchiolitis. Later, chronic inflammatory cells are seen in the interstitium, together with non-caseating granulomas. The inflammatory process may resolve on withdrawal of the antigen but if there is chronic exposure then pulmonary fibrosis will develop.

Clinically, there is acute dyspnoea and cough a few hours after inhalation of the antigen. Corticosteroid treatment helps to ameliorate the inflammatory reaction and to prevent the onset of pulmonary fibrosis.

Sarcoidosis

Sarcoidosis is a multisystem inflammatory disorder which most commonly involves the mediastinal lymph nodes and lung. The aetiology is unknown but it is possible that the granulomas arise as a result of an aberrant immune response due to abnormal T-cell–macrophage interactions. The possibility of an infective aetiology has been considered for many years but no convincing demonstration of an infective agent has been found. Clinical symptoms are variable depending on the extent of the disease. Many patients may be asymptomatic while others may have systemic upset with tiredness and cough. Common extrapulmonary manifestations include erythema nodosum, iritis and arthralgia. In most cases the disease is either self-limiting or responds to steroid therapy. In a minority of cases progression to end-stage pulmonary fibrosis occurs. Involvement of other organs, including the heart and central nervous system, occurs more rarely and can cause severe morbidity and death.

Histologically, sarcoid in the lung is characterised by the presence of relatively discrete non-caseating granulomas (Fig. 14.24) which may coalesce to form larger nodules. Predominantly they are found in relation the bronchovascular bundles, septae and the pleura. The principal differential diagnosis is that of infective disorders such as tuberculosis and histoplasmosis.

Cryptogenic organising pneumonia (COP)

COP (or bronchiolitis obliterans organising pneumonia, BOOP) is a clinical syndrome characterised by mild systemic upset with possible cough, low-grade fever and breathlessness which radiologically shows evidence of focal lung consolidation that may 'flit' within the lungs over time. The pathogenesis is poorly understood. Pathologically, the lungs show nodular foci of organising exudates within alveolar spaces and terminal bronchioles, and variable, usually mild, interstitial inflammation. In most cases the condition responds well to steroid therapy and there is resolution with no significant fibrosis. Some patients may, however, relapse and more progressive cases with lung fibrosis have been described.

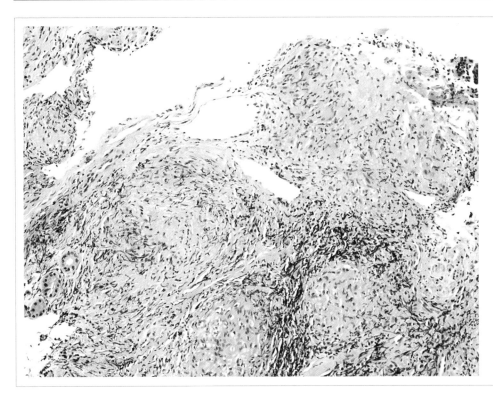

Fig. 14.24 Sarcoid. The histological feature of sarcoid is the presence of non-caseating granulomas in the lung.

Langerhans' cell histiocytosis (LCH)

Langerhans' cell granulomatosis (previously known as *histiocytosis X*) is a disease principally of smokers, characterised by the proliferation of Langerhans' cells. This is believed to occur as a response to cigarette smoke and increased numbers have been described in the lungs of smokers compared with non-smokers, even in the absence of LCH. The Langerhans' cells are specialised histiocytes which are involved in antigen presentation. Inflammatory infiltrates are seen in the pulmonary interstitium with the Langerhans' cells admixed with lymphocytes and eosinophils. These may form nodular masses with areas of cystic change. In most cases smoking cessation results in complete resolution of the nodules or healing, leaving small areas of fibrosis. In some cases, however, the disease may be progressive and result in end-stage pulmonary fibrosis.

Alveolar lipoproteinosis

Alveolar lipoproteinosis (or proteinosis) is a rare condition characterised by the accumulation of eosinophilic material within alveoli. In most instances the aetiology is unknown and the pathogenesis is uncertain but there appears to be an association with haematological disorders in some patients. Symptoms include dyspnoea and cough, when gelatinous material may be expectorated.

Connective tissue disorders and interstitial lung disease

Patients with connective tissue disorders such as rheumatoid arthritis and scleroderma may show a variety of pulmonary complications which fall into the ILD categories described above. The commonest pattern associated with these conditions is non-specific interstitial pneumonitis but patients may also develop cryptogenic organising pneumonia and usual interstitial pneumonitis. Drug treatments may also be associated with acute interstitial pneumonitis/ARDS (e.g. methotrexate), hypersensitivity reactions or opportunistic infection following immunosuppression. Other lung manifestations include rheumatoid nodules, Caplan's syndrome, vasculitis and obliterative bronchiolitis.

LUNG TUMOURS

Lung tumours may be primary or secondary. Both are common.

Primary carcinoma of the lung

- ▶ Most common primary malignant tumour in the world
- ▶ Directly related to cigarette smoking
- ▶ Associated with occupational exposure to carcinogens
- ▶ Overall 5-year survival rate of 4–7%
- ▶ Squamous cell, small cell, adenocarcinoma, and large cell undifferentiated types

Over 90% of primary lung tumours are carcinomas. Lung cancer is the leading cause of death from cancer in the world, with a poor overall prognosis—typically around 5% 5-year survival. This is due to the average age of the patients, a high incidence of comorbid disease (e.g. ischaemic heart disease, COPD) and late presentation with advanced dissemination at the time of diagnosis. In the UK only about 10% of cases are operable at the time of diagnosis.

About one-third of all cancer deaths in males in the UK are due to lung cancer. The disease is also increasing in incidence among women; it now ranks as the commonest lethal cancer in females in the UK. Typically, patients are aged between 40 and 70 years; the disease rarely affects those less than 30 years of age.

Aetiology

Major risk factors for the development of lung cancer are:

- cigarette smoking
- occupational hazards, e.g. asbestos, uranium mining
- environmental exposures, e.g. radon gas from rock
- pulmonary fibrosis.

Cigarette smoking

There is overwhelming evidence implicating cigarette smoking as the major risk factor for the development of lung cancer (Ch. 11). The rise in the incidence of lung cancer over the last century has closely paralleled the increase in cigarette smoking. Similar changes in the incidence of lung cancer have occurred in the developing world with an incidence of <5 per 100 000 population 50 years ago, rising to 14 per 100 000 by the end of the 20th century. Two-thirds of the world's smokers reside in China and it is estimated that by the mid 21st century the annual death toll from lung cancer in China alone may run into millions.

Occupational hazards

There are several occupational hazards associated with an increased incidence of lung cancer. The most important are:

- *Asbestos*. There is a significantly increased risk of lung cancer in those exposed occupationally to asbestos. If an individual also smokes, the risk is greatly increased, possibly 20–100-fold. A latent period of about 20 years is usual between exposure and the development of carcinoma.
- *Other inhaled dusts*. There is no evidence that lung cancer is associated with coal-worker's pneumoconiosis. However, a significant proportion of haematite miners die from lung cancer.
- *Radioactive gases*. In the 19th century, the Schneeberg mines in Saxony produced rock rich not only in numerous metals but also in radon; many of the workers died from lung cancer. Survivors of the atomic bombs dropped on Japan in 1945 showed an increased incidence of lung cancer, presumably related to radiation.
- *Other factors*. There is an increased risk of lung cancer in workers in industries involved with nickel, chromates, mustard gas, arsenic and coal-tar distillates.

Fibrosis

Some peripheral lung cancers (usually adenocarcinomas) apparently arise in areas of fibrous scarring, e.g. wounds, old tuberculous foci or infarcts. The theory is that metaplastic and dysplastic changes occur in pneumocytes within the scar. Such ideas have recently been challenged, the so-called 'scar cancers' being considered carcinomas with a pronounced central desmoplastic (fibroblastic) reaction. Despite this argument, there is undoubtedly a significant increase of lung adenocarcinoma in patients with pulmonary fibrosis and honeycomb lung.

Clinical features

Weight loss, cough and haemoptysis are common presenting features. Weight loss is often severe and may be due to humoral factors from the tumour. Dyspnoea and chest pain are also common; the latter is often pleuritic and due to obstructive changes. Patients may present with, or ultimately develop, metastases; common sites include lymph nodes, bone, brain, liver and adrenals. Paraneoplastic effects are common and are due to ectopic hormones: ACTH and ADH from small cell lung carcinomas, PTH from squamous cell carcinomas. Finger-clubbing and hypertrophic pulmonary osteoarthropathy are common (Fig. 14.25).

Lung carcinomas may arise centrally in the lung or towards the periphery. Central tumours may cause airway obstruction with collapse or distal consolidation of a lobe or the whole lung. These tumours may infiltrate medially into the mediastinum at a relatively early stage and patients can present as a result of this rather than the lesion in the lung (e.g. hoarseness from involvement of the left recurrent laryngeal nerve). More peripheral tumours are often asymptomatic but pleural involvement may lead to pleural effusion or the tumour may extend into the chest wall causing pain. Larger tumours, especially squamous carcinomas, often cavitate. Small cell carcinoma has usually disseminated by the time of diagnosis and the primary lesion in the lung may be small compared to the bulky nodal deposits in the mediastinum and liver.

Morphology

Most tumours arise from bronchi close to the hilum (Fig. 14.26); usually an upper lobe or main bronchus is involved. Ulceration is common, so the sputum may be blood-stained and contain malignant cells which can be detected cytologically (Fig. 14.27) or by biopsy at bronchoscopy (Fig. 14.28). Distally, the lung may be consolidated with foamy macrophages, the usual result of proximal obstruction, and patients may present with what appears to be a pneumonia.

Histological classification

There are four major types of lung cancer, classified according to their appearance on light microscopy; their approximate incidences are:

- squamous cell carcinoma (SqCC): 20–30%
- small cell lung carcinoma (SCLC): 15–20%
- adenocarcinoma (AC): 30–40%
- large cell undifferentiated carcinoma (LCUC): 10–15%
- carcinoid tumours: 5%.

The lung cancers are discussed below according to this classification. For practical purposes the tumours are often divided into non-small cell carcinomas (SqCC, AC and LCUC) and small cell carcinomas as this distinction largely directs management. About 20% of lung carcinomas may show evidence of a mixed pattern of differentiation, e.g. SqCC and SCLC, or AC and SqCC.

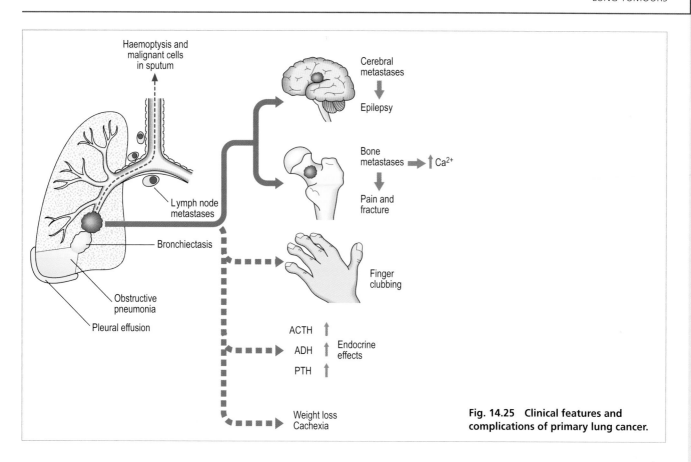

Fig. 14.25 Clinical features and complications of primary lung cancer.

Squamous cell carcinoma. This is the type of lung cancer most closely associated with cigarette smoking although the relative incidence has been decreasing over the last few years. The tumours are usually central in location and are thought to arise from areas of squamous metaplasia through increasing grades of dysplasia. There is often haemorrhage and necrosis with cavitation. Tumours may be well, moderately or poorly differentiated. SqCC tends to metastasise locally to hilar lymph nodes; distant metastases are a later feature.

Small cell lung carcinomas. These tumours were previously also known as 'oat cell' carcinoma because the small nuclei were thought to resemble oat grains; SCLC usually arise in a hilar bronchus. Unlike non-small cell carcinomas, they metastasise very early, producing widespread bulky secondary deposits. Sometimes, the primary tumour can be small and difficult to find. The histology is of a highly cellular tumour composed of small cells with hyperchromatic nuclei and indistinct nucleoli. The cells are very delicate and the chromatin may appear smudged. The cells commonly express neuroendocrine markers, suggesting that this is a form of very poorly differentiated neuroendocrine carcinoma.

Adenocarcinomas. These may be central or peripheral and can show a wide range of morphological patterns. The relative incidence of adenocarcinoma has been increasing over the last two decades and this type of tumour has overtaken squamous carcinoma as the most common subtype. Adenocarcinomas are usually single lesions but they can arise in a multifocal pattern, sometimes bilaterally. In this situation the tumour usually has a broncho-alveolar configuration where the cells grow along the alveolar walls, giving rise to areas

that appear consolidated (Fig. 14.29). There is now some evidence to suggest that most peripheral adenocarcinomas may arise from an area of broncho-alveolar carcinoma and that this may therefore represent an early form of these tumours.

Large cell undifferentiated carcinomas. Usually central, these are highly aggressive and destructive lesions with necrosis and haemorrhage. Histologically, there is often gross nuclear pleomorphism with numerous bizarre mitoses. By definition no squamous or glandular differentiation is seen on light microscopy, although such evidence is often found ultrastructurally. Some of these tumours may have features suggesting neuroendocrine differentiation and the term large cell neuroendocrine carcinoma has been adopted to distinguish them from SCLC and carcinoid tumours.

Bronchial carcinoid tumours. These are low-grade malignant tumours arising usually in the central airways. They are highly vascular and commonly present with haemoptysis or result in bronchial obstruction. These tumours generally have a good prognosis and, whilst metastatic spread to hilar lymph nodes can occur, this is rare and resection is usually curative. Some of these tumours may produce ACTH and are a rare cause of Cushing's syndrome.

Staging and treatment

As with all tumours, the stage of the tumour at presentation is of great prognostic significance. Lung cancers are staged pathologically using the TNM system although clinically the Mountain classification is also widely used to group patients together for trials (Table 14.5). The main chance of survival in

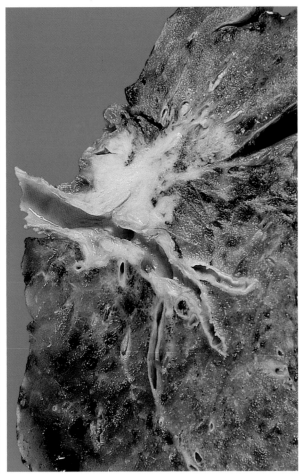

Fig. 14.26 Carcinoma of the lung. The tumour is arising at the hilum of the affected lobe and is invading the adjacent lung tissue.

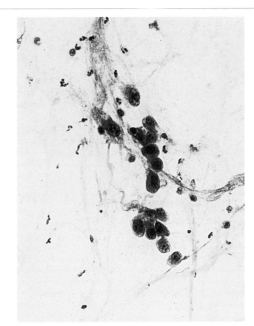

Fig. 14.27 Carcinoma of the lung. Tumour cells found in diagnostic bronchial washings, the appearances of which are consistent with non-small cell carcinoma of the lung.

Benign tumours

Adenomas may arise from bronchial mucous glands. They present as polypoid or sessile lesions in a bronchus. Symptoms are related to obstruction.

Benign mesenchymal tumours may arise anywhere that mesenchyme (connective tissue) occurs. Thus, neurofibromas, lipomas, etc. may be found in the lung. More common is the chondroma. The lesion is hard, white and well circumscribed, and is discovered as an isolated 'coin' lesion on chest X-ray. It is composed of nodules of cartilage with infoldings and clefts lined with bronchial or bronchiolar epithelium.

Malignant tumours

Malignant mesenchymal tumours (sarcomas) are extremely rare but the commonest primary type is angiosarcoma.

Primary pulmonary lymphomas are rare tumours presenting as pulmonary disease with or without hilar lymph node involvement, but without clinical evidence of disease elsewhere. HIV/AIDS patients have an increased incidence of pulmonary lymphoma. These tumours arise from bronchus- and bronchiole-associated lymphoid tissue.

non-small cell carcinoma is complete surgical resection which is achievable only in tumours confined to the lung or with limited hilar node involvement. Spread to mediastinal nodes, direct invasion of mediastinal structures or metastatic spread to other sites is usually a contraindication. Chemotherapy and radiotherapy may be used radically or palliatively in patients who have either inoperable disease or who are unfit on medical grounds for resection. As previously indicated, SCLC has almost always metastasised at the time of diagnosis and is therefore not usually amenable to surgery. Combination chemotherapy/radiotherapy can induce remission in SCLC, but this is sustained in only in a few patients.

Other primary tumours

Primary tumours other than carcinomas are rare. They can be classified as:

- benign, e.g. bronchial gland adenomas, benign mesen-chymal tumours
- malignant, e.g. sarcomas, adenoid cystic carcinomas, lymphomas.

Secondary lung tumours

Secondary lung tumours are more common than primary tumours, although a patient presenting first with a lung tumour is more likely to have a primary. Metastases may arise from blood or lymphatic spread. Usually, discrete nodules are seen scattered throughout both lungs; however, the lymphatics may be diffusely involved, leading to the appearance of lymphangitis carcinomatosa. Sarcomas, carcinomas and

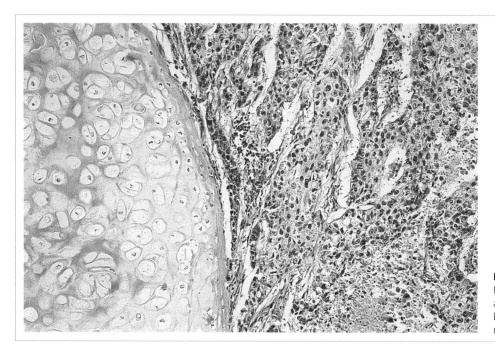

Fig. 14.28 Lung carcinoma. Histology of a poorly differentiated squamous cell carcinoma. Bronchial cartilage (left) is relatively resistant to neoplastic invasion.

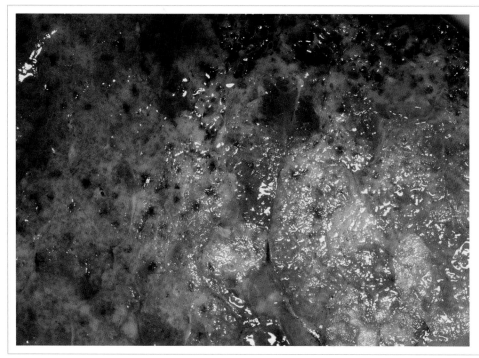

Fig. 14.29 Broncho-alveolar adenocarcinoma. The tumour cells diffusely infiltrate the alveolar spaces mimicking a pneumonic process clinically, radiologically and grossly.

lymphomas can lead to pulmonary metastases. Carcinomas that commonly give rise to lung secondaries include those from the breast, kidney and gastrointestinal tract.

PLEURA

The pleura is composed of connective tissue lined with mesothelial cells forming two apposing surfaces; the *visceral pleura* covers the lungs and the *parietal pleura* covers the thoracic cage wall, diaphragm, heart and mediastinum.

EFFUSIONS AND PNEUMOTHORAX

Various fluids (effusions) and air (pneumothorax) can collect between the two layers of pleura (Table 14.6).

Patients with pleural effusions or pneumothorax suffer shortness of breath and respiratory distress; these symptoms can be relieved by draining the fluid or air from the pleural cavity. Clinically, an effusion is dull to percussion; this is in contrast to a pneumothorax, which is hyper-resonant. To investigate the possibility that a pleural effusion might be due

Table 14.5   Staging systems for lung cancer

TNM staging system for lung cancer	
Tx	Size of tumour cannot be assessed
T0	No evidence of primary tumour
Tis	Carcinoma in situ only
T1	Primary tumour ≤ 3 cm
T2	Primary tumour > 3 cm, or Involving main bronchus > 2 cm from main carina, or Invades visceral pleura, or Partial collapse of the lung extending to the hilum
T3	Tumour of any size invading chest wall, diaphragm, mediastinal pleura or parietal pericardium, or Tumour in the main bronchus not involving the main carina but extending to within < 2 cm of it, or Collapse of an entire lung
T4	Tumour of any size invading mediastinum, heart, great vessels, trachea, oesophagus, vertebral body or main carina or Separate tumour nodules in the same lobe, or Presence of a confirmed malignant pleural effusion
Nx	Lymph node status not assessed
N0	No lymph node metastases
N1	Metastatic carcinoma in ipsilateral intrapulmonary or hilar lymph nodes
N2	Metastatic carcinoma in ipsilateral mediastinal or subcarinal nodes
N3	Metastatic carcinoma in contralateral mediastinal or hilar nodes, or Ipsilateral or contralateral scalene nodes, or Supraclavicular nodes
Mx	Distant metastases cannot be assessed
M0	No distant metastases
M1	Distant metastases or Separate tumour nodules in different lobe (ipsilateral or contralateral)

Mountain staging system for lung cancer			
Stage 0	Tis	N0	M0
Stage 1A	T1	N0	M0
Stage 1B	T2	N0	M0
Stage 2A	T1	N1	M0
Stage 2B	T2	N1	M0
	T3	N0	M0
Stage 3A	T1	N2	M0
	T2	N2	M0
	T3	N1/N2	M0
Stage 3B	Any T	N3	M0
	T4	Any N	M0
Stage 4	Any T	Any N	M1

Table 14.6 Disorders due to collection of fluid and air in the pleural cavities

Disorder	Collection	Causes
Haemothorax	Blood	Chest injury; ruptured aortic aneurysm
Hydrothorax	Low protein fluid (transudate)	Liver failure; cardiac failure; renal failure
	High protein fluid (exudate)	Tumours; infection; inflammation
Chylothorax	Lymph	Neoplastic obstruction of thoracic lymphatics
Pneumothorax	Air	Spontaneous, following rupture of alveolus or bulla in emphysema or tuberculosis
		Traumatic, e.g. following penetrating injuries of the chest
		Spontaneous idiopathic (in young healthy people without pulmonary disease); cause unknown
Pyothorax (empyema)	Pus	Infection

to primary or metastatic neoplasia, it is essential to perform a cytological examination of the cells within the fluid, with possible pleural biopsy.

INFLAMMATORY DISORDERS

Inflammation of the pleura (pleuritis or pleurisy) is common. It can be seen with:

- connective tissue disease: rheumatic fever, rheumatoid disease, systemic lupus erythematosus (SLE)
- infections: any pneumonia, tuberculosis, lung abscess
- pulmonary infarcts
- lung neoplasms.

The inflammation is nearly always accompanied by an effusion. Symptoms are usually of sharp, localised chest pain, worse on breathing. Treatment is of the underlying disorder causing the pleurisy. Depending on the degree of inflammation, pleurisy may resolve or organise to leave an area of fibrosis, sometimes with dystrophic calcification.

Pleural plaques are markers of asbestos exposure. They are asymptomatic patches of thickened fibrotic pleura on the diaphragm and posterior thoracic wall. Histologically, they consist of hyaline acellular connective tissue with a few inflammatory cells at the periphery. *Diffuse pleural fibrosis* and *pleural effusions* may both be related to asbestos exposure in the absence of lung cancer, mesothelioma or asbestosis.

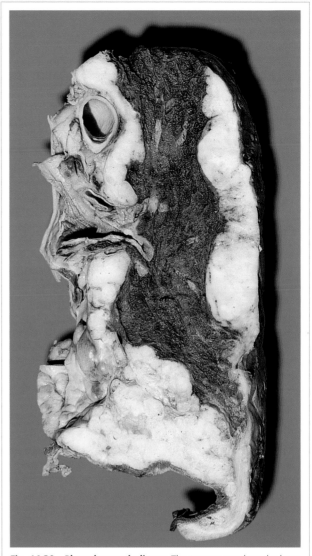

Fig. 14.30 Pleural mesothelioma. The tumour envelops the lung.

TUMOURS

Benign tumours of the pleura are rare. The *solitary fibrous* tumour is composed of a tangled network of fibroblast-like cells in a collagenous stroma. It grows as a solitary lump in the pleura, sometimes becoming very large. Hypertrophic pulmonary osteoarthropathy is a frequent association.

Malignant tumours are most often secondary deposits from primary lung adenocarcinomas and breast carcinomas, although other sites may also spread to involve the pleura. These secondary deposits may grow and encase the lung, thus mimicking a mesothelioma (pseudo-mesothelioma).

Mesothelioma

Primary malignant mesothelioma is strongly associated with occupational exposure to asbestos, especially fibres such as crocidolite ('blue' asbestos) and amosite ('brown' asbestos).

Commonly confused conditions and entities relating to respiratory tract pathology	
Commonly confused	Distinction and explanation
Emphysema and *empyema*	Pulmonary *emphysema* is characterised by large thin-walled bullae formed from fusion of alveolar spaces, and is entirely unrelated to *empyema,* which is the name given to a pus-filled cavity (e.g. pleura) or hollow organ (e.g. gallbladder).
Bronchitis and *bronchiectasis*	Both conditions affect bronchi. *Bronchitis* is simply bronchial inflammation, acute or chronic. *Bronchiectasis* is permanent abnormal dilatation of bronchi.
Bronchopneumonia and *lobar pneumonia*	In *bronchopneumonia* the inflammation is centred on airways, may be due to a wide range of bacteria, and is common in patients debilitated through age or serious disease. *Lobar pneumonia* affects diffusely an entire lobe, is due to a smaller range of bacteria (e.g. *Strep. pneumoniae, Klebsiella),* and often appears without antecedent cause.
Primary and *secondary tuberculosis*	Both are due to *Mycobacterium tuberculosis,* but the differences are determined by the host reaction. *Primary tuberculosis* is a benign self-limiting condition typically affecting the mid-zones in children. *Secondary tuberculosis* occurs in adults in whom a hypersensitivity reaction to *M. tuberculosis* results in extensive tissue destruction and fibrosis.

Other non-asbestos fibres, such as volcanic silicate erionite in Turkey, may also cause mesothelioma. The latent interval between exposure and the development of mesothelioma is often about 30 years. There has been a large increase in the incidence of mesothelioma in the Western world over the last decade, reflecting asbestos use and thus exposure in the previous decades. This is, however, expected to fall in the next decade or so following increasing restriction of its use in the 1970s and 1980s.

The tumour begins as nodules in the pleura which extend as a confluent sheet to surround the lung and extend into fissures (Fig. 14.30). The chest wall is often invaded, with infiltration of intercostal nerves, giving severe intractable pain. Lymphatics may be invaded, giving hilar node metastases. Distant metastases may be found in up to 30% of patients at autopsy.

Histology is varied; most commonly the appearance is of a mixed epithelial and spindle cell tumour although pure epithelial or spindle cell (sarcomatous) mesotheliomas can occur. Special histological techniques are often necessary to distinguish between mesothelioma and adenocarcinoma.

There is no proven effective treatment for malignant mesothelioma, and the median survival from diagnosis is around 11 months.

FURTHER READING

Britton M 2002 The epidemiology of mesothelioma. Seminars in Oncology 29: 18–25

Corrin B, Nicholson A G 2006 Pathology of the lungs, 2nd edn. Churchill Livingstone, Edinburgh

Hill A T, Wallace W A H, Emmanuel X 2004 An atlas of investigation and therapy. Pulmonary infection. Clinical Publishing, Oxford

Katzenstein A A 2006 Katzenstein and Askin's surgical pathology on non-neoplastic lung disease, 4th edn. Saunders, Philadelphia

Khalil N, Churg A, Muller N, O'Conner R 2007 Environmental, inhaled and ingested causes of pulmonary fibrosis. Toxicology and Pathology 35: 86–96

MacNee W 2005 Pathogenesis of chronic obstructive airways disease. Proceedings of the American Thoracic Society 2: 258–266

National Institute for Health and Clinical Excellence 2005 Lung cancer diagnosis and treatment. NICE, London. http://www.nice.org.uk

Nicholson A G 2002 Classification of the idiopathic interstitial pneumonias: making sense of the alphabet soup. Histopathology 41: 381–391

Scottish Intercollegiate Guidelines Network 2005 SIGN 80. Management of patients with lung cancer. A national clinical guideline. SIGN, Edinburgh. http://www.sign.ac.uk

Travis W D, Colby T V, Koss M N, Rosada-de-Christenson M L, King T E 2002 Non-neoplastic disorders of the lower respiratory tract. Fascicle 2. Armed Forces Institute of Pathology, Washington, DC

Travis W D, Brambilla E, Muller-Hermelink H K, Harris C C 2004 WHO classification of tumours. Tumours of the lung, pleura, thymus and heart. IARC Press, Lyons

Tweedle G 2002 Asbestos and its lethal legacy. Nature Reviews. Cancer 2: 311–315

World Health Organization 2008 Burden of disease statistics. WHO, Geneva. http://www.who.int/healthinfo/bod/en/index.html

Alimentary system

COMMON CLINICAL PROBLEMS FROM ALIMENTARY SYSTEM DISEASE

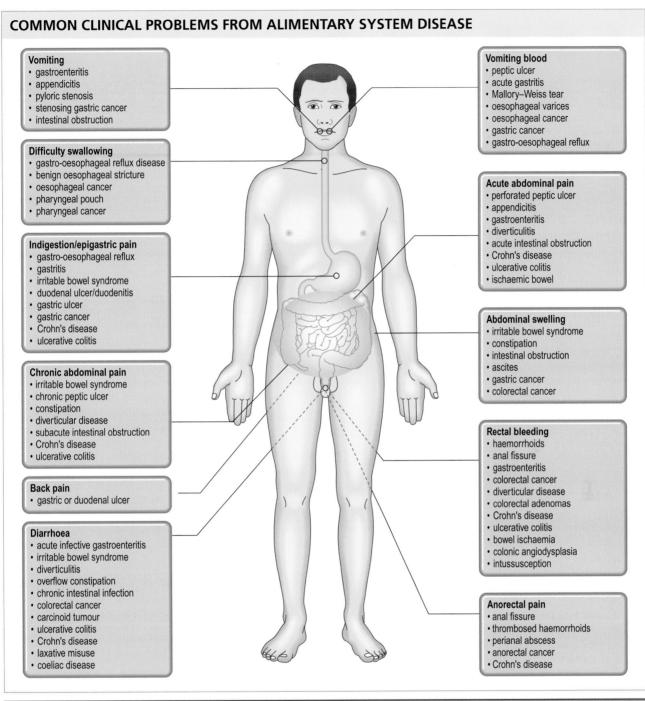

Vomiting
- gastroenteritis
- appendicitis
- pyloric stenosis
- stenosing gastric cancer
- intestinal obstruction

Difficulty swallowing
- gastro-oesophageal reflux disease
- benign oesophageal stricture
- oesophageal cancer
- pharyngeal pouch
- pharyngeal cancer

Indigestion/epigastric pain
- gastro-oesophageal reflux
- gastritis
- irritable bowel syndrome
- duodenal ulcer/duodenitis
- gastric ulcer
- gastric cancer
- Crohn's disease
- ulcerative colitis

Chronic abdominal pain
- irritable bowel syndrome
- chronic peptic ulcer
- constipation
- diverticular disease
- subacute intestinal obstruction
- Crohn's disease
- ulcerative colitis

Back pain
- gastric or duodenal ulcer

Diarrhoea
- acute infective gastroenteritis
- irritable bowel syndrome
- diverticulitis
- overflow constipation
- chronic intestinal infection
- colorectal cancer
- carcinoid tumour
- ulcerative colitis
- Crohn's disease
- laxative misuse
- coeliac disease

Vomiting blood
- peptic ulcer
- acute gastritis
- Mallory–Weiss tear
- oesophageal varices
- oesophageal cancer
- gastric cancer
- gastro-oesophageal reflux

Acute abdominal pain
- perforated peptic ulcer
- appendicitis
- gastroenteritis
- diverticulitis
- acute intestinal obstruction
- Crohn's disease
- ulcerative colitis
- ischaemic bowel

Abdominal swelling
- irritable bowel syndrome
- constipation
- intestinal obstruction
- ascites
- gastric cancer
- colorectal cancer

Rectal bleeding
- haemorrhoids
- anal fissure
- gastroenteritis
- colorectal cancer
- diverticular disease
- colorectal adenomas
- Crohn's disease
- ulcerative colitis
- bowel ischaemia
- colonic angiodysplasia
- intussusception

Anorectal pain
- anal fissure
- thrombosed haemorrhoids
- perianal abscess
- anorectal cancer
- Crohn's disease

Pathological basis of gastrointestinal signs and symptoms

Sign or symptom	Pathological basis
Dysphagia (difficulty swallowing)	Impaired neuromuscular function (e.g. multiple sclerosis) Obstruction (intrinsic or extrinsic)
Heartburn (indigestion)	Oesophageal/gastric mucosal irritation, often with inflammation and ulceration
Abdominal pain • Visceral • Peritoneal	Spasm (colic) of muscular layer in gut wall Irritation or inflammation of peritoneum
Diarrhoea	Excessive secretion or impaired absorption of fluid within lumen of gastrointestinal tract

(Continued)

Pathological basis of gastrointestinal signs and symptoms—cont'd	
Sign or symptom	Pathological basis
Steatorrhoea (fatty stools)	Impaired absorption of fat due to reduced lipase secretion or reduced mucosal surface area for absorption
Blood loss • In vomit (haematemesis) • Through anus	Ruptured blood vessel in oesophagus (e.g. varices) or stomach (e.g. erosion by ulcer) Ulceration or inflammation of colorectal mucosa, or oozing from surface of a tumour, or ruptured blood vessel (e.g. haemorrhoid, angiodysplasia)
Weight loss	Impaired food intake Malabsorption of food Catabolic state associated with a malignant neoplasm
Anaemia	Blood loss (e.g. tumour, ulcer) or impaired absorption of iron, folate or B_{12} due to mucosal disease

The alimentary system is constantly in contact with dietary contaminants, especially infective agents and environmental toxins, so it is not surprising that it is affected by many diseases. This chapter examines these diseases and, in those of major importance, attempts to relate them to the potentially pathogenic factors present in the human diet.

MOUTH, TEETH, PHARYNX AND SALIVARY GLANDS

NORMAL STRUCTURE AND FUNCTION

The mouth and teeth masticate the food prior to swallowing and digestion. At the same time digestion is initiated by the addition of salivary amylases and lipases.

The *mouth* is lined by stratified squamous epithelium overlying richly vascular connective tissue. The epithelium is of variable thickness, being thickest over the tongue where there are also papillary projections which account for its rougher texture. The epithelium is mostly non-keratinised, except over the lips, gums and hard palate where slight keratinisation occurs. Elsewhere pathological keratinisation (keratosis) results in the formation of white plaques on the mucosa; this is termed leukoplakia.

The *teeth* consist principally of *dentine*, which is similar to bone; it is composed of a collagen matrix mineralised by calcium phosphate (apatite) crystals. It differs from bone, however, in that its cellular constituents (odontoblasts) form a layer over the surface of the dentine, from which long tubular processes ramify through the tissue. The dentine is covered over the exposed part of the tooth (crown) by enamel, which is composed almost entirely of inorganic material arranged in stacked crystalline rods. The dentine of the root is covered by a thin layer of *cementum* which, as its name implies, attaches the tooth to the periodontal 'ligament' lining the socket. Centrally, the tooth has a connective tissue core, the *pulp*, which links with the narrow root canal.

The *salivary glands* are usually categorised as either major or minor. The major glands are the parotid, submandibular and sublingual glands; minor glands are scattered throughout the oral cavity. The parotids enclose branches of the facial nerve and a few lymph nodes. The glandular tissue comprises multiple small secretory acini lined by plump cells containing zymogen granules and surrounded by supporting myoepithelial cells. The secretion has a low protein content, hence these glandular units are referred to as *serous* acini. Small ducts lined by cuboidal epithelium drain the glandular lobules and unite to form the main secretory (Stensen's) duct. The submandibular glands contain both serous and mucus-secreting cells in mixed acini; the sublingual and minor salivary glands are predominantly or entirely mucus-secreting. The main ducts of the submandibular glands (Wharton's ducts) are lined by partly ciliated epithelium to facilitate drainage of the more viscid mucous secretion.

CONGENITAL DISORDERS OF THE MOUTH

Hare-lip and cleft palate

Hare-lip may appear as a sporadic defect of development but may also occur as an inherited condition exhibiting male sex linkage. The inherited form occurs both with and without a cleft palate. Where a cleft palate exists alone, a proportion of the cases are due to a dominant gene of low penetrance. Other cases are not genetically determined, as for example in the rubella syndrome (Ch. 5).

Hare-lip may be unilateral or bilateral; it may involve the lip only, or extend upwards and backwards to include the floor of the nose and the alveolar ridge. Cleft palate may vary considerably, from a small defect in the soft palate, which causes little disability, to a complete separation of the hard palate combined with hare-lip. With extensive lesions, there may be considerable difficulty with feeding as the child is unable to suck.

DISEASES OF THE TEETH AND GUMS

While of paramount importance to the dental student, diseases of the mouth, teeth and gums are soon evident to both patient and doctor, and frequently reflect generalised disorders. Their recognition and an understanding of the processes involved are therefore also of wider importance in clinical medicine.

Dental caries

Caries ('tooth decay') is the result of acid destruction of the calcified components of the teeth (Fig. 15.1). These structures are in a dynamic equilibrium between de- and re-mineralisation. When the pH falls below 5.5, de-mineralisation outstrips re-mineralisation; erosion of enamel is followed by loss of dentine. The acid is produced by bacteria, usually specific strains of *Streptococcus mutans*, acting mainly on refined sugar which is trapped in contact with the enamel by 'plaque'—a mixture of adhesive sugar residues and bacteria. Thus, a lack of oral hygiene, excessive consumption of sugars and under-development of dentine contribute to the development of caries. Penetration of the dentine is followed by bacterial invasion; this can infect the pulp, causing *pulpitis*.

Gingivitis

Acute gingivitis (inflammation of the gums) is an uncommon infection caused by the anaerobic *Borrelia vincentii* and fusiform bacilli. It is a severe ulcerative disease, formerly referred to as Vincent's infection, which can spread widely along the gum margins and deeply to destroy bone.

Chronic gingivitis, by contrast, is a very common condition which represents the response of the gum to adjacent bacterial plaque. Proliferation of anaerobic bacteria, and possibly their production of proteolytic enzymes, leads to chronic periodontitis and gradual destruction of the supporting tissues of the teeth. This results in loosening and eventual loss of teeth.

DISEASES OF THE ORAL MUCOSA

Inflammatory disorders

The oral mucous membrane is affected in a wide variety of mucocutaneous inflammatory disorders such as acute erythema multiforme, lichen planus, Behçet's syndrome and many others. However, some conditions (discussed below) are restricted to the oral mucosa.

Herpetic stomatitis

Herpetic stomatitis is a very common manifestation of infection by herpes simplex virus. It is characterised by vesiculation and ulceration of the oral mucosa and is usually acquired during childhood. Many patients develop recurrences in later life, appearing as similar lesions on the lips (herpes labialis).

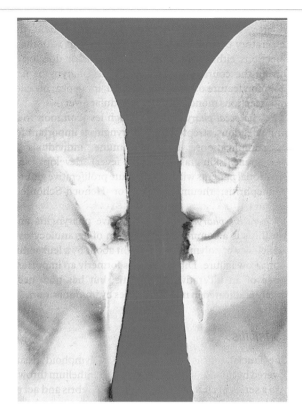

Fig. 15.1 Dental caries. Longitudinal sections of adjacent teeth showing characteristic erosion of enamel and dentine. (Courtesy of Professor C J Smith, Sheffield.)

Oral candidiasis

Oral candidiasis (thrush) is caused by the yeast-like fungus *Candida albicans*. It appears as white plaques on the oral mucosa consisting of enmeshed fungal hyphae, which invade the epithelium, together with polymorphs and fibrin. The infection is more common in neonates, in patients receiving broad-spectrum antibiotics and in immunocompromised individuals.

Aphthous stomatitis

Aphthous stomatitis is a very common disorder in which single or, more usually, multiple small ulcers appear in the oral mucosa. They are shallow, with a grey, necrotic base and a haemorrhagic rim. Many patients suffer from recurrent crops of ulcers which heal spontaneously after several days. The aetiology is unknown but assumed to be immunological; some patients have an associated gastrointestinal disorder, such as coeliac disease or inflammatory bowel disease.

Reparative lesions

The oral mucosa is frequently subjected to minor trauma. In some individuals the reparative processes that follow prove excessive, and the surplus fibrovascular tissue appears as a polyp. Such a reparative lesion in the mouth is termed an *epulis*, of which 'congenital' and giant cell forms are recognised.

There is also a similar angiomatous 'tumour' of pregnancy, and many of the so-called haemangiomas and fibromas of the mouth have the same histogenesis.

Oral leukoplakia and epithelial dysplasia

Leukoplakia ('white plaque') is a clinical term for patches of keratosis on the squamous epithelium that cannot be categorised as any other definable lesion, e.g. lichen planus or frictional keratosis. These lesions may be pre-cancerous: up to 18% of leukoplakias become oral cancer. Thus, in leukoplakia there is hyperkeratosis and hyperplasia of the squamous epithelium with, in some cases, dysplastic changes that herald the onset of malignant change. The finding of dysplasia on histological assessment is currently the best predictor of progression.

In the UK and USA, leukoplakia is associated with heavy cigarette smoking, excessive alcohol consumption and poor dental hygiene. The high incidence in India and Sri Lanka is attributed to the habit of chewing 'quids' made up of tobacco dust, areca nut and lime wrapped in a betel leaf.

Tumours

Cancer of the lip is more common than intra-oral cancers and occurs mainly in elderly people. It has a definite relationship to sunlight exposure; therefore, it is much more common on the lower than the upper lip. Lip cancers are usually well-differentiated squamous carcinomas which spread directly into surrounding tissues, and through lymphatics to the regional nodes.

Intra-oral cancers most frequently affect the tongue and commonly develop in areas of leukoplakia (Fig. 15.2); many oral carcinomas are associated with leukoplakia when diagnosed. The predisposing causes are therefore the same as those for leukoplakia but with the possibility that human

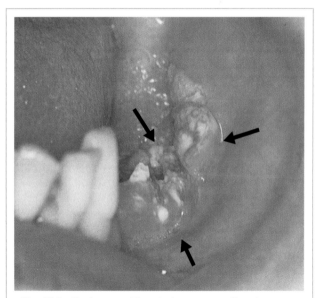

Fig. 15.2   Oral cancer. Ulcerated squamous cell carcinoma (arrowed) arising from buccal mucosa. (Courtesy of Mr P McAndrew, Rotherham.)

papillomavirus (HPV) could also be implicated. 'High-risk' HPVs (mainly type 16 or 18) are more frequently associated with oral squamous carcinoma than low-risk HPVs. Like lip cancers, oral cancers are usually squamous carcinomas. Initially they are painless and can remain undetected, especially if situated on the posterior third of the tongue, until fixation and swelling interfere with swallowing and speech. Late presentation with nodal metastases and direct spread to vital structures explains the much poorer prognosis of cancer of the tongue compared to that of cancer of the lip.

DISEASES OF THE PHARYNX

Pharyngitis

Viral pharyngitis

The commonest cause of pharyngitis is viral infection, but the causative virus is rarely identified. Most cases are thought to be caused by adeno- and rhinoviruses, but other viral infections, notably those directed at the respiratory tract, can be responsible. Patients with these infections either start with a pharyngitis or develop it during the illness. Thus pharyngitis is a common feature of the common cold, influenza, measles and infectious mononucleosis (glandular fever).

Streptococcal pharyngitis

Although less common than viral infections, streptococcal pharyngitis is important for its complications. In non-immune individuals a widespread skin rash (scarlet fever) develops and occasional patients will develop acute proliferative glomerulonephritis, rheumatic fever or Henoch–Schönlein purpura.

Ulcerative pharyngitis

An ulcerative pharyngitis and tonsillitis is a common complication of agranulocytosis (deficiency of polymorphs) due to a leukaemia or marrow failure. Diphtheria was formerly an important cause of an ulcerative pharyngitis, but has now been largely eradicated in many countries by immunisation.

Tonsillitis

The faucial tonsils are collections of lymphoid tissue covered by non-keratinising squamous epithelium thrown into a series of clefts; these can harbour debris and act as a nidus for infection. The tonsils are thus a frequent site for bacterial infection, producing either an acute inflammation or, more frequently, recurring chronic inflammation leading to tonsillar enlargement (through lymphoid hyperplasia) and general debility.

Tumours

The pharynx can be the site of squamous carcinoma and of intermediate or 'transitional' cell carcinomas, the latter exhibiting features of epithelium transitional between squamous and columnar, respiratory-type epithelium. However, most carcinomas in this site are anaplastic (undifferentiated). In addition, the tonsils may be involved by lymphomas.

Nasopharyngeal carcinoma is of interest because of the wide geographical variation in its incidence. It is an uncommon

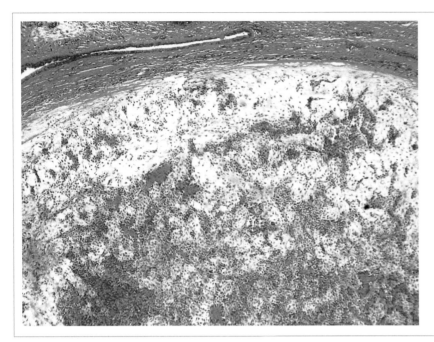

Fig. 15.3 Pleomorphic salivary adenoma. These benign neoplasms consist of a mixture of proliferating epithelium and mucinous connective tissue resembling cartilage surrounded by a capsule of fibrous and compressed salivary tissue.

carcinoma in Caucasians, but in some parts of China (particularly Canton) the frequency is 100-fold higher than in European populations. Males are more frequently affected than females. There appears to be a link with prior infection with Epstein–Barr (EB) virus, and the susceptible Chinese show a relatively higher frequency of the histocompatibility haplotypes HLA-A2 and -Bw46.

DISEASES OF THE SALIVARY GLANDS

Sialadenitis

Acute bacterial sialadenitis (inflammation of the salivary glands) is uncommon. It arises by ascending infection from the mouth and occurs in patients with abnormal dryness of the mouth (*xerostomia*), either as part of a generalised dehydration or as a result of an autoimmune-induced atrophy of the salivary glands (*Sjögren's syndrome*). Acute enlargement of the salivary glands is usually due to mumps virus infection.

Recurrent sialadenitis is seen in patients who have some degree of duct obstruction, hyposecretion of saliva and ascending infection. Duct obstruction can be due to a stone (calculus) or to fibrosis. Hyposecretion may be a direct consequence of duct obstruction but may also be due to the acinar atrophy resulting from sialadenitis itself. Bacterial infection leads to recurrent acute inflammation and also acts as a nidus for stone formation.

Tumours

▶ Pleomorphic adenoma: a benign mixed tumour
▶ Warthin's tumour (adenolymphoma): a benign tumour
▶ Muco-epidermoid tumour: both benign and malignant forms exist
▶ Adenoid cystic carcinoma: has a tendency for perineural invasion

Pleomorphic adenoma

At least two-thirds of all salivary tumours are accounted for by the pleomorphic adenoma or 'mixed tumour', and over 80% occur in the parotid gland. As the name implies, this has a varied histological appearance and is composed of a mixture of stromal and epithelial elements (Fig. 15.3). The myxoid stroma, which is rich in proteoglycans, is thought to be produced by myoepithelial cells; thus, despite its biphasic appearance, it is a purely epithelial neoplasm. Occasionally the stroma has a cartilaginous appearance. Pleomorphic adenomas are essentially benign tumours but are prone to local recurrence if surgical removal is incomplete. The facial nerve is vulnerable during attempts at surgical removal. A very small proportion undergo malignant change and are capable of metastasising; these are termed *malignant mixed tumours*.

Warthin's tumour

Warthin's tumour or adenolymphoma is a relatively common salivary gland tumour (5–10% of total). It has a very characteristic appearance: tall columnar epithelial cells line convoluted cystic spaces separated by a dense lymphoid stroma. The term adenolymphoma, with its connotations of lymphoid malignancy, is a misnomer; this is an entirely benign tumour.

Muco-epidermoid tumour

Muco-epidermoid tumour consists of mucus-secreting cells—cells showing squamous differentiation and intermediate cells (small cells that are probable precursors of the mucus-secreting and squamous cells). All should be considered as at least low-grade malignancy but those tumours with a greater proportion of intermediate and squamous cells compared to mucous cells have a more aggressive behaviour.

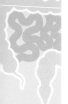

Muco-epidermoid tumours comprise about 10% of all parotid tumours.

Adenoid cystic carcinoma

Adenoid cystic carcinoma is a distinctive malignancy that is relatively more common in the minor salivary glands. It is composed of small epithelial cells arranged in islands showing microcystic change. This tumour has a propensity for perineural spread and is particularly difficult to eradicate surgically.

OESOPHAGUS

NORMAL STRUCTURE AND FUNCTION

The oesophagus is a muscular tube lined mostly by squamous epithelium. It extends from the pharynx to the cardia of the stomach and is about 25 cm long in the adult. At the upper end there is the *cricopharyngeal sphincter;* close to the lower end there is a functional sphincter whose position can be determined only by manometry. The upper sphincter contains striated muscle fibres enabling voluntary control over the initiation of swallowing, whereas the remainder of the muscular tube is composed of smooth muscle which propels the food bolus by peristalsis and is under autonomic control. Entry of food into the stomach is facilitated by relaxation of the distal sphincter. Protection of the lower oesophagus against regurgitation of gastric contents is achieved by the distal sphincter assisted by constricting muscle bands in the diaphragm, and an acute valve-like angle of entry into the stomach. The distal 1.5–2 cm of the oesophagus is situated below the diaphragm and is lined by columnar mucosa of cardiac type. The squamo-columnar junction is clearly visible on endoscopy and is usually found at about 40 cm (measured from the incisor teeth). Proximal extension of this junction is found in hiatus hernia or when there is columnar metaplasia.

The squamous lining of the oesophagus consists of a layer of non-keratinising squamous epithelium overlying connective tissue papillae containing blood vessels and lymphatics. A narrow layer one to two cells thick at the base of the epithelium forms the proliferative compartment from where cells migrate upwards, mature and desquamate at the surface (Fig. 15.4). These cells acquire an increasing glycogen content as they mature. Scattered argyrophil (neuroendocrine) cells and melanoblasts can also be found in the basal layer.

CONGENITAL AND MECHANICAL DISORDERS

Heterotopic tissue

Patches of fundic-type gastric mucosa are occasionally found above the distal sphincter and separated from the columnar lining of the distal oesophagus. These are assumed to be congenitally misplaced (heterotopic) gastric tissue rather than an acquired change; they can lead to ulceration and stricturing due to local acid/pepsin secretion.

Atresia

Atresia is a failure of embryological canalisation. It is more frequent than agenesis of the oesophagus, which is extremely rare. Atresia is usually associated with an abnormal connection (fistula) between the patent part of the oesophagus and the trachea. The affected child cannot swallow and develops an aspiration bronchopneumonia. Urgent surgical correction is required.

Diverticula

Diverticula are outpouchings of the wall of a hollow viscus. Some represent a saccular dilatation of the full thickness of the wall; others are formed by herniation of mucosa through a defect in the muscle coat. Diverticula are more common in the pharynx but can develop in the oesophagus by either *traction* (external forces pulling on the wall) or *pulsion* (forcible distension). These diverticula differ from congenital forms in lacking a muscle coat in their wall. They frequently become permanently distended with retained food and cause difficulties in swallowing (dysphagia).

Hiatus hernia

Defined as the presence of part of the stomach above the diaphragmatic orifice, hiatus hernia is the commonest mechanical disorder of the oesophagus and is found in c. 25% of people undergoing investigation for dyspepsia. The herniation of the stomach with subsequent retraction of the oesophagus is largely due to increased intra-abdominal pressure and loss of diaphragmatic muscular tone with ageing. Predisposing factors include obesity, lifting heavy loads, frequent coughing fits, tight-fitting clothes and frequent bending. The consequent incompetence of the oesophageal sphincter results in regurgitation of gastric contents leading to gastro-oesophageal reflux disease (GORD). Hiatus hernia of itself is usually asymptomatic; the condition presents with the symptoms and complications of GORD.

Achalasia

Achalasia is an uncommon condition in which the contractility of the lower oesophagus is lost and there is a failure of relaxation at the sphincter (cardiospasm).

Normal functioning of the oesophagus is dependent upon the integrity of its co-ordinated muscular activity, which in turn relies on normal neuronal transmission of peristaltic signals. Thus dysphagia may arise from fibrosis and atrophy of the smooth muscle, as occurs in progressive systemic sclerosis, or by destruction or degeneration of the intrinsic nerves. The latter can occur in neurotropic infections such as Chagas' disease (South American trypanosomiasis), or by unknown mechanisms as in the condition of achalasia.

Achalasia results in slowing or retention of the food bolus with increasing obstruction and dilatation of the oesophagus. The cause of this condition is unknown, but there are reduced numbers of ganglion cells in the myenteric plexus, and both myelinated and unmyelinated axons of the extra-oesophageal vagus nerves show Wallerian degeneration (Ch. 6).

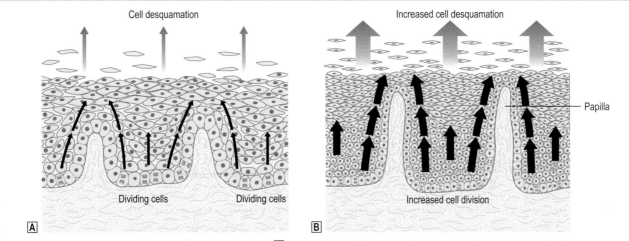

Fig. 15.4   Basal cell hyperplasia in reflux oesophagitis. **A** Normal cell proliferation and migration in the squamous epithelium. **B** In reflux oesophagitis, increased proliferation to compensate for increased cell desquamation results in basal zone hyperplasia and elongation of connective tissue papillae.

Oesophageal varices

Varices are localised dilatations of veins. The veins of the lower oesophagus are a potential site for porto-systemic shunting of blood when portal venous flow through the liver is impaired. Therefore, in portal hypertension (most commonly resulting from cirrhosis of the liver) the submucosal veins of the oesophagus become congested and dilate (Ch. 16). These enlarged veins elevate the mucosa and protrude into the oesophageal lumen where they are easily traumatised by the passage of food. Haemorrhage is thus a frequent complication and, because of the relatively high pressure within the vascular bed, can be torrential and life-threatening.

Mallory–Weiss tears

Two American physicians' names are associated with rupture of the oesophageal mucosa resulting from repeated retching or vomiting. The mucosa tears in the distal oesophagus close to the gastro-oesophageal junction. This is an important cause of upper gastrointestinal haemorrhage. Bleeding usually stops after 24–48 hours and the tears heal within 10 days or so.

INFLAMMATORY DISORDERS

Oesophagitis

Acute oesophagitis

Acute oesophagitis is clinically of only minor importance. Spread of bacterial infection from the nasopharynx to involve the oesophagus is a rare occurrence. More important are viral and fungal infections in immunocompromised individuals; for example, herpes simplex and cytomegalovirus infections are occasionally encountered in patients with leukaemias, lymphomas or AIDS. *Candidiasis* is a more common infection which may give rise to difficulties in swallowing; it is endoscopically recognisable as white plaques with haemorrhagic margins. Candidiasis is also opportunistic in immunodeficiency states and in diabetes mellitus, but can sometimes be found in otherwise healthy individuals. A further cause of acute inflammation and ulceration is the ingestion of *corrosive substances*; this may be either accidental (as when children swallow chemicals from unlabelled bottles) or taken with suicidal intent.

Chronic oesophagitis

As with chronic inflammation in any site, chronic oesophagitis may be either specific or non-specific. Specific causes are rare, but involvement by tuberculosis and Crohn's disease are recognised. Non-specific oesophagitis is very common and usually results from regurgitation of gastric contents into the lower oesophagus; this is *reflux oesophagitis*.

Reflux oesophagitis

Gastro-oesophageal reflux disease (GORD) is very common and is diagnosed when regurgitation causes symptoms or damages the mucosa. There is poor correlation between symptoms and oesophagitis; some patients with severe symptoms have little or no damage to the oesophageal lining whereas others with obvious inflammation on endoscopy may be asymptomatic. Clinically, GORD should be diagnosed on the basis of symptoms alone; the characteristic complaint is an awareness of acid regurgitation with central chest pain or discomfort—'heartburn'. A defective sphincter mechanism at the cardia predisposes to this gastro-oesophageal reflux, which is therefore an invariable accompaniment of hiatus hernia. Smokers are more likely to have GORD, as are obese people.

Morphology

Exposure of the squamous mucosa to refluxed acid leads to cell injury and accelerated desquamation. The increased cell loss is compensated for by increased proliferation of the germinative cells of the epithelium (basal cell hyperplasia; see Fig. 15.4); this results in fewer mature cells occupying most of the epithelial thickness and is accompanied by elongation of the connective

tissue papillae. Such elongation permits extension of the basal layer and possibly reflects an interaction between the proliferating epithelial cells and underlying mesenchyme. The epithelial injury is accompanied by a low-grade inflammatory cell response so that, in general, relatively small numbers of polymorphs (including eosinophils) and lymphocytes are seen within the epithelium and in the underlying connective tissue. Thus the response to reflux embraces both:

- an epithelial reaction—basal cell hyperplasia and elongation of papillae
- a conventional chronic inflammatory cell reaction.

Where reflux is severe, cell proliferation cannot keep pace with cell desquamation and ulceration occurs. These areas of ulceration can be the source of haemorrhage, and may even perforate in the most severe cases. Healing is achieved by epithelial regeneration and underlying fibrosis; subsequent shrinkage of fibrous tissue can produce a segmental narrowing (*benign oesophageal stricture*) in the area of healed ulceration.

Restoration of epithelial continuity is usually achieved by proliferation of squamous cells, but in some patients the lost squamous epithelium is replaced by columnar, intestinal-type epithelium, giving rise to a condition known as 'Barrett's oesophagus'.

BARRETT'S OESOPHAGUS

- ▶ Long-term consequence of reflux
- ▶ Metaplasia from squamous to columnar epithelium
- ▶ Increased risk of oesophageal adenocarcinoma
- ▶ Epithelial dysplasia precedes malignancy
- ▶ Regular surveillance by biopsy indicated

As a result of longstanding reflux, the lower oesophagus comes to be lined by columnar, intestinalised mucosa, an appearance referred to as Barrett's oesophagus. Opinions vary as to whether this is due to epithelial 'substitution'—migration of columnar epithelium from the distal 2 cm or from the ducts of submucosal mucous glands—or to an effect on the differentiation of progeny cells from a common stem cell (metaplasia). The latter is held to be the main mechanism at work.

In a patient with Barrett's oesophagus, the endoscopist sees proximal extension of pink columnar mucosa replacing the pearly white squamous epithelium. This extension is seen first as 'tongues' extending up from the cardia, and later as a complete 'cylinder' of columnar epithelium that can occupy much of the distal half of the oesophagus. Histologically, the epithelium may resemble that of the gastric cardia, but the characteristic 'specialised' Barrett's metaplasia consists of columnar epithelium, with goblet cells and tall intervening mucus-producing cells both secreting intestinal-type mucins—a form of intestinal metaplasia. Metaplasias arise in response to an adverse micro-environment and can be regarded as a defensive response in which the new cell lineage has a survival advantage over the 'native' epithelium it has replaced. Thus, an initial change from squamous epithelium to a columnar, gastric-type mucosa is readily understood as a response to acid reflux in that it provides a more resistant

mucosa. However, the change to epithelium with *intestinal* features cannot be explained solely as a defence response to acid. Other factors, such as bile reflux, may play a part, but it may be that patients who develop Barrett's metaplasia have a different phenotypic response to acid injury from the outset.

Barrett's oesophagus has become increasingly important following its recognition as a premalignant condition. Although the risk of malignancy is about 100 times higher among patients with Barrett's oesophagus than in the general population, the absolute risk of developing adenocarcinoma remains small. Only 2–3% of affected patients die from adenocarcinoma and overall life expectancy is unchanged. Nevertheless, it is considered best practice to undertake regular surveillance once Barrett's oesophagus has been diagnosed. If dysplasia, particularly high-grade dysplasia, is found on biopsy, then the risk of malignancy is greatly increased.

TUMOURS

Benign tumours

Benign tumours are uncommon and comprise about 5% of all neoplasms of the oesophagus; the type most frequently encountered is a *leiomyoma*. The behaviour of smooth muscle tumours in the alimentary tract is generally difficult to predict (see below) but those arising in the oesophagus are almost invariably benign. Other benign non-epithelial tumours—lipomas, haemangiomas and fibromas—are rare. The only benign epithelial tumour of note is *squamous papilloma*. Compared with squamous carcinoma (see below) these are rare lesions, certainly in terms of clinical presentation, but are of interest because they are likely to share a common pathogenesis with squamous papillomas at other sites being linked to human papillomavirus (HPV) infection.

Carcinoma

- ▶ Wide geographic variation in incidence
- ▶ Links with environmental factors
- ▶ Two main types: squamous carcinoma and adenocarcinoma
- ▶ Most adenocarcinomas arise from metaplastic columnar epithelium (Barrett's oesophagus)

There are two main types of oesophageal carcinoma—*squamous* and *adenocarcinoma*. These differ markedly in their aetiology and epidemiology.

Squamous carcinoma

Squamous carcinoma is much more common in males than in females and shows marked geographical variation in incidence. In European countries, the age-standardised annual incidence is around 5 per 100 000 population in males and 1 per 100 000 in females. However, there are some well-defined high-risk areas, such as north-west France and northern Italy, where the incidence rises to 30 per 100 000 in males and 2 per 100 000 in females. Globally there are more striking differences. Regions with very high incidence have been identified in Iran, South Africa, Brazil and Central China. In Henan Province in China the mortality rate from carcinoma of the oesophagus exceeds 100 per 100 000 in males and 50 per 100 000 in females.

Epidemiological studies in high-incidence areas have indicated that a high dietary intake of tannic acid, in the form of strong tea or sorghum wheat, or dietary deficiencies of riboflavin, vitamin A and possibly zinc may be important, but other factors such as fungal contamination of foodstuffs, opium usage and thermal injury may also be involved. In Western countries, cigarette smoking and the drinking of alcoholic spirits are associated with a higher incidence.

A factor of current interest is the possible involvement of HPV. Some oesophageal squamous cancers contain HPV in their cells, and viruses of similar subtype can be found in intact and apparently normal oesophageal mucosa. It is therefore possible that virus integrated into the host genome can bring about oncogene activation and carcinogenesis. The involvement of papillomaviruses in the development of bovine oesophageal carcinoma is well established.

Non-specific chronic oesophagitis is common among the general population in high-incidence areas, and biopsies will frequently reveal dysplasia. The squamous epithelium shows cellular pleomorphism: there is disordered maturation with immature cells and mitotic activity appearing close to the surface. The degree of atypia can be categorised as low- or high-grade dysplasia; the latter condition will proceed to invasive carcinoma if surgical resection is not performed. As in the oropharynx, dysplasia is sometimes associated with abnormal keratosis—leukoplakia.

Adenocarcinoma

In the lower third of the oesophagus, *adenocarcinomas* are the predominant type. They usually develop on the basis of a Barrett's oesophagus. The incidence has risen dramatically in recent years among white, middle-aged men in European countries and the USA; the reported annual increase in the white male population of the USA is close to 10% which exceeds that of any other malignancy in that population. Although the incidence of adenocarcinoma has increased, it is still a rare disease; in the year 2000 the numbers of new cases in Western countries varied between 1 and 5 per 100 000 white males. Nevertheless this incidence approaches, and in some areas exceeds, that of squamous carcinoma of the oesophagus.

Carcinoma of the oesophagus, either *squamous* or *adenocarcinoma*, usually commences as an ulcer, but spreads to become annular and constricting so that the patient develops dysphagia (difficulty in swallowing) (Fig. 15.5). However, by the time most patients present, direct spread outside the oesophagus has occurred and the surgical resection rate is only about 40%. Resectability and ultimate survival can be improved by pre-operative chemo-irradiation. Those patients who cannot be surgically treated may undergo chemo- or radiotherapy alone, or receive palliative laser therapy. Unfortunately, a substantial proportion of patients are simply intubated to facilitate adequate nutrition. The long-term outlook is therefore very poor; only 5% survive for 5 years. Most patients die from local disease and bronchopneumonia exacerbated by malnutrition. Unlike many forms of cancer, metastases are uncommon at autopsy.

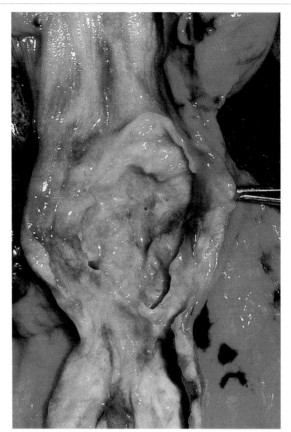

Fig. 15.5 Carcinoma of the oesophagus. The oesophagus has been opened to reveal an ulcerated tumour partly obstructing its lumen. Blood loss from the ulcerated surface can lead to anaemia, and the partial obstruction causes dysphagia.

Other tumours

Other rare malignant tumours arising in the oesophagus include malignant melanoma (from the melanocytes that are present in very small numbers in normal mucosa), small cell anaplastic carcinoma from neuroendocrine precursors, mixed adenosquamous carcinomas and sarcomas.

STOMACH

NORMAL STRUCTURE AND FUNCTION

The stomach acts essentially as a 'mixing' reservoir for food during acid–pepsin digestion. Hydrochloric acid and pepsin are, however, only two of many products of the gastric mucosa.

Histologically, the stomach can be divided into three regions—the *cardia, body* and *antrum*. The surface of the gastric mucosa and its pits (*foveolae*) are lined throughout by columnar mucus-secreting epithelium. The mucus secreted by these cells, together with contributions from the antral mucous glands, forms a viscid gel covering the mucosa—the *gastric mucus barrier* (Fig. 15.6). Bicarbonate and sodium ions, also

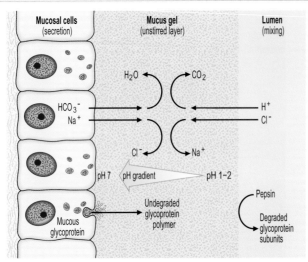

Fig. 15.6 The gastric mucus barrier. The surface epithelial cells (supplemented by foveolar and glandular mucous cells) secrete viscid mucus which forms an unstirred layer between the epithelium and the gastric lumen. The surface cells also secrete sodium and bicarbonate ions into the mucus gel and a pH gradient is established. This constitutes the major defence against acid attack.

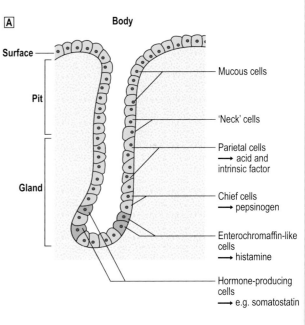

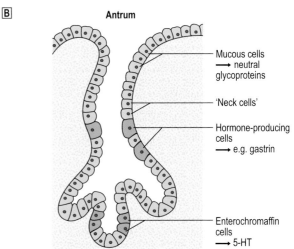

Fig. 15.7 Structure of the gastric mucosa. **A** Body (corpus) mucosa where the tubular glands contain specialised secretory cells. The 'neck' cells represent the proliferative compartment of the gastric pit from where the majority of cells migrate upwards to replenish exfoliated surface cells, and a minority move downwards to replace glandular cells. **B** Antral mucosa, predominantly composed of mucus-secreting cells but with scattered endocrine cells.

secreted by surface epithelial cells, diffuse into the unstirred gel and buffer the hydrogen ions entering from the luminal aspect. A pH gradient is thus established, ranging from 1 or 2 at the luminal surface of the barrier, to neutrality at the plasma membrane of the epithelium. The glandular component varies from region to region.

The *cardiac* (or *junctional*) *mucosa* is a narrow zone immediately below the termination of the squamous-lined oesophagus; it comprises simple tubular or cystic glands, lined by mucus-secreting cells, in which endocrine cells are scattered.

Body mucosa lines the proximal two-thirds of the stomach and consists of tightly packed tubular glands, the upper parts of which are lined by parietal cells (acid producing) and the lower parts by chief cells (pepsinogen) (Fig. 15.7A). In addition to acid, the parietal cells secrete intrinsic factor, essential for vitamin B_{12} absorption. Other cells present in body mucosa are mucous neck cells and endocrine cells. The neck cells are found at the bases of the gastric pits, i.e. at the junction between foveolar lining cells and glandular cells, and contain the stem cells of the mucosa together with some immature foveolar cells. The majority of the endocrine cells are so-called enterochromaffin-like (ECL) cells which are readily identifiable by silver staining (argyrophil) techniques. These cells modulate parietal cell activity by releasing histamine in response to stimulatory hormones such as gastrin.

Antral (or *pyloric*) *mucosa* occupies a roughly triangular region proximal to the pylorus, with its base about one-third of the distance along the lesser curvature and its apex a few centimetres from the pylorus on the greater curve. The antral glands are more branched, tortuous and less tightly packed than those in the body (Fig. 15.7B). The glands are lined by mucus-secreting cells with faintly granular cytoplasm and basal nuclei, together with endocrine cells. There may be occasional parietal cells. The endocrine cells of the antrum produce several hormones:

G cells secreting gastrin are the most numerous, but others include D cells (which secrete somatostatin), EC cells (5-hydroxytryptamine, 5-HT), P cells (bombesin) and S cells (secretin).

CONGENITAL DISORDERS

Congenital abnormalities, apart from hypertrophic pyloric stenosis, are rare. They include accessory structures lined by gastric mucosa, which are referred to as 'cysts' when saccular and not communicating with the gastric lumen, 'duplications' if tubular and non-communicating, and 'diverticula' if they communicate.

Diaphragmatic hernia

Maldevelopment of the diaphragm can lead to defects though which the stomach, together with parts of the intestine and the spleen, herniate into the left thoracic cavity. Usually only part of the stomach is dislocated into the thorax, but after birth it may become expanded by swallowed air and can rapidly compress the lungs and, very rarely, cause death from respiratory failure.

Pyloric stenosis

An abnormal hypertrophy of the circular muscle coat at the pylorus can cause outflow obstruction from the stomach. The condition, found in approximately 4 per 1000 live births, usually presents 2–3 weeks after birth with projectile vomiting. It is four to five times more common in males than in females. The primary abnormality appears to lie in the enteric nervous system at this site; the interstitial cells of Cajal (see p. 378) are either absent or abnormal.

INFLAMMATORY DISORDERS

▶ Acute gastritis is commonly due to chemical injury (e.g. alcohol, drugs)
▶ Commonest form of chronic gastritis results from *Helicobacter pylori* infection
▶ Chronic gastritis can also result from an autoimmune process, often causing vitamin B$_{12}$ deficiency
▶ Chemical (reactive) gastritis is caused by biliary regurgitation or drug-induced damage

Inflammation of the stomach, as with other organs, is usually considered as either acute (often described as 'haemorrhagic' or 'erosive') or chronic gastritis. One form of chronic gastritis, formerly designated type A, has long been recognised as an autoimmune disorder, but this type is uncommon. The major form of chronic gastritis (type B) is the result of infection with the bacterium *Helicobacter pylori*. Finally, longstanding bile reflux gives rise to a third major category—a 'chemical' type gastritis—which could therefore be termed 'type C'.

Acute gastritis

Acute gastritis is almost invariably an acute response to an irritant 'chemical' injury by drugs or alcohol. The principal drugs involved are non-steroidal anti-inflammatory drugs (NSAIDs), including aspirin, but many others have been implicated. These agents cause a prompt exfoliation of surface epithelial cells and diminished secretion of mucus such that the protective barrier against acid attack (see below) may be compromised. Many of their effects are probably mediated by an inhibition of prostaglandin synthesis.

Depending on the severity of the injury, the mucosal response varies from vasodilatation and oedema of the lamina propria, to erosion and haemorrhage. An erosion is an area of partial loss of the mucosa, as opposed to an ulcer where the full thickness, i.e. below the muscularis mucosae, is lost. The erosions in acute gastritis are frequently multiple and the resultant haemorrhage can be severe and life-threatening. Fortunately, the lesions are transient and heal rapidly by regeneration, so that erosions may well have disappeared 24–48 hours after the bleeding episode.

An acute neutrophilic gastritis (i.e. one in which polymorph infiltration is a dominant feature) is characteristic of the initial response to *Helicobacter pylori* infection. Acute *Helicobacter* gastritis is a transient phase which in the majority of individuals is subclinical and over the course of 3–4 weeks gives way to chronic gastritis. In a minority of individuals the infection is spontaneously eradicated and the inflammatory response resolves. The pathological features of acute bacterial gastritis are summarised in Table 15.1.

Chronic gastritis

Autoimmune chronic gastritis

A few patients with chronic gastritis are found to have antibodies in their serum directed against gastric parietal cells and intrinsic factor binding sites. These patients exhibit varying degrees of hypochlorhydria (they are often achlorhydric), and have a macrocytic anaemia resulting from vitamin B$_{12}$ deficiency; this association of autoimmune gastritis with macrocytic anaemia is called *pernicious anaemia*.

Histologically, the body of the stomach is maximally affected: there is marked loss of parietal cells (glandular atrophy) and replacement fibrosis of the lamina propria, together with an infiltrate of lymphocytes and plasma cells. In addition, the surface and pit-lining epithelium may show *intestinal metaplasia* (IM), a change common to all forms of longstanding chronic gastritis. In this form of metaplasia, the neutral, mucin-secreting cells characteristic of the stomach are replaced by goblet cells containing acidic glycoproteins typical of the intestine. In well-developed cases there may also be absorptive cells and Paneth cells. Intestinal metaplasia is generally regarded as a premalignant condition; however, the risk is low and cancer develops in only a very small proportion of people with IM.

Another type of metaplasia in the stomach could be more important in cancer development: parietal gland atrophy is accompanied by a multifocal proliferation of mucous glands—usually referred to as *pyloric gland metaplasia*—and this is more strongly associated with gastric cancer than IM. However, neither IM nor pyloric gland metaplasia is sufficiently closely related to cancer development to be useful for identifying 'high-risk' patients.

Helicobacter-associated chronic gastritis

The commonest cause of chronic gastritis is bacterial infection by *Helicobacter pylori*. This is a Gram-negative organism that inhabits a peculiarly protected niche closely applied to the surface epithelium beneath the mucous barrier where the pH approaches neutrality. Besides taking advantage of this acid-protected niche, the organism has its own intrinsic acid buffering mechanism using its urease and ammonia production to neutralise hydrogen ions gaining access to its periplasmic space. The organism binds to the surface cells and, depending on its virulence, exerts cytopathic effects that lead to accelerated cell exfoliation and a polymorph and chronic inflammatory cell response (Fig. 15.8). *H. pylori* is found in over 90% of biopsies showing active chronic (type B) gastritis but is very uncommon in the autoimmune type. The gastritis resolves after successful eradication of infection with antibiotics. Interestingly, the organism is found only on gastric epithelium and does not colonise duodenal (or any other intestinal) epithelium.

The neutrophil polymorph response provoked by *H. pylori* is mediated partly by leukotactic complement components liberated through activation of the alternative pathway (Ch. 9), but principally by bacteria-induced production of interleukin-8 by epithelial cells, macrophages and endothelial cells. Polymorphs subsequently release proteases, reactive oxygen metabolites (ROMs) and reactive nitrogen species into the mucosa. ROM production by leukocytes is enhanced by cytokines, such as tumour necrosis factor-alpha (TNF-alpha), and their cytopathic effects may be responsible for the glandular loss (atrophy) that characterises longstanding chronic gastritis. Anti-*H. pylori* IgA, IgG and IgM antibodies are produced locally by plasma cells in the lamina propria as part of a Th2-mediated response (Ch. 9); these antibodies have a role in the prevention of

Table 15.1   Pathological features of *Helicobacter*-associated gastritis

Pathological feature	Classification	
Surface epithelial degeneration Regenerative hyperplasia of pit-lining epithelium Vasodilatation/congestion Neutrophil polymorph response	**Acute gastritis**	'Active' chronic gastritis
Lymphocyte and plasma cell response Glandular atrophy Lamina propria fibrosis Intestinal metaplasia	**Chronic gastritis**	

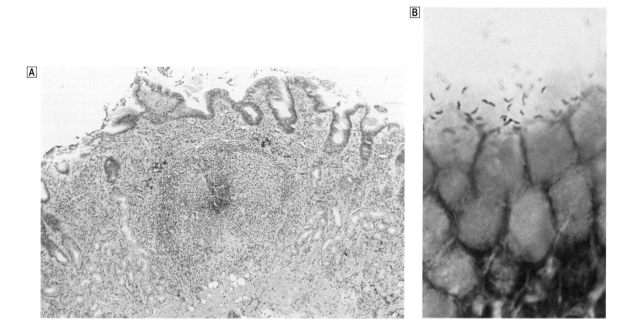

Fig. 15.8   Gastritis resulting from *Helicobacter pylori* infection. **A** At low magnification, the biopsy reveals an influx of chronic inflammatory cells into the mucosa and lymphoid follicle formation. **B** A section specially stained to reveal numerous minute curved *Helicobacter* adherent to the mucosal surface.

bacterial adhesion and in opsonisation, but fail to eliminate the infection.

Histologically, *Helicobacter*-associated gastritis affects the entire stomach mucosa but to a variable degree. The majority of patients have diffuse involvement of the antrum and body with gradual glandular atrophy, replacement fibrosis and intestinal metaplasia. The loss of parietal cells leads to hypochlorhydria and a reduction in the secreted signals that modulate the growth and differentiation of progenitor cells in the gastric mucosa; this could explain the link between atrophy and metaplasia. Patients with widespread gastritis have an increased risk of gastric ulcer and carcinoma compared with uninfected individuals. A second main pattern is where the antrum is markedly inflamed but with little involvement of body mucosa. These individuals have increased acid output rendering the body mucosa more hostile to *H. pylori* colonisation. Patients with this antrum-predominant gastritis have a greater risk of duodenal ulcer. Overall, however, only 10–15% of individuals infected with *H. pylori* develop peptic ulcer disease, and the risk of gastric cancer is about 1–3%. The histological features of acute and chronic gastritis are summarised in Table 15.1.

Chemical (reflux) gastritis

The presence of regurgitated bile and alkaline duodenal juice in the stomach provokes epithelial cell loss, compensatory hyperplasia of the proliferative compartment in the gastric foveolae, and vasodilatation and oedema of the lamina propria; this is reflux gastritis. In 'normal' people there is little or no regurgitation of duodenal contents into the stomach. Reflux gastritis is seen in the post-operative stomach following operations that destroy or bypass the pylorus, as a result of secondary motility disturbances in patients with gallstones and after cholecystectomy, and in some patients who appear to have a disturbance of antro-duodenal motility or co-ordination. Unoperated patients with bile reflux appear to have a failure in pyloric competence resulting from a disturbance in pyloro-antral motor function; this may be either a primary disturbance, or a defective response to hormones, such as cholecystokinin and secretin, which normally increase pyloric tone during duodenal acidification. The ensuing reflux gastritis stimulates production of gastrin by the antral mucosa; this may also block the effects of cholecystokinin and secretin on the pyloric muscles.

Reflux gastritis may present with bilious vomiting or less severe dyspeptic symptoms; repeated damage to the mucosa may lead to the development of a gastric ulcer.

A similar histological picture to that found with bile reflux can result from long-term usage of NSAIDs; the common denominator is repeated chemical injury. The various types of chronic gastritis are compared in Table 15.2.

Other forms of gastritis

Less common forms of chronic gastritis have been distinguished from the three major types discussed above.

In *lymphocytic gastritis* the main histological feature is the presence of numerous mature lymphocytes within the surface epithelium. This form is occasionally seen in patients who have peculiarly heaped-up erosions running along prominent rugal folds. Most patients are histologically *H. pylori*-negative at the time of diagnosis but most show serological evidence of infection. Some cases are related to villous atrophy and altered small intestinal function.

Eosinophilic gastritis is characterised by oedema and a large number of eosinophils in the inflammatory cell infiltrate. It is thought to be an allergic response to a dietary antigen to which the patient has become sensitised, or in some countries to parasitic infestation.

Granulomatous gastritis is a rare form of gastritis in which epithelioid cell granulomas are found. Such granulomas can be part of Crohn's disease (p. 385) or sarcoidosis, but after exclusion of these causes there remains an isolated granulomatous gastritis of unknown aetiology.

PEPTIC ULCERATION

Peptic ulceration is a breach in the mucosa lining the alimentary tract as a result of acid and pepsin attack. Gastric and duodenal ulcers differ in their epidemiology, incidence and pathogenesis (Table 15.3). They arise as either acute or chronic ulcers.

- ▶ Major sites: first part of duodenum, junction of antral and body mucosa in stomach, distal oesophagus and gastro-enterostomy stoma
- ▶ Main aetiological factors: hyperacidity, *Helicobacter* gastritis, duodeno-gastric reflux, NSAIDs, smoking and genetic factors
- ▶ Ulcers may be acute or chronic
- ▶ Complications include haemorrhage, penetration of adjacent organs, perforation, anaemia, obstruction due to fibrous strictures, and malignancy

Acute ulcers

Acute peptic ulcers develop:

- as part of an acute *gastritis*
- as a complication of a severe *stress response*
- as a result of extreme *hyperacidity*.

Deeper extension of the erosions in acute gastritis resulting from NSAIDs or acute alcohol overdosage can produce frank ulcers. Acute ulcers occur also in a heterogeneous group of conditions where stress seems to be the common denominator. For example, ulcers may be found following severe burns (Curling's ulcer), major trauma or cerebrovascular accidents. Such ulcers probably arise as a consequence of mucosal ischaemia, which lowers the mucosal resistance to acid. Extreme hyperacidity, as seen for example in patients with gastrin-secreting tumours (Zollinger–Ellison syndrome), can lead to multiple acute ulcers in the antrum, the duodenum and even the jejunum.

Chronic ulcers

Chronic peptic ulcers (Fig. 15.9) seem to occur most frequently at mucosal junctions. Thus gastric ulcers are often found where antral meets body-type mucosa on the lesser curvature;

Table 15.2 Types of chronic gastritis*

Aetiology	Pathogenic mechanisms	Histological findings	Clinical consequences
Autoimmune	Anti-parietal cell and anti-intrinsic factor antibodies Sensitised T-lymphocytes	Glandular atrophy in body mucosa Intestinal metaplasia	Pernicious anaemia
Bacterial infection (*H. pylori*)	Cytotoxins	Active chronic inflammation	Peptic ulceration (duodenal/gastric ulcer)
	Liberation of chemokines Mucolytic enzymes ?Ammonia production by bacterial urease Tissue damage by immune response	Multifocal atrophy: antrum > body Intestinal metaplasia	?Gastric cancer
Chemical injury NSAIDs Bile reflux ?Alcohol	Direct injury Disruption of the mucus layer Degranulation of mast cells	Foveolar hyperplasia Oedema Vasodilatation Paucity of inflammatory cells	Gastric erosions Gastric ulcer

* The order is to facilitate learning and does not reflect their frequency—*H. pylori gastritis* is by far the commonest cause.

Table 15.3 Comparison of the epidemiology, incidence and aetiology of gastric and duodenal ulcers

Feature	Gastric ulcer	Duodenal ulcer
Incidence (relative)	1	3
Age distribution	Increases with age	Increases up to 35 years of age
Social class	More common in low socio-economic classes	Even distribution
Blood group	A	O
Acid levels	Normal or low	Elevated or normal
Helicobacter **gastritis**	About 70%	95–100%

duodenal ulcers are found in the proximal duodenum close to the pylorus; oesophageal peptic ulcers are found in the squamous epithelium just above the cardio-oesophageal junction; and stromal ulcers—those occurring following construction of a gastro-enterostomy linking stomach and jejunum—are found in the jejunal mucosa immediately adjacent to the gastric mucosa of the stromal margin. This suggests that ulceration is most likely to occur where acid and pepsin first come into contact with a susceptible mucosa.

Pathogenesis

For many years peptic ulceration has been attributed to excessive acid production. However, there are many problems with this hypothesis. People with gastric ulcers frequently have normal or even subnormal acid production, and over one-half of duodenal ulcer patients do not have hyperacidity. Conversely, many people who are hypersecretors of acid do not get ulcers. Furthermore, while most ulcers respond initially to anti-acid treatment there are frequent relapses. It has therefore become increasingly apparent that mucosal defence against acid attack is of considerable importance (Fig. 15.10). Failure of the mucosal defence mechanisms means that ulcers can result from normal or even decreased quantities of acid.

Gastric ulcers

The pH of the gastric juice under fasting conditions is extremely acidic (between 1 and 2) so that any unprotected gastric mucosa would rapidly undergo auto-digestion.

The mucosal defences against acid attack consist of:

- a mucus–bicarbonate barrier
- the surface epithelium.

The *mucus barrier* is the more important of the two lines of defence. The pit-lining and surface epithelial cells of the stomach secrete viscid neutral glycoproteins which form a layer of unstirred mucus on the surface. The mucus itself has acid-resistant properties, but its protective power is greatly enhanced by the establishment of a buffering gradient within the layer brought about by bicarbonate ions.

The *surface epithelium* constitutes a second line of defence; for its proper functioning it requires integrity of both the apical plasma membrane as a barrier to ion transfer, and cellular metabolic functions, including the production of bicarbonate. These functions are dependent upon an adequate mucosal blood supply.

Ulceration can follow either destruction or removal of the mucus barrier, or a loss of integrity of the surface epithelium. Dissolution of the mucus layer can occur as a primary event as a consequence of duodeno-gastric reflux. The regurgitated bile from the duodenum strips off the mucus barrier and paves the way for acid attack. Acid and bile in combination damage the surface epithelial cells, increasing the permeability of the mucosa. This causes the congestion and oedema of the lamina propria seen in reflux gastritis.

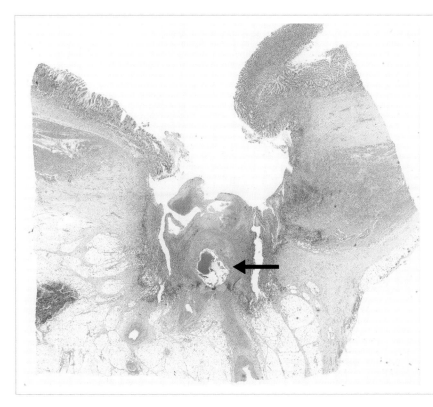

Fig. 15.9 Chronic gastric ulcer. Histological section through the ulcer revealing a deep breach of the main muscle layers and haemorrhage around an artery (arrowed) in the ulcer base. The patient presented with a profuse haematemesis (vomiting blood) and underwent emergency partial gastrectomy.

The epithelial barrier may be damaged by the effect of NSAIDs blocking the synthesis of the prostaglandins that normally protect the epithelium. Epithelial injury is also a consequence of *H. pylori* infection, produced either directly by cytotoxins and ammonia or indirectly as a result of the inflammatory reaction. Thus, in peptic ulcers in the stomach, breakdown of mucosal defence is much more important than excessive acid production.

Duodenal ulcers

Increased production of acid assumes more importance in the pathogenesis of duodenal ulceration; about one-half of such patients have an elevated maximal acid secretion, and even those with a normal maximal acid output may have inappropriately sustained acid secretion without the normal sharp fall-off of acid production during sleep. It has been shown that *H. pylori*-infected individuals secrete two to six times as much acid as non-infected controls when stimulated by gastrin-releasing peptide. Nevertheless, excess acidity is not the entire explanation and mucosal defence is also important.

The factors causing lowered resistance in the stomach do not usually apply in the duodenum: *Helicobacter* does not colonise normal duodenal epithelium; the duodenal mucosa is tolerant of bile and pancreatic alkaline secretions; and drugs are generally diluted or absorbed before reaching the duodenum. Nevertheless, *Helicobacter* is involved in duodenal ulceration because there is gastric metaplasia in response to excess acid. Gastric metaplasia (i.e. a change from intestinal absorptive cells to gastric surface mucous cells) paves the way for colonisation by *Helicobacter*, which in turn sets up chronic inflammation in the duodenum (duodenitis) and predisposes to ulceration. Furthermore, NSAID-induced ulcers can arise in the duodenum with, or without, pre-existing duodenitis.

Morphology

Grossly, chronic peptic ulcers are usually less than 20 mm in diameter but they may be larger and can exceed 100 mm in diameter. The edges are clear-cut and overhang the base. Microscopically, the base consists of necrotic tissue and polymorph exudate overlying inflamed granulation tissue which merges with mature fibrous (scar) tissue. The latter frequently occupies the remainder of the wall, with the muscularis propria completely replaced by fibrous tissue. Arteries within this fibrous base often show extreme narrowing of their lumina by intimal proliferation (*endarteritis obliterans*).

Ulcers heal by a combination of epithelial regeneration, which reconstitutes the mucosa, and progressive fibrosis. Later, shrinkage of the fibrous tissue (*cicatrisation*) may lead to pyloric stenosis or a central narrowing of the stomach, the so-called *hour-glass deformity*.

More immediate complications of peptic ulcers include:

- *perforation*, giving rise to spillage of gastric contents into the peritoneal cavity and peritonitis
- *penetration*, whereby the ulcer erodes into an adjacent organ such as the liver or pancreas
- *haemorrhage*, from eroded vessels in the ulcer base (Fig. 15.9).

Although malignant change is claimed to occur in gastric peptic ulcers, this is a very uncommon event: as far as duodenal ulcers are concerned it can be assumed that they never become malignant.

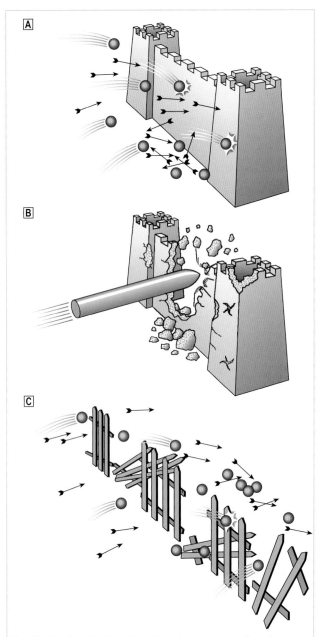

Fig. 15.10 Peptic ulceration. 'An ulcer represents the adverse outcome of a conflict between aggressive forces in the stomach or duodenum and the defence mechanisms.' (Sir Francis Avery-Jones) **A Normal.** Acid/pepsin attack is balanced by the mucus barrier and other defence mechanisms. **B Increased attack.** Hyperacidity (as in the Zollinger–Ellison syndrome) or NSAIDs may bring about the ulceration of 'normal' mucosa in the stomach and duodenum. **C Weakened mucosal defence.** This is the major factor in peptic ulceration. Chronic inflammation in the gastric and duodenal mucosa resulting from *Helicobacter pylori* infection can lead to ulceration in the presence of normal or even reduced levels of acid. Duodenal inflammation results from infection of patches of acid-induced gastric metaplasia in the first part of the duodenum.

BENIGN TUMOURS AND POLYPS

A polyp is simply a protuberant mass of tissue; it can either be neoplastic or form as a result of an excessive reparative or regenerative process. The commonest form of polyp involves simple elongation of the gastric pits separated by fibrous tissue or mildly inflamed lamina propria. These are *hyperplastic* or *regenerative* polyps and are generally found against a background of *Helicobacter*-associated gastritis in the gastric antrum. A similar variety is seen in body-type mucosa, but in this instance the main feature is enlargement by cystic dilatation of the specialised fundic glands. These were originally thought to be hamartomatous, but this is questionable and they are best termed *simple fundic polyps*. Much more rarely, true *hamartomas* occur, either as *adenomyomas*, which, as the term implies, are overgrowths of glandular and smooth muscle elements, or as part of the Peutz–Jeghers syndrome, an autosomal dominant disorder where the patient has multiple gastrointestinal hamartomatous polyps and circumoral, macular pigmentation. A further rare cause of a polypoid mass in the stomach is *heterotopic pancreas*, i.e. the presence of pancreatic tissue separate from the main gland.

Adenomas (i.e. benign epithelial neoplasms) are uncommon in most Western countries but are a relatively frequent finding in Japan and other countries with a high incidence of gastric cancer. When polypoid, these tumours have a strong potential for malignant change and, if subjected to multiple sectioning, around 40% will be found to contain carcinoma on microscopic examination. However, 'flat adenomas' with lower malignant potential are increasingly recognised and have to be distinguished from the higher-risk multifocal epithelial dysplasias (see below).

There are two main benign mesenchymal tumours, the *leiomyoma* and the *Schwannoma* or nerve sheath tumour. Both are rare. The majority of 'connective tissue tumours' in the stomach are stromal tumours. *Gastric stromal tumours* have a largely unpredictable behaviour and from a management point of view are best considered as 'low-grade' malignancy (see below).

MALIGNANT TUMOURS OF THE STOMACH

Carcinoma of the stomach

- ▶ Majority are adenocarcinomas
- ▶ Many arise on a background of chronic gastritis and intestinal metaplasia
- ▶ Most cases present when clinically advanced
- ▶ Early cases (carcinoma confined to mucosa or submucosa) have a good prognosis
- ▶ All gastric ulcers must be regarded as potentially malignant

The incidence of gastric carcinoma, like that of carcinoma of the oesophagus, varies widely both between and within countries. There is a notably high incidence in Japan, China, Colombia and Finland, but even in these countries, as elsewhere in the

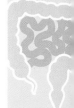

world, the incidence of carcinoma of the stomach is declining. Despite this fall, gastric cancer is still the second most common fatal malignancy (after lung cancer) in the world, accounting for around 10% of all cancer deaths, with an estimated 750 000 new cases diagnosed annually.

Aetiology

For many years, a sequence of events, starting with chronic gastritis and passing through atrophy and intestinal metaplasia to premalignant dysplasia, has been recognised as the precursor to cancer of the stomach. Given that *H. pylori* is now known to be the major cause of chronic gastritis, it is logical to implicate this infection in the causation of gastric cancer. The prevalence of *H. pylori* infection frequently runs parallel with the incidence of gastric cancer in the same populations, and epidemiological studies have shown that patients with antibodies to *H. pylori* have a higher risk of gastric cancer. The strength of the epidemiological links is such that the International Agency for Research into Cancer has declared that *H. pylori* is a gastric carcinogen, that is, the infection initiates the events leading to cancer. Given the high prevalence of infection and the comparative rarity of cancer it is highly unlikely that the organism or its products are direct-acting mutagens.

There are several possible indirect mechanisms linking *H. pylori* infection to gastric cancer. Long-term infection leads to glandular atrophy, which leads to a gradual decline in acid secretion. Hypochlorhydria allows other bacteria to proliferate in the gastric juice; these bacteria are capable of reducing nitrate ions to nitrite and can catalyse nitrosation of amines and amides present in the diet to give rise to potentially carcinogenic *N*-nitroso compounds. A more likely source of genomic DNA damage in *H. pylori* gastritis, however, are reactive oxygen metabolites produced by activated polymorphs and macrophages. Interestingly, nitrosation and oxidative damage is minimised by anti-oxidant vitamins, among which ascorbic acid is the most important, and diets rich in fresh fruit and vegetables have long been recognised as protective against gastric cancer. Ascorbic acid secretion into gastric juice is severely compromised in *H. pylori* gastritis.

When considering the role of *H. pylori*, several paradoxes have to be explained. First, there is a male preponderance of gastric cancer yet infection rates are similar in females; second, there is a low risk of cancer associated with the longstanding antral gastritis found in duodenal ulcer subjects; and third, some countries have a high rate of infection but a low incidence of gastric cancer ('the African enigma'). Possible explanations lie in the interplay between an individual's inflammatory response and the genotype of the infecting bacterium. Regarding the former, interleukin-1 beta (IL1-beta) is a powerful pro-inflammatory cytokine with acid-suppressive actions that governs many aspects of the response to *H. pylori*. Polymorphisms in the IL1-beta gene cluster allied to infection by more virulent strains of *H. pylori* could explain widely different risks of cancer development, even within populations. The balance between Th1- and Th2-mediated responses could also play a part (Ch. 9). Th1 cell immune responses are known to encourage the progression of pre-neoplastic changes like atrophy and metaplasia, relative to Th2 responses. Concurrent intestinal helminth infection alters the immune response to *H. pylori* infection away from a Th1- towards a Th2-mediated reaction and this may be protective against gastric cancer. Thus, in some developing countries, co-infection with intestinal parasites could explain the disparity between *H. pylori* infection and gastric cancer rates.

Several molecular genetic changes occur in gastric cancer. These include loss of expression of cell adhesion molecules including E-cadherin and beta-catenin, mutations and deletions of tumour suppressor genes, notably *TP53*, K-*ras* and the *APC* gene, and over-expression of oncogenes like c-*myc* and *erb*B-2. However, while some of these mutations are consistent with exogenous chemical carcinogens or exposure to endogenous free-radical injury, the nature of the mutational agent cannot be deduced from the genetic lesions with any certainty.

Overall, the evidence points to an unequivocal link between *H. pylori* infection and gastric cancer. In the year 2000, it was estimated that about 340 000 gastric adenocarcinoma deaths were attributable to *H. pylori*. The implications for the prevention of this major cancer are clear. Eradication of this infection or vaccination in childhood (when a vaccine becomes available) will have a profound effect on the incidence of gastric cancer.

However, *H. pylori* is not the only infectious agent to have a role in gastric cancer; over the past 10 years it has become clear that Epstein–Barr virus (EBV) infection is also linked to gastric adenocarcinoma. Worldwide about 10% of gastric cancers are associated with EBV but there is considerable geographical variation; the highest frequency (up to 17%) is found in Latin America. Gastric cancer has been associated with a distinctive strain of EBV, and global DNA methylation with gene 'silencing' occurs in EBV-related cancers.

About 8–10% of gastric cancers appear to have an inherited familial component, and in 1–3% of cases germline mutations inactivating the gene (*CDH1*) encoding the cell-adhesion protein E-cadherin lead to an autosomal dominant predisposition.

Dysplasia and early gastric cancer

The dysplasia–carcinoma sequence is thought to characterise the development of most gastric cancers, but the finding of dysplasia is relatively uncommon in low-incidence countries such as the UK and USA. Most cancers are advanced at the time of initial diagnosis; in the USA 65% of cases present at an advanced stage (pT3/T4) with nearly 85% of tumours accompanied by lymph node metastases at diagnosis. This accounts for the poor prognosis of gastric cancer, which generally has only a 10–15% survival rate at 5 years after diagnosis. Much better results, however, are obtained when patients undergo radical operations with extensive lymph node clearance. Patients who have such 'potentially curative resections' with removal of all regional nodes have a 60% chance of surviving 5 years.

Gastric cancers are classified as either 'early' or 'advanced' on their depth of invasion into the stomach wall (Fig. 15.11). *Early gastric cancer* (pT1) is confined to either the mucosa (intra-mucosal carcinoma) or submucosa; *advanced gastric cancer* extends into or beyond the main muscle coats (pT2–4). Cancers

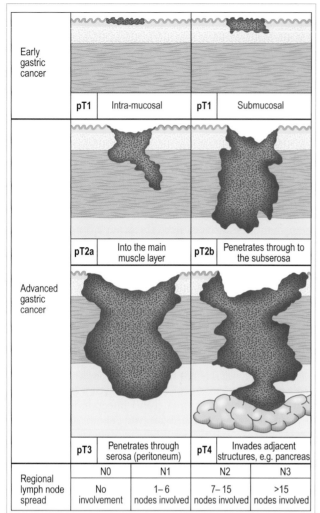

Early gastric cancer	**pT1**	Intra-mucosal	**pT1**	Submucosal
Advanced gastric cancer	**pT2a**	Into the main muscle layer	**pT2b**	Penetrates through to the subserosa
	pT3	Penetrates through serosa (peritoneum)	**pT4**	Invades adjacent structures, e.g. pancreas
Regional lymph node spread	**N0** No involvement	**N1** 1–6 nodes involved	**N2** 7–15 nodes involved	**N3** >15 nodes involved

Fig. 15.11 The spread of gastric cancer. Direct spread and lymph node metastases categorised according to the TNM scheme. Spread confined the mucosa or submucosa is classified as 'early', whereas any degree of spread into, or beyond, the main muscle layer is 'advanced'. The prognosis is highly dependent upon the extent of direct spread.

can still be 'early' even if lymphatic spread has occurred to regional lymph nodes. The importance of this categorisation lies in their differing prognosis: patients with early gastric cancer have a 5-year survival in excess of 90%. The prognosis of advanced cases rests largely on whether surgery has been truly 'curative' in removing the entire tumour. Thus, involvement of the resection margins by carcinoma carries a dire prognosis, as does the presence of covert hepatic or distant lymph node metastases. The best guide to prognosis in potentially curative cases appears to be the number of involved lymph nodes and, to some extent, the histological type of carcinoma.

Morphology

Foci of high-grade dysplasia and intra-mucosal carcinoma may be endoscopically visible as slightly elevated plaques or shallow depressions. Histologically, they may be distinguished according to whether invasion of the lamina propria has occurred, but

this can be excluded in high-grade dysplasia only by examination of multiple sections from the entire area of involvement. From a practical point of view the distinction is academic; if either of these lesions is diagnosed in a gastric biopsy, resection is essential. With increasing size, the elevated lesions develop into *polypoid* and later into *fungating* carcinomas, while the depressed areas present an excavated *ulcerated* appearance mimicking that seen in chronic peptic ulcer. The distinction between carcinoma and chronic peptic ulcer cannot be made with certainty on clinical, endoscopic or radiological grounds, so that all gastric ulcers should be subjected to cytology or multiple biopsies both before and after therapy.

Carcinomas of the stomach are almost exclusively *adenocarcinomas* derived from mucus-secreting epithelial cells. Like other carcinomas, they can be graded according to their degree of differentiation; poorly differentiated carcinomas behave more aggressively than well-differentiated types. However, a better guide to histogenesis results from division into either 'intestinal' or 'diffuse' types according to the scheme devised by Lauren (Fig. 15.12).

- *Intestinal-type carcinomas* show glandular formations lined by mucus-secreting cells with plentiful cytoplasm; in other words they resemble colorectal adenocarcinomas. They tend to have an expansile growth pattern with a well-demarcated 'pushing' border.
- *Diffuse carcinomas*, on the other hand, consist of chains of non-cohesive, single cells infiltrating the wall with a poorly demarcated invasive margin. Mucus secretion is generally less apparent, and usually takes the form of intracytoplasmic vacuoles which may compress the nucleus to form so-called 'signet ring' cells.

Intestinal-type gastric carcinomas carry a better prognosis than the diffuse type, but this is largely explained by the greater extent of spread of diffuse carcinomas at the time of diagnosis. Interestingly, the intestinal form predominates in high-incidence countries and has a strong correlation with pre-existing *Helicobacter*-associated chronic gastritis. Diffuse carcinomas predominate in low-incidence countries; this may reflect the increased contribution of genetic factors or EBV infection to cancer development among these populations. Certainly, both autosomal dominant hereditary gastric cancer and EBV-associated cancers are of diffuse type.

Carcinomas spread directly to involve the serosa (pT3), which can lead to peritoneal dissemination. This can result in the formation of a malignant effusion (ascites) or involvement of other organs by transcoelomic spread, of which metastases in the ovaries (Krukenberg tumours) are a classic example. Depending upon the site of the tumour, direct spread can also occur into the pancreas, transverse colon (when fistulation can occur), liver and spleen (pT4). Lymphatic spread is initially to perigastric nodes along both curvatures of the stomach, then to nodes along the right and left gastric, coeliac and splenic arteries (pN1–3). Spread to non-regional nodes such as retropancreatic, mesenteric and para-aortic groups is considered to be distant metastasis (M1). Rarely, spread to even more distant nodes is encountered, like the classical involvement of left supraclavicular nodes (Troisier's sign). Blood-stream spread occurs via the portal vein; liver metastases are frequently evident at the time of presentation.

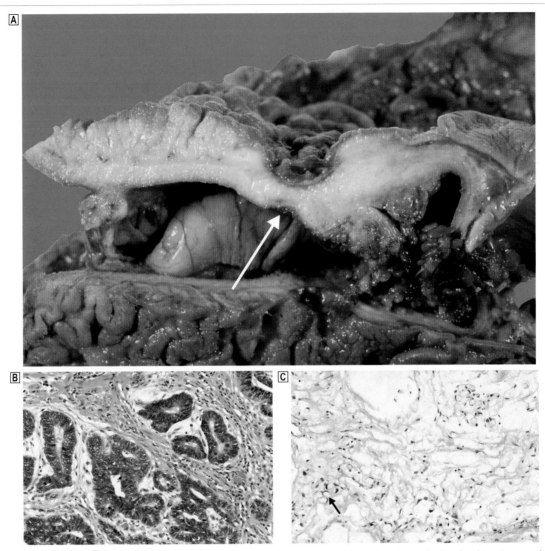

Fig. 15.12   Gastric cancer. [A] An ulcerated cancer of the stomach, initially thought to be a chronic peptic ulcer but biopsies revealed adeno-carcinoma. The carcinoma has spread through the wall and breached the peritoneal surface (pT3; arrowed). The two main histological types of gastric adenocarcinoma are: [B] *intestinal-type* comprising tubular or glandular formations of cohesive cells, and [C] *diffuse-type* composed of scattered clusters of non-cohesive cells which, in this example, contain a large clear mucin vacuole with compressed nuclei, so-called signet-ring cells (arrowed).

Other malignant tumours

Adenocarcinomas comprise over 90% of all gastric malignancies. Other malignant tumours include neuroendocrine (carcinoid) tumours (p. 396), malignant stromal tumours and lymphomas.

Stromal tumours

The stomach is the commonest site for gastrointestinal stromal tumours (GIST); approximately 45% of these are malignant and can metastasise. The component spindle cells originate from the interstitial cells of Cajal (see p. 378), and can be identified immunohistochemically by their CD117 (receptor tyrosine kinase) positivity. Affected patients present with symptoms referable to secondary ulceration—haemorrhage, anaemia, anorexia and weight loss. Endoscopically, the tumour protrudes into the lumen and often has a central deep ulcer crater. Stromal tumours behave unpredictably: it is difficult to distinguish between benign and malignant tumours on histological criteria. Features indicating a benign course are small size, encapsulation, very low mitotic activity and absence of necrosis. Malignancy is recognised by the presence of metastases at the time of surgery and can be predicted, to some extent, by an invasive margin and high mitotic activity.

Lymphomas

The stomach is the commonest site for primary lymphomas to arise in the gastrointestinal tract, accounting for around 40% of all cases, and the incidence is steadily increasing. Lymphomas

of the stomach represent about 5% of all gastric malignancies and are most frequently of the non-Hodgkin B-cell type; they are closely related to preceding *H. pylori* infection.

The normal gastric mucosa is virtually devoid of lymphocytes. *H. pylori* infection provokes an influx of lymphocytes and plasma cells in an active chronic inflammatory reaction. In keeping with a Th2-mediated response, lymphoid follicles with germinal centres appear in the gastric mucosa together with an increase in intra-epithelial lymphocytes in the immediately overlying epithelium. These features recapitulate those of a mucosa-associated lymphoid tissue (MALT); this acquired MALT provides the tissue of origin for gastric B-cell lymphomas. As with gastric carcinoma, epidemiological studies reveal a much increased risk for the subsequent development of gastric lymphoma when *H. pylori*-infected individuals are compared with uninfected controls. Indeed, patients with these low-grade B-cell lymphomas (*marginal zone lymphomas*) are almost always *H. pylori*-positive. A few cases will result from longstanding *H. heilmannii* gastritis, a much less common infection contracted from pet cats. In these cross-species *Helicobacter* infections, the predominant Th2 response favours lymphoma development over adenocarcinoma.

The emergence of a monoclonal proliferation of B-lymphocytes associated with aggressive features, evinced by invasion and destruction of epithelium (*lympho-epithelial lesions*) and replacement of germinal centres by atypical centrocyte-like B-cells, is characteristic of a low-grade malignant MALT lymphoma (Fig. 15.13). Monoclonality is detected using the polymerase chain reaction to show that a significant proportion of the lymphoid cells contain identically rearranged immunoglobulin heavy chain genes.

High-grade (large-cell) lymphomas consist of dense sheets of large 'blast' cells and are almost invariably of B-cell lineage. The transition from chronic gastritis to low-grade and then to high-grade lymphoma is associated with specific, reproducible genetic changes, but the cause remains unknown. Interestingly, the low-grade B-cell lymphomas appear to require the continuing antigenic stimulation of Th2 cells to maintain B-cell proliferation. As a consequence, these lymphomas can show complete regression following successful elimination of *H. pylori* infection. Deeply infiltrating (pT2–4) low-grade tumours and all high-grade lymphomas require treatment with chemo- and/or radiotherapy. Even so, high-grade lymphomas have a relatively good prognosis (compared to adenocarcinoma) when confined to the stomach (50% survival at 5 years), but the outlook worsens considerably when penetration of the serosa (pT3–4) or involvement of regional lymph nodes has occurred. The stomach may also be involved by lymphomas that have arisen elsewhere; the outlook in these systematised cases depends upon the overall extent, histological type and grade of the lymphoma.

INTESTINE

NORMAL STRUCTURE AND FUNCTION

Small intestine

The main functions of the small intestine are:

- enzymatic digestion
- absorption of nutrients.

By providing a vast surface area of specialised epithelium, the villous structure of the mucosa optimises absorption; this can be either passive or under active control. The *villi* are covered by tightly packed absorptive cells (*enterocytes*), which themselves

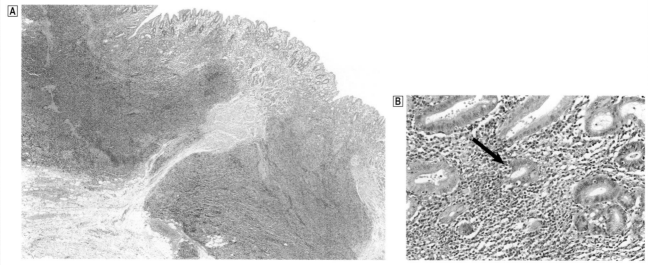

Fig. 15.13 *H. pylori*-related low-grade (marginal zone) lymphoma in the stomach. **A** A dense infiltrate of lymphocytes occupies the mucosa and extends deeply into the submucosa. **B** At high magnification, glands and the deep parts of the gastric pits are surrounded and infiltrated by lymphocytes including atypical forms. These lympho-epithelial lesions (arrowed) are a precursor to destruction of glands by the malignant infiltrate.

have *microvilli* on the luminal surface along their plasma membranes. This microvillous or 'brush' border further increases surface area and, together with the adherent glycoproteins of the glycocalyx, is also the site of hydrolytic enzyme activity, for example disaccharidases and peptidases.

Endocrine cells

Scattered among the absorptive cells are mucus-secreting goblet cells and endocrine cells; the latter are part of the diffuse neuroendocrine system and there are more than 14 different types producing a wide variety of gut hormones, including enteroglucagon, cholecystokinin, gastrin, motilin, secretin and vasoactive intestinal polypeptide (VIP). Neuroendocrine cells are also found among the proliferating cells (*enteroblasts*) of the intestinal crypts and these produce serotonin (5-HT), which has an important role in the control of gut motility and blood supply. Tumours originating from neuroendocrine cells are discussed further on page 396.

Paneth cells

These are distinctive granulated cells also found at the bases of the small intestinal crypts. Paneth cells are a rich source of defensins, peptides that are important in protecting the intestinal epithelium against microbes. Paneth cells store defensins as inactive propeptides within granules containing inactive forms of the processing enzymes, trypsin and trypsinogen. Upon granule release into the lumen, activated trypsinogen cleaves prodefensin to release the biologically active peptide alpha-defensin 5. Defensins act like broad-spectrum antibiotics with activity against Gram-positive and -negative bacteria, fungi, viruses and parasites.

Brunner's glands

The duodenal submucosa contains Brunner's glands, collections of mucus-secreting acini most plentiful proximally. They are much less frequent in the jejunum. Brunner's glands produce an alkaline mucous secretion that is also rich in epidermal growth factor (EGF). The secretion not only neutralises acidic gastric juice entering the duodenum but, through its high content of luminally active EGF, promotes mucosal regeneration after injury.

Mucosa-associated lymphoid tissue

The connective tissue of the mucosa (lamina propria) contains prominent lymphatics (lacteals), blood capillaries, and a cellular infiltrate comprising lymphocytes, plasma cells, eosinophils and mast cells. The lymphoid cells form an important arm of mucosal immunity, and most of those in the lamina propria are T-helper cells, whereas the intra-epithelial lymphocytes are predominantly T-suppressor cells thought to be important in maintaining tolerance to food antigens. Lymphoid aggregates or follicles with germinal centres are found throughout the intestinal mucosa; they frequently straddle the muscularis mucosae and extend into the superficial submucosa. Dense aggregates are found in the terminal ileum where they form *Peyer's patches*. The flattened epithelium over these aggregates contains *M-cells*, specialised cells capable of antigen binding and processing; they pass antigenic material to underlying helper T-lymphocytes.

Large intestine

The large intestine has several functions:

- the storage and elimination of food residues
- the maintenance of fluid and electrolyte balance
- the degradation of complex carbohydrates and other nutrients by luminal bacteria.

The large intestine can be divided into six parts—caecum, ascending colon, transverse colon, descending colon, sigmoid and rectum. These divisions are imprecise, but are useful for describing the sites and extent of disease.

Mucosa

The mucosa of the large bowel is devoid of villi. Instead, it comprises perpendicular crypts extending from the flat surface down to the muscularis mucosae, separated by a little lamina propria. Numerically, the predominant cell is of columnar absorptive type, but in tissue sections such cells often appear less numerous than the intervening goblet cells. As in the small intestine, several types of neuroendocrine cell are present, but in health Paneth cells are confined to the right side of the colon and then only sparsely. Also, in contrast to the small intestine, large bowel mucosa has only scanty lymphatics which are concentrated towards the muscularis mucosae. This restricts the metastatic potential of intra-mucosal malignant cells.

Vascular supply

The vascular supply to the colon derives from the superior and inferior mesenteric arteries:

- The caecum, ascending and proximal transverse colon are supplied by branches of the superior mesenteric artery.
- The distal transverse, descending, sigmoid colon and upper rectum are supplied by branches of the inferior mesenteric artery.
- The remainder of the rectum is supplied by the middle and inferior rectal arteries, which are branches of the internal iliac and internal pudendal arteries respectively.

These patterns of blood supply are important in determining the sites and consequences of ischaemia (for example, the 'watershed' territory around the splenic flexure is especially vulnerable) and, because lymphatic drainage follows similar patterns, in predicting the likely distribution of lymph node metastases from the site of the tumour.

Nerve supply

The intestine has a complex nerve network comprising autonomic motor and sensory neurones and a separate enteric nervous system. The sympathetic supply originates from ganglia outside the gut in the coeliac and mesenteric plexuses. The parasympathetic ganglia are found within the gut wall, and these, together with the associated neurones, form two nerve networks: the submucosal (Meissner's) plexus and the myenteric (Auerbach's) plexus. The nerve plexuses create and conduct the basic electrical rhythm of the gut. Stimulation of parasympathetic nerves increases muscular contraction (particularly in the inner circular layer), blood supply and secretory activity; stimulation of the sympathetic supply has the opposite effects.

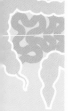

The enteric nervous system has sensory receptors in the mucosa and bowel wall that respond to changes in volume and composition of the bowel contents, and through neuronal connections elicits the appropriate response in the effector system. These activities are mediated by a wide variety of neurotransmitters, such as vasoactive intestinal polypeptide, cholecystokinin and somatostatin, some of which were formerly thought to be gut hormones.

The interstitial cells of Cajal (ICC) were until recently obscure and neglected partners in the neural control of the gut. These cells are of mesenchymal, non-neural origin and are found intercalated between elements of the enteric nervous system and smooth muscle cells. Some ICC act as a source of spontaneous electrical slow-waves responsible for paced contractions of the musculature ('intestinal pacemakers') while others appear to modulate neurotransmission in the gastrointestinal tract.

Appendix

The appendix arises from the caecum. It is a blind-ended structure lined internally by colonic-type mucosa, surrounded by submucosa and muscle coats. In children and young adults the mucosa contains numerous prominent lymphoid follicles. In the elderly, the lumen often shows fibrous obliteration.

CONGENITAL DISORDERS

The duodenum derives from the distal end of the primitive foregut; the jejunum, ileum and proximal colon from the midgut; and the distal colon and rectum from the hindgut. Proper development involves canalisation (development of a lumen), temporary herniation into the extra-embryonic coelom, rotation, and eventual retraction back into the abdominal cavity. Defects arising in the course of this complex process are relatively common.

Atresia and stenosis

Atresia represents either a failure of the gut to canalise or a failure of a segment to develop during fetal growth. A congenital stenosis is a constriction of the bowel arising during fetal development. These lesions are most commonly found in the duodenum or small intestine, and are rare in the colon. Duodenal atresia seems to be a failure of organ development, and around 30% of affected children also have Down's syndrome; jejuno-ileal atresia commonly appears to be the result of an intra-uterine accident, such as incarceration of the midgut in the physiological umbilical hernia or some other form of vascular occlusion.

Malrotation

The commonest type of malrotation occurs when the large bowel fails to descend into the right iliac fossa after emerging from the physiological umbilical hernia. This means that the caecum remains high in the abdomen and the bands that should fix it in the right iliac fossa (Ladd's bands) cross the duodenum and compress it, causing extrinsic obstruction.

Duplication and diverticula

Duplication of the bowel may either present as a tubular double-barrelled appearance, or form a cyst in the mesentery. These anomalies can produce an abdominal mass, cause intestinal obstruction, or initiate a volvulus (p. 392). Congenital diverticula are outpouchings of the full thickness of the bowel wall and are found mainly in the duodenum and jejunum. These rarely have clinical consequences, but some patients develop bacterial overgrowth, steatorrhoea and vitamin B_{12} malabsorption. The diverticula can also undergo perforation and haemorrhage.

Meckel's diverticulum

Meckel's diverticulum arises as a result of incomplete regression of the vitello-intestinal duct, such that a tubular diverticulum is present in the ileum. The diverticulum is usually lined by normal small-intestinal mucosa, but occasionally it may contain heterotopic gastric or pancreatic elements. If gastric elements are present, acid and peptic secretion may lead to ulceration at the mouth of the diverticulum and give rise to haemorrhage and perforation. The diverticulum may also become inflamed and present as an acute abdomen which can mimic appendicitis.

Meconium ileus

The term meconium ileus refers to small-intestinal obstruction resulting from thickening and desiccation (inspissation) of the viscid meconium produced by children with cystic fibrosis (Ch. 7). It is seen in about 15% of affected babies and may be complicated by perforation, secondary atresia or volvulus.

Hirschsprung's disease

Hirschsprung's disease, or aganglionosis of the intestine, results from a failure of migration of neuroblasts from the vagus into the developing gut, such that the intramural parasympathetic nerve plexuses fail to develop. The distal colon and rectum have an additional parasympathetic supply from extramural nerves derived from the sacral plexus. Under normal circumstances the parasympathetic tone, which controls the contraction of the circular muscle coat, is modulated at the ganglia by the sympathetic innervation. However, in the absence of the myenteric ganglia, the intact extramural parasympathetic supply is unchecked by sympathetic modulation and results in spasm of the circular muscle leading to intestinal obstruction. There is a proliferation of cholinergic nerves derived from this extramural supply throughout the affected segment, and their high content of acetylcholinesterase can be utilised to diagnose Hirschsprung's disease in frozen sections of rectal mucosa.

Hirschsprung's disease affects the distal large intestine, extending proximally from the anorectal junction for a variable distance. The rectum and distal colon are usually involved, but the extent varies from 1–2 cm to total colonic aganglionosis, or even extension into the small intestine. The effects of the aganglionosis vary from life-threatening total obstruction to mild cases causing chronic constipation. The main cause of death in Hirschsprung's disease is the development of an acute enterocolitis with endotoxaemia.

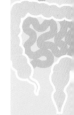

Anorectal anomalies

A large variety of malformations have been described that affect the termination of the large bowel. These include:

- a *primitive cloaca,* where the alimentary, urinary and genital tracts open into a single orifice
- *anorectal agenesis* and *rectal atresia,* where there is a failure of development or canalisation from above the level of the levators
- an *ectopic* or *imperforate anus.*

Anorectal anomalies occur in approximately 1:5000 live births. Most are amenable to surgical correction.

MALABSORPTION

Malabsorption can result from pancreatic disease or various biochemical disorders such as lactase and sucrase–isomaltase deficiency, as well as from small-intestinal diseases. Small-intestinal causes include:

- *coeliac disease,* the major small-intestinal cause of malabsorption in Western countries
- extensive *surgical resection,* for example in patients with Crohn's disease
- *lymphatic obstruction,* which gives rise to a protein-losing state
- *'blind loop syndrome',* where bacterial overgrowth in partly obstructed or bypassed loops robs the patient of vital nutrients.

Coeliac disease

> - Results from sensitivity to gluten components in cereals
> - Toxic components act largely indirectly through the immune reaction
> - Diagnosis by finding villous atrophy and crypt hyperplasia on duodenal or jejunal biopsy
> - Clinically, results in malabsorption but may present with 'non-specific' symptoms or anaemia
> - Complicated by splenic atrophy and, less commonly, lymphoma and small-intestinal ulceration

Coeliac disease is due to an abnormal reaction to gluten, a constituent of wheat, rye and barley, which results in damage to the surface enterocytes of the small intestine and severely reduces their absorptive capacity.

Incidence and clinical manifestations

Overt coeliac disease affects about 1 in 2000 individuals in the UK, but in the west of Ireland this rises to 1 in 300. Surveys in Europe, South America, Australasia and the USA have shown that approximately 0.5–1% of these populations have undetected coeliac disease. Although coeliac disease can be diagnosed at any age, it presents most frequently in either early childhood or in the third or fourth decades. In contrast to the equal sex distribution in children, there are twice as many females diagnosed as adults. Although the classical features of 'malabsorption syndrome'—diarrhoea, steatorrhoea, weight loss and fatigue—are seen in severe cases, most patients have milder, less easily recognised, symptoms such as bloating and indigestion, or are largely asymptomatic and present with an unexplained iron-deficiency anaemia. In the UK, the diagnosis is made increasingly in patients with atypical symptoms or anaemia.

Aetiology and pathogenesis

The toxic components of gluten are gliadin and glutenin, but the mechanism by which they induce tissue damage remains uncertain. Gluten is partially digested in the small intestine, but many gluten peptides are resistant to intestinal peptidases like pepsin and chymotrypsin. Although these toxic peptides have direct effects on intestinal permeability through the disruption of tight junctions between enterocytes, it seems increasingly likely that tissue injury is more a consequence of the immune response than a direct effect. A long-established factor in the immune reaction to gluten components is the possession of particular HLA (human leukocyte antigen) genes. Nearly all patients with coeliac disease possess either the HLA-DQ2 or the HLA-DQ8 heterodimer. However, HLA-DQ2 is present in approximately one-third of non-affected Caucasian populations, demonstrating that it contributes to, but is not sufficient for, disease development. The potential importance of HLA-DQ2 lies in its ability to bind the toxic gluten peptides and present them to T-cells.

Evidence of the importance of perturbed T-cell function comes from the recent identification of a disease-related region at 4q27; this harbours the genes for interleukin (IL)-2 and IL-21. IL-2, secreted in an autocrine manner by antigen-stimulated T-cells, is a key cytokine for T-cell activation and proliferation, while IL-21 enhances T-, B- and NK-cell proliferation and interferon-gamma production. One of the gluten peptides (part of alpha gliadin) appears to induce IL-15 production by enterocytes and dendritic cells. IL-15 is also important in T-cell activation and may induce expression of a major histocompatability complex chain-related molecule (MICA) on enterocytes as well as upregulating NKG2D, an activating receptor on intra-epithelial lymphocytes (IELs). The interaction between activated IELs and enterocytes expressing MICA results in direct enterocyte killing.

Morphology

Under normal circumstances, enterocytes are constantly shed from the tips of the villi and replenished by migration of cells up the villi from the proliferative compartment in the crypts (Fig. 15.14). The entire cycle from cell birth through functional maturation to extrusion takes about 72 hours. Moderately accelerated cell loss can be compensated for by increased cell proliferation. With higher rates of cell loss, a stage is soon reached when the increased proliferative compartment cannot maintain a normal number of maturing and functioning 'end cells', the size of this compartment diminishes, and villous atrophy results. Shrinkage of villi and reduction in epithelial surface area are thus inevitable consequences of any injury causing a high rate of cell loss in the small intestine. In coeliac disease the ultimate stage of this process is seen; despite a marked increase in size of the proliferative compartment, evidenced by elongation, hypercellularity and high mitotic activity of the crypts (crypt hyperplasia), there is a flat surface (total villous atrophy; Fig. 15.15) and even this is populated by immature cells incapable of

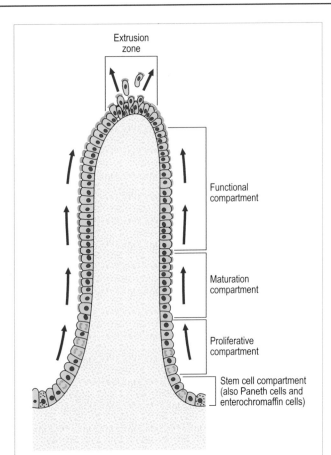

Fig. 15.14 Cell proliferation and maturation in the small intestine. See text for details.

of proper absorptive activity. Fully developed coeliac disease is therefore characterised by a total malabsorption, affecting sugars, fatty acids, monoglycerides, amino acids, water and electrolytes; the failure to absorb fat is the dominant abnormality in most cases. The loss of mature surface epithelial cells also causes disaccharidase deficiency, so that patients become intolerant of lactose and other sugars. The degenerate surface epithelium is infiltrated by large numbers of T-lymphocytes (IELs). Damaged epithelial cells may release TNF-alpha; this enhances the proliferation and migration of IELs (Fig. 15.16).

The lesion is more severe in the proximal small intestine—the duodenum and proximal jejunum—and may spare the ileum, although the latter is susceptible to injury if exposed to gluten. In addition to malabsorption, intestinal hormone production from the proximal small bowel is impaired; there may be secondary reduction in pancreatic secretion and bile flow as a result of reduced production or release of pancreozymin, secretin and cholecystokinin. Thus gallstones are commonly present in older patients.

Lesser degrees of gluten intolerance short of classical coeliac disease are increasingly recognised. Investigation of older patients with unexplained weight loss or anaemia sometimes brings to light an increase in IELs with or without mild villous atrophy in duodenal biopsies. Such patients also respond to gluten withdrawal.

Complications

Now that the primary lesion and clinical consequences of coeliac disease can be managed by gluten-free diets, the later effects of the disease are becoming of greater concern. Osteoporosis and sub-fertility have been attributed to coeliac disease but the increase in frequency is small. Of more importance, there is a low but definitely increased risk of malignant lymphoma in the small intestine, and a modest increase in other gastrointestinal

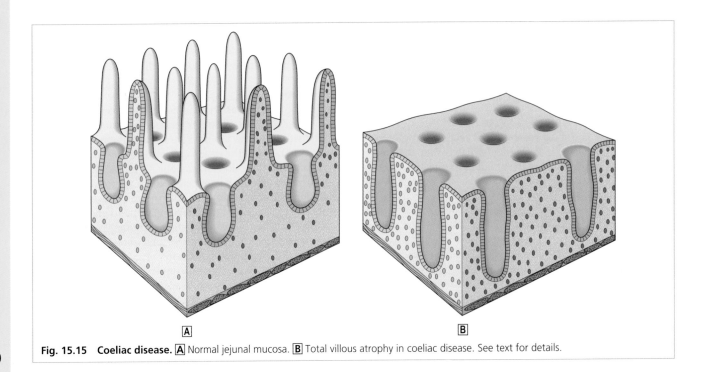

Fig. 15.15 Coeliac disease. [A] Normal jejunal mucosa. [B] Total villous atrophy in coeliac disease. See text for details.

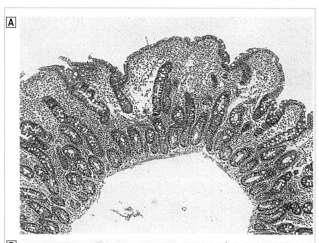

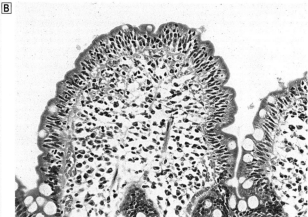

Fig. 15.16   Coeliac disease. **A** Jejunal biopsy from a patient with coeliac disease showing severe villous atrophy and crypt elongation (hyperplasia). **B** Higher power view of shortened villus showing increased numbers of lymphocytes in the surface epithelium and lamina propria.

cancers. Outside of coeliac disease, the majority of small bowel lymphomas are of B-cell lineage, but in coeliacs they are frequently of a large cell type derived from T-cells (enteropathy-associated T-cell lymphoma). The patient presents with haemorrhage, perforation, small-bowel obstruction or systemic symptoms. A few patients with coeliac disease develop ulceration of the small intestine which is non-lymphomatous; microscopic examination simply reveals non-specific chronic inflammation (chronic ulcerative enteritis).

Tropical sprue

Pathological changes identical to those found in coeliac disease (but usually less severe) are evident in tropical sprue, a form of malabsorption found, as the name indicates, in the tropics and sub-tropics but not apparently in Africa. It occurs most frequently in South-East Asia and the Caribbean. Tropical sprue is characterised by chronic diarrhoea, weight loss and a macrocytic anaemia due to folate or vitamin B_{12} deficiency. A gluten-free diet has little or no benefit, but the condition may be relieved by broad-spectrum antibiotics. The cause of the disease remains uncertain, but abnormal bacterial colonisation

of the upper small bowel is probably involved. Plasma levels of the gut hormones enteroglucagon and motilin are increased, the former slowing intestinal transit.

Repeated bacterial and viral infections are virtually the norm in tropical countries and these may lead to mucosal changes falling short of those seen in tropical sprue. In tropical Africa, for instance, jejunal biopsies from apparently healthy subjects will reveal reduced villous height and increased inflammatory cells when compared to normal Europeans. These minor morphological abnormalities found in asymptomatic residents of tropical countries have been called 'tropical enteropathy' but from a local perspective could be considered 'normal'.

Giardiasis

Mild malabsorption sometimes occurs in giardiasis (see p. 384).

BACTERIAL INFECTIONS

Bacterial infections of the intestinal tract are a major cause of morbidity and mortality throughout the world. Bacterial contamination of water supplies and the consequent diarrhoeal diseases are the major cause of infant mortality in developing countries. From a pathological viewpoint, diarrhoeal pathogens can be separated into those causing an inflammatory diarrhoea with a polymorph exudate, and those causing a secretory diarrhoea with no faecal leukocytes. Bacterial pathogens associated with secretory diarrhoea (e.g. *Vibrio cholerae*, enterotoxigenic and enterohaemorrhagic *Escherichia coli*) are generally non-invasive whereas those causing inflammatory diarrhoea (enteroinvasive *E. coli*, *Shigella*, *Campylobacter* or non-typhoidal *Salmonella* species) readily invade the intestinal epithelium and provoke an intense polymorph reaction.

Salmonella

Food poisoning by *Salmonella* organisms is a common and increasing problem in many countries. *Salmonella* infection of food poisoning type (salmonellosis) is generally confined to the gastrointestinal tract. In some patients this results in vomiting and profuse watery diarrhoea, usually with colicky, peri-umbilical pain suggesting predominantly gastric and small-intestinal involvement. However, in others the features relate to the large intestine, with frequent, small-volume, bloody motions, tenesmus and tenderness over the sigmoid colon. In the latter cases, sigmoidoscopy discloses a range of abnormalities varying from mucosal oedema and hyperaemia, to mucosal friability with slough formation and contact or spontaneous haemorrhage. The histological appearances are similarly varied. Some biopsies show oedema, focal interstitial haemorrhage and a mild increase in neutrophil polymorphs; more severe cases show a marked increase in polymorphs, with occasional crypts distended by polymorphs and mucus in the lumen ('mucoid crypt abscesses'). The crypt pattern, however, remains normal. The disease usually resolves within 10 days as the immune response clears the infection.

Typhoid fever is caused by *Salmonella enterica* serotype Typhi (*S. typhi*), and remains a major public health problem in many regions of the world; over 16 million cases are reported each year worldwide. In contrast to the gastroenteritis caused by most *Salmonella* species, typhoid fever is not a typical diarrhoeal disease and the intestinal pathology is characterised by a macrophage, not a polymorph, infiltrate. Patients usually present with prolonged fever, headache, abdominal discomfort and general debility. Around 10% of these develop severe complicated disease and without specific treatment 5–30% of all patients may die. *S. typhi* is ingested in contaminated food or water, passes through the stomach and then invades the gut epithelium, possibly in the distal ileum. After penetration through the epithelium, *Salmonella* are ingested by macrophages and several pro-inflammatory reactions are initiated (e.g. production of cytokines, increased expression of adhesion molecules and upregulation of genes involved in apoptosis). There is further recruitment of macrophages and these may facilitate systemic spread of the bacteria as *Salmonella*-infected macrophages can survive for several hours. In this way, infected cells pass into the liver and spleen and can be found also in bone marrow and blood. Some find their way back to the intestine. Shedding of *S. typhi* in the faeces of an infected individual is an essential step in the transmission of typhoid fever.

Bacillary dysentery

Bacillary dysentery is an acute infection of the large intestine characterised by painful diarrhoea, often with blood and mucus in the stools. *Shigella sonnei* is the commonest cause; it produces relatively minor lesions and seldom causes ulceration. However, *Sh. flexneri* and *Sh. dysenteriae* can produce necrosis, sloughing and haemorrhage, giving rise to a picture closely resembling ulcerative colitis.

Campylobacter colitis

Since the early 1900s *Campylobacter* organisms have been known to cause dysentery and abortion in cattle and domestic animals, but recognition of their role in human disease is relatively recent. Contamination of milk and water supplies with *C. jejuni* and *C. coli* is now recognised as a frequent cause of severe gastroenteritis and colitis, particularly in debilitated and malnourished individuals. The histological changes seen in rectal biopsies are non-specific, and are similar to those seen in other forms of infective colitis.

Cholera

Cholera is a form of secretory diarrhoea resulting from infection with *Vibrio cholerae*. The cholera toxin binds to a specific receptor on epithelial cells which leads to increased adenylate cyclase activity; this in turn results in high cyclic AMP levels in the intestinal mucosa. The affected enterocytes secrete fluid and sodium ions, and the ensuing watery diarrhoea can be extreme, with overwhelming fluid loss and a rapidly fatal outcome. Because the effects are mediated by an exotoxin and there is no bacterial invasion of host tissues, the histological changes are remarkably slight; the mucosa shows mild oedema and goblet cell depletion.

Neonatal diarrhoea

In some of the diarrhoeas of neonates and infants, various strains of *Escherichia coli* can be isolated. Such infections are more common in bottle-fed infants, and epidemics may occur in children's wards. Certain defined enteropathogenic serotypes are involved, and these differ from non-pathogenic types in their powers of adhesion to colonocytes and their ability to invade the mucosa. Diarrhoea may be severe, leading to dehydration and death. At autopsy, the small- and large-intestinal mucosa shows mucosal congestion and oedema with focal ulceration.

Staphylococcal enterocolitis

Enterocolitis due to staphylococcal infection is rare, but potentially fatal. The injudicious use of broad-spectrum antibiotics may alter the normal ecology of the intestinal bacterial flora so that the way is open for invasion by organisms that are either completely foreign to the bowel or normally present only in small numbers. The most dangerous of these is *Staphylococcus aureus*, which, when present in large numbers, can produce sufficient endotoxin to cause a severe enterocolitis. Staphylococcal enterocolitis is usually the result of cross-infection, and typically affects the hospital inpatient who has had contact with an antibiotic-resistant staphylococcus, in particular meticillin-resistant *S. aureus* (MRSA).

Patients present with sudden onset of severe diarrhoea, accompanied by shock and dehydration. The course can be relatively mild and respond to treatment, but with MRSA is often severe and carries a high mortality. There is widespread superficial ulceration predominantly affecting the small intestine. Microscopically there is acute inflammation of the mucosa with intense congestion and widespread necrosis. The surface of the mucosa is covered by an exudate containing numerous staphylococci.

Gonococcal proctitis

Gonococcal proctitis (inflammation of the rectum) is an acute exudative inflammatory condition which develops by genito-anal spread in females, and results from anal intercourse in males. The histological changes are non-specific, but the demonstration of numerous Gram-negative diplococci in the exudate leads to a presumptive diagnosis. As with other forms of infective colitis, definitive diagnosis depends on culture of the organisms.

Tuberculosis

Tuberculosis is almost entirely confined to the small intestine. In primary infection, an inconspicuous intestinal lesion is accompanied by gross enlargement of mesenteric nodes. This was the form of infection characteristic of bovine tuberculosis, a variety now virtually eliminated from the UK through the introduction of tubercle-free herds of cattle and the pasteurisation of milk.

Secondary tuberculous enteritis is a complication of extensive pulmonary tuberculosis which results from the swallowing of infected sputum. The typical alimentary lesion is ulceration of the ileum, the ulcer having formed by coalescence of caseous foci in the mucosa and submucosa. As the ulcers enlarge they follow the path of the lymphatics around the circumference of the intestine and eventually encircle the bowel. Healing is by fibrosis, and strictures may result from subsequent cicatrisation. The inflammatory exudate on the serosal aspect of the bowel may organise and form fibrous adhesions.

Ileo-caecal tuberculosis is a distinctive form of infection consisting of an ulcerative, granulomatous and fibrotic process occurring around the ileo-caecal valve, with variable extension into both ileum and caecum. The thickening and stenosis present a picture that is frequently indistinguishable from Crohn's disease, although, in tuberculosis, distinct pale tubercles can be seen in the serosa. Patients recognised as having active intra-abdominal tuberculosis are treated by chemotherapy, but surgery may be required for the treatment of complications or for diagnosis. The major complications are intestinal obstruction by strictures and adhesions, perforation of ulcers (although this is uncommon because of the marked fibrous reaction), and malabsorption resulting from widespread mucosal involvement or blockage to lymphatic drainage.

Actinomycosis

Actinomycosis usually presents as a localised chronic inflammatory process most commonly related to the appendix or caecal area. The organism, *Actinomyces israelii*, is a normal commensal of the mouth, and when swallowed may resist acid digestion and infect the bowel. The infection is protracted and characterised by chronic suppuration and the formation of sinuses (openings on to the skin) and fistulae (abnormal connections with other hollow viscera). Histology reveals inflamed granulation tissue, and foci of suppuration containing the characteristic colonies of organisms visible to the naked eye as 'sulphur granules' in the watery pus.

Whipple's disease

Whipple's disease is a rare bacterial infection usually involving the small intestine. The causative organism has been identified as *Tropheryma whippelii*, and this infection, in combination with alterations in immune responsiveness, produces multisystem involvement with joint pains, weight loss, pigmentation, lymphadenopathy and malabsorption. The mucosa from affected individuals shows infiltration of the lamina propria by numerous granular macrophages containing abundant glycoprotein. On electron microscopy, the Whipple bacillus and granular material derived from the bacterial cell wall can be found in these macrophages. Patients usually respond to prolonged treatment with tetracyclines.

Clostridium difficile enteritis

Some patients taking a broad-spectrum antibiotic develop diarrhoea resulting from overgrowth of the intestinal commensal bacterium, *C. difficile*. In most patients this is not severe and responds to withdrawal of the antibiotic; this is generally referred to as *antibiotic-associated colitis*. However, in a small proportion (generally elderly or post-operative subjects) a fulminant enteritis with profuse diarrhoea and dehydration can lead to death in the more debilitated patients. On biopsy, there is superficial loss of epithelial cells and a volcano-like eruption of mucin, polymorphs and fibrin forming a pseudo-membrane on the surface; this is *pseudomembranous colitis*. *C. difficile* is a Gram-positive bacillus that is non-invasive but produces a highly cytopathic toxin (toxin A) which is responsible for the enteritis.

Lymphogranuloma venereum

Proctitis due to lymphogranuloma venereum is principally a disease of females. This chlamydial infection begins in the genital tract and is thought to spread to the rectum via lymphatics. The deeper tissues are most heavily involved, and rectal stricture is the likely clinical problem. While non-specific chronic inflammation is usually pronounced, granulomas are a characteristic histological finding and these may show central necrosis when the disease is active.

VIRAL INFECTIONS

In many cases of presumed infective gastroenteritis or colitis no bacteria are isolated, and viral infection is probably responsible. Acute viral gastroenteritis is a major public health problem and as a cause of illness is second only to the common cold. However, the positive identification of viruses in contaminated food is difficult. The minute infecting dose required and the insensitivity of the available tests mean that laboratory identification is not always possible. The principal agents are rotaviruses, parvoviruses and 'small round structured' viruses including calicivirus. The most prevalent examples of the latter are the so-called 'Norwalk-like' viruses, a common cause of non-bacterial acute gastroenteritis resulting from contamination of food. In the small intestine these viruses produce degenerative changes in absorptive cells, minor shortening of villi and crypt hyperplasia, and inflammatory cell infiltration of the lamina propria.

Rare viral infections of the large bowel include *cytomegalovirus* colitis. Cytomegalovirus colitis has been described both as a primary infection and as a complication of ulcerative colitis. Infection is readily recognised by the presence of large intranuclear inclusions in cells within the mucosa.

FUNGAL INFECTIONS

Fungal infections of the alimentary tract are rare. Histoplasmosis may produce a striking picture of multiple inflammatory polyps in the small and large intestines, and on microscopy the intracellular *Histoplasma capsulatum* can be identified.

Mucor and *Rhizopus* are phycomycetes with non-septate hyphae that are widely distributed in nature. Although these organisms are usually non-pathogenic, gastrointestinal involvement in debilitated or immunosuppressed patients is becoming increasingly common. The oesophagus, stomach and colon are most frequently involved, and in addition to ulceration there is thrombosis of submucosal vessels with intravascular growth of the fungi. Despite this propensity for vascular infection, distant spread is surprisingly rare.

PARASITIC DISEASES

Giardiasis

Infection with the protozoan parasite *Giardia lamblia* produces a generally mild malabsorption state. It is a cause of 'traveller's diarrhoea' and of diarrhoea in childhood, in people with IgA deficiency, and following gastric surgery. It has been suggested that the malabsorption state is due to heavy infestation blocking access of nutrients to the surface epithelium; however, this is unlikely, as the numbers of organisms are rarely sufficient.

Amoebiasis

Amoebiasis is a disease of the large intestine resulting from infection with the protozoan *Entamoeba histolytica*. It is world-wide in its distribution, though more prevalent in the tropics than in temperate climates. Vegetative forms are present in the large bowel in infected individuals; these are passed in the stools, encyst into a more resistant form, and may survive in food and fluid and be re-ingested later. The cysts pass unharmed through the stomach; on reaching the intestine the cyst wall is dissolved, liberating the active amoebae (Fig. 15.17). These secrete a cytolytic enzyme which enables them to pass through the intestinal epithelium and, in disrupting the mucosa, release red blood cells which they then ingest. Contamination of food and water is brought about by human carriers, infected rats, or flies. Carriers may either be individuals known to have suffered an attack in the past, or be apparently healthy people, some of whom may have symptomless lesions in the bowel. Direct spread via anal intercourse is another recognised route of infection.

The disease can lead to discrete oval ulcers, which are characteristically 'flask-shaped' in section, or to a diffuse colitis. Blood-stream spread can result in liver abscesses, a potentially fatal complication.

Balantidiasis

Balantidiasis is a rare form of colitis caused by the ciliated protozoan *Balantidium coli*. It may be acute or chronic. Most cases are found in tropical or sub-tropical countries among debilitated, malnourished individuals. Gross and microscopic findings in the tissues are much like those in amoebiasis. The organism is readily detected by microscopy in both the lumen and the mucosa: it is so large as to dwarf the surrounding host cells.

Schistosomiasis

Infestation of the large intestine by *Schistosoma* occurs most commonly with *S. mansoni* and *S. japonicum* but can also be found with *S. haematobium*. Humans may become infected while wading or bathing in water contaminated with the second larval stage (cercaria) of the fluke. The cercariae penetrate the skin, enter venules, and are carried through the circulation to the portal veins in the liver, where they mature to form the adult flukes (Fig. 15.18). The adults migrate to either the submucosal veins of the gut or the venous plexus in the bladder, where

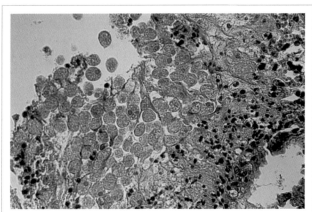

Fig. 15.17 Amoebiasis. High-power view of disintegrating colonic mucosa covered in an exudate in which there are large numbers of trophozoites. Some of these contain ingested red blood cells.

they lay their eggs. The ova pass through the intestinal wall into the faeces or through the bladder wall into the urine. The cycle is completed in water contaminated with egg-containing urine or faeces. The eggs hatch out, liberating miracidia (first larval stage) which infect a snail, the intermediate host within which the second larval stage of cercariae develop, later to emerge in their free-swimming form.

The pathological changes in schistosomiasis are essentially the result of an inflammatory reaction to the eggs in the tissues of the intestinal wall. Lesions are commonest in the rectum and left colon and are then nearly always due to *S. mansoni*; *S. haematobium* may be responsible if the lesions are in the right side of the colon and the appendix.

Cryptosporidiosis

Cryptosporidiosis is caused by a coccidial organism of the genus *Cryptosporidium*. These are common parasites in a variety of reptiles, birds and mammals. They are a frequent cause of diarrhoea in children, and are increasingly encountered in AIDS sufferers. Infection usually results from drinking contaminated water. Severe acute colitis with surface exudation and ulceration may result. Cryptosporidia cannot be recognised in stool specimens, so a biopsy or mucosal scraping is needed to make the diagnosis.

DRUGS AND THE INTESTINE

Many drugs adversely affect the gastrointestinal tract but, given their widespread use, non-steroidal anti-inflammatory drugs (NSAIDs) are the most important. The effects of aspirin and NSAIDs on the stomach and their association with gastro-duodenal ulceration are well known. Less attention has been given to their effects on the intestinal tract. Examination by capsule endoscopy (a pill-sized camera that is swallowed and passes through the intestine naturally) reveals visible small bowel lesions in the majority of people taking NSAIDs. Longer-term use can lead to small bowel ulceration, strictures

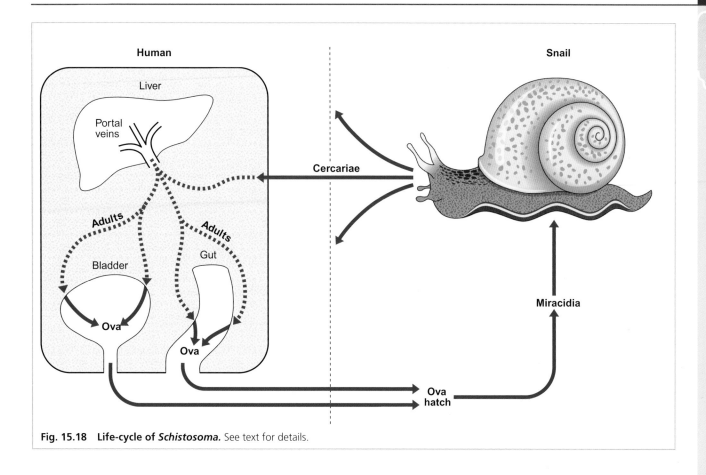

Fig. 15.18   Life-cycle of *Schistosoma*. See text for details.

and peculiar membranous mucosal 'diaphragms' that partly occlude the lumen. NSAID-related ulceration occurs occasionally in the caecum and proximal colon, but more subtle effects are usual in the large intestine. These include various forms of *microscopic colitis* where chronic inflammation is found histologically but there are no endoscopic abnormalities. These patients usually present with watery diarrhoea. Interestingly, the COX-2-selective agents protect both the stomach and intestine from NSAID injury.

Other drugs that affect the intestine include agents causing diarrhoea either by interfering with fluid absorption (secretagogues) or by an osmotic effect, and laxative abuse can lead to diarrhoea. A few drugs, such as neomycin and colchicine, directly damage the mucosa and cause malabsorption, and colitis can be a side-effect of gold salts and penicillamine used in the treatment of rheumatoid arthritis. Drugs used for chemotherapy in cancer treatment can cause ulcers and perforations.

CHRONIC INFLAMMATORY DISORDERS

Although several chronic inflammatory conditions affect the intestinal tract, by convention the term 'inflammatory bowel disease' (IBD) is used to cover two diseases that exhibit overlapping clinical and pathological features: Crohn's disease and ulcerative colitis. Crohn's disease most commonly affects the small bowel, but, when it involves the colon, the differential

diagnosis from ulcerative colitis can be a problem. The main distinguishing features are listed in Table 15.4.

Crohn's disease

▶ Chronic inflammatory disorder of unknown aetiology
▶ Small bowel most commonly affected, but any part of the gut may be involved
▶ Characterised by transmural inflammation with granulomas
▶ Thickened and fissured bowel leads to intestinal obstruction and fistulation

In 1932, Burrill Bernard Crohn and his colleagues established regional enteritis as a distinct entity. Previously, the condition had been confused with intestinal tuberculosis, then a common disease in Western countries. The chronic inflammation and ulceration in Crohn's disease predominantly affect the terminal ileum, but all parts of the alimentary tract from the mouth to the anus may be involved and more than one site may be affected. 'Satellite' lesions can also occur in skin remote from the peri-anal area. However, involvement outside the small and large intestine is uncommon. About two-thirds of patients have only small-intestinal involvement, about one-sixth only large-intestinal involvement, and in one-sixth of patients both small and large bowel are affected.

Crohn's disease usually presents with either small-intestinal obstruction or abdominal pain which may mimic

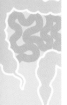

acute appendicitis; other presentations can relate to its complications (see below). The course of the disease is chronic, with exacerbations and remissions not always linked to therapy. Onset is usually in early adult life, with about half of all cases beginning between the ages of 20 and 30 years and 90% between 10 and 40 years. Slightly more males than females are affected.

Table 15.4 Chronic (idiopathic) inflammatory bowel disease: distinguishing features of Crohn's disease and ulcerative colitis		
Feature	Crohn's disease	Ulcerative colitis
Distribution	Commonly terminal ileum, but may occur anywhere from mouth to anus	Colon and rectum
Skip lesions	Common	Rare
Affected bowel	Thickened wall and narrowed lumen	Mucosal ulceration and dilated lumen
Extent of inflammation	Transmural	Mainly mucosal
Granulomas	Often present (c. 60%)	Absent
Fissures and fistulae	Common	Rare
Cancer risk	Slightly raised	Significantly raised

Morphology

Intestinal involvement by Crohn's disease is frequently segmental; that is, lengths of diseased bowel are separated by apparently normal tissue. Such separated segments of disease are referred to as 'skip lesions'.

The earliest evidence of involvement visible with the naked eye is the presence of small discrete shallow ulcers with a haemorrhagic rim. These ulcers have been likened to the common aphthous ulcers of the mouth and are thus often described as 'aphthoid'; however, there is no aetiological link between the two conditions. Later, the more characteristic longitudinal ulcers develop which progress into deep fissures (Fig. 15.19). The process comes to involve the full thickness of the wall and subsequent fibrosis leads to considerable narrowing in the diseased segments (Fig. 15.20). This produces a characteristic radiological sign where only a trickle of contrast medium passes through the affected segment (the 'string sign'). Where longitudinal fissures cross oedematous transverse mucosal folds, a 'cobblestone' appearance results. The mesenteric lymph nodes are enlarged by reactive hyperplasia and may also contain granulomas.

Microscopy reflects the gross appearances. Inflammatory involvement is discontinuous: it is focal or patchy. Collections of lymphocytes and plasma cells are found, mainly in the mucosa and submucosa, but usually affecting all layers (transmural inflammation). The classical microscopic feature of Crohn's disease is the presence of granulomas. These consist of epithelioid macrophages and giant cells surrounded by a cuff of lymphocytes. The giant cells are usually of the Langhans' type, but may resemble foreign body giant cells.

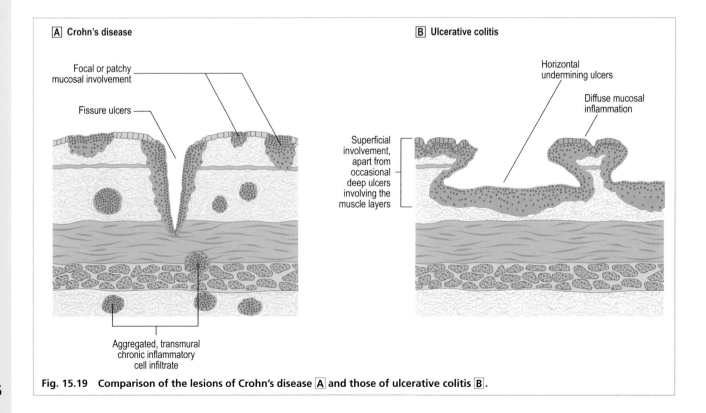

Fig. 15.19   Comparison of the lesions of Crohn's disease A and those of ulcerative colitis B.

Fig. 15.20 Crohn's disease. The terminal ileum is severely narrowed due to thickening of the bowel wall by the chronic inflammatory process. On the right, the lumen is passively dilated in response to the presence of the obstructive lesion.

Table 15.5 Complications of Crohn's disease

Complication	Comment/example
Malabsorption syndrome	Often iatrogenic ('short bowel syndrome')
Fistula formation	Causes malabsorption when loops of bowel are bypassed
Anal lesions	Skin tags, fissures, fistulae
Acute complications	Perforation (haemorrhage, toxic dilatation—rare)
Malignancy	Increased risk—adenocarcinoma
Systemic amyloidosis	Rare

The granulomas are distinguished from those of tuberculosis by the absence of central caseous necrosis. While they are virtually diagnostic of the condition, granulomas are found in only 60% of cases of Crohn's disease; in their absence the diagnosis must be based on a summation of the less specific histological changes. In addition to the aggregated transmural pattern of inflammation, these changes include the finding of vertical fissure ulcers and marked submucosal oedema, lymphangiectasia, fibrosis and neuromatoid hyperplasia (enlargement and proliferation of submucosal nerves).

Complications

The complications of Crohn's disease are summarised in Table 15.5. Widespread involvement of the small intestine can lead to a malabsorption syndrome, but the commonest cause of malabsorption in Crohn's disease is iatrogenic. Repeated resections of small intestine can lead to a 'short bowel syndrome' in which adequate nutrition can be maintained only by intravenous or intraperitoneal alimentation. Fistula formation is a frequent complication; deep penetration by ulcers produces fistulae between adherent loops of bowel and, particularly after surgical intervention, leads to enterocutaneous fistulae.

Approximately 60% of patients have anal lesions. These include simple skin 'tags', fissures, and fistulae into the anal canal or peri-anal skin. Acute complications such as perforation, haemorrhage and toxic dilatation do occur but are seen much less frequently seen in Crohn's disease than in ulcerative colitis. In the long term, there is an increased risk of malignancy, particularly in the small intestine, but the overall risk is less than in patients with ulcerative colitis because more people with Crohn's disease have the affected areas resected. Interestingly, there are reports of an increase in malignancy outside the digestive tract in patients with longstanding Crohn's disease. Systemic amyloidosis is a rare, long-term complication that results from excessive production of serum amyloid A protein (Ch. 7).

Ulcerative colitis

▶ Chronic relapsing inflammatory disorder, but may have an acute fulminating presentation
▶ Aetiology is unknown
▶ Affects only colon and rectum, sometimes confined to the latter
▶ Diffuse superficial inflammation
▶ Acute complications include toxic dilatation, perforation, haemorrhage and dehydration; the chronic complications are anaemia, liver disease and malignant change

In temperate climates ulcerative colitis is the commonest cause of diarrhoea associated with the passage of blood, mucus and pus. It is a non-specific inflammatory disorder of the large intestine, usually commencing in the rectum and extending proximally to a varying extent. Unlike Crohn's disease, ulcerative colitis is confined to the large intestine. Involvement of the terminal ileum in a so-called 'backwash ileitis' is occasionally seen, but this is thought to represent chronic inflammation provoked by incompetence of the ileocaecal valve, rather than an actual part of the disease.

Morphology

Ulcerative colitis is continuous in its distribution. Thus the disease, which is typically maximal in the rectum, extends proximally and continuously to involve the colon. Some cases are confined to the rectum (proctitis), others to the rectum and sigmoid (distal colitis), while others may exhibit a total colitis extending into the caecum. The disease does not involve the mucosa of the anal transitional zone or the anal canal, but a small proportion of patients do have anal tags and fissures.

The ulcers are irregular in outline and orientation and become confluent (Fig. 15.21); they extend horizontally to undermine adjacent, less involved, mucosa which remains as discrete islands. Usually the ulceration remains superficial (see Fig. 15.19), involving mucosa and submucosa, but in severe cases there is extension into the main muscle coats and perforation is likely. There is intense hyperaemia of the intact mucosa and haemorrhage from the ulcers.

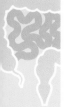

Fig. 15.21 Ulcerative colitis. The colonic mucosa is extensively ulcerated and haemorrhagic.

Table 15.6 Complications of ulcerative colitis	
Complication	Comment/example
Blood loss	May be acute (haemorrhage) or chronic, leading to anaemia
Electrolyte disturbances	Due to severe diarrhoea in acute phase
Toxic dilatation	May develop insidiously
Colorectal cancer	Overall incidence 2%
Skin involvement	Pigmentation, erythema nodosum, pyoderma gangrenosum
Liver involvement	Fatty change, chronic pericholangitis, sclerosing cholangitis, cirrhosis, hepatitis
Eye involvement	Iritis, uveitis, episcleritis
Joint involvement	Ankylosing spondylitis, arthritis

Microscopically, there is diffuse infiltration of the mucosa by mixed acute and chronic inflammatory cells. Polymorphs are seen in the interstitium, but are particularly evident as aggregates within distended crypts (crypt abscesses). There are widespread degenerative changes in surface and crypt lining epithelium, with marked depletion of their mucin content. Crypts undergo destruction during the acute phase, and when regeneration occurs they are frequently distorted by branching or dilatation. This disturbance of the crypt pattern is a useful diagnostic pointer in quiescent cases, when the inflammatory features may have totally subsided. Thus, in longstanding disease, rectal biopsy will reveal crypt atrophy and distortion, and there may be metaplastic features such as the acquisition of Paneth cells. Ulcerative colitis is a recognised premalignant condition, and a few cases will reveal epithelial dysplasia.

Complications

The complications of ulcerative colitis are summarised in Table 15.6.

Local complications

Haemorrhage is occasionally massive and life-threatening, but more often occurs as chronic blood loss leading to iron-deficiency anaemia. In the acute phase, severe diarrhoea with a markedly increased loss of water and mucus can lead to serious electrolyte disturbances. A further hazard of the acute phase is so-called toxic dilatation. Toxic dilatation occurs when ulceration affects large areas of the muscle coats and their viability and contractile strength are impaired. The resultant adynamic segment—commonly the transverse colon—becomes progressively distended, and the consequent thinning of the wall predisposes to perforation. Since there are few adhesions to localise its spread, perforation into the peritoneal cavity results in generalised faecal peritonitis and a fatal outcome is likely. Frequent radiographs should be taken in the seriously ill patient, as toxic dilatation may develop insidiously.

Systemic complications

Patients with ulcerative colitis are at risk of developing systemic problems (Table 15.6). These include:

- skin—*erythema nodosum* (subcutaneous inflammation) and *pyoderma gangrenosum* (sterile dermal abscesses)
- liver—*pericholangitis* (inflammation around bile ducts), *sclerosing cholangitis* (fibrous constriction and obliteration of bile ducts), *cholangiocarcinoma*, and *chronic active hepatitis*
- eyes—*iritis, uveitis* and *episcleritis*
- joints—increased incidence of *ankylosing spondylitis*.

Malignancy

The overall incidence of colorectal cancer in ulcerative colitis is low, around 2%, but this rises to about 10% in patients who have had the disease for 25 years. The increased risk over that for the general population warrants colonoscopic surveillance of longstanding cases. The clinical factors apparently associated with a higher cancer risk are:

- onset of the disease in childhood
- clinically severe first attack
- total involvement of the colon
- continuous rather than intermittent symptoms.

In practice, patients with extensive colitis of longer than 8–10 years' duration are usually admitted into surveillance programmes and undergo regular (usually annual) colonoscopy and multiple biopsy. If high-grade (severe) dysplasia is seen, then the development of carcinoma is considered imminent and total resection is warranted.

Pathogenesis of inflammatory bowel disease

▶ Genetically determined over-reaction by immune system to gut bacterial components
▶ Bacterial antigens gain access via increased mucosal permeability
▶ Failure to downregulate cytokine production
▶ Th1 type cell-mediated reaction in Crohn's disease; Th2 type cell-mediated reaction in ulcerative colitis
▶ Blocking of interleukins is leading to novel therapies

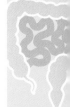

Epidemiological factors

The geographical incidence of IBD (Crohn's disease and ulcerative colitis) varies considerably. These diseases are much more common in northern Europe and the USA than in countries of southern Europe, Africa, South America and Asia, although increasing urbanisation and prosperity is leading to a higher incidence in parts of southern Europe and Japan. Even within Europe and the USA the incidence of Crohn's disease varies widely from around 4 up to 65 affected persons per 100 000 population. In northern Europe and the USA the incidence of ulcerative colitis varies between 12 and 140 per 100 000 population, but lower rates occur in underdeveloped countries with warmer climates. In low-incidence countries there may be diagnostic confusion with chronic infective colitis. The epidemiological data combined with twin studies and patterns within families indicate that IBD combines both genetic and environmental influences in its pathogenesis.

Environmental factors

The most clearly determined environmental influence on the susceptibility to IBD is that of cigarette smoking. Smokers have an increased risk of developing Crohn's disease, whereas they are apparently protected against ulcerative colitis. While this is an intriguing finding, it gives little clue to the aetiology of IBD. More interest has focused on infective agents.

Ever since a Scottish surgeon and farmer, Dr T Kennedy Dalziel, recognised the similarity between a mycobacterial infection—Johne's disease—affecting his pedigree cattle and (presumed) Crohn's disease affecting some of his patients, there has been varying interest in the role of *Mycobacterium paratuberculosis*. These mycobacteria can be frequently identified in milk samples destined for human consumption so infection is entirely possible, but tests for mycobacterial DNA by the polymerase chain reaction in affected tissues have produced conflicting results. Likewise, trials of anti-mycobacterial treatment in Crohn's disease have been equivocal. The case for *M. paratuberculosis* as an aetiological agent in Crohn's disease remains unproven. Even more controversial is the putative role of measles virus and the MMR (measles, mumps and rubella) vaccine in IBD; the majority view disputes this possibility.

The most compelling evidence for the involvement of microbial agents implicates the gut flora. Diversion of the faecal stream brings about improvement in segments affected by Crohn's disease; likewise antibiotic and probiotic treatment can lead to remissions in IBD, and animal models of colitis require the presence of gut flora for the disease to become manifest. Of itself, however, the composition of the flora cannot be the critical factor. Current interest is centred on the underlying genetic changes that determine how an individual reacts to the ingress of bacteria (or bacterial antigens) into the intestinal mucosa.

Genetic factors

The first breakthrough came in 1996: a gene conferring susceptibility to Crohn's disease (designated *IBD1*) was identified on chromosome 16 in families with multiple affected members. Five years later, the *IBD1* gene was identified as nucleotide oligomerisation domain (NOD)-2, and more recent studies have confirmed that *NOD2* mutations are associated with susceptibility to Crohn's disease but may protect against ulcerative colitis.

NOD2 is expressed in dendritic cells, macrophages and intestinal epithelial cells, but the greatest concentration is found in Paneth cells, where NOD2 is also an inducer of alpha-defensins. Thus, a mutation resulting in defective NOD2 activity could lead to an increase in bacterial density or a qualitative change in the gut flora consequent upon reduced alpha-defensin production. Furthermore, the *NOD2* gene has a leucine-rich domain at its C-terminal that is important for binding a dipeptide derived from the breakdown of bacterial peptidoglycans by mucosal dendritic cells. This dipeptide binding activates NOD2 and initiates a mechanism leading to inhibition of nuclear factor kappa B, a key transcription factor in pro-inflammatory responses. In normal dendritic cells, therefore, NOD2 activation down-modulates cytokine production resulting from exposure to bacterial components.

More recently, studies in patients with Crohn's disease have revealed further relevant loci related to genes that control IL-23 production and genes involved in autophagy that could influence antigen delivery to immune cells, and in the generation of free radicals essential for effective bacterial killing.

Immunopathology

Inappropriate and persistent T-cell activation may be the basis of both ulcerative colitis and Crohn's disease. Under normal circumstances the mucosal immune system is tolerant of luminal bacterial antigens, and this tolerance is dependent upon the relationship between intestinal epithelium and suppressor T-cells. Classically, antigen handling is attributed to M-cells over the mucosal lymphoid follicles, but direct luminal antigen sampling by dendritic cell processes extending through intact surface epithelium is another possibility. Increased mucosal permeability to antigens in IBD is more likely to be a consequence of the inflammatory response rather than the initiating event, and the cytokine TNF-alpha has been implicated through its action on epithelial tight junctions. In ulcerative colitis, increased permeability and ingress of bacterial antigens may lead to immune complex phenomena and some of the extra-intestinal complications.

In IBD, one or more genetically determined defects result in a mucosal immune system that overreacts to normal constituents of the gut flora. Despite this common basis, Crohn's disease and ulcerative colitis are immunologically distinct entities. Crohn's disease is associated with a Th1 cell-mediated response characterised by elevated production of interferon-gamma and TNF-alpha. The Th1 response is governed by the interleukins (IL)-12 and, to a lesser degree, by IL-23. The prominence of IL-12 in the induction of a Th1 response has an important bearing on the role of *NOD2* gene mutations in Crohn's disease. IL-12 production is a consequence of the activation of nuclear factor kappa B that follows stimulation of so-called Toll-like receptors on the surface of dendritic cells by bacterial peptidoglycans. We have seen (above) that NOD2 activation is necessary for the negative regulation of nuclear factor kappa B. Thus, enhanced IL-12 production and Th1 cell activation in Crohn's disease may be due to a failure of mutated NOD2 to downregulate Toll-like receptor signalling.

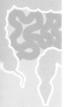

Although helper T-cells isolated from the colonic mucosa of ulcerative colitis patients produce interferon-gamma, they produce much more IL-5 than patients with Crohn's disease, suggesting that a Th2 response is of more importance in ulcerative colitis. Other cytokines characteristic of the Th2 response are increased in ulcerative colitis, including IL-13. Indeed, IL-13 produced by natural killer T-cells is thought to be central to the immunopathology of ulcerative colitis; IL-13 impairs intestinal barrier function by affecting tight junctions, increasing epithelial apoptosis and slowing epithelial restitution.

Despite these two distinctive patterns of response, it is acknowledged that the Th1 and Th2 routes converge into a common pathway of tissue injury. Mucosal damage in IBD is now accepted to occur as a result of sustained interactions between immune and non-immune cells. For example, in both diseases, IL-1-beta and TNF-alpha enhance the expression of adhesion molecules on vascular endothelium and increase chemokine production, thereby attracting blood-borne inflammatory cells into the tissues. These cytokines also stimulate mucosal myofibroblasts to synthesise matrix-degrading enzymes that contribute to mucosal damage. Pro-inflammatory responses in myofibroblasts are also induced by IL-22, a cytokine produced in excess by helper T-cells in active IBD. The similarity of the consequent events in Crohn's disease and ulcerative colitis explains the response of both diseases to certain therapies—e.g. corticosteroids and immunosuppressants—but more success is likely to be achieved by agents aimed at specific immunological targets. Already, blockade of IL-12 has been shown to be effective in Crohn's disease, while strategies to block IL-13 in ulcerative colitis are a challenge for the future.

VASCULAR DISORDERS

Ischaemic injury to the intestine occurs either as a consequence of obstruction to the mesenteric arterial supply (*occlusive ischaemia*) or in circumstances where, despite patency of the vessels, the blood supply falls to a level at which the nutrition of mucosa cannot be maintained (*non-occlusive ischaemia*). Thus, in the territory supplied by the superior mesenteric artery, occlusive ischaemia results either from embolism originating from atrial or ventricular mural thrombosis (about 50% of cases) or from thrombosis, usually on the basis of atherosclerosis (in about 25%). Non-occlusive ischaemia is a consequence of systemic hypotension, vasoconstriction, viscosity disturbances, arterial narrowing and certain drugs, such as digitalis and cocaine (in about 20%).

An uncommon cause of acute intestinal ischaemia (less than 5%) is mesenteric venous thrombosis which, by preventing outflow of blood, causes infarction by intense congestion. Predisposing factors include hypercoagulability states, portal hypertension, intra-abdominal inflammation and previous surgery or abdominal trauma.

Pathogenesis

Total vascular occlusion results in segmental anoxic or hypoxic injury, the extent depending on the adequacy of the collateral supply; cell death appears to ensue from a lethal ingress of calcium ions through the damaged plasma membrane. However,

much of the mucosal injury in non-occlusive ischaemia develops after the period of hypoperfusion, i.e. when normal perfusion and oxygenation have been restored. This is an example of a 'reperfusion injury' of the kind seen after myocardial and cerebral ischaemia and following iatrogenic ischaemia, as occurs during aortic aneurysm repair or in organ transplantation. Reperfusion injuries are mediated by free radical formation (Ch. 6), TNF-alpha and arachidonic acid metabolites; these are responsible for the membrane injuries that bring about mucosal disintegration in the reperfusion phase.

Acute ischaemia

Acute mesenteric ischaemia is a life-threatening emergency with mortality rates between 60% and 100%. Sudden ischaemia results in varying degrees of infarction of the bowel wall. Such infarcts can be classified, according to the depth of involvement, as mucosal, mural or transmural (Fig. 15.22).

Mucosal infarction
Mucosal infarction is usually considered transient or reversible because the lesion can be followed by complete regeneration. However, mucosal damage leads to release of chemokines that cause an influx of polymorphs and their adhesion to

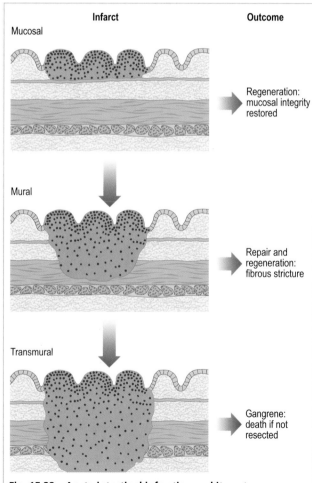

Fig. 15.22   Acute intestinal infarction and its outcome.

vascular endothelium coupled with platelet aggregation further compromise the microcirculation. Furthermore, the 'leaky' mucosa allows potentially toxic agents to enter the circulation; this can bring about further systemic cardiovascular deterioration ('shock') and gradual progression of the intestinal lesion to transmural infarction.

Mural infarction

Mural infarction reaches into the submucosa or into, but not through, the muscularis propria. The mucosa is variably ulcerated and, where intact, is haemorrhagic and elevated by marked submucosal oedema. As with mucosal infarction, this stage can progress to full-thickness infarction. The deeper extent of necrosis with involvement of connective tissues necessitates healing by granulation tissue formation and a more prolonged process of repair. If the patient recovers, this is likely to lead to fibrous stricture formation.

Transmural infarction

Transmural infarction of the intestine is the most common consequence of acute ischaemia. The infarct extends through the muscularis propria to the serosa, and is synonymous with gangrene (death of tissue together with bacterial infection). The bowel becomes flaccid and dilates, and the serosal aspect is deeply congested and coated in a thin layer of fibrin. The wall becomes friable and liable to perforation. The infarct is usually widespread, affecting several loops of small intestine, but can be segmental. Segmental infarction results either from occlusion of distal mesenteric vessels, or by mechanical obstruction of the supply to a loop of intestine. This type of involvement is amenable to surgical treatment, but many patients already have peritonitis, endotoxaemia and severe circulatory problems at the time of diagnosis, so operative results remain poor. Massive infarction, most commonly seen in the small intestine following complete occlusion of the superior mesenteric artery, has a hopeless prognosis.

Chronic ischaemia

Chronic ischaemia leads to two main problems:

- fibrous stricture formation following segmental mural infarction
- chronic mesenteric insufficiency.

Strictures are encountered most often in the large intestine, particularly in the 'watershed' area around the splenic flexure of the colon. The patients generally present with the consequences of large bowel obstruction. Chronic mesenteric insufficiency is used to describe a condition in which there is insufficient blood flow to the small intestine to satisfy the demands of increased motility, secretion and absorption that develop after meals. The insufficiency is usually manifest as pain (so-called 'mesenteric angina'), but patients may also have diarrhoea and malabsorption.

Necrotising enterocolitis

Necrotising enterocolitis (NEC) is an uncommon condition arising from a combination of ischaemia and infection. NEC is the most serious acquired gastrointestinal disease in the newborn, accounting for 1–3% of neonatal intensive care unit admissions. It carries a high risk of death with mortality rates between 20% and 50%. The disease manifests as abdominal distension and bloody stools with respiratory and circulatory disturbances. No single bacterial pathogen has been consistently identified, but organisms are frequently isolated and include *E. coli*, *Klebsiella*, *C. difficile* and *Clostridium perfrigens*. Prematurity is the only consistent risk factor; an immature mucosal barrier coupled with an impaired humoral (secretory IgA) and cellular immune response to bacteria are the suggested mechanisms. A substantially higher incidence of NEC has been found in formula-fed infants compared with exclusively breast-fed babies, suggesting that the former lack a degree of immunoprotection.

The disease can also (rarely) affect adults where it is caused by infection with *Clostridium perfringens* Type C, which produces a powerful beta-toxin. A peculiar form of NEC was that found among natives of Papua New Guinea after ceremonial feasting on huge quantities of sweet potato and inadequately cooked pork, including pig intestines. This condition was referred to as 'pigbel', pidgin English for abdominal pain after eating pig!

Adults with NEC present with severe abdominal pain and diarrhoea. Paralytic ileus develops and progresses to intestinal infarction, sepsis and shock. The appearances are typically those of gas gangrene, with either segmental or total involvement of the small and large intestines by coagulative necrosis and intramural gas bubble formation.

Vascular anomalies

Vascular anomalies in the gut are uncommon but enter into the differential diagnosis of gastrointestinal haemorrhage. Their classification is confused; some are congenital malformations that form part of recognised syndromes, while other, possibly identical, lesions are claimed to be acquired. Congenital types include arteriovenous malformations and telangiectasias; acquired forms are usually termed angiodysplasias. *Angiodysplasia* of the colon is an occasional cause of blood loss from the large bowel. This condition is more common in the elderly and can be diagnosed by mesenteric angiography.

DISORDERS RESULTING FROM ABNORMAL GUT MOTILITY

Diverticular disease

Diverticula are herniations of mucosa into the intestinal wall. The herniations are of the pulsion type and form at sites of potential weakness, notably where lymphoid aggregates breach the muscularis mucosae. They extend through the muscularis propria at the point of entry or exit of blood vessels and bulge into the subserosa.

Diverticula can be found anywhere in the intestinal tract, but the colon, and particularly the sigmoid, is by far the commonest site (Fig. 15.23). Most diverticula occur between the mesenteric and anti-mesenteric longitudinal muscle bands—the taenia coli. The affected segment of colon shows

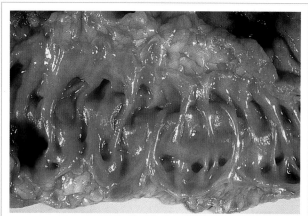

Fig. 15.23   Diverticulosis of the sigmoid colon. The mucosal surface is ridged due to hypertrophy of the underlying muscle. The openings of the diverticula can be seen between the mucosal ridges.

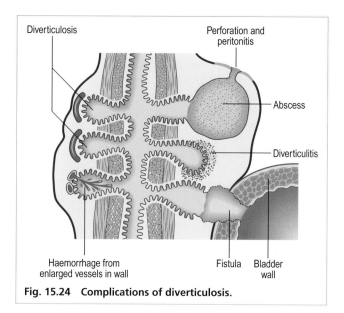

Fig. 15.24   Complications of diverticulosis.

thickening of the muscularis propria, and prominence of the mucosal folds so that they almost occlude the lumen and have a 'concertina-like' appearance. The disease is generally acknowledged to result from a deficiency of fibre in the diet. Sigmoid motility is peculiarly sensitive to the bulk of the colonic contents and when this is low, as with a low-fibre diet, abnormally high intra-luminal pressures are generated which push the mucosa into the wall.

Complications

Diverticular disease presents as abdominal pain and altered bowel habit, but it is also prone to develop some serious complications, the most common being *diverticulitis* (Fig. 15.24) The faecal contents can lead to abrasion of the herniated mucosa, or a microscopic perforation in the apex of a diverticulum can occur, which allows infection by faecal organisms and the development of a suppurative diverticulitis. This in turn can cause a peri-colic abscess and a *fistula* may form into the bladder, vagina or small intestine; more seriously, a peri-diverticular abscess may perforate and produce a generalised faecal peritonitis.

Diverticula can be the source of *haemorrhage* from the colon. This usually arises from areas of granulation tissue in an inflamed diverticulum, but the precise source is sometimes difficult to identify.

Intussusception

An intussusception is an invagination of one segment of bowel into another, thus causing intestinal obstruction. A lesion in the wall of the bowel disturbs normal peristaltic contractions, forcing the lesion and a segment of proximal bowel into a distal segment. Several lesions can act as the apex of an intussusception, including polyps, ingested foreign bodies, a Meckel's diverticulum, an area of intramural haemorrhage (e.g. in Henoch–Schönlein purpura; Ch. 23) and lymphoid hyperplasia. Such hyperplasia close to the ileo-caecal valve is the cause of the ileo-colic intussusception, the most common form of this disorder.

Volvulus and strangulation

Intestinal obstruction can result from a twist in the bowel that occludes its lumen (*volvulus*) or when a segment of bowel becomes trapped in a defect in either the posterior peritoneum or mesentery (internal herniation), or herniates into an inguinal or para-umbilical peritoneal sac. The neck of the sac may then constrict the bowel and compromise its blood supply (*strangulation*). Volvulus occurs around a 'fulcrum' such as a Meckel's diverticulum or a congenital band of fibrous tissue, or around an abnormally long mesentery. About two-thirds of cases affect the small intestine; most of the remaining one-third affect the sigmoid colon.

TUMOURS OF THE INTESTINE

Paradoxically, the small intestine, with its vast surface area and a cell turnover rate higher than that of any other tissue in the body, is an uncommon site for primary neoplasms. Adenomas and adenocarcinomas are distinctly rare in the small intestine, yet the much shorter large bowel is a very common site of neoplasia. The low incidence of carcinoma means that other neoplasms, such as neuroendocrine cell tumours and lymphomas, assume more importance in the small intestine where they are relatively more common than in the large bowel.

Polyps

A polyp is simply a protuberant growth and there is thus a wide variety of histological types. These can be broadly divided into *epithelial* and *mesenchymal* polyps (of which the latter are distinctly uncommon), and into benign and malignant categories (Table 15.7). Even epithelial polyps are rare in the small intestine and some, such as metaplastic polyps, are confined to the large bowel. Thus, the following account is confined to large-intestinal polyps.

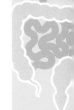

Table 15.7 Polyps of the large intestine		
Type of polyp	Benign	Malignant
Epithelial	Neoplastic • adenoma	Polypoid adenocarcinomas
	Inflammatory (e.g. in inflammatory bowel disease)	Carcinoid polyps
	Hamartomatous • juvenile polyp • Peutz–Jeghers syndrome	
	Metaplastic (or hyperplastic)	
Mesenchymal	Lipoma	Sarcomas
	Lymphangioma	Lymphomatous polyps
	Haemangiomas	
	Fibromas	
	Leiomyoma	

Benign epithelial polyps

Benign epithelial polyps fall into four categories: adenomas, and inflammatory, hamartomatous and metaplastic polyps.

Adenomas

Adenomas are very common; there is an increased incidence with age so that at 60 years they are found in about 20% of the population. There are two main histological types—*tubular* (75%) and *villous* (10%); the remaining 15% are intermediate in pattern and are designated *tubulo-villous*.

Tubular adenomas are generally small (usually less than 10 mm in diameter), and macroscopically resemble a raspberry. Most have a stalk (pedunculated) and a minority have a broad base (sessile). Microscopically, they consist of numerous cross-sectioned crypt profiles lined by mucus-secreting epithelium showing varying degrees of dysplasia.

Villous adenomas are usually sessile; they are often over 20 mm in diameter and some extend over a wide area as a thick, carpet-like growth. Microscopically, they consist of elongated villi in a papillary growth pattern; the villi are again lined by columnar epithelium showing dysplasia. Large adenomas may secrete copious electrolyte-rich mucus, leading in rare instances to hypokalaemia and acute renal failure, but their real importance lies in their propensity for malignant change.

However, not all adenomas are polypoid. *Non-polypoid* ('flat') *adenomas* are defined as adenomas whose height is less than twice the thickness of the adjacent normal mucosa, and are increasingly recognised as an alternative source of colorectal carcinomas.

Inflammatory polyps

These usually arise in the context of inflammatory bowel disease, and represent excessive reparative and regenerative tissue formed in the aftermath of mucosal ulceration. In most cases there is a preponderance of granulation or mature fibrovascular tissue, so their categorisation as epithelial is somewhat debatable.

Hamartomatous polyps

These rare polyps may be solitary, like the majority of so-called 'juvenile' polyps, or be multiple and occur throughout the gastrointestinal tract, as in *Peutz–Jeghers syndrome*. These multiple polyp syndromes carry a substantial risk of malignancy.

Metaplastic (or hyperplastic) polyps

These polyps are of unknown histogenesis, but the surface cells are hypermature compared to normal epithelium. They are common lesions, being found with increasing age, and are most frequently situated in the rectum. Microscopically they are sessile with elongated crypts, but the majority show no dysplasia. Their characteristic feature is the 'serrated' appearance of the cells lining the upper crypt and at the surface. In contrast to adenomas, these polyps have little or no malignant potential.

There is a category of polyp, however, that has appearances intermediate between metaplastic polyp and adenoma and is termed a 'serrated adenoma'. Although of low malignant potential, such polyps exhibit a distinct pathway of genetic changes leading to adenocarcinoma.

Malignant epithelial polyps

Examples of malignant epithelial polyps are polypoid carcinomas and 'carcinoid' polyps. Some adenocarcinomas develop as protuberant growths and appear endoscopically as polyps, hence the term 'polypoid carcinoma'. The vast majority of adenocarcinomas, however, arise within pre-existing adenomas (polypoid or 'flat') and these constitute the bulk of 'malignant polyps'. A very small minority of polyps are neoplasms derived from neuroendocrine cells (see p. 396); such carcinoid polyps have a low malignant potential and only give rise to metastases late in their course. Thus, complete local removal is usually curative.

Benign mesenchymal polyps

Mesenchymal polyps are uncommon. The benign forms are lipomas, haemangiomas, lymphangiomas and fibromas. Stromal tumours (GIST) are less likely to present as polyps, and are of uncertain malignant potential.

Malignant mesenchymal polyps

Malignant varieties include the sarcomas equivalent to the benign tumours, and malignant lymphomatous polyps.

The adenoma–carcinoma sequence

Adenomas are probably the precursors of most, if not all, colorectal cancers. Evidence in favour of a link comes from a number of sources, but the strongest is the hereditary condition of *familial adenomatous polyposis* (FAP). FAP is a rare autosomal disease carried by either parent and transmitted as a Mendelian dominant. Both sexes are equally affected. Adenomas, mainly in the large intestine (Fig. 15.25) but also in the small bowel, develop during the second and third decades and subsequently undergo malignant change, with an almost inevitable progression to adenocarcinoma by the age of 35 years. The gene responsible for FAP is on the long arm of chromosome 5; interestingly, a somatic mutation

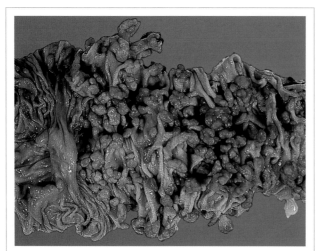

Fig. 15.25 Familial adenomatous polyposis. The colonic mucosa is studded with numerous adenomatous polyps. These are premalignant.

has been identified on chromosome 5 in cases of sporadic (non-inherited) colorectal cancer (see below).

Histologically, the finding of residual adenomatous tissue in some cancers, and the observation of early invasive malignancy developing in adenomas, is further evidence supporting the adenoma–carcinoma sequence. Examination of adenomas showing early malignancy has demonstrated an association with increasing size, villous growth pattern and more severe dysplasia, although non-polypoid (flat) adenomas frequently show high-grade dysplasia in spite of their small size. Adenomas and carcinomas are frequently found together in a resected segment of bowel. Such patients have an increased risk of developing a second cancer in the remaining large intestine, compared with patients having carcinoma alone.

Recently, genome-wide scans have revealed a colorectal cancer susceptibility locus on chromosome 8q24 that is common to some sporadic adenomas, providing genetic evidence of the link and indicating that the locus is involved in tumour initiation rather than progression.

Molecular pathology of the adenoma–carcinoma sequence

In no other tumour system are the genetic events underlying the development of carcinoma as clearly understood as they are in colorectal cancer. In recent years, however, it has become increasingly clear that acquired epigenetic changes are of major importance. The genetic/epigenetic abnormalities are:

- activation of oncogenes
- loss or mutations of tumour suppressor genes
- defective genes of the DNA repair pathway leading to genomic instability.

Activation of oncogenes
The oncogenes most frequently altered in colorectal cancer are c-Ki-*ras* and c-*myc*. Point mutations in Ki-*ras* mean that the protein can no longer hydrolyse bound GTP to GDP.

Persistence of GTP-ras, the active form of the protein, results in continual signalling of cell division. Overexpression of c-*myc* is a feature of most colorectal cancers; c-*myc* encodes a nuclear phosphoprotein that is required for DNA synthesis, and increased expression may well be followed by increased cellular proliferation. While mutations are a proven cause of activation of oncogenes, they are not necessarily the main mechanism. Epigenetic change in DNA methylation is likely to be the key event; in particular, age-related DNA hypomethylation may contribute to oncogene activation.

Loss or mutations of tumour suppressor genes
Tumour suppressor genes appear to be very important in colorectal carcinoma. FAP results from point mutations in a tumour suppressor gene, the *APC* (adenomatous polyposis coli) gene on chromosome 5q, and subsequent deletion of the accompanying normal allele results in the loss of tumour suppressor function that leads to colorectal cancer. Mutations and deletions of the *APC* gene, and of other tumour suppressor genes, have also been identified in sporadic (i.e. non-hereditary) colorectal cancer. Other genes implicated are *MCC* (mutated in colorectal cancer) whose gene product is involved in cell cycle control, *DCC* (deleted in colorectal cancer) involved in the control of apoptosis, and *TP53*. The *TP53* gene product (p53) is a nuclear protein that can hold the cell cycle at the G_1/S checkpoint and allow time for successful DNA repair, or initiate apoptosis if the DNA damage is irreparable. Finally, deletions affecting the *nm23* gene may facilitate metastasis.

Just as with oncogene activation, mutations are not the only mechanism leading to loss of function of tumour suppressor genes. Hypermethylation of CpG dinucleotides (cytosine and guanine linked by a phosphodiester bond) has been incriminated. CpG islands—DNA segments with increased concentration of this dinucleotide—are found at transcriptional start sites and close to promoter regions, and hypermethylation has been linked to the transcriptional silencing of tumour suppressor genes. Interestingly, CpG island hypermethylation is found in about a third of metaplastic polyps; it is likely that these are the polyps with malignant potential.

Defects in DNA repair
Mutation or loss of function of the *TP53* gene is not the only way in which DNA repair can be compromised. Highly conserved genes have been discovered that recognise mismatched nucleotides in complementary DNA strands and orchestrate the enzymes that effect repairs. Defects in these genes and the ensuing replication errors are manifest as microsatellite instability. Alterations in two mismatch repair genes, *hMLH1* and *hMSH2*, have been identified in most kindreds with hereditary non-polyposis colorectal cancer (HNPCC, Lynch syndrome). Similar alterations in these and other 'housekeeper' genes are found in sporadic cancers, with around 15% of cases showing high microsatellite instability.

The sequence of these genetic events in causing colorectal cancer is not as critical as the overall accumulation of changes, but the different prevalences of mutations and deletions between adenomas and invasive carcinoma do suggest that there is a preferred order (Fig. 15.26).

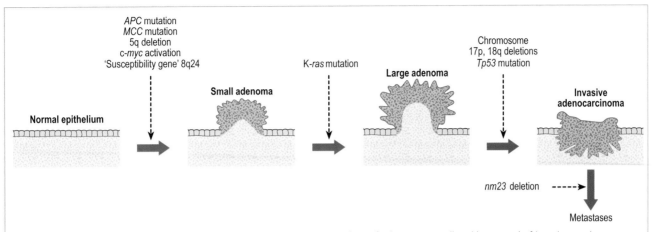

Fig. 15.26 Molecular genetics of adenoma–carcinoma sequence. Analysis of adenomas, small and large, and of invasive carcinomas and their metastases reveals a cascade of gene mutations, deletions and activations corresponding to the altered behaviour of the tumour cells. However, epigenetic changes are also of critical importance.

Colorectal cancer

▶ Common malignancy in developed countries
▶ All are adenocarcinomas
▶ Increased risk in patients with adenomatous polyps and longstanding ulcerative colitis
▶ Dukes' staging, based on local extent and metastatic status, is the best guide to prognosis

Cancer of the colon and rectum is one of the commonest forms of malignancy in developed countries. For example, it accounts for about 10% of all cancer registrations in the UK, where the death rate is second only to that of lung cancer, with gastric cancer a close third. The incidence appears to be rising.

Aetiology
Apart from the role played by inherited genetic factors, and a few cases developing in the unstable mucosa of ulcerative colitis, the most important factor in the aetiology of colorectal cancer appears to be environmental. Epidemiological evidence indicates that this is dietary. Diet affects the bacterial flora of the large bowel, the bowel transit time, and the amount of cellulose, amino acids and bile acids in the bowel contents. Some types of bacteria, the nuclear dehydrogenating clostridia (NDC), can act on bile acids to produce carcinogens. Similarly, bacterial transformation of amino acids may result in carcinogen (or co-carcinogen) production. On the other hand, a high content of fermentable cellulose leads to high levels of volatile fatty acids which appear to be 'protective' in that they provide nutrition and aid maturation of the epithelial cells. Thus, the type of diet that has been linked to colorectal cancer is a high-fat, high-protein, low-fibre diet. High fat leads to an increase in bile salt production and higher load of faecal bile acids to react with NDC; high protein favours the transformation of amino acids by bacteria; low fibre reduces volatile fatty acids and prolongs intestinal transit so that there is more time for bacterial action on the contents and more prolonged contact between any carcinogen generated and the mucosa. These factors, more than anything else, account for the high incidence of colorectal cancer in developed countries.

Clinicopathological features
Approximately 50% of cancers occur in the rectum, where they are equally divided between the upper, middle and lower thirds; about 30% occur in the sigmoid colon and the rest are equally distributed in the ascending, transverse and descending colon. This anatomical distribution is of practical importance, as about 50% of large bowel cancers can be reached with the examining finger and 80% with the sigmoidoscope.

In the rectum, the majority of cancers are of the ulcerating type (Fig. 15.27) and usually present with rectal bleeding. The stenosing type is more common in the descending colon and sigmoid, where it usually produces obstruction relatively early because of the narrowing of the lumen and the solid consistency of the faeces at this site. Polypoid and larger fungating cancers are more common in the right colon, where they tend to give rise to recurrent occult bleeding and the patient develops iron-deficiency anaemia. By virtue of the fluid bowel contents and the greater distensibility of the caecum and ascending colon, these tumours are more likely to be advanced at the time of presentation.

Microscopically the cancers are adenocarcinomas, showing varying degrees of mucin production and glandular differentiation. These histological features are of little or no value in patient management, however, and the role of the pathologist after cancer surgery is to determine the completeness of excision and the extent of spread. If microscopic examination of the resection margins (especially the circumferential margin) establishes that all the tumour has been removed and the operation has been potentially curative, then the extent of spread through the bowel wall and the presence of lymph node metastases are the major prognostic determinants. The extent of spread is given by the Dukes' and/or TNM stage (Fig. 15.28). Unfortunately, only about 70% of patients with colorectal cancer undergo a potentially curative operation; in about 15–25% of patients only a palliative operation is possible because they have

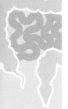

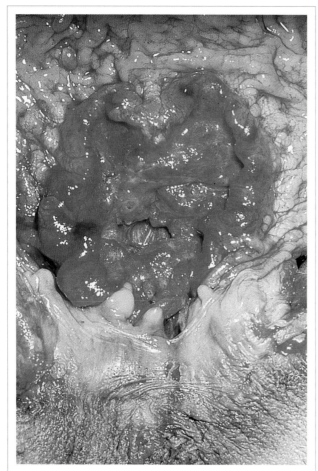

Fig. 15.27 Carcinoma of the rectum. Ulcerated carcinoma arising in the lower rectum close to and invading the anal canal.

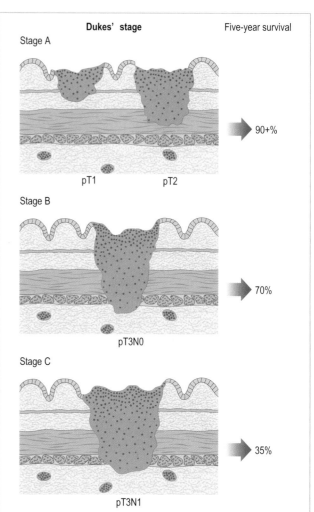

Fig. 15.28 The spread of colorectal cancer; Dukes' stage and equivalent TNM stage, together with average 5-year survival. *Dukes' A:* The tumour is confined to the submucosa (pT1) or muscle layer (pT2). *Dukes' B:* The tumour has spread through the muscle layer, but does not yet involve the lymph nodes (pT3 N0). *Dukes' C:* Any tumour involving lymph nodes irrespective of extent of direct spread. Here, spread has progressed through the main muscle coats into the subserosa and involves local lymph nodes (pT3 N1) but has not breached the peritoneal surface or invaded an adjacent organ (pT4).

widespread peritoneal deposits or liver secondaries, and the remainder are totally inoperable. However, with pre-operative radiotherapy the proportion of potentially curative operations is set to increase, and patients formerly considered inoperable because of liver metastases are now undergoing partial liver resections. Overall, the outlook for patients with colorectal cancer has improved remarkably in recent years.

Neuroendocrine tumours

Neuroendocrine tumours of the gastrointestinal tract are widely known as *carcinoid tumours* but, as they originate from the diffuse neuroendocrine system, they are better termed neuroendocrine tumours. Basically, there are two microscopic types. Some are composed of solid nests of regular cells with lightly staining nuclei and express immunochemical neuroendocrine markers; this is the typical carcinoid pattern. The second type, rare in the gastrointestinal tract, is an undifferentiated small- or large-cell tumour indistinguishable from their counterparts in the lung (Ch. 14) and more explicitly termed a *neuroendocrine carcinoma*. Both types occur as rare neuroendocrine tumours of the oesophagus where the undifferentiated types have to be distinguished from direct involvement by a primary lung tumour.

Gastric neuroendocrine tumours are relatively frequent, comprising up to 30% of all gastrointestinal neuroendocrine tumours. Two forms are encountered. More common are multiple small polypoid tumours found in association with autoimmune chronic gastritis. A second form is a solitary and, usually, larger polyp which is a sporadic finding with no associated disease. In the former, the glandular atrophy leads to achlorhydria which stimulates antral G-cells to produce gastrin. Persistent hypergastrinaemia leads to hyperplasia of the ECL cells (see p. 366) in the body of the stomach from which, after a latent period of many years, multiple tumours arise. This clinicopathological distinction is important in terms of behaviour. Neuroendocrine tumours associated with autoimmune gastritis do not metastasise and can be considered benign; thus, only the larger polyps need to be removed.

In contrast, the sporadic tumours carry a definite risk of metastasis and require complete removal whatever their size.

Most duodenal neuroendocrine tumours are *gastrinomas*, i.e. gastrin-producing tumours, and are associated with the Zollinger–Ellison syndrome, but they can also be somatostatinomas, calcitonin-producing tumour, non-functioning or poorly differentiated neuroendocrine carcinomas.

Neuroendocrine tumours of the distal jejunum and ileum account for about 25% of these lesions. They are often over 20 mm in diameter and have frequently spread to the mesenteric lymph nodes at the time of diagnosis. Indeed, about 20% of patients will have liver metastases at presentation. These tumours contain serotonin (5-hydoxytrytamine; 5-HT), substance P, kallikrein and catecholamines. 5-HT released by the tumour exerts local effects on the intestine but is inactivated in the liver by monoamine oxidases to form 5-hydroxyindole acetic acid (5-HIAA); this is excreted in the urine. The local effects are diarrhoea and borborygmi (excessive bowel sounds) because 5-HT stimulates intestinal contractility. Once metastases have formed in the liver, the tumour products (5-HT and kinins) are released directly into the hepatic veins and can affect the right side of the heart and the lungs before oxidation takes place in the pulmonary vasculature; this results in the *carcinoid syndrome*. The patient develops cyanotic flushing of the face, and there can be stenosis or incompetence of the pulmonary and tricuspid valves. The heart shows smooth muscle proliferation within the endocardium; this may result from bradykinin stimulation of mesenchymal cells which undergo differentiation to muscle cells. The spread of mid-gut neuroendocrine tumours and their effects are summarised in Figure 15.29.

Neuroendocrine tumours in the appendix are generally small (less than 20 mm in diameter), situated at or near the tip, and are discovered incidentally in specimens removed for abdominal pain. Such small tumours can be considered benign, and no further treatment is necessary. Larger tumours do occasionally metastasise and post-appendicectomy investigation and follow-up is advisable for tumours over 20 mm in diameter.

Colonic neuroendocrine tumours are rare but those in the rectum account for up to 20% of these gastrointestinal lesions. Histologically, colonic neuroendocrine tumours are usually poorly differentiated neuroendocrine carcinomas that have often metastasised at the time of diagnosis. The more common rectal neuroendocrine tumours are usually small and found incidentally at endoscopy. Histologically, they have a typical carcinoid appearance and a generally benign nature; metastases occur only when they are over 20 mm in diameter or have extended into the main muscle coat.

Lymphomas

Lymphomas are the commonest malignant tumours in the small intestine but are rare in the large bowel. Mention has already been made of the development of malignant lymphoma in coeliac disease—enteropathy-associated T-cell lymphoma—but this accounts for only a small proportion of the total; the majority of cases in developed countries have no predisposing cause. In the Middle East and South Africa, however, lymphoma of the small intestine frequently follows

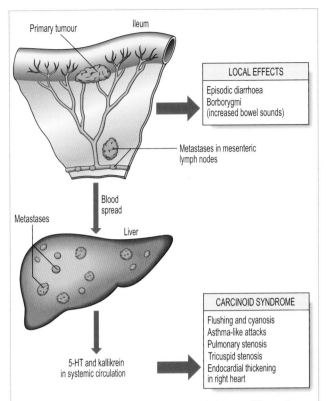

Fig. 15.29 Neuroendocrine tumours of the small intestine and their effects. See text for details.

alpha heavy chain disease, a condition in which there is initially a benign proliferation of plasma cells secreting incomplete immunoglobulins.

In Western countries, non-enteropathy-associated lymphomas account for 60–80% of intestinal lymphomas and are most commonly of diffuse large B-cell type. They appear as plaques or polypoid masses that may be multiple, and give rise to abdominal pain, obstruction (either directly or by intussusception) and anaemia through intestinal blood loss. Other specific types are Burkitt's lymphoma, mantle-cell lymphoma and follicle-centre lymphoma but these are all rare.

APPENDIX

The appendix can be the site for neuroendocrine (carcinoid) tumours, adenocarcinomas and lymphomas, but these are rare compared with the frequency of non-specific suppurative inflammation.

APPENDICITIS

- ▶ Common cause of the 'acute abdomen'
- ▶ Inflammation often precipitated by obstruction due to faecolith, lymphoid hyperplasia or tumour
- ▶ Complications include peritonitis, portal pyaemia and hepatic abscesses

Aetiology

Several factors are claimed to predispose to acute inflammation of the appendix, including faecoliths (hard pellets of faeces arising from dehydration and compaction) and food residues, lymphoid hyperplasia (as occurs in childhood and with some viral infections), diverticulosis of the appendix, and the presence of a carcinoid tumour.

Specific inflammations can also affect the appendix, and very occasional cases are due to *Yersinia pseudotuberculosis*, typhoid, tuberculosis and actinomycosis. The appendix is also involved by ulcerative colitis and Crohn's disease.

Pathogenesis

Acute inflammation commences in the mucosa following a breach in the epithelium that permits infection by bowel flora. Infection leads to mucosal ulceration and a polymorph response, with exudation of cells and fibrin into the lumen. Further spread involves all the layers of the appendix and eventually causes a peritonitis over the serosal aspect. The build-up of fluid exudate within the wall increases tissue pressure and this, together with toxic damage to blood vessels and subsequent thrombosis, can lead to superimposed ischaemia. In this way the distal part of the appendix can become gangrenous and perforate.

Complications

Complications of acute appendicitis include those arising from perforation, such as generalised peritonitis, abscess and fistula formation, and the consequences of blood spread, suppurative pyelophlebitis (inflammation and thrombosis of the portal vein), liver abscess and septicaemia. The inflammation may become chronic, or obstruction to the neck of the appendix may lead to mucus retention in its lumen causing a *mucocele*. This does not often give rise to clinical problems but, on rare occasions, may rupture and disseminate mucus-secreting epithelial cells into the peritoneal cavity—pseudomyxoma peritonei.

ANUS AND ANAL CANAL

NORMAL STRUCTURE AND FUNCTION

The anal canal begins at the upper border of the internal sphincter at the level of the insertion of the puborectalis portion of levator ani (the so-called anorectal ring), and extends down to the groove between the terminal ends of the internal and external sphincters. It is 30–40 mm long.

Histologically, the upper part of the canal is lined by rectal-type glandular mucosa, the lower part by non-keratinising squamous epithelium. The upper end of the squamous portion is clearly delineated by the pectinate (or dentate) line. Proximal to this is a narrow zone of 'transitional' mucosa, consisting of columnar epithelium with multilayered small basal cells, which merges with the rectal-type mucosa of the upper segment.

The sensory nerves of the anal canal and the muscle sphincters are of vital importance in the control of defecation.

DISEASES OF THE ANUS AND ANAL CANAL

Fissures, fistulae and abscesses are common anal conditions that arise either in isolation or as part of Crohn's disease. Anorectal tuberculosis is very rare in the UK, but is common in countries with a high incidence of pulmonary tuberculosis. Lesions of syphilis and other sexually transmitted diseases may occur at the anus.

Haemorrhoids ('piles')

Haemorrhoids are varicosities resulting from dilatation of the internal haemorrhoidal venous plexus. The mechanisms involved in their formation are not clearly understood, although chronic constipation with straining at stool is most commonly invoked. As such they are largely a consequence of the low-residue 'Western' diet and are relatively uncommon in developing countries.

Haemorrhoids present with rectal bleeding as streaks of blood on the outside of the stool. They may prolapse through the anal verge and can undergo secondary thrombosis and inflammation, whereupon they become acutely painful.

Tumours

Warts

Warts (*condyloma acuminata*) are the commonest benign tumours of the anus. They are often multiple and are almost always attributable to human papillomavirus (HPV) infection. Approximately 90% are related to HPV types 6 or 11. Their high incidence in homosexual males suggests venereal transmission through anal intercourse. There is also an increased risk of anal squamous carcinoma; those infected with HPV 16 and 18 have the highest risk of malignant change.

Carcinoma

There are three categories of carcinoma corresponding to the three kinds of epithelium found in the anal canal:

- squamous carcinoma
- basaloid carcinoma arising from the transitional zone
- adenocarcinoma arising from rectal type epithelium or from anal glands.

Squamous carcinomas at the anal verge and arising in peri-anal skin tend to be well differentiated. They appear as ulcerated lesions with rolled margins, and cause pain or bleeding. Those in the anal canal tend to be poorly differentiated squamous carcinomas and spread upwards into the lower rectum, outwards to involve the sphincters, and along lymphatics to involve the lateral pelvic and inguinal nodes. Anal carcinomas have a higher incidence in homosexual males, particularly those infected with HIV. Some are known to have developed in pre-existing anal intra-epithelial neoplasia and viral warts, and in particular in so-called giant condyloma acuminata.

Basaloid carcinomas are now considered to be a subtype of squamous carcinoma and, stage for stage, have the same prognosis. Irradiation and chemotherapy alone or in combination achieve at least 70% survival at 5 years. Surgery is usually reserved for large tumours that fail to respond to irradiation.

Adenocarcinomas at the upper end of the anal canal are treated as for low rectal tumours.

Melanoma

The anus and anal canal are also rare sites for a malignant melanoma.

Commonly confused conditions and entities relating to alimentary pathology			
Commonly confused	Distinction and explanation	Commonly confused	Distinction and explanation
Barrett's oesophagus and hiatus hernia	Barrett's oesophagus is a metaplastic change in the distal oesophagus resulting in conversion of the normal stratified epithelium into a glandular mucosa. Hiatus hernia also results in glandular mucosa lining the intrathoracic portion of the alimentary tract, but this is due to herniation of the stomach through the oesophageal opening of the diaphragm.	Diverticulosis and diverticulitis	Diverticulosis is an acquired condition characterised by mucosal herniation through the muscularis propria of the colon. When the resulting diverticula are inflamed, a common complication, it is referred to as diverticulitis.
Intra-mucosal carcinoma and carcinoma in situ	Because it is difficult reliably to identify carcinoma in situ (i.e. non-invasive carcinoma) in glandular mucosa (the structure is more complex than, for example, squamous epithelium), the term intra-mucosal carcinoma is used for superficial carcinomas that have not invaded beyond the mucosa, except in the large intestine where invasion beyond the mucosa is, by convention, required before the lesion is regarded as a 'carcinoma'.	Coeliac disease and intestinal malabsorption	Coeliac disease (gluten-sensitive enteropathy) is one cause of intestinal malabsorption.
		Addison's disease and Addisonian pernicious anaemia	Addison's disease is adrenal failure, usually due to autoimmune destruction. Addison also described pernicious anaemia, also an autoimmune disease, in which the gastric parietal cells are destroyed and hence fail to secrete intrinsic factor which is required for absorption of vitamin B_{12}.
		Fistulae, fissures and sinuses	Fistulae are abnormal, usually inflammatory, connections between either two hollow structures (e.g. loops of bowel) or one hollow structure and the skin surface. Pathological fissures are penetrating ulcers forming grooves or clefts. Both occur in Crohn's disease. Sinuses are cavities or blind-ended channels (e.g. pilonidal sinus).
Chronic inflammatory bowel disease, Crohn's disease and ulcerative colitis	Chronic inflammatory bowel disease includes Crohn's disease and ulcerative colitis. Crohn's disease is characterised by transmural chronic (often granulomatous) inflammation and may affect any part of the alimentary tract, whereas ulcerative colitis is characterised predominantly by mucosal inflammation and ulceration and involves only the colon and rectum.	Ulcers and erosions	A mucosal ulcer is a full-thickness loss of the mucosa. Erosions are characterised by loss of only the superficial layer of a mucosal surface and will, therefore, heal more rapidly.

FURTHER READING

Correa P, Schneider B G 2005 Etiology of gastric cancer: what is new? Cancer Epidemiology Biomarkers and Prevention 14: 1865–1868
Day D W, Jass J R, Price A B et al (eds) 2003 Morson and Dawson's gastrointestinal pathology, 4th edn. Blackwell, Oxford
Fortun P J, Hawkey C J 2007 Nonsteroidal anti-inflammatory drugs and the small intestine. Current Opinion in Gastroenterology 23: 134–141
Fox J G, Wang T C 2007 Inflammation, atrophy and gastric cancer. Journal of Clinical Investigation 117: 60–69
Fox M, Forgacs I 2006 Gastro-oesophageal reflux disease. British Medical Journal 332: 88–93
Gordon P H, Nivatvongs S 2007 Neoplasms of the colon, rectum and anus. 2nd edn. Informa Healthcare, New York
Iacobuzio-Donahue C A, Montgomery E A 2006 Gastrointestinal and liver pathology. Foundations in diagnostic pathology. Churchill-Livingstone, Edinburgh

Kemp Z, Thirwell C, Sieber O, Silver A, Tomlinson I 2004 An update on the genetics of colorectal cancer. Human Molecular Genetics 13: R177–185
Klöppel G, Anlauf M 2005 Epidemiology, tumour biology and histopathological classification of neuroendocrine tumours of the gastrointestinal tract. Best Practice and Research. Clinical Gastroenterology 19: 507–517
Kucharzik T, Maaser C, Lügering A et al 2006 Recent understanding of IBD pathogenesis: implications for future therapies. Inflammatory Bowel Disease 12: 1068–1083
Lagergren J 2005 Adenocarcinoma of oesophagus: what exactly is the size of the problem and who is at risk? Gut 54(suppl 1): i1–i5
Lock G 2001 Acute intestinal ischaemia. Best Practice and Research. Clinical Gastroenterology 15: 83–98
Monteleone G, Fina D, Caruso R, Pallone F 2006 New mediators of immunity and inflammation in inflammatory bowel disease. Current Opinion in Gastroenterology 22: 361–364

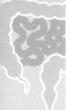

Raffatellu M, Chessa D, Wilson R P, Tükel C, Akçelik M, Bäumler A J 2006 Capsule-mediated immune evasion: a new hypothesis explaining aspects of typhoid fever pathogenesis. Infection and Immunity 74: 19–27

Reibel J 2003 Prognosis of oral pre-malignant lesions: significance of clinical, histopathological, and molecular biological characteristics. Critical Reviews in Oral Biology and Medicine 14: 47–62

Russell R K, Wilson D C, Satsangi J 2004 Unravelling the complex genetics of inflammatory bowel disease. Archives of Disease in Childhood 89: 598–603

Ryan D P, Mayer R J 2000 Anal carcinoma: histology, staging, epidemiology, treatment. Current Opinion in Oncology 12: 345–352

Strober W, Fuss I, Mannon P 2007 The fundamental basis of inflammatory bowel disease. Journal of Clinical Investigation 117: 514–521

Tamura G 2002 Genetic and epigenetic alterations in tumor suppressor and tumor-related genes in gastric cancer. Histology and Histopathology 17: 323–329

van Heel D A, West J 2006 Recent advances in coeliac disease. Gut 55: 1037–1046

16

Liver, biliary system and exocrine pancreas

COMMON CLINICAL PROBLEMS FROM LIVER AND BILIARY SYSTEM DISEASE

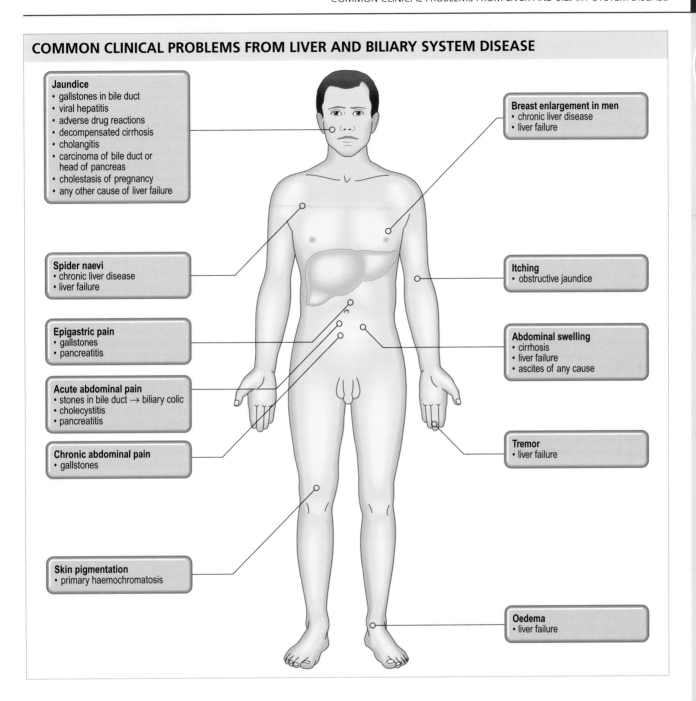

Jaundice
- gallstones in bile duct
- viral hepatitis
- adverse drug reactions
- decompensated cirrhosis
- cholangitis
- carcinoma of bile duct or head of pancreas
- cholestasis of pregnancy
- any other cause of liver failure

Spider naevi
- chronic liver disease
- liver failure

Epigastric pain
- gallstones
- pancreatitis

Acute abdominal pain
- stones in bile duct → biliary colic
- cholecystitis
- pancreatitis

Chronic abdominal pain
- gallstones

Skin pigmentation
- primary haemochromatosis

Breast enlargement in men
- chronic liver disease
- liver failure

Itching
- obstructive jaundice

Abdominal swelling
- cirrhosis
- liver failure
- ascites of any cause

Tremor
- liver failure

Oedema
- liver failure

Pathological basis of hepatic signs and symptoms	
Sign or symptom	Pathological basis
Jaundice	Haemolysis (increased formation of bilirubin), liver disease (impaired conjugation and/or excretion) or biliary obstruction
Dark urine	Conjugated hyperbilirubinaemia (water-soluble)
Pale faeces	Biliary obstruction causing lack of bile pigments

(Continued)

Pathological basis of hepatic signs and symptoms—cont'd	
Sign or symptom	Pathological basis
Spider naevi Gynaecomastia	Secondary to hyperoestrogenism
Oedema	Reduced plasma oncotic pressure due to hypoalbuminaemia
Xanthelasma	Cutaneous lipid deposits due to hypercholesterolaemia in chronic biliary obstruction
Steatorrhoea	Malabsorption of fat due to lack of bile (e.g. biliary obstruction)
Pruritus	Biliary obstruction resulting in bile salt accumulation
Ascites	Combination of hypoalbuminaemia, portal hypertension and secondary hyperaldosteronism
Bruising or bleeding	Impaired hepatic synthesis of clotting factors
Hepatomegaly	Increased size of liver due to inflammation (e.g. hepatitis), infiltration (e.g. amyloid, fat) or tumour (primary or secondary)
Haematemesis	Ruptured oesophageal varices due to portal hypertension
Encephalopathy	Failure of liver to remove exogenous or endogenous substances mimicking or altering balance of neurotransmitters

LIVER

NORMAL STRUCTURE AND FUNCTION

Forming the interface between the gastrointestinal tract and the rest of the body, the liver is of crucial importance in metabolising, storing or excreting the absorbed products of digestion. The liver has numerous other vital functions; therefore, the clinical consequences of liver disease are often wide-ranging and, if severe, life-threatening. However, considerable functional reserve and reparative capacity enables many patients to tolerate cellular injury or losses that, in other organs, would imperil their survival.

This wedge-shaped organ, weighing approximately 1.5 kg in the adult, is situated in the right hypochondrial region of the abdominal cavity. It has four lobes: the right is larger than the left; the smaller caudate lobe is situated posteriorly and the quadrate lobe is more anterior. The liver receives blood from two sources:

- *arterial blood* from the right and left hepatic arteries, which are branches of the coeliac axis
- *venous blood* from the hepatic portal vein, which drains much of the alimentary tract, from the stomach to the rectum, and the spleen.

Blood leaves the liver through the hepatic veins, which drain into the inferior vena cava.

Bile is formed in the liver and drains from it into the right and left hepatic ducts; these fuse to form the common bile duct to be joined by the cystic duct, which communicates with the gallbladder where the bile is stored and concentrated.

Most of the liver comprises liver cells (*hepatocytes*). These are arranged in plates one cell thick, bordering the vascular sinusoids through which flows hepatic arterial and portal venous blood. The blood flowing through the vascular sinusoids is separated from the liver cells by a thin fenestrated (porous) barrier of cells (*endothelial cells* and *phagocytic Kupffer cells*) and the *space of Disse*. Within the space of Disse the basement membrane is interrupted, thus allowing free exchange of molecules at the liver cell membrane. Blood flowing through the vascular sinusoids drains into hepatic vein branches (central veins or terminal hepatic venules). Bile formed by the liver cells is secreted from them into minute canaliculi which run along the centre of the liver cell plates to drain into the bile duct branches in the portal tracts. Close to the vascular sinusoids in the vicinity of the terminal hepatic venules are stellate cells called the *perisinusoidal cells of Ito*; these are involved in hepatic fibrosis by synthesising collagen.

The *portal tracts* each contain three tubular structures, which are branches of:

- the bile duct
- the hepatic artery
- the portal vein.

These constitute the *portal triad* and are supported by collagen-rich connective tissue.

The microanatomy of the liver can be regarded conceptually as either *acinar* or *lobular* (Fig. 16.1):

- *Acini* are centred on the axial vessels, arising from the hepatic artery and portal venous channels in the adjacent portal tract. Their periphery is demarcated by the surrounding hepatic veins.

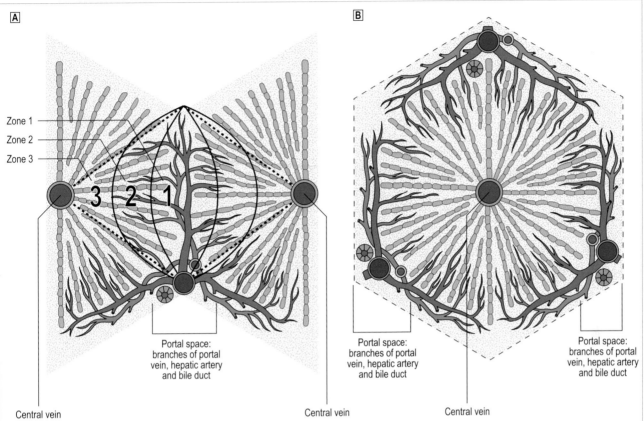

Zone 1
Zone 2
Zone 3

Portal space:
branches of portal
vein, hepatic artery
and bile duct

Portal space:
branches of portal
vein, hepatic artery
and bile duct

Portal space:
branches of portal
vein, hepatic artery
and bile duct

Central vein

Central vein

Central vein

Fig. 16.1 **Comparison of acinar and lobular concepts of the microanatomical units of the liver.** **A** The acinar concept explains better the pathophysiology of the liver. Cells in acinar zone 3, being the most remote from the vascular supply in the hilum of the acinus, are consequently the most vulnerable to injury. Death of liver cells in zone 3 results in the observed necrosis bridging between portal tracts and central veins in severe liver injury. **B** Lobular units are, however, often easier to perceive in histological sections.

- *Lobules* are centred on terminal hepatic venules ('central veins'). Their periphery is demarcated by imaginary lines joining each of the surrounding portal tracts.

Of the two microanatomical concepts—acinar or lobular—the 'acinar concept' is now considered to be more useful because it explains better many of the pathophysiological disturbances in liver disease. The zone of liver cells most remote from the axial vessels in the centre of the acinus (acinar zone 3) is the most susceptible to injury resulting from vascular insufficiency, as in circulatory shock or cardiac failure. As adjacent zones 3 are contiguous, liver cell death in this zone is often confluent.

The portal tracts are circumscribed by a boundary of liver cells, known as the *limiting plate*, which is breached in some forms of chronic liver inflammation; disruption of the limiting plate, when seen in biopsies, denotes that progression to cirrhosis is likely. The liver cells at the portal tract boundary can, in response to bile duct injury or obstruction, undergo a metaplastic change and proliferate to form new bile ductules.

Liver cells are rich in organelles, including numerous mitochondria, lysosomes, peroxisomes (microbodies), and rough and smooth endoplasmic reticulum, reflecting their wide range of metabolic functions. The cytoplasm is also laden with glycogen; this glycogen can be excessive in diabetes and

in congenital deficiencies of glycogen debranching enzymes (the glycogenoses).

Liver cells synthesise albumin, clotting factors including fibrinogen, some complement components, alpha-1 antitrypsin, etc., and remove from the body many waste products and potentially toxic substances. Through the expression of specific receptors on the liver cells, the liver—the site of action of statins, the cholesterol-lowering drugs—has a major role in the uptake and metabolism of the low-density lipoproteins involved in atheroma (Ch. 13). Liver cells also metabolise or activate many other drugs. Extensive disease of the liver therefore affects many vital functions and has profound effects on the body.

Liver cells contain many enzymes, some of which are diagnostically important. Their release from damaged or dying liver cells into the blood, where their activity can be measured, indicates the presence and severity of liver disease (Table 16.1). These enzymes include:

- aspartate aminotransferase (AST)
- alanine aminotransferase (ALT)
- gamma-glutamyltransferase (GGT).

All cells in the liver are capable of regeneration. The liver cells are classified as stable—that is, they are not normally replicating but will do so if the liver is injured. This regenerative capacity is vital in the recovery of patients with liver damage

Table 16.1   Diagnostic usefulness of serum analyses in liver disease

Test	Deviation from normal	Interpretation
Albumin Normal 35–50 g/l	↓	Liver failure
Prothrombin time Normal < 15 s	↑	Liver failure
Alanine aminotransferase (ALT) Normal < 40 IU/l	↑	Hepatocellular injury
Aspartate aminotransferase (AST) Normal < 40 IU/l	↑	Hepatocellular injury
Gamma-glutamyltransferase (GGT) Normal < 50 IU/l	↑	Hepatocellular injury (centrilobular)
Alkaline phosphatase Normal < 100 IU/l	↑	Biliary obstruction Hepatic metastases
Bilirubin Normal 5–12 µmol/l	↑	Hepatocellular injury Biliary obstruction Liver failure Congenital hyperbilirubinaemia Haemolysis
IgM anti-HAV antibody	Present	Hepatitis A
HBsAg	Present	Hepatitis B or carrier
HBeAg	Present	Active hepatitis B infection
Anti-HCV antibody	Present	Hepatitis C virus exposure
HCV RNA	Present	Active hepatitis C infection
Caeruloplasmin	↓	Wilson's disease
IgA	↑	Alcoholic cirrhosis
IgG	↑	Autoimmune hepatitis
IgM	↑	Primary biliary cirrhosis
Anti-mitochondrial antibody	Present	Primary biliary cirrhosis
Anti-smooth muscle, antinuclear or anti-LKM antibodies	Present	Autoimmune hepatitis
Ferritin	↑	Haemochromatosis
Alpha-1 antitrypsin	↓	Alpha-1 antitrypsin deficiency
Alpha-fetoprotein (AFP) (normally undetectable)	↑	Liver cell carcinoma

HAV, hepatitis A virus; HBsAg, hepatitis B surface antigen; HCV, hepatitis C virus; LKM, liver and kidney microsomal antigen.

due to viruses, drugs or trauma, but if the damage is persistent or occurs repeatedly, it can result in loss of the normal acinar or lobular structure and its replacement by regenerative liver cell nodules which are functionally inefficient. This is the condition called *cirrhosis*.

Some changes occur naturally in the liver with age. In the fetus, the liver is a relatively larger organ compared to the rest of the body. It is a major site of haemopoiesis and the adult liver can revert to this activity in some haematological disorders. The fetal liver synthesises alpha-fetoprotein, a fetal serum protein, and this is replaced by albumin towards the end of gestation. Alpha-fetoprotein synthesis by the adult liver usually denotes the presence of a primary liver cell carcinoma. With advancing age, the liver shrinks and becomes dark brown due to an increased amount of lipofuscin pigment in the liver cells ('brown atrophy').

INVESTIGATION OF LIVER DISEASE

The investigation of a patient with liver disease commonly includes:

- analysis of serum concentrations of bilirubin, hepatic enzymes, albumin, clotting factors, etc.
- immunological testing for auto-antibodies and for viral antigens and antibodies
- imaging techniques
- liver biopsy.

These investigations complement careful history-taking and a thorough clinical examination.

Biochemistry

Bilirubin

Bilirubin pigment is a breakdown product of the haem moiety of haemoglobin (Fig. 16.2). It is produced at sites of red cell destruction (e.g. spleen) and circulates in the blood in an unconjugated water-insoluble form bound to albumin. In the liver it is conjugated to glucuronic acid by the enzyme glucuronyl transferase. Conjugated bilirubin is water-soluble and can therefore appear in the urine if the outflow of bile from the liver is interrupted; the patient's urine then becomes stained with conjugated bilirubin. Bilirubin is converted by bacteria in the intestine to faecal urobilinogen (stercobilinogen), some of which is absorbed and then excreted, mostly in the bile to complete its enterohepatic circulation or, in only trace amounts normally, by the kidneys to appear in the urine as urobilinogen. Stercobilinogen is oxidised to stercobilin (faecal urobilin), the principal faecal pigment.

In early or recovering viral hepatitis, impaired biliary excretion results in preformed stercobilinogen appearing in the urine in excess as urobilinogen; this is one sensitive marker of early liver injury. In well-established biliary obstruction, the urinary urobilinogen concentration falls, because the cessation of biliary excretion into the gut results in sustained absence of synthesis of faecal urobilinogen.

Enzymes

In liver cell injury, damage to the membranes of cells and their organelles allows intracellular enzymes to leak into the blood, where the elevated concentrations can be measured. Examples include ALT, AST and GGT. Their diagnostic usefulness is summarised in Table 16.1.

The enzyme alkaline phosphatase is normally present in bile. Obstruction to the flow of bile, by gallstones for example, causes regurgitation of alkaline phosphatase into the blood, resulting in increased serum concentrations.

Many of these enzymes are not exclusively specific to the liver; therefore the results of diagnostic serum assays need careful interpretation.

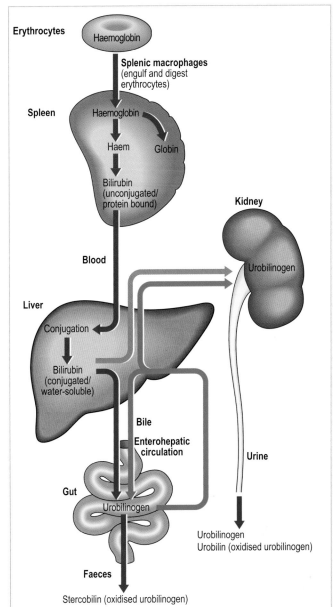

Fig. 16.2 Simplified pathways of bilirubin metabolism. Excessive breakdown of haemoglobin, as in haemolytic anaemias, will lead to increased biliary excretion of bilirubin. Biliary obstruction will cause regurgitation of conjugated water-soluble bilirubin into the blood which is then excreted in the urine, causing it to darken. Liver cell damage in hepatitis will cause impaired biliary excretion of urobilinogen and conjugated bilirubin; these are excreted in the urine, causing it to darken. The enterohepatic circulation, which involves urobilinogen, also returns cholic acid and chenodeoxycholic acid to the liver; this enhances bile secretion.

Albumin

Albumin is a major serum protein synthesised by the liver cells. It has a relatively long half-life, compared to that of clotting factors (see below), so liver damage has to persist before decreased serum levels are found. In chronic liver disease, such as cirrhosis, a low serum albumin concentration is an important manifestation of liver failure, which results in peripheral oedema and contributes to the presence of ascites due to a reduction in plasma oncotic pressure.

Clotting factors

Liver cells synthesise the vitamin K-dependent clotting factors, deficiency of which results in a bleeding tendency. This can be detected in the laboratory by measuring the prothrombin time. A prolonged bleeding and prothrombin time is a further manifestation of liver failure and, because these clotting factors have a relatively short half-life, deficiency may be found quite early in the course of the illness. The prothrombin time should be measured before performing a liver biopsy or undertaking surgery on a patient with liver disease to avoid the risk of unexpected haemorrhage. These clotting factor deficiencies can be corrected by administration of high doses of vitamin K or of the clotting factors themselves.

Immunology

Although insignificant amounts of immunoglobulins are synthesised in the liver, immunological abnormalities often accompany liver disease and are useful diagnostic markers. These abnormalities include the appearance in the patient's blood of auto-antibodies to normal tissue antigens. The antibodies are not responsible for the tissue damage in the liver diseases with which they are associated. Examples include:

- anti-mitochondrial antibodies in primary biliary cirrhosis
- antinuclear antibodies and anti-smooth muscle antibodies in autoimmune hepatitis.

Polyclonal immunoglobulin elevations also occur:

- raised IgG in autoimmune hepatitis
- raised IgM in primary biliary cirrhosis
- raised IgA in alcoholic cirrhosis.

Antibodies to hepatitis viruses are, in some instances (e.g. hepatitis A), clinically useful markers of these infections. Viral antigens or nucleic acids can also be tested for.

Imaging

Techniques used to visualise the liver and detect lesions within it include:

- ultrasonography
- cholangiography (often together with pancreatography), to visualise the biliary system
- scintigraphy after the injection of ^{99m}Tc-labelled colloids, which are taken up by the phagocytic Kupffer cells
- computed tomography (CT)
- magnetic resonance imaging (MRI).

Biopsy

The two common types of liver biopsy are:

- wedge biopsies, taken during an abdominal operation
- needle biopsies, which are much more frequent and are done percutaneously.

Both procedures carry a small but significant risk of haemorrhage and biliary leakage from the biopsy site. Bile duct obstruction is a contraindication to liver biopsy because of the increased risk of biliary peritonitis from bile leakage from the biopsy site. The risk must be outweighed by the likely therapeutic benefit to the patient resulting from an accurate assessment of their liver disease.

Most liver diseases produce diffuse abnormalities in the organ; a biopsy from any part of it will therefore be representative. Focal lesions such as tumours may be missed, particularly by percutaneous needle sampling, but the biopsy needle can be guided to them by using imaging techniques such as ultrasonography.

Liver biopsies are examined by light microscopy after sectioning and staining. Unlike renal biopsies, little additional clinically useful information is obtained by examining liver biopsies with the electron microscope.

JAUNDICE

Jaundice (or icterus) is the name given to yellowing of the skin and mucosal surfaces due to the presence of bilirubin. Usually jaundice is observable when the serum bilirubin concentration exceeds 40 micromol/l. Note, however, that:

1. Many patients with significant liver disease, often severe, are not jaundiced.
2. Liver disease is not the only cause of jaundice.

The accumulation of bilirubin in the skin may cause some embarrassment to the patient and, often if due to biliary obstruction, discomfort due to pruritus.

Jaundice in infants

Physiological neonatal jaundice is relatively common, particularly in premature infants. Although it causes understandable parental anxiety, the jaundice is rarely severe and it fades as liver function matures. However, high bilirubin levels in infancy can be directly harmful. Because the neonatal blood–brain barrier is relatively permeable, unconjugated bilirubin can accumulate in the lipid-rich brain tissue, causing *bilirubin encephalopathy* or *kernicterus*; this can be avoided by phototherapy or, in severe cases, exchange transfusion.

Worsening jaundice may be one of the clinical features alerting to the presence of a congenital abnormality within the hepato-biliary system. Such abnormalities may be:

- structural
- functional.

Structural congenital abnormalities include:

- *biliary atresia*, characterised by failure of bile duct development during embryogenesis
- *biliary hypoplasia* (Alagille's syndrome), an autosomal dominant syndrome in which paucity of bile ducts is accompanied by dysmorphic facies, skeletal abnormalities and mental retardation

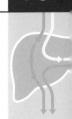

- *congenital hepatic fibrosis*, an autosomal recessive disorder in which hepatic fibrosis is often associated with cystic kidneys
- *choledochal cysts*, more common in Japan than in Western Europe, and in girls than boys.

Functional abnormalities include congenital metabolic defects involving the liver (see Ch. 7) and *congenital hyper-bilirubinaemias*.

Classification of jaundice

Jaundice may be classified as *pre-hepatic, intrahepatic* or *post-hepatic*, depending on the site of the lesion, or *conjugated* and *unconjugated*, based on chemical analysis of the bilirubin in the blood or by deduction from the colour of the patient's urine. Only conjugated bilirubin is sufficiently water soluble to be excreted in the urine.

Pre-hepatic jaundice

The main cause of pre-hepatic jaundice is *haemolysis*, due for example to hereditary spherocytosis or autoimmune red cell destruction (see Ch. 23). In these conditions there is excessive production of bilirubin from the haemoglobin released from lysed red cells. Because the excess bilirubin is unconjugated, it is not excretable in the urine; the urine colour is normal (hence the synonym 'acholuric jaundice'). The bile, however, may contain so much bilirubin that there is a risk of pigment gallstone formation.

Intrahepatic jaundice

Hepatic disorders in which jaundice may be a feature include:

- acute viral hepatitis
- drug-induced liver injury
- alcoholic hepatitis
- decompensated cirrhosis
- intrahepatic bile duct loss (e.g. primary biliary cirrhosis, sclerosing cholangitis, biliary hypoplasia)
- in pregnancy, intrahepatic cholestasis and acute fatty liver.

In these conditions there is accumulation of bilirubin within the liver (intrahepatic cholestasis), often histologically evident in biopsies as plugs of bile pigment distending canaliculi. The excess bilirubin is predominantly conjugated, is therefore water soluble and is excreted in the urine, causing darkening; this is a simple but diagnostically useful observation.

Congenital hyperbilirubinaemia
Congenital metabolic defects in the intrahepatic conjugation, transport or excretion of bilirubin are relatively rare causes of jaundice. These include:

- Gilbert's syndrome (predominantly unconjugated)
- Crigler–Najjar syndrome (predominantly unconjugated)
- Dubin–Johnson syndrome (predominantly conjugated)
- Rotor syndrome (predominantly conjugated).

Post-hepatic jaundice

Obstruction of the extrahepatic bile ducts is an important cause of jaundice necessitating urgent investigation and alleviation in order to prevent serious damage to the liver. Important causes are:

- congenital biliary atresia—often accompanied by a reduction in the number of intrahepatic ducts
- gallstones—usually associated with biliary colic and a non-distendable chronically inflamed gallbladder
- strictures—often following previous biliary surgery
- tumours—notably carcinoma of the head of the pancreas compressing the common bile duct.

As with intrahepatic causes, some of which also directly interfere with biliary drainage (e.g. primary biliary cirrhosis, sclerosing cholangitis), the excess bilirubin is conjugated and darkens the urine. Conversely, the patient's faeces are pale. Pruritus is a common and troublesome symptom, probably due to bile salt accumulation.

ACUTE LIVER INJURY

- ▶ May present with acute onset of jaundice
- ▶ Causes include viruses, alcohol, drugs, bile duct obstruction
- ▶ Possible outcomes include complete recovery, chronic liver disease, or death from liver failure

Liver injury is conveniently divided into acute and chronic for the purposes of description and clinical management. However, in practice, the same cause may produce either an acute or a chronic illness, in the latter event not necessarily with any preceding clinically evident acute phase. For example, viral hepatitis is considered here under the heading of acute liver injury, but it can lead to chronic liver damage.

Aetiology

The major causes of acute liver injury are:

- viral infections
- high alcohol consumption
- adverse drug reactions
- biliary obstruction, commonly due to gallstones.

Direct physical injury to the liver, such as laceration in a road traffic accident, is another important form of acute liver injury, but the focal nature of the injury contrasts with the diffuse injury produced by the agents listed above. Recovery from acute liver injury, focal or diffuse, is attributable to the capacity of the organ for cellular regeneration.

Clinicopathological features

The clinical and laboratory manifestations of acute liver injury are:

- malaise
- jaundice

Table 16.2   Differential diagnosis of jaundice from bile abnormalities in urine and faeces, and from serum

Colour		Serum biochemistry*	Interpretation
Faeces	Urine		
Dark	Normal	Unconjugated hyperbilirubinaemia	Haemolysis
Pale	Dark	Conjugated hyperbilirubinaemia and raised alkaline phosphatase	Cholestasis Biliary obstruction
Pale	Dark	Mixed hyperbilirubinaemia and raised transaminases	Acute hepatitis
Variable	Variable	Unconjugated or conjugated hyperbilirubinaemia; other tests normal; no evidence of haemolysis	Congenital hyperbilirubinaemia (e.g. Gilbert's syndrome)

*Dominant abnormalities are listed; cholestasis and hepatitis are usually associated with other abnormalities of serum biochemistry.

- raised serum bilirubin and transaminases
- in severe cases, evidence of liver failure.

Most of the signs and symptoms of acute liver damage are predictable from the known functions of the liver. The best known is jaundice (or icterus) due to failure of the liver to secrete bile at the rate at which it is formed in the body from the destruction of red cells. Severe acute liver damage can lead to bruising and haemorrhage, due to clotting factor deficiency, and coma due to the accumulation of toxic metabolites that mimic neurotransmitters ('false neurotransmitters').

Laboratory investigations

Laboratory investigations will reveal evidence of liver cell damage, in that there will be elevated levels of serum enzymes, particularly the transaminases, and bilirubin. Liver cell damage results in some impairment of bilirubin conjugation, but also failure to excrete conjugated bilirubin and any stercobilinogen absorbed from the gut. Consequently, the urine is darkened by the presence of excess conjugated bilirubin and urobilin (derived by oxidation from urobilinogen) that cannot be excreted by the liver (Fig. 16.2). Eventually, as the liver damage persists, urobilinogen disappears from the urine because little or no bilirubin is being excreted by the liver. Jaundice due to bile duct obstruction—commonly by gallstones—also results in dark urine due to excess conjugated bilirubin that cannot be excreted by the liver; urobilinogen is usually absent, unless the obstruction is of very recent onset or intermittent, because no bilirubin reaches the intestine. Examination of urine and faeces (for colour) can therefore assist in the differential diagnosis of jaundice (Table 16.2).

Histology

In almost all cases of acute liver injury there will be liver cell degeneration or death and an inflammatory reaction. Superimposed on this uniform reaction to acute injury are, in many cases, diagnostic changes specific to the causative agent.

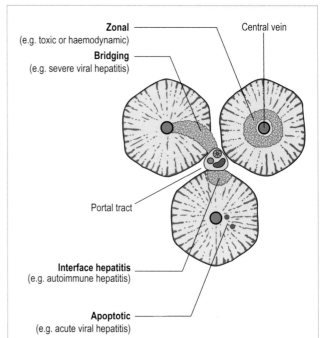

Fig. 16.3   Patterns of liver cell death and their clinicopathological significance. Death of the liver cells immediately surrounding central veins denotes cardiac failure, some other impediment to venous drainage, or some toxic cause (e.g. paracetamol overdose). Bridging necrosis (in acinar zone 3) is a feature of severe hepatitis. Interface hepatitis is death of liver cells at the margin of the portal tracts; this is a feature of chronic hepatitis due to a variety of causes. Apoptotic death of single cells is typical of acute viral hepatitis.

Also evident in liver biopsies will be the pattern of cell damage, from which the prognosis can be deduced (Fig. 16.3):

- Death of individual liver cells (*apoptosis*) is the most frequent pattern in viral hepatitis and usually denotes certain recovery with no long-term sequelae.
- Death of periportal hepatocytes at the limiting plate (*interface hepatitis*) or entire acinar zones, usually zone 3 (*bridging necrosis*), disrupts the hepatic architecture and leads to a risk of cirrhosis developing.

Table 16.3 Hepatitis viruses: their characteristics and associated diseases (delta agent, a defective virus, is not included)

Virus	Type of virus	Incubation period (days)	Illness	Carriers	Serological markers	Patient susceptibility	Transmission
HAV	ssRNA enterovirus	15–40	Mild; very low mortality	No	IgM anti-HAV antibody	Young	'Faecal–oral'
HBV	dsDNA	50–180	Significant risk of chronic hepatitis and cirrhosis	Yes	HBsAg, HBeAg	Any age	Blood and blood products; needles; venereal
HCV	ss+RNA flavivirus	40–55	Fluctuating; significant risk of chronic hepatitis and cirrhosis	Yes	Anti-HCV antibody, HCV RNA	Any age	Blood and blood products; needles; possibly venereal
HEV	ssRNA virus	30–50	No risk of chronicity; high mortality in pregnancy	No	Anti-HEV antibody	Any age	'Faecal–oral'

HAV, hepatitis A virus; HBV, hepatitis B virus; HCV, hepatitis C virus; HBsAg, hepatitis B surface antigen; HEV, hepatitis E virus; ss, single stranded; ds, double stranded; +, positive sense.

- Liver cell death substantially affecting entire acini (*panacinar necrosis*) leads to liver failure and a significant risk of imminent death.

Viral hepatitis

- ▶ Common cause of acute liver injury
- ▶ Hepatitis viruses A, B, C and E, and delta agent
- ▶ Other viruses causing liver damage include Epstein–Barr virus, yellow fever virus, herpes simplex virus and cytomegalovirus

Hepatitis viruses

The main hepatitis viruses (Table 16.3) are:

- hepatitis A virus (HAV)
- hepatitis B virus (HBV)
- hepatitis C virus (HCV)
- hepatitis E virus (HEV)
- delta agent, a defective virus requiring HBV for pathogenicity.

These hepatitis viruses are immunologically distinct. Infection usually confers life-long immunity to the infecting virus but not to the others.

The clinical features range from a trivial illness without jaundice (*anicteric hepatitis*) which may escape detection (this is a common result of HAV infection) to a more significant illness with jaundice and other clinical evidence of disturbed liver function. Sometimes the illness is dominated by jaundice, with little elevation of serum transaminases (*cholestatic hepatitis*). Severe infection leads to overt liver failure.

Yellow fever, caused by a group B arbovirus, shares many clinical and histological features with the illness usually designated viral hepatitis, but it is not normally included within this group for the purposes of description, mainly because its geographical distribution is very restricted.

The liver may also become infected by many other viruses, but these are not regarded as 'hepatitis viruses' because the infection is not confined to the liver. Examples include:

- infectious mononucleosis due to Epstein–Barr virus
- herpes simplex virus 1
- cytomegalovirus.

Hepatitis A virus
The main characteristics of hepatitis A are:

- 'faecal–oral' spread
- relatively short incubation period
- sporadic or epidemic
- directly cytopathic virus
- no carrier state
- mild illness, full recovery usual.

Infection by HAV used to be called 'infectious hepatitis' because of its common occurrence in epidemics, though it also occurs sporadically. In most countries, infection by the virus is common, usually in youth; the resulting illness is often very mild and jaundice absent or so slight that it escapes notice. Overt jaundice and clinical recognition of the infection is less common. Hepatitis sufficiently severe to warrant hospital admission is unusual, and long-term sequelae or death are exceptional rarities. It is therefore a relatively benign infection.

HAV passes from one individual to another by 'faecal–oral' transmission—usually indirectly, such as by the contamination of food and drinking water with sewage. Because the virus is excreted in the faeces before jaundice appears, thus leading to the recognition of the illness and isolation of the patient, many other individuals can be rapidly exposed to the hazard of infection. The incubation period is relatively short. HAV produces liver cell damage by a direct cytopathic effect.

Specific diagnosis is made by seeking an IgM-class antibody to HAV in the patient's serum; this indicates recent infection. A carrier state does not exist.

Hepatitis B virus

The main characteristics of hepatitis B are:

- spread by blood, blood-contaminated instruments, blood products and venereally
- relatively long incubation period
- liver damage by antiviral immune reaction
- carrier state exists
- relatively serious infection.

Infection by HBV used to be called 'serum hepatitis' because it was known to be transmitted by blood and blood products. This is because infected, but apparently healthy, individuals can carry the virus in their blood and pass it on to others by the transfusion of blood or its products. This mode of transmission is much less common now that blood donors are screened by testing for the presence of the virus. However, the term 'serum hepatitis' has been abandoned because it misleadingly excludes transmission of the virus by other methods, notably venereally; the disease is often transmitted between homosexual males. HBV can also be transmitted by contaminated needles, such as may be used for tattooing or by drug addicts. There is a relatively high incidence of the carrier state in underdeveloped countries and the virus can be transmitted vertically from mother to child—in utero, during delivery or through intimate post-natal contact.

Specific diagnosis is made by seeking the hepatitis B surface antigen (HBsAg, formerly known as 'Australia antigen' because it was first detected in the serum of an Australian aborigine). The presence of the 'e' antigen (HBeAg) in the patient's serum indicates active viral replication.

HBV produces liver cell damage not by a direct cytopathic effect but by causing viral antigens to appear on the cell surface (HBsAg); these are then recognised by the body's immune system and the infected liver cells are destroyed (Fig. 16.4). Thus, if immunity is generally impaired or there is specific tolerance to the antigen, the virus can survive in the liver cells without causing damage; such patients become asymptomatic carriers of the virus and their body fluids are a hazard to other individuals. Liver biopsies of HBV-infected carriers show that the liver cells have a ground-glass texture to their cytoplasm due to the abundance of virus particles.

HBV infection is much more serious than HAV. Infection is more likely to produce a clinical illness and jaundice, and it is more likely to result in long-term sequelae such as chronic hepatitis and cirrhosis, or even death due to fulminating acute infection causing extensive hepatic necrosis. HBV is also involved in the pathogenesis of liver cell carcinoma.

Hepatitis C virus

Hepatitis C virus was characterised in the late 1980s. Its main features are:

- spread by blood, blood-contaminated instruments, blood products and possibly venereally
- relatively short incubation period
- often asymptomatic

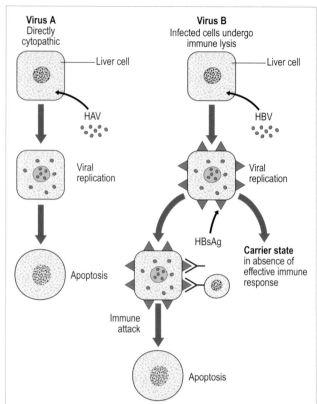

Fig. 16.4   Comparison of the pathogenesis of HAV and HBV hepatitis. The A virus, in contrast to the B virus, appears to be directly cytopathic. The B virus evokes liver cell injury by causing viral antigens to be expressed on the liver cell surface (HBsAg, hepatitis B surface antigen). The infected cells are eliminated immunologically, but an asymptomatic carrier state can ensue in the absence of specific immunity. The pathogenesis of other hepatitis viral infections is less certain.

- fluctuating liver biochemistry
- tendency to chronicity.

HCV has been an important cause of hepatitis following blood transfusion and the administration of clotting factor concentrates. Indeed, its existence was first suspected after HBV had been excluded as a possible cause by blood donor screening; it used to be known as 'non-A, non-B' hepatitis. In many countries, transmission of HCV by blood transfusion and blood product administration is much less common now that donors are screened for HCV.

The initial illness is often asymptomatic and the abnormalities of liver biochemistry (e.g. raised serum transaminases) are usually fluctuant. However, despite these misleadingly benign signals, the infection is prone to chronicity and cirrhosis is a frequent consequence.

Hepatitis E virus and other 'non-A, non-B' viruses

There are other authentic hepatitis viruses. The best characterised is a water-borne agent, distinct from HAV; it has been designated hepatitis E virus (HEV). Fortunately, the disease rarely progresses to chronicity and, as with HAV, full recovery is usual except in pregnancy, when it is associated with a high mortality rate.

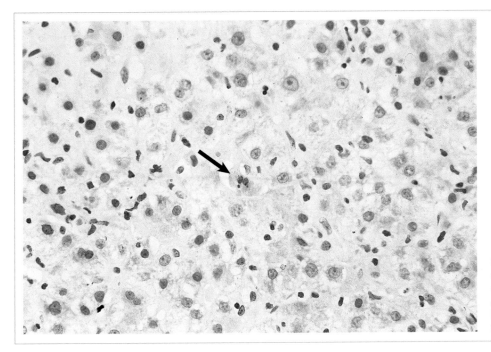

Fig. 16.5 Liver histology in acute viral hepatitis. There is disarray of the liver cell plates, accompanied by an inflammatory infiltrate and liver cell apoptosis (arrowed).

Other 'non-A, non-B' viruses associated with blood transfusions and blood products include *hepatitis G virus* and the *TT virus*. Their role in liver disease appears to be relatively minor.

Delta agent (hepatitis D virus)

Delta agent is a defective RNA virus that requires the presence of HBV, which supplies the outer layers of the viral coat, for its replication and assumed role as a pathogen. Its main effect is to aggravate the consequences of HBV infection.

Histology

Histological features of acute viral hepatitis are:

- apoptotic liver cell death
- portal tract inflammation
- cholestasis.

Although the pathogenesis of the liver cell damage resulting from HAV and HBV infection is different, the changes in the liver in a typical case are very similar (Fig. 16.5). The principal features are:

- cytoplasmic swelling of liver cells
- apoptotic death of individual liver cells
- infiltration of portal tracts by mixed inflammatory cells and expansion by oedema
- hyperplasia of Kupffer cells; in the later stages of the disease, during recovery, cellular debris (ceroid) accumulates in their cytoplasm
- accumulation of bile in liver cells, which are often swollen, and within the intercellular canaliculi, where it is sometimes misleadingly referred to as 'bile thrombi'; this pooling of bile within the liver cells and the canaliculi is called *cholestasis*.

The swelling of liver cells, portal oedema and the infiltration by inflammatory cells are responsible for hepatomegaly in viral hepatitis.

In severe viral hepatitis there may be confluent liver cell death, resulting in liver failure. At autopsy the liver will be small, have a wrinkled instead of a smooth capsule, and show extensive necrosis on the cut surfaces.

HCV infection often results in numerous lymphocytes within the vascular sinusoids and fatty change in the hepatocytes, sometimes with relatively little evidence of active liver cell death. This combination of features is unusual in HAV or HBV infection.

Alcoholic liver injury

- ▶ Common cause of acute and chronic liver disease
- ▶ Liver may show fatty change, hepatitis, fibrosis or cirrhosis, or a combination of these features
- ▶ Mechanisms include diversion of metabolic resources, direct hepatotoxicity, and stimulation of collagen synthesis

Alcohol (ethyl alcohol) is a common cause of acute and chronic liver injury. The spectrum of alcoholic liver injury includes:

- fatty change in liver cells, a relatively benign abnormality
- acute hepatitis with Mallory's hyalin
- architectural damage ranging from portal fibrosis to cirrhosis.

Histology

The fatty change (*steatosis*) is evident as fat globules within the cytoplasm of the liver cells; those in the centrilobular or acinar zone 3 areas are usually most severely affected.

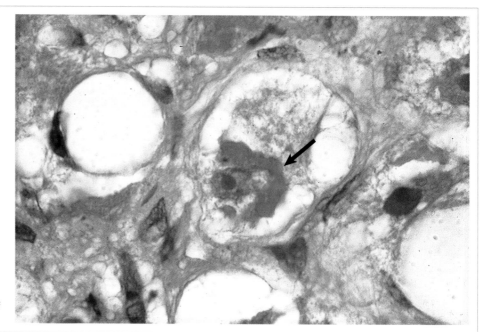

Fig. 16.6 Histology of alcoholic liver disease. Fatty change is conspicuous, and there is Mallory's hyalin (arrowed) in the cytoplasm of an injured hepatocyte.

Fatty change by itself is a relatively non-specific event because it is seen in many disorders. More specific, but not exclusive, to alcoholic liver injury is *Mallory's hyalin*; this is an intracytoplasmic aggregate of ubiquinated intermediate filaments in the liver cells (Fig. 16.6). This is usually accompanied by acute inflammation and, in contrast to pure fatty change, denotes an appreciable risk of progression to irreversible architectural disturbance and possibly cirrhosis.

Pathogenesis

Alcohol produces liver injury by a variety of mechanisms (Fig. 16.7):

- Cellular energy is diverted from essential metabolic pathways, such as fat metabolism, to the metabolism of alcohol, so fat accumulates in the liver cells.
- Acetaldehyde, the main product of alcohol metabolism, binds to liver cell proteins, resulting in injured hepatocytes and an inflammatory reaction.
- Alcohol stimulates collagen synthesis in the liver, leading to fibrosis and eventually cirrhosis.

Sustained alcoholic liver injury results in irreversible architectural disturbance, initially the linking of portal tracts and/or terminal hepatic venules by fibrous tissue, and ultimately nodular regeneration of the liver cells; this is alcoholic cirrhosis.

Recommended safe limits for alcohol continue to be debated. However, the current consensus is that, in men, up to 21 units of alcohol per week is unlikely to be harmful. In women, the safe limit is usually regarded as 14 units of alcohol per week. (One unit of alcohol is 10 ml by volume, equivalent to: half a pint, or c. 300 ml, of beer; or 25 ml of spirits. A small glass of wine contains 1.5 units.)

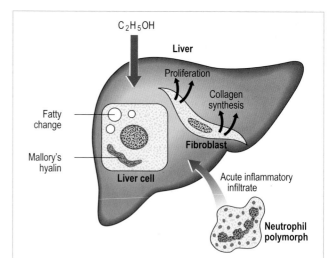

Fig. 16.7 Pathogenesis of alcoholic liver disease. There is increased peripheral release of fatty acids, and increased synthesis of fatty acids and triglycerides within the liver cells. Acetaldehyde, a product of alcohol metabolism, is probably responsible for liver cell injury, manifested by the formation of Mallory's hyalin. There is increased collagen synthesis by fibroblasts and by the perisinusoidal cells of Ito.

Drug-induced liver injury

- ▶ At least 10% of drug reactions involve the liver
- ▶ May be cholestatic or hepatocellular
- ▶ Pathogenesis may be dose-related (predictable) or idiosyncratic (unpredictable)

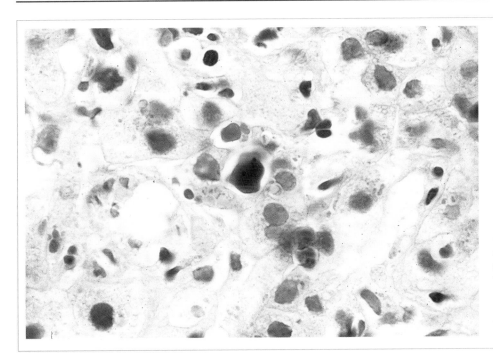

Fig. 16.8 Histology of intrahepatic cholestasis in biliary obstruction. The bile canaliculi are stuffed with stagnant brown bile that cannot be discharged from the liver because the common bile duct is blocked by a gallstone. Similar appearances result from viral hepatitis and some adverse drug reactions.

Approximately 10% of all adverse reactions to drugs involve the liver. This is not surprising in view of the central role played by the liver in metabolism and in the conjugation and elimination of toxic substances from the body. A full drug history should therefore be taken from any patient presenting with liver disease, and any suspected or proven association reported to the appropriate body (in the UK, the Commission on Human Medicines).

Adverse drug reactions may be predictable or unpredictable (Ch. 2). They may be caused by injury to the liver cells (hepatocellular) that is pathologically indistinguishable from viral hepatitis, or to bile production or excretion (cholestatic). Predictable reactions will occur in any individual if exposed to a sufficient dose; examples include coagulative centrilobular necrosis due to paracetamol overdose and cholestatic jaundice due to methyl testosterone. Unpredictable reactions include an idiosyncratic response to a drug and are not necessarily dose-related; examples include cholestatic jaundice due to chlorpromazine.

Acute biliary obstruction

> ▸ Usually due to gallstones
> ▸ Clinically characterised by colicky pain and jaundice
> ▸ May be complicated by infection (cholangitis)
> ▸ Liver shows portal tract oedema and inflammation, and cholestasis

Acute obstruction of the main bile ducts is most commonly due to gallstones. Clinically, it usually results in colicky pain and jaundice. If there is superimposed infection of the biliary tract, the ducts become inflamed (*cholangitis*) and the patient develops a fever. Cholangitis can lead to the formation of liver abscesses.

Bile accumulates within the liver, initially in the canaliculi (Fig. 16.8) and later within the intrahepatic bile ducts.

Rupture of these may result in extravasation of bile into the adjacent liver tissue; the resulting necrosis has been misnamed as a '*bile infarct*'. The portal tracts are oedematous and infiltrated with neutrophil polymorphs. The hepatocytes at the edge of the portal tract undergo ductular metaplasia. Cholangitis is recognised histologically by the presence of neutrophil polymorphs in the bile ducts.

Repeated episodes of biliary obstruction lead to portal tract fibrosis and nodular regeneration of the liver cells—*secondary biliary cirrhosis*.

CHRONIC LIVER DISEASES

Chronic liver diseases, of which there are many, are a common clinical problem. Some follow a clinically evident episode of acute liver injury; others present insidiously and may be asymptomatic until the later stages. Many forms of chronic liver disease culminate in hepatic cirrhosis.

Chronic hepatitis

> ▸ Defined as clinical or biopsy evidence of hepatitis lasting more than 6 months
> ▸ Causes include hepatitis viruses, drugs, alcohol, autoimmune hepatitis
> ▸ Biopsy appearances are graded according to severity of inflammation and staged according to degree of architectural disturbance

Chronic hepatitis is generally defined as inflammation of the liver lasting at least 6 months without evidence of resolution. The inflammation and consequent liver cell injury cause a sustained elevation of the serum transaminases, but confirmation of the diagnosis and precise classification of the disease in an individual patient usually requires a liver biopsy.

Aetiology

Chronic hepatitis is due to a variety of causes. Important causes include:

- hepatitis viruses, principally HBV and HCV
- alcohol
- drugs
- autoimmune hepatitis.

Classification

Classification of chronic hepatitis involves assessment of:

- the aetiological *type* of hepatitis
- the histological *grade* of severity of the liver cell damage and inflammation
- the histological *stage* of the degree of architectural disturbance.

Clues to the aetiological *type* of chronic hepatitis can be discovered from examination of the liver biopsy (Table 16.4), but in most cases the cause of the liver disease is already known from previous investigations (e.g. markers of HBV or HCV infection). The main purpose of the biopsy is to assess the severity of the liver damage and thereby to guide decisions about the patient's clinical management.

The *grade* of severity of the liver cell damage and inflammation is based on assessment of:

- the extent of interface hepatitis (Fig. 16.9)
- the degree of bridging or confluent necrosis
- the frequency of intralobular apoptotic hepatocytes
- the density of the inflammatory infiltrate in portal tracts.

Each of these features is scored using published protocols, such as those devised by Ishak and others, to derive a total *histological activity index*. This numerical score can then be translated into a named grade of severity, which may be minimal, mild, moderate or severe chronic hepatitis (Fig. 16.10). The greater the severity, the greater the risk of progression to significant architectural disturbance or, eventually, cirrhosis.

The *stage* of the architectural disturbance is also assessed histologically and ranges from normal architecture, fibrous enlargement of portal tracts, bridging fibrosis, to cirrhosis. The greater the disturbance, the less likely it is to be reversible when the inflammatory activity has subsided.

Iron overload and the liver

- ▶ Excessive accumulation of iron, as haemosiderin, in the liver causes it to appear dark brown
- ▶ Haemosiderosis: excess iron with normal architecture
- ▶ Haemochromatosis: excess iron with consequent cirrhosis
- ▶ Primary haemochromatosis (congenital): excess iron absorption, deposited in liver (cirrhosis) and endocrine glands (e.g. 'bronze diabetes')
- ▶ Secondary haemochromatosis (acquired): excess dietary iron or parenteral administration (e.g. multiple blood transfusions)

In haemosiderosis (or 'siderosis' of the liver) and haemochromatosis, the liver is dark brown due to the deposition of excess iron in the form of haemosiderin (an iron-rich protein). The haemosiderin is visible in histological sections as light brown granules; its identity can be confirmed by Perls' stain for iron.

Table 16.4 Principal diagnostic features of chronic disease

Disease	Distinctive features		
	Serological	Biochemical	Biopsy
Autoimmune hepatitis	Anti-smooth muscle antibody and antinuclear factor	Raised IgG and transaminases	Liver cell rosettes and abundant plasma cells
Chronic virus B hepatitis	HBsAg, HBeAg	Raised transaminases	Interface hepatitis
Chronic virus C hepatitis	Anti-HCV HCV RNA	Raised transaminases	Fatty change and sinusoidal infiltration
Primary biliary cirrhosis	Anti-mitochondrial antibody	Raised IgM and alkaline phosphatase	Depleted interlobular bile ducts and granulomas
Alcoholic cirrhosis		Raised IgA and GGT	Mallory's hyalin and fat
Wilson's disease		Low caeruloplasmin	Excess copper
Alpha-1 antitrypsin deficiency		Low alpha-1 antitrypsin	Hyaline globules in liver cells
Haemochromatosis		Raised ferritin	Haemosiderin
HBsAg, hepatitis B surface antigen; GGT, gamma-glutamyltransferase.			

The distinction between these two entities is as follows:

- *Haemosiderosis* is the name given to the mere presence of excess iron, in the form of haemosiderin, in the liver. The liver architecture is usually normal.
- *Haemochromatosis* is a more serious disorder in which the presence of excess iron, as haemosiderin, is associated with a risk of progression to cirrhosis.

Haemosiderosis

Haemosiderosis usually results from parenteral iron overload, as in the case of a patient with aplastic anaemia treated with blood transfusions. In this instance, the iron liberated from eventual lysis of the transfused blood cells cannot be reutilised in the patient for haemoglobin synthesis because of absence of haemopoiesis,

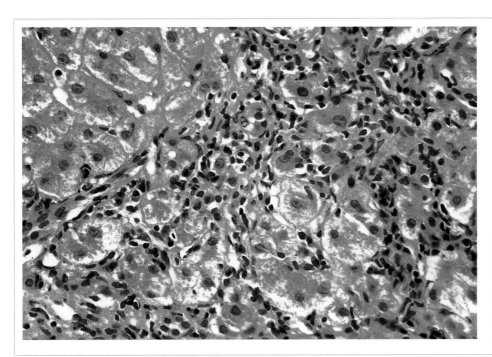

Fig. 16.9   Histology of interface hepatitis. Degenerate liver cells adjacent to the edge of a portal tract are associated with dense inflammatory cell infiltration. This leads to progressive erosion of liver architecture, frequently culminating in cirrhosis.

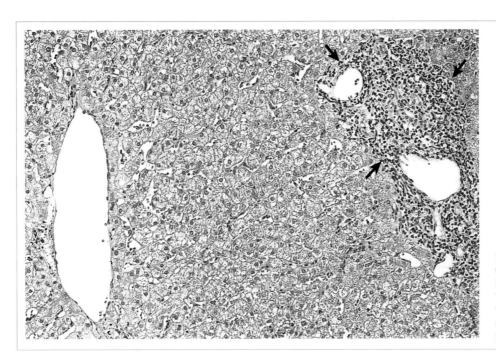

Fig. 16.10   Histology of mild chronic hepatitis. The dense lymphocytic infiltrate is confined to the portal tract (arrowed) and there is no erosion of hepatic architecture. This grade of activity progresses only rarely to cirrhosis.

so it accumulates in various organs, notably in the liver where it is stored as haemosiderin, mainly in Kupffer cells. Haemosiderosis is not commonly associated with significant liver damage or progression to cirrhosis; however, if cirrhosis does develop as a result of massive iron overload by this mechanism, the condition is referred to as *secondary haemochromatosis*.

Haemosiderosis can also occur in alcoholic liver disease because alcohol enhances iron absorption from the gut. Any hepatic architectural disturbance is more likely to be due to the alcohol than the iron in these cases.

Primary (genetic) haemochromatosis

Primary haemochromatosis is the most common form of iron overload. It is an inherited autosomal recessive (except for a rare autosomal dominant type) disease usually due to *HFE* gene defects (most commonly a C282Y mutation) on chromosome 6 near the HLA-A locus. Heterozygotes have increased absorption of iron, but only in homozygotes does this reach dangerous levels. The defect causes excessive absorption of iron in the small intestine even when transferrin, the iron-binding protein in the blood, is fully saturated. By adult life the total body iron stores may reach as high as 40–60 g (normal about 4 g). The disease is clinically manifested more commonly in men than women; pre-menopausal women compensate for the excessive iron absorption through natural iron loss due to menstrual bleeding.

For many years the iron is deposited, as haemosiderin, in the hepatocytes without any clinical effects. Eventually, however, the iron deposition becomes more extensive, involving Kupffer cells, bile duct epithelium and portal tract connective tissue (Fig. 16.11). Hepatic fibrosis ensues, followed by cirrhosis. In advanced cases the haemosiderin is deposited in other tissues, notably in endocrine organs; the clinical syndrome of 'bronze diabetes' is due to concomitant iron-induced damage to the pancreatic islets (resulting in diabetes) and the effect of raised melanotrophin levels on the skin (resulting in bronze coloration). Cardiac failure and impotence may also result.

If the condition is diagnosed in the pre-cirrhotic phase, the process may be arrested by depleting the body's iron stores by regular venesection or by the administration of desferrioxamine, a chelating agent. The genetic aetiology of primary haemochromatosis means that it is important to screen first-degree relatives to identify those at risk from this potentially treatable liver disease.

Secondary haemochromatosis

Unlike primary haemochromatosis, secondary haemochromatosis is not a single discrete disease entity. It may be due to increased iron in the diet (e.g. excessive medicinal iron tablets) or to parenteral iron loading. For example, secondary haemochromatosis may be seen in patients with aplastic anaemia and haemoglobinopathies who have received multiple transfusions. It is possible, however, that the liver damage in some cases is due to co-existent post-transfusion viral hepatitis rather than iron overload.

Wilson's disease (hepatolenticular degeneration)

▶ Inherited disorder of copper metabolism
▶ Copper accumulates in liver and brain
▶ Kayser–Fleischer rings at corneal limbus
▶ Low serum caeruloplasmin

Wilson's disease is a rare but treatable inherited autosomal recessive disorder in which copper accumulates in the liver and in the basal ganglia of the brain. The underlying

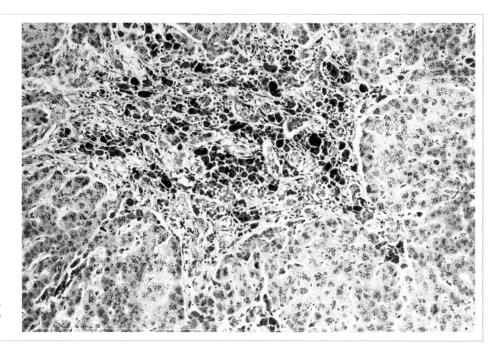

Fig. 16.11 Histology of haemochromatosis. The portal tract and the liver cells contain brown granules of haemosiderin. This has caused portal fibrosis and, if untreated, will eventually lead to cirrhosis.

defect is failure of the liver to excrete copper in the bile. Copper accumulation in the liver causes chronic hepatitis and, ultimately, cirrhosis. Copper deposition in the brain causes severe progressive neurological disability. Surplus copper released into the blood may cause episodes of haemolysis.

Clinically Wilson's disease is recognised by the combination of hepatic and neurological abnormalities and from the presence of characteristic brown Kayser–Fleischer rings at the corneal limbus. Diagnosis is confirmed by finding a low concentration of caeruloplasmin (a copper-containing protein) in the serum and an excess of copper in the liver biopsy. It is treated with penicillamine, a chelating agent that binds the copper and eliminates it in the urine.

Alpha-1 antitrypsin deficiency

▶ Congenital defect of synthesis
▶ Hyaline globular inclusions in liver cells
▶ Risk of emphysema and cirrhosis

Alpha-1 antitrypsin is a serum protein with alpha mobility on electrophoresis. It is normally synthesised in the liver and is immediately secreted into the blood, where it has antiproteolytic properties. Several phenotypes occur in the population. The normal phenotype is referred to as MM.

Phenotypes of alpha-1 antitrypsin associated with low serum levels are not uncommon. They are characterized in the laboratory by their unusually fast or slow electrophoretic mobility. Heterozygous states, such as MZ or MS, are not considered to have any significance, but homozygous states, such as ZZ, are associated with a predisposition to pulmonary emphysema and hepatic cirrhosis. These unusual phenotypes of alpha-1 antitrypsin are not readily released from the liver cell after synthesis; low serum levels are therefore found and the unreleased protein accumulates in the cytoplasm of periportal hepatocytes as hyaline intracytoplasmic globules.

Autoimmune liver disease

There are two main chronic liver diseases with an autoimmune basis:

● autoimmune hepatitis
● primary biliary cirrhosis.

In most cases these autoimmune diseases are distinguishable on investigation, including liver biopsy. However, in a small proportion, there appears to be some overlap and a clear-cut distinction may not be possible. Like almost all other autoimmune diseases, they are more common in females.

Autoimmune hepatitis

▶ Females > males
▶ Liver biopsy shows chronic hepatitis, often with plasma cells and liver cell rosettes
▶ Anti-smooth muscle, antinuclear or anti-LKM antibodies, raised IgG and transaminases

Autoimmune hepatitis occurs more commonly in females and is characterised histologically by the appearance of chronic hepatitis, often dominated by numerous plasma cells and rosette-like arrangements of swollen liver cells. Formerly called 'lupoid' hepatitis, it is not related to systemic lupus erythematosus, although it shares the presence of antinuclear antibodies in the serum with that condition. Auto-antibodies to smooth muscle antigens or to nuclear DNA or to liver–kidney microsomal (LKM) antigens are also often present. Associated biochemical factors include raised serum IgG and transaminases. Patients often benefit from treatment with steroids.

Primary biliary cirrhosis

▶ Females > males
▶ Liver biopsy shows bile duct destruction, granulomas, ductular proliferation, fibrosis, and eventual cirrhosis
▶ Raised IgM and alkaline phosphatase, anti-mitochondrial antibody, pruritus, jaundice, xanthelasmas

Primary biliary cirrhosis is misleadingly named because cirrhosis is a late manifestation of the disease and many patients have the condition diagnosed before this stage is reached.

The stages in the development of the disease are:

● autoimmune destruction of bile duct epithelium, particularly that of the smaller intrahepatic ducts; histologically, the damaged ducts are surrounded by a dense lymphocytic infiltrate and granulomas are often present (Fig. 16.12)
● later proliferation of small bile ductules, perhaps in a vain attempt to replace those that have been deleted by the autoimmune process
● architectural disturbance due to portal and bridging fibrosis
● cirrhosis.

Copper accumulates in the liver cells because it can no longer be adequately excreted in the bile.

In addition to the biopsy appearances, which may not be absolutely diagnostic in the later stages, other important features of primary biliary cirrhosis include:

● elevated serum alkaline phosphatase and IgM levels
● an anti-mitochondrial auto-antibody in the serum
● pruritus, jaundice and xanthelasmas (yellow deposits of lipid-laden macrophages in the skin around the eyes).

Sclerosing cholangitis

Primary sclerosing cholangitis is a chronic inflammatory process affecting intrahepatic, and sometimes extrahepatic, bile ducts. Initially, the ducts are surrounded by a mantle of chronic inflammatory cells, but this is eventually replaced by fibrosis and obliteration of the ducts. In *c.*10% of patients, cholangiocarcinoma (bile duct carcinoma) develops.

There is an association with chronic inflammatory bowel disease, particularly ulcerative colitis.

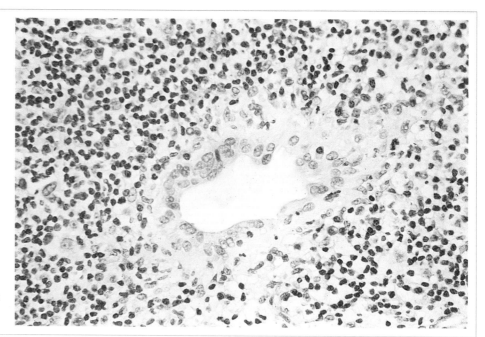

Fig. 16.12 Histology of primary biliary cirrhosis. Lymphocytes surround a bile duct, the epithelium of which is damaged as a result of the autoimmune process.

Non-alcoholic fatty liver disease

The precise diagnosis of fatty liver disease is a common problem. Alcohol is a major cause of a fatty liver, the fat accumulating as globules within the cytoplasm of the liver cells. Non-alcoholic fatty liver disease (NAFLD) occurs in the metabolic syndrome that is characterised by the presence of any three of the following conditions: central obesity, type 2 diabetes mellitus, low levels of HDL cholesterol, hypertriglyceridaemia, and hypertension (Ch. 7). In such patients, if a liver biopsy reveals fat within hepatocytes accompanied by inflammation, the liver lesion can be described as *primary non-alcoholic steatohepatitis (NASH). Secondary NASH* is due to a wide range of other causes, such as drugs (e.g. methotrexate).

Acute fatty liver of pregnancy is a rare but serious condition occurring in the third trimester or in the immediate post-natal period.

CIRRHOSIS

▸ Diffuse and irreversible process
▸ Characterised by fibrosis and nodular regeneration
▸ Classified morphologically and aetiologically
▸ Causes include HBV, HCV, alcohol, autoimmune liver disease and haemochromatosis
▸ Complications are liver failure, portal hypertension and liver cell carcinoma

The liver has considerable powers of regeneration such that quite severe loss of liver cells can be restored and normal architecture retained. However, if the loss of liver cells is recurrent or takes place against a background of severe architectural disturbance (e.g. bridging necrosis) then cirrhosis can result.

Cirrhosis is not a specific disease; it is the end result of a variety of diseases causing chronic liver injury. It is an irreversible disturbance of hepatic architecture, affecting the entire liver, and is characterised by:

● fibrosis
● nodular regeneration.

The amount of fibrous tissue greatly exceeds that in the normal liver and the liver cells are no longer arranged in acini or lobules, but regenerate after various forms of injury in a nodular pattern (Fig. 16.13).

The regeneration nodules lack the well-organised zonal structure of the normal liver lobules or acini. The blood perfuses them in a haphazard fashion, resulting in a relatively inefficient organ that is prone to failure.

Classification

Cirrhosis is classified in two ways:

● morphologically
● aetiologically.

The two classification systems are complementary and not mutually exclusive. The aetiological classification has much greater clinical importance.

Morphological classification

Classified by the average size of the regeneration nodules, cirrhosis may be:

● *micronodular*—nodules up to 3 mm in diameter
● *macronodular*—nodules greater than 3 mm in diameter.

A cirrhotic liver intermediate between these two categories is described as 'mixed'.

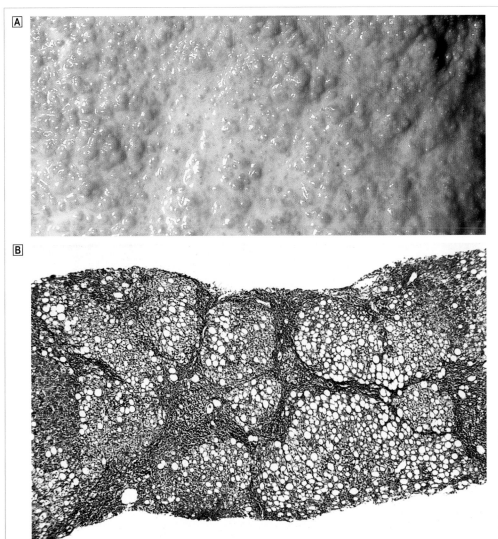

Fig. 16.13 Cirrhotic liver.
A External surface of a cirrhotic liver studded with regeneration nodules about 2 mm in diameter. B Histology of a needle biopsy of a cirrhotic liver revealing regeneration nodules surrounded by dense connective tissue. (Masson trichrome stain in which connective tissue is green.)

One of the commonest causes of micronodular cirrhosis is alcoholic liver disease. The significance of macronodular cirrhosis, irrespective of cause, is that it is believed to carry a greater risk of complication by liver cell carcinoma. Macronodular cirrhosis may also be difficult to diagnose with certainty in needle biopsies because the abnormal architecture is not often revealed fully in such small tissue samples.

Aetiological classification

The aetiological classification of a cirrhotic liver can often be deduced from clinical, biochemical, immunological or biopsy features (Fig. 16.14). Important causes include:

- viral hepatitis (HBV and HCV)
- alcohol
- haemochromatosis
- autoimmune liver disease (autoimmune hepatitis and primary biliary cirrhosis)
- recurrent biliary obstruction (e.g. gallstones)
- Wilson's disease.

In countries such as the UK, alcohol is one of the commonest causes. If the cause is unknown, then the cirrhosis is labelled cryptogenic (hidden cause) or idiopathic, although with modern investigations the proportion of cases thus designated is falling.

Complications

The major complications of cirrhosis are:

- liver failure
- portal hypertension
- liver cell carcinoma.

Liver failure

Liver failure results in:

- inadequate synthesis of albumin, clotting factors, etc.
- failure to eliminate endogenous products such as bilirubin, hormones, nitrogenous waste, etc.

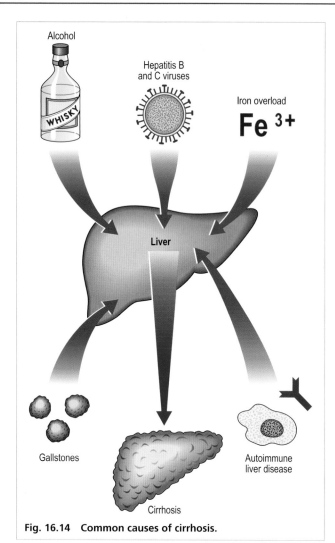

Alcohol

Hepatitis B
and C viruses

Iron overload

Fe^{3+}

Liver

Gallstones

Cirrhosis

Autoimmune
liver disease

Fig. 16.14   Common causes of cirrhosis.

Table 16.5   Pathophysiological basis of clinical features of chronic liver disease

Clinical feature	Explanation
Oedema	Reduced albumin synthesis resulting in hypoalbuminaemia
Ascites	Hypoalbuminaemia, secondary hyperaldosteronism, portal hypertension
Haematemesis	Ruptured oesophageal varices due to portal hypertension
Spider naevi Gynaecomastia	Hyperoestrogenism
Purpura and bleeding	Reduced clotting factor synthesis
Coma	Failure to eliminate toxic gut bacterial metabolites ('false neurotransmitters')
Infection	Reduced Kupffer cell number and function

characteristics and gynaecomastia due to hyperoestrogenism. 'Spider naevi' are small vascular lesions on the skin, commonly seen in pregnancy, associated with hyperoestrogenism in cirrhosis.

Defective Kupffer cell function may be responsible for the increased incidence of bacteraemia in patients with cirrhosis, sometimes in the absence of other manifestations of liver failure.

Portal hypertension

Cirrhosis is the commonest cause of portal hypertension (Fig. 16.15). In cirrhosis, the increased blood pressure (>7 mmHg) in the hepatic portal vein is due to a combination of:

- increased portal blood flow
- increased hepatic vascular resistance
- intrahepatic arteriovenous shunting.

Portal hypertension leads to oesophageal varices (Fig. 16.16) and haemorrhoids (because normal anastomoses between the portal and systemic venous systems at these sites are enlarged) and also contributes to the development of ascites. Oesophageal varices are a particularly serious complication because these thin-walled dilated veins are prone to rupture, causing massive haematemesis which can be fatal. Other manifestations of portal hypertension include the less common 'caput medusae' around the umbilicus. Portal hypertension may be further complicated by portal vein thrombosis; this complication can lead to sudden clinical deterioration.

Cirrhosis may be functionally compensated or decompensated. Indeed, if the disease process that led to the cirrhosis is now inactive, then there may be no detectable abnormalities of liver function. Liver failure is a manifestation of decompensation (Table 16.5) and is characterised clinically by:

- hypoalbuminaemia, causing oedema due to reduced plasma oncotic pressure
- clotting factor deficiencies, causing bruising, etc.
- ascites
- encephalopathy, sometimes leading to coma.

Hepatic encephalopathy is due to the failure of the liver to eliminate toxic nitrogenous products of gut bacteria; some of these mimic the effect of neurotransmitters (i.e. they are 'false neurotransmitters'). Renal failure may also occur with hepatic failure (hepato-renal syndrome). The patient's breath has a characteristic odour (fetor hepaticus).

Failure to eliminate endogenous steroid hormones results in secondary hyperaldosteronism, causing sodium and water retention and, in the male, loss of secondary sexual

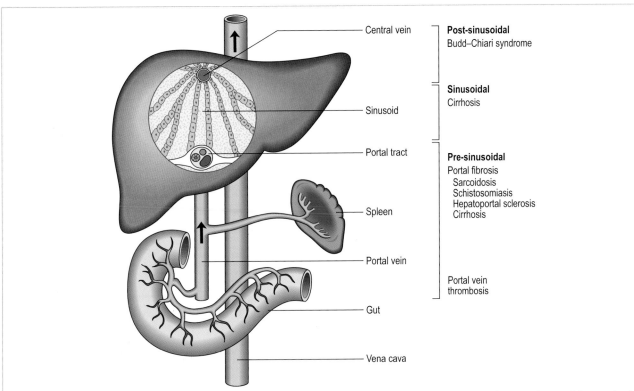

Fig. 16.15 Causes and pathogenesis of portal hypertension. Portal hypertension may be due to haemodynamic abnormalities proximal or distal to the sinusoids or at the sinusoidal level. Increased portal vascular resistance and intrahepatic shunting between high-pressure hepatic arterial and low-pressure portal venous channels are postulated explanations for portal hypertension in cirrhosis.

Liver cell carcinoma

Cirrhosis is a premalignant condition; it is associated with liver cell dysplasia and an increased risk of liver cell carcinoma. The tumour often appears to be multifocal, arising at multiple sites within the liver. The risk is greatest in macronodular cirrhosis and applies to all aetiological types. Liver cell carcinoma is considered in more detail below.

TUMOURS OF THE LIVER

▶ Benign tumours are rarely of clinical significance
▶ Metastatic carcinoma is the most common hepatic tumour
▶ Primary malignant tumours include liver cell carcinoma, cholangiocarcinoma, angiosarcoma and hepatoblastoma

Benign tumours

Benign tumours of the liver rarely give rise to serious clinical problems, except when they cause confusion with their malignant counterparts. Benign tumours of the liver include:

- liver cell adenoma
- angioma
- bile duct hamartoma
- focal nodular hyperplasia.

Liver cell adenoma

Liver cell adenoma is a benign, well-differentiated neoplasm of liver cells. It forms a well-circumscribed nodule, with a texture and colour resembling that of the normal liver. Adenomas may arise spontaneously, but an increased incidence occurs in patients taking anabolic, androgenic or oestrogenic steroids. They may be clinically silent or cause hepatomegaly. Occasionally haemoperitoneum due to spontaneous rupture may be the first manifestation.

Angioma

Angioma, a benign vascular neoplasm, is sometimes multiple, rarely exceeding a few centimetres in diameter. Angiomas are rarely of clinical significance, but they may be mistaken for something more sinister when found unexpectedly during a laparotomy.

Bile duct hamartoma

Bile duct hamartomas are not strictly tumours but are tumour-like congenital malformations. They are usually small and often multiple, sometimes referred to as *von Meyenberg*

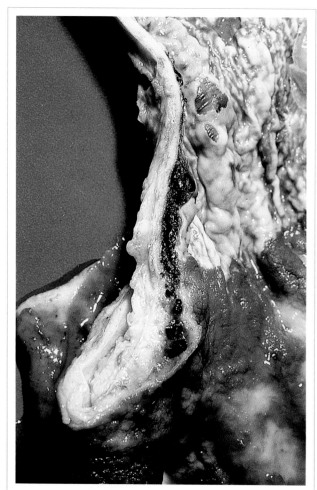

Fig. 16.16   Oesophageal varices. The gastro-oesophageal junction has been sliced to reveal numerous dilated, thin-walled veins in a cirrhotic patient who died from a massive haematemesis.

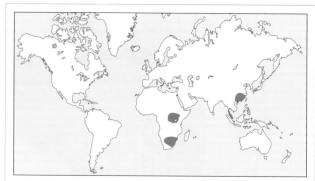

Fig. 16.17   Geographic areas of high incidence of liver cell carcinoma. The tumour occurs in all countries, particularly in patients with cirrhosis. Regions with a well-documented, very high incidence are shaded.

Primary malignant tumours of the liver include:

- liver cell carcinoma (hepatocellular carcinoma)
- cholangiocarcinoma (adenocarcinoma of bile ducts)
- angiosarcoma (malignant neoplasm of vascular endothelium)
- hepatoblastoma (primary liver tumour in childhood).

Metastases

The commonest malignant neoplasms in the liver are metastases from primary lesions in another organ. These metastases usually form multiple deposits with central necrosis, causing an umbilicated appearance when they are visible on the liver surface. They are usually white unless they are derived from a malignant melanoma, in which case they may be dark brown or black. Common primary origins for hepatic metastases include the entire gastrointestinal tract, including pancreas and bowel, the lung and the breast.

Metastases receive their vascular supply from the hepatic arterial system. This is sometimes selectively perfused with cytotoxic drugs or artificially embolised to induce infarction.

Liver cell carcinoma

Liver cell carcinoma (hepatocellular carcinoma) is one of the commonest tumours in some parts of the world (Fig. 16.17). Known or suspected aetiological factors include:

- aflatoxins, carcinogenic mycotoxins produced by the fungus *Aspergillus flavus*, which contaminates food stored in humid conditions
- hepatitis B and C viruses
- hepatic cirrhosis, irrespective of its cause (Fig. 16.18).

Various growth patterns are recognised, resembling to a variable extent the normal trabecular arrangement of liver cells. If the tumour is sufficiently well differentiated it retains the capacity to secrete bile, so that the tumour and any metastases from it appear bile-stained. In cirrhotic livers, liver cell carcinomas are often multifocal.

A type of liver cell carcinoma with specific features is the *fibrolamellar variant* in which the neoplastic liver cells

complexes. They are often seen in association with congenital hepatic fibrosis.

Focal nodular hyperplasia

Focal nodular hyperplasia is neither a true neoplasm nor, despite its name, a hyperplastic disorder; it is thought to be hamartomatous. It is usually solitary and up to 50 mm in diameter. At its centre is a stellate mass of fibrous connective tissue in which there are numerous small bile ducts. The rest of the lesion comprises liver cells and vascular sinusoids. These lesions are usually clinically silent, but they can become abnormally vascular, enlarge and rupture in patients receiving oestrogenic steroids such as oral contraceptives.

Malignant tumours

Malignant tumours in the liver often present with jaundice and weight loss. Most often they are metastases from other organs.

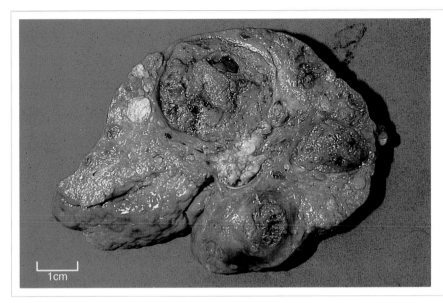

Fig. 16.18 Liver cell carcinoma arising in a cirrhotic liver. Cirrhosis is a pre-neoplastic condition. Several tumour nodules are present, perhaps reflecting the multifocal origin in cirrhotic livers.

are arranged in broad bands or lamellae separated by dense fibrous tissue. This variant occurs most often in young women, without cirrhosis as a predisposing cause.

Liver cell carcinomas often produce alpha-fetoprotein. This is a normal serum protein of the fetus, synthesis of which declines towards the end of gestation when it is replaced by albumin. Alpha-fetoprotein is secreted by the tumour cells into the patient's blood, where it is a useful diagnostic marker.

Cholangiocarcinoma

Cholangiocarcinoma is an adenocarcinoma of bile duct epithelium. In liver biopsies this gland-forming neoplasm can be extremely difficult to distinguish from metastatic adenocarcinoma from some other organ. Known aetiological factors include infestation with the Chinese liver fluke *Clonorchis sinensis* and with *Opisthorchis viverrini*, both of which induce recurrent pyogenic cholangitis ('oriental cholangitis'). There is also an increased incidence of cholangiocarcinoma in patients with ulcerative colitis, particularly in those who have developed sclerosing cholangitis.

Angiosarcoma

This highly malignant neoplasm originates from the endothelium of the vascular sinusoids and infiltrates the liver by spreading along the vascular sinusoids. Known aetiological factors include vinyl chloride, used in the manufacture of polyvinyl chloride (PVC), and administration of the now-obsolete alpha-emitting radiological contrast medium Thorotrast (Ch. 11).

Hepatoblastoma

Hepatoblastoma is a rare malignant neoplasm of the liver occurring almost exclusively in children below the age of 5 years. In a significant proportion of cases it is associated with various developmental abnormalities. Histologically, its growth pattern resembles some features of the embryonic liver, but it

is not uncommon to find unexpected tissues such as muscle. The prognosis is poor.

LIVER CYSTS

Liver cysts can often be distinguished from solid tumours by modern imaging techniques, although some malignant tumours may be so necrotic in the centre that they mimic cysts.

The main varieties are:

- simple cysts
- hydatid cysts
- choledochal cysts.

Simple cysts

Simple cysts are common, relatively small (10–20 mm in diameter), and often multiple. Sometimes they are associated with lesions elsewhere, as in the rare von Hippel–Lindau syndrome. They have little or no intrinsic clinical importance.

Hydatid cysts

Hydatid cysts are due to the parasite *Echinococcus granulosus*. They are usually many centimetres in diameter, have a fibrous laminated wall and contain numerous daughter cysts (Fig. 16.19). Great care must be taken during surgical removal, because spillage of the cyst fluid into the peritoneum may precipitate anaphylactic shock due to the presence of hydatid antigens in a patient already sensitised to them.

Choledochal cysts

Choledochal cysts are uncommon congenital cysts of the bile ducts which may be intra- or extrahepatic. Their presence predisposes to cholangitis.

Fig. 16.19 Hydatid cyst of the liver. The surgically resected cyst has been opened to reveal the enclosed daughter cysts.

LIVER INVOLVEMENT BY SYSTEMIC DISEASE

The liver is commonly affected by disease primarily arising in other organs or systems; this often causes hepatomegaly. Examples include:

- centrilobular congestion and liver cell death in right ventricular heart failure
- granulomas in sarcoidosis
- infiltration by amyloid
- metastatic solid tumours
- infiltration by leukaemic cells in leukaemias
- extramedullary haemopoiesis in myelofibrosis
- fatty change as a non-specific feature in patients ill from a variety of causes.

Liver biopsy is often done in the diagnosis and investigation of systemic diseases such as suspected sarcoidosis or carcinomatosis. The biopsy may be diagnostic of the systemic problem.

The commonest liver involvement by systemic disease occurs in cardiac failure. At autopsy in such cases, the liver appears to have a finely mottled surface due to central acinar congestion surrounded by fatty change. This is the so-called 'nutmeg liver'.

TRANSPLANTATION AND THE LIVER

The pathology of transplantation and the liver is important for two reasons. First, although liver transplants are relatively well tolerated, immunological rejection of the grafted organ can occur. Second, the liver is frequently affected by graft-versus-host disease following allogeneic bone marrow transplantation.

Liver transplants

Liver transplants have been performed successfully since the 1960s. Common indications include congenital abnormalities, advanced hepatitis C and primary biliary cirrhosis. The 5-year survival in experienced centres exceeds 60%.

Although the immunogenicity of the liver is relatively low, for example compared with the kidney, in clinical practice there is still a significant risk of rejection. The most vulnerable cells are biliary epithelium and vascular endothelium; these express MHC class II antigens. Rejection may be:

- *acute*—occurring within 2 weeks of transplantation in most cases and characterised by a mixed inflammatory cell infiltrate in portal tracts and in the endothelial layer of portal and hepatic vein branches (endotheliitis)
- *chronic*—characterised by cell-mediated destruction of intrahepatic bile ducts (vanishing bile duct syndrome) and occlusion of hepatic arteries by macrophages with lipid-laden cytoplasm accumulating in the intima.

Fortunately, close monitoring of liver transplants and improvements in immunosuppressive therapy are gradually reducing the probability of graft loss by rejection.

Graft-versus-host disease

Patients with leukaemia or lymphoma may be treated by allogeneic bone marrow transplantation after whole-body irradiation to eliminate the neoplastic cells. Although every effort is made to find a closely matched donor by histocompatibility testing, there is a risk that the lymphocytes in the marrow allograft will recognise and react to the normal antigens on the host's tissues; the result is graft-versus-host disease. Skin, gut epithelium and the liver are especially vulnerable. In the liver, the principal target for the immune reaction is biliary epithelium. If the condition is untreated, many bile ducts will be destroyed, resulting in jaundice.

BILIARY SYSTEM

NORMAL STRUCTURE AND FUNCTION

The biliary system comprises the intra- and extrahepatic bile ducts and the gallbladder. The system is lined by a glandular mucus-secreting epithelial cell layer. Bile is secreted by the liver into the right and left hepatic ducts which fuse to form the common bile duct. The bile consists of micelles of cholesterol, phospholipid and bile salts, and of course bilirubin.

Bile enters the gallbladder through the cystic duct; it is then stored and concentrated in the gallbladder. In response to the ingestion of food, particularly with a high fat content, the gallbladder contracts by stimulation with cholecystokinin and expels the concentrated bile into the second part of the duodenum, through the ampulla of Vater as the sphincter of Oddi relaxes.

Fig. 16.20 Gallstones and chronic cholecystitis. The thickened gallbladder has been opened to reveal several large cholesterol-rich stones.

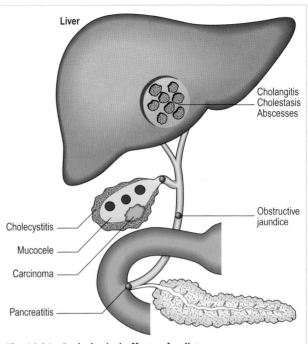

Fig. 16.21 Pathological effects of gallstones.

CONGENITAL ABNORMALITIES

Malformations of the biliary system include:

- *biliary atresia*, in which there is failure of the biliary tree to develop and anastomose normally with intrahepatic structures
- *choledochal cysts* (see above), sometimes associated with *congenital hepatic fibrosis*.

Intrahepatic malformations of the biliary system are inaccessible to surgical correction and, if life-threatening, may be an indication for liver transplantation.

In addition to these malformations, the liver is often affected by the production of abnormally viscous bile in patients with cystic fibrosis (mucoviscidosis) (Ch. 7).

DISEASES OF THE GALLBLADDER

Gallbladder disease is extremely common and in almost every case it is associated with or due to the presence of gallstones.

Cholelithiasis (gallstones)

▶ Risk factors include female gender, obesity, diabetes mellitus
▶ Gallstones consist of pure cholesterol, bile pigment or a mixture
▶ Complications include cholecystitis, obstructive jaundice, carcinoma of the gallbladder

Cholelithiasis is the name given to the common condition in which *gallstones* form within the biliary system. Risk factors for cholesterol-rich stones include female gender and obesity (hence 'fat, fair, forty, fertile, female', an alliterative description of the typical patient) and diabetes mellitus. Stones are prone to occur if there is a relative excess of cholesterol in the bile. Gallstones are usually composed of a mixture of cholesterol and bile pigment (Fig. 16.20), although almost pure cholesterol or pigment stones are occasionally found. Pure pigment gallstones occur notably in patients with haemolytic anaemia where there is consequent excessive excretion of bilirubin. Calcium carbonate stones are also found rarely.

The stones often have a laminated internal structure and, if multiple (as they commonly are), have faceted surfaces.

Pathogenesis

Cholesterol stones may form if there is an imbalance between the ratio of cholesterol and bile salts; normally, the latter form micelles which have a hydrophilic exterior enclosing the hydrophobic cholesterol. Thus, gallstones can result from:

- an excess of cholesterol
- a deficit of bile salts.

Pathological effects

The pathological effects of gallstones include (Fig. 16.21):

- inflammation of the gallbladder (cholecystitis)
- mucocele

- predisposition to carcinoma of the gallbladder
- obstruction of the biliary system resulting in biliary colic and jaundice
- infection of static bile, causing cholangitis and liver abscesses
- gallstone ileus due to intestinal obstruction by a gallstone that has entered the gut through a fistulous connection with the gallbladder
- pancreatitis.

Cholesterosis

Cholesterosis is the name given to the clinically unimportant occurrence of cholesterol-laden macrophages in the lamina propria of the gallbladder mucosa. This occurrence gives the mucosa a yellow-speckled appearance known as 'strawberry gallbladder'.

Cholecystitis

Cholecystitis is an inflammatory condition of the gallbladder. It is almost always associated with gallstones and occurs as an acute or chronic condition. It is a common cause of abdominal pain in the right hypochondrium.

Acute cholecystitis

- ▸ Usually associated with gallstones
- ▸ Initially sterile, then infected
- ▸ Complications include empyema and/or rupture

Acute cholecystitis is usually due to obstruction of the outflow from the gallbladder by a gallstone. The initial inflammatory reaction is due to the irritant effects of bile and is therefore usually sterile at this stage. However, stasis of bile predisposes to infection, which then stimulates a more vigorous and often pyogenic acute inflammatory response. The gallbladder wall becomes oedematous, due to increased vascular permeability, and infiltrated with acute inflammatory cells. The lumen distends with pus, and stretching of the wall already weakened by inflammation leads to a risk of perforation and peritonitis. Alternatively, a fistula may form with the second part of the duodenum and allow stones to enter the bowel lumen. Large stones may occasionally lodge at the ileocaecal valve and cause intestinal obstruction (gallstone ileus).

An inflamed gallbladder grossly distended with pus is called an *empyema*.

Chronic cholecystitis

- ▸ Invariably associated with gallstones
- ▸ Fibrosis and Aschoff–Rokitansky sinuses

Chronic cholecystitis may develop insidiously or after repeated episodes of acute cholecystitis.

The gallbladder wall is thickened by fibrosis and is relatively rigid. Thus obstructive jaundice due to gallstones is not usually associated with a palpable gallbladder because the stones will be associated with chronic cholecystitis and therefore a rigid gallbladder. Conversely, obstructive jaundice due to carcinoma of the head of the pancreas often results in a palpable distended gallbladder; this is the pathological basis of *Courvoisier's law*.

The thick gallbladder wall has within it Aschoff–Rokitansky sinuses, mucosal herniations (diverticula) often containing inspissated bile or even small stones. The wall bears an infiltrate of chronic inflammatory cells and the blood vessels often show endarteritis obliterans (Fig. 16.22). A stone is often found in Hartmann's pouch, a pathological dilatation in the neck of the gallbladder formed by increased intraluminal pressure or impaction of the stone.

A rare variant is *xanthogranulomatous cholecystitis* in which lipid-laden macrophages and giant cells accumulate in large numbers; this mimics a neoplasm grossly and, specifically, a clear-cell carcinoma histologically. The lesion, like its more common renal counterpart, xanthogranulomatous pyelonephritis, is prone to cause fistulae.

Mucocele

A mucocele of the gallbladder is the result of sterile obstruction of the neck by a gallstone. The lack of inflammation permits the gallbladder to distend with mucus without rupturing. The mucocele has a thin wall and demands careful handling during surgical removal to avoid the risk of spillage of mucus

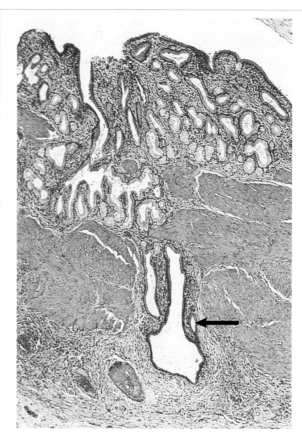

Fig. 16.22 Histology of chronic cholecystitis. A thickened gallbladder with diffuse chronic inflammatory infiltration and Aschoff–Rokitansky sinuses (arrowed).

into the peritoneal cavity and thus the risk of pseudomyxoma peritonei, a rare complication in which the peritoneum becomes seeded with mucus-producing epithelial cells and the cavity fills with mucus.

Carcinoma of the gallbladder

▶ Usually an adenocarcinoma
▶ Invariably associated with gallstones

Carcinoma of the gallbladder is almost always associated with the presence of gallstones; this relationship may be causal. The tumour is most often an adenocarcinoma, although squamous cell carcinoma is also seen. As the gallbladder is not a vital organ, the tumour is often advanced at the time of clinical presentation, and invasion of the liver and other adjacent structures defeats attempts at operative removal. It therefore has a poor prognosis.

Carcinoma of the bile duct

▶ Adenocarcinoma
▶ Increased incidence in ulcerative colitis
▶ Presents with jaundice

Carcinoma of the bile duct is most commonly an adenocarcinoma. There is an increased incidence in patients with chronic ulcerative colitis. It tends to present at a relatively early stage with obstructive jaundice.

Biliary obstruction

Bile duct obstruction is a fairly common event and may be due to:

- gallstones
- carcinoma of the common bile duct
- carcinoma of the head of the pancreas
- inflammatory stricture of the common bile duct
- accidental surgical ligation of the common bile duct.

The patient becomes jaundiced, deeply so if the obstruction is not relieved, with a raised conjugated serum bilirubin, pale stools and dark urine. A raised serum alkaline phosphatase with only modest elevation of transaminases is usual.

If the biliary obstruction persists, there is a risk that the static bile becomes infected, causing acute *cholangitis* and eventually liver abscesses. Lack of bile in the small intestine compromises the absorption of fat and fat-soluble substances (e.g. some vitamins).

Diseases of intrahepatic bile ducts

A clinical picture similar to that of biliary obstruction can result from diseases of intrahepatic bile ducts such as:

- biliary atresia
- primary biliary cirrhosis
- sclerosing cholangitis.

These conditions can usually be distinguished by careful clinical assessment, liver biopsy and imaging techniques.

EXOCRINE PANCREAS

NORMAL STRUCTURE AND FUNCTION

The pancreas is a retroperitoneal organ, the head and uncinate process lying within the duodenal loop, the body crossing the aorta and inferior vena cava, and the tail abutting onto the splenic hilum.

The pancreas is a mixed exocrine and endocrine organ. Scattered through the gland are the islets of Langerhans consisting of endocrine cells producing peptide hormones, the most important of which are insulin and glucagon (Ch. 17); their secretion drains directly into the blood and ultimately into the liver through the hepatic portal vein.

The exocrine pancreas comprises the bulk of the organ and is composed of glands and ducts with a lobular arrangement, the latter fusing to form the pancreatic and accessory ducts which convey the exocrine secretions into the duodenum. The exocrine glands contain numerous zymogen granules and produce trypsin, lipase, phospholipase, amylase and elastase; these enzymes require activation, normally in the duodenum. The pancreas also secretes a bicarbonate-rich alkaline medium.

Some of the exocrine glands are perfused with blood that has already perfused islets in the vicinity (i.e. they have a portal blood supply). This almost certainly provides some physiological advantages, but it does mean that these glands are especially vulnerable to ischaemia if the circulation is impaired.

INVESTIGATION OF PANCREATIC DISEASE

Disorders of the exocrine pancreas can be investigated radiologically by the technique of ERCP (endoscopic retrograde cholangiopancreatography) or MRCP (magnetic resonance cholangiopancreatography). These techniques reveal any deformities due to inflammatory fibrosis or tumours. Pancreatic juice can be collected through the cannula and examined biochemically for enzymes, or cytologically for abnormal cells such as may be shed from a carcinoma.

Operative biopsies of the pancreas are hazardous because there is a significant risk of precipitating acute pancreatitis (inflammation of the pancreas) due to leakage of exocrine secretions. Nevertheless, an intra-operative frozen section diagnosis may be required in cases of suspected pancreatic carcinoma before attempting to remove the lesion, a procedure with a relatively high post-operative complication rate. Fine-needle aspiration cytology is possible through the unopened abdomen under ultrasonographic or computed axial tomography (CAT) guidance.

Serum amylase is an important marker of pancreatic inflammation. The concentration is greatly elevated in acute pancreatitis; lesser elevations may occur following a perforated peptic ulcer.

CONGENITAL ABNORMALITIES

Congenital abnormalities of the pancreas include:

- *annular pancreas* encircling, and sometimes obstructing, the duodenum
- *pancreas divisum* due to failure of fusion of the two embryological anlagen
- *ectopic pancreatic tissue* (in the stomach or in a Meckel's diverticulum)
- *cysts*.

In addition, the pancreas is severely affected in cystic fibrosis (mucoviscidosis), a congenital disorder of exocrine secretions in which they are abnormally viscous (Ch. 7). The mucus plugs the pancreatic ducts, resulting in retention of secretions and damage to the exocrine glands.

DISEASES OF THE PANCREAS

Pancreatitis

Pancreatitis (inflammation of the pancreas) can be classified into acute and chronic forms. There is, however, overlap in that patients with chronic pancreatitis may have acute exacerbations.

Acute pancreatitis

> - Aetiological factors include duct obstruction, shock, alcohol, etc.
> - Amylase is released into blood (diagnostically useful)
> - Often haemorrhagic
> - Fat necrosis in surrounding tissue binds calcium

Aetiology
Acute pancreatitis (Fig. 16.23) may be due to:

- obstruction of the pancreatic duct
- bile reflux
- alcohol, particularly acute intoxication
- vascular insufficiency (e.g. shock)
- mumps virus infection
- hyperparathyroidism
- hypothermia
- trauma
- iatrogenic factors (e.g. after ERCP).

Although many cases are mild, acute pancreatitis is often a serious disorder with a high mortality. It is more common in adults than in children. The condition is serious because the gland, once injured, releases its lytic enzymes into the blood, contributing to the severe shock, and into the surrounding tissue, causing tissue digestion.

Clinical features
Patients present with a sudden onset of severe abdominal pain, often radiating into the back, and nausea and vomiting. The upper abdomen is tender. The clinical deterioration may

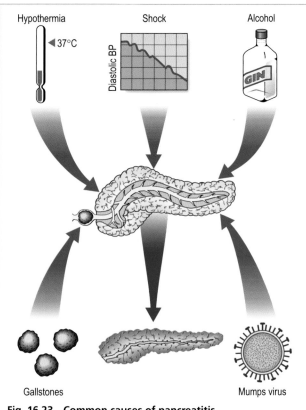

Fig. 16.23　Common causes of pancreatitis.

be rapid, the patient becoming severely shocked. Diagnosis is made by finding a greatly elevated serum amylase concentration.

Pathogenesis
The pathogenesis of the early stages varies according to the aetiology. For example, when the pancreatic duct is obstructed by a gallstone at the ampulla of Vater, or where there is biliary reflux into the pancreatic duct for any other reason, the duct epithelium is damaged, particularly if the bile is infected or admixed with trypsin. The damage extends into the gland and results in the leakage and activation of pancreatic enzymes. In contrast, when pancreatitis is attributable to vascular insufficiency, the hypoxic injury due to reduced blood flow occurs first in the acini at the periphery of the lobules; they are precariously remote from the vascular supply and some are fed by portal vessels from islets in the vicinity. Irrespective of the initiating event, the liberation of lytic enzymes causes further damage and diffuse pancreatitis develops rapidly.

The gland becomes swollen and often haemorrhagic if the inflammation is severe. Proteases digest the walls of blood vessels, causing extravasation of blood. Amylase is released into the blood, where measurement of its concentration is an important diagnostic marker of the condition.

Lipolytic action causes fat necrosis, which can be quite extensive within the abdomen and subcutaneous tissue. Sometimes the necrosis extends anteriorly around the abdominal wall to produce discoloration of the skin (Grey Turner's

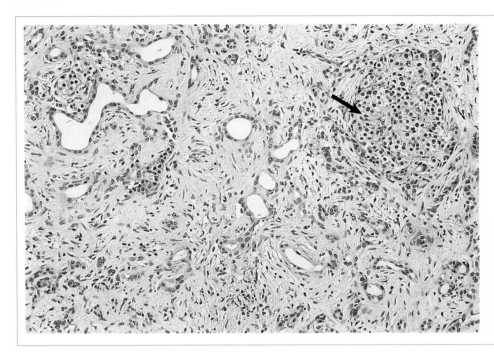

Fig. 16.24 Histology of chronic pancreatitis. There is considerable loss of acini and replacement by fibrosis. Inflammatory cells are relatively inconspicuous at this late stage. Islets of Langerhans (one is arrowed) sometimes escape destruction, but their loss can result in diabetes mellitus.

sign). The released fatty acids bind calcium ions, forming white precipitates in the necrotic fat; severe fat necrosis can bind so much calcium that hypocalcaemia results, sometimes causing tetany.

Concomitant destruction of the adjacent islets can result in hyperglycaemia.

Other complications include the formation of abscesses and cysts within the pancreas or adjacent tissues. These often necessitate surgical drainage.

Chronic pancreatitis

▶ Commonest cause is alcohol (long-term excess)
▶ Pancreas shows fibrosis and exocrine atrophy
▶ May result in intestinal malabsorption due to loss of pancreatic secretions

Aetiology
Chronic pancreatitis is a relapsing disorder that may either result from repeated episodes of clinically evident acute pancreatitis or develop insidiously without previous symptoms of pancreatic disease. The commonest cause is chronic excessive alcohol consumption. A much less common, but increasingly recognised, *autoimmune pancreatitis* also occurs. Chronic pancreatitis is also a feature of cystic fibrosis (mucoviscidosis). There is also a rare familial pancreatitis inherited as an autosomal dominant trait, in some cases associated with aminoaciduria or hyperparathyroidism.

Clinicopathological features
Chronic pancreatitis is more common in adults than in children, and presents with intermittent upper abdominal and back pain and weight loss. A plain X-ray of the upper abdomen often reveals flecks of calcification due to previous fat necrosis. ERCP or MRCP often shows that the pancreatic ducts are distorted by scar tissue resulting from the chronic inflammatory process.

The exocrine tissue is eventually replaced by fibrosis (Fig. 16.24) and, if localised, its hard texture mimics that of a carcinoma when the gland is palpated during laparotomy. The endocrine component of the gland is relatively unaffected except at an advanced stage.

Pancreatic malabsorption
Chronic pancreatitis, with loss of exocrine secretions, results in malabsorption of fat because of the relative lack of lipases. The patient's faeces contain abnormally high quantities of fat (steatorrhoea), and absorption of fat-soluble substances such as vitamins A, D, E and K is impaired.

Carcinoma of the pancreas

▶ Usually adenocarcinoma
▶ May present with obstructive jaundice
▶ Very poor prognosis

Aetiology
Pancreatic carcinoma is increasing in incidence in many countries. Over 7000 cases occur annually in the United Kingdom. There is an association with cigarette smoking and with diabetes mellitus. There appears to be an increased risk in the rare entity of familial pancreatitis. The prognosis is poor even in operable cases.

Weight loss is a common presenting feature; other symptoms are attributable to the precise location of the tumour. Some cases develop flitting venous thromboses (thrombophlebitis migrans): this is *Trousseau's sign*.

Clinicopathological features

Most pancreatic carcinomas are adenocarcinomas with a marked desmoplastic stromal reaction (Fig. 16.25), making them very firm on palpation during surgery. They arise most commonly in the head of the organ, where they tend to compress the common bile duct and cause obstructive jaundice. Elsewhere in the gland, they can present at a relatively late stage because they cause few signs or symptoms. Extensive replacement of the gland by carcinoma can lead to diabetes mellitus due to destruction of the islets of Langerhans.

Pancreatic adenocarcinomas spread by direct invasion, by lymphatics to lymph nodes and by the blood stream to the liver (Fig. 16.26). Prognosis is relatively poor because metastases are often present at the time of surgery. If surgical removal is attempted, it involves excision of at least part of the pancreas, the duodenum and regional nodes with anastomotic restoration of intestinal, biliary and residual pancreatic flow; this procedure is associated with a high risk of operative complications and death.

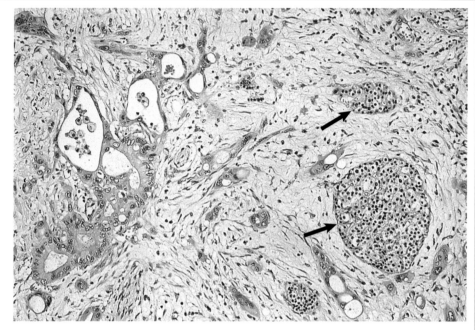

Fig. 16.25 Histology of pancreatic adenocarcinoma. The neoplastic glands with pleomorphic atypical nuclei are invested by dense fibrous connective tissue, thus mimicking the texture of chronic pancreatitis when the gland is palpated during surgery. Islets of Langerhans (arrowed) survive at the edge of the tumour.

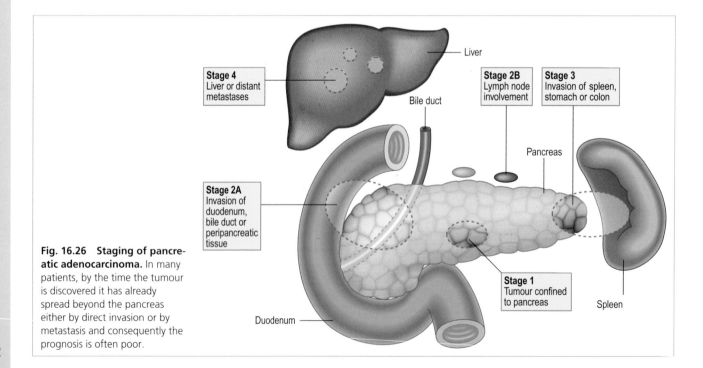

Fig. 16.26 Staging of pancreatic adenocarcinoma. In many patients, by the time the tumour is discovered it has already spread beyond the pancreas either by direct invasion or by metastasis and consequently the prognosis is often poor.

Stage 4
Liver or distant metastases

Stage 2B
Lymph node involvement

Stage 3
Invasion of spleen, stomach or colon

Liver

Bile duct

Pancreas

Stage 2A
Invasion of duodenum, bile duct or peripancreatic tissue

Stage 1
Tumour confined to pancreas

Spleen

Duodenum

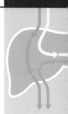

Cysts and cystic tumours

Pancreatic cysts are of two types:

- *true cysts*, which are lined by epithelium and may be congenital

- *pseudocysts*, which lack an epithelial lining and are often the result of acute pancreatitis; they can be drained surgically.

True cystic tumours also occur—the benign *cystadenoma* and its malignant variant, *cystadenocarcinoma*.

Commonly confused conditions and entities relating to liver, biliary and pancreatic pathology	
Commonly confused	Distinction and explanation
Cholestasis and *jaundice*	*Cholestasis* is stagnation of bile, usually within the liver where, histologically, it is seen in liver cells or in the canaliculi between them or in bile ducts. *Jaundice* is yellowness of the tissues due to abnormally high levels of bilirubin.
Cholestasis and *cholangitis*	*Cholestasis* is stagnation of bile, usually within the liver where, histologically, it is seen in liver cells or in the canaliculi between them or in bile ducts. *Cholangitis* is inflammation of the bile ducts, usually precipitated by biliary obstruction with secondary bacterial infection. However, in sclerosing cholangitis the inflammatory activity may be minor.
Lupoid hepatitis and *systemic lupus erythematosus* (SLE)	*Lupoid hepatitis*, better known as autoimmune hepatitis, is 'lupoid' only because it shares with SLE a tendency to affect young adult women and the presence of anti-DNA auto-antibodies.
Haemosiderosis and *haemochromatosis*	*Haemosiderosis* means only the presence of excess iron, as haemosiderin, in the liver. This is a feature of *haemochromatosis* (genetic or acquired) characterised by excessive iron deposition accompanied by fibrosis and, eventually, cirrhosis.
Gallbladder empyema and *emphysema*	*Empyema* is the presence of pus in a hollow organ or body cavity. *Emphysema* (pulmonary or interstitial) is the presence of abnormal gas-filled spaces.
Cholecystitis and *cholesterosis*	*Cholecystitis* (acute or chronic) is inflammation of the gallbladder. *Cholesterosis* is the presence of lipid-filled histiocytes in the lamina propria of the gallbladder mucosa; it is clinically insignificant.
Pancreatic cysts and *pseudocysts*	*Cysts* have an epithelial lining and are developmental or neoplastic, in contrast to *pseudocysts* which are devoid of an epithelial lining and commonly develop in the pancreas after pancreatitis.

FURTHER READING

Ala A, Walker A P, Ashkan K et al 2007 Wilson's disease. Lancet 369: 397–408

Burt A D, Portmann B C, Ferrell L D 2006 MacSween's pathology of the liver. Churchill Livingstone, Edinburgh

Cruickshank A H, Benbow E W 1995 Pathology of the pancreas. Springer Verlag, Berlin

Davis B H, Kresina T E 1996 Hepatic fibrogenesis. Clinics in Laboratory Medicine 16: 261–275

Desmet V J, Rosai J 2004 Liver. In: Rosai J (ed) Rosai and Ackerman's surgical pathology. Mosby, St Louis, pp 917–1033

Di Bisceglie A M 1998 Hepatitis C. Lancet 351: 351–355

Goodman Z D 2002 Drug hepatotoxicity. Clinics in Liver Disease 6: 381–397

Haugk B, Burt A D 2005 Non-alcoholic fatty liver disease. In: Pignatelli M, Underwood J C E (eds) 2005 Recent advances in histopathology, Vol 21. RSM Press, London, pp 1–17

Herzer K, Sprinzl M F, Galle P R 2007 Hepatitis viruses: live and let die. Liver International 27: 293–301

Ishak K, Baptista A, Bianchi L et al 1995 Histological grading and staging of chronic hepatitis. Journal of Hepatology 22: 696–699

Kaplan M M, Gershwin M E 2005 Primary biliary cirrhosis. New England Journal of Medicine 353: 1261–1273

Kasai Y, Takeda S, Takagi H 1996 Pathogenesis of hepatocellular carcinoma: a review from the viewpoint of molecular analysis. Seminars in Surgical Oncology 12: 155–159

Krawitt E L 2006 Autoimmune hepatitis. New England Journal of Medicine 354: 54–66

Neoptolemos J, Lemoine N 1995 Pancreatic cancer: molecular and clinical advances. Blackwell Science, Oxford

Pietrangelo A 2006 Molecular insights into the pathogenesis of hereditary haemochromatosis. Gut 55: 564–568

Rosai J 2004 Gallbladder and extrahepatic bile ducts. In: Rosai J (ed) Rosai and Ackerman's surgical pathology. Mosby, St Louis, pp 1035–1060

Rosai J 2004 Pancreas and ampullary region. In: Rosai J (ed) Rosai and Ackerman's surgical pathology. Mosby, St Louis, pp 1061–1114

Sanders G, Kingsnorth A N 2007 Gallstones. British Medical Journal 335: 295–299

Scheuer P J 2003 Assessment of liver biopsies in chronic hepatitis: how is it best done? Journal of Hepatology 38: 240–242

Scheuer P J, Lefkowitch J H 2006 Liver biopsy interpretation. W B Saunders, London

Teckman J, Perlmutter D H 1995 Conceptual advances in pathogenesis and treatment of childhood metabolic liver disease. Gastroenterology 108: 1263–1279

Tsukamoto H, Lu S C 2001 Current concepts in the pathogenesis of liver injury. FASEB Journal 15: 1335–1349

17

Endocrine system

COMMON CLINICAL PROBLEMS FROM ENDOCRINE DISEASE

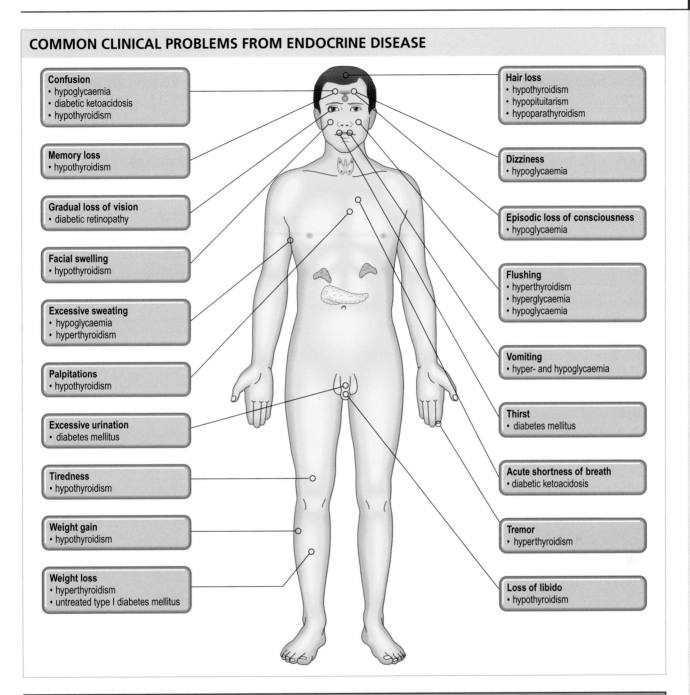

Confusion
- hypoglycaemia
- diabetic ketoacidosis
- hypothyroidism

Memory loss
- hypothyroidism

Gradual loss of vision
- diabetic retinopathy

Facial swelling
- hypothyroidism

Excessive sweating
- hypoglycaemia
- hyperthyroidism

Palpitations
- hypothyroidism

Excessive urination
- diabetes mellitus

Tiredness
- hypothyroidism

Weight gain
- hypothyroidism

Weight loss
- hyperthyroidism
- untreated type I diabetes mellitus

Hair loss
- hypothyroidism
- hypopituitarism
- hypoparathyroidism

Dizziness
- hypoglycaemia

Episodic loss of consciousness
- hypoglycaemia

Flushing
- hyperthyroidism
- hyperglycaemia
- hypoglycaemia

Vomiting
- hyper- and hypoglycaemia

Thirst
- diabetes mellitus

Acute shortness of breath
- diabetic ketoacidosis

Tremor
- hyperthyroidism

Loss of libido
- hypothyroidism

Pathological basis of endocrine signs and symptoms	
Sign or symptom	Pathological basis
Signs or symptoms of hormone excess (hyperfunction)	Endocrine gland hyperplasia caused by increased trophic stimulus to secretion
	Functioning neoplasm of endocrine gland
Signs or symptoms of hormone deficiency (hypofunction)	Endocrine gland atrophy due to loss of trophic stimulus to secretion
	Destruction of endocrine gland by inflammation, ischaemia or non-functioning tumour
Diffuse enlargement of gland	Inflammatory cell infiltration
	Hyperplasia

(Continued)

Pathological basis of endocrine signs and symptoms—cont'd	
Sign or symptom	Pathological basis
Nodular enlargement of gland	Tumour (benign or malignant)
Some organ-specific features	
• Headache, bitemporal hemianopia	Pituitary tumour
• Anxiety, sweating, tremor	Increased thyroid hormone secretion due to hyperplasia or neoplasia of gland
• Exophthalmos	Autoimmune involvement of retrobulbar connective tissue in Graves' disease
• Hypertension	Adrenocortical hyperplasia or neoplasia
	Adrenal medullary neoplasm (phaeochromocytoma)
• Excessive growth (features vary according to whether pre- or post-pubertal)	Growth hormone-secreting pituitary tumour
• Glycosuria	Absolute or relative deficiency of insulin (diabetes mellitus)

NORMAL STRUCTURE AND FUNCTION

An *endocrine gland* secretes hormones directly into the blood stream to reach distant 'target organs' where the secretory products exert their effects. Endocrine glands are thus distinguished from *exocrine glands*, whose secretions pass into the gut or respiratory tract, or on to the exterior of the body; examples of exocrine glands include the exocrine pancreas and the bronchial mucous glands. Closely related to the endocrine system is the *paracrine (diffuse endocrine) system*, consisting of regional distributions of specialised cells producing locally acting hormones, such as those regulating gut motility, and forming part of the neuroendocrine system (Ch. 15); *autocrine effects* are those acting on the cell producing the hormone (Fig. 17.1).

Hormones exert their effects on the target organs by binding to receptors, protein molecules with high and specific affinity for the hormone. These hormone receptors may be either on the cell surface (for example, thyroid-stimulating hormone receptors on the thyroid epithelium) or intracellular (for example, nuclear receptors for steroid hormones). The binding of a hormone to its cell surface receptor sets off a series of intracellular signals via secondary 'messenger' molecules (cyclic nucleotides), which results in changes in metabolic activity, differentiation or mitosis of the stimulated cell.

ENDOCRINE PATHOLOGY

The major disorders of an endocrine gland are:

- hyperfunction
- hypofunction
- benign and malignant tumours, which themselves may cause disordered function.

There are several important general considerations in endocrine pathology. First, disease of one endocrine gland cannot usually be considered in isolation, because

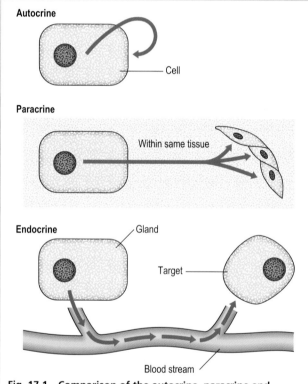

Fig. 17.1 Comparison of the autocrine, paracrine and endocrine systems. See text for details.

it almost always has implications for other endocrine glands:

- Many glands are interdependent, for example hypersecretion of a hormone by one gland may stimulate a target endocrine gland into overactivity.
- Tumours or hyperfunction of one endocrine gland may be associated with similar disease in other glands in the multiple endocrine neoplasia (MEN) syndromes (Fig. 17.2).

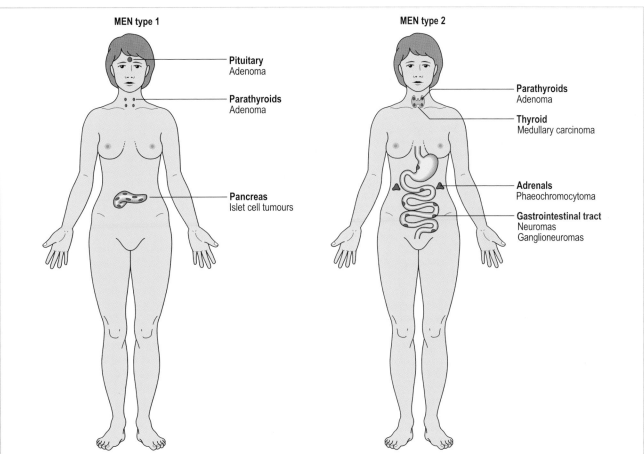

Fig. 17.2 Multiple endocrine neoplasia (MEN) syndromes. MEN syndromes are characterised by the occurrence of tumours in more than one endocrine organ. MEN types 1 and 2 can be distinguished by the organs commonly involved.

- Organ-specific autoimmune disease may affect more than one endocrine gland.

Second, one hormone may have many diverse clinical effects, so that malfunction of one endocrine gland may produce numerous clinical features.

Third, the same hormone may be produced in more than one site; thus, ectopic hormone production by tumours of non-endocrine tissues may simulate primary endocrine disease.

PITUITARY

The pituitary is a small gland, weighing only 500–1000 mg. It is situated in the sella turcica of the skull beneath the hypothalamus. Despite its small size, it exerts many essential control functions over the rest of the endocrine system, earning it the title 'conductor of the endocrine orchestra'. It consists of two parts (Fig. 17.3), each with separate functions. The anterior pituitary, the adenohypophysis, is developed from Rathke's pouch, an outpouching of the roof of the embryonic oral cavity; it comprises about

75% of the bulk of the gland. The posterior pituitary, the neurohypophysis, is derived from a downgrowth of the hypothalamus.

ADENOHYPOPHYSIS

Classification of cell types

Modern histological classification of the types of hormone-secreting cell is based on immunohistochemistry, a technique in which antibodies raised to a hormone bind to the cells containing that hormone in tissue sections, leading to a coloured stain (Fig. 17.4). This has enabled the true hormone content of the cells to be determined, and has rendered obsolete the traditional classification of the cells into eosinophil, basophil and chromophobe types according to their staining by haematoxylin and eosin (H&E). By electron microscopy, the cells of the adenohypophysis are seen to contain electron-dense granules ranging from 50 to 500 nm in diameter (Fig. 17.5); these contain stored secretory products. The six types of hormone-secreting cell are shown in Table 17.1.

Control of hormone secretion

Hormonal control factors

The adenohypophysis lacks any direct arterial supply. Blood from the hypothalamus passes down venous portal channels in the pituitary stalk (Fig. 17.3) into sinusoids which ramify within the gland. In this way hormonal control factors produced by neurosecretory cells in the hypothalamus are carried directly to the hormone-producing cells of the adenohypophysis. The known hormonal control factors and their effects are listed in Table 17.2. In general, these factors stimulate the particular secretory cells under their control into activity; the exception is prolactin-inhibiting factor, whose effect on the lactotrophs is inhibitory.

Secretion of these hormonal control factors by the hypothalamus is under two types of control: neural and hormonal. *Neural control* is via nerves from other parts of the central nervous system, and is important in reactions to stress and in changes during sleep. *Hormonal control* is a negative feedback mechanism in which the hypothalamus monitors the level of adenohypophysial hormones in the blood and adjusts its output of hormonal control factors accordingly, so as to stabilise the level of each adenohypophysial hormone at the optimum level. This is called the *hypothalamic–hypophysial feedback control*.

Feedback control

In addition to control via the hypothalamus, a more direct method of control of the adenohypophysis also exists, whereby its cells respond directly to the levels of hormones and metabolites in the blood. Most adenohypophysial hormones stimulate another endocrine gland, termed the 'target' gland; for example, ACTH stimulates the adrenal cortex to produce steroid hormones, and TSH stimulates the thyroid to produce thyroxine.

In these examples, the level of hormone from the target gland is monitored for feedback control. However, in the case of growth hormone, which has no single target gland, it is the level of metabolites such as glucose that is monitored. A general scheme of the feedback control mechanisms operating in the regulation of a hypophysial hormone is shown in Figure 17.3.

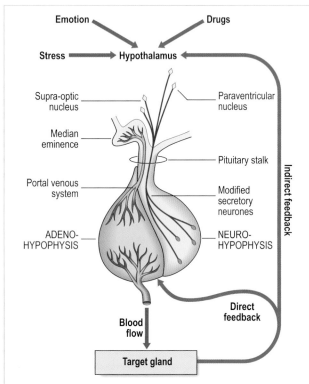

Fig. 17.3   The pituitary and its physiological relationships. The pituitary is controlled both by hormones from its target glands, and via the hypothalamus.

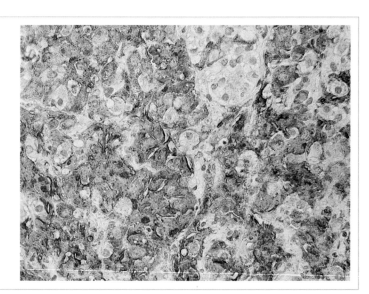

Fig. 17.4   Growth hormone-containing cells in an adenoma of the adenohypophysis. Immunoperoxidase localisation of growth hormone. Cells containing growth hormone are stained brown by this technique.

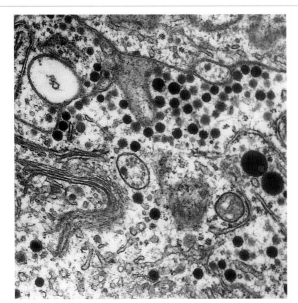

Fig. 17.5   Electron micrograph of a secretory cell of the adenohypophysis. The hormonal products are stored as electron-dense membrane-bound cytoplasmic granules (× 300 000).

Table 17.1	Hormone-secreting cells of the adenohypophysis	
Cell type	Staining reaction with H&E	Hormonal product
Corticotroph	Basophilic	Adenocorticotrophic hormone (ACTH)
Thyrotroph	Basophilic	Thyroid-stimulating hormone (TSH)
Gonadotroph	Basophilic	Follicle-stimulating hormone (FSH) Luteinising hormone (LH)
Somatotroph	Eosinophilic	Growth hormone (GH)
Lactotroph	Eosinophilic	Prolactin (PL)
Chromophobe	Pale	Unknown

Adenohypophysial hormones

Adrenocorticotrophic hormone

Adrenocorticotrophic hormone (ACTH), a peptide consisting of 39 amino acids, causes increased cell numbers (hyperplasia) and increased secretory activity in the adrenal cortex. Glucocorticoid output is elevated, but there is no effect on the output of mineralocorticoids, such as aldosterone, that are not under anterior pituitary control. ACTH levels show a marked circadian variation, being highest early in the morning.

Table 17.2	Hormonal control factors and their effects on the adenohypophysis	
Hormonal control factor		Effect
Corticotrophin-releasing factor (CRF)		Corticotrophs release ACTH
Thyrotrophin-releasing factor (TRF)		Thyrotrophs release TSH
Gonadotrophin-releasing factor (FSH/LH-RF)		Gonadotrophs release FSH/LH
Growth hormone-releasing factor (GHRF)		Somatotrophs release GH
Prolactin-inhibiting factor (PIF)		Lactotrophs inhibited from releasing PL

Thyroid-stimulating hormone

Thyroid-stimulating hormone (TSH) is a glycoprotein that induces proliferation of the follicular cells of the thyroid, synthesis of thyroxine (T_4) and tri-iodothyronine (T_3), and secretion of these into the blood. Measurement of TSH levels provides information on the state of the control system of the thyroid and is valuable in the diagnosis of thyroid malfunction.

Gonadotrophic hormones

In the female, follicle-stimulating hormone (FSH) induces growth of Graafian follicles in the ovaries; these secrete oestrogens, which in turn cause endometrial proliferation. After rupture of the follicle at ovulation, luteinising hormone (LH) causes a change in the follicle cells known as luteinisation, whereby their secretory product changes from oestrogens to progesterone which induces secretory changes in the endometrium. Both gonadotrophic hormones are glycoproteins.

The hypothalamus monitors circulating levels of the sex steroids including oestrogens and progesterone, and releases probably a single hormonal control factor, FSH/LH-releasing factor (FSH/LH-RF), to control the adenohypophysial gonadotrophs. Their response to this factor depends on the prevailing levels of sex steroids. Cyclical changes in this feedback loop form the hormonal basis for the menstrual cycle.

In the male, FSH and LH both exist but, in the absence of ovaries as the target organ, their names are inappropriate to their actions. LH stimulates testosterone production by the interstitial cells of Leydig in the testes, while FSH stimulates spermatogenesis.

The circulating levels of FSH and LH vary markedly with age: they increase at puberty and are very high in females after the menopause.

Growth hormone

Growth hormone (GH) is a protein containing 191 amino acids; it binds to receptors on the surface of various cells and thus causes increased protein synthesis, accelerates

breakdown of fatty tissue to produce energy, and tends to raise the blood glucose. It is vital for normal growth; deficiency causes dwarfism. Part of its action at tissue level is mediated by a group of peptide growth factors known as somatomedins. The hypothalamic control of GH release from the hypothalamus is complex, there being both a growth hormone-releasing factor (GH-RF) and an inhibitory factor, somatostatin.

Prolactin

Prolactin (PL) is a protein hormone with a structure very similar to that of GH. Although it is present in individuals of both sexes, its function in males remains uncertain. In females, it can produce lactation, provided that the breast has already been prepared during pregnancy by appropriate levels of sex steroids. Prolactin release is a good example of the neural form of hypothalamic control: the sensation of suckling causes reduction in hypothalamic prolactin-inhibiting factor (PIF) release and a consequent rise in PL levels.

Hypofunction

▶ Most cases due to destruction by tumour or extrinsic compression
▶ Causes include adenomas, craniopharyngiomas and ischaemic necrosis
▶ Leads to secondary hypofunction of adenohypophysial-dependent endocrine glands

Like other endocrine organs, the adenohypophysis has considerable reserve capacity, and deficiency of its hormones becomes manifest only after extensive destruction; hypofunction is therefore uncommon. Since the pituitary is tightly encased within the sella turcica, any expansile lesion, such as an adenoma, produces compression damage to the adjacent pituitary tissue, in addition to any effect from its own hormonal production. Damage to the hypothalamus or pituitary stalk may also produce adenohypophysial hypofunction through failure of control. Table 17.3 sets out the main causes of hypofunction. These conditions lead to a deficiency of all adenohypophysial hormones, a state known

as *panhypopituitarism*. This is a life-threatening condition, as deficiency of ACTH leads to atrophy of the adrenal cortex and failure of production of vital adrenocorticoids. Diagnosis of hypopituitarism is by measurement of the individual hormones. The commonest causes of pituitary hypofunction are compression by metastatic carcinoma or by an adenoma, but two specific rarer syndromes will be mentioned because they illustrate how congenital and acquired disease may affect the pituitary.

Pituitary dwarfism

Pituitary dwarfism is due to deficiency of GH, sometimes associated with deficiency of other adenohypophysial hormones. The child fails to grow, although remaining well proportioned. There is a variety of known causes including adenomas, craniopharyngiomas (rare tumours derived from remnants of Rathke's pouch) and familial forms.

Post-partum ischaemic necrosis

During pregnancy, the pituitary enlarges and becomes highly vascular. Hypotensive shock due to haemorrhage at the time of birth, compounded by the lack of direct arterial supply to the adenohypophysis, may cause ischaemic necrosis. This specific cause of necrosis is known as *Sheehan's syndrome* and the effects of the resulting adenohypophysial hypofunction are termed *Simmond's disease*. The neurohypophysis is usually spared. The first symptom following delivery is failure of lactation due to PL deficiency; the effects of lack of FSH/LH, TSH and ACTH then follow—loss of sexual function, hypothyroidism, and the diverse effects of glucocorticoid deficiency. Improvements in obstetric management mean that Sheehan's syndrome is now rare, although hypotensive shock due to trauma may produce similar effects.

Tumours: adenomas

▶ Primary pituitary tumours are almost always benign
▶ May be derived from any hormone-producing cell
▶ If functional, the clinical effects of the tumour are secondary to the hormone being produced (e.g. acromegaly, Cushing's disease)
▶ Local effects are due to pressure on optic chiasma or adjacent pituitary cells

Pituitary tumours account for approximately 10% of primary intracranial neoplasms. They may be derived from any of the hormone-secreting cells and thus may be clinically manifest by virtue of single hormone overproduction, destruction of surrounding normal pituitary and consequent hypofunction, and mechanical effects due to intracranial pressure rise and specific location.

Adenomas are the commonest adenohypophysial tumours; carcinomas are rare. Small adenomas may be asymptomatic and found only at postmortem. Histologically, adenomas consist of nodules containing cells similar to those of the normal adenohypophysis, with many small blood vessels between them. They may produce clinical disease in two ways: excess hormone production and pressure effects.

Table 17.3	Causes of adenohypophysial hypofunction
Site	Lesions
Pituitary	Adenoma
	Metastatic carcinoma
	Trauma
	Post-partum ischaemic necrosis (Sheehan's syndrome)
	Craniopharyngioma
	Infections
	Granulomatous diseases
	Autoimmunity
	Iatrogenic
Hypothalamus	Craniopharyngioma
	Gliomas

Excess hormone production. Adenomas may produce any adenohypophysial hormone, depending on their cell of origin (Table 17.4); thus presentation may be via excess production of one of the hormones, for example acromegaly due to excess growth hormone production in an adult (Fig. 17.6), or gigantism if this occurs during childhood.

Table 17.4 Types of adenohypophysial adenoma	
Type	**Remarks**
Prolactinoma (chromophobe)	Commonest type
	Produces galactorrhoea and menstrual disturbances
GH-secreting (eosinophil)	Produces gigantism in children and acromegaly in adults
ACTH-secreting (basophil)	Produces Cushing's disease
Other	Exceptionally rare

Pressure effects. These may be either on the surrounding pituitary to produce hypofunction, or on the overlying optic chiasma (Fig. 17.7), producing a characteristic visual field defect called bitemporal hemianopia. Further growth may compress the hypothalamus.

Types of adenoma

All the following adenomas comprise, histologically, nests and cords of a monotonous single cell type, the islands of cells being supported on a richly vascular sinusoidal framework. Amyloid deposition is not infrequent and calcification may occur.

Chromophobe adenoma. The commonest tumour is one derived from apparently inactive cells; thus hormonal manifestations may be absent but more sensitive biochemical assessments suggest that prolactin may be produced by many of these adenomas. The clinical effects may therefore be limited to infertility and be discovered only because of failed conception in the female.

Eosinophil adenoma. Approximately one-third of lesions are derived from the growth hormone-producing cells and are

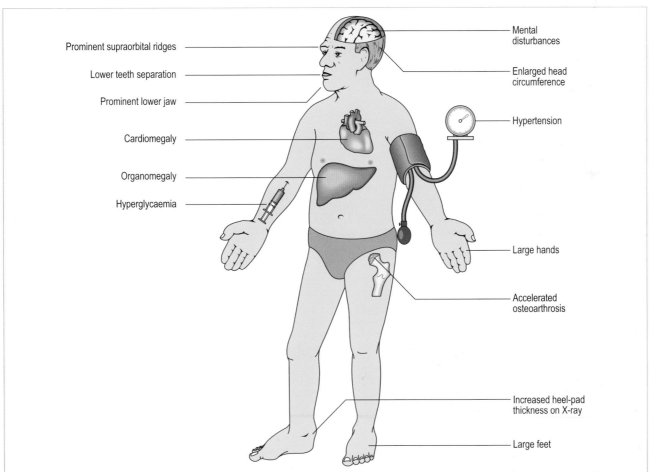

Fig. 17.6   Systemic features of acromegaly. Acromegaly is the clinical syndrome resulting from growth hormone excess in adult life. The chief presenting features are enlargement of the hands, feet and head, but it may also present with secondary diabetes. The cardiovascular effects may be life-threatening.

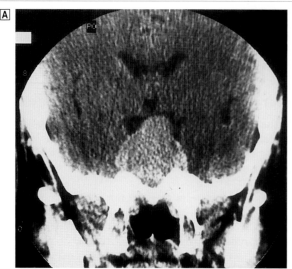

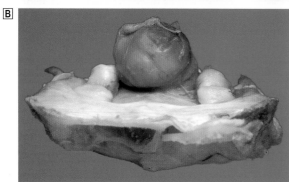

Fig. 17.7 Pituitary adenoma. Ⓐ Coronal plane CT scan of the pituitary fossa showing the sella turcica widened by a pituitary adenoma, which is compressing the optic chiasma and hypothalamus. Ⓑ Pituitary adenoma revealed at autopsy, protruding above the sella turcica.

thus manifest by gigantism in the pre-pubertal patient and acromegaly in the adult.

Basophil adenoma. The rarer ACTH-producing adenoma has its effects by stimulating bilateral adrenocortical hyperplasia and hyperfunction, resulting in Cushing's syndrome. Though rare, this remains the commonest cause of Cushing's syndrome in the adult.

Microadenoma. The microadenoma is a small neoplasm, measuring less than 10 mm in diameter, with no mechanical effects and usually discovered only during intensive investigation of infertility; the lesion often produces prolactin in excess.

NEUROHYPOPHYSIS

Neurosecretory cells in the supra-optic and paraventricular nuclei of the hypothalamus give rise to modified nerve fibres which carry the two neurohypophysial hormones—antidiuretic hormone and oxytocin—into the posterior lobe of the pituitary (Fig. 17.3); both hormones are nonapeptides, and are stored until released in response to hypothalamic stimuli.

Antidiuretic hormone

Antidiuretic hormone (ADH) controls plasma osmolarity and body water content by increasing the permeability of the renal collecting ducts; this means that more water is reabsorbed and the urine becomes more concentrated. ADH release is stimulated by increased plasma osmolarity and by hypovolaemia.

Damage to the hypothalamus, for example through trauma or tumours, causes deficiency of ADH, leading to production of large volumes of dilute urine accompanied by compensatory polydipsia (excess drinking). This is called *diabetes insipidus*, from the days when tasting of the patient's urine was part of the diagnostic process: the urine is tasteless in this condition, whereas in diabetes mellitus it is sweet due to its high glucose content.

Excess ADH is occasionally produced by the neurohypophysis in response to head injury or meningitis, but most clinical cases of ADH excess are due to its ectopic production by tumours, including bronchial carcinomas. The tumours are almost certainly of neuroendocrine origin and thus equipped for the synthesis of peptide hormones.

The rarity of any neurohypophysial tumour secreting ADH (or oxytocin) is perhaps due to the incapacity of the neurones producing these hormones to undergo mitotic division.

Oxytocin

Oxytocin is an aptly named hormone (it is the Greek word for quick birth) as it stimulates the uterine smooth muscle to contract. Interestingly, it is oxytocin from the fetal pituitary that plays the greater role in initiating parturition, suggesting that the fetus orders its own birth. Oxytocin also causes ejection of milk during lactation. The hormone is present in males, although its function, if any, is unknown.

PINEAL GLAND

The pineal gland is a tiny organ lying above the third ventricle of the brain. Little is known of its function, although its secretory product, melatonin, is thought to be involved in circadian rhythm control and gonadal maturation. The most important tumours of the pineal gland are *malignant germ cell tumours* (teratomas and seminomas) and *pinealoblastomas*, resembling neuroblastomas.

ADRENALS

The adrenals consist essentially of two separate endocrine glands within a single anatomical organ. The *medulla*, of neural crest embryological origin, is part of the sympathetic nervous system; it secretes catecholamines, which are essential in the physiological responses to stress, e.g. infection, shock or injury. The *cortex*, derived from mesoderm, synthesises a range of steroid hormones with generalised effects on metabolism, the immune system, and water and electrolyte balance.

ADRENAL MEDULLA

Histologically, the adrenal medulla consists of chromaffin cells (so called because they produce brown pigments when fixed in solutions of chrome salts) and sympathetic nerve endings. The adrenal medulla is the main source of adrenaline (epinephrine), as it is produced there from noradrenaline (norepinephrine) by the enzyme phenyl-ethanolamine-N-methyl transferase. Elsewhere in the body, sympathetic nerve endings lack this enzyme and their secretory product is thus noradrenaline. Electron microscopy reveals electron-dense granules in the chromaffin cells (Fig. 17.8), similar to those found in other tissues of the so-called amine precursor uptake and decarboxylation (APUD) system. Islands of similar tissue, known as the organs of Zuckerkandl, are sometimes found in other retroperitoneal sites; these have similar functions and a similar pattern of diseases to that seen in the adrenal medulla. Catecholamines are secreted in states of stress and of hypovolaemic shock, when they are vital in the maintenance of blood pressure by causing vasoconstriction in the skin, gut and skeletal muscles. At tissue level, these hormones bind to cell surface receptors, altering cellular levels of a second messenger, cyclic AMP, which brings about rapid functional changes in the cell.

Tumours

Phaeochromocytoma

▶ Derived from adrenal medullary chromaffin cells
▶ Symptoms due to excess catecholamine secretion (e.g. hypertension, sweating)
▶ May be familial and associated with other endocrine tumours
▶ Occasionally malignant
▶ A curable cause of secondary hypertension

A phaeochromocytoma is derived from the adrenal medullary chromaffin cells (or from those lying in other sites); it is classified as a paraganglioma. The tumour presents through the effects of its catecholamine secretions: hypertension (which is sometimes intermittent), pallor, headaches, sweating and nervousness. Its presence should be suspected especially in younger hypertensive patients. Although it is a rare cause of hypertension, phaeochromocytoma must not be overlooked as it is one of the few curable causes of elevated blood pressure; other causes include adrenal cortical adenoma, renal artery stenosis and aortic coarctation.

The diagnosis of phaeochromocytoma is usually based on estimating the urinary excretion of vanillylmandelic acid (VMA), a catecholamine metabolite, which is generally at least doubled in the presence of the tumour. Localisation of the tumour is assisted by computed tomography of the abdomen and by radio-isotope scanning with ^{131}I-mIBG, a catecholamine precursor that accumulates in the tumour.

Phaeochromocytoma may be familial, associated with medullary carcinoma of the thyroid or with hyperparathyroidism as part of a multiple endocrine neoplasia (MEN) syndrome. The familial cases are frequently bilateral. Other associations are with neurofibromatosis and the rare von Hippel–Lindau syndrome.

Phaeochromocytomas are brown, solid nodules, usually under 50 mm in diameter, often with areas of haemorrhagic necrosis (Fig. 17.9). Histologically, they consist of groups of polyhedral cells which give the chromaffin reaction, and are highly vascular (Fig. 17.10).

Although most are benign, a few phaeochromocytomas pursue a malignant course. It is not generally possible to predict this behaviour from the histological appearance.

Neuroblastoma

Neuroblastoma is a rare and highly malignant tumour found in infants and children. Derived from sympathetic nerve cells it may, like phaeochromocytoma, secrete catecholamines,

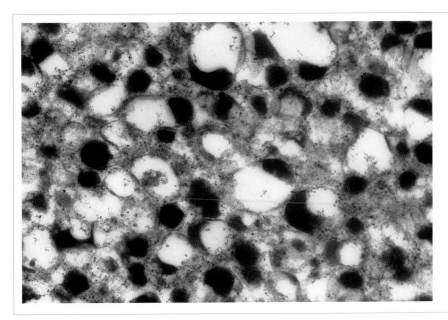

Fig. 17.8 Electron micrograph of noradrenaline granules in a chromaffin cell. The granules characteristically have eccentric electron-dense cores (× 75 000).

Fig. 17.9 Phaeochromocytoma. The adrenal medulla is expanded by a dark-coloured tumour with areas of degeneration and haemorrhage.

1cm

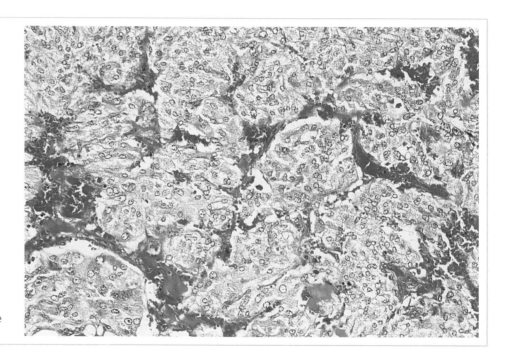

Fig. 17.10 Chromaffin cells in a phaeochromocytoma. There are groups of cells with granular cytoplasm, amidst which there are numerous branching capillaries.

and there may be elevated levels of their metabolites in the urine. Neuroblastomas may also originate from parts of the sympathetic chain outside the adrenal medulla. Secondary spread to liver, skin and bones (especially those of the skull) is common. Surprisingly, neuroblastoma may occasionally mature spontaneously to ganglioneuroma, a benign tumour.

ADRENAL CORTEX

Histologically, the adrenal cortex has three zones (Fig. 17.11). Beneath the capsule lies the *zona glomerulosa*, so called because the cells are grouped into spherical clusters superficially resembling glomeruli. This zone produces mineralocorticoid steroids such as aldosterone. Most of the adrenal cortex comprises the middle and inner zones—*zona fasciculata* and *zona reticularis*, respectively. The middle zone is rich in lipid. The inner zone cells convert lipid into corticosteroids, principally glucocorticoids and sex steroids, for secretion.

Steroid hormones

Glucocorticoids

The glucocorticoids have important effects on a wide range of tissues and organs. At physiological levels they:

- inhibit protein synthesis
- increase protein breakdown
- increase gluconeogenesis.

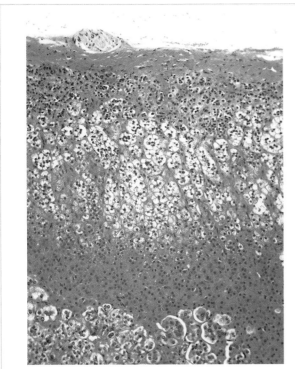

Fig. 17.11 Adrenal cortex. The normal zones are: zona glomerulosa (top), zona fasciculata (middle) and zona reticularis (bottom).

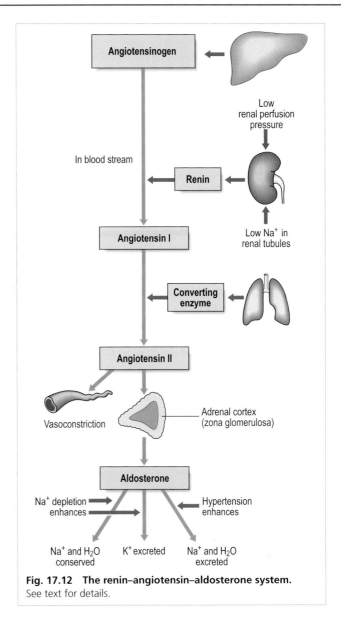

Fig. 17.12 The renin–angiotensin–aldosterone system. See text for details.

In excess, as a result of therapeutic administration or high levels of endogenous secretion, they cause:

- adiposity of face and trunk
- hypertension
- impaired wound healing
- anti-inflammatory effects
- immunosuppression
- growth inhibition
- osteoporosis
- peptic ulceration
- a diabetic state.

The most important of the hormones is cortisol (hydrocortisone), but other steroid metabolites have similar effects. The synthesis and secretion of glucocorticoids are controlled by ACTH from the pituitary.

Mineralocorticoids

The most important of the mineralocorticoids, aldosterone, acts on the renal tubules to increase reabsorption of sodium and chloride, reducing their loss in urine at the expense of potassium exchange. Unlike the production of glucocorticoids, the synthesis and release of aldosterone is not under pituitary control, but is regulated instead by the renin–angiotensin system (Fig. 17.12). Low perfusion pressure in the kidney stimulates release of renin, an enzyme, from the juxtaglomerular apparatus of the kidney. This converts angiotensinogen into angiotensin I. Angiotensin I

is then converted to angiotensin II (an octapeptide) by angiotensin converting enzyme, mainly in the lung. Angiotensin II stimulates secretion of aldosterone from the adrenal cortex. Thus, aldosterone is released to combat fluid depletion.

Sex steroids

The production of sex steroids in the adrenal cortex is low compared with that in the gonads and may not be physiologically important. However, virilising androgens may be produced in conditions such as certain congenital enzyme defects and adrenal cortical tumours, especially if these are malignant.

Hyperfunction

Hyperfunction of the adrenal cortex produces generalised effects, the nature of which depends on whether glucocorticoids, mineralocorticoids or sex steroids are produced in excess.

Cushing's syndrome

▶ Due to excess glucocorticoids
▶ Main features include central obesity, hirsutism, hypertension, diabetes and osteoporosis
▶ Main causes are excess ACTH secretion from the pituitary, adrenal cortical neoplasms, or the iatrogenic effects of ACTH or steroid administration

Cushing's syndrome refers to the constellation of bodily responses to excess glucocorticoids, whatever the underlying cause. Exogenous administration of glucocorticoids or ACTH is a common iatrogenic cause of Cushing's syndrome. The syndrome occurs most commonly in adult women, and sometimes there is also excess androgen production causing virilisation. The main physical features of the syndrome in an adult are shown in Figures 17.13 and 17.14. In children, there is also growth retardation.

Diagnosis

Diagnosis is by demonstration of glucocorticoid excess, either as elevated plasma levels of cortisol or as elevated urinary excretion of 17-hydroxysteroids, degradation products of glucocorticoids. Further tests, such as measurement of plasma ACTH levels, are essential to determine the cause of the Cushing's syndrome (see below).

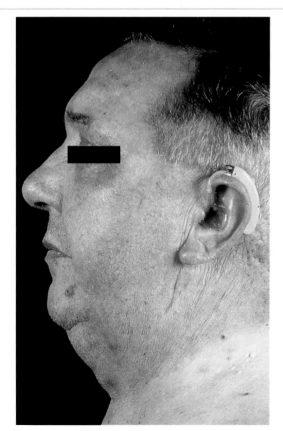

Fig. 17.13   Cushing's syndrome. There is rounding of the face, acne and central obesity causing double chin.

Pathogenesis

Iatrogenic disease.   The therapeutic administration of glucocorticoids to the patient is by far the commonest cause of the features of Cushing's syndrome.

In addition, three different types of natural disease can cause the syndrome:

● excess ACTH secretion by the adenohypophysis
● adrenal cortical neoplasms
● ectopic ACTH secretion.

Excess ACTH secretion by the adenohypophysis.   This was the cause of the syndrome originally described by Harvey Williams Cushing, a Boston neurosurgeon with an interest in the pituitary. Hypersecretion of ACTH by an adenoma of the corticotrophs leads to bilateral adrenal cortical hyperplasia; this combination is termed *Cushing's disease*. Histologically, the cells of the adrenal cortex may appear depleted of lipid, indicating that they have discharged their secretions into the blood. Plasma ACTH is raised, and if the dexamethasone suppression test is performed—administration of the synthetic potent steroid, dexamethasone—a fall in cortisol levels will result due to the suppression of pituitary ACTH secretion.

The ideal treatment of this common cause of Cushing's syndrome is surgical removal of the pituitary adenoma; this not only abolishes the excess ACTH secretion, but also avoids the serious pressure effects that may be produced by a pituitary space-occupying lesion. Removal of the adrenals (once the main form of treatment) is unsatisfactory because the adenohypophysial tumour is left to grow and, in addition to secreting ACTH, may produce a peptide (melanocyte-stimulating hormone) with an amino acid sequence similar to that of the ACTH molecule. In 20% of cases this leads to marked enlargement of the pituitary adenoma (Nelson's syndrome). Skin pigmentation will occur in most cases.

Adrenal cortical neoplasms.   These may secrete cortisol autonomously, independently of ACTH control; low ACTH levels are then found in the presence of elevated cortisol. This is the commonest cause of Cushing's syndrome in children. The neoplasm is usually an adenoma, but in 5–10% of cases it is a carcinoma, in which case virilising steroid production may be prominent. Treatment is by excision of the neoplasm.

Ectopic ACTH secretion.   Certain tumours unrelated to the adenohypophysis may secrete ACTH. Small cell (oat cell) carcinoma of the bronchus (Ch. 14) is the commonest example, although carcinoids, pancreatic islet cell tumours and renal adenocarcinoma (hypernephroma) may occasionally be responsible. Plasma ACTH levels are very high and are not suppressed in the dexamethasone suppression test.

Hyperaldosteronism

Primary hyperaldosteronism (Conn's syndrome).   This is the autonomous secretion of excess aldosterone. The usual cause is an adenoma of the zona glomerulosa, but generalised hyperplasia of the zona is sometimes responsible. The resulting renal retention of sodium and water leads to hypertension, while potassium loss leads to muscular weakness and cardiac arrhythmias. The hypokalaemia is associated with metabolic alkalosis, causing tetany and paraesthesiae.

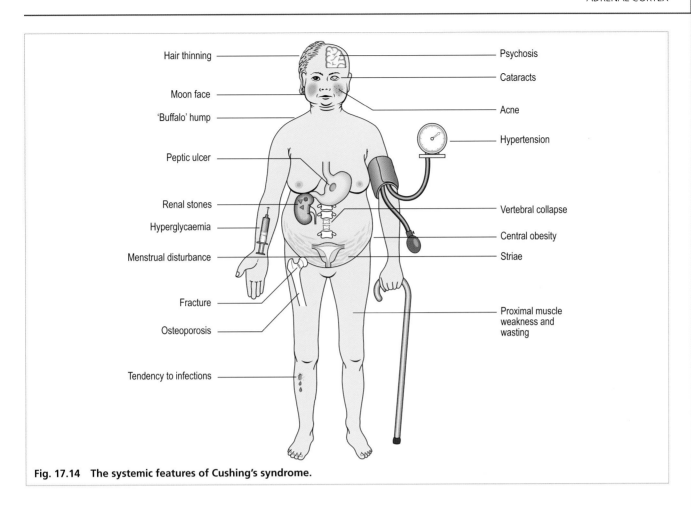

Hair thinning

Moon face

'Buffalo' hump

Peptic ulcer

Renal stones

Hyperglycaemia

Menstrual disturbance

Fracture

Osteoporosis

Tendency to infections

Psychosis

Cataracts

Acne

Hypertension

Vertebral collapse

Central obesity

Striae

Proximal muscle weakness and wasting

Fig. 17.14   The systemic features of Cushing's syndrome.

Secondary hyperaldosteronism. When renal glomerular perfusion is reduced, for example through a fall in blood volume, the *renin–angiotensin system* (Fig. 17.12) stimulates aldosterone secretion from the zona glomerulosa in an attempt to correct this. This physiological response is known as secondary hyperaldosteronism, which is by far the commonest type of hyperaldosteronism.

Diagnosis

The diagnosis of primary hyperaldosteronism rests on two criteria: plasma aldosterone must be raised while renin is low. This is to distinguish it from secondary hyperaldosteronism, in which aldosterone levels are raised but are an appropriate response to high renin levels.

Hypersecretion of sex steroids

Some adrenal cortical adenomas secrete sex steroids, most commonly androgens. In Cushing's syndrome, quantities of androgens are occasionally secreted along with the glucocorticoids, causing virilisation of females, especially those with adrenocortical carcinomas.

Rarely, congenital enzyme defects of the pathways of steroid synthesis may result in excess production of sex steroids. The least rare example is 'congenital adrenal hyperplasia' due to deficiency of the enzyme 21-hydroxylase, needed for the synthesis of both cortisol and aldosterone (Fig. 17.15).

Failure of cortisol production leads to increased ACTH secretion, resulting in hyperplasia of the adrenal cortex. The production of androgens occurs before the metabolic block caused by the enzyme deficiency, and their excessive secretion results in masculinisation of females and precocious puberty in males. 21-Hydroxylase deficiency is serious because deficiency of mineralocorticoids causes life-threatening salt loss unless replacement therapy is given.

Tumours

Adenoma. In addition to those 'functioning' adrenal cortical adenomas that present by causing Cushing's or Conn's syndromes, a clinically unsuspected 'non-functioning' adenoma occurs in about 2% of adults. The adenoma is a pale yellow circumscribed nodule, perhaps 20–30 mm in diameter (Fig. 17.16). The cells have clear cytoplasm owing to their high lipid content (Fig. 17.17).

Carcinoma. Adrenal cortical carcinoma is rare; these tumours are usually hormone-secreting, with a tendency to produce androgens. They are commonly large (over 100 g) and exhibit invasive growth. Examination of the adjacent adrenal cortex and that of the opposite gland may give a clue as to the function of the neoplasm; glucocorticoid-secreting tumours will suppress ACTH, resulting in atrophy of the non-neoplastic adrenal cortex.

Adrenal cortical insufficiency

> ▶ Clinical effects are due to lack of mineralocorticoids and glucocorticoids
> ▶ Main features include weight loss, lethargy, hypotension, pigmentation and hyponatraemia
> ▶ Causes include autoimmune adrenalitis, tuberculosis and Waterhouse–Friderichsen syndrome

Adrenocortical hypofunction can be *primary*, due to lesions within the adrenal gland, or *secondary*, due to failure of ACTH secretion by the adenohypophysis. Acute primary insufficiency is called *Waterhouse–Friderichsen syndrome*. Causes of chronic primary insufficiency include:

- tuberculosis
- autoimmune adrenalitis
- amyloidosis
- haemochromatosis
- metastatic tumours
- atrophy due to prolonged steroid therapy.

Autoimmune adrenalitis selectively damages and destroys the adrenal cortex, sparing the medulla; tuberculosis destroys the cortex and medulla.

Acute insufficiency

Acute insufficiency ('adrenal apoplexy') was first noted in children by Waterhouse and Friderichsen who, in 1911 and 1918 respectively, independently described acute haemorrhagic necrosis of the adrenals in the course of meningococcal septicaemia. Other acute septicaemias, especially those due to Gram-negative bacteria, may cause a similar effect. The adrenal cortices are necrotic and the medullae contain acute haemorrhage (Fig. 17.18). The adrenal necrosis is probably due to disseminated intravascular coagulation (DIC). The symptoms are attributable to lack of mineralocorticoids (salt and water loss with hypovolaemic shock) and of glucocorticoids (failure of gluconeogenesis resulting in hypoglycaemia).

Chronic insufficiency

Thomas Addison first described an association between destruction of the adrenal cortex and the constellation of symptoms caused by the resulting chronic insufficiency of adrenal cortical hormones (*Addison's disease*). The effects are due to a combined lack of mineralocorticoids and glucocorticoids:

- anorexia, weight loss, vomiting
- weakness
- lethargy
- hypotension
- skin pigmentation
- hyponatraemia with hyperkalaemia
- chronic dehydration
- sexual dysfunction.

Patients with chronic adrenocortical insufficiency may develop an acute Addisonian crisis, in which even minor illnesses such as infections may cause vomiting, fluid loss, electrolyte disturbances and circulatory collapse.

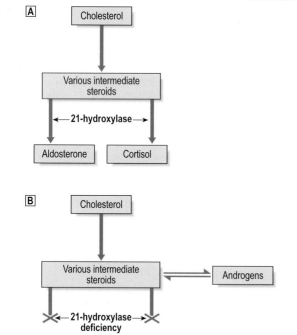

Fig. 17.15   21-Hydroxylase deficiency: the commonest cause of congenital adrenal hyperplasia. A Normal metabolism. B 21-Hydroxylase deficiency. Failure of aldosterone production leads to salt-wasting, while cortisol lack causes the anterior pituitary to release ACTH, resulting in adrenal cortical hyperplasia. The resulting excess intermediate steroids are converted to androgens, leading to virilisation.

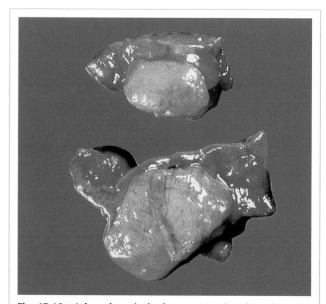

Fig. 17.16   Adrenal cortical adenoma. A pale-coloured fleshy nodule in the adrenal cortex is displacing the medulla and stretching out the rest of the cortex.

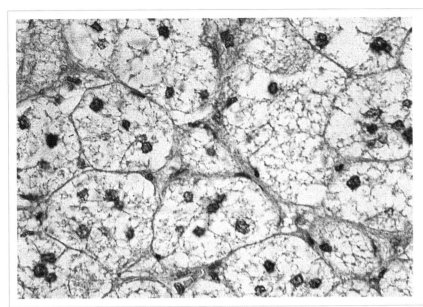

Fig. 17.17   Cells in an adrenal cortical adenoma. The cells are large with clear cytoplasm and compact nuclei.

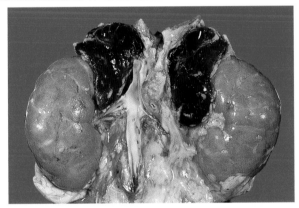

Fig. 17.18   Adrenals in Waterhouse–Friderichsen syndrome. The adrenals from a child dying from meningococcal septicaemia are destroyed by haemorrhage.

The commonest cause of Addison's disease was once caseous necrosis of the adrenal cortices due to tuberculosis. Autoimmune destruction of the cortex is now a commoner cause; this is associated with other 'organ-specific' autoimmune diseases, such as pernicious anaemia (also described by Addison), thyroiditis, insulin-dependent diabetes mellitus and parathyroid failure.

In all cases of Addison's disease, plasma cortisol levels are low. Estimation of ACTH levels enables a distinction to be made between primary adrenocortical insufficiency (ACTH raised) and secondary insufficiency (ACTH low).

THYROID

The thyroid gland (normal weight 20–30 g) is composed of follicles that are lined by cuboidal epithelial cells (Fig. 17.19) and contain a proteinaceous stored secretion ('colloid'). The main function of the thyroid epithelial cells is the synthesis of the iodinated amino acids, thyroxine (T_4) and tri-iodo-thyronine (T_3).

The secretion of T_3 and T_4 is under negative feedback control by TSH from the anterior pituitary. For example, a fall in the plasma level of these thyroid hormones causes increased TSH secretion by both direct effects on the adeno-hypophysis and effects on the hypothalamus.

The thyroid also contains a population of cells known as C-cells; these are sparsely scattered throughout the gland and secrete calcitonin, a peptide hormone involved in calcium metabolism. Medullary carcinoma, a tumour of these cells, is discussed on page 455.

There are three main types of clinical thyroid disease:

- *secretory malfunction*: hyper- or hypothyroidism
- *swelling of the entire gland*: goitre
- *solitary masses*: one large nodule in a nodular goitre, adenoma or carcinoma.

SECRETORY MALFUNCTION

Hyperthyroidism

▶ Syndrome due to excess T_3 and T_4
▶ Very rarely due to excess TSH
▶ Commonest cause is Graves' disease, in which there is a long-acting thyroid-stimulating immunoglobulin (LATS)
▶ May also be due to functioning adenoma

Thyrotoxicosis is the clinical syndrome resulting from the effect on the tissues of excess circulating T_3 and T_4; the overall result is an increased metabolic rate. Hyperthyroidism, the commonest cause of thyrotoxicosis, denotes that the source of the high circulating T_3 and T_4 is a lesion within the thyroid gland. The features are summarised in Figure 17.20. Hyperthyroidism may result from three main pathological lesions:

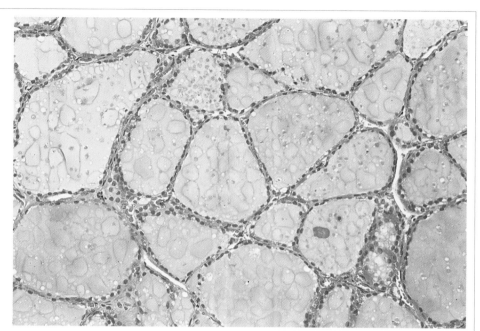

Fig. 17.19   Normal thyroid histology. Colloid-filled follicles are lined by regular cuboidal epithelium.

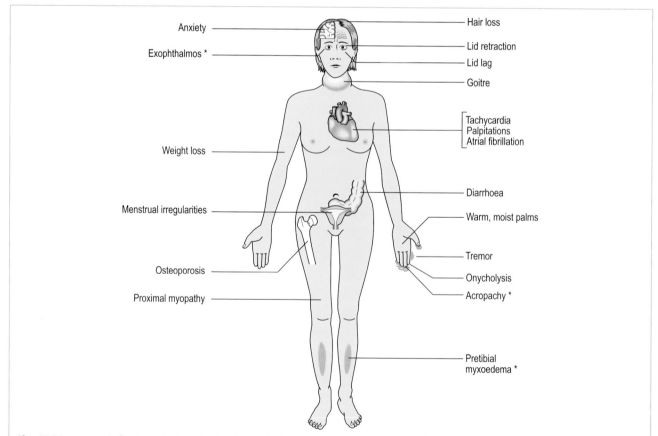

Anxiety

Exophthalmos *

Weight loss

Menstrual irregularities

Osteoporosis

Proximal myopathy

Hair loss

Lid retraction

Lid lag

Goitre

Tachycardia
Palpitations
Atrial fibrillation

Diarrhoea

Warm, moist palms

Tremor

Onycholysis

Acropachy *

Pretibial
myxoedema *

Fig. 17.20   Systemic features of thyrotoxicosis. The features marked * are seen only in thyrotoxicosis due to Graves' thyroiditis.

- Graves' thyroiditis
- functioning adenoma
- toxic nodular goitre.

More rarely, thyrotoxicosis may result from exogenous thyroid hormones taken by the patient or from ectopic secretion by some rare tumours such as struma ovarii, which is a monophyletic teratoma of the ovary comprising thyroid tissue.

Graves' thyroiditis

Graves' thyroiditis is the commonest cause of thyrotoxicosis, usually associated with a diffuse goitre. The thyroid is moderately enlarged, firm and beefy-red due to increased

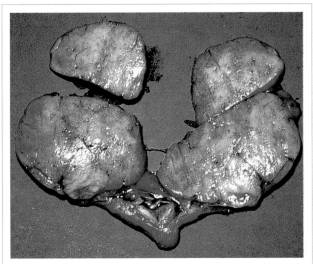

Fig. 17.21 Graves' thyroiditis. The gland is diffusely enlarged, fleshy and dark-coloured due to increased vascularity.

vascularity (Fig. 17.21). Histologically, the gland shows hyperplasia of the acinar epithelium, reduction of stored colloid, and local accumulations of lymphocytes with lymphoid follicle formation (Fig. 17.22). This full spectrum of features is now rarely seen in subtotal thyroidectomy specimens of the condition, because antithyroid drugs are given before surgery.

Graves' thyroiditis is one of the so-called 'organ-specific' autoimmune diseases. The pathogenesis is the production of an auto-antibody of the IgG class which binds to the thyroid epithelial cells and mimics the stimulatory action of TSH. The auto-antibody is known as long-acting thyroid stimulator (LATS) and its effect on the thyroid can be classed as a form of hypersensitivity reaction, 'stimulatory hypersensitivity'. LATS stimulates the function and growth of thyroid follicular epithelium. In addition to showing the usual features of thyrotoxicosis, patients with Graves' thyroiditis may also show exophthalmos, pretibial myxoedema (accumulation of mucopolysaccharides in the deep dermis of the skin) and finger-clubbing. The latter two signs are rare effects, but exophthalmos is common. It results from infiltration of the orbital tissues by fat (interestingly, adipocytes have been shown to have cell surface TSH receptors), mucopolysaccharides and lymphocytes, and may be due to an additional auto-antibody reacting with these tissues.

Functioning adenoma

Functioning adenomas of the thyroid may cause thyrotoxicosis, but less than 1% of adenomas show enough secretory activity to do so. Histologically, the tumour is composed of thyroid follicles and is sometimes so small that it is visualised only on an ^{131}I radio-isotope scan. Occasionally it may present as a solitary thyroid mass.

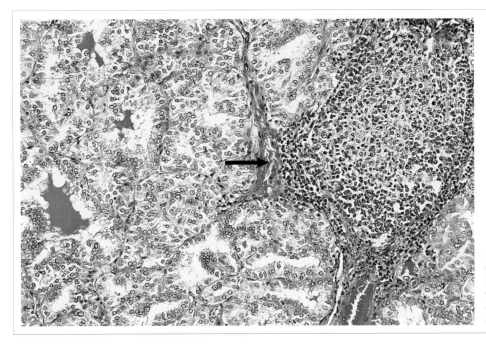

Fig. 17.22 Histological features of Graves' thyroiditis. There is hyperplasia of the follicular epithelium with nuclear irregularity, depletion of colloid and focal lymphoid aggregates (arrowed).

Toxic nodular goitre

Rarely one or two nodules in a nodular goitre may develop hypersecretory activity, a condition termed toxic nodular goitre.

Hypothyroidism

> ▶ Syndrome due to insufficient circulating T_3 and T_4
> ▶ If congenital, causes cretinism
> ▶ Commonest cause is Hashimoto's thyroiditis, an autoimmune disorder

Hypothyroidism (myxoedema) is the clinical syndrome resulting from inadequate levels of circulating T_3 and T_4. The metabolic rate is lowered and mucopolysaccharides accumulate in the dermal connective tissues to produce the typical myxoedema face (Fig. 17.23). The general features of hypothyroidism are summarised in Figure 17.24. If hypothyroidism is present in the newborn, physical growth and mental development are impaired, sometimes irreversibly; this condition is known as cretinism. Cretinism may be endemic in geographical areas where the diet contains insufficient iodine for thyroid hormone synthesis. Sporadic cases are usually due to a congenital absence of thyroid tissue, or to enzyme defects blocking hormone synthesis.

The commonest cause of acquired hypothyroidism in adults is *Hashimoto's thyroiditis* (see below), but occasional cases are iatrogenic, for example due to surgical removal of thyroid tissue or to certain drugs that cause unwanted hypothyroidism, such as sulphonylureas, resorcinol, lithium and amiodarone.

Hashimoto's thyroiditis

Hashimoto's thyroiditis may initially cause thyroid enlargement, but later there may be atrophy and fibrosis. The gland appears firm, fleshy and pale (Fig. 17.25). Histologically, the

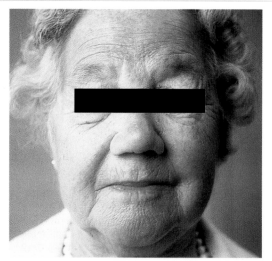

Fig. 17.23 Myxoedemic face. The skin is coarse and puffy due to accumulation of mucopolysaccharides; the outer third of the eyebrows is lost.

gland is densely infiltrated by lymphocytes and plasma cells, with lymphoid follicle formation. Colloid content is reduced, and the thyroid epithelial cells show a characteristic change in which they enlarge and develop eosinophilic granular cytoplasm due to proliferation of mitochondria; they are then termed Askanazy cells, Hürthle cells or oncocytes (Fig. 17.26). In advanced cases there may be fibrosis. Paradoxically, in the early stages of Hashimoto's thyroiditis, the damage to the thyroid follicles may lead to release of thyroglobulin into the circulation, causing a transient phase of thyrotoxicosis.

Like Graves' thyroiditis, Hashimoto's thyroiditis is one of the 'organ-specific' autoimmune diseases (Ch. 9). Two auto-antibodies can be detected in the serum of most patients with Hashimoto's thyroiditis, one reacting with thyroid peroxidase and the other reacting with thyroglobulin. These auto-antibodies are probably formed locally by the plasma cells infiltrating the thyroid, and are possibly the result of a loss of specific suppressor T-lymphocytes. In common with other organ-specific autoimmune diseases, there is a female preponderance, and certain HLA antigens (Ch. 3) are commonly found in affected individuals—especially HLA-B8 and -DR5.

GOITRE (ENLARGEMENT OF THE WHOLE GLAND)

The term goitre denotes an enlargement of the thyroid without hyperthyroidism.

Simple goitre

A spectrum of pathological changes may occur, ranging from parenchymatous goitre to colloid goitre.

In *parenchymatous goitre* there is at first hyperplasia of the thyroid epithelium with loss of stored colloid, but eventually less active areas appear and are compressed by the hyperplastic areas. Tracts of fibrosis may separate these areas, resulting in *multinodular goitre* (Fig. 17.27). The multiple nodules of this type of goitre can usually be palpated clinically, but occasionally one large nodule may be noted and give rise to suspicion of neoplasia.

In *colloid goitre* there is no epithelial hyperplasia, but follicles accumulate large volumes of colloid (Fig. 17.28), and coalesce to form colloid-filled cysts. There may be areas of haemorrhage, fibrosis and dystrophic calcification. The thyroid may be diffusely enlarged or multinodular. A complication of this condition is haemorrhage into a cyst, giving rise to rapid enlargement of the cyst, which may cause tracheal compression and stridor.

Aetiology

The aetiology of simple goitre is thought to involve a phase of relative lack of T_3 and T_4 so that TSH rises and causes hyperplasia of the thyroid epithelium. This lack of T_3 and T_4 can be brought about in three main ways:

- iodine deficiency, due to endemic goitre or food faddism
- rare inherited enzyme defects in T_3 and T_4 synthesis
- drugs that induce hypothyroidism.

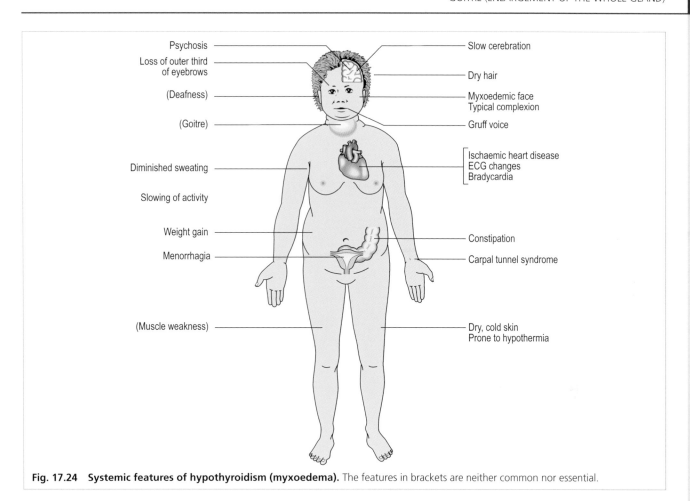

Psychosis	Slow cerebration
Loss of outer third of eyebrows	Dry hair
(Deafness)	Myxoedemic face / Typical complexion
(Goitre)	Gruff voice
	Ischaemic heart disease / ECG changes / Bradycardia
Diminished sweating	
Slowing of activity	
Weight gain	Constipation
Menorrhagia	Carpal tunnel syndrome
(Muscle weakness)	Dry, cold skin / Prone to hypothermia

Fig. 17.24 Systemic features of hypothyroidism (myxoedema). The features in brackets are neither common nor essential.

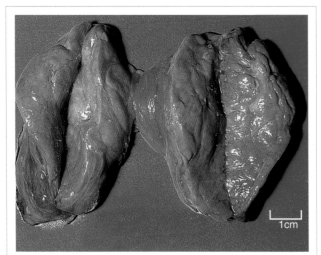

Fig. 17.25 Hashimoto's thyroiditis. The gland is slightly enlarged and the lobes have been sliced to show the uniformly pale and fleshy cut surface.

Endemic goitre was formerly common in areas remote from the sea, where the soil contains little iodine, for example in the Derbyshire hills (UK), parts of Switzerland and mountainous regions. The addition of iodine to the diet by iodination of table salt has reduced the incidence of goitre in some areas.

Rare causes of goitre

Giant cell thyroiditis

Giant cell thyroiditis (de Quervain's thyroiditis) is a distinctive form of slight thyroid swelling with tenderness on palpation, and fever, usually with fairly abrupt onset. Histologically, the gland is infiltrated by a mixture of neutrophil polymorphs and lymphocytes, with a focal giant cell reaction possibly due to epithelial cell fusion. The disease is thought to be induced by viral infections such as mumps, but the reason why only a few individuals develop this rare disease is not known.

Riedel's thyroiditis

Riedel's thyroiditis is an exceptionally rare cause of thyroid enlargement with dense fibrosis which may involve adjacent muscles; this renders the thyroid firm and immobile on palpation, thus mimicking carcinoma. Histologically, there is dense fibrous replacement of the gland and, characteristically, occlusion of thyroid veins by fibrosis. The condition is of unknown aetiology, but may be associated with retroperitoneal fibrosis.

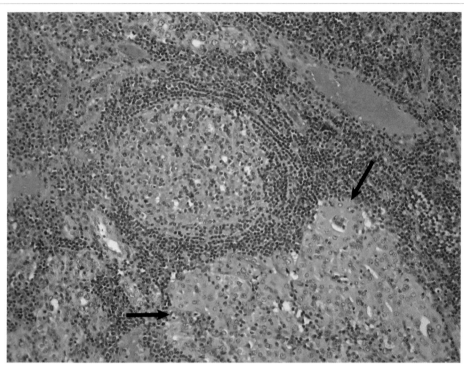

Fig. 17.26 Histological features of Hashimoto's thyroiditis. There is destruction of follicles by a dense lymphocytic infiltrate with germinal centre formation. Some of the surviving epithelial cells show Hürthle cell change (arrowed).

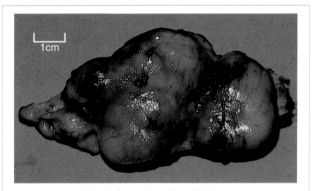

Fig. 17.27 Multinodular goitre. Thyroid lobectomy tissue showing irregular nodular enlargement due to hyperplasia, fibrosis and focally excessive colloid.

SOLITARY MASSES

The patient with a solitary mass in the thyroid presents a common clinical problem. The investigation of such a patient, following clinical examination, first involves checking the thyroid secretory status (serum T_3, T_4 and TSH).

Diagnostic imaging of the thyroid gland may be performed with ^{99m}Tc, which localises to the gland in a similar distribution to iodine (Fig. 17.29). 'Cold' lesions (which do not take up the radio-isotope) may be cysts or solid tumours; these can be distinguished by ultrasonography, which is gradually superseding ^{99m}Tc scanning (Fig. 17.30), or by fine-needle aspiration cytology. Cytology enables a pre-operative diagnosis of thyroid neoplasia to be made and has revolutionised the management of thyroid nodules.

Many apparently solitary nodules turn out to be merely one large nodule in an otherwise multinodular goitre. Others, however, are neoplastic.

Tumours

- ▶ Usually benign (follicular adenoma)
- ▶ Malignant forms include carcinomas and lymphoma:
  - – papillary adenocarcinoma (often multifocal, lymphatic spread)
  - – follicular adenocarcinoma (usually solitary, thaematogenous spread)
  - – medullary carcinoma (derived from calcitonin-producing C-cells, sometimes associated with multiple endocrine neoplasia syndromes)
  - – lymphoma (usually non-Hodgkin's lymphoma of B-cell type)

Tumours of the thyroid are generally benign. Carcinomas are rare at this site, and lymphomas rarer still. Those tumours that are malignant have a variable behaviour that dictates the clinical management. Histological classification is, therefore, of vital importance.

Benign tumours

Follicular adenoma is a common cause of a solitary thyroid nodule. It usually consists of a solid mass within a fibrous capsule, compressing the adjacent gland (Fig. 17.31), but the

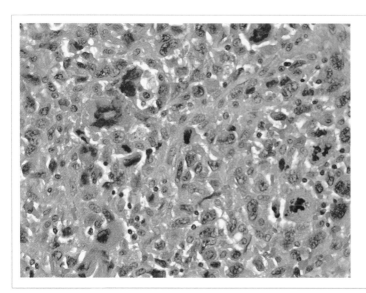

Fig. 17.36   Anaplastic carcinoma of the thyroid.
High-power photomicrograph showing pleomorphic
hyperchromatic nuclei, some lying in tumour giant cells.

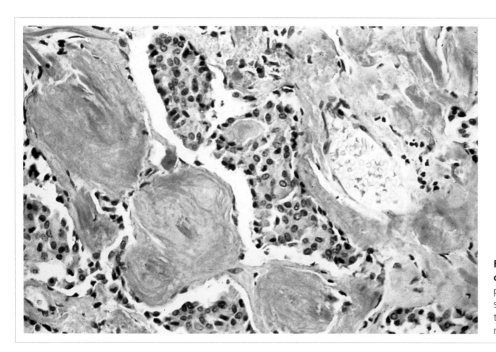

**Fig. 17.37   Medullary carcinoma
of the thyroid.** High-power
photomicrograph showing small
spherical tumour cells adjacent
to masses of amorphous hyaline
material; the latter is amyloid.

DISEASES OF THE PARATHYROIDS

The most important diseases of the parathyroids are hyperparathyroidism, hypoparathyroidism and tumours.

Hyperparathyroidism

- Primary: usually due to parathyroid adenoma
- Secondary: a physiological response to hypocalcaemia (e.g.
  malabsorption, renal failure)
- Tertiary: adenoma rarely arising in patients with secondary
  hyperparathyroidism
- Manifestations include bone resorption and, if primary or
  tertiary, the consequences of hypercalcaemia

Hyperparathyroidism is classified into primary, secondary
and tertiary types according to the circumstances in which
it occurs (Table 17.8). Primary and tertiary hyperparathyroidism are pathological states with inappropriate excess
PTH secretion for the prevailing plasma calcium levels.
Secondary hyperparathyroidism, however, is an appropriate
physiological response to hypocalcaemia, for example in renal
failure.

Primary hyperparathyroidism

Primary hyperparathyroidism is a fairly common condition,
occurring in almost 0.1% of the population, most frequently in
post-menopausal females. It presents through the symptoms
of hypercalcaemia:

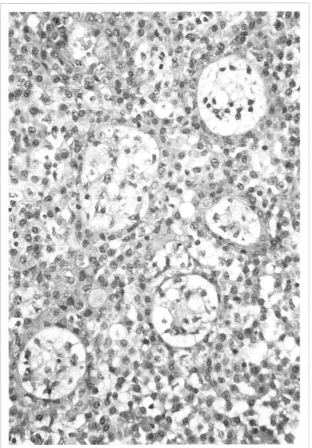

Fig. 17.38 Non-Hodgkin's lymphoma of the thyroid. High-power photomicrograph showing infiltration of the thyroid tissue by lymphocytes which invade through follicular epithelium.

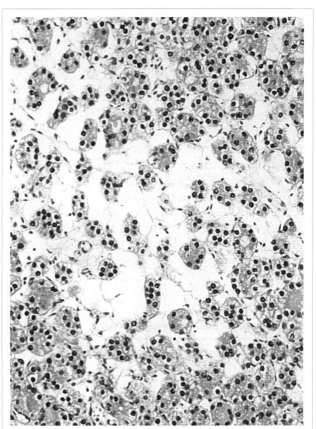

Fig. 17.39 Normal parathyroid gland. Low-power photomicrograph showing groups and small acini of the different types of parathyroid cells, between which there are islands of adipose tissue.

Table 17.6	The chief actions of PTH
Site	Action
Bone	Stimulates osteoclastic resorption Inhibits osteoblasts from forming bone matrix Releases calcium from bone
Kidney	Acts on renal tubular epithelium to cause reabsorption of calcium while inhibiting phosphate reabsorption Increases 1-hydroxylation in the epithelium of the proximal convoluted tubule of 25-hydroxyvitamin D to yield 1,25-dihydroxyvitamin D, the most active form

Table 17.7	The actions of vitamin D
Site	Action
Intestine	Increases calcium absorption
Bone	In conjunction with PTH, releases calcium into the circulation Is essential for normal mineralisation of osteoid

- renal stones, due to hypercalciuria
- muscle weakness
- tiredness
- thirst and polyuria
- anorexia and constipation
- rarely, peptic ulceration (gastrin secretion is enhanced).

In rare cases the effects of hyperparathyroidism on bone—osteitis fibrosa and brown tumour (Ch. 25)—are also apparent clinically.

Hyperparathyroidism is only one of several important possible causes of hypercalcaemia. The commonest causes of hypercalcaemia are:

- disseminated malignancy in the bones
- hyperparathyroidism
- vitamin D intoxication
- milk–alkali syndrome
- sarcoidosis

- multiple myeloma
- rarely, PTH production by malignant tumours.

In the investigation of a patient with hypercalcaemia, the results that point to hyperparathyroidism as the cause are:

- a raised plasma calcium with a lowered plasma phosphate (due to the phosphaturic effect of PTH)
- mild metabolic acidosis
- importantly, raised PTH levels measured by radio-immunoassay.

In about 80% of cases, primary hyperparathyroidism is due to a secretory *adenoma* of one of the parathyroid glands; this consists of a neoplastic mass of functioning parathyroid cells surrounded by a compressed rim of inactive parathyroid tissue (Fig. 17.40). The remaining of cases are usually due to *hyperplasia* of all the parathyroid glands, especially when hyperparathyroidism forms part of one of the MEN syndromes (Ch. 11).

The management of hyperparathyroidism usually consists of operative inspection of all four parathyroid glands wherever possible, followed by removal of any suspected adenoma

which is then submitted for intra-operative diagnosis by rapid frozen section.

Hypoparathyroidism

Hypoparathyroidism results in a fall in plasma calcium levels accompanied by elevated plasma phosphate levels. The patient presents with the clinical features of hypocalcaemia:

- tetany (spasm of the skeletal muscles)
- convulsions
- paraesthesiae
- psychiatric disturbances
- rarely, cataracts and brittle nails.

Diagnosis is confirmed by low or absent plasma PTH levels in the presence of hypocalcaemia.

In addition to hypoparathyroidism, other important causes of hypocalcaemia include:

- hyperphosphataemia occurring in chronic renal failure
- rickets due to vitamin D deficiency (Ch. 25)
- excessive loss during lactation.

Even when the total plasma calcium levels are normal, symptoms of hypocalcaemia, such as tetany, may be produced by alkalosis; this lowers the proportion of plasma calcium in the ionised state, an important factor in the control of muscle excitability.

The leading causes of hypoparathyroidism are:

- removal of or damage to the parathyroid glands during thyroidectomy
- idiopathic hypoparathyroidism
- congenital deficiency (DiGeorge syndrome; Ch. 9).

Iatrogenic disease, such as accidental removal of the parathyroid glands during thyroidectomy, remains a common cause. Idiopathic hypoparathyroidism is now known to be due to destruction of the parathyroid cells by an auto-antibody. It is associated with other 'organ-specific' autoimmune diseases (Ch. 9).

Table 17.8 Classification of hyperparathyroidism	
Hyperparathyroidism	Cause
Primary	Hypersecretion of PTH by an adenoma or hyperplasia of the gland
Secondary	Physiological increase in PTH secretions in response to hypocalcaemia of any cause
Tertiary	Development of an autonomous hypersecreting adenoma in longstanding secondary hyperparathyroidism

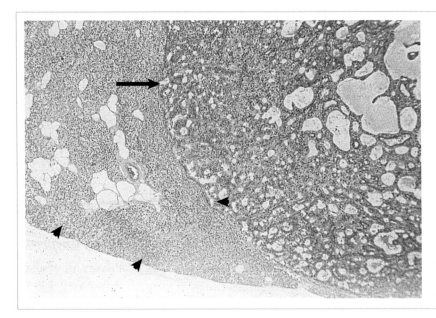

Fig. 17.40 Parathyroid adenoma from a patient with primary hyperparathyroidism. The adenomatous nodule (arrowed) is surrounded by a compressed rim of parathyroid tissue (arrowheads).

Tumours

The commonest tumours, adenomas, are benign neoplasms of one of the three types of parathyroid cell. They are usually small (less than 50 mm in diameter) and only become clinically apparent through hypersecretion of PTH. Very rarely, they may occur in more than one parathyroid gland. Adenocarcinoma of the parathyroid glands is rare.

ENDOCRINE PANCREAS

The pancreas consists of two functionally distinct components:

- the *exocrine* pancreas, which secretes digestive enzymes into the duodenum (Ch. 16)
- the islets of Langerhans, scattered within the tissues of the exocrine pancreas act together as an *endocrine* gland.

Numbering about a million, the islets of Langerhans are derived from endoderm bordering the pancreatic ductal system. Although they comprise only 1–1.5 g of the pancreatic tissue (about 1% of its mass), their endocrine secretions have profound metabolic effects and are essential for life.

The islets consist of clusters of compact cells interspersed with small blood vessels (Fig. 17.41); they contain at least four distinct cell types, classified according to their hormone content as demonstrated by immunohistochemistry (Fig. 17.42). There are regional differences in hormone content of the islet cells in different parts of the pancreas, but the average hormonal composition is as shown in Table 17.9.

On electron microscopy, these endocrine cells contain membrane-bound electron-dense granules, some of which have characteristic shapes revealing their hormone content, and they have the histochemical features of neuroendocrine (APUD) cells (Ch. 15).

The effects of two of the islet hormones, insulin and glucagon, are virtually antagonistic (Table 17.9). It seems that the secretion of pancreatic hormones is controlled locally; for example, a rising blood glucose level appears to stimulate the beta-cells to secrete insulin directly.

The principal diseases of the endocrine pancreas are hypofunction, especially of the beta-cells (diabetes mellitus), and tumours of the islet or other neuroendocrine (APUD) cells, which may produce widespread effects due to hormone hypersecretion.

Diabetes mellitus

> ▶ Abnormal metabolic state characterised by glucose intolerance due to inadequate insulin action
> ▶ Type 1 (juvenile onset) due to destruction of beta-cells (probably a result of virus infection and genetic factors); insulin-dependent
> ▶ Type 2 (maturity onset) due to defective insulin action; treatment by weight reduction and oral hypoglycaemic agents
> ▶ Complications include accelerated atherosclerosis, susceptibility to infections, and microangiopathy affecting many organs

Diabetes mellitus is a disease state rather than a single disease, because it may have several causes. It is defined as an abnormal metabolic state in which there is glucose intolerance due to inadequate insulin action. Diagnosis is based on the clinical demonstration of glucose intolerance (Table 17.10).

Insulin is unique, in that it is the only hormone with a hypoglycaemic effect; there are five hormones that tend to exert a hyperglycaemic effect—glucagon, glucocorticoids, growth hormone, adrenaline (epinephrine) and noradrenaline (norepinephrine). Thus, the hyperglycaemic effects of these hormones cannot be counterbalanced if there is inadequate insulin action.

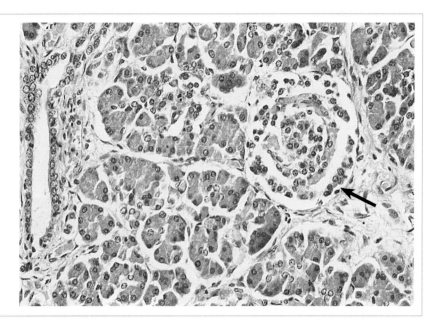

Fig. 17.41 Normal pancreas. An islet of Langerhans (arrowed) is surrounded by exocrine pancreatic acini and a duct.

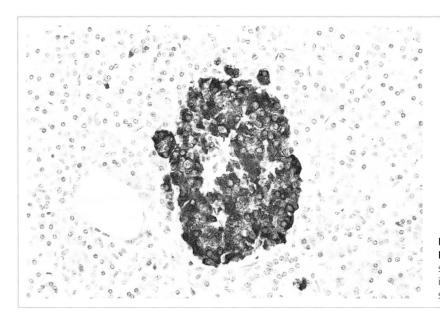

Fig. 17.42 Beta-cells in an islet of Langerhans. This normal pancreas has been stained by the immunoperoxidase technique for insulin. The insulin-containing cells are darkly stained.

Table 17.9	Cell types in the islets of Langerhans		
Cell type	Average prevalence (%) in islets	Hormone produced	
		Identity	Actions
Beta	70	Insulin	Promotes glucose entry into cells, glycogen synthesis (and inhibits breakdown), lipogenesis (and inhibits lipolysis) and protein synthesis (together with growth hormone)
Alpha	20	Glucagon	Promotes breakdown of glycogen (only in liver) and gluconeogenesis (from proteins)
Delta	8	Somatostatin	Inhibits insulin and glucagon secretion
PP	2	Pancreatic polypeptide	Function in humans unknown

Pathogenesis

The actions of insulin (Table 17.9) are all *anabolic,* that is, they promote the laying down of tissue stores from circulating nutrients. The consequences of insulin deficiency are therefore *catabolic,* that is, there is breakdown of tissue energy stores.

The major features of diabetes mellitus are:

- inability to utilise, and overproduction of, glucose (hyperglycaemia)
- diminished protein synthesis

- lipolysis resulting in hyperlipidaemia, hence there is rapid wasting and weight loss. This state has been aptly described as 'starvation in the midst of plenty'.

In hyperglycaemia the renal threshold for glucose conservation is exceeded, so that there is osmotic diuresis resulting in polyuria, dehydration and thirst. Lipolysis may also have serious consequences. Free fatty acids are converted in the liver to ketone bodies, such as acetoacetate, acetone and beta-hydroxybutyrate. These dissociate to release hydrogen ions, and a profound metabolic acidosis may ensue.

The combined result of severe ketosis, acidosis, hyperglycaemia, hyperosmolarity and electrolyte disturbance is to impair cerebral function, producing *diabetic ketoacidotic coma*. This is quite distinct from the *hypoglycaemic coma* that may also be found in diabetic patients; this is due to insulin overdosage, and has entirely different clinical features.

Classification

The two major types of diabetes mellitus are defined according to the clinical setting in which they occur. Research into pathogenesis of the disease has reinforced this classification, as the two types appear to have distinct pathogeneses. In addition, diabetes sometimes appears as a secondary consequence of other diseases.

Type 1 (juvenile-onset, insulin-dependent diabetes)

Type 1 diabetes mellitus (also called juvenile-onset, or insulin-dependent diabetes) typically presents in childhood. The patient usually shows the catabolic effects described above and is prone to develop ketoacidosis. The central defect is inadequate insulin secretion by the beta-cells of the pancreas, and this can be corrected only by the life-long administration of exogenous insulin.

Postmortem examination of the pancreas in patients who had recently developed type 1 diabetes but died from other causes (e.g. road traffic accident) shows lymphocytic

infiltration of the islets with specific destruction of the beta-cells. There are three major theories concerning the aetiology of these changes: autoimmune destruction, genetic factors and viral infection.

Autoimmune destruction. The majority of patients who have recently developed type 1 diabetes have circulatory antibodies to several different types of islet cell. Patients with this type of diabetes are also prone to develop other 'organ-specific' autoimmune diseases (Ch. 9).

Genetic factors. As with other 'organ-specific' autoimmune diseases, there is an association with certain HLA types (Ch. 3), notably HLA-DR4, especially if HLA-B8 or -DR3 is also present. It seems that environmental factors also play a role, as identical twins show only 40% concordance in development of the disease.

Viral infection. Titres of antibodies to viruses such as Coxsackie B types and mumps are elevated in some patients developing this type of diabetes; these viruses may act as a trigger for direct or autoimmune destruction of the islets.

Type 2 (maturity-onset, non-insulin-dependent diabetes)

Type 2 diabetes mellitus (also called maturity-onset, or non-insulin-dependent diabetes) is more common than type 1 and usually presents in middle age, being commonest in the obese. Patients are not prone to ketoacidosis, but occasionally develop a non-ketotic coma in which there is extreme hyperosmolarity of the plasma. Insulin secretion is normal or increased and the central defect may therefore be a reduction in the number of cell surface receptors for insulin.

Genetic factors clearly play an important part in the aetiology of type 2 diabetes, as identical twins show nearly a 100% concordance in development of the disease. No clear Mendelian pattern of inheritance can be recognised. The evidence is against this being an autoimmune disease.

Treatment is usually by weight reduction coupled with orally administered drugs that potentiate the action of insulin.

Secondary diabetes

Hypersecretion of any of the hormones that tend to exert a hyperglycaemic effect may cause glucose intolerance. Thus Cushing's syndrome, phaeochromocytoma, acromegaly and glucagonomas may cause secondary diabetes. Generalised destruction of the pancreas (Ch. 16) by acute and chronic pancreatitis, haemochromatosis and, occasionally, carcinoma may cause insulin deficiency.

Complications

The major complications of diabetes mellitus are shown in Table 17.11. The commonest complications are seen in blood vessels. Atheroma, often ultimately severe and extensive, develops at an earlier age than in the non-diabetic population. Small blood vessels show basal lamina thickening and endothelial cell proliferation (diabetic microangiopathy), frequently causing retinal and renal damage. About 80% of adult diabetics die from cardiovascular disease, while patients with longstanding diabetes, especially type 1, frequently develop serious renal and retinal disease. Improved metabolic control through modern insulin regimens has only partially reduced the incidence of such serious complications.

Tumours

> ▸ Less common than pancreatic adenocarcinoma
> ▸ Present with endocrine effects and may be malignant
> ▸ Insulinoma: causes hypoglycaemia
> ▸ Glucagonoma: causes secondary diabetes and skin rash

Adenomas and carcinomas derived from the islet cells are quite rare. They usually present clinically through hypersecretion of their normal hormonal product, producing widespread symptoms; consequently these tumours may be small at the time of presentation. Most consist of cellular nodules within

Table 17.10 Diagnosis of diabetes

Test	Diagnosis		
	Normal	Impaired GT	Diabetes
Random glucose	2.2–11.1	>10.0 on more than one occasion implies impaired GT or diabetes mellitus	
Fasting glucose	2.2–6.7	6.7–10.0	>10.0
2 hours after 75 g glucose	6.7	6.7–10.0	>10.0
Samples taken from venous blood; measurements in mmol/l; all values apply to non-pregnant adults. GT, glucose tolerance.			

Table 17.11 Complications of diabetes

Situation	Complication
Large blood vessels	Accelerated atheroma, leading to: • myocardial infarction • cerebrovascular disease • ischaemic limbs • 80% of adult diabetic deaths
Small blood vessels	Endothelial cells and basal lamina damage Retinopathy (a major cause of blindness) Nephropathy, including Kimmelstiel–Wilson lesion (Ch. 21)
Peripheral nerve	Neuropathy, possibly due to disease of small vessels supplying the nerves
Neutrophils	Susceptibility to infection
Pregnancy	Pre-eclamptic toxaemia Large babies Neonatal hypoglycaemia
Skin	Necrobiosis lipoidica diabeticorum Granuloma annulare Gangrene of extremities

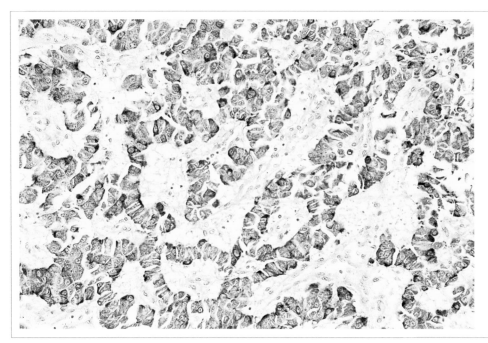

Fig. 17.43 Insulinoma. This tumour has been stained by the immunoperoxidase technique for insulin. Ribbons of brown-stained cells resemble those of the normal islet of Langerhans.

the pancreatic tissue. Histologically, they are composed of cells resembling normal islet cells (Fig. 17.43) and immunohistochemistry may be used to identify the hormonal content of the cells. Like other tumours of APUD tissues (Ch. 11), they contain dense-core secretory granules on electron microscopy. It is usually not possible to predict whether an islet cell tumour will pursue a benign or malignant course on the basis of histological appearance.

Insulinoma

Insulinoma is the commonest islet cell tumour and produces hypoglycaemia through hypersecretion of insulin. During hypoglycaemic attacks, the patient develops confusion, psychiatric disturbances and possibly coma. Diagnosis is urgent because hypoglycaemia may produce permanent cerebral damage.

Glucagonoma

Glucagonoma is much less common; it leads to hypersecretion of glucagon, producing secondary diabetes and a distinctive skin rash known as necrolytic migratory erythema.

Other islet cell tumours

Other islet cell tumours are very rare, but include somatostatinomas and tumours secreting vasoactive intestinal peptide (VIP), which leads to watery diarrhoea.

Gastrinomas

Although gastrin is usually produced in the G-cells of the stomach, tumours of the G-cells, called gastrinomas, most commonly originate in the pancreas. These APUD tumours lead to intractable hypersecretion of gastric acid due to the action of gastrin, resulting in widespread severe peptic ulceration (Zollinger–Ellison syndrome). Most gastrinomas are malignant.

Islet cell tumours and gastrinomas may occur as part of one of the MEN syndromes (Ch. 11), most commonly MEN type 1.

Commonly confused conditions and entities relating to endocrine pathology	
Commonly confused	Distinction and explanation
Gigantism and *acromegaly*	Both due to excess GH secretion. *Gigantism* is the result before epiphyseal closure. *Acromegaly* is the result in adults, with fused epiphyses.
Renin and *rennin*	*Renin* cleaves angiotensinogen into angiotensin I. *Rennin* (rennet, chymosin) is a proteinase, usually derived from the mucosa of calf's stomach, which curdles milk; used in the cheese industry.
Addison's disease and *Addisonian pernicious anaemia*	*Addison's disease* is adrenal failure, usually due to autoimmune destruction. Addison also described *pernicious anaemia,* also an autoimmune disease, in which the gastric parietal cells are destroyed and hence fail to secrete intrinsic factor, which is required for absorption of vitamin B_{12}.

(Continued)

Commonly confused conditions and entities relating to endocrine pathology —cont'd	
Commonly confused	**Distinction and explanation**
Primary hypertension and *secondary hypertension*	*Primary hypertension* is the commonest (99%) type of hypertension; it has no definite single cause. *Secondary hypertension* (< 1% of cases) is secondary to other disease (e.g. phaeochromocytoma) and is therefore potentially curable.
Graves' thyroiditis and *hyperthyroidism*	*Graves' thyroiditis* is an organ-specific autoimmune disease; antibodies to TSH receptors cause thyroid hyperfunction. *Hyperthyroidism* is thyroid hyperfunction from any cause.
Hashimoto's thyroiditis and *hypothyroidism*	*Hashimoto's thyroiditis* is autoimmune thyroid destruction. *Hypothyroidism* is a generic term for thyroid hypofunction from any cause.
Exophthalmos and *lid retraction*	*Exophthalmos* is eye protrusion specific to Graves' thyroiditis, caused by expansion of the retro-orbital tissues by adipose tissue (which also contains TSH receptors). Hyperthyroidism from any cause may also cause *lid retraction*.
Myxoedema and *pretibial myxoedema*	*Myxoedema* is generalised deposition of mucopolysaccharides in hypothyroidism. *Pretibial myxoedema* is also mucopolysaccharide deposition, but confined to the pretibial region and specifically associated with Graves' thyroiditis.
Medullary carcinoma of the thyroid and *medullary carcinoma of the breast*	*Medullary carcinoma of the thyroid* is derived from the C-cells and is an endocrine neoplasm making calcitonin. *Medullary carcinoma of the breast* is a type of adenocarcinoma that is soft on gross examination and has no connection with the thyroid tumour.
Exocrine and *endocrine*	*Exocrine* glands secrete into the gut or onto the surface of the body. *Endocrine* glands secrete hormones into the blood.
Type 2 diabetes and *secondary diabetes*	*Type 2 diabetes* is maturity-onset (non-insulin-dependent) diabetes mellitus, so called to distinguish it from type 1 juvenile-onset (insulin-dependent) diabetes mellitus. *Secondary diabetes* is distinct from both of these: it is the development of glucose intolerance secondary to another disease (e.g. Cushing's syndrome).
Insulin and *inulin*	*Insulin* is the hypoglycaemic peptide hormone secreted by the beta-cells of the islets of Langerhans. *Inulin* is a storage polysaccharide found in Jerusalem artichokes, once used in the investigation of renal clearance, and in some 'diabetic' dietary products.

FURTHER READING

Al-Shraim M, Asa SL 2006 The 2004 World Health Organisation classification of pituitary tumors: what is new?. Acta Neuropathologica 111: 1–7

Asa SL 2004 My approach to oncocytic tumours of the thyroid. Journal of Clinical Pathology 57: 225–232

Balotti S, Chiarelli F, de Martino M 2006 Autoimmunity: basic mechanisms and implications in endocrine diseases. Hormone Research 66: 132–141

Bishop A E, Polak J M 1996 Gastrointestinal endocrine tumours. Pathology. Baillière's Clinical Gastroenterology 10: 555–569

Boyages S C, Cheung W 1995 Goitre in Australia. Medical Journal of Australia 162: 487–489

Dahia P L M 2006 Evolving concepts in phaeochromocytoma and paraganglioma. Current Opinion in Oncology 18: 1–8

DeLellis R A 1993 Tumors of the parathyroid gland. In: Rosai J (ed) Atlas of tumor pathology, 3rd series. Fascicle 6. Armed Forces Institute of Pathology, Washington, DC

Fassnacht M, Kenn W, Allolio B 2004 Adrenal tumors: how to establish malignancy? Journal of Endocrinological Investigation 27: 387–399

Fonseca E, Sobrinho-Simões M 1995 Diagnostic problems in differentiated carcinomas of the thyroid. Pathology, Research and Practice 191: 318–331

Gepts W, Pepeleers D 1976 The endocrine pancreas. Functional morphology and histopathology. Acta Medica Scandinavica Supplementum 601: 9–52

Goldstone A P, Scott-Coombes D M, Lynn J A 1996 Surgical management of gastrointestinal endocrine tumours. Baillière's Clinical Gastroenterology 10: 707–736

Grimelius L, Johansson H 1997 Pathology of parathyroid tumors. Seminars in Surgical Oncology 13: 142–154

Julie C, Vieillefond A, Desligneres S, Schaison G, Grunfeld J P, Franc B 1997 Hashimoto's thyroiditis associated with Riedel's thyroiditis and retroperitoneal fibrosis. Pathology, Research and Practice 193: 573–577

Kovacs K, Asa S L 1998 Functional endocrine pathology, 2nd edn. Blackwell Science, Oxford

Lack E E 1997 Tumors of the pancreas. In: Rosai J (ed) Atlas of tumor pathology, 3rd series. Fascicle 19. Armed Forces Institute of Pathology, Washington, DC

Lahita R G 1997 Predisposing factors to autoimmune disease. International Journal of Fertility and Women's Medicine 42: 115–119

Lansford C D, Teknos T N 2006 Evaluation of the thyroid nodule. Cancer Control 13: 89–98

Lewis P D 1996 The endocrine system. symmers textbook of pathology. Churchill Livingstone, Edinburgh

LiVolsi V A, Asa S L 2002 Endocrine pathology. Churchill Livingstone, Edinburgh

Lloyd R V, Douglas B R, Young W F 2000 Endocrine diseases, 1st series. Fascicle 1. In: King D W (ed) Atlas of nontumor pathology. Armed Forces Institute of Pathology and American Registry of Pathology, Washington, DC

CLINICAL FEATURES OF BREAST LESIONS

▶ Physiological changes must be distinguished from pathological lesions
▶ Many breast conditions present as a lump or lumps
▶ Always note the characteristics of the lump and the age of the patient
▶ Discharge from the nipple occurs with some conditions

Most pathological lesions of the breast present as a lump or lumps. These can vary in their nature depending on their cause: well-circumscribed or ill-defined; single or multiple small nodules; soft or firm; mobile or attached to skin or underlying muscle. These features assist in the clinical distinction between benign breast lesions and breast carcinomas, but they are relatively weak discriminators on their own. Below the age of about 35, benign breast lumps are much more common than carcinomas. Most women with breast cancer are peri- or post-menopausal. The most likely type of lesion will vary with the age of the patient, although overlaps occur (Table 18.1). However, there can be exceptions and histological examination is mandatory for a definite diagnosis.

Physiological conditions can be confused with, or mimic, pathological conditions. A degree of tenderness and swelling of the breast in the premenstrual phase is common. Some women have naturally 'lumpy' breasts and this may become exaggerated in this phase of the menstrual cycle. Uneven proliferation of the glandular substance during pregnancy, and irregular involution after pregnancy and during and after the menopause, can result in lumps that are the outcome of physiological and not pathological events. Other manifestations of a pathological lesion within the breast are discharge from the nipple, eczema and ulceration of the skin of the nipple.

DIAGNOSTIC METHODS

Several methods are used to investigate breast lesions. The aim is to get a diagnosis and either negate surgery or be able to discuss management with the patient (i.e. pre-operative diagnosis). They include:

● imaging—mammography and ultrasonography
● fine-needle aspiration cytology
● core biopsy.

Mammography and ultrasonography
Radiography of the breasts (mammography) is used to help in the diagnosis of both palpable and impalpable lesions, looking for deformities and/or calcifications. This technique forms the basis of screening programmes. It is of less value in younger women due to the dense nature of their breasts. Ultrasound imaging is of value for younger patients for defining the edge of lesions, e.g. cysts. Both investigations should be undertaken before a needle is inserted.

Fine-needle aspiration cytology
This technique is used in the clinic. A needle is inserted into the lump or area in the breast with the abnormality (guided if necessary by ultrasonography or mammography). Cells are aspirated, and after staining are examined by a pathologist; if

Table 18.1 The probable pathological causes of presenting clinical lesions at different ages in women

| Clinical presentation | Probable pathological cause | | | |
	<25 years	25–35 years	35–55 years	>55 years
Mobile lump	Fibroadenoma	Fibroadenoma Phyllodes tumour	Fibroadenoma	Phyllodes tumour
Ill-defined lump or lumpy areas	Uncommon	Fibrocystic change Sclerosing adenosis	Fibrocystic change	Uncommon
Firm lump ± tethering	Uncommon	Carcinoma*	Carcinoma	Carcinoma Fat necrosis
Nipple discharge				
Clear	Uncommon	Uncommon	Duct ectasia	Duct ectasia
Bloody	Uncommon	Uncommon	Duct papilloma In situ carcinoma	Duct papilloma In situ carcinoma
Nipple ulceration, eczema	Nipple adenoma	Nipple adenoma	Paget's disease Nipple adenoma	Paget's disease Nipple adenoma

*Carcinoma is relatively uncommon in this age group.

the sample is adequate a diagnosis can be made. Women with benign conditions can be reassured and surgery may not be necessary. It is possible to prepare slides and a report while the patient is in the clinic.

Core biopsy

A core of tissue is removed from the lump/lesion using a biopsy needle, under local anaesthetic. This can be done under mammographic control and is of particular value for diagnosis of calcifications seen on mammograms. It can also be ultrasonographically guided. Core biopsies are of value when sufficient cells cannot be obtained or a diagnosis cannot be made on cytology; for calcifications; if a patient has an obvious cancer and is going to be treated with chemotherapy prior to surgery, as marker studies can be done. Some centres prefer core biopsies to cytology.

Other

If a diagnosis cannot be made then the patient will have a larger piece of tissue removed, under general anaesthetic. It is uncommon nowadays for frozen sections to be performed. This involves a small sample of tissue being frozen, sectioned, stained and interpreted by a pathologist at the time of surgery, while the patient is under general anaesthetic. It is only considered if a diagnosis cannot be made pre-operatively and there are medical reasons for the patient not to have two anaesthetics.

Screening for breast cancer

In several developed countries with a high incidence of breast cancer, such as the UK, screening programmes for the detection of early breast cancer have been introduced. Trials in Sweden and the USA strongly suggest that women whose cancers have been detected by regular mammographic screening have an increased survival rate. This is because the tumours are detected when they are either pre-invasive (in situ carcinoma) or invasive but small, with less risk of metastasis. Unscreened women present when the tumour has grown to a size sufficient to be felt, at which stage there is a higher probability of metastases.

In the UK, women between the ages of 50 and 69 are invited to attend for breast screening by mammography every 3 years. Suspicious features on the mammographic image, such as microcalcification and localised densities, are further investigated by ultrasonography and clinical examination, with histology of biopsy samples, and very occasionally cytology, providing the definitive diagnosis. Impalpable lesions detected in this way require an X-ray-directed guidewire to be inserted into them before surgery to help the surgeon find the right area.

Besides being smaller, the invasive tumours have a higher frequency of being of a more favourable histological type and lower grade. This, along with the lower incidence of lymph node metastasis, will contribute to the improved prognosis. The surgery for these early lesions is more likely to be conservative.

The greater density of the pre-menopausal breast means that mammography may be less reliable for screening women under 50 years.

INFLAMMATORY CONDITIONS

▶ Infections of the breast are uncommon, usually complications of lactation
▶ Duct ectasia can cause nipple discharge, uncommon in younger women
▶ Fat necrosis is due to trauma, more frequent in the obese

Acute pyogenic mastitis

Acute pyogenic mastitis is a painful acute inflammatory condition which usually occurs in the first few weeks after delivery, and *Staphylococcus aureus* is the commonest organism. The usual portal of entry is a crack in the nipple, although persistence of the keratotic plug at the orifice of a duct may be a factor. The organisms spread via the lymphatics, and the infection tends to be confined to one segment of the breast, resulting in localised swelling and erythema. The infection can spread to other segments and, if *Streptococcus pyogenes* is the causative organism, a more widespread inflammation occurs with systemic symptoms. If antibiotics are given but there is inadequate drainage, a localised breast abscess will result.

Other infections

Tuberculosis

This is rare and usually results from haematogenous spread. The infection results in a fibrocaseous mass with the formation of sinuses, although a marked fibrous reaction can occur, giving a firm mass that will mimic a carcinoma.

Actinomycosis

Also rare, actinomycosis can be due to extension of infection from the lung through the thoracic cage, or occur as a primary infection. The usual presentation is as a hard lump beneath the nipple, which may be painful, but with no temperature change, so mimicking a tumour. It results in abscess formation, within which are the bacterial colonies.

Mammary duct ectasia

Mammary duct ectasia involves the larger ducts within the breast but, in severe cases, can also extend to the smaller interlobular ducts. It occurs predominantly in women in the second half of reproductive life and after the menopause, and mild degrees of the condition are often an incidental finding in breast tissue excised for other conditions. Severe forms, in which it is the primary presenting condition, are less frequent. Severe cases can be mistaken clinically for a carcinoma as there may be a discharge from the nipple which may be bloodstained. Fibrosis around the ducts may result in nipple retraction, and there may be a firm palpable mass. However, mammary duct ectasia is a purely inflammatory condition with no relationship to malignancy.

The aetiology is unknown but the affected women are usually parous. The ducts are dilated and filled with white–green viscid matter; this material may be discharged from the nipple. The matter can usually be seen with the naked eye in excised tissue. The tissue around the ducts contains lymphocytes, plasma cells and macrophages, with a significant degree of fibrosis. Due to the inflammatory reaction, the condition is sometimes known as *periductal mastitis*.

Fat necrosis

Trauma, e.g. seat belt injury, is thought to be the cause of fat necrosis, although a history is not always obtained. It is more frequent in obese women and after the menopause, when the breast has a proportionally greater amount of adipose tissue. It usually presents as a discrete lump and can therefore mimic a carcinoma clinically.

Macroscopically, the tissue is yellow and haemorrhagic, with flecks of calcification. Fibrous tissue is also present, the amount depending on the duration of the condition.

Histologically, the appearances are the same as those of any adipose tissue that undergoes necrosis (Ch. 6): collections of macrophages and giant cells containing lipid material may be seen, and there is an associated reaction with lymphocytes, fibroblasts and small vascular channels. The necrotic fat acts as a persistent irritant, resulting in a chronic inflammatory process and hence fibrous tissue formation.

Similar foreign body reactions can occur in the breast around ruptured prosthetic implants, in which silicone fluid is frequently used; a very dense fibrous tissue reaction can result, causing considerable distortion.

PROLIFERATIVE CONDITIONS OF THE BREAST

- ▶ Increase in frequency towards menopause, then rapid decrease
- ▶ Present as diffuse granularity, ill-defined lump or discrete swelling
- ▶ Variety of histological changes
- ▶ Adenosis commoner in younger age group, cysts commoner nearer the menopause
- ▶ Women with atypical hyperplasia are at increased risk of developing breast cancer
- ▶ Gynaecomastia is enlargement of breasts in men

Proliferative conditions of the breast include a wide variety of morphological changes with consequently varied clinical features; because of this there has been much confusion about the terminology and significance of these conditions.

Fibrocystic change

The commonest proliferative condition of the breast is fibrocystic change. Although benign and non-neoplastic, it is important because:
- in many women, it causes severe periodic discomfort
- one component, epithelial hyperplasia, is associated with an increased breast cancer risk
- it causes palpable lumps, mimicking breast cancer.

Terminology

The old term for proliferative conditions of the breast was 'chronic mastitis'; this is incorrect, as these are not inflammatory conditions, but the name may have arisen because of the tenderness that can occur in some cases. Other names include fibroadenosis, epithelial hyperplasia, fibrocystic disease, cystic hyperplasia and mammary dysplasia. Since some of the features are similar to physiological changes the term 'fibrocystic change', rather than 'disease', is now used.

The terms *fibroadenosis* and *epithelial hyperplasia* describe the proliferative changes that occur in the condition (see below), and are appropriate terms for the changes that occur in the 30–45-year age group. Fibrocystic change and cystic hyperplasia are descriptive of the changes that occur from 40–45 years to the menopause, when cysts are more prominent. The term 'mammary dysplasia' is not really correct, as true dysplasia occurs only in a few cases.

Incidence

Estimates indicate that at least 10% of women develop clinically apparent benign proliferative breast disease, although breast tissue from women at postmortem shows such changes to be present in 50% or more, suggesting that lesser degrees of change are much more common.

Aetiology and pathogenesis

Although benign proliferative breast disease is not uncommon, the aetiology is poorly understood. There is no doubt that ovarian hormones participate in its causation but the means by which the changes are produced are still obscure.

The fact that the incidence of benign proliferative changes increases as the menopause gets nearer, and that failure of ovulation also increases in this time period, suggests that the relative imbalance between oestrogen and progesterone in each menstrual cycle could be an important aetiological factor. The disturbance may involve interaction of the pituitary and the ovaries. Alternatively, the fault may lie in the responsiveness of the breast tissue to the hormonal influences. Not all parts of the breast are equally affected by the hormonal changes occurring in each menstrual cycle, and this may account for the focal nature of the changes.

Cystic change is considered to be due to an imbalance between epithelial hyperplasia, together with ductal and lobular dilatation, that occurs with each menstrual cycle, and subsequent regressive changes. The cystic dilatation thus occurs because of a distortion of cyclical changes rather than as a consequence of obstruction, which is the usual cause in other organs.

Clinical and gross features

Proliferative lesions and their associated tissue responses generally occur between the ages of 30 and 55, with a marked decrease in incidence after the menopause. The incidence reaches a maximum in the years just before the menopause (Fig. 18.6).

The clinical features tend to vary with the age of the patient and the underlying pathological changes. In younger women, there is usually a diffuse granularity in one or more segments of the breast, with nodules up to 5 mm in diameter. The area may be tender, particularly in the premenstrual period. In women nearer the menopause, there is usually an ill-defined rubbery mass. The finding of discrete swelling indicates the presence of cysts. If fibrosis is a component of the proliferative lesion, the lump will be firm and therefore more difficult to differentiate clinically from carcinoma.

Surgery for benign conditions is now uncommon. If undertaken it is more common to find nodules of soft pink or grey tissue, up to 3 mm in diameter in younger women, whereas in women nearer the menopause cysts are frequently seen. These cysts can vary in size from 2 to 20 mm (Fig. 18.7) and, rarely, a solitary large cyst can be seen. The small cysts are often multiple. They frequently have a dark blue surface and, on opening, contain clear, yellowish or blood-stained fluid.

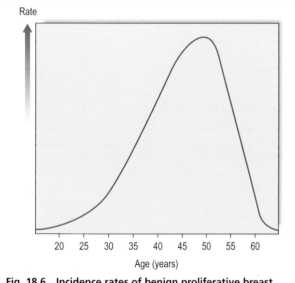

Fig. 18.6 **Incidence rates of benign proliferative breast changes occurring in women at different ages.**

The intervening tissue is usually firm due to the increase in fibrous tissue but the softer foci of epithelial proliferation can be seen and felt.

Histological features

A variety of histological changes can occur (Fig. 18.8). These are:

- adenosis
- sclerosing adenosis
- epithelial hyperplasia
- papillomatosis
- cysts
- apocrine metaplasia
- fibrosis.

An individual woman may show one, some or all of these changes. However, the types of change do tend to vary with the age of the patient.

Adenosis

Adenosis is enlargement of the lobules which contain many, up to hundreds, of acini. In other respects they are structurally normal. The term is often used to refer to blunt duct adenosis in which the acini of the lobules are larger than normal and are lined by cells that are increased in size and may also be more numerous, although the acinar lumen is always clearly seen. The lobular stroma may also increase. The changes are not confined to the epithelium and can involve the surrounding myoepithelium. Such areas correspond to the grey–pink nodules seen macroscopically and the fine nodules felt clinically.

Sclerosing adenosis

In sclerosing adenosis there is lobular proliferation but the acini become distorted. The proliferation involves both epithelium and myoepithelium, but the latter tends to predominate. Large amounts of collagen can intervene between the glandular components, although the extent of this varies both within the same breast and between patients (Fig. 18.9). Due to the collagen component these lesions can mimic carcinomas clinically, and on mammograms where the associated calcification can be seen.

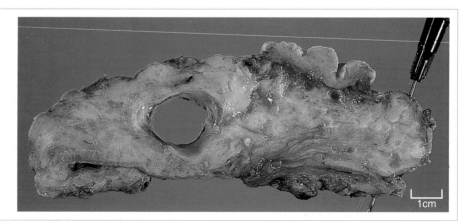

Fig. 18.7 **Fibrocystic change: cysts.** Breast tissue from a 48-year-old woman showing one large cyst and multiple smaller ones, with areas of fibrosis.

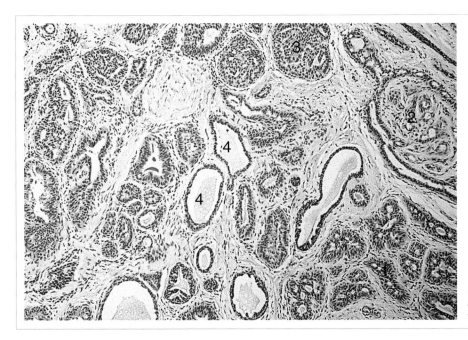

Fig. 18.8 Fibrocystic change. There is adenosis (1), papilloma formation (2), epithelial hyperplasia (3) and small cysts (4).

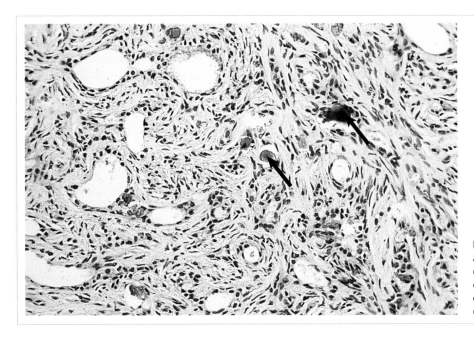

Fig. 18.9 Sclerosing adenosis. There are glandular structures with intervening cords of cells in a fibrous stroma. Areas of calcification (arrowed) are also present; these would render the lesion visible on mammography.

Epithelial hyperplasia

Epithelial hyperplasia, previously called epitheliosis, is the proliferation of epithelial cells that occurs in the small interlobular ducts, the intralobular ducts and the acini, resulting in a solid or almost solid mass obliterating the lumens (Fig. 18.10).

Papillomatosis

Papillomatosis comprises simple papillary processes projecting into the lumens of dilated ducts or small cysts. The papillae have a fine connective tissue core and are covered by one or two layers of epithelium; they may undergo branching.

Cysts

Cysts develop through dilatation of the acini of the lobules and the terminal ducts. These cysts may remain small, or enlarge to sizes up to 20–30 mm. They may be fairly evenly distributed, with little variation in size, or show quite marked variation in size, shape or number. They may be lined by simple cuboidal or flattened epithelium, or focal proliferative change may occur. Occasionally cysts can rupture, causing an inflammatory reaction.

Apocrine metaplasia

Frequently the cysts, both large and small, are lined entirely or partly by cells that resemble the epithelium of the apocrine sweat glands. This condition is called apocrine

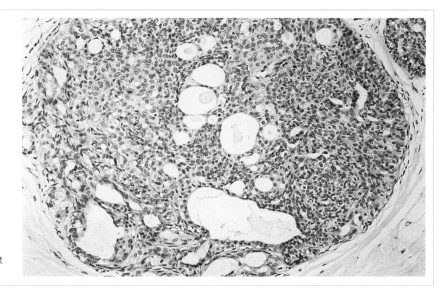

Fig. 18.10 Epithelial hyperplasia. The duct lumen is filled by hyperplastic epithelium.

metaplasia. The lining cells are large columnar cells with pink-staining (eosinophilic) cytoplasm, hence the alternative name 'pink cell metaplasia'. It has no special clinical or prognostic significance.

Fibrosis

Fibrosis can occur in association with the various proliferative conditions, or as an isolated lesion. When associated with proliferative conditions it is probably due to the hormonal imbalances causing changes in the typical loose connective tissue of the lobules, making it denser with fewer glycosaminoglycans. The solitary form of fibrosis produces a poorly defined area of rubbery consistency consisting of dense connective tissue with few atrophic epithelial areas. This condition is found mainly in women with a clear history of hormone imbalance.

Atypical hyperplasia

The epithelial hyperplasia that can result in total or partial occlusion of the acini and small ducts may sometimes show abnormalities of cellular growth, with disordered orientation of cells, nuclear pleomorphism and occasional mitotic figures. This is termed either atypical ductal or atypical lobular hyperplasia, depending on its situation. It is important for the pathologist to identify these cellular changes (see below).

Lesions in women aged 30–45 years

In the 30–45-year age group, lesions are more likely to consist of areas of adenosis, possibly with epithelial hyperplasia, and a mild degree of fibrosis. Sclerosing adenosis may also be present. Microcysts with apocrine metaplasia start to develop in the late thirties, but are generally not a major feature. Between 40 and 45 years the changes may be predominantly proliferative, with adenosis and epithelial hyperplasia, or may be more cystic.

Lesions in women aged 45–55 years

Cysts are the more prominent feature in this age group and can be quite large. The terms 'blue domed cyst' and 'Bloodgood's cyst' used to be applied. Apocrine metaplasia is often present. Proliferative features, such as adenosis, epithelial hyperplasia and papillomatosis, can be seen, and fibrosis is quite common.

Radial scars

Radial scars are benign focal lesions commonly detected by mammography. They are stellate fibrous structures with foci of ductal epithelial proliferation. Their structure mimics radiologically the appearance of invasive carcinoma. When larger than 10 mm, they are named *complex sclerosing lesions*.

Significance of proliferative lesions

Clinically, the presence of a lump can cause anxiety in the patient, who may believe it is a cancer when it is benign; diagnostic investigations can reassure her.

Previous studies have shown that up to 70% of women who undergo breast biopsy for benign fibrocystic change are not at an increased risk of developing cancer. However, if the biopsy contains areas of atypical hyperplasia, the woman has a risk of developing cancer five times higher than that of a woman with non-proliferative lesions, and the risk increases if there is a family history of breast cancer. Cysts alone do not appear to increase the risk.

Lesions in men: gynaecomastia

The breast tissue in men contains only ductular structures with no evidence of acini; it is similar in appearance to the pre-pubertal female breast.

Gynaecomastia is benign enlargement of the male breast tissue. The breast may resemble that of a young adolescent

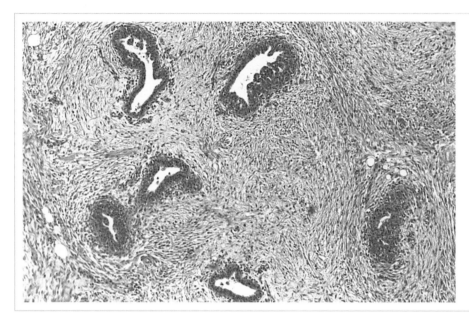

Fig. 18.11 Gynaecomastia. Male breast in which the ducts are lined by an increased number of cells, and are surrounded by loose connective tissue.

female in appearance and consistency, or there may be a firm, mobile disc beneath the nipple. The condition is unilateral in 75% of cases. The ducts are dilated and there is a variable degree of epithelial proliferation. The stroma around the ducts is often oedematous and myxoid, but in longstanding cases the stroma becomes dense and hyalinised (Fig. 18.11).

Gynaecomastia occurs most commonly in adolescence and in older age groups. In both of these groups it is probably due to some hormonal effects relating to oestrogens, possibly a result of endocrine disturbances such as hyperthyroidism, pituitary disorders and tumours of the adrenals and testis. Both of the latter can secrete oestrogens. In the older age group, diethylstilbestrol therapy of prostatic carcinoma can cause gynaecomastia. Other causes include Klinefelter's syndrome, malnutrition and cirrhosis, as well as the drugs chlorpromazine and spironolactone, and digitalis therapy.

BENIGN TUMOURS

Unlike the situation in other glandular tissues, the commonest type of benign tumour of the breast is a combined product of both connective tissue and epithelial cells; purely epithelial tumours are less frequent.

The benign breast tumours comprise:

- fibroadenomas
- duct papillomas
- adenomas
- connective tissue tumours.

Fibroadenoma

> ▶ Commonest type of benign tumour, mainly in young women
> ▶ Arises from connective tissue and epithelium
> ▶ Clinically, mobile on palpation

Fibroadenomas are the commonest type of benign tumour of the breast, and are the commonest primary tumour in younger age groups. In a study in New York, fibroadenomas were seen with a quarter of the frequency of carcinomas, but six times more frequently than duct papillomas. However, not all fibroadenomas are excised, so their actual frequency may be higher.

The greatest incidence of fibroadenomas is in the third decade, although they can occur at any time from puberty onwards. The tumours are usually solitary, although some women do develop multiple fibroadenomas.

Fibroadenomas arise from the breast lobule, from both the loose connective tissue stroma and the glands. As they are mixed tumours, fibroadenomas will undergo some of the same hormonally induced changes as the surrounding breast. Thus, during pregnancy the glands will show lactational changes, and in older women the stroma will become more dense and fibrous. During pregnancy, fibroadenomas may grow rapidly in size, but this is due to hormonal effects and is not a sign of malignancy.

Gross appearance

Fibroadenomas are well circumscribed with a lobulated appearance (Fig. 18.12), and range in size from 10 to 40 mm in diameter, although larger tumours can occur in juvenile fibroadenoma (see below). The surrounding breast tissue can become compressed, but the tumour is not tethered; this lack of fixation accounts for its mobility on clinical examination, and the nickname of 'breast mouse'. In young women, the tumours are soft and have a slightly gelatinous cut surface due to the loose connective tissue component; however, in older women they tend to be firmer as the connective tissue becomes more fibrous and sometimes calcified.

Histology

Fibroadenomas show duct-like structures or elongated and thinned ductular structures associated with overgrown connective tissue masses (Fig. 18.13). Fibroadenoma does not progress to malignancy, although very occasionally a tumour, such as lobular carcinoma, will involve a fibroadenoma.

Juvenile fibroadenoma

Large (50–100 mm in diameter) fibroadenomas can occur in the breast of girls, the tumours growing quite rapidly. They are more frequent in Africans and West Indians than in Caucasians. The tumours are benign and should not be confused with phyllodes tumour.

Fig. 18.12 Fibroadenoma. The outer surface is smooth, well circumscribed, and has a lobulated appearance.

Duct papilloma

> ▶ Less common, occurring in middle-aged women
> ▶ Presents as blood-stained nipple discharge
> ▶ Usually solitary lesion, occurring in large ducts
> ▶ Papillary structures, with fibrovascular core covered by benign epithelium

Duct papillomas are considerably less frequent than fibroadenomas. They also differ in several other respects. Although they can occur in the young and the elderly, they more frequently arise in middle-aged women. Duct papillomas are the commonest cause of nipple discharge. About 80% of patients present with a discharge, which is often blood-stained, and a mass can often be felt. The tumours arise from ductal epithelium.

Duct papillomas arise as a solitary lesion within a large duct, up to 40 mm from the nipple. They appear either as an elongated structure extending along a duct, or as a spheroid which causes distension of the duct, making it cyst-like. The tumours have soft, pink or white outgrowths except when haemorrhage has occurred, in which case the surface will be brown from altered blood. Duct papillomas consist of branching fibrovascular cores covered by epithelium, which is cytologically benign (Fig. 18.14). Solitary duct papillomas are not premalignant; there is no increased risk of carcinoma.

There is a rare condition in which multiple ductal papillomas occur, but these arise in the smaller ducts, away from the nipple, and so present as a mass rather than as nipple discharge. These tend to occur in a younger age group than do solitary papillomas and there is an increased risk of carcinoma developing.

Adenomas

> ▶ Rare, arise only from epithelium
> ▶ Tubular and lactating adenomas occur in young women
> ▶ Nipple adenomas occur at all ages; there is a mass beneath the nipple which can ulcerate the skin

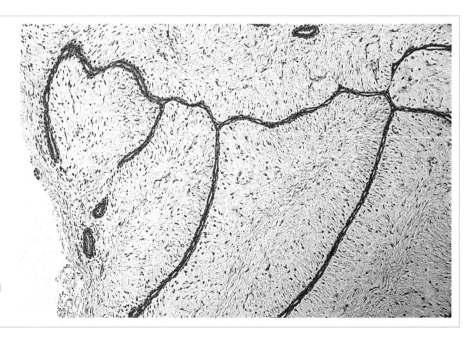

Fig. 18.13 Fibroadenoma. Elongated duct-like structures are surrounded by loose connective tissue.

Adenomas are much rarer than fibroadenomas and duct papillomas. *Tubular adenomas* are well-circumscribed tumours between 10 and 40 mm in diameter, occurring mainly in women in their early twenties. They are composed of closely packed, uniform tubular structures with little connective tissue in between; hence the only tumorous component is the glands.

Lactating adenomas are tubular adenomas that undergo secretory changes during pregnancy.

Nipple adenomas occur as a nodule under the nipple, usually less than 15 mm in diameter, in women of any age. The overlying skin is often ulcerated, and there may be a blood-stained discharge, so that clinically nipple adenomas may be mistaken for Paget's disease. They are well circumscribed, and contain small and larger ducts filled with masses of cells and surrounded by a dense stroma.

Connective tissue tumours

Lipomas and haemangiomas can occur in the breast, but are often hamartomas. Leiomyomas may occur deep in the breast or in the nipple, arising from the smooth muscle that is abundant there.

BREAST CARCINOMA

▸ 31% of all cancers in women
▸ Commonest cause of death in women in 35–55-year age group
▸ In the UK, any woman has a 1 in 9 chance of developing breast cancer

In North America, north-west Europe and Australia, breast cancer is the commonest type of malignancy in women. In the UK it accounts for 31% of all cancers, with 80% occurring in women aged above 50 years. It is the commonest cause of death among women in the 35–55-year age group. Recent reports (2004) show there are 44 659 new cases each year in the UK. It is estimated, in the high-risk areas, that any individual woman has a 1 in 9 chance of developing the disease in her lifetime.

Many risk factors have been identified, and these, together with advances in the analysis of genetic and hormonal factors, have resulted in several aetiological hypotheses (Fig. 18.15). An understanding of these can help in the development of programmes directed towards the prevention of breast cancer. Schemes aimed at the early detection of breast cancer have been introduced in several countries.

Risk factors

The risk factors identified to date are:

● female sex; risk increases with age
● long interval between menarche and menopause
● older age at first full-term pregnancy
● obesity and high-fat diet
● radiation
● family history of breast cancer
● geographic factors
● atypical hyperplasia in previous breast biopsy.

Female sex and age

Around 1% of all breast cancers occur in men, so being female is an important risk factor. As with all carcinomas, increasing age is another significant factor. Up to the age of 50 years, the rate of increase is steep; it then slows down, although the incidence of breast cancer continues to increase into old age (Fig. 18.16).

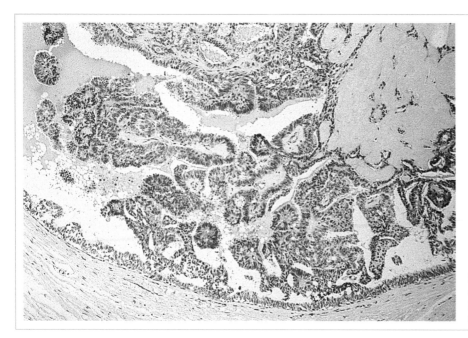

Fig. 18.14 Duct papilloma. A duct containing finger-like projections covered by a layer of epithelial and underlying myoepithelial cells, with a fibrous core.

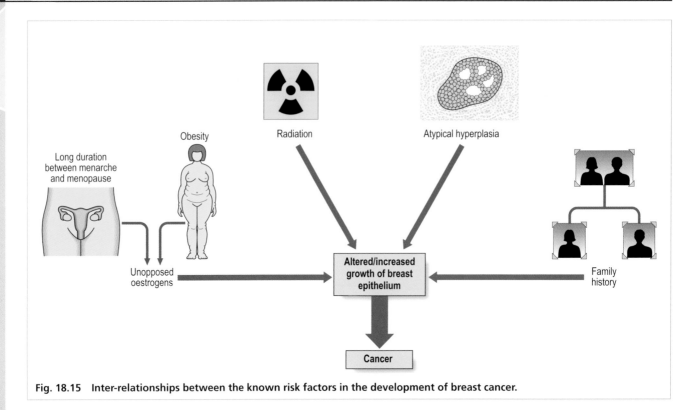

Fig. 18.15 Inter-relationships between the known risk factors in the development of breast cancer.

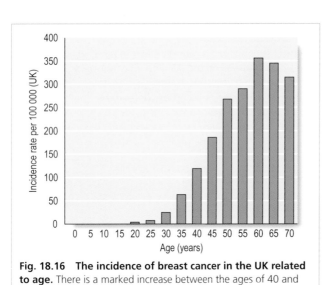

Fig. 18.16 **The incidence of breast cancer in the UK related to age.** There is a marked increase between the ages of 40 and 50, but the highest incidence is in those aged 60–70 years.

Age at menarche and menopause

There is a significantly higher risk of developing breast cancer among women with an early age at menarche. At the other end of the reproductive life, women whose natural menopause occurs before 45 years have only half the breast cancer risk of those whose menopause occurs after 55 years. Therefore women with 40 or more years of active menstruation have twice the breast cancer risk of those with fewer than 30 years of menstrual activity.

Age at first full-term pregnancy

Nulliparous women have an increased risk of developing breast cancer. However, among parous women protection is related to early age for the first full-term pregnancy. If the first birth is delayed to the mid or late thirties, the woman is at a greater risk of developing breast cancer than is a nulliparous woman.

Weight and diet

For women of above average weight but below 50 years of age there is little or no increased risk of developing breast cancer. However, women aged 60 or over whose weight is increased have a higher cancer risk. Diet, obviously, can be a determinant for weight. In rodents, a high-fat diet increases the incidence of breast tumours, and international breast cancer incidence rates correlate with the consumption of fat. Although these observations suggest that a high-fat diet may be a risk factor, the evidence is not as clear as it is for weight.

Radiation

Women treated for Hodgkin's disease by mantle radiation are at an increased risk of developing breast cancer and now undergo surveillance.

Family history and genetic factors

Breast cancer is common, thus a history of a relative having breast cancer can be found in at least 10% of new cases. However, a proportion of these will be sporadic cancers and not due to familial (inherited genetic) factors. The risk of developing breast cancer is increased in first-degree relatives (e.g. sister, daughter) of breast cancer cases, particularly if that person is pre-menopausal. For example, the risk increases to nine-fold for first-degree relatives of pre-menopausal women with bilateral breast cancer. Up to five-fold increases in risk have been found for women with multiple first-degree relatives with breast cancer.

There are rare familial syndromes such as Li–Fraumeni, in which there is an association between sarcomas, brain tumours and breast cancer at a young age. This is linked in some families to abnormalities of the *p53* gene. Approximately 4–6% of breast cancers are associated with a very strong family history and in certain families there is breast and ovarian cancer. Inherited mutations of a gene on the long arm of chromosome 17 (*BRCA1*) are responsible for families with susceptibility to female breast and ovarian cancer. Another susceptibility gene, *BRCA2,* located on chromosome 13q12–13, is linked to families with early-onset breast cancer, including male breast cancer. Products of both genes are involved in DNA repair mechanisms. An inherited deletion in *CHEK2* increases breast cancer risk.

There are likely to be yet more moderate- or low-risk genes that confer susceptibility. It must be remembered that this explains only a small proportion of breast cancers.

Geographic variation

There is a marked variation in breast cancer rates between different countries. The highest rates are in North America, north-west Europe, Australia and New Zealand, with the lowest in South-East Asia and Africa. Several factors probably contribute to this difference: age at menarche, age at first full-term pregnancy, age at menopause and post-menopausal weight. The length of time between age at menarche and first pregnancy may be quite short in some of these low-incidence countries.

Atypical hyperplasia

Women with benign breast disease whose breast biopsies show atypical epithelial hyperplasia have a definite increased risk of developing breast cancer. Ordinary epithelial hyperplasia is associated with a slightly increased risk. The risk is augmented by a family history of breast cancer.

Aetiological mechanisms

> ▸ Overexposure to oestrogens and underexposure to progesterone important
> ▸ Limited relationship to oral contraceptives, more with hormone replacement therapy
> ▸ Many tumours contain receptors for oestrogen and progesterone and may respond to hormone manipulation
> ▸ No good evidence for viral involvement

Hormones

The association of breast cancer risk with menarche, menopause and first full-term pregnancy indicates that hormones must have some role in the development of carcinomas, but they are more likely to be promoters than initiators.

Oestrogen activity appears to be important, with overexposure to oestrogens and underexposure to progesterone being significant. Early menarche and late menopause will result in a higher number of menstrual cycles, with repeated surges of oestrogen having a stimulatory effect on breast epithelium. The beneficial effect of early full-term pregnancy could be due to the high concentrations of progesterone and/or prolactin protecting the breast cells against oestrogens in the long term. The risks associated with obesity may be partly due to the ability of fat cells to synthesise oestrogens, or to altered levels of sex hormone-binding protein levels.

Oral contraceptives/hormone replacement therapy

There is a slightly increased risk for current and recent users of oral contraceptives but no long-term increase. Combined oestrogen and progesterone hormone replacement therapy increases the relative risk of developing breast cancer for current users by two-fold, and is greater the longer the duration of treatment. The risk decreases with cessation. Oestrogen-only preparations have a lower risk.

Hormone receptors

Hormones have an effect on cells only after interacting with specific receptors present on or in their target cells. The sex steroid, oestrogen, interacts with a nuclear receptor. Subsequent interaction with DNA results in the formation of differentiation- and proliferation-associated factors. Prolactin and other polypeptides interact with receptors on the cell surface (Fig. 18.17).

Oestrogen receptors can be detected in varying amounts in about 75% of breast cancers. The progesterone receptor, which can normally be formed only when the oestrogen receptor is present and active, is present in about 50% of tumours, and women whose tumours contain both types of receptor are more likely to respond to some form of hormone manipulation therapy. This suggests that hormones are important in the growth and maintenance of these carcinomas.

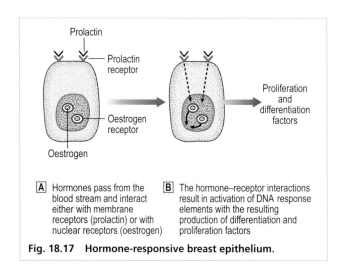

| A | Hormones pass from the blood stream and interact either with membrane receptors (prolactin) or with nuclear receptors (oestrogen) | B | The hormone–receptor interactions result in activation of DNA response elements with the resulting production of differentiation and proliferation factors |

Fig. 18.17   Hormone-responsive breast epithelium.

Viruses

In mice a tumorigenic virus is transmitted via milk (the Bittner factor). However, no similar agent has been found for human breast cancer.

Non-invasive carcinomas

> ▸ Tumour is confined to ducts (ductal carcinoma in situ) or acini (lobular carcinoma in situ)
> ▸ Ductal carcinoma in situ is unilateral in pre- and post-menopausal women, has several forms and can become invasive
> ▸ Lobular carcinoma in situ is commoner in pre-menopausal women, has no clinical features, is often bilateral, can be multifocal and is a risk marker

Virtually all breast carcinomas are *adenocarcinomas* derived from the epithelial cells of the ducts or glands.

The term 'non-invasive' means that the malignant cells are confined to either the ducts or the acini of the lobules, with no evidence of penetration of the tumour cells through the basement membranes around these two types of structure into the surrounding fibrous tissue. There are two forms of non-invasive carcinoma:

- ductal carcinoma in situ
- lobular carcinoma in situ.

Ductal carcinoma in situ

Ductal carcinoma in situ can occur in both pre- and post-menopausal women, usually in the 40–60-year age group. It can present as a palpable mass, especially if extensive and associated with fibrosis. If the larger ducts are involved, presentation can be as a nipple discharge, or as Paget's disease of the nipple. The disease can be found incidentally in surgical biopsies or be detected by mammography screening due to the presence of calcification. Pure ductal carcinoma in situ accounts for about 5% of breast carcinomas that present clinically.

The size of the area involved in the breast can range from 10 to 100 mm in length. It is usually unifocal, being confined within one quadrant of the breast, although multicentricity can occur with larger lesions. Bilateral disease is uncommon. The macroscopic appearances depend on the architecture of the ductal carcinoma in situ. Creamy necrotic material can exude from the cut surface of the breast, rather similar in appearance to comedones.

Histologically, the changes are to be found in the small and medium-sized ducts, although, in older women, the larger ducts can be involved. The ducts contain cells that show cytoplasmic and nuclear pleomorphism to varying degrees. Mitotic figures may be frequent and can be abnormal. These features are used to classify ductal carcinoma in situ into high grade (more aggressive features) and non-high grade lesions. The ducts may be completely filled with cells (solid pattern), or have central necrosis (comedo pattern; Fig. 18.18) which may calcify, rendering the lesion mammographically detectable. The cribriform pattern of ductal carcinoma in situ has numerous gland-like structures within the sheets of cells. Ductal carcinoma in situ can spread along the duct system or into the lobules.

The previous management of ductal carcinoma in situ was generally mastectomy, so it is difficult to know the fate of these lesions if left. Estimates of residual carcinoma changing from non-invasive to invasive range from one-third to one-half, based on studies where there was local incomplete excision. If the tumour is completely removed the woman's prognosis is excellent.

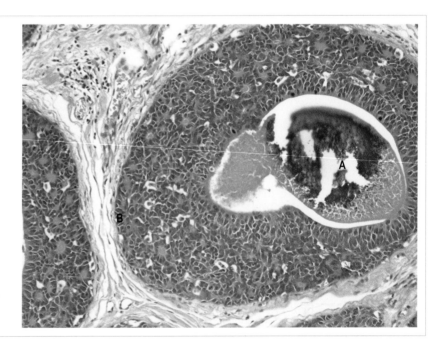

Fig. 18.18 Ductal carcinoma in situ. Both ducts are expanded. One has (A) a central necrotic area which has calcified and would show on a mammogram. The basement membrane (B) is intact.

Lobular carcinoma in situ

Lobular carcinoma in situ occurs more frequently in pre-menopausal women, but can be found in biopsies taken to investigate mammographic (screening) abnormalities. A major problem is that it does not present as a palpable lump and is usually found in biopsies removed for other reasons. A further important clinical feature is that it is often multifocal within the one breast and is frequently bilateral. Not surprisingly, there are no specific radiological or macroscopic features.

Histologically, the changes are found in the acini—hence the term 'lobular'—although they may extend into extralobular ducts and replace ductal epithelium (Fig. 18.19). Within the acini, the normal cells are replaced by relatively uniform cells with clear cytoplasm that appear loose and non-cohesive. The overall size of the acini increases, but the lobular shape is retained. Unlike the situation in ductal carcinoma in situ, necrosis is unusual.

About one-quarter to one-third of all patients with lobular carcinoma in situ who are treated by biopsy alone will go on to develop an invasive carcinoma. This may occur in either or both breasts and there may be a long time interval.

Invasive carcinomas

> ▶ Occur in pre- and post-menopausal women
> ▶ Most are infiltrating ductal of no special type
> ▶ Infiltrating lobular carcinomas can be multifocal
> ▶ Less common types include mucinous, medullary, papillary and tubular carcinomas

An 'invasive' tumour is one whose cells have broken through the basement membrane around the breast structure in which they have arisen, and spread into the surrounding tissue. Invasive carcinomas are categorised into different histological types, but the name given to them does not always mean that the tumour arises only from that site; for example, invasive (infiltrating) duct or ductal carcinomas and invasive (infiltrating) lobular carcinomas may both arise from the cells at the junction of the extralobular and intralobular ducts. If an invasive tumour develops in a patient with previous lobular carcinoma in situ it can be ductal in morphology.

The histological types of invasive carcinoma and their relative incidence for palpable tumours are:

- infiltrating ductal of no special type (75%)
- infiltrating lobular (10%)
- mucinous (3%)
- tubular (2%)
- medullary (3%)
- papillary (2%)
- others (5%).

There is a higher frequency of tubular carcinoma in mammographically detected tumours.

Carcinomas vary in size from less than 10 mm in diameter to over 80 mm, depending on whether detected by mammography or presenting clinically, but with the latter are often 20–30 mm in diameter. Clinically, they are firm on palpation and may show evidence of tethering to the overlying skin (Fig. 18.20) or underlying muscle. The skin may also show 'peau d'orange'—dimpling due to lymphatic permeation. The nipple may be retracted due to tethering and contraction of the intramammary ligaments.

Gross features

The macroscopic appearance of the tumours tends to depend on the amount or type of stroma within the carcinoma. It is this that gave rise to the terms previously applied to tumours: scirrhous, medullary (or encephaloid) and mucinous (or colloid).

The term *scirrhous* implies that there is a prominent fibrous tissue reaction, usually in the central part of the tumour. This

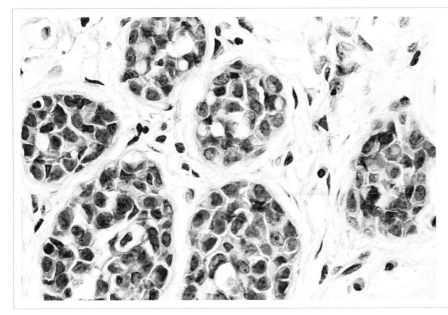

Fig. 18.19 Lobular carcinoma in situ.
A breast lobule in which the acini are expanded. There is complete loss of the lumen and of the two-cell layer.

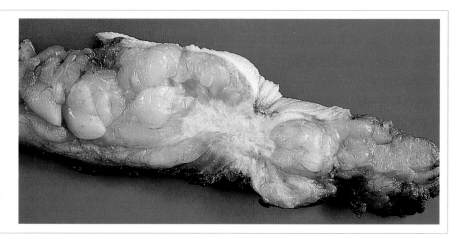

Fig. 18.20   Invasive carcinoma of breast. Mastectomy covered by skin and including the nipple. Beneath the nipple there is an irregular white area which has caused contraction. This is a carcinoma and the white tissue represents the fibrous (scirrhous) reaction. The rest of the breast is fat.

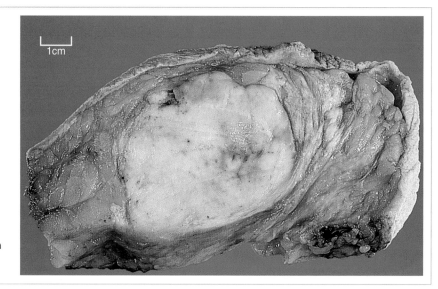

1cm

Fig. 18.21   Medullary carcinoma. Breast tissue containing a 60 mm diameter carcinoma with a rounded edge, and no evidence of a fibrous reaction.

results in the carcinoma having a dense white appearance, which grates when cut. Yellow streaks may be seen; these are due to the presence of elastic tissue within the tumour. Carcinomas with a prominent stromal reaction usually have irregular edges, extending into the adjacent fat or other structures (Fig. 18.20).

Medullary (brain-like) tumours are very cellular with little stroma. The edges of the carcinoma are often more rounded and discrete than those of the scirrhous tumours (Fig. 18.21). Necrosis is common. When palpated the tumours feel much softer.

Mucinous carcinomas have a predominance of mucin, or jelly-like, material within them. They usually have a well-defined edge.

Some of the changes that occur within carcinomas explain their clinical features, for example skin and nipple retraction due to the fibrous reaction.

Infiltrating ductal carcinomas

Infiltrating duct or ductal carcinomas of no special type comprise the majority (up to 75%) of infiltrating breast carcinomas. Macroscopically, they usually have a scirrhous consistency. The size of the tumours varies between patients. They can occur in both pre- and post-menopausal women.

Histologically, the tumour cells are arranged in groups, cords and gland-like structures. Quite marked variations can be seen between different carcinomas even though they are of the same type (Fig. 18.22). For example, the size of the solid groups of cells can be variable, and ductal carcinoma in situ is often present. The amount of stroma between the tumour cells can also vary, but in those carcinomas in which it is prominent it is most marked at the centre, with the periphery being more cellular. Collections of elastic tissue (elastosis) around ducts or within the stroma are common in tumours with a scirrhous reaction.

The degree of differentiation or grade of the tumour is based on the extent to which it resembles non-tumorous breast: whether the cells are in a gland-like pattern or as solid sheets; the degree of nuclear pleomorphism; and the number of mitotic figures present. A well-differentiated (grade I) infiltrating duct carcinoma tends to behave less aggressively than a poorly differentiated (grade III) tumour, which is composed of sheets of pleomorphic cells with large numbers of mitotic figures.

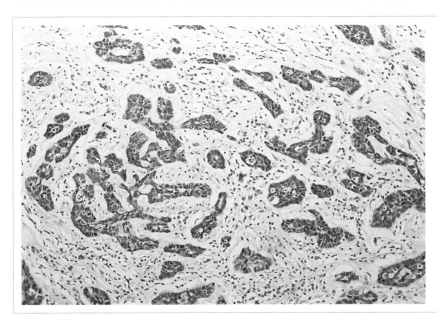

Fig. 18.22   Infiltrating ductal carcinoma.
The lesion is composed of irregular solid groups
of cells in a dense fibrous stroma, with an
associated lymphocytic infiltrate.

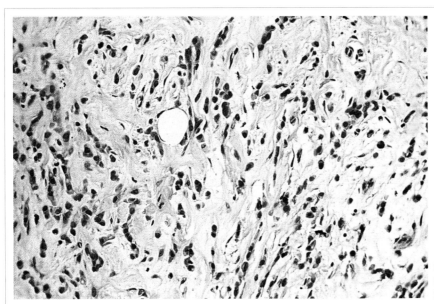

Fig. 18.23   Infiltrating lobular carcinoma.
Strands of single cells (Indian file) invade
fibrous stroma.

Infiltrating lobular carcinomas

While lobular carcinoma in situ usually occurs in pre-
menopausal women, the infiltrating lesion can also occur in
post-menopausal women. In the UK, infiltrating lobular carcinomas constitute about 10% of invasive breast carcinomas,
but the incidence may vary in other parts of the world.

Infiltrating lobular carcinomas have abundant fibrous
stroma, so that macroscopically they are always scirrhous.
While infiltrating ductal carcinomas usually form at one
focus in the breast, infiltrating lobular carcinomas can be
multifocal throughout the breast.

Histologically the cells are small and uniform and are
dispersed singly, or in columns one cell wide ('Indian files';
Fig. 18.23), in a dense stroma. Elastosis can be present. The
cells infiltrate around pre-existing breast ducts and acini,
rather than destroying them as occurs with invasive duct
carcinomas. This method of infiltration may account for the
occasional multifocal nature of the tumours. The cells in
some carcinomas may appear signet-ring in shape due to the
accumulation of mucin within an intracytoplasmic acinus,
displacing the nucleus to one side. A characteristic feature
of these tumours is that the cells lack the cell adhesion
molecule E-cadherin, which may account for their pattern of
spread. Residual lobular carcinoma in situ can sometimes be
found in the invasive tumours.

Mucinous carcinomas

Mucinous carcinomas (also known as colloid, mucoid and
gelatinous carcinomas) usually arise in post-menopausal
women and comprise 2–3% of invasive carcinomas.

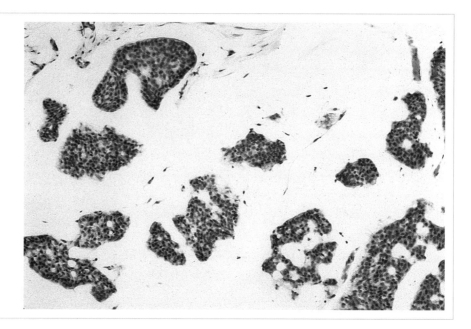

Fig. 18.24 Mucinous carcinoma.
Small solid and tubular groups of cells lie in pools of mucin, or jelly-like material.

Macroscopically, the tumours are well circumscribed and have a soft, grey, gelatinous cut surface. They vary in size from 10 to 50 mm in diameter. Since there is no dense stroma and the edges are rounded, these tumours do not cause retraction of the nipple or tethering of the skin.

These carcinomas comprise small nests and cords of tumour cells, which show little pleomorphism, embedded in large amounts of mucin (Fig. 18.24). The latter is composed of neutral or weakly acidic glycoproteins, which are secreted by the tumour cells and are different from the proteoglycans of the stroma.

The survival of women with mucinous carcinomas is better than that of those having invasive duct or lobular carcinomas.

Tubular carcinomas

As the name implies, tubular carcinomas are well-differentiated carcinomas composed of cells arranged as tubules. They are often small lesions, less than 10 mm in diameter, and are firm, gritty tumours with irregular outlines. Tubular carcinomas form 1–2% of invasive carcinomas but constitute a higher proportion of screen-detected tumours.

Histologically, they are composed of well-formed tubular structures, the cells of which show little pleomorphism or mitotic activity. The stroma is dense, often with elastosis (Fig. 18.25).

Patients with tubular carcinomas do extremely well—better than those with well-differentiated invasive duct carcinomas.

Medullary carcinomas

The incidence of medullary carcinomas is difficult to assess because not all of the criteria for diagnosis have been strictly adhered to in some studies; hence figures have ranged from very rare to 5%. These tumours usually occur in post-menopausal women.

Medullary carcinomas are circumscribed and often large. Histologically, they are composed of large tracts of confluent cells with little stroma in between them. The cells show quite marked nuclear pleomorphism, and mitotic figures are frequent. There is never evidence of gland formation. These cytological appearances put them into the 'poorly differentiated' category. Around the islands of tumour cells there is a prominent lymphocytic infiltrate, predominantly T-lymphocytes, with macrophages (Fig. 18.26).

Despite the aggressive cytological features of these tumours, the patients have a significantly better 10-year survival than women with invasive duct carcinomas. It may be that the lymphocytic and macrophage infiltrate has a beneficial effect, and this has stimulated much research into the immunological responses to tumours generally.

Papillary carcinomas

Papillary carcinomas are rare tumours that occur in post-menopausal women. They are usually circumscribed and can be focally necrotic, with little stromal reaction. The tumours are in the form of papillary structures, and areas of intraductal papillary growth are usually found.

The prognosis of patients with these carcinomas is probably better than that of the much more common invasive duct carcinoma.

Other types

Much rarer types of breast carcinoma include: adenoid cystic carcinomas; secretory carcinomas, which occur predominantly in juveniles; apocrine carcinomas, which are composed of cells with abundant eosinophilic cytoplasm; and

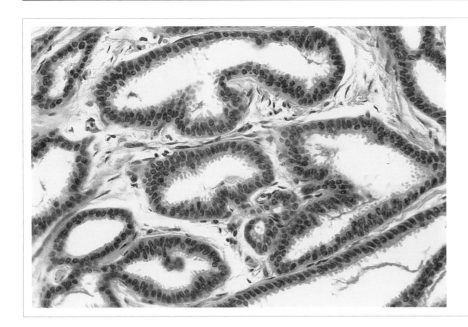

Fig. 18.25 Tubular carcinoma. Tubular profiles lie in a fibrous stroma.

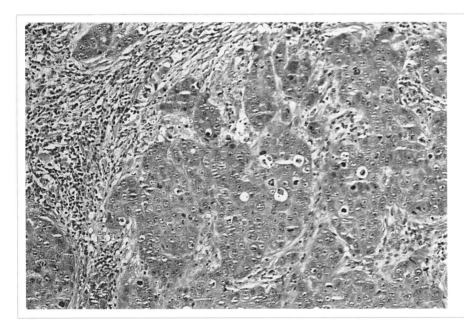

Fig. 18.26 Medullary carcinoma. Large groups of irregularly shaped tumour cells are surrounded by an infiltrate of lymphocytes.

carcinomas showing metaplasia, e.g. squamous, spindle cell, cartilaginous and osseous features.

Paget's disease of the nipple

▶ Erosion of the nipple clinically resembling eczema
▶ Associated with underlying ductal carcinoma in situ or invasive carcinoma

Paget's disease of the nipple was first described by Sir James Paget in 1874. Clinically, there is roughening, reddening and slight ulceration of the nipple, similar to the skin changes of eczema. Recognition is important, as it is associated with an underlying carcinoma, mainly in the subareolar region. Paget's disease of the nipple occurs with about 2% of all breast carcinomas, and is associated with a higher frequency of multicentric breast carcinomas.

Within the epidermis of the nipple, large, pale-staining malignant cells can be seen histologically and these cause the changes seen clinically. The malignant cells are derived from the adjacent breast carcinomas. A direct connection may not be seen. The relationship between Paget's disease of the nipple and an underlying carcinoma is shown in Figure 18.27.

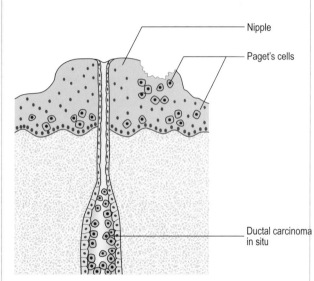

Fig. 18.27   Relationship between Paget's disease of the nipple and underlying ductal carcinoma in situ. Note the epidermis infiltrated by individual tumour (Paget's) cells.

Spread of breast carcinomas

▸ Directly into skin and muscle
▸ Via lymphatics to axillary and other local lymph nodes
▸ Via blood stream to lungs, bone, liver and brain
▸ May be considerable delay before metastasis occurs

Breast carcinomas can infiltrate locally (direct spread) or metastasise to more distant sites via lymphatics and the blood stream and to pleura (Fig. 18.28).

Direct spread.   Local infiltration (direct spread) into the underlying muscles and the overlying skin can be detected clinically, the latter because of ulceration or tethering.

Via lymphatics.   Permeation of the lymphatic channels of the skin results in the clinical sign of 'peau d'orange'. The axillary lymph nodes are the commonest initial site of metastasis via lymphatics, and between 40% and 50% of women with symptomatic breast carcinoma will have axillary lymph node metastases at the time of presentation. Figures will differ for those detected by mammography. It is important that the lymph nodes are examined histologically, as clinical palpation is not always reliable. Sentinel node removal is an increasingly used method for determining node status. Metastasis to intramammary, supraclavicular and tracheobronchial lymph nodes also occurs.

Via blood stream.   Blood-borne metastasis most frequently involves the lungs and bones, but the liver, adrenals and brain are also common sites. The pleura on the same side as the breast carcinoma can be a site of metastasis, causing an effusion.

Infiltrating lobular carcinomas can metastasise to more unusual sites, and this may be due to their single-cell method of spread as seen within the breast.

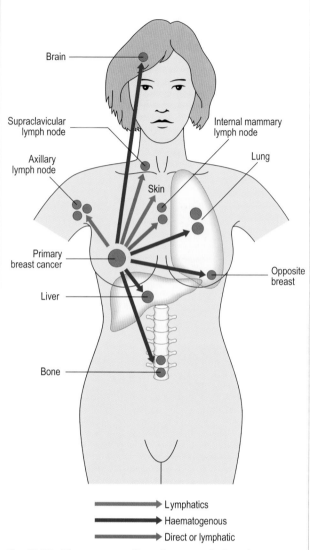

Fig. 18.28   The common sites of metastasis from breast carcinoma via the lymphatic system or blood stream.

Extensive infiltration of bone marrow can cause leuko-erythroblastic anaemia. Destruction of bone can result in hypercalcaemia, with renal complications.

Breast carcinomas exhibit quite marked variation in the length of time between presentation of the primary carcinoma and the appearance of recurrent/metastatic disease. Some breast carcinomas never recur; in some patients reappearance of the disease may not be until as much as 20 years after the original excision, while for others it can be within 2–5 years. Tumour can recur at the site of the original excision and/or as distant metastases. The mechanisms by which a metastasis becomes clinically apparent after a long time interval are not known. They may relate to changes in tumour cells that have been lying dormant at that site, causing them to alter their behaviour, and/or to changes in the host response to the tumour.

Prognostic factors

▶ These can be gross and histological features—type, grade, size
▶ Spread, local to lymph nodes or distant
▶ Behavioural characteristics of carcinomas, such as growth rates and hormone receptor status

Some women have carcinomas for several years before seeking medical help; in this time the tumour may ulcerate into the skin and become large. However, despite the horrifying features the tumour may present, such patients may survive for many years after treatment. Other women seek medical help promptly after palpating a lump but die from the disease within a short time. There are thus obviously quite marked differences between individual breast carcinomas and in the host response of patients to them.

Several factors have been identified that may help to predict how an individual carcinoma will behave, and may help in planning therapy. However, despite the great effort expended in this area, the only major changes made clinically have been in lengthening the disease-free interval (time before development of recurrence/metastasis) rather than in improving patient survival.

Type of carcinoma

Medullary, mucinous, tubular and, possibly, invasive lobular carcinomas generally behave less aggressively than other types, but these constitute the minority of types so that this knowledge is of value to only a few patients.

Histological grade

As described above, tumours can be graded for their degree of differentiation. Patients whose tumours are well differentiated (grade I), showing greater resemblance to non-malignant breast, do better, while those whose tumours are poorly differentiated (grade III) do worse; however, prediction of how the group with moderately differentiated carcinomas will do is more difficult.

Stage

When a woman presents with a breast carcinoma, staging is undertaken so as to assess the absence or presence and extent of spread both locally and distantly. The management of the patient will depend on the stage of the disease. The two main systems used are the International Classification of Staging and the TNM (Tumour, Node, Metastasis) system (Table 18.2).

If there is evidence of metastatic spread to axillary lymph nodes when the patient presents with the primary carcinoma, both the 5- and 10-year survival figures are worse than in those with no evidence of metastasis. The outlook for the patient is also worse if there is evidence of more distant spread.

Oestrogen receptors

The presence of oestrogen receptors within a carcinoma indicates that the tumour cells have a higher degree of functional differentiation. It is thus not surprising that women whose

Table 18.2 The main staging systems used to assess the extent of spread of breast carcinomas

Stage	Extent of spread
International classification	
I	Lump with slight tethering to skin, but node negative
II	Lump with lymph node metastasis or skin tethering
III	Tumour that is extensively adherent to skin and/or underlying muscles, or ulcerating or lymph nodes are fixed
IV	Distant metastases
TNM	
T1	Tumour 20 mm or less; no fixation or nipple retraction. Includes Paget's disease
T2	Tumour 20–50 mm, or less than 20 mm but with tethering
T3	Tumour greater than 50 mm but less than 100 mm; or less than 50 mm but with infiltration, ulceration or fixation
T4	Any tumour with ulceration or infiltration wide of it, or chest wall fixation, or greater than 100 mm in diameter
N0	Node-negative
N1	Axillary nodes mobile
N2	Axillary nodes fixed
N3	Supraclavicular nodes or oedema of arm
M0	No distant metastases
M1	Distant metastases

tumours are oestrogen receptor-positive have better survival figures than those whose carcinomas are oestrogen receptor-negative. More importantly, they are more likely to benefit from tamoxifen, an oestrogen receptor antagonist.

Growth kinetics

The growth activity of carcinomas can be measured by several methods; that of breast carcinomas may be low, medium or high. Tumours with lower cell growth rates tend to behave better clinically. It must be remembered that tumours with a high rate of division may also have a high cell death rate by apoptosis, and that not all cell divisions result in doubling of the population as the division may be abnormal.

HER-2

The oncogene c-erbB-2/HER-2 is altered in approximately 20% of invasive breast carcinomas. There is amplification of the gene with resultant overexpression of the membrane-related protein. Patients whose carcinomas have this alteration have a poorer prognosis. A humanised monoclonal antibody,

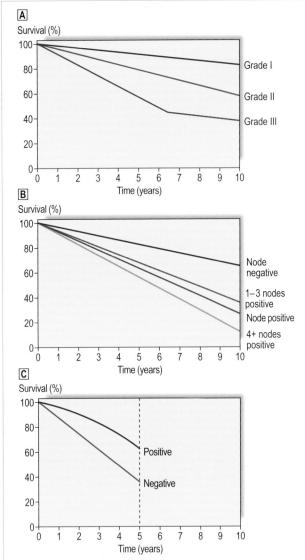

Fig. 18.29 Relationship of various prognostic factors with survival for patients with operable breast cancer. **A** Grade or degree of tumour differentiation (grade I = well differentiated; grade II = moderately differentiated; grade III = poorly differentiated). 10-year survival. **B** Presence or absence of lymph node metastasis, and relationship to number of lymph nodes involved. 10-year survival. **C** Presence or absence of oestrogen receptor within the tumours. 5-year survival (less significant after this period).

trastuzumab (Herceptin) has been developed, which can be used as adjuvant treatment and to treat women with metastatic disease, if the cancers have the molecular alteration.

Examples of the effects some of these prognostic factors may have on survival are shown in Figure 18.29.

Breast carcinomas in men

About 1% of breast carcinomas occur in males, but the incidence varies throughout the world. The tumour is rare in young men. There is an increased risk in patients with Klinefelter's syndrome, and for carriers of *BRCA2* mutations.

The tumour usually presents as a lump, but there can be nipple discharge or retraction. Paget's disease is relatively commoner in men, probably because of the small size of the male breast.

Ductal carcinoma in situ and all types of invasive carcinoma can occur, although lobular carcinoma in situ has not been reported. The prognosis in males is similar to that in females, and is affected by such factors as lymph node status and size. Oestrogen receptors can be detected in male breast carcinomas.

OTHER TUMOURS

▶ Phyllodes tumours used to be called 'giant fibroadenoma' and 'cystosarcoma phyllodes'
▶ The stroma of phyllodes tumours is the part that becomes aggressive if the tumours recur
▶ Cutaneous angiosarcomas can occur after radical mastectomy, but can arise spontaneously in younger women

Phyllodes tumours

Phyllodes tumours can occur at any age, but the median age is 45 years. This is older than for fibroadenoma and the incidence of phyllodes tumours is considerably lower. Phyllodes tumours present clinically as a discrete lump. Macroscopically, they are circumscribed and vary in size up to as much as 60 mm in diameter. They may have both soft and firm areas.

Phyllodes tumours have two characteristic parts, epithelium and stroma. The epithelium covers large, club-like projections which push into cystic spaces. The stroma is much more cellular than that of fibroadenomas (Fig. 18.30) and can vary in type within the same tumour. The cells may resemble fibroblasts, or they may show marked pleomorphism with mitotic figures. In some tumours, the stromal changes are so marked that they have the appearances of sarcomas.

Recurrence is a major problem with phyllodes tumours. The risk of recurrence is less if the tumours are small, with a low mitotic rate and minimal cellular atypia, and have a rounded rather than an infiltrative edge. With each recurrence, the stroma of the tumour tends to become more atypical with a higher mitotic rate. The chance of metastasis then increases, and this is usually via the blood stream to lung and bones; lymph node involvement is rare. In one series of cases, recurrence occurred in 30% of cases and 16% died from metastatic disease; however, these patients were a pre-selected group whose original tumours had a more aggressive-looking stroma.

Angiosarcomas

Angiosarcomas are rare tumours that can occur at any time from adolescence to old age but are commoner in young women. Although most cases occur spontaneously, angiosarcomas can arise in irradiated mastectomy scars and in lymphoedematous arms after radical mastectomy for breast cancer (Stewart–Treves syndrome).

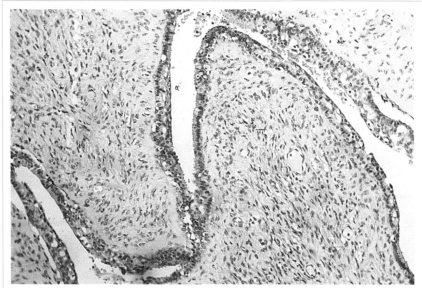

Fig. 18.30 Phyllodes tumour. The stroma is cellular and it is forming club-like fingers covered with epithelium.

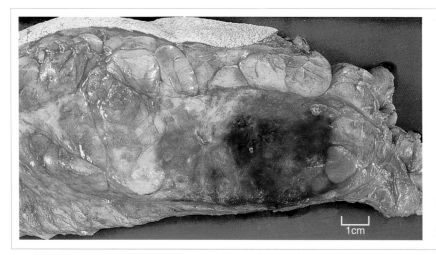

Fig. 18.31 Angiosarcoma of the breast. There is a large haemorrhagic tumour in the breast.

Angiosarcomas can present as a lump, or cause a diffuse enlargement of the breast. Discoloration of the overlying skin can be seen in some cases. Macroscopically, they can be haemorrhagic or appear as ill-defined areas of induration (Fig. 18.31).

Histologically, the tumours consist of numerous vascular channels that infiltrate into fat and around normal breast structures. The channels are lined by endothelial cells which have hyperchromatic nuclei. Papillary areas can be present and, in the more undifferentiated tumours, there can be sheets of large, pleomorphic endothelial cells with little evidence of vascular channels.

The clinical outcome tends to parallel the histological appearances. Those tumours with well-formed vascular spaces and little atypia of the endothelium are less aggressive. Metastasis is by the blood stream to lungs, bone, liver and brain.

Other sarcomas

Fibrosarcoma, liposarcoma and leiomyosarcoma can all occur in the breast but are rare.

Lymphomas

Lymphomas may be primary, but are more usually secondary to disease elsewhere in the body.

493

Commonly confused conditions and entities relating to breast pathology			
Commonly confused	Distinction and explanation	Commonly confused	Distinction and explanation
Fibroadenoma and *fibroadenosis*	*Fibroadenoma* is a localised circumscribed benign neoplasm comprising epithelial cells and specialised fibrous tissue. *Fibroadenosis* is an obsolete name for fibrocystic change, a hyperplastic lesion.	*Radial scar* and *complex sclerosing lesion*	*Radial scars* and *complex sclerosing lesions* differ only in size: the latter are >10 mm in diameter. Both mimic carcinomas radiologically and histologically, but they are benign non-neoplastic lesions.
Fibroadenoma and *phyllodes tumour*	*Fibroadenoma* and *phyllodes tumour* both comprise neoplastic epithelial and fibrous tissue components. However, in phyllodes tumours the fibrous tissue component is more cellular and abundant, and the lesion has less well defined margins; borderline and malignant variants occur.	*Medullary carcinoma of the breast* and *of the thyroid*	The term *medullary* refers only to the soft consistency (resembling the medulla of the brain). There is no other relationship between these lesions.
Ductal epithelial hyperplasia and *ductal carcinoma in situ*	*Ductal epithelial hyperplasia* is a benign proliferation of duct epithelium, whereas *ductal carcinoma in situ* has undergone neoplastic transformation, although it is not yet invasive. These lesions can have morphological similarities. A proportion share genetic alterations.	*Paget's disease of the nipple* and *of bone*	Both lesions were described by Sir James Paget (1814–1899). There is no other relationship between these lesions.

FURTHER READING

Dixon J M 2000 ABC of breast diseases, 2nd edn. BMJ, London

Elston C W, Ellis I O 1998 The breast. Churchill Livingstone, Edinburgh

Harris J R, Morrow M, Lippman M E 2004 Diseases of the breast, 3rd edn. Lippincott, Williams & Wilkins, Philadelphia

Nathanson K L, Wooster R, Weber B L 2000 Breast cancer genetics: what we know and what we need. Nature Medicine 7: 552–556

Rosen P P 2001 Rosen's breast pathology, 2nd edn. Lippincott-Raven, Philadelphia

Sloane J P 2001 Biopsy pathology of the breast, 2nd edn. Arnold, London

World Health Organization 2003 WHO classification of tumours. Pathology and genetics of the breast and female genital tract. IARC, Lyons

http://www.cancerresearchuk.org
http://www.breastcancercampaign.org
http://ww5.komen.org
http://www.nlm.nih.gov/medlineplus/breastcancer.html

Female genital tract

COMMON CLINICAL PROBLEMS FROM FEMALE GENITAL TRACT DISEASE

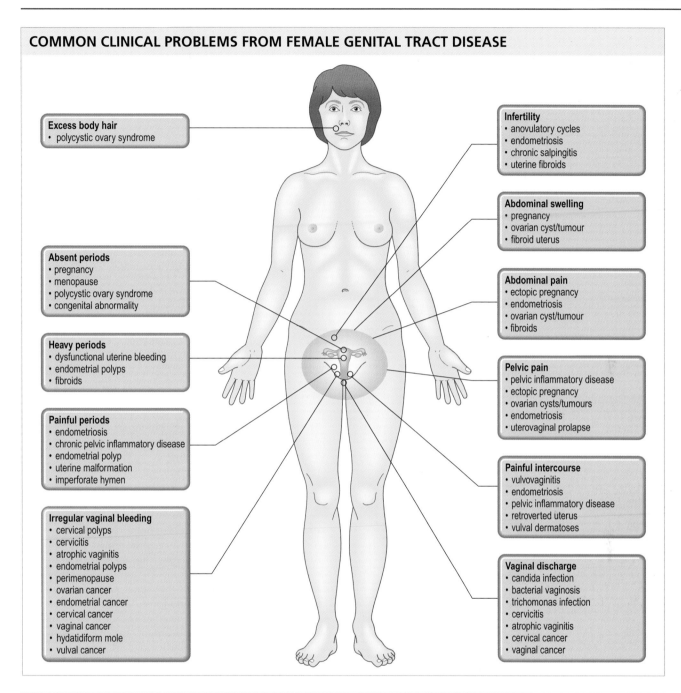

Excess body hair
- polycystic ovary syndrome

Absent periods
- pregnancy
- menopause
- polycystic ovary syndrome
- congenital abnormality

Heavy periods
- dysfunctional uterine bleeding
- endometrial polyps
- fibroids

Painful periods
- endometriosis
- chronic pelvic inflammatory disease
- endometrial polyp
- uterine malformation
- imperforate hymen

Irregular vaginal bleeding
- cervical polyps
- cervicitis
- atrophic vaginitis
- endometrial polyps
- perimenopause
- ovarian cancer
- endometrial cancer
- cervical cancer
- vaginal cancer
- hydatidiform mole
- vulval cancer

Infertility
- anovulatory cycles
- endometriosis
- chronic salpingitis
- uterine fibroids

Abdominal swelling
- pregnancy
- ovarian cyst/tumour
- fibroid uterus

Abdominal pain
- ectopic pregnancy
- endometriosis
- ovarian cyst/tumour
- fibroids

Pelvic pain
- pelvic inflammatory disease
- ectopic pregnancy
- ovarian cysts/tumours
- endometriosis
- uterovaginal prolapse

Painful intercourse
- vulvovaginitis
- endometriosis
- pelvic inflammatory disease
- retroverted uterus
- vulval dermatoses

Vaginal discharge
- candida infection
- bacterial vaginosis
- trichomonas infection
- cervicitis
- atrophic vaginitis
- cervical cancer
- vaginal cancer

Pathological basis of signs and symptoms in the female genital tract	
Sign or symptom	Pathological basis
Vaginal bleeding • In pregnancy	Haemorrhage from placenta (e.g. placenta praevia), placental bed (e.g. miscarriage) or decidua (e.g. ectopic pregnancy)
• Post-coital	Haemorrhage from lesion on cervix (e.g. carcinoma)
• Post-menopausal	Haemorrhage from uterine lesion (e.g. polyp, carcinoma)
Abnormal menstruation (timing or volume of loss)	Psychological disturbance Hormonal dysfunction Defects in local haemostasis Fibroids

497

(Continued)

Pathological basis of signs and symptoms in the female genital tract—cont'd	
Sign or symptom	Pathological basis
Pain	Pathological distension or rupture (e.g. tubal ectopic pregnancy) Muscular spasm (e.g. uterine contractions) Ischaemia or inflammation (e.g. ovarian torsion) Menstrual pain due to adenomyosis
Abdominal distension	Ascites (e.g. peritoneal involvement by ovarian carcinoma) Uterine enlargement (e.g. pregnancy) Ovarian cyst

Diseases of the female genital tract include inflammation, neoplasia, hormonal disturbances and complications of pregnancy. The commonest disorders are discussed here on a topographical basis.

NORMAL DEVELOPMENT

Female sexual development

Female development does not require the presence of a gonad, and the ovary plays no part in primary sexual development. This means that a neuter embryo will always develop along female lines. The testis-determining factor is the *SRY* gene carried in the sex-determining region of the Y chromosome. The indifferent gonad develops into an ovary when no Y chromosome is present, although two functional X chromosomes are usually required for normal ovarian differentiation. Disorders of female sexual development are listed in Table 19.1.

Embryological development

Germ cells arise in the wall of the yolk sac, and migrate to the region of the coelomic germinal epithelium. In the sixth week cords of cells appear within the indifferent gonad, but it is not until after the seventh week that ovarian differentiation is apparent and by 14 weeks these cell cords surround the primordial follicles.

The paired paramesonephric Müllerian ducts arise as an invagination of the coelomic epithelium of the mesonephric ridge lateral to the mesonephric duct. The paramesonephric duct follows the mesonephric duct. Near the cloaca, the paramesonephric ducts cross from the lateral to the medial side of the mesonephric ducts (Fig. 19.1A); together they carry with them some mesoderm from the side walls of the pelvis to create the transverse bar which helps to form the septum dividing the rectum from the urogenital sinus.

At the 30-mm stage (8 weeks), fusion of the paramesonephric ducts creates the utero-vaginal canal, which ultimately forms the uterus and proximal part of the vagina (Fig. 19.1B); the unfused parts form the uterine tubes. The trans-pelvic bar, which is a continuation of the mesonephric mesentery, forms the broad ligament; the ovary, projecting medially from the mesonephric ridge in the early stage, comes to lie posterior to the broad ligament. The inferior free end of the fused paramesonephric ducts (utero-vaginal canal) is still solid, and the sino-vaginal bulbs grow out from the posterior wall of the urogenital sinus to fuse with it and, later, give rise to the lower part of the vagina. The hymen occupies the position where the sino-vaginal bulb and urogenital sinus meet. The gonads are at first elongated and lie in the long axis of the embryo. Later, each gonad assumes a transverse lie. The gubernaculum is formed in the inguinal fold as a fibromuscular band which burrows from the gonad to gain attachment to the genital swelling; thus the caudal pole of the gonad becomes relatively fixed. The gubernaculum persists as the round ligament of the uterus. The ovaries retain attachment to the posterior aspect of the broad ligament. The genital swellings form the labia majora, the genital folds form the labia minora, and the genital tubercle forms the clitoris.

Table 19.1 Abnormalities of female sexual development		
Sex chromosomes	Gonads	Possible abnormalities
Normal XX	Bilateral normal ovaries	Congenital adrenal hyperplasia Maternal androgen or progestagen administration in pregnancy Maternal virilising tumour in pregnancy
Normal XX or XY	Abnormal (streak gonads)*	Gonadal dysgenesis
	Ovaries (XY) or testes (XX)*	Inappropriate gonads for chromosomes
Abnormal		Turner's syndrome Mixed gonadal dysgenesis True hermaphroditism
*Diagnosis of a specific type of intersex requires histological confirmation of gonadal status; ovotestis can look macroscopically exactly like a normal ovary, or the patient could have one macroscopically normal testis on one side and an ovary on the other.		

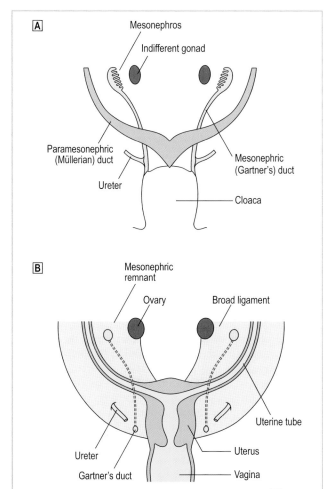

Fig. 19.1 Development of the female genital tract. [A] Frontal view of the posterior wall of 7-week embryo showing the mesonephric and paramesonephric ducts during the indifferent stage of development. [B] Female genital tract in a newborn infant.

VULVA

A variety of skin disorders, including inflammatory lesions, may manifest themselves in the vulva. Candidal infection may occur, particularly in diabetics. These disorders are discussed in Chapter 24. Vulval condylomata (viral warts) are discussed below.

Herpes virus infection

Sexually transmitted herpes virus infection is usually due to herpes simplex type 2, and produces painful ulceration of the vulval skin. Histologically, intra-epithelial blisters are seen, accompanied by specific cytopathic effects characterised by intranuclear viral inclusions and eosinophilic cytoplasmic swelling.

Syphilis

Primary and secondary syphilitic lesions may affect the vulva. The condyloma latum of secondary syphilis is characterised by oedematous, acutely inflamed, hyperplastic epithelium with underlying chronic inflammation, including prominent plasma cells. Hypertrophy of endothelial cells ('endarteritis obliterans') may occur. A silver stain may be used to demonstrate spirochaetes.

Granuloma inguinale (donovanosis)

This sexually transmitted disease caused by the Gram-negative bacillus *Calymmatobacterium granulomatis* is found throughout the tropics. It commonly causes chronic vulval ulceration but may spread to other sites in the female genital tract. Characteristically, large macrophages with clear or foamy cytoplasm containing bacilli (Donovan bodies) are seen, demonstrated with the help of Giemsa or silver stains.

Lymphogranuloma venereum

This sexually transmitted disease is caused by *Chlamydia trachomatis* and is most prevalent in the tropics. The earliest lesion is a vesicle which breaks down to form a punched-out painless ulcer. The primary lesion may become secondarily infected with abundant granulation tissue, fibrosis, fistula formation and lymphatic obstruction characterising the chronic form of the disease. Necrotising granulomas may occur in inguinal lymph nodes.

Candidiasis

Candida may cause chronic irritation and inflammation of the vulva that may be associated with vaginitis. The diagnosis may be made by microscopic examination of skin scrapings or culture. The histological features are non-specific, although the fungi may be identified within the keratin layer or superficial epithelium with the use of silver stains.

Cysts and tumours

Any benign cyst or tumour of the skin may be seen in the vulva. Two uncommon benign tumours are worthy of comment because of their distinct histological appearance: papillary hidradenoma and granular cell tumour.

Papillary hidradenoma

Papillary hidradenoma is a benign skin adnexal tumour. It presents as a localised lump, and is composed of interlacing papillae lined with epithelium.

Granular cell tumour

Granular cell tumour presents as a well-circumscribed vulval lump. It is composed of uniform large cells with pink granular cytoplasm. This neoplasm is currently thought to be derived from Schwann cells.

Bartholin's glands

Bartholin's glands are common sites of cysts and of abscesses secondary to infection of a cyst. Bartholin's gland adenoma is uncommon, and adenocarcinoma arising at this site is rare.

NON-NEOPLASTIC EPITHELIAL DISORDERS

The term 'non-neoplastic epithelial disorders' (Fig. 19.2) encompasses a group of vulval disorders of uncertain aetiology which affect all age groups, although predominantly peri- and post-menopausal women. In the past, these disorders have been given a confusing variety of clinical labels. They often appear clinically as 'leukoplakia', a term that refers to the white appearance of the skin and which should never be used in a pathological context. The clinical appearance of 'leukoplakia' is due to hyperkeratosis. In about 5% of cases there is a risk of squamous carcinoma, so that the presence or absence of cytological atypia (vulval intra-epithelial neoplasia) in biopsies should always be reported. There are two basic types of non-neoplastic epithelial disorder of the vulva: squamous hyperplasia and lichen sclerosus; these may sometimes co-exist.

Squamous hyperplasia

Vulval squamous hyperplasia is characterised by hyperkeratosis, irregular thickening of the epidermal rete ridges, and chronic inflammation of the superficial dermis.

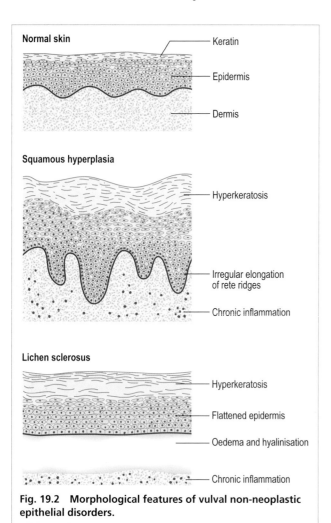

Fig. 19.2 Morphological features of vulval non-neoplastic epithelial disorders.

Lichen sclerosus

Lichen sclerosus, like hyperplasia, shows hyperkeratosis, but there is thinning of the epidermis with flattening of the rete ridges. The most characteristic feature is a broad band of oedema and hyalinised connective tissue in the superficial dermis. Beneath this, there may be mild chronic inflammation. Lichen sclerosus has a lower neoplastic potential than squamous hyperplasia.

NEOPLASTIC EPITHELIAL DISORDERS

Intra-epithelial neoplasia

The term *intra-epithelial neoplasia* refers to the spectrum of pre-invasive neoplastic change affecting the vulva. Its classification is the same as that of similar lesions in the cervix, although it may be incorrect to draw too close an analogy with the cervix as far as natural history is concerned. It is a condition that predominantly affects young women, and is associated with high-risk human papillomavirus infection (see below). In severe cases, there may be extensive involvement of the perineum, including the peri-anal area. The incidence of malignant change occurring in these lesions is low compared with that for the cervix. There is a tendency for intra-epithelial neoplasia to occur multifocally, with synchronous or metachronous involvement of vulva, vagina and cervix.

Squamous carcinoma

Squamous carcinoma (Fig. 19.3) is a tumour predominantly affecting elderly women in whom it is not usually associated with human papillomavirus infection. The recognition of

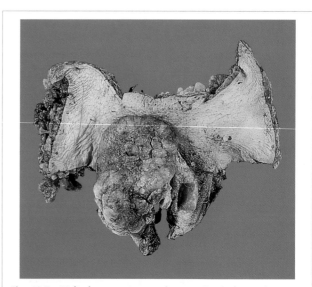

Fig. 19.3 Vulval squamous carcinoma. Surgical resection showing a large, fungating and invasive tumour on the vulva of an elderly patient.

associated intra-epithelial neoplasia may be difficult as it may occur in a so-called 'differentiated' form. The appearances are those of squamous carcinoma in any site; thus the tumour may be well, moderately or poorly differentiated. The prognosis is determined by the size, depth of invasion and degree of histological differentiation of the tumour, and the presence and extent of lymph node metastases, which predominantly affect the inguinal lymph nodes.

In contrast to squamous carcinoma of the cervix, even minimally invasive disease in the vulva is associated with a risk of local lymph node metastasis, although this risk seems to be negligible for carcinoma invading to a depth of less than 1 mm. Tumour thickness greater than 5 mm and positive lymph nodes are associated with a poor prognosis.

Paget's disease

The rare occurrence of mucin-containing adenocarcinoma cells within the squamous epithelium of the vulva is analogous to Paget's disease of the breast (Ch. 18). Paget's disease of the vulva tends to be chronic, with multiple recurrences. It may be indicative of an underlying invasive adenocarcinoma (in about 25% of cases), usually of skin adnexal origin, although, unlike the equivalent breast lesion, this is not usual. Adenocarcinomatous differentiation within the squamous epithelium has also been proposed as a possible explanation.

Other malignant tumours

Other malignant tumours of the vulva are rare. The most important of these are *basal cell carcinoma*, for which local excision is usually curative, and *malignant melanoma* which, as in other sites, generally has a poor prognosis.

VAGINA AND CERVIX

The commonest diseases affecting the vagina and cervix are infections, many of which are transmitted sexually. Tumours and pre-neoplastic lesions of the cervix, of which squamous cell carcinoma is the most important, are associated with human papillomavirus infection.

Infections

Vaginal infections are common and often sexually transmitted. The organisms of most importance are: *Gardnerella vaginalis, Neisseria gonorrhoeae, Candida albicans* and *Trichomonas vaginalis*.

Vaginal adenosis

The occurrence of glands within the subepithelial connective tissue of the vagina is uncommon, and is believed to be due to a defect in embryological development. The lining of these glands is usually a mucinous cuboidal epithelium which may undergo squamous metaplasia. Vaginal adenosis particularly affected young females who were exposed to diethylstilbestrol in utero. This synthetic oestrogenic agent was used in the 1950s in the treatment of threatened miscarriage in the USA and, to a lesser extent, in the UK. Clear cell adenocarcinoma of the vagina may rarely complicate adenosis.

Vaginal intra-epithelial neoplasia

Vaginal intra-epithelial neoplasia is much less common than cervical intra-epithelial neoplasia but the same diagnostic criteria are applied. The lesion may co-exist with similar lesions of the vulva and cervix (reflecting the multicentric origin of squamous neoplasia).

Vaginal squamous carcinoma

Vaginal squamous carcinoma is an uncommon tumour predominantly occurring in older women. Pathologically, the tumour resembles squamous carcinoma of the cervix but it has a propensity to local invasion and radical surgery may be necessary.

Cervicitis

Non-specific acute and/or chronic inflammation is common in the cervix, particularly in the presence of an intra-uterine contraceptive device, ectopy (see below) or prolapse.

Chlamydiae are obligate intracellular organisms containing DNA and RNA, and are larger than viruses. *Chlamydia trachomatis* is a common sexually transmitted infection which is often recognised by its persistence following treatment for gonorrhoea in males (post-gonococcal urethritis). Chlamydiae can be isolated from the cervices of about 50% of asymptomatic female partners of these infected males and from women with chronic cervicitis. Chlamydial infection may produce subepithelial reactive lymphoid follicles, a condition sometimes given the label of 'follicular cervicitis'.

Cervical polyps

Benign polyps of the cervix are common. They are composed of columnar mucus-secreting epithelium and oedematous stroma. Vessels may be prominent and there may be acute or chronic inflammation of varying severity. These polyps have no malignant potential.

Cervical microglandular hyperplasia

Cervical microglandular hyperplasia is a commonly seen complex glandular proliferation that may be confused with carcinoma. Small, tightly packed glands, lined by low columnar or cuboidal epithelium, may form polypoid projections into the endocervical canal. Accompanying acute inflammation and reserve cell hyperplasia (see below) are often seen. These changes may be seen in pregnancy and in users of the oral contraceptive pill, where they are the result of high levels of progestogen. Microglandular hyperplasia may also rarely be seen in post-menopausal women. It appears to have no malignant potential.

CERVICAL SQUAMOUS NEOPLASIA

- ▶ Incidence associated with sexual intercourse (especially number of male partners)
- ▶ Human papillomavirus postulated as main causative factor, with cigarette smoking as independent risk factor
- ▶ Pre-invasive phase of intra-epithelial neoplasia can be detected by cervical cytology
- ▶ Cervical intra-epithelial neoplasia (CIN) graded from 1 to 3 according to severity of abnormality

Aetiology

Squamous neoplasia of the cervix is associated with sexual activity; early age at first intercourse, frequency of intercourse and number of sexual partners are all risk factors. The sexual behaviour of the male partner is probably also of importance. There is probably no one single cause of cervical cancer or pre-cancer, but epidemiological evidence points to a sexually transmitted agent or agents. There is now compelling evidence that human papillomaviruses are implicated in the aetiology of cervical squamous neoplasia. Cigarette smoking is an independent risk factor; some contents of cigarette smoke, which can be detected in cervical mucus, may act as co-carcinogenic agents. The polycyclic aromatic hydrocarbons in cigarette smoke form damaging adducts with DNA; these have been demonstrated in cervical tissue at higher levels in current smokers.

Human papillomaviruses and neoplasia of the lower female genital tract

Genital warts or condylomata have been recognised for centuries. Only comparatively recently, however, has their viral aetiology been established. Electron microscopy showed the presence of viral particles, and immunohistochemistry (using antibodies to viral capsid antigen) and in situ hybridisation (using DNA probes) also confirmed their viral nature. Warts may affect the vulva but may also involve the cervix (Fig. 19.4). Moreover, it is now appreciated that human papillomaviruses (HPV) may infect the vulva, vagina and cervix in a non-condylomatous manner. Such infections show characteristic morphological features; most important of these is a specific cytoplasmic vacuolation called koilocytosis (Fig. 19.5). The features associated with human papillomavirus infection are:

- koilocytosis
- hyperkeratosis
- parakeratosis
- papillomatosis
- individual cell keratinisation (dyskeratosis)
- multinucleation.

These morphological features are also common accompaniments of vulval, vaginal and cervical intra-epithelial neoplasia.

There are now more than 100 subtypes of human papillomavirus recognised and certain of these show a particular predilection for the lower female genital tract, notably HPV 6, 11, 16 and 18. HPV 6 and 11 are found in benign condylomata and are only rarely implicated in malignant transformation. HPV 16 and, to a lesser extent, 18 are found in cervical intra-epithelial neoplasia and in nearly 100% of cervical carcinomas. Other types, such as HPV 31 and 33, have also been reported in carcinoma. These are the oncogenic HPV types. Infection of the male genitalia by HPV is also seen; similar lesions to those seen on the cervix occur on the glans penis and prepuce, and may also be associated with neoplastic change.

Papillomavirus DNA may be present either extrachromosomally (episomal) or integrated into the host DNA. Integration of the viral genome into host DNA is usual in high-grade cervical intra-epithelial neoplasia (see below) and invasive cervical squamous carcinoma. The protein coding sequences of the viral early (E) or late (L) open reading frames appear to have a major role in oncogenesis. Most interestingly, the E6 protein of HPV type 16 is capable of binding to the cellular p53 protein to form a complex that neutralises the normal response of cervical epithelial cells to DNA damage (apoptosis mediated by p53), which may thereby allow the accumulation of genetic abnormalities. E6 protein of low-risk HPV types (e.g. 6 and 11) does not appear to form a complex with p53.

These events may explain why, unlike many other solid tumours, mutation of the *p53* gene is an uncommon event in cervical carcinogenesis, as there is an alternative mechanism for its inactivation.

HPV 16 and 18 E7 proteins also have the ability to bind to the product of the retinoblastoma gene (*RB1*), thus affecting its tumour suppressor role.

HPV vaccination is now being implemented in many countries. The vaccine comprises virus-like particles produced by recombinant DNA technology.

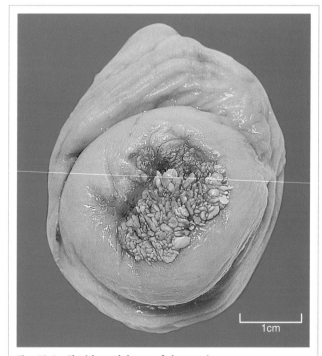

Fig. 19.4 Florid condyloma of the cervix.

Physiological and neoplastic changes in the cervical transformation zone

Before puberty, the squamo-columnar junction lies within the endocervical canal (Fig. 19.6). With the onset of puberty and in pregnancy, there is eversion of the columnar epithelium of the endocervix so that the squamo-columnar junction comes to lie beyond and on the vaginal aspect of the external os. This produces the clinical appearance of a cervical 'erosion', an unfortunate term, as the change is physiological. The term

ectopy is more appropriate. The columnar epithelium is then exposed to the low pH of the vaginal mucus and undergoes squamous metaplasia. This is a physiological phenomenon, and takes place through the stages of reserve cell hyperplasia and immature squamous metaplasia. Reserve cells undermine the columnar mucus-secreting cells and multiply. This labile epithelium is called the transformation zone and is the predominant site for the development of cervical neoplasia.

Cervical intra-epithelial neoplasia (CIN) refers to the spectrum of epithelial changes that take place in squamous epithelium

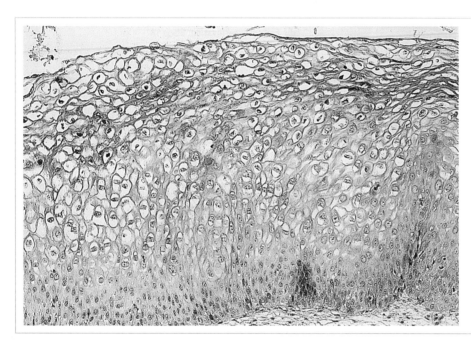

Fig. 19.5 Koilocytosis. Cytoplasmic vacuolation and pyknotic nuclei indicative of human papillomavirus infection of the cervix.

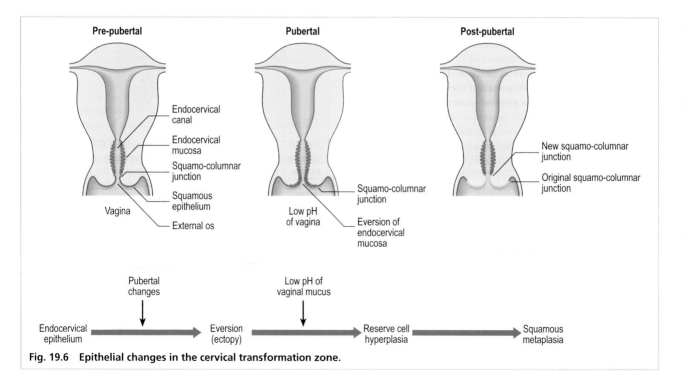

Fig. 19.6 Epithelial changes in the cervical transformation zone.

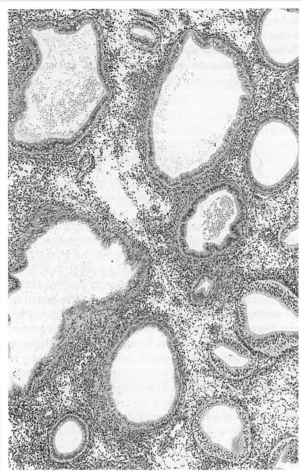

Fig. 19.13 Simple hyperplasia of the endometrium. There is prominent cystic dilatation of glands.

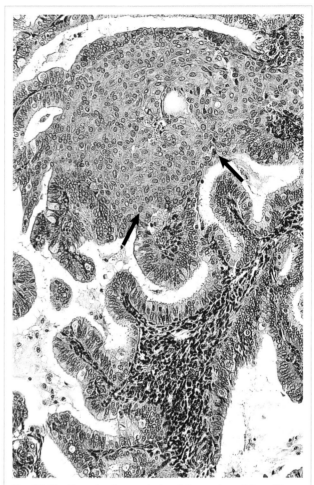

Fig. 19.14 Complex hyperplasia of the endometrium. There is architectural, but no cytological, abnormality. Note the associated squamous metaplasia (arrowed).

Atypical hyperplasia

In atypical hyperplasia (endometrial intra-epithelial neoplasia) architectural and cytological changes are combined. The nuclei of the epithelial cells may show a variable degree of cytological atypia (Fig. 19.15). There is a close correlation between the risk of malignant change and the severity of the atypia. Thus, for atypical hyperplasia showing a severe degree of cytological atypia, the risk is probably about 25% after 3 years.

Endometrial adenocarcinoma

▸ May result from unopposed oestrogenic action or in atrophic post-menopausal endometrium
▸ Spreads via lymphatic and haematogenous routes

There are two clinicopathological types of endometrial adenocarcinoma.

The first type is endometrioid adenocarcinoma and is usually due to unopposed oestrogenic stimulation and arises from endometrial intra-epithelial neoplasia (EIN). This type of tumour characteristically occurs in young women with the polycystic ovary syndrome or in association with obesity.

It also affects peri-menopausal women, and may complicate post-menopausal oestrogen replacement therapy. It is generally associated with a good prognosis.

The second type of endometrial adenocarcinoma is non-endometrioid, affects elderly post-menopausal women, is not associated with oestrogenic stimulation, and probably arises on the basis of a pre-existing inactive or atrophic endometrium. High-grade serous and clear cell carcinoma are in this category and are associated with a poor prognosis.

Recently it has been shown that the molecular profiles of these two basic types of endometrial adenocarcinoma (endometrioid and non-endometrioid) are quite different (Table 19.4). The lack or presence of *p53* mutation is the most important distinguishing molecular feature.

Endometrial adenocarcinoma may be confined to the endometrium. Since the endometrium is composed of glands and stroma, it is possible for a carcinoma to invade its own stroma and still be intra-endometrial. Alternatively, there may be invasion of the myometrium (Fig. 19.16). The extent of myometrial invasion at the time of diagnosis is the single most important prognostic factor. Involvement of the endocervix also has an adverse effect on prognosis. Thereafter, spread of the tumour occurs via the lymphatic

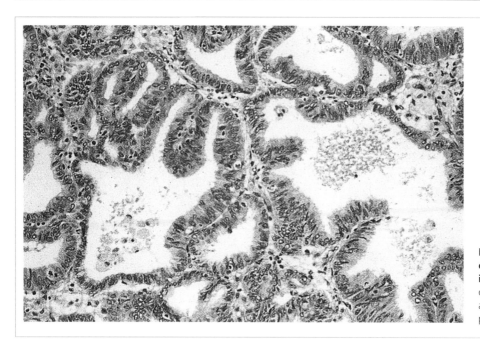

Fig. 19.15　Atypical hyperplasia of the endometrium (endometrial intra-epithelial neoplasia). There is a combination of architectural abnormality and cytological abnormality (nuclear pleomorphism).

Table 19.4　Molecular profile of endometrial carcinoma		
	Endometrioid	Serous
ER/PR	+	–
p53 mutation	–	+
Microsatellite instability	++ (20–30%)	+ (11%)
PTEN mutation	+ (34–83%)	–
k-*ras* mutation	+ (10–30%)	–
Beta-catenin mutation	+ (28–35%)	–

and venous routes to the vagina and pelvic and para-aortic lymph nodes.

Endometrial stromal sarcoma

Neoplastic change can occur in the endometrial stroma as well as the endometrial glands, but stromal neoplasms are much less common. Low-grade stromal sarcoma occurs in the uterus of peri- and post-menopausal women and may be diagnosed as an incidental finding in a hysterectomy specimen or following a clinical diagnosis of fibroids. Nodules of bland-looking stroma infiltrate the myometrium, with little or no mitotic activity. The natural history of these tumours is one of local recurrence, sometimes after many years. Histologically, these recurrences resemble the original tumour. High-grade uterine sarcoma is a highly malignant tumour which may show extensive invasion of the myometrium at the time of diagnosis, with high mitotic activity and focal necrosis.

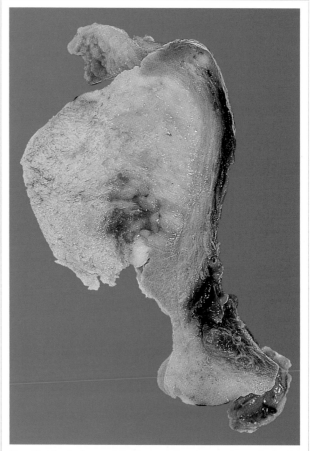

Fig. 19.16　Endometrial adenocarcinoma. Uterine wall sliced to reveal extensive myometrial invasion by endometrial adenocarcinoma.

Mixed Müllerian neoplasia

Not only do both glandular and stromal components of the endometrium have the propensity to undergo neoplastic change, but they may do so concurrently. This gives rise to the spectrum of mixed Müllerian (mesodermal) neoplasia. Either component may be benign or malignant. Several variants are recognised, but carcinosarcoma or malignant mixed Müllerian tumour is the most important type and is discussed in more detail below.

Malignant mixed Müllerian tumour (carcinosarcoma)

Malignant mixed Müllerian tumour is a highly malignant tumour with a poor prognosis that occurs in elderly women. Clinically, it presents in the same way as endometrial adenocarcinoma, but the tumour is usually advanced with extensive myometrial invasion at the time of diagnosis. Diagnosis can usually be made on an endometrial biopsy or curettage specimen, where obviously malignant glands and stroma are characterised by cellular pleomorphism, increased mitotic activity and abnormal mitoses. The tumours are usually polypoid and fill the endometrial cavity (Fig. 19.17). If the tumour shows only those components derived from endometrium or myometrium, it is of homologous type. Often, other components foreign to the uterus are seen, including cartilage and bone; it is then of *heterologous type*. Recent molecular genetic evidence suggests a monoclonal origin of these tumours, which should probably be regarded as 'metaplastic carcinomas'.

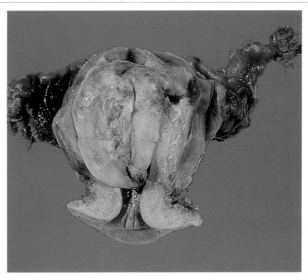

Fig. 19.17   Malignant mixed Müllerian tumour. This polypoid tumour fills the uterine cavity of an elderly patient.

ABNORMALITIES OF THE MYOMETRIUM

Adenomyosis

Adenomyosis is a common finding in hysterectomy specimens and refers to the presence of endometrial glands and stroma deep within the myometrium. It characteristically occurs in peri-menopausal multiparous women and is of uncertain aetiology. It may be regarded as a form of 'diverticulosis', as there is continuity between adenomyotic foci and the lining endometrium of the uterine cavity. Neoplastic change may occur within these foci but should not be regarded as evidence of myometrial invasion.

Smooth muscle tumours

> ▸ Uterine leiomyomas (fibroids) are the commonest benign tumours
> ▸ Associated with infertility
> ▸ Leiomyosarcomas have varying malignant behaviour correlated with their mitotic activity

The commonest tumour of the female genital tract is the benign fibroid or *leiomyoma*. These commonly present in later reproductive life and around the time of the menopause. They are associated with low parity, although it is uncertain whether this is a common cause or an effect. The precise aetiology of leiomyomas is unknown. They may present clinically with:

- abdominal mass
- urinary problems due to pressure on the bladder
- abnormal uterine bleeding.

Characteristically, they are multiple, round, well-circumscribed tumours varying in diameter from 5 mm to, in some cases, 200 mm or more (Fig. 19.18). They may show cystic change or focal necrosis. On section, they have a white, whorled appearance. Histologically, they are composed of complex interlacing bundles of smooth muscle fibres showing little or no mitotic activity. Sometimes, nodules of tumour may be seen within veins (intravenous leiomyomatosis); this is not a sinister feature. Smooth muscle tumours contain steroid hormone receptors, and at least a proportion are oestrogen-dependent.

The crucial factor in the assessment of malignancy in smooth muscle tumours is their mitotic activity. There is a very good correlation between clinical behaviour and the mitotic count but malignancy is always associated with other features, including nuclear pleomorphism, an irregular tumour margin, haemorrhage and necrosis. The mitotic count is usually expressed in terms of numbers of mitoses per 10 high-power fields (hpf) of the microscope (the field area should always be stated). Leiomyomas contain 0–3 mitoses/10 hpf. If there are 10 or more in association with nuclear pleomorphism, then a tumour must be regarded as a leiomyosarcoma and will behave as a malignant tumour, with all the risks of recurrence and metastases. If there are between 3 and 10 mitoses/10 hpf, the behaviour of smooth muscle tumours is unpredictable. They are referred to as 'smooth muscle tumours of uncertain malignant potential', and the patients must be placed under periodic surveillance. Although these criteria may appear arbitrary, their application has proved useful in practice.

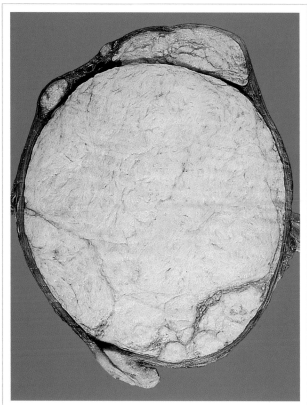

Fig. 19.18   Benign fibroid or leiomyoma. Note the typical white whorled appearance of its cut surface. This is an enormous example, 160 mm in diameter; the remaining uterus is small by comparison.

OVARY

Ovarian lesions present either with pain due to inflammation or swelling of the organ, or with the remote effects of an endocrine secretion.

OVARIAN CYSTS

Ovarian cysts may be non-neoplastic or neoplastic; many ovarian tumours are partially cystic. The various types of non-neoplastic cyst are:

- mesothelial-lined
- epithelial inclusion
- follicular
- luteinised follicular
- corpus luteum
- corpus albicans
- corpus luteum cyst of pregnancy
- endometriotic.

Inclusion cysts occur in the ovarian cortex probably as a result of surface trauma at the time of ovulation; they may be lined by original peritoneal mesothelium or metaplastic epithelium. This is discussed in more detail below. The

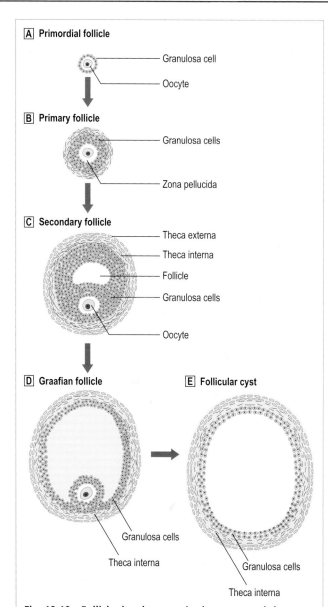

Fig. 19.19   Follicle development in the ovary and the origin of a follicular cyst. A Primordial follicle. B Primary follicle. The primordial follicle responds to follicle stimulating hormone (FSH) to form a primary follicle comprising the oocyte, a mucopolysaccharide layer (zona pellucida) and proliferating granulosa cells. **C and D Secondary and Graafian follicles.** With continuing FSH stimulation a secondary or Graafian follicle is produced, comprising an eccentrically placed oocyte, a cavity containing clear liquid (the antrum), surrounding granulosa cells and condensed ovarian stromal cells, the theca interna and theca externa. The maximum diameter should be 25–30 mm. **E Follicular cysts,** which are probably due to disordered hormonal function, are larger than 30 mm.

nature and origin of many of the non-neoplastic cysts that occur in the ovary can only be appreciated with knowledge of the normal histology of the ovary, as well as of the development of the follicle (Fig. 19.19) and corpus luteum.

Polycystic ovary syndrome

The polycystic ovary syndrome is the association of amenorrhoea, hyperoestrogenism and multiple follicular cysts of the ovary. There is usually stromal hyperplasia and little evidence that ovulation has occurred. The syndrome, which is related to defective insulin metabolism, is an important cause of infertility, endometrial hyperplasia and, rarely, endometrial adenocarcinoma in young women.

Ovarian hyperstimulation syndrome

This may be induced by gonadotrophins or clomifene used in the treatment of infertility. It is characterised by bilateral ovarian enlargement due to multiple luteinised follicular cysts. The condition may be complicated by ascites and pericardial effusion, hypovolaemic shock and renal failure.

OVARIAN STROMAL HYPERPLASIA AND STROMAL LUTEINISATION

The stroma of the ovary is unlike stromal tissue at other sites because, in addition to a general metabolic and supportive function, the cells may also be directly involved in the endocrine activity of the organ. Ovarian stromal hyperplasia is a proliferative change seen to some extent in the ovaries of many peri- and post-menopausal women. It is characterised by the non-neoplastic proliferation of stromal cells resulting in varying degrees of bilateral ovarian enlargement. In old age there is a tendency towards atrophy. Atrophic ovaries tend to be small, wrinkled, hard and pearly white.

Hyperplastic ovarian stroma is associated with increased levels of androgens and oestrogens. Thus there is an association between stromal hyperplasia and endometrial hyperplasia, carcinoma and polyps. Other steroidogenic cells may be scattered throughout the stroma; such 'luteinised' cells may secrete androgens and may cause virilism. Stromal hyperplasia and luteinisation may also be observed in ovaries containing primary or secondary neoplasms.

ENDOMETRIOSIS

Endometriosis is the presence of endometrial glands and stroma in sites other than the uterine corpus. It is a very important cause of morbidity in women and may be responsible for pelvic inflammation, infertility and pain. The common sites include the pouch of Douglas, the pelvic peritoneum and the ovary. Endometriosis may also involve the serosal surface of the uterus, cervix, vulva and vagina, and extragenital sites such as the bladder and the small and large intestines. The occurrence of endometriosis in extra-abdominal sites is very rare.

The aetiology of endometriosis is unknown, but retrograde menstruation into the peritoneal cavity along the fallopian tube, and metaplasia of mesothelium to Müllerian-type epithelium, are possible explanations. The glands and stroma are usually subject to the same hormone-induced changes that occur in the endometrium. Thus, haemorrhage in endometriotic foci may cause pain. In the ovary especially, recurrent haemorrhage may

produce cysts containing altered blood, so-called 'chocolate cysts'. Uncommonly, hyperplastic or atypical changes may be seen in the epithelial component, with appearances similar to those that affect the endometrium. At least a proportion of endometrioid tumours of the ovary (see below) arise from pre-existing foci of endometriosis. Recently, similar patterns of chromosomal abnormalities (loss of heterozygosity) have been demonstrated in endometriosis and endometrioid adenocarcinoma. Individual endometriotic foci have been shown to be monoclonal.

OVARIAN NEOPLASMS

▶ May be solid or cystic, benign or malignant
▶ Borderline lesions have low risk of malignant behaviour
▶ Nomenclature based on cellular origin
▶ Some produce oestrogens
▶ Commonest fatal gynaecological malignancy in many countries

Ovarian tumours may be divided into five broad categories:

● epithelial
● germ cell
● sex cord stromal
● metastatic
● miscellaneous.

The further subdivisions of these categories are shown in Table 19.5.

Epithelial tumours

Epithelial tumours are believed to arise from the mesothelial cell layer covering the peritoneal surface of the ovary and associated inclusion cysts. This mesothelium has the propensity to undergo metaplasia to Müllerian epithelium, as, indeed, does the entire mesothelial lining of the peritoneal cavity. Thus, differentiation may take place to resemble tubal mucosa (serous tumours), endocervical mucosa (mucinous tumours) or endometrium (endometrioid tumours). Transitional cell tumours do not fit neatly into this histogenetic theory as they resemble the transitional epithelium of the bladder. Each of these tumours may be benign or malignant (Fig. 19.20), but there is a third category of *borderline tumour*. These tumours show some of the features associated with malignancy, such as irregular architecture, nuclear stratification and pleomorphism and mitotic activity, but lack the most important criterion of invasion. Their biological behaviour is intermediate between that of clearly benign and overtly malignant tumours (Figs 19.21 and 19.22).

Aneuploid tumours are more likely to behave in a malignant manner. A significant proportion of mucinous tumours, particularly in the borderline category, contain intestinal-type rather than endocervical-type epithelium. These tumours may be complicated by peritoneal implants producing copious amounts of mucus (*pseudomyxoma peritonei*). This condition has a poor prognosis and is often complicated by intestinal obstruction. However, recent evidence suggests that when pseudomyxoma peritonei is associated with appendiceal and

Table 19.5 Classification of ovarian neoplasms

Origin	Tumour	
	Types	Subtypes
Epithelium	Serous Mucinous Endometrioid* Transitional cell	Benign, borderline or malignant

Germ cells	Dysgerminoma
	Teratoma
	
	Extraembryonic
	
	Malignant mixed germ cell tumours
		
		Mature cystic, immature solid or monodermal
		  (e.g. carcinoid, struma ovarii)
		Yolk sac (endodermal sinus tumour),
		  choriocarcinoma

Sex cord stroma	Thecoma Granulosa cell tumour Sertoli–Leydig cell tumour Mixed germ cell stromal tumour (gonadoblastoma) Steroid cell tumour	
Metastatic	Various (most commonly from the gastrointestinal tract)	
Miscellaneous	Haemangioma, lipoma, etc.	

*Clear cell carcinoma is a variant of endometrioid tumour.

ovarian disease, the peritoneal and ovarian lesions are, in fact, metastases from a primary appendiceal tumour.

The diagnosis of borderline tumour is made on the primary tumour but associated peritoneal implants may be borderline or invasive. The latter are associated with an adverse prognosis (60–70% 5-year survival).

Benign mucinous and serous tumours are commonly smooth-walled and cystic (Fig. 19.23), while benign transitional cell (Brenner) tumours are solid but may show cystic areas. Endometrioid tumours of the ovary may show the full range of mixed Müllerian neoplasia already referred to in the context of uterine tumours, such as endometrioid adenofibroma and carcinosarcoma.

The aetiology of epithelial ovarian cancer remains uncertain but certain facts are known. First, ovarian cancer is a disorder of developed societies and shows a higher incidence among women of higher social classes. Second, the oral contraceptive pill and pregnancy offer a protective effect; these probably act by reducing ovulation, although the reduced risk conferred by one pregnancy is much greater than would be expected. Thus, repeated ovulatory trauma to the surface epithelium seems to be a crucial factor.

Studies of ovarian cancer in families have shown that sisters and mothers of affected individuals have an approximately five-fold increased risk of ovarian cancer. Among all of the common cancers this is the largest excess risk to relatives and implies genetic susceptibility. Family studies also show that first-degree relatives are at an increased risk of breast cancer. Mutations of a rare dominant gene, *BRCA1*, localised on chromosome 17q, increase the risk of cancer at both sites. Familial ovarian cancer related to *BRCA1* accounts for only 5–10% of ovarian cancers; they are predominantly of serous type. There is growing awareness that similar familial tumours can arise from the fallopian tube rather than the ovary.

Ovarian cancers show complex genetic abnormalities with a high incidence of *p53* point mutations. Loss of heterozygosity has been demonstrated at a number of other chromosomal sites close to known tumour suppressor genes. Amplification of the *erbB-2* (*HER-2/neu*) oncogene is associated with a poor prognosis.

Ovarian cancer is responsible for more deaths than any other gynaecological malignancy (Table 19.6). This is largely because it often presents at an advanced stage, due to its anatomically obscure site. Malignant tumours may be solid and/or cystic and there may be areas of haemorrhage and necrosis, with the tumour projecting into the lumen of a cyst or projecting exophytically into the peritoneal cavity. Tumour spread occurs predominantly intra-abdominally. The clinical staging of ovarian cancer is shown in Figure 19.24. The ovarian cancer-related protein CA125 is used routinely as a serum tumour marker, particularly to aid in the recognition of early relapse.

Germ cell tumours

A potentially confusing range of tumours may arise from germ cells in the ovary. These may be benign or malignant.

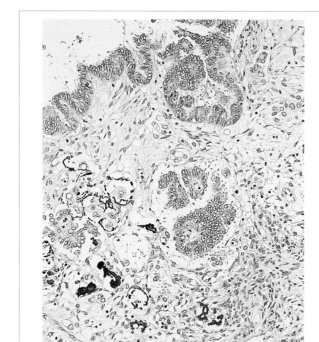

Fig. 19.20   **Papillary serous adenocarcinoma.** Note the presence of microcalcification (psammoma body formation).

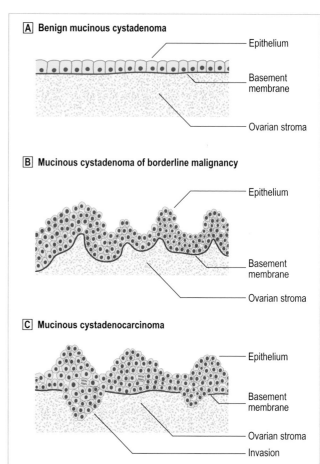

Fig. 19.21   **Epithelial morphology of ovarian mucinous neoplasms.** [A] **Benign mucinous cystadenoma.** Note the monolayer of cuboidal mucinous cells and basally located nuclei. [B] **Mucinous cystadenoma of borderline malignancy.** There is irregular architecture, multilayering of cells and mitotic activity, but the basement membrane is intact. [C] **Mucinous cystadenocarcinoma.** There is invasion through the original basement membrane.

[A] Benign mucinous cystadenoma — Epithelium, Basement membrane, Ovarian stroma

[B] Mucinous cystadenoma of borderline malignancy — Epithelium, Basement membrane, Ovarian stroma

[C] Mucinous cystadenocarcinoma — Epithelium, Basement membrane, Ovarian stroma, Invasion

Fig. 19.22   **Serous cystadenoma of borderline malignancy.** An ovarian cyst containing abundant papillary tumour that was found on subsequent histological examination to be a serous borderline tumour.

Fig. 19.23   **Mucinous cystadenoma of the ovary.**

Table 19.6 Gynaecological cancer in the UK		
	Cases*	Deaths†
Ovary	6615	4447
Uterus	6438	1637
Cervix	2726	1061
Vulva	1022	332
Vagina	246	107

*New cases in 2004. †Deaths in 2005.
Data from Cancer Research UK (http://info.cancerresearchuk.org/cancerstats)

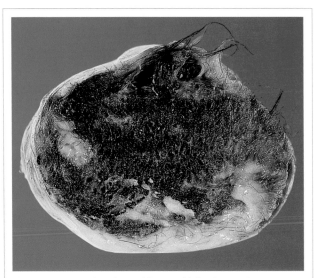

Fig. 19.25 Ovarian dermoid cyst. This benign cystic teratoma is filled with matted hair.

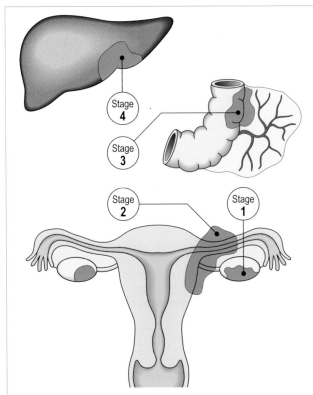

Fig. 19.24 Simplified clinical staging of ovarian cancer.
Stage 1: Tumour limited to ovary. **Stage 2:** Involvement of other pelvic structures. **Stage 3:** Intra-abdominal spread beyond pelvis. **Stage 4:** Distant metastases.

Dysgerminoma

The fundamental or undifferentiated female ovarian germ cell tumour is the dysgerminoma, which is the exact counterpart of the seminoma arising in the male testis. It is a rare malignant tumour arising predominantly in young females; it is usually confined to one ovary and has a fleshy cut surface. Histologically, it shows a uniform appearance of germ cells admixed with lymphocytes. Occasional giant cells containing human chorionic gonadotrophin may be present, but these do not imply a poorer prognosis. These tumours are highly radiosensitive.

Teratomas

When germ cells differentiate along embryonic lines they give rise to teratomas, that is, a tumour that contains elements of all three germ cell layers—ectoderm, endoderm and mesoderm.

Mature cystic teratoma

The commonest germ cell tumour and, indeed, the commonest ovarian tumour, is the benign or mature cystic teratoma (dermoid cyst). The majority of ovarian mature cystic teratomas arise from an oocyte that has completed the first meiotic division, in a manner analogous to parthenogenesis. It may present at any age, although usually in younger patients, as a smooth-walled, unilateral ovarian cyst. These tumours characteristically contain hair, sebaceous material and teeth (Fig. 19.25). Histologically, they show a wide range of tissues which, although haphazardly arranged, are indistinguishable from those seen in the normal adult. Squamous epithelium, bronchial epithelium, cartilage and intestinal epithelium may all be seen. These tumours are benign, although in elderly women malignancy (usually squamous carcinoma) may develop very rarely.

Immature teratoma

In contrast to the mature cystic type, teratomas may also be predominantly solid and composed of immature tissues similar to those seen in the developing embryo. These tumours are potentially malignant, and the predominant components are immature neural tissue and immature mesenchyme. They occur in young patients, and the prognosis is related to the amount of immature neural tissue present. Such tumours may metastasise to the peritoneum, where the assessment of tissue maturity is crucial, particularly in assessing response to chemotherapy. Immature neural tissue within the peritoneum

may mature, or mature glial tissue may be present from the outset (gliomatosis peritonei).

Monodermal teratoma

Germ cell tumours may be composed entirely, or almost entirely, of tissue derived from one germ cell layer; these are monodermal teratomas. The best known examples are struma ovarii, composed of thyroid tissue which may be benign or malignant and rarely cause thyrotoxicosis, and carcinoid tumours, which are similar to carcinoid tumours arising in the gut. The carcinoid syndrome may occur even with benign tumours, as metabolic products are released directly into the systemic circulation and are therefore not denatured by hepatic enzymes.

Extra-embryonic germ cell tumours

Differentiation of germ cells may take place along extra-embryonic (as opposed to embryonic) lines to form the neoplastic counterparts of the non-fetal parts of the conceptus (the primitive yolk sac and the trophoblast of the placenta). These elements may give rise to yolk sac tumours (also known as endodermal sinus tumours because of their resemblance to the endodermal sinuses of Duval in the developing rat placenta) and choriocarcinoma. These are highly malignant tumours which may be associated with other germ cell elements.

Yolk sac tumours

Yolk sac tumours usually affect young females below the age of 30 years. The tumours are cystic and solid and often haemorrhagic. Histologically, characteristic structures (Duval–Schiller bodies), composed of central vessels with a rosette of tumour cells, may be seen. Alpha-fetoprotein may be demonstrated immunohistochemically and is used as a serum marker. Intra-abdominal metastasis occurs, and the prognosis for untreated patients is poor. Modern combination chemotherapy, however, has considerably improved the outlook for patients with this tumour, and subsequent pregnancy following conservative surgery and chemotherapy is now possible.

Choriocarcinoma

Pure choriocarcinoma of the ovary is extremely rare and is associated with beta human chorionic gonadotrophin production. Theoretically, it could occur either as a germ cell tumour or as a primary or secondary gestational neoplasm (see below), in which case the tumour would contain the paternal haplotype on chromosomal analysis. When choriocarcinoma is seen, it is more usually one component of a malignant mixed germ cell tumour.

Sex cord-stromal tumours

During the fourth month of fetal life and onwards cell cords grow down from the surface epithelium of the ovary to surround the primordial follicles. Sex cord-stromal tumours comprise a range of ovarian neoplasms which frequently produce steroid hormones and are considered to arise from the cells that are the adult derivatives of these primitive sex cords in the fetal ovary. The detailed classification of these tumours is complex, but there are five broad groups (see Table 19.5).

Thecoma

Thecoma is the commonest sex cord-stromal tumour. It presents in the reproductive years as an abdominal mass, and is a benign tumour of the ovarian stroma. It is usually unilateral and well-circumscribed with a pale, fleshy cut surface. Histologically, it is a cellular, spindle-celled tumour containing abundant lipid. Its particular importance clinically is that it may be associated with the production of oestrogens.

Granulosa cell tumour

Granulosa cell tumour can occur at any age and all cases are potentially malignant, although there is a close correlation between large size at presentation and malignant behaviour. It is particularly associated with oestrogenic manifestations, and may therefore give rise to abnormal uterine bleeding, endometrial hyperplasia or, uncommonly, endometrial adenocarcinoma. (It should, however, be remembered that granulosa cells do not synthesise oestrogens, but merely convert hormonal precursors to oestrogens.) They present as unilateral multicystic tumours that may be focally haemorrhagic or necrotic. Histologically, they are composed of nests and cords of granulosa cells with characteristically grooved nuclei. Often, cells surround a central space containing eosinophilic hyaline material; this structure is called the Call–Exner body. Granulosa cell tumours are characterised by their propensity for late recurrence, in some cases many years after removal of the original tumour. Granulosa cells produce *inhibin* which is used as a serum or immunohistochemical marker for the tumour.

Sertoli–Leydig cell tumours

Sertoli–Leydig cell tumours are rare tumours composed of a variable mixture of cell types normally seen in the testis. Pure Sertoli and Leydig cell tumours may also occur. The tumours may be well, moderately or poorly differentiated and may present with androgenic signs and symptoms. Leydig cells may be identified by the presence of Reinke's crystals within their cytoplasm.

Gonadoblastoma

Gonadoblastoma is a rare lesion, which may not be a true neoplasm, in which primitive germ cells and sex cord-stromal derivatives are present. The latter usually resemble immature Sertoli cells and granulosa cells. These lesions typically develop in the dysgenetic streak gonads of phenotypic females carrying a Y chromosome. The germ cell component may undergo malignant change, usually to form a dysgerminoma.

Steroid cell tumours

Steroid cell tumours are uncommon and are usually benign and unilateral. In many cases the patient presents with virilisation due to androgen production (Fig. 19.26). Microscopically, the tumour is well circumscribed and composed of cells that resemble adrenal cortical cells and contain abundant intracellular lipid. The precise origin of these tumours is still debated. Although other sex cord-stromal

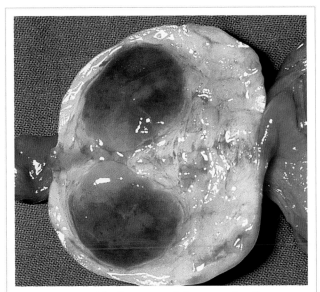

Fig. 19.26 Steroid cell tumour of the ovary. A well-circumscribed benign ovarian stromal tumour that caused virilisation in the patient.

infection is now an important cause of chronic inflammation and subsequent secondary infertility due to loss of tubal patency. Anaerobic organisms, such as *Bacteroides*, are also important as causes of salpingitis, whereas gonococcal infection is uncommon. Infection may be complicated by the accumulation of pus within the lumen of the tube (*pyosalpinx*). Longstanding chronic inflammation may lead to distension of the tube, loss of mucosa and the accumulation of serous fluid within the lumen (*hydrosalpinx*).

Cysts and tumours

Benign fimbrial cysts and *paratubal cysts* are common. They are usually lined by tubal-type epithelium. Rarely, *benign papillary serous neoplasms* may arise in paratubal or para-ovarian cysts.

Tumours of the fallopian tube are uncommon. Of most clinical importance is *primary adenocarcinoma of the fallopian tube epithelium* which, in some cases, may have a familial basis related to inherited *BRCA1* mutation. This tumour has a similar appearance to that of papillary serous adenocarcinoma of the ovary, for which it may be mistaken. The mode of spread is via lymphatics and the peritoneum. The tumour usually has a poor prognosis.

tumours may secrete steroids, the term 'steroid cell tumour' is conventionally reserved for this particular variant.

Metastatic tumours

Tumour metastatic to the ovary may be genital or extragenital. Endometrial adenocarcinoma may spread to the ovary, but it should be remembered that primary endometrial adenocarcinoma may co-exist with primary endometrioid adenocarcinoma of the ovary and be associated with a favourable prognosis. Large intestine, stomach and breast adenocarcinomas are the most important extragenital tumours. Metastatic colonic adenocarcinoma may be confused with primary mucinous cystadenocarcinoma or endometrioid adenocarcinoma. The term 'Krukenberg tumour' refers to bilateral ovarian neoplasms composed of malignant, mucin-containing, signet-ring cells, usually of gastric origin. Breast carcinoma frequently metastasises to the ovary, but usually these metastases do not manifest themselves clinically. Metastatic malignant melanoma may first present as an ovarian tumour.

FALLOPIAN TUBES

The fallopian tubes may be the site of inflammation, pregnancy, cysts or neoplasia. Inflammatory lesions and tubal ectopic pregnancies commonly present clinically with acute lower abdominal pain, mimicking, for example, acute appendicitis. Loss of tubal patency is an important cause of female infertility.

Inflammation (salpingitis)

Inflammation of the fallopian tube (salpingitis) is usually secondary to endometrial infection or the presence of an intra-uterine device; it may be acute or chronic. Chlamydial

PATHOLOGY OF PREGNANCY

There is a high rate of fetal loss in early pregnancy, and many early miscarriages are subclinical. Clinical miscarriage is usually the result of chromosomal abnormalities (Ch. 3). The chorionic villi of the immature placenta may be oedematous (hydropic change), or the stroma may be fibrotic, which is an involutional change following fetal death.

HYDATIDIFORM MOLE

▶ Characterised by swollen chorionic villi and trophoblastic hyperplasia
▶ Associated with high hCG levels
▶ Partial mole: triploid karyotype; fetus may be present
▶ Complete mole: 46XX karyotype; no fetus
▶ May be complicated by choriocarcinoma

Hydatidiform mole is a disorder of pregnancy affecting approximately 1 in 1000 pregnancies in the Western world and is much commoner in the Far East. It is characterised by swollen, oedematous chorionic villi, trophoblastic hyperplasia and the irregular distribution of villous trophoblast. Macroscopically, the placenta appears to be composed of multiple cystic, 'grape-like' structures (Fig. 19.27). A hydatidiform mole usually grows faster than a normal pregnancy, and the patient may present either with a 'large for dates' pregnant uterus, or with bleeding in early pregnancy. If an ultrasound scan is performed, the abnormal cysts can be clearly seen and uterine evacuation is indicated. There are two types of hydatidiform mole—complete mole and partial mole (Fig. 19.28)—which are genetically quite different.

519

Fig. 19.27   Hydatidiform mole. Note the characteristic 'grape-like' clusters.

Partial mole

The partial mole is triploid, and may not be diagnosed clinically but only identified histologically in miscarriage material. Most contain one maternal and two paternal haploid sets of chromosomes, with all three sex chromosome patterns possible (XXY, XXX and XYY). It must be remembered, however, that not all triploids are partial moles. A fetus may be present and only a proportion of the villi are abnormal; the rest may be fibrotic or may simply be hydropic without trophoblastic hyperplasia. Stromal vessels are present.

Complete mole

The chromosomal constitution of the complete mole is androgenetic (i.e. of paternal origin), characteristically 46XX, and is probably due to the fertilisation of an anucleate ovum either by a spermatozoon carrying an X chromosome which is then replicated or by two X-bearing spermatozoa. Grossly, the placenta is obviously abnormal with swollen villi. Histologically, the oedema is confirmed; there is an absence of stromal vessels and circumferential trophoblastic hyperplasia affecting all villi. The constituent trophoblast may show varying degrees of cytological atypia.

*p57*kip2

*p57*kip2 is a maternally expressed imprinted gene. Its protein product is expressed by the villous cytotrophoblast of partial moles but not androgenetic complete moles.

Complications

The importance of correctly diagnosing hydatidiform mole is that, in a small number of cases, the disorder may be complicated by *gestational trophoblastic neoplasia* (persistent trophoblastic disease). This term encompasses two main pathological entities with similar clinical manifestations, diagnosed by persistently elevated or rising urinary hCG levels following evacuation of molar tissue.

- *Invasive mole*: chorionic villi are present within the myometrium and myometrial vessels. The main complication is uterine perforation.
- *Choriocarcinoma*: this is a rare, malignant neoplasm of trophoblast with a propensity to systemic metastasis. Although there is usually a preceding history of hydatidiform mole, choriocarcinoma may follow a miscarriage or very rarely an apparently normal pregnancy. It is more common in the Far East and, without treatment, has a high mortality. A biphasic pattern of invading cyto- and syncytiotrophoblast is the characteristic appearance of this tumour.

Cases of hydatidiform mole are monitored by estimation of the serum and urinary hCG. If the level rises, or does not fall, then the patient will receive chemotherapy irrespective of the precise pathological diagnosis. The role of the pathologist in the management of gestational trophoblastic neoplasia is thus limited. The neoplastic potential of complete mole is greater than that of partial mole. Therefore, all cases of molar disease are followed up, although this may prove to be unnecessary in many cases. Patients are advised not to become pregnant during follow-up as this would cause a confusing rise in hCG levels.

PATHOLOGY OF THE FULL-TERM PLACENTA

The pathology of the full-term placenta is a large complex topic, the details of which are beyond the scope of this book. Only the commoner and/or clinically significant lesions are mentioned here. These may be considered under the following headings:

- abnormalities of placentation
  — extrachorial (may be circumvallate or circum-marginate)
  — accessory lobe
  — placenta accreta
- inflammation (villitis)
- vascular lesions
  — perivillous fibrin deposition
  — fetal artery thrombosis
  — placental infarct
  — haemangioma
- immaturity of villous development.

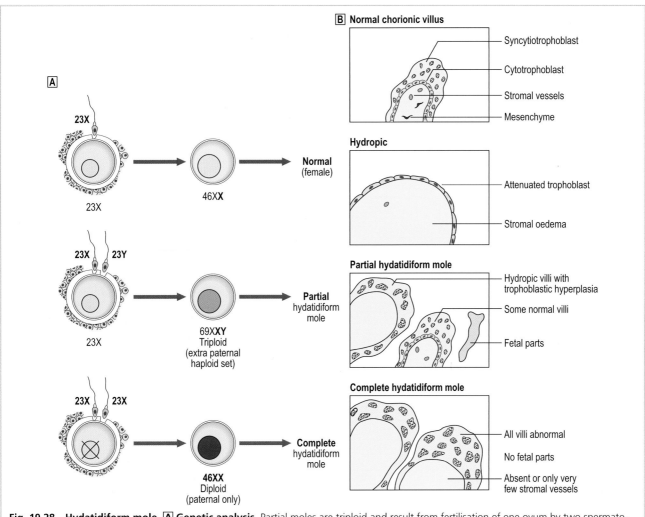

Fig. 19.28 Hydatidiform mole. **A** **Genetic analysis.** Partial moles are triploid and result from fertilisation of one ovum by two spermatozoa. Complete moles are diploid, but comprise only paternal chromosomes. **B** **Morphology.** See text for details.

Fascinatingly, long-term follow-up of offspring whose placental weights were accurately recorded in the early to mid 20th century has shown a strong correlation between low placental weight and subsequent adult (e.g. cardiovascular) disease.

Abnormalities of placentation

Abnormalities of placental shape are usually of no clinical significance. Placenta accreta is an abnormality of implantation.

Extrachorial placentation

Extrachorial placentation is a developmental abnormality in which the fetal surface of the placenta from which the chorionic villi arise (the chorionic plate) is smaller than the maternal surface attached to the uterine decidua (the basal plate). Thus, the border between the extravillous chorionic membrane and chorionic villi is not at the placental margin but is present circumferentially on the fetal surface of the placenta (Fig. 19.29). This border may be flat ('circum-marginate') or raised ('circumvallate'). Circum-marginate

placentation is of no clinical significance, but circumvallate placentation is associated with a higher incidence of low birthweight babies, although the causal relationship between the two is still obscure.

Accessory lobe

An accessory lobe to the placenta is usually of no clinical importance, but occasionally the lobe may be retained in utero after delivery of the main placenta.

Placenta accreta

Placenta accreta is a rare disorder in which the chorionic villi are immediately adjacent to, or penetrate, the myometrium to a varying degree. This is associated with a deficiency of decidua, and may be the result of previous operative intervention, such as curettage or caesarean section, infection or uterine malformation. The main clinical significance is the risk of ante-partum bleeding. Post-partum bleeding may also occur due to a failure of placental separation resulting from the abnormally adherent chorionic villi.

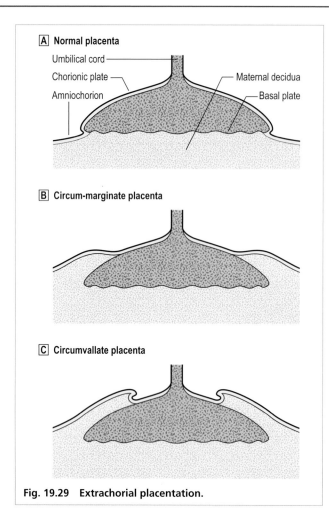

Fig. 19.29 Extrachorial placentation.

Inflammation

Inflammation of the placental tissues may involve either the chorionic villi (villitis) or the extraplacental membranes (chorioamnionitis). Inflammation of chorionic villi is usually due to infection through the maternal blood stream. Specific infections, such as listeriosis, toxoplasmosis or cytomegalovirus, are responsible for only a small proportion of cases (Fig. 19.30). Most examples are of unknown aetiology, and are seen in approximately 5% of all pregnancies as a focal infiltrate of lymphocytes and histiocytes. Villitis is associated with an increased incidence of fetal intra-uterine growth retardation but, again, the pathogenesis is unclear.

Vascular lesions

Several vascular lesions may occur in the placenta. They are usually of no clinical significance.

Perivillous fibrin deposition

Perivillous fibrin deposition occurs to some extent in all placentae and quite commonly is macroscopically apparent as a firm white plaque. The lesion is of no clinical significance.

Fetal artery thrombosis

Thrombosis of a fetal villous stem artery will produce a well-circumscribed area of avascular chorionic villi, which may be apparent macroscopically as an area of pallor. The inter-villous space appears normal. The aetiology is unknown, although there is an association with maternal diabetes mellitus. Although usually of no clinical significance, extensive thrombosis of fetal villous stem vessels can, rarely, be responsible for fetal death.

Placental infarct

A placental infarct is a localised area of ischaemic villous necrosis due to thrombotic occlusion of a maternal uteroplacental (spiral) artery. (It must be remembered that chorionic villi have a dual blood supply.) Macroscopically, fresh infarcts are red but progressively undergo fibrosis. When extensive, placental infarction is a manifestation of maternal vascular disease and is thus particularly associated with hypertensive disorders of pregnancy.

Haemangioma

Haemangiomas are uncommon tumours that occur as well-circumscribed, dark nodules. They are of no clinical significance except when large or multiple. They may then be associated with polyhydramnios, premature labour and intra-uterine growth retardation due to diversion of blood through the tumour rather than through normal placental tissue.

Immaturity of villous development

Maturation of the placenta during pregnancy is associated with increased branching of chorionic villi with the production of small terminal villi to maximise the surface area available for materno-fetal transfer. Syncytiotrophoblast at the tips of villi thins to form vasculosyncytial membranes closely apposed to fetal stromal vessels. These are important sites of oxygen transfer between mother and fetus. Immaturity of chorionic villi and inadequate formation of vasculosyncytial membranes may be associated with intra-uterine fetal hypoxia, low birth-weight and perinatal death.

PATHOLOGY OF THE UMBILICAL CORD AND MEMBRANES

Umbilical cord

Mechanical lesions of the umbilical cord include knots, rupture, torsion and stricture, all of which may lead to fetal complications. Abnormal (velamentous) insertion of the cord into the membranes, rather than the chorionic plate, may lead to serious haemorrhage during pregnancy or labour, as unprotected vessels run from the membranes to the surface of the placenta. A single umbilical artery is often accompanied by congenital fetal malformation. Visible oedema of the cord is associated with a relatively high incidence of fetal respiratory distress, although the reason for this is unclear.

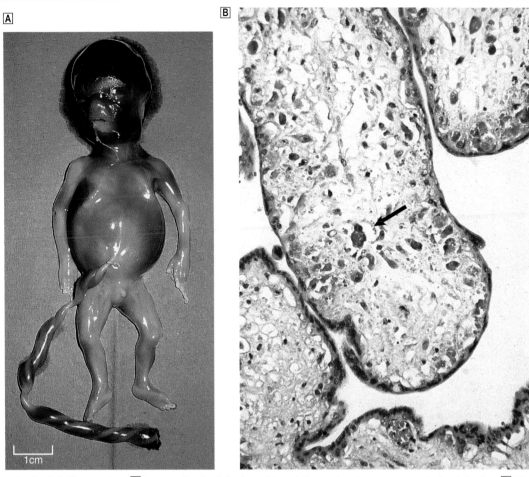

Fig. 19.30 Chorionic inflammation. A Intra-uterine fetal death at 17 weeks' gestation due to cytomegalovirus infection. B Chorionic villi from the placenta showing the characteristic large cells (arrowed) typically containing inclusion bodies resulting from cytomegalovirus infection.

Membranes

Amnion nodosum is the occurrence of nodules on the fetal surface of the amnion, particularly around the site of the insertion of the cord. Histologically, these are composed of amorphous material in which cell fragments, and sometimes fetal hair, are embedded. The lesion is usually associated with oligohydramnios.

Chorioamnionitis, or acute inflammation of the membranes, is usually the result of ascending bacterial infection from the vagina and cervix. It may be associated with prolonged rupture of membranes before delivery.

PATHOLOGY OF THE PLACENTAL BED

Within the placental bed there is an intimate admixture of maternal and fetal cells. The former comprise the decidua, residual endometrial glands and a population of macrophages and stromal granulated lymphocytes. The cells of fetal origin are composed of the various populations of non-villous trophoblast. These cells develop from the proliferating cytotrophoblast columns of the implanted blastocyst in the early weeks of pregnancy, and invade maternal decidua in a manner reminiscent of a malignant neoplasm. However, this biologically unique and physiologically controlled invasion is essential for the establishment of normal placentation.

The most important types of non-villous trophoblast are the interstitial trophoblast cells, some of which fuse to form giant cells (Fig. 19.31), and the endovascular trophoblast, which invades maternal spiral arteries, destroying their muscular media and replacing it with a fibrinoid matrix. In this way, these vessels lose their elasticity and become of wide calibre to meet the growing nutritional demands of the developing feto-placental unit. The invasion of non-villous trophoblast occurs in two waves, the first wave occurring in the first weeks of pregnancy and the second between 14 and 16 weeks.

Pre-eclampsia and fetal intra-uterine growth retardation

Pre-eclampsia is a common syndrome of pregnancy characterised by maternal hypertension and proteinuria. It is potentially dangerous for both mother and fetus.

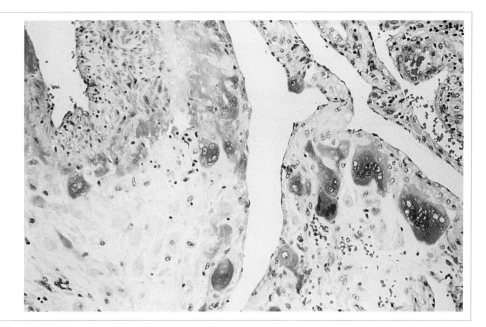

Fig. 19.31 Placental bed. Typical appearance showing interstitial trophoblast giant cells.

In pre-eclampsia, especially when associated with intra-uterine fetal growth retardation, there is a failure of the second wave of endovascular trophoblast migration into the myometrial segments of the spiral arteries. This may also occur in intra-uterine growth retardation uncomplicated by hypertension. Examination of the placental bed shows that the physiological changes mediated by endovascular trophoblast are confined to the intradecidual segments of the spiral arteries. The pathogenesis of pre-eclampsia is still uncertain; a toxic effect of oxygen free radicals and lipid peroxides on endothelial cells is implicated.

Acute atherosis

Acute atherosis is a necrotising lesion of the uterine spiral arteries characterised by infiltrates of foam cells. It occurs in the hypertensive disorders of pregnancy—pre-eclampsia and eclampsia—either alone or superimposed on other hypertensive disorders, such as renal disease.

Post-partum haemorrhage

There are three main causes of post-partum haemorrhage associated with significant histopathological findings:

- retained chorionic villi
- infection
- inadequate involution of placental bed vessels.

Retained chorionic villi are unusual after normal pregnancy, but are more common following miscarriage or termination of pregnancy. Normally, after parturition, the myometrial segments of the uteroplacental spiral arteries are left behind, and rapidly undergo thrombosis to prevent torrential haemorrhage. Other involutionary changes then take place, and over the course of a few weeks the vessels resume their non-pregnant appearance. However, in a substantial number of cases of post-partum haemorrhage, the vessels are seen to be still distended and only partially thrombosed, so-called *inadequate involution* (Fig. 19.32).

The control mechanisms of normal involution and the causes of its failure are unknown.

ECTOPIC PREGNANCY

▸ Pregnancy outside uterine cavity
▸ Fallopian tube is commonest site
▸ Leads to pain and haemorrhage when it ruptures
▸ Pregnancy-associated changes in endometrium

An ectopic pregnancy is the occurrence of pregnancy outside the uterine cavity; its incidence is increasing. The incidence of ectopic pregnancy in the UK is 10–12 per 1000 pregnancies; 65% of cases occur in the 25–34-year age range. After one ectopic pregnancy the risk of recurrence is 10–20%. By far the commonest site of ectopic pregnancy is the fallopian tube (Fig. 19.33); the ovary is a much rarer site. Occasionally, there is evidence of a fallopian tube abnormality such as chronic inflammation. The apparently increasing incidence of ectopic pregnancy may be related to increasing tubal infection. In most cases, however, there is no obvious cause, and a functional defect in tubal transport is assumed. Whether the presence of an intra-uterine device leads to a real increased risk of ectopic pregnancy is controversial.

The presenting symptoms are due to the physical expansion of the developing pregnancy within the limited space of the tube. Thus pain, with or without rupture, and haemoperitoneum are the commonest presenting features. In most cases, the pregnancy and fetus per se are not abnormal, and the same physiological changes associated with implantation can be seen in the fallopian tube as are seen in the uterus. The finding of pregnancy-associated changes in the endometrium (Arias-Stella phenomenon) in the absence of trophoblast or a fetus should always alert the pathologist to the possibility of an ectopic pregnancy.

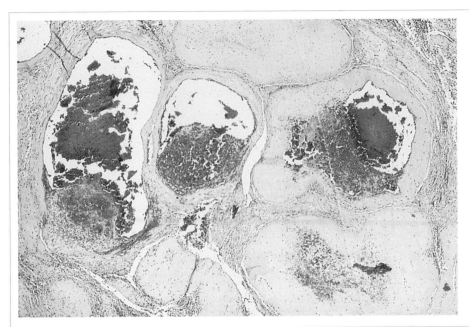

Fig. 19.32 Inadequate involution of placental bed vessels. Widely patent, only partially thrombosed uteroplacental (spiral) arteries in a case of post-partum haemorrhage.

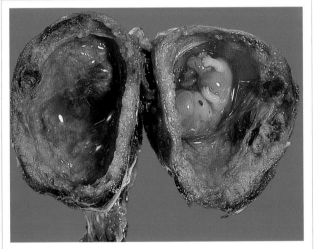

Fig. 19.33 A tubal ectopic pregnancy.

MATERNAL DEATH

The maternal mortality rate in the UK is 11 per 100 000 live births. There are, however, widespread and huge international variations in maternal mortality; for example, in Africa, the maternal mortality rate averages 910 per 100 000 live births. The main causes of direct maternal death are:

- thrombosis and thrombo-embolism (including amniotic fluid embolism)
- hypertensive disorders of pregnancy
- haemorrhage.

Early pregnancy deaths are usually due to ectopic pregnancy and abortion, which includes rare cases of legal termination of pregnancy and spontaneous miscarriage. Other causes of maternal mortality include anaesthetic-related deaths, uterine rupture and genital tract sepsis.

Commonly confused conditions and entities relating to female genital pathology	
Commonly confused	**Distinction and explanation**
Moles and *hydatidiform moles*	The pathological term *mole* (Latin: moles = mass) is used for the common melanocytic naevus or mole occurring in skin. However, a *hydatidiform mole* is a placental lesion characterised by swollen chorionic villi and trophoblastic hyperplasia.
Dyskaryosis and *dysplasia*	*Dyskaryosis* is a term used for nuclear abnormalities (e.g. enlargement, hyperchromasia) in cervical cytology, and can be categorised into mild, moderate or severe according to the degree of abnormality. *Dysplasia* is disordered differentiation and is seen in histological sections of cervical epithelium as loss of stratified structure; dysplasia and carcinoma in situ are merged into 'cervical intra-epithelial neoplasia (CIN)'. A cervical cytology specimen from a woman with CIN will show dyskaryosis.
Adenomyosis and *endometriosis*	*Adenomyosis* refers to the presence of endometrial glands and stroma in the myometrium, in continuity with the endometrium. In contrast, *endometriosis* is the presence of endometrial glands and stroma outside the body of the uterus, discontinuous with the endometrium.
Benign, borderline and *malignant ovarian tumours*	*Benign* and *malignant* tumours are, by definition, non-invasive and invasive, respectively. In the ovary, a third category of *borderline* tumour is recognised; these lesions exhibit some features commonly seen in malignant tumours (e.g. pleomorphism, mitotic activity) but lack invasion. Their behaviour is intermediate between that of benign and malignant tumours.

FURTHER READING

Bosch F X, Castellsagué X, de Sanjosé S 2008 HPV and cervical cancer: screening or vaccination? British Journal of Cancer 98: 15–21

Fox H, Wells M 2003 Haines and Taylor: Obstetrical and gynaecological pathology, 5th edn. Churchill Livingstone, Edinburgh

Wells M 2004 Recent advances in endometriosis with emphasis on pathogenesis, molecular pathology, and neoplastic transformation. International Journal of Gynecological Pathology 23: 316–320

Wells M 2007 The pathology of gestational trophoblastic disease: recent advances. Pathology 39: 88–96

Wells M, Östör A G, Crum C P et al 2003 Epithelial tumours and related lesions of the uterine cervix. Tumours of the uterine cervix. In: Tumours of the breast and female genital tract. World Health Organization, Geneva

Mutter G L (a website devoted to endometrial hyperplasia and endometrial cancer): http://www.endometrium.org.

20

Urinary and male genital tracts

COMMON CLINICAL PROBLEMS FROM DISEASES OF THE URINARY AND MALE GENITAL TRACTS

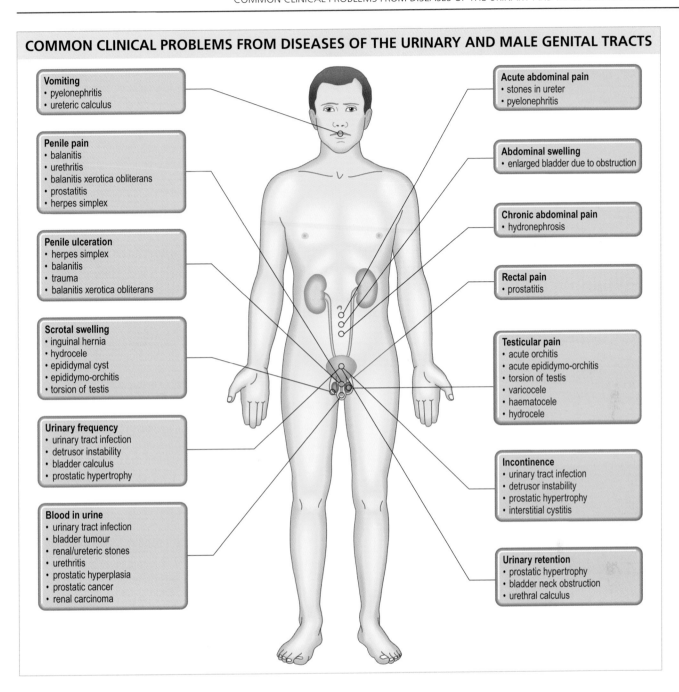

Vomiting
- pyelonephritis
- ureteric calculus

Penile pain
- balanitis
- urethritis
- balanitis xerotica obliterans
- prostatitis
- herpes simplex

Penile ulceration
- herpes simplex
- balanitis
- trauma
- balanitis xerotica obliterans

Scrotal swelling
- inguinal hernia
- hydrocele
- epididymal cyst
- epididymo-orchitis
- torsion of testis

Urinary frequency
- urinary tract infection
- detrusor instability
- bladder calculus
- prostatic hypertrophy

Blood in urine
- urinary tract infection
- bladder tumour
- renal/ureteric stones
- urethritis
- prostatic hyperplasia
- prostatic cancer
- renal carcinoma

Acute abdominal pain
- stones in ureter
- pyelonephritis

Abdominal swelling
- enlarged bladder due to obstruction

Chronic abdominal pain
- hydronephrosis

Rectal pain
- prostatitis

Testicular pain
- acute orchitis
- acute epididymo-orchitis
- torsion of testis
- varicocele
- haematocele
- hydrocele

Incontinence
- urinary tract infection
- detrusor instability
- prostatic hypertrophy
- interstitial cystitis

Urinary retention
- prostatic hypertrophy
- bladder neck obstruction
- urethral calculus

Pathological basis of clinical signs and symptoms in the urinary and male genital tracts	
Sign or symptom	Pathological basis
Abnormal micturition	
• Dysuria (pain)	Inflammation of the urethra, often accompanying a urinary tract infection
• Hesitation, poor stream and dribbling	Obstructed urinary outflow, usually due to prostate gland enlargement
• Frequency	Incomplete bladder emptying due to obstructed urinary outflow
• Urinary retention	Severe obstruction to bladder outflow, usually due to prostate gland enlargement
Urethral discharge	Urethritis, possibly due to sexually transmitted infections (e.g. gonorrhoea)

(Continued)

Pathological basis of clinical signs and symptoms in the male genital tracts—cont'd	
Sign or symptom	Pathological basis
Scrotal swelling	
• Painful	Inflammation or ischaemia of the testis
• Painless	Enlargement of scrotal contents due to hernia, fluid (e.g. hydrocele), varicocele or tumour
Genital ulceration	Often sexually transmitted infection (e.g. syphilis)
Bone pain	If associated with male genital tract disease, possibly due to metastases from prostatic adenocarcinoma
Raised serum prostate specific antigen	Secreted by prostatic carcinoma
Raised serum alpha-fetoprotein and/or human chorionic gonadotrophin	Testicular germ cell neoplasia, particularly teratoma/non-seminomatous germ cell tumour
Gynaecomastia	Possible manifestation of Leydig cell or germ cell tumour of testis
Infertility	Impaired spermatogenesis due to endocrine disorders or to testicular lesions, or impaired ejaculation due to obstruction or to neurological disorders

Fig. 20.1 'Staghorn' calculus. The shape of the stone is moulded to that of the pelvis and calyceal system in which it has formed.

URINARY CALCULI

Urinary calculi (stones) occur in 1–5% of the population in the UK, mainly those aged over 30 years, and with a male preponderance. They may form anywhere in the urinary tract, but the commonest site is within the renal pelvis. They present as:

- renal colic, an exquisitely painful symptom due to the passage of a small stone along the ureter
- a dull ache in the loins
- recurrent and intractable urinary tract infection.

Calculi form in the urine either because substances are in such an excess that they precipitate, or because other factors affecting solubility are upset. Factors influencing stone formation include the pH of the urine, which can be influenced by both bacterial activity and metabolic factors. Substances in the urine normally inhibit precipitation of crystals, notably pyrophosphates and citrates. The mucoproteins in the urine are thought to provide the organic nidus on which the crystals focus.

Calculi are classified according to their composition. The categories are:

- calcium oxalate, often mixed with calcium phosphate and uric acid (75–80% of all calculi)
- triple (struvite) stones composed of magnesium ammonium phosphate (15%); these form the large 'staghorn' calculi (Fig. 20.1)
- uric acid stones (6%)
- calculi in cystinuria and oxalosis (1%).

Only 10% of patients with *calcium-containing stones* have hyperparathyroidism or some other cause of hypercalcaemia. However, most have increased levels of calcium in the urine, attributable to a defect in the tubular reabsorption. In the remaining patients, with idiopathic hypercalciuria, no known cause has been identified. The association of uric acid with calcium stones is probably because urates can initiate precipitation of oxalate from solution.

Magnesium ammonium phosphate stones are particularly associated with urinary tract infections with bacteria, such as *Proteus*, that are able to break down urea to form ammonia. The alkaline conditions thus produced, together with sluggish flow, cause precipitation of these salts, and large staghorn calculi form a cast of the pelvicalyceal system. Staghorn calculi remain in the pelvis for many years and may cause irritation, with subsequent squamous metaplasia or, in some cases, squamous carcinoma.

Uric acid stones occur in patients with gout (Ch. 7). Uric acid precipitates in acid urine. The stones are radiolucent.

RENAL TUMOURS

▶ Renal cell carcinoma is the only common renal tumour. It presents with haematuria. Cigarette smoking, obesity and rare inherited disorders (such as von Hippel–Lindau disease) are the main risk factors

▶ Nephroblastoma (Wilms' tumour) is an uncommon tumour of childhood showing embryonal cell differentiation. Modern therapy has produced 5-year survival rates of over 80% despite a biologically aggressive behaviour

RENAL CELL CARCINOMA

Incidence

Renal cell carcinoma arises from epithelial cells in the kidney. About 7400 new cases a year are diagnosed in the UK, 3% of all cancers, with around 4000 deaths a year. The incidence in the UK is gradually increasing but this may be due to higher detection rates by improved imaging techniques. There is a male:female ratio of 3:2. Renal cell carcinoma is rare before the age of 40 years and the peak incidence occurs between the ages of 65 and 80 years.

Predisposing factors

Tobacco smoking, obesity, radiation and acquired renal cystic disease are the main environmental risks for renal cell carcinoma. On average, current smokers have a 50% increased risk and about 25% of all renal cell carcinoma cases can be attributed to smoking. Renal cell cancer risk increases by 7% for each unit increase in body mass index, and overall the obesity risk accounts for about 25% of cases. The radiation risk is usually acquired through treatment of other cancers such as cervical and testicular cancer. Acquired cystic kidney disease, commonly seen in patients with renal failure on dialysis, results in a three- to four-fold increased risk of renal cell cancer.

Most cases of renal cell cancer are sporadic but there are some rare inherited disorders that predispose to development of this tumour. The most illustrative is von Hippel–Lindau (VHL) disease where there are mutations in the *VHL* gene, which normally produces a protein responsible for degrading proteins of the hypoxia-inducible factor (HIF) family. In the

absence of this functioning protein there is accumulation of the HIF family of proteins, which in turn results in increased transcription of hypoxia-associated genes which promote cell growth, survival and angiogenesis. In VHL disease the risk of developing renal cell cancer is 70% by the age of 60 years with multiple and bilateral tumours; these patients are also at risk of epididymal, cerebral and other tumours (Ch. 26). The largest subgroup of sporadic renal cell carcinoma (clear cell carcinoma) has loss of expression of the *VHL* gene.

Presentation

Some 50% of renal cell cancers present with haematuria as the tumour invades and bleeds into the renal collecting system. Other presentations may be due to distant effects of the tumour—polycythaemia due to tumour production of erythropoietin, or hypercalcaemia due to lytic bone metastases. A substantial proportion of cases are identified almost incidentally by ultrasonography or computed tomography while investigating a wide range of non-specific symptoms. This results in the diagnosis of many small tumours amenable to curative treatment, often conserving the rest of the kidney.

Appearances

Macroscopically, the kidney is distorted by a large tumour, found most often at the upper pole (Fig. 20.2). The cut surface reveals a solid yellowish-grey tumour with areas of haemorrhage and necrosis. The margins of the tumour are usually well demarcated, but some breach the renal capsule and invade the perinephric fat. Extension into the renal vein is sometimes seen grossly; occasionally, a solid mass of tumour extends into the inferior vena cava and, rarely, into the right atrium.

Microscopically there are distinctive different tumours with very different cytogenetic abnormalities (and by inference differing pathogenesis). Clear cell (conventional) renal cell carcinoma has *VHL* gene abnormalities and is the largest group. Next is papillary renal cell carcinoma which has trisomies of chromosomes 7 and 17; this has papillary structures lined by cuboidal cells and is the variant associated with acquired cystic disease in renal failure. The third largest group is chromophobe renal

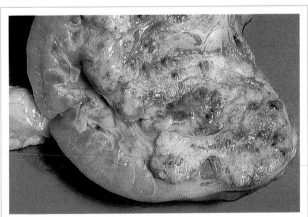
Fig. 20.2 Renal cell carcinoma (hypernephroma). Renal cell carcinoma (hypernephroma).

cell carcinoma, which has large eosinophilic cells often similar to renal oncocytoma, a benign tumour.

Prognosis and treatment

Current overall 5-year survival rates in the UK are 50%. Prognosis worsens with increased stage (5-year survival rate of 10% for those with metastatic disease at presentation, but of 90% for early-stage disease) and increased age at presentation. Treatment is primarily by surgical excision, which is usually a complete nephrectomy. However, partial nephrectomy or local oblation by cryosurgery or other means is often done and conserves renal capacity. If the disease is metastatic there may still be some benefit in removing the primary tumour for control of local symptoms such as loin pain and haematuria. Renal cell carcinoma is not sensitive to conventional chemotherapy but there may be some response with interferon or newer oral tyrosine kinase inhibitors such as sunitinib.

NEPHROBLASTOMA

Nephroblastoma (*Wilms' tumour*) is a kidney tumour derived from embryonal tissue. It is rare, with 45 cases per year in the UK, and has a peak incidence between the ages of 1 and 4 years. Although it is usually biologically aggressive, often with lung metastases at presentation, combined chemoradiotherapy and

Fig. 20.3 Carcinoma of the renal pelvis. These malignant tumours arise from the transitional cell epithelium (urothelium) lining the renal pelvis. These patients commonly develop synchronous or metachronous urothelial tumours elsewhere in the ureters or bladder.

surgery has improved the 5-year survival rate from 35% in the 1970s to over 80% at present. The Wilms' tumour gene (*WT1*) has long been known to be abnormal in nephroblastoma, but the molecular mechanisms of this have still not been coherently elucidated.

CARCINOMA OF THE RENAL PELVIS

The renal pelvis is lined by transitional cell epithelium and so transitional cell carcinomas can arise at this site, accounting for 5–10% of all renal tumours. As they project into the pelvicalyceal cavity, they present early with haematuria or obstruction (Fig. 20.3). Their risk factors, histology and treatment are similar to those for transitional cell carcinomas of the ureters and bladder described below.

BENIGN RENAL TUMOURS

Renal oncoctyoma is composed of large eosinophilic cells, sometimes difficult to distinguish from renal cell carcinoma. Its imaging features also overlap with those of renal cell carcinoma, so, even though benign, is it usually diagnosed after surgical removal.

Angiomyolipoma typically has a combination of abnormal blood vessels, smooth muscle and adipose tissue. This gives it a characteristic radiological appearance, so small masses need not be resected; however, large masses have a risk of spontaneous haemorrhage. Some 20% of cases arise in patients with tuberous sclerosis complex, an inherited disorder involving the central nervous system, skin and other viscera.

URETERS

NORMAL STRUCTURE AND FUNCTION

The ureters form in continuity with the calyceal system and collecting ducts from an outgrowth of the Wolffian duct. Urine is conveyed to the bladder by peristaltic activity; this activity is reduced in pregnancy, predisposing to stasis and infection.

The lumen is lined by urothelium; the muscle layer is predominantly circular with a thin, inner longitudinal layer, and is invested in a fibrous adventitia. The ureteric orifice is slit-like, and the course of the terminal part of the ureter through the bladder wall is oblique to form a valve (see Fig. 21.14B, p. 591).

CONGENITAL LESIONS

A congenitally short terminal segment of the ureter, which is not oblique, results in vesico-ureteric reflux, an important cause of renal infection and scarring. *Hydroureter* is dilatation and often tortuosity of the ureter; this condition may occur as a congenital lesion, when it is thought to reflect a neuromuscular defect. The most frequent causes of hydroureter in the adult are low urinary obstruction and pregnancy.

OBSTRUCTION

Obstruction of the ureter is the most frequent problem requiring clinical attention. Acute ureteric obstruction causes intense pain known as renal colic. The consequences of chronic ureteric obstruction are hydroureter and hydronephrosis. In both acute and chronic ureteric obstruction there is an increased risk of ascending infection, causing pyelonephritis. Ureteric obstruction may be either intrinsic or extrinsic.

Intrinsic lesions are within the ureteric wall or lumen; the most common is a urinary calculus. Calculi become impacted where the ureter is normally narrowed, that is at the pelvi-ureteric junction, where it crosses the iliac artery, and where it enters the bladder. Strictures may be congenital, when they occur at the pelvi-ureteric junction or in the transmural terminal segment of the ureter. Acquired strictures occur as a result of trauma and involvement by adjacent inflammatory conditions such as diverticulitis and salpingitis. Severe haematuria may cause obstruction due to blood clot.

Extrinsic factors cause pressure from without, and include primary tumours of the bladder and rectum, metastatic carcinoma in pelvic lymph nodes and benign hyperplasia of the prostate. Aberrant renal arteries may compress the ureter. Retroperitoneal fibrosis causes narrowing and medial deviation of the ureters and may either be due to drugs, such as methysergide, or be idiopathic.

Primary tumours of the ureter are transitional cell carcinomas. They may be multiple and are associated with urothelial tumours in the renal pelvis and bladder.

BLADDER

NORMAL STRUCTURE AND FUNCTION

The urinary bladder is a cavity lined by transitional cell epithelium—the urothelium, surrounded by connective tissue—the lamina propria, and smooth muscle. Histologically, the normal bladder urothelium is seven to eight cells thick and has three zones: basal, intermediate and a surface layer of umbrella cells. The smooth muscle is arranged in bundles that interlace rather than form defined layers. Urine drains into the bladder from the kidneys, via the ureters, for storage until a convenient time and place is found for its discharge through the urethra. The bladder responds to obstruction to the outflow by undergoing muscular hypertrophy. The proximity of the bladder to the genital tract in females, to the prostate in males, and to the bowel in both sexes, means that it is often invaded by tumours arising in, or affected by other changes in, these nearby organs.

DIVERTICULA

Diverticula are outpouchings of the bladder mucosa. Bladder diverticula are either congenital or acquired. They are clinically important because urinary stasis within them predisposes to calculus formation and infection.

Congenital diverticula are usually solitary. They arise from either a localised developmental defect in the muscle or urinary obstruction during fetal life.

Acquired diverticula are small and multiple. They are most often associated with outflow obstruction, and the high incidence in elderly males correlates with prostatic enlargement. They occur between the bands of hypertrophic muscle, known as trabeculae, which form in response to obstruction.

CONGENITAL LESIONS

Exstrophy of the bladder is a serious developmental defect affecting the anterior abdominal wall, bladder and, in some cases, the symphysis pubis. The bladder opens directly on to the external surface of the lower abdomen. Infection and pyelonephritis, together with a predisposition to adenocarcinoma, are important sequelae.

Vesico-ureteric reflux (VUR) is an important consequence of a developmental abnormality of the terminal part of the ureter that appears to correct itself as the patient matures. However, during early childhood reflux occurs, which results in substantial scarring of the renal parenchyma. This condition is an important cause of renal impairment and infection in adult life.

Persistence of the urachus may be partial or complete. Retention of the entire structure results in a fistula connecting the bladder with the skin at the umbilicus. Partial retention results in a diverticulum arising from the dome of the bladder. Alternatively the central area may persist and present as a cyst. Adenocarcinomas may develop in these urachal remnants.

CYSTITIS

Inflammation of the bladder (cystitis) is a common occurrence as part of a urinary tract infection. The causative organism is usually derived from the patient's faecal flora. Unusual organisms do occur; for example, *Candida* is seen in patients on prolonged antibiotic therapy, and tuberculous cystitis almost always reflects tuberculosis elsewhere in the urinary tract. Radiation and trauma due to instrumentation cause cystitis, which is often sterile.

Cystitis presents with frequency, lower abdominal pain and dysuria (scalding or burning pain on micturition), and occasionally haematuria. In some patients there is general malaise and pyrexia. Cystitis usually responds readily to treatment. However, its clinical importance lies in the predisposition to pyelonephritis, a serious complication.

Schistosomiasis causes a granulomatous cystitis, in which the parasite ova are demonstrable; it is notable for the increased risk of squamous cell carcinoma.

BLADDER CALCULI

Diverticula, obstruction and inflammation are all important in the development of stones within the bladder. Alternatively, calculi may be passed down the ureter from the kidney. Bladder stones may be asymptomatic, but eventual chronic irritation and infection lead to frequency, urgency, dysuria and sometimes haematuria. There is an increased risk of bladder carcinoma; this is often of squamous type, arising from metaplastic squamous epithelium.

FISTULAE

Fistulae between the bladder and adjacent structures occur as a result of:

- invasion by a malignant neoplasm
- radiation necrosis
- inflammatory bowel lesions (diverticulitis of the colon, Crohn's disease)
- surgical complications
- obstetric trauma.

TUMOURS OF THE BLADDER

- ▶ In Europe and North America, transitional cell carcinoma of the bladder accounts for 90% of bladder tumours
- ▶ Risk factors include cigarette smoking and exposure to chemicals such as aromatic amines and polycyclic aromatic hydrocarbons
- ▶ Most transitional cell carcinomas are superficial and can be treated by cystoscopic resection
- ▶ There is often a field change of dysplasia in the bladder of people with transitional cell carcinoma, so they require follow-up to detect and treat future tumours
- ▶ In countries with endemic schistosomiasis, squamous cell carcinoma of the bladder is common

TRANSITIONAL (UROTHELIAL) CELL CARCINOMA OF THE BLADDER

Incidence

Transitional cell carcinoma accounts for 90% of bladder cancer in North America and Europe. In the UK about 10 500 new cases are diagnosed each year, 4% of all cancers, with around 5000 deaths a year. The incidence in the UK is gradually decreasing from a peak in the early 1990s. There is a male: female ratio of 5:2. Transitional cell bladder cancer is rare before the age of 50 years and the peak incidence occurs between the ages of 70 and 80 years.

Predisposing factors

Tobacco smoking and occupational exposures are the main environmental risks for transitional cell bladder cancer. On average, current smokers have a 300% increased risk and about 50% of all transitional cell bladder cancers can be attributed to smoking. This risk is due to the absorption of aromatic amines from cigarette smoke and their excretion in the urine. Aromatic amines have historically been present in industrial processes used to produce dyes, drugs and rubber, and a significant amount of bladder cancer could be

attributed to industrial exposure to these chemicals. Most of these compounds were withdrawn from these processes in the 1950s, but there was a lag phase of new cancers developing from this exposure. Exposure to polycyclic aromatic hydrocarbons is a risk factor and these by-products of combustion are present in many industrial processes. It is estimated that 4% of European bladder cancer cases are due to this exposure, and this effect might be higher in countries with less regulated industries.

Genetic risk factors fall into two groups: genetic deficiencies of enzymes that would otherwise metabolise chemicals that are risk factors for bladder cancer (e.g. *N*-acetyl transferase), and genetic alterations in the tumours themselves. Although an oversimplification, there are two distinct genetic patterns in urothelial carcinoma. *Papillary superficial tumours* have relatively few and stable abnormalities. In contrast, *solid invasive tumours* have different alterations and tend to accumulate multiple abnormalities as they progress. However, molecular or genetic testing is not yet sufficient for diagnosis or follow-up.

Presentation

Some 80% of transitional cell bladder cancers present with painless haematuria. Other presenting symptoms may include urinary frequency and pain on micturition.

Appearances

At presentation most bladder tumours are low-grade and papillary, with fronds lined by a slightly thickened urothelium showing little cytological abnormality (Fig. 20.4). Usually there is no invasion of the lamina propria. Papillary tumours are frequently multiple, consistent with a widespread field change throughout the urothelium including the upper tract, even though it is histologically normal.

In contrast, about 20% of tumours are solid and invasive at presentation extending into the detrusor muscle, and if beyond they render the tumour fixed clinically. These tumours are high grade with marked cytological abnormalities; aberrant squamous or adenocarcinoma differentiation may be seen, and there are other histological variants too. The background urothelium often shows carcinoma in situ, which is considered to be the precursor lesion, and may give rise to further high-grade invasive tumours.

Between these two extremes of tumour type there are some high-grade papillary tumours; these may have background carcinoma in situ, and are more likely to progress to invasive carcinoma.

Prognosis and treatment

Prognosis is closely related to the stage of the tumour. Superficial tumours (without muscle invasion) can be removed by transurethral resection and have an excellent prognosis. These patients are likely to have a field change and so require regular follow-up cystoscopy as about 70% of patients will develop further tumours. Progression to more invasive tumours occurs in around 20% of patients. Intra-vesical treatment with BCG or chemotherapy can be used for multiple superficial tumours or carcinoma in situ. Tumours which have invaded muscle

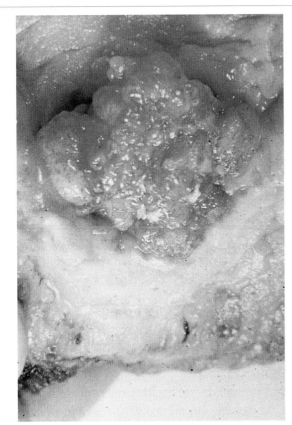

Fig. 20.4 Transitional cell carcinoma of the bladder. These common tumours usually project into the bladder lumen before invading the underlying bladder wall.

require more intensive therapy. A radical cystectomy will remove the tumour and all the dysplastic bladder epithelium but it is a large operation which results in the patient having an ileal bladder, either isotopic or with a stoma. Radiotherapy is another possible treatment modality.

SQUAMOUS CELL CARCINOMA OF THE BLADDER

As the bladder is normally lined by transitional epithelium, squamous cell carcinoma can arise only from metaplastic squamous epithelium in the bladder. This metaplasia commonly occurs with chronic infection with schistosome parasites. In countries where schistosomiasis is endemic, such as Egypt, squamous cell bladder cancer is the most common tumour in men, presenting in the fifth decade, usually at a more advanced tumour stage with corresponding worse prognosis. Long-term catheterisation following paraplegia carries similar risks.

ADENOCARCINOMA OF THE BLADDER

Adenocarcinoma of the bladder is uncommon. It can arise from:

- urachal remnants at the bladder apex

- cystitis glandularis
- glandular metaplasia in a transitional carcinoma.

PROSTATE GLAND

NORMAL STRUCTURE AND FUNCTION

The prostate gland surrounds the bladder neck and proximal urethra (Fig. 20.5). It consists of five lobes, separated by the urethra and ejaculatory ducts. Two lateral lobes and an anterior lobe enclose the urethra. The two lateral lobes are marked by a posterior midline groove, palpable on rectal examination. The middle lobe lies between the urethra and ejaculatory ducts and the posterior lobe lies behind the ejaculatory ducts. The normal gland weighs about 20 g and is enclosed in a fibrous capsule.

From a pathology perspective, it is more useful to divide the prostate into zones. In early adult life the peripheral zone accounts for 70% of the organ, the transition zone (both sides of the proximal urethra) 5% and the central zone 20%. Prostate cancers arise almost exclusively from the peripheral zone. The transition zone gradually enlarges with age, and is the site of considerable enlargement in benign prostatic hyperplasia. Concentric groups of glands in all zones converge on ducts and open in the urethra.

Individual glandular acini have a convoluted outline, the epithelium varying from cuboidal to a pseudostratified columnar cell type depending upon the degree of activity of the prostate and androgenic stimulation. The epithelial cells produce *prostate-specific antigen* (PSA), acid phosphatase and the prostatic secretion that forms a large proportion of the seminal fluid for the transport of sperm. The normal gland acini often contain rounded concretions of inspissated secretions (corpora amylacea). The acini are surrounded by a stroma of fibrous tissue and smooth muscle.

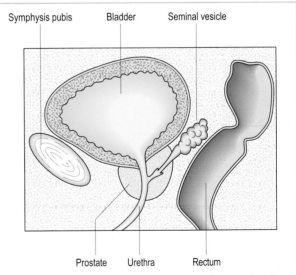

Fig. 20.5 Male pelvic organs. Sagittal section showing that the prostate can be palpated easily by inserting a finger into the rectum.

The blood supply to the prostate gland is from the internal iliac artery by the inferior vesical and middle rectal branches. The prostatic veins drain to the prostatic plexus around the gland and then to the internal iliac veins. The nerves are from the pelvic plexus.

INCIDENCE OF PROSTATIC DISEASE

Diseases of the prostate are common causes of urinary problems in men, the incidence of which increases with age, particularly beyond 60 years. Most prostatic diseases cause enlargement of the organ resulting in compression of the intraprostatic portion of the urethra; this leads to impaired urine flow, an increased risk of urinary infections, and, in some cases, acute retention of urine requiring urgent relief by catheterisation. The most important and common causes of these signs and symptoms are prostatic hyperplasia and prostatic carcinoma. Inflammation of the prostate gland—prostatitis—is also common, but it less often gives rise to serious clinical problems; indeed, small foci of prostatic inflammation are not uncommon coincidental findings in prostatic tissue removed because of hyperplasia or carcinoma.

The principal clinicopathological features of the common types of prostatic pathology are compared in Table 20.1.

PROSTATITIS

Prostatitis means inflammation of the prostate; however, it is a confusing subject because of the substantial lack of correlation between the clinical symptoms, detection of neutrophils in prostatic secretions and an inflammatory infiltrate in histological samples. A causative organism is found in only 5–10% of cases; symptoms overlap with those of benign prostatic hyperplasia. The US National Institutes of Health (NIH) has published a consensus categorisation of prostatitis, and also a chronic prostatitis symptom index to tighten up clinical diagnosis:

- Category I: Acute bacterial prostatitis
- Category II: Chronic bacterial prostatitis
- Category III: Chronic pelvic pain syndrome
  — A Inflammatory
  — B Non-inflammatory
- Category IV: Asymptomatic inflammatory prostatitis.

In addition, there are patients with granulomatous inflammation of the prostate.

Category I: Acute bacterial prostatitis

Patients will be ill and febrile, and have difficulty with voiding, dysuria, frequency and urgency. On palpation the prostate is firm, indurated and tender. The usual cause is *Escherichia coli*, and infection may follow instrumentation. The glands and adjacent stroma show neutrophil infiltration, which may progress to an abscess.

Category II: Chronic bacterial prostatitis

This may follow inadequately treated acute prostatitis; the symptoms are similar, though the patients are not so ill. The causative organism can be cultured from appropriate specimens.

Category III: Chronic pelvic pain syndrome

The presence or absence of neutrophils in specimens distinguishes the subtypes. Symptoms may relate to urination or there may be pain on ejaculation. No organisms can be cultured by usual methods, so the causes are uncertain. However, bacterial DNA has been detected in patients, and some respond to prolonged antibiotic treatment, so infection by novel pathogens is a plausible cause.

Category IV: Asymptomatic inflammatory prostatitis

Though patients have no symptoms, leukocytes or bacteria are identified from investigations. About 70% of biopsies taken for the investigation of possible cancer show an inflammatory cell infiltrate at least focally.

Granulomatous prostatitis

Granulomatous prostatitis is a heterogeneous group of lesions, all of which may cause enlargement of the gland and urethral obstruction. The inflammatory component and associated fibrosis produce a firm, indurated gland on rectal examination which may mimic a neoplasm clinically, thus highlighting the importance of correctly diagnosing this uncommon group of conditions.

Table 20.1 Differences between the three most common types of prostate pathology					
Condition	Incidence	Location in gland	Morphology	Serum prostate-specific antigen	Metastases
Prostatitis	Common, particularly asymptomatic	Any site	Inflammatory infiltrate	Slight to moderate elevation	Not applicable
Benign prostatic hyperplasia	75% of men over 70 years	Peri-urethral transition zone	Nodular hyperplasia of glands and stroma	Slight to moderate elevation	Not applicable
Prostatic carcinoma	Commonest male cancer, peak 60–75 years	Peripheral zone	Infiltrating adenocarcinoma	Slight to gross elevation (depends on stage). May be normal	Lymph nodes Bone Liver Lung

Idiopathic prostatitis may result from leakage of material from distended ducts in a gland enlarged by nodular hyperplasia. There is a periductal inflammatory infiltrate which includes macrophages, multinucleated giant cells, lymphocytes and plasma cells, with associated fibrosis.

The prostate is often involved in cases of genito-urinary *tuberculosis*. This condition is usually secondary to tuberculous cystitis or epididymitis, the infection spreading along the prostatic ducts or vas deferens. The histological features are of caseating granulomas distributed among the prostatic glands and through the stroma.

Some patients may require a second transurethral resection for benign nodular hyperplasia or carcinoma if the first operation fails to relieve the obstructive symptoms. The second biopsy often contains granulomas with necrosis; this lesion may be *ischaemic,* related to damaged blood vessels.

BENIGN PROSTATIC HYPERPLASIA

▶ A common non-neoplastic lesion
▶ Involves peri-urethral transition zone
▶ Nodular hyperplasia of glands and stroma
▶ Not premalignant

Benign prostatic hyperplasia (BPH) is the histological basis of a non-neoplastic enlargement of the prostate gland, benign prostatic enlargement (BPE), which occurs commonly and progressively after the age of 50 years. About 75% of men aged 70–80 years are affected and develop variable symptoms of urinary tract obstruction, benign prostatic obstruction (BPO). If severe and untreated, the hyperplasia may lead to recurrent urinary infections and, ultimately, impaired renal function.

Aetiology

The glands and stroma of the transition zone proliferate, sometimes substantially. The driver is dihydrotestosterone, which is derived from testosterone by the action of 5-alpha reductase, acting via testosterone receptors; after binding, the complex relocates to the nucleus to bind to DNA where it acts as a gene transcription regulator to promote growth, cell survival and other functions. The underlying cause is not known, but there is some evidence to suggest that persistent inflammation results in the secretion of growth-promoting cytokines. As well as the increased bulk of the prostate gland around the urethra, the smooth muscle tone, mediated via alpha-adrenergic receptors, may make a significant contribution to the symptoms. Although benign prostatic hyperplasia is not premalignant, there are some epigenetic abnormalities, particularly gene methylation, and the gene expression profile is different from normal.

Morphology

The hyperplastic process usually involves both lateral lobes of the gland. In addition, there may be a localised hyperplasia of peri-urethral glands posterior to the urethra and projecting into the bladder adjacent to the internal urethral meatus (Fig. 20.6). This hyperplasia is described as 'median' lobe enlargement but does not correspond to the anatomical middle lobe.

The cut surface of the enlarged prostate shows multiple circumscribed solid nodules and cysts (Fig. 20.7). Histological examination reveals two components: hyperplasia both of glands and of stroma. The acini are larger than normal (some may be cystic) and are lined by columnar epithelium covering papillary infoldings (Fig. 20.8). The acini may contain numerous corpora amylacea. Phosphates and oxalates may be deposited around these to form prostatic calculi.

The stromal hyperplasia includes both smooth muscle and fibrous tissue. Some of the nodules are solid, being composed predominantly of stroma, and others also contain hyperplastic acini. Stromal oedema and periductal inflammation are common and may contribute to the urinary obstruction. Areas of infarction commonly occur, evident as yellowish necrotic areas with a haemorrhagic margin; these may result from obstruction to the blood supply by the hyperplastic nodules. There is often squamous metaplasia of prostatic ducts and acini at the edges of the infarct. Benign nodular hyperplasia is not a premalignant lesion.

Clinical features

There are four main factors in the development of obstructive symptoms:

● The hyperplastic nodules compress and elongate the prostatic urethra, distorting its course.
● Involvement of the peri-urethral zone at the internal urethral meatus interferes with the sphincter mechanism.
● Contraction of hyperplastic smooth muscle in stroma.
● Inflammatory cell infiltration.

The resulting obstruction to the bladder outflow produces various lower urinary tract symptoms (LUTS), which can be grouped as bladder sensation symptoms, storage symptoms

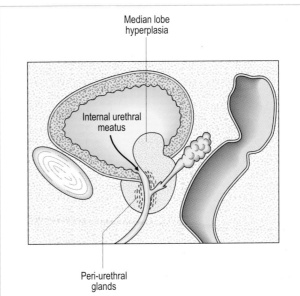

Fig. 20.6 Prostatic hyperplasia. Sagittal section showing the hyperplastic median lobe protruding into the bladder.

and voiding symptoms; these have been incorporated into an International Prostate Symptom Score. Bladder sensation may be normal, increased or decreased. Storage symptoms include daytime frequency, nocturia, urgency and incontinence. Voiding symptoms include hesitancy, poor or intermittent stream, straining and dribbling.

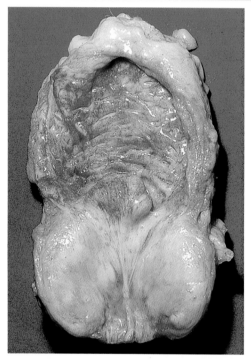

Fig. 20.7 Prostatic hyperplasia. The prostatic lobes are symmetrically enlarged and nodular. The bladder mucosa has a trabecular pattern due to hypertrophy of the underlying muscle bundles.

Digital examination of the gland per rectum reveals enlargement of the lateral lobes, often asymmetrical. The gland has a firm, rubbery consistency, and the median groove is still palpable.

Acute urinary retention may develop in a man with previous LUTS; the bladder is palpably enlarged and tender, requiring catheterisation. This condition may be precipitated by voluntarily withholding micturition for some time, by recent infarction causing sudden enlargement of a hyperplastic nodule, or by exacerbation of local inflammation.

Chronic retention of urine is relatively painless. There may be increasing frequency and overflow incontinence, usually at night. The bladder is distended, often palpable up to the umbilicus, but is not tender since the distension is more gradual.

Complications

Continued obstruction of the bladder outflow results in gradual *hypertrophy* of the bladder musculature. *Trabeculation* of the bladder wall develops due to prominent bands of thickened smooth muscle between which *diverticula* may protrude. This compensatory mechanism eventually fails, with resulting dilatation of the bladder. The ureters gradually dilate (*hydroureter*), allowing reflux of urine; if untreated, bilateral hydronephrosis may develop, with dilatation of renal pelvis and calyces (Fig. 20.9).

As the bladder fails to empty completely after micturition a small volume of urine remains in the bladder. This *residual urine* is liable to *infection,* usually by coliform organisms. The resulting cystitis is characterised by painful micturition with increased frequency and haematuria. An ascending infection in the presence of an obstructed urinary tract may result in *pyelonephritis* and *impaired renal function.* Repeated infections predispose to the development of *calculi,* often containing phosphates, within the bladder. *Septicaemia* may complicate pyelonephritis.

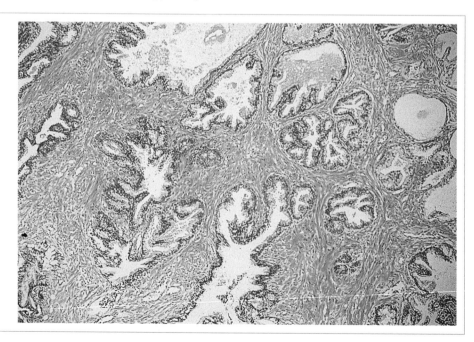

Fig. 20.8 Prostatic hyperplasia.
The acini are lined by columnar epithelium with numerous infoldings. The muscular stroma is abnormally abundant.

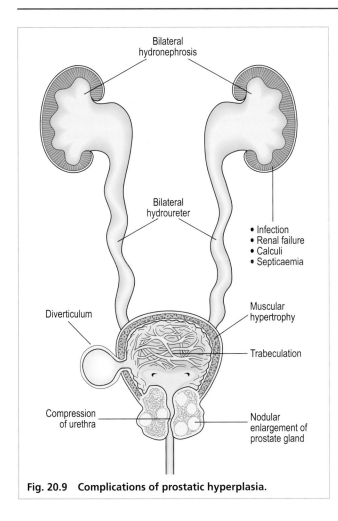

Fig. 20.9   Complications of prostatic hyperplasia.

Bilateral hydronephrosis

Bilateral hydroureter

- Infection
- Renal failure
- Calculi
- Septicaemia

Diverticulum

Muscular hypertrophy

Trabeculation

Compression of urethra

Nodular enlargement of prostate gland

interventions are the usual initial treatment, using alpha-adrenergic blockers (to reduce smooth muscle tone) or 5-alpha reductase inhibitors (to reduce dihydrotestosterone drive). Anti-inflammatory drugs and antibiotics may also be appropriate.

Some patients will require surgical intervention, typically transurethral resection of the hyperplastic prostate tissue. Multiple other methods of selective tissue destruction are possible including heat (using microwaves or other media), lasers, electromagnetic radiation and ultrasound.

IDIOPATHIC BLADDER NECK OBSTRUCTION

Idiopathic bladder neck obstruction, an uncommon obstructive lesion at the bladder outlet, usually occurs in young men. Its cause is unknown. A prominent transverse ridge develops at the internal urethral meatus, resulting from a localised hypertrophy of smooth muscle.

The clinical symptoms are similar to those of benign nodular hyperplasia. As the pathological lesion is very localised, the gland is not palpably enlarged on rectal examination. Treatment is by bladder neck incision.

PROSTATIC CARCINOMA

▶ Commonest cancer in men
▶ Adenocarcinoma occurring usually at >50 years of age
▶ Investigation and management of asymptomatic men is problematic
▶ Metastasises to lymph nodes and bone (osteosclerotic metastases)
▶ Many are hormone (androgen)-dependent

Clinical diagnosis and management

A careful history of LUTS in the usual basis for a diagnosis of benign prostatic hyperplasia.

Further investigation may include:

- microbiological examination of the urine to detect any infection requiring treatment
- blood urea, electrolytes and creatinine to assess renal function
- urinary tract ultrasonography to provide an assessment of the upper urinary tract, indicating the severity of obstruction; it may demonstrate an enlarged prostate as a filling defect in the bladder. Ultrasonography also provides an assessment of the quantity of residual urine after micturition
- cystoscopy to reveal median lobe enlargement not palpable on rectal examination
- histological examination of prostatic tissue removed either for diagnosis (i.e. biopsy) or to restore flow.

Serum PSA may be elevated in benign prostatic hyperplasia, but this is not usually used in the diagnosis or assessment of it, but rather as an explanation of elevated PSA after prostate cancer has been excluded.

Many patients will not be sufficiently troubled by their symptoms to request treatment. For those that are, pharmacological

Carcinoma of the prostate is one of the commonest forms of malignant disease and is the second leading cause of male death from malignancy in Europe and the USA. The UK incidence has increased during the last two decades to about 93 per 100 000 males, giving about 29 000 new cases, and 9000 deaths in 2005 in England (13% of male cancer deaths). The tumour is rare below 50 years of age; the peak incidence is between 65 and 75 years. From these data it is apparent that prostate cancer is a substantial burden of disease with many deaths, though many men are cured. However, there are also many people who require no treatment, who in retrospect have only the disadvantages and none of the benefits of making the diagnosis.

Aetiology

The aetiology of prostatic carcinoma is unknown, although a substantial proportion are dependent on androgens. Most tumours arise in the peripheral zone, though intriguingly this zone also undergoes some involution with advancing age. A family history of the disease is relevant: there is a two- to three-fold risk of the tumour developing in men with a first-degree relative in whom prostatic carcinoma was diagnosed at under 50 years of age. There is a three-fold risk for African or Caribbean men compared to whites; the risk in China and Japan is lower. Some dietary studies have shown possible associations, but these do not fully explain the racial difference.

The molecular genetic basis of prostate cancer is complex, and so far lacks clinical application. Benign prostatic hyperplasia is not considered a pre-neoplastic lesion although it is often found coincidentally in the same gland as a carcinoma, as both lesions are common. Operations for hyperplasia do not remove the peripheral zone, so carcinoma can arise after such a 'prostatectomy' (Fig. 20.10).

Pathology

There may be very little to see on macroscopic examination, particularly for organ-confined disease, though sometimes the tumour is slightly yellow. Locally advanced disease may be more obvious, with invasion of the seminal vesicles or bladder, or fixation to the pelvic wall.

The great majority of tumours are *adenocarcinoma*, often described as microacinar, though much variety of histological pattern is recognised, and the tumours often show more than one pattern. Rare subtypes include an aggressive small cell carcinoma, which is similar to small cell lung cancer (Ch. 14), and large duct carcinoma, which arises centrally from the large ducts; these are not discussed further.

The Gleason grading system describes the usual patterns taken by the tumour. Gleason pattern 3 is the commonest pattern, and comprises separated, somewhat irregular, gland or acinar profiles, that infiltrate into normal glands at the edge of the mass. Gleason pattern 4 has fused glands or cribriform structures (Fig. 20.11), while in pattern 5 acinar

differentiation is no longer apparent in strands of tumour cells, or there may be cribriform structures with central necrosis. It is now widely acknowledged that Gleason pattern 1 is probably not carcinoma, while pattern 2 is a generally small, well-circumscribed mass of regular glands; it is of limited clinical significance. The grading system is to note the dominant (primary) pattern and add the next most frequent (secondary) pattern to give a combined score; where only one pattern is seen (as often applies in a small biopsy) the number is doubled. Thus, the majority of prostate cancers are graded as Gleason 3+3=6; many are Gleason 3+4=7, while a particularly aggressive tumour would be Gleason 5+5=10.

Prostatic intra-epithelial neoplasia (PIN)
This is a common precursor lesion which may be present for many years before invasive carcinoma develops, if ever. Like carcinoma in situ at other sites, it comprises cytologically malignant cells confined within the ductal system, with no invasion of stroma. If PIN is discovered in a biopsy it is not yet clear what the management should be—whether to re-biopsy or when.

Mode of spread

Spread of prostatic carcinoma may be:

- *direct*—stromal invasion, prostatic capsule, urethra, bladder base, seminal vesicle
- *via lymphatics* to sacral, iliac and para-aortic nodes.
- *via blood* to bone (pelvis, lumbosacral spine, femur), lungs and liver.

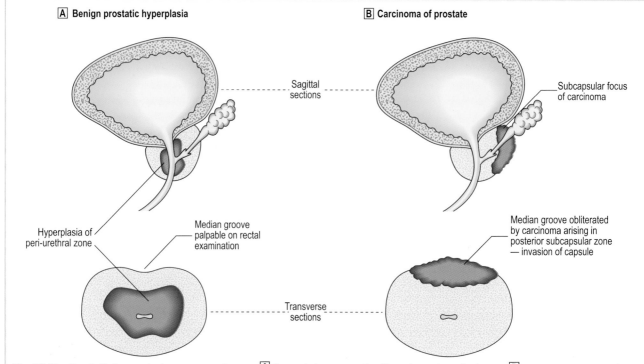

Fig. 20.10 Prostatic hyperplasia versus carcinoma. A Hyperplasia commonly affects the peri-urethral zone. **B** In contrast, most carcinomas are peripheral.

Direct spread

Direct spread of the prostatic tumour occurs both within the gland and to extracapsular adjacent structures. There is invasion of the prostatic stroma towards the peri-urethral tissues and the base of the bladder is also commonly involved. Extension through the prostatic capsule is common, involving the seminal vesicles. The rectal wall is rarely invaded, being protected by the recto-vesical fascia. This extracapsular invasion results in the prostate becoming fixed to adjacent tissues.

Spread via lymphatics

Lymphatics provide an important route of dissemination of prostatic carcinoma, producing metastases in the sacral, iliac and para-aortic nodes. These may result in lymphatic obstruction and oedema of the legs. Less often, the inguinal nodes are involved.

Spread via blood

Vascular invasion by the tumour results in blood-borne metastases, most commonly to bone, lungs and liver. The most frequent sites of bone metastases are the pelvis, lumbosacral spine and proximal femur, less frequently the ribs and skull. Tumour emboli may reach the vertebrae by venous spread to the lung, then by passing through the pulmonary capillaries to enter the arterial circulation. An alternative mechanism is by retrograde venous spread through the vertebral venous plexus, because the blood flow in these veins may reverse due to physiological variation in the intra-abdominal pressure.

Bone metastases are usually *osteosclerotic*, with proliferation of osteoblasts and areas of new bone formation occurring in association with the neoplastic cells (Fig. 20.12). The osteoblast proliferation results in a raised serum alkaline phosphatase level.

Clinical features

The clinical presentation and features of prostatic carcinoma include:

- urinary symptoms—difficulty or increased frequency of micturition, urinary retention
- rectal examination revealing hard craggy prostate
- bone metastases—presenting with pain, pathological fracture, anaemia
- lymph node metastases.

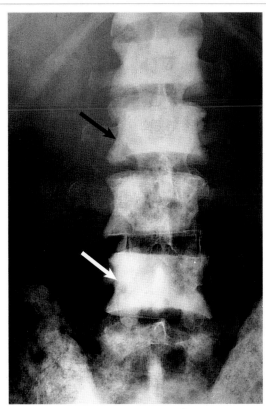

Fig. 20.12 Metastases from carcinoma of the prostate. X-ray of lumbar spine, including part of iliac bones, showing numerous sclerotic (white) metastases (arrowed).

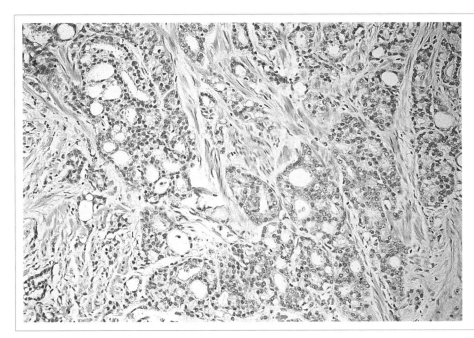

Fig. 20.11 Histology of prostatic carcinoma. The tumour is an adenocarcinoma consisting of neoplastic glands infiltrating a fibrous stroma.

Many men are unaware of their prostate cancer, or may have a tumour diagnosed and remain asymptomatic. This situation can last for years. Other men have a tumour that will progress and is potentially fatal.

Urinary outflow obstructive symptoms caused by prostatic carcinoma usually progress more rapidly than those due to benign hyperplasia.

Digital rectal examination is a very important clinical procedure, revealing a hard nodule of tumour in the posterior lobe; the induration is due to the fibrous stromal reaction to the adenocarcinoma cells. The gland may be enlarged. If capsular invasion has occurred, the capsule is irregular and the median groove is obliterated. Less often, the rectal mucosa is fixed to the prostate. Induration may, however, be due to a non-neoplastic lesion such as prostatic calculi or granulomatous prostatitis. With many small tumours there is no palpable abnormality. Many patients will have benign prostatic hyperplasia.

Bone metastases often present as *localised bone pain,* back pain from vertebral metastases being a common initial manifestation of the tumour. *Pathological fracture* is another clinical presentation. Anaemia may result from extensive neoplastic infiltration of several bones with replacement of haemopoietic tissue.

Finally, peripheral *lymphadenopathy* due to metastatic carcinoma is occasionally the initial presentation.

Diagnosis

There are four common ways to diagnose localised or non-metastatic prostate cancer:

- digital rectal examination
- serum prostate-specific antigen
- transrectal ultrasonography
- needle biopsy.

With symptomatic men, all four modalities are likely to be used. With or without a palpable abnormality it will be usual to take blood for prostate-specific antigen (PSA) estimation. If this is elevated the patient will be offered needle biopsy under transrectal ultrasonographic guidance. It is rare for there to be a lesion to target on biopsy, so usually a standard set of 10 to 12 cores is taken from all accessible parts of the gland, preferentially sampling the periphery. If adenocarcinoma is found, it is possible to get an estimate of the Gleason grade and extent of tumour. If no tumour is found it is necessary to discuss with the patient whether to repeat the biopsy series after a short interval or to monitor serum PSA pending further decisions.

With asymptomatic men the situation is rather different. It is important to discuss with the man the merits and disadvantages of being investigated, to enable him to make choices that fit his lifestyle priorities.

Prostate-specific antigen
PSA is a glycoprotein produced by prostate epithelium which has a physiological role in the liquefaction of semen. Normally, very little is detectable in serum; however, prostatic inflammation, hyperplasia and neoplasia can all result in elevated levels. As a consequence, serum levels tend to rise with age, probably reflecting hyperplasia, and may fluctuate in a short time frame, presumably reflecting inflammation. There is no threshold value below which cancer is excluded, or above which cancer is likely. Taking values in the range 4–10 ng/ml, only 30% of men will have prostate cancer detected on biopsy, but 15% of men tested with a PSA value below 4 ng/ml will have cancer; occasional prostate cancers do not secrete PSA.

Further investigations
Further investigations include:

- magnetic resonance imaging (MRI)
- isotope bone scan.

Patients considered for curative treatment will usually have MRI of the pelvis, looking for evidence of lymph node metastasis and locally advanced disease with invasion beyond the prostate. If the PSA is above 10 ng/ml an isotope bone scan will be offered to seek evidence of skeletal metastasis. With widespread carcinomatous infiltration of the bone marrow a *leukoerythroblastic* anaemia develops, evinced by the presence of primitive red and white cell precursors in the peripheral blood (Ch. 23). If routine blood tests suggest renal impairment, then causes such as ureteric obstruction by the tumour will need to be investigated.

The diagnosis of metastatic prostate cancer will depend upon the presenting symptoms. Pain or fracture related to skeletal metastases is investigated radiologically, with biopsy as appropriate. Immunohistochemical staining for PSA would confirm origin from the prostate.

Clinical management

There are many challenges in the management of prostate cancer, and much uncertainty about what is best. This is a brief outline of some of these issues. Expert counselling of the man is critically important.

Initiating diagnostic tests

As alluded to above, whether to embark on a diagnostic pathway or whether to perform a needle biopsy cannot be assumed. Whilst many men will benefit, some will be disadvantaged, so the issues must be discussed.

Localised prostate cancer

At diagnosis about 70% of men will have the cancer apparently confined to the prostate gland. Though these men are potentially curable by local treatment (surgery or radiotherapy), not all will benefit from treatment. The issue is that some tumours grow slowly and remain asymptomatic, so the person eventually dies with their tumour, but not from it; radical treatment in this situation gives the risks and potential morbidity, but not the benefit. However, identifying such indolent or low- risk tumours cannot, at present, be done at diagnosis with sufficient accuracy. So if after discussion a man elects not to proceed directly to radical treatment, but does not wish to abandon the possibility later, it would be essential to monitor the situation; the window of opportunity for curative treatment may close, leaving only palliative options.

Those tumours that are localised but of a higher Gleason score or higher PSA are still potentially curable, so radical prostatectomy and radiotherapy are the usual treatment options offered; discussion is again important as the morbidity varies with the treatment.

Locally advanced prostate cancer

About 20% of cases present with disease no longer confined to the prostate, but still within the pelvis. Curative surgery is not likely to be an option; radiotherapy has a place. The mainstay of treatment is hormone manipulation to reduce the androgen tumour drive. This can be by removing the supply of androgens or by androgen receptor blockade (e.g. bicalutamide), or a combination of both.

Androgen withdrawal can be achieved by pharmacological means such as luteinising hormone-releasing hormone agonists (LHRHa), or surgically by bilateral orchidectomy. Historically, Huggins in Chicago introduced oestrogens in 1941 for the same purpose.

Metastatic prostate cancer

About 10% of patients present with disseminated cancer. Hormone treatment is the usual way forward, as above. There is also a role for bisphosphonates in the management of bone metastases, though the specific indications are still contentious.

Hormone refractory disease

There is a general tendency for prostate cancer eventually to escape from androgen dependency as the disease progresses, often as a result of mutations in the androgen receptor gene. Initially changes to the method of androgen deprivation being used may help; eventually only chemotherapy remains as an option and has limited success.

Screening and prevention of prostatic cancer

With the current tests available and level of knowledge, the criteria for population cancer screening are not met. Though PSA is widely used for case detection, it has serious shortcomings because of the absence of a reliable threshold between tumour and non-tumour bearers, as outlined above. There is also the major uncertainty about how to manage incidentally discovered cancers. However, as the prostate is dependent on dihydrotestosterone there have been studies showing that 5-alpha reductase inhibitors reduced the incidence, though this can be considered only in specific high-risk individuals, for example those with a strong family history.

PENIS AND SCROTUM

Diseases affecting the penis, ranked in order of frequency, are:

- sexually transmitted infections
- congenital malformations
- tumours.

It is common practice to examine carefully the external genital region of male neonates to detect major malformations; minor abnormalities may remain undetected until the prepuce can be fully retracted. In adolescents and adults, sexually transmitted infections (e.g. gonorrhoea) constitute a major public health problem in many countries; the penis is also one route of transmission of other serious infections, notably HIV—the cause of AIDS. The commonest tumours are benign warts, occurring usually in young adults; carcinomas are relatively uncommon.

CONGENITAL LESIONS

Congenital lesions of the penis and scrotum include:

- hypospadias
- epispadias.

Hypospadias

Hypospadias is the commonest congenital abnormality of the male urethra, resulting from a failure of fusion of the urethral folds over the urogenital sinus. Normal fusion of these folds starts at the posterior end and extends forward along the penile shaft to the tip. If fusion is incomplete, the urethra does not reach the tip of the penis, but opens on to its inferior aspect. The commonest site is a meatus on the inferior aspect of the glans. Less often, the meatus is on the penile shaft, and is associated with a downward curvature of the penis (congenital chordee). Rarely, there is a complete hypospadias with the urethral opening on the perineum behind the scrotum.

Epispadias

The congenital abnormality epispadias is much less common than hypospadias. The urethra opens on to the dorsum of the penis, the commonest site being at the base of the shaft near the pubis. This lesion results in urinary incontinence and infections. Epispadias is sometimes associated with exstrophy of the bladder.

INFLAMMATION AND INFECTIONS

Balanoposthitis

Inflammation of the inner surface of the prepuce (posthitis) is usually accompanied by inflammation of the adjacent surface of the glans penis (balanitis). Such a balanoposthitis is often associated with a tight prepuce (*phimosis*). Sebaceous material and keratin may accumulate beneath the prepuce, which may become infected by pyogenic bacteria. These bacteria include staphylococci, coliforms or gonococci. In diabetic patients, *Candida* infection is a further risk.

There is redness and swelling of the prepuce and glans with an associated purulent exudate. If treatment is delayed or there are recurrent episodes of infection, fibrous scarring can occur with the formation of preputial adhesions or severe phimosis.

Phimosis

Phimosis, and the closely related condition of paraphimosis, are the commonest medical indications for male circumcision.

In phimosis, the prepuce cannot be retracted over the glans penis. In most cases this is an acquired lesion, being the late sequel of an ammoniacal preputial dermatitis in infancy. Ammonia is formed by the action of some bacteria on the urine, producing blisters over the glans and inner aspect of the prepuce. This blistering results in the formation of numerous minute skin ulcers with associated acute inflammation and eventual fibrosis, narrowing the opening in the prepuce.

Paraphimosis

If a tight prepuce is retracted behind the glans it may obstruct the venous return from the glans and prepuce. The resulting oedematous swelling of the glans and prepuce produces a paraphimosis in which the prepuce cannot be returned easily to its normal position.

Balanitis xerotica obliterans

Balanitis xerotica obliterans is an uncommon penile lesion characterised by thickened white plaques and fissures on the glans and prepuce. The symptoms are of a non-retractile prepuce or preputial discharge, often necessitating circumcision. Similar lesions may develop around the urethral meatus with resulting scarring. The condition most commonly affects men aged 30–50 years.

The histological features are of hyperkeratosis and atrophy of the epidermis with basal layer degeneration. The papillary dermis shows hyalinisation of the collagen with an underlying infiltrate of lymphoid cells. Similar changes are seen in lichen sclerosus of the vulval skin; some people thus also refer to the penile lesion as lichen sclerosus.

Genital herpes

Aetiology

Herpes is an acute infectious disease caused by herpes simplex virus (HSV). There are two antigenic types of the virus: HSV types 1 and 2. Most genital tract lesions are caused by type 2 as a sexually transmitted disease. HSV type 2 produces a recurrent, acute vesicular eruption on the skin, usually around the mouth or on the genitalia. The incidence of genital herpes is increasing.

The majority of *primary herpes infections* are subclinical, but sometimes there is a febrile illness followed by the vesicles; following this initial infection the virus may remain latent for many years. The virus may remain either locally in the skin or in the nerve ganglion supplying that skin segment, by migrating along the axons to the ganglia. *Recurrent herpes infections* are caused by reactivation of the virus and may be precipitated by a febrile illness, immune suppression, emotional stress or by ultraviolet light.

Clinicopathological features

The primary lesion of herpes genitalis in the male is preceded by itching followed by the appearance of several closely grouped *vesicles* surrounded by erythema on the glans penis or the coronal sulcus. The acute skin lesion is an intra-epidermal vesicle with evidence of cellular damage associated with the virus. There may be vacuolation of the epidermal cells, some of which are multinucleated and contain viral inclusions. The vesicles soon burst to produce shallow painful *ulcers*. Less often, there is a more diffuse balanitis which may heal with a resulting phimosis, and occasionally vesicles develop on the shaft of the penis or on the scrotum. Herpetic lesions are less common in circumcised men. In some patients, the infection is asymptomatic with no visible lesions, although these patients may still transmit the disease.

The clinical features may be sufficient to enable a diagnosis but laboratory confirmation can be obtained by isolation of the virus from vesicular fluid. A swab or scrape from this source, collected in a suitable viral transport medium, can be used to demonstrate a cytopathic effect in tissue culture. Viral particles may also be identified by examining vesicle fluid by electron microscopy. The polymerase chain reaction (PCR) to identify viral DNA is rapid, and has a high diagnostic yield.

Genital warts

Genital warts are increasing in prevalence and are now probably the commonest type of lesion seen in patients attending departments of genito-urinary medicine.

Aetiology

Genital warts are caused by the human papillomavirus (HPV), a DNA virus of the papovavirus group. The HPV types causing genital warts (HPV 6 and 11) differ from those causing the common skin wart (HPV 1, 2 and 4). HPV types 16 and 18 are incriminated in the aetiology of squamous carcinoma of the penis, and also cervical cancer (Ch.19).

Clinicopathological features

In the male, the characteristic lesion is a hyperplastic, fleshy wart or *condyloma acuminatum*. This wart occurs most commonly on the glans penis and inner lining of the prepuce or in the terminal urethra. Less often, lesions develop on the shaft of the penis, the peri-anal region or the scrotum.

Histologically, the epidermis shows papillomatous hyperplasia. Many of the epidermal cells show cytoplasmic vacuolation, a feature indicating a viral aetiology. There is no epidermal dysplasia and these lesions are not premalignant.

The clinical diagnosis is usually obvious and laboratory diagnosis is rarely required. The clinical management is complicated by a high infectivity and a tendency to multiple recurrences.

Syphilis

▸ Causative organism is a spirochaete: *Treponema pallidum*
▸ Primary chancre on penis: ulcerated nodule and endarteritis with lymphocytes and plasma cells; associated inguinal lymphadenitis
▸ Secondary stage: condylomata lata, generalised lymphadenitis
▸ Tertiary stage: gumma, often in the testis

Aetiology

Syphilis is now a less prevalent sexually transmitted infection in the developed world. It is caused by a spirochaete, *Treponema pallidum*. In the male, the primary lesion develops between 1 and 12 weeks after infection, usually on the penis at the site of inoculation. The organism probably enters the tissues through a mucosal abrasion and, by the time the primary lesion develops, the organism has already disseminated via lymphatics.

Clinicopathological features

The *primary chancre* usually develops on the inner aspect of the prepuce, the glans penis or corona. It forms a painless indurated nodule which soon becomes an ulcer with rounded margins. There is regional lymphadenopathy. Examination by dark-ground microscopy of the serous exudate in the base of the ulcer reveals numerous spirochaetes. Initially, the tissue response consists of oedema with necrosis and an associated exudate of fibrin and polymorphs. At a later stage there is an endarteritis with a perivascular infiltrate of lymphocytes and plasma cells. Thrombotic occlusion of these vessels produces necrosis and ulceration of the epidermis. There is usually an associated unilateral or bilateral inguinal lymphadenitis. Without treatment the primary chancre heals in a few weeks, leaving an atrophic scar.

The secondary and tertiary stages of syphilis develop later as a result of dissemination of the infection and are accompanied by an immunological reaction. Secondary syphilis develops within 2 years of the primary lesion and may include several different cutaneous manifestations. One of these is the development of *condylomata lata* on the prepuce and scrotum—proliferative epithelial lesions containing numerous spirochaetes. There is a generalised lymphadenitis in many cases.

The tertiary stage of syphilis may involve the formation of a *gumma* in the testis, but is also associated with thoracic aortic aneurysms and central nervous system changes.

Clinical diagnosis and management

Syphilis is diagnosed in the primary stage by microscopy of the exudate in the chancre or ulcer; the characteristic spirochaetes can be seen by dark-ground illumination. In this and later stages, the diagnosis is confirmed serologically by seeking specific antibodies in the patient's blood; the fluorescent treponemal antibody absorption (FTA-Abs) test and the *Treponema pallidum* haemagglutination assay (TPHA) are the most specific.

Treatment is usually with penicillin, but it is essential to trace and possibly treat the patient's sexual partners.

Lymphogranuloma venereum

▸ Caused by *Chlamydia trachomatis*, serotypes L1–L3
▸ Primary genital lesion
▸ Inguinal lymphadenitis: acute suppurative inflammation with necrosis; chlamydial inclusions

Lymphogranuloma venereum is a sexually transmitted disease seen more commonly in the tropics. Infections seen in the UK, for example, have usually been acquired abroad.

Aetiology

The disease is caused by the bacterium *Chlamydia trachomatis*, serotypes L1–L3 (different from those associated with non-specific urethritis).

Clinicopathological features

Following a short incubation period of 2–5 days, about 50% of infected males give a history of a *primary genital lesion*. This lesion is a painless papule on the penis which may ulcerate but usually heals within a few days.

Between 1 and 4 weeks later the patient develops an *inguinal lymphadenitis* and this is the usual manifestation of the disease in the male. There is usually unilateral enlargement of the inguinal lymph nodes. The nodes are tender and initially discrete, becoming matted together as a result of pericapsular inflammation. The nodes may also become fluctuant. This lymphadenitis is often accompanied by constitutional symptoms with pyrexia and malaise. If untreated, the lymphadenitis may resolve but with some residual local lymphoedema.

The histological features are of an acute inflammation of the node with foci of necrosis surrounded by a margin of polymorphs, histiocytes and plasma cells. This inflammatory infiltrate extends through the capsule of the lymph node into the perinodal adipose tissue and may result in the development of sinuses to the overlying skin.

Clinical diagnosis

Surgical biopsy of the lymph node may be performed if the diagnosis is unsuspected; the histological features are almost pathognomonic. The diagnosis may also be made by aspirating pus from the lymph node and examining smears by specific immunofluorescence or stained by the Giemsa technique for the presence of chlamydial inclusions. A serum complement fixation test is also available.

Elephantiasis

In elephantiasis, the skin of the penis, scrotum and legs is greatly thickened by chronic oedema resulting from lymphatic obstruction. Two main groups can be distinguished:

● non-tropical elephantiasis
● tropical elephantiasis.

The tropical form is relatively common in parts of Africa and other countries with a similar climate in which the causative parasite is prevalent.

Non-tropical elephantiasis

In non-tropical elephantiasis, an earlier inflammatory process such as a recurrent cellulitis results in obliteration of the lymphatics in the skin. Another cause is disruption of lymphatic flow after surgical dissection of the inguinal lymph nodes as treatment for metastatic carcinoma of the penis or scrotum.

Tropical elephantiasis

Tropical elephantiasis is a late sequel of infection by the nematode parasite *Wuchereria bancrofti*. The adult worm lives in the lymphatic spaces, where the female produces microfilariae which re-enter the blood. These are ingested by blood-sucking mosquitoes, developing further in the insects' salivary glands. They re-infect humans at the time of a further bite, passing back to the lymphatics. In this site the parasite induces a granulomatous inflammation with associated fibrosis, leading to lymphatic obstruction. Mechanical blockage of the lymphatic lumen by numerous parasites contributes to the oedema.

Peyronie's disease

Peyronie's disease is a rare penile lesion presenting usually in the fifth and sixth decades with painful curvature of the penis on erection and, sometimes, difficulty in micturition. The lesions may gradually progress for a few years, and some later resolve spontaneously.

One or more ill-defined plaques of fibrous tissue develop along the dorsal aspect of the shaft of the penis, initially involving the corpora cavernosa. Histological examination shows fibroblast proliferation, with increasing amounts of collagen as the lesion progresses. In the early stages of Peyronie's disease, there is also an inflammatory component with an infiltrate composed predominantly of lymphocytes and plasma cells.

The nature of the lesion is uncertain. Some cases are associated with palmar fibromatosis (Dupuytren's contracture), although the inflammatory component is unlike most fibromatoses. Peyronie's disease may be related to idiopathic retroperitoneal fibrosis.

Idiopathic gangrene of the scrotum (Fournier's syndrome)

Idiopathic gangrene of the scrotum (Fournier's syndrome) is a rare necrotising subcutaneous infection that involves the scrotum and sometimes extends to involve the penis, perineum and abdominal wall. It usually affects middle-aged to elderly men.

Aetiology

Several predisposing factors may be associated with Fournier's syndrome: local trauma, anal fistula or ischiorectal abscess. There is an increased risk in patients with diabetes mellitus. The common aetiological factor of local tissue trauma allows bacteria to enter the subcutaneous tissue. The causative organisms are of the faecal flora, including coliforms and anaerobes such as *Bacteroides,* some of which are gas-forming organisms. A mixed infection is common.

Clinicopathological features

The scrotum is red and swollen with crepitus on palpation due to the presence of subcutaneous gas. This initial stage is soon followed by necrosis of the skin and subcutaneous tissue, eventually exposing the testes. Later, the tissue slough separates, sharply demarcated from the adjacent viable skin. There is a high risk of death from multi-organ failure. Antibiotics and surgical debridement are the mainstay of treatment. Finally, if the patient survives, there is regeneration of the skin.

Thrombosis of blood vessels in the scrotal skin results in necrosis of the subcutaneous tissue and dermal gangrene.

TUMOURS OF THE PENIS

Tumours of the penis are of two types:

- intra-epidermal carcinoma (Bowen's disease)
- invasive squamous carcinoma.

Intra-epidermal carcinoma

A localised area of intra-epidermal carcinoma (Bowen's disease; see Ch. 24) may develop on the penis as on other sites on the body surface, presenting as a sharply delineated erythematous patch with a moist keratotic surface. On the glans penis this lesion is sometimes termed *erythroplasia of Queyrat,* with the appearance of a well-defined, slightly raised, red plaque.

The histological features are of a pre-invasive squamous cell carcinoma. The epidermis is thickened with loss of cellular polarity and stratification. There is cellular and nuclear pleomorphism with hyperchromatic nuclei and an increased number of mitoses. Many of these abnormal cells keratinise at deeper levels within the epidermis (dyskeratosis). The basal layer of the epidermis remains sharply demarcated from the dermis at this stage, although this lesion carries a significant risk of progression to invasive squamous carcinoma.

Invasive squamous carcinoma

Carcinoma of the penis is rare in the UK although common in parts of Africa, Latin America and the Far East, where it accounts for 10% of cancers in men. It occurs predominantly in uncircumcised men and is associated with phimosis, chronic balanoposthitis, balanitis xerotica obliterans and PUVA-treated psoriasis. Human papillomavirus infection (HPV 16 and 18) is an aetiological factor in a substantial proportion of cases.

The usual site at which the tumour develops is on the glans penis or inner aspect of the prepuce, forming an indurated nodule or plaque which later ulcerates. It rarely develops on the outer surface of the prepuce or on the shaft of the penis.

The tumour is usually a well-differentiated squamous carcinoma and invades the corpora cavernosa. Metastases may develop in the inguinal lymph nodes.

CARCINOMA OF THE SCROTUM

Carcinoma of the scrotum was the first recognised example of a tumour caused by occupational exposure to carcinogens. In 1775, Percival Pott recognised this association in chimney sweeps. During the sweeps' work, soot containing carcinogens became retained in the rugose skin of the scrotum, later inducing a tumour. Since that time, other occupational factors have been identified in the development of this type of tumour, such as exposure to mineral oils. Workers handling arsenic or tar are also at risk.

Nevertheless, this tumour is now rare in the UK. It develops in elderly men, often many years after possible exposure to industrial carcinogens. It presents as a nodular, often ulcerated mass which may involve an extensive area of the scrotal skin. The tumour is a squamous carcinoma, usually well differentiated with keratinisation. The inguinal lymph nodes may be enlarged by metastatic carcinoma or as a result of reactive changes resulting from ulceration of the primary tumour.

URETHRA

URETHRAL OBSTRUCTION

The commonest cause of urethral obstruction is extrinsic compression due to prostate gland enlargement. Intrinsic lesions include:

- congenital valves
- rupture
- stricture.

Congenital urethral valves

Congenital urethral valves are a rare cause of urinary tract obstruction in the male neonate. In most cases this presents acutely with urinary obstruction and resulting bladder distension and muscle hypertrophy. The causative lesion is single or paired mucosal folds in the prostatic part of the urethra. Less often, a milder degree of this abnormality is first diagnosed in early adult life.

Traumatic rupture of the urethra

Traumatic rupture of the urethra is a rare event confined to males, and results from trauma such as a fall astride a hard object or complicating a fractured pelvis. The resulting damage to the wall of the urethra may involve its whole circumference or only part of it and may involve both the mucosa and muscle layers. Any part of the urethra may be involved.

The rupture leads to *extravasation of urine* into the peri-urethral tissues, which may later become the site of a *secondary infection*. There is *difficulty in passing urine* with *bleeding* from the urethral orifice and *localised pain*. A late complication of this lesion is the development of a *urethral stricture*.

Urethral stricture

A urethral stricture is usually an acquired lesion developing secondary to some other pathological condition of the urethra. The commonest cause is a *post-inflammatory stricture* following a *gonococcal urethritis*. This infection usually involves the peri-urethral glands and, if treatment is delayed, this condition may be associated with fibrosis around the glands and a fibrous stricture that encircles the urethra. Proximal to the stricture, the urethra becomes dilated, with hypertrophy of bladder muscle and urinary obstruction. The patient complains of difficulty in micturition with a poor stream and dribbling of urine. The retention of urine may be complicated further by the development of cystitis.

Urethral strictures may also be *post-traumatic*, complicating a rupture of the urethra, or develop after transurethral instrumentation or resection. A congenital stricture of the urethra occurs more rarely.

URETHRITIS

Urethritis (inflammation of the urethra) may occur in association with a more proximal infection in the urinary tract or adjacent to a local urethral lesion such as a calculus or an indwelling urinary catheter. The commonest causes, however, are the following specific primary infections of the urethra occurring as a sexually transmitted infection:

- gonococcal urethritis (gonorrhoea)
- non-gonococcal (non-specific) urethritis.

Gonococcal urethritis (gonorrhoea)

In gonococcal urethritis, the bacterial organism *Neisseria gonorrhoeae* (syn. gonococcus) produces an acute inflammation of the urethra. Following a short incubation period of 2–5 days after intercourse, a purulent urethral discharge develops, with pain on passing urine. If the infection spreads to the proximal urethra there may also be increased frequency of micturition. About 90% of males develop such symptoms as a result of infection, in contrast to females in whom about 70% of gonococcal infections are asymptomatic.

The gonococcus can penetrate an intact urethral mucosa, producing an infection in the submucosa that extends to the corpus spongiosum. This is an acute suppurative inflammation with increased vascularity, oedema and an infiltrate of polymorph leukocytes.

The inflammation commonly involves the *peri-urethral* glands and may also extend to the *prostate* and *epididymis* (Fig. 20.13). In all these sites abscesses may develop containing numerous polymorphs and bacteria with localised tissue destruction. A *urethral stricture* may develop many years after the initial infection as a result of fibrosis in relation to damaged peri-urethral glands. Gonorrhoea is a common infection, mainly occurring in young adults, and has a high infectivity.

Diagnosis

The gonococcus is a delicate organism and careful collection and transport of specimens is required for a laboratory diagnosis. A swab from the urethral mucosa may give a rapid diagnosis of gonococcal urethritis in the clinic, enabling immediate antibiotic treatment of the infection to be started.

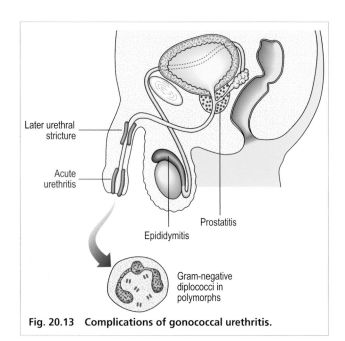

Fig. 20.13 Complications of gonococcal urethritis.

Later urethral stricture

Acute urethritis

Prostatitis

Epididymitis

Gram-negative diplococci in polymorphs

Microscopy demonstrates Gram-negative gonococci within polymorphs (Fig. 20.14).

Microbiological culture of the organism requires urethral swabs to be transferred promptly to the laboratory. Such a culture will provide confirmation of the diagnosis. Laboratory *antibiotic sensitivity tests* may also be required because of the recent emergence of strains of gonococci resistant to penicillin due to penicillinase (beta-lactamase) production.

Non-gonococcal (non-specific) urethritis

Non-gonococcal urethritis (synonymous with non-specific urethritis) is the commonest sexually transmitted disease. In males, a mucopurulent urethral discharge and dysuria develop within a few days to a few weeks of the infecting intercourse. The discharge contains pus cells but gonococci cannot be detected by microscopy or culture.

Aetiology

In about 40% of cases the cause is *Chlamydia trachomatis*; *Ureaplasma urealyticum* and *Histoplasma genitalium* are responsible for about a further 40%, while in the remainder no organism can yet be identified.

Chlamydia trachomatis is an obligate intracellular organism which structurally resembles a bacterium. Serotypes D–K are associated with genital tract infections. The infectious form of the agent, the elementary body, enters the urethral mucosal cells, enlarging to produce an initial body which is metabolically active. This body multiplies to form more organisms within a vacuole, seen on microscopy as a basophilic cytoplasmic inclusion. These organisms are released by cell rupture to infect adjacent cells.

Ureaplasma urealyticum and *Histoplasma genitalium* are similar Gram-negative organisms that lack a cell wall.

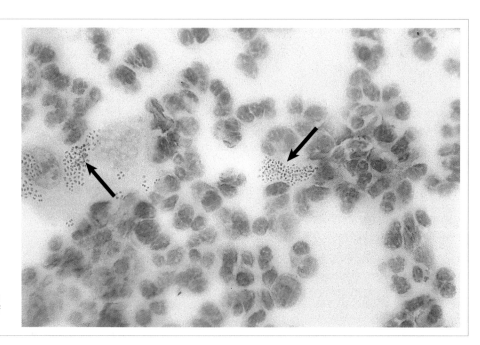

Fig. 20.14 Gonococcal urethritis.
Gram-stained pus showing numerous neutrophil polymorphs and clusters of gonococci (arrows).

TUMOURS

Tumours of the urethra include:

- viral condyloma
- transitional cell carcinoma.

Viral condyloma

These are analogous to the genital warts seen externally on the penis, and follow infection by human papilloma-viruses, mainly HPV 6 and 11; there is no particular risk of malignancy.

Transitional cell carcinoma

A papillary transitional cell carcinoma may rarely develop in the urethra, in association with a similar tumour in the bladder. This condition may be a separate, multifocal tumour of the urothelium, or may develop occasionally as a result of tumour implantation in the urethra following instrumentation of the bladder.

TESTIS

NORMAL STRUCTURE AND FUNCTION

During its development, each testis descends from the posterior abdominal wall to the scrotum, carrying with it a covering layer of peritoneum which forms the *tunica vaginalis,* a closed serous cavity around the testis (Fig. 20.15). Blood vessels and lymphatics enter and leave the testis on its posterior surface at the hilum, which is not covered by tunica vaginalis.

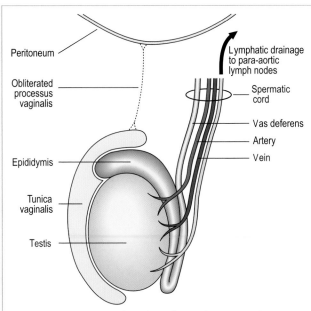

Fig. 20.15 Anatomy of testis and vascular connections.
Note that the lymphatic drainage of the testis is to the para-aortic lymph nodes.

Blood is supplied by the *spermatic artery,* a branch of the aorta, which passes along the spermatic cord. The venous return surrounds the spermatic artery as a network of intercommunicating veins, the *pampiniform plexus.* This plexus becomes the main testicular vein which, on the right side, drains to the inferior vena cava and, on the left, joins the left renal vein. Lymphatic drainage of the testis is to the *para-aortic lymph nodes.*

The testis has a fibrous capsule, the *tunica albuginea.* From this capsule, fibrous septa divide the testis into about 250 lobules, each containing up to four convoluted *seminiferous tubules.* These tubules converge on to a network of spaces, the rete testis, at the hilum, from where 10 to 12 *efferent ductules* lead to the *epididymis.* The rete testis and the efferent ductules are both lined by a ciliated epithelium.

The epididymis lies along the posterior aspect of the testis and is the main storage site for freshly formed sperm. The epididymis is a convoluted tubular structure lined by columnar epithelium.

The seminiferous tubules are each lined by a layer of *germinal epithelium* four or five cells thick; the more immature spermatogonia are situated close to the basement membrane. During spermatogenesis, meiotic division occurs at the spermatocyte stage; maturation of spermatids into sperm occurs near the tubular lumen. *Sertoli cells* lie in contact with the tubular basement membrane and insinuate between the germinal epithelial cells, providing local support and phagocytic function. In the interstitium between the seminiferous tubules, *Leydig cells* occur in small groups. These cells produce the hormone testosterone, which promotes spermatogenesis and the development of secondary sex characteristics, in response to stimulation by the pituitary gonadotrophic hormone, luteinising hormone.

From birth until puberty, the seminiferous tubules are small, being lined by Sertoli cells and primitive germ cells only. Spermatogenic activity starts at puberty.

INCIDENCE OF TESTICULAR LESIONS

Most testicular lesions are non-neoplastic disorders (e.g. mumps orchitis, torsion), but the possibility of a tumour must be considered fully in each case of testicular swelling or pain. Many testicular lesions present with a hydrocele, an accumulation of fluid around the testis; when this has been drained the testis must be examined carefully by palpation and, if necessary, by ultrasound imaging to exclude the possibility of an underlying testicular tumour.

The incidence of testicular tumours is rising slowly in many countries, but improvements in therapy are having a beneficial impact on patient survival.

DEVELOPMENTAL AND CYSTIC LESIONS

Undescended testis (cryptorchidism)

During fetal development, the testis descends from the posterior abdominal wall to the scrotum and in most cases is intrascrotal at birth. In about 5% of boys, one or both testes are undescended at birth, although many descend by the first birthday.

An undescended testis cannot be palpated in the scrotum because the testis is situated in the inguinal canal or in the abdominal cavity. This condition must be distinguished clinically from a retractile testis, in which a normally situated testis is drawn up into the inguinal canal by contraction of the cremaster muscle.

If an undescended testis is not surgically drawn down to the scrotum before puberty, adequate spermatogenic activity does not develop. The seminiferous tubules remain small and spermatogonia are progressively lost until the tubules are lined by Sertoli cells only. There is associated peritubular fibrosis. A longer-term risk of undescended testis is neoplasia from residual spermatogonia; an undescended testis carries a higher risk of tumour development than a normally situated testis, and an enhanced risk remains after surgical correction, and also applies to the opposite testis.

Hydrocele

The commonest intrascrotal swelling is a hydrocele, an accumulation of serous fluid within the tunica vaginalis of the testis. The smooth, pear-shaped swelling may be tense but is usually fluctuant and can be transilluminated. The contained testis is not palpable as it is surrounded by a layer of fluid (Fig. 20.16).

A *congenital hydrocele,* appearing in the first few weeks of life, results from persistence of the processus vaginalis, the channel between the peritoneal cavity and the tunica.

A *secondary hydrocele* may be associated with an underlying lesion of the testis or epididymis. This may be either *inflammatory,* such as mumps orchitis or gonococcal epididymitis, or *neoplastic.* The accompanying inflammation of the mesothelial lining of the tunica vaginalis results in the overproduction of fluid which cannot be drained adequately by the lymphatics in the tunica outer layer.

An *acute inflammatory hydrocele* accumulates rapidly and may produce pain. The straw-coloured fluid contains protein, fibrin, erythrocytes and polymorphs. A *chronic hydrocele,* however, causes only gradual stretching of the tunica and, although it may become large and produce a dragging sensation, it rarely produces pain. In this instance the fluid may also contain cholesterol crystals. A rough exudate of fibrin lines the hydrocele sac with an associated proliferation of mesothelial cells and the wall of the sac gradually becomes thickened by fibrosis.

Haematocele

A haematocele is haemorrhage into the tunica vaginalis. The usual cause is local trauma to the scrotal contents; this includes trauma to a blood vessel in a hydrocele sac as a result of a therapeutic tap. Another cause is an underlying testicular neoplasm.

In this condition, the tunica is lined by a shaggy layer of organising blood clot (Fig. 20.17). Microscopy of the tunica reveals fibrosis, haemosiderin-containing macrophages and an associated reactive proliferation of mesothelial cells.

ORCHITIS

Orchitis is the name given to any inflammatory condition of the testes.

Mumps orchitis

Mumps is an acute infectious febrile illness with parotitis, usually occurring in children. In adults, about 25% of cases are complicated by an orchitis, which develops as the parotitis begins to subside, though may appear without it. The condition is usually unilateral. The testis is enlarged and very tender.

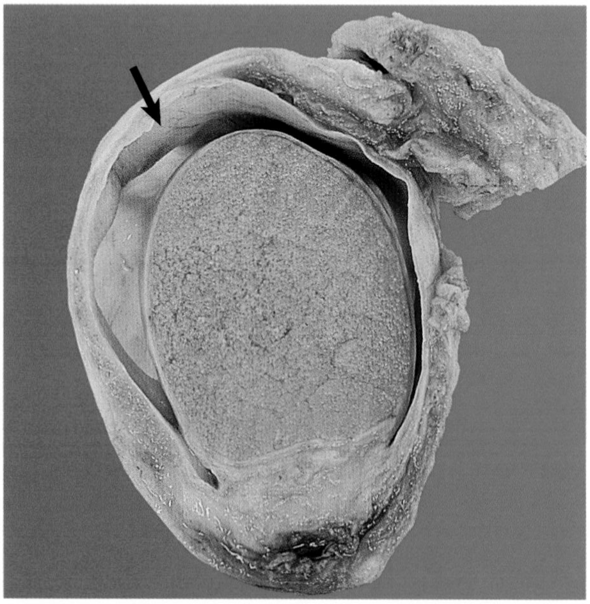

Fig. 20.16 Hydrocele. The tunica vaginalis is dilated (arrow). In this case, the testis was normal.

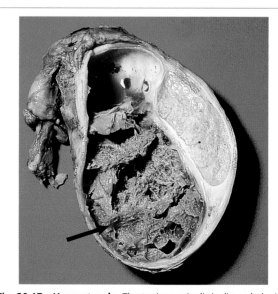

Fig. 20.17 Haematocele. The tunica vaginalis is distended with blood clot (arrowed) compressing the testis.

There is vascular dilatation and oedema of the interstitium of the testis, with an infiltrate of lymphocytes. Increasing pressure within the swollen testis produces ischaemia from blood vessel compression and necrosis of seminiferous tubules.

If the inflammation is mild, resolution may be complete. In other cases, however, the testis becomes atrophic with reduced spermatogenesis and increased fibrosis in the interstitium. If the involvement is bilateral, this scarring may result in subfertility, though this is rare.

Idiopathic granulomatous orchitis

Granulomatous orchitis is an uncommon chronic inflammatory lesion of the testis of unknown aetiology. The peak age incidence is 45–60 years. Granulomatous orchitis produces a firm, unilateral testicular enlargement which may mimic a neoplasm clinically.

The testis is enlarged with a firm or rubbery consistency and a lobulated appearance on its cut surface; there may also be a secondary hydrocele. Histology reveals loss of the germinal epithelium in the seminiferous tubules. The tubular architecture remains recognisable, but there is a dense granulomatous inflammatory infiltrate centred on the tubules and extending into the interstitium. This infiltrate comprises lymphocytes, plasma cells, macrophages and giant cells.

Although the aetiology is unknown, there is often a history of a *urinary tract infection*, suggesting that reflux of urine along the vas may be an aetiological factor. A reaction to *extravasated sperm* in the interstitium is another possible explanation.

Syphilitic orchitis

Although the lesion is now rarely seen, the testis was a common site for the development of a *gumma* in the tertiary stage of syphilis. There is unilateral painless enlargement of the testis which may mimic a neoplasm clinically. There is an irregular area of necrosis on the cut surface of the body of the testis and there may be a hydrocele. Histology shows tissue necrosis, although the architectural outline of the seminiferous tubules remains. At the edge of the necrotic area, there is an infiltrate of lymphocytes and plasma cells with an endarteritis.

TESTICULAR TUMOURS

The distinctive features of testicular tumours are that they are the commonest tumours of young males, they are generally curable, and the incidence has risen steeply over the past 50 years. There are about 2000 cases per annum in the UK, representing 1–2% of male cancers, with about 70 deaths. Nearly all the tumours are germ cell tumours.

Aetiology

Maldescent of the testis is the only certain risk factor for germ cell tumours, and accounts for about 10% of them. An undescended testis is 10 times more likely to develop a tumour than an intrascrotal testis; much of this risk remains after surgical correction, and the opposite testis also has an increased risk. Some patients have a positive family history.

Post-pubertal tumours have a consistent gain of the short arm of chromosome 12, often with an isochromosome (two copies back to back) i(12p). This is apparent from the first trimester onwards, though tumour development starts after puberty, initially as intratubular germ cell neoplasia before the invasive tumours develop. In contrast, pre-pubertal tumours are diploid.

The incidence has risen amongst whites in the USA and Europe, by up to 6% per annum, doubling in the last 30 years; in world terms the incidence is about 0.5–1 per 100 000 in Africa, 6.8 in the UK and 11 in Denmark. The cause for this increase is not known, though there has been much speculation about the role of environmental oestrogens.

Clinical features

Testicular tumours (Fig. 20.18) may present with:

- painless unilateral enlargement of testis
- secondary hydrocele
- symptoms from metastases
- retroperitoneal mass
- gynaecomastia.

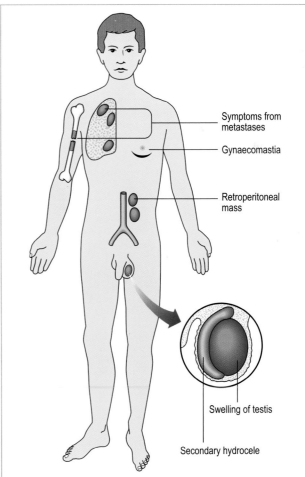

Fig. 20.18 Presenting features of testicular tumours.

The majority of testicular tumours present as slow, painless enlargement of one testis. On examination, there is a smooth or irregular firm enlargement of the testis. There may be a loss of testicular sensation on palpation. Less often, the patient notices a more rapidly enlarging scrotal swelling due to a secondary hydrocele around the tumour.

Some of the more malignant tumours may produce symptoms from metastases initially, for example haemoptysis from lung deposits, or pain from hepatomegaly.

A retroperitoneal mass may be the presenting feature. This mass may be a para-aortic lymph node metastasis from either a small viable primary tumour in the testis or a regressed testicular primary leaving a small hyaline scar.

Gynaecomastia is occasionally the initial feature, either because of sex hormones from Leydig cell tumours, or due to grossly elevated serum human chorionic gonadotrophin (hCG) from choriocarcinoma.

Classification of testicular tumours

Testicular tumours may have different origins (Fig. 20.19), the broad categories being:

- germ cell tumours (85–90% of cases)
- sex cord-stromal cells; Leydig or Sertoli cell tumours
- miscellaneous others such as lymphoma
- tumours of other structures; epididymis, cord.

Germ cell tumours may show a wide variety of histological patterns, and the classification has been confused by the British and WHO systems using the term 'teratoma' to convey different meanings. The main histological variants will be presented according to the WHO names, and then the different classification of germ cell tumours drawn together.

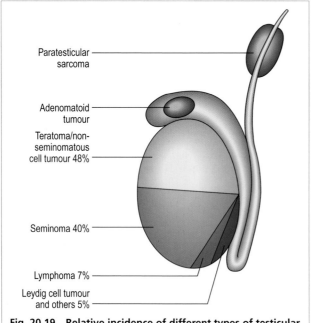

Fig. 20.19   Relative incidence of different types of testicular tumour.

Labels: Paratesticular sarcoma; Adenomatoid tumour; Teratoma/non-seminomatous cell tumour 48%; Seminoma 40%; Lymphoma 7%; Leydig cell tumour and others 5%

Germ cell tumours

- ▶ Commonest types of testicular tumour
- ▶ Commonest tumours of young adult males
- ▶ Seminoma peak incidence 30–50 years; show lymphatic spread
- ▶ Other germ cell tumours (teratoma) peak incidence 20–30 years; show vascular and lymphatic spread, and have tumour markers AFP and hCG
- ▶ Germ cell tumours are chemosensitive and generally curable

Intratubular germ cell neoplasia

The precursor of post-pubertal germ cell tumours, this comprises enlarged and pleomorphic spermatogonia partly or completely filling seminiferous tubules; residual Sertoli cells may be present. Positive staining for Oct4, CD117 or placental-like alkaline phosphatase (PLAP) can aid their identification. This 'carcinoma in situ' phase can last for many years, and there is usually evidence of it in residual tubules at the periphery of established tumours; this can be helpful in confirming the germ cell origin of a tumour in cases of doubt. Occasionally testis biopsy investigation of infertility reveals intratubular germ cell neoplasia.

Seminoma

Incidence
Seminoma is the largest single category of germ cell tumour, comprising 40%. It has a peak incidence between 30 and 50 years (Fig. 20.20), and is the usual tumour to arise in a maldescended testis.

Gross and microscopic features
The testis is enlarged by a homogeneous firm white solid tumour (Fig. 20.21). This tumour replaces all or part of the body of the testis. A rim of residual testis may be compressed at one edge of the tumour.

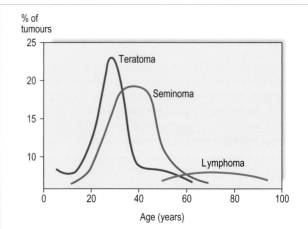

Fig. 20.20   Age incidence of testicular tumours (British classification).

Axis labels: % of tumours; Age (years). Curves: Teratoma, Seminoma, Lymphoma

Fig. 20.21 Seminoma. The testis is replaced by a solid and relatively homogeneous neoplasm.

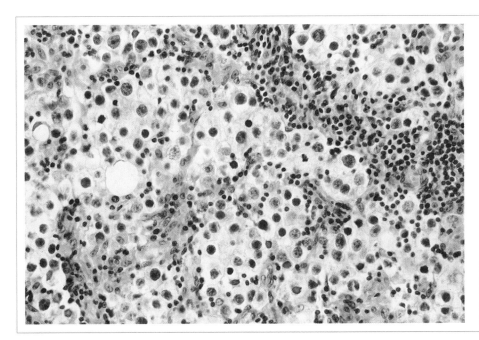

Fig. 20.22 Seminoma. Histology showing the characteristic combination of the large neoplastic cells with clear cytoplasm and the lymphocyte-rich stroma.

It is composed of uniform cells with well-defined cell borders. The cytoplasm is vacuolated and contains glycogen. In most of these tumours the stroma contains a variable lymphocytic infiltrate (Fig. 20.22), and some tumours may have a histiocytic granulomatous response in the stroma with fibrosis. About 10% of seminomas have scattered syncytiotrophoblast giant cells; these secrete human chorionic gonadotrophin (hCG) which can be demonstrated in tissue sections (Fig. 20.23) and serum, producing modest elevations.

Spermatocytic seminoma

Despite the similarity in name, this is completely different from classical seminoma. With its characteristic histology, spermatocytic seminoma is a tumour of older men, does not

arise from intratubular germ cell neoplasia, and has losses of chromosome 9 and not i(12p) gains. Most significantly, apart from a rare subtype with a sarcomatous component, it is benign.

Teratoma

These tumours show multiple different patterns of differentiation corresponding to ectoderm, mesoderm and endoderm, a reflection of their origin from pluripotent germ cells. Usually there are epithelial-lined cystic structures, somewhat organoid in nature, mimicking gut, bronchus or other organs (Fig. 20.24). Islands of cartilage are common; sometimes there is neural tissue. However, in contrast with ovarian teratomas (Ch. 19), highly organoid dermoid cysts are very rare. Exceptionally, a second neoplasm can arise in a teratoma.

Embryonal carcinoma

Solid, tubular and papillary configurations are present, composed of pleomorphic epithelial cells; necrosis is common (Fig. 20.25). Positive staining for Oct4 attests the pluripotent nature of these cells, and is very useful to identify a metastatic tumour as of germ cell origin. These tumours also express CD30 and cytokeratins.

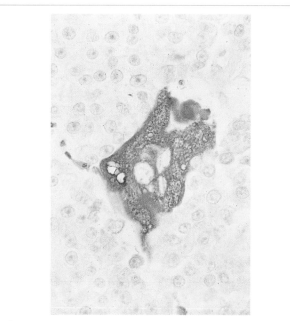

Fig. 20.23   Seminoma. Immunohistology showing a trophoblastic giant cell containing human chorionic gonadotrophin (brown).

Yolk sac tumour

Several varieties of histology are likened to yolk sac, with oedematous to myxoid stroma of varying cellularity and strands, cystic and solid formations of relatively regular, sometimes cuboidal, epithelial cells. Sometimes these are arranged around a blood vessel giving a Schiller–Duval body (Fig. 20.26). Yolk sac tumour cells secrete alpha-fetoprotein (AFP), which can be stained in sections and detected in serum.

Choriocarcinoma

This tumour is histologically similar to the gestational tumour of the same name (Ch. 19). There are bilaminar arrangements of mutually oriented syncytiotrophoblast giant cells overlying cytotrophoblast cells (Fig. 20.27). Extensive haemorrhage is usual, and it may be necessary to search carefully to find the trophoblast. Sections can be stained to show hCG, and serum levels can be very greatly raised, giving gynaecomastia or thyrotoxicosis by cross-reaction with pituitary hormone receptors. This tends to be a particularly aggressive tumour, often with widespread metastases at presentation.

As a separate issue relating to trophoblast, there may be isolated syncytiotrophoblast cells scattered or clustered within the context of other patterns of germ cell tumour. These cause moderate elevation of serum hCG, and are much more frequent than choriocarcinoma.

Combinations of histological patterns

Apart from seminoma, which is usually present in pure form, all the other patterns of malignant germ cell tumour tend to be present in combinations and are less often in pure form; the gross appearance is correspondingly a varied cystic and solid mass with necrosis (Fig. 20.28).

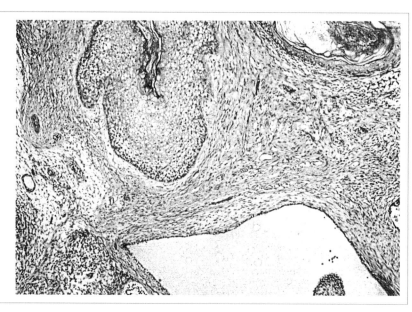

Fig. 20.24   Teratoma. Histology showing neoplastic epithelium and stroma forming organoid structures.

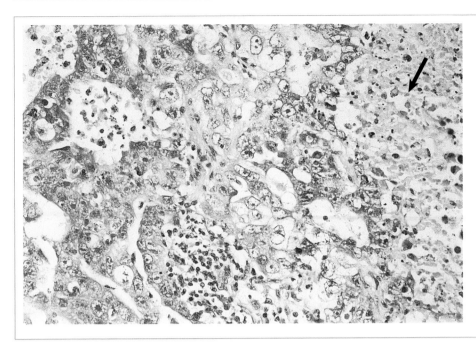

Fig. 20.25 Embryonal carcinoma. This lesion lacks recognisable organoid structures and shows extensive tumour necrosis (arrowed).

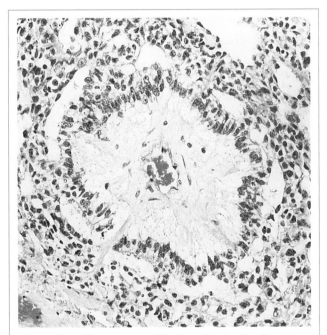

Fig. 20.26 Yolk sac tumour. Histology showing the characteristic arrangement of tumour cells around a blood vessel (Schiller–Duval body).

Classification of germ cell tumours

The more frequent germ cell tumours in the WHO classification are listed below; spermatocytic seminoma has been excluded for simplicity, and because of its substantial differences from the malignant germ cell tumours.

WHO classification of germ cell tumours (extract)

Tumours of one histological type

- Seminoma
- Embryonal carcinoma (EC)
- Yolk sac tumour (YST)
- Choriocarcinoma
- Teratoma

Tumours of more than one histological type

- Mixed germ cell tumour (noting the types and proportions)

The possible profusion of names of these tumours means that they are often described generically as seminoma versus non-seminomatous germ cell tumours.

The British classification has two broad categories of seminoma and teratoma; it uses the term teratoma to indicate all the tumours with any combination of embryonal carcinoma, yolk sac tumour, choriocarcinoma and teratoma as described above. The histological pattern is indicated by describing it as below.

British Testicular Tumour Panel classification

- Seminoma (same as WHO)
- Teratoma differentiated (WHO teratoma)
- Malignant teratoma intermediate (WHO mixed, teratoma and EC or YST)
- Malignant teratoma undifferentiated (WHO one type EC or YST, or mixed EC and YST)
- Malignant teratoma trophoblastic (WHO chorio alone or mixed with any other)
- Combined tumour, seminoma and teratoma (WHO mixed seminoma and any other)

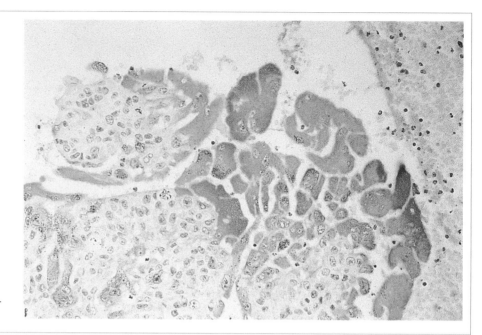

Fig. 20.27 Malignant teratoma trophoblastic. Immunohistology for human chorionic gonadotrophin (brown) revealing evidence of trophoblastic differentiation.

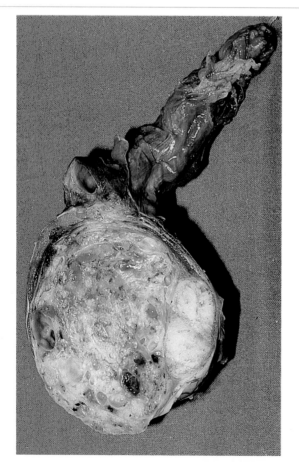

Fig. 20.28 Mixed germ cell tumour (malignant teratoma intermediate). A cystic and haemorrhagic tumour replaces the testis. Contrast this with the more uniform appearance of a seminoma (Fig. 20.21).

A combined tumour is defined as having a separate mass of seminoma; small foci of seminoma are permitted in all the malignant teratomas.

Extragonadal germ cell tumours

Tumours identical to those usually found in the testis may be primary at other sites in the body, notably the retroperitoneum, mediastinum and brain. This is attributed to aberrant migration of primordial germ cells in early gestation. Although the prognosis is not quite as good as for testicular tumours, the principles of management are the same.

Pre-pubertal germ cell tumours

Germ cell tumours in infancy and early childhood are distinct, and have a different pathogenesis. They are typically diploid, and not associated with antecedent intratubular germ cell neoplasia. There are two varieties: yolk sac tumour and teratoma.

Infantile yolk sac tumours are histologically similar to their counterparts in older men. Teratomas tend to be relatively highly differentiated and organoid, but there is also a tendency to have immature tissue components, for example neuroblastic tissue which can behave as a tumour in its own right.

Sex cord-stromal tumours

Leydig cell tumours

Leydig cell tumours arise from the sex hormone-secreting interstitial cells located between the tubules. They comprise about 2% of adult testis tumours and can arise at any age, with a peak at 30–45 years. They usually secrete androgens, so can cause precocious sexual development in boys; paradoxically, gynaecomastia may be the initial presentation. Leydig cell tumours form a yellow–brown rounded mass in the testis composed of eosinophilic cells. Most of these tumours are benign, but prediction of malignancy from the histology is imprecise. The differential diagnosis includes hyperplastic nodules of Leydig cells as well as other tumours.

Sertoli cell tumours

Sertoli cell tumours are much less common; they are also usually benign.

Malignant lymphoma

Lymphoma comprises about 7% of testicular tumours, with a peak incidence from 60 to 80 years when they are more frequent than germ cell tumours. Most testis lymphomas are diffuse large B-cell lymphoma (Ch. 22), giving a homogeneous, rubbery pale mass of large lymphoid cells sub-totally obliterating the tubules. The tumour is frequently disseminated beyond the testis at presentation. The differential diagnosis includes spermatocytic seminoma.

Other tumours

As well as rare tumours of testicular structures, the testis can be involved in dissemination of malignancy from other sites including bronchus, prostate or melanoma. Acute lymphoblastic leukaemia has a particular risk of recurring in the testis.

Dissemination and staging of germ cell tumours

After initial growth in the body of the testis, the tumours invade the rete and epididymis; invasion of the tough tunica albuginea is late. Invasion of lymphatics gives para-aortic node deposits and subsequently mediastinal or cervical node disease; there may be transit deposits in the spermatic cord. Vascular invasion may be evident at the periphery of the tumours, leading to lung metastases in particular; less often there is hepatic, cerebral or skeletal spread. All germ cell tumours may give lymphatic deposits, but vascular dissemination is rare in seminoma.

The staging can be categorised on the TNM system, or the Royal Marsden staging below can be used:

Stage I—tumour confined to the testis
Stage II—involvement of testis and para-aortic lymph nodes
Stage III—involvement of mediastinal and/or supraclavicular nodes
Stage IV—pulmonary or other visceral metastasis
(Stages II to IV are subdivided to indicate the volume of metastatic disease.)

Histological examination of metastatic disease may reveal components not observed in the primary tumour. After chemotherapy, resected nodal disease may be purely differentiated teratoma, reflecting preferential cell killing of more primitive histological patterns.

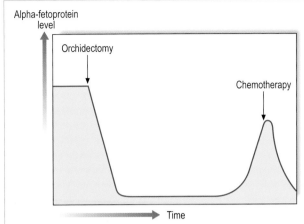

Fig. 20.29 Monitoring tumour growth by serum markers. The blood level of the tumour marker (alpha-fetoprotein in this instance) is high at presentation but falls when the tumour is removed. Regular monitoring, however, shows a rise in blood levels of alpha-fetoprotein corresponding to a tumour recurrence. The levels again fall with chemotherapy.

Tumour markers

The vast majority of teratomas (British usage) are associated with release of either alpha-fetoprotein (AFP) or human chorionic gonadotrophin (hCG), or both, into the serum in quantities that generally reflect the volume of disease. In this respect they act as markers of the presence of tumour, and as such are invaluable as an aid to diagnosis and for monitoring therapy (Fig. 20.29). Regular monitoring can enable a conservative approach to initial treatment, in the knowledge that residual or recurrent disease can be treated promptly. Apart from some seminomas with elevated hCG, there is no usable marker for the others.

Clinical management

If a testicular neoplasm is suspected clinically the first investigation is ultrasound examination followed by serum for tumour markers. Demonstration of a mass by clinical or ultrasound techniques requires surgical exploration and orchidectomy by an inguinal approach, taking the spermatic cord too. A scrotal incision or testis biopsy can risk local recurrence of tumour, or alter the pattern of lymphatic dissemination.

Pathological examination of the specimen needs to be sufficiently thorough to reflect the potential histological variability of germ cell tumours. Tumour type, extent of local spread and the presence of vascular invasion are the key data.

After confirmation of the diagnosis by microscopy, the patient should be offered a CT scan to search for metastatic disease, and attribution to a Royal Marsden stage. Regular monitoring of tumour markers is commenced as appropriate for the tumour.

In outline, patients with stage I teratoma can go on a surveillance protocol, with the option to use chemotherapy later if tumour markers or periodic CT indicate disease. Seminoma patients with stage I disease are rarely just monitored, and usually have prophylactic para-aortic radiotherapy (it is very radiosensitive) or a single dose of chemotherapy. All patients with higher stage disease are offered chemotherapy, with the expectation that the great majority will be cured.

MALE INFERTILITY

Male infertility may be due to:

- endocrine disorders—e.g. gonadotrophin deficiency; oestrogen excess—e.g. hepatic cirrhosis
- testicular lesions—cryptorchidism; Klinefelter's syndrome; maturation arrest of spermatogenesis—idiopathic, varicocele, pyrexial illness; irradiation; defective spermatozoa—e.g. immotile cilia
- post-testicular lesions—blockage of efferent ducts, congenital or secondary to an inflammatory process; impotence—neurological disorders.

The clinical assessment of infertile men includes thorough investigation to determine the precise nature of the problem. This may include a testicular biopsy to assess the integrity of the seminiferous tubules and the degree of spermatogenesis.

EPIDIDYMIS AND CORD

Congenital anomalies

In about 10% of men, the epididymis is situated anterior to a normal intrascrotal testis, instead of in its usual posterior position. This abnormality may cause diagnostic problems in palpation of other lesions. *Maldescent* of the testis may be accompanied by an abnormality in the position of the epididymis, which then lies along the course of the spermatic cord.

Rarely, an *extra vas deferens* is present on one side, or one may be *absent*. This latter condition may be associated with absence or hypoplasia of the corresponding epididymis. These abnormalities are of practical importance to the surgeon at vasectomy.

Several vestigial structures adjacent to the epididymis or mesorchium may become enlarged and cystic. These include aberrant ductules and the appendix of the epididymis. They usually remain small but may undergo torsion, with resulting infarction, presenting as an acute painful swelling.

Epididymal cysts and spermatoceles

Acquired cysts of the epididymis are more common than the congenital types. An obstruction to the passage of sperm along the narrow lumen of the vas or obstruction of an epididymal tubule results in cystic dilatation of the duct system in the epididymis and efferent ductules of the testis. The resulting *spermatocele* forms a swelling in the epididymis, above and behind the testis on palpation (Fig. 20.30). It is usually a multilocular cyst with opalescent fluid containing sperms.

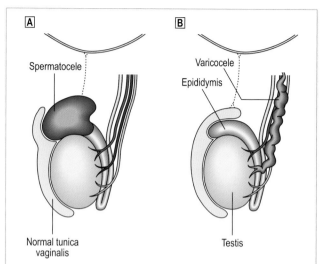

Fig. 20.30 Spermatocele and varicocele. [A] Spermatoceles are derived from the epididymis. [B] Varicoceles are lesions of the pampiniform venous plexus in which there is excessive tortuosity and dilatation.

Varicocele

A varicocele is varicosity of the pampiniform plexus of veins around the spermatic cord (Fig. 20.30). This may be a *primary varicocele* with no obvious underlying cause, more common on the left side. It may be related to maldevelopment of valves in the pampiniform veins or the testicular vein; on the left side the testicular vein drains into the left renal vein almost at 90°.

A *secondary varicocele* is the result of venous obstruction and occurs with equal frequency on both sides. One cause is a carcinoma of the kidney invading the renal vein and obstructing the testicular vein.

A varicocele may raise the intrascrotal temperature as a result of increased blood flow, reducing spermatogenesis and causing *subfertility*.

Torsion of the spermatic cord

Torsion of the spermatic cord involves twisting of the testis and epididymis together on their axis. It is an acute surgical emergency, presenting as a swollen, hard, painful testis. The patient is usually aged 13–16 years. An earlier peak incidence occurs under the age of 1 year. Torsion of the spermatic cord is often precipitated by exertion, which causes contraction of the cremaster muscle. There is sometimes a history of preceding minor, less painful episodes of testicular pain.

Several anatomical abnormalities, often bilateral, predispose to this lesion. They include maldescent of the testis, an abnormally long spermatic cord, or an abnormally long mesorchium. The torsion usually occurs within the tunica vaginalis, involving only the testis and epididymis. If it occurs above the level of the tunica it involves all structures in that side of the scrotum.

Torsion produces an initial occlusion of the venous return from the testis, although the arterial flow continues for a time. There is congestion of the testis followed by haemorrhagic infarction as the arterial supply becomes impaired with rising pressure within the tunica. If treatment is delayed, the infarction progresses, finally resulting in a shrunken, fibrotic testis and epididymis.

Inflammatory lesions

Acute epididymo-orchitis

An acute inflammation of the body of the testis (*orchitis*) most frequently develops in association with an initial *epididymitis* which later spreads to the testis. The commonest underlying cause is a *urinary tract infection* with coliform organisms; it may also develop after a *prostatectomy*. A *urethritis*, either gonococcal or non-specific, may be complicated by an epididymo-orchitis. In all these instances, the infection spreads along the vas deferens or the lymphatics of the spermatic cord to the epididymis.

The process may be unilateral or bilateral. The epididymis and testis are enlarged, warm and painful. These signs are accompanied by fever and malaise. Histology shows an acute inflammatory process. There may be a secondary hydrocele. The inflammation is usually mild and resolves either spontaneously or with antibiotic therapy; in severe cases it may, however, progress to suppuration.

Less often, an epididymo-orchitis may complicate a septicaemia (e.g. meningococcal).

Tuberculous epididymo-orchitis

Tuberculous infection of the male genital tract is now rare but the epididymis used to be the commonest site of involvement in the male. Infection of the epididymis is secondary to a tuberculous lesion elsewhere in the urinary tract, such as the kidney or bladder, with extension of the infection along the vas deferens.

In about one-third of cases the infection is bilateral, resulting in nodular enlargement of the epididymis. There may be a secondary hydrocele and, in an advanced infection, the inflamed epididymis becomes adherent to the scrotal skin with the formation of sinuses. The infection may spread directly to the *testis* with the formation of areas of caseation necrosis and the characteristic granulomatous inflammation. There may also be extension to the prostate or seminal vesicles. Microscopy of the urine shows a 'sterile' pyuria with acid–alcohol-fast bacilli.

Sperm granuloma

Sperm granuloma is an uncommon chronic inflammatory lesion involving the epididymis and resulting from extravasation of sperm from the tubules into the interstitium. There is an associated inflammatory reaction composed mainly of histiocytes and polymorphs, with secondary fibrosis. The process results in the formation of a firm swelling in the epididymis. The cause is uncertain, although there may be a preceding history of an epididymitis.

A similar cellular response to extravasated sperm may sometimes be seen in the spermatic cord at the site of recent vasectomy, forming a localised nodule at the operation site.

Tumours

Tumours of the epididymis and spermatic cord are relatively rare, together forming only 1–2% of the total group of testicular tumours. They include:

- adenomatoid tumour
- paratesticular sarcoma.

Adenomatoid tumour

Adenomatoid tumour is an uncommon, benign neoplasm of the epididymis, which may develop over a wide age range, and presents as a slowly enlarging painless firm nodule in the epididymis. Examination reveals a circumscribed solid nodule 10–20 mm in diameter, composed of irregular clefts and spaces lined by flattened or cuboidal cells. These cells merge with an intervening stroma of fibrous tissue and smooth muscle. A similar neoplasm may occur in the female over the uterine serosa or in the fallopian tube. The phenotype of this lesion is mesothelial, but the localisation to the genital tract has led to speculation that these tumours arise from Müllerian remnants.

Commonly confused conditions and entities relating to urinary and male genital pathology	
Commonly confused	**Distinction and explanation**
Phimosis and *paraphimosis*	Both are due to chronic inflammation of the prepuce. In *phimosis* the prepuce cannot be retracted over the glans penis, whereas in *paraphimosis* the retracted prepuce cannot be returned to its normal position.
Hydrocele, *spermatocele* and *varicocele*	A *hydrocele* is formed by serous fluid accumulating in the tunica vaginalis surrounding the testis. A *spermatocele* is an epididymal cyst containing opalescent (due to spermatozoa) fluid. A *varicocele* contains blood because it is due to varicosity of the pampiniform venous plexus.
Prostatism and *prostatitis*	*Prostatism* is a term sometimes used for lower urinary tract symptoms suggesting urethral obstruction due to prostatic enlargement. In contrast, *prostatitis* is inflammation of the prostate—one of several causes of prostatism.
Orchitis and *epididymo-orchitis*	*Orchitis* is inflammation of the testis alone, while in *epididymo-orchitis* infection spreads from epididymis to adjacent testis.
Teratoma, WHO and British usage	Both describe a germ cell tumour. The WHO restricts the term to differentiated tissues, while the British usage also includes undifferentiated tumours.

Paratesticular sarcoma

Paratesticular sarcomas of the spermatic cord are rare neoplasms which present as an inguinal or scrotal swelling, the tumour forming a mass separate from the body of the testis and epididymis. The types of tumour that occur vary with age: in children and adolescents, the majority are rhabdomyosarcomas; these give lymph node metastases, and have a relatively favourable outcome. In adults, liposarcoma is the most frequent.

FURTHER READING

Costa L J, Drabkin H A 2007 Renal cell carcinoma: new developments in molecular biology and potential for targeted therapies. Oncologist 12: 1404–1415

De Mulder P H M 2007 Targeted therapy in metastatic renal cell carcinoma. Annals of Oncology 18: 98–102

Dobosy J R, Roberts J L, Fu V X, Jarrard D F 2007 The expanding role of epigenetics in the development, diagnosis and treatment of prostate cancer and benign prostatic hyperplasia. Journal of Urology 177: 822–831

Epstein J I, Allsbrook W C, Amin M B, Egevad L L, ISUP Grading Committee 2005 The 2005 International Society of Urological Pathology (ISUP) consensus conference on Gleason grading of prostatic carcinoma. American Journal of Surgical Pathology 29: 1228–1242

Hohenstein P, Hastie N D 2006 The many facets of the Wilms' tumour gene *WT1*. Human Molecular Genetics 15: 196–201

Horwich A, Shipley J, Huddart R 2006 Testicular germ-cell cancer. Lancet 367(9512): 754–765. Erratum in Lancet 367(9520): 1398

Izzedine H, Billemont B, Thibault F, Rixe O 2007 New challenges in kidney cancer therapy: sunitinib. Annals of Oncology 18: 83–86

Knowles M A 2006 Molecular subtypes of bladder cancer: Jekyll and Hyde or chalk and cheese?. Carcinogenesis 27: 361–373

Ludwig M 2008 Diagnosis and therapy of acute prostatitis, epididymitis and orchitis. Andrologia 40: 76–80

Metzger M L, Dome J S 2005 Current therapy for Wilms' tumor. Oncologist 10: 815–826

Moreau J-P, Delavault P, Blumberg J 2006 Luteinizing hormone-releasing hormone agonists in the treatment of prostate cancer: a review of their discovery, development, and place in therapy. Clinical Therapeutics 28: 1485–1508. Erratum in Clinical Therapeutics 28: 1970

Naber K G 2008 Management of bacterial prostatitis: what's new? British Journal of Urology International 101(Suppl 3): 7–10

National Institute for Health and Clinical Excellence 2008 Prostatic carcinoma: diagnosis and treatment. NICE, London. http://www.nice.org.uk/CG058

Reuter V E 2005 Origins and molecular biology of testicular germ cell tumors. Modern Pathology 18 (Suppl 2): S51–S60

Scottish Intercollegiate Guidelines Network 1998 Management of adult testicular germ cell tumours. SIGN, Edinburgh. http://www.sign.ac.uk/pdf/qrg28.pdf

Tindall D J, Rittmaster R S 2008 The rationale for inhibiting 5alpha-reductase isoenzymes in the prevention and treatment of prostate cancer. Journal of Urology 179: 1235–1242

Cancer Research UK. UK bladder cancer statistics: http://info.cancerresearchuk.org/cancerstats/types/bladder/

Cancer Research UK. UK kidney cancer statistics: http://info.cancerresearchuk.org/cancerstats/types/kidney/

21

Kidney diseases

COMMON CLINICAL PROBLEMS FROM KIDNEY DISEASE

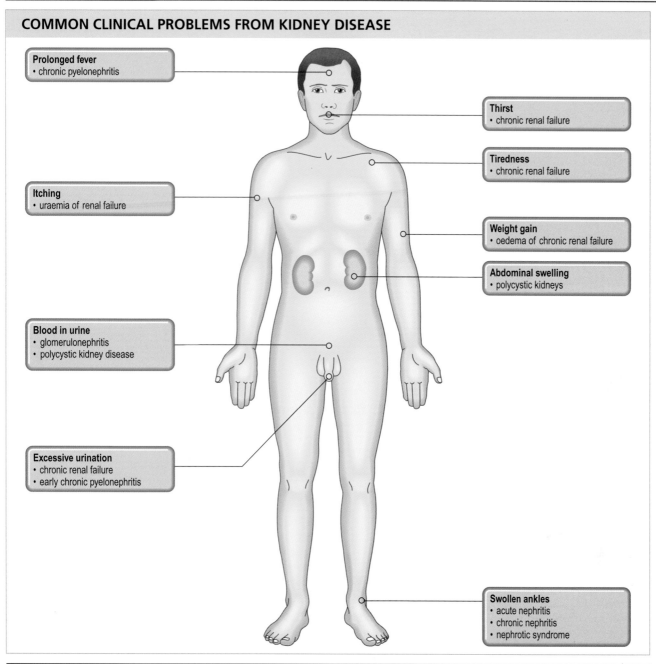

Prolonged fever
• chronic pyelonephritis

Thirst
• chronic renal failure

Tiredness
• chronic renal failure

Itching
• uraemia of renal failure

Weight gain
• oedema of chronic renal failure

Abdominal swelling
• polycystic kidneys

Blood in urine
• glomerulonephritis
• polycystic kidney disease

Excessive urination
• chronic renal failure
• early chronic pyelonephritis

Swollen ankles
• acute nephritis
• chronic nephritis
• nephrotic syndrome

Pathological basis of renal symptoms and signs	
Symptom or sign	Pathological basis
Proteinuria	Increased permeability of the glomerular basement membrane
Uraemia	Renal failure
Haematuria	Severe glomerular injury (red cell casts on urine microscopy) Renal tumours or trauma Bladder tumours or trauma
Urinary casts • Hyaline casts • Granular casts • Red cell casts	Formed in tubules as a result of protein loss from glomeruli Formed in tubules from aggregates of inflammatory cells Formed in tubules from red cells in filtrate from severely damaged glomeruli

(Continued)

Pathological basis for urinary tract symptoms and signs—cont'd	
Symptom or sign	Pathological basis
Hypertension	Sodium and fluid retention (see Oedema) Renal ischaemia releasing renin in some cases (renal artery stenosis)
Oliguria or anuria	Severe renal failure (acute or chronic), obstruction or dehydration
Polyuria	Excessive fluid intake (e.g. beer) Osmotic diuresis (e.g. diabetes mellitus) Impaired tubular concentration (e.g. diabetes insipidus, recovering acute tubular necrosis)
Renal (ureteric) colic	Calculus, blood clot or tumour in ureter
Oedema	Primary renal abnormality leading to sodium and fluid retention
Dysuria	Stimulation of pain receptors in urethra due to inflammation

NORMAL STRUCTURE AND FUNCTION OF THE KIDNEYS

The kidneys contribute to the body's biochemical homeostasis by:

- eliminating metabolic waste products
- regulating fluid and electrolyte balance
- influencing acid–base balance.

The kidneys also produce:

- *prostaglandins,* which affect salt and water regulation and influence vascular tone
- *erythropoietin,* which stimulates red cell production
- *1,25-dihydroxycholecalciferol,* which enhances calcium absorption from the gut and phosphate reabsorption by the renal tubules
- *renin,* which acts on the angiotensin pathway to increase vascular tone and aldosterone production.

The kidneys have a large functional reserve; the loss of one kidney produces no ill-effects. However, in renal disease waste products can accumulate, causing a condition known as *uraemia.* If the glomerular filters become excessively leaky, large protein molecules are lost in the urine—*proteinuria.* If the glomeruli are severely damaged, erythrocytes pass through causing *haematuria.*

The basic unit of the kidney is the nephron; each nephron comprises a glomerulus connected to a tubule. Each kidney contains approximately 1 million nephrons. These form in the embryonic metanephros, after the physiological involution of the pronephros and mesonephros. The ureter, calyceal system and collecting ducts form from the ureteric bud arising from the original duct of the pronephros—the Wolffian duct.

Glomerular structure and function

The formation of urine begins in the glomeruli, where the filtration of approximately 800 litres of plasma each day results in 140–180 litres of filtrate, most of which is reabsorbed by the tubules. Each glomerulus comprises a tuft of capillaries projecting into Bowman's space (Fig. 21.1A).

Blood enters and leaves the glomerular capillaries by arterioles. In contrast to all other systemic capillaries in which there is a fall in pressure towards the venous end, the hydrostatic pressure within the glomerular capillary remains high throughout its length, thus enabling efficient filtration.

The glomerular capillary comprises:

- endothelial cells
- basement membrane
- epithelial cells.

All components of the capillary wall contribute to the *filtration barrier,* which is entirely extracellular and has two complementary aspects:

1. a charge-dependent barrier to anionic molecules, including most proteins, comprising:
   - polyanionic glycosaminoglycans (e.g. heparan sulphate and sialoproteins) in the fenestrae of the endothelial cells
   - proteins in the basement membrane

2. a size-dependent barrier for large molecules which are neutral or cationic, comprising
   - filtration slit diaphragms between the epithelial cells
   - matrix proteins of the basement membrane.

The integrity of the filtration barrier is disturbed in glomerular disease.

The attenuated endothelial cytoplasm lining the luminal aspect of the glomerular capillary has numerous holes or fenestrae, 70–100 nm diameter. Functionally the endothelial cells:

- play an important role in the charge-dependent filtration barrier. The cell surfaces, covered by podocalyxin and other polyanionic sialoproteins and glycosaminoglycans, will repel anionic molecules such as albumin. In addition the fenestrae are filled with polyanionic glycoproteins and represent the first channel through which plasma components must pass in the process of ultrafiltration
- synthesise, release and bind coagulation factors
- participate in antigen presentation along with monocytes and macrophages by expressing class II histocompatibility antigens on their surface
- synthesise and release a relaxing factor.

The basement membrane is a mesh of filamentous matrix proteins, including collagen IV, laminin and fibronectin, many of which are anionic, through which the ultrafiltrate must pass.

The external aspect of the basement membrane bears epithelial cells with complex interdigitating cellular processes, termed foot processes, enveloping the capillary loops. Modified adherens-type junctions (filtration slit diaphragms) occur where the foot processes meet and are essential to the function of the epithelial cell (Fig. 21.1C). The integrity of the slit diaphragm is maintained by the complex inter-relationship of numerous proteins including nephrin, podocin and CD2-associated protein (CD2AP). Other proteins, such as integrins, span the membrane and anchor the actin cytoskeleton to the collagen IV in the lamina rara externa of the basement membrane. Therefore, changes in these proteins modify the configuration of the foot process, and defects in the genes encoding these proteins result in simplification of the foot processes.

The glomerular capillary tufts are supported centrally by *mesangial cells,* which proliferate and become more prominent in some diseases. Surrounded by a loose network of fibrillary material — the mesangial matrix — the mesangial cells comprise two types. One type of mesangial cell contains actin filaments and is contractile. They attach to the capillary basement membrane at the point where it is reflected over the mesangial matrix, thus anchoring the capillary to the central structure. Contraction of these cells therefore pulls on the glomerular basement membrane and will alter the shape and calibre of the capillary. Damage to this area reduces the strength of the capillary with the formation of a micro-aneurysm. The other type of mesangial cell resembles a monocyte and is analogous to a tissue macrophage. Both types of cell are involved in the mesangial reaction in glomerular disease by synthesising new matrix material and secreting cytokines responsible for cell proliferation and attraction of inflammatory cells.

The *basement membrane* is reflected over the mesangial area to extend onto the adjacent capillary, which means endothelium is attached to the mesangial matrix in the central core area (Fig. 21.1B). This allows access of immune complexes to the mesangium and the ability of mesangial cells to probe the capillary lumen.

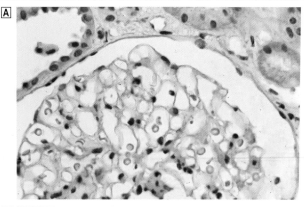

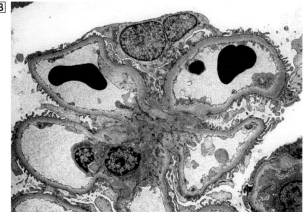

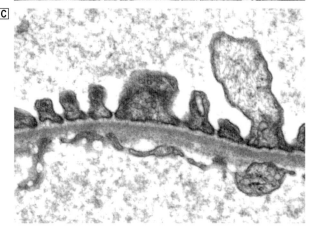

Fig. 21.1   Normal glomerulus. **A** Each glomerulus consists of capillaries invested by epithelial cells and is surrounded by Bowman's space. **B** Low-power electron micrograph showing capillary loops clustered around the mesangium. The basement membrane does not surround the capillary loop completely but is reflected onto the adjacent loop in the region of the mesangium, leaving the mesangial area covered only by the endothelium. **C** High-power electron micrograph showing ultrastructure of the glomerular capillary. The wall of each glomerular capillary comprises an inner thin layer of fenestrated vascular endothelium, the basement membrane and an outer epithelial layer characterised by cytoplasmic ('foot') processes. Slit diaphragms span the gap between adjacent epithelial cells. In electron micrographs the basement membrane has a central dense zone, the lamina densa, surrounded on either side by the less densely packed lamina rara interna and externa.

Glomerular filtration rate

Blood flow through the kidneys produces 130–180 l/day of ultrafiltrate which is termed the glomerular filtration rate (GFR). The GFR reflects the permeability of the capillary wall, together with the hydrostatic and osmotic gradients between the capillary lumen and the Bowman's capsular fluid. The hydrostatic pressure within the glomerular capillary is determined by the calibres of the feeder afferent and draining efferent arterioles.

The GFR is modified by three important mechanisms, all of which are closely inter-related and involve the juxtaglomerular apparatus (JGA):

- autoregulation within the glomerulus
- tubuloglomerular feedback
- neurohormonal influences.

Autoregulation and tubuloglomerular feedback

The JGA, situated at the hilum of the glomerulus, comprises the afferent and efferent arterioles and the modified tubular cells of the thick loop of Henle, the *macula densa* (Fig. 21.2), and enables autoregulation and tubuloglomerular feedback. The specialised cells of the macula densa monitor the level of chloride in the tubular luminal fluid, reflecting the amount of chloride reabsorbed by the tubule. A reduced GFR leads to a fall in the luminal chloride level. This results in dilatation of the afferent arteriole, together with constriction of the efferent arteriole, resulting from the release of renin. These two changes increase the hydrostatic pressure within the glomerular capillary and restore the GFR. Autoregulation and tubuloglomerular feedback are important for normal renal function, and are disturbed in patients with systemic hypertension due to renal artery stenosis.

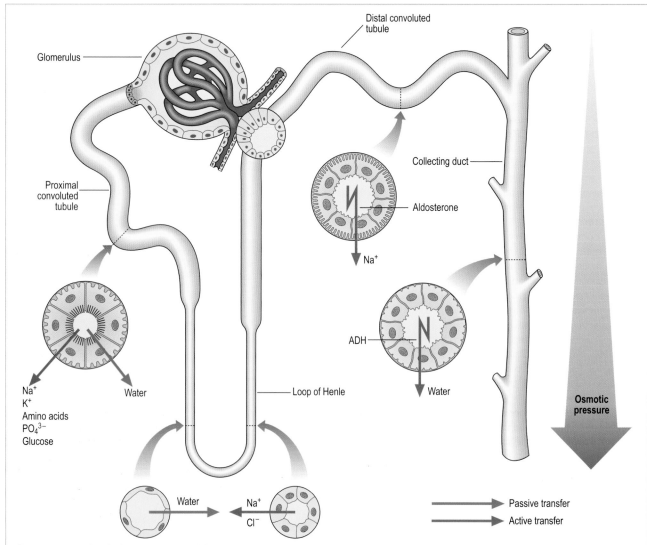

Fig. 21.2   Renal tubular structure and function. Representation of a single nephron showing the function of each part of the tubule. The composition of the glomerular filtrate is modified as it flows along the tubule to form urine.

Neurohormonal factors

Neurohormonal influences operate in patients who have systemic hypotension due to heart failure, or fluid depletion in gastroenteritis.

Both angiotensin II and noradrenaline (norepinephrine) from the adrenal are involved. Angiotensin II constricts the efferent more than the afferent arteriole, and noradrenaline constricts both vessels to the same degree, which preserves the GFR. Both angiotensin II and noradrenaline stimulate prostaglandin synthesis, which by reducing arteriolar tone prevents excessive renal ischaemia. Since non-steroidal anti-inflammatory drugs inhibit the synthesis of prostaglandin, in patients who are hypoperfused they block the potential protective effect of the prostaglandins and can result in acute renal failure.

By liberating angiotensin II, renin also causes the adrenal cortex to produce aldosterone which, in turn, leads to increased reabsorption of sodium by the distal tubular epithelium.

The glomerular filtrate, which is isotonic with the plasma, has to be substantially modified osmotically so that water and electrolytes are conserved and the waste metabolites are concentrated. This occurs as the filtrate flows through the tubules (Fig. 21.2).

Tubular structure and function

Epithelial cells modify the filtrate by transferring electrolytes and solutes aided by a series of carrier proteins or transporters within the apical (luminal) cell membrane. Transfer from the cytoplasm to the interstitial and peritubular fluid is performed by an energy-dependent ATPase pump situated on the basolateral membrane of the cell. The epithelial cells are separated from each other by tight junctions that contain claudins, membrane proteins that prevent the unregulated passage of electrolytes, water and solutes through the epithelial layer between the cells.

In the *proximal tubule* approximately 50–55% of the sodium in the filtrate is reabsorbed through selective sodium transporters, together with specific transmembrane co-transporters linked separately to glucose, phosphate or amino acids. In this way nearly all of the glucose, phosphate and amino acids are reabsorbed by the proximal tubule, thus altering the osmolality of the tubular fluid and causing water to flow into the cytoplasm through specialised water channels termed aquaporins. Some of the sodium transporters are linked with hydrogen exchange, whereby sodium is reabsorbed and hydrogen is excreted. Consequently, c. 80% of all the bicarbonate filtered is reabsorbed by the proximal tubules.

The *loop of Henle,* situated in the medulla and doubling back on itself, is the next part of the nephron through which the now reduced volume of the filtrate must pass. The two limbs have quite different physiological properties. The descending loop is permeable to water but not to ions, whereas the ascending limb is permeable to ions but, lacking aquaporins, is impermeable to water. Thus, the interstitium of the medulla becomes hypertonic. The filtrate in the loop lumen equilibrates with this, because of the permeability to water in the descending limb.

The *distal tubule* is continuous with the ascending limb of the loop of Henle. The epithelial cells of this segment lack aquaporins, making this segment impermeable to water. Sodium

and chloride are reabsorbed by a co-transporter, the activity of which is governed by the concentration of chloride in the luminal fluid. Transport of sodium and chloride in the loop of Henle and distal convoluted tubule is flow-dependent, an important concept in the context of understanding the action of loop diuretics which tend to increase the rate of flow. Calcium transport, under the influence of parathyroid hormone and 1,25-dihydroxycholecalciferol (vitamin D_3), occurs in the distal convoluted tubule and adjacent segments.

The distal convoluted tubule continues into the collecting duct. Two main cell types are present:

- principal cells fund mainly in the cortical collecting duct and inner medullary collecting duct are concerned with sodium and water reabsorption, both of which are influenced by hormones
- intercalated cells are found in the cortex and outer medulla and are involved with acid–base balance.

Aldosterone increases the number of open sodium channels, thus increasing the reabsorption of sodium in the event of volume depletion. The principal cells of the collecting ducts are relatively impermeable to water due to the paucity of aquaporins on the apical membrane. However, under the influence of antidiuretic hormone (ADH) produced by the pituitary, a complex sequence of changes occurs within the cell. This culminates in the fusion of intracytoplasmic vesicles containing preformed aquaporins with the apical membrane so that water can be cleared into the circulation.

The intercalated cells are concerned with hydrogen ion excretion. The excreted hydrogen combines with ammonia in the lumen to form ammonium. Ammonia, formed in the proximal tubule by the metabolism of glutamine and by diffusion from the interstitial fluid, is freely diffusible in contrast to ammonium which is lipid insoluble and cannot pass back into the tubular cytoplasm.

The vasa recta is the delicate meshwork of capillaries that invests the tubules and is derived from the efferent glomerular arteriole. The configuration of the vascular network complements that of the tubule and plays an integral role in the functioning of the countercurrent mechanism.

Countercurrent mechanism

The countercurrent mechanism ensures urine of variable osmolarity forms in response to a variable water intake. The hairpin configuration of the loop of Henle, the complementary vasa recta, coupled with the selective permeabilities to ions and water of the different segments of the loop, the distal tubule and collecting tubules, are all pivotal to the countercurrent mechanism. The active transport of sodium by the thick ascending limb increases the osmolarity of the interstitium. As a result of this, water diffuses from the filtrate in the lumen of the descending limb, which is permeable to water but not to ions. With progress towards the tip of the loop, osmolarity of the filtrate and interstitium increases, particularly in the longer loops derived from the juxtamedullary glomeruli. The principal cells of the collecting tubules display a variable permeability to water under the influence of ADH, achieving urine of variable osmolarity by passing through this hyperosmolar environment on the way to the papillae.

Tamm–Horsfall protein (uromodulin) is a large mucoprotein produced exclusively by the cells of the thick ascending limb of the loop of Henle. It is the main constituent of all tubular casts and may help prevent infections of the urinary tract, but other functions are uncertain. Mutations in the gene encoding this protein are associated with medullary cysts, hyperuricaemia and progressive renal failure.

Renal papillae and urinary reflux

The collecting ducts open onto the surface of the renal papillae projecting into the calyces. The shape of the duct orifice is relevant to the development of reflux and pyelonephritis. Two patterns have been described:

- In the *mid-zone papillae,* the ducts open obliquely onto the surface. In the event of urinary reflux from the bladder, these duct orifices will close under the increased pressure in the pelvicalyceal system, acting effectively as a one-way valve.
- In contrast, the *polar papillae* are more frequently compound. These are formed as a result of fusion of lobes of renal parenchyma during fetal development. They have a flattened or slightly depressed summit (see Fig. 21.14). The collecting ducts in this central area open vertically onto the surface of the papilla; they have no valve effect and remain widely patent, thus allowing the refluxed urine and any bacteria within it to flow into the kidney.

Physiological changes

During pregnancy

During pregnancy the size and weight of the kidneys increases and the glomeruli enlarge. These changes are reflected in the raised GFR and renal plasma flow which reach a peak by 16 weeks and persist until the end of pregnancy.

Ageing

The size of the kidneys falls abruptly after the age of 60 years. Gradual shrinkage of the tubules commences at about 40 years. Arteries display intimal thickening, with progressive reduplication of elastic laminae. Small arteries develop medial hypertrophy and hyalinosis. The number of sclerosed or scarred glomeruli increases with age, thus reducing renal reserve. Drugs usually excreted by the kidneys must, therefore, be used cautiously in the elderly to avoid toxic accumulation.

RENAL DISEASE

Clinicopathological features

Diseases of the kidney can present with a variety of features, alone or in combination. As the kidneys are so often affected by a primary disease elsewhere in the body, a simple urine examination (e.g. colour, glucose, protein, haemoglobin) is routine practice in patients being investigated for a variety of disorders.

Investigation

The investigation of patients with renal disease is multidisciplinary (Table 21.1). Urine and blood analyses are essential; imaging, biopsies and cystoscopy are optional depending on the nature of the clinical problem. Tests with the greatest general clinical utility are urine testing for glucose (to exclude uncontrolled diabetes mellitus), protein (to determine the permeability characteristics of the glomerular basement membrane), and determination of blood concentrations of urea and/or creatinine, the latter being the more reliable indicator of renal function. The GFR is an important expression of renal function and is a useful parameter for monitoring the severity and progress of renal disease.

Renal biopsy is performed only when clinically justified, because of the risk of haemorrhage. The biopsy is examined by light microscopy with additional information revealed by immunofluorescence and electron microscopy in some cases.

Accurate information about the incidence of diseases of the urinary tract is available from transplant and dialysis registries. However, two important factors conspire to make the true incidence of renal disease almost impossible to ascertain. First, not all countries have registries for the accurate recording of cases. Second, transplantation and dialysis registries record severe and end-stage disease only,

Table 21.1 Investigation of patients with urinary tract disease

Investigation	Diagnostic utility
Urine analysis Volume Specific gravity Culture Protein content Glucose Haemoglobin Microscopy (casts, etc.)	Determination of urine production rate and concentrating power of the kidneys; investigation of urinary tract infections; urinary protein indicates integrity of glomerular filter; exclusion of diabetes mellitus; investigation of glomerular or tubular lesions
Blood analysis Urea Creatinine Electrolytes	Determination of integrity of renal function; glomerular filtration rate can be calculated from urinary and plasma creatinine concentration and urine flow rate
Imaging Plain X-ray Ultrasound Contrast urography Angiography	Determination of kidney size and symmetry; investigation of suspected tumours, cysts, etc.; detection of calculi; position and integrity of ureters
Cystoscopy	Investigation of haematuria and other symptoms; biopsy of bladder lesions
Renal biopsy Histology Electron microscopy Immunofluorescence	Diagnosis of glomerular, tubular and interstitial renal diseases

making no allowance for mild and subliminal disease. Clinical experience suggests that the prevalence of post-infectious glomerulonephritis is much higher in Africa and India than in Europe and North America.

Pathophysiological basis of renal disease

Two main clinical syndromes occur in renal disease: nephritis (also referred to as the nephritic syndrome) and the nephrotic syndrome. As part of these, patients present with either acute or chronic renal failure.

Nephritis

Nephritis is characterised by an 'active' urinary sediment comprising red cells, white cells and urinary casts. The clinical manifestations are variable depending on the degree of damage ranging between intermittent painless (asymptomatic) haematuria, acute renal failure and rapidly progressive glomerulonephritis. The unifying feature of the diseases that cause nephritis is endothelial damage and inflammation. In cases of severe nephritis where the inflammatory infiltrate is intense and widespread (i.e. diffuse), there is a substantial reduction in the GFR. The diseases causing nephritis fall into three broad groups:

- immune complex deposition as in post-infective glomerulonephritis or lupus nephritis
- antibodies against the glomerular basement membrane, anti-GBM disease
- systemic vasculitis in which antibodies against neutrophil cytoplasmic antigens (ANCA) are identified.

Nephrotic syndrome

The nephrotic syndrome is due to excessive leakiness of the glomerular filter and comprises:

- proteinuria
- hypoalbuminaemia
- oedema
- hyperlipaemia
- lipiduria.

The unifying abnormality in patients with the nephrotic syndrome is damage to the epithelial cells resulting in 'effacement', 'fusion' or 'simplification' of the foot processes. It results from molecular alterations at the base of the cells and the filtration slit diaphragms. Nephrin and podocin, amongst other proteins, span the cell membrane and effectively hold the cells together in the region of the filtration slit diaphragm. Similarly, integrins anchor the cell surface to the underlying lamina rara externa of the basement membrane, and these proteins in turn connect to the actin-based cytoskeleton of the cell. Thus, when these proteins are altered, through either mutation or damage, the cell cytoplasm retracts, resulting in simplification or effacement, and leading in some cases to focal epithelial separation from the basement membrane.

Diseases causing the nephrotic syndrome fall into four broad groups:

- damage to the integrity of the epithelial cells, as in minimal change disease or focal segmental glomerulosclerosis
- damage to the integrity of the basement membrane by excessive accumulation of abnormal membrane-like material, as in diabetes mellitus
- immune deposition within the capillary wall, as in membranous glomerulonephritis
- deposition of extraneous substances within the wall, as in amyloid deposition.

Proteinuria and oedema

Proteinuria

Three types of proteinuria occur in patients with renal disease emanating from:

- the glomeruli
- the tubules
- overflow proteinuria—when excessive quantities of protein are presented to the kidney, exceeding its capacity to deal with them.

Proteinuria arising from the glomeruli implies severe damage leading to loss of the slit diaphragms and effectively reducing the filtration surface. This results in a major change in the character of the resistance to macromolecules, with ensuing substantial leakage of proteins. A degree of vasoconstriction of the efferent arteriole occurs in response to proteinuria and this serves to increase the intraglomerular hydrostatic pressure which exacerbates the passage of protein through the wall. Therefore, reducing the hydrostatic pressure in the capillary will have a beneficial effect and rationalises the use of antihypertensive therapy in chronic renal disease. The terms selective and non-selective proteinuria refer to the degree and composition of the proteinuria which corresponds to the degree of damage to the filter. Selective proteinuria is seen mostly in minimal change disease.

The tubular epithelial cells reabsorb most of the smaller low molecular weight proteins normally escaping from the glomeruli. Tubulo-interstitial diseases therefore will impede this reabsorption and result in loss of small proteins. In patients with multiple myeloma and other plasma cell dyscrasias, excessive quantities of immunoglobulin light chains are produced and appear in the urine.

Detection of microalbuminuria is particularly important in the management of diabetes and indicates very early increases in permeability. The urinary loss of albumin in these cases amounts to 30–300 mg/day. Routine 'dipstick' testing of urine will not detect microalbuminaemia and is therefore unsuitable for managing diabetics.

Oedema

Oedema is common in renal disease, especially in patients with the nephrotic syndrome, and also in some severe forms of nephritis. Sodium retention by the damaged kidney is the fundamental event, but the mechanism is not known. Oedema in renal disease relates therefore to sodium retention and fluid retention rather than alterations in plasma proteins and plasma osmotic pressure.

Renal failure

Renal failure, 'impairment' or 'insufficiency' are terms used when the kidneys are unable to excrete waste products and fail to manage electrolytes and water in the usual way.

Acute renal failure

Acute renal failure is said to occur when the plasma creatinine concentration has increased by at least 0.5 mg/dl within the past month. The causes of acute renal failure fall into three main groups:

- pre-renal in which the kidneys are inadequately perfused
- intrinsic renal disease which may be glomerular, tubulo-interstitial or vascular
- post-renal or obstructive.

Chronic renal failure

Chronic renal failure (CRF) leads to clinical features often referred to as uraemia, which reflect a severe reduction in functioning renal mass. The development of the clinical changes in uraemia results from:

- reduced excretion of electrolytes and water
- reduced excretion of organic solutes termed uraemic toxins
- impaired renal hormone synthesis.

Alterations in electrolyte excretion are minimal initially because of adaptive mechanisms involving reducing tubular reabsorption and do not become evident until the GFR reduces by c. 80%. Conversely, organic solutes are excreted primarily by glomerular filtration and will accumulate when the GFR falls. Although individual proteins and metabolites cannot be linked to specific uraemic symptoms, they are known collectively as uraemic toxins.

Hormone production by the severely damaged kidney is impaired. The consequences include renal osteodystrophy and secondary hyperparathyroidism, hypertension and anaemia.

Renal osteodystrophy and secondary hyperparathyroidism
Phosphate retention occurs with mild reductions of GFR and is important in CRF. Whilst calcium and phosphate are inversely related, the role of phosphate retention in CRF is pivotal. By attaching to specific receptors, calcitriol (vitamin D_3), produced predominantly by the proximal tubular epithelial cells, appears to be the main regulator of phosphate and exerts a negative feedback on the parathyroids, reducing both production and release of parathyroid hormone (PTH). In CRF, a rise in phosphate inhibiting the secretion of calcitriol may in turn reduce the inhibitory effect on PTH release. The reduced level of calcitriol continues as renal damage proceeds and GFR falls. Eventually the inhibitory effect by PTH on phosphate reabsorption by the proximal tubule will be saturated and hyperphosphataemia and hyperparathyroidism will persist, with two important clinical consequences:

- osteitis fibrosa due to the prolonged bone resorption leading to characteristic cystic changes in the bones
- metastatic calcification due to calcium phosphate deposition in arteries, soft tissues and viscera.

The effects of hyperparathyroidism in patients with CRF can be minimised by a low phosphate diet or the administration of a phosphate-binding agent. Calcitriol is also used but is associated with hypercalcaemia due to the effect on bone. Calcimimetics, which bind to the receptors on the surface of the parathyroid cell, reduce the synthesis and release of PTH. However, oversuppression of PTH may result in adynamic bone disease.

Hypertension
Hypertension occurs in c. 90% of patients with CRF, due mostly to fluid retention; it responds to diuretics. Auto-regulation in response to the reduced GFR releases renin and consequently angiotensin II. Renal scarring and subsequent focal renal ischaemia is thought to be a cause of increased renin secretion. The management of hypertension in patients with chronic renal disease is very important since persistent high blood pressure will exacerbate glomerular damage and further reduce GFR.

Anaemia
Anaemia is common in patients with CRF and accounts for their lethargy and general lack of well-being which worsen with deteriorating renal function. Anaemia results from inadequate renal production of erythropoietin (EPO). The precise site of EPO formation is uncertain but the endothelial cells of the peritubular capillaries have been suggested. Red cell survival is reduced; bleeding tendencies consequent on altered platelet function and iron deficiency are also associated with CRF.

Recombinant EPO treatment corrects most of these changes with marked symptomatic improvement. Iron supplements are required to keep pace with the red cell production as stores can become depleted. Importantly, about one-third of patients develop hypertension, which may be severe. Increased viscosity of the blood and reversal of the peripheral vasodilatory effect of the anaemia have both been implicated.

MECHANISMS OF GLOMERULAR DAMAGE

Glomeruli can be damaged by immunological or non-immunological mechanisms.

Immunological mechanisms

Immune glomerular injury

Immunological damage causes most human glomerular disease. There are two mechanisms:

- nephrotoxic antibody, as in anti-glomerular basement membrane (anti-GBM) disease
- immune complex deposition/activation.

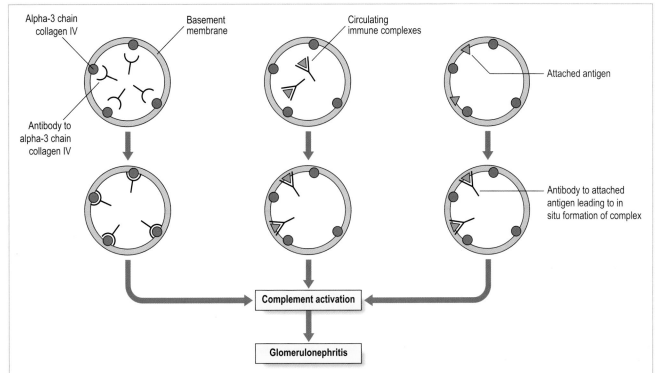

Fig. 21.3 Immunological mechanisms of glomerulonephritis. Glomerulonephritis is due to an antibody reaction to glomerular antigen (alpha-3 chain of collagen IV), to circulating immune complexes that become deposited in the glomeruli, or to antibody reacting to a foreign antigen that has become attached to the basement membrane. The final common pathway of glomerular injury is complement activation resulting in varying degrees of cell damage and inflammatory cell recruitment.

The resulting disease is called glomerulonephritis (in some cases, glomerulopathy). Genetic factors influence susceptibility and prognosis.

Nephrotoxic antibody

In anti-GBM disease, an IgG antibody forms against the alpha-3 chain in the collagenase-resistant component of collagen IV within the basement membrane, binds to it and activates the complement cascade. Renal biopsy reveals, in glomeruli, a linear pattern of immunofluorescent staining for IgG and granular staining for C3. Polymorphs are attracted and a florid proliferative glomerulonephritis results (Fig. 21.3).

Anti-GBM disease is an uncommon cause of glomerulonephritis and in some cases is associated with pulmonary haemorrhages (Goodpasture's syndrome), because the antigen also occurs in the alveolar basement membrane. Clinical and histological features of anti-GBM disease are discussed below.

Immune complex deposition/activation

An immune complex develops when an antibody binds to its soluble specific antigen. The antigen may be extrinsic, e.g. derived from an infective agent, or endogenous, e.g. DNA in lupus; the latter is said to be autoimmune. Some immune complexes form large lattice structures within the circulation and are eliminated by the reticuloendothelial system; others are smaller and initiate glomerular damage by either deposition or in-situ formation (Fig. 21.3). The complexes seen in the glomeruli are termed 'deposits'. The glomeruli are vulnerable because the kidneys filter large volumes of blood. Immune complex damage occurs by:

- entrapment of antigen or complexes, leading to mesangial and subendothelial deposits, or subendothelial deposits
- in-situ formation, following antigen binding to glomerular proteins or by antigenic cross-reaction with basement membrane constituents.

The interaction of antigen and antibody within the deposit activates the complement cascade with the production of the C5b-9 membrane attack complex. In addition, C3a and C5a are chemotactic and recruit polymorphonuclear leukocytes, macrophages and monocytes.

The site of the interaction determines the type of glomerular lesion and the clinical features. Thus, deposits within the mesangium or subendothelial lamina rara interna have access to the circulating blood, and complement activation elicits a proliferative reaction and an active nephritis with haematuria. Both membrano-proliferative glomerulonephritis and IgA disease have this pattern.

In contrast, deposits within the subepithelial lamina rara externa will also activate complement, but the reactants are sequestered from the circulation by the basement membrane. There is therefore no evidence of inflammatory reaction; an example of this pattern is seen in membranous glomerulo-nephritis (glomerulopathy).

Participation by glomerular cells in glomerular disease

Cells within the glomerulus participate in the reaction and consequently to the development of the lesion and the fate of the glomerulus. These cells produce a variety of cytokines and locally influence the coagulation cascade.

Epithelial cells overlying subepithelial deposits are stimulated to produce basement membrane material, mostly laminin. This overproduction results in irregular projections which separate and then partially surround the deposits. These projections, called 'spikes', are characteristic of membranous glomerulopathy. The accumulation of extracellular matrix material is an important aspect of the evolution of glomerular lesions having a wide aetiological background. This accumulation of matrix material is a balance between production, degradation and remodelling and it contributes to the development of glomerulosclerosis.

Endothelial cells lose their natural thromboresistance leading to platelet deposition on the endothelial cell surface and further damage. This is relevant in conditions such as hypertension, diabetes and the inflammatory diseases of blood vessels (vasculitis).

Mediators of glomerular damage

Glomerular cells are affected by a wide variety of substances:

- Complement activation (Ch. 9) has a major role in glomerulonephritis of both anti-GBM and immune complex types. All complement pathways activate C3 and yield C5b-9, the membrane attack complex.
- Nephritic factors (NeFs) or C3 nephritic factors (C3Nefs) are immunoglobulins that inactivate inhibitors of the converting enzymes of the complement cascade. Consequently, the breakdown of C3 remains unchecked, resulting in the depletion of C3 from the plasma, a situation termed hypocomplementaemia.
- Polymorphonuclear leukocytes are attracted by C3a and C5a. The polymorphs bind to the immune complexes by their C3 and Fc receptors. They release their lysosomal enzymes in the vicinity of the complexes, augmenting the damage to the glomerular basement membrane.
- Reactive oxygen species derived from recruited leukocytes and native glomerular cells enhance degradation of the basement membrane and influence arachidonic acid metabolism, thus promoting thrombus formation within the glomerulus.
- Clotting factors also mediate glomerular damage. Fibrin entraps platelets which, because of their C3 and Fc receptors, form microthrombi, degranulate and release their vasoactive peptides, thereby increasing vascular permeability. Platelet-derived growth factor encourages mesangial migration, proliferation, matrix production and thus glomerulosclerosis.

The contribution of the individual mediators varies in each case.

Non-immunological mechanisms

Non-immunological mechanisms include:

- genetic factors: defects in the genes that encode the proteins of the epithelial cell membrane result in simplification of the foot processes, leading to proteinuria
- basement membrane abnormalities, as occur in hereditary nephritis
- vascular lesions which result from endothelial damage and occur in hypertension and thrombotic microangiopathies
- metabolic changes in basement membrane matrix materials induced by hyperglycaemia, which characterise diabetic nephropathy
- accumulation of abnormal proteins in the basement membrane, e.g. amyloid.

CONGENITAL DISEASES

Approximately 10% of individuals have a congenital abnormality of the urinary tract, some of which are hereditary:

- developmental abnormalities related to volume of renal tissue formed or its differentiation
- anatomical abnormalities including abnormal position of vascular or ureteric connections
- defects in the genes encoding enzymes affecting tubular transport (e.g. cystinuria and renal tubular acidosis), proteins of the filtration slit diaphragm (e.g. congenital nephrotic syndrome) and collagen and intercellular matrix proteins (e.g. hereditary nephritis).

Developmental abnormalities

Conditions affecting the volume of renal tissue
Renal agenesis (absence of the kidney) may be unilateral or bilateral.

Bilateral agenesis results from failure of initiation of the pronephros–metanephros sequence; the ureteric bud fails to develop. It occurs in c. 0.04% of all pregnancies and is associated with a severe reduction in amniotic fluid (oligohydramnios) resulting in neonatal death due to lung hypoplasia. The majority of cases are stillborn. There are also developmental abnormalities of other tissues derived from the mesonephros, e.g. bladder and genitalia. Accompanying spinal cord abnormalities with involvement of the hind gut and fused lower extremities is termed sirenomelia (mermaid syndrome).

Unilateral agenesis of a kidney is common, affecting up to 0.1% of the population. The opposite kidney undergoes marked hypertrophy and is prone to trauma and to reflux nephropathy since it is often associated with pelvi-ureteric or ureterovesical junction obstruction. The relatively high incidence of a solitary kidney in the general population means it is imperative to confirm the presence of a second kidney before renal biopsy or nephrectomy.

Disorders of differentiation
Renal dysplasia may present in childhood as an abdominal mass simulating a tumour. It is characterised by islands of undifferentiated mesenchyme or cartilage within the parenchyma.

The pathogenesis is failure of induction of both the ureteric bud and mesenchymal tissues leading to abnormal development of the collecting ducts and subsequent loss of potential nephrons with the formation of cysts. The prognosis is good if the lesion is unilateral with no obstruction.

Anatomical abnormalities

Ectopic kidneys form in an abnormal site, usually the pelvis, and may be associated with intestinal malrotation. They may present as a suspicious pelvic mass and there is a risk of infection due to the ureteric kinking that often accompanies this condition.

Horseshoe kidney results from fusion of the two nephrogenic blastemas during fetal life. Most are fused at the lower pole. The condition is not rare and renal function is usually normal.

Genetic abnormalities leading to enzyme abnormalities

Cystinuria

Cystinuria (Ch. 7) results from defective tubular reabsorption of several dibasic amino acids including cystine, lysine, ornithine and arginine. There is mutation in the genes for the amino acid transporters. Cystine crystals are found in the urine; stones may develop by the second or third decade.

Renal tubular acidosis

Two forms of renal tubular acidosis affect different tubular segments. Type 1 ('distal') causes metabolic acidosis and a persistent urinary pH of 5.5 because the hydrogen-ATPase pump in the apical membrane is deficient due to acquired or genetic factors. Type 2 ('proximal') causes a metabolic acidosis associated with a low plasma bicarbonate; there is impaired reabsorption of bicarbonate by the proximal tubular cells.

Genetic abnormalities leading to abnormal proteins

Congenital nephrotic syndrome

This is a rare autosomal recessive condition. There are mutations of the gene for nephrin (*NPHS1*) on chromosome 19. Consequently, the nephrin formed is defective and, being an integral part of the filtration slit diaphragm of the podocyte, there is effacement of the foot processes and proteinuria which is present before birth. The kidneys are enlarged and appear microcystic due to dilatation of the proximal tubules and Bowman's capsule. Affected infants have additionally the characteristic Potter facies and marked motor and mental retardation, and are particularly vulnerable to pneumococcal infection. There is no treatment, but the lesion does not recur in a transplanted kidney.

Hereditary nephritis

Hereditary nephritic syndromes result from mutations in the genes encoding alpha chains in the collagen IV molecule and result in abnormal basement membranes which feature collagen IV. The least severely affected patients have an autosomal recessive form of inheritance. Two forms are recognised: thin basement membrane disease and persistent haematuria.

Thin basement membrane disease

Thin basement membrane disease is identified ultrastructurally when patients are investigated for chronic haematuria. Also known as benign familial haematuria, the condition is common, occurring in some 25% of patients investigated for haematuria, and may be present in about 1% of the population. The clinical importance lies in excluding more serious causes of haematuria and differentiating it from the early stages of Alport's disease.

Alport's disease

Alport's disease is recognised clinically by the triad of:

- nephritis
- deafness
- ocular lesions.

The most common form (90%) is X-linked, due to a mutation of the gene encoding the alpha-5 chain of collagen IV. The mutation causes an inability to form normal basement membranes which feature collagen IV, notably in the kidney, eye and ear, thus explaining the clinical triad. Males are affected more frequently and more severely; the eventual outcome is renal failure by the second decade. In contrast, renal function may be preserved in females until the fifth decade. The deafness, which is for high frequencies, is often difficult to demonstrate. Ocular disease occurs in severely affected patients and involves dislocation of the lens, cataracts and corneal dystrophy.

Microscopic changes are most noticeable in the late stages when glomerulosclerosis develops. Electron microscopy reveals an irregular thinned and reduplicated basement membrane giving rise to the 'basket weave' pattern characteristic of the disease.

CYSTIC DISEASE

- ▶ Cysts may be solitary or multiple, congenital or acquired
- ▶ A solitary cyst may simulate a tumour
- ▶ Congenital polycystic disease may not present until adult life
- ▶ Acquired cysts may be due to renal scarring

Cystic disease of the kidney comprises a heterogeneous group of conditions which are genetic or acquired. Accurate diagnosis is essential so that, where the disease is genetically transmitted, the appropriate genetic counselling can be given to patients and their relatives.

Formerly, renal cystic disease was classified morphologically, but with improved imaging and characterisation of genetic factors the pathogenesis of these conditions is being clarified. The current classification of cystic disease, correlating morphological features and genetic factors, will almost certainly be revised as further information becomes available (Table 21.2).

Pathogenesis of cysts

The development of cysts is thought to involve several processes involving the development and polar differentiation of the epithelial cells. Reversal of the polarity of transporter proteins results in transport of fluid via the sodium pump into the tubular lumen which then becomes cystic. There are also changes in the primary cilia where all of the major proteins relevant to cystic disease are normally expressed.

Autosomal dominant polycystic kidney disease (ADPKD)

ADPKD is the primary renal disease in 8% of adult patients in the European Dialysis and Transplantation Registry. The condition is always bilateral; the kidneys are grossly enlarged, each commonly weighing 1000 g or more (Fig. 21.4). The kidneys are distorted by numerous cysts, from a few millimetres up to c. 100 mm in diameter, with thin bands of renal parenchyma compressed between them. Most cysts contain clear fluid, but previous haemorrhage can result in the contents being brown due to haemosiderin. The cysts are formed at all levels of the nephron.

ADPKD is inherited as an autosomal dominant trait with a high degree of penetrance; this is relevant to genetic counselling and screening. Most cases are linked to the alpha-globin cluster on the short arm of chromosome 16 (PKD 1) which encodes polycystin-1; the remainder are due to mutations on chromosome 4 (PKD 2) which encodes polycystin-2. This condition presents at any age from childhood to late adult life. Renal function is maintained until the enlarging cysts press on the adjacent parenchyma, causing ischaemic changes leading to hypertension or renal failure. There is an association with berry aneurysms of the circle of Willis, a frequent source of often fatal subarachnoid haemorrhage (Ch. 26). Cysts also occur within the liver, pancreas and lungs, but have no functional significance in these organs.

Autosomal recessive polycystic kidney disease (ARPKD)

Autosomal recessive polycystic disease (ARPKD) is a rare condition which has a recessive pattern of inheritance. All of these patients have mutations in a single gene known as the 'polycystic kidney and hepatic disease gene 1' (*PKHD1*) on chromosome 6 which encodes for the protein fibrocystin/polyductin. Fibrocystin is a transmembrane receptor located in the cilia of the renal epithelial cells and is involved in the differentiation of renal collecting ducts and bile ducts.

Clinical presentation depends on the severity of involvement and occurs in neonates, children and young adults. The antenatal or perinatal patient has the characteristic Potter facies associated with oligohydramnios and is either stillborn or develops respiratory distress soon after birth. The kidneys are enlarged and show a characteristic radial pattern of fusiform

Table 21.2   Cystic disease: classification
Simple cysts
Polycystic kidney disease • Autosomal dominant (ADPKD) • Autosomal recessive (ARPKD) • Glomerulocystic disease

Renal medullary cysts
• Nephronophthisis (NPH)
   — juvenile
   — infantile
   — adolescent
• Medullary cystic disease (MCKD)
• Medullary sponge kidney

Renal cysts associated with genetic diseases affecting multiple systems • Tuberose sclerosis • von Hippel–Lindau disease
Acquired (dialysis related) cysts

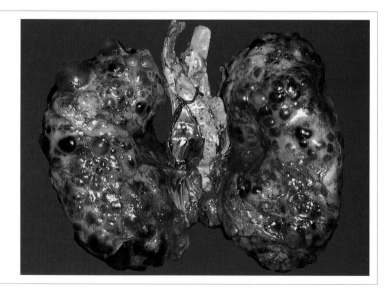

Fig. 21.4 Autosomal dominant polycystic disease (ADPKD). Both kidneys are greatly enlarged by numerous cysts of varying sizes.

cysts which are dilated collecting ducts. The enlarged kidneys are usually palpable and may impair birth.

Patients who survive to childhood or adult life develop abnormalities of the liver, ranging from bile duct proliferation and cysts, to substantial hepatic fibrosis and cirrhosis which will eventually interfere with hepatic function and produce portal hypertension (Ch. 16). In addition, chronic lung disease, growth retardation and urinary tract infections are recorded. The median survival is 27 years for patients who survive the first month.

Renal medullary cysts

Medullary cystic diseases (nephronophthisis and medullary cystic kidney disease) have been categorised and clarified using genetic and molecular biological features. Clinical and pathological features are shared, but they have different patterns of inheritance and are associated with different extrarenal conditions. Medullary cysts develop as the diseases progress so they are not reliable early diagnostic features.

Nephronophthisis (NPH) encompasses a group of autosomal recessive inherited conditions. These are related to mutations in different NPH genes, which encode important proteins for renal development. They affect different age groups.

- Mutation of the *NPH1* gene, which encodes for nephrocystin-1, causes the *juvenile form*. Patients lose salt and cannot form concentrated urine, with polyuria and polydipsia. Renal failure ensues by the age of c. 13 years.
- The *infantile form*, involving *NPH2* which encodes for inversin, results in anaemia with growth retardation and renal failure by the age of 1–3 years.
- In the *adolescent form* the genetic defect involves *NPH3* and the protein nephrocystin-3, with renal failure developing by the age of c. 19 years. Some patients (c. 10%) develop extrarenal lesions including retinitis pigmentosa, mental retardation, cerebral, optic and bone lesions.

Medullary cystic kidney disease (MCKD) is rare, usually presents in adults and has an autosomal dominant inheritance. These patients fail to concentrate urine and lose salt, with polyuria and polydipsia in most cases. Two genes are involved: the more damaging, *MCKD2*, is situated on chromosome 16 and encodes for uromodulin (Tamm–Horsfall protein). Patients with this anomaly develop renal failure during the third decade of life.

Medullary sponge kidney

Medullary sponge kidney is a disease of adults resulting from dilated collecting ducts in the medulla, causing cysts mainly in the papillae. Renal function is usually normal but large calculi form within the cysts, causing pain, haematuria, infections and obstruction.

Dialysis-associated cysts

Dialysis-associated cysts occur in the kidneys of patients in chronic renal failure who have been dialysed long term. The cysts vary in size and number, frequently show intracystic haemorrhage and contain oxalate crystals. The epithelial lining forms micropapillary proliferations and c. 5% of patients with acquired cystic disease develop renal cell carcinoma; therefore patients with acquired cystic disease should be monitored.

GLOMERULAR DISEASE

> ▶ Glomerular disease may be classified by pathogenesis or histological pattern
> ▶ Pathogenic classification includes immunological and non-immunological injury
> ▶ Immunological injury may be due to anti-glomerular basement membrane antibody (anti-GBM) or to immune complex deposition
> ▶ In immune complex glomerular injury, antigens may be derived from bacteria, parasites, drugs, etc.
> ▶ Histological classification is based on the reaction of the glomerulus to injury (e.g. proliferative, membranous thickening)
> ▶ Histological features assist in the identification of aetiology and in prognostic and therapeutic decisions

Classification

Classification of glomerular disease usually presents difficulties for students of renal disease. As with many aspects of human disease, it is impossible to provide a satisfactory classification of glomerular disease on the basis of one set of features. There are three parallel and complementary classifications:

- aetiological
- immunological
- morphological.

Clinicopathologically, diseases affecting the glomeruli are best grouped initially into two broad categories:

- *primary glomerular lesions*—in which the kidney is the prime target
- *secondary glomerular lesions*—in which the glomerular injury is secondary to events elsewhere in the body.

Either of these may involve:

- *immunological reactions* involving either
  — glomerular antigens (e.g. anti-glomerular basement membrane glomerulonephritis), or
  — non-glomerular antigens (e.g. immune complex glomerulonephritis)
- *non-immunological disorders* (e.g. diabetes mellitus and inherited disorders)

Nomenclature of glomerular injury

Glomeruli show a limited range of reactions to injury. The following nomenclature is used to describe the pattern of injury:

- *diffuse:* a lesion affecting > 50% of the glomeruli
- *focal:* a lesion involving < 50% of the glomeruli
- *global:* affecting the whole glomerulus
- *segmental:* affecting only part of the glomerulus.

Additional terms are used to describe the character of the light microscopic changes within the glomeruli:

- *proliferative:* increased numbers of cells within the glomerulus; due to proliferation of indigenous cells and to recruitment of polymorphs and macrophages from the circulation as a consequence of activation of the complement cascade
- *membranous change:* the peripheral loops are thickened due to basement membrane expansion
- *membrano-proliferative:* a combination of the two preceding features, often with accentuation of the lobular architecture
- *crescentic:* florid proliferation of cells including macrophages lining Bowman's capsule, often compressing the glomerulus.

Recognition of these changes and the use of this nomenclature have important clinical implications; for example, the presence of crescents in >50% of glomeruli corresponds to rapidly progressive glomerulonephritis, which heralds a poor prognosis unless it is treated effectively.

Morphology alone gives little indication of the precise nature of the underlying or primary abnormality. Similar morphological features occur in entirely different conditions. To establish an accurate diagnosis, immunological and ultrastructural assessment is needed.

Clinical presentations

Patients with glomerular disease usually present with one of five conditions.

1. *Recurrent painless haematuria* which varies considerably in degree, ranging from macroscopic haematuria to that which may be detected only at a medical examination.
2. *Asymptomatic proteinuria,* varying in severity, and detected at a routine or insurance medical examination.
3. *Acute nephritis,* characterised by haematuria, oliguria and hypertension. Loin pain and headache may be present and the patient will often feel unwell. In post-infective cases the relation to the preceding infection can usually be ascertained.
4. *Nephrotic syndrome,* characterised by heavy proteinuria and severe oedema. There is hypoalbuminaemia and hypercholesterolaemia.
5. *Chronic renal failure,* is characterised by elevated blood urea (uraemia) and other features including anaemia, nausea, vomiting, gastrointestinal bleeding and itching; there is often polyuria and nocturia. The gradual loss of nephrons leads initially to a reduction in renal reserve, so that a relatively minor insult, such as an episode of diarrhoea and vomiting, will reveal renal impairment in an otherwise healthy patient. The consequences of chronic renal failure are discussed above (p. 570).

There is considerable overlap of the conditions within these clinical states (Table 21.3). Several diseases, therefore, may give rise to the same clinical picture; conversely, many diseases fall into more than one of the presenting clinical conditions.

Table 21.3 Glomerular disease: clinical presentations

Recurrent painless haematuria:
- exercise haematuria
- mesangial IgA nephropathy (Berger's disease)
- Henoch–Schönlein purpura
- bacterial endocarditis
- systemic lupus erythematosus (SLE)
- vasculitis–polyarteritis.

Asymptomatic proteinuria:
- Henoch–Schönlein purpura
- SLE
- polyarteritis
- bacterial endocarditis
- shunt nephritis
- focal segmental glomerulosclerosis
- mesangiocapillary glomerulonephritis (MCGN).

Acute nephritis:
- post-streptococcal glomerulonephritis
- idiopathic rapidly progressive glomerulonephritis (RPGN)
- post-infectious RPGN
- Goodpasture's syndrome (anti-glomerular basement membrane disease)
- SLE
- polyarteritis
- Wegener's granulomatosis
- Henoch–Schönlein purpura
- essential cryoglobulinaemia.

Nephrotic syndrome:
- primary glomerular diseases
  — minimal change disease
  — membranous glomerulonephritis
  — membrano-proliferative GN (mesangiocapillary GN)
  — focal glomerulosclerosis
  — mesangial IgA nephropathy
  — bacterial endocarditis
  — shunt nephritis
- secondary glomerular disease
  — SLE
  — Henoch–Schönlein purpura
  — immune complex disease related to tumours, e.g. carcinoma of bronchus, lymphomas
  — diabetes mellitus
  — amyloid
  — drugs, e.g. penicillamine, gold, 'street heroin', phenytoin, captopril
  — infections—malaria, syphilis, leprosy, hepatitis B
  — cardiovascular—constrictive pericarditis
  — bee sting allergy
- inherited disease
  — congenital nephrotic syndrome (Finnish type).

Chronic renal failure:
- those with known renal disease which has caused gradual parenchymal destruction
- those who present de novo, the initial disease having been undetected in its active stage.

PRIMARY GLOMERULAR DISEASES

Anti-glomerular basement membrane disease

Anti-glomerular basement membrane (anti-GBM) disease is uncommon and occurs predominantly in young men. The mechanism of this disease is discussed above. The usual presenting feature is rapidly progressive renal failure. Haemoptysis may be present as part of the pulmonary–renal (Goodpasture's) syndrome. The prognosis is poor without treatment, but plasma exchange (plasmapheresis) substantially improves the outlook, particularly in patients treated early.

Histologically, the characteristic lesion is a focal and segmental glomerulonephritis. With increasing severity, segmental necrosis with fibrin deposition, and a florid crescentic glomerulonephritis occurs (Fig. 21.5).

Immune complex-mediated lesions

Immune complex-mediated glomerular injury (for mechanism, see above) results in a variety of glomerular reactions depending on the nature and site of the complexes.

Diffuse proliferative glomerulonephritis

Acute diffuse proliferative glomerulonephritis is one of the patterns of glomerular damage associated with a post-infective aetiology. It is usually an acute lesion following a transient infection. For many years it has been associated with a preceding beta-haemolytic streptococcal infection (post-streptococcal glomerulonephritis). However, a variety of other causative organisms produce this change, including:

- staphylococci
- meningococci
- pneumococci
- viruses
- malaria
- toxoplasmosis
- schistosomiasis.

Post-streptococcal glomerulonephritis

Beta-haemolytic streptococci of Lancefield group A, Griffith's subtypes 12, 4 and 1, cause post-streptococcal glomerulonephritis. The primary infection usually causes pharyngitis but may also involve the middle ear or skin. There are considerable geographical differences in the incidence and severity of post-streptococcal glomerulonephritis; for example, it is the commonest renal disease in India, but its incidence is falling in the UK.

Clinical features. Post-streptococcal glomerulonephritis affects all ages, but children are more commonly affected, with the onset of malaise, fever and nausea 7–14 days after a sore throat. There is oliguria (a significant reduction in urine volume), and the urine is dark or 'smoky' due to the presence of microscopic haematuria. Facial oedema, often periorbital, and a mild degree of hypertension are apparent on examination. A raised anti-streptolysin O (ASO) titre and a significant reduction in complement (C3) levels are present.

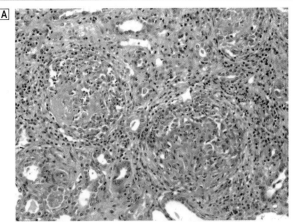

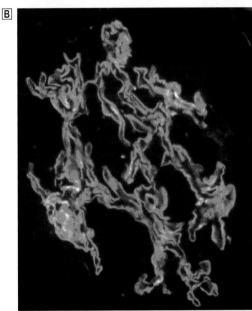

Fig. 21.5   Anti-glomerular basement membrane disease. The glomerular injury in this case is due to anti-glomerular basement membrane antibody. **A** The resulting damage causes obliteration of the Bowman's space by macrophages, inflammatory cells and epithelial cells forming a crescent. **B** Immunofluorescence reveals linear deposition of immunoglobulin on the glomerular basement membrane.

Urine analysis reveals haematuria, together with white cells and casts, with a variable degree of proteinuria.

Histological features. The glomeruli are distended and hypercellular (Fig. 21.6A). All of the glomeruli are involved, hence the use of the term 'diffuse'. The increase in cellularity is due to the proliferation and swelling of mesangial, endothelial and epithelial cells, together with polymorphonuclear leukocytes. Some glomeruli may show proliferation of cells lining Bowman's capsule to form a crescent; the presence of crescents in 60% or more of the glomeruli indicates a rapidly progressive disease and heralds a poor prognosis. There is usually interstitial oedema and a variable inflammatory cell infiltrate. The tubules contain red cell casts and the tubular epithelial cells may show degenerative changes.

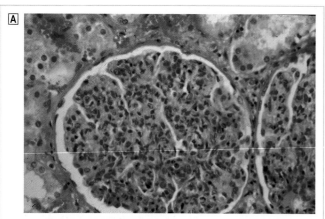

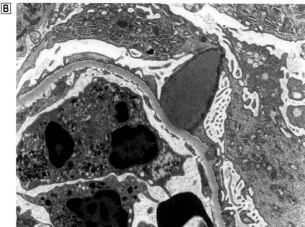

Fig. 21.6   Diffuse proliferative glomerulonephritis. **A** The glomerular injury in this case, characterised by hypercellularity owing to cellular proliferation and acute inflammatory cell infiltration, is due to immune complex deposition. **B** Ultrastructure of diffuse proliferative glomerulonephritis. The principal abnormality is the presence of electron-dense immune complexes deposited between the epithelial cells and the basement membrane. The cells with the granular cytoplasm in the lumen are neutrophil polymorphs attracted by the activation of complement in the loose subendothelial material.

Using immunofluorescence techniques, granular deposits of IgG and C3 are identified on the peripheral basement membranes. Ultrastructurally, subepithelial deposits correspond to the granular IgG and C3 demonstrated by the immunological techniques (Fig. 21.6B).

Pathogenesis.   The precise streptococcal antigen is not yet known—one is antigenically similar to streptokinase, others are cationic: streptococcal M protein, for example, cross-reacts with basement membrane antigens. Current evidence suggests an in-situ antigen–antibody reaction in post-streptococcal glomerulonephritis.

Prognosis.   This is good in children, but only 60% of adults recover fully. Acute post-streptococcal glomerulonephritis is usually treated conservatively; renal biopsy is not usual unless the anticipated improvement fails to occur. In most cases the characteristic morphological changes will have resolved

by 6–8 weeks after the onset of the illness. All that remains is mild mesangial hypercellularity, which may persist for many months or even years. The relationship between post-streptococcal glomerulonephritis and subsequent chronic glomerulonephritis remains controversial.

Focal proliferative glomerulonephritis

'Focal' implies uneven involvement of the glomeruli with some affected and the majority normal. In addition, involvement of only parts of individual glomeruli is usual, and the term 'segmental' is also appropriate. Thus, focal and segmental lesions are often found together. A focal glomerulonephritis is a fairly common pattern of reaction which is found in a variety of systemic diseases including:

● systemic lupus erythematosus
● Henoch–Schönlein purpura
● infective endocarditis
● microscopic polyarteritis
● Goodpasture's syndrome
● Wegener's granulomatosis.

The unqualified term 'focal glomerulonephritis' is not helpful clinically. The immunological and ultrastructural profile of the glomerular lesion in the renal biopsy must be ascertained for a more precise diagnosis.

There is one significant condition having a focal pattern that affects the kidney primarily: IgA disease. IgA deposition also occurs systemically, giving rise to Henoch–Schönlein purpura, a systemic vasculitis with involvement of the kidney.

IgA disease

IgA disease is now recognised as a major cause of chronic renal failure and insufficiency. The features include:

● children and young adults affected
● racial differences (Asian and Native Americans > Caucasians > Africans)
● males more susceptible
● episodic haematuria or asymptomatic haematuria, often coinciding with an upper respiratory infection
● mild proteinuria: nephrotic syndrome in 10%
● hypertension
● raised IgA1 levels.

Histological features.   A wide spectrum of changes occurs. Mild focal mesangial proliferation is associated with a good prognosis. In contrast, at the other end of the spectrum, a mesangiocapillary pattern, sometimes with segmental necrosis, is associated with a more rapid deterioration of renal function. IgA disease is often accompanied by a brisk interstitial inflammatory component, and established interstitial fibrosis is an ominous feature.

Aetiology.   Most IgA is produced by mucosa-associated plasma cells. IgA nephropathy is associated with inflammatory bowel disease and an increased turnover of IgA complexes occurs. IgA nephropathy also occurs in patients with hepatic cirrhosis due to impaired clearance of complexes.

Prognosis and treatment.   The prognosis is better in young patients with IgA disease. Adverse clinical prognostic indicators include age, renal impairment at presentation, persistent proteinuria and hypertension.

Membranous glomerulopathy

Membranous glomerulopathy (membranous glomerulo-nephritis, MGN), a chronic immune complex-mediated disorder, has a distinctive histological picture but many causes. It is an important cause of nephrotic syndrome.

Aetiology. In approximately 85% of patients with membranous glomerulopathy there is no identifiable cause; it is idiopathic. Other cases have an identifiable cause; these are secondary membranous glomerulopathies:

- *infective*—syphilis, malaria, hepatitis B
- *drugs*—penicillamine, gold, mercury, heroin
- *tumours*—lymphomas, melanomas, carcinoma of the breast and bronchus.

These patients are important to identify because the renal lesions may subside when the causative factor is removed. Approximately 10% of patients with systemic lupus erythematosus have membranous change.

Clinical features and prognosis. MGN affects all ages, but more commonly adults, with the highest incidence in the fifth to seventh decades. Males are affected more frequently. The presenting feature is either proteinuria or nephrotic syndrome. Hypertension occurs in about half of the patients. Treatment is controversial; most cases are unresponsive to steroids. Adult patients progress over a variable and unpredictable period; the 10-year survival is c. 75% and c. 30% will develop CRF due to glomerulosclerosis. The prognosis in children is much better, particularly when there is proteinuria alone. In these cases, only 10% develop renal failure, and some 50% remit.

Histological features. Capillary wall thickening, without proliferation or inflammation, and characteristic spikes occur in all glomeruli (Fig. 21.7). There are granular immune deposits of IgG and C3 in the thickened capillary walls. Electron microscopy reveals immune complexes deposited on the outer aspect of the basement membrane beneath the epithelial cells and there is effacement of the foot processes. The epithelial cells overlying the deposits produce new basement membrane, forming the spikes seen light microscopically; this encircles the deposits which undergo degradation and lysis. Eventually the affected glomeruli become sclerosed.

Pathogenesis. The features of membranous glomerulopathy suggest a chronic immune complex disease, but the precise molecular target is still debated. Possibilities include glycoproteins (megalin) on the surface of the epithelial cells.

Membrano-proliferative glomerulonephritis

Membrano-proliferative glomerulonephritis (MPGN), a glomerular lesion with many causes, features both membrane thickening and proliferation (Fig. 21.8A). In addition, there is accentuation of the lobular architecture of the glomerulus. The thickened capillary walls, which have a duplicated 'tram track' appearance of the basement membrane revealed by silver staining (Fig. 21.8B), prompt the alternative name of mesangiocapillary glomerulonephritis (MCGN). This duplication is due to a new layer of basement membrane laid down by cell processes interposed between the endothelium and the basement membrane (Fig. 21.8C). Two main types are recognised.

Type I MPGN
Type I MPGN is an immune complex-mediated lesion. Patients with this condition fall into two groups:

- those with mixed cryoglobulinaemia—c. 80% have hepatitis C
- those without cryoglobulinaemia, occurring in a wide range of conditions including infections, tumours, collagen vascular diseases, hereditary and acquired complement deficiencies, drug reactions and genetic disorders (e.g. sickle cell disease).

Most patients present with nephrotic syndrome, but some have haematuria. A persistently low serum complement C3 (hypocomplementaemia) occurs in two-thirds of patients. There is progressive deterioration over 10 or more years.

Type II MPGN
Type II MPGN is characterised by markedly thickened capillary walls expanded by a discontinuous linear deposition of altered basement membrane material and C3. Ultrastructurally, large electron-dense ribbon-like deposits give rise to the preferable alternative name—dense deposit disease (Fig. 21.9).

The lesion results from self-perpetuating activation of the alternative pathway of the complement cascade by a C3 nephritic factor (C3NeF), now termed NeFa, and explains the hypocomplementaemia.

Type III MPGN
A third rare variant of MPGN is not related to immune complex deposition but is thought to be related to another nephritic factor (NeFt) involving the terminal pathway of the complement cascade.

Crescentic glomerulonephritis

Crescentic glomerulonephritis, which equates clinically to rapidly progressive glomerulonephritis (RPGN), is a manifestation of severe glomerular damage characterised by the presence of >50% cellular crescents that eventually compress the glomeruli (Fig. 21.10). There is a florid necrotising glomerulonephritis with fibrinoid necrosis and breaks in the basement membrane.

Crescentic glomerulonephritis may be limited to the kidneys or be part of a systemic small vessel vasculitis. Three main categories lead to this histological appearance:

- immune complex-mediated (45%)
- pauci-immune glomerulonephritis (50%)
- anti-GBM disease (5%).

Immune complex-mediated represents a heterogeneous group in which crescentic nephritis complicates a known

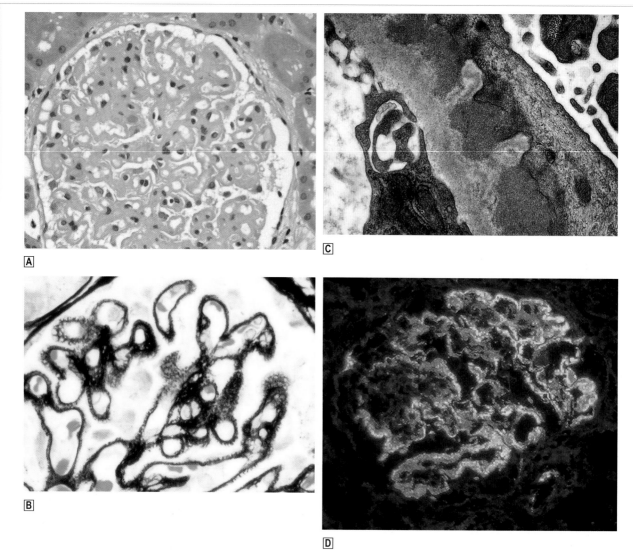

Fig 21.7 Membranous glomerulopathy. [A] Membranous glomerulopathy is characterised by thickened glomerular capillary walls.
[B] Histological staining by a silver impregnation method reveals minute 'spikes' on the outer aspects of the capillary wall. [C] An electron micrograph shows the capillary wall to be thickened by the deposition of electron-dense deposits beneath the epithelial cells and between them new basement membrane corresponding to the 'spikes' seen histologically. [D] Immunofluorescence microscopy reveals granular deposition of IgG in the glomerular basement membranes, corresponding to the electron-dense deposits ultrastructurally.

form of glomerulonephritis, e.g. IgA, Henoch–Schönlein purpura (HSP), lupus nephritis, MPGN, etc.

Pauci-immune glomerulonephritis is characterised by few or no immunoreactants on immunofluorescent staining. Some 85% of these patients have demonstrable antineutrophil cytoplasmic antibody (ANCA). ANCA has been shown to damage the glomerular capillaries and small renal vessels by interacting with and activating neutrophils.

Anti-GBM disease has already been discussed (p. 577). In c. 50% of cases the lesion is restricted to the kidneys. When the renal disease is accompanied by haemoptysis and pulmonary haemorrhages it is part of the pulmonary–renal (Goodpasture's) syndrome, which accounts for the remainder. This disease is commoner in young men; the causative factor is unknown although both a recent flu-like illness and

exposure to hydrocarbons feature in the clinical history in some patients.

Anti-GBM disease is the most aggressive lesion and requires vigorous immunosuppression augmented by plasma exchange (plasmapheresis) at a very early stage. Nevertheless, there is a high risk of permanent scarring of the kidney with subsequent hypertension.

Minimal change disease

Minimal change disease (MCD) is an important cause of nephrotic syndrome, particularly in children. With a light microscope the glomeruli are normal; the extensive effacement of the epithelial foot processes is evident only by electron microscopy.

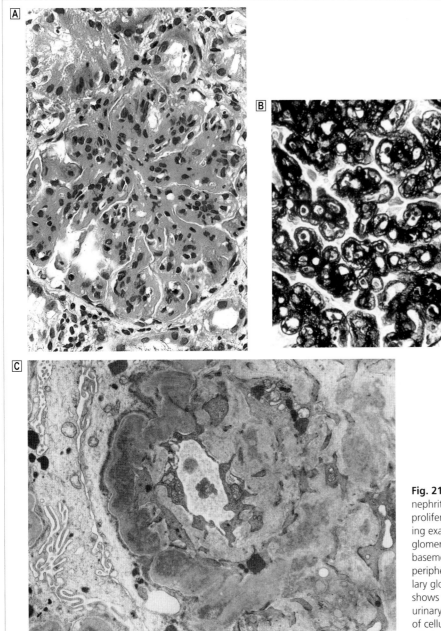

Fig. 21.8 Membrano-proliferative glomerulonephritis. **A** The combination of mesangial cell proliferation and basement membrane thickening exaggerates the lobular architecture of the glomerulus. **B** MST stain shows the new layer of basement membrane giving rise to the reduplicated peripheral profiles characteristic of mesangiocapillary glomerulonephritis. **C** Electron microscopy shows the wall between the capillary lumen and urinary space to be thickened by the interposition of cellular processes and electron-dense deposits in relation to them.

Pathogenesis. This is still not clear. The association of MCD with drug sensitivities, stings, venoms and Hodgkin's disease has suggested immune mechanisms influencing the permeability of the capillary wall.

Clinical features and prognosis. Minimal change disease affects all ages, but is much more common in children, with a peak age incidence below 5 years and with a male preponderance. In a few patients it follows an upper respiratory infection or prophylactic immunisation. Nephrotic syndrome responsive to steroid therapy is the classical presentation. The prognosis in children is good with no permanent renal damage, but in adults the outlook is variable.

Focal glomerulosclerosis

Focal segmental glomerulosclerosis (FSGS) is an important cause of nephrotic syndrome; the incidence is increasing in adults. It accounts for c. 10% of children with nephrotic syndrome. This pattern of glomerular damage results from a variety of pathogenic and aetiological factors such as in diabetic nephropathy, HIV infection, heroin abuse and reflux nephropathy. It occurs not uncommonly in the late stages of immune complex-induced lesions, e.g. IgA nephropathy.

Aetiology and pathogenesis. There is good evidence (e.g. recurrent FSGS in transplanted kidneys) for a circulating factor

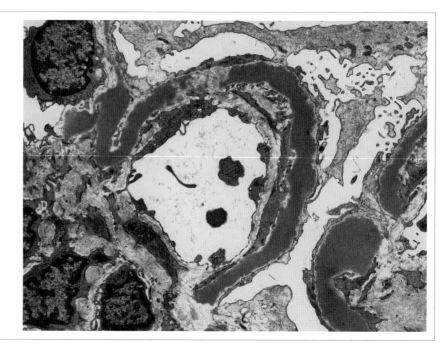

Fig. 21.9   Dense deposit disease. Electron micrograph showing the irregular ribbon-like deposits in dense deposit disease.

having an aetiological role in FSGS but this has not yet been fully characterised.

Congenital nephrotic syndrome features focal and segmental glomerulosclerosis, one cause of which has been identified in the mutation of the gene for nephrin (*NPHS1*). Gene aberrations for the associated proteins in the slit diaphragm are associated with familial FSGS, each family showing an individual mutation.

Histologically, sclerosis is recognised by expansion of the matrix together with obliteration of the capillary lumen, sometimes involving only part of the glomerulus (segmental). Hyalinosis of the capillary loops is present in some cases of FSGS. Vascular hyalinosis is also seen and there is interstitial fibrosis and tubular atrophy. Electron microscopy shows foot process effacement, but there are no deposits to correspond to the non-specific entrapment of IgM and C3 seen immunohistochemically.

SECONDARY GLOMERULAR DISEASES

▶ Many systemic disorders result in glomerular damage
▶ Immune complexes in autoimmune disease (e.g. SLE) can damage basement membranes
▶ Diabetes mellitus may be complicated by glomerulopathy and renal papillary necrosis
▶ Glomerular vascular lesions can result from systemic vasculitis and hypertension

Secondary glomerular disease implies renal damage occurring as part of a systemic condition. These systemic conditions may be:

- immune complex-mediated
- metabolic
- vascular.

Immune complex-mediated conditions

Immune complex-mediated systemic conditions that may involve renal damage include:

- systemic lupus erythematosus
- Henoch–Schönlein purpura
- infective endocarditis.

Systemic lupus erythematosus

Renal involvement occurs in about 70% of lupus patients. The lesions are varied and represent a spectrum with increasing degrees of damage. The glomeruli contain granular immune deposits typically comprising all of the immunoglobulins (IgG, IgM, IgA) with C3 and C1q. A diffuse proliferative glomerular reaction is the most frequently occurring histological picture. Membranous change occurs in c. 20% of cases and is associated with marked proteinuria or nephrotic syndrome.

Henoch–Schönlein purpura

Henoch–Schönlein purpura (HSP) is a systemic vasculitis affecting the skin, joints, intestine and kidneys and occurs most commonly in childhood before the age of 10 years. A purpuric rash typically affects the extensor aspects of the arms and legs and buttocks. This is due to leukocytoclastic angiitis in the dermal capillaries and is related to IgA deposits within them. Joint pains and abdominal pains, with or without intestinal haemorrhage, are also related to involvement of small blood vessels. Most patients with HSP have one episode which completely resolves. However, recurrences occur but are usually milder and shorter than the initial episode.

The proportion of patients with renal involvement is difficult to assess. Significant renal damage occurs in over one-third

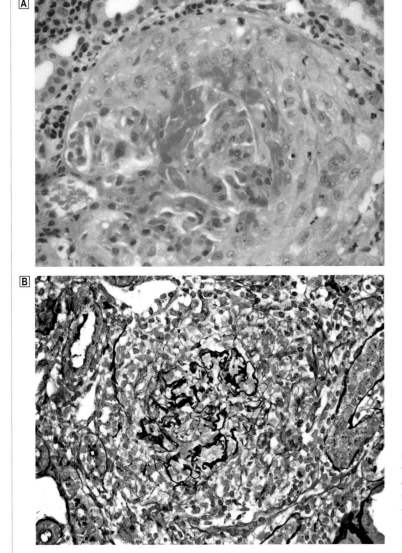

Fig 21.10 Crescentic glomerulonephritis, in this case due to pauci-immune ANCA-associated glomerulonephritis. A The glomerulus, which is partially necrotic, is surrounded by an exuberant crescent. **B** Silver stains emphasise the disruption of the Bowman's capsule and the compression of the glomerulus by the crescent.

of cases, ranging from proteinuria with nephrotic syndrome, to rapidly progressive glomerulonephritis.

Infective endocarditis

Renal complications of infective endocarditis (Ch. 13) are:

- infarcts due to embolic vegetations from the heart valves
- focal and segmental glomerulonephritis ('focal embolic nephritis')
- diffuse proliferative glomerulonephritis.

The last two complications are due to immune complex deposition.

In cases with a focal and segmental glomerulonephritis the kidney shows multiple haemorrhagic foci throughout the cortex and beneath the capsule; it is one of the causes of a 'flea-bitten' kidney. The renal lesions subside when the bacterial source of the antigen is removed by intensive antibiotic therapy or removal of the valve.

Metabolic conditions

Metabolic conditions involving renal damage include:

- changes in the basement membrane in diabetes mellitus
- accumulation of abnormal proteins proteins in the basement membrane, e.g. myeloma.

Diabetes mellitus

Diabetes mellitus is associated with damage to large and small vessels throughout the body. Severe atheroma involving the renal artery may cause renal ischaemic lesions and hypertension. Involvement of the microcirculation, in addition to causing lesions in the retina, nerves and skin, significantly affects the kidneys, leading to glomerulopathy, arteriolar hyalinosis and tubulo-interstitial lesions. The combination of changes that occur in individual cases is varied and referred to collectively as diabetic nephropathy.

Diabetic glomerulopathy

Glomerular disease in diabetics causes proteinuria, which becomes heavier as the disease progresses, leading to nephrotic syndrome and chronic renal failure. The clinical importance of diabetic glomerulopathy is exemplified by the fact that diabetes is the commonest cause of end-stage renal failure in the United States, Europe and Japan. In comparison to patients with insulin-dependent diabetes (type 1), those with non-insulin-dependent diabetes (type 2) have a shorter course to end-stage renal failure and a higher mortality. Being older they have more cardiovascular disease—myocardial infarcts and congestive cardiac failure. In contrast, patients with type 1 diabetes have a higher incidence of microvascular lesions causing retinopathy and neuropathy.

Histologically, three types of glomerular lesion occur—a spectrum of increasing severity:

- Capillary wall thickening is the initial change.
- Mesangial matrix expansion encroaches on the capillaries, causing diffuse diabetic glomerulosclerosis.
- Nodular expansion of the mesangium, beginning in the centre of the mesangium and encroaching on the capillaries, causes nodular glomerular sclerosis or Kimmelstiel–Wilson lesion (Fig. 21.11).

The glomerular lesions are accompanied by arteriolar hyalinosis affecting both the afferent and efferent arterioles. Tubular basement membrane thickening, analogous to the glomerular changes with tubular atrophy and interstitial fibrosis, completes the picture of diabetic nephropathy.

Pathogenesis of diabetic nephropathy. Hyperglycaemia has a central role in the pathogenesis of diabetic nephropathy and is prominent when control is poor. The effects of

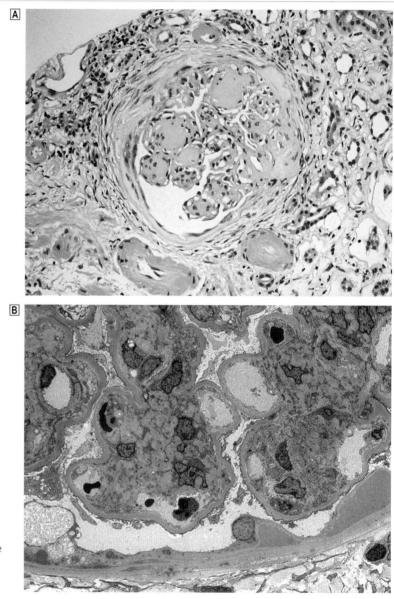

Fig. 21.11 Diabetic glomerulopathy (nodular glomerulosclerosis). **A** This lesion features hyaline sclerotic nodules, thickened capillary walls and hyaline arteriolar change. **B** An electron micrograph shows an early mesangial nodule and the thickened basement membrane characteristic of this condition.

hyperglycaemia are mediated by several metabolic pathways, the most important of which are the accumulation of advanced glycation end products (AGEs) and increased glucose flux through changes in the polyol–inositol pathway. Hyperglycaemia thereby induces morphological changes and matrix protein production. The resultant imbalance between synthesis and degradation explains the accumulation of matrix material. The basement membrane becomes more permeable.

Renal papillary necrosis

Renal papillary necrosis occurs frequently in diabetics with acute pyelonephritis. The blood supply to the renal papillae via the vasa recta is tenuous, and the vasculopathy together with the effects of the inflammation result in ischaemia of the papillae, which become infarcted. The necrotic papillae may then become detached (Fig.12.12) and either cause an obstruction or are passed in the urine.

Accumulation of abnormal proteins in the basement membrane

Renal amyloidosis

Renal involvement is present in 80–90% of cases of secondary amyloidosis (Ch. 7). The affected patients have heavy proteinuria or the nephrotic syndrome. Renal involvement is the presenting feature in over 50% of patients, and leads inevitably to chronic renal failure, with extensive glomerulosclerosis within 1–2 years.

Multiple myeloma

Renal damage occurs frequently in patients with multiple myeloma. Renal failure may be the presenting feature. The most significant lesions are tubulo-interstitial, characterised by proteinaceous casts to which there is a giant cell reac-

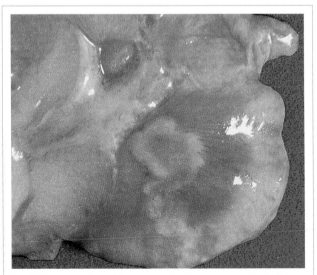

Fig 21.12 Renal papillary necrosis. The renal papillae in this diabetic patient's kidney appear yellow and structureless due to necrosis. Necrotic papillae may detach and cause ureteric colic or obstruction.

tion. Glomerular involvement is uncommon in myeloma, but includes amyloid infiltration in about 10% of cases and the deposition of monoclonal cryoglobulin in a smaller proportion.

Vascular damage

Diseases causing vascular damage resulting in glomerular lesions include:

- vasculitides
- thrombotic microangiopathies.

Vasculitides

The vasculitides are a group of conditions in which there is acute or chronic inflammation of the blood vessel wall. There is considerable overlap between these conditions and, so that an appropriate diagnosis is made, the clinical, immunological and pathological findings are all relevant. Glomerular changes occur in those cases involving small blood vessels and are considered in detail in the section on crescentic glomerulonephritis and other ANCA-associated lesions.

Polyarteritis nodosa

Polyarteritis nodosa (Chs 13 and 25) involves medium-sized vessels throughout the body. Involvement of renal vessels involves the interlobular to arcuate arteries mainly and does not cause small vessel involvement or glomerulonephritis. When these arteries are inflamed, patients experience haematuria and loin pain due to renal infarcts. Hypertension is a common feature.

Wegener's granulomatosis

Wegener's granulomatosis is a rare necrotising vasculitis affecting the nose and upper respiratory tract (Ch. 14) in addition to the kidneys. It occurs more commonly in males in their fourth and fifth decades, although it can occur at any age. The clinical indicators of renal involvement vary from microscopic haematuria to rapidly progressive renal failure. If the condition remains untreated, progressive renal impairment is inevitable, but cyclophosphamide induces a remission in the majority of patients, with complete resolution of the glomerular lesions if treated early enough.

Thrombotic microangiopathies

Thrombotic microangiopathies are characterised by the deposition of thrombi within the capillaries, arterioles and small arteries of a variety of organs. There are two major conditions in this group: haemolytic uraemic syndrome and thrombotic thrombocytopenic purpura, with considerable clinical overlap.

The extensive deposition of thrombi within the microvasculature leads a microangiopathic haemolytic anaemia. The circulating erythrocytes are deformed and fragmented (helmet cells, burr cells, schistocytes) by the strands of fibrin. The haemolytic anaemia is accompanied by a thrombocytopenia due in part to the excessive deposition of platelets, but damage to the platelets also occurs.

Pathogenesis and aetiology. Endothelial damage, the unifying feature of thrombotic microangiopathies, may be induced by genetic or acquired factors:

- verotoxin in haemolytic uraemic syndrome
- bacterial and viral neuraminidase, especially from *Streptococcus pneumoniae* and *Salmonella typhi*
- complement abnormalities
- drugs, e.g. quinine and ciclosporin
- acquired or hereditary deficiency of a von Willebrand factor-cleaving factor produced by the endothelial cells, especially in thrombotic thrombocytopenic purpura.

Haemolytic uraemic syndrome

Haemolytic uraemic syndrome (HUS) is a complex condition in which there is:

- acute nephropathy
- haemolysis
- thrombocytopenia.

The classical or epidemic form of haemolytic uraemic syndrome is accompanied by diarrhoea, often due to verotoxin-producing *Escherichia coli* infections from eating contaminated meat or dairy products. Patients without diarrhoea (diarrhoea-negative) have the atypical form of haemolytic uraemic syndrome; these cases are a heterogeneous group which is further subdivided according to aetiology; for example, infections with non-verotoxin-producing organisms, secondary to systemic diseases (particularly autoimmune disorders), drugs and pregnancy.

Thrombosis occurs in the renal arteries more frequently in patients with the atypical form and consequently there is a higher mortality.

Histological features of HUS. The glomeruli contain thrombi within the capillary lumen and there is swelling and separation of the endothelial cells. Mesangial interposition is also seen with double contouring of the basement membrane. Arteriolar changes are more often seen in diarrhoea-negative cases with swelling of the endothelial cells and subendothelial space. The lumen of the vessel is compromised and fibrin and fragmented red cells are seen in the vessel walls; this is termed 'fibrinoid necrosis'. Similar changes are seen in the interlobular arteries which may severely narrow the lumen. This results in ischaemic changes in the glomeruli supplied by the vessel and explains the poor prognosis seen in patients with diarrhoea-negative HUS.

Thrombotic thrombocytopenic purpura

The histological changes in the kidney are less marked than in haemolytic uraemic syndrome. Thrombi are present in the glomerular capillaries. The afferent arterioles characteristically feature eosinophilic granular thrombus and may become aneurysmally dilated. Cellular proliferation may be a prominent feature in some cases.

Disseminated intravascular coagulation

Disseminated intravascular coagulation (DIC) (Ch. 23) is a systemic problem involving activation of the coagulation cascade by a variety of extraneous factors.

Fibrin thrombi are identified within the glomerular capillaries, but the condition is characterised by a marked reduction in the levels of fibrinogen and factors V and VII, and is termed a consumptive coagulopathy, in contrast with the thrombotic microangiopathies where endothelial damage is the initiating factor.

RENAL DISEASE IN ASSOCIATION WITH SPECIFIC INFECTIONS

Viral infections involving the kidney are becoming increasingly important. They involve the glomeruli, tubules and interstitium by a variety of mechanisms.

Hepatitis B virus (HBV) is associated with several renal diseases. It is important to diagnose these forms of glomerulonephritis since the usual treatment for idiopathic forms is not appropriate and may be detrimental in HBV-induced disease. The renal conditions include:

- membranous nephropathy, with e antigen (HBeAg) in the subepithelial deposits
- membrano-proliferative glomerulonephritis, from deposition of both HBsAg and HBeAg in the mesangium and subendothelial space
- polyarteritis nodosa.

Hepatitis C virus (HCV) is associated with mixed cryoglobulinaemia, membranoproliferative glomerulonephritis and membranous nephropathy with or without cryoglobulinaemia. HCV-containing immune complexes are identified in the capillary walls and mesangium of the glomeruli. The recommended treatment is with interferon-alpha and ribaflavin, although the later is not tolerated when there is renal impairment. Rituximab is used in patients who do not respond or for whom other treatments are inappropriate.

HIV-associated nephropathy occurs in patients before the development of AIDS and is therefore distinct from any infective aspects of the latter disease. Clinically, in untreated individuals, there is an abrupt onset of heavy non-selective proteinuria and progressive deterioration in renal function to renal failure within months. Histologically, all of the major compartments of the kidney are involved:

- Glomerular involvement features the collapsing variant of focal segmental glomerulosclerosis. The epithelial cells are severely damaged with vacuolation and separation from the basement membrane.
- Tubular epithelial cells are degenerate and the tubular lumens are dilated with the formation of small cysts which may be identified macroscopically. The dilated tubules contain pale casts which do not include Tamm–Horsfall protein.
- There is interstitial oedema with a variable infiltrate of lymphocytes. Interstitial fibrosis and tubular atrophy feature at a later stage.

Polyomavirus-induced nephropathy is endemic and causes disease in immunocompromised individuals. The two polyoma viruses known (BK and JC) share 70% of their sequence homology with the SV40 virus. They have been implicated in a variety of conditions including Guillain–Barré syndrome, hepatitis and SLE. BK virus displays tropism for the urogenital epithelium and causes interstitial nephritis in HIV-infected patients and renal transplants. It is an important cause of graft failure.

RENAL TRANSPLANTATION

Patients in chronic renal failure, who in the past would have died, are now effectively maintained on either peritoneal dialysis or haemodialysis, both of which place restrictions on the patient's lifestyle. For young and otherwise fit patients with domestic and occupational responsibilities, renal transplantation offers freedom from the restrictions of regular dialysis and has transformed the quality of their lives.

Cadaveric kidneys are most frequently used, but because suitable donors are scarce there is increasing use of living donors, both related and unrelated. The long-term survival of the grafts from unrelated donors, e.g. spouse or friend, is almost as good as from parent or sibling. Graft survival is affected by the source of the kidney, histocompatibility match, the number of episodes of acute rejection, delayed graft function, pre-sensitisation, recipient race (poor in blacks) and age of the recipient.

Changes resulting from procedural events

Events during the process of renal transplantation can lead to delayed graft function. Preservation injury results from renal anoxia during harvesting or transport. Perfusion injury occurs as a result of the graft being perfused with storage solution which is too cold during preparation; this causes endothelial damage and consequent microthrombi form in the glomerular capillaries and small arteries.

Allograft rejection

Two distinct types of graft rejection can damage the kidney during the first days or weeks after transplantation. Both are immunologically mediated and involve different aspects of the immune system: acute cellular rejection involves the cell-mediated system and features a T-cell response; acute antibody-mediated rejection involves activation of the complement cascade.

Chronic allograft rejection—seen after some years and responsible for long-term graft loss—involves both mechanisms.

Graft rejection must be distinguished from graft ischaemia (e.g. due to stenosed or occluded vascular anastomosis) and from drug-induced pathology (e.g. due to immunosuppressive agents such as ciclosporin and tacrolimus).

Acute cellular rejection (ACR)

A gradual rise in the serum creatinine, weight gain, fever and tenderness over the grafted kidney alert to acute cellular rejection, the most common form of rejection, usually in the first 6 weeks. The interstitium, tubules, arteries and glomeruli are all affected. A brisk interstitial infiltrate of activated lymphoblasts and T-cells features most frequently in ACR (Fig. 21.13). Damage to arterial and arteriolar endothelium occurs in more severe cases. In most cases, glomerular damage is minimal and limited to occasional segmental mononuclear cells. The T-cell infiltrate is thought to be promoted by a concurrent cytomegalovirus infection. Acute cellular rejection usually responds to pulses of steroids, ciclosporin or OKT3 treatment.

Acute humoral rejection (AHR) or acute antibody-mediated rejection

The clinical features of AHR are more dramatic and acute than with ACR. Acute and severe graft dysfunction due to AHR may occur at any time after transplantation. AHR is

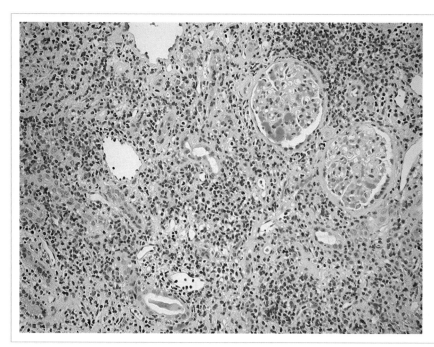

Fig 21.13 Acute cellular rejection in a renal transplant. The renal architecture is overwhelmed by infiltrating T-cells which also infiltrate the tubules (tubulitis).

less responsive to therapy and carries a worse prognosis for the kidney than ACR. Histological changes range from acute tubular injury with no cellular infiltrate, through infiltration of the peritubular capillaries by neutrophils, to frank necrosis of the arteries. Complement activation is an integral part of the immunological response in AHR.

Presensitisation (e.g. previous transplantation) increases the risk of AHR. Antibodies to donor-specific human leukocyte class I antigens are responsible for AHR due to either undetected presensitisation or an occult antigen.

Hyperacute rejection

Hyperacute rejection is due to preformed complement-fixing antibodies in the blood stream of the recipient, usually to human leukocyte or ABO antigens. The immune damage is directed at the endothelial cells of the graft, and the speed of onset is related to the antibody concentration. In some cases the reaction is immediate, and is apparent to the surgeon on establishing a flow of blood through the graft, when the kidney becomes flaccid, cyanosed and mottled, suggesting intrarenal vasoconstriction. This compares with an onset at 1–2 days when the levels are low. Thrombi form in arteries and glomeruli accompanied by interstitial haemorrhages. Cortical infarcts occur as a result of vascular thrombosis.

Chronic rejection

Chronic rejection, an important cause of graft failure months or years after transplantation, is heralded by an insidious increase in creatinine, often associated with proteinuria and hypertension. Vascular changes dominate the histology with marked fibrous intimal thickening of arteries by myointimal cells and a variable T-cell infiltrate and foamy macrophages. The glomerular changes are less impressive with mild mesangial thickening. Ultrastructurally, however, there is foot process effacement and loss of endothelial fenestrae. The basement membrane of the peritubular capillaries is reduplicated. There is progressive interstitial fibrosis and tubular atrophy.

Banff classification

Transplant rejection is classified according to two working schemes, the first devised internationally at Banff, the second the Collaborative Clinical Trials in Transplantation. The two are congruent and seek to grade each histological aspect of rejection. Adoption of these schemes aims to improve the consistency of reporting between centres and thus enable more meaningful conclusions on a larger group of patients, particularly in the context of multicentre therapeutic trials.

Recurrent disease

Recurrent disease is seen more frequently in transplants for:

- immunologically mediated renal disease, e.g. lupus nephritis, IgA nephropathy and anti-GBM disease
- metabolic abnormalities, e.g. diabetes, oxalosis and amyloid
- disease of uncertain aetiology, e.g. focal segmental glomerulosclerosis and dense deposit disease.

DISEASES AFFECTING BLOOD VESSELS

In addition to the conditions mentioned above, the renal vasculature may be damaged in:

- progressive systemic sclerosis (scleroderma; Ch. 25)
- systemic hypertension (Ch. 13).

Renal infarction

Two mechanisms of infarction are recognised:

- embolic infarction
- diffuse cortical necrosis.

Embolic infarction

Most renal infarcts result from embolisation of:

- *atheromatous material,* responsible for the small subcapsular pits in benign-phase hypertension
- *thrombotic material* arising from the left side of the heart
- *bacterial vegetations* from infective endocarditis.

Many renal infarcts are clinically silent, but some result in haematuria and loin pain.

Renal infarcts are pale or white, and have a characteristic wedge shape with the apex directed towards the hilum.

Diffuse cortical necrosis

Diffuse cortical necrosis is a rare condition complicating pregnancy or trauma associated with severe haemorrhage or severe sepsis. Profound hypotension occurs in these situations, but there is considerable controversy relating to the pathogenesis of this condition. Vasoconstriction is important because infarction can be avoided by the use of angiotensin antagonists.

Diffuse cortical necrosis is a cause of acute anuric renal failure. The prognosis is poor when the infarction is generalised, but is less ominous when the infarction is focal.

Macroscopically, the appearance is striking: the external surface bears irregular yellowish areas with intervening congestion and haemorrhage. The cut surface shows the infarction to be confined to the cortex.

RENAL DISEASE IN PREGNANCY

The kidneys undergo morphological and functional changes during pregnancy. Some of these changes affect the renal response to disease and influence the interpretation of function tests. Whatever the cause, renal impairment at the beginning of pregnancy has important implications; the risks to the mother and fetus are significant. The risk of deteriorating renal function and hypertension increases and fetal morbidity and mortality rise. Pregnancy is likely to exacerbate active and proliferative systemic lupus. Maternal diabetes is associated with prematurity and neonatal complications when there is established nephropathy and renal impairment. The risk of pre-eclampsia is also increased in these patients. In general, however, there are no long-term adverse effects of pregnancy on diabetic nephropathy.

Infection

Infection is the most frequent urinary tract abnormality in pregnant women and is usually detected on routine antenatal urine testing. Asymptomatic bacteriuria occurs in up to 10% of pregnant women, and such patients are at risk of acute pyelonephritis. Prompt diagnosis and early treatment are essential. Renal abnormalities such as the coarse polar scarring of vesicoureteric reflux are detected radiologically in a high proportion of these patients. In addition, physiological changes occur in the smooth muscle cells of the lower urinary tract in pregnancy, with slower ureteric peristaltic activity and pelvi-ureteric dilatation. This leads to stasis which, combined with infection, particularly with urea-splitting organisms, predisposes to stone formation; existing stones may enlarge considerably during pregnancy.

Hypertension

Hypertension is an important complication of pregnancy. The patient may have latent essential hypertension or concurrent renal disease. Alternatively, pre-eclampsia or eclampsia may be present. *Pre-eclampsia* is characterised by hypertension, proteinuria and oedema; *eclampsia* supervenes when fits occur. In severe cases the glomeruli are large and relatively bloodless due to marked swelling of the endothelial and mesangial cells. Arteries and arterioles display endothelial swelling and myointimal proliferation. The vascular and glomerular lesions are reversible when the hypertension has been corrected. However, a thrombotic microangiopathy may be superimposed during the course of pre-eclampsia, and persistent hypertension may ensue when fibrinoid necrosis of the arterioles has occurred.

TUBULO-INTERSTITIAL DISORDERS

In tubulo-interstitial conditions there is damage to the tubular epithelial cells and the interstitium. These disorders account for a significant proportion of patients presenting with impaired renal function.

Infections of the kidney affect the tubules and the interstitium, and may present as acute renal failure if there are complications such as tubular or papillary necrosis. These are discussed separately because of their clinical importance.

Acute tubular epithelial cell damage causes the condition known as acute tubular necrosis.

Acute tubular necrosis

> ▸ Important cause of acute renal failure
> ▸ May be due to toxic or haemodynamic causes (e.g. shock)
> ▸ Regeneration of renal tubular epithelium often permits clinical recovery

Acute tubular necrosis (ATN) is a very important cause of acute renal failure; patients often present with extreme oliguria (less than 100 ml of urine each 24 h). The importance of ATN is that it is fully recoverable if the patient is given adequate supportive fluid and electrolyte therapy. Following the initial oliguria, there is a later diuretic phase due to the loss of urinary concentration. In the oliguric phase, hyperkalaemia with the risk of cardiac arrhythmias presents a serious threat to life. This situation contrasts with hypokalaemia which can occur in the early diuretic phase.

The histological features range from sublethal injury, which is often difficult to identify morphologically, to necrosis of the epithelial cells. In most cases a severe metabolic disturbance is the essential change and the term 'necrosis' is not entirely appropriate. The oliguria comes about in these cases because the cells of the proximal tubules and loops of Henle are rendered unable to reabsorb sodium chloride. Thus the luminal fluid at the macula densa contains too much chloride and the tubuloglomerular feedback system is activated, reducing the GFR.

The principal causes of acute tubular necrosis are:

- ischaemia
- toxins.

Ischaemic ATN

Ischaemic ATN follows a variety of clinical situations, such as trauma, burns and infections in which the patient becomes shocked. Profound hypotension is usually responsible for the hypoperfusion of the peritubular circulation. The kidneys are pale and swollen. Histology reveals patchy epithelial cell injury along the entire length of the tubules; the cells are flattened and vacuolated, making distinction between proximal and distal tubules very difficult histologically. Inflammatory cells pack the vasa recta in response to the necrotic cells; the interstitium is oedematous. Casts occur frequently in the distal tubules and collecting ducts; they are composed of cellular debris and protein, including Tamm–Horsfall protein. In the case of ATN resulting from a crush injury, myoglobin is present in the casts. Following a mismatched blood transfusion, haemoglobin would be present.

Toxic ATN

Toxic ATN results from a wide variety of substances, the kidney being vulnerable because of the high metabolic activity of the epithelial cells and the high perfusion rate. The causes are:

- *heavy metals* (lead, mercury, arsenic, gold, chromium, bismuth and uranium)
- *organic solvents* (carbon tetrachloride, chloroform)
- *glycols* (ethylene glycol, propylene glycol, dioxane and diethylene glycol)
- *therapeutic substances* (antibiotics—meticillin, sulphonamides, gentamicin, polymyxin, cephalosporins; nonsteroidal anti-inflammatory drugs; mercurial diuretics; anaesthetics—methoxyflurane)
- *iodinated radiographic contrast medium*
- *phenol*
- *pesticides*
- *paraquat.*

The kidneys are swollen and red. Histologically, there is often marked vacuolation of the tubular epithelial cytoplasm. The damage is characteristically restricted to the proximal tubular cells, those of the distal tubule being spared. This situation contrasts with the picture in ischaemic ATN in which the tubular cells along the entire length of the tubule are affected. Recovery is indicated in biopsies by the presence of mitotic figures within the flattened cells.

Interstitial nephritis

Interstitial nephritis is a heterogeneous group of conditions involving the interstitium that have a profound effect on renal function. The interstitium contains a complex network of capillaries, derived from the efferent arterioles of the glomeruli. In addition, the blood supply to the medulla emanates from the vasa recta arising from the efferent arterioles of the juxtamedullary glomeruli. Thus, damage to the glomerular vessels will cause tubular dysfunction. Therefore, damage to the interstitium, by either inflammation or fibrosis, will affect the peritubular capillary network and cause profound disturbance in renal function.

Acute interstitial nephritis

Acute interstitial nephritis is an important cause of acute renal failure which is often oliguric; c. 60% require dialysis initially. Acute interstitial nephritis is a complication of severe systemic bacterial infections. Most cases of acute renal failure due to acute interstitial nephritis are due to drugs, most commonly penicillins, sulphonamides and non-steroidal anti-inflammatory drugs (NSAIDs). The kidneys are large and swollen due to oedema. The interstitium is oedematous and infiltrated by lymphocytes, macrophages and eosinophils with infiltration of the tubules (tubulitis). This explains the urinary finding of white cell casts in these cases. The renal changes will resolve completely if the drug is discontinued, often with little lasting damage. The reaction is idiosyncratic and not dose-related, but will recur if the patient is re-exposed to the offending drug.

Chronic interstitial nephritis

Patients with chronic interstitial nephritis present in chronic renal failure; establishing a cause is often difficult.

Vesico-ureteric reflux

Vesico-ureteric reflux is the commonest cause of chronic interstitial nephritis (Fig. 21.14). Organisms enter the kidney from the bladder. The primary abnormality is the angle at which the terminal ureteric segment traverses the bladder wall. Normally the ureter is at an acute angle to the mucosal surface, so that contraction of the bladder wall during micturition closes the orifice. In patients with reflux, the terminal portion is short and oriented at approximately 90° to the mucosal surface; contraction of the bladder holds the orifice open and facilitates reflux of urine. Reflux into the kidney itself occurs through compound papillae (Fig. 21.14).

The appearance of reflux nephropathy is characteristic. Deep irregular scars occur towards the poles of the kidney. Involvement may be unilateral or, if bilateral, is characteristically asymmetrical. Microscopically, there is interstitial fibrosis with atrophic and dilated tubules containing eosinophilic casts ('thyroidisation' of the kidney, so called because of the histological resemblance to thyroid).

Analgesic nephropathy

Analgesic nephropathy is an adverse reaction to analgesics which is now less frequent since combined aspirin and phenacetin preparations are no longer available. The phenacetin and its toxic metabolites concentrate in the medulla. The aspirin is thought to induce medullary ischaemia by inhibiting the synthesis of vasodilatory prostaglandins. The effect is on the medullary capillaries and vasa recta which develop thickening of the basement membranes. The toxic and ischaemic effects are synergistic, leading eventually to renal papillary necrosis. The prognosis is good if the analgesic abuse is terminated at an early stage; however, if continued, progressive fibrosis ensues.

Transitional cell carcinomas of the renal pelvis and ureter occur more frequently in patients with analgesic nephropathy.

Lesions associated with metabolic disorders

A variety of metabolic diseases and disturbances affect the tubules and interstitium. These include:

- hypokalaemia
- urate nephropathy
- hypercalcaemia
- oxalosis.

Hypokalaemic nephropathy

Persistently low plasma levels of potassium occur in:

- chronic diarrhoea
- hyperaldosteronism, either primary or secondary
- chronic abuse of laxatives or diuretics.

Hypokalaemia causes coarse vacuolation of the tubular epithelial cells principally in the proximal tubules, but in severe states those of the distal tubules are also involved; the medullary tubules are spared.

Urate (gouty) nephropathy

Renal damage due to elevated levels of uric acid in the blood occurs in gout (Ch. 7). Additionally, patients with chronic renal damage due to pyelonephritis or glomerulonephritis have impaired filtration and reduced tubular secretion of uric acid; this leads to retention of uric acid and its subsequent deposition in the kidney. Uric acid crystallises in an acid environment such as that found in the distal tubules, collecting ducts and interstitium of the papillae.

Acute urate nephropathy

Acute urate nephropathy presents as acute renal failure. It occurs principally in patients with myeloproliferative or solid tumours and is precipitated by chemotherapy, when extensive breakdown of cells releases vast quantities of nucleic acids. The cut surface of affected kidneys displays yellow streaks within the medulla due to precipitation of urate crystals filling the tubular lumina; this precipitation causes obstruction and tubular dilatation.

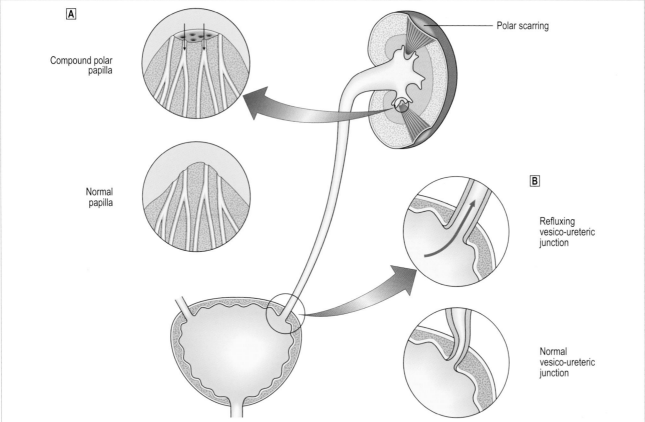

Fig. 21.14 Chronic interstitial nephritis due to urinary reflux. Urinary reflux can occur due to either obstruction of urinary flow or, as shown in this diagram, congenital anomalies. **A** Compound polar papillae. Contrasting with the normal convex papilla, compound papillae have concave tips without valve-like openings of the collecting ducts which enable intraparenchymal reflux. **B** Refluxing vesico-ureteric junction. Normally, the terminal ureter runs through the bladder wall beneath the surface and enters the lumen at an angle forming a valve; refluxing junctions result from the absence of the valve-like structure.

Chronic urate nephropathy

Chronic urate nephropathy is more insidious and occurs in patients with persistently elevated uric acid levels, as in gout. Urate crystals precipitate in the tubular lumina causing chronic obstruction and tubular damage with a granulomatous tubulo-interstitial nephritis. The kidneys become reduced in size and the cortex becomes atrophic and thinned.

Urate stones may occur in both acute and chronic nephropathy, and there is an increased incidence of pyelonephritis.

Hypercalcaemic nephropathy (nephrocalcinosis)

Calcium deposition in the kidneys occurs when there is hypercalcaemia: this is 'metastatic' calcification (Ch. 7). The onset of renal symptoms is insidious; the tubular disturbance results in an inability to concentrate urine, with consequent polyuria often causing the patient to complain of nocturia. The kidney is often scarred and focally calcified. The cut surface of the kidneys reveals stones within the pelvicalyceal system, and linear white streaks and flecks. There is interstitial fibrosis, a non-specific inflammatory infiltrate and tubular atrophy in relation to the calcification.

Oxalate nephropathy

Calcium oxalate deposition occurs systemically in the tissues when blood levels are high. Increased urinary excretion of oxalate also occurs and the kidneys may be damaged. Hyperoxalaemia and the resulting hyperoxaluria are either primary or secondary. The primary form is due to deficiencies of hepatic enzymes, which are concerned with the decarboxylation of glyoxylate, which accumulates and is oxidised by an alternative pathway to oxalate. Hepatic together with renal transplantation are required to replace the deficient hepatic enzyme. Oxalate accumulates in many tissues (e.g. myocardium), causing systemic problems after the onset of renal failure, and transplantation before that stage is recommended. Secondary hyperoxaluria is seen in poisoning with ethylene glycol (antifreeze) or the anaesthetic agent methoxyflurane, and in pyridoxine (vitamin B_6) deficiency. Oxalate deposition is also seen in the kidneys in a variety of chronic renal disorders.

In advanced cases, the kidneys are small, granular and scarred, the thinned cortex reflecting the fibrosis and tubular disruption that occurs with the deposition of oxalate. Stones are often present in the pelvis and calyceal system.

Lesions due to physical agents

Obstructive uropathy

Obstructive uropathy is an important cause of interstitial nephritis; the causes include:

- *congenital anomalies* (uretero-pelvic stenosis, vesico-ureteric reflux)
- *tumours* (carcinoma of the bladder and prostate)
- *hyperplastic lesions* (benign prostatic hyperplasia)
- *calculi.*

Clinical features. The signs, symptoms and prognosis depend on the level of the obstruction. Thus, a renal calculus or a fragment of sloughed papilla will cause renal colic, whereas obstruction due to carcinoma of the bladder or benign prostatic hyperplasia will be accompanied by bladder symptoms. Acute obstruction in the lower urinary tract will result in anuria and pain, and if not relieved is incompatible with survival.

Pathogenesis. The pelvis and calyceal system become dilated due to back pressure; the dilatation is mild in cases of acute obstruction. The peristaltic activity of the ureters is increased in obstruction; this raises the intrapelvic pressure, which in turn is transmitted into the renal parenchyma. Initially, the filtrate formed is reabsorbed through lymphatic and vascular channels. The continued rapid rise in pressure, however, reduces glomerular and medullary blood flow and eventually impairs glomerular filtration.

Gross dilatation occurs as a result of prolonged back pressure. The kidney becomes a dilated sac-like structure: this is *hydronephrosis* (Fig. 21.15).

Pyelonephritis

> ▸ A common and important cause of renal disease
> ▸ Causative bacteria may reach the kidneys either through the blood (as in septicaemia) or by reflux of contaminated urine from the bladder
> ▸ Acute pyelonephritis is characterised by pus in the tubules and by abscess formation
> ▸ Chronic pyelonephritis is characterised by coarse scarring and contraction of the kidneys

Pyelonephritis is an infection in the kidney that may arise by haematogenous or retrograde ureteric routes. Due to their rich blood supply, the kidneys are often involved in severe systemic infections by direct spread of organisms through septicaemia. The commonest infecting organisms are bacteria. Urinary tract infections are common within the community, second only to upper respiratory infections. However, not all urinary tract infections are associated with pyelonephritis; organisms can gain access to the kidney only if there is vesico-ureteric reflux.

The incidence of pyelonephritis parallels that of obstructive uropathy. In infancy, boys are mainly affected because of anatomical abnormalities. From puberty to middle age, females show the highest incidence, related to urethral trauma and pregnancy. After 40 years, prostatic disease provides an obstructive aetiology in ageing men. Other factors include instrumentation (e.g. catheterisation, cystoscopy) and diabetes mellitus.

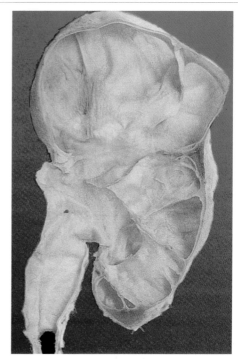

Fig. 21.15 Hydronephrosis. The renal pelvis and calyces are grossly dilated, causing compression atrophy of the renal tissue. In this case, hydronephrosis is due to blockage of the ureter by a stone.

The clinical distinction between acute and chronic pyelonephritis is quite clear.

Acute pyelonephritis

Acute pyelonephritis, due to infection of the kidney by pyogenic organisms, presents with malaise and fever, and pain and tenderness in the loins. Dysuria and urgency of micturition indicate an associated infection in the lower urinary tract. Finding pus cells in the urine (pyuria) is helpful, but white cell casts provide unequivocal evidence of pyelonephritis. Urine culture in suspected cases is imperative, but bacteriuria is regarded as significant only when in excess of 10^5 culture-forming units/ml; this result eliminates cases of extraneous bacterial contamination.

Pathogenesis

The pathogenesis of acute pyelonephritis is either:

- haematogenous spread
- retrograde ureteric spread.

Haematogenous spread can occur in a patient with infective endocarditis or bacteraemia from other sources; the spectrum of organisms can be wide, including bacteria, fungi, rickettsia and viruses. Previous renal damage or structural abnormality predisposes to organisms localising in the kidney.

More commonly, pyelonephritis results from organisms gaining access from the lower urinary tract, known as an ascending infection, in association with reflux of urine. In

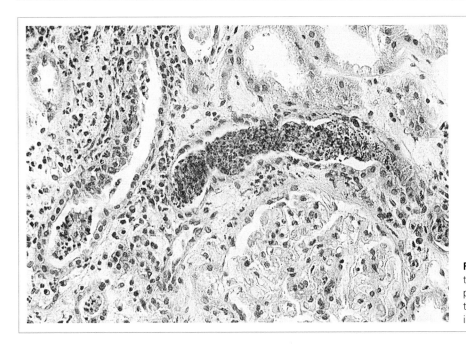

Fig 21.16   Acute pyelonephritis. The tubules contain casts consisting of neutrophil polymorphs; the intertubular connective tissue is oedematous and infiltrated by inflammatory cells.

these cases the infecting organisms are Gram-negative bacilli (e.g. *E. coli*, *Proteus* spp. and *Enterobacter*) from the patient's faecal flora. This occurs frequently in young women; predisposing factors include the short urethra, urethral trauma during sexual intercourse, and pregnancy. Instrumentation of the urinary tract in both sexes increases both the incidence and the variety of infecting organisms.

Morphology

There are either abscesses throughout the cortex and medulla or wedge-shaped confluent areas of suppuration. Minute abscesses are randomly distributed when the infection is blood-borne, but tend to be located at the upper and lower poles when associated with urinary reflux. A lower urinary tract infection may be associated with inflammation of the pelvic and calyceal mucosa, and pus may be present in the pelvis.

Histology reveals intratubular polymorphs together with interstitial oedema and inflammation (Fig. 21.16). These white cell 'granular' casts pass into the bladder and are evident on microscopy of the urine. With healing, fibrosis occurs in the interstitium and the inflammatory infiltrate becomes dominated by lymphocytes and plasma cells.

Complications

Three important complications may develop in acute pyelonephritis:

- *Renal papillary necrosis.* As a result of the inflammation, the medullary blood supply is compromised and renal papillary necrosis may ensue, particularly in diabetics or where there is obstruction (Fig. 21.12).
- *Pyonephrosis.* This arises when there is complete obstruction high in the urinary tract near the kidney. The stagnant fluid in the pelvis and calyceal system suppurates. Eventually, the kidney becomes grossly distended with pus.

- *Perinephric abscess.* When the infection breaches the renal capsule and extends into the perirenal tissues, it gives rise to a perinephric abscess.

Chronic pyelonephritis

Chronic pyelonephritis is associated with obstruction developing during adulthood, the site of which determines whether or not one or both kidneys are involved. In contrast to reflux nephropathy, the obstruction leads to dilatation of the renal pelvis and calyceal system with widespread atrophy of the overlying parenchyma. The papillae are stretched and distorted, enabling intraparenchymal reflux to occur. Histologically, atrophic changes with 'thyroidisation' are seen together with inflammatory cells. Obstruction is the predominant aetiological factor together with persistent bacteria and an altered host response.

Renal tuberculosis

The kidneys can be affected by tuberculosis as part of generalised miliary spread from an active tuberculous lesion elsewhere (usually in the lungs); the kidneys become dotted with numerous minute white granulomas.

Solitary tuberculous lesions occur in the kidneys of adults. These may or may not be associated with other active tuberculous lesions elsewhere; they may represent reactivation of a dormant lesion. The kidney contains an irregular white mass filled with caseous material. This arises within the renal parenchyma but may eventually rupture into the calyceal system, leaving an open, ragged cavity and enabling tubercle bacilli to seed along the ureter and into the bladder. Severe and longstanding tuberculosis may produce a tuberculous pyelonephrosis with complete destruction of the kidney. 'Sterile' pyuria is an important feature in renal tuberculosis and should stimulate an active search for the acid–alcohol-fast bacilli in the urine.

Commonly confused conditions and entities relating to renal and urinary tract pathology	
Commonly confused	**Distinction and explanation**
Glomerulonephritis and *glomerulopathy*	*Glomerulonephritis* is strictly inflammation (hence '-itis') of glomeruli. However, the term is also used for some forms of glomerular injury (e.g. membranous glomerulonephritis) lacking inflammatory features; *glomerulopathy* is a better term, and is becoming more widely used.
Creatinine and *creatine*	*Creatinine* is relevant to renal pathology; its blood concentration is used to assess glomerular function. Creatinine is the anhydride of *creatine* (*N*-methyl-guanidinoacetic acid); when phosphorylated, it is an important storage form of high-energy phosphate.
Membranous and *proliferative*	Both terms are used to describe the histology of glomerulonephritis (GN). In *membranous* GN the dominant feature is basement membrane thickening. In *proliferative* GN the dominant feature is glomerular hypercellularity.
Focal, segmental, global and *diffuse*	These terms are used to describe, first, whether most *(diffuse)* or some *(focal)* glomeruli are abnormal, and, second, whether the abnormality affects the entire glomerulus *(global)* or only a segment *(segmental)*. Recognition of these patterns is useful in diagnosis and prognosis.
Haematuria and *haemoglobinuria*	*Haematuria* is the presence of red blood cells in the urine, indicating severe glomerular injury (in which case red cell casts, formed in the tubules, may be found on urine microscopy) or a tumour or trauma in the urinary tract. *Haemoglobinuria* is due to intravascular haemolysis and can occur in the absence of urinary tract disease.

FURTHER READING

Avner E D, Sweeney W E 2006 Renal cystic disease: new insights for the clinician. Pediatric Clinics of North America 53: 889–909

Blumenthal I 2006 Vesicoureteric reflux and urinary tract infection in children. Postgraduate Medical Journal 82: 31–35

Eaton D C, Pooler J 2004 Vander's renal physiology, 6th edn. McGraw-Hill Medical, Columbus, Ohio

Pannu N, Klarenbach S, Wiebe N et al 2008 Renal replacement therapy in patients with acute renal failure: a systematic review. Journal of the American Medical Association 299: 793–805

Rennke H G, Denker B M, Burton D R 2006 Renal pathophysiology, 2nd edn. Lippincott Williams & Wilkins, Philadelphia

Steddon S, Ashman N, Cunningham J, Chesser A 2006 Oxford handbook of nephrology and hypertension. Oxford University Press, Oxford

Lymph nodes, thymus and spleen

COMMON CLINICAL PROBLEMS FROM DISEASE OF THE LYMPH NODES, THYMUS AND SPLEEN

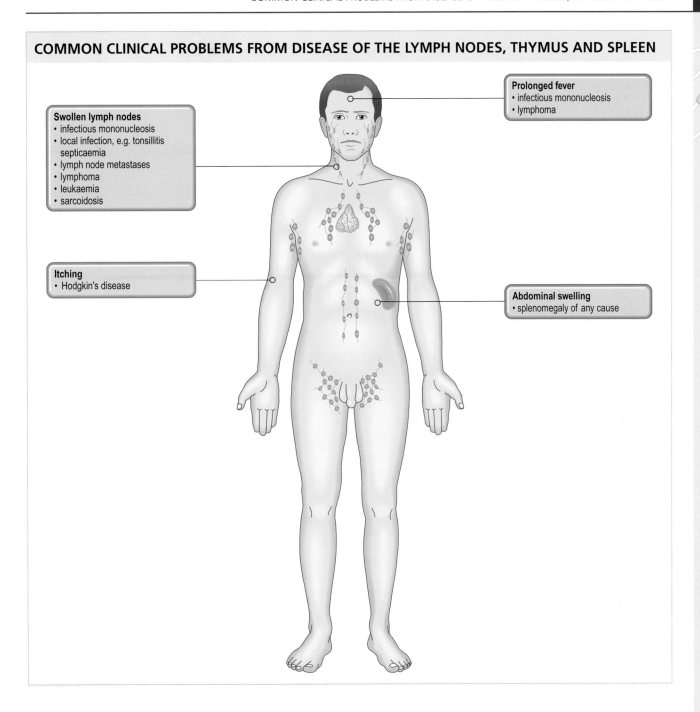

Swollen lymph nodes
• infectious mononucleosis
• local infection, e.g. tonsillitis septicaemia
• lymph node metastases
• lymphoma
• leukaemia
• sarcoidosis

Itching
• Hodgkin's disease

Prolonged fever
• infectious mononucleosis
• lymphoma

Abdominal swelling
• splenomegaly of any cause

Pathological basis of signs and symptoms attributable to the lymphoreticular system	
Sign or symptom	Pathological basis
Enlarged lymph nodes	Neoplastic infiltration • primary (lymphoma) • secondary (metastases) Specific infections (e.g. tuberculosis, toxoplasmosis, infectious mononucleosis) Reactive hyperplasia
Enlarged spleen	Congestion (heart failure, portal hypertension) Storage disorder Neoplastic infiltration (leukaemia, lymphoma)

(Continued)

Pathological basis of signs and symptoms attributable to the lymphoreticular system—cont'd	
Sign or symptom	Pathological basis
Susceptibility to infection	Immune deficiency • congenital • acquired (lymphoma, leukaemia, AIDS, iatrogenic)
Weight loss/pyrexia	Interleukins produced by inflammatory or lymphomatous (i.e. type B symptoms) tissue acting on thermoregulatory centre in hypothalamus
Muscle weakness (myasthenia gravis)	Thymic hyperplasia or neoplasia
Howell–Jolly inclusions in red cells	Persistence of DNA fragments in red cells due to splenic atrophy

LYMPH NODES

NORMAL STRUCTURE AND FUNCTION

Lymph nodes are discrete encapsulated structures, usually ovoid and ranging in diameter from a few millimetres to several centimetres. They are situated along the course of lymphatic vessels and are more numerous where these vessels converge (e.g. roots of limbs, neck, pelvis and mediastinum).

Micro-architecture and functional anatomy

Lymph nodes are surrounded by a connective tissue capsule, with trabeculae that extend into the substance of the node and provide a framework for the contained cellular elements. Beneath the capsule is a slit-like space, the subcapsular sinus, into which the afferent lymphatics drain after penetrating the capsule. Lymph from the subcapsular sinus passes via the medullary cords to the hilum of the lymph node from which the efferent lymphatic drains.

Three distinct micro-anatomical regions can be recognised within normal lymph nodes (Ch. 9). These regions are:

• the *cortex*, which contains nodules of B-lymphocytes either as primary follicles or as germinal centres
• the *paracortex* or *deep cortex*, which is the T-cell-dependent region of the lymph node
• the *medulla*, containing the medullary cords and sinuses which drain into the hilum.

The micro-anatomical regions of the lymph nodes are populated by a variety of specialised cells with different functional characteristics.

Germinal centres

The germinal centre is the principal site of B-cell activation in response to antigenic challenge. Antigen, bound to antibody, entering the lymph node via the afferent lymphatics is trapped upon the surface of specialised antigen-presenting cells called *dendritic reticulum cells* (DRCs) by their Fc receptors. DRCs are restricted to primary follicles and germinal centres and are binucleate cells with long cytoplasmic processes linked by desmosomes which form a network throughout the germinal centre. Antigen trapped on the surface of the DRC is presented to 'virgin' B-lymphocytes in the presence of T-helper cells (T-cell co-operation) and these B-cells subsequently undergo a series of morphological and functional changes (Table 22.1). After antigenic challenge, the initial step in B-cell transformation is the formation of the *centroblast*, which is a rapidly dividing cell that is responsible for expansion of the antigen-reactive B-cell clone; this then develops into a *centrocyte* (Fig. 22.1). During the germinal centre reaction the B-cell immunoglobulin genes undergo hypermutation to produce higher affinity immunoglobulin molecules; B-cells in which hypermutation does not achieve this undergo apoptosis. The number of B-cells that act as progenitors for the fully mature germinal centre is remarkably small and the mass of the germinal centre B-cell population is made up by the extensive proliferative activity of a small number of progenitor cells.

The function of germinal centres is to generate immunoglobulin-secreting plasma cells in response to antigenic challenge. Within the lymph node, plasma cells are located principally within the *medullary cords*.

The fully formed germinal centre is seen histologically as a rounded, pale structure in the cortex of the lymph node, surrounded by a rim of small, round lymphocytes termed the *mantle zone*. Distinct zonation may be seen within the germinal centre: a pale zone faces towards the subcapsular sinus, is rich in centrocytes and T-cells, and contains the greatest density of DRCs; at the opposite pole of the germinal centre is a dark zone rich in rapidly dividing centroblasts mixed with tingible body macrophages which phagocytose the cellular debris generated by apoptosis of B-cells secondary to unsuccessful immunoglobulin gene hypermutation (Fig. 22.2). In florid B-cell reactions a population of post-germinal centre B-cells may accumulate adjacent to the mantle zone; these are termed marginal zone B-cells.

Paracortex

The paracortex is the T-cell-dependent region of the lymph node and accordingly contains large numbers of T-lymphocytes with a predominance of the helper/inducer subset (CD4+). The cluster of differentiation (CD) 4 antigen is expressed by helper/inducer T-cells. As in the germinal centre, specialised antigen-presenting cells are present in the paracortex; these are called *interdigitating reticulum*

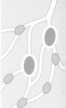

Table 22.1 Characteristics and nomenclature (Kiel scheme) of follicle centre cells and therefore B-cell lymphomas derived therefrom

Cell features	Nomenclature
Small lymphocyte with round nucleus	**Lymphocyte**
Small or large cell with indented nucleus	**Centrocyte**
Large cell with round nucleus and usually multiple nucleoli	**Centroblast**
Large cell with round nucleus and large nucleolus	**Immunoblast**

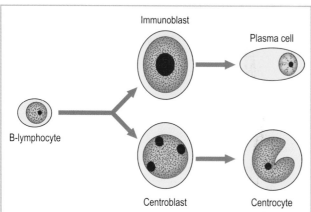

Fig. 22.1 Morphological changes of the germinal centre B-cell. Hypothetical follicle centre B-cell transformation. The virgin B-lymphocyte has two activation pathways. The first involves direct transformation to an immunoblast following exposure to an antigen, with subsequent differentiation to an immunoglobulin-secreting plasma cell; this pathway is independent of the germinal centre. The second pathway occurs within the germinal centre and involves the generation of a centroblast as the initial reaction to antigen exposure, with subsequent differentiation to a centrocyte.

cells (IDCs) and are different morphologically and functionally from the DRCs. IDCs possess abundant cytoplasm with complex membrane profiles which interdigitate with surrounding T-cells. Large amounts of class II human leukocyte antigen (HLA) substances are expressed on the surface of the IDC and this is important for interactions between immune cells, especially in antigen presentation to T-cells (particularly the helper T-cells).

Medulla

Lymph enters the marginal sinus of the node and drains to the hilum through sinuses that converge in the medullary region. The sinuses are lined by macrophages which phagocytose particulate material within the lymph. Between the sinuses in the medulla lie the medullary cords, which contain numerous plasma cells and are one of the main sites of antibody secretion within the lymph node.

LYMPH NODE ENLARGEMENT

▸ Localised or generalised
▸ Diagnosis often requires lymph node biopsy
▸ May be due to inflammatory, reactive or neoplastic disorders
▸ Neoplastic disorders may be primary (e.g. lymphoma) or secondary (e.g. metastatic carcinoma)

Lymph node enlargement (lymphadenopathy) may be localised or widespread and is a common clinical problem that frequently requires a biopsy to establish a diagnosis. The causes of lymphadenopathy are varied and include:

● infection (both local and systemic)
● autoimmune disorders
● neoplasms (either primary or metastatic).

NON-NEOPLASTIC LYMPHADENOPATHY

Lymph nodes respond to a wide variety of inflammatory stimuli by cellular proliferation which leads to node enlargement. The cell type that proliferates is dependent upon the antigenic stimulus, which may elicit:

● a predominantly *B-cell response* with germinal centre hyperplasia which may be associated with marginal zone hyperplasia
● a predominantly *T-cell response* with paracortical expansion
● a *macrophage response* which is associated with sinus hyperplasia
● most commonly, a *mixed response* in which all the cellular elements of the lymph node are activated and proliferate.

Non-specific reactive hyperplasia

The pattern of cellular proliferation within a lymph node may give some clue to the aetiology of the lymphadenopathy (see below); however, in many instances these clues are absent and the features are termed *non-specific reactive hyperplasia*. On occasions the node enlargement may reach a considerable size and be difficult to distinguish clinically and macroscopically from neoplastic disorders. Microscopically, numerous enlarged germinal centres are seen; these may be present throughout the node and are not restricted to the outer cortex as in the normal state. The germinal centres are active, with a predominance of large blast cells, a high mitotic rate, and often contain numerous tingible body macrophages. There may be an expanded marginal zone which may form a thick rim around the germinal centre. The paracortex usually shows some degree of hyperplasia characterised by the presence of transformed, large lymphoid cells and vessels lined by large endothelial cells (high endothelial venules). The sinuses often show hyperplasia of the lining macrophages, termed *sinus histiocytosis*.

Non-specific reactive hyperplasia may occur in lymph nodes draining sites of infection and, in some cases, pathogenic organisms may cause inflammatory changes within the substance

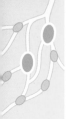

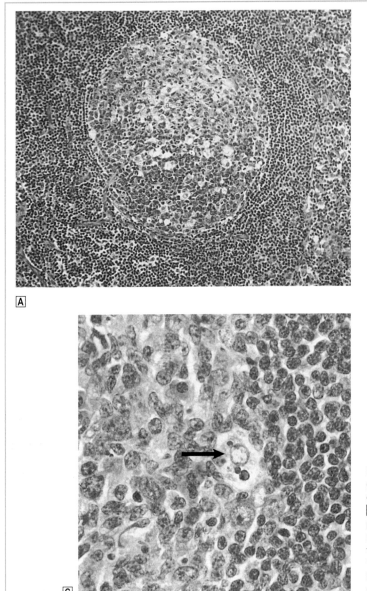

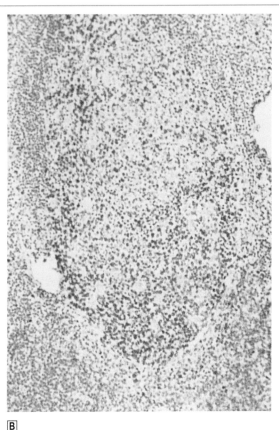

Fig. 22.2   Lymph node germinal centre. [A] Normal germinal centre showing distinct zoning, the lower half containing closely packed and rapidly dividing centroblasts. [B] A germinal centre stained with monoclonal antibody to proliferating cells (Ki-67). Numerous dividing cells (brown nuclei) are seen in the lower, centroblast-rich, region of the germinal centre. [C] High-power view of phagocytic or 'tingible body' macrophage (arrowed) engulfing apoptotic lymphoid cells. These are concentrated in the most proliferative part of the germinal centre.

of the node, termed *lymphadenitis*, which may progress to abscess formation.

Specific disorders

Some types of non-neoplastic lymphadenopathy exhibit histological features that allow the pathologist to make an exact diagnosis. These may be grouped into the following categories:

- granulomatous lymphadenitis
- necrotising lymphadenitis
- sinus histiocytosis
- paracortical hyperplasia.

Granulomatous lymphadenitis

Granulomatous lymphadenitis can occur in a variety of clinical settings such as mycobacterial infection (Ch. 14), sarcoidosis (Ch. 14) and Crohn's disease (Ch. 15). These are described elsewhere and will not be detailed here.

Infection with *Toxoplasma gondii*, a protozoal organism, in the immunocompetent host produces a flu-like illness of short duration and localised lymphadenopathy, usually occipital or high cervical, which persists for some weeks. The affected lymph node is enlarged and shows germinal centre hyperplasia with formation of ill-defined granulomas adjacent to them. In addition, there is florid marginal zone B-cell hyperplasia characterised by a proliferation of medium-sized, monomorphic

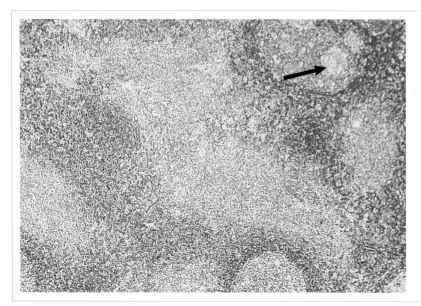

Fig. 22.3   Toxoplasmic lymphadenitis. There is follicular hyperplasia with epithelioid granulomas (arrowed) adjacent to germinal centres. A perifollicular proliferation of uniform B-cells, termed marginal zone B-cells, is also present.

B-cells. This histological triad of follicular hyperplasia with adjacent granulomas and marginal zone B-cell hyperplasia suggests a diagnosis of toxoplasmic lymphadenitis which should be confirmed serologically (Fig. 22.3).

Lymph nodes draining tumours occasionally show a granulomatous reaction in the absence of metastatic involvement, possibly a reaction to tumour antigens. It is particularly common in Hodgkin's lymphoma. Lymph nodes may develop a granulomatous response to foreign particulate material; this most often occurs as a response to silicone compounds used in plastic surgery and joint replacement.

Necrotising lymphadenitis

A variety of diseases caused by infectious agents may lead to necrosis within lymph nodes. Examples are lymphogranuloma venereum and cat scratch disease. *Lymphogranuloma venereum* is a sexually transmitted chlamydial disease and most commonly affects the groin nodes. *Cat scratch disease* follows a bite or scratch from an infected cat. Days to weeks later, tender lymphadenopathy develops in the cervical or axillary regions; the groin is less commonly affected. Two organisms have been shown to be responsible for cat scratch disease: both are extracellular, pleomorphic coccobacilli. The commoner is *Bartonella henselae*, which causes up to 75% of cases; less common is *Afipia felis*. In immunosuppressed patients, particularly those with AIDS, infection with *B. henselae* may cause an unusual vascular proliferation termed *bacillary angiomatosis*. This may affect lymph nodes or extranodal sites. Lymphogranuloma venereum and cat scratch disease show histological similarities, with formation of stellate abscesses within the lymph node, surrounded by palisaded histiocytes (Fig. 22.4).

A rare form of necrotising lymphadenitis is *Kikuchi's disease*, in which tender cervical or occipital lymphadenopathy develops, most commonly in young adult women. The aetiology is unknown. Systemic lupus erythematosus may cause a necrotising lymphadenitis which is histologically very similar to Kikuchi's disease.

Sinus histiocytosis

Sinus histiocytosis with massive lymphadenopathy (SHML or Rosai–Dorfman syndrome) is a rare condition of unknown aetiology which is more common in black populations than in others. It presents typically with bulky cervical lymphadenopathy in the first and second decades of life and may persist for several years. SHML may, however, affect any age and any organ. Histologically, the lymph node sinuses are grossly distended by an infiltrate of large histiocytic cells whose morphology is quite distinctive; admixed with these cells are lymphocytes and plasma cells, which are often seen in the cytoplasm of the histiocytes. Molecular analysis of SHML has shown it to be a polyclonal disorder. The disease often follows a benign course and may regress spontaneously. Some patients with extensive nodal and extranodal disease have pursued an aggressive course and fatalities due to SHML have occurred.

Langerhans' cell histiocytosis (histiocytosis X) may affect lymph nodes and characteristically involves the sinuses initially, where clusters of typical, pale Langerhans' cells with folded nuclei may be seen among giant cells and eosinophils. Langerhans' cell histiocytosis is a clonal neoplastic disease which may present as a variety of clinical syndromes with uni- or multi-focal disease.

Paracortical hyperplasia

Paracortical hyperplasia is a prominent feature in many cases of lymphadenopathy. Two entities deserve special mention: dermatopathic lymphadenopathy and infectious mononucleosis.

Patients with exfoliative chronic skin conditions such as severe eczema or psoriasis, and patients with cutaneous T-cell lymphoma, quite commonly develop enlarged lymph nodes in the groin and axilla. This condition is *dermatopathic lymphadenopathy*. The enlarged lymph nodes may have a yellow or brown cut surface and, microscopically, the paracortex is expanded by pale histiocytes with the cytological features of

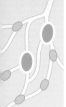

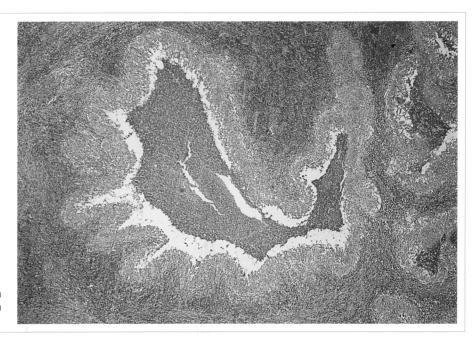

Fig. 22.4 Cat scratch disease. Lymph node showing central abscess formation surrounded by palisaded histiocytes.

interdigitating reticulum cells and Langerhans' cells; lipid droplets and melanin pigment may also be apparent.

Infectious mononucleosis is due to Epstein–Barr virus. This causes widespread lymphadenopathy and is characterised, certainly in the later stages, by paracortical hyperplasia with numerous, large, transformed T-cells. The histological picture may be mistaken for high-grade non-Hodgkin's lymphoma or Hodgkin's lymphoma by the unwary pathologist.

Human immunodeficiency virus infection

The human immunodeficiency virus (HIV) specifically binds to the cluster of differentiation (CD) 4 antigen, which is expressed by helper/inducer T-cells and by cells of the mononuclear phagocytic system, and to a member of the chemokine receptor family CXCR4. The destruction of cells bearing the CD4 antigen causes a severe immune dysregulation, which ultimately leads to a profound immunodeficiency state called the *acquired immune deficiency syndrome* (AIDS).

Lymphadenopathy is extremely common in HIV infection and may be observed in association with systemic symptoms in the AIDS-related complex (Ch. 9) and in the persistent generalised lymphadenopathy (PGL) syndrome (defined as persistent, extra-inguinal lymphadenopathy, in two or more non-contiguous sites, of greater than 3 months' duration and of no known aetiology other than HIV infection).

Morphology
Lymph node biopsies from patients infected with HIV show a spectrum of appearances that, although not absolutely specific, are virtually diagnostic in the appropriate clinical setting. Initially the follicles are hyperplastic and often markedly irregular in shape. Ultrastructurally, a proliferation of dendritic reticulum cells is observed, with complex branching of their processes. In between the DRC processes, retroviral particles can be identified. In some follicles there is focal destruction of

the follicular dendritic cell (FDC) meshwork. This is associated with an infiltrate of small CD8+ T-lymphocytes and focal haemorrhage into the germinal centres ('follicular lysis'). The paracortical reaction is usually disproportionately less than the degree of follicular activation and only scattered immunoblasts and transformed lymphocytes are observed. There is also a reversal of the normal CD4:CD8 ratio of T-cells, often with a preponderance of CD8+ cells. The sinuses may be filled with marginal zone B-cells.

In the later stages of HIV infection, involutional changes are apparent. There is loss of germinal centre B-cells and depletion of paracortical T-cells; sinus histiocytosis may be prominent. These involutional changes are a poor prognostic sign and portend the development of AIDS.

Complications
Lymphadenopathy in HIV infection may not be due solely to immune dysregulation and aberrant lymphocyte proliferation; a variety of neoplastic and infective conditions may also affect the lymph node. Lymphadenopathic Kaposi's sarcoma and high-grade B-cell non-Hodgkin's lymphoma (often with Burkitt-like morphology) are common. A wide variety of infectious agents may cause lymph node enlargement, of which atypical mycobacterial infection is frequently encountered (Fig. 22.5). *Pneumocystis jiroveci* may also be encountered in the lymph nodes of severely immunosuppressed patients.

NEOPLASTIC LYMPHADENOPATHY

Neoplastic lymph node enlargement may occur in:

- malignancies of the immune system (Hodgkin's lymphoma and the non-Hodgkin's lymphomas)
- metastatic spread of solid tumours and involvement by leukaemia.

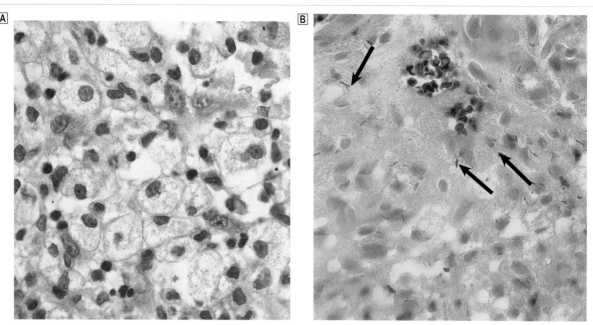

Fig. 22.5 Mycobacterial infection of a lymph node in AIDS. Ⓐ Aggregates of large histiocytes with foamy cytoplasm. Ⓑ A similar area stained for acid-fast bacilli (Ziehl–Neelsen stain), demonstrating numerous mycobacteria (stained red; arrowed).

Hodgkin's lymphoma

The first detailed account of the pathology of Hodgkin's lymphoma was given by Thomas Hodgkin in 1832 in which he described the morbid anatomical appearances of lymph nodes. Earlier descriptions of a similar disease process exist but these lack sufficient detail to categorise them as a distinctive clinicopathological entity. The eponymous term Hodgkin's disease was generously applied by Wilks in 1865 after he had discovered Hodgkin's original paper. Hodgkin's observations were based purely on the macroscopic appearances of the disease at postmortem and it was some years before microscopic studies were undertaken. Over the ensuing decade a gradual awareness of the histopathological features of Hodgkin's lymphoma emerged with descriptions of the typical giant cell by Sternberg and Reed.

Many attempts were made to classify Hodgkin's disease into clinically meaningful groups, the most successful of which was proposed by Lukes and Butler in 1966. This classification was felt to be too complicated for clinical use and was simplified at the Rye Conference. The essential concept of the Lukes and Butler classification was that nodular sclerosis was a distinctive entity and separate from other types of Hodgkin's disease and that lymphocyte predominant, mixed cellularity and lymphocyte depleted represented a spectrum of disease of varying clinical aggressiveness which was reflected in the histopathological picture.

More recent studies have demonstrated that lymphocyte predominant nodular Hodgkin's lymphoma is distinctive and that nodular sclerosis and mixed cellularity are closely related. This view is reflected in the World Health Organization classification, which clearly separates nodular lymphocyte predominant from other forms of Hodgkin's lymphoma, which are collectively termed 'classical Hodgkin's lymphoma':

- classical Hodgkin's lymphoma
  — nodular sclerosis grades 1 and 2
  — mixed cellularity
  — lymphocyte-rich classical Hodgkin's lymphoma
  — lymphocyte depleted
- nodular lymphocyte predominant Hodgkin's lymphoma.

The malignant cell of Hodgkin's lymphoma forms only a small percentage of the cellular population within affected lymph nodes, the bulk of the tissue being made up of reactive lymphocytes, macrophages, plasma cells and eosinophils attracted into the cellular milieu by a variety of cytokines secreted by the Hodgkin's and Reed–Sternberg (H-RS) cells. The relative paucity of the H-RS cell population has hampered efforts to define its origin. Many cell lineages have been postulated for the H-RS cell, including macrophages, follicular dendritic cells, interdigitating reticulum cells and, most recently, lymphocytes. Elegant microdissection studies have isolated single H-RS cells which have then been subjected to molecular biological analysis; this has shown that, in the vast majority of cases studied, the H-RS cells have a clonal immunoglobulin gene rearrangement, indicating that they are derived from B-lymphocytes. In addition, there is evidence of somatic hypermutation of the immunoglobulin genes which indicates that the cells are of germinal centre origin. The majority of cases of classical Hodgkin's lymphoma have defects in the critical transcription factors required for immunoglobulin production, either OCT 2 or BOB 1 or both. Approximately 25% of patients with classical Hodgkin's lymphoma acquire crippling mutations in their immunoglobulin genes. Both the

lack of transcription factors and crippling mutations in the immunoglobulin genes prevent the production of a functional immunoglobulin molecule.

Nodular lymphocyte predominant Hodgkin's lymphoma differs from classical Hodgkin's lymphoma in having intact immunoglobulin transcription factors and an absence of crippling mutations. This form of Hodgkin's lymphoma also shows the presence of ongoing immunoglobulin gene hypermutation in an identical form to that seen in the follicle centre cell non-Hodgkin's lymphoma and again emphasises the difference between lymphocyte predominant and classical Hodgkin's lymphoma.

The clear demonstration of a lymphoid cell of origin for classical Hodgkin's lymphoma as well as the nodular lymphocyte predominant type has prompted replacement of the term Hodgkin's disease with Hodgkin's lymphoma.

Classical Hodgkin's lymphoma

Clinical features

Hodgkin's lymphoma shows a peak incidence in the third and fourth decades and is relatively rare in childhood and old age.

The commonest clinical presentation is one of lymphadenopathy, most often in the upper half of the body, with involvement of cervical and/or axillary lymph nodes. The enlarged nodes are typically rubbery, discrete and mobile, and may achieve a considerable size. Radiological evidence of mediastinal involvement is present in over half of patients and on occasion may be massive, causing respiratory embarrassment. A third of patients with Hodgkin's lymphoma have systemic symptoms (weight loss greater than 10%, unexplained pyrexia of 39°C or more, and drenching night sweats) and in a small proportion the clinical picture will be dominated by these symptoms. Classical Hodgkin's lymphoma appears to arise in lymph nodes or the thymus, and spreads, certainly in its early stages, via the lymphatics in a contiguous and predictable fashion. Involvement of the liver and bone marrow is rarely seen in the absence of splenic involvement and thus the spleen appears to be the key to haematogenous dissemination.

Stage is an important determinant in the treatment and prognosis of patients with Hodgkin's lymphoma; the staging system currently used is that proposed at the Ann Arbor workshop in 1971 and modified at the Cotswolds meeting in 1989.

- *Stage I.* Involvement of a single lymph node region.
- *Stage II.* Involvement of two or more lymph node regions on the same side of the diaphragm.
- *Stage III.* Involvement of lymph node regions on both sides of the diaphragm (III), subdivided into III₁ = upper abdominal disease (splenic, hilar, coeliac or portal disease) and III₂ = lower abdominal disease (para-aortic, iliac and mesenteric disease).
- *Stage IV.* Disseminated involvement of one or more extra-lymphatic organs such as liver, lung and bone marrow, with or without lymph node involvement.

The absence or presence of the systemic symptoms described above is indicated by the suffix A or B respectively;

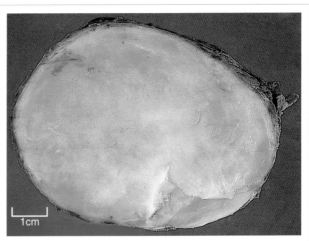

Fig. 22.6   Mixed cellularity Hodgkin's lymphoma. Macroscopic appearances of an axillary lymph node from a 32-year-old man with mixed cellularity Hodgkin's lymphoma. There is a homogeneous white cut surface. The capsule is not involved and there is no infiltration of surrounding fat.

E indicates involvement of a single extranodal site contiguous with or proximal to a known nodal site; X denotes the presence of bulky disease, > one-third widening of the mediastinum at T5–6 or >10cm maximum dimension of a nodal mass. The survival of patients declines with advancing stage, bulky disease (X) and the presence of systemic (B) symptoms.

Classical Hodgkin's lymphoma is also associated with a variety of haematological and biochemical abnormalities such as anaemia, lymphocytopenia, a raised erythrocyte sedimentation rate (ESR) and a low serum albumin. These abnormalities are also indicators of a reduced survival.

Morphology

Classical Hodgkin's lymphoma is principally a disease of lymph nodes. A lymph node biopsy is usually done to establish the diagnosis.

Macroscopically, affected lymph nodes are enlarged, with a smooth surface. Classical Hodgkin's lymphoma, unlike the non-Hodgkin's lymphomas, rarely breaches the lymph node capsule, a fact that accounts for the discrete nature of the lymphadenopathy upon palpation. The cut surface is usually homogeneously white (Fig. 22.6), although in some histological subtypes a nodular or fibrotic appearance may be present.

Microscopically, affected lymph nodes show a partial or complete effacement of their normal architecture by a mixed infiltrate containing lymphocytes, histiocytes, plasma cells and eosinophils as well as the malignant cells of classical Hodgkin's lymphoma; these are large cells and take the form of mononuclear Hodgkin's cells or of Reed–Sternberg cells, which have a large, pale, multilobed nucleus and a prominent eosinophilic nucleolus about the size of a red blood cell (Fig. 22.7).

Nodular sclerosis.   The term nodular sclerosis describes many of the histological features of this, the commonest subtype

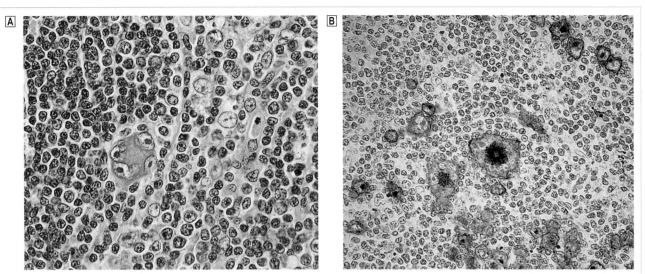

Fig. 22.7   Hodgkin's lymphoma. [A] A classical Reed–Sternberg cell shows multiple nuclei with prominent nucleoli. [B] Reed–Sternberg cells identified by immunohistochemical staining for CD30 (Ki-1 antigen).

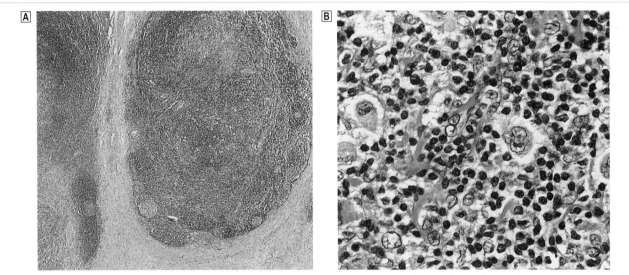

Fig. 22.8   Nodular sclerosing Hodgkin's lymphoma. [A] The cellular nodules are surrounded by thick collagen bands. [B] Lacunar cells (Hodgkin's cell surrounded by a clear space) are characteristic of nodular sclerosing Hodgkin's lymphoma.

of classical Hodgkin's lymphoma (75% of cases). The normal lymph node architecture is replaced by cellular nodules which are separated by bands of collagen (Fig. 22.8). Within the cellular nodules is a mixed infiltrate similar to other types of Hodgkin's lymphoma but containing a distinctive Hodgkin's cell variant termed the lacunar cell. The lacunar cell is so named because it appears to sit in a space or 'lacuna', caused by the disappearance of its lipid-rich cytoplasm during the process of creating a paraffin block of the tissue. It possesses the large nucleus and prominent eosinophilic nucleolus seen in other Hodgkin's cells.

Nodular sclerosis is a distinctive form and does not transform into any of the other subtypes of classical Hodgkin's lymphoma. However, the cytological composition of the cellular nodules may vary from one in which the predominant cell is the small lymphocyte, with only scanty lacunar and Reed–Sternberg cells, to a histological picture that is dominated by Hodgkin's cells with depletion of lymphocytes. This latter form has been correlated with an aggressive natural history and is termed grade 2 nodular sclerosis; all other histological subtypes are classified as grade 1 nodular sclerosis.

Nodular sclerosis displays distinct clinical differences from other subtypes of Hodgkin's lymphoma, having an almost equal sex ratio (most forms of Hodgkin's lymphoma show a marked male predominance), a striking propensity for mediastinal involvement at presentation (50% of patients) and an association with the bizarre syndrome of alcohol

intolerance (5% of patients). There is now strong evidence from gene expression profiling studies that nodular sclerosing classical Hodgkin's lymphoma shares many features in common with a subtype of large B-cell lymphoma presenting in the mediastinum, termed mediastinal large B-cell lymphoma. The similarities are further highlighted by the occurrence of composite tumours containing nodular sclerosing Hodgkin's lymphoma and mediastinal large B-cell lymphoma within the same lymph node and by the presence of grey zone cases which share morphological and phenotypic similarities of both entities. There are also marked similarities in the patient population affected and the clinical distribution of disease.

Mixed cellularity. Mixed cellularity is the second commonest subtype of classical Hodgkin's lymphoma (18% of cases). As the name suggests, the histological picture is an admixture of lymphocytes, histiocytes, plasma cells, eosinophils, Hodgkin's cells and Reed–Sternberg cells; the latter are relatively abundant compared to lymphocyte-rich classical Hodgkin's lymphoma.

Mixed cellularity is a rather aggressive form of classical Hodgkin's lymphoma when compared to grade 1 nodular sclerosis: it presents at an advanced stage relatively frequently (stages III and IV in > 50% of patients) and with systemic (B) symptoms (35% of patients) and a poor overall survival.

Lymphocyte-rich classical Hodgkin's lymphoma. Lymphocyte-rich classical Hodgkin's lymphoma (LRCHL) is a relatively recently described histological variant of classical Hodgkin's lymphoma characterised by the presence of morphologically and phenotypically characteristic H-RS cells in a lymphocyte-rich cellular background. There may be a nodular or diffuse growth pattern. When nodular it is composed predominantly of mantle zone B-lymphocytes with scattered and sometimes scanty classical H-RS cells within the nodules. When diffuse there is a T-cell predominance. There is a close morphological overlap between LRCHL and nodular lymphocyte predominant Hodgkin's lymphoma—the term is designed to alert the pathologist that everything that is lymphocyte rich is not lymphocyte predominant and that the clinical behaviour of LRCHL differs greatly from nodular lymphocyte predominant.

Lymphocyte depleted. Two histological patterns of lymphocyte depleted Hodgkin's lymphoma may be recognised:

- reticular, which is characterised by numerous Hodgkin's and Reed–Sternberg cells with depletion of lymphocytes
- diffuse fibrosis, where the lymph node architecture is replaced by a hypocellular infiltrate containing bizarre Reed–Sternberg cells and associated with non-collagenous fine fibrosis.

These two patterns of lymphocyte depletion may co-exist in the same lymph node and are closely allied conditions. Extensive necrosis is common in both subtypes.

Lymphocyte depletion is rare (< 1% of all cases of classical Hodgkin's lymphoma) and carries the worst prognosis. Patients often present acutely with systemic (B) symptoms and usually at an advanced stage, with a high frequency of involvement of liver (60% of patients) and bone marrow (40% of patients). Lymphocyte depleted classical Hodgkin's

lymphoma appears to be becoming extremely rare in the developed world and cases are seldom seen outside the setting of immunodeficiency states.

Nodular lymphocyte predominant Hodgkin's lymphoma

Clinical features

Nodular lymphocyte predominant Hodgkin's lymphoma (N-LP) differs markedly in clinical presentation from classical Hodgkin's lymphoma. There is a marked male predominance, over 80% of patients being men. The peak age incidence is a decade older for N-LP than for patients with classical Hodgkin's lymphoma; most patients are in their thirties and forties. The majority of patients (nearly 90%) present with localised, asymptomatic disease (stages I and IIA) and the lymphadenopathy occurs in unusual locations such as the suprahyoid neck and inguinal regions, sites rarely involved by classical Hodgkin's lymphoma. Mediastinal disease is rare. Late relapse is common in N-LP and may occur even after 20 years; the vast majority of relapses with classical Hodgkin's lymphoma occur within 3 years. Relapses of N-LP occur at the site of original disease or in other typical N-LP locations. Patients with N-LP are at increased risk of developing secondary high-grade non-Hodgkin's lymphoma (4% at 25 years), which is usually of B-cell lineage and may be clonally related to the original N-LP. The overall survival of patients with N-LP is excellent and superior to that in classical Hodgkin's lymphoma.

Histologically, lymphocyte predominant Hodgkin's lymphoma is characterised by a paucity of typical Hodgkin's and Reed–Sternberg cells and abundant lymphocytes, sometimes admixed with bland histiocytes. There is a nodular growth pattern but occasionally diffuse areas may be present. Collagen band formation is not a feature. Nodular lymphocyte predominant Hodgkin's lymphoma contains a distinctive Reed–Sternberg cell variant which is called the 'popcorn' cell because of its excessively lobulated nucleus. Phenotypically and genotypically the popcorn cell has been shown to be derived from a neoplastic germinal centre B-cell.

Survival in Hodgkin's lymphoma

The overall survival figures for Hodgkin's lymphoma vary between different treatment centres, but results from a British multi-centre trial show that approximately 75% of patients were still alive 5 years after diagnosis (Fig. 22.9). As relapse tends to occur early in the course of the disease (usually within 3 years), the majority of these patients are probably cured. It is now clear that treatment-related causes of death are becoming increasingly important for patients with Hodgkin's lymphoma. Second epithelial malignancies and cardiovascular disease now rival the mortality from Hodgkin's lymphoma itself.

Factors that adversely affect survival are:
- advanced age
- systemic (B) symptoms
- abnormal haematological parameters
- advanced stage
- aggressive histopathological subtype.

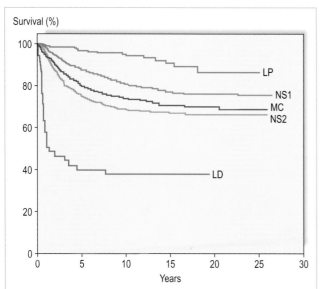

Fig. 22.9 Actuarial survival of patients with Hodgkin's lymphoma. The data are subdivided according to a modified Rye histological classification with subdivision of nodular sclerosis (NS) into grades 1 and 2. (LP, lymphocyte predominant; MC, mixed cellularity; LD, lymphocyte depleted) (Data from the British National Lymphoma Investigation.)

Table 22.2   World Health Organization classification of neoplastic diseases of the haematopoietic and lymphoid tissues (summary of main entries)
B-cell neoplasias
B-cell lymphoblastic leukaemia/lymphoma
B-cell chronic lymphocytic leukaemia/small lymphocytic lymphoma
B-cell prolymphocytic leukaemia
Lymphoplasmacytic lymphoma
Mantle cell lymphoma
Follicular lymphoma
Marginal zone B-cell lymphoma of mucosa-associated lymphoid tissue
Nodal marginal zone lymphoma
Splenic marginal zone B-cell lymphoma
Hairy cell leukaemia
Diffuse large B-cell lymphoma
Diffuse large B-cell lymphoma, subtypes:
Burkitt's lymphoma
Plasmacytoma
Plasma cell myeloma
T-cell neoplasias
Precursor T-cell leukaemia/lymphoma (T-cell lymphoblastic leukaemia/lymphoma)
Peripheral T/NK cell neoplasms, predominantly leukaemic/disseminated (e.g. adult T-cell lymphoma/leukaemia)
Peripheral T-cell and NK cell neoplasms, predominantly nodal
Peripheral T-cell and NK cell neoplasms, predominantly extranodal (e.g. mycosis fungoides, Sézary syndrome, enteropathy-type intestinal T-cell)

Non-Hodgkin's lymphomas

▸ Lymphomas other than Hodgkin's lymphoma
▸ Classified according to anatomical origin (central, peripheral), histological architecture and predominant cell: follicular or diffuse; centrocytic; centroblastic; immunoblastic, etc.
▸ Majority are of B-lymphocyte origin
▸ T-cell lymphomas are less common; two types involve the skin: mycosis fungoides and Sézary syndrome

The non-Hodgkin's lymphomas (NHLs) are malignant tumours of the immune system other than Hodgkin's lymphoma. The vast majority are derived from lymphoid cells; solid tumours of the mononuclear phagocytic system (termed histiocytic lymphoma) are extremely rare.

NHLs form a wide spectrum of disease both clinically and biologically, ranging from slowly progressive neoplasms to rapidly growing destructive tumours. This diversity of clinical behaviour is reflected in the wide range of histological appearances exhibited by NHLs. Classification of NHL is based on the cell lineages in the normal immune system in which precursor lymphoid cells are processed in the thymus and bursa equivalent tissue and into lymphoid cells which are located in peripheral sites such as lymph nodes, spleen and mucosa-associated lymphoid tissue; these are termed peripheral T- and B-cells respectively (Table 22.2).

Precursor lymphoid neoplasms

These are high-grade NHLs composed of diffuse sheets of medium-sized lymphoid cells possessing a high nucleocytoplasmic ratio. They may be of T-cell or B-cell lineage and express the nuclear antigen TdT (terminal deoxynucleotidyl transferase, an enzyme involved in amplification of antigen receptor diversity). These tumours form the spectrum of disease termed *lymphoblastic lymphoma* and *lymphoblastic leukaemia,* and these appear to be biologically the same disease process.

Lymphoblastic lymphomas are commonest in childhood but also occur in adults. Bone marrow infiltration is frequent and a leukaemic phase is often seen; this presents difficulties in separating acute lymphoblastic leukaemia (ALL) from lymphoblastic lymphoma. By convention, an arbitrary subdivision is made on the percentage of lymphoblasts present in the bone marrow (< 25% is lymphoma; >25% is ALL).

Precursor T-cell lymphomas/leukaemias tend to involve the mediastinum of adolescent boys; histologically, the lymphoblasts may have a distinct convoluted nuclear morphology (Fig. 22.10). Precursor B-cell lymphoma/leukaemia may present in leukaemic phase or have solid tumour deposits involving nodal and extranodal sites.

Peripheral non-Hodgkin's lymphoma

Unlike the precursor or lymphoblastic lymphoma/leukaemia, the peripheral NHLs form a heterogeneous group of neoplasms with a wide range of histological appearances. They represent biologically distinctive tumours derived from B-cells, T-cells and natural killer (NK) cells and may arise in nodal or extranodal sites. As more is understood about the biology of the peripheral NHLs, so the complexity of this

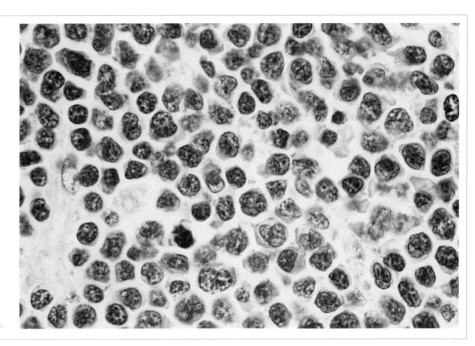

Fig. 22.10 T-cell lymphoblastic lymphoma. Medium-sized cells with a high nucleo-cytoplasmic ratio and convoluted nuclear morphology are shown.

group of neoplasms increases; this is reflected in the proposed classification schemes (Table 22.2). The common subtypes of nodal, peripheral NHLs are:

- B-cell chronic lymphocytic leukaemia/small lymphocytic lymphoma
- follicular lymphoma
- mantle cell lymphoma
- diffuse large B-cell lymphoma
- Burkitt's lymphoma
- peripheral T-cell lymphoma
- anaplastic large cell lymphoma.

B-cell chronic lymphocytic leukaemia/small lymphocytic lymphoma

B-cell chronic lymphocytic leukaemia/small lymphocytic lymphomas are tumours of immature small round lymphocytes. They are of B-cell lineage. The borderline between lymphocytic lymphoma and chronic lymphocytic leukaemia is blurred; there is close morphological and immunophenotypic homology between the neoplastic cells of the two conditions. Most now regard B-cell small lymphocytic lymphoma as a tissue manifestation of B-cell chronic lymphocytic leukaemia (CLL).

Affected lymph nodes are enlarged and usually smooth surfaced, with a homogeneous white cut surface. The normal nodal architecture is replaced by a monotonous infiltrate of small lymphocytes with scattered larger cells (called prolymphocytes) which may form aggregates termed pseudofollicles.

The disease is almost invariably disseminated, with a high frequency of splenic, liver and bone marrow infiltration.

B-CLL is exclusively a disease of adults. It is now clear that there is clinical and biological heterogeneity within B-CLL. In many it runs an indolent course with patients dying from unrelated causes; these cases are associated with immunoglobulin gene hypermutation. In some patients the disease is much more aggressive and these are commonly associated with unmutated immunoglobulin genes.

As the disease progresses it may cause death by extensive bone marrow infiltration and bone marrow failure. In 5–10% of patients the disease will transform into a high-grade pleomorphic large cell lymphoma (*Richter's syndrome*) which is refractory to treatment and has a poor prognosis. Patients with B-CLL are frequently hypogammaglobulinaemic and are particularly susceptible to bacterial infections.

Follicular lymphoma

Follicular lymphomas are tumours derived from (or differentiated towards) germinal centre B-cells. These lymphomas contain an admixture of centroblasts and centrocytes and may have a purely follicular growth pattern or may have a mixed pattern with follicular and diffuse areas. In addition to the neoplastic B-cells, non-neoplastic T-lymphocytes and dendritic reticulum cells are also present within the neoplastic follicle, having been recruited by the neoplastic B-cell clone.

Important in the pathogenesis of follicular lymphoma is a specific chromosomal translocation involving the immunoglobulin heavy chain promoter region on chromosome 14 and the anti-apoptotic gene *bcl*-2 on chromosome 18 (t(14;18)(q32;q21)). This translocation causes the constitutive overexpression of bcl-2 protein, rendering follicular lymphoma cells relatively resistant to apoptosis.

Lymph nodes replaced by follicular lymphoma are usually enlarged and smooth surfaced. Cut surfaces are homogeneous grey/white with occasional areas of haemorrhage and necrosis. A faintly nodular pattern may be seen with a magnifying glass. Microscopically, the normal lymph node architecture is replaced by closely packed neoplastic follicles, often extending through the lymph node capsule into perinodal fat (Fig. 22.11); diffuse areas may also be present. The neoplastic

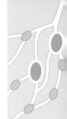

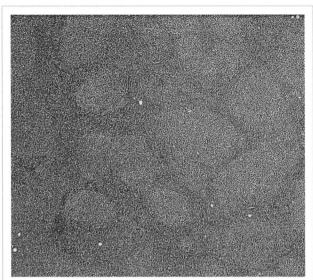

A

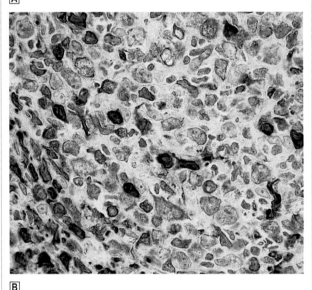

B

Fig. 22.11 Follicular lymphoma. A Numerous rounded lymphoid aggregates are seen throughout the lymph node. B Immunohistochemical evidence of overexpression of bcl-2, an inhibitor of apoptosis.

follicles contain a mixture of centroblasts and centrocytes; the relative proportion of these cells forms the basis of grading these lymphomas. Tumours with relatively large numbers of centroblasts have a worse prognosis.

Follicular lymphoma is one of the commonest types of non-Hodgkin's lymphoma and is a disease of late adult life with a peak age incidence in the sixth and seventh decades. It is exceptionally rare in children and young adults. Most patients with follicular lymphoma will present with painless, slowly progressive lymphadenopathy, usually with disseminated disease (stages III and IV); 40% of patients will have systemic symptoms.

Involvement of bone marrow, spleen and liver is common in follicular lymphoma. The earliest morphological manifestations of marrow infiltration are localised collections of irregular small lymphoid cells adjacent to bone trabeculae (termed paratrabecular infiltration). Extensive bone marrow replacement may occur with consequent marrow failure. A leukaemic phase of follicular lymphoma is seen in a significant percentage of patients, when neoplastic B-cells may be found in peripheral blood.

Splenic involvement may either be minimal or cause massive splenomegaly with hypersplenism. The neoplastic cells of follicular lymphoma maintain some degree of physiological homing function and selectively infiltrate the B-cell areas of the white pulp of the spleen, progressively replacing and expanding these structures such that the cut surface of the organ may be seen to contain numerous discrete white nodules separated by normal red pulp.

Follicular lymphoma is an indolent disease but it is generally regarded as incurable when disseminated, and the majority of patients die as a direct result of their lymphoma. The exact mode of death is sometimes difficult to determine but in at least 30% of patients the disease will transform into a diffuse large B-cell lymphoma. This lymphoma behaves aggressively and is usually refractory to treatment. In the remainder, following a clinical course of multiple remissions and relapses, the tumour becomes unresponsive to further chemotherapy, with a progressively increasing tumour burden leading to death.

Although it is difficult to determine prognosis for an individual patient with follicular lymphoma, factors that are associated with a reduced survival are rapid disease progression, the presence of systemic (B) symptoms and infiltration of vital organs. There is now good evidence that the non-neoplastic constituents of the follicles of follicular lymphoma are important determinants of prognosis. Follicles that contain a high percentage of reactive T-cells are associated with a favourable prognosis and those containing large numbers of macrophages are associated with a reduced survival. This important role of 'bystander' elements in determining the biological behaviour of tumours may be recognised in other lymphoma subtypes in the future.

Mantle cell lymphoma

Mantle cell lymphoma is the term currently used for a low-grade B-cell lymphoma that is derived from or differentiates towards the mantle zone of the germinal centre. The term encompasses entities such as centrocytic lymphoma and intermediately differentiated lymphocytic lymphoma in previous classification schemes.

Mantle cell lymphoma may have a nodular or diffuse architecture and is composed of a mixture of irregular small B-cells, follicular dendritic cells and T-cells; the B-cell component is monoclonal.

Mantle cell lymphoma has a distinctive chromosomal translocation—t(11;14)(q13;q32). This leads to the deregulation of the *PRAD*-1 gene with subsequent overexpression of the important cell cycle control protein cyclin D1.

Mantle cell lymphoma is not uncommon (6% of all NHLs) and has a peak age incidence in the seventh decade. It is generally regarded as a low-grade lymphoma but its natural history appears to be more aggressive than other low-grade NHLs and it has the ability to transform into a 'blastoid' form which has a very poor survival. The disease usually presents with lymphadenopathy but a distinctive pattern is seen in the

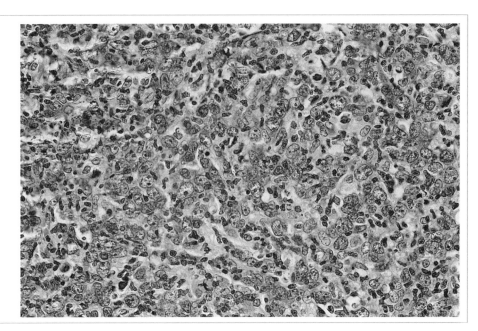

Fig. 22.12 Diffuse large cell lymphoma. The majority of the cells, growing in a diffuse pattern, are large B-cells (centroblasts) with multiple nucleoli often peripherally located.

gastrointestinal tract, where it is termed *lymphomatous polyposis.* Most patients have advanced stage and symptomatic disease. Leukaemic overspill is quite common.

Diffuse large B-cell lymphoma

Diffuse large B-cell lymphoma forms the commonest type of high-grade NHL; it may arise de novo or as a result of the transformation of a low-grade B-cell lymphoma (usually follicular lymphoma). As the name implies, this lymphoma is characterised by a diffuse outgrowth of large B-cells which may display centroblastic or immunoblastic cytology (Fig. 22.12).

Diffuse large B-cell lymphoma is usually a disease of adults but may occur in childhood. The majority of patients present with rapidly progressive nodal disease but extranodal involvement is common; involvement of the gastrointestinal tract and Waldeyer's ring is most frequent.

Unlike the low-grade lymphomas, diffuse large B-cell lymphoma is frequently localised (stages I and II in 45% of patients) and curable even when advanced (5-year survival for patients with stage III and IV disease is approximately 35%). A variety of cytogenetic abnormalities are seen in diffuse large B-cell lymphoma; the commonest are the t(14;18) translocation resulting in deregulation of the *bcl*-2 gene and translocations involving the 3q27 breakpoint with overexpression and mutations of the *bcl*-6 gene. Gene expression profiling in diffuse large B-cell lymphoma has led to the identification of two potentially distinct biological forms of this disease, one termed germinal centre-like large B-cell lymphoma and one activated B-cell-like large B-cell lymphoma. The latter is associated with a relatively poor survival. Abnormalities of the *bcl*-6 gene have been associated with extranodal presentations and a more favourable clinical course.

Burkitt's lymphoma

Burkitt's lymphoma is a distinctive type of B-cell lymphoma, associated with a specific chromosomal translocation involving the c-*myc* gene at 8p24. The translocation involving

c-*myc* usually occurs into the immunoglobulin heavy chain gene locus at 14q32 (t(8;14)(p24;q32)) but variant translocations involving the kappa and lambda light chain gene loci also occur. Three categories of Burkitt's lymphoma are recognised: endemic, sporadic and immunodeficiency-associated. Endemic Burkitt's lymphoma occurs in paraequatorial Africa and New Guinea and occurs much less commonly in other regions. The disease affects children and adolescents, is associated with Epstein–Barr virus infection and malaria (Ch. 11), and involves extranodal sites, particularly the jaw, gastrointestinal tract and gonads. The histological appearances are distinctive, with tightly packed medium-sized lymphoid cells interspersed with phagocytic macrophages which impart a 'starry sky' appearance to histological sections. There is a very high proliferation rate, with almost 100% of cells being in cycle. The histological and phenotypic features of sporadic and immunodeficiency-associated Burkitt's lymphoma are identical. They have a propensity to involve the gastrointestinal tract and oropharynx.

Peripheral T-cell lymphoma

T-cell lymphomas are relatively uncommon in Europe and America, making up no more than 10% of NHL cases. In Japan and the Caribbean region they are much more common. This increased disease prevalence is due to the presence of an endemic retrovirus, the human T-cell leukaemia/lymphoma virus (HTLV-I), which appears to be a causative agent in some forms of T-cell malignancy.

The spectrum of T-cell NHL appears as broad as that of B-cell tumours and complicated classification schemes have been proposed. More recently it has been appreciated that the histological recognition of different subtypes of nodal peripheral T-cell lymphoma is difficult to perform reliably and that morphology is not a good indicator of clinical behaviour. For this reason the majority of these tumours have been categorised as *peripheral T-cell lymphoma unspecified.* Within this group of tumours there is wide variation in the size and shape

of the neoplastic T-cells and they are frequently mixed with other non-neoplastic components of the paracortex, such as interdigitating reticulum cells and high endothelial venules; aggregates of epithelioid histiocytes and an eosinophil infiltrate may also be prominent.

Within the heterogeneous group of T-cell lymphomas there are several distinctive clinicopathological entities:

- cutaneous T-cell lymphomas (CTCL; mycosis fungoides and Sézary syndrome)
- adult T-cell lymphoma/leukaemia (ATLL)
- angioimmunoblastic T-cell lymphoma (AILD)
- anaplastic large cell lymphoma (ALCL).

Mycosis fungoides (MF) and *Sézary syndrome* are closely allied cutaneous T-cell lymphomas. The neoplastic T-cells usually have a 'helper' cell phenotype (CD4) and form a band-like upper dermal infiltrate with a moderate degree of epidermal infiltration, often forming small aggregates of cells within the epidermis (termed *Pautrier's micro-abscesses*), usually in association with epidermal Langerhans' cells. The neoplastic T-cells are larger than normal lymphocytes and usually have a markedly irregular nuclear profile imparting a cerebriform appearance.

Cutaneous T-cell lymphoma is a disease of adult life with a tendency to involve older age groups.

Mycosis fungoides clinically progresses through three stages:

- the *patch stage*, characterised by erythematous macules usually occurring on areas not exposed to sunlight
- the *plaque stage*, with elevated scaly plaques which may be pink or red/brown and are often intensely pruritic
- the *tumour stage*, with dome-shaped firm tumours which may ulcerate.

The density of the lymphoid infiltrate increases from the patch to the tumour stage and in some cases of tumour stage MF there may be transformation to a large-celled cytological pattern. Although MF is initially confined to the skin, lymph node and visceral organ involvement become clinically apparent later in the course of the disease and are particularly common in the tumour stage. This is a bad prognostic feature with a median survival of only 2.5 years compared to a 12-year median survival for patients with limited extent cutaneous disease.

The Sézary syndrome variant of CTCL is characterised by the presence of generalised erythroderma, lymphadenopathy and at least 10% of peripheral blood mononuclear cells having an atypical cerebriform morphology. The prognosis of patients with the Sézary syndrome is poor.

Adult T-cell leukaemia/lymphoma (ATLL) is one of the few human malignancies for which there is strong evidence of a viral aetiology. The disease is endemic in the islands of southern Japan, the Caribbean basin, the tropical islands of the Pacific Ocean and in the Seychelles. Outside endemic areas the majority of affected patients have been black. The disease is associated with the retrovirus *HTLV-I* whose p40 tax protein leads to transcriptional activation of a range of genes in infected T-cells that confer a survival advantage. The disease presents with lymphadenopathy and a leukaemic blood picture, often associated with cutaneous infiltration and hypercalcaemia (secondary to the production of parathyroid hormone-related peptide). Low-grade and chronic forms of ATLL have a more indolent course. The affected lymph nodes are infiltrated by a pleomorphic T-cell proliferation, indistinguishable from other non-virus-associated T-cell lymphomas. The disease has a poor prognosis, with a median survival of less than 1 year; most patients die from opportunistic infection due to severe immunosuppression.

Angioimmunoblastic T-cell lymphoma (AILD) is a rare but distinctive form of T-cell lymphoma. Although originally it was not thought to be neoplastic, the demonstration of T-cell receptor gene rearrangement in the majority of cases studied has indicated that this lesion should be regarded as a lymphoma. Patients usually present with widespread lymphadenopathy, systemic symptoms, skin rashes, polyclonal hypergammaglobulinaemia and evidence of immunosuppression. The prognosis for AILD is poor, although occasional spontaneous or steroid-induced remissions are described.

Anaplastic large cell lymphoma (ALCL) is a recently described high-grade NHL that is often of T-cell lineage but may fail to express lineage-associated markers; the latter are usually genotypically T-cell in origin. ALCL may arise de novo or may be a high-grade transformation of a low-grade NHL. Primary ALCL is most common in children and young adults, although any age may be affected. The disease may be nodal but there is frequently extranodal disease as well. Common sites of extranodal disease include the skin, gastrointestinal tract and Waldeyer's ring. Histologically, ALCL shows a wide spectrum of appearances, and many different subtypes have been described, including common, small cell, lymphohistiocytic, giant cell and sarcomatoid. Despite this marked divergence in appearance, ALCL appears to be a unified biological entity and all cases contain a characteristic cell termed by some the 'hallmark' cell (Fig. 22.13). ALCL is associated with a particular chromosomal translocation, t(2;5)(p23;q35), which leads to the aberrant expression of a fusion protein containing a tyrosine kinase called *anaplastic lymphoma kinase* (ALK) and a 'housekeeping' protein, nucleophosphomin; this translocation occurs in 70–80% of ALK protein-expressing ALCLs. Variant translocations also occur in 20–30% of ALCLs, which fuse the *ALK* gene with other partners. Despite its very aggressive histological appearance, primary ALCL has a relatively good overall survival (approximately 80% of patients alive at 5 years). This favourable survival appears independent of traditional prognostic factors.

Extranodal lymphoma

Extranodal lymphoid tissue is widely distributed in the body, often located adjacent to mucosal surfaces (e.g. Peyer's patches in the terminal ileum). The structure of this mucosa-associated lymphoid tissue (MALT) differs from that in peripheral lymph nodes and there are differences in function and patterns of lymphocyte recirculation. Many extranodal lymphomas show features in common with MALT and it is now clear that these are distinctive forms of NHL. They are currently termed extranodal marginal zone lymphoma.

Extranodal lymphomas make up at least a quarter of all NHLs and occur most commonly in the gastrointestinal tract (Ch. 15); other common sites include skin, salivary gland, thyroid and orbit. Most extranodal lymphomas occur in sites normally devoid of lymphoid tissue; the acquisition of

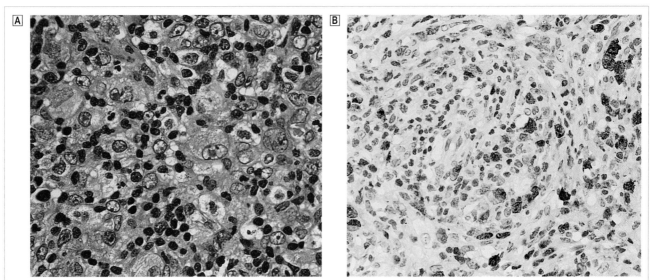

Fig. 22.13 Anaplastic large cell lymphoma. A Pleomorphic large cells infiltrate this lymph node. B Expression of anaplastic lymphoma kinase, a fusion protein associated with the characteristic chromosomal translocation.

lymphoid tissue as the result of either an autoimmune (such as Hashimoto's thyroiditis) or infective (as seen in *Helicobacter* gastritis) process is the essential forerunner to the development of lymphoma in these locations.

Extranodal lymphomas of marginal zone type share common histological and cytogenetic features wherever they occur. Histologically, they are characterised by the presence of reactive germinal centres surrounded by a population of neoplastic B-cells which show cytological similarities to lymph node marginal zone B-cells. These marginal zone B-cells infiltrate epithelial structures to form *lympho-epithelial lesions* which are characteristic of extranodal marginal zone lymphomas (Fig. 22.14). These lymphomas often show impressive degrees of plasma cell differentiation, usually adjacent to the mucosal surface. Many extranodal lymphomas are low grade but some show features of high-grade lymphoma, usually of diffuse large B-cell type. These high-grade lymphomas may arise de novo or be associated with a low-grade extranodal marginal zone component.

MALT lymphomas lack the common cytogenetic abnormalities seen in nodal lymphomas (t(14;18) and t(11;14)) and are associated with novel karyotypic changes such as t(11;18) and t(1;14); both of these translocations are associated with overactivity of the NF kappa B transcription factor which appears important in the pathogenesis of this lymphoma subtype.

There are marked differences in the clinical behaviour of extranodal marginal zone lymphomas compared with that of nodal lymphomas. They appear to remain localised for long periods and have an indolent natural history, often with a very good prognosis. The pattern of relapse is also different, with a tendency to recur in extranodal locations.

The remarkable similarities in histology, cytogenetics and clinical course of extranodal lymphomas from different sites strongly suggest that they represent a common biological entity. The recognition and characterisation of the extranodal

marginal zone lymphoma group is an important advance in lymphoma pathology.

Not all extranodal lymphomas correspond to the extranodal marginal zone pattern; some are identical to nodal lymphomas and some are distinctive clinicopathological entities that present in extranodal locations.

Lymphomatous polyposis is a manifestation of mantle cell lymphoma in the gastrointestinal tract. It is characterised by the presence of multiple mucosal polyps throughout the alimentary system; these may range in size from half a millimetre to many centimetres in diameter and tend to centre around the ileocaecal valve (Fig. 22.15). This is an aggressive lymphoma which frequently becomes leukaemic at some point in its natural history.

Enteropathy-type T-cell lymphoma is a pleomorphic T-cell lymphoma that develops in some patients with coeliac disease. Enteropathy-type T-cell lymphoma has a predilection for jejunal involvement, where it often presents as multifocal lesions—ulcers, fissures and perforation. The tumour is probably derived from intramucosal T-cells. This is an aggressive lymphoma with a poor survival.

Classification of the non-Hodgkin's lymphomas

The classification of malignant lymphoma has undergone dramatic changes in recent years, which have come to fruition with the publication of the new WHO classification of tumours of haematopoietic and lymphoid tissues. This classification is based on the previously published Revised European–American Lymphoma classification and classifies lymphomas according to lineage. Within each category, distinct diseases are defined according to a combination of morphology, phenotype, and genetic and clinical features with the aim of identifying lymphoma entities that can be recognised by pathologists and have clinical relevance (see Table 22.2).

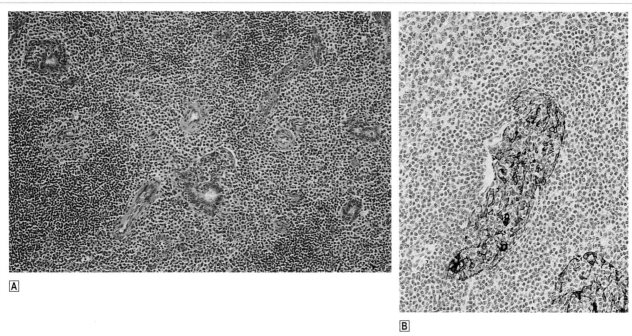

Fig. 22.14   Low-grade MALT lymphoma of the salivary gland. [A] Centrocyte-like cells infiltrate the glands and form lympho-epithelial lesions characteristic of low-grade MALT lymphoma. [B] Immunohistochemical demonstration of cytokeratin in the surviving glandular epithelium infiltrated by lymphoma cells.

THYMUS

NORMAL STRUCTURE AND FUNCTION

The thymus develops from the third and occasionally the fourth pharyngeal pouches. It is a pyramidal, bilobed, encapsulated organ situated in the anterior superior mediastinum. The relative weight of the thymus in comparison to body weight is greatest in the neonate (20–30 g). The absolute thymic weight peaks around puberty (40–50 g) and thereafter declines such that in the elderly adult the thymus is atrophic and composed largely of adipose tissue. The significance and the mechanisms of thymic atrophy are largely unknown.

The lobes of the thymus are divided into lobules by connective tissue septa which grow in from the fibrous capsule. Subdivision of the thymus into an outer, dark cortex and inner, pale medulla is apparent macroscopically.

The thymus is a central lymphoid organ and is responsible for the induction of cell-mediated immune function in developing lymphoid cells (Ch. 9). Most of this inductive activity appears to be located in the cortex, which contains densely packed medium-sized lymphoid cells, scattered epithelial cells and abundant interdigitating reticulum cells. The thymic epithelial cells are responsible for the secretion of thymic hormones, such as thymosin and thymopoietin, and critical cytokines which are necessary for T-cell lineage commitment and maturation. During the acquisition of immunocompetence the cortical lymphoid population is rapidly dividing, but many cells die in situ and relatively few migrate to the medulla and then to peripheral lymphoid organs. The thymic medulla is far less cellular than the cortex. In addition, the thymic medulla contains structures termed *Hassall's corpuscles*, which are concentrically arranged squamous epithelial cells with central keratinisation; their function is unknown. A small and morphologically inconspicuous population of B-cells is present within the medulla and may be important in the pathogenesis of myasthenia gravis and mediastinal B-cell lymphoma.

DISORDERS OF THE THYMUS

Agenesis and hypoplasia

Agenesis and hypoplasia may occur because of a failure of either the epithelial or the lymphoid component of the thymus to develop properly.

In the *DiGeorge* and *Nezelof syndromes* there is defective development of the epithelial component of the thymus from the third pharyngeal pouch. The DiGeorge syndrome has, in addition, defective development of the fourth pharyngeal pouch, which results in an absence of the parathyroid glands. It is associated with deletion of the 22q11.2 chromosomal region. The thymus is either completely absent in these two syndromes or is represented by a fibrous streak.

Abnormalities of lymphoid colonisation of the thymus occur in the severe combined immune deficiency syndromes, *ataxia–telangiectasia* and *reticular dysgenesis*. In reticular dysgenesis the thymus is small, weighing little more than a few grams, and is composed of disordered aggregates of epithelial cells.

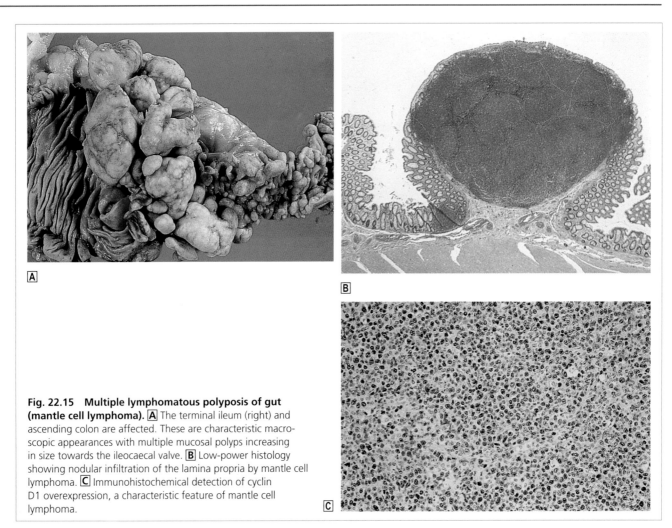

Fig. 22.15 Multiple lymphomatous polyposis of gut (mantle cell lymphoma). **A** The terminal ileum (right) and ascending colon are affected. These are characteristic macroscopic appearances with multiple mucosal polyps increasing in size towards the ileocaecal valve. **B** Low-power histology showing nodular infiltration of the lamina propria by mantle cell lymphoma. **C** Immunohistochemical detection of cyclin D1 overexpression, a characteristic feature of mantle cell lymphoma.

Acquired hypoplasia may be seen as a natural ageing phenomenon, as a response to stress and in the acquired immune deficiency syndrome following infection with HIV.

Hyperplasia

Thymic hyperplasia is strongly associated with autoimmune disease (in particular, *myasthenia gravis*). Hyperplasia is difficult to diagnose from the thymus size or weight alone, owing to extreme variation in these indices in the general population. The most reliable criterion is the formation of germinal centres within the thymus. The germinal centres are located principally in the medulla, from which they expand and may cause cortical atrophy. They are identical to the germinal centres in peripheral lymphoid sites.

Neoplasms

A wide variety of neoplasms occur within the thymus:

- epithelial—thymoma, thymic carcinoma
- lymphoid—Hodgkin's lymphoma; non-Hodgkin's lymphoma

- germ cell—seminoma; teratoma
- stromal—thymolipoma
- others—thymic carcinoid; small cell carcinoma.

Thymic epithelial tumours

A variety of epithelial tumours arise from thymic epithelial cells. Those that appear histologically benign are termed thymomas. A percentage of thymomas, despite appearing histologically bland, may demonstrate an invasive growth pattern and are termed invasive thymomas.

Thymic carcinomas show the cytological features of malignancy in addition to usually having an invasive growth pattern.

Thymomas

Only those neoplasms in which the neoplastic cell is derived from thymic epithelium and appears histologically benign are termed thymomas. The vast majority of thymomas arise within the thymus, but thymomas from ectopic thymus tissue have been described in the soft tissues of the neck, hilum of the lung, other sites within the mediastinum and, rarely, the thyroid.

In addition to the neoplastic epithelial component, thymomas contain variable numbers of lymphoid cells; those that contain large numbers are termed 'lymphocyte-rich' and those with scanty numbers are termed 'lymphocyte-poor'. The lymphocyte-rich thymomas to some extent recapitulate the structure of the cortical thymus in their microscopic appearances and the phenotype of the lymphoid cells present. Conversely, the lymphocyte-poor thymomas show similarities with the thymic medulla. In addition to variations in the degree of lymphocytic infiltration, there are also variations in the cytological appearances of the neoplastic epithelial cells, which may range from round to spindle-shaped.

Many thymomas are asymptomatic and are detected by chest X-ray performed for other reasons; some present with signs of local disease such as dyspnoea, cough and stridor, and the remainder present with autoimmune disease. The majority of thymomas (60–80%) are benign and complete surgical excision is curative. The remaining cases are termed invasive thymomas. There is a good correlation between survival and the extent of spread or presence of metastases in malignant thymomas.

Thymomas may be associated with a variety of disorders, including myasthenia gravis, pure red cell aplasia, neutropenia, thrombocytopenia, hypogammaglobulinaemia and systemic lupus erythematosus.

Thymic carcinoma

A variety of histological patterns of thymic carcinoma have been recognised and include squamous cell, basaloid, large cell and lympho-epithelioma-like carcinomas. They are all aggressive tumours and are associated with a poor survival.

Other thymic neoplasms

Thymic involvement by *Hodgkin's lymphoma* is relatively common and occurs particularly in the nodular sclerosing subtype.

Non-Hodgkin's lymphomas originating in the thymus tend to be high-grade tumours of either T-lymphoblastic or large B-cell types. The T-lymphoblastic lymphomas of the thymus occur in young and adolescent boys, often possess a characteristic convoluted nuclear morphology, and usually develop a leukaemic phase. Their phenotype shows similarities to the cortical thymic lymphoid cell. The large B-cell lymphomas of the thymus tend to occur in women in the second and third decades of life. It has been postulated that they arise from thymic medullary B-cells. The biological similarities between mediastinal large B-cell lymphoma and nodular sclerosing classical Hodgkin's lymphoma have been discussed previously. The prognosis of mediastinal large B-cell lymphoma, when accurately classified, appears to be more favourable than other variants of diffuse large B-cell lymphoma. Low-grade NHLs with histological features of extranodal marginal zone lymphoma of MALT type also occur in the thymus.

The same spectrum of germ cell neoplasia is apparent in the thymus as in the gonad and accounts for 10–15% of all primary mediastinal tumours. These neoplasms are thought to arise from primitive germ cells that have become misplaced during migration to the developing gonadal anlage. Mediastinal germ cell tumours are also rarely associated with haemopoietic neoplasms such as acute myeloid leukaemia, myelodysplasia, systemic mastocytosis and malignant histiocytosis. The mature teratomas are benign and complete surgical excision is curative. Teratomas with an immature component are usually of low stage and have a good prognosis. Seminomas are radio- and chemosensitive and have a relatively good prognosis. Non-seminomatous malignant germ cell tumours of the thymus have a significantly worse prognosis than their testicular counterparts.

A variety of benign and malignant mesenchymal tumours may originate in the thymus and these are identical to their counterparts outside the thymus; the commonest are lipomas. Thymolipomas are unique to the thymus and are circumscribed stromal tumours composed of an admixture of mature fat and thymic tissue. They are benign but may reach a substantial size, often weighing over half a kilogram. They may be associated with paraneoplastic syndromes such as myasthenia gravis, pure red cell aplasia and hypogammaglobulinaemia.

Thymic carcinoids and *small cell carcinomas* are rare neoplasms thought to arise from neuroendocrine cells scattered in the organ. About a third of thymic carcinoids are associated with Cushing's syndrome. Both thymic carcinoids and small cell carcinomas are aggressive malignant neoplasms.

SPLEEN

NORMAL STRUCTURE AND FUNCTION

The spleen is an encapsulated organ normally weighing 100–150 g in the adult; it is situated in the left upper quadrant of the abdomen, mostly concealed by the lower ribs. It first appears in the fifth gestational week and is mesodermally derived. The spleen has two functions: it is a lymphoid organ, and it has a great capacity for phagocytosing particulate material in the circulation and culling senescent red cells. These two functions of the spleen are architecturally distinct: the lymphoid function occurs in the *white pulp* and the phagocytic activity resides in the *red pulp*.

White pulp

The splenic artery is derived from the coeliac axis and enters the spleen at the hilum, then branches and follows the trabeculae of the fibrous capsule into the substance of the organ. Leaving the trabeculae as central arteries and arterioles, these branches become ensheathed in lymphoid cells. These aggregates of lymphoid cells are termed the white pulp and can be seen on the cut surface of the spleen as 1–2 mm diameter white nodules in the deep-red background of the red pulp. As in lymph nodes, the lymphocytes within the white pulp of the spleen show distinct micro-architectural segregation of different functional subsets. T-cells are found in the immediate vicinity of the central arterial vessel of the white pulp and are termed the *peri-arteriolar lymphoid sheath*. The B-cell follicle is eccentrically placed within the white pulp and may

be composed predominantly of small lymphocytes, or may form a germinal centre when stimulated. At the junction of the red and white pulp, and surrounding the peri-arteriolar lymphoid sheath and the B-cell follicle, is a group of specialised B-cells termed marginal zone lymphocytes; their precise function is unknown. The white pulp is a major site of antibody production.

Red pulp

Most of the spleen is occupied by the red pulp, whose main function appears to be destruction of senescent red cells and phagocytosis of particulate material. The red pulp has a dual circulation, with a 'closed' sinusoidal pathway and an 'open' system through the splenic pulp cords.

The splenic arterial supply, having traversed the white pulp, flows through the penicillary arteries into the splenic sinuses or pulp cords. The sinuses are narrow channels with a discontinuous endothelial lining which allows adjacent macrophages access to the red cells as they traverse sinuses and drain into the trabecular veins. The open pulp-cord circulation places the red cells in prolonged intimate contact with serried ranks of macrophages before entering the splenic sinuses. Within the pulp cords, macrophages remove any intracytoplasmic inclusions (such as Howell–Jolly bodies—a process termed pitting) and excess surface membrane from the red blood cells. The environment within the pulp cords is hostile and the red cells must possess marked deformability and intact metabolic machinery to survive. Those cells that do not survive are phagocytosed and broken down.

DISORDERS OF THE SPLEEN

Congenital abnormalities

Congenital abnormalities in the form of accessory spleens or splenunculi are relatively common, occurring in about 10% of the population. They are rounded, encapsulated structures up to several centimetres in size and usually located near the spleen. Congenital asplenia and polysplenia are rare and often associated with other congenital malformations, particularly of the cardiovascular system.

Hypersplenism

The term 'hypersplenism' is applied to the association between a peripheral blood pancytopenia and splenic enlargement. It may be primary or secondary to a wide variety of pathological processes.

Primary hypersplenism is a poorly understood condition of unknown aetiology, characterised by marked and often massive splenomegaly and pancytopenia, in which leukopenia is particularly pronounced. Within the spleen there is marked lymphoid hyperplasia. The haematological response to splenectomy is excellent, although some patients may remain leukopenic.

Secondary splenomegaly (see below) may also be associated with hypersplenism.

Splenomegaly

> ▸ Many causes, including vascular congestion, inflammatory and reactive disorders, leukaemias and lymphomas, and storage disorders
> ▸ Enlarged spleen may rupture after only minor trauma
> ▸ Secondary splenomegaly (due to above causes) may result in hypersplenism

The causes of secondary splenomegaly are numerous and include the following basic pathological processes:

- congestion
- infection
- immune disorders
- primary or metastatic neoplasms
- storage disorders
- amyloidosis (Ch. 7).

Congestive splenomegaly

Conditions that lead to a persistent elevation of splenic venous blood pressure are capable of causing splenomegaly. The splenic venous pressure may be raised due to pre-hepatic, hepatic and post-hepatic causes.

Pre-hepatic causes include thrombosis of the extrahepatic portion of the portal vein or of the splenic vein.

Very marked splenomegaly occurs in longstanding portal hypertension associated with cirrhosis (Ch. 16).

Post-hepatic causes of congestive splenomegaly are associated with a raised pressure in the inferior vena cava, which is transmitted to the spleen via the portal system. These are usually associated with ascites and hepatomegaly. Decompensated right-sided heart failure and pulmonary or tricuspid valve disease are the usual post-hepatic causes of congestive splenomegaly.

The spleen in congestive splenomegaly is variably enlarged and may reach a massive size, weighing a kilogram or more. The capsule may be thickened and fibrotic, but it is in the red pulp that the major pathological alterations occur. The cut surface of the spleen has a beefy-red colour with an inconspicuous white pulp, often containing scattered, firm brown nodules; these are Gamna–Gandy nodules and represent areas of healed infarction, composed of fibrous and elastic tissue with abundant haemosiderin and dystrophic calcification. In the early stages of congestive splenomegaly, the sinusoids are distended with red cells. Later, fibrosis occurs around the sinusoids, which appear ectatic and empty. Foci of extramedullary haemopoiesis may be seen and it is postulated that these are secondary to local hypoxia within the spleen.

Infection

Systemic infection may cause moderate splenomegaly characterised by congestion and macrophage hyperplasia within the red pulp. The white pulp is usually prominent macroscopically and shows reactive changes microscopically, often with germinal centre formation.

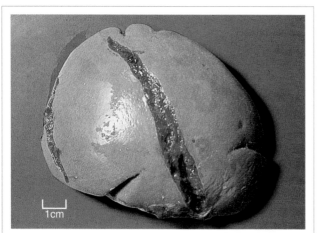

Fig. 22.16 Splenic rupture in infectious mononucleosis. This spleen was removed from an adolescent with infectious mononucleosis who sustained minor abdominal trauma.

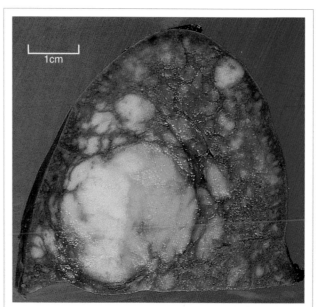

Fig. 22.17 Spleen infiltrated by Hodgkin's lymphoma. Note the discrete white nodules of tumour ranging in size from a few millimetres to several centimetres.

Some viral diseases, in particular infectious mononucleosis, may produce more severe splenomegaly. In addition to the changes described above, the splenomegaly may also show immunoblastic infiltration of the red pulp. In infectious mononucleosis, the spleen is susceptible to rupture (Fig. 22.16).

Chronic malarial infection may lead to massive splenomegaly. The splenic capsule is thickened and fibrotic and the cut surface has a slate-grey coloration due to the abundant, iron-containing malarial pigment. Microscopically there is pronounced red pulp macrophage hyperplasia containing malarial parasites.

Immune disorders

A variety of immune disorders may lead to splenomegaly, in particular rheumatoid disease and systemic lupus erythematosus. Hypersplenism may ensue, and, in the case of rheumatoid disease in adults, is called Felty's syndrome.

Neoplasms

Splenic infiltration is a common feature of a wide variety of haematological neoplasms including:

- acute and chronic leukaemias
- myeloproliferative disorders
- Hodgkin's lymphoma
- non-Hodgkin's lymphomas.

The pattern of splenic involvement is characteristic of each group of neoplasms.

Acute leukaemias preferentially infiltrate the red pulp, although minor degrees of white pulp involvement may be seen, particularly in acute lymphoblastic leukaemia. The splenic red pulp cords and sinuses are filled with numerous primitive haemopoietic blast cells.

Chronic myeloid leukaemia (CML) and the myeloproliferative syndromes may lead to massive degrees of splenomegaly. In CML, the red pulp is filled with myeloid precursors which are predominantly mature and, in the myeloproliferative disorders, the red pulp contains areas of extramedullary haemopoiesis. The red pulp expansion in these disorders gradually effaces

the white pulp, such that the cut surface of the spleen has a homogeneous brick-red appearance. In contrast, chronic lymphocytic leukaemia infiltrates both the red and white pulp.

Classical Hodgkin's lymphoma preferentially invades the white pulp and forms expansile nodules which encroach upon the red pulp. These may be single or multiple and range in size from a few millimetres to several centimetres in diameter (Fig. 22.17). The earliest site of involvement in the white pulp is the T-cell-dependent region of the peri-arteriolar lymphoid sheath, which progressively expands to obliterate the normal white pulp architecture.

Non-Hodgkin's lymphomas also principally affect the white pulp, but their pattern of disease varies. The low-grade lymphomas form multiple small and medium-sized nodules that expand and replace the normal white pulp; the cut surface of the spleen is seen to be studded with numerous relatively even-sized nodules (Fig. 22.18). In contrast, high-grade lymphomas form small numbers of large destructive nodules. These differences in the pattern of splenic involvement by low- and high-grade NHLs are probably due to the physiological homing of the recirculating lymphoid cells of low-grade lymphomas to their natural milieu within the white pulp.

Although haemopoietic malignancies frequently involve the spleen, other tumours rarely metastasise to the spleen, and then only as part of a widely disseminated malignancy. Primary tumours of the spleen are rare and include hamartomas, benign and malignant vascular tumours and occasionally other mesenchymal neoplasms.

Storage disorders

Several storage disorders may cause splenomegaly: these include Niemann–Pick disease, Gaucher's disease and the mucopolysaccharidoses (Ch. 7). Characteristically, there is

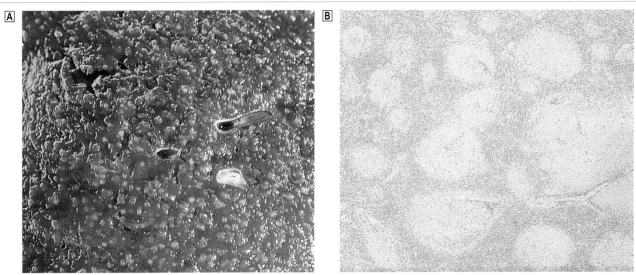

Fig. 22.18   Spleen infiltrated by low-grade non-Hodgkin's lymphoma. **A** Macroscopic appearance. The cut surface is studded by small white nodules which stand out against the red pulp. **B** Low-power view showing numerous lymphoid aggregates with adjacent unaffected red pulp.

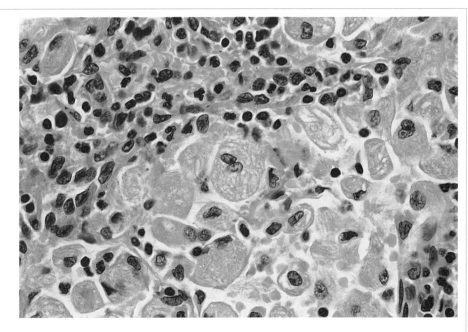

Fig. 22.19   Gaucher's disease. Characteristic histiocytes of Gaucher's disease contain abundant glucocerebroside which accumulates due to a deficiency of the enzyme glucocerebrosidase.

marked red pulp expansion by macrophages whose cytoplasm is distended with the abnormal storage product (Fig. 22.19).

Splenic infarction

Splenic infarction follows occlusion of the splenic artery or its branches and is usually secondary to emboli that arise in the heart (Ch. 8). Occasionally, splenic infarction may be due to local thrombosis, as in sickle cell disease, myeloproliferative disorders and malignant infiltrates.

Splenic infarcts are macroscopically pale and wedge-shaped with the base adjacent to the splenic capsule. They may be single or multiple, and heal forming depressed scars.

Rupture of the spleen

Rupture of the spleen is usually caused by blunt abdominal trauma, particularly automobile accidents. Massive, life-threatening intraperitoneal haemorrhage may follow splenic rupture, necessitating emergency splenectomy.

Spontaneous rupture of the spleen may occur, particularly in infectious mononucleosis and in spleens enlarged by haemopoietic proliferations such as myelofibrosis.

Splenic atrophy

Splenic atrophy may occur in association with intestinal malabsorption states such as coeliac disease. In splenic atrophy, the spleen is small and weighs less than 50 g. There is evidence of hyposplenism with numerous target cells and Howell–Jolly inclusion bodies in red cells.

Patients with sickle cell disease suffer multiple splenic infarcts and the spleen is greatly reduced in size and function.

Commonly confused conditions and entities relating to the lymph nodes, thymus and spleen	
Commonly confused	**Distinction and explanation**
Mantle cell and *marginal zone lymphomas*	Both are B-cell lymphomas and both can occur in the gastrointestinal tract. *Mantle cell lymphomas* have features of the cells in the mantle zone of germinal centres and a characteristic chromosomal translocation resulting in overexpression of cyclin D1. *Marginal zone lymphomas,* the most common type of extranodal lymphoma, contain cells resembling those in the marginal zone of lymph nodes, often with plasma cell differentiation.
Mycosis fungoides and *Sézary syndrome*	Both are cutaneous T-cell lymphomas (and have nothing to do with fungal infection). In *mycosis fungoides* the neoplastic T-cells are initially confined to focal skin lesions, whereas in *Sézary syndrome* there is more generalised involvement including atypical cells in the blood.
Thymoma and *thymic lymphoma*	Although *thymomas* often contain numerous lymphocytes, they are usually benign lesions derived from thymic epithelium. *Thymic lymphomas* may be of Hodgkin's or non-Hodgkin's type.
Hypersplenism and *splenomegaly*	*Splenomegaly* is enlargement of the spleen. If this is accompanied by blood pancytopenia, then the combination of splenic enlargement and functional disturbance is called *hypersplenism*.

FURTHER READING

De Paepe P, De Wolf-Peeters C 2007 Diffuse large B-cell lymphoma: a heterogeneous group of non-Hodgkin lymphomas comprising several distinct clinicopathological entities. Leukemia 21: 37–43

Ekström-Smedby K 2006 Epidemiology and etiology of non-Hodgkin lymphoma. Acta Oncologica 45: 258–271

Higgins R A, Blankenship J E, Kinney M C 2008 Application of immunohistochemistry in the diagnosis of non-Hodgkin and Hodgkin lymphoma. Archives of Pathology and Laboratory Medicine 132: 441–461

Kapatai G, Murray P 2007 Contribution of the Epstein–Barr virus to the molecular pathogenesis of Hodgkin lymphoma. Journal of Clinical Pathology 60: 1342–1349

Marcus R, Sweetenham J W, Williams M E 2007 Lymphoma: pathology, diagnosis and treatment. Cambridge University Press, Cambridge

Martin P, Leonard J P 2007 Targeted therapies for non-Hodgkin lymphoma: rationally designed combinations. Clinical Lymphoma and Myeloma 7 (Suppl 5): S192–198

Tward J, Glenn M, Pulsipher M, Barnette P, Gaffney D 2007 Incidence, risk factors, and pathogenesis of second malignancies in patients with non-Hodgkin lymphoma. Leukemia and Lymphoma 48: 1482–1495

Blood and bone marrow

COMMON CLINICAL PROBLEMS FROM BLOOD AND BONE MARROW DISEASE

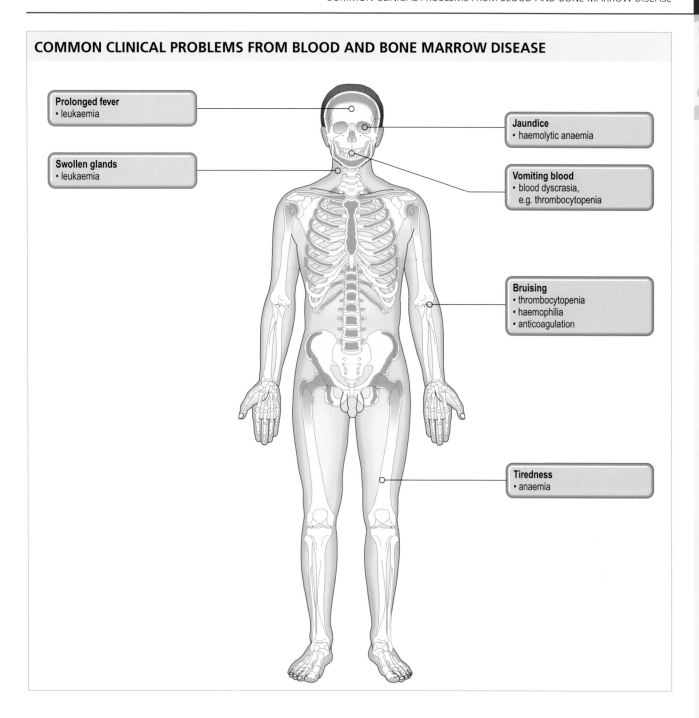

Prolonged fever
• leukaemia

Swollen glands
• leukaemia

Jaundice
• haemolytic anaemia

Vomiting blood
• blood dyscrasia,
  e.g. thrombocytopenia

Bruising
• thrombocytopenia
• haemophilia
• anticoagulation

Tiredness
• anaemia

Pathological basis of haematological signs and symptoms	
Sign or symptom	Pathological basis
Tiredness, dyspnoea	Reduced oxygen-carrying capacity of blood due to anaemia
Mucosal pallor	Anaemia
Glossitis (sore mouth, smooth tongue)	Mucosal effects of haematinic deficiency
Spoon-shaped nails	Due to iron deficiency

(Continued)

Pathological basis of breast signs and symptoms—cont'd	
Sign or symptom	Pathological basis
Jaundice	Bilirubin accumulation from haemolysis
Abnormal tendency to infections	Neutropenia, e.g. in leukaemia or hypoplastic anaemia
	Immune deficiency, e.g. in myeloma, and due to chemotherapy in leukaemia and lymphoma
Splenomegaly	Due to expansion of haemopoiesis in myeloproliferative disorders, red cell pooling and destruction in haemolytic anaemias, infiltration in leukaemias and lymphomas
	Also non-haematological causes, e.g. portal hypertension
Lymphadenopathy	Non-neoplastic causes, e.g. infectious mononucleosis
	Infiltration with leukaemia or lymphoma
Bone pain and fractures	Osteoclast activation in myeloma
Purpura, bruising, mucosal or traumatic bleeding	Thrombocytopenia or platelet dysfunction
Bruising, muscle and joint bleeding, and traumatic bleeding	Coagulation factor deficiency

COMPOSITION, PRODUCTION AND FUNCTIONS OF BLOOD

Blood is a unique organ: it is fluid and comes into contact with almost all other tissues. The blood cells are non-cohesive and supported in the fluid medium of blood—the plasma. The blood cells comprise the non-nucleated erythrocytes and platelets, and the nucleated cells or leukocytes.

In addition to primary disease of the blood-forming organ—the bone marrow—many disease states produce secondary changes in the blood. For this reason, the counting and morphological examination of blood cells is routine in the clinical assessment of disease, frequently providing valuable diagnostic information.

CELLULAR COMPONENTS

The peripheral blood is investigated by microscopy of a droplet spread evenly over the surface of a glass slide—the blood film. Routinely, the blood film is treated with a combination of stains which allow identification of nuclear and cytoplasmic detail (Fig. 23.1).

Quantitation of blood cells is essential; in modern laboratories this is routinely performed by automated cell-counting equipment. The size and concentration of erythrocytes, and the leukocyte and platelet concentrations are measured. Haemoglobin is automatically measured. Also, the proportion of leukocytes of each category—the differential white cell count—is measured from cell size and granule content.

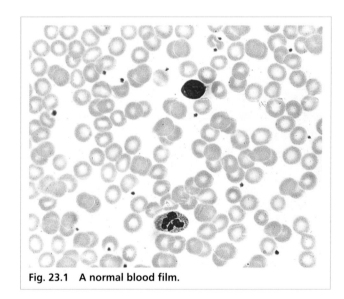

Fig. 23.1 A normal blood film.

Erythrocytes

Erythrocytes (red blood cells) are deformable, non-nucleated and biconcave discs (Fig. 23.2). They are the most abundant blood cell. When blood is separated, by centrifugation, into cellular and plasma components, the red cell portion is approximately 45% of the total volume: this is the 'packed cell volume' or *haematocrit*.

The erythrocyte is a special oxygen-carrying cell because it is rich in haemoglobin. The cell membrane is composed of a phospholipid bilayer with integral proteins. The shape of the cell is maintained by structural proteins, such as spectrin, which form a cytoskeleton. Enzyme systems protect the haemoglobin from irreversible oxidation. The mature erythrocyte has no nuclear material, so new protein cannot be synthesised. The mature erythrocyte circulates for around 120 days before it is removed by the reticulo-endothelial system.

Absolute values

The absolute values are measures of red cell size and haemoglobin content which provide valuable information in the assessment of anaemia, as they provide diagnostic clues as to the likely cause. Absolute values are calculated from the red cell concentration, haemoglobin concentration and haematocrit as follows:

$$\textit{Mean corpuscular volume (MCV) in femtolitres (fl)}$$
$$= \frac{\text{Haematocrit (g/l)}}{\text{Red cell concentration (per litre)}}$$
$$\textit{Mean corpuscular haemoglobin (MCH) in picograms (pg)}$$
$$= \frac{\text{Haemoglobin concentration (g/dl)}}{\text{Red cell concentration (per litre)}}$$
$$\textit{Mean corpuscular haemoglobin concentration (MCHC) (g/dl)}$$
$$= \frac{\text{Haemoglobin concentration (g/dl)}}{\text{Haematocrit (l/l)}}$$

In the modern laboratory, automated cell counters provide these data on each blood sample analysed.

Morphology

The biconcave erythrocyte shape provides a large surface area for oxygen diffusion. By light microscopy erythrocytes appear as uniform round cells with central pallor. Up to 1% of cells stain with a purplish tinge and are of rather greater diameter. These are polychromatic cells; this purple staining is due to the residual ribonucleic acid (RNA) of the immature erythrocyte. These young cells become indistinguishable from the mature red cell population after 48 hours in the blood. When stained with a supravital stain (such as methylene blue) polychromatic cells are more easily identified by the presence of characteristic inclusions; they are then termed *reticulocytes*. The inclusions are remnants of RNA. When bone marrow production of erythrocytes is increased, the proportion of polychromatic cells, or reticulocytes, in the peripheral blood becomes greater than 1% or 100×10^9/l. This occurs most commonly in recovery from acute haemorrhage or when there is an increased rate of destruction of red cells, which is called haemolytic anaemia. Failure to produce a reticulocyte response to anaemia suggests that the patient has bone marrow failure or haematinic deficiency.

Changes in disease

Anaemia is present when the haemoglobin concentration is less than approximately 130 g/l in a male or 115 g/l in a female (Table 23.1); the haematocrit is also reduced. Conversely, polycythaemia describes an increased red cell concentration; it is usually accompanied by a raised haemoglobin concentration and haematocrit.

Anaemias may be simply classified according to red cell size (MCV) and haemoglobin content (MCH). This classification is of great diagnostic value in most common types of anaemia (Table 23.2). Further diagnostic information is obtained by the microscopic examination of the red cell morphology on a blood smear. Disease of the blood is frequently associated with increased variation in red cell size—*anisocytosis*—and the presence of erythrocytes of abnormal shape—*poikilocytosis* (Fig. 23.3). Increased erythrocyte anisocytosis and poikilocytosis are non-specific abnormalities present in many

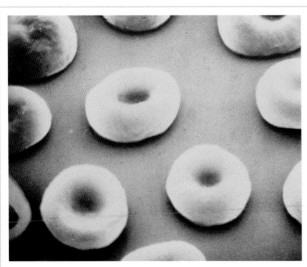

Fig. 23.2   Scanning electron micrograph of red blood cells.

Table 23.1 Normal red cell values			
Value	Male	Both sexes	Female
Haemoglobin (g/l) Adult Newborn 3 months 12 months	130–170	135–195 95–135 105–135	115–160
Haematocrit (l/l)	0.39–0.50		0.34–0.47
Red cell count (×10¹²/l) **MCH** (pg) **MCV** (fl) **MCHC** (g/dl)	4.3–5.7	26–33 78–98 30–35	3.9–5.1
These values will vary slightly between laboratories. All laboratory ranges include values for 95% of the normal population; 5% of normal subjects will therefore have values slightly outside the range quoted. MCH, mean corpuscular haemoglobin; MCV, mean corpuscular volume; MCHC, mean corpuscular haemoglobin concentration.			

Table 23.2 Morphological classification of anaemia		
Morphology	Absolute values	Common causes
Microcytic **Hypochromic**	MCV < 78 MCH < 26	Iron deficiency Thalassaemia
Macrocytic	MCV > 98	Megaloblastic anaemias, myelodysplasias
Normocytic **Normochromic**	MCV MCH } Normal	Acute blood loss Most haemolytic anaemias Anaemia of chronic disorders* Bone marrow failure
*There may be slight microcytosis.		

haematological and systemic disorders. An example is the marked aniso-poikilocytosis that occurs in the absence of a functioning spleen, due to surgical removal or secondary to disease. In this situation there are also inclusions in red cells. They are called Howell–Jolly bodies (Fig. 23.4) and are remnants of nuclear material that would normally be removed when newly formed erythrocytes released from bone marrow circulate for the first time through the spleen.

In addition to Howell–Jolly bodies, red cells may contain other inclusions (Fig. 23.4) under certain circumstances. The basophilic stippling of the 'stipple cell' is due to the presence of residual RNA; stipple cells may be present in several anaemias, especially thalassaemia. Siderotic granules contain iron and may occur in states of iron overload, for example in chronically anaemic subjects who have received treatment by frequent transfusion of red cells. Occasionally, nucleated red cell precursors may escape into the peripheral blood; when these normoblasts are accompanied by immature neutrophil leukocytes the film is described as *leukoerythroblastic*. A leukoerythroblastic blood film results from gross marrow disturbance such as infiltration by malignancy, or fibrous tissue (myelofibrosis) or in severe anaemia due to deficiency of vitamin B_{12} or folate (megaloblastic anaemia).

Supravital staining is used to detect the presence of reticulocytes, as described above. This technique also identifies another type of red cell inclusion—Heinz bodies. These inclusions represent denatured haemoglobin and are seen typically in certain haemolytic anaemias, especially those due to a deficiency in the protective enzyme systems such as glucose-6-phosphate dehydrogenase deficiency.

Leukocytes

The nucleated cells of the peripheral blood are termed white blood cells or leukocytes. Their primary role is protection against infection or infestation of the body. Morphologically, on a stained blood film, five varieties of leukocyte are identified.
The normal concentrations of these are:

- neutrophil granulocytes $2.0–7.5 \times 10^9/l$
- lymphocytes $1.0–3.0 \times 10^9/l$
- monocytes $0.15–0.6 \times 10^9/l$
- eosinophil granulocytes $0.05–0.3 \times 10^9/l$
- basophil granulocytes $0.01–0.10 \times 10^9/l$.

These are typical values for healthy adults and older children. The normal counts differ in infants, who have a higher proportion of lymphocytes, for example.

Also, it is important to appreciate how such laboratory normal ranges are established in order to avoid misinterpretation. Cell counts are performed on a large number of healthy subjects and the range is determined from the population mean and two standard deviations above and below the mean. This dictates that, for a particular measurement, 2.5% of healthy subjects have a count just below the lower limit of 'normal' and a further 2.5% just above.

The granulocytes and monocytes are phagocytic leukocytes produced from precursor cells in the bone marrow. The lymphocytes are broadly composed of B-cells which mediate humoral immunity via the maturation to immunoglobulin-producing plasma cells; they are produced initially in the bone marrow and subsequently mature by antigen selection in the germinal centres of secondary lymphoid tissues; and T-cells which provide cell-mediated immunity such as killing virally infected cells. T-cells are produced and selected for antigen in the thymus gland. B- and T-cells circulate in the blood as small lymphocytes.

Neutrophil granulocytes

Neutrophils are the most numerous leukocytes in the blood of the healthy adult. The nucleus of the neutrophil granulocyte is characteristically segmented into up to five lobes and the nuclear chromatin stains densely (Fig. 23.1). The abundant cytoplasm stains pink and contains characteristic granules. Within the granules are enzymes, including myeloperoxidase, alkaline phosphatase and lysozyme. Neutrophils have a scavenging function and are of particular importance in defence against bacterial infection.

Neutrophil precursors and neutrophils spend 14 days in the bone marrow, whereas the half-life of neutrophils in the blood is only 6–9 hours. Peripheral blood counts therefore measure less than 10% of the total body neutrophils. Within the circulation the cells move between a circulating and a 'marginating' pool, margination being attachment to vascular endothelial cells. To perform their scavenging

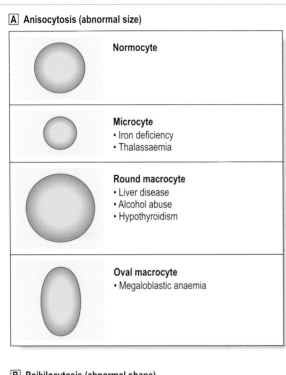

A Anisocytosis (abnormal size)

Normocyte

Microcyte
• Iron deficiency
• Thalassaemia

Round macrocyte
• Liver disease
• Alcohol abuse
• Hypothyroidism

Oval macrocyte
• Megaloblastic anaemia

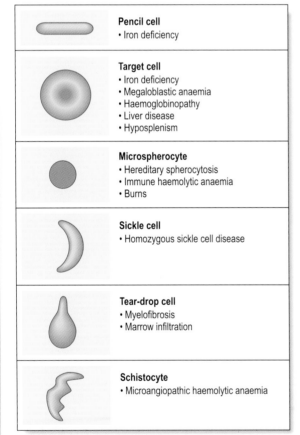

B Poikilocytosis (abnormal shape)

Pencil cell
• Iron deficiency

Target cell
• Iron deficiency
• Megaloblastic anaemia
• Haemoglobinopathy
• Liver disease
• Hyposplenism

Microspherocyte
• Hereditary spherocytosis
• Immune haemolytic anaemia
• Burns

Sickle cell
• Homozygous sickle cell disease

Tear-drop cell
• Myelofibrosis
• Marrow infiltration

Schistocyte
• Microangiopathic haemolytic anaemia

Fig. 23.3   Abnormalities of red cell size and shape.
A Increased variation in size: anisocytosis. B Variation in shape: poikilocytosis.

A Visible on a Romanowsky-stained film

Erythrocyte containing a **Howell–Jolly body**
• Hyposplenism
• Megaloblastic anaemia

Normoblast
(with immature leukocytes in a leukoerythroblastic film)
• Massive haemorrhage or haemolysis
• Marrow infiltration
• Myelofibrosis

Stipple cell
• Lead poisoning
• Haemoglobinopathy
• Megaloblastic anaemia
• Myelodysplastic syndromes

Erythrocyte containing **siderotic granules**
• Hyposplenism
• Iron overload

B Visible only after supravital staining

Reticulocyte
increased in
• Haemorrhage
• Haemolysis
• Response to haematinic replacement

Erythrocyte containing **Heinz bodies**
• Glucose-6-phosphate dehydrogenase deficiency
• Poisoning with oxidative agents
• Some haemoglobinopathies
• Hyposplenism

Fig. 23.4   Red cell inclusions.

function, granulocytes irreversibly enter the tissues by penetrating endothelial cells modified by inflammatory mediators. Cytokine-stimulated endothelial cells present adhesion molecules which interact with neutrophils and facilitate their passage: one such is ICAM-1 (intercellular adhesion molecule 1).

Lymphocytes
The peripheral blood lymphocytes are small leukocytes with a round or only slightly indented nucleus and scanty sky-blue-staining cytoplasm which may contain an occasional pink- or red-staining granule. Circulating B- and T-cells are not distinguishable by morphology alone. Immunological staining shows that in health approximately 70% of circulating small lymphocytes are T-cells and 30% B-cells.

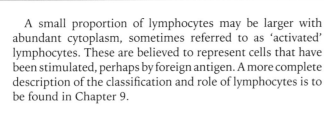

A small proportion of lymphocytes may be larger with abundant cytoplasm, sometimes referred to as 'activated' lymphocytes. These are believed to represent cells that have been stimulated, perhaps by foreign antigen. A more complete description of the classification and role of lymphocytes is to be found in Chapter 9.

Monocytes

Monocytes are the largest blood cells. The nucleus is oval or reniform but not lobed. The abundant cytoplasm stains pale blue and often contains pink granules; vacuoles are often present. The function of monocytes is similar to that of neutrophil granulocytes: they enter the tissues and, as tissue macrophages, are responsible for the phagocytosis and digestion of foreign material and dead tissue.

Eosinophil granulocytes

Eosinophil granulocytes have much larger red-staining granules. They contain enzymes, including a peroxidase. The nucleus is lobulated, but usually only two or three lobes are seen. The eosinophil is important in the mediation of the allergic response and in defence against parasitic infestation.

Basophil granulocytes

Basophil granulocytes are the least frequent leukocytes in normal blood. The granules are large, blue–black and obscure the bilobed nucleus; they contain heparin and histamine. Basophils are closely related to tissue mast cells but their function has not been determined precisely. They appear to be key mediators of immediate hypersensitivity reactions, involving release of histamine.

Changes in disease

Changes may be *quantitative* or *qualitative;* the former are more important and often of diagnostic value. Knowledge of the causes of increased numbers of the various leukocytes in the peripheral blood is useful clinically.

Quantitative changes

Leukocytosis means an increase in numbers of circulating white blood cells. Depending on the cause, there may be a polymorphonuclear leukocytosis (neutrophilia—increased neutrophil leukocytes), monocytosis, eosinophil leukocytosis (eosinophilia), basophil leukocytosis (basophilia) or lymphocytosis.

Causes of reactive neutrophil leukocytosis include:

- sepsis (e.g. acute appendicitis, bacterial pneumonia)
- trauma (e.g. major surgery)
- infarction (e.g. myocardial infarction)
- chronic inflammatory disease (e.g. systemic lupus erythematosus (SLE), rheumatoid disease)
- malignant neoplasms
- steroid therapy
- acute haemorrhage or haemolysis.

Monocytosis may be reactive to:

- sepsis

- chronic infections (e.g. tuberculosis)
- malignant neoplasms.

Eosinophil leukocytosis may be reactive to:

- allergy (e.g. asthma)
- parasites (e.g. tapeworm infestation)
- malignant neoplasms (e.g. Hodgkin's lymphoma)
- miscellaneous conditions (e.g. polyarteritis nodosa).

Lymphocytosis is most commonly associated with an infection such as infectious mononucleosis, tuberculosis, etc.

In some disorders the leukocytosis may be extreme (for example $100 \times 10^9/l$), particularly in children. There may also be a tendency for immature leukocytes, particularly myelocytes and metamyelocytes, to appear in the peripheral blood. Severe bacterial infection may result in such an extreme reactive picture, which has in the past been referred to as a 'leukaemoid reaction' because of the similarity of the blood picture, with immature forms present, to that of chronic myeloid leukaemia. Occasionally, the lymphocyte series may be involved in such an extreme reactive process, especially during childhood viral infection.

A characteristic leukocytosis composed of 'atypical' lymphocytes is a feature of *infectious mononucleosis* (glandular fever). The infection is common in young adults and often manifests as a sore throat with enlarged lymph nodes and spleen and skin rash. It is due to infection with Epstein–Barr (EB) virus and is common between 15 and 25 years of age in developed countries, but occurs in young children in heavily populated developing countries. The major additional features are:

- infection of B-lymphocytes with EB virus
- T-lymphocytosis with morphologically atypical forms in the blood
- hepatitis often present
- development of antibodies reactive with non-human erythrocytes (heterophile antibodies)
- development of antibodies to EB virus.

The atypical cells in peripheral blood are recognisable as lymphocytes but are much larger and have abundant cytoplasm and nuclear irregularities (Fig. 23.5). They are probably reactive T-lymphocytes responding to B-lymphocytes containing the virus, are detectable in blood about 7 days after the onset of illness and may persist for 6 weeks or more. Apparently fortuitously, but usefully, antibodies reactive against horse, sheep and ox red cells (heterophile antibodies) typically develop during the second week and may persist for a few months; they are detected in the Paul–Bunnell test or by more convenient commercial screening slide tests such as the 'Monospot' test, and are of diagnostic value. A very similar clinical and haematological (but not serological) picture can develop as a result of other infections, especially with human immunodeficiency virus (HIV), cytomegalovirus and toxoplasma.

All of the above are examples of reactive leukocytosis. Increased white cell counts in peripheral blood, often with immature forms present, are also a typical feature of some primary disorders of the bone marrow, especially leukaemias and myeloproliferative disorders.

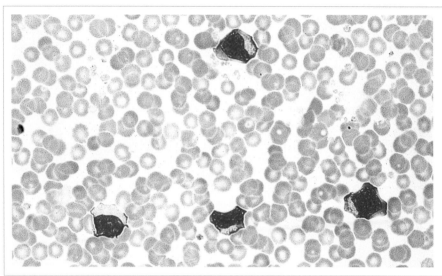

Fig. 23.5 Atypical mononuclear cells in infectious mononucleosis. These large T-lymphocytes have copious basophilic cytoplasm with irregular cell outline.

A reduction in circulating leukocytes is termed *leukopenia*. Most important is a deficiency of neutrophil granulocytes—neutropenia. Neutropenia is commonly seen in association with a reduction in other blood cells, that is, as part of a pancytopenia. Important causes of pancytopenia are:

- bone marrow failure (e.g. hypoplastic anaemia; marrow infiltration with leukaemia or carcinoma; due to cyto-toxic drug therapy; due to irradiation)
- megaloblastic anaemia (in which deficiency of vitamin B_{12} or folate impairs DNA synthesis and thereby slows cell replication)
- hypersplenism (in which an enlarged spleen in disease causes pooling of blood cells within the splenic vasculature, e.g in portal hypertension due to liver disease).

Important causes of selective neutropenia are:

- overwhelming sepsis (e.g. septicaemia, miliary tuberculosis)
- racial (in African races the normal neutrophil count is lower)
- autoimmune (e.g. due to auto-antibody, often in association with other autoimmune disease such as rheumatoid arthritis)
- drug-induced (as an idiosyncratic reaction, for example to anti-thyroid drugs like carbimazole)
- cyclical.

In cyclical forms the neutropenia is temporary and recurrent, often with a periodicity of 3–4 weeks. It is an uncommon condition.

Neutropenia with counts of less than $0.5 \times 10^9/l$ may result in severe sepsis, especially of the mouth, pharynx (Fig. 23.6) and peri-anal regions, and also in disseminated infection. This clinical picture is now most commonly seen in patients receiving drug or irradiation therapy for malignant disorders.

Qualitative changes

Qualitative leukocyte changes are less important than quantitative abnormalities. Defects of phagocytic cell function resulting in an increased tendency to bacterial infection are recognised, particularly as acquired defects after splenectomy,

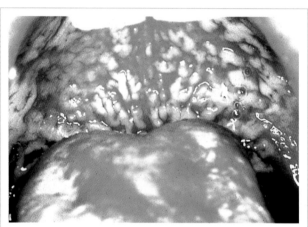

Fig. 23.6 Oral infection with *Candida albicans* ('thrush') in a neutropenic patient.

in leukaemic disorders and due to corticosteroid therapy. Congenital abnormalities of leukocyte function are uncommon. 'Atypical' lymphocytes in infectious mononucleosis have been described earlier. Other abnormalities of neutrophil morphology are also recognised (Fig. 23.7).

Deficiency of lymphocytes in blood is termed lymphopenia. It is often due to medication with immunosuppressive or cytotoxic drugs, for example. Lymphopenia is an important feature of infection with HIV.

Platelets

On a stained blood film platelets appear as non-nucleated fragments of granular cytoplasm, approximately one-fifth the diameter of erythrocytes and in a concentration of $150–400 \times 10^9/l$. Platelets are contractile and adhesive cells, the function of which is the maintenance of vascular integrity. Exposure of vascular subendothelial structures results in rapid adhesion of platelets to the exposed area and aggregation of platelets to each other in the formation of a primary haemostatic plug

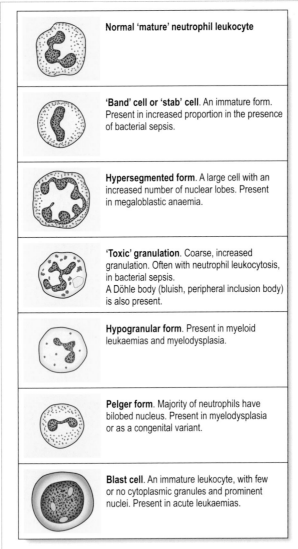

Normal 'mature' neutrophil leukocyte

'Band' cell or 'stab' cell. An immature form. Present in increased proportion in the presence of bacterial sepsis.

Hypersegmented form. A large cell with an increased number of nuclear lobes. Present in megaloblastic anaemia.

'Toxic' granulation. Coarse, increased granulation. Often with neutrophil leukocytosis, in bacterial sepsis.
A Döhle body (bluish, peripheral inclusion body) is also present.

Hypogranular form. Present in myeloid leukaemias and myelodysplasia.

Pelger form. Majority of neutrophils have bilobed nucleus. Present in myelodysplasia or as a congenital variant.

Blast cell. An immature leukocyte, with few or no cytoplasmic granules and prominent nuclei. Present in acute leukaemias.

Fig. 23.7   Abnormalities of neutrophil morphology.

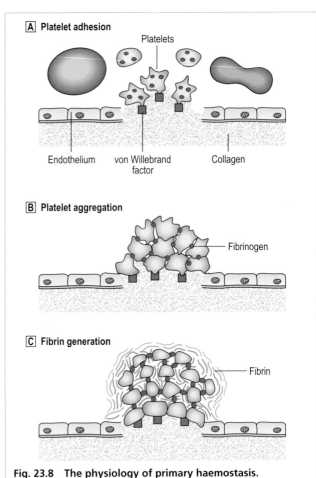

A **Platelet adhesion**

B **Platelet aggregation**

C **Fibrin generation**

Fig. 23.8   The physiology of primary haemostasis.
A **Platelet adhesion.** Exposure of subendothelial material causes activation of platelets, which change shape and produce pseudo-podia, and rapidly adhere to the area via receptor sites which interact with *von Willebrand factor* (vWF). vWF is a multimeric protein synthesised by endothelial cells and megakaryocytes. It associates with a coagulation factor, factor VIII, in plasma.
B **Platelet aggregation.** Platelets interact with each other via receptor sites which use *fibrinogen* as an intercellular bridge. Platelets contract and release granules which contain pro-aggregatory substances that promote the aggregation response. These include ADP, 5-hydroxytryptamine, fibrinogen and vWF. Metabolism of arachidonic acid, a fatty acid of the cell mem-brane, to the prostaglandin-like metabolite thromboxane A_2 also promotes aggregation and, in addition, vasoconstriction.
C **Fibrin generation.** Exposure of tissue factor activates the extrinsic coagulation system. *Thrombin* generation augments the platelet activation and activated platelets provide phospholipid, which is an essential co-factor at several points in the coagulation cascade.

(Fig. 23.8). Platelets are rich in intracellular granules, which are released during stimulation. The most abundant granules, alpha granules, contain proteins and peptides, including von Willebrand factor, some coagulation factors and growth factors. Platelets deliver these to sites of vascular injury, where they contribute to clot formation and the repair process. Dense bodies are less abundant platelet granules and are rich in calcium, serotonin and adenine nucleotides.

A deficiency of blood platelets is termed *thrombocytopenia,* the causes and consequences of which are described on page 670. Thrombocytosis, or increased platelet numbers, may be due to a primary bone marrow problem or may be reactive. Examples of reactive thrombocytosis are seen in:

- acute or chronic blood loss (e.g. from peptic ulcer, menorrhagia)
- iron deficiency (e.g. dietary deficiency, chronic blood loss)
- chronic inflammatory disease (e.g. rheumatoid arthritis)
- neoplastic disease (e.g. bronchial carcinoma, lymphoma)
- tissue trauma (e.g. post-operative state, especially splenectomy).

Thrombocytosis may also occur in primary disorders of bone marrow—the myeloproliferative diseases and chronic myeloid leukaemia. Morphological platelet abnormalities are of minor importance, although 'giant' platelets, with a diameter exceeding that of an erythrocyte, are a feature of the myeloproliferative disorders rather than reactive thrombocytosis. Giant platelets are also a feature of some inherited syndromes, including those associated with mutations of the myosin heavy chain gene.

Blood count and morphology in disease

Changes in the blood are present in a wide range of diseases of other organs. These changes are most commonly reactive or secondary but may be useful in providing a clue to the presence and type of underlying disease, e.g. polymorphonuclear leukocytosis in bacterial sepsis; eosinophilia in some parasitic infections. In other cases the abnormalities of cell number and morphology are due to a primary haematological disorder.

BLOOD PLASMA

Plasma amounts to greater than 50% of blood volume. While changes in the innumerable constituents of plasma are outside the scope of this text, consideration of certain major plasma proteins is necessary for an understanding of the pathology of some blood and systemic disorders. The plasma proteins that are components of the blood coagulation and fibrinolytic systems are considered first.

Blood coagulation

For normal homeostasis, blood must be fluid; however, the capacity to minimise loss of blood through breaches of the vascular system is essential. The rapid plugging of defects in small vessels is the function of platelets (primary haemostasis, Fig. 23.8) but a more permanent and secure seal results from the generation of insoluble fibrillar fibrin from its soluble plasma protein precursor fibrinogen in the process of blood coagulation. Failure of primary haemostasis, due to platelet disorders, or of coagulation due to clotting factor deficiency or presence of a coagulation inhibitor, can each result in life-threatening haemorrhage. In contrast, inappropriate activation of platelets or blood coagulation may result in vascular occlusion, ischaemia and tissue death. A complex system of activators and inhibitors in plasma has therefore evolved in order to allow localised clot formation at sites of injury but to minimise the risk of inappropriate and undesirable clotting, i.e. thrombosis. These are the coagulation and fibrinolytic factors and their inhibitors (Fig. 23.9).

Important features of the haemostatic mechanism are as follows.

- The components interact in a biological amplification system.
- Thrombin is a key enzyme in coagulation because it acts in a feedback loop to activate several of the other coagulation factors and is therefore pivotal in the amplification system (Fig. 23.9). In addition it activates platelets through a specific receptor, ensures clot stabilisation by activating factor XIII and helps to address the degree of clot formation by activating the natural anticoagulant activated protein C (aPC).

- Almost all of the coagulation factors and inhibitors are synthesised in the liver. Liver disease is therefore a cause of abnormal bleeding.
- Factors II, VII, IX, X, XI and XII are serine proteases, i.e. enzymes in which the presence of serine at the active site is necessary for their action in hydrolysing peptide bonds.
- Factors II, VII, IX and X require vitamin K for post-translational modification into their functional forms. This is clinically important: vitamin K inhibitors known as coumarins are among the main anticoagulant drugs used in clinical practice; warfarin is an example.
- Many of the interactions involved in coagulation require assembly of the components on an appropriate surface, for example the generation of thrombin from prothrombin by activated factor X. In vivo, this surface is provided by platelet membranes which become reconfigured during platelet activation to promote the binding of coagulation factors.

Coagulation inhibitors limit unwanted clotting and protect against vessel occlusion, especially in veins:

- In common with clotting factors, the principal inhibitors are synthesised in the liver. Proteins C and S require vitamin K for their complete synthesis.
- Antithrombin is a serine protease inhibitor which acts at several sites to inhibit activated coagulation factors. Inhibition of the key coagulation enzymes thrombin and activated factor X are most important. Antithrombin requires glycosaminoglycan 'heparans', present on the vascular endothelial cell surface, for full inhibitory activity. In clinical practice the glycosaminoglycan heparin is a widely used antithrombotic which enhances the inhibitory activity of antithrombin several thousand fold.
- Protein C requires a co-factor, protein S, for full activity. When activated, protein C inhibits activated factors V and VIII.
- Protein C requires thrombin bound to an endothelial protein, thrombomodulin, for its activation. Thrombin therefore not only acts to promote fibrin formation but also has a crucial role as part of a negative feedback loop to inhibit clot formation.
- Another inhibitor, tissue factor pathway inhibitor, acts early in the process of coagulation activation.
- The fibrinolytic mechanism acts as a further check on uncontrolled clot formation. Plasminogen activators are released from endothelial cells. They cleave plasminogen to produce plasmin which rapidly digests fibrin clot. This fibrinolytic activity is partially balanced by the thrombin activated fibrinolytic inhibitor (TAFI). Several components of the fibrinolytic system (Fig. 23.9) also originate in the liver.

Although the scheme for the initial stages of coagulation activation can be conveniently divided into extrinsic and intrinsic pathways (Fig. 23.9), this is a simplification. Coagulation activation in vivo is initiated through tissue factor, an integral cell membrane protein which is not expressed by vascular endothelial cells in an unstimulated state but is expressed by subendothelial cells and smooth muscle as well as other cells. As soon as blood leaks from a vessel it is exposed to

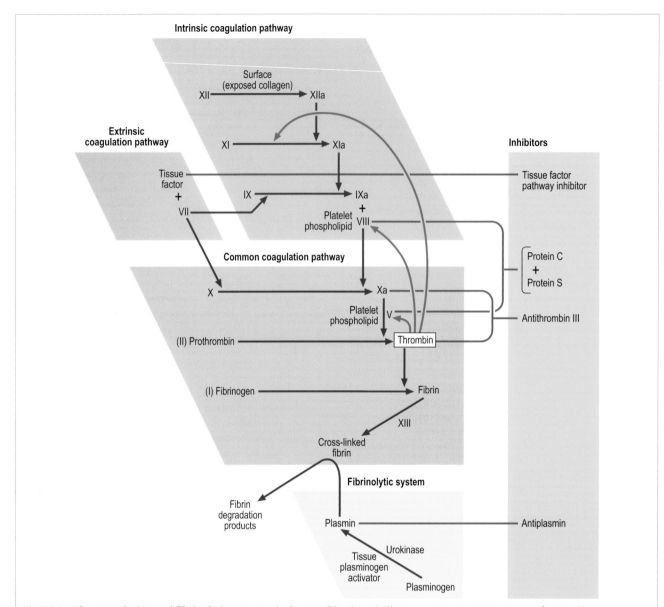

Fig. 23.9 **The coagulation and fibrinolytic systems. Activators** (blue boxes). These are enzyme precursors or co-factors. The nomenclature uses Roman numerals, the suffix 'a' designating the active enzyme. Ca^{2+} is required at several points in the cascade, as is phospholipid surface provided by activated platelets. **Inhibitors.** These have an anticoagulant action. **Fibrinolytic system.** This leads to plasmin generation. Plasmin has its own principal inhibitor, antiplasmin.

tissue factor. Tissue factor activates factor VII. The much slower pathway for fibrin generation through activation of factor XII on contact with subendothelial components is of minor importance. This partially explains the absence of any increased tendency to haemorrhage in subjects who are congenitally deficient in factor XII. It is the tissue factor–activated factor VII complex that rapidly activates factors X and IX, leading to thrombin generation. When the procoagulant stimulus is sufficiently strong, the degree of amplification through thrombin activation of factors V and VIII overcomes inhibition by activated protein C and fibrin generation proceeds.

The final step in clot formation is the stabilisation of fibrin by cross-linking through the activity of factor XIII.

In the laboratory, the function of the components of the coagulation system can be assessed by the time required for clotting of recalcified plasma prepared from a blood sample anticoagulated with sodium citrate. The citrate binds calcium ions, which are required at several points in the mechanism. Recalcification allows fibrin formation to take place. The two principal screening tests used in clinical practice are:

• Activated partial thromboplastin time (APTT). In the APTT, the intrinsic pathway is activated by contact activation, for example by addition of kaolin (chalk powder, which provides a massive surface area for contact). Phospholipid is added to substitute for the role of platelets

in coagulation. The APTT therefore involves all clotting factors other than factor VII and factor XIII.
- Prothrombin time (PT). In the PT, tissue factor and phospholipid are added. The PT therefore assesses factors VII, V, X, II and fibrinogen only.

The pathology and consequences of deficiency of the components of the coagulation and fibrinolytic system are described on page 673.

Rheological considerations

Blood is a viscous fluid and changes in its physical properties accompany some diseases. The major determinant of blood viscosity is the *haematocrit*.

The plasma *fibrinogen* concentration is the major determinant of red cell aggregation and is second only to haematocrit as a factor in determination of blood viscosity. Other plasma protein molecules tend to be smaller and more symmetrical than fibrinogen and consequently have a much lesser effect on viscosity. However, when they are present in increased concentrations, blood viscosity may be affected. This may result in a *hyperviscosity syndrome*, in which there is stasis within the microcirculation and tissue anoxia. Cerebral dysfunction, with headache, visual disturbance and drowsiness progressing to coma may result. Very high plasma immunoglobulin concentration, which is a common feature of the malignant disorders multiple myeloma and macroglobulinaemia, is a common cause of the hyperviscosity syndrome. Numbers of leukocytes and platelets have little influence on blood flow in health. However, when leukocyte counts exceed 300×10^9/l, usually in leukaemia, flow may be adversely affected, resulting in clinical hyperviscosity.

The hyperviscosity syndrome represents an extreme abnormality of blood flow producing organ dysfunction. However, epidemiological studies suggest that even minor increases in blood viscosity, due to increased haematocrit or fibrinogen concentration, may result in a tendency to vascular occlusion, manifesting as an increased incidence of myocardial infarction and cerebral infarction. The concentration of plasma fibrinogen is a risk factor for atherosclerosis and arterial thrombosis that is at least as potent as the level of serum cholesterol. The interplay between rheological and haemostatic changes in thrombotic disease is not yet fully understood.

Erythrocyte sedimentation rate
The erythrocyte sedimentation rate (ESR) measures the rate at which red cells sediment by gravity in plasma in 1 hour and is a widely used laboratory test. Increased aggregation and sedimentation occur in the presence of high concentrations of immunoglobulin and fibrinogen. As the latter is an acute phase reactant, the ESR is increased in a wide variety of inflammatory and neoplastic conditions. It is an entirely non-specific test and a normal value for ESR can never be used to exclude the presence of significant disease. Direct measurement of plasma viscosity provides equally useful data and has replaced ESR measurement in some diagnostic laboratories.

HAEMOPOIESIS AND BLOOD CELL KINETICS

Haemopoiesis is the formation of blood cells.

Sites of haemopoiesis

In the adult, all blood cells are produced in the red marrow, which is restricted to the bones of the axial skeleton—vertebrae, ribs, sternum, skull, sacrum, pelvis and proximal femora. In these regions the bone marrow is composed of approximately 50% fat, within adipocytes, and 50% blood cells and their precursors (Fig. 23.10). The fatty marrow of other bones is

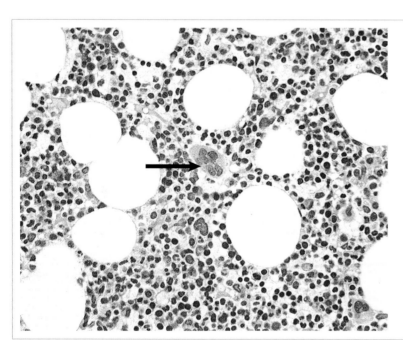

Fig. 23.10 Normal bone marrow. From a section of a bone marrow biopsy from the pelvis. Marrow cells are interspersed between fat spaces. The arrow points to a megakaryocyte.

capable of haemopoiesis when requirements for blood cells are increased in some diseases.

In the infant and young child, practically all of the bones contain haemopoietically active marrow.

In fetal life, the liver and spleen are the major haemopoietic organs between about 6 weeks and 6–7 months' gestation; the yolk sac is the main site before 6 weeks. In disease, the liver and spleen can again become haemopoietic organs, even in adult life; this development is referred to as *extramedullary haemopoiesis* and is particularly associated with the progressive fibrosis of bone marrow seen in the myeloproliferative disorders.

The bone marrow is examined histologically in two ways. Marrow can be aspirated through a needle inserted into a marrow cavity (usually sternum or pelvis), smeared on a slide and stained in a method similar to that for peripheral blood. Further information, particularly on the structure and cellularity of the marrow, can be obtained by preparation of sections of a marrow trephine biopsy: this is a core of tissue obtained using a wide-bore needle (Fig. 23.10).

Additional investigations carried out on bone marrow samples include staining of individual cells with monoclonal antibodies (immunophenotyping and immunohistochemistry) and genetic analysis including karyotyping, fluorescent in situ hybridisation (FISH) and molecular analysis of individual genes.

Haemopoietic stem cells

Studies of bone marrow in culture lead to the conclusion that erythrocytes, leukocytes (including lymphocytes) and platelets are derived from a common, self-replicating precursor cell or 'pluripotential stem cell'. By a series of cell divisions, cells committed to each line are produced and further divisions result in mature cells—erythrocytes, granular leukocytes, megakaryocytes and T- and B-lymphocytes (Fig. 23.11). The pluripotential stem cells possess the ability to renew in addition to the capacity to differentiate. It is now clear that bone marrow also contains mesenchymal stem cells which can give rise to connective tissues such as fat cells, fibroblasts, bone and cartilage. The development and preferential survival of a malignant clone of haemopoietic cells, derived from mutated bone marrow stem cells, explains the pathological features of the leukaemias and myelodysplastic syndromes.

If human bone marrow is infused intravenously into a subject without functioning marrow, as during bone marrow transplantation treatment, normal blood cell production returns after a period of several weeks. This finding confirms the presence of pluripotential stem cells in bone marrow and also indicates that the microenvironment of the bone marrow is central to normal blood production; stem cells do not tend to thrive in other sites, and blood production resumes only in the marrow cavities after marrow infusion. Stem cells can be made to circulate in the peripheral blood. This is most conveniently achieved by the administration of one of the cytokines (most commonly G-CSF) responsible for stimulation of haemopoiesis—the colony stimulating factors. Using an extracorporeal centrifugation technique these cells can be harvested and used as an alternative to bone marrow cells in transplantation therapy—a 'peripheral blood stem cell transplant'. Peripheral blood is used as a source of haemopoietic stem cells more commonly now than bone marrow because engraftment is

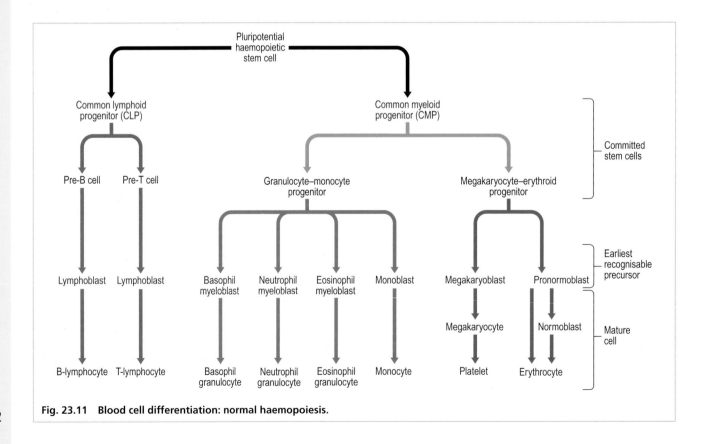

Fig. 23.11 Blood cell differentiation: normal haemopoiesis.

faster and procurement of peripheral blood stem cells does not require the donor to have a general anaesthetic.

There is great interest in the possibility that marrow stem cells may be able to differentiate into diverse tissue types, including neuronal, muscle, liver and vascular cells. This is referred to as transdifferentiation or stem cell plasticity. Although definitive proof of this is still lacking, should it be confirmed it offers exciting new possibilities for treatment of common disorders through transfer of stem cells. Such studies are ongoing and to date show some benefit in treating damaged myocardium and improving blood flow to ischaemic limbs.

Erythropoiesis

The pronormoblast is the earliest red cell precursor that can be identified in the bone marrow. It is a large cell with prominent nucleoli within the nucleus. By a series of four cell divisions a fully haemoglobinised, non-nucleated erythrocyte is produced. During differentiation the nucleus becomes increasingly condensed and the cytoplasm contains increasing amounts of haemoglobin and less RNA; the early, intermediate and late normoblasts can be distinguished morphologically through the increasing haemoglobin content and progressive nuclear condensation (Fig. 23.12). The nucleus is eventually extruded, leaving a 'polychromatic' erythrocyte which remains in the marrow for a further 48 hours; it then circulates for approximately 48 hours before maturing in the spleen to an erythrocyte.

Only polychromatic erythrocytes and mature erythrocytes normally circulate. However, nucleated red cell precursors are present in the peripheral blood in some marrow disorders.

Leukopoiesis

The normal bone marrow contains many more myeloid than nucleated erythroid cells (around 5:1). In the granulocyte series these include the myeloblast, promyelocyte and myelocyte, which are capable of cell division, and the metamyelocyte and band cell, which are undergoing maturation without further division (Fig. 23.12). Maturation of granulocyte precursors involves a reduction in cell size, development of cytoplasmic granules, increased condensation of nuclear chromatin, and irregularity of nuclear outline.

Monoblasts cannot easily be distinguished from myeloblasts. They mature in the bone marrow to monocytes via a promonocyte stage. Peripheral blood contains mature granulocytes and monocytes only, in health. However, as previously mentioned, their precursors may enter the circulation in the presence of severe infection or bone marrow disease.

Megakaryocytopoiesis

Megakaryocyte maturation is unique. The earliest identifiable precursor, the megakaryoblast, is a large cell that undergoes nuclear replication without cell division, the cytoplasmic volume increasing as the nuclear material increases, in multiples of 2, up to 32N (Fig. 23.12). Cytoplasmic maturation occurs, often at the 8N stage, and platelets are released. Megakaryocytes are not seen in peripheral blood by routine methods.

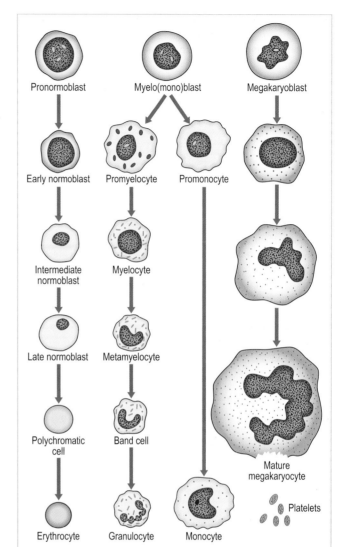

Fig. 23.12 Haemopoiesis. The later morphological stages of erythrocyte, megakaryocyte and myeloid cell development from the committed progenitor cell stage.

Blood cell kinetics

Erythrocytes circulate for an average of 120 days and are then destroyed, predominantly in the bone marrow, but also in liver and spleen. There is no significant storage pool of erythrocytes in humans. In contrast, some 10 times more granulocytes are present in the bone marrow than in the peripheral blood, constituting a storage pool of leukocytes which can be mobilised rapidly in response to some stimuli, such as infection or tissue damage. Granulocytes spend only a few hours in the circulation before they enter the tissues, where they act as phagocytes, surviving for several days under normal circumstances. Monocytes also spend a limited time in the circulation, after which they enter the tissues and become tissue macrophages; they may survive for many months.

Platelets circulate for approximately 10 days. The spleen acts as a reservoir of platelets; some 30% are present in the spleen at any time.

Control of haemopoiesis

Peripheral blood cell counts are normally maintained within close limits. However, the ability of each cell line to respond appropriately to increased requirement is exemplified by the increased red cell production after haemorrhage, the granulocyte leukocytosis in response to sepsis and the enhanced platelet production that results from chronic bleeding.

Erythropoietin is a glycoprotein hormone, produced by peritubular fibroblasts in the kidney, that increases erythropoietic activity. The production of erythropoietin is increased in response to a reduced oxygen tension in the blood reaching the kidney. It results in an increase in the number of cells committed to the erythroid line, reduced maturation time and early release of erythrocytes from the bone marrow. Erythropoietin mediates the physiological response of the bone marrow to anaemia or hypoxia. In pathological states, failure of erythropoietin production is a major contributor to the anaemia of chronic renal failure and this can be corrected by erythropoietin administration; inappropriate erythropoietin production by some renal cysts and tumours results in secondary polycythaemia.

Numerous growth factors have been found to govern production of leukocytes in the bone marrow. They are synthesised mainly by T-lymphocytes, monocytes/macrophages, endothelial cells and fibroblasts of the bone marrow stroma. Examples are interleukins 1, 3 and 6 and the *colony stimulating factors*. GM-CSF increases stem cell commitment to granulocyte and monocyte production, G-CSF to granulocytes and M-CSF to monocytes. Recombinant forms of some of these cytokines are now in therapeutic use, particularly in cancer chemotherapy, where the duration of drug-induced neutropenia can be limited by cytokine administration.

Thrombopoietin, capable of the stimulation of platelet production, is synthesised principally in the liver. Analogues of thrombopoietin may be of use in stimulating platelet production in bone marrow failure states and as shown recently in immune thrombocytopenic purpura (ITP).

Haemoglobin

Structure, synthesis and metabolism

Some knowledge of haemoglobin structure and metabolism is necessary for an understanding of the pathology of the anaemias. Haemoglobin is the oxygen-carrying pigment. The haem group of haemoglobin is responsible for oxygen carriage and is composed of a protoporphyrin ring structure with an iron atom.

By 1 month of age red cell precursors synthesise predominantly haemoglobin A, composed of four haem groups and four polypeptide (globin) chains (Fig. 23.13), of which two molecular forms are present: alpha and beta chains. Haemoglobin A thus has the structure $\alpha_2\beta_2$. Up to 2.5% of the haemoglobin in adults has delta chains ($\alpha_2\delta_2$)—haemoglobin A_2; and up to 1% of the haemoglobin in adults has gamma chains ($\alpha_2\gamma_2$)—haemoglobin F. Adult blood therefore has predominantly haemoglobin A with some A_2 and F (Table 23.3).

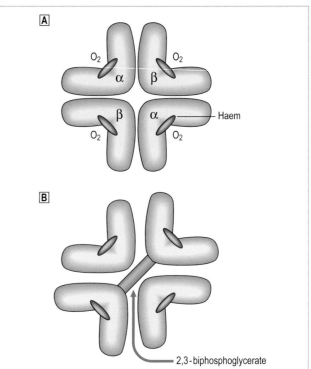

Fig. 23.13 Oxygenated [A] and deoxygenated [B] adult haemoglobin. Uptake and release of oxygen (O_2) is associated with movement of the globin chains. On release of O_2 the beta chains are moved apart, allowing entry of 2,3-BPG and a reduction in the affinity of the haemoglobin molecule for O_2.

Table 23.3	Human haemoglobins	
Type	Chains	Nomenclature
Adults	$\alpha_2\beta_2$	A
	$\alpha_2\delta_2$	A_2
Fetal	$\alpha_2\gamma_2$	F
Embryonic	$\alpha_2\varepsilon_2$	'Gower 2' } Present in
	$\zeta_2\varepsilon_2$	'Gower 1' } early fetal
	$\zeta_2\gamma_2$	Portland } life only
After 1 year of life and in the adult, less than 1% haemoglobin is F and less than 2.5% is A_2.		

In later fetal and early neonatal life haemoglobin F predominates. In early fetal life three other haemoglobins are present: Gower 1, Gower 2 and Portland (Table 23.3).

The whole haemoglobin molecule is thus composed of a tetramer of globin chains, each with a haem group. The complex structure of the molecule is responsible for its oxygen (O_2) binding characteristics, the globin chains moving against each other during transfer of O_2. The affinity of the haemoglobin molecule for O_2 is also controlled by its ability to bind the metabolite 2,3-biphosphoglycerate (2,3-BPG) produced during anaerobic respiration. When 2,3-BPG enters the haemoglobin molecule as the beta chains pull apart during release of O_2, the affinity for O_2 of the haemoglobin–2,3-BPG complex is reduced, allowing O_2 to be given up more readily. Haemoglobin F cannot bind 2,3-BPG and thus has a relatively high O_2 affinity, facilitating O_2 transfer from maternal blood across the placenta.

At the end of the erythrocyte life-span haemoglobin is metabolised, with conservation of iron and amino acids. Iron is carried by plasma transferrin to the bone marrow and utilised in the synthesis of haem. Globin is degraded to its constituent amino acids, which enter the general pool. Liver, gut and kidneys are all involved in excretion of products of haem breakdown as derivatives of bilirubin.

In the congenital disorders collectively known as *haemoglobinopathies,* the rate of synthesis of one globin chain type is defective (the *thalassaemias*) or an abnormal chain is synthesised (the *sickle haemoglobinopathies* and other haemoglobin variants).

FUNCTIONS OF THE BLOOD

From a consideration of the preceding sections the functions of blood and the major pathological consequences of blood and marrow disease will be apparent.

Oxygen transport is the primary function of the red blood cells. Failure of red cell production, or loss or dysfunction thereof, results in tissue hypoxia affecting the metabolism of all organs.

The cells responsible for host defence against infection are carried, in the blood, from the bone marrow to sites of infection. Infections with bacteria, viruses and fungi are the predictable results of a failure to produce normal leukocytes in adequate numbers.

The primary haemostatic and coagulation mechanisms allow the transport functions of blood to operate without risk of exsanguination from breaches of the vascular compartment. Failure of these leads to spontaneous haemorrhage, whereas a defect in the control mechanisms can result in thrombosis and vascular occlusion.

The diseases that interfere with the function of the blood and their pathological consequences are now described.

ANAEMIAS

▶ Defined as when the haemoglobin is less than 130 g/l in a male or 115 g/l in a female adult
▶ Usually represent a reduction in the body red cell mass
▶ Result in tissue hypoxia
▶ Are due to failure of erythrocyte production or loss or destruction of erythrocytes

Anaemia is present when the haemoglobin level falls below around 130 g/l in a male or 115 g/l in a female. The different lower limits of normal haemoglobin concentration for neonates, infants and children should be noted (Table 23.1).

The consequences of anaemia are dependent upon the speed of onset. Thus the rapid loss of 10% or more of the circulating blood volume through haemorrhage will result in shock, i.e. the failure of adequate perfusion of all tissues and organs, with consequent hypoxia. In this situation the subject may not initially be anaemic, as both red cells and plasma are lost through haemorrhage. The plasma component is more rapidly replaced, however, and anaemia will be present after several hours have elapsed.

Anaemia that develops more gradually is better tolerated. A haemoglobin concentration as low as 20 g/l may be consistent with survival if it develops over a protracted period. The inevitable result of anaemia, however, is a reduction in the oxygen-carrying capacity of the blood and thus chronic tissue hypoxia.

The general consequences of anaemia are due to the tissue hypoxia, which can result in fatty change, especially in the myocardium and liver, and even infarction. Lethargy, increased breathlessness on exertion, and new or worsened ischaemic phenomena are typical clinical features. Breathlessness at rest implies the development of heart failure, a result of severe anaemia. Expansion of the red marrow is present in those anaemias where a marrow response is possible—generally the haemolytic anaemias. Other features are specific to anaemias resulting from a particular mechanism, such as the jaundice of haemolytic anaemias, or are specific to anaemia of a particular type, such as the nail changes of iron deficiency anaemia. Such pathological features are described in the relevant sections.

A low haemoglobin concentration usually reflects a reduction in the body red cell mass. An important exception is pregnancy, when both red cell mass and plasma volume increase, but the latter to a greater degree. This process results in a haemoglobin concentration in blood that is lower than in the non-pregnant state in the presence of a relatively increased red cell mass and overall oxygen-carrying capacity; this condition is often referred to as the physiological 'anaemia' of pregnancy. The increased red cell mass during pregnancy is necessary to support the increased metabolic requirement of the mother and fetus. The reason for the expansion of the plasma compartment is obscure, but it may be explained in part by a need for increased skin perfusion for heat loss due to the increased metabolic rate.

Expansion of the plasma volume, resulting in dilutional anaemia, may also occur when the spleen is pathologically enlarged. (The spleen appears to exert a controlling influence on plasma volume.) Other mechanisms also operate in this situation, however, as described under hypersplenism (p. 654).

Classification

Table 23.4 outlines a classification of anaemias. Anaemias are divided into two categories: those where anaemia is due to failure to produce erythrocytes, and those in which erythrocyte loss is increased but production is normal (or usually increased, in response to the anaemia). While useful, this categorisation is an oversimplification, as both mechanisms are present in some anaemias. Thus, in the megaloblastic states, cell production is defective due to lack of vitamin B_{12} or folic acid for nucleic acid synthesis

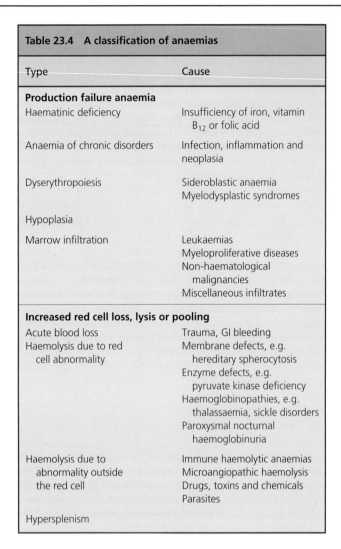

Table 23.4 A classification of anaemias

Type	Cause
Production failure anaemia	
Haematinic deficiency	Insufficiency of iron, vitamin B$_{12}$ or folic acid
Anaemia of chronic disorders	Infection, inflammation and neoplasia
Dyserythropoiesis	Sideroblastic anaemia Myelodysplastic syndromes
Hypoplasia	
Marrow infiltration	Leukaemias Myeloproliferative diseases Non-haematological malignancies Miscellaneous infiltrates
Increased red cell loss, lysis or pooling	
Acute blood loss	Trauma, GI bleeding
Haemolysis due to red cell abnormality	Membrane defects, e.g. hereditary spherocytosis Enzyme defects, e.g. pyruvate kinase deficiency Haemoglobinopathies, e.g. thalassaemia, sickle disorders Paroxysmal nocturnal haemoglobinuria
Haemolysis due to abnormality outside the red cell	Immune haemolytic anaemias Microangiopathic haemolysis Drugs, toxins and chemicals Parasites
Hypersplenism	

but, in addition, the erythrocytes that are produced are abnormal and of diminished survival. In thalassaemia, cell production is not optimal due to abnormal haemoglobin synthesis, and there is also increased erythrocyte destruction.

The myeloid and megakaryocytic lines are also involved in some anaemias due to failure of haemopoiesis (megaloblastic anaemia, hypoplastic anaemia) but not in others (iron deficiency anaemia).

Despite these qualifications, the classification described is useful as an aid to determining the cause of the anaemia.

PRODUCTION FAILURE ANAEMIAS

The most commonly encountered anaemias are in the production failure group.

Haematinic deficiency

Haematinics are dietary factors essential for either haemoglobin synthesis or erythrocyte production.

Iron deficiency

> ▸ A production failure anaemia
> ▸ The commonest cause of anaemia
> ▸ Results in a microcytic hypochromic blood picture
> ▸ Usually indicative of chronic blood loss
> ▸ Frequently indicative of an occult, bleeding lesion of the gastrointestinal tract

Iron deficiency is the commonest cause of anaemia worldwide. It is also the commonest cause of a microcytic hypochromic blood picture, the others being thalassaemias and (rarely) sideroblastic anaemias.

Iron metabolism

Iron is an essential requirement. It is also one of the commonest elements present in the Earth's crust. Excessive iron deposited in the tissues is, however, toxic, causing damage to the myocardium, pancreas and liver in particular (Ch. 16). As the body has no active method for iron excretion, iron status is controlled largely by its absorption; the capacity to absorb iron is, however, limited and any tendency to increased loss of iron, due to haemorrhage, is highly likely to result in a negative iron balance and iron deficiency. These factors explain the high prevalence of iron deficiency.

Normally, at least 60% of the body iron is in the haemoglobin of erythroid cells. Approximately 30% is stored within the reticulo-endothelial system (also known as the mononuclear phagocyte system), especially in the bone marrow, as *ferritin* and *haemosiderin*. A small proportion of total body iron is present in other tissues, especially muscle, and iron-containing enzymes. This tissue iron is relatively conserved during states of iron deficiency. Only a small fraction of the total body iron is in transport, attached to the carrier protein *transferrin*.

Ferritin is a protein–iron complex. The protein, apoferritin, is a shell made up of 22 subunits. The core is composed of ferric oxyhydride. Haemosiderin consists of partially degraded ferritin aggregates. Ferritin is present in all tissues, but especially in the macrophages of the bone marrow and spleen and in hepatocytes. A small amount is detectable in plasma and, as it is derived from the storage pool of body iron, its concentration is thus an accurate indicator of body iron stores. Low serum ferritin concentration is a useful confirmatory test for iron deficiency. However, because ferritin is an acute phase response protein, the concentration in plasma is not a reliable guide to body iron stores in the presence of infection, inflammation and neoplasia. In those situations serum ferritin may be normal or high despite tissue iron depletion.

Ferritin is water soluble and not visible by light microscopy; haemosiderin is insoluble and forms yellow granules. When exposed to potassium ferrocyanide (Perls' stain) the granules are blue–black. Examination of aspirated bone marrow stained with Perls' stain can therefore be used to assess body iron stores reliably. When iron stores are normal, haemosiderin is visible, mainly in the reticulo-endothelial cells of the bone marrow. In iron overload, most of the iron is in the form of haemosiderin and can be easily identified.

Transferrin is an iron-binding beta-globulin responsible for iron transport and delivery to receptors on immature erythroid cells. Each molecule of transferrin can bind two atoms of iron, but normally the transferrin is only one-third saturated (thus the serum iron concentration is normally one-third of the total serum iron-binding capacity). Transferrin is reutilised after delivering its iron. A low transferrin saturation is therefore diagnostic of iron deficiency while high levels are a feature of iron overload with deposition of iron in tissues.

In order to maintain iron balance, sufficient iron must be absorbed to replace that lost from the urinary and gastrointestinal tracts as shed cells and in sweat, together with any extra requirements.

Daily iron requirements are:

- adult male   1.0 mg
- child   1.5 mg
- pregnant female   1.5–3.0 mg
- menstruating female   2.0 mg.

Thus, requirements vary with circumstances, extra iron being required for growth during childhood, for the fetus and placenta and expansion of maternal red cell mass during pregnancy, and to compensate for menstrual loss of women of child-bearing age.

As a Western diet contains only 10–20 mg of iron per day and only a maximum of one-third of this can be absorbed, excess losses of iron of just a few milligrams will inevitably result in negative iron balance and eventual depletion of iron stores. One millilitre of blood contains 0.5 mg iron. Thus, loss of 10 ml of blood daily will inevitably exceed the capacity to absorb sufficient iron, even from a good diet. This explains the finding of some degree of iron depletion in 25% or more of menstruating women.

Iron absorption takes place in the duodenum and upper jejunum. Haem iron is present in meat and readily absorbed, with little effect from other dietary components. Inorganic iron in vegetables and cereals is mostly trivalent and may be complexed to amino acids and organic acids, from which it must be released and reduced to the divalent state for absorption. HCl produced by the stomach and ascorbic acid in food favour its absorption. In contrast, phosphates and phytates in some foods form precipitates and prevent absorption.

Mechanisms controlling the rate of iron absorption are becoming better understood. Major influences are the total body iron stores and rate of erythropoiesis. Thus, if iron stores are replete a smaller proportion of available iron is absorbed; when erythropoiesis is more active, due to premature red cell destruction for example, extra iron is absorbed even though total stores may be high. This is a feature in thalassaemia, and iron overload may ensue. A major regulator of iron balance is the liver protein hepcidin. Iron loading leads to rapid production of hepcidin by the liver which, in turn, inhibits intestinal iron absorption and movement of iron from stores. This is achieved by hepcidin downregulating the plasma membrane transfer protein ferroportin. Iron is consequently trapped in iron-exporting cells, including duodenal enterocytes. Plasma iron levels subsequently fall. Conversely, low iron levels lead to downregulation of liver hepcidin and increased iron transfer from the gut and iron-exporting cells so that plasma iron levels rise (Fig. 23.14).

Mechanisms of iron deficiency
In developed countries, iron deficiency in the non-menstruating and non-pregnant adult most frequently results from chronic blood loss, often from the gastrointestinal tract. As it is possible to lose several millilitres of blood daily into the gut lumen without marked change in appearance of the stool, such blood loss is frequently occult. Iron deficiency anaemia is thus commonly a presenting feature of lesions within the gastrointestinal tract (Fig. 23.15). In clinical practice, when iron deficiency anaemia occurs in the face of a reasonable diet and no excessive menstrual loss it is mandatory to perform a careful assessment of the gastrointestinal tract.

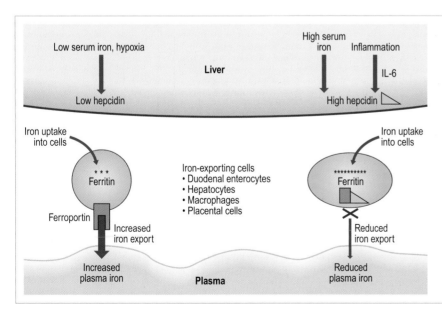

Fig. 23.14 The role of hepatic hepcidin in regulating iron stores. Hepcidin binds to ferroportin and internalises it, trapping iron within iron-exporting cells. (IL-6, interleukin 6.)

Causes of iron deficiency are:

- chronic blood loss (e.g. peptic ulcer; carcinoma of stomach, caecum, colon or rectum; menorrhagia)
- increased requirements (e.g. in childhood and pregnancy)
- malabsorption (due to gastrectomy, coeliac disease)
- malnutrition.

More than one factor may operate concurrently. Thus a poor-quality vegetarian diet is highly likely to result in iron deficiency in a menstruating female. In a male or post-menopausal female, failure to ingest or absorb any iron would result in complete depletion of iron stores only after 3 or more years (1 mg/day). Malnutrition or malabsorption is thus rarely the sole cause of iron deficiency, although it may be an important contributory factor.

The microcytic hypochromic anaemia is a late stage in iron deficiency; it does not occur until iron stores are severely depleted. The microcyte results from an extra cell division, in addition to the normal four, during red cell production. Increasing cytoplasmic haemoglobin concentration normally acts as an inhibitor of normoblast division. The failure of haemoglobin synthesis that results from iron deficiency therefore allows extra mitoses to occur, with the production of small erythrocytes. The same mechanism is responsible for the microcytes in thalassaemia, another disorder of haemoglobin synthesis.

Blood and bone marrow changes

The typical blood picture is one of microcytic, hypochromic red cells, with increased anisocytosis and poikilocytosis; elongated 'pencil' or 'cigar' cells are typically present (Figs 23.3 and 23.16). The proportion of polychromatic cells (or reticulocytes) is low for the degree of anaemia, indicating an inability of the bone marrow to respond due to lack of iron for haemoglobin synthesis. The platelet count is often raised, especially if chronic bleeding is present. The leukocytes are typically normal.

Occasionally, a mixture of microcytic, hypochromic erythrocytes and macrocytic cells is seen. This is termed a dimorphic picture and occurs in mixed deficiency of iron and folic acid or vitamin B_{12}. The MCV and MCH may be misleadingly normal.

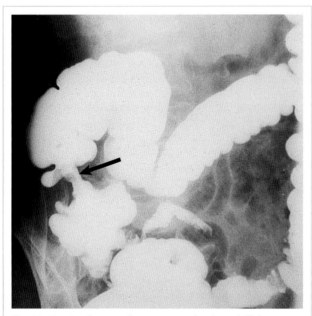

Fig. 23.15   Carcinoma of caecum causing iron deficiency anaemia. An annular carcinoma can be seen as a lesion that causes narrowing of the barium-filled bowel (arrowed) and from which blood loss has occurred.

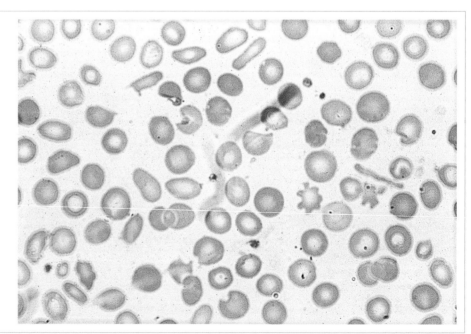

Fig. 23.16   The blood in iron deficiency: microcytic hypochromic anaemia. There is central pallor of the erythrocytes and poikilocytosis with elongated (pencil or cigar) cells.

A mixture of microcytic, hypochromic cells and normocytes is present in iron deficiency responding to iron replacement or after transfusion of a subject with iron deficiency anaemia (Fig. 23.17). In the former circumstance, mildly increased polychromasia (and reticulocytosis) may be present.

Abnormalities are also present in the bone marrow. The nucleated red cell precursors are small in diameter and the cytoplasm is frequently ragged—micronormoblastic erythropoiesis. Staining for haemosiderin (Perls' stain) reveals its absence from macrophages and normoblasts.

Important biochemical changes in the blood are a fall in serum iron and increase in total iron-binding capacity (representing a compensatory increased transferrin concentration). Saturation of iron-binding capacity is thus reduced to 10% or less, from the normal 33%. The serum ferritin is generally markedly reduced, corresponding to severely depleted body iron content. This situation contrasts with the anaemia associated with chronic inflammatory disease or neoplasia ('anaemia of chronic disorders'), where red cells are often normocytic but may be mildly microcytic. The serum iron may also be low but this is misleading as iron stores are normal. In contrast to iron deficiency, total iron-binding capacity is usually reduced in anaemia of chronic disorders, and serum ferritin is often raised due to the presence of inflammation or malignancy.

Changes in other organs and tissues

In addition to the manifestations of chronic anaemia, a variety of epithelial changes may be present in chronic iron deficiency:

- angular cheilitis
- atrophic glossitis
- oesophageal web
- gastric achlorhydria
- brittle nails
- koilonychia.

The cause of these phenomena is unknown. Angular cheilitis (Fig. 23.18), painful fissuring of the mouth corners, is common but not specific: it occurs in dental malocclusion, most often due to poorly fitting dentures. Smooth tongue is also common (Fig. 23.18). Gastric achlorhydria appears to be an occasional result, as well as a contributory cause, of iron deficiency.

Dysphagia (difficulty in swallowing) due to the presence of a web or fold of mucosa in the post-cricoid region is an uncommon association of iron deficiency. The combination has been termed Paterson–Kelly or Plummer–Vinson syndrome and is important mainly because the mucosal abnormality is premalignant, carcinoma occasionally developing at the site.

Koilonychia (spoon-shaped nails) of chronic tissue iron depletion is typical but only rarely seen.

The pathological changes of iron deficiency are reversed by adequate replacement therapy by the oral route.

Vitamin B$_{12}$ and folate deficiency

- ▶ Result in a macrocytic anaemia with marrow megaloblasts
- ▶ Nucleic acid synthesis for cell division is defective
- ▶ B$_{12}$ deficiency is most commonly due to Addisonian pernicious anaemia
- ▶ Folate deficiency is most commonly due to poor diet or increased requirements
- ▶ Pancytopenia is common
- ▶ Neurological involvement (subacute combined degeneration of the spinal cord, peripheral neuropathy) in B$_{12}$ deficiency only

Vitamin B$_{12}$ and folic acid are essential co-factors for blood cell production. Deficiency of either results in macrocytic anaemia with characteristic pathological appearances in the bone marrow described as *megaloblastic haemopoiesis*. Megaloblastic anaemias are common, being second in incidence only to iron deficiency and the so-called anaemia of chronic disorders among production failure anaemias. Some other disorders may be associated with macrocytosis

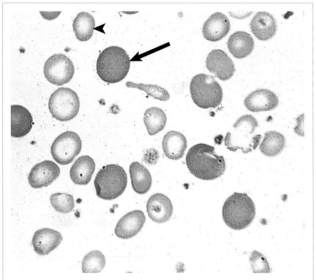

Fig. 23.17 A dimorphic blood film in iron deficiency anaemia responding to oral iron therapy. Hypochromic microcytes (arrowhead) and normocytes (arrow) are present.

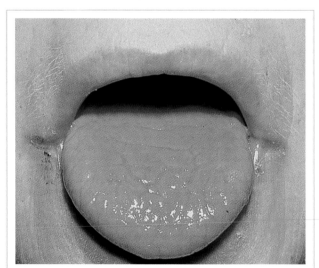

Fig. 23.18 Angular cheilitis and smooth tongue in iron deficiency.

(Fig. 23.3) but megaloblastic haemopoiesis is most commonly due to deficiency of vitamin B_{12} or folate.

Vitamin B_{12} deficiency

Vitamin B_{12} metabolism

Vitamin B_{12} is necessary for DNA synthesis. Deoxyadenosylcobalamin is the main form of vitamin B_{12} in tissues and methylcobalamin is the main form in plasma. These forms differ only in the type of chemical group (deoxyadenosyl or methyl) attached to the cobalt atom which is located at the centre of a corrin ring, to which a nucleotide portion is attached. (The corrin ring is similar to the porphyrin ring of haem.) The vitamin is known to be a coenzyme in the methylation of homocysteine to methionine and also in conversion of methylmalonyl CoA to succinyl CoA. During the former reaction, methylcobalamin loses its methyl group and this is replaced from methyltetrahydrofolic acid, the principal form of folic acid in plasma. The tetrahydrofolic acid is essential for the generation of deoxythymidine monophosphate, a precursor of DNA. Metabolism of vitamin B_{12} and of folate are thus closely related and essential for nucleic acid production (Fig. 23.19).

Vitamin B_{12} is present in foods of animal origin. It cannot be synthesised by higher animals but is produced by micro-organisms. Animals obtain the vitamin from bacterially contaminated foods. Cereals, fruit and vegetable foods contain no vitamin B_{12} unless they have undergone bacterial contamination. Milk and eggs contain sufficient vitamin B_{12} for human needs (1–2 mg daily) and thus dietary deficiency can occur only if a strictly vegetarian (vegan) diet is consumed. Nutritional vitamin B_{12} deficiency (in contrast to dietary folate deficiency) is thus rarely encountered.

Vitamin B_{12} released from food in the stomach becomes bound to a glycoprotein produced by gastric parietal cells —intrinsic factor. The complex of cobalamin and intrinsic factor binds to receptors on the mucosal cells of the terminal ileum, where vitamin B_{12} is absorbed and intrinsic factor remains in the lumen of the bowel. In the absence of intrinsic factor, cobalamin cannot be absorbed.

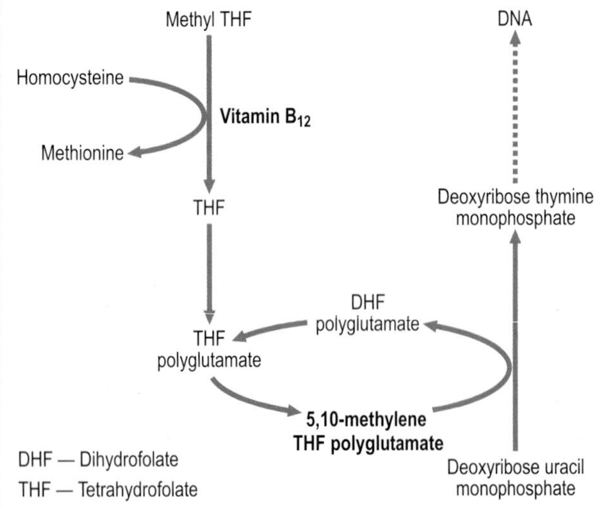

Vitamin B_{12} is transported to the tissues attached to a plasma-binding protein—transcobalamin II. Another transcobalamin (transcobalamin I), synthesised by neutrophil granulocytes, binds the greater proportion of plasma vitamin B_{12} but does not liberate it efficiently. The function of transcobalamin I-bound vitamin B_{12} is unknown.

Body stores of vitamin B_{12} amount only to some 2–3 mg. However, only 1 μg daily is required for normal DNA synthesis. Several years must therefore have elapsed before a deficiency state develops, even in the absence of absorption of the vitamin. Twenty micrograms or more per day is available in a mixed diet.

Mechanisms of vitamin B_{12} deficiency

Causes of vitamin B_{12} deficiency are:

- pernicious anaemia due to lack of intrinsic factor
- gastrectomy resulting in lack of intrinsic factor
- congenital due to lack of intrinsic factor
- blind-loop syndrome due to bacterial overgrowth competing for vitamin B_{12}
- ileal resection resulting in lack of absorption site
- Crohn's disease resulting in lack of absorption site
- tropical sprue
- malnutrition (e.g. dietary deficiency of vitamin B_{12} in veganism).

Addisonian pernicious anaemia accounts for by far the majority of cases of megaloblastic anaemia due to deficiency of vitamin B_{12}. Other causes are uncommon. Some cases occur after gastric resection, usually total gastrectomy. Blind loops of bowel have previously been the result of gastric surgery and this is now a rare cause of vitamin B_{12} deficiency, with improvements in the medical and surgical management of gastric and duodenal disease.

Addisonian pernicious anaemia is a common disorder in which chronic atrophic gastritis and failure of intrinsic factor synthesis lead to malabsorption of vitamin B_{12} and, after several years, the development of megaloblastic anaemia. Untreated, this was severe and eventually fatal; the condition was indeed 'pernicious' but is now easily corrected by injections of vitamin B_{12}.

Pernicious anaemia is due to an autoimmune process, resulting in atrophy of the chief and parietal glands of the stomach, with consequent failure of acid and intrinsic factor production. An auto-antibody to parietal cells is present in the serum in the majority of cases, but is not specific to this disorder. Antibodies to intrinsic factor are present in 50–70% of cases and much more specific to pernicious anaemia. Absence of anti-intrinsic factor antibodies does not exclude the diagnosis of pernicious anaemia; however, in cases where it is not identified, malabsorption of vitamin B_{12} can be detected by the Schilling test which measures absorption of an oral dose both in isolation and combined with intrinsic factor. Malabsorption that is corrected by the addition of intrinsic factor is due to pernicious anaemia; malabsorption that is not corrected is due to another cause.

The disease is rather more common in females and rarely presents before 30 years of age, although an uncommon

Fig. 23.19 The roles of vitamin B_{12} and folate in DNA synthesis.

childhood form is occasionally seen. The patient may have another autoimmune disorder such as thyroid disease or vitiligo. There is an association with blue eyes and premature greying of hair.

Blood and bone marrow changes

In contrast to iron deficiency, the defect in DNA synthesis affects all cell lines, and pancytopenia is frequently present. The MCV is high, and oval macrocytes are visible on the blood film (Figs 23.3 and 23.20). In megaloblastic anaemia, a reduction in the number of mitoses during red cell development, due to impaired DNA synthesis with normal RNA and protein synthesis, results in the production of macrocytes. The degree of polychromasia on the blood film is not appropriate to the severity of anaemia, because the marrow is unable to respond.

A proportion of neutrophil leukocytes have exaggerated lobulation of the nucleus and are often large (neutrophil hypersegmentation). Rarely, the blood picture is leukoeryth-roblastic.

The bone marrow is hypercellular and the stained smears reveal the characteristic megaloblastic change of the developing red cells (Fig. 23.21): the red cells are larger than normal at each stage of development; nuclear chromatin has a very open appearance, with little condensation, and nuclear development lags behind that of the cytoplasm; thus well-haemoglobinised cells with an immature nucleus are a feature. Multilobed polymorphonuclear leukocytes may be seen, as well as particularly large metamyelocytes and band cells. Megakaryocytes may also appear abnormal.

Biochemical abnormalities detectable in the serum include unconjugated hyperbilirubinaemia and increased concentration of lactic dehydrogenase. These changes are due to increased cell breakdown within the marrow, called ineffective erythropoiesis, and the premature removal of macrocytes, in the reticulo-endothelial system. The serum concentration of vitamin B_{12} is reduced.

Changes in other organs and tissues

Lesions of the nervous system are a frequent feature of vitamin B_{12} deficiency from any cause. Myelin degeneration of the posterior and lateral columns of the spinal cord is typical and often associated with a peripheral neuropathy affecting sensory neurones. This *subacute combined degeneration of the cord* causes spasticity, reduced coordination and impaired sensation in the lower limbs and may be present despite normal haemoglobin levels, although the megaloblastic erythropoiesis is always detectable. Conversely, extreme megaloblastic change and profound pancytopenia may be present without evidence of damage to the nervous system from vitamin B_{12} deficiency. Optic atrophy and cerebral changes resulting in psychiatric disease are less common accompaniments of deficiency of vitamin B_{12}. The cause may be failure of synthesis of S-adenosyl methionine necessary for myelin formation. Deficiency of folate is *not generally* associated with the neurological features seen in

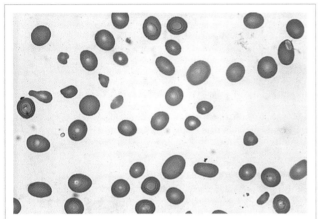

Fig. 23.20 A macrocytic blood film in megaloblastic anaemia. Oval macrocytes and neutrophil nuclear hypersegmentation (Fig. 23.7) are typical.

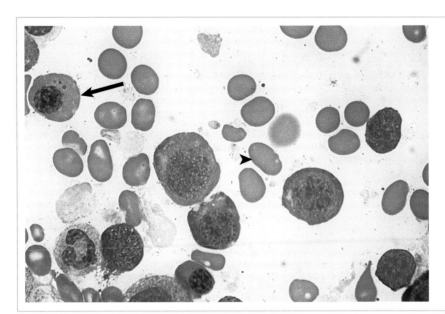

Fig. 23.21 Bone marrow appearances in megaloblastic anaemia from a vitamin B_{12}-deficient patient. The megaloblasts are extremely large red cell precursors and the nucleus has a very open, speckled pattern. Although some of the megaloblasts are well haemoglobinised, the nucleus is still present, suggesting nuclear/cytoplasmic developmental asynchrony (arrow). The more mature non-nucleated red cells are also large and oval in shape—oval macrocytes (arrowhead).

cobalamin deficiency, although psychiatric abnormalities may occur.

Mucosal abnormalities may be present. Atrophic glossitis is a common feature. In pernicious anaemia there is atrophy of the glands of the gastric body affecting chief cells and parietal cells; there is replacement by mucus-secreting goblet cells. The intestinal epithelial cells are often larger than normal, reflecting megaloblastic change akin to that in the bone marrow.

In addition to the above, changes may be present in the heart and elsewhere due to the chronic hypoxia of severe anaemia. Cardiomyopathy is a particularly important feature; transfusion is tolerated badly due to volume overload and may result in fatal cardiac failure.

The clinical features of B_{12} deficiency are explained by the pathology, although it is unusual for all features to be present together:

- lethargy, breathlessness and cardiac failure due to megaloblastic erythropoiesis with anaemia
- bruising and mucosal haemorrhage due to thrombocytopenia in severe cases
- weight loss due to malabsorption resulting from mucosal changes
- sore mouth due to mucosal changes
- sensory impairment in the feet, altered gait, visual disturbance and dementia due to demyelination and axonal degeneration.

Treatment is by parenteral (intramuscular) administration of vitamin B_{12}. Oral replacement is ineffective in pernicious anaemia due to the deficiency of intrinsic factor.

The haematological abnormalities are completely reversed by vitamin B_{12} replacement; however, the neuropathology and associated clinical features may only be partly corrected. The gastric atrophy and achlorhydria are primary features in pernicious anaemia, not secondary to the deficiency state, and as such do not reverse on treatment of the deficiency. There is a life-long slightly increased risk of carcinoma of the stomach.

The haematological response is manifested by a marked increase in the reticulocyte count 2–3 days after administration of vitamin B_{12} and maximal at 7 days; the rise is proportional to the severity of the anaemia. White cell and platelet counts recover within several days and haemoglobin increases at about 10 g/l each week, with an accompanying fall in the MCV to normal values. Erythropoiesis is already normoblastic within 48 hours of starting replacement therapy.

Folic acid deficiency

Deficiency of folic (pteroylglutamic) acid, the parent compound of folates, causes a macrocytic anaemia with megaloblastic haemopoiesis identical to that resulting from deficiency of cobalamin.

Folate metabolism
Folates are required for DNA synthesis. Folate polyglutamates (pteroylglutamic acid with extra glutamic acid residues) are the main intracellular forms. However, all dietary folates are metabolised to the monoglutamate methyltetrahydrofolate during absorption from the gut and are transported in this form. Folates are necessary for single carbon unit transfer reactions in amino acid interconversions, in purine synthesis and, crucially, in the thymidylate synthetase reaction.

Humans cannot synthesise folates de novo. Vegetables and fruits are especially rich in folates as polyglutamate conjugates, but most foods contain some folate. Absorption occurs in the proximal jejunum. Dietary polyglutamates are, however, very sensitive to heat, and cooking can markedly deplete foods of their available folate.

Body stores of folate, mainly in the liver, are modest, amounting to some 10 mg. As up to 200 μg is required daily, a deficiency state can develop within weeks, in contrast to deficiency of vitamin B_{12}. Furthermore, folate requirements are markedly increased in pregnancy and in some diseases associated with increased cell turnover, such as chronic haemolysis.

Mechanisms of folic acid deficiency
Causes of folate deficiency are:

- malnutrition (e.g. poor diet, overcooking of food, alcoholism)
- malabsorption (e.g. coeliac disease, tropical sprue, Crohn's disease)
- increased requirements (e.g. pregnancy and lactation, haemolytic anaemias, myelofibrosis, malignancy, extensive psoriasis or dermatitis)
- drugs (e.g. anticonvulsants).

Whereas malnutrition is an unusual cause of deficiency of vitamin B_{12}, it is the most common mechanism of folate deficiency. It is most prevalent in the elderly. Overcooking of food and lack of fresh foods contribute.

During pregnancy, folate and iron deficiency may occur if no supplements are given. In contrast, vitamin B_{12} deficiency is almost unknown, as fertility is impaired in vitamin B_{12} deficiency and the commonest cause, pernicious anaemia, is a disease of late middle age and after.

In some disorders the folate deficiency is likely to be multifactorial, as in malignant disease, where lack of appetite with resultant malnutrition may aggravate folate deficiency secondary to increased utilisation of folate by the malignant tissues.

Phenytoin and phenobarbital used long term as anticonvulsants probably impair folate absorption and may interfere with folate metabolism.

Some anti-cancer drugs act as folic acid antagonists. Methotrexate inhibits the enzyme dihydrofolate reductase, thus depleting tetrahydrofolate. The antimalarial pyrimethamine acts similarly. Trimethoprim acts as a folate inhibitor in bacteria but is ineffective as an inhibitor in humans.

Blood and bone marrow
In folic acid deficiency, blood and bone marrow changes are indistinguishable from those in vitamin B_{12} deficiency. The concentration of folic acid in serum and erythrocytes (red cell folate) is reduced.

Oral folic acid supplements result in a complete reversal of the pathological features. Even in malabsorption states, sufficient folate can be absorbed from pharmacological doses. The time course of the response is identical to that in vitamin B_{12} deficiency.

Table 23.5 Comparison of features of vitamin B$_{12}$ and folic acid deficiency states

Feature	Cobalamin (vitamin B$_{12}$) deficiency	Folate deficiency
Nutritional deficiency	Uncommon	Common
Onset	Slow (years)	More rapid (weeks)
Revealed by increased demands	Never	Frequently
Absorption	In terminal ileum as a complex with intrinsic factor. Gastric and terminal ileal disease (e.g. autoimmune gastritis, Crohn's disease) may cause deficiency	In jejunum. Jejunal disease (e.g. coeliac disease) may cause deficiency
Drug-related	Never	May be due to anticonvulsant therapy. Anti-metabolites induce a similar deficiency
Spinal cord and peripheral nerve degeneration	Frequent	None

Contrasting features of vitamin B$_{12}$ and folate deficiency are listed in Table 23.5.

Megaloblastic anaemia is the result of deficiency of vitamin B$_{12}$ or folate in the vast majority of instances. However, other causes include drugs and congenital defects. Prolonged anaesthesia with N$_2$O causes inactivation of vitamin B$_{12}$ by oxidising the cobalt moiety and has resulted in pancytopenia with megaloblastic erythropoiesis. Cases of congenital deficiency of enzymes involved in cobalamin or folate metabolism or purine or pyrimidine synthesis are extremely rare. However, several anti-neoplastic drugs act by inhibition of synthesis of purine or pyrimidine (hydroxyurea, cytosine arabinoside) and can cause reversible marrow pathology similar to megaloblastic haemopoiesis.

Anaemia of chronic disorders

Anaemia of chronic disorders is one of the most common anaemias. It is found in association with a range of chronic inflammatory diseases, especially connective tissue disorders, chronic infections such as osteomyelitis or tuberculosis, and malignancies such as carcinoma and lymphoma. Anaemia is not severe; the haemoglobin concentration is 80 g/l or greater and the red cells are normocytic and normochromic. A degree of microcytosis and hypochromia may be present, but never to the degree seen in iron deficiency. Bone marrow iron is plentiful. If the underlying chronic disorder remits, the anaemia resolves. It may also respond to pharmacological doses of erythropoietin.

The disorder may represent a cytokine-induced failure of transfer of iron from reticulo-endothelial cells to normoblasts. This is supported by recent evidence showing that the inflammatory cytokine IL-6 stimulates the production of hepcidin from the liver which then inhibits release of iron from iron-exporting cells (Fig. 23.14). It has also been shown that some cytokines, such as tumour necrosis factor (TNF), can induce apoptosis of erythroblasts. Indeed, treatment of rheumatoid disease with anti-TNF leads to improvement in anaemia. This type of anaemia occurs in disorders frequently associated with other types of anaemia, resulting in a complicated picture. For example, in rheumatoid arthritis iron deficiency often accompanies anaemia of chronic disorders due to the gastric irritation and bleeding caused by anti-inflammatory medications. There may be folate deficiency due to poor diet, and hypersplenism and immune haemolytic anaemia may also be present.

Dyserythropoietic anaemias

The term dyserythropoietic anaemias is used to describe disorders where anaemia is at least in part due to production failure, but haematinic deficiency is not present and marrow cellularity is normal or increased. There are prominent morphological abnormalities of bone marrow cells, often affecting erythroid, myeloid and megakaryocytic cell lines. Most of these conditions are classified as myelodysplastic syndromes (MDS) and described in the section on MDS below.

Sideroblastic anaemias

The term sideroblastic anaemias describes a rather diverse and uncommon group of anaemias in which a defect of haem synthesis is present and a characteristic cell is seen in the bone marrow—the *ring sideroblast*. This cell is a nucleated red cell precursor that has granules of haemosiderin within mitochondria surrounding the nucleus, visible on staining with Perls' reagent. Causes include:

- refractory anaemia with ring sideroblasts (RARS) and refractory cytopenia with multi-lineage dysplasia and ring sideroblasts (RCMD-RS); these are acquired clonal abnormalities of the bone marrow
- secondary in patients with a bone marrow malignancy (e.g. myeloma, myeloid leukaemia, etc.)
- those due to drugs and toxins (e.g. vitamin B$_6$ antagonism by isoniazid; lead poisoning which inhibits synthesis of haem; alcoholism)
- hereditary due to enzyme defect in haem synthesis.

Although deficiency of vitamin B_6 (pyridoxine) causes a similar anaemia in animals, it is never the cause in humans. However, vitamin B_6 antagonism can result from antituberculous therapy, and other sideroblastic anaemias occasionally respond partially to pharmacological doses of vitamin B_6.

RARS/RCMD-RS are primary acquired sideroblastic anaemias which are classified among the myelodysplastic syndromes. These are neoplastic disorders of bone marrow in which dyserythropoiesis is prominent. They are described on page 663.

Hypoplastic anaemia

Hypoplastic (aplastic) anaemia is pancytopenia (anaemia, neutropenia and thrombocytopenia) resulting from bone marrow hypoplasia of variable severity. Hypoplastic anaemia probably results from failure or suppression of pluripotent stem cells. Very occasionally, the defect appears to affect cells committed to the erythroid series only, when 'pure red cell aplasia' results.

The cause is often unknown; however, it is occasionally congenital or due to poisoning, an associated viral infection or to iatrogenic causes. Thus, hypoplastic anaemia may be:

- idiopathic
- due to chemical agents (e.g. benzene, cytotoxic drugs, chloramphenicol)
- due to ionising radiation
- due to infection such as hepatitis virus and parvovirus
- congenital (Fanconi anaemia).

Most cases caused by anti-neoplastic drugs are reversible. Aplasia is also often a feature of the rare disorder paroxysmal nocturnal haemoglobinuria, a clonal disorder of bone marrow.

In idiopathic forms of hypoplastic anaemia there is strong evidence that T-lymphocytes are involved in the suppression of stem cells. As such idiopathic aplastic anaemia is recognised as a form of autoimmune disease. Some 15% of patients have an associated hepatitis as demonstrated by rises in liver transaminases, also thought to be autoimmune. Immunosuppressive therapy with anti-thymocyte globulin (ATG) is successful in idiopathic aplastic anaemia and is the mainstay of treatment for most patients.

The reason for an idiosyncratic response to some drugs is unknown. Chloramphenicol, an antibiotic, and gold, used in treatment of rheumatoid arthritis, are especially likely to produce marrow aplasia, often irreversible. Infection with parvovirus causes a transient suppression of erythropoiesis; this suppression is brief and clinically insignificant in otherwise healthy subjects. However, where red cell survival is markedly shortened, as in sickle cell disease, such infection may cause a catastrophic fall in haemoglobin. Aplastic anaemia is a rare late complication of viral hepatitis.

There is anaemia (normocytic or slightly macrocytic), leukopenia (including lymphopenia in severe cases) and thrombocytopenia. There is reduced polychromasia, especially in relation to the degree of anaemia, and the reticulocyte count is very low. Morphologically abnormal cells are not a feature.

Marrow aspiration often fails. Trephine biopsy reveals increased fat spaces and little residual marrow activity, although a few small clusters of haemopoietic cells occasionally remain.

Clinically, anaemia, infections and bleeding due to thrombocytopenia occur. Splenomegaly and lymphadenopathy are absent. Without successful treatment of the aplasia, severe forms are fatal within months. Spontaneous remission occasionally occurs. Immunosuppression is the mainstay of treatment for idiopathic aplastic anaemia. Bone marrow transplantation can be curative but is generally reserved for children and young adults with severe aplasia.

Anaemia due to bone marrow infiltration

Not infrequently, carcinoma and lymphoma involve the bones and bone marrow (Fig. 23.22). A leukoerythroblastic blood picture may result. In carcinomatosis, numerous other factors

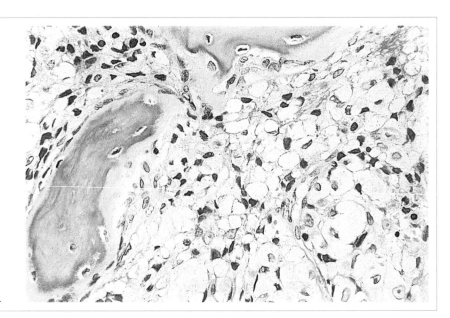

Fig. 23.22   Carcinoma cells infiltrating bone marrow. Sheets of non-haemopoietic carcinoma cells replace normal bone marrow.

are likely to be contributory to the anaemia, such as bleeding from carcinoma of the gastrointestinal tract, folate deficiency and chemotherapy.

In myelofibrosis the marrow is replaced by reticulin and collagen. Fibrosis of the marrow is also a feature of other myeloproliferative disorders and some other malignant marrow infiltrates.

Other causes of marrow infiltration are very uncommon, e.g. Gaucher's disease, a metabolic defect where glucocerebroside accumulates in the reticulo-endothelial cells of many organs (Ch. 7).

ANAEMIAS DUE TO INCREASED CELL LOSS, LYSIS OR POOLING

The haemolytic states are the main members of the group of anaemias due to increased cell loss, lysis or pooling. However, anaemia due to acute blood loss and the pancytopenia of hypersplenism are also conveniently included.

A fall in haemoglobin of much greater than 10 g/l per week must indicate the presence of haemorrhage or haemolysis, as complete cessation of erythropoiesis would result in a rate of fall of no more than 10 g/l per week. An exception is the rapid fall in haematocrit due to infusion of cell-free fluids in a dehydrated subject.

Acute blood loss anaemia

Chronic haemorrhage, usually gastrointestinal, causes anaemia by depletion of iron stores. Acute blood loss may result initially in a state of cardiovascular collapse, as described in an earlier section. Following adjustment to the plasma volume over a period up to 48 hours, anaemia will be apparent. The blood picture is normocytic and normochromic, and an increased number of polychromatic erythrocytes and reticulocytes in the days following a brisk haemorrhage reflects increased haemopoiesis. Transient leukocytosis and thrombocytosis commonly occur.

Haemolytic anaemias

> ► Characterised by a reduction in red cell life-span
> ► Classified into hereditary red cell disorders and acquired haemolytic states due to a defect outwith the red cell
> ► Important hereditary haemolytic disorders include sickle cell disease, thalassaemias and spherocytosis
> ► Important acquired haemolytic disorders include autoimmune haemolytic anaemias, malaria and microangiopathic haemolytic anaemias
> ► Normocytic anaemia with increased reticulocytes and hyperbilirubinaemia is typical
> ► Splenomegaly is commonly present

The haemolytic anaemias are those in which a major feature is a reduction in red cell life-span. In severe haemolysis red cell survival may be reduced from the normal 120 days to less than 1 day. Although erythropoiesis will increase, anaemia is inevitable under such circumstances. Even in the presence of normal marrow function and adequate supplies of haematinics, the maximum potential increase in red cell production is some six times the normal rate. In the presence of a defect of red cell production, as in folate deficiency or thalassaemia major, the severity of the anaemia is increased in relation to the degree of shortening of red cell survival.

Classification and incidence

Haemolytic anaemias can be divided usefully into those due to a defect of the red cell itself and those due to an abnormality outside the red cell (Table 23.4). Almost all of the former are hereditary; an exception is the uncommon acquired disease paroxysmal nocturnal haemoglobinuria (PNH). Those due to mechanisms 'outside' the red cell are acquired disorders.

The relative incidence of haemolytic anaemias is highly variable geographically. In the UK the acquired haemolytic states, especially autoimmune haemolytic anaemias, are relatively common disorders. Worldwide, however, thalassaemia, sickle cell disease and malaria are of major importance.

Consequences of haemolysis

In addition to the particular pathological and clinical features of the various haemolytic diseases, certain consequences of the haemolytic process and the response to it are common to all types of haemolytic disorder. These consequences are:

- raised serum bilirubin (unconjugated) resulting in the formation of pigment gallstones
- raised urine urobilinogen
- raised faecal stercobilinogen
- absent serum haptoglobin, which binds haemoglobin; the complex is removed by the liver
- splenomegaly
- reticulocytosis in peripheral blood
- erythroid hyperplasia in bone marrow, causing bone deformity in children in extreme cases, especially thalassaemia.

Red cell destruction occurs predominantly in the reticulo-endothelial tissues of the spleen and liver. Splenomegaly is therefore common in chronic haemolytic anaemia, and hepatomegaly may also be present. Within the spleen there is congestion within the cords and deposition of haemosiderin.

Less commonly, the red cells are destroyed within the circulation. Examples are haemolytic red cell antibody in major blood group mismatch, the presence of a foreign surface such as a (malfunctioning) artificial heart valve, malaria and glucose-6-phosphate dehydrogenase deficiency. Particular features of intravascular haemolysis are the presence of free haemoglobin in plasma and urine (haemoglobinaemia, haemoglobinuria), of methaemalbumin in plasma (oxidised haem bound to albumin) and of haemosiderin in urine (in shed renal tubular cells that have reabsorbed haemoglobin from the tubular contents; the haem is incorporated into haemosiderin).

Haemolytic anaemia due to red cell defects

The major components of the erythrocyte are haemoglobin, enzymes involved in protection of haemoglobin from oxidant stress, and the plasma membrane. Abnormalities of each of these components can be a cause of chronic haemolytic anaemia.

Defects of the red cell membrane

Hereditary spherocytosis and *hereditary elliptocytosis* include several disorders in which diminished red cell survival is due to a defect in one of the structural proteins of the erythrocyte membrane such as *spectrin*. Inheritance is dominant. Spherocytosis is the most common cause of hereditary haemolytic anaemia among Caucasians in the UK. Spherocytes are not confined to hereditary spherocytosis however; they are also present in the blood film in immune haemolytic anaemia (p. 639).

In hereditary spherocytosis, biconcave erythrocytes are released from the marrow but they rapidly lose membrane and therefore assume a spherical shape. Spherocytes are of reduced deformability, which impedes their traverse through the splenic microcirculation. The cells are retained for long periods in the splenic cords. They become metabolically stressed by glucose lack and acidosis, and are eventually prematurely phagocytosed. The abnormal red cells in these disorders are more sensitive than normal to lysis under osmotic stress. This increased osmotic fragility is of diagnostic value.

Anaemia is usual but varies in severity between affected kindreds. The blood film has many spherocytes (Fig. 23.23); they appear smaller than normocytes and denser, with loss of the central pallor. Polychromatic cells are increased. General features of chronic haemolysis are also present. Haemolysis tends to be less severe in elliptocytosis.

The clinical features are variable and are those of chronic extravascular haemolysis. Pigment gallstones commonly develop. The disorder can be subclinical. Occasionally, transient red cell aplasia secondary to parvovirus infection can develop, when several family members may be affected by aplasia simultaneously.

Removal of the spleen results in resolution of the anaemia, confirming the role of the spleen in the haemolytic process. Splenectomy is reserved for cases in which symptoms of anaemia are intolerable.

Defects of red cell enzymes

Defects of red cell enzymes render the erythrocyte susceptible to damage by oxidant compounds. The generation of reduced glutathione by the metabolic activity of the red cell normally inactivates oxidants. Reduced glutathione is generated by the hexose monophosphate shunt of the Embden–Meyerhof glycolytic pathway, which is the source of: energy, as ATP, necessary for maintenance of red cell shape, volume and flexibility; NADH for reduction of oxidised haemoglobin; and 2,3-biphosphoglycerate (2,3-BPG) for the regulation of the oxygen affinity of haemoglobin.

Deficiency of several of the enzymes involved in these reactions has been identified. Only two are of pathological and major clinical significance: glucose-6-phosphate dehydrogenase deficiency and pyruvate kinase deficiency.

Glucose-6-phosphate dehydrogenase deficiency

Deficiency or defect of glucose-6-phosphate dehydrogenase (G6PD) results in impaired reduction of glutathione. Reduced glutathione protects haemoglobin and red cell membrane from oxidative damage. Inherited G6PD deficiency is an uncommon cause of anaemia in the UK but is among the most common genetic disorders worldwide. It is a sex-linked disorder: female heterozygotes are usually asymptomatic and may have some protection from falciparum malaria; this probably explains the high prevalence of the disorder in many parts of the world.

The common isoenzymes are traditionally designated 'type B', the most common, 'type A' and 'type A-minus', found among American blacks (30% and 11% respectively). Type A differs from type B by a single amino acid substitution and is

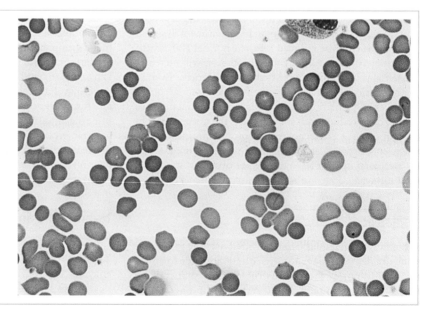

Fig. 23.23 Hereditary spherocytosis. Densely staining spherocytic erythrocytes predominate.

functionally normal. Type A-minus has an additional amino acid substitution resulting in decreased red cell enzyme activity and disease. Typically there is a tendency to the development of an acute haemolytic episode associated with the ingestion of an oxidant drug (for example some antimalarials and anti-biotics) and with other stresses such as surgery or infection. Clinically, a self-limiting episode of anaemia and jaundice develops. Treatment centres on avoidance of exposure to known oxidant drugs.

A further variant is found in Mediterranean populations and is associated with the acute haemolytic tendency known as *favism,* where ingestion of the fava (broad) bean results in acute haemolysis. The responsible oxidant compound has not yet been identified. Again, oxidant drugs, surgical stress and infections may also lead to haemolysis.

Many other less common genetic variants have been recognised. Some result in a more chronic haemolytic state or neonatal jaundice due to haemolysis.

The blood picture during haemolytic crisis includes increased poikilocytosis with contracted red cells, 'bite' cells and 'blister' cells (poikilocytes with bite-shaped defects or surface blebs). Oxidised, denatured haemoglobin is seen as red cell inclusions (Heinz bodies) attached to the cell membrane, when blood is stained supravitally as in the reticulocyte preparation. Haemolysis is generally self-limiting because of the rapid outpouring of new red cells, with higher G6PD content, from the marrow in response to the falling haemoglobin. The blood picture is normal between haemolytic episodes.

Treatment consists essentially of avoidance of known precipitating factors for haemolysis. Health is generally good between haemolytic episodes.

Pyruvate kinase deficiency

Pyruvate kinase (PK) deficiency is an autosomal recessive disorder which results in congenital chronic haemolytic anaemia. The blood film has increased poikilocytosis. The chronic anaemia is associated with increased erythrocyte 2,3-BPG because of the site of the metabolic block. This situation results in reduced oxygen affinity of haemoglobin and increased oxygen delivery to the tissues; the anaemia is thus less symptomatic than would be expected from its severity. No specific treatment is available.

Haemoglobinopathies (abnormal haemoglobins)

Abnormal haemoglobins are caused by a single point mutation in the genetic code resulting in an amino acid substitution in the alpha or beta globin chain of haemoglobin A. Variant haemoglobins can be readily identified by their electrophoretic mobility (Fig. 23.24). Several hundred variant haemoglobins have been identified but few are clinically significant and almost all of those involve beta chain substitutions. Depending on the site of the substitution, four main types of functional defect result:

- a haemoglobin that becomes crystalline at low oxygen tension, e.g. HbS, causing haemolysis and microvascular occlusion
- an unstable haemoglobin causing chronic haemolysis with Heinz bodies (red cell inclusions composed of denatured haemoglobin)

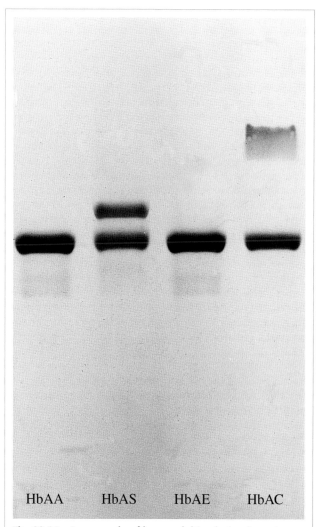

Fig. 23.24 An example of haemoglobin electrophoresis: acid haemoglobin electrophoresis (pH 6.0). This procedure clearly separates haemoglobins S and C from A. The carrier for haemoglobin E cannot be distinguished from AA but would be by performing the procedure at alkaline pH.

- a haemoglobin of increased oxygen affinity causing polycythaemia
- a haemoglobin that tends to the oxidised state (methaemoglobin) causing cyanosis.

The first defect is the most common. HbS is very common worldwide, as are three related haemoglobins: C, D and E.

Sickle cell disease

▶ Due to homozygous inheritance of a gene coding for a haemoglobin variant that becomes crystalline at low oxygen tensions
▶ Characterised by episodes of tissue infarction and chronic haemolysis
▶ The heterozygous state (sickle cell trait) is associated with normal full blood count and no symptoms

Substitution of valine for glutamic acid in position 6 in the beta chain of globin results in a haemoglobin (HbS) that undergoes aggregation and polymerisation at low oxygen tensions. In the homozygote for sickle cell disease, where the majority of the haemoglobin content of the erythrocytes is HbS, this results in distortion of the red cells, which acquire a sickle shape. The consequence of this distortion and the predominant features of sickle cell disease are a chronic haemolytic anaemia and microvascular occlusion, causing ischaemic tissue damage. The results of the latter dominate the clinical picture.

The gene for HbS is common in the West and Central African populations, the Mediterranean, Middle East and some parts of the Indian subcontinent. Carriage of the gene may confer some protection against falciparum malaria. The gene is carried by 8% of black Americans and 30% of black Africans. The heterozygous state, or *sickle cell trait*, results in less than 40% HbS, the remainder being mostly normal HbA. Two major bands are therefore present on electrophoresis of haemoglobin: one corresponding to HbS and one to HbA. The carrier is clinically and haematologically essentially normal, sickling occurring only very uncommonly and only under conditions of severe hypoxia. Haematuria is an occasional feature, due to renal papillary necrosis from focal sickling in the renal medulla. Hypoxic sickling in heterozygotes is an avoidable risk of general anaesthesia.

In the homozygote the haemoglobin concentration is low (70–90 g/l). Sickle cells and target cells are present on the blood film, as are features of hyposplenism in the adult (Fig. 23.25). (Splenomegaly due to chronic haemolysis is present during childhood but the spleen shrinks progressively due to microvascular occlusion and infarction.) Even in infancy children with sickle cell disease are functionally hyposplenic with an increased risk of capsulate organism infection. The bone marrow is hyperplastic with erythroid hyperplasia. Extramedullary erythropoiesis in the liver and, occasionally, other sites is a minor feature. Pathological changes in other organs result from the effects of local ischaemia (Fig. 23.26). Haemoglobin electrophoresis reveals a characteristic single band of HbS.

Clinical features. These are predictable from the above. There is anaemia and jaundice from infancy. Sickle 'crises' of various clinical types occur from an early age. Vascular occlusion with resultant ischaemia causes severe pain, often in the long bones, abdomen or chest. Ischaemic stroke is common. There is convincing evidence that transcranial arterial Doppler ultrasonography can identify children at increased risk of stroke manifested by increased Doppler flow rates. Introduction of an exchange red cell transfusion programme can reduce this risk. Acute sequestration of sickle cells in the liver or (in children) spleen may cause pain and acute exacerbation of anaemia. Between episodes of crisis, health may be good. Cholecystitis, due to the presence of pigment stones, is a frequent occurrence. As in pyruvate kinase deficiency, oxygen affinity of the haemoglobin is low and symptoms of anaemia mild, due to the relatively enhanced O_2 delivery to tissues. Premature death, often from respiratory complications, may occur in early middle age, but longer survival is a feature in some populations.

Treatment. This is essentially conservative, with avoidance of factors known to precipitate crises, especially hypoxia, and provision of warmth and rehydration during crises. Pregnancy may be complicated by an increased tendency to acute sickle crises. Use of vasoconstrictor drugs is contraindicated—this is an issue when local anaesthetic containing adrenaline (epinephrine) is being considered. Exchange transfusion of red cells to reduce the proportion of cells capable of sickling is a useful treatment in severe exacerbations such as acute chest syndrome where lung tissue is often sequestered following the development of infection. In sickle cell disease, a relatively high proportion of HbF in erythrocytes is associated with a less severe clinical course. Hydroxyurea is a drug used in chemotherapy of some malignancies that increases

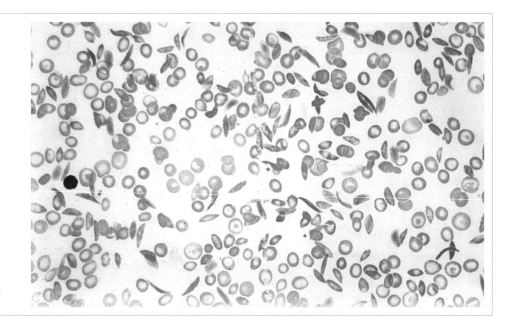

Fig. 23.25   Sickle cell disease (homozygous).

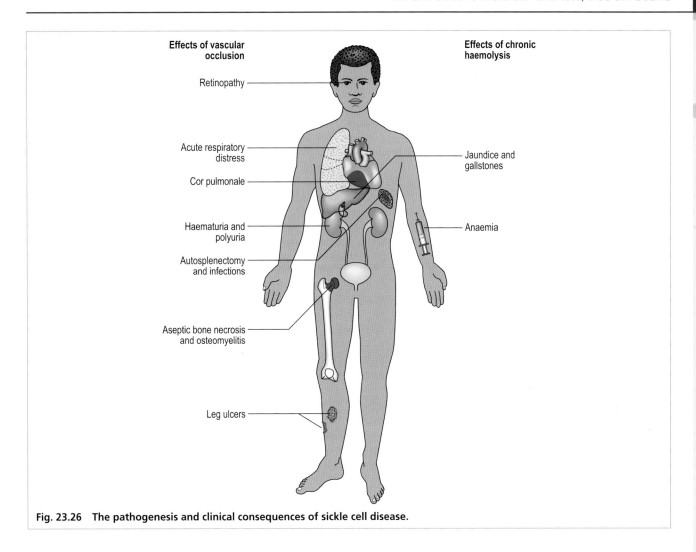

Fig. 23.26 **The pathogenesis and clinical consequences of sickle cell disease.**

HbF. It reduces the tendency to acute sickle crises in some patients with sickle cell disease.

Haemoglobin C, D and E. These are also the result of point mutations in the beta chain gene. In the homozygous state they produce mild chronic haemolysis with splenomegaly but without the occlusive manifestations of sickle cell disease. They are commonly found in West Africa, India and South-East Asia respectively. Due to their geographical distribution, the gene for HbC is often inherited with that for HbS. HbS-C disease behaves as a mild sickle disease with a particular tendency to venous thrombosis.

Thalassaemias

- ▶ Due to abnormalities of (alpha or beta) globin chain synthesis
- ▶ Characterised by a microcytic, hypochromic blood picture
- ▶ Beta-thalassaemia major results in severe anaemia from infancy, splenomegaly, marrow expansion with bony deformities and premature death
- ▶ Beta-thalassaemia minor is clinically mild
- ▶ Alpha-thalassaemias include disorders resulting in intra-uterine death from severe anaemia and heart failure and those producing clinically insignificant disease

In contrast to the abnormal haemoglobin states described above, where a structurally abnormal globin is synthesised but at a normal rate, in thalassaemia the globin chains are of normal composition, but the rate at which one of the globin chains (alpha or beta) is synthesised is reduced. In alpha-thalassaemia the alpha globin chain synthesis is so affected; in beta-thalassaemia the beta chain is affected. Accumulation of an excess of the unaffected globin chains results in damage to the developing and mature erythrocytes.

Again, in contrast to 'variant haemoglobin' conditions (such as sickle cell disease) where point mutations affecting coding regions underlie the disorders, in thalassaemias the genetic lesions are of a regulatory nature, affecting the normal *expression* of the globin structural genes.

Each chromosome 16 has a pair of alpha globin genes, thus each cell has four genes coding for alpha globin, all of them functional. The genes for beta globin, as well as those for gamma and delta, are located in close linkage on chromosome 11.

In the alpha-thalassaemia syndromes there is deletion of all four genes or of three of the four. In alpha-thalassaemia trait, there is deletion of two or only one gene (Table 23.6).

More than 200 genetic defects responsible for beta-thalassaemia have now been described, predominantly point mutations, in contrast to the deletions that cause much alpha-thalassaemia. The type of defect tends to vary between racial groups. Some defects result in an absence of chain synthesis (β^0); in others, chain synthesis is severely restricted but present (β^+).

Alpha-thalassaemia. This is an uncommon cause of anaemia in the UK. Red cells are microcytic. Haemoglobin H disease (Table 23.6) is seen mainly in Asian populations. HbH is identifiable on electrophoresis in the 3-gene deletion disorder and HbH inclusion bodies are visible in red cells stained supravitally (as in the reticulocyte preparation) in the 3- and 2-gene deletion forms. Electrophoresis is normal in alpha-thalassaemia trait and the conditions can be confirmed only by direct measurement of rate of synthesis of alpha and beta chains.

Beta-thalassaemia major (Mediterranean or Cooley's anaemia). This is a severe disorder due to the inheritance of two genes for beta-thalassaemia—β^+/β^+, β^0/β^0 or occasionally β^+/β^0. The beta-thalassaemia genes are most frequent in Mediterranean countries, the Middle East and parts of Africa and South-East Asia.

The blood picture is that of a severe microcytic, hypochromic anaemia (haemoglobin concentration 30–60 g/l) developing from 3 to 6 months of age, when beta-chain production would have normally replaced the great majority of gamma chain production, leading to the dominance of Hb A ($\alpha_2\beta_2$) and only 1% residual fetal haemoglobin ($\alpha_2\gamma_2$).

In response to the defective haemoglobin synthesis and haemolysis the red bone marrow is dramatically expanded with gross erythroid hyperplasia. As a result, cortical bone is thinned and new bone deposits on the outer aspect, especially in the skull vault, maxilla and frontal facial bones (Fig. 23.27). Cortical thinning and fractures may develop in the long bones, vertebrae and ribs. The spleen is grossly enlarged, with expansion of the reticulo-endothelial elements and extramedullary erythropoiesis. The liver is similarly affected. Iron overload is apparent and often gross.

Haemoglobin electrophoresis reveals absent or markedly reduced haemoglobin A. Small (normal) amounts of haemoglobin A_2 are present and the remainder of the haemoglobin is F.

Table 23.6 The alpha-thalassaemia disorders

Number of globin genes deleted	Syndrome	Clinicopathological features
4	**Hydrops fetalis**	Death in utero. Congestive cardiac failure secondary to an extreme degree of anaemia. Free gamma chains form tetramers (γ_4, Hb Bart's)
3	**Haemoglobin H disease**	Free beta chains form tetramers (HbH, β_4). Moderate microcytic, hypochromic anaemia. HbH inclusions visible in erythrocytes on supravital staining. Splenomegaly
2	**Alpha-thalassaemia trait**	Normal haemoglobin concentration. Low MCV and MCH. Occasional HbH inclusion visible. A subclinical disorder, resembling beta-thalassaemia minor
1	**Alpha-thalassaemia trait**	Normal haematology or slightly reduced MCV

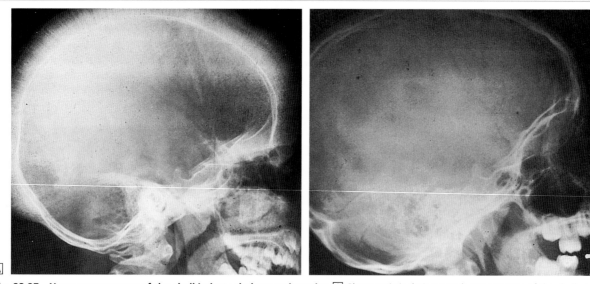

Fig. 23.27 X-ray appearances of the skull in beta-thalassaemia major. **A** Characteristic 'hair-on-end' appearances of the skull vault due to marrow expansion. **B** Normal subject.

Predictably, the clinical features are those of severe anaemia, including growth retardation, and iron overload secondary to red cell transfusion and a tendency to absorb excess iron as a result of the dyserythropoietic state. Secondary iron overload may result in failure of sexual development due to iron deposition in the pituitary and endocrine organs, as well as diabetes mellitus, liver and heart failure. Facial deformities result from the bone changes. Iron chelation therapy to reduce tissue iron is a crucial part of management and has been shown to prolong life when used in trials in thalassaemia major patients. Commonly, it is introduced once serum ferritin has reached 1000 mg (approximately 20–25 units of red cells transfused). Until recently iron chelation could only be efficiently delivered by near continuous subcutaneous infusion of the iron-chelating drug desferrioxamine. However, there are now two orally administered iron chelators available: deferiprone and deferasirox. Bone marrow transplantation has been curative.

Beta-thalassaemia minor. This is mild and most commonly subclinical. The characteristic pathology is gross microcytic and hypochromic change on the blood film with normal or slightly raised red cell count and normal haemoglobin concentration. Mild anaemia may be present during pregnancy, when the condition is often first diagnosed, as it is often the first occasion when the healthy carrier undergoes a routine blood count. The blood picture is very similar to that of iron deficiency but the MCV and MCH are disproportionately low for the level of haemoglobin. Iron stores are normal or high. Bone changes and hepatosplenomegaly are absent. Haemoglobin electrophoresis reveals a raised haemoglobin A_2 concentration (>2.5%). Diagnosis is important in order that genetic counselling can be offered.

Thalassaemia intermedia. The term thalassaemia intermedia describes disease of intermediate severity, often not requiring transfusion and compatible with prolonged survival. Hepatosplenomegaly and iron overload are present. It is genetically heterogeneous, some cases being severely affected heterozygotes, others homozygotes with an unusually mild beta-chain deficiency.

Occasional patients are doubly heterozygous for beta-thalassaemia and HbS. These patients have a variant of sickle cell disease, often with prominent and persisting splenomegaly.

Paroxysmal nocturnal haemoglobinuria

Paroxysmal nocturnal haemoglobinuria is an acquired disorder in which chronic haemolysis is due to a clonal abnormality of erythrocytes that renders them abnormally sensitive to complement lysis. Due to an acquired mutation of the *PIG-A* gene within a stem cell clone, blood cells lack an enzyme required for the synthesis of a phosphatidyl inositol which anchors several proteins to the red cell membrane, including some responsible for complement degradation. Leukocytes and platelets are also affected. The condition is rare and often chronic. Aplastic anaemia, chronic haemolytic anaemia and venous thrombosis in the portal, hepatic or cerebral veins are major features. Haemoglobinuria occurring at night or in early morning is not a common feature, despite the name

(nocturnal) of the disorder. It seems to result from a decrease in plasma pH during the night which promotes complement activation.

The presence of haemosiderinuria and tendency of erythrocytes to lyse at low pH, which activates complement (acid lysis or Ham's test), are useful diagnostically. More commonly nowadays flow cytometry is used to demonstrate the missing phosphatidyl inositol-anchored proteins on cell surfaces, e.g. absence of CD59 or CD55 on red cell surfaces or absence of CD14 on monocyte surfaces. Until recently treatment has been supportive. However, there has been success using an anti-complement (C5) humanised monoclonal antibody (eculizumab). Recent trials of this antibody have shown that it decreases the rate of haemolysis, decreases the red cell transfusion requirement and improves patient quality of life. Historically, death is often ultimately due to sepsis or thrombosis.

Haemolytic anaemia due to a defect outside the red cell

Haemolytic anaemias due to a defect outside the red cell are all acquired disorders.

Immune haemolytic anaemias

> ▸ Red cell damage is immune-mediated
> ▸ Direct antiglobulin (Coombs') test is positive, indicating erythrocyte sensitisation with immunoglobulin or complement
> ▸ In the autoimmune types an auto-antibody causes haemolysis and the clinical features depend on the thermal characteristics of the antibody ('warm' or 'cold' reacting); the disorder may be idiopathic or symptomatic of underlying disease
> ▸ In mismatched blood transfusion and in haemolytic disease of the newborn an allo-antibody causes haemolysis

Immune haemolytic anaemias are due to red cell damage by an antibody. The phenomenon may be *autoimmune,* as in idiopathic and drug-induced autoimmune haemolytic anaemias and cold antibody disorders, or *alloimmune* (where the antibody forms to an antigen foreign to that individual), as in haemolysis due to mismatched blood transfusion and that in haemolytic disease of the newborn (Table 23.7). In all cases the presence of antibody or complement on the red cell surface is confirmed by the direct antiglobulin (or Coombs') test which uses antibodies to human immunoglobulin or complement raised in an animal to cause in vitro agglutination of red cells sensitised with antibody or complement in vivo.

In some (the more common) instances of autoimmune haemolysis the auto-antibody is IgG and most reactive at 37°C—'warm antibody' autoimmune disorders. In 'cold antibody' autoimmune disorders an IgM antibody is active at 4°C, becoming less active at higher temperatures, but is still able to bind complement and agglutinate red cells at the temperature (c. 30°C) of the peripheral tissues (hands, feet, nose, ears).

Antibody-coated cells bind to macrophages of the reticuloendothelial system via Fc receptors. Partial phagocytosis results and the erythrocyte loses some membrane. In order to maintain cellular integrity after this reduction of surface area, a sphere

Table 23.7   The immune haemolytic anaemias

Autoimmune		Alloimmune
'Warm antibody'	'Cold antibody'	
Idiopathic Autoimmune haemolytic anaemia	**Idiopathic** Chronic haemagglutinin disease	Mismatched blood transfusion
Secondary Chronic lymphocytic leukaemia Lymphoma Systemic lupus erythematosus and other autoimmune disorders	**Secondary** Infectious mononucleosis Mycoplasma pneumonia Lymphoma Carcinoma	Haemolytic disease of the newborn
Drug-related e.g. methyl dopa		

is formed. Such spherical red cells are less deformable than normal; they eventually become trapped in the spleen and are removed by phagocytosis.

'Warm antibody' immune haemolytic anaemia

In 'warm antibody' immune haemolytic anaemia, the autoantibody is usually IgG and may or may not bind complement. Red cell destruction occurs in the cells of the reticulo-endothelial system, especially the spleen. Most cases are idiopathic, occurring at any age. There may be a family history of autoimmune disease. In about one-third of instances the process is initiated by a drug or it occurs in association with some other disease, particularly a lymphoproliferative disorder, or collagen vascular disease such as systemic lupus erythematosus or rheumatoid arthritis (Ch. 25).

Drugs can cause the disorder by one of three mechanisms (Fig. 23.28). Withdrawal of the drug results in resolution of the disorder.

The blood picture in warm antibody haemolysis is that of a chronic anaemia with microspherocytes and increased polychromasia (and reticulocytosis). The degree of anaemia is very variable within and between cases but may be extremely severe. Erythroid hyperplasia is marked in the bone marrow; megaloblastic erythropoiesis may supervene, as in all haemolytic anaemias, due to increased folate requirements. The spleen is moderately enlarged and congested. Features of an underlying disorder, such as lymphoma, may also be present.

Clinical features and treatment. The clinical features are those of haemolytic anaemia—pallor, jaundice and splenomegaly. In those instances where a drug cannot be implicated and withdrawn, treatment by immunosuppression with corticosteroids and other immunomodulatory drugs is employed. In some cases splenectomy is successful in reducing the rate of haemolysis.

'Cold antibody' immune haemolytic anaemias

In 'cold antibody' immune haemolytic anaemias, the IgM antibody attaches to red cells in the peripheral circulation and complement is bound. On re-entering the central circulation

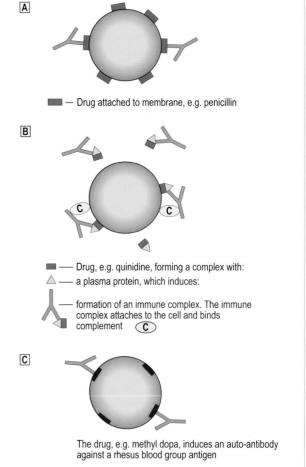

A ▬ — Drug attached to membrane, e.g. penicillin

B ▬ — Drug, e.g. quinidine, forming a complex with:
△ — a plasma protein, which induces:
— formation of an immune complex. The immune complex attaches to the cell and binds complement C

C The drug, e.g. methyl dopa, induces an auto-antibody against a rhesus blood group antigen

Fig. 23.28   Three mechanisms of drug-induced immune haemolysis. **A** The drug acts as a hapten. **B** The drug forms an immune complex which attaches non-specifically to red cells. **C** The drug induces an auto-antibody.

the IgM antibody may become detached, but complement activation leads to red cell destruction in the reticulo-endothelial system. The main consequences of this sequence of events are agglutination of erythrocytes in cooler areas which causes sluggish flow and reduced oxygen saturation, and chronic haemolysis. Severity relates particularly to the thermal amplitude of the antibody, that is its activity at temperatures up to 30°C.

The pathological features are those of chronic haemolysis with a tendency to marked agglutination of red cells on the blood film. If the film is prepared at 37°C the agglutination is no longer present. The reticulocyte count is increased.

Clinical features and treatment. The clinical features are of anaemia and of discoloration (blueness) and coldness of the fingers, toes, nose and ears, occasionally progressing to ischaemia and ulceration. Many cases occur spontaneously in older adults. The disorder is chronic and often mild. It occurs as an unusual complication of lymphoma, and also, rarely and transiently, in infectious mononucleosis (glandular fever) and mycoplasma pneumonia.

The degree of haemolysis can be reduced by maintenance of a warm environment. Steroids and splenectomy are rarely successful, probably because complement-sensitised cells tend to be destroyed at other sites, especially the liver.

Haemolytic disease of the newborn

Haemolytic disease of the newborn, a previously common disorder, is due to passage across the placenta of maternal IgG antibodies which are reactive against, and cause destruction of, the fetal red cells. This disorder requires the inheritance by the fetus of a red cell antigen from the father which is not present on the maternal red cells, thus provoking antibody development in the mother. Antibodies against the D antigen of the rhesus blood group system are most commonly implicated, but with improvements in management classical rhesus haemolytic disease is now much less common and an increased proportion of cases are due to antibodies to other antigens in the rhesus system, to the A antigen of the ABO system or occasionally to other antibodies.

The prevalence of negativity for the rhesus D antigen varies according to race: approximately 15% for Caucasians, 8% for African–Americans, 4% for Africans, 1% for Native Americans and < 1% for Asians. Such individuals who are negative for the rhesus D antigen can become sensitised to produce anti-D. Passage of fetal red cells into the maternal circulation occurs normally at delivery or as a result of miscarriage or operative intervention during pregnancy and these D-positive cells sensitise a D-negative mother. Further stimulation of antibody production occurs in subsequent pregnancies with a D-positive fetus. IgG antibody then crosses the placenta from mother to fetus and causes immune destruction of fetal red cells. Thus, the disorder does not manifest in the first pregnancy. The pathogenesis is similar for other antibodies; however, the fetus may be affected in the first pregnancy in ABO haemolytic disease of the newborn, where IgG antibody to A or B on fetal red cells develops in a group O mother.

Clinicopathological features. The pathological features are those of a haemolytic anaemia of variable severity occurring in utero. In the most severe cases, associated with a high titre of anti-D, the result is death in utero from 'hydrops fetalis'; the fetus is extremely pale and oedematous and has gross hepato-splenomegaly, the result of severe anaemia with cardiac and hepatic failure and increased extramedullary erythropoiesis. In less severe examples the neonate is pale and jaundiced at birth, with hepatosplenomegaly.

The blood picture is that of anaemia, polychromasia with increased reticulocytes and often nucleated red cells in the peripheral blood. The direct antiglobulin test on the neonatal red cells is positive, indicating that they are coated with antibody. When unconjugated bilirubin levels are very high, bile pigment becomes deposited in the central nervous system, especially the basal ganglia, causing severe damage, known as *kernicterus*. The bilirubin levels rise rapidly after birth due to immaturity of the liver, with further central nervous system damage. Spasticity and mental retardation may be the clinical consequences of this damage.

In some cases of haemolytic disease of the newborn due to anti-D, and most due to anti-A, the disease is mild, with neonatal anaemia and mild jaundice.

Management. The incidence of the disorder has been reduced by the prophylactic removal of fetal cells entering the maternal circulation before sensitisation can occur. This is achieved by injection of anti-D into the D-negative mother.

Management of the affected fetus centres on provision of unsensitised red cells by intra-uterine transfusion and removal of bilirubin by exchange blood transfusion postnatally. Mildly affected neonates are treated by phototherapy, in which exposure to light of an appropriate wavelength degrades bilirubin.

Haemolysis due to mismatched blood transfusion

Haemolytic transfusion reaction constitutes a second type of alloimmune haemolysis. Severe reactions result from transfusion of red cells possessing an antigen (e.g. ABO group antigens) to which the recipient possesses complement binding antibody of IgG or IgM class.

Microangiopathic haemolytic anaemia

The term microangiopathic haemolytic anaemia describes the dramatic haematological picture that occurs when haemolysis is caused by physical trauma to erythrocytes as they are forced through narrow or damaged areas in the microvasculature. Characteristic cells are present on the blood film, especially schistocytes (Fig. 23.3). This type of process is commonly present in disseminated intravascular coagulation (p. 663); the erythrocytes are damaged on fibrin strands deposited in small blood vessels. It is also a feature of the haemolytic uraemic syndrome, thrombotic thrombocytopenic purpura (p. 671), malignant hypertension and of the extensive vasculitis in systemic lupus erythematosus. In many of these conditions, thrombocytopenia is also present, due to platelet consumption in microthrombi formed on damaged endotheium.

Similar erythrocyte damage without microvascular lesions occurs in march haemoglobinuria, originally described in soldiers after prolonged marching; red cell damage presumably occurs in the feet. An analogous situation has

been described in marathon runners, bongo drummers and exponents of karate! In most of these situations the haemolysis is not chronic, and splenomegaly and other features of chronic red cell destruction are absent. The direct antiglobulin test is negative, as antibody is not involved in the pathogenesis.

Schistocytes and haemolysis, sometimes catastrophic, are occasionally the result of red cell injury from a malfunctioning mechanical heart valve or other vascular prostheses.

Other causes of haemolytic anaemia

Extensive burns are associated with haemolysis, in part due to direct heat damage of erythrocytes in blood vessels of the burned areas, and in part due to a microangiopathic mechanism. Snake bites, spider bites and chemicals are occasional causes.

Infection with clostridia is a rare cause of haemolysis. Malarial infection is common and results in haemolytic anaemia (Fig. 23.29). Schizonts escape by rupturing the erythrocytes in which they have matured. In chronic malarial infection, extreme splenomegaly is often present. Histologically, there is marked congestion and expansion of reticuloendothelial cells; macrophages contain parasites and red cells, and are laden with malarial pigment.

Hypersplenism

Hypersplenism is defined as anaemia (often accompanied by leukopenia and thrombocytopenia) secondary to splenic enlargement (Ch. 22). This anaemia is in part due to a haemolytic component, presumed to be due to increased red cell sequestration in the enlarged spleen, with enhanced phagocytosis by macrophages. However, other mechanisms contribute: the plasma volume increases in proportion to the degree of splenic enlargement, for reasons that are not understood. This results in a dilutional anaemia. Pooling of blood cells also occurs within the spleen.

Hypersplenism is associated with splenomegaly from any cause, such as portal hypertension and collagen vascular disease. Hypersplenism in rheumatoid arthritis has the eponym *Felty's syndrome*. The blood picture in hypersplenism is that of a pancytopenia with no specific features. The haemoglobin concentration would rarely be less than 80 g/l and the platelet count less than 60×10^9/l due to hypersplenism alone.

NEOPLASTIC DISORDERS OF THE BONE MARROW

Classification of bone marrow malignancies

Bone marrow malignancies are classified according to their presentation (acute or chronic), their tissue distribution (e.g. leukaemia in blood and marrow or lymphoma in lymph nodes and other tissues) and their histogenesis (e.g. myeloid, lymphoid). The World Health Organization has refined the classification of tumours of the haemopoietic and lymphoid tissues. The objectives of the WHO classification are to offer pathologists, haematologists, oncologists and geneticists worldwide a system of classification of human haemopoietic neoplasms that is based on their histopathological and genetic features. This classification takes into account tissue and cell morphology, immunological characteristics of the malignant cells and, where known, specific acquired genetic aberrations associated with the malignancies. The advantages of this approach to classification are improved reliability in diagnosis, better prognostic information with the possibility of tailored therapy for a given prognostic group and, finally, more reliable characterisation of patients entered into trials of therapy.

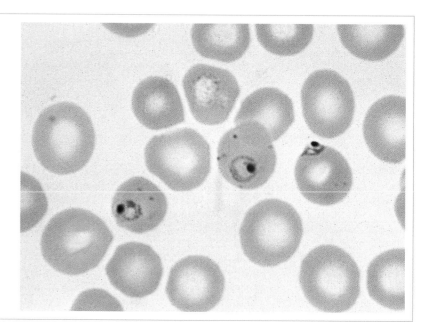

Fig. 23.29 The blood in falciparum malaria.
Ring forms of the parasite are visible in several of the erythrocytes.

Summary of the major WHO subtypes of tumours of haematopoietic and lymphoid tissues

▶ Chronic myeloproliferative diseases
▶ Myelodysplastic/myeloproliferative—crossover syndromes
▶ Myelodysplastic syndromes
▶ Acute myeloid leukaemia
  – with recurrent cytogenetic abnormalities
  – with multilineage dysplasia
  – therapy related
  – ambiguous lineage
  – not otherwise characterised
▶ B-cell neoplasms
  – precursor B-lymphoblastic leukaemia/lymphoma
  – mature B-cell neoplasms (B-non-Hodgkin's lymphomas and plasma cell neoplasms)
▶ T-cell and natural killer (NK)-cell neoplasms
  – precursor T-lymphoblastic leukaemia/lymphoma
  – blastic NK-cell lymphoma
  – mature T-cell and NK-cell neoplasms
▶ Hodgkin's lymphoma
▶ Histiocytic and dendritic cell neoplasms
▶ Malignant mastocytosis

The lymphomas are described in Chapter 22. The myelodysplastic syndromes are described on pages 663–664.

LEUKAEMIAS

Leukaemias are neoplastic proliferations of white blood cell precursors. This proliferation results in the common features of leukaemia:

- diffuse replacement of normal bone marrow by leukaemic cells with variable accumulation of abnormal cells in the peripheral blood
- infiltration of organs such as liver, spleen, lymph nodes, meninges and gonads by leukaemic cells.

Bone marrow failure with anaemia, neutropenia and thrombocytopenia is the most important consequence, particularly in the acute leukaemias.

Aetiology

In the majority of cases the cause is unknown. Leukaemias represent neoplastic monoclonal proliferations of cells within the bone marrow and blood. Whether or not the cell of origin is a pluripotent stem cell or a more committed cell in each type remains contentious. However, current evidence suggests that in most cases of acute myeloblastic leukaemia (AML) a pluripotential stem cell is mutated. The exception to this is acute promyelocytic leukaemia (APL), which seems to arise from a more committed myeloid progenitor cell. In acute lymphoblastic leukaemia (ALL) the transforming events occur in a very primitive B-cell that has not yet developed the capacity to produce immunoglobulin; most cases of chronic myeloid (or granulocytic) leukaemia (CML), where megakaryocytes and erythroid cells are involved as well as leukocytes, derive from a pluripotent stem cell. Most cases of chronic lymphocytic leukaemia (CLL) are of B-cell origin, but these cells are more differentiated than those in ALL.

In acute leukaemia the typical cells—'blast' cells—accumulate as a result of a combination of proliferation but failure of maturation (Fig. 23.30). In CML the abnormal myeloid stem cells also accumulate, but maturation still occurs, with increased numbers of mature myeloid cells in blood and bone marrow, as well as blast cells.

It seems likely that several predisposing factors acting together trigger the onset of the disease in most cases. These triggers act by inducing a series of mutations in certain key genes involved in regulating cell proliferation and differentiation. Such genes are known as oncogenes if they promote tumour development and as tumour suppressor genes if their normal, un-mutated form protects against tumour development. In some leukaemias genetic material is exchanged between two genes (translocation), leading to the development of a novel

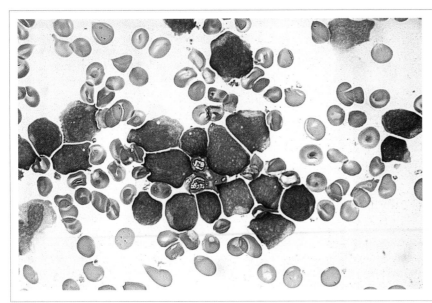

Fig. 23.30 Blast cells in acute lymphoblastic leukaemia. Blast cells are relatively large leukocytes with fine chromatin, nucleoli and basophilic cytoplasm.

fusion gene which acts as an oncogene. The best understood examples of these types of mutation in leukaemogenesis include the t(9;22) translocation in CML, in which the fusion gene is a tyrosine kinase, BCR-ABL (Fig. 23.31), and the t(15;17) translocation in acute promyelocytic leukaemia. Such genetic mutations are often first recognised by the identification of gross cytogenetic abnormalities at the chromosome level, for example the Philadelphia chromosome is the small chromosome 22 produced by the exchange of genetic material with chromosome 9. With more sophisticated molecular techniques such as fluorescent in situ hybridisation (FISH) and gene array technology it is becoming clear that all leukaemias have altered genes. Already such abnormalities are being used to produce targeted therapies, for example imatinib mesilate (Glivec) in CML (p. 649), and to identify patients with a good prognosis who do not necessarily need a stem cell transplant, for example AML patients with t(15;17) or t(8;21).

Certain factors known to initiate leukaemic transformation are:

- irradiation (e.g. atomic bomb survivors, spinal irradiation in ankylosing spondylitis, ^{32}P therapy in myeloproliferative disease)
- drugs (e.g. alkylating agents in treatment of lymphomas)

- other chemicals (e.g. benzene exposure)
- viruses (e.g. leukaemia in some animals; HTLV-I in adult T-cell leukaemia/lymphoma)
- genetic factors (e.g. increased incidence in Down's syndrome).

Acute leukaemias

Acute leukaemias arise from mutations in haemopoietic stem cells. The leukaemic clone of cells proliferates but loses the ability to differentiate into mature blood cells. This imbalance between proliferation and differentiation in acute leukaemia leads to the accumulation of blast cells in the bone marrow and the hallmark clinical features of bone marrow failure. Two broad types of acute leukaemia are recognised: acute lymphoblastic leukaemia (ALL), most common in childhood, and acute myeloblastic leukaemia (AML), most common in adults. The incidence of ALL and AML with age is shown in Figure 23.32.

Acute lymphoblastic leukaemia
ALL is most common between 2 and 4 years of age. It is the commonest cause of cancer death in childhood. Recent data suggest that one of the predisposing genetic mutations for

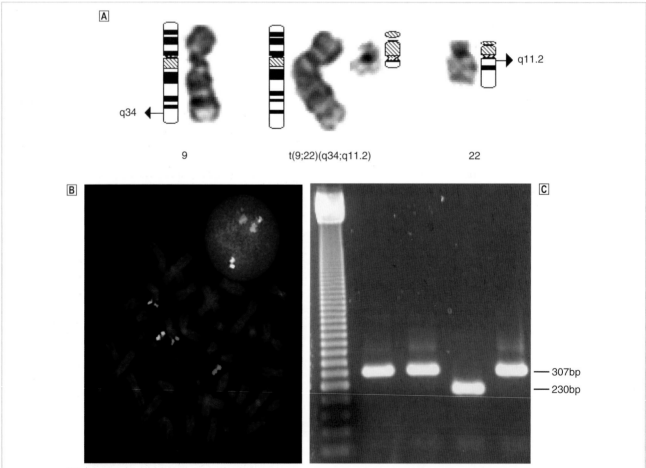

Fig. 23.31 **A Philadelphia chromosome.** The Philadelphia chromosome produced by t(9;22) (the small derivative chromosome centre right). **B** BCR-ABL rearrangement identified by FISH (yellow) because of co-localised BCR (red) and ABL (green), and **C** as a single band of 230 kb by PCR. (FISH, fluorescent in situ hybridisation.) (Courtesy of David Stevenson.)

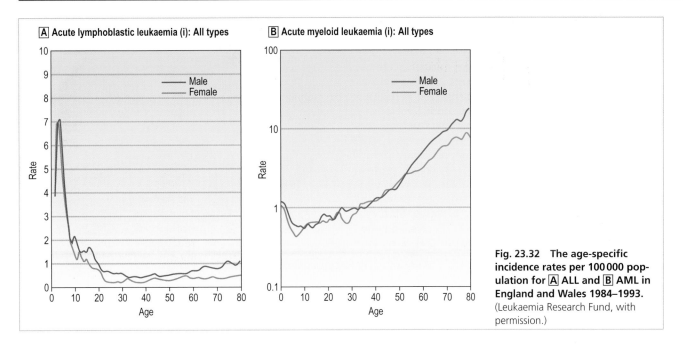

Ⓐ Acute lymphoblastic leukaemia (i): All types

Ⓑ Acute myeloid leukaemia (i): All types

Fig. 23.32   The age-specific incidence rates per 100 000 population for Ⓐ ALL and Ⓑ AML in England and Wales 1984–1993. (Leukaemia Research Fund, with permission.)

childhood ALL actually occurs in utero and that further genetic mutations in the first years of life lead to the disease.

ALL blasts were described morphologically by the French–American–British (FAB) classification according to their size, nuclear:cytoplasmic ratio and whether or not there is marked cytoplasmic vacuolation, as L1, L2 or L3 cells. Routine use of panels of monoclonal antibodies has shown that the majority of cases of ALL derive from B-cell precursors, and the use of these antibodies can classify ALL according to the degree of maturation along the B-cell pathway, i.e. common ALL and pre-B ALL, which can be of L1 or L2 morphology, or B-ALL which is of L3 morphology and now known as Burkitt's leukaemia because of its biological similarity to Burkitt's lymphoma. The WHO classification distinguishes cases as precursor B-lymphoblastic leukaemia/lymphoma and precursor T-lymphoblastic leukaemia/lymphoma. A number of acquired genetic abnormalities are recognised in ALL. These include the occurrence of a Philadelphia chromosome caused by the t(9;22) translocation in 2% of children but 20–30% of adults with ALL, hypodiploid or hyperdiploid (> 50) numbers of chromosomes, t(1;19), t(12;21) and rearrangements of the myeloid/lymphoid or mixed lineage leukaemia (MLL) gene on chromosome 11q.

Acute myeloblastic leukaemia

The incidence of AML increases steadily with age. In older people AML is more likely to develop from an existing bone marrow disorder such as myelodysplastic syndrome (MDS), whereas the majority of younger patients present with de novo AML.

The WHO classification of AML distinguishes subtypes based on biological homogeneity and clinical relevance. As such there are four major categories:

1. AML with recurrent genetic abnormalities (including t(8;21), t(15;17), deletion 11q and inversion 16)
2. AML with multilineage dysplasia

3. AML, therapy related (including following exposure to alkylating agents or topoisomerase II inhibitors)
4. AML not otherwise categorised (including cases with evidence of some myeloid, monocytic, erythroid or megakaryocytic differentiation).

In all cases there must be at least 20% blast cells in the bone marrow for AML to be diagnosed.

Prognosis in AML is related to acquired cytogenetic abnormalities. As acknowledged in the WHO classification, some of these abnormalities occur in specific subtypes of AML. Patients with balanced translocations t(15;17) in acute promyelocytic leukaemia (APL), t(8;21) and inversion of chromosome 16 respond very well to treatment and have a long-term cure rate of 70–80%. Much is now known about the genes altered by these chromosome rearrangements. For example, in APL with t(15;17) the genes rearranged are *PML/RARA*. The retinoic acid receptor alpha gene (*RARA*) in its fused form with *PML* leads both to the development of this leukaemia and its response to pharmacological doses of all-trans-retinoic acid (ATRA), which is now part of standard therapy for this subtype of AML. At the other end of the spectrum are cytogenetic abnormalities that carry a very poor prognosis with cure rates of less than 20%. These include loss of a whole chromosome 5 or 7 or complex multiple cytogenetic abnormalities. These cases occur more commonly in elderly people, following on from MDS or in so-called treatment-related AML after exposure to chemotherapy for previous cancers. A significant majority of patients have no detectable chromosomal abnormality. However, genetic abnormalities are increasingly recognised in this group of patients using molecular techniques. Examples include internal tandem duplication of the *FLT3* gene in 30% of cases which carries a poor prognosis, and a mutation in the nucleophosmin gene which leads to the aberrant location of the protein in the cytoplasm rather than the nucleolus and which carries a relatively favourable prognosis.

Blood and bone marrow changes in acute leukaemia

In peripheral blood the white cell count is usually increased but can be decreased or normal despite massive marrow infiltration with blast cells. Counts greater than $100 \times 10^9/l$ can occur. Irrespective of the total white cell count, a majority of nucleated cells in the blood are leukaemic blasts. In AML, cells containing diagnostic rod-like granular structures (Auer rods) may be present, as may hypogranular polymorphonuclear variants and pseudo-Pelger cells (Fig. 23.7). Anaemia is present, usually normocytic and normochromic. Thrombocytopenia is marked, particularly in AML.

Bone marrow cellularity is markedly increased. Blast cells constitute at least 20% of nucleated cells present, and often greater than 80%. Extension into areas of previously fatty marrow may occur. Gross bone erosion with fractures is not generally a feature of acute leukaemia. Karyotype analysis reveals abnormalities in the leukaemic blasts, with gains and losses of whole chromosomes as well as translocations.

Changes in other organs

Lymph nodes, liver and spleen may be infiltrated with leukaemic blast cells in all types of acute leukaemia. Lymph node enlargement is generally mild and nodes remain discrete, although in some cases of ALL massive involvement of mediastinal lymph nodes is a feature. Splenic enlargement, where present, is also minor in contrast to that in chronic leukaemias. Histologically, there is effacement of normal node architecture by sheets of leukaemic blasts and focal or diffuse infiltration of the spleen.

A diffuse infiltrate of leukaemic cells may also be present in most other organs. Evidence of bacterial, fungal or viral infection may be apparent, as may haemorrhage secondary to thrombocytopenia.

Meningeal infiltration in ALL is an important feature. Leukaemic blasts within the central nervous system are protected from chemotherapeutic agents by the blood–brain barrier. Perivascular aggregates of blast cells later form diffuse lesions and plaques which may result in compression of adjacent nerve tissue.

Infiltration of the gums (Fig. 23.33) and skin is a peculiar feature of the monocytic types of AML.

Severe, life-threatening coagulation failure occurs in APL, probably due to coagulation activation and consumption of clotting factors by activators released from the granules of the leukaemic promyelocytes and excess fibrinolysis.

Clinical course

The onset is often very rapid and progression to death from anaemia, haemorrhage or infection occurs within weeks if no treatment is given. The features are those of marrow failure, with anaemia, infection due to neutropenia and mucocutaneous bleeding due to severe thrombocytopenia (Fig. 23.34).

Infections are typically with bacteria and fungi. Septicaemias, pneumonia and skin sepsis are common (Fig. 23.35). Fungal infections can be local, such as in the oral cavity (Fig. 23.6),

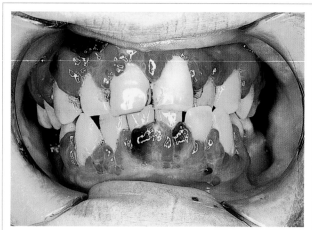

Fig. 23.33   **Gum hypertrophy and haemorrhage in acute monocytic leukaemia.**

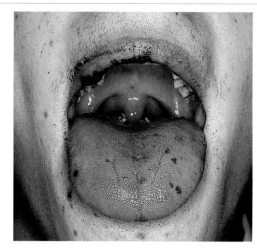

Fig. 23.34   **Mucosal haemorrhage due to severe thrombocytopenia in acute leukaemia.**

but fungal septicaemia and organ invasion occur. Systemic fungal infection is often fatal (Fig. 23.36). The situation may be exacerbated, especially in AML, by transient but prolonged aplasia induced by highly myelotoxic chemotherapeutic agents. The clinical course is, however, often less catastrophic in childhood ALL.

Treatment

Treatment of acute leukaemia is directed by individual prognostic assessment. The aim is to offer curative treatment where possible and minimise the long-term complications in groups of patients who have a high cure rate, while intensifying the treatment or using new modes of treatment in those groups of patients who presently do badly. Therefore, as an example of this principle, children and young adults with good prognosis ALL or AML will not be routinely offered bone marrow transplantation, while those with poor prognosis disease may be offered bone marrow transplantation as part of initial treatment. Treatment is by chemotherapeutic agents in combination to

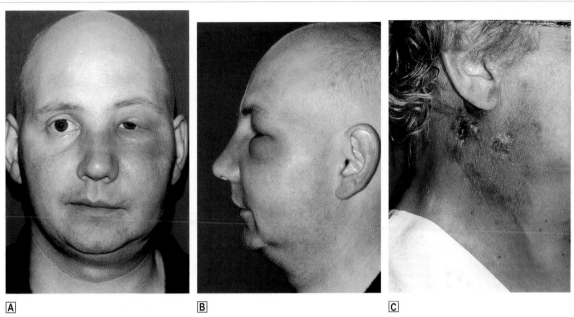

Fig. 23.35   Bacterial infection in AML. Ⓐ and Ⓑ Peri-orbital cellulitis caused by *Pseudomonas aeruginosa* (with permission) and Ⓒ streptococcal cellulitis.

Table 23.8 Acute versus chronic leukaemia	
Acute	**Chronic**
Leukaemic cells do not differentiate	Leukaemic cells retain ability to differentiate
Bone marrow failure	Proliferation without bone marrow failure
Rapidly fatal if untreated	Survival for a few years
Potentially curable	Not presently curable without bone marrow transplant

clear the blood, bone marrow and other sites of leukaemic blasts as far as is possible. The first one or two courses of treatment are aimed at producing a state of remission, in which the blood counts are normal and there are less than 5% blast cells in the bone marrow as identified by light microscopy. However, light microscopy is not very sensitive and in remission there can still be in the order of 10^9 leukaemic cells in the marrow. Further courses of chemotherapy are given to consolidate the remission and reduce this leukaemic burden further.

In poor prognostic disease it seems chemotherapy alone cannot overcome the leukaemic burden and the additional allogeneic immune attack provided by a stem cell transplant is required to eradicate the disease. This attack is called graft-versus-leukaemia and is mediated by the donor's engrafted T-lymphocytes. New approaches to leukaemia management include more accurate monitoring of minimal residual disease (disease that cannot be detected by conventional microscopy) by PCR or flow cytometry and acting on the results of such tests. This has been particularly successful in childhood ALL

and in APL. New modes of therapy, such as the addition of antibodies targeted against the leukaemia cells, e.g. calicheamicin bound to anti-CD33 (gemtuzumab ozogamicin) in AML, and techniques to harness the graft-versus-leukaemia effect whilst reducing the toxicity of the transplant procedure by using intense T-cell immunosuppression and less myelosuppression (so-called reduced intensity conditioned allografts) are showing promise.

Intensive support by transfusion of blood products and use of antibacterial and antifungal agents is necessary to support the patient during the treatment while bone marrow function is suppressed. Survival is months or a few years in adults, with an increasing proportion of long-term survivors with advances in therapy. The outlook is much better in childhood ALL and in adults with good prognosis AML, where significant cure rates are now achieved.

Chronic leukaemias

The important differences between chronic and acute leukaemia are shown in Table 23.8.

Chronic myeloid (granulocytic) leukaemia

Although a 'chronic' leukaemia, the natural history of CML is that of a fatal disorder with a median survival in the pre-imatinib era of about 5 years in patients not eligible for allogeneic bone marrow transplantation. It occurs in all age groups. Normal bone marrow is replaced by an abnormal clone derived from a pluripotential stem cell which, in the majority of cases, is characterised by the presence of a karyotypic abnormality, the Philadelphia chromosome (reciprocal translocation of part of the long arm of chromosome 22 to another chromosome, usually 9) (Fig. 23.31). Erythroid, megakaryocytic and B-lymphocyte cell lines all carry the

659

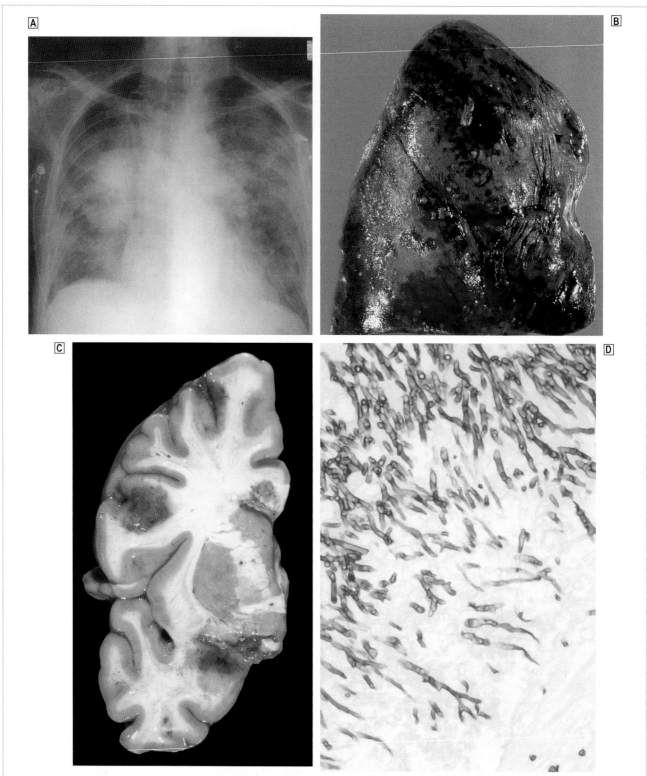

Fig. 23.36 Fatal disseminated fungal infection in AML. [A] Fungal pneumonia. [B] and [C] Multiple lung and brain fungal abscesses. [D] *Aspergillus fumigatus* grown from lung abscess.

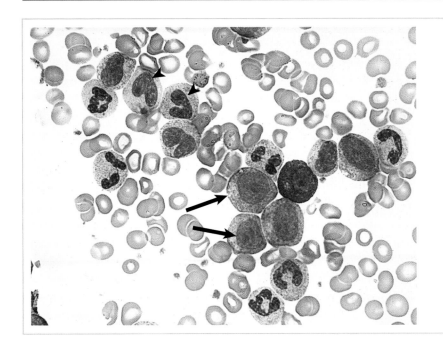

Fig. 23.37 The blood in chronic myeloid leukaemia. Myelocytes (arrows) and metamyelocytes (arrowheads) enter the circulation.

defect, as well as the granulocytic series. In most cases the disease eventually enters a more aggressive phase due to the emergence and dominance of a clone of myeloid cells that have now lost the ability to differentiate. The disease, called blast crisis, then bears a close resemblance to AML (or less commonly ALL) and is fatal.

Blood and bone marrow changes

Leukocytosis is a uniform feature, with occasional cell counts in excess of $300 \times 10^9/l$. The cell picture in the blood can superficially resemble that in a bone marrow aspirate, with myelocytes, promyelocytes, myeloblasts and normoblasts present as well as large numbers of band cells and mature polymorphonuclear granulocytes (Fig. 23.37). Basophilia is common. Platelets are increased (sometimes over $1000 \times 10^9/l$), normal or reduced. A normochromic anaemia is often present.

The leukocytes are abnormal, as exemplified by an absence or severe reduction of their content of alkaline phosphatase, a feature unique to CML and of diagnostic value. Serum vitamin B_{12} is elevated due to production of binding protein by the granulocyte series.

The bone marrow is hypercellular with marked reduction of fat spaces; granulocytopoiesis predominates. In the acute, terminal phase increased numbers of blast cells become evident in blood and bone marrow, and anaemia and thrombocytopenia are more marked.

Changes in other organs

The spleen is enlarged, often massively, due to infiltration by CML cells (Fig. 23.38); it may fill the abdominal cavity and extend into the pelvis. Areas of infarction are present due to the rapid enlargement outstripping the available blood supply. Hepatomegaly is also frequently present. Infiltration in other organs is an occasional feature. Infection and bleeding are not common in the chronic phase.

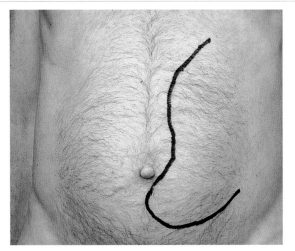

Fig. 23.38 Massive splenomegaly in chronic myeloid leukaemia. The palpable margins of the spleen are indicated.

Clinical course

Symptoms may be mild in the chronic phase and are essentially those of anaemia and massive splenomegaly (abdominal fullness and pain from splenic infarction). Rarely, a hyperviscosity state may develop when the white count is greater than $300 \times 10^9/l$. In the acute phase the clinical features are those of acute leukaemia.

Treatment

The treatment of BCR-ABL-positive CML has seen a remarkable change in recent times. With detailed understanding of the molecular structure of the causative oncogene *BCR-ABL*, a drug called imatinib mesilate—trade name Glivec—has been developed. The drug is a small molecule that binds to the ATP-binding site of BCR-ABL and inhibits the function of the protein. In a large randomised clinical trial (IRIS), this oral drug has had very dramatic positive results with > 95% of patients achieving complete haematological remission within 12 months and 87% achieving a complete cytogenetic remission by 60 months. After 5 years of follow-up, the estimated overall survival is 89% of patients treated with imatinib. A trial of imatinib with monitoring of response milestones is now regarded as the standard therapy for all patients newly diagnosed with BCR-ABL-positive chronic phase CML. Some patients will fail to meet the response milestones whilst on imatinib and some who do respond subsequently develop resistance to the drug because of mutations in the ATP-binding site or multiple copies of the *BCR-ABL* gene. Such patients who are young enough, fit enough and have a suitable donor can be cured by an allogeneic stem cell transplant.

Newer tyrosine kinase inhibitors with a broader range of cellular targets (dasatinib) or more potent anti-BCR-ABL activity (nilotinib) are being introduced for patients who fail imatinib therapy and for whom stem cell transplantation is not available. Imatinib and the newer tyrosine kinase inhibitors are also more effective in treating patients in blast crises than conventional chemotherapy. It is too early to know if imatinib or its successors will cure patients with CML; however, the introduction of imatinib is a landmark event and marks the proof of principle that a clear understanding of the pathogenesis of a disease at a molecular level can lead to the design of effective targeted treatment. If tyrosine kinase inhibitor therapy is not available, the proliferative features of CML can be controlled with oral hydroxycarbamide and the chronic phase prolonged with the use of alpha-interferon with or without cytosine arabinoside.

Chronic lymphocytic leukaemia

Aetiology

CLL is a chronic lymphoproliferative disorder with features similar to those of a low-grade lymphoma but with predominant blood and marrow involvement. During the last few years there has been significant new understanding of the pathology of this disease. The disease process is a relentless accumulation of B-lymphocytes that appear resistant to apoptosis. In the majority of cases it is a considerably less aggressive disorder than are the other leukaemias. This common form of the disease is a disease of the elderly. It is slowly progressive, usually following a predictable clinical course (Fig. 23.39) with a median survival of 25 years and often does not require therapy.

In this form of the disease the malignant B-cell has undergone rearrangement of its immunoglobulin genes and the cell has also passed through the germinal centre of the lymph node and been selected for antigen by hypermutation of its rearranged immunoglobulin genes. Such cells therefore are the leukaemic equivalent of memory B-cells. In a proportion of patients the disease is much more aggressive in its behaviour with resistance to chemotherapy and a much shortened median survival of 8–9 years. In these cases the leukaemic B-cell has not been selected for antigen by hypermutation of the immunoglobulin genes and is the leukaemic equivalent of a naive B-cell. In both forms of the disease lymphocytes accumulate in blood, marrow, liver and spleen until the total lymphoid mass is expanded up to 100-fold.

Blood and bone marrow changes

Leukocytosis is present; up to 99% of nucleated cells are small lymphocytes (Fig. 23.40) of B-cell origin in most instances. The lymphocyte count is between $5 \times 10^9/l$ and more than $300 \times 10^9/l$. The CLL cells tend to fragment during preparation of the blood film, producing many 'smear cells' (Fig. 23.40). Anaemia (normocytic) and thrombocytopenia are late developments (Fig. 23.39). However, in up to 10% of cases a secondary autoimmune haemolytic anaemia develops, with reticulocytosis and microspherocytes and a positive direct antiglobulin test result. Serum immunoglobulins are low in the later stages of the disease.

The bone marrow is hypercellular, with progressive replacement of normal tissue by small lymphocytes, resulting eventually in anaemia and thrombocytopenia.

Advanced stage non-Hodgkin's lymphoma (NHL) may result in blood and marrow involvement superficially resembling CLL. However, extensive involvement usually occurs late in the course of the disease and the lymphoma cells are morphologically distinct from the lymphocytes of CLL. Immunophenotyping of B-CLL cells shows a distinct pattern of antigen staining, with the leukaemic cells staining positively for the B-cell antigen CD19 and also for CD5 and CD23. This pattern of staining is useful for helping to distinguish CLL from other cases of B-NHL appearing in the blood which lack staining for CD5 and/or CD23. Cases of

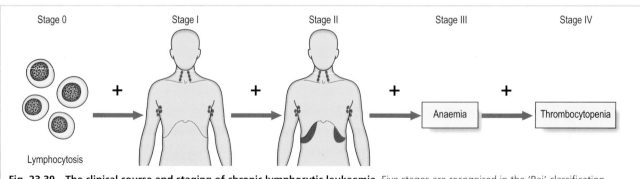

Fig. 23.39 The clinical course and staging of chronic lymphocytic leukaemia. Five stages are recognised in the 'Rai' classification.

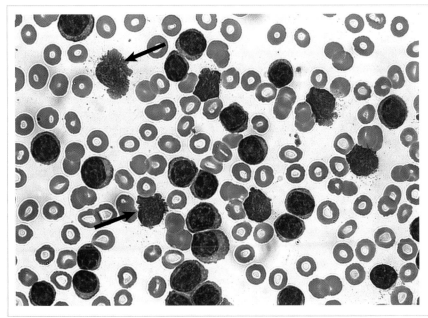

Fig. 23.40 The blood in chronic lymphocytic leukaemia. Numerous small lymphocytes and 'smear' cells (arrows) are characteristic.

CLL, as with other leukaemias, have acquired cytogenetic abnormalities within the leukaemic cells. The common ones are deletions of 13q, 11q and 17p (loss of p53) and trisomy 12. As with acute leukaemia, these abnormalities have prognostic significance, with deletion of 11q and of p53 carrying a poorer prognosis.

Changes in other organs

The lymph nodes, liver and spleen are characteristically involved. In nodes and spleen the normal architecture becomes completely effaced by the infiltrate of monomorphic small lymphocytes, and similar cells are present in the portal tracts of the liver. Occasionally, the predominant presentation is with lymph node involvement with little or no evidence of disease in the blood and marrow, when it is termed small cell lymphocytic lymphoma (WHO-CLL/SCLL).

Clinical course and treatment

For the good prognostic form of the disease the clinical course is protracted; it is summarised in Figure 23.39. The protracted course means that many cases are diagnosed as a result of routine blood tests or clinical examination for some other reason. Elderly patients with this form of the disease often die from an unrelated cause. Many of these patients do not require treatment at all or for many years. Treatment is indicated for the development of significant cytopenias, bulky lymphadenopathy or hepatosplenomegaly, or systemic symptoms such as loss of weight or night sweats. Successful first-line treatment options include single agent chlorambucil or fludarabine alone or in combination with cyclophosphamide.

For the aggressive form of the disease occurring in younger patients and in patients with relapsed disease the outlook is less favourable. Treatment should still be initiated only when there are clinical indications, and treatment regimens involving intensive combinations of chemotherapy, such as fludarabine and cyclophosphamide with the anti-CD20 antibody rituximab,

CHOP combination chemotherapy, stem cell transplantation, and the anti-CD52 monoclonal antibody alemtuzumab are therapeutic options to be considered.

Patients with autoimmune manifestations including autoimmune haemolysis and immune thrombocytopenic purpura are treated with corticosteroids.

Other leukaemias

The *prolymphocytic variant of CLL* is more aggressive and responds poorly to therapy. Splenomegaly is massive. The leukaemic cells in blood and bone marrow are larger and of more primitive appearance than is the case in CLL. *T-PLL* (T-cell prolymphocytic leukaemia) occurs in younger subjects than does the more common B-cell CLL described above. Skin involvement is common. T-PLL has been shown to respond well to alemtuzumab.

Hairy-cell leukaemia is a rare B-cell leukaemia of the middle-aged and elderly. The characteristic cells in the blood have cytoplasmic projections or 'hairs'. Pancytopenia is typical, as is splenomegaly, which may be gross. A characteristic feature of the peripheral blood count is a marked monocytopenia. The marrow is diffusely infiltrated by the malignant cells and marrow fibrosis is present. The disorder may run a chronic course and is of particular interest because there are a number of very effective treatments, including interferon, cladribine and deoxycoformycin. Splenectomy is also useful in management and can relieve cytopenias, but is used less frequently now with these newer effective therapies.

MYELODYSPLASTIC SYNDROMES

This is a group of neoplastic conditions of bone marrow in which there is dysplastic haemopoiesis, resulting in marked morphological abnormalities in blood cells, and a tendency to progress to AML. As such they are pre-leukaemic disorders. Their hallmark is the presence of a cellular bone marrow with cytopenias in the peripheral blood. The pathogenesis appears to be an abnormal clone arising from a mutated stem cell. The combination of the high marrow cellularity and blood cytopenias may be explained by development of a mutated clone with predisposition to apoptosis. In some cases the myelodysplastic syndrome is secondary to stem cell damage from prior treatment of unrelated malignancies with chemotherapy or radiotherapy and is therefore iatrogenic.

Blood and bone marrow changes

There is anaemia, usually macrocytic, with leukopenia and thrombocytopenia. Abnormal cells such as poikilocytes and neutrophils with poorly developed or absent cytoplasmic granules are commonly present (Fig. 23.7). Bone marrow appearances are dysplastic with changes resembling those seen in megaloblastic anaemia—megaloblastoid change. Typical appearances include binucleate normoblasts, ring sideroblasts, megakaryocytes with a single round nucleus and neutrophils with absent granules and poorly developed nuclear segmentation including bilobed forms (pseudo-Pelger–Huet cells). Leukaemic blast cells may be present but constitute less than 20% of the marrow cells, unless there has been progression to acute leukaemia. Dysplasia is considered to be significant in a given cell line if 10% of the marrow nucleated cells are dysplastic. Abnormalities of marrow chromosomes are commonly present, consistent with the malignant and clonal nature of the disorders.

Subclassification is possible depending on the number of cell lineages involved, the presence of ring sideroblasts at greater than 15% of nucleated erythroblasts and whether or not there are increased leukaemic blasts. The WHO classification, therefore, recognises subtypes involving the red cell lineage without increases in blast cells; refractory anaemia (RA) or refractory anaemia with ring sideroblasts (RARS) as distinct from those involving two or more cell lineages without increases in blast cells; refractory cytopenias and multilineage dysplasia (RCMD) and refractory cytopenias with multilineage dysplasias and ring sideroblasts (RCMD-RS). If blasts are increased the term refractory anaemia with increased blasts is used: RAEB-1 (blasts 5–9%), RAEB-2 (blasts 10–19%). In another variant of myelodysplasia there is a marked excess of monocytes in the blood—chronic myelomonocytic leukaemia (CMML). Because of the combination of features of myeloproliferative disease and myelodysplasia the WHO uses the term 'MDS/myeloproliferative crossover syndrome' for CMML and some other variants of myelodysplasia.

Clinical features

Myelodysplasia occurs in the elderly most commonly—median age over 65 years. Anaemia is usually the most troublesome problem and occurs in some 80% of patients. Infections and bleeding also occur. Splenomegaly is rare, except in CMML. Progression to acute leukaemia occurs in around 30%. The mainstay of treatment is largely supportive with red cell transfusions and treatment of infections. In some cases the anaemia responds to treatment with recombinant erythropoietin with or without granulocyte colony-stimulating factor (G-CSF).

AML-type chemotherapy is used for some patients with excess blasts and can achieve transient remissions. Increasingly, allogeneic stem cell transplantation offers a hope of cure, with reduced intensity conditioning regimens allowing older patients to benefit from this approach. Important new developments include the recognition that patients with the cytogenetic abnormality of del 5q rerspond very well to the drug lenalidomide with relief of anaemia and transfusion dependence and the achievement of cytogenetic remissions. In addition, the demethylating agents azacitidine and decitabine improve cytopenias and survival, perhaps by switching on differentiating genes inhibited by DNA methylation. Overall, survival varies with the subtype, ranging from a few years for RA and RARS to less than 1 year in those with excess blasts.

NON-LEUKAEMIC MYELOPROLIFERATIVE DISORDERS

▸ Malignant proliferations of myeloid cells with differentiation to mature forms
▸ In polycythaemia rubra vera (PRV), a pancytosis is accompanied by splenomegaly and hyperviscosity
▸ In essential thrombocythaemia (ET), a predominant thrombocytosis is accompanied by splenomegaly and by bleeding or thrombosis
▸ In myelofibrosis (MF), anaemia and marrow fibrosis are accompanied by massive hepatosplenomegaly due to extramedullary haemopoiesis

The non-leukaemic myeloproliferative disorders are listed in Table 23.9. This list is something of an oversimplification as intermediate forms exist. More importantly, progression in an individual from one such disorder to another within the group is well recognised.

Myeloproliferative disorders most often represent a neoplastic proliferation of a marrow myeloid stem cell with differentiation to the mature form(s) (in contrast to the acute myeloid leukaemias, where maturation is very limited). The normal control mechanisms governing the cell line(s) involved are no longer active, allowing accumulation of erythrocytes, platelets or leukocytes. Proliferation of megakaryocytes produces growth factors causing a secondary overgrowth of fibroblasts (myelofibrosis).

The molecular basis of the myeloproliferative diseases has recently been significantly clarified by the recognition of the common occurrence of point mutations in the cell signalling gene *JAK2* kinase. This leads to stem cells proliferating independently of the normal regulatory signals (e.g. erythropoietin). Some 95% of cases of polycythaemia rubra vera carry the mutation and this is rapidly becoming a crucial diagnostic tool. The other myeloproliferative diseases carry the mutation less frequently: essential thrombocythaemia ~40% and myelofibrosis ~40%. Interestingly, cases of ET that are *JAK2* mutation-positive tend towards having a higher red cell count and haematocrit and this supports the notion that the mutations favour a polycythaemic phenotype.

Table 23.9   The non-leukaemic myeloproliferative diseases

Disorder	Pathology of bone marrow	Clinical features
Myelofibrosis	Increased reticulin/collagen Mutation in *JAK2* kinase ≅ 40%	Leukoerythroblastic blood picture Anaemia with tear-drop poikilocytes Gross hepatosplenomegaly due to myeloid metaplasia
Polycythaemia rubra vera	Increased cellularity, particularly of the erythroid series Mutation in *JAK2* kinase ≅ 95%	Erythrocytosis, often neutrophilia and thrombocytosis Plethora Pruritus Thrombosis or haemorrhage Splenomegaly
Essential thrombocythaemia	Increased megakaryocytes Mutation in *JAK2* kinase ≅ 40%	Thrombocytosis Thrombosis or haemorrhage Sometimes splenomegaly

Polycythaemia rubra vera

Polycythaemia is an increase in the concentration of red cells above normal, usually with a corresponding increase in haemoglobin concentration and haematocrit. In polycythaemia rubra vera (PRV) it is an idiopathic, primary condition.

The body red cell mass and plasma volume can be accurately assessed by isotopic labelling techniques. Normal ranges are 25–35 ml/kg for red cell mass (22–32 ml/kg in females) and 35–45 ml/kg for plasma volume.

Blood and bone marrow changes

The haemoglobin concentration is raised, often to 200 g/l or more, with haematocrit values of up to 75%. Red cell mass may be as high as 80 ml/kg. However, iron deficiency is not uncommon, partly due to increased requirements and partly to a bleeding tendency with chronic gastrointestinal blood loss due to production of functionally abnormal platelets. In such circumstances of iron-deficient polycythaemia, haemoglobin and haematocrit may be normal or even low, but the red cell count is still high.

Thrombocytosis and neutrophil leukocytosis are present in up to 50% of cases. Serum vitamin B_{12} and uric acid are increased, the former due to production of binding protein by myeloid cells, the latter due to increased cell turnover. The bone marrow is hypercellular. Erythroid hyperplasia is present. Megakaryocytes may be prominent and increased reticulin deposition is common. Molecular analysis reveals the *V617F* mutation in the JAK2 kinase gene in virtually all cases with the full-blown PRV phenotype. Some cases in which only pure erythrocytosis exists harbour an alternative mutation in the JAK2 kinase gene.

Changes in other organs

The spleen is enlarged in 75% of cases, usually to a moderate extent. Splenic sinuses are engorged. Extramedullary haemopoiesis may be present: normoblasts and cells of the developing myeloid series are present in the spleen and often the liver. Infarction of heart, brain and spleen is common due to the high blood viscosity and poor flow.

Haemorrhagic lesions may be a feature, especially in the gastrointestinal tract. Peptic ulceration is common in PRV, for unknown reasons.

Clinical features

Clinical features correspond to the pathological changes described above. The skin is plethoric and cyanosis is common. Itching is typical and usually exacerbated by changes in temperature, as after bathing. The conjunctival vessels appear congested, as are retinal vessels. Hyperviscosity results in headache and lethargy. The spleen is palpable. Acute gout may be a presenting feature. Evidence of mucosal bleeding or of thrombosis (particularly arterial) may be present. Myeloproliferative PRV must be distinguished from other causes of polycythaemia, in which splenomegaly and pancytosis are not features (see below).

Treatment is by venesection and/or myelosuppression with hydroxycarbamide or, less commonly nowadays, the alkylating agent busulfan. Aspirin is of proven benefit in reducing all-cause mortality. In the elderly radiophosphorus (^{32}P) is still occasionally used. Survival is for many years. Progression to a myelofibrotic state is common and transformation to acute myeloid leukaemia may occur, especially following ^{32}P treatment.

Secondary and low plasma volume polycythaemias

Polycythaemia is considered significant when the haematocrit is above 0.52 for a man or above 0.47 for a woman. Most cases of polycythaemia are due not to PRV, but to secondary causes that result in appropriate increases in erythropoietin production:

- high altitude
- cyanotic heart disease
- respiratory disease
- smoking
- high-affinity haemoglobinopathy.

Any disorder resulting in chronic hypoxia results in stimulation of erythropoietin production and secondary polycythaemia, as in severe chronic bronchitis, emphysema or alveolar hypoventilation for any reason. Congenital heart disease in which a right-to-left shunt is present is a potent cause; haemoglobin concentrations of 200 g/l are not uncommon. Cigarette smokers have a higher haematocrit than non-smokers, due in part to the carbon monoxide in tobacco smoke. In these situations the polycythaemia is frequently not symptomatic and the blood and bone marrow are otherwise normal. Treatment is rarely necessary.

Very rarely the following renal disorders and tumours are associated with inappropriate erythropoietin production and secondary polycythaemia:

- renal carcinoma or cysts
- renal artery stenosis
- massive uterine fibroids
- hepatocellular carcinoma
- cerebellar haemangioblastoma.

Polycythaemia may also result from a reduction in the plasma volume with normal red cell mass (low plasma volume polycythaemia). This situation occurs chronically in so-called *stress polycythaemia*, also known as Gaisbock's syndrome, where the plasma volume may be 30 ml/kg or less. It is a common disorder, especially in middle-aged, overweight male heavy smokers. It is associated with an increased risk of arterial occlusion causing myocardial infarction and stroke. The pathogenesis is obscure.

Myelofibrosis

Also known as myelosclerosis, myelofibrosis (MF) is characterised by the predominant features of gross marrow fibrosis with massive extramedullary haemopoiesis in liver and spleen. The fibrosis is reactive (a polyclonal proliferation of fibroblasts is present). Factors released from pathological megakaryocytes which proliferate in the bone marrow are thought to be the stimulus to the fibroblastic response. It is a chronic disorder of late middle age and beyond.

Blood and bone marrow changes

Anaemia is usually present; platelets and leukocytes are often increased, but become subnormal eventually. The blood film is typically leukoerythroblastic. Characteristic poikilocytes with a tear-drop shape are a consistent finding (Fig. 23.3).

Bone marrow cannot be aspirated. Trephine biopsy reveals variable cellularity with increased reticulin, progressing to massive deposition of collagen. Megakaryocytes are often increased. Bony trabeculae may be expanded.

Changes in other organs

The spleen is invariably enlarged, often to a massive degree. Lymphoid follicles are preserved but the red pulp is expanded with diffuse areas of extramedullary haemopoiesis. The liver is often enlarged, with obvious foci of haemopoiesis present. Occasionally, lymph nodes are also involved. The liver involvement may result in portal hypertension, causing oesophageal varices and ascites.

Clinical features

Symptoms are caused by the anaemia and massive splenomegaly. Symptoms of hypermetabolism may also be present, especially weight loss and night sweats. Sclerosis of bones may be apparent on X-ray examination. Many patients have a history of polycythaemia rubra vera or essential thrombocythaemia; in others, the onset is insidious. With supportive therapy (blood transfusion), survival is often a few years. If the enlarged spleen is troublesome, splenectomy can be safely performed, surprisingly without exacerbation of the anaemia, though sometimes leading to significant hepatomegaly. There are reports of improved blood counts and reduction in splenic size with thalidomide. Some patients have achieved a remission with resolution of marrow fibrosis following allogeneic stem cell transplantation, suggesting a graft-versus-disease effect.

Essential thrombocythaemia

Essential thrombocythaemia, a myeloproliferative disorder, is an important cause of thrombocytosis. The diagnosis is being made more frequently as an incidental finding now that automated cell counters are routinely used.

Blood and bone marrow changes

The platelet count is raised, often to $1000 \times 10^9/l$ and even to $3000 \times 10^9/l$. Neutrophil leukocytosis may also be a feature. 'Giant' platelets and megakaryocyte fragments may be present. Anaemia, when present, is due to iron deficiency from chronic blood loss. Howell–Jolly bodies and other features of hyposplenism may be apparent due to splenic infarction. Bone marrow cellularity is normal or increased, megakaryocytes predominate and some increase in marrow reticulin is common. Mutations in the *JAK2* kinase gene are found in about 40% of cases.

Changes in other organs

The spleen may be enlarged but is usually normal or reduced in size due to infarction. Ischaemic changes in the area supplied by digital arteries may be present, as may evidence of infarction in other organs. Paradoxically, haemorrhagic lesions also occur, often in the gastrointestinal tract.

Clinical features

The disorder may be asymptomatic for many years. Painful ischaemic lesions of the digits are an occasional feature. Paradoxical haemorrhage, which may be serious, occurs particularly in association with platelet counts over $1000 \times 10^9/l$. Treatment with aspirin and hydroxyurea or the megakaryocyte-suppressing drug anagrelide is effective and survival prolonged. Progression to myelofibrosis may occur.

PLASMA CELL NEOPLASMS

Plasma cells are the immunoglobulin-producing cells resulting from terminal differentiation of B-cells and are normally identifiable in the bone marrow. Diffuse neoplastic, monoclonal proliferation of plasma cells throughout the red marrow is characteristic of the disorder *multiple myeloma*. When the proliferation is more localised an apparently discrete plasma cell tumour develops, usually in bone, but also in soft tissue of the airways and head and neck—*solitary plasmacytoma*. Monoclonal proliferation of IgM-producing plasma cells and lymphoplasmacytoid cells in the reticulo-endothelial organs, bone marrow, liver and spleen is present in a subgroup of non-Hodgkin's lymphoma (NHL) called lymphoplasmacytic lymphoma—the combination of NHL (usually lymphoplasmacytic type) with an IgM paraprotein, with or without signs of hyperviscosity, is known as *Waldenström's macroglobulinaemia*.

Multiple myeloma

- ▶ Malignant proliferation of plasma cells in bone marrow
- ▶ Occurs in older age groups
- ▶ Usually associated with the accumulation of a monoclonal immunoglobulin or light chains (Bence Jones protein) in plasma
- ▶ Often causes renal failure
- ▶ Results in bone destruction in the axial skeleton, with pain and fractures

Multiple myeloma is a common neoplastic disease affecting especially the elderly; almost all cases occur after the age of 40 years. Multifocal plasma cell tumours erode the bones of the axial skeleton; the plasma cells synthesise a monoclonal immunoglobulin or light chain, referred to as the *M-component* or paraprotein in plasma. The M-component is present in over 99% of cases of multiple myeloma; it is most commonly IgG (60% of cases) but may be IgA or immunoglobulin light chains only (kappa or lambda). IgD and IgE M-components are unusual and IgM types are much more commonly a feature of Waldenström's macroglobulinaemia. In two-thirds of cases of IgG and IgA myeloma, a large excess of free light chains is produced in addition to the complete immunoglobulin molecule, presumably due to a functional defect in the malignant plasma cells. While immunoglobulins cannot pass the glomerular filter, free light chains are small enough to enter the urine, where they are called *Bence Jones protein*.

Free light chains can now be measured accurately in serum and urine by nephelometric methods. The result expressed as a serum free light chain ratio (kappa/lambda) is a useful tumour marker in assessing response to treatment. The plasma concentration of the unaffected immunoglobulins is often markedly suppressed ('immune paresis').

Paraprotein formation is not unique to multiple myeloma; a monoclonal immunoglobulin is present occasionally in CLL and lymphomas and, rarely, in carcinomatous disease. Furthermore, a proportion of elderly subjects are found to have a stable paraprotein without immune paresis and without the other features of multiple myeloma or lymphoproliferative disease—so-called 'monoclonal gammopathy of uncertain significance' (MGUS). Only 1% per year of patients with MGUS progress to multiple myeloma.

The pathology of the bone disease in myeloma is becoming better understood and leading to improved treatments for this catastrophic manifestation of the disease (Fig. 23.41). The osteolytic destruction of the axial skeleton (sites of haemopoiesis in adults) results from malignant plasma cells stimulating osteoclasts to erode bone. This leads to lytic lesions, pathological fractures, generalised osteoporosis and hypercalcaemia. For some time it has been recognised that chemical messengers (cytokines) produced from the interaction of malignant plasma cells with their microenvironment stimulate the osteoclast activity. Such cytokines were known as osteoclast activating factors (OAFs) and are now known to include interleukin-1 and -6.

Recently another system of messengers has been shown to be important in the development of the bone disease in myeloma. A protein called RANKL is expressed by osteoblasts and plasma cells; it binds to its ligand RANK on the osteoclast surface and stimulates the osteoclast to erode bone. A second protein called osteoprotegerin (OPG) normally blocks this interaction. However, in myeloma, it is suggested that the levels of OPG are reduced and this RANKL stimulation of bone erosion goes unchecked. This understanding has produced successful treatments to limit the bone disease. A group of drugs called bisphosphonates (e.g. clodronate and pamidronate) directly inhibit osteoclasts and are used routinely in myeloma. Recombinant OPG is being used in trials.

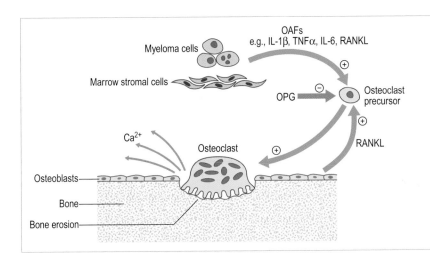

Fig. 23.41 The pathogenesis of bone disease in multiple myeloma. (OAF, osteoclast activating factors; OPG, osteoprotegerin.)

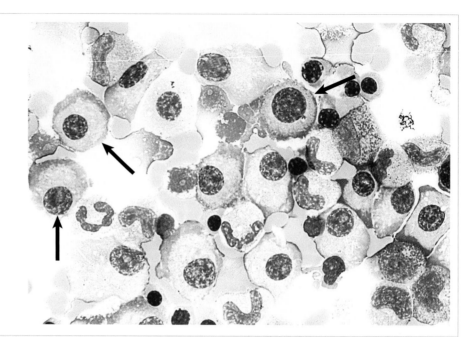

Fig. 23.42   The bone marrow in multiple myeloma. An infiltrate of atypical plasma cells (arrows) is a major diagnostic criterion.

Blood and bone marrow changes

Anaemia is common. The blood film often has rouleaux formation: a tendency for the erythrocytes to adhere to each other and form columns one cell across in the blood film, due to the presence of a high concentration of immunoglobulin. The anaemia is normocytic, but automated cell counters may suggest a high MCV, probably due to rouleaux formation. In advanced disease, pancytopenia is present. Abnormal plasma cells are only occasionally seen in the peripheral blood.

The marrow is hypercellular; 10–90% of the cells are morphologically abnormal plasma cells, including multinucleate forms (Fig. 23.42). Increased numbers of osteoclasts actively resorbing bone may be seen on trephine biopsy.

The plasma cell infiltrate and discrete tumours are present in those bones normally containing red marrow, especially the skull, ribs, vertebrae and pelvis (Fig. 23.43). The distal long bones and those of the extremities are rarely involved. Generalised osteoporosis is common.

Changes in other organs

Renal involvement is present in over half of the cases. The most common abnormality is the presence of protein casts in the distal convoluted and collecting tubules with surrounding giant cells and atrophy of tubular cells—'Bence Jones or myeloma kidney'. Metastatic calcification, changes of pyelonephritis and primary amyloid may also be present in the kidneys. Systemic amyloidosis (Ch. 7) is present in 10% of cases, particularly in the tongue, heart and peripheral nerves, as well as the kidneys.

Clinical features

The clinical features in multiple myeloma are outlined in Figure 23.44. Not all are present in every case. Bone pain is present in the majority and is often severe. Renal failure is

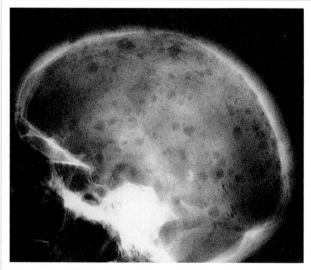

Fig. 23.43   Skull radiograph in multiple myeloma. There are numerous osteolytic bone lesions.

common and prognostically sinister. Hyperviscosity is especially associated with IgA paraproteins because of the physical characteristics of IgA.

Treatment involves management of acute problems, including hypercalcaemia, cord compression and renal failure, and the routine use of bisphosphonates to limit bone disease. The disease is not curable but significant improvements in therapy have occurred in recent times. A number of initial approaches to therapy are successful and include single agent chemotherapy (melphalan) or combination chemotherapy such as vincristine, doxorubicin (Adriamycin), dexamethasone (VAD) or cyclophosphamide, thalidomide, dexamethasone (CTD). These are presently being compared in the UK

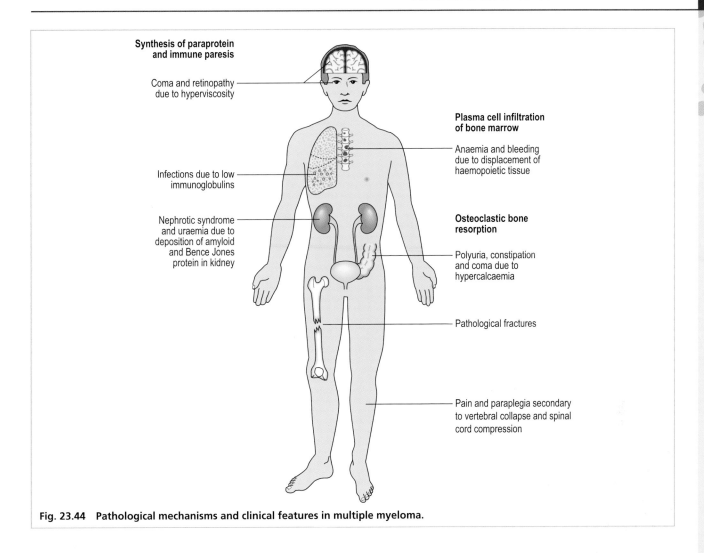

Fig. 23.44 Pathological mechanisms and clinical features in multiple myeloma.

Synthesis of paraprotein and immune paresis

Coma and retinopathy due to hyperviscosity

Infections due to low immunoglobulins

Nephrotic syndrome and uraemia due to deposition of amyloid and Bence Jones protein in kidney

Plasma cell infiltration of bone marrow

Anaemia and bleeding due to displacement of haemopoietic tissue

Osteoclastic bone resorption

Polyuria, constipation and coma due to hypercalcaemia

Pathological fractures

Pain and paraplegia secondary to vertebral collapse and spinal cord compression

Myeloma IX trial. Radiotherapy provides effective control of localised bone pain.

Randomised data have shown a survival advantage for high-dose melphalan therapy and autologous stem cell transplantation which is now offered routinely to younger patients. Relapsed disease has been successfully treated with thalidomide and new agents including the proteasome inhibitor bortezomib and lenalidomide. Survival is improving with these innovations in treatment to a median of 4–5 years.

Solitary plasmacytoma

Solitary tumours composed of malignant plasma cells identical in morphology to those in multiple myeloma occasionally arise in bone or extra-osseous sites. A paraprotein may be synthesised by the cells of the tumour. Solitary plasmacytoma of the bone may progress to multiple myeloma in some 60% of cases.

Waldenström's macroglobulinaemia

In Waldenström's macroglobulinaemia the marrow, lymph nodes, liver and spleen are infiltrated by cells with morphology between lymphocytes and plasma cells, which synthesise a monoclonal IgM. The disorder is uncommon and tends to occur in the later years. It is recognised as a low-grade NHL (lymphoplasmacytic) with moderate lymph node enlargement and hepatosplenomegaly, and does not produce the characteristic osteolytic bone lesions and hypercalcaemia of multiple myeloma. Hyperviscosity is common and occurs at lower paraprotein concentrations than is the case in myeloma, due to the physical characteristics of the IgM molecule. Visual deterioration, lethargy, bleeding tendency and disturbance of consciousness result. Hyperviscosity is treated with plasma exchange.

Survival for many years follows treatment with alkylating agents. Newer treatments include cladribine and rituximab.

DISORDERS OF BLOOD COAGULATION AND HAEMOSTASIS

The components of the haemostatic system are described on page 629. Although it is convenient to describe separately the intrinsic and extrinsic pathways of blood coagulation, platelet adhesion and aggregation, and activation of the fibrinolytic system, there are numerous points of interaction.

Disturbances of blood coagulation and haemostasis produce excessive haemorrhage or thrombosis, or occasionally both, as

Table 23.10   Features that may distinguish bleeding in coagulation defects from that in platelet disorders*

Feature	Platelet defect	Severe coagulation defect
Purpura	Very common	Absent
Mucosal bleeding	Common from mouth, gut and nose	Relatively uncommon except from urinary tract
Joint bleeding	Absent	Very common in severe congenital factor deficiencies
Muscle haematomas	In response to trauma	Spontaneous
Bleeding after surgery	Immediate	Often delayed several hours

*Severe thrombocytopenia and severe haemophilia are taken as examples.

in the acquired disorder *disseminated intravascular coagulation*. As described below and in Table 23.10, the patterns of bleeding differ somewhat between disorders of primary haemostasis (platelet disorders) and defects of blood coagulation. Also, as a general rule, disorders that allow the unchecked generation and deposition of fibrin tend to be associated with thrombosis in the venous circulation (red thrombus), whereas inappropriate platelet activation tends to result in vascular occlusion in arteries and arterioles (white thrombus), although this is by no means a rigid distinction.

DISORDERS OF PRIMARY HAEMOSTASIS

Theoretically, primary haemostasis could be defective as a result of platelet abnormalities or defects of the small blood vessels. In fact, vascular disease is rarely the cause of clinically important haemorrhage. Bleeding due to primary haemostatic defects is most commonly secondary to acquired platelet disorders such as thrombocytopenia or disturbance of platelet function.

In bleeding due to disorders of primary haemostasis the skin and mucous membranes are especially involved (Table 23.10 and Fig. 23.34).

Thrombocytopenias

▶ Cause spontaneous bleeding when the blood platelet count falls below 20×10^9/l
▶ Due to failure of platelet production or increased destruction/sequestration
▶ When due to production failure, thrombocytopenia is usually accompanied by other evidence of marrow dysfunction: anaemia, leukopenia, leukocytosis or atypical cells
▶ When due to increased destruction, immune mechanisms and disseminated intravascular coagulation are common causes

Although a bleeding tendency results from thrombocytopenia, there must be a substantial reduction in platelet numbers before this occurs. No clinical defect of primary haemostasis occurs with platelet counts greater than 80×10^9/l if they function normally. Increased bleeding after trauma is present with counts of $40–50 \times 10^9$/l, but spontaneous skin and mucosal haemorrhage occur only when platelet counts fall to 20×10^9/l. The time to cessation of bleeding from skin incisions increases progressively as the platelet count falls below 80×10^9/l and, when performed in a standardised manner in the bleeding time test, is a good guide to the efficiency of primary haemostasis. The bleeding time is not usually affected by deficiencies of clotting factors because it relies on adequate platelet numbers and function rather than fibrin formation.

Classification
Thrombocytopenia can be conveniently classified according to pathogenesis:

- failure of platelet production
  — megaloblastic anaemia
  — haematological malignancy, including leukaemias, myelodysplasia, myelofibrosis, myeloma and marrow involvement in lymphoma
  — other marrow infiltration, e.g. carcinoma
  — hypoplastic/aplastic anaemia
  — chemotherapeutic agents and occasionally other drugs
  — alcohol
  — some viral infections
  — congenital absence of megakaryocytes

- increased platelet destruction
  — acute and chronic autoimmune thrombocytopenic purpura
  — drug-induced immune thrombocytopenia
  — neonatal and post-transfusion purpura (alloimmune)
  — massive blood loss and transfusion (dilutional and consumptive)
  — disseminated intravascular coagulation
  — thrombotic thrombocytopenic purpura/haemolytic uraemic syndrome

- platelet sequestration
  — hypersplenism.

Where thrombocytopenia is an isolated finding, with normal haemoglobin and white cells, increased platelet destruction is most likely. Failure of platelet production due to a bone marrow abnormality is most commonly associated with a pancytopenia, a leukocytosis or the presence of circulating blast cells in the leukaemias.

Of the causes of thrombocytopenia due to platelet production failure, those due to thiazides, viral infection and congenital megakaryocyte abnormalities are very uncommon. The other disorders resulting in marrow failure have been described earlier.

Autoimmune thrombocytopenic purpura and disseminated intravascular coagulation are the most common disorders in which thrombocytopenia is due to increased destruction or utilisation of platelets.

Autoimmune thrombocytopenic purpura

In autoimmune thrombocytopenic purpura platelets are destroyed in the reticulo-endothelial system, especially the spleen, due to coating with auto-antibody. The disorder is analogous to autoimmune haemolytic anaemia. It occurs in an acute, spontaneously remitting form in children, as a chronic idiopathic state at all ages, and as a drug-induced phenomenon. The acute childhood variety may follow a viral infection. The chronic type is occasionally symptomatic of a disorder such as chronic lymphocytic leukaemia, or lymphoma, may occur in association with other autoimmune disease such as SLE and rheumatoid arthritis, or may present without an associated disorder. It has been recognised that a form of immune-mediated thrombocytopenia occurs in HIV-infected individuals, usually at a point in the disease where there is relative preservation of immune function. Drugs associated with idiopathic thrombocytopenic purpura (ITP) include quinine, heparin and sulphonamides; in most cases, an immune complex mechanism is involved, similar to that in some cases of drug-induced immune haemolytic anaemia.

Blood and bone marrow changes

Thrombocytopenia is present; severity is variable. Platelet counts of less than $10 \times 10^9/l$ are not uncommon. Erythrocytes and leukocytes are usually normal. Iron deficiency anaemia may be present due to chronic mucosal bleeding. In the bone marrow there is a non-specific increase in megakaryocyte size and number. It may be possible to detect the auto-antibody in serum by tests analogous to the antiglobulin test used in the investigation of haemolytic anaemias, but poor sensitivity and specificity of these assays limit their clinical utility.

Changes in other organs

Changes in other organs are those of haemorrhage. Bleeding into the skin in the form of purpura is common. Purpura (petechiae) of thrombocytopenic type is due to apparently spontaneous leakage of red cells from capillaries and arterioles in the skin. It is usually most prominent in the skin of the lower legs and feet, suggesting that hydrostatic pressure may play a role. Areas of skin trauma may also be affected. Histological evidence of capillary bleeding may also be present in the serosal linings, mucosae of gastrointestinal and urinary tracts, and the central nervous system. The spleen is usually of normal size or only moderately enlarged, not extending below the costal margin. The sinusoids are congested and splenic follicles reactive. Megakaryocytes may be present in the spleen, a response to the increased platelet turnover.

Clinical features

Clinical features are restricted to excessive haemorrhage. Purpuric rash, skin bruising, epistaxis, menorrhagia and gastrointestinal haemorrhage are common. The presence of mucosal bleeding is relevant in the clinical evaluation of patients with severe thrombocytopenia indicating a more severe bleeding disorder. In severe cases retinal haemorrhage is present and, although it is unusual, fatal intracerebral bleeding is described.

The acute form in childhood is transient and often requires no treatment. Drug-induced ITP responds to withdrawal of the offending medication. Chronic 'idiopathic' ITP often responds to immunosuppressive therapy, for example with corticosteroids. Intravenous infusion of a concentrate of normal human IgG prepared from plasma is also often effective. It may act through blockade of the reticulo-endothelial Fc receptors responsible for binding of antibody-coated platelets, or possibly through anti-idiotype activity. Surgical removal of the spleen (splenectomy) may result in long-term remission. Thrombopoietin analogues (discussed above) may also have a role in the treatment of ITP. Prognosis is good.

Other immune thrombocytopenias

The immune thrombocytopenia that is occasionally associated with exposure to the anticoagulant drug heparin is unusual, as it is often accompanied by thrombosis rather than haemorrhage. It results from the development of an immune complex formed between heparin, platelet factor 4 (a peptide secreted from the cytoplasmic granules of stimulated platelets) and the auto-antibody to heparin–platelet factor 4. Binding of the complex to platelet Fc receptors causes platelet activation and consumption with thrombocytopenia. Thrombosis occurs—for example deep vein thrombosis or arterial thrombosis—resulting in myocardial or cerebral infarction. Heparin must be withdrawn and replaced with a non-cross-reacting anticoagulant such as lepirudin or danaparoid.

Neonatal thrombocytopenia due to placental transfer of the platelet-reactive IgG auto-antibody can occur in infants of women with chronic ITP. Also, a condition analogous to rhesus haemolytic disease, due to transplacental passage of an antibody, is occasionally recognised as a cause of neonatal thrombocytopenia—neonatal alloimmune thrombocytopenia (NAIT). The pathogenesis is comparable to that of haemolytic disease of the newborn, the fetus possessing a platelet antigen lacking in the mother, usually HPA1a (p. 653).

Post-transfusion purpura is a very uncommon immune thrombocytopenia typically seen in parous women 10 days or so following transfusion of platelets or occasionally red cell concentrate. It is also due to formation of an allo-antibody to a foreign antigen on transfused platelets, usually HPA1a, although the mechanism by which it results in destruction of the woman's HPA1a-negative platelets is not clear.

Thrombotic thrombocytopenic purpura and haemolytic uraemic syndrome

In thrombotic thrombocytopenic purpura (TTP) and haemolytic uraemic syndrome (HUS) the dominant features are thrombocytopenia due to platelet consumption in microvascular occlusive platelet plugs and a microangiopathic haemolytic anaemia. Characteristic fragmented erythrocytes—schistocytes—are present on the blood film (Fig. 23.3). Glomerular lesions are characteristic, especially in HUS (Ch. 21), but vascular lesions in other organs, especially the central nervous system, are a feature in TTP.

In children, HUS may occur in epidemics, suggesting an infectious origin. When it is associated with an acute haemorrhagic colitis, production of verocytotoxin by *Escherichia coli*, usually strain O157, from contaminated food has been shown to be the cause.

TTP is usually sporadic, but can be relapsing and may be familial. It appears to be due to platelet aggregation by very high molecular weight multimers of von Willebrand factor. Such multimers are normally secreted by endothelial cells but are rapidly degraded into smaller multimers, which are less reactive with platelets, by a protease called ADAMTS 13 (A Disintegrin And Metalloproteinase with a ThromboSpondin type 1 motif). In all forms of TTP there is deficiency of ADAMTS 13: in sporadic TTP there is development of an auto-antibody that interferes with the protease activity, whereas in familial TTP there may be a deficiency of the enzyme due to underproduction or abnormalities in its secretion.

Clinically, organ dysfunction due to the microvascular lesions predominates. Renal failure is present. Neurological abnormalities, which may be transient or permanent, including stroke, characterise TTP and distinguish it from HUS. The disease runs a subacute or chronic course. Spontaneous remission is not uncommon in the childhood form, but chronic renal impairment may result. Renal support, including dialysis therapy, may be required in HUS. In TTP, high volume plasma exchange is effective, presumably through removal of auto-antibody and replacement of the cleaving protease in the transfused plasma. Recent data suggest that the therapeutic monoclonal antibody rituximab is of value in the management of TTP due to an auto-antibody.

Qualitative disorders of platelets

Disorders of platelet function result in excessive bleeding of platelet type and prolonged skin bleeding time, usually in the presence of normal platelet numbers.

Acquired disorders of platelet function

Acquired disorders of platelet function are due to:

- drugs (e.g. aspirin, clopidogrel, anti-GP IIb/IIIa drugs (abciximab, tirofiban, eptifibatide), anti-inflammatory drugs)
- metabolic disorders (e.g. uraemia, hepatic failure)
- myeloproliferative disorders (essential thrombocythaemia, polycythaemia rubra vera)
- plasma cell disorders (e.g. multiple myeloma, Waldenström's macroglobulinaemia).

Aspirin and anti-inflammatory drugs block the cyclo-oxygenase enzyme necessary for platelet synthesis of pro-aggregatory thromboxane. Clopidogrel inhibits ADP-mediated platelet activation while abciximab, tirofiban and eptifibatide interfere with glycoprotein IIb/IIIa function. In general any bleeding tendency is mild, but there may be increased skin bruising and bleeding after surgery. Gastric haemorrhage from acute mucosal erosions may be life-threatening. Following percutaneous coronary intervention (PCI) and myocardial infarction, these drugs are being increasingly used in combination with other antithrombotics, thus increasing the bleeding risk. In uraemia and liver failure, platelet interactions with subendothelium are abnormal and bleeding may be severe. In myeloproliferative disease, the clonal defect gives rise to functionally abnormal platelets, and in myeloma platelets become coated with immunoglobulin, which blocks surface receptors and prevents platelet aggregation.

Congenital disorders of platelet function

Hereditary platelet disorders causing life-threatening haemorrhage, such as those where the platelet glycoprotein receptors for von Willebrand factor (Fig. 23.8) (Bernard–Soulier syndrome) or fibrinogen (Glanzmann's disease) are absent, are extremely rare autosomal recessive diseases. Life-threatening haemorrhage may occur. Mild defects of platelet function, causing easy bruising and bleeding after trauma, are more common. In some, a familial pattern is apparent. Various metabolic disturbances of platelets may be responsible, such as a deficiency of adenine nucleotides due to an abnormality of a type of platelet storage granule known as dense bodies (platelet storage pool deficiency).

Bleeding due to vascular disorders

Vascular disorders do not usually cause serious bleeding. Skin haemorrhage and occasional mucosal haemorrhage may occur. In some disorders, the collagen that supports vessel walls is abnormal. This mechanism probably accounts for the bruising of Cushing's syndrome and the bruising, mucosal bleeding and perifollicular skin haemorrhages of scurvy (Ch. 7).

Hereditary haemorrhagic telangiectasia

Telangiectases (microvascular dilatations) accumulate from childhood on mucous membranes, in liver and lungs, and on the skin of hands and face (Fig. 23.45). The condition is inherited as an autosomal dominant trait and involvement

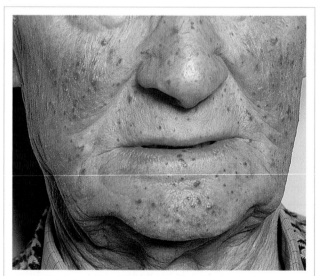

Fig. 23.45 Hereditary haemorrhagic telangiectasia. Typical vascular lesions on the lips and facial skin.

of abnormalities in the genes expressing *alk-1* or *endoglin* are described. Nosebleeds and gastrointestinal bleeding may be severe, but bleeding occurs only from telangiectases; coagulation and platelet numbers and function are normal.

Henoch–Schönlein purpura

In Henoch–Schönlein purpura no systemic bleeding tendency is present. It is an immune complex hypersensitivity reaction, usually in children. A rash, superficially similar to thrombocytopenic purpura but with localised oedema causing the lesions to be raised above the skin level, is present on buttocks and lower legs. Arthralgia, abdominal pain and haematuria may occur. It is usually self-limiting. Although the skin rash resembles thrombocytopenic purpura, the platelet count and skin bleeding time are normal.

Platelet disorders causing thrombosis

HUS and TTP have been described; however, the abnormality causing increased platelet reactivity does not lie within the platelet itself in these disorders. Thrombosis is a feature of myeloproliferative disease with thrombocytosis, especially essential thrombocythaemia and polycythaemia rubra vera. Laboratory evidence for increased platelet reactivity can be found in subjects with coronary thrombosis, cerebral thrombosis, diabetes mellitus and other disorders.

Paradoxically, the heparin-induced immune thrombocytopenia that occasionally develops on exposure to this anticoagulant drug may be associated with extensive arterial and venous thrombosis, due to platelet activation by the auto-antibody (p. 659).

DISORDERS OF BLOOD COAGULATION

▶ Coagulation or fibrinolytic disorders may cause thrombosis or haemorrhage
▶ Can be congenital or acquired
▶ Acquired disorders are common, due to anticoagulant drugs, vitamin K deficiency, liver disease and disseminated intravascular coagulation
▶ The most important congenital bleeding disorders are von Willebrand disease and haemophilia

Diseases of the coagulation/fibrinolytic system causing thrombosis as well as those causing haemorrhage are recognised. In practice, the majority of bleeding disorders are acquired and due to anticoagulant drugs or to liver disease, or to clotting factor consumption in disseminated intravascular coagulation. Vitamin K deficiency in the neonatal period has become uncommon due to routine vitamin K administration in neonates; where this is omitted the child is at risk of developing haemorrhagic disease of the newborn which may result in catastrophic intracranial haemorrhage. The severe congenital haemorrhagic diatheses are uncommon but clinically important disorders due to inherited defects of production of a coagulation factor.

Congenital clotting factor deficiencies

Deficiencies of most of the coagulation factors have been described, but deficiency of factor VIII (haemophilia A) and factor IX (haemophilia B or Christmas disease), and of von Willebrand factor (von Willebrand disease) are the clinically most important disorders in the group. Haemophilia A and B are X-linked conditions, whereas deficiencies of the other coagulation factors are autosomal recessive conditions. The latter are therefore rare, but are seen more commonly in populations where consanguineous marriage is a feature.

Factor VIII is a co-factor for factor IX allowing activation of factor X and therefore fibrin generation via the intrinsic coagulation pathway (Fig. 23.9); it is probably synthesised predominantly by hepatocytes. In order to circulate in plasma with a normal half-life of 12 hours it requires a carrier protein—von Willebrand factor (vWF) (Fig. 23.46). vWF is a large multimeric protein synthesised and assembled by vascular endothelial cells and megakaryocytes. It has no role in the coagulation cascade but is an essential co-factor for interaction of platelets with exposed subendothelium in primary haemostasis (Fig. 23.8). It has binding sites for factor VIII, platelet glycoprotein Ib and collagen, and thus its role in haemostasis is apparent.

Haemophilia

Haemophilia A and B are identical clinically and pathologically, differing only in the deficient factor. In each case the disorder is due to sex-linked recessively inherited deficiency of the clotting factor, or synthesis of a defective clotting factor. Males are affected. Female carriers have approximately 50% of the normal factor level and may occasionally be mildly clinically affected as a result of the process of lyonisation toward the abnormal X chromosome. Mild, moderate and severe forms of haemophilia are recognised, depending on the residual clotting factor activity (Table 23.11); degree of severity is constant within a kindred. Predictably, from the place of factors VIII and IX in the coagulation mechanism, the APTT is prolonged and the PT is normal

The pattern of bleeding is of the coagulation factor deficiency type (Table 23.10). Purpura is not a feature. In severe disease, bleeding from wounds persists for days or weeks. Control

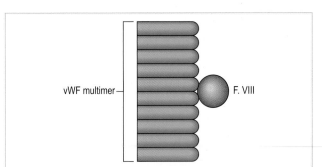

Fig. 23.46 The factor VIII:von Willebrand factor (vWF) complex in plasma. Each unit has antigenic properties identifiable as vWF antigen but only the multimeric structure possesses the ability to bind platelets to subendothelium.

Table 23.11	Classification of haemophilia A	
Category	Factor VIII % of normal	Features
Severe	<1	Frequent and spontaneous haemorrhage into joints and soft tissues from birth Degenerative joint disease
Moderate	1–5	Bleeding after trauma, including dental and other surgical trauma Bruising
Mild	>5–30	Bleeding after trauma only May be subclinical in mildest form

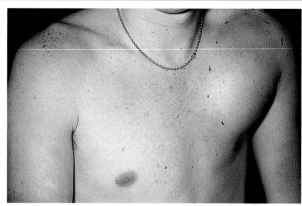

Fig. 23.47   Muscle haematoma in severe haemophilia. The left pectoral muscle is the site of haemorrhage, which developed spontaneously.

can be achieved by coagulation factor replacement by the intravenous route, but this must be administered 12-hourly or by continuous infusion to maintain adequate factor VIII or IX levels. Modern management of severe haemophilia is by prophylaxis administered two or three times per week to convert severe into moderate phenotypes.

Molecular genetics
Molecular genetic studies have recognised a variety of defects in haemophilia, including large deletions of the factor VIII gene, as well as single base changes, which create either a translational stop signal (so-called nonsense mutations), with the consequent synthesis of a truncated protein that is ineffective functionally and rapidly degraded, or single amino acid substitutions that alter the stability and function of the proteins. Inversions in intron 22 and intron 1 are common causes of severe haemophilia A. Large deletions are less common in haemophilia B. Mutations occurring de novo account for a substantial proportion of affected subjects (around 30%).

Clinical features and treatment
Spontaneous haemorrhage into a major joint, especially knees, hips, elbows and shoulders, occurring several times each month is typical of the untreated severe disease. Without factor replacement therapy bleeding continues until the intra-articular pressure rises sufficiently to prevent further haemorrhage. Slow resolution of this exquisitely painful acute haemarthrosis then occurs. Recurrent bleeds within a joint produce massive synovial hypertrophy, erosion of joint cartilage and para-articular bone and changes of a severe osteoarthritis (Ch. 25).

Bleeding into muscles (Fig. 23.47), retroperitoneal tissues and the urinary tract also occurs. Pressure necrosis of adjacent structures such as peripheral nerves may result.

The clinical picture in severe haemophilia is one of recurrent spontaneous haemarthrosis and soft tissue haemorrhage from around 6 months onwards. External bleeding from the urinary tract and epistaxis are also common. By

self-administration of clotting factor concentrate at the first symptoms of haemorrhage, or use of prophylactic factor replacement, many of the disabling consequences of haemophilia can now be avoided. The life expectancy in severe haemophilia rose spectacularly as a result of the introduction of coagulation factor concentrates but replacement therapy with these products prepared from pooled human plasma has led to other diseases in subjects receiving such treatment due to virus transmission. Liver disease due to hepatitis C (Ch. 16) is universal in haemophiliacs treated with concentrates prior to the introduction of virucidal preparation using heat and solvents. This disease may be progressive, with changes of cirrhosis and hepatocellular carcinoma eventually ensuing and resulting in the death of a proportion of patients. Many haemophiliac subjects have also contracted hepatitis B, although only 5% of them are persistently HBsAg positive.

Many UK haemophiliacs were infected with HIV and developed the pathological features of the acquired immune deficiency syndrome (AIDS), including *Pneumocystis jiroveci* pneumonia, toxoplasmosis and systemic candidiasis. Modern virucidally treated factor concentrates appear to be free of hepatitis viruses and HIV, and recombinant factor VIII and IX is now available. The description of transmission of variant Creutzfeldt–Jakob disease (vCJD) by blood transfusion has alerted clinicians to the possibility of passage of this agent by pooled plasma products, although no case has yet been described in an individual with haemophilia.

In around 12% of severe haemophilia A and less than 1% of haemophilia B patients, exposure to therapeutic factor VIII or IX leads to development of antibody to the clotting factor. The presence of such inhibitors makes management of affected individuals very difficult, as infused clotting factor is rendered ineffective by the antibody. Rarely subjects without a congenital bleeding disorder develop comparable clotting factor inhibitors, usually directed against factor VIII. The factor VIII concentration in plasma is markedly reduced and bleeding is often spontaneous and life-threatening in these cases of acquired haemophilia.

Other coagulation factor deficiencies

Deficiency of factor XII is common. Although the APTT is prolonged, there is no bleeding tendency, as factor XII is not essential for normal coagulation in vivo (p. 616). Factor XI deficiency is a relatively common disorder in some populations. Again, the APTT is prolonged but the bleeding tendency is variable and often subclinical. Recessively inherited deficiencies of factor V, VII, X and XIII are very uncommon but severe bleeding diathesis often presents with umbilical stump or intracranial bleeding in the neonatal period.

von Willebrand disease

von Willebrand disease (vWD) is most commonly a mild bleeding disorder. It is due to synthesis of vWF in reduced amounts or production of functionally abnormal vWF. It is transmitted as an autosomal dominant disorder in most kindred, and epidemiological studies suggest it may be common in mild or subclinical form.

The majority of cases have a quantitative deficiency of vWF (Type 1), but in around 20% a dysfunctional vWF is synthesised and in these the multimeric structure of vWF (Fig. 23.46) is often abnormal, with a reduction in the large multimers (Type 2A and 2B). Types 2M and 2N have a normal multimeric pattern but have abnormalities in binding to platelets and factor VIII respectively. There is marked genetic heterogeneity. The homozygous disease (Type 3) is a serious bleeding diathesis but is extremely uncommon. In the more usual heterozygous form the main manifestations are easy bruising, bleeding after trauma and menorrhagia in females. Haemarthrosis and muscle haematomas are not common features of vWD.

The plasma concentration of vWF is reduced, and, because of the requirement for vWF as a carrier protein, factor VIII activity is reduced in parallel; levels of less than 10–20% of normal are unusual, however. The bleeding time is prolonged due to the defect of platelet interaction with exposed subendothelium which arises from a reduced availability of vWF. The APTT is prolonged due to factor VIII deficiency. vWF-rich concentrate prepared from plasma is used for treatment of severe haemorrhage. In many patients the vWF level can be temporarily increased by stimulating its release from endothelial cells by administration of an analogue of vasopressin—desmopressin. This is also effective in mild haemophilia.

Acquired disorders of coagulation

Bleeding due to acquired platelet disorders has been described above. A haemorrhagic diathesis due to coagulation factor deficiency is present in liver disease, disseminated intravascular coagulation and vitamin K deficiency due to immaturity (haemorrhagic disease of the newborn), obstructive jaundice, pancreatic disease or small bowel disease.

Bleeding may also be a feature of therapy with anticoagulant and fibrinolytic drugs and is occasionally due to the development of an acquired inhibitor to factor VIII which develops in isolation or in individuals with B-cell malignancy, autoimmune disease or rarely pregnancy.

Vitamin K deficiency

Vitamin K is obtained from green vegetables and by bacterial synthesis in the gut. It is a fat-soluble vitamin and requires bile for its absorption. Vitamin K is essential for the gamma-carboxylation of clotting factors II, VII, IX and X (and the natural anticoagulants protein C and protein S); in the absence of vitamin K, these factors are released from the liver in an incomplete and inactive form. The PT is particularly prolonged as a result.

A coagulopathy due to vitamin K deficiency occurs when absorption is defective, particularly in obstructive jaundice. In addition, the neonate tends to have vitamin K deficiency due to poor transplacental passage of maternal vitamin K, lack of gut bacteria and low concentrations of the vitamin in breast milk. This exacerbates the inefficient coagulation resulting from low levels of clotting factors secondary to liver immaturity and may produce life-threatening haemorrhage during the first week of life—*haemorrhagic disease of the newborn*. Vitamin K supplementation corrects the defect.

The oral anticoagulant drug warfarin is a vitamin K antagonist and acts by inhibiting the complete synthesis of coagulation factors II, VII, IX and X. Its use is therefore associated with an increased risk of haemorrhage.

Liver disease

Severe hepatocellular disease is commonly associated with coagulation defects due to failure of clotting factor synthesis, including fibrinogen, and production of abnormal fibrinogen—dysfibrinogenaemia. This is often compounded by thrombocytopenia due to hypersplenism, which complicates portal hypertension, and a qualitative platelet disorder. The skin bleeding time may be prolonged, as is the PT, and often the APTT. Life-threatening haemorrhage may result, particularly from oesophageal varices.

Disseminated intravascular coagulation

Disseminated intravascular coagulation (DIC) is a common state in which a combination of haemorrhage and thrombosis complicates another disorder. Activation of coagulation leads to the formation of microthrombi in numerous organs and to the consumption of clotting factors and platelets in the process of clot formation, in turn leading to a haemorrhagic diathesis. There are several potential triggers to coagulation activation in DIC (Fig. 23.48) and a wide range of disorders can be complicated by this phenomenon:

- infection (e.g. septicaemia, malaria)
- neoplasm (e.g. mucin-secreting adenocarcinoma)
- tissue trauma (e.g. burns, major accidental trauma, major surgery, shock, intravascular haemolysis, dissecting aortic aneurysm)
- obstetric complications (e.g. abruptio placentae, retained dead fetus, amniotic fluid embolism, toxaemia)
- liver disease.

The pathogenesis of DIC is complex and centres on the enhanced generation of thrombin. Factors that contribute to the process include increased tissue factor expression, suboptimal function of natural anticoagulants, dysregulation of fibrinolysis and the increased availability of anionic phospholipids. Thus, in obstetric disorders, tissue factor release into the maternal circulation from the placenta or fetus, or in amniotic fluid, may trigger coagulation. Many tumours are also rich in procoagulant substances. Septicaemia may also cause coagulation activation by damage to vascular endothelium and induction of tissue factor expression by endothelial cells and monocytes. In liver disease there is reduced clearance of activated clotting factors.

Dysregulated fibrinolytic activity results in the production of plasmin which causes digestion of fibrin and fibrinogen-generating split products (fibrinogen and fibrin degradation products; FDP), which themselves have an anticoagulant and anti-platelet effect and contribute to the haemorrhagic diathesis (Fig. 23.48).

Thrombi, composed of platelets and fibrin, may be found in the microvasculature of brain, lungs, kidneys, heart, spleen and liver. Other organs may also be affected. The distribution of affected organs is variable. Micro-infarcts or more major areas of infarction such as renal cortical necrosis or hepatic necrosis may result. Areas of haemorrhage may also be apparent histologically and on gross examination; any organ may be affected.

The blood platelet count is often low and the PT and APTT prolonged; the fibrinogen concentration may be reduced. Coagulation factors V and VIII are consumed during fibrin

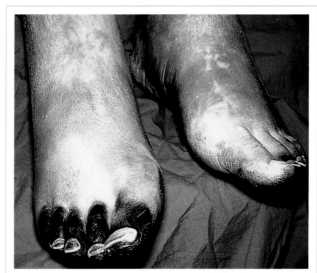

Fig. 23.49 Disseminated intravascular coagulation. There is peripheral gangrene due to small vessel thrombosis.

generation, and plasma levels may be severely reduced. FDP are present in high concentration. Red cells become damaged as they pass through partially occluded small vessels, and the blood changes of a microangiopathic haemolytic anaemia may be present. The above changes are present in florid DIC. In some cases the course is more chronic and the blood changes considerably more subtle.

Clinical features

These include haemorrhage, which may be torrential, multi-organ failure due to ischaemia, and haemolytic anaemia. Bleeding is from mucous membranes, and into skin, serosal cavities and internal organs. Organ dysfunction may manifest as hepatic or renal failure, neurological disturbance or cardiac and respiratory failure. In some cases a predominantly haemorrhagic picture dominates; in others, thrombotic peripheral ischaemia and gangrene are the major features (Fig. 23.49). Chronic 'low-grade' DIC may be only mildly symptomatic. Treatment is largely removal of the underlying cause and clotting factor and platelet replacement. Mortality is high in severe cases.

Coagulation disorders associated with a thrombotic tendency

Familial thrombophilia

Control mechanisms for the prevention of inappropriate fibrin deposition are an important feature of the coagulation system. These mechanisms include the rapid lysis of fibrin by plasmin generated at the site of a thrombus, neutralisation of thrombin by antithrombin, and inactivation of factors Va and VIIIa by activated protein C with its co-factor, protein S (Fig. 23.9). Hereditary defects of these control mechanisms have been described which lead to a life-long tendency to thrombosis—*thrombophilia*. The thrombosis in these familial thrombophilic states is almost always in the venous system: deep venous thrombosis of the limbs and

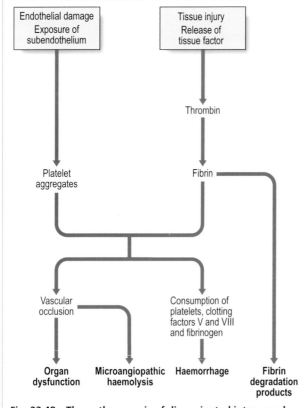

Fig. 23.48 The pathogenesis of disseminated intravascular coagulation.

pulmonary embolism. Thrombotic events rarely manifest before adulthood and usually occur when a second risk factor is also present, commonly pregnancy, exposure to female hormones in the combined oral contraceptive or hormone replacement therapy, immobilisation or surgery. The recognised familial abnormalities associated with such a thrombotic tendency are:

- *antithrombin deficiency* resulting in failure of thrombin neutralisation
- *protein C and protein S deficiency* resulting in failure of neutralisation of activated factors Va and VIIIa
- *activated protein C resistance*, the commonest cause of familial thrombophilia, where a point mutation in the factor V gene leads to synthesis of a factor V variant that has normal procoagulant activity but which is not inhibited by activated protein C; this variant, called factor V Leiden, is present in 5% or more of northern European subjects
- a point mutation in the *prothrombin gene* resulting in an increased plasma concentration of prothrombin, present in around 2% of northern Europeans
- *dysfibrinogenaemia* resulting in abnormal fibrinogen.

Individuals with antithrombin deficiency are heterozygous for the defect. Over 30 mutations leading to deficiency of the protein have been discovered, mostly caused by frameshifts or base changes resulting in a protein that is not secreted or is rapidly removed from the circulation. This type of deficiency is designated 'Type 1'. In Type 2 a dysfunctional protein is produced due to one of several single base changes that alter the amino acid sequence of the synthesised antithrombin.

Subjects deficient in protein C or protein S are also heterozygous, the homozygous condition producing a severe thrombotic disease often manifesting in the neonate. Type 1 and Type 2 (dysfunctional) defects are also found in protein C deficiency. Several mutations in the genes for protein C and protein S have been identified.

One or more of these genetic thrombophilias, most commonly factor V Leiden, can be found in around 30% of subjects with deep vein thrombosis, and affected family members are also at increased risk of venous thromboembolism compared with the background population.

Acquired prothrombotic states

Acquired coagulation disorders causing thrombosis are also recognised. In systemic lupus erythematosus (SLE) a predisposition to arterial and venous thrombosis is associated with a paradoxical prolongation of the APTT, apparently due to the development of auto-antibodies which interact with phospholipid-bound proteins involved in coagulation activation ('antiphospholipid antibodies'). Stroke and deep venous thrombosis are common. These antibodies are also associated with major thrombotic disease in subjects without other evidence of SLE. Women with such antibodies are prone to pregnancy failure due to recurrent miscarriage, possibly secondary to placental thrombosis or poor implantation.

The term *antiphospholipid syndrome* describes those patients with thrombosis or pregnancy failure associated with persistent antiphospholipid antibody. The mechanisms underlying thrombosis in this disorder are not yet known. Long-term therapy with anticoagulant drugs is often indicated, as the risk of recurrent thrombosis is high. The antibodies can be detected in the laboratory through the ability to prolong clotting times in coagulation tests that involve low concentrations of phospholipid, when the term *lupus anticoagulant* is used, or through binding to negatively charged phospholipid, such as cardiolipin—the *anticardiolipin* antibody.

Thrombosis risk is also increased in a range of other conditions, including myeloproliferative diseases (p. 664), cancer, nephrotic syndrome, congestive cardiac failure, atrial fibrillation and paroxysmal nocturnal haemoglobinuria (p. 651).

An increased plasma concentration of homocysteine is also associated with a tendency to thrombosis. The homocysteine level is partly genetically determined, but is also influenced by the dietary content of vitamin B_{12}, folate and pyridoxine (Fig. 23.19). This raises the intriguing possibility of reducing thrombosis risk by dietary manipulation and this approach is currently under investigation.

ANTENATAL DIAGNOSIS OF BLOOD DISORDERS

Several of the more serious haematological disorders can be diagnosed in the fetus. Fetal blood can be obtained from the placenta or umbilical vein with imaging using ultrasound scanning techniques from around the middle of the second trimester. This material can be used for detection of abnormalities of red cells, white cells or platelets and for diagnosis of clotting factor deficiencies. For example, thalassaemia can be identified by measuring relative rates of globin chain synthesis. Alternatively amniotic fluid cells can be obtained by aspiration of the amniotic fluid, and techniques have been developed by which fetal material can be safely obtained by biopsy of chorionic villi, this being performed as early as 9–11 weeks' gestation.

Fetal DNA can be analysed by restriction endonuclease mapping and RFLP linkage analysis but increasingly direct sequencing for known mutations is used. Using these techniques, first trimester prenatal diagnosis of beta-thalassaemias and of haemophilia has become possible. Gene probes for the diagnosis of red cell enzyme defects are also becoming available.

New non-invasive methods utilising the detection of fetal cells in maternal blood are now starting to be offered in clinical practice.

BLOOD TRANSFUSION

Donor blood, or fractions of blood, can be safely and beneficially administered intravenously. Transfusion of red cells is valuable in the management of some anaemias and in resuscitation after acute haemorrhage, and is essential for the safe performance of many surgical procedures. Other cellular components of blood, especially platelets, can be usefully transfused, for example to treat bleeding in severely thrombocytopenic subjects. Blood plasma is fractionated to provide albumin, immunoglobulin and coagulation factors or can be used as a complete entity as 'fresh-frozen plasma'. In red cell transfusion it is essential that compatibility is ensured between antigens on the donor erythrocytes and antibodies present in the recipient's plasma in order to avoid acute haemolysis of the donor cells which may be fatal. The cross-match procedure is used to determine compatibility. The red cells from the donor unit are incubated with the recipient's serum under a range of conditions that enhance sensitivity to any antibody present. Agglutination or lysis of the red cells indicates the presence of clinically important red cell antibody and that the donor unit is incompatible and cannot be safely administered to the recipient.

Red cell antigens and antibodies

Although there are about 400 red blood cell antigens, most inherited in Mendelian dominant fashion, only a minority are clinically important. An individual lacking a particular antigen may develop an antibody after exposure to red cells carrying that antigen. Exposure occurs by transfusion of red cells or by passage of fetal red cells into the maternal circulation during pregnancy, the fetal cells carrying paternal antigens foreign to the mother. The important clinical consequences of the development of such an 'immune' antibody are the development of a *haemolytic transfusion reaction* on further exposure to red cells carrying the antigen, and *haemolytic disease of the newborn* due to transplacental passage of maternal IgG antibody against fetal red cell antigens.

The most important *'immune' antibody* is anti-D, an antibody to the major antigen of the rhesus blood group system (Table 23.12). It is a major cause of haemolytic disease of the newborn.

As well as 'immune' antibodies, *'naturally occurring'* antibodies to red cell antigens are also important. In contrast to the IgG immune antibodies, they are predominantly IgM and require no previous red cell antigen exposure. They occur in the ABO blood group system, where naturally occurring anti-A and anti-B are present in subjects whose red cells lack the corresponding antigen (Table 23.13).

In addition to the ABO and rhesus blood group systems the major red cell antigen systems of clinical importance are Kell, Duffy and Kidd, as, with ABO and rhesus, their antibodies are responsible for most cases of haemolytic transfusion reaction.

Clinically important platelet antigens are also recognised. Human platelet antigen 1a (HPA1a) is present on platelets in around 98% of Caucasians. Subjects lacking the antigen are at risk of allo-antibody development from exposure to HPA1a platelets during pregnancy or blood transfusion. Anti-HPA1a is responsible for most cases of post-transfusion purpura and neonatal alloimmune thrombocytopenic purpura (p. 671).

Haemolytic transfusion reactions

Immediate reactions

Massive intravascular haemolysis occurs when complement-activating antibodies, such as anti-A and anti-B, interact with the relevant antigen on transfused red cells. There is typically collapse, with hypotension and pain in the lumbar region. Haemoglobin-stained urine may be passed and oliguric renal failure may ensue. Red cell lysis may trigger disseminated intravascular coagulation. This clinical scenario can develop after transfusion with only a few millilitres of incompatible red cells. Treatment includes immediate interruption of the transfusion, resuscitation with intravenous fluid, immunosuppression with corticosteroid therapy and management of the renal failure. Fatalities still occur. The cross-match procedure should prevent exposure to such incompatible blood. However most cases result from clerical error through mislabelling of the cross-match sample or transfusion to the wrong recipient.

Because antibodies to the rhesus system are not complement-fixing, cell lysis occurs in the reticulo-endothelial system and reactions are generally milder, although they can still be life-threatening.

Delayed reactions

Occasionally a low titre antibody is too weak to be detectable in the cross-match and is unable to cause lysis at the time of transfusion. Transfusion of red cells carrying the relevant antigen leads to a gradual increase in the titre of the antibody, developing over a period of a few days. Delayed, gradual red cell lysis occurs, producing anaemia and jaundice; this is a delayed transfusion reaction.

Table 23.12 The rhesus blood group system

Allelic genes at closely linked loci code for paired antigens designated C and c, E and e and D. Absence of D is termed d. A set of genes and hence antigens is inherited from each parent and the presence of D determines rhesus 'positivity'.

Genotype	Rhesus status	% Frequency (UK)
cde\cde	Negative	15
CDe\cde	Positive	32
CDe\CDe	Positive	17
cDe\cde	Positive	13
CDe\cDE	Positive	14
Others	Positive	9

Table 23.13 The ABO blood group system

There are three allelic genes A, B and O. A and B genes control the synthesis of enzymes that modify the red cell membrane glycolipid. The unmodified molecule is known as H substance and is not modified in the presence of the O gene alone, which is an amorph. Thus there are six genotypes and four phenotypes.

Genotype	Phenotype	Natural antibodies	% Phenotypic frequency (UK)
OO	O	Anti-A, -B	46
AA or AO	A	Anti-B	42
BB or BO	B	Anti-A	9
AB	AB	None	3

Other adverse effects of transfusion

Most nucleated cells, including leukocytes, carry antigens of the HLA (human leukocyte antigen) or major histocompatibility complex system. Prior exposure to human leukocyte antigens by transfusion or pregnancy may lead to development of antibody capable of causing fever and rigors on subsequent exposure to the antigens present on leukocytes in transfused blood. This can be avoided by using filters to remove donor leukocytes prior to transfusion. Such *non-haemolytic transfusion reactions* are unpleasant but rarely dangerous. Allergic reactions may also develop in a recipient because of hypersensitivity to a protein present in the donor plasma. Fever, urticaria and oedema may result.

Virus transmission by blood transfusion was previously a major problem but this has been largely overcome by processes of deferral of donors identified as being at increased risk for certain virus infections including the hepatitis viruses and HIV, combined with increasingly sensitive methods of testing donated blood for antibodies, antigens or nucleic acid indicative of infection with these agents. Nevertheless, transmission of viruses for which screening is not possible or feasible, such as parvovirus and cytomegalovirus, does occur and, although transmission rates for the previously mentioned agents are low, transmission can theoretically still occur. Increased foreign travel has led to more donor exposure to other pathogens and has resulted in the need to defer donors returning from parts of the world where infections such as malaria and West Nile fever are endemic. It is likely that the prion responsible for variant Creutzfeld–Jakob disease can be transmitted by transfusion of blood and as a result potential donors who have been previously transfused are now excluded.

Circulatory overload may result from transfusion of excessive volume. Because bank blood is devoid of functioning platelets, transfusion of large volumes can cause thrombocytopenia and haemorrhage.

Repeated red cell transfusion without blood loss, usually in the management of chronic anaemias such as thalassaemia, inevitably leads to *tissue iron overload*. A unit of blood contains 200 mg of iron, in haemoglobin. Although, initially, deposition occurs in reticulo-endothelial tissues without toxic results, iron later accumulates in skin, liver, myocardium and pancreas. Pigmentation, liver cirrhosis (Ch. 16), heart failure and diabetes mellitus are the consequences. Iron chelating compounds, such as desferrioxamine and deferasirox, are administered by subcutaneous infusion to minimise iron accumulation in tissues.

Transfusion-related acute lung injury (TRALI), which presents with non-cardiac pulmonary oedema within 6 hours of transfusion, most commonly of fresh frozen plasma, is an immunological complication of transfusion mediated by anti-leukocyte antibodies. The main intervention is supportive care. Finally, transfusion-associated graft-versus-host disease is seen following the transfusion of competent lymphocytes into an immuno-incompetent recipient. The transfused cells engraft over around 10 days and then mount an immune attack on the donor due to histo-incompatibility which results in fever, skin rash, pancytopenia and liver failure, which is usually fatal. This occurs in patients with congenital and acquired cell-mediated immune dysfunction—for example, severe combined immunodeficiency (SCID), lymphoma, allogeneic bone marrow transplant and the use of purine analogue drugs. It is prevented by supplying these patients with irradiated cellular blood products.

Commonly confused conditions and entities relating to the blood and bone marrow	
Commonly confused	Distinction and explanation
Pernicious and *megaloblastic anaemia*	*Pernicious anaemia* is a specific example of *megaloblastic anaemia* in which autoimmune gastritis results in loss of intrinsic factor and failure to absorb vitamin B_{12}. *Megaloblastic anaemia* can also be due to folate deficiency and to other causes of B_{12} deficiency.
Polycythaemia rubra vera and *secondary polycythaemia*	Both are characterised by an increased concentration of red blood cells. *Polycythaemia rubra vera* is a clonal myeloproliferative condition, whereas *secondary polycythaemia* is usually a physiological response to hypoxia or to inappropriately excessive erythropoietin production.
Myelodysplasia, myelofibrosis and *myeloproliferative diseases*	The *myelodysplastic syndromes* are neoplastic bone marrow disorders at the stem cell level, affecting all myeloid lines, with characteristic morphological changes in the marrow and a tendency to progress to acute leukaemia. *Myelofibrosis* is characterised by marrow fibrosis and the emergence of extramedullary haemopoiesis. *Myeloproliferative diseases,* a group of disorders with abnormal proliferation of one or more cell lines, including myelofibrosis, chronic myeloid leukaemia, polycythaemia rubra vera and essential thrombocythaemia, are grouped together because intermediate forms exist and progression from one to another is common.

FURTHER READING

Hehlmann R, Hochhaus A, Baccarani M 2007 European LeukemiaNet. Chronic myeloid leukaemia. Lancet 370: 342–350

Hoffbrand A V, Tuddenham E G, Catovsky D (eds) 2005 Postgraduate haematology, 5th edn. Blackwell Publishing, Oxford

Hoffbrand A V, Pettit J, Moss P (eds) 2006 Essential haematology, 5th edn. Blackwell Publishing, Oxford

Melo J V, Barnes D J 2007 Chronic myeloid leukaemia as a model of disease evolution in human cancer. Nat Rev Cancer 7: 441–453

24

Skin

COMMON CLINICAL PROBLEMS FROM SKIN DISEASE

Macule(s)
- viral exanthems
- drug rashes
- freckles
- lentigo
- actinic keratosis
- Bowen's disease
- melanocytic naevus
- malignant melanoma

Papule(s)
- acne vulgaris
- acne rosacea
- urticaria
- lichen planus
- molluscum
- melanocytic naevus
- seborrhoeic keratosis
- viral wart
- dermatofibroma
- actinic keratosis
- basal cell carcinoma
- malignant melanoma

Nodule
- cyst
- lipoma
- pyogenic granuloma
- basal cell carcinoma
- squamous cell carcinoma
- malignant melanoma

Plaque(s)
- psoriasis
- eczema
- lichen simplex chronicus
- cutaneous T-cell lymphoma

Leg ulcer
- venous–varicose
- arterial–atheroma
- diabetes mellitus
- pyoderma gangrenosum
- squamous cell carcinoma
- basal cell carcinoma

Alopecia
- male pattern baldness
- alopecia areata
- tinea
- lichen planus
- lupus erythematosus

Scale(s)
- eczema
- psoriasis
- pityriasis rosea
- actinic keratosis
- Bowen's disease

Pustule(s)
- acne vulgaris
- impetigo
- herpes
- pustular psoriasis

Itching
- eczema
- urticaria
- psoriasis
- scabies
- lice

Abnormal nails
- trauma
- onychogryphosis
- lichen planus
- fungi

Blisters
- heat/friction
- eczema
- herpes
- pemphigoid
- dematitis herpetiformis
- pemphigus

Purpura
- trauma
- senile purpura
- haematological disease
- vasculitis

Pathological basis of dermatological signs	
Clinical sign	Pathological basis
Scaling	Parakeratosis
Erythema	Dilatation of skin vessels
Blisters	Separation of layers of the epidermis or epidermis from dermis
Bruising	Leakage of blood into dermis

(Continued)

Pathological basis of dermatological signs—cont'd	
Clinical sign	Pathological basis
Pigmentation	Increased activity of melanocytes Increased numbers of melanocytes Endogenous pigment, e.g. ochronosis Exogenous pigment, e.g. tattoo
Plaques	Increase in epidermal and dermal thickness with cells
Macules	Dilated blood vessels Inflammatory cells Altered pigmentation
Papules	Inflammatory cells Oedema Tumour
Nodules	Epidermal tumours Adnexal tumours Dermal tumours (fibroblasts, vessels, etc.) Cysts
Rashes restricted to exposed areas	Photosensitivity Contact eczema
Nail abnormalities	Trauma to nail bed Psoriasis Fungi

NORMAL STRUCTURE AND FUNCTION

The two major layers of the skin—the superficial *epidermis* and deeper *dermis*—are derived from different embryonic components and retain a radically different morphology (Fig. 24.1). The epidermis is highly cellular, avascular, lacks nerves, sits on a basement membrane and shows marked vertical stratification (Fig. 24.2). It produces a complex mixture of proteins collectively termed *keratin*. A series of specialised *adnexa* extend from the epidermis into the dermis. The density of these adnexa varies from site to site on the body, as does the thickness of the epidermis and the structure of the keratin layer. This site-to-site variation means that the histological interpretation of diagnostic biopsies has to take into account the area of the body from which the biopsy was taken; what may constitute severe hyperkeratosis (excess keratin) on the forehead may be normal for the sole of the foot.

Although the epidermis consists mostly of epithelial cells in various stages of maturation, from the mitotic pool in the basal layer through the various post-mitotic squamous cells to fully formed keratin, there are other, non-epithelial, cells present. Like the melanocytes described below, some of these cells—*Langerhans' cells*—are dendritic and their function is to present antigen to lymphocytes. They are members of the monocyte/macrophage series and contain a subcellular organelle found in no other cell—the Birbeck granule. Similar cells are found in the lymph node presenting antigen to T-lymphocytes, and in the thymus. Indeed, there are many similarities between skin and thymus: the thymus contains keratinised structures termed Hassall's corpuscles, and the same mutation that results in athymic mice also renders them hairless ('nude' mice).

The *dermis* is relatively acellular and is recognisably divided into two zones: the upper zone comprises extensions of the dermis (dermal papillae) between the downward projecting rete ridges ('pegs') of the epidermis and is called the *papillary dermis*; beneath this zone is the *reticular dermis*. Both regions of the dermis contain blood and lymph vessels as well as nerves. The intervening connective tissue consists of the characteristic dermal proteins collagen and elastin, together with various glycosaminoglycans. These proteins and complex carbohydrates are secreted by the principal cells of the dermis, the fibroblasts. Although the proteins of the dermis appear to be arranged in a haphazard fashion when viewed in standard histological preparations, they are in fact arranged in specific patterns that are characteristic of different sites in the body; these patterns are the *Langer's lines*. The significance of this knowledge is that if incisions are made in the skin along the long axis of the dermal collagen fibres then little permanent scarring will occur. If, however, incisions are made across the fibres and disrupt them, then in the effort to repair the damage scarring is bound to result. A considerable part of the surgeon's skill relies on knowing the characteristic orientation of these fibres and in making incisions that generate the minimum risk of permanent scars. Scattered within the dermis and often clustered about blood vessels are the *mast cells*. The nerves of the dermis approach close to

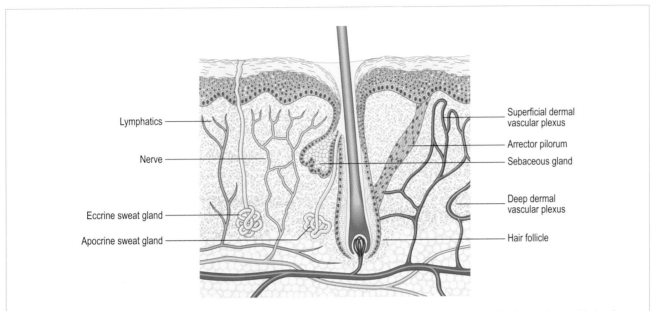

Fig. 24.1   Normal skin. There are two main regions: the superficial epidermis with adnexal extensions into the deeper dermis. Notice that there are no blood vessels, lymphatics or nerves in the epidermis.

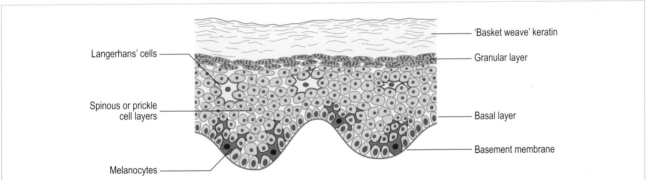

Fig. 24.2   Normal epidermis. The cells in the basal layer divide and a daughter cell progresses through the epidermis and eventually dies and contributes to the outer, keratin layer. At the base there are dendritic melanocytes producing and donating pigment to surrounding epidermal cells. Scattered through the epidermis are dendritic Langerhans' cells which are part of the antigen-presenting system of the body.

the epidermis and often end in specialised sensory structures such as *Pacinian corpuscles*. Similarly, the dermal blood vessels run close to the underside of the epidermis, although they are organised into two recognisable structures—the *superficial* and *deep vascular plexuses*.

At the dermo-epidermal junction are pigmented dendritic cells—the *melanocytes*. There is about one to every six basal epithelial cells, regardless of race or degree of pigmentation. On electron microscopy, their dendritic processes can be seen to be closely applied to the surrounding basal cells, to which they transfer packets of preformed *melanin*. The donated melanin forms a cap over the nucleus, protecting it from damage by the ultraviolet light in sunlight. Racial differences in pigmentation result from the amount and distribution of this pigment.

Below the dermis is a layer of fat (panniculus adiposus or subcutaneous fat) and in most mammals, but not in humans, there is also a layer of muscle (panniculus carnosus). In

humans, the only remnants of this are the platysma muscle in the neck and the dartos muscle in the scrotum. The only other muscles found in human skin are those associated with hair follicles—the *arrector pili*.

Skin as a barrier

The most important function of the skin is to serve as a barrier between the individual and the external environment. Organisms must overcome this barrier to gain access to the individual's internal environment. This is important because burns victims die from their loss of barrier function through water loss and bacterial invasion.

The other way in which the barrier is often breached is at the weak points where there are natural holes in the barrier, such as the sweat glands and hair ducts, and organisms may use these portals of entry.

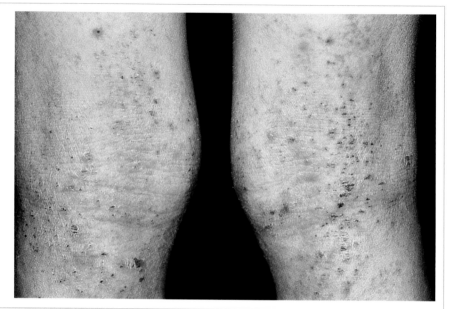

Fig. 24.3 Eczema. This scaly eruption can occur as a reaction to many triggering factors. There is marked oedema within the epidermis and the lesions are often very itchy. This is a case of atopic eczema, in which there is an inherent predisposition to eczema as well as to allergic rhinitis and asthma.

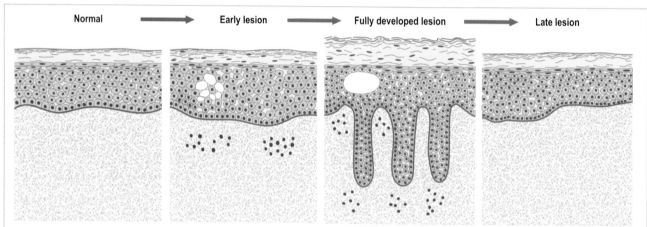

Normal	Early lesion	Fully developed lesion	Late lesion

Fig. 24.4 Eczema. This inflammatory skin condition may have a great variety of precipitating factors. The progression from normal skin to healed lesion is shown diagrammatically from left to right.

Failure of the barrier (eczema and immersion)

The barrier function of the skin can be either damaged (as in eczema) or overwhelmed (as in immersion).

Eczema/dermatitis

▸ A reaction pattern, not a single disease
▸ Several causes
▸ Varied clinical patterns
▸ Characterised histologically by inflammation and spongiosis

The word *eczema* comes from the Greek meaning to 'bubble up'; this meaning conveys well the clinical development of the lesions. The word *dermatitis* is often used in an interchangeable manner, in particular when referring to the histopathological changes. The skin becomes reddened (erythematous) and tiny vesicles may develop (pompholyx); the surface develops scales, and cracking and bleeding can cause great discomfort (Fig. 24.3). The skin becomes tender and secondary infection may occur. The clinical pattern is very varied and there are several different types of eczema. Sometimes the variation is due to the cause of the eczema, such as contact with a toxic or allergenic material; sometimes the site of the lesion or the age of the patient is sufficient to make the disease a clinical entity. For example, chromate hypersensitivity causes eczema in cement workers and discoid/atopic eczema occurs in atopic individuals. Seborrhoeic eczema has a tendency to involve the scalp, face, axillae and groins. Whatever the cause, the underlying pathological processes are recognisably similar and can be seen as a stereotyped reaction pattern to a variety of different stimuli.

The earliest histological change in eczema is swelling within the epidermis (Fig. 24.4). This swelling is due to separation of the keratinocytes by fluid accumulating between them and this appearance is known as spongiosis. Later, there

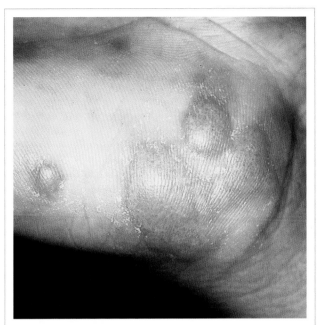

Fig. 24.5 Pompholyx. The extreme form of epidermal oedema (spongiosis) can express itself as intra-epidermal blisters.

may be *hyperkeratosis* (an increase in the thickness of the stratum corneum) and *parakeratosis* (retention of nuclei in the stratum corneum), which give rise to the clinical scales. Various degrees of inflammation also give rise to the classical inflammatory signs and symptoms (Ch. 10). In severe cases the intercellular oedema can then join up to form foci of fluid within the epidermis, recognised clinically as blisters or vesicles (pompholyx) (Fig. 24.5).

In all forms of eczema the barrier is damaged and water loss can occur, but material can also pass the other way and allergens may enter the skin, elicit an allergic response and produce a superimposed allergic eczema. People with long-standing eczema commonly have hypersensitivities to numerous materials that the eczema has allowed to penetrate, particularly medicaments that have been used to treat it.

The treatment of eczema includes reducing the inflammation by topical steroids, attending to the water loss in dry skin and the use of barrier creams.

Prolonged itching (pruritus) of the skin and rubbing can give rise to thickened/lichenified skin called *lichen simplex chronicus*.

Immersion

▶ Prolonged immersion in water may overwhelm the barrier
▶ May be used for topical therapy

The barrier function of the skin, although efficient, can be overwhelmed. This occurs particularly after prolonged immersion in water.

Various groups of patients are occupationally exposed to immersion; the most common are housewives. They are in daily skin contact with large amounts of water, often containing agents capable of removing the skin barrier, such

as detergents. This situation has led to the development of numerous synthetic barrier creams, containing water repellents such as silicone, which mimic the action of the physiological barrier.

Localised swelling can be seen with the use of occlusive dressings for burns or under surgical dressings. Use is made of this phenomenon, of breakdown of the skin barrier, in the application of topical pharmacological agents beneath occlusive dressings to aid penetration.

CLINICAL ASPECTS OF SKIN DISEASES

Any component of the skin can be affected by any category of disease, whether it be inflammatory or neoplastic, but some components are affected more often and more characteristically by particular processes than are others. For instance, the epidermis frequently produces both benign and malignant tumours (neoplasms), whereas a malignant tumour of the sweat glands is a rarity. Similarly, with age, some diseases are more likely than others: blisters in the young are likely to be infective, in the younger adult they are likely to be dermatitis herpetiformis, while in the elderly they are more likely to be pemphigoid.

There are several reasons why the skin seems to produce such a wide variety of pathological conditions. One reason is that it is so visible and the quality of the skin is a major contribution to a person's appearance.

A second reason is that the skin has three layers, so that there are diseases of the epidermis, dermis and subcutaneous fat. Added to all of this are the effects of the mechanical, chemical, thermal, radiant, parasitic, cosmetic and therapeutic environments. Its appendages are dyed, permed, deodorised and varnished in accordance with fluctuations in fashion and new generations of micro-organisms attack it daily.

The great advantage of the skin from the point of view of the pathologist and dermatologist is that the gross pathology is always visible and does not have to be inferred from stethoscopes, or imaging, and that its accessibility means that it can be readily biopsied.

Incidence of skin diseases

Skin diseases, like all diseases, vary in their distribution according to a wide range of factors (Table 24.1), but they also vary markedly in the experience of particular doctors. A hospital dermatologist running a pigmented skin lesion clinic will see many melanomas in a year, depending on the population make-up of the catchment area and its size, whereas a general practitioner in the same area may expect to see only one every 2 years. A dermatologist will see only the difficult cases of acne and pityriasis rosea but a general practitioner will see many more straightforward ones. With these reservations in mind, skin diseases can be categorised according to their frequency:

● common—acne, psoriasis, eczema, varicose leg ulcers, moles, seborrhoeic and viral warts, actinic keratoses, basal cell carcinoma, squamous cell carcinoma

Table 24.1 Incidence of skin diseases	
Variable	**Associations**
Age	Impetigo in children Acne in adolescence Pemphigus in old age
Sex	Acne commoner in boys Bullous pemphigoid of pregnancy ('herpes gestationis')
Anatomical site	Psoriasis and dermatitis herpetiformis common on elbows and knees Atopic eczema (lichenified) in antecubital fossae Scabies in finger webs
Geography	Parasites in developing world Psoriasis in Faroe Islands (inbred community)
Exposure	Basal cell carcinoma and squamous cell carcinoma common on sun-exposed sites
Race	Basal cell carcinoma and squamous cell carcinoma and melanoma rare in blacks (protected by pigmentation)

- uncommon—pemphigoid, pemphigus, melanoma, scabies
- rare—xeroderma pigmentosum, dermatitis artefacta, mycosis fungoides.

DISORDERS INVOLVING INFLAMMATORY AND HAEMOPOIETIC CELLS

Many of the characteristics of inflammation (Ch. 10) were first observed and studied in the skin. The various phases and types of inflammation are characterised by a particular spectrum of cells that mediate the inflammatory response. Because the types of cell in a particular lesion are there in response to the initiating factor, a careful analysis of the composition of a particular lesion will significantly narrow down the differential diagnosis. Thus, cuffing of vessels by plasma cells would strongly suggest syphilis and the presence of granulomas with caseous centres would suggest tuberculosis.

Because inflammatory cells must enter tissues from the blood stream, the epidermis, which lacks blood vessels, must receive its inflammatory infiltrate secondarily from the dermis. The only cells that are an exception in this situation are the Langerhans' cells and these antigen-presenting cells in the epidermis are in a prime position to encounter new antigens. Langerhans' cells are intimately involved in the development of those contact hypersensitivities whose clinical expression is one form of eczema.

As in other body sites, there can also be an aberrant response by the body when an inflammatory reaction occurs as a result of autoimmune disease. In other cases, the inflammatory cells themselves may become abnormal and the skin may become the site for neoplastic lesions composed of these cells.

The nature of the infiltrating cells within the skin is a reflection of the complex interactions of cytokines and adhesion molecules.

Polymorph infiltrates

> ▶ Pustules contain polymorphs
> ▶ May contain organisms (impetigo)
> ▶ May be sterile (psoriasis)

Neutrophil polymorphonuclear leukocytes (polymorphs) can accumulate in the skin in response to infection by pyogenic bacteria (e.g. *Staphylococcus aureus*) as in *impetigo* (p. 688).

Several conditions are characterised by polymorph infiltrations, although no infective process can be identified. *Psoriasis* is a very common disease which is thought to be a disorder of epidermal turnover and is considered fully below. However, psoriasis is also characterised by neutrophil migration from dilated superficial dermal vessels in such numbers that the disease may sometimes be dominated by the presence of numerous sterile pustules within the epidermis (pustular psoriasis).

Some diseases, such as *Sweet's disease* and *pyoderma gangrenosum* (skin lesions that may occur in association with various internal diseases such as chronic inflammatory bowel diseases; Ch. 15), show massive infiltration by polymorph neutrophils in the dermis.

In some cases, polymorphs are attracted by the deposition of auto-antibodies (Ch. 9) and in these cases the resulting damage often causes blistering. Antibodies to the basement membrane on which the epidermis sits and to proteins in the papillary dermis cause pemphigoid and dermatitis herpetiformis respectively (see below). The presence of one type of polymorph rather than another suggests different aetiological processes and dermatitis herpetiformis can sometimes be distinguished from bullous pemphigoid by the relative excess of neutrophil polymorphs in the former and eosinophil polymorphs in the latter. Eosinophil polymorphs are a frequent reflection of allergic diseases (such as eczema) and parasitic infestation.

Very rarely, deposits of leukaemic cells may occur in the skin, but the cells are often immature and generally do not resemble those seen within inflammatory pustules.

Lymphocytic infiltrates

> ▶ Most chronic inflammatory skin diseases contain lymphocytes of T-cell type
> ▶ Eczema is characterised by lymphocytes and spongiosis
> ▶ Neoplastic lymphoid lesions can be primary or secondary

Any chronic inflammation of the skin will eventually come to be dominated by lymphocytes, but there are many skin conditions that are primarily due to lymphocyte accumulation and whose distinctive clinical character is due to the disposition and behaviour of these cells. The lymphocytes present in inflammation are usually of T-cell type and most commonly of CD4/helper phenotype.

In *eczema* the epidermis is penetrated by lymphocytes that with spongiosis eventually can accumulate in sufficient numbers to form an intra-epidermal abscess. In *lupus erythematosus* the lymphocytes cluster about the hair follicles and the base of the epidermis, resulting in atrophy of the skin and scarring alopecia (baldness). In other cases, such as *lichen planus*, the attack on the base of the epidermis can be so aggressive that histologically it begins to separate from the dermis.

Cutaneous lymphomas

Secondary deposits of systemic lymphomas and primary lymphomas may occur within the skin. Both are relatively rare. Any of the lymphomas and leukaemias that occur systemically (Ch. 22) can give secondary deposits in the skin, but usually only in advanced cases. The primary lymphomas include *mycosis fungoides* which is a T-cell lymphoma and which, as it develops, can spill over into the blood to give an associated T-cell leukaemia, called the *Sézary syndrome*.

Mycosis fungoides provides a good example of the progression of a malignant lymphoid condition. Initially, the infiltrate is sparse and the only clinical sign is the presence of red patches of skin. As the lymphocytes begin to accumulate, raised plaques become visible. These become more and more pronounced until they form frank, ulcerating tumour nodules. Sézary syndrome can give rise to the clinical picture of the red man (l'homme rouge).

Occasionally, skin lymphomas also result from B-cell lymphocytes.

Histiocytic infiltrates

These usually present as granulomatous skin disease. In most instances, there must be a careful clinical search for infective causes, including mycobacteria, fungi and parasites. Not infrequently, the granulomas can be a manifestation of a systemic disease such as sarcoidosis. In other instances, the granulomas are indicative of primary skin disease, such as granuloma annulare, acne rosacea or necrobiosis lipoidica. At times histiocytes phagocytose lipid from the dermis with resulting yellow skin lesions called xanthoma and xanthelasma.

INFECTIONS

The clinical appearance depends on:

- site within the skin
- nature of the organism
- nature of the body's response to the organism.

There are two routes by which infection may arrive in the skin:

1. internally via some route such as the blood stream
2. externally by penetrating the skin barrier.

In practice, most infections arise via the latter route.

Another possible mechanism whereby infections can cause skin lesions is where the organism infects some other part of the body but produces a skin rash in which it is impossible to identify any organisms; this mechanism, for example,

occurs in acute rheumatic fever and is similar to the effects on the heart also seen in this condition (Ch. 13). *Staphylococcus* can produce a toxin and give rise to a blistering disorder called the staphylococcal scalded skin syndrome.

Infections may be due to a variety of different organisms—fungi, viruses, bacteria, protozoa and various metazoa. Many organisms live on or even in the skin but cause no harm to the host; these are called *commensals*, or, if they merely consume dead material, they may be called *saprophytes*.

The precise clinical nature of an infective skin disease depends not only on the nature of the infecting organism, but also on the precise nature of the host response to it.

Viral infections

Viruses are obligate intracellular organisms that usurp the replicative processes of the cell for their own replication. In the skin, they tend to parasitise the metabolically active basal cells of the epidermis which are producing new DNA and RNA; these processes are taken over by the virus for its own reproduction. The actual assembling and packaging of total virions occurs higher in the epidermis and this process is complete by the time they reach the surface, where they are released to be passed on to another host. Consequently, they are easiest to detect in the upper layers of the epidermis where they are fully formed and present in large numbers.

Human papillomavirus (HPV) (a DNA virus of which there are numerous subtypes) has attracted interest because of its role in the development of cervical cancer in the human (Chs 11 and 19). In human skin these viruses are responsible for squamous cell papillomas (warts or verrucae). The precise clinical appearance of the wart depends on the particular HPV type concerned and the body site involved. The keratotic, exophytic growths of *verrucae vulgaris* may occur anywhere on the skin or oral mucosa while the flat *verruca plana* occurs more commonly on the face and the backs of the hands. Another form, *verruca palmaris* or *plantaris* is much deeper and causes the bothersome lesions on the soles of the feet of children and of individuals who share communal washing facilities. Genital warts are large, fleshy polyps called *condyloma acuminatum* and are located at those sites where person-to-person contact is most likely to promote effective spread.

Molluscum contagiosum is a very characteristic umbilicated self-limiting lesion in children produced by a DNA pox virus.

Herpes viruses are DNA viruses often responsible for skin disease. Herpes zoster virus is responsible for the relatively benign infectious disease of childhood known as *chickenpox*, but it can also take refuge in the dorsal root ganglia and lie dormant for many years. As the patients become older and develop some degree of immune paresis, or if they develop some disease that produces or is treated by immunosuppression, the virus may escape its host restraints, travel down the nerves and manifest as *shingles*. This is a rash of herpetic blisters in a single nerve root distribution with severe pain and discomfort that may persist even after the blisters have healed and the viruses returned to their ganglionic hiding place.

Other herpes viruses are responsible for *cold sores* (HSV1) and for *genital herpes* (HSV2). The great problem with these kinds of herpetic infections is that they are infections for life.

Human immunodeficiency virus (HIV) infection in the skin can cause a transient itchy eruption. Most significant, however, in patients with HIV infection is the development of the blood vessel tumour, Kaposi's sarcoma, due to co-infection with *human herpes virus type 8*.

Virtually all common childhood viral infections (so-called exanthems) can present with maculo-papular eruptions, including glandular fever due to Epstein–Barr virus.

Bacterial infections

Bacteria are responsible for a wide range of skin infections. *Impetigo* is a staphylococcal infection in young children but is more commonly streptococcal in older patients. The organisms penetrate only a little way into the epidermis and form subcorneal pustules (collections of pus just beneath the stratum corneum). Because the pustules are so superficial, they rupture rapidly and the clinical picture of impetigo is a mixture of yellow pustules and crusted lesions, usually in a child. A complication in the streptococcal lesions is an immune reaction resulting in glomerulonephritis about 3 weeks after the onset of the skin rash. This reaction is thought to be the body's antibody response to an antigen in the kidney that cross-reacts with a streptococcal antigen.

Cellulitis is often caused by *Streptococcus pyogenes* and its particular mode of spread within the superficial dermis results from its production of a 'spreading factor' (hyaluronidase) that enzymatically breaks down the glycosaminoglycan component of connective tissue of the dermis and allows the organism to spread. The affected area is diffusely swollen, hot, red and painful, thus demonstrating the cardinal features of acute inflammation (Fig. 10.1, p. 201). The rapidly progressive and often fatal condition of *necrotising fasciitis* is due to mixed synergistic bacterial infections.

Abscesses of various sorts occur in the skin as elsewhere, but their clinical picture often depends upon the adnexa involved; a *furuncle* is a deep abscess of a single hair follicle, often with extensive necrosis, while a *carbuncle* involves several contiguous hair follicles. Obviously, the hair follicle is an effective hole in the skin barrier and so it comes as no surprise that bacteria may use it as a portal of entry into the host.

Tuberculosis of the skin ('lupus vulgaris') is uncommon in developed countries but still occurs. The offending organism may be either the human form of *Mycobacterium tuberculosis* or the bovine organism *Mycobacterium bovis*. A classical presentation is involvement of the overlying skin from a subcutaneous tuberculous lymph node, a condition named *scrofuloderma*. The basic pathology is of typical caseous granulomas as described in Chapter 10. Atypical mycobacterial infection can occur in HIV-positive patients and its occurrence in non-immunocompromised individuals is a cause of so-called fish tank granuloma on the finger.

Leprosy is still a cause of considerable morbidity worldwide: estimates suggest about 10 million patients in total. In developed countries the disease is very rare and usually imported. It is caused by *Mycobacterium leprae* and a variety of clinical forms are described. The differences between these clinical forms are determined by the host immune response. In *lepromatous leprosy* the host seems to mount little response to the infection and bacteria are numerous in the skin and in nasal secretions. In the *tuberculoid* form the host develops a strong immunological reaction and the lesions tend to contain very few organisms and eventually heal spontaneously. The lepromatous form is often progressive and fatal as the host is not mounting an effective response. However, in the tuberculoid form, it is the immune response itself that destroys tissues and nerves to produce the classical, mutilated leonine facies and auto-amputations of digits that have caused lepers to be so feared and shunned.

Fungal infections

Various fungi attack the skin, usually living in the upper keratinised layers and spreading outwards in a ring of erythematous scaling dermatitis that is commonly known as *tinea* (ringworm). In other sites the lesions are somewhat different in appearance: between the toes the lesions appear as *tinea pedis* (athlete's foot) and in the groins as *tinea cruris*. The organisms responsible for these infections vary but the commonest are various *Trichophyton* species.

Pityrosporum species are responsible for various superficial fungal infections of the skin; the most common is tinea versicolor in which pigment changes are very characteristic.

A different type of organism, *Candida*, which is a yeast, is responsible for another group of fungal infestations, most commonly of mucosal and adjacent areas. This infection causes the clinical condition of *thrush*, commonly seen in babies' mouths and in the adult vagina. *Candida* can also affect the nails and cause inflammation of the adjacent soft tissue (paronychia).

Fungal lesions are rarely biopsied because they are usually diagnosed clinically. The diagnosis can be made in difficult cases by the direct microscopy of a potassium hydroxide digest of skin scrapings. Histologically, fungi are often revealed only when stains that react with their cell walls are used, such as silver stains or stains for neutral polysaccharides (periodic acid–Schiff; PAS). Under these circumstances the diagnosis is best achieved when the pathologist is alerted by the clinical history, illustrating the importance of providing full clinical details with all biopsies.

Deeper fungal infections tend to cause chronic abscesses, often with severe destruction. They are common in tropical conditions but are also seen particularly as opportunistic infections in the immunosuppressed. *Blastomyces, Actinomyces* and *Nocardia* may all be encountered now outside their traditional endemic areas due to foreign travel and immunosuppression.

Protozoal infections

Protozoal infections are rare in temperate climates, but worldwide *leishmaniasis, amoebiasis* and *trypanosomiasis* form a significant volume of suffering and in some areas of the world will be the predominant dermatological conditions encountered by physicians. Many of these conditions, like many other tropical diseases, are spread by arthropod parasites and the most effective means of control has proven to be elimination of the vector rather than treatment of the disease.

Leishmaniasis is an infection caused by *Leishmania tropica* which is transmitted by sandflies. The organisms have

developed a mechanism for subverting the body's defences and can be found living in abundance within the host macrophages.

Metazoan parasites

Metazoan parasites are mainly worms or arthropods; the former tend to invade and parasitise, while the latter are more common as 'predators'. The worms are again a tropical problem primarily and include *onchocerciasis, larva migrans, strongyloidiasis, ancylostomiasis, filariasis* and *schistosomiasis*. Again, the skin presentations of these lesions may be spectacular and may form a dominant proportion of tropical dermatological practice.

Apart from the arthropod vectors of disease, many of these ubiquitous animals live in intimate contact with human hosts: fleas, bedbugs and lice (pediculosis) have generated a huge technical and popular literature. There are poems, operatic songs and books of philosophical speculation devoted to the flea, not to mention the blame for spreading the Black Death. The louse lives on its human host and attaches its eggs to the hair, where they are seen as small bead-like 'nits'. The scabies mite is recorded in Anglo-Saxon poetry and the female burrows into the skin to lay eggs, leaving a little track by which its progress can be observed; when a pin is stuck into the end of the track the mite clings to the tip and can be extracted to demonstrate the infestation, a performance that never fails to enliven a dermatology clinic. Hypersensitivity to the mite causes widespread itching (pruritus). Other mites (*Demodex folliculorum*) have adapted so well to living within the hair follicle that they can be found in the majority of the normal population living as simple commensals and, as far as we know, causing no host response and therefore no disease. The house dust mite, on the other hand, lives free in our bed linen in even the cleanest homes and ekes out a blameless existence consuming shed keratin skin flakes. However, the end products of this diet are excreted into our environment and, in susceptible individuals, produce the chronic skin rash of atopic eczema mediated by a hypersensitivity response.

NON-INFECTIOUS INFLAMMATORY DISEASES

Many skin diseases are characterised by inflammatory reactions without an obvious cause. Some diseases, such as lupus erythematosus, have a well-established autoimmune component, while others are known to arise as a result of drug sensitivities or insect bites (urticaria). Why some people develop these diseases, and others do not, lies principally in the innate genetic constitution of the individuals.

Urticaria

▶ Urticaria (hives and wheals) is a reaction pattern
▶ The basic lesion is oedema of the dermis
▶ Characterised clinically by itching and swelling

When classified according to their causes there are many types of urticaria, but the final common pathway of expression in this condition is always the same. An urticarial lesion results from a sudden marked increase in the permeability of small vessels, resulting in oedema of the dermis or subcutis and the production of a clinically erythematous and/or oedematous papule (a small elevated skin lesion of less than 5–10 mm). The classical lesion is seen in nettle rash or hives. Extreme forms involving the mouth and upper respiratory passages may follow insect stings and may be life-threatening.

Histologically, the collagen bundles of the dermis are separated by the oedema and a sparse infiltrate of polymorphs, often including eosinophils and an increased numbers of mast cells. The most important mediator of this process is histamine but other substances such as kinins and various circulating globulins, mainly IgE, play a role (Ch. 10). Agents causing urticaria include:

- plant and animal toxins
- physical stimuli such as pressure or heat or cold
- various drugs (including aspirin and antibiotics).

Lupus erythematosus

▶ Autoimmune disease affecting connective tissue
▶ Systemic form can involve kidneys
▶ Skin lesions involve epidermis and adnexa

Lupus erythematosus (LE) is a failure in immune self-tolerance. This failure results in the production of a large range of auto-antibodies directed at a wide variety of tissue components; the disease is, therefore, an autoimmune disease. The most important antibodies are those directed against DNA.

Clinicopathological features

Clinically, LE is a multisystem disease which may present with symptoms associated with almost any organ; in practice, skin and renal (Ch. 21) involvement are among the commonest. In many cases the skin appears to be the only organ involved and the disease is then called *discoid LE*. The *systemic* variant may or may not involve the skin. However, the fact that the lesions in discoid and systemic cases are often indistinguishable, and the occurrence of serological abnormalities in systemic and some discoid cases, suggest that the relationship is close.

The skin lesions are initially erythematous, scaly and indurated and slowly progress to atrophic scarred patches, often with hyperpigmented edges in the older lesions. They are often symmetrical on the face in a butterfly distribution over the nose and cheeks, and on the scalp may be associated with a scarring alopecia. These features are explained by the histology, which shows a dilatation of superficial vessels with a dense accumulation of lymphocytes around them, leading to the observed erythema. The infiltrate also involves the dermo-epidermal interface and damages the melanocytes. The melanocytes lose their melanin to dermal macrophages in which the pigment accumulates, accounting for the hyperpigmentation in older lesions. The persistent junctional inflammation results in damage to hair follicles, with the formation of follicular plugs (tin-tacks) and eventually atrophy of hair follicles and the epidermis itself.

Immunofluorescence reveals deposits of IgG and IgM at the epidermal basement membrane. This is the 'lupus band test', a helpful diagnostic feature in doubtful cases.

Psoriasis

▶ Genetically determined disease
▶ Silvery-grey scales of parakeratosis
▶ Polymorphs enter epidermis but abscesses are sterile

Psoriasis is a common, genetically determined disease associated with human leukocyte antigen (HLA) haplotypes Cw6, B13 and B17. The appearance of the disease is often triggered by environmental factors such as various drugs. It pursues a chronic course and, in 5–10% of cases, is complicated by a very destructive arthropathy.

Clinicopathological features
The lesions are commonest on the extensor surfaces (Fig. 24.6), such as the knees and elbows, and the first appearance may be in a site of trauma such as a surgical wound—a phenomenon known as the *Koebner effect*. The clinical lesions are termed plaques, meaning slightly palpable and elevated areas, often measuring over 50mm. The individual lesions are covered with a silvery scale and scraping the scale off reveals a series of small bleeding points *(Auspitz's sign)*.

Histologically (Fig. 24.7), the normal pattern of rete ridges becomes thickened (acanthotic) and the dermal papillae are covered only by a thin layer of epidermis two or three cells thick. This accounts for the bleeding points seen when the scale is scratched off. The progress of the epidermal cells through the epidermis is speeded up and maturation is incomplete. This is reflected in the accumulation of abnormal keratin with nuclear fragments (parakeratosis) in the form of the silvery scales. The maturation of the keratin is so disturbed that the normal granular layer of the epidermis is lost (Fig. 24.7). The erythema is caused by dilated vessels in the upper dermis and these can be seen to contain numerous polymorphs which migrate from the vessels into the epidermis, sometimes in sufficient numbers to form actual pustules. These sterile pustules may dominate the clinical picture in one variant of the disease (pustular psoriasis) and this presentation is often marked when the disease appears on the palms of the hands or soles of the feet.

Pathogenesis and treatment
There have been many theories regarding the pathogenesis of psoriasis and, although there is a certain genetic component, the precise mechanism is not fully understood.

Some clue as to the cause of psoriasis can be found in the therapy of the disease. Almost anything that inhibits the growth of the epidermis will alleviate the disease; such therapies include coal tar, methotrexate and heavy-metal poisons such as arsenic. A very effective current therapy is with analogues of the retinoid subunit of vitamin A, overdose of which causes loss of the keratin layer of the normal skin. So from the therapeutic point of view it seems that psoriasis is a disease of epidermal proliferation and excess keratin production, a description that fits the clinical and histopathological observations very well.

The excessive epidermal proliferation appears to be driven by cytokines released from activated T-cells in the dermis.

Lichen planus

▶ Polygonal, itchy papules
▶ Band-like chronic inflammatory infiltrate
▶ Centred on dermo-epidermal junction

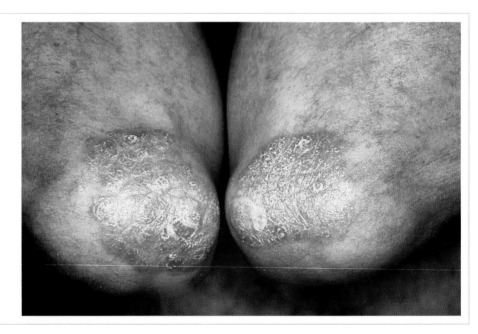

Fig. 24.6   Psoriasis. This inflammatory condition has a strong genetic tendency. It is characterised by silvery scales of parakeratosis and bleeding when scratched superficially. The lesions show a predilection for extensor surfaces and are uncommon on the face.

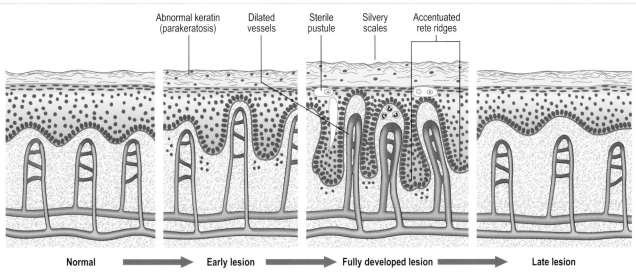

Fig. 24.7 Psoriasis. A common, inherited inflammatory condition of the skin, of unknown aetiology. The progression of the lesion from normal skin to the healed lesion is shown from left to right.

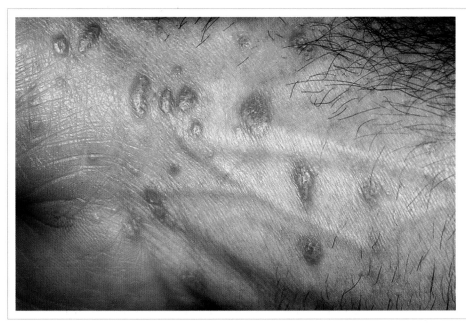

Fig. 24.8 Lichen planus. The lesions are violaceous, flat-topped and polygonal. White lines on the surface (Wickham's striae) are very characteristic.

Lichen planus is a non-infectious inflammatory disease characterised by destruction of keratinocytes, probably mediated by interferon-gamma and tumour necrosis factor from T-cells in the dermal infiltrate. Usually there is no precipitating factor but some drug eruptions may be indistinguishable. It affects the skin, often the inner surfaces of the wrists (Fig. 24.8), and the mucosae, where it appears as a white lacy lesion. On the skin it presents as small, intensely itchy, polygonal, violaceous papules that may develop into blisters, particularly on the palms of the hands or soles of the feet. As the eruption heals, which it usually does spontaneously, it may leave behind hyper- or hypopigmented patches.

Clinicopathological features
Histology reveals a lymphohistiocytic infiltrate in a band-like distribution at the dermo-epidermal junction. The basal layer of the epidermis comes under lymphocytic attack and foci of degeneration, apoptosis and regeneration are seen; this eventually gives the epidermis a characteristic saw-tooth profile. Little splits also occur at the junction and, rarely, these may coalesce to form bullae (Fig. 24.9). Lichen planus constitutes the classical so-called *lichenoid reaction*. In contrast to psoriasis there is an increase in the granular layer; the scale is consequently different and presents as tiny white lines running over the papules. During the active phase of the eruption papules can be induced by minor trauma such

691

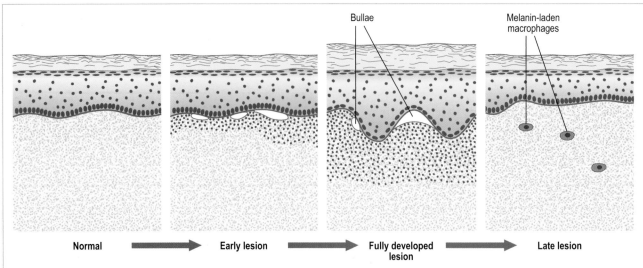

Bullae

Melanin-laden macrophages

Normal → Early lesion → Fully developed lesion → Late lesion

Fig. 24.9 Lichen planus. An inflammatory skin disease of unknown aetiology. The progression from normal skin to healed lesion is shown diagrammatically from left to right.

as scratching. Treatment is with steroids, and in those cases in which a precipitating cause can be identified this can then be withdrawn.

Pityriasis rosea

This is a not uncommon self-limiting disease that starts as a small oval 'herald' scaly patch and then becomes more extensive. Histologically there is mild spongiosis and inflammation.

Panniculitis

This is inflammation of the subcutaneous fat. The commonest type is erythema nodosum, where painful red nodules appear on the shins, often following a streptococcal infection or in association with inflammatory bowel disease or tuberculosis.

EPIDERMAL CELLS

Normal structure and function

The epidermis consists of a stratified squamous epithelium attached to a basement membrane. The cells are recognisably different from each other in the various layers of the epidermis; at the base they are modified for attachment to the dermis via the basement membrane and hemidesmosomes—this layer is called the *stratum basale* or *basal layer*. Cells in this layer and in the layer immediately above may often be seen in division and provide the replicative pool of cells that regenerates the epidermis as cells grow up through it to form the overlying keratin layer. The cells in the mid zone of the epidermis are the recognisable squamous cells (keratinocytes) and they, like the rest of the epidermal cells, are held together by desmosomes. In histological preparations there is generally some shrinkage of the cells and the desmosomal

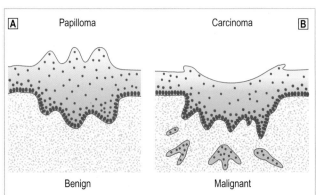

A Papilloma   Carcinoma B

Benign   Malignant

Fig. 24.10 Common tumours (neoplasms) of epidermal cells. A Benign neoplasm (papilloma). B Malignant neoplasm (carcinoma).

bridges draw out small spines of cytoplasm from the cells, giving them their typical spinous or prickle appearance, from which they derive their name of *stratum spinosum or prickle cell layer*. As the cells move up through the stratum spinosum they become simplified and their metabolism becomes totally directed to producing the components of the eventual horny layer. The last cellular layer contains many granules of pre-keratin called *keratohyaline granules*. Eventually, the cells die and leave a highly structured keratin layer behind—the *stratum corneum*.

Although the epidermis is involved in the pathogenesis of numerous diseases, such as lichen planus or eczema, the main diseases of significance that involve the epidermis primarily are disorders of keratinisation (such as ichthyosis when the keratin layer is thickened due to gene mutations) and various neoplasms, both benign and malignant. The cellular layers of the epidermis are also the main site of viral infections, because viruses require living cells for their replication. The range of epidermal neoplasms that have been described is very wide, but the majority are rare and those described below are common or important clinical problems (Fig. 24.10).

Benign epidermal neoplasms and tumour-like conditions

Skin tags (fibroepithelial polyps)

These pedunculated lesions with a fibrovascular core and a benign epidermal covering occur more frequently in the elderly and are common in the axillae. They may be a reaction to friction on the skin, rather than a true neoplasm. Their main significance is cosmetic or catching on clothes.

Seborrhoeic wart/keratosis (basal cell papilloma)

▶ Common in the elderly
▶ Benign
▶ Cells resemble those in the basal layer of the epidermis

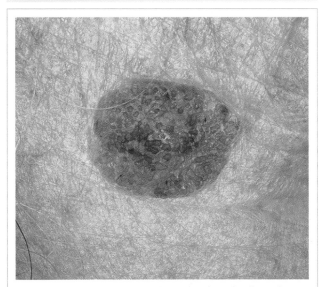

Fig. 24.11 Seborrhoeic wart/keratosis (basal cell papilloma). A symmetrical, benign lesion. It may occur anywhere on the skin and is commoner in the elderly.

Seborrhoeic warts/keratoses are much more common in the elderly and, despite their name, have nothing to do with sebaceous glands. They are also called basal cell papillomas but seborrhoeic wart/keratosis is the preferred name to avoid confusion with the term basal cell carcinoma. They are dark, greasy-looking (hence 'seborrhoeic') nodules with an irregular surface (Fig. 24.11). They can occur on most parts of the skin surface and rarely turn malignant. Histologically they consist of a proliferation of cells with similar appearances to the basal cells in the epidermis (Fig. 24.12). They have a very convoluted surface with keratin tunnels extending deeply from the surface inwards (horn cysts). In some cases they may become inflamed, due to irritation or attempts by the body to remove the lesion (regression). Although they have little biological significance, they are often removed for cosmetic purposes or to exclude melanoma. In one very rare condition a sudden, widespread, pruritic crop of these lesions may be a sign of internal malignancy, usually in the gastrointestinal tract (the sign of Leser–Trélat).

Squamous cell papilloma

These are benign neoplasms of the squamous epithelium. They are invariably HPV-related and commonly called verrucae or condylomata.

Cysts

▶ Classified from their linings
▶ Benign in almost all cases

Various benign cysts occur in the skin, the commonest being:

- *epidermal (infundibular) cysts*
- *sebaceous (pilar or tricholemmal) cysts.*

They occur in the dermis and contain keratin, not sebum. The distinguishing feature is the nature of the cyst lining. In epidermal cysts, the lining is identical to normal epidermis.

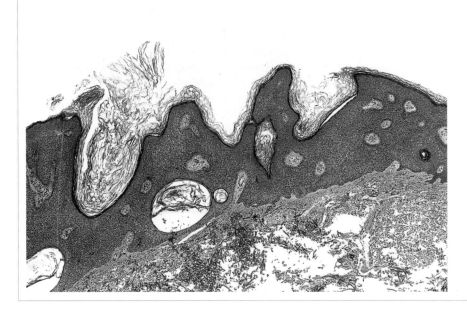

Fig. 24.12 Seborrhoeic wart. This shows a proliferation of basal cells with thickened epidermis (acanthosis) and projection above the surface (papillomatosis). The lesion seems 'stuck' on the dermis.

Table 24.2 Main features of common malignant skin tumours (including keratoacanthoma)				
Lesion	Usual site	Gross features	Histology	Behaviour
Keratoacanthoma	Sun-exposed hair-bearing skin	Symmetrical Central keratin plug	Symmetrical Invades dermis but no deeper than sweat glands	Rapid initial growth Involutes within several months
Basal cell carcinoma	Face	Ulcer Irregular rolled edges	Small basophilic cells	Slow growing Rarely metastasises
Squamous cell carcinoma	Face and hand	Asymmetrical	Asymmetrical growth Capable of invading deeply Nuclear pleomorphism Variable keratinisation	Slow growing Metastasises late
Malignant melanoma	Legs in young women Back in young men Face in elderly	Asymmetrical, bleed, variable pigmentation, enlarge May ulcerate	Melanin pigment in cells Nuclear pleomorphism	Prognosis depends on thickness (>1.0 mm indicates significant risk of metastasis)

In sebaceous cysts, the lining is identical to the middle part of the hair follicle. Consequently, it is believed that epidermal cysts arise from the upper part of the hair follicle, where it is lined by normal epidermis, and that sebaceous cysts arise from the deeper part.

One lesion that may cause problems is the so-called *proliferating pilar tumour*. This tumour usually arises on the scalp and in essence is a low-grade squamous cell carcinoma. In common with many neoplasms, they can cause nodules, which are loosely defined as elevated lesions over 5–10 mm in diameter.

Malignant epidermal neoplasms

Malignant skin tumours are among the commonest neoplasms but only malignant melanomas account for a significant number of deaths. The main features are summarised in Table 24.2.

Molecular biology

Increasing molecular biological information is now emerging with regard to the cause of common malignant epidermal neoplasms. Some of these result, in part, from exposure to ultraviolet radiation in the 290–320 nm spectrum, resulting in free-radical photoproducts that cause DNA damage. This includes mutations to tumour suppressor genes such as *p53* in squamous cell carcinoma and some melanomas. Mutations of the *BRAF* and *NRAF* genes have also been identified in 70% of melanomas and result in dysregulation of the mitogen-activated protein kinase (MAPK) pathway

Basal cell carcinoma

▶ Very common skin malignancy
▶ Related to chronic sun exposure
▶ Occurs most commonly on the face
▶ Locally very invasive
▶ Metastasis extremely rare

Basal cell carcinomas (BCCs) are the commonest skin tumour and they are closely associated with chronic sunlight

exposure. They are, therefore, most common on the face of elderly people. Clinically, they are often ulcerated irregular lesions, hence their common name of *rodent ulcers*, with a raised pearly border, often with tiny blood vessels visible on the border (Fig. 24.13).

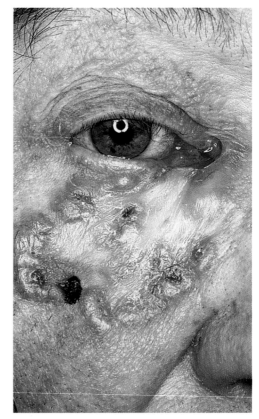

Fig. 24.13   Basal cell carcinoma. This invasive neoplasm occurs most commonly on the face. Note the raised border. Metastases are rare.

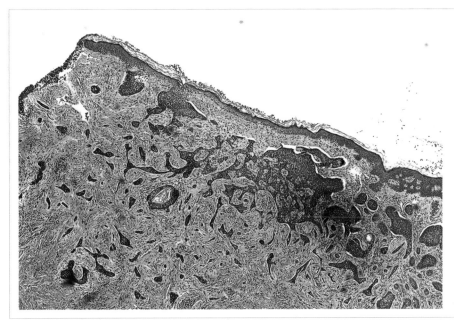

Fig. 24.14   Basal cell carcinoma. This shows a 'high-risk' infiltrating type of BCC with irregular invasion in the dermis.

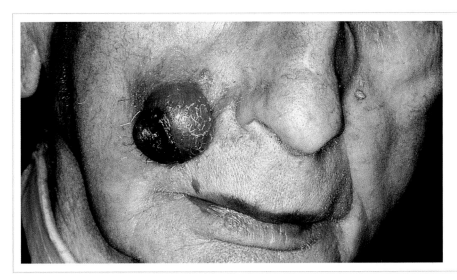

Fig. 24.15   Squamous cell carcinoma. This asymmetrical lesion often occurs on sun-damaged skin. It grows slowly and metastasises late.

Histologically, they are formed of clumps of small cells surrounded by a rim of cells whose nuclei line up like a picket fence (palisading) (Fig. 24.14). Mitoses are frequent and ulceration is common. The cells are very similar in appearance to those of the normal basal layer of the epidermis; the tumours are believed to arise from this layer and from hair follicles.

Their behaviour is interesting because, although they may be very invasive and locally destructive, they rarely metastasise. Consequently they can be quite adequately treated by local excision or by radiotherapy. The extent of local excision, to a degree, depends on whether the BCC is of low risk (nodular or superficial) or high risk (micronodular or morphoeic/infiltrative) histological type.

Many BCCs are associated with mutations in the human homologue of the *Drosophila gene patched* (*PTCH1*). This is a tumour suppressor gene and a member of the sonic hedgehog signalling pathway.

Squamous cell carcinoma

▶ Malignant skin neoplasm
▶ Associated with chronic sun exposure
▶ Locally invasive
▶ Metastasises late

Invasive squamous cell carcinomas are common and are aetiologically related to chronic sunlight exposure, immunosuppression or to chemical carcinogens such as arsenic, tar and machine oil. They also occur in the site of previous X-irradiation. They are much more common in the elderly on sun-exposed areas. Clinically, they may be roughened keratotic areas, papules, nodules, ulcers or horns (Fig. 24.15). They are difficult to distinguish from keratoacanthomas except by their behaviour.

Histologically, they are composed of disorganised keratinocytes with typical malignant cytology. They also show

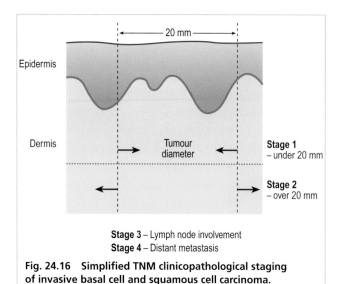

Fig. 24.16 Simplified TNM clinicopathological staging of invasive basal cell and squamous cell carcinoma.

foci of keratinisation within the tumour and thus appear to echo the behaviour of the normal upper layers of the epidermis but in a disordered and malignant fashion.

Although they show obvious invasion, their behaviour is usually fairly indolent and metastasis, when it occurs, is a late and relatively uncommon complication. Treatment is by surgical excision, as they are more resistant to radiation than are basal cell carcinomas.

Rarely, squamous cell carcinomas arise at the edge of chronic skin ulcers (Marjolin's ulcer).

The staging of basal cell carcinoma and squamous cell carcinoma is shown in Figure 24.16.

Actinic keratosis and Bowen's disease

Invasive squamous cell carcinoma of the skin often originates through the spectrum of premalignant dysplastic epithelium and in situ squamous cell carcinoma (*Bowen's disease*). The dysplastic epithelium usually overlies dermal damage due to actinic (solar) damage and the lesions are termed *actinic keratoses*.

Keratoacanthoma

▸ Clinically benign and regresses
▸ Crater-like symmetrical architecture
▸ Face is commonest site

This curious lesion appears, often on sun-damaged skin, grows very rapidly for several months and then regresses. The lesion is typically symmetrical and highly keratotic and may even develop a horn of keratin in its centre. Histologically, it is indistinguishable from a well-differentiated squamous cell carcinoma, but it never invades deeply and does not metastasise. One clue to the diagnosis is the crater-like architectural symmetry of the lesion, but this can only be seen in intact lesions and not in curettings or punch or incisional biopsies. This lesion may be a special form of squamous cell carcinoma originating from hair follicles and is clinically benign due to its ability to regress totally.

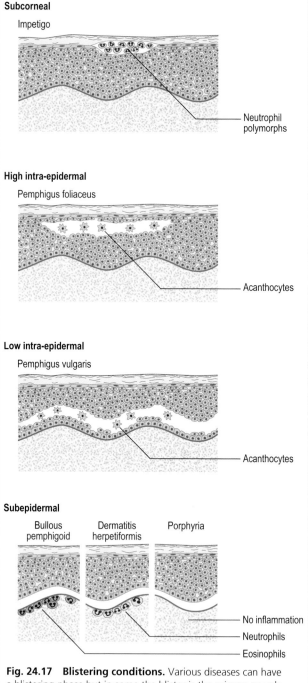

Fig. 24.17 Blistering conditions. Various diseases can have a blistering phase but in some the blister is the primary or only feature. The clinical presentation depends on the level in the skin at which the blisters form. The precise diagnosis often requires special diagnostic techniques such as immunofluorescence. (Porphyria is described in Ch. 7.)

Blisters

Blisters are fluid-filled spaces within the skin due to separation of two layers of tissue and the leakage of plasma into the space. When over 5 mm they are called bullae, and under 5 mm vesicles.

Table 24.3 Clinicopathological features of bullous disorders			
Disease	Location of bullae	Immune reactants	Clinical features
Pemphigus	Intra-epidermal	IgG on intercellular junctions	High mortality
Pemphigoid	Subepidermal	IgG on basement membrane	Elderly patients
Dermatitis herpetiformis	Subepidermal	IgA on papillary dermis	Associated with coeliac disease

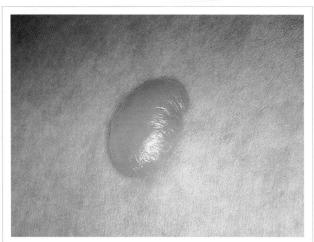

Fig. 24.18 Bullous pemphigoid. The subepidermal blisters are often larger and less itchy than dermatitis herpetiformis. They show no particular site of predilection.

The most common forms of blister are thermal burns and friction blisters. The latter occur commonly on the foot, due to shearing forces set up within the skin as a result of poorly fitting footwear. Such blisters form at the dermo-epidermal junction but other blisters may form at any level within the skin and the precise site of blisters gives a very good clue as to their nature (Fig. 24.17). Many blisters form because an antibody attacks some skin component that has a discrete distribution within the skin and this attack causes separation at that point. Subsequent damage to the blister roof causes it to be shed; the barrier function is lost and secondary infection may ensue.

There are several distinct mechanisms of blister formation:

1. The bonds between epidermal cells may be destroyed directly, as in pemphigus.
2. The cells may be forced apart by oedema fluid, as in eczema.
3. The cells themselves may be destroyed, leaving gaps, as in herpetic blisters.
4. The basement membrane or its attachments to the epidermis or dermis may be altered, as in pemphigoid.

With the help of immunofluorescence techniques, it is possible to diagnose these types histologically (Table 24.3).

Some diseases (such as impetigo and sunburn) have blisters as an incidental part of their clinical presentations.

Erythema multiforme is a maculo-papular rash that is often associated with herpes simplex infection or drugs. The centre

of the target-like lesions can blister and when extensive and involving mucosal surfaces is called the Stevens–Johnson syndrome. The latter can be life-threatening.

Pemphigus

- ▶ More common in middle-aged to elderly people
- ▶ Fatal if untreated
- ▶ Intra-epidermal blister

Pemphigus is a disease of the middle-aged to elderly and, before the introduction of steroid therapy, many patients died within a year from the complication of serum electrolyte loss or from secondary infections. Even now, it is a serious disease with a significant mortality. The disease is caused by circulating auto-antibodies directed at components of the intercellular bridges (desmosomes) within the epidermis. The commonest antibody is against desmoglein 3. The bridges are lysed and the epidermis falls apart, leaving loose keratinocytes within the blister cavity. These keratinocytes are no longer held in shape by the surrounding cells and consequently round up (acanthocytes); the whole process is known as *acantholysis*.

There are several varieties of the disease, depending upon the precise site within the epidermis at which the blisters occur. Superficial blistering occurs in the sub-corneal region in *pemphigus foliaceus* and more deeply in the more common form, *pemphigus vulgaris*. In the superficial form the blisters are so near the surface that their roof is very fragile and intact blisters are seldom seen. In vulgaris, where the split is located more deeply, the blisters are more persistent. In all varieties of the disease the skin is very fragile due to the weakening of the intercellular bridges and firm, sliding pressure on apparently normal skin will precipitate a blister (*Nikolsky's sign*).

Bullous pemphigoid

- ▶ More common in the elderly
- ▶ Often self-limiting disease
- ▶ Blister forms at dermo-epidermal junction

This disease is more common than pemphigus, although still rare, and occurs mainly in those aged over 60 years (Fig. 24.18). It is generally self-limiting but may be associated with a long period of pruritus, even after the blisters have healed. In this disease the split occurs at the dermo-epidermal junction and is due to circulating antibodies to the lamina lucida layer (immediately adjacent to the basal

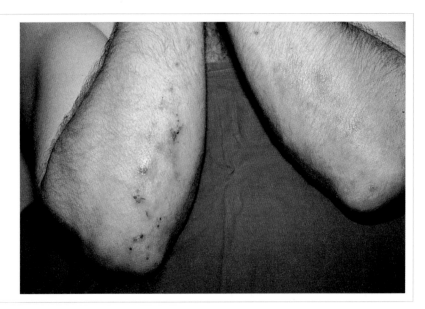

Fig. 24.19 Dermatitis herpetiformis. This is characterised by small, subepidermal, very itchy blisters that occur most commonly on elbows and knees. They are so pruritic that they are seldom seen intact. There is an association with gluten-sensitive enteropathy.

cells) of the epidermal basement membrane. Immunofluorescence reveals a linear deposition of antibody, generally IgG, along the basement membrane. The antigen–antibody complex causes the release of various complement factors which can also be demonstrated by immunofluorescence and the whole reaction causes degranulation of mast cells. This accounts not only for the pruritus but also for the characteristic presence of eosinophils, which are the common accompaniment of mast cell activation in any condition. Being deeper, the blisters are more persistent, although the severe pruritus often results in them being destroyed by scratching.

Dermatitis herpetiformis

▶ Most common in young adults
▶ Blister forms at dermo-epidermal junction
▶ May be associated with coeliac disease

This blistering condition is characterised by small, intensely itchy blisters occurring mainly on the extensor surfaces of knees and elbows of young adults (Fig. 24.19). The blisters are so pruritic that it is often difficult for the patient to keep one intact for the clinician to recognise. They occur at the dermo-epidermal junction, but in this case the immunoglobulin deposit is granular rather than continuous in distribution and it is almost always IgA. Curiously, although the lesions are very pruritic, the characteristic inflammatory cell seen in the infiltrates is the neutrophil polymorph and not the eosinophil. The disease is also remarkable for the fact that the response to therapy with dapsone is usually so dramatic as to be diagnostic. A significant number of these patients are shown to have some degree of gluten sensitivity (coeliac disease; Ch. 15).

Ulcers

An ulcer is a defect in an epithelial surface. Ulcers in the skin are usually attributable to vascular insufficiency or trauma. In the elderly, where there is often impaired blood flow, minor trauma can often result in severe, persistent ulceration requiring hospitalisation.

Venous (varicose) ulcers

▶ Lower legs in the elderly
▶ Associated with varicose veins and varicose eczema
▶ Due to venous stasis

Venous ulcers commonly arise from chronic venous congestion in the lower legs of the elderly due to incompetence of the valves in the small veins connecting the deep and superficial venous systems of the leg.

Pathogenesis

The congestion results in the shunting of the deep venous pressure, generated by muscular contractions around veins, to the superficial veins which are not designed to withstand such high pressures. These veins dilate *(varicose veins)* and venous pooling occurs, resulting in venous stasis within the skin. This presents as a discoloured, often eczematous area of skin, frequently in the region of obvious varicose veins. Eventually, the venous drainage of the skin becomes too poor to support the metabolism of the epidermis, which dies and is sloughed off leaving a venous ulcer. This may happen spontaneously or be accelerated as a result of relatively minor trauma.

Treatment

Patients often attempt a variety of irrelevant topical medications and their ulcers are aggravated, and possibly maintained, by the superimposition of a wide range of topical hypersensitivities that perpetuate the local skin irritation with a mixture of venous and contact eczemas.

Mechanical therapies are the most favoured and include: compressive bandages, which prevent the pressure transfer to the skin, or surgical removal of incompetent vessels before ulceration occurs. Local grafting of the patient's own

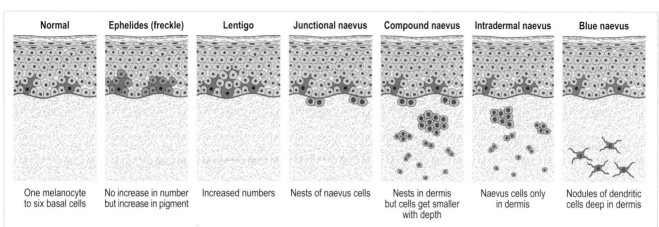

Normal	Ephelides (freckle)	Lentigo	Junctional naevus	Compound naevus	Intradermal naevus	Blue naevus
One melanocyte to six basal cells	No increase in number but increase in pigment	Increased numbers	Nests of naevus cells	Nests in dermis but cells get smaller with depth	Naevus cells only in dermis	Nodules of dendritic cells deep in dermis

Fig. 24.20 Melanocytic naevi. Normal melanocytes occur in the basal layer (about one melanocyte to six basal cells). The various patterns of abnormality are illustrated and are described in detail in the text.

healthy epidermis into the ulcer with the leg elevated to reduce venous pressure is also effective.

However, all treatment is difficult in these cases as healing depends on a good circulation and that is what is defective in the first place.

Arterial ulcers

> ▶ On the legs, commonly in diabetics and patients with severe atheroma
> ▶ Usually associated with poor foot pulses and claudication

Arterial ulcers are more shallow, undermined and painful than their venous counterparts. They result from failure of the arterial supply to that region of skin. For this reason the common treatment used for venous ulcers, that of compressive bandaging, is a disaster because it reduces even further the arterial supply and large areas of skin may become necrotic before the error is appreciated.

Diabetic ulceration, like most of the long-term effects of diabetes, is mediated through the final common pathway of arterial damage.

Other ulcers

Many other conditions cause ulcers, in particular many tropical infections such as *yaws* and *leishmaniasis,* but ulcers can occur as non-specific lesions complicating conditions such as *herpes. Pyoderma gangrenosum* is a specific entity with violaceous, undermined ulcers that may present as a lesion complicating inflammatory bowel disease.

Behçet's syndrome is a rare condition, of unknown aetiology, with ulcers of the mucosae and a variety of systemic lesions.

Persistent ulcers provide a long-term irritation and a cause of continuous epithelial regeneration. In this sort of situation there is an increased tendency for malignant transformation to occur and squamous cell carcinoma may be a late complication of skin ulcers. Such malignant ulcers are called *Marjolin's ulcers.*

MELANOCYTES

Normal structure and function

At about the 13th week of embryonic life, cells migrate from the neural crest and come to lie at the dermo-epidermal junction. These cells become the pigmented melanocytes and are distributed among the cells of the epidermal basal layer. Within the cytoplasm of the melanocytes are organelles (melanosomes) that are specialised for the production of the black pigment melanin, a condensation product of dihydroxyphenylalanine (DOPA).

The melanocytes transfer melanin to the basal keratinocytes where it comes to lie above the nucleus, protecting the nucleus from solar irradiation. The protective importance of melanin can be deduced from the high rate of skin cancers found in those people who lack melanin (albinos) or those exposed to higher levels of sunlight. The melanocyte system is very responsive to changes in exposure to sunlight and vast amounts of time and money are expended on driving these cells to the limits of their productiveness in pursuit of a tan, although medically unhealthy in view of the high risk of skin cancer.

Although variations in skin colour are produced by variations in the activity of melanocytes and not by variations in their numbers, focal areas of increased activity may occur as a result of sun exposure in some individuals and these foci appear as *freckles* (ephelides).

It is a poignant fact that, although the role of melanocytes is to protect the skin against the development of relatively indolent skin cancers such as basal cell carcinomas and squamous carcinomas, the cancers that arise from melanocytes are amongst the most malignant of skin tumours. A reduction of melanocytes in the skin results in the disease *vitiligo.*

Lentigo and melanocytic naevi

Lentigos are characterised by an increase in single melanocytes in the basal epidermis. Melanocytic (naevocellular) naevi ('moles') are nests of melanocytes; the nest can lie:

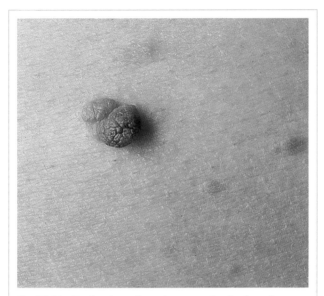

Fig. 24.21 Benign intradermal naevus. A collection of pigmented naevocellular naevus cells is situated in the dermis. There is no junctional component, the lesion is symmetrical and there is little risk of malignancy.

- at the dermo-epidermal junction (*junctional naevus*)
- at the junction and in the dermis (*compound naevus*)
- in the dermis (*intradermal naevus*).

These clinical types of naevus are all believed to be stages in the evolution of the same pathological entity (Fig. 24.20). This is not to say that any one lesion must pass through all of these stages, for their development may cease at any point.

Clinicopathological features

The earliest clinical feature is a small, pigmented macule (a flat skin lesion) caused by an increase in the number of individual melanocytes at the dermo-epidermal junction. At this stage the melanocytes appear completely normal; they are pigmented and dendritic and transfer their pigment to the surrounding keratinocytes, but because their numbers are increased the degree of skin pigmentation is increased. This lesion is called a *lentigo*.

In the next stage the melanocytes proliferate to form nests clustered at the dermo-epidermal junction. This clustering may cause the clinical lesion to become very slightly raised (papule), but it is often impossible to distinguish this stage from the preceding one. The cells are still pigmented but are now losing their dendrites and becoming rounded, true 'naevus' cells. At this stage the lesion is termed a *junctional naevus* since all of the naevus cells remain at the dermo-epidermal junction.

With further development the junctional naevus cells seem to detach from the dermo-epidermal junction, become smaller and rounder and less metabolically active, and lose the ability to divide (post-mitotic cells). The lesion now has two components histologically—a junctional component and an intradermal component—and is therefore called a *compound naevus*. Clinically these are pigmented papules or nodules and are so common as to be found in most normal subjects.

The last stage in the evolution of these naevi is reached when all of the junctional melanocytes have gone and only the intradermal naevus cells remain. These lesions are often pink papules or nodules because the intradermal cells produce little or no pigment and because the overlying epidermis contains only normal numbers of normally active melanocytes. It has become an *intradermal naevus* (Fig. 24.21) and its evolution is complete.

There seems to be some interaction between the naevus cells and the epidermis: in junctional and subsequent naevi there may be a very marked increase in the growth of the epidermis, either outwards to form a rough, papillary lesion, or inwards to form a highly reticulated naevus growth pattern. This pattern of growth involving both keratinocytes and melanocytes has led some pathologists to assert that melanocytic naevi are not benign neoplasms at all, but are hamartomas, that is to say, congenital areas of malformation with the same genome as the rest of the individual's somatic cells.

Blue naevi

The blue naevus is a benign lesion which occurs as a deep dermal papule or nodule on any area of the skin and which, as its name suggests, often has a bluish tinge. They are usually solitary and malignant transformation is very rare.

Histologically, they consist of deeply pigmented, dendritic melanocytes lying deep in the dermis. The combination of heavy pigmentation and the deep situation beneath the superficial dermal vascular plexus gives them their characteristic blue colour due to the Tindall effect. There is usually no epidermal component to these tumours, although combinations with other types of naevus can sometimes occur.

The fact that the cells of this tumour retain their dendrites and that they sit so deeply in the dermis has led to the attractive proposition that they are melanocytes arrested in their embryonic migration to the dermo-epidermal junction.

Malignant melanoma

- ▶ Tumour is composed of malignant melanocytes
- ▶ Usually pigmented, but may be amelanotic
- ▶ Prognosis depends on thickness
- ▶ Aetiologically associated with fair skin and sunburn

The malignant tumours of melanocytic origin are called *melanomas*; more properly they should be called 'melanocarcinomas' since the term *melanoma* implies a benign tumour (Ch. 11), which these lesions certainly are not. In general, malignant melanomas are tumours of the skin, but since melanocytes may be found in central nervous sites such as the leptomeninges and the retina, primary malignant melanomas can arise there also.

The great clinical tragedy of malignant melanoma is that it is visible from its earliest stages and if excised before it has begun to invade the dermis it is totally curable. This is the clinical basis behind programmes encouraging self-examination and the identification of changing dysplastic (atypical) moles or early 'thin' melanoma. Nevertheless,

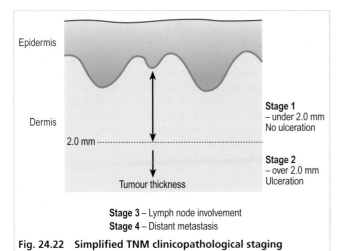

Fig. 24.22 **Simplified TNM clinicopathological staging of invasive malignant melanoma.**

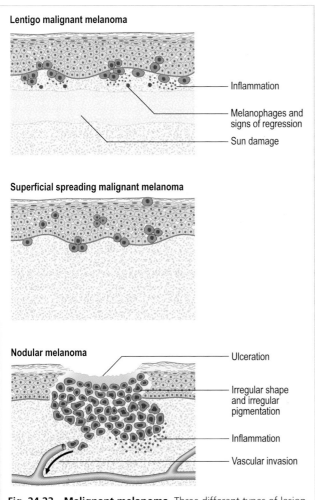

Fig. 24.23 **Malignant melanoma.** Three different types of lesion are shown and are discussed fully in the text.

each year many patients die from disseminated malignant melanoma and the incidence is increasing steadily. Clinically malignant melanoma can appear as pigmented macules, papules or nodules, and may ulcerate.

Pathogenesis
The most important aetiological factor is UV light. Melanomas occur most commonly in fair-skinned people (e.g. Caucasians) living sunny climates. Sunbeds are also thought to be a significant factor.

Theoretically, malignant melanomas can arise from any melanocyte, whether it be one of the normal junctional melanocytes or a melanocyte present in a benign naevus. Statistically, we might expect at least some malignant melanomas to arise in benign naevi simply because they contain so many melanocytes. However, many of the cells in a benign compound naevus are post-mitotic, and all of those in an intradermal naevus are post-mitotic and we should not expect these cells to produce malignant melanomas. Clinical experience tends to bear this out: those melanomas that are thought to have arisen in pre-existing benign naevi do so only in those classes of naevi with an active junctional component. However, a large number of malignant melanomas appear to arise de novo and they may well pass through a stage where it is difficult to know whether or not they are true malignant melanomas, so the precise fraction that arises in naevi or de novo is difficult to determine.

Clinicopathological features
Prognosis of malignant melanoma depends predominantly on the thickness of the lesion at the time of primary excision and the presence or absence of surface ulceration. The former parameter is termed the *Breslow thickness* and is expressed in millimetres. The cure rate for completely excised non-ulcerated melanomas below 1mm can approach 100% and the extent of excision depends on Breslow thickness. The staging of malignant melanoma is shown in Figure 24.22.

Clinicians and histopathologists recognise several subtypes of malignant melanoma. Although this distinction is useful for diagnostic purposes, it is somewhat artificial as the prognosis of all subtypes is essentially the same for the same Breslow thickness. This division, however, is supported by different molecular mechanisms for the subtypes.

The main variants of invasive malignant melanoma are (Fig. 24.23):

- lentigo maligna melanoma
- acral lentiginous melanoma
- superficial spreading melanoma
- nodular melanoma.

Lentigo maligna melanoma usually occurs on the sun-damaged skin of the face in the elderly. The development of lentigo maligna melanoma invariably occurs in a pre-existing in situ lesion termed lentigo maligna (Hutchinson's melanotic freckle). This is like the benign lentigo described previously, but in which the lentigo cells appear cytologically atypical.

Acral lentiginous malignant melanoma arises on the palms and soles, most commonly at their junction with the volar surface. The lesions are uncommon in Europeans but are the commonest form of malignant melanoma in non-Caucasians.

Superficial spreading melanoma (Fig. 24.24) is the commonest type in people of European descent. The epidermal spread produces a very recognisable pattern, variably described as pagetoid spread (so named because of the resemblance histologically to Paget's disease of the nipple) or, more colourfully, as 'buck shot scatter' (Fig. 24.25).

Nodular melanomas retain no features to identify a pre-existing in situ lesion.

The excision margins for invasive melanoma vary according to the Breslow thickness, but in general are no more than 10–30 mm.

Clinical course

The final common pathway for malignant melanoma is metastatic spread. This occurs early in the development of the tumour. It seems that the tumour cells have a great capacity for metastatic spread and begin to show this as soon as they come into contact with the superficial dermal vessels. The tumour spreads to all parts of the body, with a predilection for skin, brain and gastrointestinal tract. Currently, there is no effective therapy for widespread disease; the only effective treatment is early excision of the primary lesion.

Lymph node biopsy is being increasingly undertaken to assess whether melanoma has spread to the nearest node draining the melanoma (so-called sentinel lymph node biopsy). This is currently used as a prognostic tool and, if the lymph node is involved, radical dissection can be undertaken. The results of more clinical trials are awaited to determine whether this procedure has definite therapeutic value, although the prognostic value of the procedure is greater than Breslow thickness.

Prevention

Because of the increasing incidence and the intractable nature of advanced disease, emphasis has come to be placed on early diagnosis and on prevention. The main factor that seems to be associated with the development of the tumour is sunlight exposure. However, the pattern is not the same as for squamous cell carcinoma and basal cell carcinoma, which are associated with chronic sun exposure. With melanomas the most important factor appears to be episodic acute exposure with burning and, as might be expected therefore, the groups most at risk are pale-skinned individuals with blue eyes who always burn and never tan (so-called skin type 1 subjects). Self-examination of moles is recommended, looking for the so-called clinical ABCD criteria (asymmetry, bleeding, irregular colour and enlarging diameter).

Dysplastic naevus syndrome

▶ Familial tendency to melanomas in some kindreds
▶ Possess atypical naevi
▶ High risk of developing melanoma

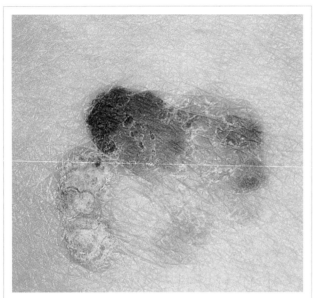

Fig. 24.24 Malignant melanoma. This asymmetrical lesion shows variable pigmentation and regression. The original lesion was a superficial spreading malignant melanoma and a nodule has now developed within it, giving it a significantly poorer prognosis.

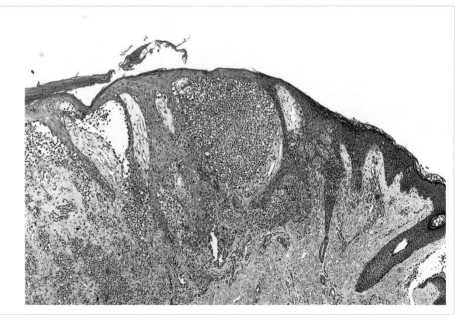

Fig. 24.25 Malignant melanoma. The malignant melanocytes in this lesion are invading the epidermis in a pagetoid manner and the nests in the dermis are expanding in size.

Recently it has become apparent that some families have a greater than normal frequency of malignant melanomas. These families are known as BK mole kindreds, the BK referring to the initials of the first recognised patients with this condition. Members of these families also have numerous atypical moles (*dysplastic naevi*) and it is from these naevi that their melanomas may develop.

Histologically, they resemble benign naevi but show asymmetry with variable cytological and architectural atypia. They display a chronic inflammatory cell infiltrate, indicating that the body is recognising their altered antigenic status and possible malignant potential.

Dysplastic naevi have the same clinical ABCD criteria as melanoma. Accordingly, when there is clinical uncertainty, they must be excised for histological examination.

Clinical and histopathological sporadic dysplastic/atypical naevi occur outside the familial situation. Depending on the number present, these are best regarded as a small risk factor for the later development of melanoma.

DERMAL VESSELS

The blood vessels of the dermis participate in inflammatory reactions; the details of this are identical to those seen in any organ of the body (Ch. 10). Discussed here are the phenomena affecting the skin vasculature that result in typical skin lesions. The skin lymphatics demonstrate a similar range of pathologies but these are much rarer and will not be discussed.

Bruises

Bruises are due to blood leaking from vessels into the dermis. Bruises can occur from:

- damaged vessels (trauma, vasculitis)
- changes in the blood (thrombocytopenia)
- changes in the dermis (old age—senile purpura and scurvy).

Bruises result when blood vessels are sufficiently damaged for red blood cells to escape into the surrounding connective tissue. The breakdown of this extravasated haemoglobin provides the attractive series of colour changes associated with the resolution of this common lesion; the initial bluish-red of haemoglobin fades to the green of biliverdin, then to the yellow of haemosiderin, and finally disappears back to the body's general iron stores.

Bruises are commonly classified according to their sizes and causes and there are long clinical lists describing such minor variations as *petechiae*, *purpura* and *ecchymoses*. Bruises may arise due to blunt trauma of sufficient power to damage normal vessels, as a result of minor trauma to fragile vessels in the elderly or in patients on steroids, as a result of inadequacy of the clotting system as in liver failure or idiopathic thrombocytopenia, or because the supporting tissue has become defective due to vitamin C deficiency; the list is lengthy, but the end effect is the same.

Telangiectasia

Telangiectasias are dilatations of capillaries often seen:

- in the elderly
- in irradiated skin
- following prolonged steroid therapy
- in patients suffering from liver failure (when they are called Campbell de Morgan spots or *spider naevi*).

Histologically, the vessels are normal but dilated.

Naevus flammeus (port-wine stain) develops on the face in early infancy in histologically normal skin. The lesion is flat and in some cases is associated with an underlying meningeal vascular malformation (Sturge–Weber syndrome) which may bleed with catastrophic neurological results. Histologically, the overlying epidermis is normal and the vessels appear to be passively dilated with no evidence of endothelial proliferation, so although it is usually categorised as a naevus (see below) it is in fact telangiectasis occurring on the basis of congenitally abnormal vessels.

Hamartomas

Hamartomas are tumour-like malformations of tissues (Ch. 11). They consist of normal tissue elements in abnormal amounts and arrangements; in the skin, they are often called naevi or birthmarks. Naevi may contain any tissue element but in the skin the commonest are vascular naevi and 1pigmented naevi. The pigmented naevi derive from melanocytes; the vascular naevi are considered below.

Vascular naevi

There is one further problem in terminology: if vascular naevi are true hamartomas then their genetic make-up is the same as that of the rest of the patient's tissues, that is to say they are not truly neoplastic. Unfortunately, they are still commonly referred to in the clinical and pathological literature as 'haemangiomas', implying erroneously that they are true benign neoplasms.

Vascular naevi, present from birth or developing soon after, may be of any size and are very common. Their differences in appearance, clinical significance and prognosis depend upon their site and the calibre of vessels involved.

Capillary haemangiomas (strawberry naevi) appear in early infancy, but in contrast to the other vascular naevi they have a brief period of growth with endothelial proliferation followed by fibrosis and regression which may be total. Because of the vascular proliferation they are raised, often lobulated masses, but they rarely give rise to anything other than cosmetic problems.

Cavernous haemangiomas lie in the deep dermis or subcutaneous tissues but may be associated with an overlying capillary haemangioma. The lesion consists of large, dilated thin-walled vessels that may contain so much blood with disturbed flow characteristics that, in rare cases, consumption coagulopathy can occur (Ch. 23).

Vasculitis

Vessels themselves may become inflamed and this results in a series of specific skin conditions, often with systemic symptoms. Conversely, the classical systemic vasculitides frequently have skin manifestations. Several skin diseases such as lupus erythematosus and hypersensitivity reactions (especially to drugs) may have a vasculitic component. Then, they are characterised by purpura in addition to their normal clinical picture, because the vessel damage allows blood to leak into the dermis. A common vasculitis of small blood vessels in children is Henoch–Schönlein purpura. In this there is considerable neutrophil breakdown (leukocytoclasis) and it often follows streptococcal infection.

Other generalised vasculitides, such as polyarteritis nodosa and Wegener's syndrome, may cause skin lesions (Ch. 25).

Tumours

Benign tumours

Haemangioma and lymphangioma

These represent benign neoplasms of vessels containing blood and lymph respectively. Distinction from the vascular hamartomas described previously is difficult and only of academic interest.

Pyogenic granuloma (lobular haemangioma)

The nomenclature 'pyogenic granuloma' is misleading because the lesions do not contain granulomas and the inflammation reflects secondary surface ulceration and inflammation rather than primary pyogenic infection.

Some of these lesions appear to be an idiosyncratic response to trauma.

Glomus tumour

This is a tiny, painful nodule which often occurs beneath the nail. It derives from the glomus apparatus, which is a contractile device governing flow in the cutaneous micro-vasculature. The tumours consist of groups of cells looking rather like epithelial cells around vascular spaces and can be shown to contain numerous nerve fibres as well as mast cells and fibroblasts.

Angiosarcoma

Malignant proliferations of blood vessels are called angiosarcomas. They are rare and many arise in sites of previous irradiation or in chronically oedematous limbs (following mastectomy with removal of axillary lymph nodes) or on the face or scalp of the elderly.

Kaposi's sarcoma

Kaposi's sarcoma, a previously rare lesion, has recently assumed much more significance due to its association with AIDS (acquired immune deficiency syndrome), of which it can be one late manifestation. Kaposi's sarcoma presents most commonly as vascular lesions on the limbs. In non-AIDS cases, 90% are found in males. Prior to the AIDS outbreak they were seen in young Africans living around Lake Victoria, in elderly patients of Jewish or Mediterranean origin, and in some patients on long-term immunosuppression. The new risk groups—chiefly male homosexuals—are associated with sexually transmitted AIDS.

The lesions may be single or multiple, may resemble bruises or be raised nodules. Their histology resembles granulation tissue with proliferation of vessels with plump endothelial cells, extravasation of erythrocytes and interstitial inflammatory cells. Human herpes virus 8 (HHV8) appears to be an important aetiological factor.

ADNEXA

The skin adnexa—the *pilosebaceous system* and the *eccrine sweat glands*—are complex structures that develop from the epidermis and remain in continuity with it but reside in the dermis. Their distribution is characteristic of the anatomical site of the body and, consequently, the distribution of diseases related to them is also anatomically characteristic. They are metabolically highly active structures and very sensitive to toxic and hormonal influences; one only has to recall the induction of sweating by anxiety or hair loss in patients subjected to chemotherapy to confirm this sensitivity.

One other set of adnexa actually protrude from the surface of the skin—the nails. These structures are also subject to a specific set of pathological conditions but, like the hair, they are non-living keratin and therefore only reflect metabolic events that happened as they were growing and which may later have ceased to operate.

In skin trauma, such as burns, the regrowth of the epidermis occurs from the viable edges of the wound but it can also occur from remnants of adnexa if the original destruction was not too deep (Ch. 6). If there is full thickness destruction including the adnexa, then epidermal regrowth will occur from the edges as usual but no adnexa will develop. This implies that the adnexal remnants have the ability to differentiate to produce epidermis but that epidermal cells have lost the ability to differentiate towards the highly specialised adnexal structures of skin grafts.

Pilosebaceous system

Acne vulgaris

- ▶ Very common in adolescence
- ▶ Clinically consists of comedones and pustules
- ▶ Often heals with scarring
- ▶ Hormone dependent; more common in males

Acne vulgaris is so common among the adolescent population that it could nearly be viewed as a normal variant. Clinically, it is characterised by pilosebaceous units that are blocked by dark plugs of keratin, called comedones or blackheads. These blocked follicles become infected and swell up to form the characteristic pustules which may discharge on to the skin surface or rupture into the dermis, with resultant scarring.

The development of acne is dependent on circulating testosterone which is converted to the active hormone by enzymes contained in the pilosebaceous system itself. Females also have significant levels of circulating testosterone, although generally at lower levels than in the male, which accounts for the lower incidence of acne in females; castrated males have no acne. Acne may also occur in pregnancy and with steroid therapy as well as a reaction to some halogens such as bromides and iodides and to various industrial oils. These secondary acnes suggest that the development of spontaneous acne vulgaris may be dependent on hormonal influences and perhaps on some toxic influences such as the products of bacterial breakdown of skin lipids. Currently, acne is very successfully treated by antibiotics or synthetic analogues of retinoids (a subunit of vitamin A) which modify keratin production, suggesting that the first step in the process may be the formation of a comedone in the form of a keratin plug.

Acne rosacea

This causes redness and papules on the cheeks and nose. Histologically, there is mild granulomatous inflammation, and the follicular parasite *Demodex* is often present.

Alopecia

> ▶ Male pattern baldness due to increased hormonal sensitivity of follicles
> ▶ Alopecia areata due to autoimmunity
> ▶ Lichen planus and lupus erythematosus can cause scarring alopecia

Hair loss for any reason is alopecia. The commonest form is *male pattern baldness*. This can be an inherited trait which affects a large proportion of the adult male population and a much smaller proportion of the female population. It is characterised by a progressive loss of hair from the temples and from the crown of the head. It is testosterone-dependent and eunuchs at least have the compensation of retaining their hair. Histologically, there is progressive reduction in size (miniaturisation) of the resting (telogen) hair follicles.

Another type of alopecia occurs as a result of autoimmune damage to the hair follicle: this is termed *alopecia areata*. Clinically, there is a circumscribed area of baldness with small exclamation-mark hairs regrowing within it. Histologically, there is a lymphocytic infiltrate around the deeper part of the follicle, which is destroyed by the infiltrate. The upper part of the follicle remains so that the appearance is of a normal number of short, stubby follicles with deep inflammation.

Hair loss can also occur in inflammatory skin conditions in which there is epidermal damage such as *lichen planus* and *lupus erythematosus*. In these conditions there is usually obvious scarring of the scalp and signs of the disease in other sites. Histologically, there is the recognisable pattern of the disease involving the epidermis, but also spreading down the hair follicle. In distinction to alopecia areata, the inflammation affects the upper part of the follicle in continuity with the epidermis, and the end effect is to leave a thinned, atrophic skin with a diminished number of growing (anagen) follicles.

Total hair loss can occur in some forms of systemic poisoning such as thallium intoxication, or from chemotherapy, in which the rapidly dividing hair cells are early victims of antimitotic agents (Ch. 5) in the same way as haemopoietic and intestinal epithelial cells.

Hirsutism

Unwanted hair is almost as much of a personal problem as baldness. Currently, our culture disapproves of facial, axillary and leg hair in women and a large amount of effort is directed towards its removal. Facial hair growth is a secondary sexual characteristic dependent upon circulating testosterone levels. It is not the testosterone that is active but a metabolite of it produced by enzymes within the hair follicle itself. There are then two factors involved: first, the level of circulating hormone, and second, the end organ sensitivity. In general it is not clear which of these is the important process in most cases of female hirsutism.

Facial hair also develops in the post-menopausal female as the small amount of testosterone produced by the adrenal glands is no longer counterbalanced by the ovarian oestrogens.

Facial hair may also develop as a result of various drug treatments and in response to virilising hormones (e.g. androgens) secreted by tumours (e.g. Cushing's syndrome).

Pilosebaceous tumours

The commonest benign pilosebaceous tumour is *pilomatrixoma* (so-called benign calcifying epithelioma of Malherbe). The commonest malignant tumour derived from the pilosebaceous system is the basal cell carcinoma and therefore purists sometimes call this trichoblastic carcinoma!

Eccrine sweat glands

A long period of evolution has provided land animals with an effective water-conserving kidney and an impermeable skin to prevent water and electrolyte loss. The value of this impermeable skin can readily be seen in the metabolic imbalance that develops in patients with severe burns. It is, therefore, rather curious that mammals have developed a system for pouring out water and electrolytes onto the skin in order to control their temperature. Long-distance athletes and newcomers to tropical climates find that they need to take in large amounts of water and salt in order to balance the losses due to eccrine gland thermal regulation. Another problem faced by unacclimatised dwellers in the tropics is that the eccrine gland pores swell up with the unaccustomed activity and block sweat excretion, causing 'prickly heat'.

Benign (poromas and hidradenomas) and malignant sweat gland tumours occur but are rare.

Nails

The nails are affected in many general skin conditions such as psoriasis and fungal infections and may also be indicators of internal disease (p. 708). In the elderly, the great toenail may be disrupted by ill-fitting footwear or other trauma and develop into a startling hoof or horn-like

protuberance *(onychogryphosis)* that is incapacitatingly difficult to deal with. In younger people, the direction of growth of the nail may be disturbed, from similar causes, resulting in *ingrowing toenail* which often needs ablation of the nail bed to cure it.

DERMAL CONNECTIVE TISSUES

The dermis contains the nerves and blood vessels that nourish and support the epidermis and its adnexa. In their turn, these dermal structures are supported by a matrix of proteins and complex sugars (glycosaminoglycans), collectively known as the connective tissue ground substance. This ground substance is secreted by fibroblasts and, to a lesser extent, by mast cells. The two characteristic proteins of the dermis are *collagen,* which provides the tensile strength of the skin, and *elastin,* which provides the elasticity. Together, these compounds make the skin tough, flexible and deformable but with the property of returning to its original shape once the deforming stresses are released. The complex sugars include *hyaluronic acid,* which binds water and provides the fluid environment in which the proteins can function. This substance seems to act as a selective filter and a barrier to the spread of organisms. Indeed, many organisms penetrate the dermis by producing an enzyme (hyaluronidase) that breaks down the hyaluronic acid. There are also various sulphated polysaccharides which act as a matrix on which the proteins are synthesised and organised three-dimensionally. These substances all seem to be synthesised by the *fibroblasts*—elongated cells scattered about the dermis. The other cell type found in the dermis, usually around blood vessels, is the *mast cell.* These are not very obvious with routine histological stains, but special techniques reveal them to be cells containing numerous granules that can be shown to contain histamine and heparin, as well as a variety of other pharmacologically active substances.

Collagen and elastin

The normal effects of wear and tear on collagen and elastin are usually made good with no evidence being left that anything has happened. Eventually, however, because of the progressive accumulation of sun damage, the fibroblasts no longer secrete the ground substance in great enough quantities to repair the ravages of time and a lax, wrinkled, poorly healing skin develops as one of the unmistakable signs of the ageing process. Sun damage seems to play a large part in this process, as can be seen by comparing, clinically or histologically, areas of skin from clothed and unclothed sites. Histologically, the collagen patterns in the upper dermis are disrupted and tangled and their staining properties change (elastosis; Ch. 12); the whole skin, including the epidermis, is thinned and many fibroblasts are lost. Old skin has great difficulty in healing, not only because of the failing circulation, but also because the dermis can no longer regenerate itself or service the epidermis. Considerable time and effort can be applied in the attempt to stop or reverse these ageing processes with expensive cosmetics, but the evidence base that many achieve their desired aim is low.

There are several inborn errors of metabolism involving the dermal proteins, the most spectacular of which results in folds of loose skin that can be hyperextended and which heal poorly *(Ehlers–Danlos syndrome).*

There is also a series of diseases in which collagen seems to be the subject of inflammatory attack by the body. *Granuloma annulare, necrobiosis lipoidica* and *rheumatoid nodules* are all characterised histologically by areas of degenerate collagen surrounded by an inflammatory infiltrate which seems to be causing the collagen destruction.

Another series of collagen diseases that are even more clearly autoimmune are the group including *dermatomyositis, scleroderma, morphoea* and *lichen sclerosus.* The latter diseases occur with a variety of other autoimmune phenomena and have recently come to light as end effects of *graft-versus-host disease* when it involves the skin. Lichen sclerosus (often occurring on the genitals) and graft-versus-host disease (following bone marrow transplantation) have some similarity with lichen planus, in that T-lymphocytes attack the more basal parts of the epidermis.

Glycosaminoglycans

The best known of the diseases involving the glycosaminoglycans (GAGs) are the range of conditions in which the enzymes involved in their breakdown are defective. Because these substances are usually being metabolised and resynthesised, when their enzymatic breakdown is inhibited, they slowly accumulate, causing monstrous deformities and a host of general body symptoms. The syndromes include Hunter's and Hurler's diseases (Ch. 7) which used to be lumped together as *gargoylism* in reference to the terrible physical effects that they produce.

Mast cells

The mast cells degranulate on stimulation to release histamine, which is noxious to metazoan parasites. It also makes the skin itch and this probably results in the parasite being dislodged when the host scratches. Histamine also causes the blood vessels to dilate, allowing the various elements of the immune response to escape into the tissue and also attack the invader (Ch. 10).

The classic histamine reaction is nettle rash where the nettle introduces its own histamine into the victim, but some subjects produce a comparable reaction to foods or drugs. This can be life-threatening if the angioedema involves the larynx.

There are some proliferative mast cell diseases, the most notable of which is *urticaria pigmentosa.* This disease occurs in various clinical forms ranging from a benign rash in childhood that may regress completely, to a severe and systemic adult form with spill-over of mast cells into the blood.

Connective tissue tumours

Most dermal connective tissue tumours are benign. The most common is a benign tumour of adipose tissue (lipoma). *Dermatofibroma* (histiocytoma) (Fig. 24.26) usually occurs on the legs and appears to be derived from a newly discovered group of dermal cells—the dermal dendrocytes. *Dermatofibrosarcoma*

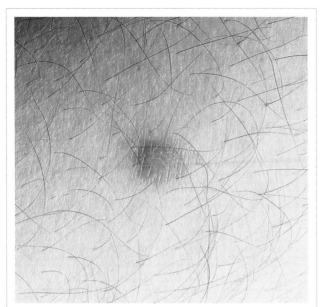

Fig. 24.26 Dermatofibroma (histiocytoma). This benign tumour of dermal cells induces epidermal hyperplasia and pigmentation over it.

protuberans is a malignant variant characterised by high cellularity, mitotic activity and a nodular/protuberant surface; it has a marked tendency to recur locally.

DEPOSITS

Various materials may be deposited in the skin for a variety of metabolic reasons. In general, the substances that accumulate do so for the same reasons that they accumulate in any other organ of the body.

In jaundice (Ch. 16), bile pigments accumulate in the blood and eventually diffuse into the tissue. All tissues are more or less stained (except for the brain in adults) but those tissues that contain the most elastin are the most heavily stained. Elastin specifically binds bile pigments and for this reason jaundice is very obvious in the skin and even more obvious in the sclera, which contains even higher amounts of elastin than does the skin.

For reasons that are mostly obscure, many drugs, or their metabolites, accumulate in the skin. Some are visible, such as amiodarone, and the presence of some can only be implied because of their effects, such as the sweat gland damage seen in barbiturate overdose or the photosensitivity seen with chlorpromazine.

Other deposits in the skin include:

- amyloid
- calcification
- porphyrins.

The skin is involved in systemic amyloidosis (Ch. 7) in the same way that other organs are affected. The skin shows raised, waxy plaques and deposition of the amorphous, eosinophilic material within the deeper dermis and subcutaneous tissue. In *localised cutaneous amyloidosis* there are several clinical variants, ranging from small discrete papules up to much larger, flat macules. The amyloid is located high in the skin, in the papillary dermis, and therefore causes the lesions to be more raised and to have sharper edges than those seen in systemic amyloidosis. The lesions are usually severely pruritic and therefore their appearance may be modified by the effects of scratching and rubbing. Recent studies have revealed that the amyloid in these lesions often contains modified keratin, which has descended from the epidermis and been rendered inert and packaged as amyloid in the upper dermis.

Calcium tends to precipitate in many post-inflammatory (dystrophic) situations (Ch. 7). While pilar cysts often contain areas of calcification, epidermal cysts rarely do; similarly, calcified nodules arise fairly commonly in the scrotum but are almost never encountered in the vulva. Several distinct clinical entities of dystrophic calcium accumulation are known, such as *scrotal calcinosis, idiopathic calcinosis cutis, tumoral calcinosis* and *subcutaneous calcified nodules,* in which no preceding cause can be identified. Other lesions, such as pilar cysts, scars and basal cell carcinomas, can have secondary deposits of calcium within them. One hair follicle tumour, the calcifying *epithelioma of Malherbe* (pilomatrixoma), is highly specific and always calcifies eventually. In all of these examples, the deposits are chemically the same and consist of calcium and phosphate.

In porphyria (Ch. 7) the various porphyrins may accumulate in different organs of the body, resulting in a variety of curious metabolic diseases. When they accumulate in the skin, as in *porphyria cutanea tarda,* they are often capable of producing a photosensitivity. The reason is that these molecules are similar in structure to plant chlorophyll and can generate very reactive free radicals when excited by short-wave ultraviolet light.

CUTANEOUS NERVES

The epidermis contains no nerves; they all lie in the dermis. Many nerve fibres approach the epidermis; some terminate in specific structures that are specialised to subserve different functions, while others end as naked fibres, generally those that respond to painful stimuli. The significance of sensation to the skin itself can be seen in those rare conditions in which pain sensation is congenitally absent; such individuals generally do not survive, as they are subject to continual wounds that are destructive but give no warning pain signals. A similar situation occurs when nerves are damaged by *diabetes or leprosy.* These patients develop skin ulcers and a variety of chronic infections in the distribution of the damaged nerves.

Tumours of cutaneous nerves

The majority of nerve tumours are benign. They are tumours of the various cells of the nerve sheath, as mature nerves are post-mitotic and incapable of mitosis (Chs 12 and 26). The Schwann cells that support and insulate myelinated nerve fibres are capable of developing benign tumours *(schwannomas).* However, the other cells within the nerve sheath that seem to be more closely related to fibroblasts are the ones involved in *neurofibromatosis,* the

congenital disease that has been identified as the cause of the Elephant Man's deformities. These tumours are usually multiple fleshy nodules that arise throughout life and which have significant eventual malignant potential. The disease is inherited as an autosomal dominant and the gene for cutaneous neurofibromatosis type 1 (*NF1*) is present on chromosome 17.

BEHAVIOUR AND THE SKIN

The skin is the surface at which the world and the individual meet. Many individuals attempt to modify their relationship with the outside world by some manipulation of the aspect that is most visible. Much socially acceptable behaviour of this sort that is perceived as 'normal' occurs in the form of cosmetics in our society or ritual scarring in other societies. However, non-acceptable self-mutilation is usually an indication of severe emotional disturbance and it has recently been observed that 'body piercing' is statistically a high risk activity for AIDS.

Tattoos

Tattooing is achieved by introducing stable, inert pigment into the upper dermis where it can be seen through the epidermis. This process can occur accidentally, in trauma cases where gravel and dirt enter wounds that subsequently heal, or in contact gunshot wounds where unburnt powder particles are driven into the skin, or deliberately as a decorative device. Clearly, any of these mechanisms is a potential route for infection, and the AIDS crisis has increased awareness of this problem. Some pigments that were formerly used were found to be less than ideally inert, and cadmium pigments, used to produce yellow colours, were found also to produce the erythema of photosensitivity as an added tinctorial bonus.

Dermatitis artefacta

There is a variety of self-inflicted skin disorders that come to the attention of dermatologists, and sometimes even pathologists. Curious patterns of baldness that do not conform to the usual clinical picture can be caused by patients habitually plucking hair (*trichotillomania*) as a nervous tic or as a more extensive behavioural activity. Curious patterns of rashes can be produced with the help of acids or caustic substances, only in the sites that can be reached by the patient and often with tell-tale drip marks. Strange stories of parasitic infestation backed up by various materials plucked from their own skins (including bits of adnexa, dermis and nerves) are offered by some patients with parasite phobias! The common feature of these conditions is the bizarre nature of the lesions, conforming to no known pattern of naturally occurring disease. The lesions occur only in the sites that the patient can reach, and the behaviour of the patient is abnormal. The pathologist is faced with an atypical clinical history and an often very destructive lesion with no abnormality in the tissue itself and with no inflammation in the early lesion to explain its genesis.

TOXINS AND THE SKIN

Almost any rash can be the result of some drug or toxin either taken internally or applied to the skin surface. Many drug eruptions are of a maculo-papular nature and often recognised clinically by appearing soon after commencing the drug and disappearing when stopped. They may be photosensitive, where the actual substance does no harm until acted upon by specific wavelengths of light. They may be allergic rashes in which the compound itself, or a normal skin protein modified by the toxic compound, elicits an immune response. The compound may itself be inert but become toxic when modified by the body's own metabolic processes.

The skin reactions themselves are often indistinguishable from the idiopathic lesions that they mimic. Thus, various drugs such as gold, antimalarials and photographic colour developers can produce very characteristic eruptions that are almost identical to lichen planus histologically. Contact dermatitis and photodermatitis are often impossible to distinguish histologically from eczema, and many drugs and toxins will produce blisters at all levels of the skin. Even malignant lymphomas may be mimicked by insect bites; often the only way to recognise the source of this lesion is to find the insect mouthparts in the skin.

In these situations the clinical history and the distribution of the lesions is a better guide to aetiology than the histological appearance.

SKIN MANIFESTATIONS OF INTERNAL AND SYSTEMIC DISEASE

Some skin conditions are pathognomonic of internal disorders, some are frequently associated with them and some are rare associations that may be no more than chance. Skin conditions are, however, very important clues that should be watched for with great attention. Nevertheless, they are mainly clinical diagnostic clues, and their histological appearance is often less dramatic than their clinical presentation. They are mentioned here for completeness and because the mechanisms by which they arise offer such fascinating speculations on pathological processes.

Metastatic (secondary) deposits of tumour in the skin can be a manifestation of internal disease. The skin is a relatively rare site for secondary tumour deposits, particularly before the primary lesion has declared itself, but it does happen and a skin biopsy can be of great diagnostic help. In general, secondary deposits retain the characteristics of the original tumour and a reasonable assessment as to its origins can be offered in most cases.

A more curious but fascinating phenomenon is the specific skin rash that accompanies the very rare tumour of the pancreas, glucagonoma. This skin lesion is *necrotising migratory erythema*; it is virtually specific and seems to be due to some mechanism on the part of tumour that deprives the skin of zinc. Other skin lesions associated with internal and systemic disease include:

- *pyoderma gangrenosum* with chronic inflammatory bowel disease

- the acral and facial skin rash associated with *dermatomyositis*
- wart-like lesions in the armpit called *acanthosis nigricans* and sudden crops of *seborrhoeic warts,* both of which may signal internal malignancies
- *necrobiosis lipoidica* and diabetes mellitus
- *xanthomas* and hyperlipidaemia
- *finger clubbing* with a variety of internal congenital, inflammatory and malignant disorders
- *tumours of the hair follicle* in association with internal malignancies such as bowel cancer (Muir–Torre syndrome).

DERMATOLOGICAL SURGERY

Dermatological surgery is now commonplace, both within and outside the hospital setting. The golden rule of good clinical practice (and to avoid potential medico-legal actions) is to submit all tissue removed for histological examination.

Any lesion clinically considered to be a skin tag, mole or cyst could in reality be any benign or malignant neoplasm. Only histopathology can establish the definitive diagnosis and thereby provide information relating to prognosis and management.

MULTIDISCIPLINARY TEAMS

Some aspects of dermatology, such as skin cancers, are best managed by multidisciplinary teams where cases are discussed and appropriate management strategies formulated. The dermatopathologist plays a major role in this setting by reviewing and presenting the histopathology and providing vital diagnostic, management and prognostic information to other clinical colleagues.

ACKNOWLEDGEMENTS

The current author acknowledges the contribution of Dr Dennis Cotton for his authorship of this chapter in initial editions. In addition, the following are acknowledged for help in providing illustrations: Professor S S Bleehen, Dr A Messenger, Dr A Wright.

Commonly confused	Distinction and explanation
Spongiosis and *acantholysis*	Both are mechanisms of vesicle or bulla formation. *Spongiosis* is produced by intercellular fluid forcing apart the epidermal cells. In *acantholysis,* the cells are separated by destruction of the intercellular desmosomes.
Acanthosis and *acantholysis*	Both affect the prickle cell (acanthocyte) layer of the epidermis. *Acanthosis* means that the prickle cell layer is thickened. *Acantholysis* means a destruction of the intercellular desmosomes leading to cellular separation.
Mycosis fungoides and *fungal infections*	*Mycosis fungoides,* a cutaneous T-cell lymphoma, has absolutely nothing to do with *fungal infections;* the nomenclature is misleading. The lesions are clinically and pathologically different.
Pemphigus and *pemphigoid*	Pemphigus and pemphigoid are both immune-mediated bullous disorders. In *pemphigus vulgaris* there is damage to the prickle cell layer of the epidermis, whereas in *bullous pemphigoid* the damage is located at the dermo-epidermal junction.
Herpes virus, herpes gestationis and *dermatitis herpetiformis*	The virus inherits its name from the herpetic (clusters of small vesicles) rash it produces, similar to the clinical features of *herpes gestationis* and *dermatitis herpetiformis,* neither of which has any causal connection with *herpes virus.*
Lichenoid and *psoriasiform*	A *lichenoid* reaction is characterised by basal cell damage resulting in a low rate of epidermal cell renewal; for example, it is a feature of lichen planus. A *psoriasiform* epidermal reaction is characterised by an increased rate of epidermal cell renewal, as in psoriasis.

FURTHER READING

Elder D 2005 Lever's histopathology of the skin, 9th edn. Lippincott-Raven, Philadelphia

LeBoit P, Burg G, Weedon D, Sarasin A 2006 World Health Organization classification of tumours. Skin tumours. IARC Press, Lyons

McKee P H, Calonje E, Granter S R 2005 Pathology of the skin with clinical correlations, 3rd edn. Mosby, Philadelphia

Miller A J, Mihm 2006 M Mechanisms of disease. Melanoma. New England Journal of Medicine 355: 51–64.

Naeyaert J M, Brochez L 2003 Dysplastic naevi. New England Journal of Medicine 349: 2233–2240.

Rubin A I, Chen E H, Ratner D 2005 Basal cell carcinoma. New England Journal of Medicine 353: 2262–2269

Slater D N, McKee P H 2002 Minimum dataset for the histopathological reporting of common skin cancers. Royal College of Pathologists, London, pp 1–25

Thompson J F, Scolyer K A, Kefford R F 2005 Cutaneous melanoma. Lancet 365: 687–703

Weedon D 2002 Skin pathology, 2nd edn. Churchill Livingstone, London

Commonly confused conditions and entities relating to skin pathology	
Commonly confused	Distinction and explanation
Eczema and *dermatitis*	*Eczema* is a clinical term used to describe the appearance of skin affected by *dermatitis* causing vesicles, scaling and exudation.

Osteoarticular and connective tissues

COMMON CLINICAL PROBLEMS FROM OSTEOARTICULAR AND CONNECTIVE TISSUE DISEASE

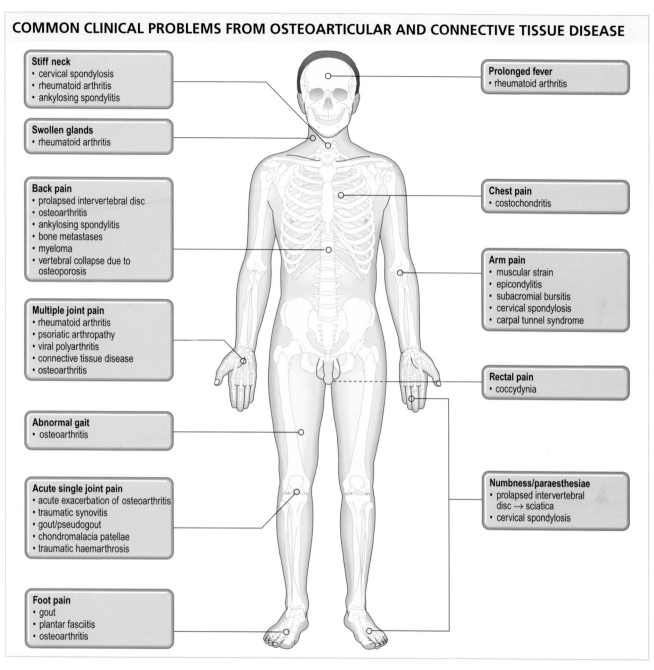

Stiff neck
- cervical spondylosis
- rheumatoid arthritis
- ankylosing spondylitis

Swollen glands
- rheumatoid arthritis

Back pain
- prolapsed intervertebral disc
- osteoarthritis
- ankylosing spondylitis
- bone metastases
- myeloma
- vertebral collapse due to osteoporosis

Multiple joint pain
- rheumatoid arthritis
- psoriatic arthropathy
- viral polyarthritis
- connective tissue disease
- osteoarthritis

Abnormal gait
- osteoarthritis

Acute single joint pain
- acute exacerbation of osteoarthritis
- traumatic synovitis
- gout/pseudogout
- chondromalacia patellae
- traumatic haemarthrosis

Foot pain
- gout
- plantar fasciitis
- osteoarthritis

Prolonged fever
- rheumatoid arthritis

Chest pain
- costochondritis

Arm pain
- muscular strain
- epicondylitis
- subacromial bursitis
- cervical spondylosis
- carpal tunnel syndrome

Rectal pain
- coccydynia

Numbness/paraesthesiae
- prolapsed intervertebral disc → sciatica
- cervical spondylosis

Pathological basis of clinical signs and symptoms of bone, joint and connective tissue diseases	
Sign or symptom	Pathological basis
Bone disease	
Pain	Stimulation of nerve endings in bone by: • inflammation • trauma (fracture) • tumour • pathological increased bone resorption (e.g. Paget's disease)
Fracture after trivial injury	Bone weakening due to: • congenital disorders of bone integrity • metabolic bone disease • erosion of bone by tumour

(Continued)

Pathological basis of clinical signs and symptoms of bone, joint and connective tissue diseases—cont'd	
Sign or symptom	Pathological basis
Deformity	Abnormal bone growth/remodelling due to: • congenital disorders of bone integrity • metabolic bone disease • malunion of a fracture
Hypercalcaemia	• Extensive bone erosion by tumour deposits • Secretion of parathyroid hormone (PTH) by parathyroid adenoma • Secretion of PTH-related peptide by visceral tumours, e.g. carcinoma of the bronchus
Joint disease	
Pain	Stimulation of nerve endings in joint capsule and synovium by inflammation (arthritis) or abnormal load bearing/joint movement
Deformity	Joint swelling due to: • synovial inflammation • effusion into joint space Erosion of articular surfaces Abnormal remodelling of subchondral bone Loss of alignment of joint surfaces by cartilage destruction and bone deformity
Restricted movement	Synovial swelling Fibrosis Limited by pain
Systemic features (e.g. subcutaneous nodules, lymphadenopathy)	Arthritis mediated by immune mechanisms
Connective tissue diseases	
Swelling	Tumour Oedema Inflammation
Joint pain	Synovial oedema and inflammation with stimulation of nerves in joint capsule
Ischaemic lesions	Vasculitis
Restricted mobility of tissues	Fibrosis or increased tissue tension due to inflammation

BONE

NORMAL STRUCTURE AND FUNCTION

Functions of bone

Bone has structural, protective and metabolic functions. The skeleton is divided into the axial (head, vertebral column, thoracic cage, shoulder and pelvic girdles) and the appendicular (limbs). The axial skeleton participates extensively in all three areas of function, whereas the appendicular skeleton has a primarily structural function. The structural functions of bone are to provide support and also insertion sites for muscles and ligaments. The skull and thoracic cage provide physical protection for the brain, thoracic and upper abdominal organs.

Bone has two major metabolic functions:

1. It provides a *reservoir of essential minerals,* most importantly calcium, phosphorus (in the form of phosphate) and magnesium. These minerals can be released from bone matrix through the process of bone resorption (see below) and are also constantly incorporated into bone matrix during the process of bone mineralisation.

2. The second metabolic function provided by bone is the *support of haemopoiesis*. This is a metabolic function rather than simply a structural function: the bone microenvironment provides growth factor support for haemopoietic precursors which, under normal circumstances, reside in no other tissue in the adult human body.

The main clinical manifestations of bone disease are:

* pain
* fractures
* deformity
* disturbances of mineral homeostasis (usually hypercalcaemia).

Structure of bone

Bone is characterised by its hard matrix. This matrix consists of two components, *matrix proteins* and *mineral*. The main structural protein in bone matrix is type I collagen. This protein provides the framework of the overall structure of bone. Within the collagen framework there is a mixture of many other proteins, some of which are thought to aid mineralisation; others mediate cell attachment. Another major group of proteins present in bone matrix are growth factors, such as the bone morphogenetic proteins and transforming growth factor beta (TGF-beta). These appear to be important in mediating the cellular events of bone remodelling. Proteoglycans are also present in bone matrix, but do not have the same major structural role in bone as they do in cartilage. The mineral component of bone matrix provides its structural resilience. Most of the mineral deposited in bone is in the form of a calcium phosphate complex known as *hydroxyapatite*. The precise mechanism by which bone mineral forms is unclear. The enzyme alkaline phosphatase, a major product of osteoblasts, and vitamin D metabolites are thought to be important in this process.

Despite its lifeless appearance, bone is a highly complex and dynamic cellular tissue. Bone contains two distinct types of cell, osteoclasts and the osteoblast family. *Osteoclasts,* the bone-resorbing cells, are mono- or multinucleated cells that are specialised members of the monocyte–macrophage lineage. These short-lived cells are recruited to the bone surface at sites of remodelling and destroy bone matrix by secreting hydrogen ions and proteolytic enzymes into a sealed space beneath the cell. The osteoblast family consists of: *osteoblasts,* which are bone forming cells; *osteocytes,* which form an interconnecting network throughout bone matrix; and *lining cells,* which cover metabolically inactive bone surfaces. Osteocytes are thought to be mechanosensory cells. The cells of the osteoblast family are unrelated to osteoclasts, being related more closely to fibroblasts, chondrocytes and adipocytes.

Osteoclasts and osteoblasts act together to control bone growth and metabolism through the *bone remodelling cycle.* This cycle, illustrated in Figure 25.1, forms the basis of bone metabolism.

Each remodelling cycle takes several weeks to complete. Approximately one million remodelling cycles are occurring within the adult human skeleton at any one time. These cycles are asynchronous, some being in resorption, some in formation. This continual process of remodelling renews the adult human skeleton approximately every 7 years. The functions of the remodelling cycle are to:

- continually release minerals to maintain appropriate levels in the circulation
- maintain structural integrity of bone
- allow changes in bone structure in response to the requirements of growth or changes in load bearing.

In the normal bone remodelling cycle, resorption and formation are *coupled,* with the same quantity of bone being formed as had been resorbed, except where extra bone matrix is called for by the requirements of growth. In pathological situations, the two processes can become *uncoupled;* for example, osteoporosis can result from uncoupled increases in bone resorption or decreases in bone formation resulting in a net loss of bone. All diseases of bone are associated with changes in bone remodelling of some type.

There are two types of mature bone, *cortical* and *trabecular* (sometimes known as cancellous bone). Cortical bone has a predominantly structural load-bearing function. It is the dense bone that forms the diaphyses (shafts) of long bones such as the femur and the outer surfaces of predominantly trabecular bones such as the vertebral bodies. Trabecular bone has some structural function, but contributes to the metabolic functions of bone far more than cortical bone. Because it is metabolically more active, it is far more prone to diseases involving or resulting from increased bone remodelling than cortical bone. For example, post-menopausal osteoporosis affects trabecular bone before it affects cortical bone, and deposits of metastatic carcinoma are far more common in sites occupied by trabecular bone.

Development and growth of bones

Most tissues and organs grow as a result of a general increase in the number of their constituent cells. Because the proteinaceous matrix is so heavily calcified, a similar process is not possible in bone. Thus the process of remodelling described above is essential for bone growth.

During development, bone is formed either directly in connective tissue, as in the skull (*intramembranous ossification*), or on pre-existing cartilage, as in the limb bones (*endochondral ossification*).

During intramembranous ossification the first bone that is laid down has a loose and rather haphazard arrangement. This 'woven bone' gradually matures into more organised and compact 'lamellar' bone.

Endochondral ossification is a much more complicated process during which a cartilagenous template is converted into a bony structure with capacity for further growth. In each bone, ossification occurs at particular sites or *centres of ossification* situated in the shaft (diaphyseal centres) or towards the ends of the bone (epiphyseal centres) (Fig. 25.2). Ossification proceeds at different, but predictable, rates in each particular bone. In long bones, a plate of epiphyseal cartilage persists into adolescent or early adult life; this allows a continual increase in bone length. Skeletal growth through the growth plates is

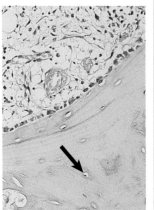

Fig. 25.1 The bone remodelling cycle. The bone remodelling cycle consists of resorption by osteoclasts (arrowheads in left-hand plate) which results in the removal of an area of bone matrix and is inevitably followed at the same site by resynthesis of bone matrix by osteoblasts (right-hand plate). Many osteoblasts become incorporated into the matrix they synthesise to become osteocytes (arrowed). Osteocytes are connected by a complex network of cytoplasmic processes not visible on these haematoxylin and eosin-stained sections.

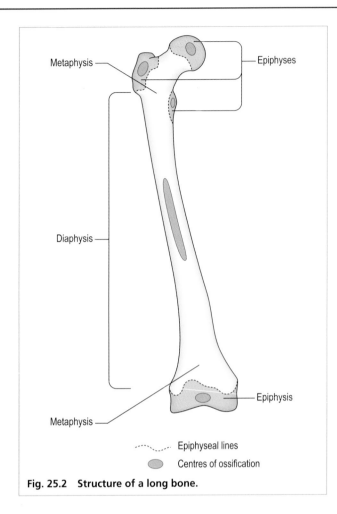

Fig. 25.2   Structure of a long bone.

controlled by growth hormone and sex steroids with parathyroid hormone-related peptide (PTHrP) and insulin-like growth factor-1 (IGF-1) acting as paracrine (locally produced) growth factors. The overall shape and size of bone changes during growth and, to some extent, in adult life. This involves both osteoclastic bone resorption and enlargement of pre-existing, or the formation of new, bony trabeculae. Cortical bone grows in an analogous way through remodelling occurring at the periosteal and endosteal surfaces and within Haversian canals.

FRACTURES AND THEIR HEALING

▶ Types of fracture: simple (clean break); comminuted (multiple bone fragments); compound (breaking through overlying skin); complicated (involving adjacent structures—blood vessels, nerves, etc.); stress fractures (small linear fractures)
▶ Pathological fracture: fracture of bone weakened by disease (e.g. tumours, osteoporosis, osteomalacia, Paget's disease)
▶ Healing requires immobilisation of approximated bone ends
▶ Healing may be impaired by movement, poor blood supply, interposition of soft tissue, infection, poor nutrition, steroid therapy

Causes of fractures

Fractures in normal bone are the result of substantial trauma, such as direct violence or a sudden unexpected fall. The precise site of fracture, the nature and direction of the fracture line, and the speed of the subsequent repair process depend very much on the age of the patient, the particular bone involved and the precise pattern of injury (Fig. 25.3).

Repeated episodes of minor trauma, for example after marching, marathon running or training for sport, can produce small but often painful *stress fractures*. These usually occur in the long bones of the lower limbs but have also been described in the metatarsals, the upper limb, pelvis and spine. They usually heal satisfactorily after a short period of rest. Even professional athletes can develop these fractures.

Fractures occur more easily in bone that is structurally abnormal. They may occur after a trivial injury or minor fall or even spontaneously during normal activity. This is particularly common in patients with osteoporosis but also occurs in most forms of metabolic bone disease (e.g. in osteomalacia and rickets), in Paget's disease and in bone infiltrated by malignant tumours. Fractures of this type are called *pathological fractures*.

Fracture healing

The first stage in fracture healing is the formation of a bony bridge between the separated fragments. When this is formed, and some rigidity has been regained, remodelling and restructuring gradually restore the normal contours of the fractured bone. This process and the factors that can interfere with it are described in Chapter 6.

The major causes of delayed fracture healing are:

1. Local factors:
   ● excessive movement of fractured bone during healing
   ● extensive damage to fractured bone, i.e. bony necrosis in a comminuted fracture
   ● a poor intrinsic blood supply, e.g. lower tibia
   ● severe local soft tissue injury or impaired blood supply
   ● interruption of blood supply following fracture, e.g. head of femur, scaphoid
   ● infection—only if overlying skin surface is broken, as in compound fracture
   ● interposition of soft tissue in fracture gap, or wide separation of fracture ends.
2. General factors:
   ● elderly patients
   ● poor general health
   ● drug therapy, e.g. corticosteroids.

All of these are well recognised by orthopaedic surgeons, who modify the treatment in individual cases in line with the particular pattern of injury, and the age and general health of the patient. For example, a fracture through the neck of the femur usually deprives the head of its normal blood supply and satisfactory fracture healing is unlikely to occur. Surgical treatment, such as excision of the head and replacement by a metallic prosthesis, is therefore essential. Fractures in which the overlying skin surface is broken (compound fractures)

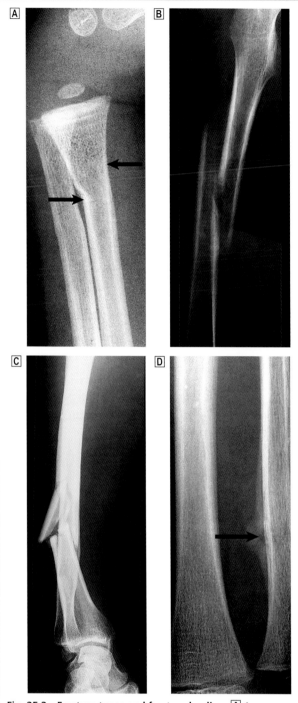

Fig. 25.3 Fracture types and fracture healing. [A] A green-stick fracture of the distal radius in a young child (arrowed). [B] A displaced spiral fracture of the femur in a child. [C] A comminuted fracture of the tibia. One fragment of bone has almost separated from the shaft. [D] A healing fracture of the ulna. The site of the break is just visible and is surrounded by callus (arrowed).

nails, plates and screws or external fixator devices to hold the fractured fragments in an appropriate position; this often allows early mobilisation. Primary callus does form but is reduced in amount. Small gaps are filled by new woven bone. Dead bone is gradually revascularised and new Haversian bone grows in.

Surgical treatment is sometimes necessary for fractures in which the healing process has been delayed. The object is to 'restart' the primary callus response. This can sometimes be achieved by lifting flaps of periosteum close to the fracture site. In addition, local 'grafting' with the patient's own bone or devitalised bone from another donor can promote bone healing, presumably through the action of bone morphogenetic proteins and other growth factors present in the graft matrix.

OSTEOPOROSIS AND METABOLIC BONE DISEASE

Normal calcium metabolism

The two major hormones that regulate calcium metabolism are *vitamin D* and *parathyroid hormone* (PTH). Vitamin D is not a vitamin in the strict sense of an essential dietary requirement, as it can also be synthesised photochemically in the skin. In reality, vitamin D is more like a steroid hormone precursor that can be derived from the diet. Its active metabolites function in a similar way to conventional hormones. Vitamin D must be metabolised by the liver to 25-hydroxyvitamin D_3, and subsequently by the kidney to the active metabolite 1,25-dihydroxyvitamin D_3. Receptors for vitamin D are present in a variety of cell types in the body; the physiological role of this vitamin may be much wider than is currently known. Expression of the receptors is subject to genetic variation within the population and may contribute to the individual differences in risk of developing metabolic bone disease. The combined effects of vitamin D and parathyroid hormone are:

- to stimulate bone calcium mobilisation
- to increase renal reabsorption of calcium in the distal tubule (chiefly PTH, but also vitamin D)
- to stimulate intestinal calcium and phosphate absorption (vitamin D).

These functions are complex and are demonstrated in Figure 25.4. This area of metabolism is still incompletely understood. There is evidence to suggest that there may be another pathway regulating phosphate transport involving fibroblast growth factor 23. PTH and 1,25-dihydroxyvitamin D_3 also have important direct effects on bone: PTH stimulates both bone resorption and formation; 1,25-dihydroxyvitamin D_3 promotes bone matrix mineralisation.

In contrast to PTH, *calcitonin*, a peptide hormone, appears to lower serum calcium, but usually only when it is pathologically elevated. The stimulus to its secretion is an increase in the serum calcium concentration; it is produced in specialised parafollicular cells (C-cells) of the thyroid. Its exact physiological action is uncertain but it has an inhibitory effect on osteoclasts.

are liable to infection, whereas this is extremely uncommon in closed fractures. Healing will be substantially delayed if a wound infection develops.

In many fractures, healing can be accelerated by prompt and appropriate surgical treatment using internal fixation by

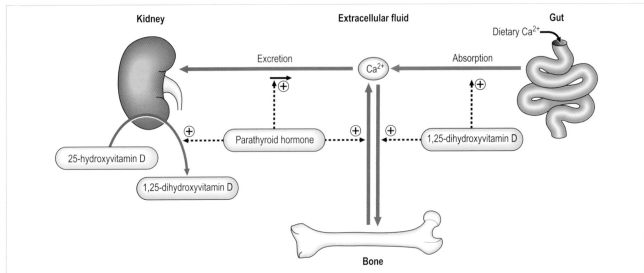

Fig. 25.4 Regulation of calcium metabolism. Calcium levels are maintained in the extracellular fluid within a narrow range of concentrations by absorption from the gut and excretion via the kidney with bone acting as a buffering reservoir. PTH raises calcium levels by inhibiting renal tubular calcium reabsorption, increasing release of calcium from bone matrix through osteoclastic resorption and indirectly increasing calcium absorption from the gut by increasing the metabolism of 25-hydroxyvitamin D to 1,25-dihydroxyvitamin D (the active form) in the kidney.

Although vitamin D, PTH and, possibly, calcitonin are the most important factors controlling calcium and phosphate concentrations, and therefore normal bone integrity, several other factors are also involved. Glucocorticoids have a role in the regulation of skeletal growth but prolonged corticosteroid therapy often induces osteoporosis. Thyroid hormone deficiency, as in cretinism, is associated with several skeletal abnormalities. Sex steroids accelerate the closure of epiphyses, and growth hormone has an effect on the development and maturation of cartilage.

Osteoporosis

- ▶ Reduction in total bone mass causing weakening
- ▶ Common in the elderly, particularly females
- ▶ Common predisposing cause of fractures, particularly neck of femur
- ▶ Complication of steroid therapy and Cushing's syndrome
- ▶ Follows any form of immobility
- ▶ Associated with alcoholism, diabetes, liver disease and smoking

Osteoporosis is a disease in which there is a reduction in bone mass in the presence of normal mineralisation. It is diagnosed by radiological assessment of bone mineral density (generally measured by dual photon absorptiometry). The usual definition of osteoporosis is a bone mineral density measurement two standard deviations below the mean value for young adults of the same sex. Clinically, osteoporosis may present as a fragility fracture, loss of height, or stooping deformity (kyphosis or 'dowager's hump') due to wedge fractures of the vertebral bodies. Sometimes osteoporosis is diagnosed, when clinically silent, by screening individuals thought to be at risk.

Clinically significant osteoporosis most often results from a combination of age-related bone loss and additional bone loss from another cause; by far the most common such cause is postmenopausal oestrogen withdrawal. Osteoporosis is a clinically silent disease until it is complicated by deformity or fractures.

Pathogenesis

Osteoporosis is caused by a loss of coupling in the bone remodelling process. This can be due to increased bone resorption, decreased bone formation, or both. The loss of coupling results in a net loss of bone volume. In contrast to osteomalacia (see below), mineralisation of bone is normal. Because of its greater metabolic activity, trabecular bone is usually affected more severely than cortical bone. This is particularly the case when increased bone resorption is the main pathogenetic mechanism.

The total bone mass of an individual is influenced by factors such as body build, race, gender, physical activity and general nutrition. Osteoporosis is more common in females than in males and is less common in blacks, who have a greater skeletal mass than whites or Asians. Osteoporosis can be assessed radiologically or by techniques based on the ability of bone to absorb photons released by a gamma-emitting isotope. These demonstrate a progressive loss of bone of 0.75–1% per annum in normal adults of both sexes from as early as 30 years of age. More importantly, there is an accelerated phase of bone loss of up to 1–3% per year in females in the 5–10 years following the menopause.

Localised osteoporosis is inevitable after immobilisation of any part of the skeleton. Even young, healthy males confined to bed after a limb fracture show substantial bone loss. Painful joints in patients with rheumatoid arthritis restrict movement, and osteoporosis often develops in adjacent bones, although this may also be the result of increased bone resorption due to inflammatory mediators produced in affected joints.

Complications

The major complications of osteoporosis are:

- skeletal deformity
- bone pain (usually due to compression fractures)
- fracture.

The commonest clinical feature of osteoporosis is the progressive loss of height that occurs with age. This is a direct result of compression of vertebrae. Sudden collapse or unequal compression of individual vertebral bodies can cause severe localised back pain and deformities such as kyphosis or scoliosis (Fig. 25.5).

Wrist and hip fractures are common in elderly patients with osteoporosis. Although osteoporosis is the major underlying cause, other factors such as an increased tendency to fall and a loss of 'protective neuromuscular reflexes' (the ability to fall over safely) are also important. Hip fractures account for numerous hospital admissions and are a major source of disability and a frequent cause of death in the elderly.

Prevention and treatment

Osteoporosis is a major social and economic problem in the elderly, and preventive measures should begin in the middle-aged. Vertebral osteoporosis is reduced in women treated with oestrogens (hormone replacement therapy—HRT).

Bisphosphonate drugs, which inhibit bone resorption, are more effective in preventing osteoporotic hip fractures. Regular exercise and an increased dietary intake of calcium also have beneficial effects.

Rickets and osteomalacia

> ▸ Inadequate mineralisation of organic bone matrix
> ▸ Rickets occurs in children and is characterised by bone deformities
> ▸ Osteomalacia occurs in adults, causing susceptibility to fracture but few deformities
> ▸ Due to deficiency of active metabolites of vitamin D
> ▸ Causes include nutritional deficiency of vitamin D, lack of sunlight, intestinal malabsorption, renal and liver disease

Osteomalacia is characterised by deficient mineralisation of the organic matrix of the skeleton. Rickets is the name given to osteomalacia affecting the growing skeleton of children; it results in characteristic deformities. Causes of osteomalacia, or rickets, include:

- dietary deficiency of vitamin D
- intestinal malabsorption
- failure to metabolise vitamin D (renal disease, congenital enzyme deficiencies).

Fig. 25.5 Vertebral osteoporosis. Ⓐ The lower thoracic vertebrae showing small protrusions of the intervertebral disc into the osteoporotic bone (arrowed). Ⓑ The lumbar spine. The vertebral body in the centre has collapsed and has a typical biconcave shape.

Aetiology

In the past, nutritional deficiency of vitamin D was a common cause of rickets in children and, occasionally, of osteomalacia in adults. In most communities, this has been eliminated by improvements in diet and by the addition of vitamin D to foodstuffs. The disease still occurs in some Asian communities in the UK; skin pigmentation impairs photochemical synthesis of vitamin D, and a constituent of chapatti flour interferes with calcium and phosphate absorption in the gut. As dietary rickets is becoming less common in Western countries, an increasing proportion of cases of rickets are due to congenital abnormalities in vitamin D metabolism. Disorders of this type are referred to as 'vitamin D-resistant rickets' because vitamin D supplements fail to generate active vitamin D metabolites.

Malabsorption of calcium and phosphate from the intestine is the commonest cause of osteomalacia in adults. The underlying cause is often coeliac disease, but occasional cases result from Crohn's disease or extensive surgical resection of the small intestine. As the liver and kidney have important roles in the metabolism of vitamin D, renal and hepatic disorders may cause osteomalacia. This is uncommon in liver disease, but a complex pattern of bone disease that includes osteomalacia is seen in renal failure. Occasional patients treated with anticonvulsants, such as phenytoin, develop osteomalacia. These drugs induce liver enzymes that degrade vitamin D to inactive metabolites.

Diagnosis

The characteristic clinical deformities of rickets include:

- bowing of the long bones of the leg
- pronounced swelling at the costochondral junctions
- flattening or 'bossing' of the skull.

Inadequate mineralisation of bone reduces its normal strength and allows deformities to develop, for example from pressure on the skull while lying in a cot, or on the limbs as they begin to bear weight. Calcification of epiphyseal cartilage is an essential step in the normal process of ossification in long bone. When the levels of vitamin D metabolites are low, calcification cannot occur and cartilaginous proliferation continues. This accounts for the enlargement of long bones and the ribs at growth plates.

The characteristic pathological feature in adults with osteomalacia is spontaneous incomplete fractures ('Looser's zones'), often in the long bones or pelvis. The main symptoms are bone pain and tenderness, and weakness of proximal limb muscles. Serum calcium levels may be reduced and serum alkaline phosphatase is increased (these biochemical abnormalities are usually absent in osteoporosis). A bone biopsy will demonstrate an increase in non-mineralised osteoid (Fig. 25.6).

Treatment and prevention

Uncomplicated rickets or osteomalacia will respond promptly to vitamin D treatment. Increased calcium intake may also be required to compensate for the flux of calcium into unmineralised bone matrix that occurs in response to vitamin D treatment. Intramuscular injection can overcome problems associated with malabsorption, and underlying disorders such as coeliac disease should be treated appropriately. A normal balanced diet will prevent rickets or osteomalacia, but many foodstuffs are now artificially supplemented with vitamin D.

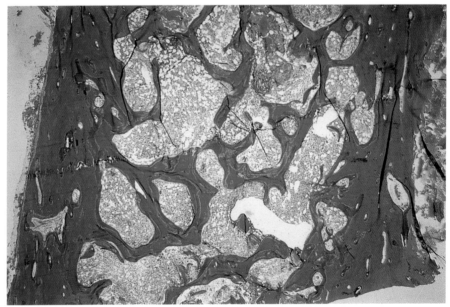

Fig. 25.6 Osteomalacia. This transiliac crest undecalcified bone biopsy, stained by the Goldner's trichrome technique, was taken from a patient on renal dialysis suffering from osteomalacia due to a combination of low 1,25-dihydroxy-vitamin D levels (a common consequence of renal failure) and aluminium toxicity (an iatrogenic complication of dialysis). Mineralised bone matrix is stained green and unmineralised matrix (osteoid) is stained red. The amount of osteoid present is approximately 20 times greater than normal.

Hyperparathyroidism and hypercalcaemia

▶ Hyperparathyroidism causes increased osteoclastic breakdown of bone
▶ Serum calcium is usually raised in primary hyperparathyroidism, but low or normal in secondary (reactive) hyperparathyroidism
▶ Bone lesions may be cystic and haemorrhagic ('brown tumours')

Persistent elevation of fasting blood calcium, after correction has been made for the serum albumin concentration, is an important indication for further investigation. The major pathological causes are:

- primary hyperparathyroidism
- bone destruction by metastatic carcinoma or myeloma
- inappropriate secretion of parathyroid hormone-related peptide (PTHrP) by malignant tumours
- sarcoidosis
- renal failure
- iatrogenic, e.g. thiazide diuretics, hypervitaminosis D.

By far the commonest causes of hypercalcaemia are primary hyperparathyroidism and hypercalcaemia of malignancy.

In hyperparathyroidism (Ch. 17), increased secretion of parathyroid hormone stimulates calcium absorption in the intestine, reabsorption in the kidney and osteoclastic breakdown of bone.

In *primary hyperparathyroidism* the usual cause is a parathyroid adenoma or, occasionally, diffuse hyperplasia of the parathyroid glands. In contrast, in *secondary hyperparathyroidism*, prolonged *hypocalcaemia* stimulates parathyroid hyperplasia and eventually produces parathyroid enlargement. This is usually the result of renal failure or malabsorption secondary to coeliac disease. In occasional patients, secondary hyperparathyroidism is associated with hypercalcaemia. This has been called *tertiary hyperparathyroidism* and usually results from inappropriately high secretion of PTH by an adenoma arising in secondary hyperparathyroidism.

When obvious causes, such as malignant disease, sarcoidosis or drug therapy, have been excluded, it must be suspected that an otherwise fit patient with hypercalcaemia has primary hyperparathyroidism (Table 25.1).

The advanced bone pathology associated with hyperparathyroidism is now rare. In the early stages there are subtle radiological changes such as subperiosteal resorption of phalangeal bone (Fig. 25.7) or characteristic changes around the teeth. As the disease progresses, cystic bone lesions may develop—*osteitis fibrosa cystica (von Recklinghausen's disease of bone)*. These are sometimes referred to as 'brown tumours', although they are not neoplasms. The brown appearance is the result of haemorrhage and there is often a marked associated osteoclastic reaction. Because PTH has anabolic as well as catabolic effects in bone, hyperparathyroidism does not usually cause generalised osteoporosis.

Bone disease in renal failure (renal osteodystrophy)

Most patients with chronic renal failure have clinical, radiological or pathological evidence of bone disease. There is no

Table 25.1 Causes of hypercalcaemia

Cause	Pathophysiology
Primary hyperparathyroidism	Abnormal PTH secretion from adenoma, hyperplasia or carcinoma of parathyroid glands
Malignant disease	• Secondary deposits producing bone destruction and calcium release • Inappropriate PTHrP secretion, usually squamous carcinoma of bronchus or carcinoma of breast • Uncoupled bone resorption due to myeloma
Sarcoidosis	Probable secretion of vitamin D metabolites from granulomas
Miscellaneous causes: Drugs, e.g. thiazide diuretics Renal failure (tertiary hyperparathyroidism) Thyrotoxicosis Hypervitaminosis D	

single bone disease that occurs in renal failure; in most patients it is a combination of *osteomalacia* with a variable degree of *hyperparathyroidism*. Other features include:

- osteosclerosis
- osteoporosis
- bone necrosis
- soft tissue calcification
- aluminium-induced osteomalacia.

The most important pathophysiological changes in renal bone disease are summarised in Table 25.2. Several mechanisms have been suggested to account for the osteomalacia. In all forms of renal failure there is a decrease in the amount of functional renal tissue, and this may be directly responsible for the inadequate production of active vitamin D metabolites. An increased blood phosphate level (hyperphosphataemia) is frequent in renal failure, and this may directly inhibit enzymes responsible for vitamin D metabolism in the kidneys. In the past, haemodialysis fluids rich in aluminium were associated with aluminium deposition in organs such as brain and bone. In bone, aluminium inhibits the calcification of osteoid and contributes to osteomalacia in renal failure (Ch. 7).

Patients with chronic renal failure may have a low serum calcium. This is partly the result of impaired vitamin D metabolism, as vitamin D metabolites are essential for the proper absorption of calcium from the small intestine. The high serum phosphate also reduces the ionised fraction of plasma calcium. This acts as a stimulus to PTH production, and a degree of hyperparathyroidism is inevitable in severe renal failure. Patients with some forms of glomerulonephritis are treated with steroids and this may induce osteoporosis or, occasionally, areas of bone necrosis. Calcification of the soft tissues, or of blood vessel walls, is a further feature of chronic renal failure, particularly after prolonged haemodialysis. Longstanding

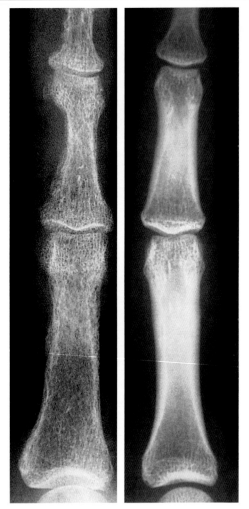

Fig. 25.7   X-ray of finger in primary hyperparathyroidism (left) and a normal patient (right). The irregular outlines of the phalanges are the result of resorption of bone.

Table 25.2   Mechanisms of renal bone disease (renal osteodystrophy)

Feature of renal failure	Pathological effect in bone
Inadequate renal tissue	Impaired conversion of 25(OH)D$_3$ to 1,25(OH)$_2$D$_3$ → *Osteomalacia*
High serum phosphate	1. Inhibition of renal enzymes catalysing formation of 1,25(OH)$_2$D$_3$ 2. Decrease in ionised Ca^{2+} in serum → *Hyperparathyroidism*
Prolonged haemodialysis	Inhibition of calcification of osteoid → *Osteomalacia*
Steroid therapy (e.g. for chronic glomerulonephritis)	Osteoporosis Avascular necrosis of bone

disordered bone remodelling due to the combination of secondary hyperparathyroidism and osteomalacia can lead to alternating areas of thickened bone (osteosclerosis) and osteoporosis. This has a characteristic appearance ('rugger jersey spine').

OSTEOMYELITIS

- ▶ Inflammatory lesion due to bacterial infection of bone
- ▶ Bacteria enter bone either from blood (septicaemia) or directly through skin wound over a compound fracture
- ▶ Necrotic bone forms inner sequestrum; reactive new bone forms outer involucrum
- ▶ Most common in children, where *Staphylococcus aureus* is the usual cause
- ▶ A complication of advanced tuberculosis
- ▶ May complicate the use of internal fracture fixation devices

Aetiology

Osteomyelitis is the result of a bacterial infection of bone. The typical patient is a young child who presents with pain in a long bone, sometimes with a misleading history of recent trauma. In the majority of cases the lesion develops in the metaphysis, the part of the shaft immediately adjacent to the epiphyseal plate. The rich capillary network and large venous channels in this area may favour the deposition of circulating micro-organisms and their subsequent growth. In children and adolescents, osteomyelitis is usually the result of *Staphylococcus aureus* bacteraemia, often secondary to a boil or other skin infections. Sometimes, the underlying cause of bacteraemia is not apparent. Osteomyelitis is also increasingly seen in elderly patients.

Before the introduction of antibiotics, tuberculous and even syphilitic osteomyelitis were common. Children with haemoglobinopathies, especially sickle cell disease, have an increased risk of osteomyelitis; unusual organisms, such as *Salmonella*, are sometimes responsible.

Osteomyelitis is a well-recognised complication of compound fractures, particularly if the wound in the overlying skin is extensive and there are necrotic bone splinters at the fracture ends. Osteomyelitis is not a complication of closed fractures.

Pathogenesis

The classical sequence of changes in osteomyelitis is as follows:

1. transient bacteraemia, e.g. *Staphylococcus aureus*
2. focus of acute inflammation in metaphysis of long bone
3. necrosis of bone fragments, forming the *sequestrum*
4. reactive new bone forms, the *involucrum* (Fig. 25.8)
5. if untreated, sinuses form, draining pus to the skin surface via *cloacae*.

The development of a sequestrum is due to necrosis of bone caused by compression of blood vessels by the inflammatory process within the Haversian canals of the cortical bone. This event rarely occurs if antibiotic treatment is initiated early in the course of the disease. However, infections in bone can be

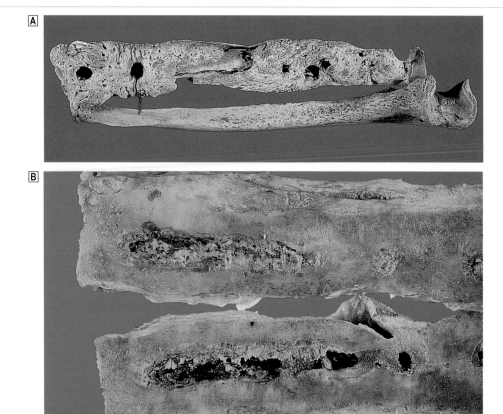

Fig. 25.8   Chronic osteomyelitis. **A** The radius and ulna of an 18th-century sailor. The 'granular bone' is the involucrum and the circular defects are 'cloacae' through which pus drained. **B** The cut surface of the femur of a 78-year-old male who received a shrapnel wound to his thigh in World War I. The pus drained through a sinus for the next 50 years! A thick bony involucrum surrounds a chronic inflammatory abscess in the marrow cavity.

difficult to eradicate, particularly if foreign material is present, for example following a penetrating injury. Commonly encountered 'foreign materials' in bone are joint prostheses, internal fracture fixation devices and other pieces of orthopaedic hardware. Bone infections associated with orthopaedic surgery are more common than primary osteomyelitis in many countries.

Brodie's abscess is a distinctive clinical form of subacute pyogenic osteomyelitis. The lesion is solitary and, as in typical acute osteomyelitis, localised to the metaphysis.

Clinical features, laboratory investigations and treatment

Most patients with acute osteomyelitis present with localised bone pain and some tissue swelling. A dull continuous back pain, which increases on straining, is typical of vertebral osteomyelitis. The radiological changes are usually characteristic. Blood cultures are positive in some patients, but open biopsy of the lesion may be needed to ensure accurate bacteriological diagnosis. The commonest organisms are *Staphylococcus aureus*, *Mycobacterium tuberculosis*, *Escherichia coli*, pneumococcus or group A streptococcus. Wherever possible

a precise bacteriological diagnosis must be made and treatment continued for several weeks.

PAGET'S DISEASE

- ▶ Common disorder of unknown aetiology in which there is a localised increase in bone turnover
- ▶ May affect part of one bone, an entire bone, or many bones
- ▶ Most affected individuals have few symptoms
- ▶ Complicated by pain, deformities, fractures, nerve compression, deafness, osteosarcoma and (rarely) heart failure

Incidence and epidemiology

Paget's disease is a disorder in which there is disorderly bone remodelling. There is considerable variation in its incidence both within and between different countries and racial groups. Despite intensive study, little is known of the cause of Paget's disease and it is not regularly associated with any other common disorder. Electron microscopic studies have demonstrated probable viral inclusions in the nuclei of osteoclasts, possibly derived from measles or canine distemper virus, but no definite proof has been obtained. Paget's disease has a distinctive epidemiology. It is most common in western Europe and those parts of the world to which western Europeans have emigrated. For unknown reasons, it is far more common in Lancashire (UK) than anywhere else in the world.

Clinicopathological features

The usual presenting complaints of patients with Paget's disease are bone pain, deformities or fractures. Although the pelvis and spine are most frequently affected, deformities are most obvious in the long bones such as the tibia, which is characteristically bowed, and in the skull.

Serum calcium concentration is usually normal, but the alkaline phosphatase is markedly elevated, reflecting the osteoblastic activity. The histological changes of Paget's disease consist of irregular trabecular bone, much of which is woven rather than lamellar, and areas of osteolysis with abnormally large osteoclasts. These changes reflect grossly disordered bone remodelling (Fig. 25.9).

Complications

The complications of Paget's disease are:

- deformities
- bone pain
- fractures
- nerve or spinal cord compression
- deafness

- osteosarcoma, occasionally other bone tumours
- heart failure.

In many patients, Paget's disease is completely asymptomatic and is unlikely to be diagnosed unless discovered as an incidental finding on X-ray. The commonest complications are deformities (Fig. 25.10) and bone pain. In some cases, the pain is the result of osteoarthritic degeneration of a related joint. The cause of the pain is uncertain, but interestingly responds well to treatments that inhibit bone resorption. Pagetoid bone is particularly susceptible to fracturing in the initial lytic phase. Enlargement in the sclerotic stage can lead to nerve or spinal cord compression. Deafness is the result of both VIIIth cranial nerve compression and distortion of the middle ear cavity. Occasional patients develop other cranial nerve palsies and, in advanced cases, paraplegia can result.

The most sinister complication of Paget's disease is osteosarcoma; the majority of elderly patients with osteosarcoma do have Paget's disease. As in younger patients, osteosarcoma develops in the long bones, particularly the humerus. The prognosis of osteosarcoma in Paget's disease is especially poor. There is also an increased incidence of other forms of sarcoma.

Patients with Paget's disease may also have heart failure. This is usually a simple coincidence of two common diseases of the elderly. However, the bone in patients with Paget's disease is extremely vascular (Fig. 25.9), and blood flow in these areas is markedly increased. This may represent an example of 'high output heart failure' (Ch. 13). Paget's disease is usually responsive to treatment with bisphosphonate drugs.

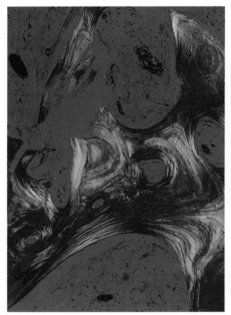 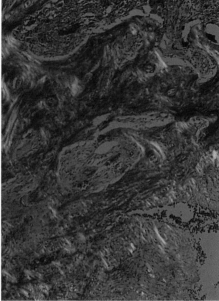

Fig. 25.9 Paget's disease. In normal trabecular bone (left) viewed by polarised light, note the regular lamellar pattern. In bone affected by Paget's disease (right) the lamellar pattern is largely replaced by irregular woven bone. Bone of this type is associated with deformity and poor mechanical function.

areas of adjacent bone of their blood supply. Necrosis is then an inevitable consequence. Surgical treatment is therefore sometimes necessary to replace the fractured head of femur. The cause of other cases of avascular necrosis is less certain. Lesions occur in patients treated with corticosteroids, in sickle cell disease and other haemoglobinopathies. Similar lesions develop in divers and are probably the result of air embolism, associated with decompression.

Fibrous dysplasia

In this benign disorder of children and young adults, lesions composed of fibrous and bony tissue develop, usually in the ribs, femur, tibia or skull. It is sometimes asssociated with precocious puberty (McCune–Albright syndrome). Histologically, these lesions are composed of irregular masses of immature woven bone separated by a richly vascular fibrous stroma. Mature lamellar bone is not formed and this suggests that the lesion is a result of an arrest of bone maturation at the woven bone stage. Lesions do not usually enlarge after puberty, though some appear to be reactivated during pregnancy. Although the clinical and radiological findings are often diagnostic, lesions in long bones are often biopsied and the affected parts of ribs can be excised. In typical cases, the histological changes can be easily distinguished from true neoplastic disorders, such as osteosarcoma, fibrosarcoma or giant cell tumours.

Hypertrophic osteoarthropathy

This is an uncommon reactive condition in which there is clubbing, pain and swelling of the wrist and ankle joints, and subperiosteal new bone formation in the distal part of long bones. In the vast majority of affected patients there is an associated pulmonary carcinoma or a pleural mesothelioma. The underlying causes of both clubbing and hypertrophic osteoarthropathy are unknown, but in both cases there is a marked increase in blood flow in the distal portions of the limbs. Occasional cases regress after surgical treatment of the primary tumour.

Osteogenesis imperfecta

Osteogenesis imperfecta is a clinical syndrome characterised by fractures occurring as a result of mild or minimal trauma. In its most severe form it is fatal in utero or in the perinatal period. Mild forms compatible with normal development also occur, but many patients are severely disabled. Many cases are associated with mutations of the genes encoding the chains of type I collagen. Inheritance is usually autosomal dominant, but many cases result from sporadic new mutations. The uveal pigment of the eye is visible through the thinned sclera, which therefore appear blue in some forms of the disease.

BONE TUMOURS

▶ Commonest tumour in bone is metastatic carcinoma (commonly from breast, kidney, thyroid, lung or prostate)
▶ Important primary malignant bone tumours are osteosarcoma, chondrosarcoma and Ewing's sarcoma

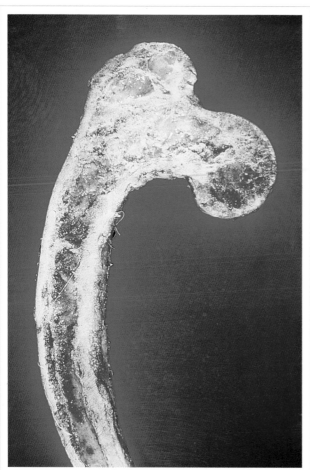

Fig. 25.10 Paget's disease. This affected femur shows characteristic thickening and deformity.

MISCELLANEOUS BONE DISORDERS

Achondroplasia

Achondroplasia is a single gene disorder transmitted as an autosomal dominant with almost complete penetrance and occurs in approximately 1 in 25 000 births. The affected gene is for fibroblast growth factor receptor. The physical appearances of the patients are characteristic. The limbs are short, particularly the proximal portions of the arms, but the trunk is of normal length. There is a failure of proper ossification in bones that have developed from a cartilaginous template (endochondral ossification). In contrast, bones that develop from connective tissue (intramembranous ossification), such as the vault of the skull, are normal. Affected patients have normal intelligence and life-span. There is a wide variety of other congenital skeletal dysplasias, many of which are lethal in utero. Achondroplasia is the commonest non-lethal form.

Avascular necrosis of bone

This usually presents with pain and limitation of joint movement. For anatomical reasons, fractures of bones such as the neck of the femur (Fig. 25.11) or the scaphoid deprive some

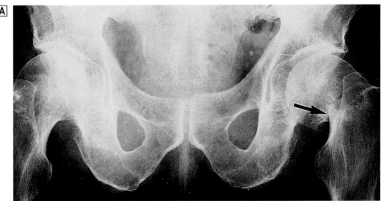

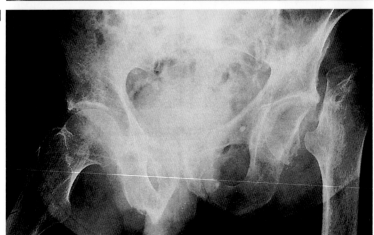

Fig. 25.11 Fracture of femoral neck. A Compare the normal contours of the femoral neck on the right with the fracture on the left (arrowed). B There is a displaced fracture of the left femoral neck (detected 8 weeks after a fall!) resulting in necrosis of the bone deprived of its blood supply.

Incidence and aetiology

Primary tumours of bone are uncommon and account for only 0.5% of all cancer deaths. Because of their rarity, these tumours are best managed in centres where there are orthopaedic surgeons, radiologists and histopathologists with sufficient experience of these lesions. Individual tumours tend to occur in particular age groups or in specific sites (Fig. 25.12).

Classification

Bone tumours are classified as follows:

1. *Benign tumours:*
   • osteochondroma (exostosis)
   • enchondroma
   • chondroblastoma
   • chondromyxoid fibroma
   • osteoma
   • osteoid osteoma
2. *Borderline tumours* (locally aggressive or recurrent):
   • giant cell tumour ('osteoclastoma')
   • osteoblastoma
   • chordoma
   • adamantinoma

3. *Malignant tumours* (locally aggressive, frequently metastasise):
   • osteosarcoma
   • chondrosarcoma
   • fibrosarcoma
   • malignant fibrous histiocytoma
   • Ewing's sarcoma
4. *Metastases,* commonly from:
   • breast
   • lung
   • prostate
   • kidney
   • thyroid
5. *Myeloma* (multiple myeloma or solitary plasmacytoma).

Benign tumours

The two commonest benign tumours of bone are the *osteochondroma (exostosis)* and the *chondroma (enchondroma)* which together make up over 50% of all benign bone tumours.

Osteochondroma

Patients with osteochondromas are usually under 20 years old and both sexes are affected. The lesions tend to develop near the epiphyses of limb bones, although they can form in

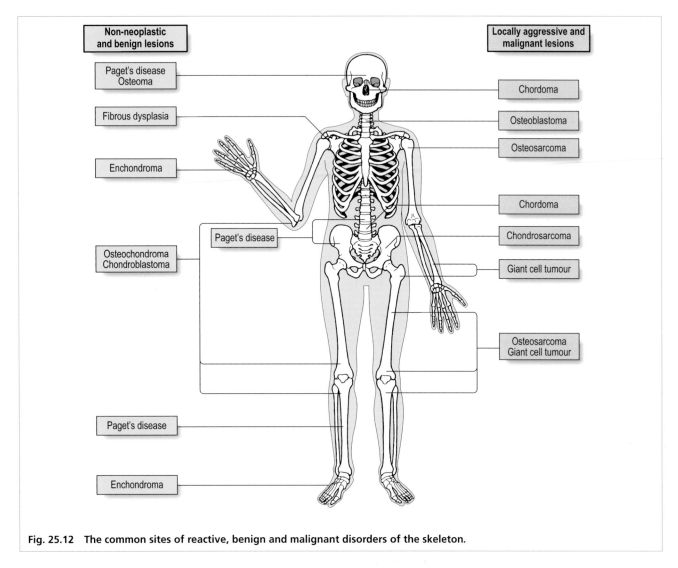

Fig. 25.12 The common sites of reactive, benign and malignant disorders of the skeleton.

any bone that develops from cartilage. Solitary lesions are benign, although they may recur if incompletely excised. Histologically, a thick cartilaginous cap is present, covering irregularly arranged bony trabeculae. There is an intermediate zone where the bone merges gradually into the overlying cartilage.

In *diaphyseal aclasis* there are multiple cartilage-capped exostoses and a substantial risk of associated chondrosarcoma. Malignancy should be suspected in any lesion that continues to grow after puberty. The incidence is approximately 1 per 2000 births and the lesion is transmitted as an autosomal dominant. Up to one-third of cases are the result of new mutations and the condition is probably a single gene disorder.

Chondroma (enchondroma)

Chondromas arise within the medullary cavity of the bones of the hands and feet and because of this are usually known as 'enchondromas'. They are thought to develop from small nests of cartilage that are sometimes found close to the metaphysis. They usually present in patients aged 20–50 years and are more common in men. There may be slight swelling

of the affected bone but the lesions are sometimes discovered incidentally on X-ray. Simple curettage of the lesion is usually curative, although some recur. *Enchondromatosis (Ollier's disease)* is the counterpart of multiple exostoses. Numerous enchondromas develop and there is a considerable risk of chondrosarcoma. This disorder has no obvious genetic basis. Multiple enchondromas may also occur in Mafucci's syndrome in association with multiple angiomas.

Other benign tumours

Other benign bone tumours are uncommon. An osteoma is a mass of abnormally dense bone, usually in the paranasal sinuses or the skull.

An *osteoid osteoma* is a solitary and characteristically painful lesion which usually affects the femur or tibia. The pain may be severe, worse at night, and characteristically relieved by aspirin. Histologically there is a central 'nidus' of vascular fibrous tissue containing bone trabeculae formed by benign osteoblasts.

Chondroblastoma and *chondromyxoid fibroma* are rare tumours of long bones with distinctive histological appearances. They are most common in the femur, tibia or humerus in patients between 10 and 30 years of age.

Locally aggressive or recurrent benign tumours

Some benign tumours of bone, such as giant cell tumour ('osteoclastoma') and osteoblastoma are locally aggressive or may recur after surgery.

Giant cell tumours make up as much as 5% of all bone neoplasms and most often occur at the end of the long bones. They probably originate from undifferentiated mesenchymal cells in the connective tissue framework of bone. Their histological appearance is distinctive. Giant cells are conspicuous and for this reason the tumour has also been known as osteoclastoma; however, these cells are not thought to be the neoplastic component but are non-neoplastic osteoclasts 'recruited' to the tumour by the neoplastic fibroblast-like component. Giant cell tumours can also be confused histologically with the bone lesions of primary hyperparathyroidism ('von Recklinghausen's disease of bone'), in which osteoclasts are plentiful.

Osteoblastomas are uncommon solitary tumours that involve vertebrae and, to a lesser extent, the long bones of the extremities, and are essentially large osteoid osteomas. The lesions are very vascular and show intense osteoblastic activity. Surgical treatment—usually by curettage—can be curative.

Chordomas arise from notochordal remnants, usually in the base of the skull or the sacral region. The constituent cells often have a characteristic 'bubbly' appearance due to cytoplasmic vacuolation. These tumours seldom metastasise but often recur locally.

Adamantinomas and *ameloblastomas* are histologically similar tumours. Ameloblastomas affect the jaw and have the capacity to produce tooth enamel but adamantinomas usually involve the tibia and do not produce enamel. The histological appearance is characteristic, with ribbons and cords of darkly staining cells arranged around a vascular fibrous stroma. Adequate surgical excision is often curative.

Malignant tumours

Although primary malignant tumours of bone are comparatively rare, they are always locally invasive and frequently metastasise. Patients are often young adults. The previously dismal prognosis of these tumours has been considerably improved in recent years with the advent of pre-operative radio- and chemotherapy, often in combination with limb-sparing surgery (Table 25.3).

Osteosarcoma

This aggressive malignant tumour usually affects adolescents and most often involves the distal femur, proximal tibia or humerus (Fig. 25.13). Occasional cases occur in the elderly, usually complicating Paget's disease or previous radiation. Other cases are associated with familial cancer syndromes, notably the retinoblastoma syndrome and the Li–Fraumeni syndrome. Somatic mutations of the tumour suppressor genes that have germline mutations in these syndromes (*RB1* and *p53*) are common in sporadic osteosarcomas. These tumours grow rapidly and often have a typical X-ray appearance. Osteosarcomas are characterised histologically by pleomorphic and mitotically active osteoblasts associated with osteoid; some variants are exceedingly vascular. Approximately 50% of patients can now be cured by a combination of surgery and intensive chemotherapy. Although amputation was previously necessary, local resection and the insertion of prosthetic joints is now usually possible.

Other malignant tumours

Chondrosarcomas, in contrast to osteosarcomas, grow slowly and arise not only in long bones but also in the pelvis, ribs and spine (Fig. 25.14). These tumours may be well differentiated and can resemble normal cartilage. Surgical excision is the treatment of choice, as radiotherapy and chemotherapy are usually ineffective.

Fibrosarcomas and *malignant fibrous histiocytomas* are spindle cell malignant tumours with characteristic histological appearances. These lesions probably arise from fibroblasts and collectively they make up the majority of soft tissue sarcomas. They also occur as primary bone lesions, with the long bones and pelvis most often affected. With adequate surgical treatment up to 40% of patients can be cured. Death is usually the result of blood-borne metastases.

Ewing's sarcoma affects children and teenagers. The tumour is composed of small, darkly staining, undifferentiated cells whose exact origin (histogenesis) has puzzled pathologists for many years. It has a characteristic chromosomal translocation—t(11;22)(q24;q12)—that is also found in an equivalent soft tissue tumour (primitive neuro-ectodermal tumour or PNET). These are now recognised as being the same type of tumour. Males are affected more often than females, and the long bones, pelvis and ribs are the most frequent sites. Widespread metastases are frequent and the bone marrow is often involved.

Metastases and multiple myeloma

The commonest malignant tumours of bone are secondary *metastatic deposits* from carcinomas in other sites. The commonest primaries to cause skeletal metastases are breast, prostate, lung, kidney and thyroid. In the case of breast and prostate carcinomas, skeletal metastases may present early in the course of the disease and be associated with prolonged survival with appropriate treatment. Widespread and extensive bony lesions are also a feature of *multiple myeloma*. Most secondary deposits in bone cause bone breakdown (osteolysis) but some, particularly from carcinoma of the prostate, stimulate bone formation (osteosclerosis; Fig. 20.12, p. 541). Secondary deposits in bone are the commonest cause of hypercalcaemia in middle-aged and elderly patients and are a frequent cause of pathological fractures. Vertebral metastases can cause spinal cord compression.

JOINTS

NORMAL STRUCTURE AND FUNCTION

Joints permit mobility, but not all junctions between bones are designed to allow movement. At one extreme, the cranial sutures in adults are rigidly fixed while, at the other, the

Table 25.3 Malignant tumours of bone

Tumour (% all primary malignant bone tumours)	Usual age (years) and male: female sex ratio	Sites affected	Behaviour	Treatment and prognosis
Osteosarcoma (c. 30%)	Adolescents 2:1	Long bones, esp. distal femur and proximal tibia	Rapid growth, pain and swelling, lung metastases	Surgery and chemotherapy 40% plus cure rate
Chondrosarcoma (c. 15%)	35–60 2:1	Pelvis, ribs, spine, long bones	Slow enlargement, eventual vascular invasion	Surgery c. 75% cure rate
Fibrosarcoma and malignant fibrous histiocytoma (c. 20%)	Any age, peak 30–40 3:2	Femur, tibia, humerus, pelvis	Local growth, vascular invasion	Surgery 40% cure rate
Ewing's sarcoma (c. 7%)	Children and teenagers 2:1	Long bones, pelvis and ribs	Widespread metastases	Surgery and chemotherapy 50% cure rate

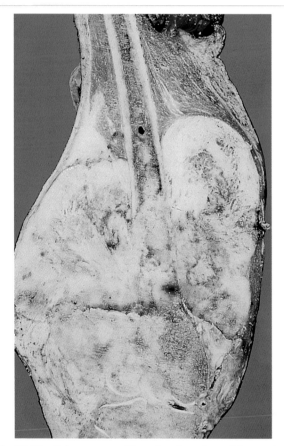

Fig. 25.13 Osteosarcoma. The cut surface of a rapidly growing tumour in the distal femur of a teenager.

shoulder joint has an almost unlimited range of movement. Joints such as the symphysis pubis and the lower tibiofibular joint have limited movement but are firmly bound by fibrous and cartilaginous tissue. In contrast, the articulating surfaces of *synovial joints* are in contact but not in continuity.

The articular surfaces of synovial joints are covered by a thin layer of hyaline or, occasionally, fibrous *cartilage*, up to 3 mm thick. In early life these surfaces are remarkably smooth, and slide and move against each other with very little friction. A viscous, clear *synovial fluid* lubricates the joint surfaces and supplies essential nutrients to the chondrocytes of the articular cartilage.

Synovial joints are enclosed by a tough fibrous capsule, which in turn is lined by a thin *synovial membrane*. Two types of cell—type A and type B—have been identified in the lining membrane. Type A synoviocytes are modified macrophages while type B are fibroblast-like cells and are responsible for synthesising and secreting the hyaluronic acid and other proteins of the synovial fluid. *Ligaments* are band-like thickenings of the joint capsule which not only provide stability, but, as with the cruciate ligaments of the knee joint, limit excessive mobility. Tendons, ligaments and joint capsules insert into bone, their collagen fibres becoming incorporated into the underlying bone. These insertions are called *entheses* and are prone to inflammation in the spondyloarthropathies (see below).

The bone immediately beneath the articular cartilage—the *subchondral bone plate*—provides the strength to withstand and cushion the repeated forces generated by joint movement. In weight-bearing joints, this plate is supported by an underlying 'scaffold' of bony trabeculae. If this supporting system is damaged, as in advanced osteoarthritis, the joint surfaces become deformed and movement is limited. The individual arteries and veins supplying joints and joint capsules have not been studied in detail and are seldom specifically named. Nevertheless, joints are richly vascular structures, particularly in acute inflammatory arthritis or during the active stages of rheumatoid disease. Joints such as the knee, the sternoclavicular and the temporomandibular have partial or complete discs of fibrocartilage called *menisci*, which either project into joint cavities or divide them into separate cavities. These may act as 'cushions' or 'shock absorbers'. When these discs are damaged or torn, there is acute limitation of joint movement and surgical removal or repair is often necessary.

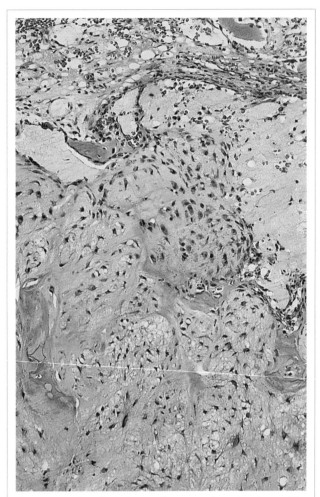

Fig. 25.14   Chondrosarcoma. The tumour has arisen in a pelvic bone of a 42-year-old female. Histologically the abnormal carti-lage is much more cellular than normal.

Joints have a rich innervation, usually derived from nerves supplying the adjacent muscular tissue. This arrangement allows a local reflex arc to be established between movement in an individual joint and the actions of surrounding muscles. There are many sensory nerve endings in the fibrous capsule of joints and in the bone underlying the articular surfaces. Any substantial pathological process involving a joint is likely to cause inflammatory cell infiltration and oedema of the adjacent joint capsule, if not of the articular surfaces themselves, and this leads to both pain and subsequent limitation of movement.

OSTEOARTHRITIS (OSTEOARTHROSIS)

▶ Common painful, disabling degenerative joint disease
▶ Primarily affects cartilage of weight-bearing joints (e.g. hips, knees)
▶ Erosion of cartilage leads to secondary changes in underlying bone
▶ Only limited inflammatory changes in synovial membrane
▶ Osteoarthritis of hip and knee can be treated surgically by joint replacement

Osteoarthritis is a remarkably common, disabling, degenerative disease which usually affects large weight-bearing joints. The inevitable pain, and limitation of movement, associated with this disease is a major cause of morbidity in almost all societies.

Epidemiology

About 20% of elderly men and women have significant osteoarthritic joint disease. Pain and limitation of movement are the most important symptoms, particularly in the hip, the knee and the joints of the cervical spine (cervical spondylosis).

Certain occupations are associated with a high incidence of osteoarthritis in particular joints. Coal miners develop osteoarthritis in elbow joints, golfers in the first metatarso-phalangeal joint of the foot, and footballers in the knees. Some patients with premature osteoarthritis of the hip have previous congenital dislocation in this joint. Similarly, any obvious deformity or previous fracture is an important predisposing cause. Patients with pre-existing bone disease, such as Paget's disease, gout or acromegaly, or other forms of arthritis such as rheumatoid disease, are at risk for secondary osteoarthritis. Nevertheless, in the majority of patients there are no obvious predisposing factors. This is particularly true of vertebral osteoarthritis, which, although often asymptomatic, can produce severe pain and disability.

Pathogenesis

The term 'osteoarthritis' is a misnomer; the role of inflammation in the pathogenesis of this disease appears to be minimal. It is primarily a degenerative disease for which the term 'osteoarthrosis' would be more appropriate. The earliest changes are fragmentation and fibrillation of the normally smooth surface of the articular cartilage (Fig. 25.15). Change of this degree is very common with ageing and may not necessarily progress to symptomatic osteoarthritis. Only in a proportion of joints does the process of degeneration progress to 'joint failure'. Progressive osteoarthritis may occur because of the predisposing factors listed above. However, in the majority of cases, the reason for progression is not clear. There is increasing evidence that genetic factors are important. As the disease progresses, there is increasing loss of articular cartilage accompanied by abortive attempts at regeneration. Because the overall structural integrity of the cartilage has been lost (Fig. 25.16), this new cartilage formation has no structural benefit and eventually the full thickness of the cartilage may be lost, resulting in bone articulating against bone (eburnation). The mechanisms underlying the cartilage degradation are still poorly understood.

The second series of changes in the development of osteoarthritis involves the subchondral bone plate. This plate not only defines the contours of the articular surface but also contributes to the strength and resilience of the joint. Loss of articular cartilage may be a stimulus to reactive proliferation of this plate. In turn, this leads to ever increasing damage to the residual articular cartilage.

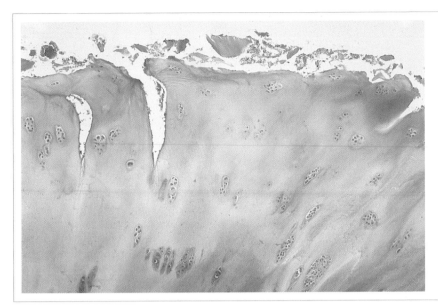

Fig. 25.15 Early osteoarthritis. Histology of a section through the articular surface showing 'fibrillation' and fissuring.

Fig. 25.16 Osteoarthritis. This view of the articular surfaces of the femoral condyles shows advanced osteoarthritis. There are areas of complete cartilage loss with eburnated subchondral bone.

Eventually, the articular surface becomes deformed and in many joints this is the major cause of limitation of movement. There is progressively more severe disorganised bone remodelling, leading to loss of the normal cortical and trabecular patterns of subchondral bone and the development of cystic lesions often visible on X-rays. Bony outgrowths (osteophytes) develop at the margins of the articular surface. These are a characteristic feature of osteoarthritis but serve no useful function. In joints such as the hip they limit the range of movement, and in the distal interphalangeal joints they produce characteristic nodular swellings called *Heberden's nodes*. In *cervical spondylosis,* a variant of osteoarthritis affecting the cervical spine, symptoms result from osteophytic outgrowths impinging on nerve roots as they leave the intervertebral foramina.

Clinicopathological features

The major symptoms of osteoarthritis are pain on joint movement, stiffness during inactivity and audible creaking of joints, often accompanied by a palpable crepitus. Although there is no primary synovial pathology in osteoarthritis, small joint effusions are common and histologically the synovium shows slight hyperplasia and focal areas of chronic inflammation, often as a reaction to calcified debris shed from the articular surfaces.

The diagnosis of osteoarthritis is made on the basis of clinical examination and characteristic radiological appearances. Almost all of the pathological features of osteoarthritis can be identified on a plain X-ray. One of the earliest changes is loss of joint space: the articular surfaces of the bone appear close together when articular cartilage has been lost. Reactive proliferation of the subchondral bone plate occurs and there are deformities of the articular surface. All routine laboratory investigations are normal.

Treatment of osteoarthritis causing the failure of major joints is by replacement of the joint by a prosthesis. Prostheses themselves can fail by loosening of their attachment to the bone into which they are inserted. This can occur as a result of infection, often by low virulence organisms such as *Staphylococcus albus,* or by aseptic loosening. Aseptic loosening is due to localised bone resorption resulting from cytokine production by macrophages activated by prosthesis debris.

RHEUMATOID DISEASE

▸ Common systemic chronic inflammatory disorder invariably involving joints
▸ Associated with rheumatoid factor, an auto-antibody reactive with altered autologous immunoglobulin
▸ Chronic inflammation and proliferation of synovium gradually erodes articular cartilage
▸ Systemic features include subcutaneous rheumatoid nodules, anaemia, lymphadenopathy and splenomegaly, serositis (e.g. pericarditis), Sjögren's syndrome, uveitis, vasculitis, pulmonary changes and amyloidosis

Rheumatoid arthritis is a common, systemic, progressive and often disabling chronic inflammatory disorder. Unlike osteoarthritis, the pathological changes are not restricted to joints. Inflammatory lesions can develop in many tissues, including the heart and pericardium, lungs, blood vessels, skin and subcutaneous tissues, eye, and salivary and lacrimal glands. For this reason, the disorder is more correctly termed rheumatoid *disease*, but the arthritis is the first and generally most disabling feature.

Aetiology and pathogenesis

The main epidemiological and pathogenetic features of rheumatoid disease are:

- females affected more often than males
- occurs in all age groups; children can be affected (Still's disease)
- prevalence in most Caucasian populations at least 1%; less common and less aggressive in blacks and Asians
- slight familial tendency, especially in severe forms
- up to 75% of patients are human leukocyte antigen (HLA)-DR4 positive (normally only 25%)
- most adults have circulating auto-antibodies (rheumatoid factors) directed against autologous (native) immunoglobulins
- multisystem disease characterised by chronic inflammatory granulomatous lesions (rheumatoid nodules).

Immunological abnormalities

Rheumatoid disease is associated with a variety of immunological abnormalities. These involve both the cellular and the humoral arms of the immune system.

Humoral

Most patients have considerably raised levels of serum immunoglobulins and have a characteristic auto-antibody directed against autologous immunoglobulin, called *rheumatoid factor*. The exact role of this antibody in the pathogenesis of rheumatoid arthritis is uncertain (it is possible that rheumatoid factors are simply markers of a loss of immunological self-tolerance) but at the least it is associated with the progression of the disease. Generally, patients with severe arthritis and evidence of multisystem disease have high titres of this antibody. In contrast, seronegative patients often have a milder form of disease. There is no definite evidence that aggregates of these immunoglobulins can act as immune complexes and trigger acute and chronic inflammatory reactions in joints and other tissues. The nature of the underlying stimulus to rheumatoid factor production is completely unknown, but many patients with severe rheumatoid disease have generalised hyperplasia of lymphoid tissue with prominent lymphadenopathy and splenomegaly.

Cellular

There is increasing evidence to suggest that rheumatoid arthritis is a disease driven by cellular, rather than humoral, immune mechanisms. The T-helper lymphocyte populations present in rheumatoid joints are oligoclonal, and may be autoreactive. These cells probably contribute to the process that causes macrophages, macrophage-like type A synoviocytes and other inflammatory cells to secrete cytokines such as tumour necrosis factor alpha and interleukin-1. Thus type IV rather than type II or type III hypersensitivity may be the predominant mechanism. Tumour necrosis factor alpha and interleukin-1 are potent stimulators of synoviocyte proliferation and cartilage resorption and are known to be present in joint fluid and pannus tissue (see below and Fig. 25.19) from rheumatoid joints. Pro-inflammatory cytokines can induce the production of other cytokines, possibly contributing to the progressive nature of rheumatoid disease. Of particular significance, these cytokines are potent inducers of proteolytic enzyme production by synoviocytes. These cytokines are of central importance in the pathogenesis of rheumatoid arthritis, and specific cytokine antagonist drugs are coming into clinical use.

Infectious agents

Although the nature of the immunological abnormalities in rheumatoid disease is becoming clearer, very little progress is being made in identifying the factors that initiate these changes. Micro-organisms have been implicated for many years and it is now beyond doubt that Lyme arthritis (see below) is infectious and that erythrovirus B19 (formerly parvovirus B19) can induce arthritis. Bacteria, viruses and mycoplasmas have been suggested as causes of rheumatoid disease but there is no conclusive proof that rheumatoid disease is caused by infection. Joints affected by rheumatoid are, however, vulnerable to secondary bacterial infection, a potentially serious complication.

Clinicopathological features

The two major changes in rheumatoid arthritis are a chronic inflammatory synovitis and progressive erosion of the articular cartilage (Figs 25.17 and 25.18). In the early stages of the disease there is pain and swelling, chiefly of the hands and the distal metatarsal joints of the foot. As the disease becomes established, the knees, ankles, hips, cervical spine and temporomandibular joints are affected. Joints are tender, and often swollen.

The synovial infiltrates include lymphocytes, plasma cells, macrophages and occasional polymorphs (Fig. 25.19). In the earlier stages there is only a mild increase in inflammatory cells, but in the established disease large nodular masses of lymphocytes and macrophages are characteristic. True granulomas are not usually identified in the synovium but may occasionally be seen in the adjacent joint capsule. A layer of chronically inflamed fibrous tissue (pannus) slowly extends from the synovial margin, eroding the articular cartilage as it spreads (Fig. 25.17).

Osteoporosis often develops in the bones immediately adjacent to affected joints, particularly in the fingers. This is often the first radiological change of rheumatoid disease, but small pocket-like erosions of the peri-articular surface are also seen (Fig. 25.20). In chronically diseased joints the articular cartilage is extensively eroded and fragmented and the resultant debris is a further source of synovial inflammation. The loss of articular cartilage, along with damage to the joint capsule and peri-articular structures, causes deformities (Fig. 25.20) and secondary osteoarthritis can develop, particularly in the knee.

Extra-articular features

The extra-articular features of rheumatoid disease are:

- subcutaneous rheumatoid nodules
- anaemia
- lymphadenopathy and splenomegaly
- pericarditis
- dry eyes and mouth (Sjögren's syndrome)
- uveitis and scleritis
- vasculitis, especially fingers and nail beds
- pulmonary changes (nodules, interstitial fibrosis, obstructive airway disease)
- amyloidosis.

Subcutaneous *rheumatoid nodules* develop in up to one-third of patients with rheumatoid disease, but most of these are severe and progressive cases. Typically, they involve the extensor surfaces of the forearm, less commonly the dorsum of the foot. These locations suggest that everyday incidental trauma contributes to their development. The nodules vary in size but are usually 20–40mm in maximum dimension.

Their histological structure is characteristic: central areas of necrotic collagen are surrounded by palisades of fibroblasts and macrophages.

Many patients with rheumatoid disease have clinically obvious *lymphadenopathy*. In some, the spleen can be felt—rheumatoid disease is one of the commoner causes of *splenomegaly*. A chronic inflammatory fibrinous *pericarditis* is a frequent

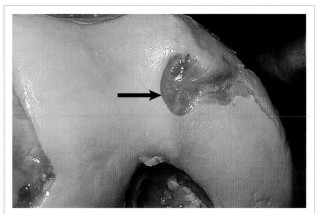

Fig. 25.17   Early rheumatoid disease. A layer of chronic inflammatory tissue ('pannus', arrowed) has eroded the articular surface of the femoral condyle.

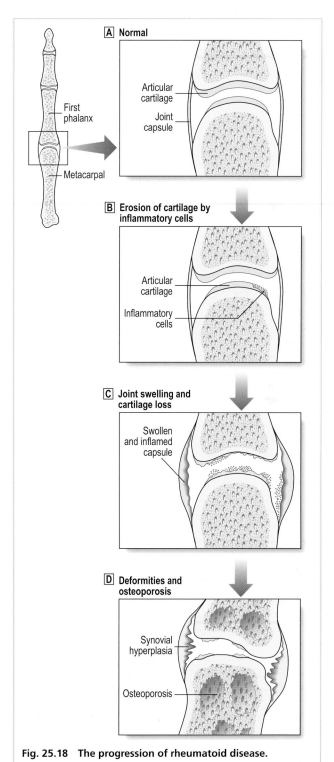

Fig. 25.18   The progression of rheumatoid disease.

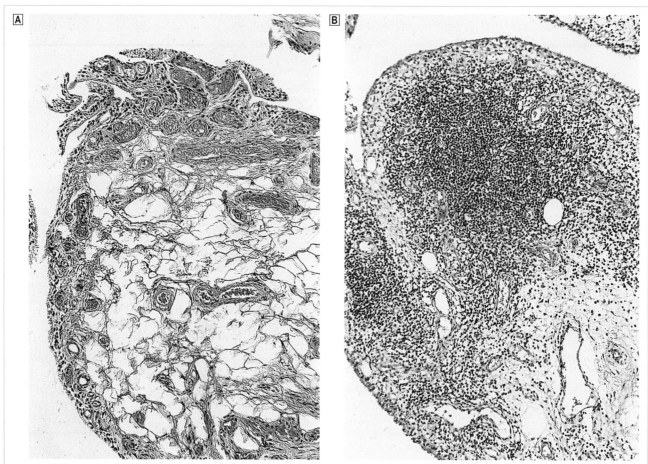

Fig. 25.19   Rheumatoid arthritis. [A] Normal synovium. [B] Note the dense lymphocytic infiltrates in the synovial biopsy from a patient with active rheumatoid arthritis.

finding in rheumatoid disease and occasionally chronic inflammatory granulomas can develop within the myocardium.

The wide range of *pulmonary pathology* includes rheumatoid nodule formation within the parenchyma of the lung and chronic interstitial fibrosis. Chronic inflammatory infiltrates can develop in both the lacrimal and salivary glands, impairing tear and saliva production. The resulting dryness in both the eyes and mouth (Sjögren's syndrome) is often persistent and irritating. Patients complain of a gritty feeling in the eyes and of photophobia. Both *uveitis* and *scleritis* are important ocular manifestations of rheumatoid disease (Fig. 25.21). The uveal tract, like the skin, the glomerulus of the kidney and the joints, has a very high blood flow per unit mass of tissue and this may contribute to the deposition of immune complexes and the subsequent inflammatory reaction. Paradoxically, uveitis can occur many years after the onset of rheumatoid arthritis, sometimes when the disease is in a quiescent phase. *Vasculitis* is a sinister feature and implies a poor prognosis. It is clinically most obvious in the fingers, particularly the nail beds.

Increasingly, treatment of rheumatoid arthritis is aimed at limiting joint damage, with immunosuppressive drugs such as methotrexate becoming the treatment of choice. Corticosteroids are also effective, but their use is limited by their many side-effects. Newly developed specific inhibitors of cytokines, such as tumour necrosis factor alpha, show considerable promise in the treatment of severe rheumatoid disease.

Laboratory investigations

In contrast to the situation in osteoarthritis, there are a wide range of haematological and immunological abnormalities in rheumatoid disease:

- normochromic, normocytic anaemia (anaemia of chronic disease)
- raised erythrocyte sedimentation rate (ESR) and acute phase proteins such as C-reactive protein
- IgG and IgM rheumatoid factors are usually present in severe cases
- auto-antibodies, such as antinuclear factor (ANF), are identified in a higher proportion of patients than in the general population.

Patients with severe symptoms in the early stages of the disease, or a poor response to anti-inflammatory drug therapy, tend to progress more rapidly. Careful evaluation of radiographs of the hand is also important, as the early development of bony

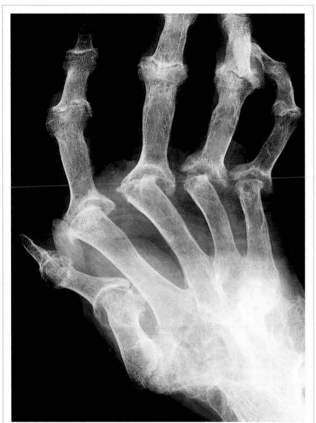

Fig. 25.20 Radiological features of rheumatoid arthritis.
There is prominent ulnar deviation in longstanding rheumatoid disease. There are erosions of the distal metacarpal bones and of most of the carpal bones.

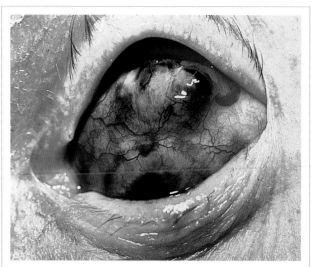

Fig. 25.21 Scleritis in rheumatoid arthritis. The inflammation has caused thinning of the scleral connective tissue, revealing the underlying pigmentation of the choroid.

Rheumatoid disease in children

At the turn of the 20th century, chronic inflammatory arthritis with systemic manifestations was described by Sir George Still (1868–1941), a paediatrician at Great Ormond Street Hospital. He emphasised that the disease occurred 'between the first and second dentition' and that there were similarities to rheumatoid disease in adults. It is now appreciated that there are many different forms of juvenile chronic arthritis and that only some of these are strictly similar to rheumatoid disease in adults.

Clinicopathological features

In juvenile chronic arthritis there are prominent systemic manifestations, often early in the course of the disease. These include pyrexia, skin rashes, lymphadenopathy, splenomegaly, pericarditis and pleurisy, and some can occur even before the onset of the arthritis. As in the classical rheumatoid arthritis of adults, several joints are affected. The joint symptoms and synovial pathology are very similar to those of adult rheumatoid arthritis. A chronic inflammatory pannus may form and erode articular cartilage. Fortunately, articular cartilage is somewhat thicker in children and this tends to protect the underlying bone.

Laboratory investigations and prognosis

As in adults, the erythrocyte sedimentation rate (ESR) is raised and a normochromic normocytic anaemia may be present. Although there may be hyperglobulinaemia, specific tests for rheumatoid factor are usually negative; this is the most important laboratory investigation distinguishing juvenile chronic arthritis from typical rheumatoid disease. A subgroup of adolescent children with chronic arthritis do have rheumatoid factor, and these children often have a progressive form of disease and require early treatment. In at least three-quarters of cases, the disease remits, either spontaneously or after drug

erosions is another poor prognostic feature. If a remission of disease can be obtained by drug treatment, it can sometimes be sustained for months or even years.

Prognosis and complications

At the onset of the disease it is very difficult to determine the prognosis for any individual patient. Approximately 10% of patients who develop rheumatoid arthritis will become severely disabled, dependent on others for some or all of their normal daily activities. In contrast, at least 20% of patients have only slight symptoms and relatively mild disability. They may have mild intermittent swelling of joints and difficulty in movements such as unscrewing lids. The remaining 70% of patients have varying degrees of disability and most will require some form of drug therapy, at least during exacerbations of disease.

Although rheumatoid disease can be relentless and progressive, it is seldom directly responsible for the death of an individual. Infections are more common in patients with rheumatoid disease than in the general population; these include septic arthritis, pneumonia, suppurative pericarditis and septicaemia. Blood culture is essential in a seriously ill patient with rheumatoid disease. Rheumatoid disease can be complicated by reactive systemic (AA) amyloidosis (Ch. 7).

treatment, and there is often no residual joint damage. In contrast, some patients may have a progressive arthritis and there can be substantial and permanent joint deformity.

Very little is known of the cause of juvenile chronic arthritis. The principles of treatment are much the same as in adult rheumatoid disease.

SPONDYLOARTHROPATHIES

This is a puzzling group of related disorders of unknown aetiology, including ankylosing spondylitis and Reiter's disease. These diseases are characterised by enthesitis and a strong association with the HLA-B27 tissue type. In classical cases of ankylosing spondylitis and Reiter's disease, there are well-defined clinical signs and symptoms and, even if the pathogenesis is obscure, pathological changes have been identified in a number of different organs. In some systemic disorders, including psoriasis, ulcerative colitis, Crohn's disease, infectious dysentery and chlamydial urethritis, there may be a chronic and disabling arthropathy resembling true ankylosing spondylitis or Reiter's disease.

Ankylosing spondylitis

> ► Relatively uncommon inflammatory disorder of spinal joints
> ► 90% of cases have the HLA-B27 haplotype
> ► Systemic features include peripheral arthritis, uveitis, aortic valve incompetence and chronic inflammatory bowel disease

The term 'spondylitis' implies an inflammatory disorder of the spine, whereas 'spondylosis' is used to describe the commoner degenerative osteoarthritic change.

Epidemiology

Fully developed ankylosing spondylitis is rare and occurs in only 1 in 1000 middle-aged male adults, and rather fewer females. About 90% of patients with unequivocal ankylosing spondylitis have the human leukocyte antigen B27—one of the strongest disease associations with a particular HLA haplotype. Once this association was established, surveys were undertaken to determine what proportion of the 5–10% of the Caucasian population who are B27 positive had signs of spondylitis. Depending on the stringency of the criteria used for diagnosis, up to 15% of these patients have some evidence of mild spondylitis but only 1–2% of severe spondylitis. The first symptoms usually occur before the age of 30 years.

Clinicopathological features

Information on the underlying pathological changes can be obtained only by sequential radiological studies or postmortem examination of the occasional patients who die in the early stages of the disease. The inflammatory process begins at the entheses where ligaments are attached to vertebral bone. As these lesions heal, there is reactive new bone formation in the adjacent ligaments and sclerosis of the underlying bone. The earliest changes are often present in the sacro-iliac joints and may be detected by careful radiological examination or computed tomography. Pain may be produced if the lower portion of the sacrum is depressed forward with the patient lying face down. Fusion of the vertebral bodies inhibits both flexion and rotation, and this is particularly disabling when the cervical segment is affected. Some patients develop fixed spinal deformities.

The symptoms and lesions strongly associated with ankylosing spondylitis are:

- pelvic and back pain; chronic inflammatory changes in entheses, progressing to bony ankylosis
- peripheral arthritis (30%), often sparing the hands
- anterior uveitis
- aortic incompetence
- inflammatory bowel disease.

At least 30% of patients with typical ankylosing spondylitis have a peripheral arthropathy. There are no specific histological features that distinguish this from other low-grade forms of arthropathy, but the clinical distribution is distinctive. Lower limb joints and the shoulders are often involved, but the lower arm, particularly the hands, is usually spared. The arthritis may begin before, together with, or some time after the first back symptoms.

Ankylosing spondylitis is one of the diseases that is associated with uveitis. In most cases, the anterior part of the eye—the iris and ciliary body—is affected, and choroidal changes are less common. The cause of the majority of cases of uveitis is unknown but between 10% and 20% will have some evidence of spondylitis. Uveitis is also associated with inflammatory bowel disease, and there is no doubt that both Crohn's disease and ulcerative colitis are more common in those with ankylosing spondylitis than in the general population. The best-recognised cardiovascular complication of spondylitis is aortic incompetence, but this is present in only 1–2% of longstanding cases. Pathologically, there is a chronic inflammatory aortitis, usually restricted to the valve ring and ascending aorta.

Reiter's disease

During World War I, a German physician, Hans Reiter, described the combination of arthritis, conjunctivitis and urethritis developing in a soldier shortly after an attack of dysentery. Most of the patients are males and the onset of the illness is usually abrupt. The arthritis usually affects lower limb joints and classically there is swelling and inflammation at the insertion of the Achilles tendon. The urethritis is usually due to chlamydial infection, and the conjunctivitis is only a minor feature of the illness.

The underlying pathological mechanisms in Reiter's disease are unknown. Chlamydial infections usually respond to tetracycline, but the arthritis can persist for months and occur at irregular intervals. Up to one-half of severely affected patients subsequently develop signs of spondylitis and, as most of these are HLA-B27 positive, it is very likely that the underlying disease process is the same as in true ankylosing spondylitis.

Psoriasis and arthritis

Psoriasis is a common and chronic skin disorder affecting up to 1% of Caucasians (Ch. 24). About 5% of patients with psoriasis have arthropathy, typically involving the distal interphalangeal joints. Again, if there is evidence of spondylitis, patients with arthropathy and psoriasis are usually HLA-B27 positive.

Arthritis and bowel disease

A low-grade peripheral arthropathy is a well-recognised, though comparatively rare, complication of *Salmonella, Shigella* and *Yersinia* gastroenteritis. HLA-B27-positive patients have a substantially increased risk of developing this complication. The underlying pathological mechanisms are unknown. Arthritis occurs in up to 20% of patients with ulcerative colitis and Crohn's disease which may manifest itself as sacro-ileitis or fully developed ankylosing spondylitis.

DEGENERATIVE DISEASE OF INTERVERTEBRAL DISCS

Degenerative softening of the fibrocartilaginous intervertebral discs is a very common cause of back pain. It usually affects adults and clinical symptoms are exacerbated by heavy straining when lifting or by poor posture. Discs in the lumbar spine are affected most commonly.

The softened nucleus pulposus can herniate vertically into an adjacent vertebral body, forming a *Schmorl's node* (Fig. 25.5) which may be radiologically evident. More seriously, the disc material may herniate posterolaterally through the surrounding annulus fibrosus, forming a protrusion that impinges upon the nerve emanating from the intervertebral foramina. This is the *prolapsed intervertebral disc,* or so-called 'slipped disc', that causes severe pain radiating into the territory supplied by the compressed nerve (e.g. 'sciatica' when the pain radiates across the buttock and down the leg); motor nerve conduction may also be impaired. In many cases the symptoms resolve with analgesia and/or physiotherapy or spinal manipulation. Recurrences are common. Surgical removal of the degenerate disc material may be necessary in some patients. The natural history of the disease is for the nucleus pulposus to degenerate spontaneously over time, thus relieving the symptoms. With increasing age the naturally restricted movement of the spine reduces the probability of disc herniation.

INFECTIVE ARTHRITIS

Most cases of septic arthritis are the result of bacterial infection. In some viral diseases there is an associated arthritis, or at least arthralgia (joint pain) is a prominent symptom. In contrast, fungal infections of joints are extremely rare.

Organisms responsible include:

- *Staphylococcus aureus*
- *Staphylococcus albus* (prosthetic joints)
- *Streptococcus pyogenes*
- *Diplococcus pneumoniae*
- *Neisseria gonorrhoeae*
- *Haemophilus influenzae* (children)
- Gram-negative organisms (drug addicts)
- *Borrelia burgdorferi* (Lyme arthritis)
- *Mycobacterium tuberculosis*
- *Brucella abortus* (intervertebral discitis).

Septic arthritis is the result of blood-borne spread from a focus of infection elsewhere. The epiphyseal plate forms a very effective barrier and it is unusual for an area of osteomyelitis in the metaphysis to spread and involve adjacent joints. This occasionally occurs in the hip, where the metaphysis may lie within the joint capsule.

As with osteomyelitis, children are affected more commonly than adults but the reasons for this are uncertain. Most cases are the result of staphylococcal or streptococcal infection. Both pneumococci and gonococci have a tendency to involve joints, and a septic arthritis can follow a bacteraemia or septicaemia associated with these organisms. *Haemophilus influenzae* arthritis is restricted to young children. Gram-negative septicaemia may cause inflammatory arthritis, particularly in drug addicts.

Diabetes mellitus, rheumatoid arthritis and immunosuppressive treatment are all risk factors for septic arthritis. Similarly, intra-articular injections of corticosteroids can be followed by inflammatory arthritis, and rigorous asepsis is essential during these procedures, particularly in patients with rheumatoid disease.

Clinicopathological features

The symptoms of infective arthritis are pain, tenderness, swelling and erythema. Although most cases of bacterial arthritis involve a single joint (monoarthritis), a small proportion of staphylococcal infections and the majority of cases of gonococcal arthritis involve two or more joints. As there is usually an associated septicaemia, patients are obviously ill, are usually pyrexial and may have rigors.

There are no diagnostic X-ray features, although radiographs are essential to exclude fractures or other bony injury. The diagnosis can be made only by aspirating and culturing the joint fluid. Special culture techniques are required for gonococci and mycobacteria, and full clinical details must therefore be given to the laboratory. Gram-stained preparations of synovial fluid may give a pointer to the causative organism and suggest appropriate antibiotic treatment before culture results are available. Initially, parenteral antibiotics should be given and oral antibiotics continued for 4–6 weeks. With adequate and prompt treatment, surgical drainage is not usually necessary, but should be considered if symptoms persist. The heavy polymorph infiltrates inevitably cause some superficial destruction of articular cartilage, and joint-space narrowing may become visible in radiographs. There may also be evidence of osteoporosis in the bones immediately adjacent to the joint.

Uncommon forms of infective arthritis

Gonococcal arthritis

This is usually a disorder of females or homosexual males, in whom the primary genital infection has been overlooked. Characteristically, it is a polyarthritis, frequently involving the hands, wrists and knees. Gonococcal arthritis is probably the commonest cause of infective arthritis in teenagers and young adults. Only in a minority of cases can gonococci be isolated from the synovial fluid.

Tuberculous arthritis

Approximately 1% of patients with tuberculosis have bony involvement as a result of spread from an established focus in the lungs or elsewhere. Involvement of the synovial membrane and peri-articular tissues produces a persistent arthritis with or without typical caseating granulomatous lesions. An inflammatory pannus may form and erode the articular cartilage. Tuberculous arthritis affects the hip and knee in children, but the vertebral column is most commonly involved in adults. In the vertebral column the associated osteomyelitis causes extensive bony destruction, and wedging or complete collapse of vertebrae may result (Pott's disease of the spine). The lower thoracic and lumbar spine are most commonly affected. Infection may spread along fascial planes, particularly around the psoas muscle, producing a full-blown psoas abscess. Synovial fluid culture may produce a diagnosis.

Arthritis due to spirochaetes

Lyme disease was first described in the eastern United States in 1977. Epidemics of the disease have now been reported in many different areas of the world. The presenting symptom is a migratory erythematous rash—erythema chronicum migrans. An arthritis follows weeks, or months, after the initial infection. Epidemiological studies have now shown that ticks of the genus *Ixodes* are responsible for transmitting the causative agent, a spirochaete named *Borrelia burgdorferi*. Immune complexes containing antibody directed against this organism have been detected in joint fluid and may play a role in the development of the arthritis. Antibiotic therapy given early in the course of the disease can prevent the joint disease.

Virus-associated arthritis

Many different virus infections are associated with a transient arthritis, or at least distinct pain within joints. In rubella infections, arthritis of the hands and wrists is common and the virus has been isolated from affected joints. A mild arthralgia may persist for several weeks. Occasionally, transient arthritis follows rubella vaccination. An arthritis may be a feature early in the course of viral hepatitis and is more severe with hepatitis B infection. Arthralgia can also be a feature of infectious mononucleosis.

Infective discitis

Occasionally, intervertebral discs can be the site of bacterial infections. This is usually due to *Staphylococcus aureus, Mycobacterium tuberculosis or Brucella abortus*. Because of the avascular nature of disc tissue, antibiotic penetration is poor and surgical removal of the disc may be necessary.

RHEUMATIC FEVER

▶ Characterised by joint pain, skin rashes and fever
▶ Due to a disordered immune reaction to a Lancefield group A beta-haemolytic streptococcal pharyngeal infection
▶ Associated with pancarditis
▶ Commonest in children aged 5–15 years, boys more than girls

Rheumatic fever is a disease of disordered immunity characterised by inflammatory changes in the heart (Ch. 13) and joints, and in some cases associated with neurological symptoms (chorea). The disease is common in India, the Middle East and Central Africa. Although it is now rare in Europe and North America, occasional clusters of cases do occur and several recent outbreaks in the United States have emphasised that the disease must be considered in any child or adolescent with joint pain, skin rashes or unexplained fever. Polyarthritis is the presenting feature in over 75% of cases and usually involves the large joints of the wrists, elbows, knees and ankles. The arthritis characteristically 'flits' from joint to joint, involving each for 2–4 days, and may cause severe pain. In the acute phase the inflammation involves the endocardium, the myocardium and the pericardium ('pancarditis'). Heart murmurs are common and children can die from cardiac failure.

Most patients have had a recent sore throat, typically a group A beta-haemolytic streptococcal infection. Disappointingly there have been no recent advances in the understanding of the underlying immunopathology. For many years it has been known that there is a strong antibody reaction to the streptococcus and it is thought that this may cross-react with as yet unknown antigens in connective tissues, especially in the heart and joints.

GOUT

▶ Painful acute inflammatory response to tissue deposition of urate crystals
▶ Most commonly affects metatarsophalangeal joint of first toe
▶ Much more common in males than in females
▶ Serum uric acid levels are raised
▶ May be associated with chronic renal damage

Gout is one of the most clearly documented conditions in medical history. Evidence of gouty arthritis has been detected in Egyptian mummies, and the condition is clearly described in the writings of Hippocrates and other Greek and Roman physicians. It appears to have been common (or perhaps a fashionable diagnosis) in the 17th and 18th centuries and in the popular imagination is associated with corpulence and alcoholism.

Pathogenesis

The underlying biochemical mechanisms in gout are well understood (Ch. 7), although the exact reasons why the majority of patients develop a raised uric acid level are uncertain. The mechanisms and causes are:

- idiopathic decrease in uric acid excretion (c. 75% of cases of clinical gout)
- impaired uric acid excretion secondary to thiazide diuretics, chronic renal failure, etc.
- increased uric acid production due to increased cell turnover (e.g. tumours), increased purine synthesis (specific enzyme defects)
- high dietary purine intake.

At least 5% of middle-aged males have a serum uric acid greater than 0.5 mmol/l, but less than 5% of these will ever develop clinical signs of gout. In over 75% of patients who present with gout, there is a decrease in uric acid clearance by the kidney but the underlying cause of this is not known. In a few patients, there appears to be an idiopathic increase in the rate of purine synthesis, leading in turn to increased uric acid production. The increased cellular turnover associated with a wide variety of different malignant disorders and other diseases is a common cause of secondary gout. Most patients receiving chemotherapy are now treated prophylactically with xanthine oxidase inhibitors in order to minimise the hyperuricaemia associated with the cellular necrosis and metabolic breakdown of nucleic acids induced by cytotoxic drugs.

The stimulus to the acute inflammatory reaction in acute gout is the deposition of monosodium urate crystals in the synovium and adjacent connective tissues of the joints. The exact mechanisms leading to this are poorly understood. Gout is most common in the metatarsophalangeal joint of the great toe, and gravitational factors could play a part in promoting crystal deposition. Acute gout also occurs in the ankle but is comparatively uncommon in the knee and hips. In acute gout, the joint fluid contains numerous polymorphs, and crystals can frequently be detected by polarised light microscopy. Microcrystals of monosodium urate can absorb a variety of immunoglobulins, complement components, fibrinogen and fibronectin, and these may encourage their phagocytosis by polymorphs. Regulatory cytokines, such as interleukin-1, almost certainly have some role in promoting inflammation. There is a rapid turnover of neutrophils within acutely inflamed gouty joints, largely because phagocytosed microcrystals have a toxic effect on cellular membranes. This is in itself a potent acute inflammatory stimulus, and in acute gout there is often an associated cellulitis.

Clinicopathological features

The clinicopathological features of gout are as follows:

- males usually affected (90%)
- onset 40–60 years, familial tendency
- acute inflammatory monoarthritis—more than one joint involved in 10%
- raised plasma uric acid (>0.5 mmol/l)

- deposition of monosodium urate crystals in joints
- variable incidence of uric acid renal calculi
- mild intermittent proteinuria with focal interstitial nephritis
- untreated patients may progress to chronic gouty arthritis and renal failure.

Gout presents as an acute inflammatory monoarthritis. In over two-thirds of patients the metatarsophalangeal joint is affected. The onset can be surprisingly abrupt. Affected joints are warm and tender and exquisitely painful (Fig. 25.22). There may be associated pyrexia, and the white cell count and ESR are generally raised. The clinical diagnosis is usually obvious, and prompt treatment with non-steroidal anti-inflammatory drugs relieves symptoms within hours. Occasionally, several joints can be involved simultaneously and this can be diagnostically misleading.

There may be long intervals between acute attacks in individual patients. Most patients are treated with allopurinol, which suppresses uric acid synthesis by inhibiting xanthine oxidase.

Renal disease is the most serious complication of gout. For poorly understood reasons, the incidence of renal calculi in gout varies from country to country. In western Europe it is of the order of 10% and gout should be considered in any patient who presents with renal colic. Mild proteinuria is found in a proportion of patients but very few progress to chronic urate nephropathy and renal failure. Those that do so have usually received inadequate treatment or have a strong familial history of severe gout. Urate crystal deposition in renal tubular epithelium induces cellular necrosis, chronic interstitial nephritis and fibrosis.

In chronic *tophaceous gout*, large deposits of uric acid occur within joints or in the soft tissues, particularly around the pinna of the ear. In these patients, there are substantial X-ray changes, with soft tissue swelling, calcification of urate deposits and even erosions of phalangeal bone.

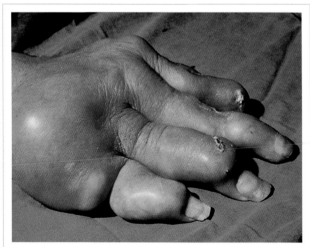

Fig. 25.22 Acute gout. Note the marked oedema and inflammation. There are areas of early ulceration at the tips of the index and ring fingers.

Gout is associated with obesity, alcoholism, hypertension, ischaemic heart disease, various forms of hyperlipoproteinaemia and impaired glucose tolerance. However, the majority of patients who have a raised blood uric acid level will never develop gout, or any of its complications.

PYROPHOSPHATE ARTHROPATHY

Pyrophosphate arthropathy, also known as 'pseudogout' or 'chondrocalcinosis', results from the deposition of calcium pyrophosphate crystals in joint cartilage. Occasionally, an acute arthritis results and this can mimic true gout.

The cause of the pyrophosphate deposition is unknown. It is very much an age-related phenomenon and is more common in the elderly. There is an association with hyperparathyroidism and haemochromatosis, and occasional familial cases are described. Pyrophosphate arthropathy can also complicate true gout.

Clinicopathological features

In most cases, pyrophosphate deposition produces no clinical symptoms. Minor degrees of cartilaginous calcification, particularly in the knee, are a common finding in X-rays taken in the elderly. In advanced cases, there is a characteristic linear area of calcification—evidence that the midzone of the articular cartilage is particularly susceptible to pyrophosphate deposition. If crystals are shed into the joint cavity in sufficient numbers, an acute inflammatory arthritis results. This can usually be distinguished from true gout: if joint fluid is examined the crystals can be distinguished from urate by their weak positive, rather than strong negative, birefringence.

There is a strong association between chondrocalcinosis and osteoarthritic joint disease. One explanation of this is that crystal deposition predisposes the articular cartilage to degenerative change and subsequent florid osteoarthritis. Alternatively, pyrophosphate crystals may be preferentially deposited in cartilage previously injured by early osteoarthritis. There is also a form of osteoarthritis associated with deposition of calcium hydroxyapatite crystals in and around knee and shoulder joints ('pseudopseudogout'). This usually affects middle-aged or elderly women.

As most cases of chondrocalcinosis are asymptomatic, no particular treatment is indicated. Acute pseudogout is best treated by intra-articular corticosteroids. Anti-inflammatory drugs and colchicine are less effective than in true gout. No prophylactic measures are available to prevent recurrent attacks but these are uncommon.

JOINT INVOLVEMENT IN SYSTEMIC DISEASE

An arthritis, or at least some degree of joint involvement, is a common feature of many systemic disorders (Table 25.4). In some of these, the arthritis is the direct result of the primary pathological process involving the synovium.

Table 25.4 Systemic diseases and joint changes		
Underlying disease	Clinical features	Pathology
Acromegaly	Episodic painful swelling of small joints, e.g. in hands	Periosteal new bone formation
Amyloidosis	Arthropathy of shoulders, knees and wrists, usually secondary to myeloma	Amyloid deposition in synovium
Behçet's disease	Inflammatory arthropathy of knee (minor criterion) Major features—oro-genital ulceration, uveitis and skin rashes	Inflammatory synovitis Underlying pathogenesis not understood
Clubbing	Characteristic swelling of nail beds	Increased blood flow to fingers and toes Associated with intra-thoracic pathology but mechanism unknown
Hypertrophic pulmonary osteoarthropathy (HPOA)	Arthropathy of wrists, ankles, feet	Periosteal new bone formation Same associations as clubbing, but less common
Haematological disorders Haemophilia	Recurrent joint haemorrhages Can progress to chronic painful deformative arthritis	Haemorrhage secondary to inherited deficiencies of factors VIII and IX
Haemoglobinopathies (esp. sickle cell disease)	Arthralgia, joint haemorrhages, aseptic necrosis of bone	Inherited defects in globin chain structure or synthesis
Acute leukaemia	Asymmetrical polyarthritis	Leukaemic infiltration of joints
Sarcoidosis	Small joint polyarthropathy, especially fingers	Sarcoidal granulomas in synovium

CONNECTIVE TISSUES

TRAUMATIC AND DEGENERATIVE CONDITIONS OF CONNECTIVE TISSUES

In contrast to the remarkable healing capacity of bone, most other connective tissues are rather limited in their ability to repair. Injuries to connective tissue structures can occur as a result of single episodes of trauma, such as a ligament rupture, or chronic damage due to overuse or repetitive stress.

Single episode trauma to connective tissue structures results either in healing by scarring, such as a skeletal muscle tear, or in a chronic injury, such as a meniscal tear or cruciate ligament rupture. Chronic trauma to tendons, ligaments or joint capsules results in neovascularisation and increased proteoglycan content in the tissue. These processes cause chronic pain and can result in impaired movement. There are several distinct clinical syndromes that result from these pathological changes such as 'tennis elbow', 'housemaid's knee' and the carpal tunnel syndrome. In some of these conditions, inflammation of bursae or tendon sheaths is the main pathological process. Where repetitive injury, usually to a tendon sheath, causes local proteoglycan accumulation, this can lead to the formation of cysts referred to as ganglia/ganglion cysts.

CONNECTIVE TISSUE DISEASES

There is no agreed definition of a 'connective tissue disease'. It is a convenient general term which covers a wide variety of disorders:

- rheumatoid arthritis
- systemic lupus erythematosus (SLE)
- polyarteritis nodosa
- ankylosing spondylitis, Reiter's disease and related disorders
- polymyositis and dermatomyositis
- polymyalgia rheumatica
- temporal/cranial (giant cell) arteritis
- systemic sclerosis (scleroderma)
- mixed connective tissue disease (MCTD).

These disorders have the following common features:

- multisystem disorders, often affecting joints, skin and subcutaneous tissues
- females preferentially affected (except in polyarteritis nodosa and ankylosing spondylitis), weak genetic tendency
- chronic clinical course, may respond to anti-inflammatory drugs
- first presentation may be during adolescence or early adult life
- immunological abnormalities often present, either circulating auto-antibodies or evidence of immune complex deposition.

These disorders were originally termed 'collagen diseases', and this emphasises that cutaneous and subcutaneous changes are often prominent clinical features. The clinical and pathological features of some of the more important connective tissue diseases are summarised in Table 25.5.

Systemic lupus erythematosus

- ▶ Systemic disorder associated with auto-antibodies to DNA and other nuclear components
- ▶ Features include arthralgia, erythematous (butterfly) skin rash, anaemia, serositis (e.g. pericarditis), glomerular injury and neurological changes
- ▶ Can be provoked by drugs, especially hydralazine and procainamide

Systemic lupus erythematosus (SLE) is, more than any other connective tissue disease, a multisystem disorder. Females are affected more often than males, in some age groups by a ratio of up to 10:1. The incidence is higher in blacks and Asians than in Caucasians. The peak age of onset is usually between 20 and 30 years.

Aetiology and immunopathology

The cause of SLE is unknown. The first immunological abnormality was detected in the 1940s. It was found that leukocytes from patients with SLE phagocytosed nuclear debris produced by agitating a sample of freshly drawn blood. It was subsequently shown that most patients with SLE have circulating auto-antibodies directed against nuclear antigens. When serum containing these antibodies is added to tissue sections, such as liver or kidney, they bind to nuclear components and this can be visualised by immunofluorescence. Many other auto-antibodies have now been detected, reacting with both nuclear and cytoplasmic antigens. As these antibodies are characterised, it is becoming clear that they are directed against a relatively small range of epitopes, components of both nucleic acids and cytoplasmic phospholipids:

- anti-DNA (double or single stranded)—only 5% of patients persistently negative
- antibodies to other nuclear components:
  — antihistones
  — anti-Ro, La and Sm (Ro La, Sm refer to the names of patients in whom the auto-antibodies were first detected)
- antiphospholipid antibodies (thrombotic tendency, recurrent abortions, false-positive tests for syphilis)
- red cell antibodies (autoimmune haemolytic anaemia)
- rheumatoid factors
- cell or organelle-specific antibodies (mitochondrial, smooth muscle, gastric parietal cell, etc.).

The immune system is capable of developing immunogenicity or tolerogenicity towards any given antigen. Which of these events occur depends upon the balance of immunogenic and tolerogenic cytokine pathways, which are poorly understood. As in rheumatoid disease, the auto-antibodies of SLE may be manifestations of a generalised loss of self-tolerance. None of these antibodies is SLE-specific and most have been detected in other forms of autoimmune disease. However, there is more evidence to suggest that immune complexes

Table 25.5 Clinical and pathological features of the major connective tissue diseases

Disease	Sex ratio	Age at onset	Main clinical features	Immunological abnormalities	Pathology
Rheumatoid arthritis	3F:1M	Young or middle-aged adults Occasionally children	Chronic polyarthritis Subcutaneous nodules Splenomegaly	Auto-antibodies against native Ig (rheumatoid factors)	Chronic inflammatory synovitis Granulomatous lesions in subcutaneous tissues Fibrinous pericarditis
Systemic lupus erythematosus (SLE)	8F:1M	Young or middle-aged adults	Skin rashes Light sensitivity Arthritis Anaemia Leukopenia Renal disease	Auto-antibodies against nuclear and cytoplasmic proteins and many other cellular components	Inflammatory synovitis Glomerulonephritis Erythematous skin rashes, etc.
Polyarteritis nodosa (PAN)	3M:1F	Any age, chiefly middle-aged adults	Arthralgia Abdominal pain Hypertension Fever Leukocytosis and eosinophilia	Some patients: antinuclear antibodies and rheumatoid factors	Necrotising vasculitis affecting medium-sized arteries
Ankylosing spondylitis	2M:1F	Young adults	Back pain Arthritis Uveitis	No consistent changes Most patients HLA-B27 positive	Inflammatory changes progressing to partial bony fusion of spine and sacro-iliac joints
Polymyositis and dermatomyositis	3F:1M	Adults	Muscle weakness, pain and tenderness Skin rashes in dermatomyositis	Only if features of other connective tissue diseases present	Inflammatory myositis underlying malignancy in some cases
Polymyalgia rheumatica	2F:1M	Elderly	Malaise and weakness Muscular aching, esp. shoulders, pelvis and hips	No consistent changes Raised ESR	Limited and non-specific muscle biopsy changes Some cases overlap with temporal arteritis
Cranial (temporal or giant cell) arteritis	2F:1M	Elderly	Headache Visual loss Tender scalp	No consistent changes Raised ESR	Chronic granulomatous arteritis chiefly in head and neck arteries
Systemic sclerosis (scleroderma)	3F:1M	30–50 years	Raynaud's phenomenon Skin thickening Polyarthritis Dysphagia and dyspnoea Hypertension	Rheumatoid factor (25%) Antinuclear antibodies (50%)	Fibrosis of subcutaneous tissues Intimal and medial fibrosis of muscular arteries

are important in the pathogenesis of SLE than there is in rheumatoid disease.

The precise trigger for loss of self-tolerance in SLE is mysterious. The antihypertensive drug hydralazine can cause an SLE-like illness.

No other environmental or occupational factors have been implicated in SLE. It is not obviously associated with any particular human leukocyte antigen but there is a strong familial tendency. Relatives of SLE patients have a substantially increased incidence of the disorder and there is a greater than 50% concordance in monozygotic twins.

Clinicopathological features

Spontaneous remissions and exacerbations are common in SLE and some patients can be managed for long periods without specific treatment. Signs and symptoms can occur in almost every system:

- mild arthralgia, especially hands, knees and ankles; low-grade inflammatory synovitis but few erosions
- erythematous ('butterfly') facial rash and alopecia; photosensitivity
- lymphadenopathy and splenomegaly

- myalgia
- anaemia and leukopenia
- pyrexia
- pleurisy and pericarditis
- glomerulonephritis with proteinuria and occasionally nephrotic syndrome
- psychiatric symptoms, headaches, fits and occasionally cerebral infarction with hemiplegia.

Arthralgia is often the presenting symptom and in the early stages may resemble rheumatoid arthritis. The hands, knees and ankles are most affected, and a series of joints may be involved in succession (flitting arthralgia). Synovial biopsy shows a low-grade inflammatory synovitis but, unlike the situation in rheumatoid disease, pannus does not form and cartilaginous erosions are rare.

The most characteristic *cutaneous change* in SLE is a symmetrical erythematous facial ('butterfly') rash (Fig. 25.23) which may be precipitated by exposure to sunlight (photosensitivity). Raynaud's phenomenon, urticaria, hyperpigmentation and cutaneous ulcers are other less common features.

Non-specific early signs in SLE include mild pyrexia, normochromic normocytic anaemia, leukopenia, muscle pain, lymphadenopathy and splenomegaly. Although pleurisy and pericarditis are common postmortem findings, they rarely produce overt clinical symptoms. Non-bacterial thrombotic vegetations (Libman–Sacks endocarditis) may form on mitral or aortic valves and can be detected by echocardiography.

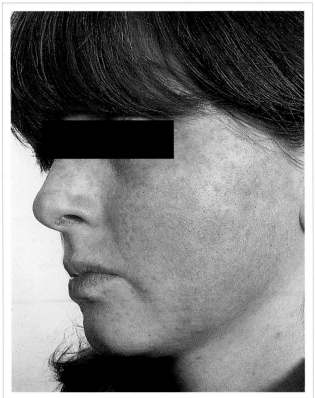

Fig. 25.23   The typical 'malar' flush of systemic lupus erythematosus.

Murmurs may result, but the vegetations seldom erode the valve leaflets or cause significant embolic disease.

Renal involvement is one of the most important features and patients should be regularly screened for proteinuria. The underlying lesion is glomerulonephritis, which may be of minimal change, focal, membranous or diffuse proliferative type (Ch. 21). Although some patients do progress to renal failure, not all forms are necessarily associated with a poor prognosis.

Neurological changes are more common in SLE than in any other connective tissue disease. Psychiatric symptoms are the commonest abnormality but some of these may be the result of treatment with steroids. Severe headaches and convulsions occur in some patients. The small sub-group who present with recurrent transient ischaemic attacks or definite episodes of cerebral infarction generally have circulating antibodies to cardiolipin—the so-called 'antiphospholipid antibody syndrome'. Anti-cardiolipin antibodies are also associated with recurrent spontaneous abortions. The neuropathological changes in SLE are rather non-specific but occasional cases have evidence of cerebral arteritis or thrombosis.

Laboratory investigations

Abnormal findings in SLE include:

- raised ESR and C-reactive protein
- mild normochromic normocytic anaemia
- leukopenia or thrombocytopenia
- circulating antinuclear antibodies
- reduced serum albumin, raised gamma globulins, low complement levels.

Polyarteritis nodosa

> ▶ Inflammatory disorder of unknown aetiology affecting medium-sized arteries
> ▶ Causes muscle and joint pain, fever, ischaemic lesions in many organs, neuropathy and renal damage

Polyarteritis nodosa (PAN) is one of the most florid of the inflammatory disorders of arteries, collectively known as arteritis (Ch. 13). The main features are:

- medium-sized muscular arteries affected
- myalgia, polymyositis and arthralgia; fever and malaise
- abdominal pain, vomiting and diarrhoea
- mucosal ulcers, occasionally intestinal or splenic infarcts
- tender subcutaneous nodules (arteritic lesions), skin rashes and digital gangrene
- hypertension and pericarditis
- peripheral neuropathy—motor, sensory or mixed; usually single nerves involved (mononeuritis multiplex)
- haematuria and proteinuria; glomerulonephritis and hypertensive renal disease
- asthmatic symptoms, often with eosinophilia; haemoptysis; pulmonary infarcts due to pulmonary arteritis.

Almost any artery can be affected but, because arthralgia and abdominal pain are frequent early symptoms, these patients are often referred to rheumatologists or gastroenterologists.

Aetiology and immunopathology

The cause of PAN is not fully understood. There is increasing evidence to suggest hepatitis B virus is important in the development of this disease, although this may not apply to all forms of PAN-like vasculitis. The incidence seems to be increasing but this may be because milder forms of vasculitis are now recognised. The florid acute inflammatory changes with associated fibrinoid necrosis resemble experimental models of immune complex vasculitis. Circulating immune complexes may be elevated in patients with vasculitis. Complement levels can be reduced and abnormal deposits of immunoglobulins are sometimes present in affected vessels in biopsy specimens. Many patients with systemic vasculitis have circulating anti-neutrophil cytoplasmic antibodies (ANCA). They are not specific for any particular disorder but are most strongly associated with Wegener's granulomatosis (a severe destructive vasculitis affecting the nasal cavity, lungs and kidneys) and PAN, and may not be present in patients in clinical remission. It is not known whether these antibodies are involved directly in the disease process or are a secondary result of the associated vascular damage.

Clinicopathological features

Most patients present with non-specific signs of a generalised illness, such as pyrexia of unknown origin (PUO), malaise and myalgia. Arthralgia, abdominal pain, vomiting and diarrhoea are common in the early stages of the disease, and other non-specific signs include hypertension and pericarditis.

The underlying vasculitic process (Ch. 13) can involve almost any medium-sized artery. The disease was originally named because of the tender nodules produced by involvement of subcutaneous arteries, but these are quite different from rheumatoid nodules and occur in only a small proportion of cases. Peripheral gangrene can result from arteritis of digital vessels. Polyarteritis nodosa is a cause of mononeuritis multiplex—a pattern of peripheral neuropathy where individual nerves are affected because of disease of the nutrient arteries (Ch. 26). Symptoms can be motor, sensory or mixed.

Renal disease is one of the leading causes of death in PAN (Ch. 21). There is a well-established association between PAN, pulmonary disease and eosinophilia (Churg–Strauss syndrome). Classically, there are prominent asthmatic symptoms, with cough and dyspnoea. In severe cases, pulmonary arteritis leads to areas of infarction and there may be haemoptysis.

In contrast to the case in SLE, central nervous system involvement is comparatively rare in PAN. Only occasional patients develop cerebral arteritis.

Laboratory investigations

Typical haematological findings in PAN include a mild normochromic normocytic anaemia, a moderate leukocytosis and an absolute eosinophilia. ESR and other acute phase reactants are raised. Although gamma globulin levels may be increased, auto-antibodies such as rheumatoid factor and antinuclear antibodies are usually negative.

A firm diagnosis can be made histologically or by arteriography. Biopsy of a skin lesion or a nerve associated with an area of cutaneous anaesthesia or a muscle biopsy may show the histological appearances of necrotising arteritis (Ch. 13). Selective angiography of the major abdominal branches, such as the coeliac axis or mesenteric artery, may reveal typical aneurysms.

The outlook in PAN is worst in patients with definite evidence of multisystem involvement. Patients with limited forms of the disease often do well and may need little or no treatment. It is quite possible that several disease processes are presently included under the label of 'polyarteritis nodosa'.

Polymyalgia rheumatica

Polymyalgia rheumatica (PMR) is an important disorder of the elderly. It is more common in females than in males, and patients usually present with persistent muscular pain in the shoulders and hips, lethargy and tiredness. These rather non-specific symptoms occur in most rheumatic disorders, and PMR may therefore be confused with rheumatoid arthritis, cranial arteritis (see below), polyarteritis nodosa or various forms of polymyositis. In most patients these disorders can be excluded, and PMR is considered to be a disease in its own right.

The underlying pathological changes are incompletely understood. Myositis does not occur, but there is evidence from magnetic resonance imaging (MRI) that bursitis occurs in active disease. In typical cases, the ESR is greater than 100 mm/h, but there are no other consistent laboratory abnormalities. There may be a mild normochromic or hypochromic anaemia and non-specific elevations of immunoglobulins. Circulating auto-antibodies, such as rheumatoid factor and antinuclear antibody, are usually absent and creatine phosphokinase levels are normal.

Although PMR is a somewhat non-specific clinical and pathological entity, it is a common and important condition which can affect up to 1% of elderly patients. Clinical benefit can be obtained with steroid treatment, but there are inevitable side-effects if this is continued for long periods. At least 15% of patients with polymyalgia rheumatica have cranial arteritis and in these patients a positive temporal artery biopsy is of great value in justifying long-term treatment. In other patients steroids are usually given for at least a year and then discontinued gradually.

Cranial arteritis

Cranial arteritis (also known as temporal or 'giant cell' arteritis) is an important, and not uncommon, disease of the elderly. It affects arteries of the head and neck region and, unlike almost all other arterial diseases, responds rapidly and predictably to treatment with anti-inflammatory drugs such as corticosteroids.

Aetiology and pathogenesis

Epidemiological surveys in different communities have demonstrated that the incidence of the disease varies between 50 and 150 cases per 100 000 population. The disease is commonest in Caucasians but occurs in all races. There is no satisfactory explanation for the preferential involvement of the arteries of the head and neck. Involvement of the superficial temporal artery is responsible for scalp tenderness, but it is disease of the ciliary and ophthalmic arteries that may produce blindness. The carotid arteries and, occasionally, the aorta may be affected but this is usually clinically silent. The disease appears to be a distinct entity, and the histological appearances and clinical course of the disorder are very different from those of other inflammatory conditions of arteries, such as polyarteritis nodosa, although there may be some relationship with Takayasu's arteritis. This is a form of arteritis, usually affecting the thoracic aorta and its branches, that is best known in Japan. Cranial arteritis has no obvious genetic basis and is not associated with auto-antibody production.

Clinicopathological features

Because the superficial temporal artery is accessible for biopsy, the histological features are well described (Ch. 13).

Most patients present with headache or scalp tenderness, and in any elderly patient these symptoms should suggest a diagnosis of cranial arteritis. Jaw claudication is another important symptom. There is a well-recognised overlap between the symptoms of cranial arteritis and polymyalgia rheumatica. Careful palpation of the temporal arteries is essential in any patient with polymyalgia and, conversely, musculoskeletal symptoms are not uncommon in cases of cranial arteritis. The precise relationship between these disorders is uncertain, particularly as the pathological changes in the two disorders are rather dissimilar. Fortunately, steroid therapy is the treatment of choice in each disorder.

Laboratory investigations

Temporal artery biopsy should be performed urgently in any patient with suspected cranial arteritis. Ideally, 20–30 mm of superficial temporal artery should be removed, preferably before steroid therapy has started. However, because of the risk of blindness due to involvement of the ophthalmic arteries, steroid therapy should not be delayed while awaiting the result of the biopsy, because of the risk of rapid progression to blindness. A high ESR is characteristic but in a few patients this may be only slightly elevated. There are no other characteristic laboratory findings, although a mild normochromic normocytic anaemia is sometimes present. Up to 40% of patients with good clinical evidence of cranial arteritis have a negative temporal artery biopsy.

Polymyositis and dermatomyositis

Polymyositis is a chronic inflammatory disorder of skeletal muscle of unknown cause. The typical patient is a female in late middle age with a history of progressive muscular weakness, often commencing in the shoulder or neck muscles. There is associated pain and tenderness but muscle wasting is not a feature in the early stages.

In active polymyositis there is a florid chronic inflammatory infiltrate in affected muscles (Fig. 25.24) with extensive associated degeneration of both type 1 and type 2 fibres (Ch. 26). Many of the clinical features suggest a viral infection but no particular virus has been consistently isolated. Auto-antibodies to a variety of nuclear antigens have been detected in up to

25% of patients. Rheumatoid factor and antinuclear antibody are usually absent. The diagnosis is best made on a combination of clinical findings, raised levels of muscle enzymes such as creatine phosphokinase (CPK), electromyography and muscle biopsy. Serial estimation of CPK may give a clue to the prognosis in individual patients. The majority make an uneventful recovery, albeit over a period of months or years. Oesophageal disease produces a troublesome dysphagia, and cardiac involvement is not uncommon. The mortality rate is between 5% and 15% and is usually the result of respiratory failure, aspiration pneumonia or, occasionally, heart failure.

In *dermatomyositis* a variety of skin changes occur in association with an otherwise typical polymyositis. There is a diffuse erythema involving the upper part of the body, prominent swelling of the eyelids and a variable purple 'heliotrope' discoloration of the eyelids (Ch. 24). The muscular symptoms are more prominent in patients with dermatological changes.

At least 10% of middle-aged or elderly patients with polymyositis have evidence of malignant disease, most commonly carcinoma of the bronchus, gastrointestinal tract or breast. The polymyositis may occur months or years before the first symptoms of the underlying carcinoma, and for this reason all patients with genuine polymyositis should be screened

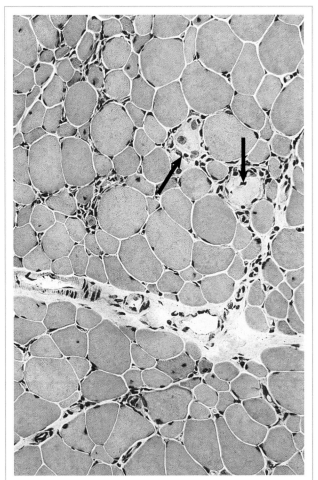

Fig. 25.24 Polymyositis. A low-power view of a muscle biopsy showing irregular infiltrates of inflammatory cells. Some muscle fibres are undergoing necrosis (arrows).

for the common malignancies. Although polymyositis and dermatomyositis are more common in females, this ratio is reversed when there is an associated malignancy.

Scleroderma

▶ Systemic disorder of unknown aetiology characterised by sclerosis (hardening) of connective tissues
▶ Early features include Raynaud's phenomenon, polyarthritis, and induration and contraction of the skin of the fingers
▶ May be limited to skin and subcutaneous tissues ('morphoea')
▶ Submucosal fibrosis may develop in gastrointestinal tract
▶ Underlying changes include vascular injury and connective tissue deposition

Scleroderma describes a spectrum of diseases of uncertain cause. The disorder is most common in young and early middle-aged females who usually present with Raynaud's phenomenon, polyarthritis and thickening and tightness of the skin (Table 25.6). This affects the hands and fingertips first, and movements of the finger joints are impaired. Facial changes are also common; the mouth appears small and the peri-oral skin is taut and creased (Fig. 25.25). Careful observation of the progress of the disease gives a good indication of the prognosis. If the disease spreads to the upper arms, legs or the flank there is a strong chance that a generalised form of disease, *systemic sclerosis,* may develop. In contrast, in other patients the disease is entirely limited to the skin and is characterised by well-defined plaques or bands of subcutaneous fibrosis ('morphoea'). The most complete manifestation of the disease is the CREST syndrome (cutaneous *c*alcinosis,

*R*aynaud's phenomenon, *o*esophgeal dysfunction, *s*clerodactyly and *t*elangiectasia).

The underlying pathological changes include vascular injury, perivascular accumulation of mononuclear cells and deposition of connective tissue. In systemic sclerosis the process may extend to the gastrointestinal tract. A frequent symptom is dysphagia and there may be submucosal fibrosis and muscular atrophy in the lower oesophagus.

Little is known of the cause of scleroderma. Some circulating auto-antibodies have now been detected but they have not been as well characterised as in diseases such as systemic lupus erythematosus or rheumatoid disease. The pathological changes in small arteries and arterioles resemble those of systemic hypertension, but only 20% of patients with scleroderma have raised blood pressure.

Mixed connective tissue disease (MCTD)

Connective tissue diseases share many common clinical and pathological features. In clinical practice, it is usually possible to attach a specific diagnostic label to the majority of patients. The term 'overlap syndrome' or mixed connective tissue disease (MCTD) is used when there are distinct overlapping features of systemic lupus erythematosus (SLE), systemic sclerosis, rheumatoid arthritis, polymyositis or even polyarteritis nodosa. The usual features are:
● occurrence in young adult females (75%)
● arthritis, suggestive of rheumatoid disease (>90%)
● Raynaud's phenomenon (>90%)
● swollen, puffy hands with skin changes suggestive of scleroderma (75%)
● anaemia and leukopenia (50%)
● disordered oesophageal motility (50%)

Table 25.6 Clinical and pathological features of scleroderma and systemic sclerosis		
Organ/system	Clinical features	Pathology
Skin	Tightness and tethering Pitting and induration, esp. fingertips Ulceration and calcification Telangiectasia, esp. face Fibrous plaques (morphoea)	Epidermal atrophy Loss of skin appendages Dense dermal fibrosis
Joints	Polyarthritis, esp. hands Lack of joint movement due to skin tethering	Low-grade inflammatory synovitis
Gastrointestinal tract	Dysphagia Occasionally malabsorption and diarrhoea	Submucosal fibrosis and muscular atrophy in lower oesophagus
Cardiovascular system	Raynaud's phenomenon Pericarditis	Intimal fibrosis of small and medium-sized arteries Pericarditis Patchy myocardial fibrosis Intimal thickening of arteries
Kidneys	Proteinuria Rapidly progressive renal failure (rare)	Ischaemic atrophy of tubules Fibrinoid necrosis of arterioles Widespread thickening of glomerular vessels
Lungs	Dyspnoea	Interstitial inflammation and fibrosis

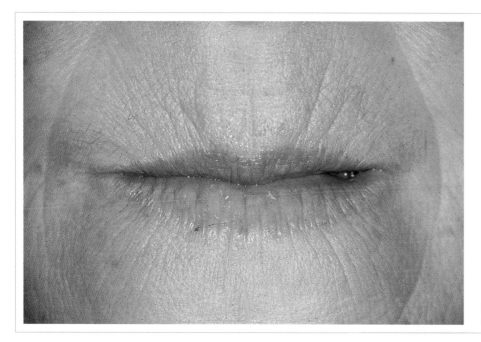

Fig. 25.25 Tightening of the peri-oral skin in scleroderma.

- lymphadenopathy, pleurisy and pericarditis (25%)
- antinuclear antibodies (100%)
- rheumatoid factor (>30%)
- no evidence of renal disease.

All patients with MCTD have a strongly positive fluorescent test for antinuclear antibodies. The exact nature of the nuclear antigen is unknown, but there is evidence that several different nuclear matrix proteins may be involved.

Because true MCTD is uncommon there is comparatively little information on clinical and pathological progression. In some patients a full clinical remission occurs, but others develop into typical scleroderma or SLE. In these patients the outlook is much the same as if an MCTD phase had not occurred.

CONNECTIVE TISSUE TUMOURS

Connective tissue tumours are, with a few exceptions, relatively uncommon. However, those classified as malignant (i.e. sarcomas) are important because they are often deeply located, for example in the retroperitoneum, resulting in late clinical presentation and difficulties in ensuring complete surgical removal. As a general rule, the more deeply a connective tissue tumour is situated, the less likely it is to be benign.

Benign connective tissue tumours

Benign connective tissue tumours include:

- lipoma
- angioma
- leiomyoma
- fibrous histiocytoma
- granular cell tumour.

Lipomas are the commonest connective tissue tumours, usually subcutaneous and comprising morphologically mature adipocytes. They are usually solitary, but may be multiple, well circumscribed and located in subcutaneous fat. Less common variants include *angiolipoma* characterised by numerous blood vessels, *spindle cell lipoma* in which there is an admixture of fibroblasts, and *myelolipoma* containing haemopoietic cells.

Although *angiomas* are benign in the sense that they do not actively invade surrounding tissues, they can be troublesome clinically and prone to recurrences requiring further surgery. These problems arise because the margins of the lesion are often blurred, merging with the surrounding normal tissue.

Leiomyomas in connective tissues (they are commoner in the uterus and gut) arise from smooth muscle cells in the walls of blood vessels and, in the skin, from arrector pili muscles.

Fibrous histiocytomas are neoplasms of fibroblast-like cells that also contain varying numbers of macrophages. Benign fibrous histiocytomas occur most commonly in the skin (dermatofibroma; Ch. 24).

Granular cell tumours are of uncertain histogenesis. Although benign, they are usually poorly circumscribed. They are generally located superficially and, curiously, when they occur beneath squamous epithelium (in skin, tongue, etc.) they often induce florid epithelial hyperplasia morphologically mimicking carcinoma.

Malignant connective tissue tumours (sarcomas)

Malignant connective tissue tumours include:

- liposarcoma
- malignant fibrous histiocytoma/undifferentiated sarcoma
- angiosarcoma
- leiomyosarcoma
- rhabdomyosarcoma

- synovial sarcoma
- epithelioid
- peripheral neuroectodermal tumour (Ewing's sarcoma of soft tissue)
- fibrosarcoma.

Liposarcomas are the commonest. The incidence of tumours designated 'malignant fibrous histiocytoma' varies according to the belief of local histopathologists in this controversial entity; in places where its existence is accepted, the incidence is often as high as that of liposarcoma. However, most of these tumours are either poorly differentiated examples of other types of sarcoma or essentially undifferentiated sarcomas.

The behaviour of sarcomas is strongly influenced by their histological grade. Low-grade sarcomas, such as well-differentiated liposarcomas, rarely metastasise. High-grade sarcomas frequently metastasise to the lungs. Overall, the long-term survival rate for soft tissue sarcomas is approximately 50%. Surgical excision, usually followed by radiotherapy, is the treatment of choice for most types of sarcoma. Many of them grow as 'spindle cell tumours' or 'small blue round cell tumours', the latter particularly in children (the 'blue' refers to their appearance with haematoxylin and eosin staining), with few identifying characteristics to betray their true

histogenesis. Immunohistochemistry may reveal the histogenesis of the tumour. However, because several of these tumours (e.g. synovial sarcoma, myxoid liposarcoma) have characteristic chromosomal translocations, cytogenetics is increasingly becoming the most important diagnostic investigation.

Some of these tumours merit specific comments. *Synovial sarcomas* usually occur, as the name suggests, close to joints and have a biphasic growth pattern comprising spindle cells and epithelial cells. They are, however, soft tissue carcinosarcomas and are not derived from synovium. *Epithelioid sarcomas* are rare tumours occurring on the limbs and have an unusual tendency to arise from and grow along fascial sheaths. *Peripheral neuroectodermal tumours* occur most commonly in children and are cytogenetically identical to Ewing's sarcoma of bone.

Tumour-like lesions of connective tissues

Some nodular connective tissue lesions are characterised by cellular proliferation but they do not fulfil all the criteria of neoplasia. These include:

- fibromatoses
- nodular fasciitis
- myositis ossificans.

Fibromatoses are tumour-like proliferations of myofibroblasts. These cells have contractile properties; this explains the puckering and tethering associated with some variants of fibromatoses. For example, *palmar fibromatosis* (Dupuytren's contracture) leads to permanent flexion of the fingers. Other variants of fibromatosis include *musculoaponeurotic fibromatosis* and *desmoid tumours*. Many examples of fibromatosis have abnormalities of the Wnt signalling pathway that can be demonstrated histologically through nuclear localisation of the signalling molecule beta-catenin. Desmoid and intra-abdominal fibromatoses can be associated with Gardner's syndrome and familial adenomatous polyposis.

Nodular fasciitis occurs superficially as a rapidly growing nodule with alarming histological appearances mimicking sarcoma. *Myositis ossificans*, as its name suggests, is characterised by inflammation in muscle and ossification. The clinical significance of these benign lesions is that they can be mistaken, both clinically and histologically, for malignant lesions, resulting in clinically disastrous overtreatment.

Commonly confused conditions and entities relating to osteoarticular and connective tissue pathology	
Commonly confused	**Distinction and explanation**
Rheumatic and *rheumatoid*	Both terms denote disorders affecting joints, but of different aetiologies. *Rheumatic* fever is an immunologically mediated post-streptococcal illness affecting the heart and joints. *Rheumatoid* disease is an autoimmune disorder causing arthritis, completely unrelated to rheumatic fever.
Osteoporosis and *osteomalacia*	Both conditions cause bone weakening. In *osteoporosis* there is a reduction in the bone protein matrix; however, that which is formed is adequately mineralised. In *osteomalacia*, the bone matrix is normal but there is insufficient mineralisation.
Osteomalacia and *rickets*	Both conditions are due to defective mineralisation of the skeleton. *Osteomalacia* is the name given to the appearances in the adult skeleton. *Rickets* occurs in children; the defective mineralisation leads to deformities of the growing skeleton.
Gout and *pseudogout*	Both are crystal arthropathies. In *gout* the crystals are urate. In *pseudogout,* the crystals are calcium pyrophosphate.
Systemic sclerosis and *multiple sclerosis*	*Systemic sclerosis* (sclerosis = hardening) is a disorder of connective tissue. *Multiple sclerosis* is a demyelinating disorder of the central nervous system.

FURTHER READING

Cope A P, Schulze-Koops H, Aringer M 2007 The central role of T cells in rheumatoid arthritis. Clinical and Experimental Rheumatology 25: S4–11

Ebeling P R 2008 Osteoporosis in men. New England Journal of Medicine 358: 1474–1482

Goldring M B, Goldring S R 2007 Osteoarthritis. Journal of Cellular Physiology 213: 626–634

Hakim A, Clunie G J A, Haq I 2006 Oxford Handbook of Rheumatology, 2nd edn. Oxford University Press, Oxford

Lane N E 2007 Osteoarthritis of the hip. New England Journal of Medicine 357: 1413–1421

Tung S, Iqbal J 2007 Evolution, aging, and osteoporosis. Annals of the New York Academy of Sciences 1116: 499–506

Weiss S W, Goldblum J R 2007 Enzinger and Weiss's soft tissue tumors, 5th edn. Mosby, St Louis

26

Central and peripheral nervous systems

COMMON CLINICAL PROBLEMS FROM CENTRAL AND PERIPHERAL NERVOUS SYSTEM DISEASE

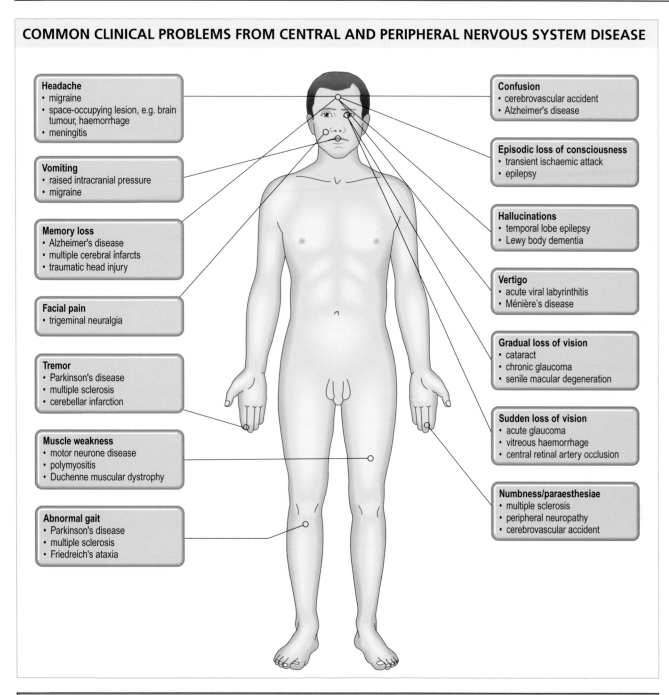

Headache
- migraine
- space-occupying lesion, e.g. brain tumour, haemorrhage
- meningitis

Vomiting
- raised intracranial pressure
- migraine

Memory loss
- Alzheimer's disease
- multiple cerebral infarcts
- traumatic head injury

Facial pain
- trigeminal neuralgia

Tremor
- Parkinson's disease
- multiple sclerosis
- cerebellar infarction

Muscle weakness
- motor neurone disease
- polymyositis
- Duchenne muscular dystrophy

Abnormal gait
- Parkinson's disease
- multiple sclerosis
- Friedreich's ataxia

Confusion
- cerebrovascular accident
- Alzheimer's disease

Episodic loss of consciousness
- transient ischaemic attack
- epilepsy

Hallucinations
- temporal lobe epilepsy
- Lewy body dementia

Vertigo
- acute viral labyrinthitis
- Ménière's disease

Gradual loss of vision
- cataract
- chronic glaucoma
- senile macular degeneration

Sudden loss of vision
- acute glaucoma
- vitreous haemorrhage
- central retinal artery occlusion

Numbness/paraesthesiae
- multiple sclerosis
- peripheral neuropathy
- cerebrovascular accident

Pathological basis of neurological signs and symptoms

Sign or symptom	Pathological basis	Sign or symptom	Pathological basis
Headache		**Abnormal reflexes**	
• Intracranial cause	Raised intracranial pressure Constriction and dilatation of intracranial vessels (migraine) Irritation or inflammation of meninges	• Exaggerated • Impaired	Upper motor neurone corticospinal tract lesion Lower motor neurone corticospinal tract lesion Compression of motor nerve roots Peripheral neuropathy
• Extracranial cause	Referred from paranasal sinuses, cervical or temporomandibular joints, teeth, ears, etc. Giant cell temporal arteritis		

(Continued)

Pathological basis of neurological signs and symptoms—cont'd			
Sign or symptom	Pathological basis	Sign or symptom	Pathological basis
Neck stiffness	Irritation or inflammation of meninges Cervical spine osteoarthritis	**Muscle deficit** • Wasting • Weakness	Loss of trophic stimulus from lower motor neurones Myopathy Disease directly or indirectly affecting function of: • upper or lower motor neurones • neuromuscular conduction • muscle fibre function
Coma or impaired consciousness	Metabolic, e.g.: • hypoglycaemia • ketoacidosis • drug-induced • hepatic failure Brainstem lesions, e.g.: • infarction • haemorrhage Cerebral hemisphere lesions, e.g.: • intracerebral or extracerebral haemorrhage • infarction • infections • trauma	**Sensory impairment and/or paraesthesiae**	Disease directly or indirectly affecting function of: • neurones in sensory cortex • corticospinal tracts • spinal sensory nerve roots • peripheral nerves
Dementia	Loss of limbic or cortical neurones due to ischaemia, toxic injury or neurodegenerative disease, e.g. Alzheimer's disease	**Visual field defects or blindness**	Disease involving the eyes, optic nerves and pathway or visual cortex (e.g. cataracts, tumours (intrinsic or extrinsic to optic neural pathway), inflammation or demyelination in the optic pathway, retinopathy, ischaemia)
Epileptic fits	Paroxysmal neuronal discharges, either idiopathic or emanating from a focus of cortical disease or damage	**Tinnitus and/or deafness**	Impaired transmission of sound through external meatus (e.g. wax) or through middle ear ossicles, or disease affecting the organ of Corti or the auditory nerve

CENTRAL NERVOUS SYSTEM

NORMAL STRUCTURE AND FUNCTION

The central nervous system (CNS) is the most anatomically complex system in the body, able to function both as a self-contained unit and as the control unit that co-ordinates the activities of the peripheral nervous system (PNS), skeletal muscle and other main organ systems.

The CNS is composed of three principal structures: the brain, brainstem and spinal cord. The brain comprises two hemispheres which are joined by a band of white matter fibres known as the corpus callosum. The grey matter known as the cerebral cortex is located on the outer surface of the hemispheres, and is composed of six layers of neurones. The cerebral cortex is divided into four anatomical regions: the frontal, temporal, parietal and occipital lobes. Each of these has distinct functions, which are summarised in Figure 26.1. The white matter beneath the cerebral cortex is composed of axons which connect the cortical neurones with neurones in other grey matter regions, including the opposite hemisphere. In the centre of the hemispheres there is a complex series of grey matter nuclei known as the basal ganglia, the thalamus and the hypothalamus. Their principal functions are summarised in Table 26.1. The cerebellum is located at the posterior surface of the brainstem, to which it is connected by white matter fibre bundles. The cortex of the cerebellum lies on its outer surface, but its structure is different from that of the cerebral cortex. The function of the cerebellum is summarised in Table 26.1.

The brainstem contains many ascending and descending white matter fibre bundles which connect the spinal cord to the brain; however, it also contains many nuclei, including cranial nerves 3–12, the substantia nigra, the respiratory centre and the vomiting centre. The spinal cord is largely composed of ascending and descending white matter fibre bundles, such as the corticospinal pathways (descending motor fibres) and the posterior columns (ascending sensory fibres). The grey matter of the spinal cord is located in the centre, and contains several groups of neurones, including the anterior horn cells, which are the lower motor neurones supplying all the skeletal muscle in the trunk and limbs. Motor nerve roots leave the anterior spinal cord to form peripheral motor nerves; sensory nerves from the skin, joints and organs enter the spinal cord by the posterior nerve roots, and then pass into the ascending posterior columns.

Despite the structural and functional complexities of the CNS, the constituent cells can be divided into just five main groups:

- neurones
- glia
- microglial cells
- connective tissue
- blood vessels.

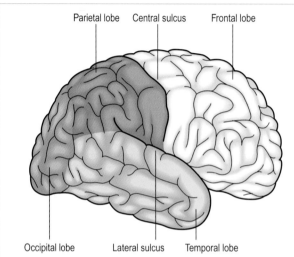

Fig. 26.1 Location and function of the lobes of the cerebral cortex. The frontal lobe is responsible for voluntary movement, intellect, personality and memory. Sensation is appreciated in the parietal cortex, which also has a major role in reading, speech and writing. The temporal lobe has an important role in memory, mood and hearing; the main function of the occipital lobe is vision.

Table 26.1 Functions of the basal ganglia, thalamus, hypothalamus and cerebellum	
Structure	**Functions**
Basal ganglia	Movement co-ordination Tone and posture regulation
Thalamus	Movement co-ordination Visual co-ordination Sensory co-ordination Memory processing
Hypothalamus	Memory processing Thirst, appetite and temperature control Autonomic regulation Control of pituitary endocrine function
Cerebellum	Movement co-ordination Stance, posture and gait regulation Storing and initiating learned movements

Neurones

Neurones are the structural and functional units of the CNS, generating electrical impulses that allow rapid cell–cell communication at specialised junctions known as synapses (Fig. 26.2). Many millions of neurones are present, arranged in layers within the cortex on the surface of the cerebellum and the cerebral hemispheres. Groups of functionally related neurones within the subcortical grey matter are known as nuclei (Table 26.1). Neurones are highly specialised post-mitotic cells which cannot be replaced after cell death. They are subject to unique metabolic demands, having to maintain an axon (which may be up to 1 m in length) by intracellular transport. This makes neurones particularly vulnerable to a wide range of insults, principally hypoxia and hypoglycaemia.

Neurones contain ion channels within the cell membrane that can be opened by either changing the voltage across the membrane or by the binding of a chemical (neurotransmitter) to a receptor in or near the ion channel. In the resting state, the neuronal cell membrane is relatively impermeable to ions. Opening of the ion channels allows an influx of sodium ions which depolarises the membrane, forming an action potential which is transmitted rapidly down the axon by saltatory conduction. Cell to cell transmission occurs at the synapse

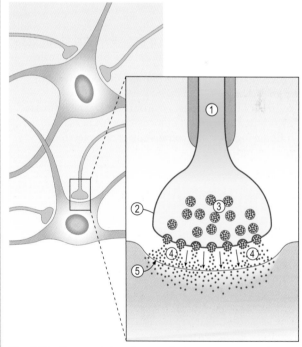

Fig. 26.2 Neuronal signal transmission at synapses. The transmission of the action potential down the axon **(1)** to the presynaptic membrane **(2)** results in opening of Ca ion channels, producing an influx of calcium. The subsequent phosphorylation of calcium-binding proteins allows the synaptic vesicles **(3)** to bind to the presynaptic membrane and release their neurotransmitter contents into the synaptic cleft **(4)**. The neurotransmitters diffuse across the synaptic cleft and bind to receptors in the post-synaptic membrane **(5)**, causing membrane depolarisation and eventually the formation of another action potential.

(Fig. 26.2). The commonest excitatory neurotransmitter in the CNS is glutamate. Excessive release of glutamate under certain conditions such as cerebral ischaemia and epilepsy can result in excitotoxic neuronal cell death.

Neurones, or nerve cells, vary considerably in size and appearance within the CNS. All possess a cell body, axons and dendrites.

The *cell body* or *perikaryon* is easily seen by light microscopy (Fig. 26.3). It contains neurofilaments, microtubules, lysosomes, mitochondria, complex stacks of rough endoplasmic reticulum, free ribosomes and a single nucleus with a prominent nucleolus. Some groups of neurones contain the pigment neuromelanin and are readily identifiable with the naked eye as darkly coloured nuclei, e.g. in the substantia nigra.

Axons and *dendrites* are the neuronal processes that convey electrical impulses from and towards the perikaryon respectively. These processes vary enormously in size and complexity, and may be difficult to identify on routine microscopy.

Glia

Glia are specialised supporting cells of the CNS comprising four main groups:

- astrocytes
- oligodendrocytes
- ependymal cells
- choroid plexus cells.

Astrocytes are process-bearing cells which are poorly visualised by light microscopy (Fig. 26.3) unless special staining techniques are used. They perform several important roles:

- provision of a supportive framework for other cells in the CNS
- control of the neuronal environment by the intimate association of astrocyte processes with perikarya, influencing local neurotransmitter and electrolyte concentrations

- regulation of the blood–brain barrier by astrocyte foot processes which are closely applied around cerebral capillaries (see below).

Oligodendrocytes are the most numerous cells in the CNS. On light microscopy, they are visible as darkly staining nuclei located around neurones and nerve fibres (Fig. 26.3). The most important function of oligodendrocytes is the synthesis and maintenance of myelin in the CNS.

Ependymal cells form the single-cell lining of the ventricular system and the central canal of the spinal cord. They are short columnar cells that bear cilia on the luminal surface. Ependymal cells may participate in the absorption and secretion of cerebrospinal fluid (CSF).

Choroid plexus cells secrete CSF and contain large quantities of mitochondria, rough endoplasmic reticulum and Golgi apparatus within the cytoplasm. They form a cuboidal epithelial covering over the ventricular choroid plexus, and bear atypical microvilli.

Microglial cells

Microglia belong to the macrophage/monocyte system of phagocytic cells. They are normally quiescent, and inconspicuous on light microscopy, but are of major importance in reactive states, for example in inflammatory and demyelinating disorders.

Connective tissue

Connective tissue in the CNS is confined to two main structural groups: the meninges and perivascular fibroblasts.

The *meninges* comprise the pia, arachnoid and dura mater, and the arachnoidal granulations which are the main sites of CSF absorption. The meninges are composed of fibroblast-like cells which also extend around meningeal and cerebral blood vessels.

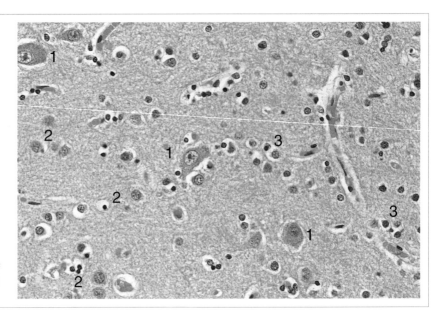

Fig. 26.3 Normal cerebral cortex. Figure shows the normal arrangement of neurones **(1)**, astrocytes **(2)**, oligodendrocytes **(3)** and capillaries in the cerebral cortex. Although the neuronal perikarya are visible, the cytoplasm of glial cells is best demonstrated by using special histological techniques.

Blood vessels

Blood vessels in the CNS are similar in structure and function to those elsewhere in the body, with the important exception of the capillaries. The capillaries within the CNS differ from most other capillaries in several respects:

- The vessels are non-fenestrated, and tight junctions are present between adjacent cells.
- The endothelial cells possess a thick layer of cytoplasm containing numerous organelles.
- Relatively few microvilli are present on the luminal surface of the endothelial cells, and only occasional pinocytotic vesicles are present in the cytoplasm.
- The endothelial cell basement membrane is intimately surrounded by a network of astrocyte processes.

These special structural features are important constituents of the *blood–brain barrier*: this is a functional unit which restricts the entry and exit of many substances—including proteins, ions, non-lipid-soluble compounds and drugs—to and from the CNS.

REACTIONS OF CNS CELLS TO INJURY

▶ Axonal damage results in central chromatolysis in neuronal peri-karya, with anterograde degeneration of the damaged axon
▶ Axonal regeneration does not occur to a significant extent in the CNS
▶ Axonal degeneration results in breakdown of the myelin sheath around damaged fibres
▶ Hypertrophy and hyperplasia of astrocytes with fibrillary gliosis results in a glial scar around areas of tissue damage
▶ Microglia and recruited blood monocytes form a popula-tion of phagocytic cells

Neurones

Neurones can undergo various reactive changes to cell injury:

- central chromatolysis
- anterograde degeneration
- atrophy.

Central chromatolysis is a distinctive reaction which usually occurs in response to axonal damage (Fig. 26.4). This reaction is maximal at around 8 days following axonal damage, and is accompanied by increased RNA and protein synthesis, suggestive of a regenerative response.

Anterograde degeneration occurs as a result of axonal transection, and is usually accompanied by central chromatolysis (Fig. 26.4). Degeneration of the distal part of the axon will occur following its separation from the intact perikaryon, e.g. by transection. Within 4 days, the distal segment degenerates and becomes fragmented. The myelin sheath surrounding the axon also fragments, but this usually occurs only after axonal degeneration is established. Axonal and myelin debris is then phagocytosed by macrophages, which often remain around the site of injury for several months. Attempts at axonal regeneration do not occur to a significant extent in the CNS.

Atrophy of neurones occurs in many slowly progressive degenerative disorders, e.g. motor neurone disease. Such neurones appear shrunken, and often contain excess lipo-fuscin pigment. Trans-synaptic atrophy occurs in neurones following loss of the main afferent connections, e.g. in neurones of the lateral geniculate body following damage to the optic nerve or retina.

Astrocytes

Astrocytes undergo hyperplasia and hypertrophy following almost all forms of CNS damage, in a response known as 'reactive gliosis'. Gliotic tissue is translucent and firm, often forming a limiting barrier to sites of tissue damage, for example at the edge of a cerebral infarct.

Microglia

Microglia are also involved in the response to many forms of CNS damage, often acting as phagocytes (as in neuronophagia). When myelin is damaged, these cells ingest the breakdown products, resulting in an enlarged rounded cell body distended with droplets of neutral lipid.

Oligodendrocytes and ependymal cells

These cells show only a limited capacity to react to injury.

DYSFUNCTION OF THE CNS

Diseases of the CNS impair the highly complex integration that is necessary for normal neurological function. The result-ing clinical abnormalities can often indicate the anatomical basis of the lesion in the CNS, and this can be investigated in greater detail by imaging of the CNS by MRI scanning. The pathological basis box (p. 749) gives an introduction to some common clinical abnormalities and their pathological basis in the CNS.

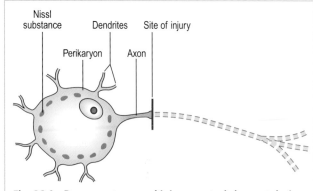

Fig. 26.4 Response to axonal injury: central chromatolysis and anterograde degeneration. Following axonal injury, the perikaryon swells and the nucleus migrates peripherally. The Nissl substance is dispersed to the periphery of the perikaryon, hence the term 'central chromatolysis'. Anterograde degeneration of the axon occurs distal to the site of injury.

INTRACRANIAL SPACE-OCCUPYING LESIONS

▶ Brain swelling may be diffuse or focal
▶ Diffuse brain swelling is usually due to vasodilatation and vascular engorgement, or oedema
▶ Focal brain swelling may be due to inflammatory, traumatic, vascular or neoplastic lesions, and is often accompanied by oedema in the adjacent tissue
▶ Result in intracranial shift and herniation (supracallosal, tentorial or tonsillar types) once a critical stage of mass expansion is reached
▶ Produce characteristic clinical signs and symptoms relating to raised intracranial pressure and intracranial shift or herniation

Intracranial space-occupying lesions may result from a variety of causes, but all share one common feature: an expansion in volume of the intracranial contents. Such brain swelling may be either diffuse or focal.

Diffuse brain swelling

Diffuse brain swelling denotes a generalised increase in the volume of the brain which results from either vasodilatation or oedema.

Vasodilatation

Vasodilatation in the brain occurs following changes in the calibre of intracerebral vessels that cause an increase in cerebral blood volume resulting in brain swelling. This occurs particularly in response to hypercapnia and hypoxia, but may also result from failure of the normal vasomotor control mechanisms, for example in severe head injuries.

Oedema

Oedema in the brain is defined as an abnormal accumulation of fluid in the cerebral parenchyma that produces an increase in cerebral volume. Cerebral oedema can be classified into three main types:

- *vasogenic:* due to increased cerebral vascular permeability (blood–brain barrier dysfunction)
- *cytotoxic:* due to cellular injury to neurones and glia
- *interstitial:* due to damage to the ventricular lining in hydrocephalus (p. 759).

In many instances, cerebral oedema occurs due to a combination of mechanisms; for example, both vasogenic and cytotoxic mechanisms are involved in ischaemia. Cerebral oedema frequently accompanies focal lesions in the brain, thereby exaggerating the mass effect.

Focal brain swelling

Focal lesions of many types can produce an increase in cerebral volume, for example cerebral abscesses, intracranial haematomas and intrinsic neoplasms. Many extrinsic intracranial lesions, for example subdural haematomas and meningiomas, exert a mass effect within the cranial cavity and so act as space-occupying lesions.

Consequences of intracranial space-occupying lesions

The consequences of intracranial space-occupying lesions may be:

- raised intracranial pressure
- intracranial shift and herniation
- epilepsy
- hydrocephalus
- systemic effects.

Raised intracranial pressure

Raised intracranial pressure is an invariable consequence of enlarging intracranial lesions, as there is very little space within the rigid cranium to accommodate an expanding mass. Initially, however, there is a phase of spatial compensation, made possible in three ways:

- reduction in the CSF space within and around the brain
- pressure atrophy of the brain, which occurs most commonly with slow-growing extrinsic lesions, e.g. meningiomas (see Fig. 26.34)
- reduction in blood volume, e.g. within the intracranial venous sinuses.

Once this phase is passed, there is a critical period in which a further increase in the volume of the intracranial contents will cause an abrupt increase in intracranial pressure. The characteristic clinical signs and symptoms of raised intracranial pressure and their likely causes are:

- papilloedema: due to accumulation of axoplasm in the optic papilla when axonal flow is impeded by pressure on the optic nerve
- nausea and vomiting: due to pressure on vomiting centres in the pons and medulla
- headache: due to compression and distortion of pain and stretch receptors around intracranial blood vessels and within the dura mater
- impairment of consciousness, ranging from drowsiness to deep coma, related to the level of increased intracranial pressure.

Intracranial shift and herniation

Intracranial shift and herniation are the most important consequences of raised intracranial pressure due to space-occupying lesions. They usually occur following a critical increase in intracranial pressure, which may inadvertently be precipitated by withdrawing CSF at lumbar puncture. Lumbar puncture is therefore contraindicated in any patient with raised intracranial pressure and a suspected intracranial space-occupying lesion to avoid the risk of precipitating a potentially fatal brainstem herniation.

Lateral shift of the midline structures is a common early complication of intracranial space-occupying lesions. However, patients with acute lateral displacement of the brain due to a hemispheric mass show a depressed level of consciousness even in the absence of an intracranial herniation. The clinical features are summarised in Table 26.2.

Table 26.2 Clinical consequences of intracranial herniation

Site of herniation	Effect	Clinical consequence
Transtentorial	Ipsilateral 3rd cranial nerve compression	Ipsilateral fixed dilated pupil
	Ipsilateral 6th cranial nerve compression	Horizontal diplopia, convergent squint
	Posterior cerebral artery compression	Occipital infarction
		Cortical blindness
	Cerebral peduncle compression	Upper motor neurone signs
	Brainstem compression and haemorrhage	Coma
		Cardiorespiratory failure
		Death
Foramen magnum	Brainstem compression and haemorrhage	Coma
		Cardiorespiratory failure
		Death
	Acute obstruction of CSF pathway	Coma
		Cardiorespiratory failure
		Death

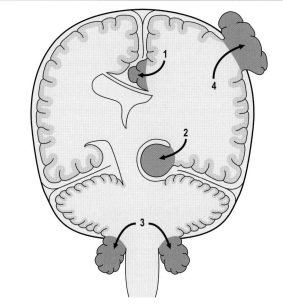

Fig. 26.5 Sites of intracranial herniation. Space-occupying lesions in the cerebral hemispheres may cause herniation of the cingulate gyrus under the falx cerebri **(1)** or of the hippocampal uncus and parahippocampal gyrus over the tentorium cerebelli **(2)**. Cerebellar tonsillar herniation through the foramen magnum **(3)** can occur with lesions in the cerebrum or cerebellum. A swollen brain will herniate through any defect in the dura and skull **(4)**.

Herniations occur at several characteristic sites within the cranial cavity, depending on the site of the space-occupying lesion (Fig. 26.5). Transtentorial herniation is frequently fatal because of secondary haemorrhage into the brainstem (Fig. 26.6). This is a common mode of death in patients with large intrinsic neoplasms or intracranial haemorrhage.

Epilepsy

Seizures (fits) may be focal or generalised (p. 775), and are particularly common in patients with raised intracranial pressure due to cerebral abscesses and neoplasms.

Hydrocephalus

Hydrocephalus is a particularly common complication of space-occupying lesions in the posterior fossa that compress and distort the cerebral aqueduct and fourth ventricle (p. 759).

Systemic effects

The systemic effects of raised intracranial pressure are of major clinical importance, as they may result in a life-threatening deterioration in an already ill patient. These are thought to result from autonomic imbalance and overactivity as a result of hypothalamic compression and include:

- hypertension and bradycardia
- pulmonary oedema
- gastrointestinal and urinary tract ulceration and haemorrhage
- acute pancreatitis.

CNS TRAUMA

- ▶ Classified as missile or non-missile injury: the latter is commoner
- ▶ CNS damage in non-missile injuries may occur as primary damage (immediate) or secondary damage (after the injury)
- ▶ Primary damage includes focal lesions (contusions and lacerations) and diffuse axonal injury
- ▶ Secondary damage includes intracranial haematomas, oedema, intracranial herniation, infarction and infection
- ▶ Important complications include epilepsy, persistent vegetative state and post-traumatic dementia

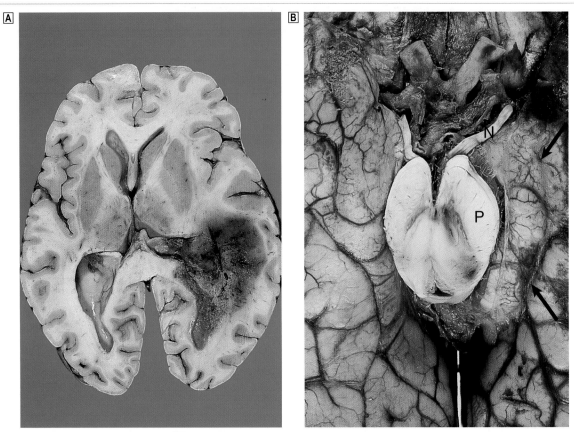

Fig. 26.6 Herniation effects in the brain. **A** A large haemorrhagic neoplasm (glioblastoma) is present in the right cerebral hemisphere, causing shift of the midline structures to the left and compression of the right lateral ventricle. **B** Transtentorial herniation at the base of the brain. A prominent groove surrounds the displaced parahippocampal gyrus (arrow). The adjacent 3rd nerve (N) is compressed and distorted and the ipsilateral cerebral peduncle (P) is distorted with small areas of haemorrhage.

In the UK, 200–300 per 100 000 population present to hospital each year with head injuries, most of which are due to road traffic accidents and falls. Head injuries can be classified according to their aetiology: missile and non-missile (blunt) injuries. The latter are more common.

Missile injury to the brain

Missile injuries to the brain are typically caused by bullets or other small objects propelled through the air. Three main types of injury are recognised:

- *depressed injuries,* in which the missile causes a depressed skull fracture with contusions, but does not enter the brain.
- *penetrating injuries,* which occur when the missile enters the cranial cavity but does not exit. Focal damage is common, and may be accompanied by infection.
- *perforating injuries,* which are caused when a missile enters and exits from the cranial cavity, usually leaving a large exit wound. Brain damage around the missile tract is severe, with extensive haemorrhage. The risk of infection and epilepsy in survivors is high.

Non-missile injury to the brain

Non-missile injuries to the brain range from relatively minor injuries with spontaneous improvement (as in concussion injuries), to severe injuries that are rapidly fatal. These injuries occur most commonly in road traffic accidents (55%) and falls (35%), when rotational forces acting on the brain may be accompanied by impact-related forces. The latter often result in a skull fracture, but it is important to note that around 20% of fatal head injuries occur without a fracture. The types of brain damage occurring in non-missile injuries may be classified as either primary or secondary.

Primary brain damage

Primary brain damage occurs at the time of injury. There are two main forms: focal damage and diffuse axonal injury.

Focal damage
The commonest type of focal damage is contusions. These often occur at the site of impact, particularly if a skull fracture is present. Contusions are commonly asymmetrical and may be more severe on the side opposite the impact—the

'*contrecoup*' lesions (Fig. 26.7). Movement of the brain within the skull brings these areas into contact with adjacent bone, resulting in local injury. Large contusions may be associated with an intracerebral haemorrhage, or accompanied by cortical lacerations. Healed contusions are represented by wedge-shaped areas of gliosis and cortical rarefaction which are yellow–brown due to the presence of haemosiderin.

Other forms of focal damage, e.g. tears of cranial nerves, pituitary stalk or brainstem, occur less frequently.

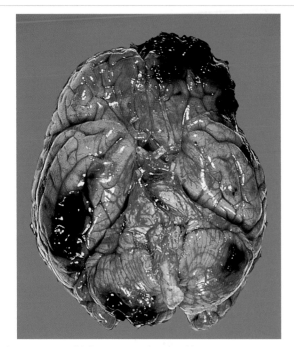

Fig. 26.7 Head injury: contusions and haematomas. A severe blow to the frontal bone has resulted in contusions and haematomas in the frontal lobes. 'Contrecoup' contusions are present in the parietal lobes, and in the cerebellum.

Diffuse axonal injury

This type of damage occurs as a result of shearing and tensile strains on neuronal processes produced by rotational movements of the brain within the skull. It often occurs in the absence of a skull fracture and cerebral contusions. Two main components exist:

- *small haemorrhagic lesions* in the corpus callosum and dorsolateral quadrant of the brainstem; these heal by reactive gliosis and are represented by gliotic scars.
- *diffuse damage to axons*, which can only be detected microscopically in the form of axonal retraction balls; in long-term survivors, damaged axons undergo anterograde degeneration, resulting in a loss of fibres in the white matter.

Modern neuropathological techniques reveal that diffuse axonal injury occurs in almost all fatal head injuries and may occur to a lesser degree in milder injuries (e.g. concussion).

Secondary brain damage

Secondary brain damage occurs as a result of complications developing after the moment of injury. These complications often dominate the clinical picture, and are responsible for death in many cases:

- *Intracranial haemorrhage.* The mechanisms and clinical manifestations of traumatic intracranial haemorrhage are summarised in Table 26.3.
- *Traumatic damage to extracerebral arteries.* Although uncommon, this is of clinical importance because some cases can be treated surgically. The injuries encountered most frequently are dissection of the internal carotid artery and rupture of the vertebral artery.
- *Intracranial herniation.* The mechanisms and consequences of intracranial herniations are described above.
- *Hypoxic brain damage.* Hypoxic brain damage with cerebral infarction can often be related to a clinical episode of hypotension, for example cardiac arrest. Hypoxic damage may also occur as a consequence of raised intracranial pressure,

Table 26.3 Mechanisms and clinical manifestations of traumatic intracranial haemorrhage

Site	Mechanism	Clinical manifestations
Extradural space	Skull fracture with arterial rupture, e.g. middle meningeal artery	Lucid interval followed by a rapid increase in intracranial pressure
Subdural space	Rupture of venous sinuses or small bridging veins due to torsion forces	Acute presentation with a rapid increase in intracranial pressure. Chronic presentation with personality change, memory loss and confusion, particularly in the elderly
Subarachnoid space	Arterial rupture	Meningeal irritation with a rapid increase in intracranial pressure
Cerebral hemisphere	Cortical contusions. Rupture of small intrinsic vessels with intracerebral haematoma. 'Burst lobe' with intracerebral haematoma contusions and subdural haematoma	May cause seizures. Increased intracranial pressure with focal deficits; usually fatal. Profound coma, usually rapidly fatal

fat emboli, traumatic damage to the main neck vessels or respiratory obstruction.
- *Meningitis.* This is a well-recognised complication of head injury, particularly in patients with an open skull fracture.

Outcome of non-missile head injury

Most patients with minor head injuries make a satisfactory recovery. However, only 20% of survivors of severe head injuries make a good recovery, while 10% remain severely disabled. Important causes of persisting debility are:

- *post-traumatic epilepsy,* which is the commonest delayed complication of non-missile head injury
- *persistent vegetative state,* in which patients remain severely neurologically impaired; this occurs most often in patients with diffuse axonal damage and hypoxic brain damage
- *post-traumatic dementia,* due to neuronal loss and axonal damage following non-missile head injury.

Spinal cord injuries

Spinal cord injuries account for the majority of hospital admissions for paraplegia and tetraplegia. Over 80% occur as a result of road traffic accidents; most of the patients are males under 40 years of age. Two main groups of injury are recognised clinically: open injuries and closed injuries.

Open injuries

Open injuries cause direct trauma to the spinal cord and nerve roots. Perforating injuries can cause extensive disruption and haemorrhage, but penetrating injuries may result in incomplete cord transection which can be manifested clinically as the Brown–Séquard syndrome (hemisection of the cord resulting in an upper motor neurone lesion and loss of position and vibration sense on the affected side with loss of pain and temperature sense on the contralateral side, below the level of the injury—see Fig. 26.20).

Closed injuries

Closed injuries account for most spinal injuries and are usually associated with a fracture/dislocation of the spinal column which is usually demonstrable radiologically. Damage to the cord depends on the extent of the bony injuries and can be considered in two main stages:

- primary damage: contusions, nerve fibre transection, haemorrhagic necrosis
- secondary damage: extradural haematoma, infarction, infection, oedema.

Complications and outcome

Late effects of cord damage include:

- ascending and descending anterograde degeneration of damaged nerve fibres

- post-traumatic syringomyelia
- systemic effects of paraplegia: urinary tract and chest infections, pressure sores and muscle wasting.

The outcome of cord injuries depends mainly on the site and severity of the cord damage. Patients with incomplete lesions in the cauda equina have an almost normal life expectancy, while patients surviving a high cervical lesion have a much higher morbidity and mortality.

SPINAL CORD AND NERVE ROOT COMPRESSION

The principal causes of spinal cord and nerve root compression are:

- intervertebral disc prolapse
- neoplasm (e.g. metastatic carcinoma, myeloma, schwannoma)
- skeletal disorder (e.g. spondylosis, rheumatoid arthritis, Paget's disease)
- infection (e.g. tuberculosis, abscess)
- vascular disease (e.g. arteriovenous malformation, haemorrhage)
- trauma.

The commonest causes of subacute or chronic nerve root and cord compression are intervertebral disc prolapse and spondylosis.

Intervertebral disc prolapse

Intervertebral disc prolapse (Ch. 25) occurs in two main ways:

- In young adults, disc rupture following strenuous exercise or sudden exertion is the main cause of disc herniation.
- In the middle-aged or elderly, disc herniation following minimal stress is due to degenerative disc disease, usually accompanied by spondylosis (see below).

In both instances, a tear in the annulus fibrosus allows the soft nucleus pulposus to herniate posteriorly. This usually takes place in a lateral direction, causing nerve root compression. Central herniation is less common, but can cause direct cord damage and may also compress the anterior spinal artery, resulting in infarction. Disc prolapse occurs most commonly at the C5/C6 and L5/S1 levels; nerve root compression in the latter results in sciatica.

Spondylosis

Spondylosis due to osteoarthritis (Ch. 25) of the vertebral column occurs commonly with age. It affects around 70% of adults over 40 years of age, and is usually accompanied by degenerative disc disease. It is characterised by bony outgrowths, known as osteophytes, on the upper and lower margins of the vertebral bodies. These may encroach upon the spinal canal or intervertebral foramina to produce nerve root pain which is exacerbated by movement.

HYDROCEPHALUS

▶ A group of disorders resulting in excess CSF within the intracranial cavity
▶ Two main groups: primary hydrocephalus, usually accompanied by increased intracranial pressure; and secondary hydrocephalus, compensatory to loss of cerebral tissue
▶ Primary hydrocephalus usually due to obstruction of the CSF pathway; divided into communicating and non-communicating types
▶ Produces irreversible brain damage unless the raised intracranial pressure is relieved by surgical drainage

The cerebrospinal fluid (CSF) is secreted by the choroid plexus epithelium in an active process which carefully regulates its biochemical composition. In adults, the total volume of CSF is around 140 ml; this volume is renewed several times daily (Fig. 26.8).

CSF resorption occurs primarily at the arachnoid villi. Hydrocephalus is the term used to describe any condition in which an excess quantity of CSF is present in the cranial cavity. These conditions can be considered in two main groups:

• primary hydrocephalus
• secondary or compensatory hydrocephalus.

Primary hydrocephalus

Primary hydrocephalus includes any disorder in which the accumulation of CSF is usually accompanied by an increase in intracranial pressure. It can be due to:

• obstruction to CSF flow (non-communicating hydrocephalus)
• impaired CSF absorption at the arachnoid villi (rare)
• excess CSF production by choroid plexus neoplasms (very rare).

Obstructive hydrocephalus

Obstructive hydrocephalus is by far the commonest form; it may be either congenital or acquired.

Congenital hydrocephalus
Congenital hydrocephalus occurs in around 1 per 1000 births and occasionally may be so marked as to enlarge the fetal head considerably and interfere with labour. The more severe forms may be diagnosed antenatally by ultrasonography. Congenital malformations, for example *Arnold–Chiari malformation* (see Fig. 26.22), are the principal causes of congenital hydrocephalus. A few cases in males are due to an X-linked disorder that results in aqueduct stenosis. Aqueduct stenosis is more commonly due to acquired disorders, for example viral infections, which affect both sexes.

Acquired hydrocephalus
Acquired hydrocephalus can result from any lesion that obstructs the CSF pathway (Fig. 26.8). Expanding lesions in the

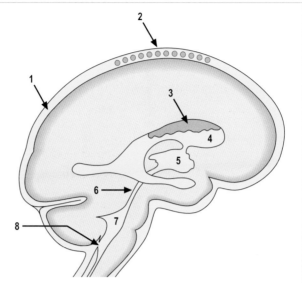

Fig. 26.8 Sites of obstruction in the cerebrospinal fluid (CSF) pathway. The circulation and absorption of CSF in the subarachnoid space **(1)** and arachnoid granulations **(2)** is readily impaired by inflammatory exudate and organising haemorrhage. CSF production in the choroid plexus **(3)** and flow through the lateral ventricles **(4)** and third ventricle **(5)** may be obstructed by intracranial or intraventricular neoplasms. The relatively narrow spaces of the cerebral aqueduct **(6)**, and the fourth ventricle **(7)** and its exit foramina **(8)**, are commonly obstructed by neoplasms, haemorrhage or inflammatory exudate.

posterior fossa are particularly prone to cause hydrocephalus, as the fourth ventricle and aqueduct are easily obstructed. Some lesions may cause intermittent obstruction, particularly colloid cysts of the third ventricle which may block the foramen of Monro. Obstructive hydrocephalus commonly results from the organisation of blood clot or inflammatory exudate in the CSF pathway following an episode of haemorrhage or meningitis (Fig. 26.9). *Intermittent pressure hydrocephalus* is thought to result from defective CSF absorption at the arachnoid villi.

Secondary hydrocephalus

In secondary or compensatory hydrocephalus the increase in CSF volume occurs following a loss of brain tissue, for example cerebral infarction or atrophy, so that overall there is no increase in either intracranial volume or intracranial pressure (see Fig. 26.26).

Complications and treatment

The complications of hydrocephalus can be averted or relieved by the insertion of a ventricular shunt with a one-way valve system to drain CSF into the peritoneum. Untreated patients may suffer irreversible brain damage (Fig. 26.9). Ventricular shunts often need to be replaced in growing children and are prone to become infected with low-virulence bacteria, for example *Staphylococcus epidermidis*. Infection may result in shunt blockage and exacerbation of symptoms attributable to raised intracranial pressure.

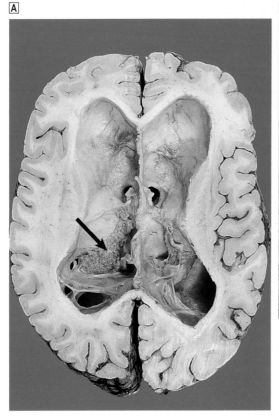

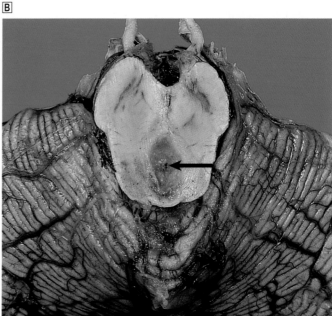

Fig. 26.9 Longstanding hydrocephalus. **A** The lateral ventricles are very dilated and contain a prominent choroid plexus (arrow). The overlying white and grey matter are atrophic. Fibrous adhesions are present in the ventricles posteriorly, suggestive of previous infection. **B** In the same case, the cerebral aqueduct in the midbrain is completely obliterated by glial tissue as a consequence of a previous viral infection (arrow). This has resulted in obstructive hydrocephalus.

SYRINGOMYELIA

Syringomyelia is an uncommon condition in which a cavity (syrinx) develops within the spinal cord, sometimes extending up into the brainstem (syringobulbia). The cavity is usually situated in the central region of the cord, posterior to the central canal. Syringomyelia occurs most frequently in the cervical region of the cord, and usually extends for several centimetres in a vertical direction. However, extensive cavities involving almost the entire length of the cord have been described. Modern radiological techniques are of great value in delineating the extent of the lesion (see Fig. 26.22).

Syringomyelia can arise in a variety of conditions, which may be considered as follows:

- *maldevelopment of the cord*, with failure of fusion of the ventral and dorsal segments
- *disorders of CSF flow*, where CSF is propelled down the central canal
- *tissue destruction* following a spinal cord injury, or as a consequence of an intrinsic neoplasm.

The cavities within the spinal cord in syringomyelia are lined by reactive astrocytes and their fibrillary processes. The CSF composition in syringomyelia is normal.

The clinical manifestations of syringomyelia usually occur in adult life, with:

- lower motor neurone lesion (muscle weakness and atrophy) in upper limbs due to compression of anterior horn cells
- dissociated anaesthesia (loss of pain and temperature sensation) due to damage to nerve fibres crossing the cord in the lateral spinothalamic tracts.

Surgery can sometimes arrest or alleviate symptoms by decompression or draining the fluid in the cystic cavity.

CEREBROVASCULAR DISEASE

- ▶ Third commonest cause of death in the UK and a major cause of morbidity in the elderly
- ▶ CNS damage occurs in cerebrovascular disease as a result of hypoxia
- ▶ Neurones are the cells most vulnerable to hypoxia; they become irreversibly damaged after 5–7 minutes
- ▶ Important risk factors are atheroma, heart disease, hypertension and diabetes mellitus
- ▶ Often presents clinically as a stroke or transient ischaemic attack
- ▶ Most strokes (82%) are due to cerebral infarction; the remainder are due to intracerebral and subarachnoid haemorrhages

Cerebrovascular disease is the third commonest cause of death in the UK, after heart disease and cancer, and is a major cause of morbidity, particularly in the middle-aged and elderly. The ultimate effect of cerebrovascular disease is to reduce the supply of oxygen to the CNS, resulting in hypoxic damage to cells.

Hypoxic damage to the CNS

Hypoxic damage to the CNS occurs when the blood supply to the brain is reduced (oligaemia) or absent (ischaemia). It may also occur:

- when the blood supply is normal but oxygen is carried at a reduced tension (hypoxia)
- in anoxia
- in rare circumstances when cellular respiratory enzyme function is impaired, such as in cyanide poisoning.

The cells most vulnerable to hypoxia are the neurones, which depend almost exclusively on the oxidative metabolism of glucose for energy. Experimental evidence suggests that the early stage of hypoxic neuronal damage (microvacuolation) is reversible; in the final stages, however, the damaged neurones shrink and exhibit nuclear pyknosis and karyorrhexis.

The neurones most vulnerable to hypoxia are those in the third, fifth and sixth layers of the cortex, in the CA1 sector of the hippocampus and in the Purkinje cells in the cerebellum. This pattern of selective vulnerability does not hold true at all ages; in infants, certain brainstem nuclei are also vulnerable. The basis of this selective vulnerability is unknown, but it may relate to differences in neuronal metabolism at these sites. Ischaemic neuronal death is characterised by activation of glutamate receptors, causing uncontrolled entry of calcium into the cell. This may be abolished or reduced in some cases by drugs that block glutamate receptors or calcium channels.

Complete cessation of the circulation, such as may occur following myocardial infarction, results in *global cerebral ischaemia*. In less severe cases, a critical reduction of cerebral blood flow may result in boundary zone infarcts, which occur in zones between territories supplied by each of the main cerebral arteries.

Stroke

The term stroke denotes a sudden event in which a disturbance of CNS function occurs due to vascular disease. The annual incidence of stroke is 3–5 per 1000 of the general population worldwide, but is much commoner in the elderly. These events can be classified clinically into *completed strokes, evolving strokes* or a *transient ischaemic attack* in which the CNS disturbance lasts for less than 24 hours. Transient ischaemic attack is a major risk factor for cerebral infarction; most attacks are due to circulatory changes in the CNS occurring as the result of disease in the heart or extracranial arteries.

The clinical features of stroke result from *focal cerebral ischaemia*, and depend on the localisation and nature of the lesion (Table 26.4). Recurrent or multiple strokes often occur in patients with certain risk factors, particularly heart disease, hypertension and diabetes mellitus.

Cerebral infarction

The site and size of a cerebral infarct depend on the site and nature of the vascular lesion. Most infarcts occur within the cerebral hemispheres in the internal carotid territory, particularly in the distribution of the middle cerebral artery. Infarction of the corticospinal pathway in the region of the internal capsule is a common event, resulting in contralateral hemiparesis. Although many infarcts produce clinical symptoms, small infarcts may not result in any apparent neurological disturbance. These micro-infarcts are often found in apparently normal elderly individuals, but are also numerous in the brains of hypertensive patients. Multiple infarcts involving the cerebral cortex may result in dementia (p. 779).

Table 26.4	Comparison of the major causes of stroke				
Cause	%	Clinical presentation	30-day mortality (%)	Pathogenesis	Predisposing factors
Cerebral infarction	82	Slowly evolving signs and symptoms	15–45	Cerebral hypoperfusion Embolism Thrombosis	Heart disease (e.g. infective endocarditis, endocardial thrombus) Hypertension Atheroma Diabetes mellitus
Intracerebral haemorrhage	15	Sudden onset of stroke with raised intracranial pressure	80	Rupture of arteriole or micro-aneurysm	Hypertension Vascular malformation
Subarachnoid haemorrhage	3	Sudden headache with meningism	45	Rupture of saccular aneurysm on circle of Willis	Hypertension Polycystic renal disease Coarctation of the aorta

Pathogenesis

The following mechanisms may be responsible for cerebral infarction:

- *arterial thrombosis* occurring as a complication of atheroma in the intracranial arterial tree or extracranial vessels supplying the CNS
- *embolic arterial occlusion* occurring as a complication of atheroma in the extracranial arterial supply (particularly around the carotid artery bifurcation) or mural thrombus in the heart following myocardial infarction. Fat and air emboli may also result in cerebral infarction following major trauma
- *head injury* may result in cerebral hypoxia, vascular occlusion or rupture, all of which may result in cerebral infarction
- *subarachnoid haemorrhage* following rupture of a saccular aneurysm may be accompanied by vascular spasm resulting in cerebral infarction
- *generalised arterial disease*, e.g. vasculitis, may affect both intra- and extracranial vessels and result in cerebral infarction
- *critical reduction of cerebral blood flow*, e.g. following cardiac arrest
- *critical reduction in arterial oxygenation*, e.g. in anoxia or profound hypoxia following respiratory arrest
- *intraventricular haemorrhage in neonates* is often accompanied by infarction in the adjacent white matter (periventricular leukomalacia)
- *venous thrombosis* as a complication of local sepsis or drugs, e.g. oral contraceptives.

Morphological features

At a very early stage after cerebral infarction, no naked-eye abnormalities are apparent. However, 24 hours after infarction the affected tissue becomes softened and swollen, with a loss of definition between grey and white matter. There may be considerable oedema around the infarct, resulting in a local mass effect. Within 4 days, the infarcted tissue undergoes colliquative necrosis. Histology shows infiltration by macrophages, which are filled with the lipid products of myelin breakdown. Reactive astrocytes and proliferating capillaries are often present at the edge of the infarct. Eventually, all the dead tissue is phagocytosed to leave a fluid-filled cystic cavity with a gliotic wall (Fig. 26.10). Some infarcts are haemorrhagic, possibly due to reflow of blood through anastomotic channels. Anterograde degeneration of nerve fibres occurs distal to the site of infarction, for example in the ipsilateral cerebral peduncle in infarcts involving the internal capsule.

Venous infarction

Venous infarction is a consequence of venous thrombosis in the cranial cavity. This can occur at localised sites, most commonly in the lateral and sagittal sinuses, or as part of a generalised cortical venous thrombosis. Venous thrombosis results in a haemorrhagic infarction of the cerebral cortex and subcortical white matter. It usually occurs secondary to other disease processes, for example local sepsis, dehydration or drugs (e.g. oral contraceptives). Extensive venous infarcts are usually fatal.

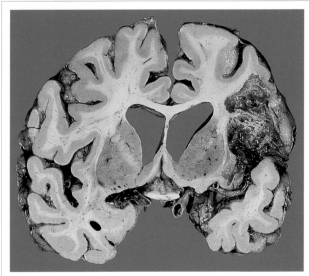

Fig. 26.10   Cerebral infarct: cystic change. In this old infarct in the territory of the right middle cerebral artery, the necrotic tissue has been phagocytosed to leave a cystic cavity lined by glial tissue.

Intracranial haemorrhage

Intracerebral and subarachnoid haemorrhage together account for around 18% of strokes. Extradural and subdural haemorrhages usually occur following trauma and are considered in Table 26.3.

Intracerebral haemorrhage

The commonest cause of intracerebral haemorrhage is hypertensive vascular disease, in which haemorrhages occur most frequently in the basal ganglia (80% of cases), the brainstem, cerebellum and cerebral cortex. Most intracerebral haemorrhages occur in hypertensive adults over 50 years of age. The haematoma acts as a space-occupying lesion, causing a rapid increase in intracranial pressure and intracranial herniation (Fig. 26.11). In survivors, resorption of the haematoma eventually occurs, and a fluid-filled cyst with a gliotic wall is formed. The mortality from spontaneous intracerebral haemorrhage is greater than 80%, and many survivors suffer severe neurological deficit.

The pathogenesis of spontaneous intracerebral haemorrhage is not fully understood. For many years, it was thought that most intracerebral haemorrhages in hypertensive patients occurred following rupture of micro-aneurysms on small arterioles, particularly on the lenticulostriate branch of the middle cerebral artery. Recent studies, however, have found that the ruptured vessels are arterioles, which show replacement of smooth muscle by lipids and fibrous tissue (lipohyalimosis), predisposing to rupture. Intracerebral haemorrhage in children and younger adults may occur as a consequence of trauma, or rupture of an arteriovenous malformation. In older adults, haemorrhage into the lobes of the brain may be due to amyloid depostion in the vessel walls (amyloid angiopathy), which is associated with Alzheimer's disease (p. 779).

Subarachnoid haemorrhage

Subarachnoid haemorrhage usually occurs following rupture of a saccular or 'berry' aneurysm on the circle of Willis. Other causes are uncommon, but include trauma, hypertensive haemorrhage, vasculitis, tumours and disorders of haemostasis.

Saccular aneurysms. Saccular aneurysms occur in 1–2% of the general population, but are commoner in the elderly. Most cases of ruptured saccular aneurysm occur between 40 and 60 years of age; males in this age group are affected twice as often as females. Several predisposing factors for saccular aneurysms have been identified.

The role of hypertension in the pathogenesis of these lesions is uncertain, but it does appear that hypertensive patients are more likely to have multiple aneurysms than are normotensive patients. Local vascular abnormalities, such as atheroma, are important in the pathogenesis of saccular aneurysms by altering haemodynamics in affected vessels.

Saccular aneurysms are usually sited at proximal branching points on the anterior portion of the circle of Willis, particularly on the internal carotid, anterior communicating and middle cerebral arteries. Most are less than 10 mm in diameter, but some may be partly filled by thrombus, which can obscure their true size on radiological studies (Fig. 26.12). Their pathogenesis is thought to relate to congenital defects in the smooth muscle of the tunica media at the site of an arterial bifurcation, where local haemodynamic factors act to produce a slowly enlarging aneurysm.

Clinicopathological features and prognosis. Subarachnoid haemorrhage often presents with the characteristic clinical history of sudden onset of severe headache. Blood accumulates in the basal cisterns and around the brainstem following rupture of a saccular aneurysm. Subarachnoid haemorrhage may be instantly fatal in as many as 15% of cases, with some patients dying later due to rebleed at the site of rupture, or arterial spasm (see below). One-third of survivors are permanently disabled as a consequence of hypoxic brain damage following haemorrhage.

Arterial spasm in the distal cerebral vasculature following rupture causes cerebral ischaemia and infarction, that is often accompanied by brain swelling due to oedema.

Hydrocephalus can occur acutely following rupture as blood accumulates in the basal cisterns, or at a later stage in survivors, where fibrous obliteration of the subarachnoid space or arachnoid granulations may occur.

Systemic hypertension and the CNS

As well as being a major risk factor for stroke, systemic hypertension causes many other changes in the CNS that result in neurological dysfunction:

- alteration in autoregulation of cerebral blood flow (e.g. a sudden drop in systemic blood pressure to normal levels may result in hypoperfusion)
- encephalopathy due to blood–brain barrier disruption and fibrinoid vascular necrosis
- vascular changes, especially atheroma

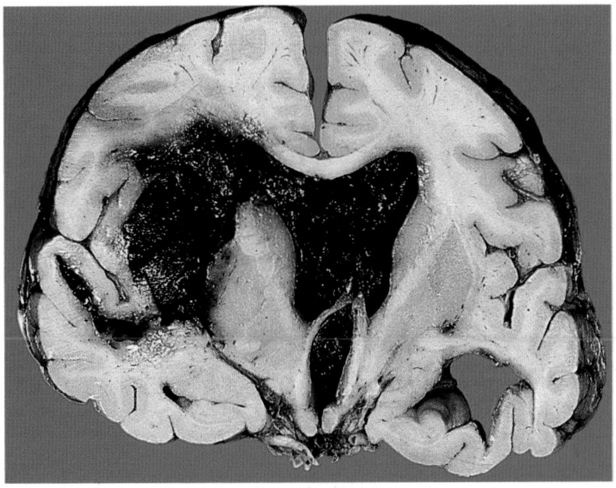

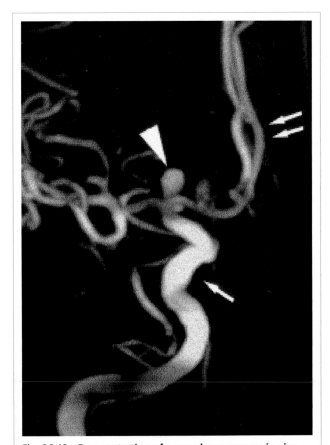

Fig. 26.12 Demonstration of a saccular aneurysm in vivo. This 3D digital subtraction angiogram shows a large grape-like saccular aneurysm (arrowhead) arising at the terminal region of the internal carotid artery (single arrow). The anterior cerebral arteries (double arrows) appear normal. (Courtesy of Dr D Summers, Edinburgh.)

Fig. 26.11 Complications of intracerebral haemorrhage. An intracranial haemorrhage originating in the internal capsule on the left has ruptured into the ventricular system, which is filled with blood. The mass effect of the haematoma has resulted in a shift of adjacent structures to the opposite side.

- aneurysms, including atheromatous aneurysms of the basilar artery, multiple saccular aneurysms on the circle of Willis, and micro-aneurysms on small arterioles in the basal ganglia
- dementia due to multiple infarcts in cerebral grey and white matter.

Spinal cord infarction

Spinal cord infarction is most often due to spinal cord trauma or compression, but may also result from ischaemia following myocardial infarction or aortic dissection. In such cases, the infarct occurs in the mid-thoracic region of the cord, in the distribution of the anterior spinal artery where the arterial blood supply is relatively poor. These infarcts result in paraplegia with a dissociated sensory loss, as the posterior columns are spared. Infarcts in the territory of the posterior spinal artery are very rare.

Intracranial haemorrhage in neonates

Intracranial haemorrhage in neonates has a markedly different pathology from intracranial haemorrhage in adults (Table 26.5). Haemorrhage from the subependymal germinal matrix is particularly important, and is the major cause of death in premature neonates.

Cerebrovascular malformations

Three main types of vascular malformation occur in the CNS:

- arteriovenous malformations
- cavernous angioma
- capillary telangiectasis.

Arteriovenous malformations are clinically the most important; these usually consist of an irregular plexus of dilated thick-walled vessels in the superficial grey matter of the cerebral hemispheres or spinal cord. Cerebral lesions may be associated with epilepsy (p. 775), or may rupture to result in a subarachnoid or intracerebral haemorrhage. Cavernous angioma and capillary telangiectasis may also be associated with epilepsy, but are often clinically unapparent.

CNS INFECTIONS

Bacterial infections

▸ Follow direct spread of infection from the skull, or haematogenous spread
▸ Leptomeningitis is the commonest form of bacterial infection in the CNS; it occurs most frequently in children and the elderly
▸ CSF in bacterial meningitis contains many neutrophil polymorphs and bacteria; the fluid has high protein and low glucose concentrations
▸ Complications of bacterial meningitis include hydrocephalus, cerebral thrombophlebitis and cerebral abscess
▸ Cerebral abscesses are encapsulated foci of suppuration which act as space-occupying lesions
▸ Tuberculous infections occur as subacute meningitis or, rarely, as intracerebral tuberculomas

The CNS is normally sterile but, once bacteria gain access to it, spread of infection can occur rapidly, resulting in widespread meningitis. Bacteria gain access to the CNS by three main routes:

- *direct spread* from an adjacent focus of infection, such as the paranasal sinuses or middle ear; infections may also be established by direct spread from outside the body, for example in cases of head injury with open skull fractures
- *blood-borne spread,* which can occur as a consequence of septicaemia or as septic emboli from established infections elsewhere, for example bacterial endocarditis and bronchiectasis
- *iatrogenic infection,* following introduction of organisms into the CSF at lumbar puncture; a low-grade meningitis may occur in up to 20% of patients with a ventriculo-peritoneal shunt, usually due to *Staphylococcus epidermidis,* a skin commensal organism.

Table 26.5 Intracranial haemorrhage in neonates		
Site	Pathogenesis	Complication
Falx cerebri **Tentorium cerebelli** **Subdural space**	Rupture of veins (birth trauma)	Acute subdural haematoma Cystic hygroma
Subarachnoid space	Capillary or arterial rupture	Hydrocephalus
Subependymal germinal matrix	Prematurity, hypoxia (hyaline membrane disease)	Intraventricular haemorrhage
	Venous congestion	Venous infarction in white matter (periventricular leukomalacia)
	Arterial spasm	Hydrocephalus

Bacterial meningitis

The clinical term 'meningitis' usually refers to inflammation in the subarachnoid space involving the arachnoid and pia mater, i.e. *leptomeningitis*. However, inflammation of the meninges may involve predominantly the dura mater (*pachymeningitis*).

Pachymeningitis

Pachymeningitis is usually a consequence of direct spread of infection from the bones of the skull following otitis media or mastoiditis, and is a well-recognised complication of skull fracture. Common bacterial pathogens include Gram-negative bacilli from the middle ear, alpha or beta haemolytic streptococci from paranasal sinuses, or mixed organisms, often with *Staphylococcus aureus,* from skull fractures. An epidural or subdural abscess may then occur.

Epidural abscess. This is the result of suppuration between the dura mater and the skull or vertebral column. Epidural abscesses can act as space-occupying lesions, and usually require surgical drainage and antibiotic therapy before healing by fibrosis can occur.

Subdural abscess. In contrast to the above, a subdural abscess is seldom a localised lesion, as pus can readily spread in the subdural space over the cerebral hemispheres to form a subdural empyema. Involvement of subdural vessels may result in cerebral cortical thrombophlebitis and arteritis with infarction. Spontaneous resolution is rare, and surgical drainage and antibiotic therapy are usually required before healing can occur.

Leptomeningitis

Leptomeningitis ('meningitis') is frequently a result of blood-borne spread of infection, particularly in children, but many cases arise from direct spread of infection from the skull bones. The most important organisms are:

- in neonates: *Escherichia coli, Streptococcus agalactiae, Listeria monocytogenes*
- 2–18 years: *Neisseria meningitidis* type B
- over 30 years: *Streptococcus pneumoniae* type 3.

Tuberculosis and syphilis are considered separately on pages 766–767.

Following successful vaccination programmes, bacterial meningitis due to *Haemophilus influenzae* is now rare. Vaccines are now also available for subgroups A and C of *Neisseria meningitidis,* and for *Streptococcus pneumoniae.* Meningococcal meningitis is the commonest variety of bacterial meningitis; it is now ususally due to the subgroup B meningococcus, which can occur as sporadic cases or as an epidemic outbreak in small communities. The organism is spread in droplets from asymptomatic nasal carriers; the carriage rate in small communities may reach over 25%. The organism reaches the CNS by haematogenous spread, and the onset of the symptoms of meningitis may follow a short history of upper respiratory tract infection. A petechial rash may herald the onset of disseminated intravascular coagulation accompanied by adrenal haemorrhage (Waterhouse–Friderichsen syndrome), which is often fatal. Vigorous antibiotic therapy is essential: incomplete or inappropriate therapy can be fatal or may result in a chronic meningitis with marked meningeal thickening.

Diagnosis and complications of bacterial meningitis

Examination of the CSF by lumbar puncture is essential in each case; the main CSF changes in the CNS infections are listed in Table 26.6. The CSF in bacterial meningitis usually contains many organisms, although these are sometimes detected only on culture. In fatal cases, pus is present in the cerebral sulci and around the base of the brain, extending down around the spinal cord (Fig. 26.13).

The meningeal and superficial cortical blood vessels are congested, often with small foci of perivascular haemorrhage. The CSF is usually turbid, even in the ventricles, which often show signs of acute inflammation with fibrin deposition. Common complications of bacterial meningitis are:

- cerebral infarction
- obstructive hydrocephalus
- cerebral abscess
- subdural empyema
- epilepsy.

Cerebral abscess

A cerebral abscess usually develops from an acute suppurative encephalitis following:

- *direct spread* of infection, usually Gram-negative bacilli, from the paranasal sinuses or middle ear
- *septic sinus thrombosis,* due to spread of infection from the mastoid cavities or middle ear via the sigmoid sinus

Table 26.6	CSF parameters in health and infection				
	Cells		Protein (g/l)	Glucose (mmol/l)	Appearance
Normal	0–4 lymphocytes/mm³		0.15–0.40	2.7–4.0	Clear and colourless
Bacterial meningitis	↑↑ polymorphs		↑	↓ or absent	Opaque and turbid
Tuberculous meningitis	↑ polymorphs initially, then lymphocytes		↑	↓ or absent	Clear or opalescent
Viral meningitis	↑ polymorphs initially, then ↑↑ lymphocytes		↑	Normal	Clear and colourless
Viral encephalitis	↑ polymorphs initially, then lymphocytes		↑	Normal	Clear and colourless

• *haematogenous spread,* for example in patients with infective endocarditis (particularly in association with congenital heart disease) or bronchiectasis. Haematogenous abscesses are most often found in the parietal lobes, but may occur in any region of the brain, and are often multiple.

Abscess formation in the brain, as in other tissues, occurs when pus formation is accompanied by local tissue destruction (Fig. 26.14). A pyogenic membrane is formed, and the abscess develops a capsule composed of granulation tissue, and reactive astrocytes and their fibrillary processes. The adjacent brain is markedly oedematous, containing a perivascular inflammatory infiltrate of lymphocytes and plasma cells. Cerebral abscesses frequently enlarge and become multiloculate.

The clinical presentation is similar to that of acute bacterial meningitis, but focal neurological signs, epilepsy and fever are common manifestations. Abscesses act as space-occupying lesions and it is important to remember that a lumbar puncture must never be performed as an initial investigation on a patient with a suspected cerebral abscess (or other space-occupying lesion) as this may precipitate a fatal intracranial herniation. Antibiotic therapy is useful in the treatment of abscesses at an early stage, but once a capsule has formed surgical aspiration or excision is usually necessary. Complications of cerebral abscesses include:

• meningitis
• intracranial herniation
• focal neurological deficit
• epilepsy.

Tuberculosis

Tuberculous infection of the CNS is always secondary to infection elsewhere in the body; the lungs are the commonest site. CNS involvement takes two main forms: tuberculous meningitis and tuberculomas.

Tuberculous meningitis

Tuberculous meningitis is usually the result of haematogenous spread from a primary or secondary complex in the lungs. Rarely, it can result from direct spread of infection from a spinal vertebral body to the meninges. The resulting meningitis is characterised by a thick gelatinous exudate which is most marked around the basal cisterns and within cerebral sulci. The exudate often contains grey tubercles adjacent to blood vessels. The findings in the CSF are listed in Table 26.6. On microscopy, the tubercles are seen to consist of granulomas with central caseation in which giant cells may be scanty or absent.

Patients usually present with signs and symptoms of a subacute meningitis, occasionally accompanied by isolated cranial nerve palsies. However, sometimes the clinical features are entirely non-specific and the diagnosis is made only following a

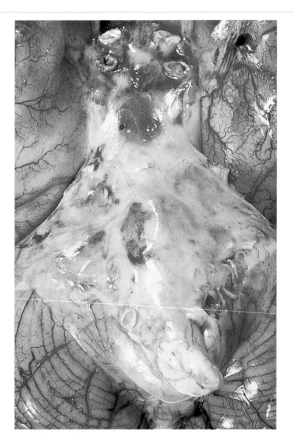

Fig. 26.13   Bacterial meningitis: basal exudate. In this example of pyogenic meningitis due to *Escherichia coli,* a dense acute inflammatory exudate is present around the brainstem, cerebellum and adjacent structures at the base of the brain. Obstruction of the fourth ventricle exit foramina resulted in acute hydrocephalus in this case.

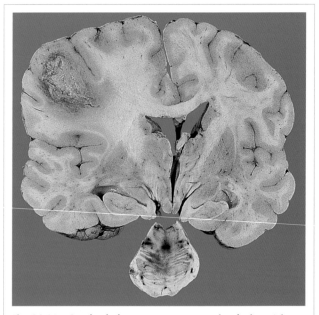

Fig. 26.14   Cerebral abscess: space-occupying lesion. A large abscess in the left parietal lobe is surrounded by oedematous white matter. This has acted as an expanding lesion and displaced the midline structures to the right. Death in this case resulted from a transtentorial brainstem herniation, with a characteristic haemorrhage in the central pons.

lumbar puncture. This disorder is frequently fatal and requires intensive antituberculous chemotherapy.

Tuberculomas

Tuberculomas are uncommon in the UK, but are still encountered in patients originating from some other countries (particularly in Asia). These lesions consist of focal areas of granulomatous inflammation with caseation, and are surrounded by a dense, fibrous capsule. Tuberculomas occur most frequently in the cerebellum and present with signs and symptoms of raised intracranial pressure; features of meningitis are rarely present. As with pyogenic cerebral abscesses, surgical excision may be required.

Syphilis

Syphilis is now rare; it occurs most frequently in male homosexuals. After the initial infection, *Treponema pallidum* gains access to the CNS by haematogenous spread. CNS involvement includes:

- clinically silent *meningitis* during primary and secondary stages
- meningeal thickening in the tertiary stage, causing *cranial nerve palsies*
- *gummas,* causing cerebral or spinal compression
- *tabes dorsalis* due to degeneration of dorsal spinal columns.

Viral infections

> ▶ Infections spread to the CNS by the haematogenous route or by retrograde neural transport
> ▶ Viral meningitis is a common, self-limiting illness with characteristic CSF changes
> ▶ Encephalitis is less frequent, but may result in death or severe disability
> ▶ Reactivation of a latent viral infection (e.g. herpes zoster) may damage the CNS
> ▶ CNS involvement in HIV infection is common and often accompanied by other viral, bacterial or parasitic infections
> ▶ 'Slow' virus infections are responsible for subacute spongiform encephalopathy, a rare cause of dementia
> ▶ Acute disseminated encephalomyelitis, a demyelinating disorder, may result from a virus-induced immune reaction

CNS infection by viruses can occur by the following mechanisms:

- *haematogenous spread* as part of a systemic infection with viraemia, usually causing meningitis or encephalitis
- *neural spread* along peripheral sensory nerves by retrograde axonal transport.

Certain viruses exhibit neurotropism—a tendency to spread specifically to the CNS from the initial site of infection, for example poliovirus from the gut. Viruses can cause neurological dysfunction either as a result of viral multiplication within cells of the CNS, or as a result of an immunological response to a viral infection (acute disseminated encephalomyelitis; see below). The former mechanism is much more common.

Viral meningitis

Although acute in onset, viral meningitis is usually clinically less severe than bacterial meningitis. In most instances, the viruses reach the CNS by haematogenous spread. Common organisms are:

- echovirus 7, 11, 24, 33
- coxsackie B1–5
- coxsackie A9
- mumps virus
- other enteroviruses.

Characteristic changes are present in the CSF (Table 26.6) and serology or PCR techniques are often used to confirm the diagnosis.

Viral meningitis is characterised by infiltration of the leptomeninges by mononuclear cells (lymphocytes, plasma cells and macrophages), along with perivascular lymphocytic cuffing of blood vessels in the meninges and superficial cortex.

Viral encephalitis

Infection of the brain is a well-recognised complication of several common viral illnesses. Most cases are mild, self-limiting conditions, but others, such as rabies and herpes simplex type I infections, result in extensive tissue destruction and are often fatal. Herpes simplex encephalitis is the commonest variety of acute viral encephalitis in the UK. Despite these differences in severity, all viral infections of the brain and spinal cord produce similar pathological changes in the CNS:

- *mononuclear cell infiltration* by lymphocytes, plasma cells and macrophages; this is often noticeable as perivascular cuffing which usually extends into the parenchyma (Fig. 26.15)
- *cell lysis* (cytolytic viral infection) and phagocytosis of cell debris by macrophages; when neurones are involved, for example as in poliovirus infection, this process is known as neuronophagia
- *viral inclusions*, which can often be detected in infected neurones or glial cells; occasionally, these can be of diagnostic value, for example 'owl-eye' inclusions in cytomegalovirus infection, or Negri bodies in rabies
- *reactive hypertrophy* and hyperplasia of astrocytes and microglial cells, often forming cell clusters
- *oedema*, which is of vasogenic type.

Latent viral infections

Herpes zoster

Herpes zoster results from reactivation of latent varicella zoster virus within sensory ganglia in the CNS, the infection having been established following chickenpox in childhood. Reactivation (resulting in shingles) usually occurs during periods of intercurrent illness or immunosuppression, particularly in the elderly. Acute inflammation of the sensory ganglion (usually a thoracic dorsal root ganglion or the trigeminal ganglion) is accompanied by pain and hyperalgesia along the nerve distribution, followed by erythema and vesicle formation.

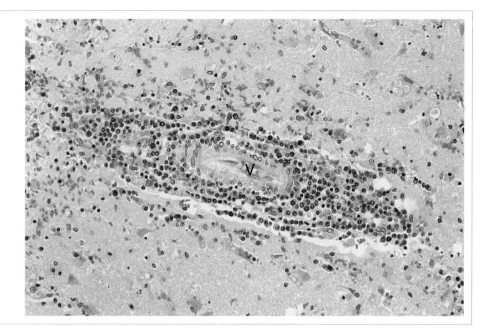

Fig. 26.15 Acute viral encephalitis due to herpes simplex virus. A blood vessel (V) in the grey matter is surrounded by a dense aggregate of lymphocytes and plasma cells, which have crossed the blood–brain barrier and migrated into the surrounding temporal lobe.

Involvement of the ophthalmic division of the trigeminal nerve may result in blindness as a consequence of corneal ulceration and scarring.

Progressive multifocal leukoencephalopathy

Progressive multifocal leukoencephalopathy results from CNS infection by the JC papovavirus. Most cases occur in immunosuppressed patients. The virus produces a cytolytic infection of oligodendrocytes, resulting in demyelination in the white matter. The disease is uniformly fatal.

Antenatal viral infections

The commonest viruses to infect the CNS in utero are cytomegalovirus and rubella virus; the latter is becoming less common following immunisation in schoolgirls. Both viruses cause a necrotising encephalomyelitis resulting in developmental malformations and microcephaly, particularly when infection has occurred during the first trimester of pregnancy.

Persistent viral infections

Persistent viral infections are extremely rare diseases in which infection of the CNS occurs in early life, with neurological disease occurring years later.

Subacute sclerosing panencephalitis

This uncommon disease usually affects children aged 7–10 years and is characterised by a progressive neurological deficit with dementia, myoclonus and focal signs leading to death. Subacute sclerosing panencephalitis is caused by the measles virus, which is usually acquired before the age of 1 year. Large numbers of measles viral inclusion bodies are present within neurones, and high titres of measles antibody can be detected in the CSF. The pathogenesis of this prolonged disorder is not fully understood.

Human immunodeficiency virus (HIV) infection

The CNS is commonly involved in HIV infection both in the acquired immune deficiency syndrome (AIDS) and in pre-AIDS stages. The mechanisms by which HIV gains access to the CNS are uncertain; many research workers believe that the virus is carried across the blood–brain barrier in monocytes or macrophages (the 'Trojan horse' theory). Once in the CNS, the virus appears to reside predominantly in microglial cells and multinucleate cells of the macrophage/microglial type (Fig. 26.16). Evidence for direct infection of nerve cells and other glia is not fully established and awaits further research.

Patients with HIV infection frequently present with neurological abnormalities and at the time of death at least 80% of AIDS patients have CNS pathology resulting from:

- cerebral HIV infection (causing progressive dementia)
- multiple opportunistic infections (e.g. *Toxoplasma*, fungi)
- other viral infections (e.g. cytomegalovirus, papovavirus)
- primary cerebral lymphoma (p. 785).

Other organisms important in infecting immunosuppressed patients are listed on page 770. Dementia may occur in the absence of overt immunodeficiency (i.e. AIDS); diagnosis can then be made by serology on the blood, or by PCR analysis of CSF.

Prion diseases

Prion diseases are a group of rare transmissible neurodegenerative disorders also known as *spongiform encephalopathies*. One of these disorders, kuru, was at one time restricted geographically to a small number of islands in the East Indies and appeared to result from ritualistic endocannibalism; eating the brain of an infected individual resulted in the onset of the disease many years later. The disease is now virtually extinct.

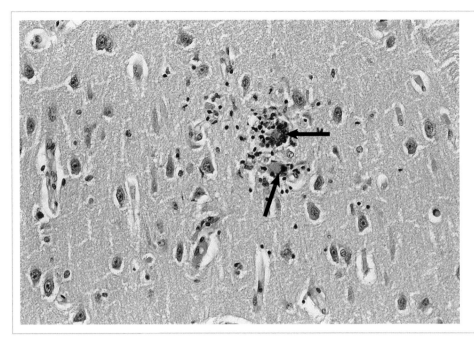

Fig. 26.16 Giant cell encephalitis in AIDS. The giant cells (arrows) in the cerebral cortex are derived from macrophages which are infected with HIV and express viral proteins on the cell surface.

Creutzfeldt–Jakob disease

Creutzfeldt–Jakob disease (CJD) usually presents in adult life as a rapidly progressive dementia often accompanied by myoclonus, visual abnormalities and ataxia. It occurs as a sporadic disorder in 1–2 in 1 000 000 per year worldwide; familial and iatrogenic (see below) forms occur more rarely. No specific treatment is available and the disease is uniformly fatal.

In 1968, the disease was found to be transmissible to primates, and further studies have found the infectious agent to be of very small size and highly resistant to heat, ultraviolet light and most chemicals. Its precise nature is as yet unknown. Increasing evidence supports the prion hypothesis, which states that the agent is composed entirely of a modified host protein, *prion protein,* which accumulates in the brain. Cases of iatrogenic human–human transmission of CJD have been recorded, attributed to implantation of intracerebral electrodes, corneal or dura mater grafts and, most recently, the administration of growth hormone extracted from human pituitary glands. These are, however, rare occurrences and the source of infection in most cases is unknown.

The brain from affected individuals often shows widespread cerebral cortical atrophy. Microscopy of the cortex shows a loss of neurones and a reactive proliferation of astrocytes. Numerous small vacuoles are present within neuronal and astrocytic processes, hence the term spongiform encephalopathy (Fig. 26.17). No inflammatory reaction occurs in this group of disorders.

Variant Creutzfeldt–Jakob disease. A new variant form of CJD was identified in the UK in 1996, affecting young patients (average age 28 years). This new disease appears to result from the transmission of the bovine spongiform encephalopathy ('mad cow' disease) agent to humans, probably via contaminated beef products. Over 160 cases of variant CJD have been identified in the UK so far, including three cases that were transmitted by blood transfusion from infected donors, but the likely number of future cases is uncertain.

Acute disseminated encephalomyelitis

Acute disseminated encephalomyelitis is an infrequent complication of measles, mumps and rubella infections, and may also occur following vaccination for smallpox and rabies. The onset of the disease is sudden, usually occurring 5–14 days after the initial infection or inoculation. This appears to be a T-cell-mediated delayed hypersensitivity response to a protein component of myelin, but the mechanism of sensitisation is unknown. The prognosis is good, with a complete recovery in 90% of cases.

Acute haemorrhagic leukoencephalitis is a related but more severe disorder which is accompanied by immune complex deposition in cerebral vessel walls and is usually rapidly fatal.

Fungal infections

Fungal infections of the nervous system are relatively uncommon; most occur as a consequence of haematogenous spread from the lungs, but direct spread of infection from the nose and paranasal sinuses also occurs. In the UK, most fungal infections of the CNS occur in immunosuppressed patients, but some organisms, for example *Cryptococcus neoformans,* are capable of producing disease in humans in the absence of any predisposing illness. Cryptococcal infection usually presents as a subacute meningitis in which the inflammatory reaction is often remarkably mild.

Opportunistic fungal infections with *Candida albicans* and *Aspergillus fumigatus* are usually accompanied by pulmonary infection. Both organisms may cause meningitis with haemorrhage due to vascular invasion, and characteristically produce multiple cerebral abscesses.

Mucormycosis is a rare fungal infection that particularly affects uncontrolled diabetics, producing a granulomatous mass in the paranasal sinuses that extends to involve directly the skull

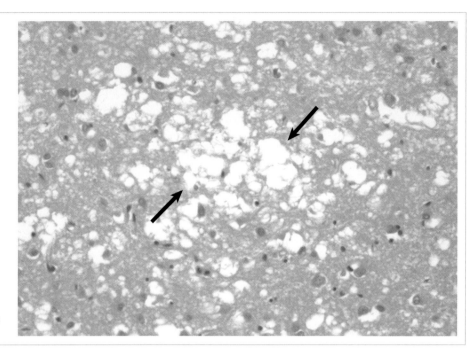

Fig. 26.17   Creutzfeldt–Jakob disease. The cerebral cortex shows a characteristic spongiform vacuolation (arrows) accompanied by neuronal loss and reactive astrocytosis.

and frontal lobes. Vascular involvement is also common with this organism, resulting in cerebral infarction.

Parasitic infections

Parasitic infections of the CNS are uncommon except in countries in which human parasites are endemic. The most frequently encountered organisms are:

- *Toxoplasma gondii*, which may be congenital
- *Plasmodium falciparum*, causing one form of malaria
- *Trypanosoma rhodesiense*, causing chronic meningoencephalitis
- *Entamoeba histolytica*, causing solitary amoebic abscess
- *Taenia solium*, causing cerebral cysticercosis
- *Echinococcus granulosus*, causing solitary hydatid cyst
- *Toxocara canis*, causing eosinophilic meningitis, with granulomas around larvae.

Infections in immunosuppressed patients

CNS infections are common in immunosuppressed patients, whatever the nature of the underlying disease. The main varieties are:

- atypical mycobacteria
- cytomegalovirus
- papovaviruses
- *Candida albicans*
- *Aspergillus fumigatus*
- *Cryptococcus neoformans*
- *Toxoplasma gondii*
- *Entamoeba histolytica*.

Many of these infections prove fatal, and a diagnosis is often difficult to establish prior to death. Multiple infections are not uncommon, particularly in the acquired immune deficiency syndrome (AIDS).

DEMYELINATING CONDITIONS

▶ Can be due to viral, chemical or immunological mechanisms
▶ Axons are preserved while myelin disintegrates
▶ Myelin fragments are phagocytosed by macrophages and esterified into neutral lipids
▶ Commonest demyelinating condition is multiple sclerosis, in which the mechanism of demyelination is unknown
▶ Remyelination does not occur to any significant extent

In the CNS, most axons and dendrites are ensheathed in myelin, which is formed from complex folds of oligodendrocyte cell membranes. CNS myelin differs slightly in structure and composition from peripheral myelin, but serves essentially the same functions:

- to protect and insulate neuronal processes
- to allow the rapid transmission of electrical impulses by saltatory conduction.

Most of the myelin in the CNS is located in the white matter, but neuronal processes in the grey matter are also surrounded by myelin.

Primary demyelination in the CNS occurs in several conditions where the myelin sheath is destroyed but the axons remain intact. Primary axonal damage results in the breakdown of myelin around damaged axons, a process referred to as *secondary demyelination*. Whenever myelin breakdown occurs, the debris is phagocytosed by macrophages. Intact myelin is rich in cholesterol and phospholipids, but following phagocytosis it is transformed into droplets of neutral lipids (mainly cholesterol esters).

Multiple sclerosis

Multiple sclerosis is the leading non-traumatic cause of neurological disability in young adults in the Europe and the USA. It is most prevalent in populations living at latitudes remote from the equator; the prevalence is particularly high in northern Europe, but is low in the tropics (Table 26.7). Individuals who migrate from a high-prevalence to a low-prevalence area after the age of 15 years remain at high risk; the disease risk is lower following migration at an earlier age. Studies of twins have shown a higher incidence of concordance in monozygous than in dizygous twins. Recent genetic studies have found an association between multiple sclerosis and the interleukin-2 and -7 receptor alpha genes, and the human leukocyte antigen (HLA) genetic locus.

Multiple sclerosis appears to be an autoimmune disorder, triggered by an environmental factor (e.g. a virus) in a genetically susceptible host. The therapeutic use of corticosteroids and cytokines, such as beta-interferon, which modulate the immune response, has reduced the frequency of disease relapse and progression in some patients.

Clinical features

Most cases present between 20 and 40 years of age. The disease is slightly more common in females than in males, and the onset is usually characterised by the sudden development of a focal neurological deficit which spontaneously recovers. The relative incidences of initial manifestations are:

- limb weakness: 40%
- paraesthesiae: 20%
- visual abnormalities: 20%
- diplopia: 10%
- bladder dysfunction: 5%
- vertigo: 5%.

The disease follows a characteristic relapsing and remitting course. Recovery from each episode of demyelination (relapse) is usually incomplete, and a progressive clinical deterioration ensues. The effects of demyelination may be detected electrophysiologically as delays in the latencies of visual and auditory evoked responses because demyelinated axons conduct nerve impulses more slowly than normal. CSF analysis in multiple sclerosis shows oligoclonal bands of IgG, which is synthesised by plasma cells in the CNS. The progress of the disease is variable. Some patients (particularly children) follow a rapidly progressive course, while others may survive for over 20 years with only minor disability. Most patients die as a result of urinary tract infections, chest infections or pressure sores rather than during an acute episode of demyelination.

Morphological features

The primary abnormalities in multiple sclerosis are confined to the CNS; the peripheral nervous system is not involved. Patients with multiple sclerosis have numerous demyelinated plaques in the brain and spinal cord (Fig. 26.18), often closely related to veins and venules. In early lesions, the plaques are soft and pink with ill-defined boundaries. Histologically, there is myelin breakdown and phagocytosis by macrophages. Oedema is usually present, suggesting a local defect in the blood–brain barrier. Perivascular cuffing with inflammatory cells (plasma cells and T-lymphocytes) is widespread in the acute plaque. The plasma cells synthesise immunoglobulins, which can be detected in the CSF (see above). T-lymphocytes have also been identified at the edges of acute plaques.

Table 26.7 Geographical variance in the prevalence of multiple sclerosis	
Area	Crude prevalence per 100 000 population
North-east Scotland	144
Northumberland, England	50
North Italy	20
Israel	13
Mexico	1.5

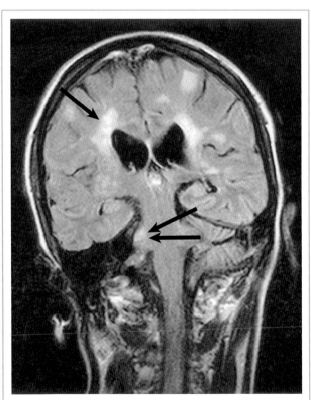

Fig. 26.18 Multiple sclerosis: demonstration of demyelination in vivo. Coronal MRI image showing the typical appearances of multiple sclerosis plaques, particularly in a periventricular location (single arrow) and in the right middle cerebellar peduncle (double arrow). (Courtesy of Dr D Summers, Edinburgh.)

As myelin breakdown eventually subsides, a reactive gliosis is established, giving rise to a chronic plaque. These lesions consist of sharply defined, grey, lucent areas of demyelination in which oligodendrocytes are scarce or absent. The inflammatory infiltrate also subsides, sometimes leaving small numbers of perivascular lymphocytes at the edge of chronic plaques (Fig. 26.19). Although it appears that oligodendrocytes have the capacity to proliferate in plaques, successful remyelination of established plaques probably never occurs. Axonal damage begins early in multiple sclerosis and correlates with the inflammatory activity in the white matter, contributing to progressive neurological debility.

Miscellaneous demyelinating conditions

Leukodystrophies

Although included as demyelinating conditions, it is known that most leukodystrophies result from a failure to synthesise normal myelin (sometimes called 'dysmyelination'). Two of these disorders—*metachromatic leukodystrophy and Krabbe's globoid cell leukodystrophy*—are due to inherited lysosomal enzyme deficiencies, and can be diagnosed antenatally. Others, such as adrenoleukodystrophy, are the result of an inherited abnormality in lipid metabolism, while in others the cause is unknown.

Metabolic disorders

In central pontine myelinolysis, which occurs most frequently in alcoholism and malnutrition, myelin breakdown occurs in the central brainstem and cerebrum. Its pathogenesis is unknown, but some cases appear to result from the rapid alterations in serum sodium levels.

Viruses

Viruses can cause demyelination, as in progressive multifocal leukoencephalopathy (p. 768), which produces a cytolytic infection of oligodendrocytes.

Immunological reactions

Immunological reactions may result in demyelination, as in acute disseminated encephalomyelitis (p. 769).

METABOLIC DISORDERS

▶ Hypoglycaemia (in diabetes mellitus) is one of the commonest metanbolic disorders affecting the CNS
▶ May be caused by toxins, deficiency states and metabolic disease
▶ Some toxins produce CNS damage directly; others produce liver damage causing secondary CNS changes
▶ Many of the metabolic CNS diseases are inherited, and can be diagnosed antenatally

Hypoglycaemia

The brain is critically dependent on a continuous supply of oxygen and glucose; hypoglycaemia (most often occurring in patients with diabetes mellitus) can result in irreversible neuronal damage and neuronal cell death unless relieved rapidly. Affected patients usually lapse into a coma, and may never recover full neurological function.

CNS toxins

The CNS can be affected by a large number of substances that act as toxins.

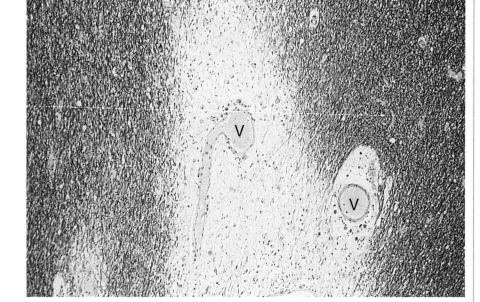

Fig. 26.19   Multiple sclerosis: chronic plaque. The chronic plaque consists of a sharply defined area of myelin loss (which appears pale in this preparation) containing fibrillary astrocytes. A few lymphocytes and macrophages are present around blood vessels (V) in the plaque. Normal myelinated white matter appears blue.

Methanol and ethanol

Both methanol and ethanol are toxic to the CNS. Acute poisoning with methanol can result in sudden death with multiple haemorrhagic lesions in the cerebral hemispheres, while chronic ingestion results in degeneration of neurones, e.g. in the retina, where loss of ganglion cells is accompanied by optic nerve atrophy. Ethanol can cause a wide range of CNS disorders (Table 26.8).

Drugs

Drugs affecting the CNS can be considered in two main groups:

- drugs affecting CNS development
- drugs affecting the mature CNS.

Drugs affecting CNS development include phenytoin and trimethadione, which can cause microcephaly and other congenital abnormalities following maternal ingestion. Drugs affecting the mature CNS include vincristine, which may cause axonal neuropathy.

Metals and industrial chemicals

Metals and industrial chemicals capable of affecting the CNS are listed in Table 26.9.

Deficiency states

In the developed countries of the world, the commonest deficiency states affecting the CNS are those involving vitamins, e.g. in chronic alcoholism. Elsewhere, the lack of an adequate food supply is responsible for a range of abnormalities that are still poorly understood in terms of their effects on the developing and mature CNS.

Malnutrition

Severe malnutrition may result in irreversible brain damage, particularly if it occurs in infancy during periods of CNS myelination, as the lack of normal myelin development cannot be reversed at a later date. Malnutrition later in life, e.g. kwashiorkor (Ch. 7), may result in encephalopathy and ultimately lead to coma. The underlying mechanisms in these

Table 26.8 Consequences of excessive ethanol intake on the CNS

Disease	Features	Mechanism
Fetal alcohol syndrome (maternal alcoholism)	Cerebral malformations Facial and somatic malformations Growth retardation	Direct toxicity
Acute intoxication	Cerebral oedema Petechial haemorrhages	Direct toxicity
Cerebral and cerebellar atrophy	Neuronal loss	Direct toxicity
Nutritional disorders	Wernicke's encephalopathy	Deficiency of vitamin B_1
Hepatocerebral syndromes	Hepatic encephalopathy Chronic hepatocerebral degeneration	Hepatic toxicity with secondary effects on CNS
Demyelinating disorders	Central pontine myelinolysis	Electrolyte disturbances

Table 26.9 Metal and industrial chemical toxins affecting the CNS

Metal/Chemical	Source	Clinical manifestations of toxicity
Aluminium	Dialysis water from mains	Progressive encephalopathy in patients undergoing renal dialysis
Manganese	Mines	Degeneration of basal ganglia
Lead (inorganic)	Paint and petrol fumes	Encephalopathy in children; peripheral neuropathy
Mercury • Inorganic • Organic	 Industrial pollution Fungicides	 Progressive dementia Peripheral neuropathy, cerebellar and optic nerve degeneration (Minimata disease)
Acrylamide monomer	Construction industry	Encephalopathy and peripheral neuropathy with axonal degeneration
Hexacarbon compounds	Solvents	'Giant axonal neuropathy' affecting the CNS and peripheral nerves
Organophosphates	Insecticides	Anticholinesterase activity and distal axonopathy in CNS and peripheral nerves

Table 26.10 Major vitamin deficiency states affecting the nervous system	
Vitamin	**Deficiency state**
A	Benign intracranial hypertension (rare)
B_1	Wernicke–Korsakoff syndrome
B_2	Peripheral neuropathy, ataxia, dementia
B_6	Convulsions in infants
B_{12}	Weakness and paraesthesiae in the lower limbs
C	Scurvy
E	Weakness, sensory loss, ataxia, nystagmus

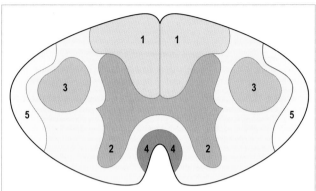

Fig. 26.20 Sites of degenerations in the spinal cord.
1. Dorsal columns, involved in subacute combined degeneration, Friedreich's ataxia and tabes dorsalis. **2. Anterior horn cells,** involved in motor neurone disease and spinomuscular atrophy.
3. Lateral corticospinal tracts, involved in motor neurone disease, subacute combined degeneration and Friedreich's ataxia.
4. Ventral corticospinal tracts, involved in motor neurone disease. **5. Spinocerebellar tracts,** involved in Friedreich's ataxia.

events are uncertain, but may result from severe electrolyte disturbances.

Vitamin deficiency

The major vitamin deficiency states (Ch. 7) affecting the nervous system are shown in Table 26.10. The most important of these are discussed below.

Vitamin B_1 (thiamine)
Vitamin B_1 deficiency is particularly common in chronic alcoholics and in patients with longstanding diseases of the upper gastrointestinal tract. Deficiency results in Wernicke's encephalopathy, which presents clinically with memory impairment, ataxia, visual disturbances and peripheral neuropathy. This disorder is often accompanied by Korsakoff's psychosis, in which case the term *Wernicke–Korsakoff syndrome* is used. Wernicke's encephalopathy is characterised by perivascular haemorrhages in the region of the fourth ventricle and aqueduct, particularly in the mammillary bodies. Fibrillary gliosis occurs in longstanding cases, when the affected structures appear shrunken. The pathogenesis of the lesions is uncertain.

Vitamin B_{12} (cyanocobalamin) deficiency
Vitamin B_{12} deficiency is an important condition that can result from a variety of disorders. The pathogenesis of the CNS damage is unknown; impairment of CNS amino acid and fatty acid metabolism has been implicated. In severe cases, there is extensive degeneration of the posterior columns and lateral corticospinal tracts in the spinal cord (Fig. 26.20); this process is referred to as *subacute combined degeneration of the spinal cord*. The cerebral hemispheres are involved to a lesser extent. If replacement therapy is commenced at an early stage, the degenerative process is reversible. Longstanding cases show irreversible axonal damage accompanied by a reactive fibrillary gliosis.

Lysosomal storage diseases

Lysosomal storage diseases are uncommon inherited disorders characterised by a deficiency of various lysosomal enzymes that results in the accumulation of stored material in cells (Ch. 7). The CNS is involved in many lysosomal storage disorders (Table 26.11).

Table 26.11 Examples of lysosomal storage diseases affecting the CNS		
Disease	**Example**	**Enzyme deficiency**
Sphingolipidosis	Tay–Sachs disease	Hexosaminidase A
	Niemann–Pick disease	Sphingomyelinase
	Metachromatic leukodystrophy	Arylsulphatase A
Mucopolysaccharidosis	Hurler's disease	Alpha-L-iduronidase
Glycogenosis	Pompe's disease	Acid maltase
Ceroid lipofuscinosis	Batten's disease	Lysosomal peptidases and esterases

Hepatic encephalopathy

Hepatic encephalopathy may occur in patients with liver damage, due to a variety of agents. Encephalopathy in severe cases may progress to coma and result in permanent CNS damage in survivors. Increased levels of ammonia in the blood are associated with encephalopathy, possibly interfering with the function of certain neurotransmitters, such as gamma aminobutyric acid. The commonest cause of hepatic encephalopathy is alcoholic liver disease.

Wilson's disease

Wilson's disease, a disorder of copper metabolism, is inherited as an autosomal recessive condition. In some patients, liver disease is severe (Ch. 16) and may result in hepatic encephalopathy. In others, neurological signs predominate with tremor, rigidity and chorea; these abnormalities result from a marked loss of neurones in the basal ganglia, particularly the putamen. Deposition of copper in the cornea results in the characteristic Kayser–Fleischer ring.

EPILEPSY

Epilepsy occurs where an individual suffers repeated seizures due to paroxysmal neurological dysfunction caused by abnormal discharges from neurones in the brain. Epilepsy is one of the commonest serious neurological conditions, with around 350 000 affected patients in the UK. Epilepsy can be classified according to the type of seizure, each of which is associated with different forms of brain pathology:

1. *Generalised epilepsy*—synchronous abnormal neuronal discharges due to generalised hyperexcitability of membranes, often for an unknown reason. This usually starts in childhood and is not associated with a structural abnormality in the brain. The prognosis is relatively good with adequate drug control.
2. *Focal epilepsy*—discharges originate from a specific cortical region, for example temporal lobe epilepsy, and can either remain localised or spread to other regions. This can start at any age and is associated with structural abnormalities in the brain, e.g. developmental abnormalities of the cerebral cortex (p. 776), contusions following head injury (p. 756) or stroke (p. 761). Focal epilepsy is a common presenting feature in patients with undiagnosed brain tumours (p. 782). Seizure control and mortality is significantly higher than for generalised epilepsy.
3. *Provoked seizures*—discharges occur due to acute damage to the brain that affects neuronal membrane stability, for example acute head injury, metabolic abnormalities (e. g. hypoglycaemia) or alcohol. The outcome is dependent on the severity of the causative condition.

CONGENITAL ABNORMALITIES

▶ Affect the CNS in 3–4 per 100 000 live births
▶ Neural tube defects and posterior fossa malformations are the most common
▶ Aetiology in most cases is unknown: genetic abnormalities and maternal infections account for many cases

Malformations of the CNS occur in 3–4 per 100 000 live births. The severe varieties cause considerable morbidity and mortality, but many of these abnormalities are of little clinical significance and may be detected only in later life as an incidental finding. Some of the known causes of CNS malformations in humans are:

- genetic factors, such as in tuberous sclerosis (autosomal dominant), aqueduct stenosis (X-linked recessive) and Down's syndrome (trisomy 21)
- maternal infections, such as rubella and cytomegalovirus
- irradiation in utero
- toxic, as in fetal alcohol syndrome

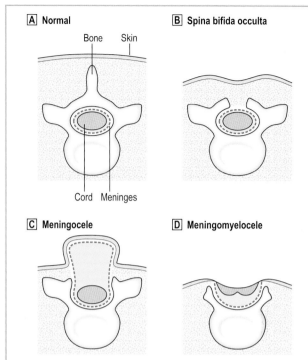

Fig. 26.21 Neural tube defects: spinal involvement.
A Normal arrangement. B Spina bifida occulta: vertebral defect with a normal cord and meninges. The overlying skin is intact. **C Meningocele:** the meningeal sac is usually covered by intact skin, but rupture of the sac may occur following birth. **D Meningomyelocele:** the skin overlying the sac frequently ruptures, exposing the abnormal meninges and spinal cord.

- dietary factors: folic acid deficiency has been implicated in neural tube defects
- metabolic, such as phenylketonuria.

In many cases, the underlying causes are unknown. The most frequent malformations are the neural tube defects and posterior fossa malformations.

Neural tube defects

Neural tube defects are the commonest and most important congenital abnormalities of the CNS, occurring in 2–3 per 100 000 live births. Failure of the neural tube to close at 28 days' gestation, or damage to its structure after closure, can be detected in utero by ultrasonography. In 90% of cases, the level of alpha-fetoprotein in the maternal serum and amniotic fluid is increased; this investigation is often used as a screening procedure.

Both cranial and spinal involvement may occur; the term *spina bifida* is often used for the latter, when the CNS malformation is usually accompanied by *rachischisis*—failure of the vertebral laminae to develop. The major types of spinal involvement are illustrated in Figure 26.21.

Neural tube defects occur most frequently in the lumbosacral region. The more severe forms result in a considerable neurological deficit with paraplegia and absence of sphincter control. The musculature of the lower limbs undergoes neurogenic atrophy, and meningitis and urinary tract infections are common. Hydrocephalus occurs in cases with an accompanying Arnold–Chiari malformation. These factors account for the generally poor prognosis in severe cases, even after early surgical repair of the spina bifida.

Cranial involvement

Encephalocele and *cranial meningocele* usually occur in the occipital region, with herniation of the posterior cerebral hemispheres and their coverings respectively through a defect in the skull.

Anencephaly is the commonest of the neural tube defects. It is thought to occur when the developing brain is exposed to amniotic fluid as its coverings fail to develop. The calvaria is usually absent, but the base of the skull is thickened and partly covered by a mass of vascular granulation tissue. The anterior pituitary gland is present but hypoplastic, and several associated visceral and limb abnormalities have been described. The condition is fatal and often results in spontaneous abortion.

Posterior fossa malformations

Arnold–Chiari malformation

Arnold–Chiari malformation is a complex disorder involving the cerebellum, brainstem and spinal cord, and is the commonest congenital malformation in the posterior fossa. It is often associated with a meningomyelocele. The main features are illustrated in Figure 26.22.

These abnormalities result in an obstructive hydrocephalus, usually of the communicating type (p. 759). There is no entirely satisfactory explanation for the Arnold–Chiari malformation.

Dandy–Walker malformation

Dandy–Walker malformation is the second most important congenital abnormality affecting the posterior fossa. The cerebellar hemispheres are of normal size, but the vermis is absent or hypoplastic. The fourth ventricle is markedly distended and forms a cyst-like structure. This results in obstructive hydrocephalus, which may be detectable antenatally by ultrasonography. The aetiology and pathogenesis of this malformation are unknown.

Other congenital malformations

Many other congenital malformations affecting the CNS have been described. Without being comprehensive, these can be considered in the following broad groups.

Agenesis and dysgenesis

Agenesis and dysgenesis may involve almost any structure within the CNS, but the commonest sites affected are the corpus callosum and the olfactory bulbs and tracts (arhinencephaly). These lesions may occur in isolation or in association with other malformations, for example agenesis of the corpus callosum with the Dandy–Walker malformation, and

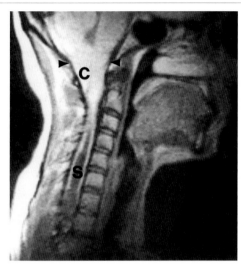

Fig. 26.22   Arnold–Chiari malformation: brain and cord abnormalities. The cerebellar tonsils (C) are displaced downwards from the shallow posterior fossa below the level of the foramen magnum (arrowheads). The brainstem is elongated and a syrinx (S) is present in the spinal cord commencing at the level of the third cervical vertebral body. (Magnetic resonance image: courtesy of Professor B S Worthington, Nottingham.)

arhinencephaly with holoprosencephaly, a complex disorder of forebrain diverticulation.

Disorders of cell migration and corticogenesis

Failure of neuronal migration during CNS development results in a number of structural disorders, of which the most important are:

- *Agyria* and *pachygyria*. These result in defective formation of the cerebral cortex with complete failure (agyria) or partial failure of gyral development.
- *Polymicrogyria*. The cortical surface bears numerous small irregular gyri, imparting a wrinkled appearance to affected areas.
- *Heterotopias*. These occur when neuronal migration is arrested, and are seen most frequently in the white matter of the CNS. They can occur as an isolated finding, but occasionally occur as part of a more complex disorder, as in Down's syndrome.

Destructive lesions

Destructive lesions occur most frequently in the developing CNS as a consequence of maternal infections and hypoxia. Extensive destruction of tissue may result in microcephaly, but focal lesions may also occur, such as *ulegyria*, with severe loss of neurones in the cerebral cortex.

Phakomatoses

Phakomatoses are a group of autosomal dominant inherited neurocutaneous disorders that result in CNS malformations. Important members of this group include neurofibromatosis, tuberous sclerosis and von Hippel–Lindau syndrome.

Chromosomal abnormalities

Chromosomal abnormalities frequently result in mental retardation. CNS malformations are often present in such cases, and are sometimes of sufficient severity to cause permanent disability or death. The best characterised of these disorders include *Down's syndrome,* the principal features of which are:

- trisomy 21
- abnormal facies and palmar creases
- mental retardation
- flattened cerebral contours
- abnormal myelination and neuronal heterotopias
- congenital heart defects
- development of Alzheimer's disease from the fourth decade.

AGE-RELATED CHANGES IN THE CNS

- ▸ Brain weight decreases slowly after the third decade and rapidly from the seventh decade
- ▸ Ageing is accompanied by cortical atrophy and loss of white matter with compensatory hydrocephalus
- ▸ The aged brain shows a variable loss of neurones with increased numbers of reactive astrocytes
- ▸ Surviving cortical neurones may exhibit a range of structural changes, e.g. neurofibrillary tangles
- ▸ Cerebrovascular disease is common, and may include amyloid angiopathy in small intracranial vessels

A wide variety of changes has been described in the CNS of normal elderly adults. The extent of these changes often relates to the age of the person, but there is considerable variation from one individual to another.

Brain weight progressively reduces from normal values of around 1450 g in males and 1300 g in females at about 40 years of age; these values decline more rapidly after the age of 60. This loss of brain substance appears to occur at an earlier age in females than in males, and is most evident in the white matter of the cerebral hemispheres. Ventricular enlargement (compensatory hydrocephalus, p. 759) is a variable finding in elderly brains and can readily be detected in life by CT scanning. On average, the volume of the ventricular system increases from 35 ml in young adults to 60 ml in those over 60 years.

Other age-related changes in the CNS include:

- progressive loss of neurones, particularly in the hippocampus and cerebral cortex
- reduction in size, numbers and dendritic branches of surviving neurones
- alterations in the quantity and distribution of neurotransmitters (e.g. acetylcholine in the cerebral cortex)
- increase in number of astrocytes
- thickening of leptomeninges
- arteriosclerosis and amyloid angiopathy.

SYSTEM DEGENERATIONS

- ▸ Characterised by progressive loss of neurones in functionally related areas of the CNS
- ▸ Neuronal death is accompanied by neuronophagia and reactive fibrillary gliosis
- ▸ Considerable overlap of clinical and pathological features, but several well-defined entities exist, e.g. Parkinson's disease and motor neurone disease
- ▸ Several disorders show characteristic neurochemical abnormalities, for which replacement therapy may be clinically beneficial, e.g. Parkinson's disease
- ▸ Aetiology in most cases unknown, although some are inherited disorders, e.g. Friedreich's ataxia

Several degenerative conditions affecting the CNS are characterised by the progressive loss of certain groups of functionally related neurones and their associated pathways. These conditions can be considered as system degenerations; these disorders may occur in isolation or as part of a multiple systems degeneration. Many of these disorders have a genetic basis and are associated with nucleotide triplet repeat expansions in the relevant genes. It is therefore important to establish a diagnosis to allow genetic counselling of an affected family. Considerable overlap of both the clinical and pathological features occurs in this group of conditions, but several well-defined examples exist (Table 26.12).

Motor neurone disease

This disorder affects 5 in 100 000 of the population, occurring most often in males over the age of 50 years; 5% of cases are familial, some of which have a mutation in the Cu/Mn superoxide dismutase gene on chromosome 21q. Three main disease patterns are recognised clinically:

- *amyotrophic lateral sclerosis,* with distal and proximal muscle weakness and wasting, spasticity and exaggerated reflexes indicative of both upper and lower motor neurone involvement
- *progressive muscular atrophy,* when predominantly lower motor neurone involvement results in weakness and wasting of distal muscles, fasciculation and absent reflexes
- *progressive bulbar palsy,* when involvement of cranial nerve motor nuclei results in weakness of the tongue, palate and pharyngeal muscles.

Most patients die 3–5 years after diagnosis due to respiratory difficulties or the complications of immobility. Examination of the CNS shows loss of motor neurones (in patterns corresponding to the clinical groups listed above) and corticospinal pathway degeneration with reactive gliosis. Occasional surviving motor neurones contain filamentous cytoplasmic inclusions of unknown aetiology; in a minority of cases these inclusions may be widespread in the cerebral cortex and are associated with dementia.

Table 26.12   Examples of central nervous system degenerations

Disease	Sites affected	Clinical features	Genetic basis
Friedreich's ataxia	Spinal cord Sensory nuclei Cerebellum	Ataxia Sensory loss Deafness Autosomal recessive inheritance	CAA triplet expansion in *frataxin* gene on 9q
Autosomal dominant cerebellar ataxia type 1	Purkinje cells Granular neurones Inferior olivary nuclei	Ataxia Nystagmus Autosomal dominant inheritance	CAG triplet expansion in *ataxin*-1 gene on 6p
Dentatorubropallidoluysial atrophy (DRPLA)	Dentate nucleus Globus pallidus Subthalamus Red nucleus	Chorea Myoclonic epilepsy Dementia Autosomal dominant inheritance	CAG triplet expansion in gene on 12p
Multiple system atrophy (Shy–Drager syndrome)	Substantia nigra Purkinje cells Pontine nuclei Spinal autonomic nuclei	Ataxia Sensory loss Tremor Orthostatic hypotension	Unknown

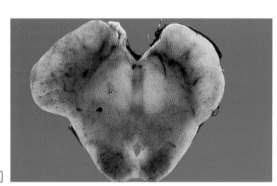 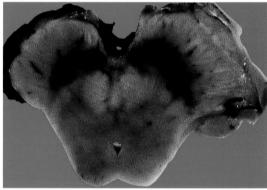

Fig. 26.23   Idiopathic Parkinson's disease. **A** The pigmented neurones in the substantia nigra within the midbrain degenerate and die off in Parkinson's disease, giving a pale appearance in comparison to **B** an age-matched normal control.

Parkinson's disease

Parkinson's disease is characterised clinically by tremor, brady-kinesia and rigidity, which usually become manifest between the ages of 45 and 60 years, affecting 1% of the population over 60. Similar clinical features may occur in unrelated conditions, such as cerebrovascular disease or phenothiazine drug therapy. This disorder results in a progressive loss of pigmented neurones in the substantia nigra (Fig. 26.23), the locus ceruleus and several other brainstem nuclei. Surviving neurones at these sites contain round eosinophilic inclusions—Lewy bodies (Fig. 26.24)—containing neuronal proteins, including alpha-synuclein. Lewy body inclusions may occasionally be widespread throughout the brain, particularly in the cerebral cortex, resulting in dementia due to 'diffuse Lewy body disease'.

The neurones of the substantia nigra synthesise dopamine, which acts as an inhibitory neurotransmitter at their axonal projection sites in the basal ganglia (putamen and globus pallidus). Loss of the pigmented neurones results in a relative deficiency of dopamine in the basal ganglia that can be overcome by replacement therapy, for example with L-dopa. This often relieves the clinical symptoms of the disease, but a permanent cure is not yet possible.

A disorder similar to Parkinson's disease can be produced experimentally by the administration of MPTP (1-methyl-4-phenyl-1,2,3,6-tetrahydropyridine). This compound has also produced a severe disorder resembling Parkinson's disease in intravenous drug addicts when it is present as a contaminant in synthetic heroin preparations. Chronic exposure to environmental toxins, including pesticides, is a risk factor for Parkinson's disease, and recent genetic studies have identified mutations in the alpha-synuclein gene in some families with an autosomal dominant form of Parkinson's disease.

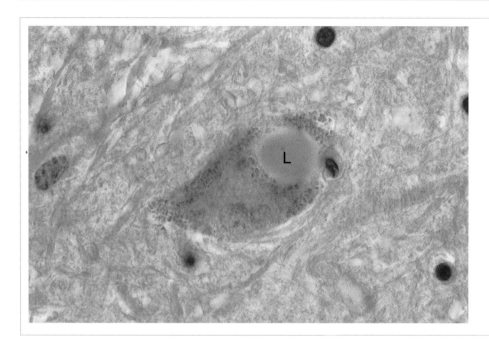

Fig. 26.24 Idiopathic Parkinson's disease. A surviving pigmented neurone in the substantia nigra contains an intracytoplasmic rounded eosinophilic inclusion known as a Lewy body (L), which contains aggregates of alpha-synuclein.

DEMENTIA

▶ Predominantly a disorder of the elderly; more than 15% of adults over 80 are demented
▶ Classified aetiologically into primary organic and secondary dementias
▶ Commonest cause of dementia in the UK is Alzheimer's disease, a progressive degenerative organic disorder
▶ Aetiology of most primary organic dementias is unknown; some are inherited as single gene defects, e.g. Huntington's disease

Dementia has been defined clinically as an acquired global impairment of intellect, reason and personality without impairment of consciousness. Emotional lability and memory dysfunction are prominent manifestations, implying a cerebral cortical disorder. Most patients with dementia exhibit both gross and histological abnormalities within the cerebral cortex, although some rarer causes of dementia appear to involve mainly subcortical structures. A variety of disorders affecting the CNS can result in dementia:

- primary neurodegenerative disorders (e.g. Alzheimer's disease, Pick's disease, Huntington's disease, diffuse Lewy body disease)
- cerebrovascular disease (e.g. multi-infarct dementia, Binswanger's disease)
- infections (e.g. Creutzfeldt–Jakob disease, neurosyphilis, HIV infection)
- intracranial space-occupying lesions (e.g. neoplasms, chronic subdural haematoma)
- hydrocephalus
- drugs and toxins (e.g. barbiturates, digoxin, anticholinergic agents, alcohol, heavy metals)

- metabolic disorders (e.g. hypothyroidism, hypoparathyroidism, uraemia, hepatic failure)
- vitamin deficiencies (e.g. B_1—Wernicke–Korsakoff syndrome, B_2, B_{12})
- paraneoplastic syndromes (e.g. limbic encephalitis).

These disorders may be considered in two main categories:

- primary neurodegenerative disorders affecting the CNS (sometimes referred to as *organic dementias*)
- other disorders producing secondary changes in the CNS that result in dementia.

The commonest cause of dementia in Western countries is Alzheimer's disease (at least 70% of cases), followed by Lewy body dementia and vascular dementia. It is important to establish the cause of dementia in each patient, as in some cases an effective treatment is available. In other cases, dementia may be due to an inherited disorder, in which case genetic counselling is required for the affected family. The major causes of organic dementia are discussed below.

Alzheimer's disease

Alzheimer's disease accounts for well over 70% of all cases of dementia in adults. In the UK, it is thought to affect 5% of people over the age of 65 years, rising to 15% of those over 80. As the number of elderly people in the population increases, so there is a concomitant increase in the number of patients suffering from Alzheimer's disease; this has been termed the 'silent epidemic'. Females are affected almost twice as frequently as males. Most cases occur sporadically, although a small proportion are inherited as an autosomal dominant disorder. Several gene loci are involved in familial cases, including the amyloid precursor protein (APP) gene on chromosome 21, the *presenilin 1* gene on chromosome 14 and the *presenilin 2* gene on chromosome 1 (Fig. 26.25). There

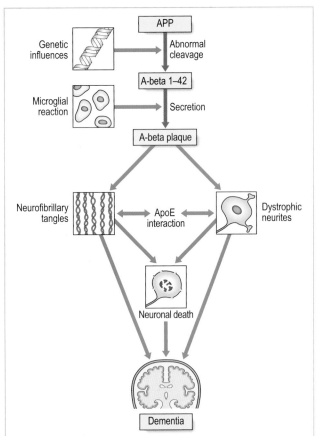

Fig. 26.25 Amyloid cascade pathway in Alzheimer's disease. This simplified diagram indicates how abnormal processing of the cell surface glycoprotein APP (coded by a gene on chromosome 21) leads to the formation of A-beta plaques, the histological hallmark of Alzheimer's disease. The mechanisms of interaction with ApoE and neurofibrillary tangle formation are not fully understood.

is an increased incidence of sporadic Alzheimer's disease in individuals with the ApoE e4 genotype on chromosome 19. The clinical presentation usually occurs after the age of 60 years, but a significant subgroup is affected between the ages of 50 and 60 years. The illness lasts from 2 to 8 years; most patients die from inanition and bronchopneumonia.

Morphological features

The brain is reduced in weight, often to 1100 g, and shows cortical atrophy which is often most marked in the frontal and temporal lobes. There is loss of both cortical grey and white matter, with compensatory dilatation of the ventricular system (secondary hydrocephalus, Fig. 26.26). The cerebellum and spinal cord appear normal.

The characteristic histological changes in Alzheimer's disease are most pronounced in the limbic system (amygdala, entorhinal cortex and hippocampus) and cerebral cortex. The severity of these changes correlates with the clinical severity of the dementia. The histological hallmarks of Alzheimer's disease are *A-beta amyloid plaques* and *neurofibrillary tangles*.

A-beta amyloid plaques

A-beta amyloid plaques are best demonstrated in specially stained histological sections of the CNS (Fig. 26.27A). They occur most frequently in the amygdala, hippocampus and cerebral cortex. These plaques can measure up to 200 μm in diameter, and in their earliest stages comprise a collection of dilated presynaptic neuronal processes, which contain many organelles, around a diffuse aggregate of amyloid material. As the plaques mature, they enlarge and develop a core of A-beta amyloid protein, which eventually forms the major component of the 'burnt-out' plaque. Reactive astrocytes and microglia are usually present at the periphery of the plaque.

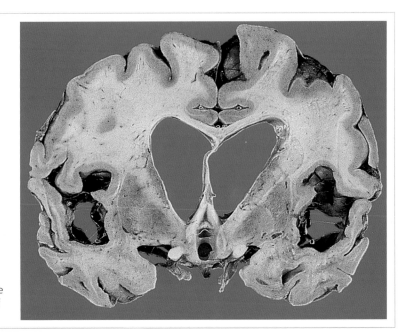

Fig. 26.26 Alzheimer's disease cortical atrophy. The brain in Alzheimer's disease shows severe cortical atrophy with narrowing of the gyri and widening of the sulci. White matter loss is accompanied by dilatation of the ventricular system (compensatory hydrocephalus).

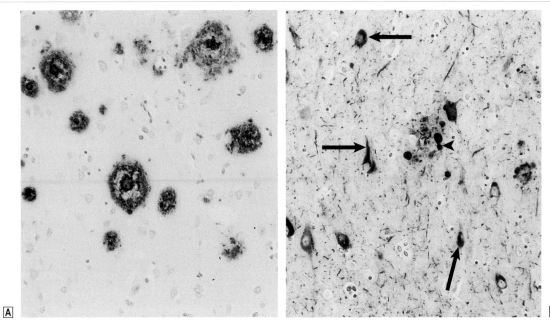

Fig. 26.27 Plaques and tangles in Alzheimer's disease. [A] The amyloid plaques in Alzheimer's disease are composed of the A-beta protein, and form irregular rounded masses (brown) in the extracellular matrix in the cerebral cortex. [B] In Alzheimer's disease, abnormally phosphorylated tau protein (brown) accumulates intracellularly in neurofibrillary tangles (arrows) and in dystrophic neurites (arrowhead).

Neurofibrillary tangles

Neurofibrillary tangles are present within the neuronal perikarya and are most easily visualised in specially stained sections (Fig. 26.27B). Affected neurones are most often found in the hippocampus, but may also occur in the cerebral cortex, subcortical grey matter and brainstem nuclei. This form of degeneration consists of a thickening of fibrils within the neuronal cytoplasm, to form a tortuous and elongated corkscrew-like structure. Electron microscopy has shown that each tangle consists of a mass of twisted tubules composed of paired helical filaments, each 10 nm in diameter, with a periodic narrowing at 80 nm. The major component of these tangles is tau, a microtubule-associated protein, which becomes hyperphosphorylated in Alzheimer's disease.

Neuronal loss

Neuronal loss is often widespread in the cerebral cortex, but is most severe in the hippocampus.

Amyloid angiopathy

A-beta amyloid may be deposited within the walls of small arterioles and capillaries in the brain in Alzheimer's disease. This is derived from abnormal cleavage of APP (Fig. 26.25), as for the A-beta amyloid in the plaques.

Neurochemical abnormalities

The functional impairment in Alzheimer's disease is accompanied by a number of neurochemical abnormalities, the best known of which involve a reduction in cholinergic activity in the cerebral cortex. Treatment with anticholinesterase inhibitors increases levels of acetylcholine in the brain and improves cognitive function in the early stages of the disease.

Aetiology and pathogenesis

Genetic factors are of major importance in the aetiology of Alzheimer's disease in both familial and sporadic forms. Increasing evidence supports a primary role for A-beta amyloid in the pathogenesis of Alzheimer's disease. A-beta amyloid is formed as part of the 'amyloid cascade' from APP (Fig. 26.25). This explains why individuals with trisomy 21 (Down's syndrome) develop accelerated Alzheimer-like changes in the CNS as a consequence of their extra APP gene load.

Frontotemporal dementia

This term covers a group of dementias associated with aphasia and behavioural disorders that are characterised by severe atrophy of the frontal and temporal lobes of the brain. This group includes disorders previously referred to as Pick's disease. Recent research has indicated that the prevalence of frontotemporal dementias is higher than previously thought, perhaps accounting for up to 10% of all cases of dementia. Most cases occur in individuals aged between 35 and 75 years, with some conditions occurring as familial disorders. The pathology is characterised by severe neuronal loss and gliosis in the frontal and temporal cortex, with neuronal inclusions present in some disorders. Treatment is aimed at alleviating symptoms for as long as possible, but death usually occurs within 3–6 years after the onset of symptoms.

Huntington's disease

The degenerative condition known as Huntington's disease is inherited as an autosomal dominant disorder. It is uncommon,

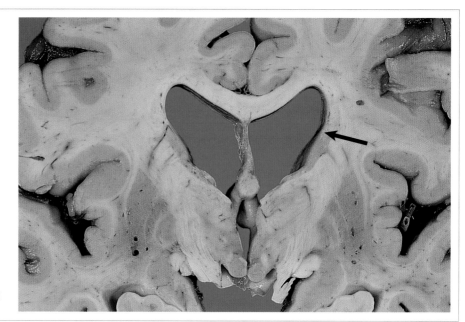

Fig. 26.28 Huntington's disease: subcortical atrophy. In Huntington's disease, cerebral atrophy is most marked in the caudate nucleus (arrow), which is markedly narrowed, and the adjacent putamen. These changes are accompanied by compensatory hydrocephalus involving the lateral ventricles.

affecting 4–7 per 100 000 in the UK. The disease does not usually become clinically apparent until the fifth decade of life, when the onset of personality change and depression are later accompanied by choreiform movements, jerking and dementia. The gene responsible for Huntington's disease, the *huntingtin* gene, has been located on chromosome 4p, allowing an effective means of preclinical and antenatal diagnosis.

The genetic abnormality is an excess number of tandemly repeated CAG nucleotide sequences. The number of repeats influences the age of onset: the more repeats, the earlier the onset.

The gross appearances are illustrated in Figure 26.28. Histology of the caudate nucleus and putamen shows a marked loss of small neurones, accompanied by a reactive fibrillary gliosis. The cerebral cortex in this disorder also shows neuronal loss, but to a variable extent.

Neurochemical abnormalities have been identified in this disorder, for example reduced levels of choline acetyltransferase and gamma aminobutyric acid in the basal ganglia. These changes are presumably secondary to the neuronal loss.

Dementia pugilistica

In the 'punch-drunk' syndrome seen in boxers, progressive dementia is accompanied by tremor and focal neurological signs. Characteristic findings in the brain are structural abnormalities of the septum pellucidum, thinning of the corpus callosum, degeneration of the substantia nigra and cerebral cortical neurofibrillary tangles. A-beta accumulation has been identified in the brain, leading to the suggestion that brain trauma may play a role in the pathogenesis of Alzheimer's disease.

PARANEOPLASTIC SYNDROMES

Paraneoplastic syndromes (PNS) are a group of rare neurological disorders that represent non-metastatic complications of malignancy in the nervous system. The commonest of these include limbic encephalitis, resulting in dementia due to inflammatory damage in the hippocampus and limbic system, and the Lambert–Eaton myasthenic syndrome, where damage to the motor end plate in muscle fibres results in weakness. Many PNS are associated with circulating antibodies against antigens expressed in both the tumour (often a small cell lung cancer) and the nervous system, suggesting that PNS may result from a misdirected immune response. Treatment of the underlying tumour often results in clinical improvement from the PNS.

CNS TUMOURS

▶ Second commonest tumours in children and the sixth commonest in adults
▶ Present clinically with localising signs due to tissue destruction, or with the non-specific effects of raised intracranial pressure
▶ Classified according to cell of origin and degree of differentiation
▶ In children, 70% are sited in the posterior fossa; most are intrinsic tumours
▶ In adults, 70% are sited supratentorially; intrinsic and extrinsic tumours both occur frequently
▶ Metastatic tumours occur more frequently with increasing age: most are carcinomas, which may form solid deposits in the CNS or spread by seeding in the CSF
▶ Survival depends on the age of the patient and the site, size and histology of the neoplasm

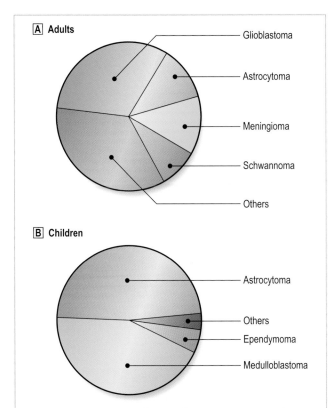

A Adults
- Glioblastoma
- Astrocytoma
- Meningioma
- Schwannoma
- Others

B Children
- Astrocytoma
- Others
- Ependymoma
- Medulloblastoma

Fig. 26.29 Relative incidence of primary CNS neoplasms. The relative incidences of the commonest primary CNS neoplasms are illustrated for adults and children. Important differences in site also occur in relation to age. **A** In adults, most neoplasms are supratentorial. **B** In children, most arise in the posterior fossa.

Primary tumours of the CNS occur in approximately 8–12 per 100 000 of the general population. Two main peaks of incidence occur: in the first decade and in the fifth or sixth decades of life. In children, CNS tumours are the second commonest group of neoplasms (after leukaemias), but in adults they rate as the sixth commonest group. The relative incidences of the main groups of primary CNS tumours in adults and in children are shown in Figure 26.29.

Pathogenesis

The pathogenesis of most CNS neoplasms is unknown, but the following factors have been studied:

- *Genetic factors.* Primary CNS tumours are major components of several disorders inherited as autosomal dominant conditions including tuberous sclerosis, neurofibromatosis and von Hippel–Lindau syndrome (see Phakomatoses, p. 776).
- *Chemical and viral factors.* In animals, chemical and viral carcinogens resulting in the development of primary CNS neoplasms have been discovered but their relationship to tumours in humans is uncertain.
- *Radiation.* In humans, irradiation of the CNS in childhood has very occasionally resulted in the development of a neoplasm in adult life. It has been suggested that exposure of the brain to radiation from mobile telephones may result in

Table 26.13 Classification of CNS tumours according to presumed cell of origin	
Cell of origin	**CNS tumour**
Glial cells	Astrocytoma, oligodendroglioma, ependymoma, glioblastoma
Primitive neuroectodermal cells	Medulloblastoma, neuroblastoma
Arachnoidal cell	Meningioma
Nerve sheath cells	Schwannoma, neurofibroma
Lymphoreticular cells	Lymphoma

brain tumours, but the evidence to support this possibility is conflicting.
- *Immunosuppression.* This is of major importance in the pathogenesis of primary CNS lymphomas.
- *Trauma.* The role of trauma in the pathogenesis of CNS neoplasms is unproven.

Classification

As in other organs, tumours of the CNS are classified according to their cellular differentiation and presumed cell of origin (Table 26.13).

Clinicopathological features

Brain tumours may present clinically in two main ways:

- *Local effects.* Focal neurological signs related to the site of the tumour in the CNS, for example epilepsy with a temporal lobe tumour or paraplegia with a spinal cord tumour.
- *Mass effects.* Many tumours present with the non-specific signs and symptoms of space-occupying lesions, without any localising signs. Vasogenic oedema around CNS neoplasms is particularly common and may greatly potentiate the mass effect. Posterior fossa tumours present with the clinical features of hydrocephalus, particularly in children. Intracranial herniation is a common mode of death in patients with CNS neoplasms (Fig. 26.6).

Unlike neoplasms arising in other tissues, primary CNS neoplasms virtually never metastasise to other organs; the reasons for this are not clearly understood. However, infiltration of adjacent tissues both within the nervous system and its coverings (including the skull) is common, for example in meningioma, and seeding to remote parts of the nervous system by the CSF pathway is an important means of spread for certain intrinsic tumours, for example medulloblastomas. Spread by seeding can sometimes occur down a ventriculoperitoneal shunt, resulting in intra-abdominal tumour deposits.

Intrinsic tumours

The commonest group of primary CNS neoplasms are the intrinsic tumours of the brain, which account for all primary CNS neoplasms in children. In adults, intrinsic tumours account

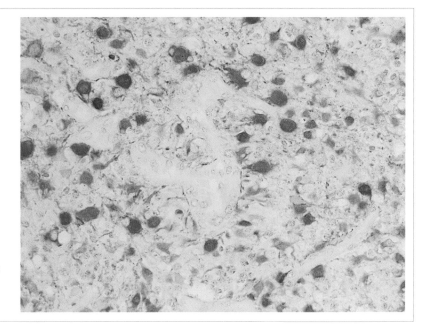

Fig. 26.30 Astrocytoma. In this well-differentiated cerebral astrocytoma, most of the cells bear numerous cytoplasmic processes which are arranged around blood vessels in a manner similar to astrocytic processes in normal grey matter.

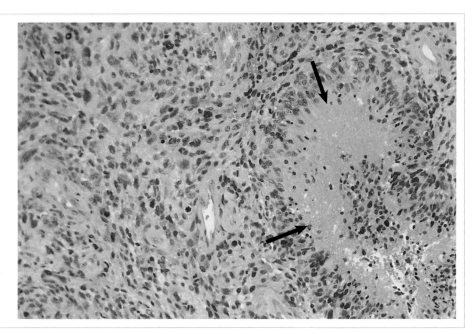

Fig. 26.31 Glioblastoma. Areas of necrosis (arrows) are a characteristic feature of this neoplasm, and are usually surrounded by the nuclei of small malignant cells. The neoplastic cell population is pleomorphic, and also includes multinucleate cells. Vascular endothelial proliferation is another characteristic histological feature.

for around 65% of primary CNS neoplasms, the majority of which are of glial origin (Fig. 26.29). Intrinsic tumours occur more frequently in male patients.

Astrocytomas

Astrocytomas account for 10% of all primary CNS tumours in adults, but are relatively more frequent in children (Fig. 26.29). They commonly arise in the cerebellum in children, and in the cerebral hemispheres in adults. Astrocytomas are usually classified according to the predominant cell type and degree of differentiation (Fig. 26.30). It is thought that many anaplastic astrocytomas arise as a consequence of

dedifferentiation within a pre-existing astrocytic neoplasm. The prognosis for patients with astrocytomas (and gliomas generally) depends on the degree of tumour differentiation, the age of the patient at diagnosis, and the site and size of the neoplasm.

Glioblastoma

Glioblastoma accounts for 30% of all primary CNS tumours in adults, but is extremely rare in children. Most arise in the white matter of the cerebral hemispheres (Fig. 26.6). As its name implies, this neoplasm is characterised histologically by a pleomorphic cell population (Fig. 26.31). Although it

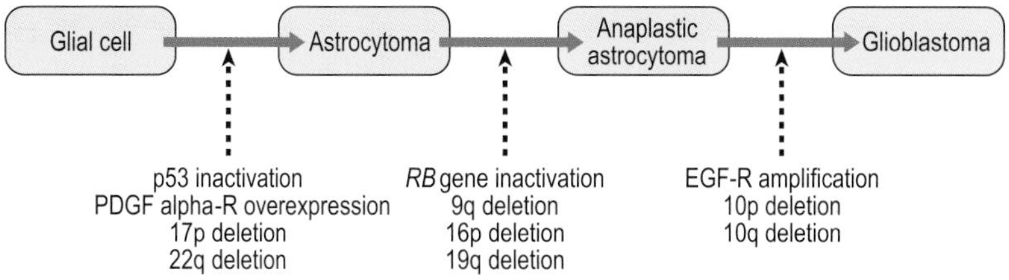

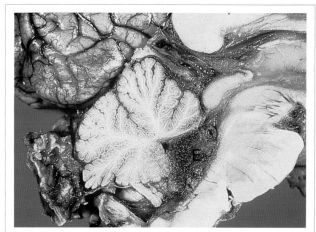

Fig. 26.32   **Molecular genetic abnormalities in glioma progression.**

is accepted that glioblastomas may arise de novo, it seems likely that many of these neoplasms arise as a consequence of dedifferentiation within a pre-existing astrocytic glioma. De-differentiation is accompanied by, or is the result of, a series of genetic events (Fig. 26.32). Mitotic activity in glioblastomas is abundant, and vascular endothelial proliferation is prominent. These features suggest a rapid growth rate; most patients die within 1 year of diagnosis.

Oligodendroglioma

Oligodendroglioma accounts for 3% of all primary CNS neo-plasms in adults, but is rare in children. Oligodendrogliomas are usually ill-defined, infiltrating neoplasms, arising in the white matter of the cerebral hemispheres. Histologically, oligodendrogliomas present a spectrum of appearances which may be graded in a similar manner to astrocytomas. In a well-differentiated tumour, the neoplastic cells are small, rounded and uniform with a clear cytoplasm and prominent cell membrane. Small foci of calcification are common, and a characteristic interweaving vascular pattern is often present. Oligodendrogliomas exhibit a different set of genetic abnor-malities to astrocytic gliomas, with losses of chromosomes 1p and 19q.

Ependymoma

An ependymoma arises from an ependymal surface, usually in the fourth ventricle, and projects into the CSF pathway (Fig. 26.33). Most ependymomas are well differentiated, and extensive invasion of adjacent CNS structures is uncommon. A special variant, the myxopapillary ependymoma, occurs in the cauda equina region in adults.

Choroid plexus papilloma

An uncommon intraventricular papillary growth, choroid plexus papilloma is most often found in a lateral ventricle and usually presents with obstructive hydrocephalus. Although showing little tendency to infiltrate locally, spread via the CSF may occur.

Primitive neuroectodermal tumours

The commonest variety of the primitive neuroectodermal group of tumours is the *medulloblastoma*, which arises in the cerebellum in children. The growth rate is rapid, and extensive local infiltration is common, often resulting in obstructive hydrocephalus. Meningeal infiltration frequently occurs and

Fig. 26.33   **Ependymoma: ventricular obstruction.** The ependymoma (E) arising from the lining of the fourth ventricle has almost totally obstructed the CSF pathway and produced obstruc-tive hydrocephalus. This results in characteristic clinical features that are common presenting symptoms for this group of neoplasms.

CSF seeding is common. As the name implies, these tumours are composed of poorly differentiated neuroepithelial cells which consist of small round nuclei surrounded by a scanty rim of cytoplasm. Mitotic figures are numerous, and evidence of differentiation into mature cell types, such as neurones or glia, is occasionally present. The prognosis for this group of tumours in children has improved in recent years as a conse-quence of improved treatment with radiotherapy; the 5-year survival rate is around 60%.

Haemangioblastoma

Haemangioblastoma is an uncommon neoplasm arising most often in the cerebellum and forming a well-defined, frequently cystic mass. Histologically, the tumour is com-posed of blood vessels, separated by stromal cells with clear cytoplasm containing lipid. CNS haemangioblastomas are an important component of von Hippel–Lindau syndrome, an autosomal dominant inherited disease with a genetic locus on chromosome 3p.

Lymphoma

Although an uncommon CNS tumour, there is much current interest in primary CNS lymphomas because of their greatly increased frequency of occurrence in immunosuppressed patients, for example in cardiac and renal transplant patients and in the acquired immune deficiency syndrome (AIDS). Recent studies have implicated the Epstein–Barr virus in the pathogenesis of these neoplasms. Most primary CNS lymphomas are ill-defined masses arising in the white matter or the cerebral hemispheres. Histologically, most are high-grade, non-Hodgkin's lymphomas of B-cell type. Accordingly, the prognosis is poor and most patients are dead within 2–3 years.

Tumours of neuronal cells

Tumours comprising neuronal elements are rare; they occur most commonly around the region of the third ventricle in children. In gangliocytomas, the neoplastic cells all resemble mature neurones, but gangliogliomas include neoplastic glial cells (usually astrocytic cells).

Miscellaneous cysts

A variety of cystic lesions occur in the CNS which, although not all neoplastic, often present clinically with symptoms and signs similar to those of CNS tumours. Examples include:

- *craniopharyngioma* in the suprasellar region, causing pituitary dysfunction and visual disturbance
- *colloid cyst* in the third ventricle in children and young adults, causing intermittent hydrocephalus and sudden death
- *dermoid cyst* in the posterior fossa and lumbar spine in children and young adults, causing cerebellar signs and symptoms, and paraplegia
- *epidermoid cyst* in the cerebello-pontine angle and pituitary region in adults, causing cerebellar signs and symptoms of pituitary dysfunction respectively.

Extrinsic tumours

Tumours arising from the coverings of the brain and spinal cord, and from cranial and spinal nerve roots, are less common than intrinsic CNS tumours. Complete surgical removal of extrinsic neoplasms often results in a clinical cure.

Meningiomas

Meningiomas account for around 18% of intracranial neoplasms in adults; female patients outnumber males by 2:1. Meningiomas arise from cells of the arachnoid cap (a component of arachnoid villi). The most frequent sites are the parasagittal region, sphenoidal wing, olfactory groove and foramen magnum. Meningiomas are smooth lobulated masses, which are broadly adherent to the dura. Infiltration of the adjacent dura and overlying bone is not uncommon, but invasion of the brain is exceptionally rare. The brain, however, may be markedly compressed by a meningioma, resulting in considerable anatomical distortion (Fig. 26.34). Histologically, meningiomas display a variety of patterns, the most characteristic of which includes sheets of fusiform cells in a composite solid and whorled pattern. Small foci of calcification (psammoma bodies) are common.

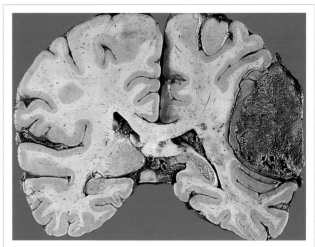

Fig. 26.34 Meningioma: cerebral compression. Meningiomas do not usually invade CNS structures, but may produce clinical manifestations by compression of the adjacent brain. This neoplasm has the lobulated surface characteristic of meningiomas, and is sharply demarcated from the cerebrum.

Occasional meningiomas are frankly malignant and may metastasise outside the CNS, for example to the lung.

Schwannoma

As the name suggests, schwannomas derive from Schwann cells in the nerve sheath of the intracranial or intraspinal roots to sensory nerves. By far the commonest site is the vestibular branch of the 8th cranial nerve in the region of the cerebello-pontine angle; such neoplasms are often known as 'acoustic neuromas'. As with meningiomas, schwannomas occur most frequently in adults, and are commoner in females. Bilateral 8th nerve tumours commonly occur in patients suffering from neurofibromatosis type 2. Histologically, schwannomas exhibit two main patterns: densely packed spindle-shaped cells with frequent nuclear palisading, and more loosely structured areas with a myxoid stroma which may contain cyst. Malignant change is very uncommon in these tumours.

Neurofibromas

In the CNS, neurofibromas usually arise on the dorsal nerve roots of the spinal cord, and occur most frequently in patients suffering from neurofibromatosis. Unlike schwannomas, neurofibromas are not encapsulated but tend to involve an entire nerve root, producing a localised or diffuse expansion (plexiform neurofibroma). Histologically, neurofibromas consist of a mixture of Schwann cells and fibroblasts, forming bundles of elongated cells with characteristically 'wavy' nuclei.

Secondary tumours

The CNS may be involved by other neoplasms in two main ways: compression and invasion, and metastasis.

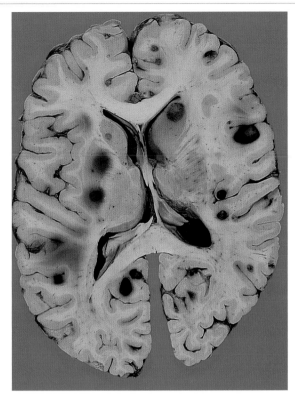

Fig. 26.35 Cerebral metastases: malignant melanoma.
The darkly pigmented metastases from a malignant melanoma are present at several sites within the brain, mostly at junctions between grey and white matter. This is a characteristic pattern for metastases within the CNS.

Compression and invasion

Tumours arising in adjacent organs may compress and invade the CNS, producing localising clinical signs, or presenting as space-occupying lesions. The commonest examples involving the brain are pituitary adenomas, which frequently cause visual impairment due to pressure on the optic chiasm.

Metastasis

The CNS is a common site for metastases, which may occur by haematogenous or direct spread. The commonest neoplasms to metastasise to the CNS are carcinomas of the breast, bronchus, kidney and colon, and malignant melanomas. Metastases often occur at the boundary between grey and white matter (Fig. 26.35) and may present as space-occupying lesions with or without focal signs. Metastatic carcinoma sometimes infiltrates the subarachnoid space producing 'carcinomatous meningitis'. Patients with this condition present with the symptoms of subacute meningitis, often with multiple cranial nerve palsies. Metastatic deposits within the spinal cord are uncommon, but extradural metastases occur frequently and may present with paraplegia. CNS involvement occurs commonly in acute leukaemias and non-Hodgkin's lymphomas (Ch. 22) with infiltration of the subarachnoid space and parenchyma. The prognosis for patients with a metastatic neoplasm within the CNS is extremely poor.

PERIPHERAL NERVOUS SYSTEM

▶ Three main reactions to cell injury: Wallerian degeneration, segmental demyelination and distal axonal degeneration
▶ Peripheral neuropathies classified clinically according to distribution of lesions, and function of the nerve involved
▶ Commonest neoplasms arising in peripheral nerves are schwannomas and neurofibromas

NORMAL STRUCTURE AND FUNCTION

Peripheral nerves may be involved in many diseases, but because they can undergo only a limited number of pathological changes, it is important to consider their normal structure and general pathology before specific disorders are mentioned.

On histology, nerve fibres can be divided into two main groups: myelinated and non-myelinated.

Myelinated fibres

Myelinated fibres range in diameter from 2 to 17 μm, with myelin sheaths proportional in thickness to the diameter of the axon. Myelin is formed by the compaction of cell membranes from multiple Schwann cells along the length of the axon, to form a lamellar structure with a periodicity of 14 nm. The node of Ranvier is the site where adjacent Schwann cells meet and where their myelin sheaths terminate. This arrangement allows the rapid transmission of electrical impulses by saltatory conduction, up to 10 m/s in the largest fibres.

Non-myelinated fibres

Non-myelinated fibres are much smaller in size (0.5–3 μm in diameter) and are surrounded by Schwann cell cytoplasm. The absence of myelin around these fibres results in slow conduction velocities (0.3–1.6 m/s).

REACTIONS TO INJURY

Although peripheral nerves may be involved by many disease processes, for example vasculitis or amyloidosis, nerve fibres exhibit only two basic reactions to disease:

● axonal degeneration
● segmental demyelination.

These reactions may occur in combination in some peripheral neuropathies; this is usually referred to as combined or mixed degeneration.

Axonal degeneration

Degeneration and loss of axons in peripheral nerves occurs by two main processes: Wallerian degeneration and distal axonal degeneration. Loss of axons in peripheral nerves results in the reduction in amplitude of the conducted impulse, which can be identified on nerve conduction studies.

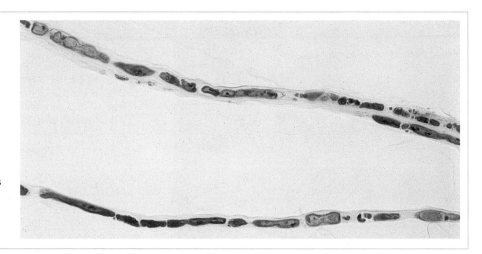

Fig. 26.36 Teased fibre preparations of peripheral nerves in Wallerian degeneration. These show a characteristic fragmentation of the myelin sheath (which appears dark) around the damaged axons.

Wallerian degeneration

Damage to the neuronal body, for example anterior horn cells, spinal nerve roots or nerve trunks, results in degeneration of the axon distal to the site of the injury. In myelinated fibres, this is accompanied by the secondary breakdown of myelin around the degenerate axons (Fig. 26.36). This process is similar to anterograde degeneration in the CNS but occurs more rapidly.

Regeneration commences 3–4 days following injury; the regenerating axonal sprouts grow at 2–3 mm/day. This is accompanied by central chromatolysis in the neuronal perikaryon, and remyelination by Schwann cells. If axonal regeneration and remyelination are successful, the re-innervation of the target organ, for example a motor end-plate of muscle, may occur. Re-innervation is hindered or prevented by factors that inhibit nerve growth, for example ischaemia or cytotoxic drugs, or disrupt the continuity of the perineurium, for example haematoma or scar tissue.

Distal axonal degeneration

The neuronal cell body is responsible for the maintenance of the axon, which often extends for a considerable distance from the perikaryon. When neuronal metabolism is disrupted, the axon often begins to degenerate at its distal end. This form of degeneration is known as a 'dying-back' process or distal axonopathy. It usually also results in secondary breakdown of the myelin sheath at the affected site. Axonal regeneration may occur if normal neuronal metabolism is restored before extensive degeneration occurs.

Distal axonal degeneration occurs in various conditions, including vitamin E and B_1 deficiencies, acute porphyria, isoniazid and hexacarbon neuropathies.

Segmental demyelination

In segmental demyelination, the continuity of the axon is maintained, but the myelin sheath is broken down over various segments corresponding to the internodes. This results in a marked slowing of impulse conduction along the nerve fibres, detectable on nerve conduction studies.

Primary segmental demyelination

Primary segmental demyelination occurs when damage to Schwann cells results in breakdown of the myelin sheath which they normally maintain. The myelin debris is eventually phagocytosed and digested by reactive macrophages. This can occur in many conditions, such as ischaemia, inherited metabolic disorders such as leukodystrophies, and the neuropathy of diphtheria.

Allergic segmental demyelination

Allergic segmental demyelination occurs when myelin sheaths are stripped and broken down by activated macrophages in the presence of lymphocytes. This mechanism is thought to operate in the Guillain–Barré syndrome. Remyelination of affected segments of nerve can occur in both allergic and primary segmental demyelination. Schwann cells in the affected internodes undergo mitosis within a few days following the injury, after which remyelination can commence.

Hypertrophic neuropathy

Certain chronic peripheral neuropathies for example leukodystrophies and hereditary sensorimotor neuropathy type III, are characterised by hypertrophic peripheral nerves. These are often thickened, with a distinctive 'onion-bulb' appearance on microscopy due to the concentric proliferation of Schwann cells around axons in response to repeated segmental demyelination and remyelination.

PERIPHERAL NEUROPATHY

Peripheral nerve disorders are often classified clinically according to the distribution of the lesions:

- *mononeuropathy*, e.g. carpal tunnel syndrome, diabetes: a single nerve is involved
- *mononeuritis multiplex*, e.g. polyarteritis nodosa, sarcoidosis: several isolated nerves are involved
- *polyneuropathy*, mainly motor, e.g. Guillain–Barré syndrome; mainly sensory, e.g. carcinomatous neuropathy; sensorimotor, e.g. alcoholism; autonomic, e.g. diabetes; or multiple nerve involvement.

Additional classifications include the predominant nerve fibre types involved, that is motor, sensory, autonomic or mixed. Many peripheral neuropathies are of a mixed type. Nerve biopsy will in some cases show diagnostic features, for example in amyloid neuropathies or polyarteritis nodosa, but in many cases the aetiology of the neuropathy is not apparent on histology.

TUMOURS AND TUMOUR-LIKE CONDITIONS

Traumatic neuroma

Traumatic neuroma is not a neoplasm but a reactive proliferation of Schwann cells and fibroblasts that occurs at the proximal severed end of a peripheral nerve. Traumatic neuromas contain disordered fascicles of twisted axons, and may produce severe pain (e.g. 'phantom limb' pain after amputation) until excised.

Schwannoma

Schwannomas are benign neoplasms that resemble their CNS counterparts histologically (p. 786).

Neurofibroma

Neurofibromas are a common manifestation of neurofibromatosis (see Phakomatoses, p. 776), when they may occur at multiple sites in large numbers and produce gross deformities.

Other tumours

Malignant peripheral nerve sheath tumours are rare; they occur most often in patients with neurofibromatosis, when they sometimes arise from a pre-existing neurofibroma. These neoplasms behave as sarcomas and are frequently fatal. Ganglion cell tumours occasionally arise from autonomic ganglia, particularly in the sympathetic chain. Phaeochromocytomas and neuroblastomas are discussed in Chapter 17.

SKELETAL MUSCLE

▶ Diagnosis of skeletal muscle disorders requires clinicopathological liaison, and cannot be made on muscle biopsy histology alone
▶ Three groups of skeletal muscle disorders: neurogenic disorders, myopathies and disorders of neuromuscular transmission
▶ Neurogenic disorders and myopathies commonly occur in both children and adults; many of the latter are inherited, e.g. muscular dystrophies
▶ Neurogenic disorders may result from lesions affecting motor neurones, nerve roots or peripheral nerves
▶ Myopathic disorders include muscular dystrophies, polymyositis and other inflammatory conditions, and congenital, metabolic and toxic disorders
▶ Commonest disorder of neuromuscular transmission is myasthenia gravis, an autoimmune disease
▶ Commonest neoplasms arising in skeletal muscle are of connective tissue origin

The diagnosis of skeletal muscle diseases requires multi-disciplinary investigation, often involving neurologists, neurophysiologists, neuropathologists, biochemists and geneticists. Muscle biopsy histology can contribute much important information, but it cannot alone be relied upon for a diagnosis. The innervation of muscle can be studied by electromyography and motor nerve conduction studies. Muscle fibres contain the enzyme creatine phosphokinase (CPK), which is released into the blood following muscle fibre damage; its measurement in serum is widely used in the investigation of muscle diseases.

Normal muscle consists of densely packed, uniformly sized myofibres (40–80μm diameter in adults) with peripheral nuclei (Fig. 26.37). The terminal axons supplying each fibre can also be studied using histochemical techniques, but the investigation of motor end plates and subcellular organelles requires electron microscopy. Muscle diseases can be classified clinically and pathologically into three main groups:
● neurogenic disorders
● myopathies
● disorders of neuromuscular transmission.

NEUROGENIC DISORDERS

Neurogenic muscle diseases all result from damage to the muscle innervation. This can occur as a consequence of lesions affecting the motor neurones in the spinal cord and brainstem, motor nerve roots or peripheral motor nerves. The denervated muscle fibres undergo atrophy and are eventually reduced to small clusters of nuclei with very little surrounding cytoplasm. Re-innervation may occur in some longstanding disorders, for example peripheral motor neuropathies, producing the histological appearance of fibre type grouping (Figs 26.37 and 26.38). In progressive disorders, for example motor neurone disease, the anterior horn cells responsible for re-innervation also eventually degenerate, resulting in atrophy of all the fibres in an affected muscle. Four main groups of disorders are responsible for neurogenic muscle disease:
● motor neurone disease
● spinal muscular atrophy
● peripheral neuropathies
● miscellaneous spinal disorders.

Motor neurone disease

Motor neurone disease is a progressive degenerative disorder affecting principally the anterior horn neurones in the spinal cord. This results in denervation atrophy (Fig. 26.38), fasciculation and weakness in affected muscles.

Spinal muscular atrophy

Spinal muscular atrophy is one of the commonest autosomal recessive disorders, occurring in 1 in 10000 live births. It results from homozygous loss of the survival motor neurone gene 1, and presents in four main forms, which represent allelic variants:

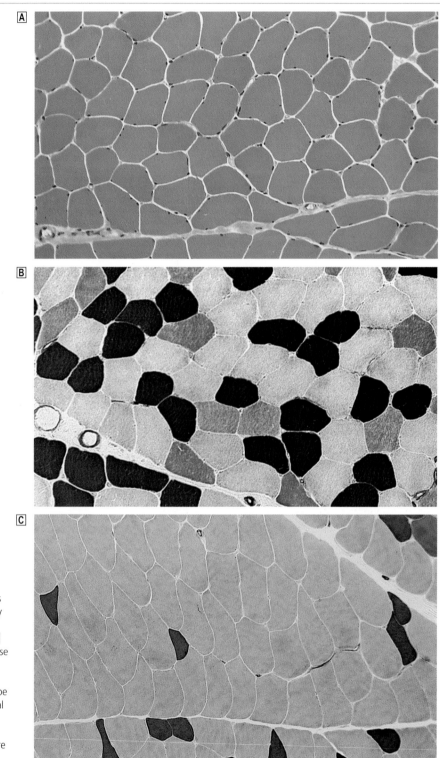

Fig. 26.37   Skeletal muscle histology.
A Normal muscle fibres within the fascicles are of relatively uniform size and are closely packed, with little intervening tissue. The nuclei are at the periphery of each fibre. **B** Histochemical preparation for myosin ATPase demonstrating the normal random mosaic pattern of fibre types within the fascicle (type 1 fibres are dark, type 2a pale and type 2b intermediate in colour). **C** Histochemical preparation for myosin ATPase in a case of chronic spinal muscular atrophy showing a loss of the normal mosaic pattern, with fibre type 2b predominance and grouping.

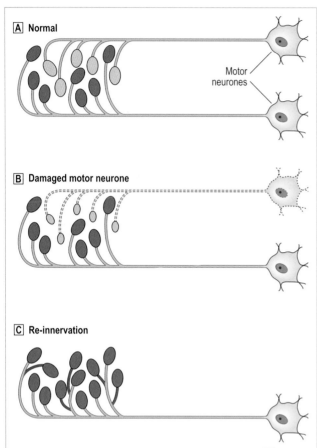

Fig. 26.38 Skeletal muscle: effects of denervation. A In normal muscle, the two main fibre types are distributed in a mosaic pattern. The muscle fibre type is determined by its innervation from a motor neurone. A single motor neurone can supply many muscle fibres. B Damage to a single motor neurone or its axon results in neurogenic atrophy of muscle fibres; each affected fibre is of the same fibre type. C The atrophied denervated fibres can be re-innervated by axons from other motor neurones supplying adjacent fibres. This process can change the fibre type of the re-innervated muscle fibres, resulting in fibre type grouping with loss of the normal mosaic arrangement (see also Fig. 26.37C).

- *Type 1 (Werdnig–Hoffmann disease)* has an onset before 3 months of age and is sometimes present at birth. This condition is rapidly progressive and usually results in death before the age of 18 months.
- *Type 2* also affects infants and children, with an onset between 6 and 12 months of age. It is more slowly progressive than Type 1, but causes severe disability with a variable life expectancy.
- *Type 3 (Kugelberg–Welander disease)* has an onset between 2 and 15 years of age. It is a slowly progressive disorder which usually allows survival into adult life with mild to moderate disability.
- *Type 4* affects adults and pursues a very slow course, often causing mild disability. Its progress may become arrested after several decades.

Peripheral neuropathies

Peripheral neuropathies involving motor nerves often present clinically with muscle wasting and weakness, accompanied by sensory loss in a 'glove and stocking' distribution. In chronic neuropathies, for example hereditary sensorimotor neuropathies, there is usually evidence of denervation and re-innervation on muscle biopsy.

Miscellaneous spinal cord disorders

There are a number of miscellaneous spinal cord disorders involving the anterior horn cells or the ventral motor nerve roots, for example poliomyelitis, syringomyelia and degenerative diseases of the vertebral column (osetoarthritis and prolapsed intervertebral discs).

MYOPATHIES

The main primary diseases of skeletal muscle may be classified as follows:

- muscular dystrophies
- inflammatory myopathies
- congenital myopathies
- metabolic myopathies
- toxic myopathies.

Muscular dystrophies

The muscular dystrophies form a group of inherited disorders that result in the progressive destruction of muscle fibres. The muscle innervation is normal in most cases. The most important examples are discussed below.

Duchenne dystrophy

Duchenne dystrophy is an X-linked disorder affecting 1 in 3000–5000 live male births. Approximately one-third of cases represent new mutations. The gene for this disorder has been located to the p21 region of the X chromosome. The gene product, *dystrophin,* is a protein normally present at the interphase between the cytoplasm and the muscle cell membrane. Gene deletions in Duchenne dystrophy result in a deficiency of dystrophin in muscle fibre membranes, causing muscle fibre damage by disruption of the cell membrane, leading to uncontrolled entry of calcium into the cell. Further understanding of the genetic defects in this disorder will allow for a fuller knowledge of its pathogenesis and hence potential for treatment.

The disease usually presents between 2 and 4 years of age, with proximal muscle weakness and pseudohypertrophy of the calves. The serum creatine phosphokinase (CPK) is elevated in the early stages of the disease, and is sometimes also elevated in female carriers. Most patients die before the age of 20, usually of the cardiomyopathy that occurs as part of this condition.

The characteristic biopsy findings are abnormal variation in the diameter of the muscle fibres, with many fibres showing

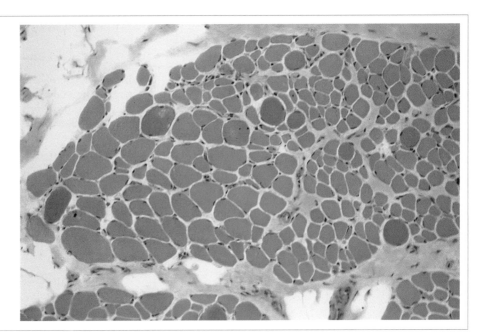

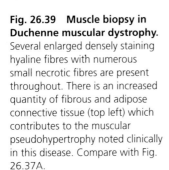

Fig. 26.39 Muscle biopsy in Duchenne muscular dystrophy. Several enlarged densely staining hyaline fibres with numerous small necrotic fibres are present throughout. There is an increased quantity of fibrous and adipose connective tissue (top left) which contributes to the muscular pseudohypertrophy noted clinically in this disease. Compare with Fig. 26.37A.

hyaline degeneration or necrosis, with attempts at regeneration (Fig. 26.39). Partial or complete absence of dystrophin can be demonstrated by immunohistochemistry or western blotting of muscle biopsies. Eventually, as the muscle fibre destruction progresses, the muscle is almost totally replaced by fat and connective tissue.

Becker dystrophy

An X-linked disorder, Becker dystrophy exhibits many similarities to Duchenne dystrophy, but the onset occurs at a later age and the progress of the disease is slower, many patients surviving into adult life. Genetic studies indicate that this disorder is an allelic variant of Duchenne dystrophy, involving deletions in the p21 region on the X chromosome.

Limb girdle dystrophy

The group of disorders known as limb girdle dystrophy are inherited as autosomal recessive conditions. The onset can occur in childhood or adult life, usually with weakness in the pelvic girdle and, later, the shoulder girdle. The progress of the disease is variable, many patients surviving with only mild to moderate disability. Muscle biopsy shows the typical dystrophic features of fibre destruction and regeneration, but to a lesser degree than occurs in Duchenne dystrophy.

Facioscapulohumeral dystrophy

Facioscapulohumeral dystrophy is an autosomal dominant disorder, the genetic locus for which is chromosome 4q35. This disease usually presents in children and young adults with weakness of the face and shoulder girdle. The rate of progress is slow, and many patients survive with only mild disability. Muscle biopsy shows the features of a slowly progressive dystrophy, in which focal lymphocytic infiltration is occasionally present.

Myotonic dystrophy

Myotonic dystrophy is also an autosomal dominant condition, the gene for which has been localised to chromosome 19. The genetic abnormality is an unstable CTG repeat sequence in a cAMP-dependent protein kinase. It usually presents between 20 and 30 years of age with weakness and wasting of facial, limb girdle and proximal limb muscles. Myotonia (persistence of contraction after voluntary effort has ceased) is common in the involved muscles, and patients usually exhibit a number of systemic disorders, including cataract, balding, gonadal atrophy and diabetes mellitus. Characteristic changes are found on electromyography. Muscle biopsy shows dystrophic changes, in which many fibres contain internal nuclei and exhibit a variety of cytoskeletal abnormalities.

Inflammatory myopathies

Muscle can be involved in a variety of infections, most of which are accompanied by a characteristic inflammatory reaction. The infecting organisms may be:

- bacteria, such as streptococci (group A), clostridia
- viruses, such as coxsackie B, influenza
- parasites, such as *Toxoplasma, Trichinella, Taenia solium*.

Several systemic inflammatory disorders frequently involve muscle, including sarcoidosis, systemic lupus erythematosus (SLE) and polyarteritis nodosa.

Polymyositis and dermatomyositis

Polymyositis is the commonest inflammatory muscle disorder, occurring most frequently in adults; females are affected more often than males. It may be associated with collagen vascular diseases (Ch. 25), for example systemic lupus erythematosus, or malignancies, for example bronchial carcinoma. Patients usually present with weakness, pain and swelling of proximal muscles. Dermatomyositis is a microangiopathy affecting skin and muscle, where complement deposition causes capillary lysis and muscle ischaemia. The serum CPK is usually elevated in the early stages of both diseases, and characteristic changes are usually present on electromyography.

Histology shows muscle fibre necrosis with phagocytosis of degenerate fibres by macrophages. T-lymphocytes are usually present within the endomysium and around blood vessels. Evidence of muscle fibre regeneration can usually be found, and fibre atrophy may be a striking feature in some cases, particularly in the perifascicular fibres in cases of childhood dermatomyositis.

The muscle fibre damage results from immunological injury by clonally expanded CD8 T-lymphocytes and macrophages. The mechanism of antigen sensitisation is unknown. Treatment with immunosuppressive drugs, such as corticosteroids and azathioprine, is beneficial in many cases.

Inclusion body myositis

Inclusion body myositis is most frequent in elderly patients and clinically resembles polymyositis. Its aetiology is unknown, but affected muscles show inflammation and fibre necrosis associated with small filamentous intracellular inclusions and vacuoles. Unlike polymyositis, it responds poorly to corticosteroids and azathioprine.

Congenital myopathies

Congenital myopathies are uncommon; many of them occur as inherited disorders. Most cases present with hypotonia and floppiness in infancy; these features may prove fatal in severe cases. The diagnosis depends largely on the muscle biopsy appearances, which are thought to reflect delayed development and maturation of the muscle fibres, for example centro-nuclear myopathy, or congenital fibre type disproportion. Hypotonia in infancy is a common manifestation of muscle disease, but may be due to other disorders, including cerebral palsy, hypothyroidism and Down's syndrome.

Metabolic myopathies

Muscle involvement occurs in many inherited metabolic disorders, such as glycogenosis, carnitine deficiency and mitochondrial disorders. Most of these exhibit other systemic manifestations, for example stroke-like episodes and lactic acidosis in mitochondrial cytopathies. Other metabolic disorders involving muscle include:

- *Malignant hyperthermia.* This uncommon, dominantly inherited disorder results in an abnormal sensitivity to certain anaesthetic agents, such as halothane, which can result in a fatal hyperpyrexia on exposure.
- *Endocrine myopathies.* A large number of endocrine disorders may involve muscle, including hyper- and hypothyroidism and Cushing's syndrome. The changes are usually reversible with appropriate therapy.

Toxic myopathies

Many drugs, for example corticosteroids and penicillamine, can produce muscle damage, which is usually reversible on withdrawal. One of the commonest toxins to affect skeletal muscle is ethanol. Two main patterns of damage are recognised:

- *Acute alcoholic myopathy* is induced by bouts of heavy drinking, which cause acute fibre necrosis. Release of myoglobin from the damaged fibres may result in acute renal failure.
- *Subacute alcoholic myopathy* occurs in chronic alcoholics, and presents with proximal muscle weakness and wasting. Biopsy shows selective atrophy of type 2b fibres, which is reversible in the early stages.

DISORDERS OF NEUROMUSCULAR TRANSMISSION

Two main conditions occur in this group: myasthenia gravis and Lambert–Eaton myasthenic syndrome.

Myasthenia gravis

Myasthenia gravis, an autoimmune disorder, usually presents in adults aged 20–40 years, with fluctuating progressive weakness involving particularly the ocular, bulbar and proximal limb muscles. Females are affected more often than males. Over 90% of patients have antibodies against acetylcholine receptor proteins which bind to the post-synaptic receptor and block neurotransmission; anti-striated muscle antibodies are present in a smaller proportion of patients. Linkage with various HLA antigens has been demonstrated, for example A1, B7 and DRw3.

The thymus is hyperplastic in over 50% of patients, and a thymoma is present in a further 15%. The thymus appears to be the site of antigen presentation in this disorder, but the mechanism of sensitisation is unknown. Treatment with cholinergic drugs, immunosuppressive agents such as corticosteroids, plasmapheresis and thymectomy may be beneficial.

Lambert–Eaton myasthenic syndrome

Lambert–Eaton myasthenic syndrome is a rare, non-metastatic complication of malignancy (usually small cell carcinoma of the bronchus) which presents with limb girdle and proximal muscle weakness. Acetylcholine release from motor nerve terminals is impaired by the binding of an abnormal IgG class antibody to presynaptic calcium ion channels.

THE EYE

- ▶ Vascular disease of the retina in hypertension and diabetes mellitus is a common cause of visual impairment
- ▶ Inflammatory conditions include infectious disorders, sarcoidosis and autoimmune diseases

▶ Cataracts result from the formation of opaque proteins in the lens
▶ Glaucoma occurs when intra-ocular pressure is increased, usually due to obstruction to the outflow of aqueous fluid
▶ Commonest primary intra-ocular neoplasms are naevi, malignant melanomas and retinoblastomas

A brief summary of the anatomical features of the eye is given in Figure 26.40. The unique anatomy and function of the eye mean that the clinical and pathological manifestations of eye diseases often present features not encountered elsewhere.

TRAUMA

Damage to the eye can occur following direct or indirect injuries to the globe. The eye is also susceptible to damage by chemicals, for example ammonia, and physical agents, for example heat and irradiation. Direct injuries to the eye are the most important clinically and may be classified according to the site and nature of the damage; in the perforating injuries, the sclera is only partially torn, but complete rupture occurs in penetrating injuries.

Penetrating and perforating injuries result in the most severe form of traumatic damage to the eye. The immediate complications of penetrating injuries include disruption of the globe, with haemorrhage and detachment of the lens and retina. Infection is a common complication, particularly if the missile is composed of organic material. *Sympathetic uveitis* and *ophthalmitis* are uncommon delayed complications of penetrating injuries (see below).

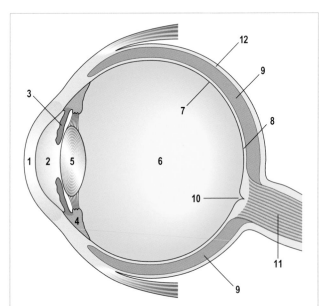

Fig. 26.40 Anatomy of the normal eye. Diagram shows cornea **(1)**, anterior chamber **(2)**, iris **(3)**, ciliary body **(4)**, lens **(5)**, vitreous humour **(6)**, retina **(7)**, macula **(8)**, choroid **(9)**, optic disc **(10)**, optic nerve **(11)** and sclera **(12)**.

VASCULAR DISEASE

Vascular diseases are a major cause of visual impairment in the middle-aged and elderly. Two main categories are recognised: retinal ischaemia and retinal haemorrhages.

Retinal ischaemia

Retinal ischaemia usually occurs due to the occlusion of a blood vessel by atheroma, vasculitis, thrombosis or embolism. If the central retinal artery is involved, the inner two-thirds of the retina will undergo ischaemic degeneration; occlusion of the posterior ciliary artery damages the photoreceptor cells in the outer retinal layers.

Vascular occlusion in the retina causes exudation of plasma from capillaries. This is seen ophthalmoscopically as 'hard' exudates, which appear as discrete, well-defined, pale yellow retinal lesions. Ophthalmoscopy may also reveal 'soft' or 'cotton wool' exudates; these represent microinfarcts of the retina, involving both ganglion cells and nerve fibres. These lesions are most frequently seen in diabetic and hypertensive retinopathies, both of which are accompanied by changes in the retinal vessels that are readily detectable on ophthalmoscopy (Fig. 26.41).

Characteristic changes in *hypertensive retinopathy* include:

- decreased arteriolar tortuosity and calibre variation
- arteriovenous nipping
- flame-shaped haemorrhages
- soft exudates.

Characteristic changes in *diabetic retinopathy* include:

- increased tortuosity and dilatation of veins
- capillary dilatation and micro-aneurysms
- 'dot and blot' haemorrhages
- hard and soft exudates
- neovascularisation.

Retinal haemorrhages

Retinal haemorrhages may occur in a number of conditions, for example trauma or infection, but are most commonly found in diabetic and hypertensive retinopathy. Two main patterns of haemorrhage are seen on ophthalmoscopy:

- flame haemorrhages, originating from arterioles
- blot haemorrhages, focal accumulations of blood in the outer plexiform layer of the retina due to capillary rupture.

Neovascularisation

Neovascularisation is an important response to retinal ischaemia and haemorrhage, resulting in the proliferation of small vessels around the edge of the lesion. As well as proliferating in the retina, these small vessels may penetrate the vitreous fluid, where the lack of supporting tissue renders them prone to rupture and haemorrhage. Neovascularisation can also occur in response to senile macular degeneration, causing a submacular fibrovascular mass which damages the overlying photoreceptor cells and results in loss of central vision.

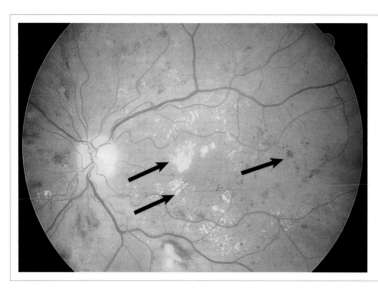

Fig. 26.41 Diabetic retinopathy. Using fundoscopy, multiple haemorrhages and exudates (arrows) are demonstrable throughout the retina in an adult with longstanding diabetes mellitus. (Courtesy of Mr B A Noble, Leeds.)

INFLAMMATORY LESIONS

Micro-organisms, an important cause of ocular inflammation, can gain access to the eye by haematogenous spread from adjacent tissues, for example the paranasal sinuses, or from the external surface of the eye.

Bacterial infections

Bacterial infections can occur at any site within the eye, but are particularly liable to spread to the vitreous fluid and lens, where the local conditions favour growth of organisms. The cellular reactions to infection in the eye are similar to those elsewhere in the body and will not therefore be described in detail.

Inflammation of the uvea and ciliary body leads to exudation of protein and inflammatory cells into the posterior cornea which can be detected on ophthalmoscopy. Local inflammatory changes can result in adhesions within the anterior chamber, causing glaucoma (see below).

Viral infections

Important viral infections include:

- adenovirus 3, 7, causing follicular conjunctivitis
- adenovirus 8, 19, causing epidemic keratoconjunctivitis
- herpes simplex type 1 virus, causing superficial punctate keratitis and dendritic corneal ulcers
- varicella zoster virus, causing corneal vesicles with scarring when the ophthalmic division of the trigeminal nerve is involved in shingles.

Chlamydial infections

Two main forms of infection occur:

- *Chlamydia trachomatis A–C* cause *trachoma,* a tropical disease that is a common cause of blindness. The organism infects the conjunctival and corneal epithelium, and can

be identified as intracytoplasmic inclusions on conjunctival smears.
- *Chlamydia trachomatis D–K* commonly infect the genital tract, but can cause a mild form *of keratoconjunctivitis.* The organism can be identified and cultured from conjunctival smears.

Parasitic infections

Acanthamoeba
Acanthamoeba is a free-living protozoan in mains water supplies. It can cause a corneal infection (keratitis) and may invade the eye, particularly in contact lens wearers. Antibiotic therapy is usually effective, although invasive infections are difficult to eradicate.

Toxoplasmosis
In congenital infections with the protozoan *Toxoplasma gondii,* the organism spreads to numerous sites in the body. Retinal involvement takes the form of chorioretinitis with extensive tissue destruction and microphthalmos in severe cases.

Toxocara canis
Toxocara canis infection is usually acquired in childhood from contact with ova from infected dogs. Ingestion of the ova is followed by liberation of larvae in the stomach and duodenum; the larvae migrate through the body but do not usually mature. A granuloma can develop in the retina around a dead larva, causing visual obstruction which clinically may mimic an intra-ocular neoplasm.

Sarcoidosis

Ocular involvement is often one of the main manifestations of sarcoidosis, along with erythema nodosum and hilar lymphadenopathy. The granulomatous inflammation characteristic of sarcoidosis occurs in three main forms:

- conjunctivitis
- iridocyclitis (the commonest form)
- retinitis, sometimes involving the optic nerve head.

Autoimmune disease

This group of uncommon disorders almost always arises as a consequence of ocular injury, particularly perforating wounds. Prompt clinical attention to such injuries has greatly reduced the incidence of these complications.

Lens-induced uveitis

Release of lens protein into the anterior chamber or vitreous (usually as a result of trauma) occasionally causes a giant cell granulomatous reaction involving the lens and uvea. This results from a delayed hypersensitivity reaction following sensitisation to lens antigens.

Sympathetic ophthalmitis

Trauma to one eye with damage to the iris or ciliary body may cause a delayed hypersensitivity reaction following sensitisation to uveal and retinal antigens. This results in a giant cell granulomatous inflammatory response in either the damaged eye or the second eye. Children are particularly susceptible to this uncommon complication.

CATARACT

The normal structure of the lens depends on the integrity of its elastic capsule, the viability of the lens fibre cells, which contain transparent proteins, and a supply of essential metabolites in the fluid.

Cataracts result from the formation of opaque proteins within the lens which usually also results in a loss of lens elasticity. This can occur in:

- rubella
- Down's syndrome
- senile degeneration
- tears in lens capsule
- irradiation
- uveitis
- diabetes mellitus
- corticosteroid therapy.

Mature cataracts can cause severe visual loss, but this can be treated surgically by removal of the affected lens and insertion of a synthetic plastic substitute. Cataracts occasionally cause glaucoma due to mechanical obstruction of the anterior chamber angle, or lens dislocation.

GLAUCOMA

The normal intra-ocular pressure is 11–21 mmHg (1.5–2.8 kPa). This pressure depends on:

- the rate of the production of aqueous fluid
- the resistance to fluid movement in the outflow system.

Glaucoma denotes a group of common disorders in which the intra-ocular pressure is increased to a level that impedes blood supply to the retina, resulting in optic nerve cupping on fundoscopy and ultimately in blindness. The increase in intra-ocular pressure is usually caused by obstruction to the outflow of aqueous fluid, for example at the trabecular meshwork, canal of Schlemm or the drainage angle of the anterior chamber (Fig. 26.40). Glaucoma affects 1–2% of adults under the age of 40 years, rising to 5% over the age of 70 years. It is commoner in black populations of African origin.

Closed-angle glaucoma

Closure of the irideocorneal angle, thus obstructing the drainage of aqueous humour from the anterior chamber, can occur when the iris is in mid-dilatation, particularly in middle-aged or elderly individuals. This results in acute glaucoma, with corneal oedema, congestion and pain. The next commonest cause of closed-angle glaucoma is neovascularisation around the irideocorneal angle (Fig. 26.42) following a variety of disorders, for example haemorrhage, ischaemia or infection.

Open-angle glaucoma

Open-angle glaucoma can occur as a primary degenerative condition in the elderly, when a progressive accumulation of collagen within the trabeculae and extracellular space of the outflow system increases resistance to the flow of aqueous fluid. This results in a slow increase in intra-ocular pressure which is often manifest clinically as a central visual field defect.

Open-angle glaucoma may also occur due to mechanical obstruction of the outflow system by inflammatory cells, haemorrhage or tumour infiltration. The effects of raised intra-ocular pressure are:

- central visual defect due to retinal ischaemia
- bullous keratopathy due to corneal oedema
- scleral bulges (staphylomas) due to scleral stretching
- in infants, expansion of the eye (buphthalmos).

MACULAR DEGENERATION

Macular degeneration is a common cause of visual loss in the elderly in the UK. Progressive damage to the macula, the most sensitive region of the light-sensitive retina (Fig. 26.40), results in a gradual loss of central and detailed vision. Macular degeneration usually occurs over the age of 60 years and is more common in females. However, rare inherited varieties occur, and may affect younger patients. The precise causes of macular degeneration are uncertain. Two main types occur:

- *Dry macular degeneration*. This accounts for 90% of cases, where retinal photoreceptor cells in the macula are gradually lost, leading to slowly progressive visual impairment. Dry macular degeneration cannot be treated.
- *Wet macular degeneration*. Macular damage occurs as a result of ingrowth of fragile new blood vessels beneath the retina that are prone to leak and haemorrhage. This leads

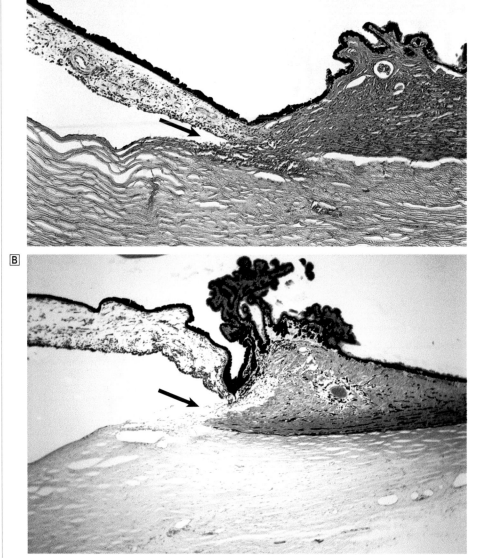

Fig. 26.42 Closed-angle glaucoma: neovascularisation. The aqueous outflow at the anterior chamber angle (arrow) is obstructed by a mass of fibrovascular tissue containing numerous capillaries **A** in contrast to a normal control **B**. The resulting increase in intra-ocular pressure caused glaucoma, which eventually necessitated removal of the eye.

to a more rapid visual loss, which can be treated by laser surgery to seal off the abnormal vessels. A new treatment involving antivascular endothelial growth factor compounds has shown promise and is becoming widely available in countries such as the UK.

OCULAR TUMOURS

A large variety of neoplasms may arise within the eye and its adnexa, tumours in the latter resembling those occurring in the skin, connective tissue and salivary glands. The most important intra-ocular tumours are naevi and malignant melanoma, and retinoblastoma.

Naevi and malignant melanoma

Naevi and malignant melanoma occur most frequently in adults, and derive from the melanocytes of the uveal tract. *Naevi* are benign melanocytic lesions akin to those commonly occurring in skin. *Malignant melanomas* occur as a solitary mass in one eye, usually arising in the posterior choroid. The neoplasm often grows rapidly to form an intra-ocular mass that causes extensive retinal detachment and secondary glaucoma (Fig. 26.43). Histologically, two main patterns are recognised:

- *Spindle cell melanoma.* This has a relatively good prognosis, greater than 50% survival at 5 years.

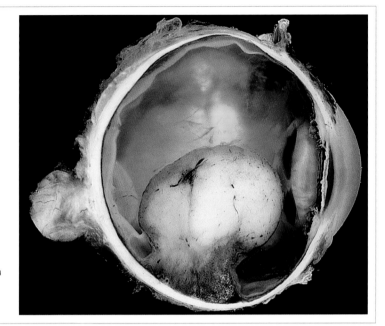

Fig. 26.43 Malignant melanoma: intra-ocular mass. In this eye, a large unpigmented malignant melanoma is arising from the choroid. The neoplasm has caused extensive retinal elevation and detachment.

- *Epithelioid melanoma.* This has a much worse prognosis. Blood spread to other organs (particularly the liver) can occur; these metastases sometimes present many years after enucleation of the affected eye.

Melanomas may also arise in the iris; these are associated with a better prognosis and seldom metastasise.

Retinoblastoma

There has been much recent interest in retinoblastoma. It is an uncommon neoplasm, with an incidence in the UK of around 1 per 20 000 live births; 5–10% of cases are familial, with affected individuals inheriting a deletion on the long arm of chromosome 13 which always involves the RB tumour suppressor gene on band q14. The same chromosomal abnormality occurs in tumour tissue (but not normal tissue) from patients with sporadic retinoblastomas (Ch. 11).

Children with retinoblastomas present with visual loss, squint or enlargement of the eye, which is occupied by a tumour within the retina. On histology, the neoplasm has the features of a primitive neuroectodermal tumour, in which the cells tend to form rosettes. Local extension along the optic nerve or through the sclera is common, but distant metastases are rare. The results of early enucleation and radiotherapy are good, with a 5-year survival rate of around 90%.

Optic nerve glioma

Optic nerve glioma is a rare neoplasm which occurs most frequently in children and young adults; it is a well-recognised complication of neurofibromatosis and tuberous sclerosis. Patients usually present with progressive visual failure, with proptosis and papilloedema. The histological features are those of a pilocytic astrocytoma. The results of surgery and radiotherapy are good, with over 90% of patients surviving for 5 years or more.

Metastatic carcinoma

Metastatic carcinomas form the largest group of intra-ocular neoplasms. The commonest primary sources are breast carcinoma in females and bronchial carcinoma in males.

THE EAR

MIDDLE EAR

The middle ear and mastoid air cells of the temporal bone are extensions of the upper respiratory tract, and are lined by ciliated epithelium. Infections in these sites are common, particularly in children, and may occur as part of a generalised upper respiratory tract infection.

Otitis media

Acute otitis media

Acute otitis media may result from primary or secondary bacterial infections; the latter occasionally complicate a viral illness. Acute bacterial otitis media is a suppurative inflammatory process most often caused by *Haemophilus influenzae* or *Streptococcus pneumoniae*. The inflammatory exudate can cause the tympanic membrane to bulge and rupture, and may spread to the mastoid air cells, causing acute mastoiditis. This condition usually responds rapidly to antibiotics.

Serous otitis media

Serous otitis media is a non-suppurative process in which fluid accumulates in the middle ear as a consequence of Eustachian tube obstruction. It is an important cause of hearing difficulties in children ('glue ear') and can be relieved by removing the Eustachian obstruction, for example in patients with tonsillar hyperplasia.

Chronic otitis media

Chronic otitis media usually results from persistent or repeated acute bacterial infections. Common complications include:

- tympanic perforation and discharge
- aural polyps: granulation tissue in the middle ear
- disarticulation and resorption of ossicles, with conductive hearing loss
- cholesteatoma: accumulation of keratin derived from squamous epithelium spreading in from the external auditory canal following tympanic perforation.

Tumours

Middle-ear neoplasms are uncommon. The most frequently encountered are:

- adenomas: derived from the lining epithelium
- squamous cell carcinomas
- jugular paragangliomas: arising from paraganglia (chemoreceptor cells) in the glomus jugulare. These slow-growing neoplasms usually occur in women aged 40–60 years, and are characterised by relentless local invasion. Metastases are uncommon.

INNER EAR

The most important clinical manifestations of inner ear disorders are deafness and dizziness. These occur in varying degrees, due to impaired cochlear and vestibular function. Among the most common disorders affecting the inner ear are labyrinthitis, Ménière's disease and otosclerosis.

Labyrinthitis

Infections of the labyrinth are usually viral: mumps, cytomegalovirus and rubella are the organisms most frequently involved. The inflammatory process usually subsides spontaneously.

Ménière's disease

Ménière's disease is an uncommon disorder characterised clinically by attacks of nausea, vertigo, nystagmus, tinnitus and hearing loss. The pathogenesis is unknown, but the disease results in distension of the endolymphatic system in the cochlear duct and saccule. The vestibular membrane of Reissner may rupture, and the distended saccule compresses adjacent structures. The aetiology of Ménière's disease is uncertain, but similar symptoms may occur in post-infectious labyrinthitis following upper respiratory tract viral infections.

Otosclerosis

Otosclerosis is one of the commonest causes of hearing loss in young adults. It affects females more often than males, and is inherited as an autosomal dominant trait with variable penetrance. The conductive hearing loss results from bone deposition around the stapes footplate, which eventually results in ankylosis. The disease can be treated surgically by stapedectomy.

Commonly confused conditions and entities relating to the central and peripheral nervous systems	
Commonly confused	Distinction and explanation
Extradural and subdural haemorrhage	Extradural haemorrhage is usually associated with a skull fracture, resulting in rupture of an artery (e.g. middle meningeal artery); the bleeding is rapid and at relatively high pressure. Subdural haemorrhage is slower venous bleeding leading to formation of a blood clot between the dura and the brain.
Saccular aneurysm and microaneurysm	Rupture of an extracerebral saccular aneurysm on the circle of Willis results in subarachnoid haemorrhage. Rupture of a (much smaller) intracerebral microaneurysm results in intracerebral haemorrhage.
Meningitis and meningism	Meningitis is inflammation of the meninges, whereas meningism is a set of symptoms and signs (headache, photophobia, neck stiffness) indicating meningeal irritation, e.g. by inflammation, subarachnoid haemorrhage.
Senile plaques and neurofibrillary tangles	Both occur in the brain in Alzheimer's disease. Senile plaques are larger and extracellular, with an amyloid protein core. Neurofibrillary tangles are smaller and intracellular and contain tau, a microtubule-associated protein.
Multiple sclerosis and systemic sclerosis	Multiple sclerosis is a demyelinating disorder of the nervous system. Systemic sclerosis is a connective tissue disorder also known as scleroderma. Both are probably autoimmune disorders, but there is no other relationship between them.

FURTHER READING

Dubowitz V, Sewery C A 2007 Muscle biopsy: a practical approach, 3rd edn. Saunders, London

Ellison D, Love S (eds) 2004 Neuropathology: a reference text of CNS pathology, 2nd edn. Mosby, Edinburgh

Fuller G, Manford M 2006 Neurology: an illustrated colour text, 2nd edn. Churchill Livingstone, Edinburgh

Graham D I, Bell J E, Ironside J W 1995 Color atlas and text of neuropathology. Mosby-Wolfe, London

Gray F, de Girolami U, Poirier J (eds) 2004 Manual of basic neuropathology, 4th edn. Butterworth-Heinemann, Philadelphia

Ironside J W, Moss T, Louis D N, Lowe J S, Weller R O 2002 Diagnostic pathology of nervous system tumours. Churchill Livingstone, Edinburgh

Lee W R 2002 Ophthalmic histopathology, 2nd edn. Springer, London

Louis D, Ohgaki H, Wiestler O, Cavanee W K (eds) 2007 WHO classification of tumours of the central nervous system, 4th edn. IARC, Lyons

Love S, Louis D N, Ellison D W (eds) 2008 Greenfield's neuropathology, 8th edn. Hodder Arnold, London

National CJD Surveillance Unit, UK: http://www.cjd.ed.ac.uk

Neuroanatomy and Neuropathology on the Internet: http://www.neuropat.dote.hu

Neuropathology: an illustrated interactive course for medical students and residents: htpp://www.neuropathologyweb.org

Neuropathology and Neuroimaging Laboratory (neuropathology slides): http://www.urmc.rochester.edu/neuroslides/index.html

The Whole Brain Atlas: http://www.med.harvard.edu/AANLIB/home.html

GLOSSARY

Abscess Localised collection of pus resulting from an inflammatory reaction, often provoked by bacteria.

Acantholysis Separation of individual cells of the epidermis, often resulting in a bulla (blister).

Acanthosis Increased thickness of the stratum spinosum of the epidermis.

Achalasia Failure of a gut sphincter (usually) to relax, causing dilatation proximally.

Achlorhydria Lack of gastric acid secretion.

Acidosis Disturbance of acid–base balance characterised by acidity (decreased pH) of body fluids (contrast with alkalosis).

Acquired Due to an event after birth (contrast with congenital).

Acute Appearing rapidly (e.g. acute inflammation), but not necessarily severe as in common usage (contrast with chronic).

Adenocarcinoma Malignant neoplasm of glandular or secretory epithelium.

Adenoma Benign glandular neoplasm.

Adenosis Glandular proliferation.

Adhesin A molecule on the surface of a microbe that binds to a tissue receptor enabling cell or tissue-specific attachment.

Adhesion Abnormal band or layer of connective tissue fixing two or more normally separate structures (e.g. between loops of bowel after peritonitis).

-aemia Suffix—of the blood.

Aetiology Cause of a disease.

Agenesis Failure of a tissue or organ to form during embryogenesis.

Agonal Terminal event, immediately prior to death.

Alkalosis Disturbance of acid–base balance characterised by alkalinity (increased pH) of body fluids (contrast with acidosis).

Allele One copy of a paired gene.

Allergy Excessive and/or inappropriate immunological reaction to an environmental antigen (allergen) as in hay fever, allergic asthma and some adverse drug reactions.

Allograft Tissue transplanted between two individuals of the same species.

Amyloid Insoluble extracellular material of variable composition (e.g. immunoglobulin light chains, amyloid protein A) causing hardening, enlargement and malfunction of the organs in which it is deposited.

Ana- Prefix—absent.

Anaemia Abnormally low blood haemoglobin concentration.

Anamnestic (response) Immunological reaction enhanced by previous exposure to the same agent.

Anaphylaxis Excessive and/or inappropriate type I immunological reaction; often used synonymously with hypersensitivity.

Anaplasia Lack of differentiated features, usually in a tumour (i.e. anaplastic tumour).

Aneuploid Abnormal chromosome numbers other than in exact multiples of the haploid state (i.e. not diploid, tetraploid, etc.); DNA aneuploidy is abnormal quantities of DNA per nucleus other than in exact multiples of the haploid quantity.

Aneurysm Abnormal permanent dilatation of a blood vessel or part of a heart chamber.

Angiitis inflammation of a blood vessel.

Anisocytosis Abnormal variation in size of red blood cells.

Ankylosis Fusion of a joint, resulting in its impaired mobility.

Annular Encircling the circumference of a hollow tube (e.g. annular carcinoma of the colon).

Anoxia Lack of oxygen.

Antibody Immunoglobulin with antigen specificity.

Antigen A substance binding specifically to an antibody or T-cell antigen receptor.

Antiserum Serum containing specific antibody.

Antitoxin Antibody capable of neutralising a bacterial toxin.

Aplasia Failure of growth of a tissue (e.g. aplastic anaemia).

Apoptosis A form of normal or pathological individual cell death characterised by activation of endogenous endonucleases.

APUDoma Neoplasm of APUD cells (APUD = amine content and/or precursor uptake and decarboxylation) (e.g. carcinoid tumour, insulinoma).

Arteriosclerosis Hardening of the arteries caused by any condition.

Arteritis Inflammation primarily within the wall of arteries (e.g. polyarteritis nodosa).

Ascites Abnormal accumulation of fluid in the peritoneal cavity.

Aseptic 1. Performed in such a way as to avoid infection (e.g. by using sterile instruments); 2. inflammatory illness not due to any identifiable bacterium (e.g. 'aseptic' meningitis).

Asphyxia Consequence of suffocation or mechanically impaired respiration.

Atelectasis Failure to expand, usually of the lung.

Atheroma Condition characterised by the focal accumulation of lipid in the intima of arteries causing their lumen to be narrowed, their wall to be weakened and predisposing to thrombosis.

Atherosclerosis Atheroma causing hardening of arteries.

Atopy Condition characterised by predisposition to allergies.

Atresia Embryological failure of formation of the lumen of a normally hollow viscus or duct (e.g. biliary atresia).

Atrophy Pathological or physiological cellular or organ shrinkage.

Atypia Departure from the typical normal appearance, usually histological, either reactive or sometimes denoting pre-neoplastic change (i.e. dysplasia).

Auto-antibody Antibody reactive with the body's own tissues or constituents.

Autocrine Characteristic of a cell responding to growth factors, cytokines, etc., produced by it (contrast with endocrine and paracrine); when unregulated, a feature of neoplasia.

Autograft Tissue transplanted in the same individual from which it is taken.

Autoimmunity Abnormal state in which the body's immune system reacts against its own tissues or constituents.

Autologous Transplantation or transfusion in which the donor and recipient are the same individual.

Autolysis Digestion of tissue by the enzymes contained within it.

Autopsy Synonymous with necropsy or postmortem examination (autopsy = 'to see for oneself' rather than relying on signs and symptoms).

Autosomal (gene) Residing on any autosome (autosomes are chromosomes other than sex chromosomes).

Bacteraemia Presence of bacteria in the blood.

Bacteriuria Presence of bacteria in the urine.

Benign Relatively harmless though usually not without risk of serious consequences if untreated; as in benign hypertension (mild blood pressure elevation associated with insidious tissue injury), and benign neoplasm (tumour that does not invade or metastasise); (contrast with malignant).

Biopsy The process of removing tissue for diagnosis, or a piece of tissue removed during life for diagnostic purposes.

'Blast' cell Any primitive cell but especially a primitive haemopoietic cell such as a myeloblast, the presence of which in the blood is suspicious of acute leukaemia.

-blastoma Suffix—tumour histologically resembling the embryonic state of the organ in which it arises and more commonly seen in young children (e.g. retinoblastoma).

Borderline (tumour) A tumour of uncertain malignant potential.

Bronchiectasis Permanent abnormal dilatation of bronchi.

Bulla An abnormal thin-walled cavity filled with liquid (e.g. bulla of skin) or gas (e.g. emphysematous bulla of lung).

Cachexia Extreme wasting of the body, often associated with a malignant neoplasm.

Cadherin Calcium-dependent cell surface adhesion molecule.

Calcification Process occurring naturally in bone and teeth, but abnormally in some diseased tissues (dystrophic calcification) or as a result of hypercalcaemia ('metastatic' calcification).

Calculus Stone (e.g. gallstone).

Callus 1. New immature bone formed within and around a bone fracture; 2. patch of hard skin formed at the site of repeated rubbing (also referred to as a 'callosity').

Cancer A general term, in the public domain, usually implying any malignant tumour.

Carbuncle Large pus-filled swelling, usually on the skin, often discharging through several openings and invariably due to a staphylococcal infection.

Carcinogenesis Mechanisms of the causation of malignant neoplasms (usually not just carcinomas).

Carcinoid Tumour of usually low-grade malignancy arising from APUD cells but not characterised by the production of a peptide hormone from which an alternative name might be derived (e.g. insulinoma); often secretes 5-hydroxytryptamine (serotonin).

Carcinoma A malignant epithelial neoplasm.

Carcinoma in situ A malignant epithelial neoplasm that has not yet invaded through the original basement membrane; synonymous with intra-epithelial neoplasia (see CIN).

Caruncle Small fleshy nodule; whether normal or pathological depends on location.

Caseation Type of necrosis, characteristically associated with tuberculosis, in which the dead tissue has a cheesy structureless consistency.

CD Cluster of differentiation (or designation); a standard numerical coding scheme for antigens borne by different types and subtypes of leukocytes and some other cells; used for identification of these cells by immunological methods.

Cellulitis Diffuse acute inflammation of the skin caused by streptococcal infection.

Centimorgan   Length of DNA estimated from exchange of homologous genetic material, between chromosomes during meiosis, averaging 1 cross-over per 100 gametes.

Centromere   Chromosomal constriction at which the chromatids are joined (contrast with telomere).

Cerebrovascular accident (CVA)   Cerebral infarction, or haemorrhage within or around the brain. Synonymous with 'stroke'.

Cestode   A tapeworm.

Chemotaxis   Migration of cells induced by some chemical influence such as complement components, and causing accumulation of leukocytes in inflamed tissues.

Cholestasis   Reduced or absent bile flow, thus leading to jaundice (cholestatic jaundice).

Chromatolysis (of nucleus)   Dissolution of the nucleus evident from the loss of its staining characteristics.

Chronic   Persisting for a long time (e.g. chronic inflammation); (contrast with acute).

CIN   Cervical intra-epithelial neoplasia, a precursor of invasive squamous cell carcinoma of the cervix uteri; graded I to III depending on the degree of severity.

Cirrhosis (liver)   Irreversible architectural disturbance characterised by nodules of hepatocytes with intervening fibrosis; a consequence of many forms of chronic liver injury.

Clot (blood)   Blood coagulated outside the cardiovascular system or after death (contrast with thrombus).

Coagulation   Solidification of material (e.g. blood coagulation, coagulative necrosis).

Coarctation   Congenital narrowing of the aorta.

Comedo(ne)   Plug of material (e.g. in some intraduct breast carcinomas, and in the lesions of acne vulgaris).

Comminuted (fracture)   Bone broken into fragments at fracture site.

Complement   Collective noun for a set of blood proteins that, when activated in cascade by, for example, antigen–antibody reactions, has various effects including leukocyte chemotaxis and cell lysis.

Complications   Events secondary to the primary disorder (e.g. complicated fracture involves adjacent nerves and/or vessels; cerebral haemorrhage is a complication of hypertension).

Compound   Involving more than one structure (e.g. compound naevus involves dermis and epidermis; compound bone fracture is associated with traumatic defect in the overlying skin).

Condyloma   Warty lesion, often on genitalia.

Congenital   Condition attributable to events prior to birth, not necessarily genetic or inherited.

Congestion   Engorgement with blood.

Consolidation   Solidification of lung tissue, usually by an inflammatory exudate; a feature of pneumonia.

Cyst   Cavity with an epithelial lining and containing fluid or other material (contrast with pseudocyst).

Cytokines   Substances (e.g. interleukins) produced by one cell that influence the behaviour of another, thus effecting intercellular communication.

Cytopathic (virus effect)   Causing cell injury, not necessarily fatal.

Cytotoxic   Causing cell injury, not necessarily fatal.

Degeneration   Disorder, not otherwise classified, characterised by loss of structural and functional integrity of an organ or tissue.

Demyelination   Loss of myelin from around nerve fibres.

Desmoid (tumour)   A tumour-like connective tissue proliferation related to fibromatosis.

Desmoplasia   Proliferation of connective tissue, typically a stromal response to tumours.

Diapedesis   Passage of blood cells between endothelial cells into the perivascular tissue; characteristic of inflammation.

Differentiation   1. Embryological—process by which a tissue develops special characteristics; 2. pathological—degree of morphological resemblance of a neoplasm to its parent tissue.

Diffuse   Affecting the tissue in a continuous or widespread distribution.

Diploid   Twice the haploid chromosome number or DNA content.

Disease   Abnormal state causing or capable of causing ill health.

Diverticulum   Abnormal hollow pouch communicating with the lumen of the structure from which it has arisen.

Dominant   Characteristic of a gene of which only one copy is necessary for it to be expressed.

Dyskeratosis   Disordered or premature keratinisation; a feature of dysplasia in squamous epithelium.

Dysplasia   Abnormal growth and differentiation of a tissue; in epithelia, often a feature of the early stages of neoplasia.

Dystrophy   Abnormal development or degeneration of a tissue (e.g. muscular dystrophy, dystrophic calcification).

Ecchymoses   Any bruise or haemorrhagic spot, larger than petechiae, on the skin (may be spontaneous in the elderly, usually due more to vascular fragility than to coagulation defects).

Ectasia   Abnormal dilatation (e.g. lymphangiectasia—dilatation of lymphatics).

Ectopic   Tissue or substance in or from an inappropriate site (but not by metastasis).

Effusion   Abnormal collection of fluid in a body cavity (e.g. pleura, peritoneum, synovial joint).

Elastosis   1. Increase in elastin in a tissue; 2. altered collagen with staining properties normally characteristic of elastin.

Embolus   Fluid (e.g. gas, fat) or solid (e.g. thrombus) mass, mobile within a blood vessel and capable of blocking its lumen.

Emphysema   Characterised by the formation of abnormal thin-walled gas-filled cavities; pulmonary emphysema—in lungs, 'surgical' emphysema—in connective tissues.

Empyema   Pre-existing cavity filled with pus (e.g. empyema of the gallbladder).

Endocrine   Characteristic of cells producing hormones with distant effects (contrast with autocrine and paracrine).

Endophytic   Tumour growing inwards from a surface, usually by invasion and thus malignant (contrast with exophytic).

Endotoxin   Toxin derived from disruption of the outer membrane of Gram-negative bacteria (contrast with exotoxin).

Epithelioid   Histologically resembling epithelium; specifically as in epithelioid cells which are derived from macrophages and a distinctive feature of granulomas.

Eponym   Name of a disease, etc., derived from its association with a place or person (e.g. Cushing's disease).

Erosion   Loss of superficial layer (not full-thickness) of a surface (e.g. gastric erosion).

Erythema   Abnormal redness of skin due to increased blood flow.

Essential (disease type)   Without evident antecedent cause; synonymous with primary and idiopathic.

Exon   Portion of a gene encoding the protein product (contrast with intron).

Exophytic   Tumour growing outwards from a surface, usually because it lacks invasive properties (contrast with endophytic).

Exotoxin   Toxin secreted by living bacteria (contrast with endotoxin).

Extrinsic   1. Outside the structure and, for example, compressing it (e.g. tumour outside the intestine, but compressing it and causing intestinal obstruction); 2. cause external to the body (e.g. extrinsic allergic alveolitis); (contrast with intrinsic).

Exudate   Extravascular accumulation of protein-rich fluid due to increased vascular permeability (contrast with transudate).

Fibrinoid   Resembling fibrin (e.g. fibrinoid necrosis).

Fibrinous   Rich in fibrin (e.g. fibrinous exudate).

Fibroid   Benign smooth-muscle tumour (leiomyoma) commonly arising from uterine myometrium.

Fibromatosis   A tumour-like infiltrative proliferation of fibroblasts and myofibroblasts.

Fibrosis   Process of depositing excessive collagen in a tissue.

Fibrous (tissue)   Connective tissue comprising predominantly fibroblasts and collagen.

Fistula   Abnormal connection between one hollow viscus and another or with the skin surface.

Fluke   A trematode (flatworm) of the order Digenea.

Focal   Localised abnormality (contrast with diffuse).

Follicular   Forming a circumscribed structure resembling a follicle (but not necessarily secretory, as would be the strict definition of follicular).

Forme fruste   Early stage of a disease, either at diagnosis or interrupted by treatment, before it has developed a complete set of characteristics.

Free radicals   Chemical radicals characterised by unpaired electrons in the outer shell and therefore highly reactive.

Fungating   Forming an elevated growth, usually neoplastic (and usually malignant).

Furuncle   A boil.

Ganglion (pathological)   Cystic lesion containing mucin-rich fluid associated with a joint or tendon sheath.

Gangrene   Bulk necrosis of tissues; 'dry' gangrene—sterile; 'wet' gangrene—with bacterial putrefaction.

Genotype   1. Genetic constitution of an individual; 2. classification of organisms according to their genetic characteristics (contrast with serotype).

Giant cell   Abnormally large cell, often multinucleated.

Gliosis   Increase in glial fibres, within the central nervous system; analogous to fibrosis elsewhere in the body.

Goitre   Enlarged thyroid gland.

Grade   Degree of malignancy of a neoplasm usually judged from its histological features (e.g. nuclear size and regularity, mitotic frequency); (compare with stage).

Granulation tissue   Newly formed connective tissue often found at the edge or base of ulcers and wounds, comprising capillaries, fibroblasts, myofibroblasts and inflammatory cells embedded in mucin-rich ground substance.

Granuloma   An aggregate of epithelioid macrophages, often including giant multinucleate cells also derived from macrophages (histiocytes).

Gumma   Focal necrotic lesion in tertiary stage of syphilis.

Haematocrit   Volume fraction of blood consisting of cells.

Haematoma   Localised collection of blood or blood clot, usually within a solid tissue.

Haemostasis   Natural ability to arrest bleeding (e.g. by vascular spasm and blood coagulation) or its arrest by artificial means (e.g. by ligating a blood vessel).

Hamartoma   Congenital tumour-like malformation comprising two or more mature tissue elements normally present in the organ in which it arises.

Haploid   Single allocation of unpaired chromosomes, as found in ova and spermatozoa.

Haplotype   Two or more gene loci inherited together, as in HLA (human leukocyte antigen) haplotype.

Hernia   Abnormal protrusion of an organ, or part of it, outside its usual compartment.

Heterologous   1. Transplantation or transfusion in which the donor and recipient are of different species (synonymous with xenogeneic); 2. tissue not normally present at that site (contrast with homologous).

Heterotopia   Presence of normal tissue in an abnormal location, usually due to an error in embryogenesis.

Histiocyte   Macrophage fixed within tissue rather than migrating through it.

Histogenesis   In the context of neoplasms, a term meaning the putative cell of origin.

Homeobox   Highly conserved DNA sequences usually present in genes controlling development.

Homograft   Transplantation from one individual to another of the same species.

Homologous   1. Transplantation or transfusion in which the donor and recipient are of the same species (synonymous with allogeneic); 2. tissue normally present at that site (contrast with heterologous).

Hyaline   Amorphous texture, sometimes due to the deposition or accumulation of intra- or extracellular material (e.g. amyloid, Mallory's hyalin).

Hydrocele   Fluid-filled cavity, especially surrounding a testis.

Hyperaemia   Increased blood flow, usually through a capillary bed as in acute inflammation.

Hyperchromatic   Increased histological staining, usually of nucleus.

Hyperkeratosis   Formation of excess keratin on the surface of stratified squamous epithelium (e.g. epidermis).

Hyperplasia   Enlargement of an organ, or a tissue within it, due to an increase in the number of cells.

Hypersensitivity   Excessive or inappropriate reaction to an environmental agent, often mediated immunologically (see allergy).

Hypertrophy   Enlargement of an organ, or part of it, due to an increase in the size of cells.

Hypoxia   Reduction in available oxygen.

Iatrogenic   Caused by medical intervention (e.g. adverse effect of a prescribed drug).

Idiopathic   Unknown cause; synonymous with primary, essential and cryptogenic.

Immunity   A body defence mechanism characterised by specificity and memory.

Incompetence (valvular)   Allowing regurgitation when valve is closed.

Infarction   Death of tissue (an infarct) due to insufficient blood supply.

Infiltrate   Abnormal accumulation of cells (e.g. leukocytes, neoplastic cells) or acellular material (e.g. amyloid) in a tissue.

Integrins   Heterodimeric molecules responsible for cell–matrix adhesion.

Interleukins   Cytokines produced by leukocytes.

Intrinsic   1. Within a structure rather than compressing it from without; 2. defect without obvious external cause (e.g. intrinsic asthma); (contrast with extrinsic).

Intron   Portion of a gene not encoding the protein product (contrast with exon).

Intussusception   Invagination or telescoping of a tubular structure, especially bowel.

Invasion   Property of malignant neoplastic cells enabling them to infiltrate normal tissues and enter blood vessels and lymphatics.

Involution   Reduction in size of an organ or part of it; may be physiological (e.g. shrinkage of thymus gland before adulthood).

Ischaemia   An inadequate blood supply to an organ or part of it.

-itis   Suffix—inflammatory.

Junctional   At the interface between two structures (e.g. junctional naevus is characterised by naevus cells at the dermo-epidermal junction).

Karyolysis   Disintegration of the nucleus.

Karyorrhexis   Nuclear fragmentation seen in necrotic cells.

Karyotype   Description of the number and shape of chromosomes within a cell, normally characteristic of a species.

Keratinisation   Production of keratin by normal or neoplastic stratified squamous epithelium.

805

Keratosis   Excess keratin.

Koilocytosis   Vacuolation of the cells of stratified squamous epithelium (e.g. skin, cervix), often characteristic of human papillomavirus infection.

Latent (interval)   Period between exposure to the cause of a disease and the appearance of the disease itself (e.g. incubation period).

Leiomyo-   Prefix—of smooth muscle (e.g. leiomyosarcoma—malignant neoplasm of smooth muscle).

Lesion   Any abnormality associated with injury or disease.

Leukaemia   Neoplastic proliferation of white blood cells; classified into acute and chronic types, according to onset and likely behaviour, and from the cell type (e.g. lymphocytic, granulocytic).

Leukocytosis   Excessive number of white blood cells (leukocytes).

Leukopenia   Lack of white blood cells.

Lipo-   Prefix—of adipose tissue (e.g. lipoma—benign adipose tumour).

-lithiasis   Formation of calculi (stones) (e.g. cholelithiasis—gallstones).

Lobar   Affecting a lobe, especially of lung as in lobar pneumonia.

Lobular   Affecting or arising from a lobule (e.g. lobular carcinoma of the breast).

Loss of heterozygosity   Loss of constitutional maternal or paternal alleles of a gene which, if lost from all abnormal cells in a lesion, indicates a monoclonal proliferation; a molecular marker of neoplasia, especially if at a tumour-suppressor gene locus.

Lymphokine   Cytokine produced by lymphocytes.

Lymphoma   Primary malignant neoplasm of lymphoid tissue classified according to cell type.

Lysis   Dissolution or disintegration of a cell, usually as a result of chemical effects.

Malformation   Congenital structural abnormality of the body.

Malignant   Condition characterised by relatively high risk of morbidity and mortality (e.g. malignant hypertension—high blood pressure leading to severe tissue damage; malignant neoplasm—invasive neoplasm with risk of metastasis); (contrast with benign).

Marantic (thrombus)   Occurring in association with severe wasting (marasmus), usually in infants.

Margination   Gathering of leukocytes on endothelial surface of capillaries and venules in acute inflammation.

Medullary (tumour)   Of a relatively soft consistency.

Melanoma   Malignant neoplasm of melanocytes (except 'juvenile' melanoma which is benign).

Metaplasia   Reversible change in the character of a tissue from one mature cell type to another.

Metastasis   Process by which a primary malignant neoplasm gives rise to secondary tumours (metastases) at other sites, most commonly by lymphatic, vascular or transcoelomic spread.

Mole   1. Common benign skin lesion composed of melanocytes and/or melanocytic naevus cells; 2. hydatidiform mole—rare benign disorder of pregnancy characterised by swollen chorionic villi and hyperplastic trophoblast.

Monoclonal   Attributable to a single clone of cells and thus more characteristic of a neoplasm than of a reactive process (contrast with polyclonal).

Mononuclear cells   Vague histological term for leukocytes other than polymorphonuclear leukocytes and not otherwise identifiable precisely.

Mucocele   Mucus-filled cyst or hollow organ (e.g. mucocele of the gallbladder).

Mural   On the wall of a hollow structure (e.g. mural thrombus on the inner wall of the left ventricle after myocardial infarction).

Mutation   Alteration in the base sequence of DNA, possibly resulting in the synthesis of an abnormal protein product; often an early stage in carcinogenesis.

Mycosis   1. Mycosis—fungal infection; 2. mycosis fungoides—cutaneous T-cell lymphoma entirely unrelated to any fungal infection.

Myxoid   Having a mucin-rich consistency.

Naevus   Coloured lesion on skin, often congenital, most commonly consisting of melanin-containing cells, but may be vascular, etc.

Necrosis   Pathological cellular or tissue death in a living organism, irrespective of cause (compare with apoptosis, gangrene and infarction).

Nematode   A roundworm.

Neoplasm   Abnormal and unco-ordinated tissue growth persisting after withdrawal of the initiating cause (synonymous in modern usage with 'tumour').

Neurogenic   Disorder attributable to interruption of nerve supply (e.g. neurogenic atrophy of muscle).

Normal   1. Statistical—distribution of a numerical variable in which the mode, median and mean are equal; 2. biological—natural state free of disease.

Nosocomial   Infection acquired in hospital or some other medical environment.

Occult   Abnormality present, but not observable.

Oedema Abnormal collection of fluid within or, more usually, between cells.

-oma Suffix—tumour (except 'granuloma', 'atheroma', 'stoma', etc.).

Oncocyte Cell with swollen cytoplasm, commonly due to numerous mitochondria.

Oncofetal Fetal characteristics expressed by tumours (e.g. carcinoembryonic antigen).

Oncogene A gene inappropriately, abnormally or excessively expressed in tumours and responsible for their autonomous growth.

Oncogenesis Mechanisms of the causation of tumours (almost synonymous with carcinogenesis).

Oncosis 1. A condition marked by the tumour formation (uncommon usage); 2. swelling of cells or tissues, more commonly the former.

Opportunist (micro-organism) Usually harmless, but causing disease in an individual with impaired immunity or some other susceptibility.

Opsonisation Enhancement of phagocytosis by factors (opsonins) in plasma.

Organisation Natural process of tissue repair.

-osis Suffix—state or condition, usually pathological (e.g. osteoarthrosis, acidosis).

p arm (of a chromosome) Short arm (p = petit; contrast with q arm).

-penia Suffix—deficiency (e.g. leukopenia—abnormally low white blood cell count).

Papillary Surface of a lesion characterised by numerous folds, fronds or villous projections.

Papilloma Benign neoplasm of non-glandular epithelium (e.g. squamous cell papilloma).

Paracrine Characteristic of neighbouring cells of different types influencing each other by secretion of cytokines, growth factors or hormones (contrast with autocrine and endocrine).

Parakeratosis Excessive keratin in which nuclear remnants persist (a histological sign of increased epidermal growth).

Paraprotein Abnormal plasma protein, usually a monoclonal immunoglobulin in multiple myeloma.

Parasite Organism living on or in the body (the host) and dependent on it for nutrition.

Parenchyma The morphologically and functionally specific cells of an organ.

Pathogenesis Mechanism through which the cause (aetiology) of a disease produces the clinicopathological manifestations.

Pathogenicity Ability (high, low, etc.) of a micro-organism to cause disease.

Pathognomonic Pathological feature characteristic of a particular disease.

Pedunculated On a stalk (contrast with sessile).

Peptic (ulcer) Due to the digestive action of gastric secretions.

Petechiae Minute haemorrhagic lesions.

Phagocytosis Ingestion of micro-organisms or other particles by a cell, especially neutrophil polymorphonuclear leukocytes and macrophages.

Phlebitis Inflammation of a vein.

Phlebothrombosis Venous thrombosis.

Pleomorphism Variation in size and shape, usually of nuclei and characteristic of malignant neoplasms.

Pleurisy Painful inflammation of the pleura.

Pneumoconiosis Lung disease due to dust inhalation.

Pneumonia Inflammation of the lung.

Poikilocytosis Abnormal erythrocyte shape.

Polyclonal Indicative of more than one cell clone; feature of reactive rather than neoplastic proliferations (contrast with monoclonal).

Polycythaemia Excessive number of red blood cells.

Polymorphic Consisting of more than one cell type.

Polyp Sessile or pedunculated protrusion from a body surface.

Polyposis Numerous polyps.

Primary 1. Initial event without apparent antecedent cause, synonymous with essential or idiopathic (e.g. primary hypertension); 2. a neoplasm arising in the organ in which it is situated (contrast with secondary).

Primer Short specific nucleotide sequence used to initiate the polymerase chain reaction.

Prion Proteinaceous infective particle.

Probe 1. Specific RNA, DNA or antibody used to locate or detect a substance or organism in a tissue; 2. mechanical device (e.g. rod) used to determine the route or patency of a track or orifice.

Prodromal Any feature heralding the appearance of a disease.

Prognosis Probable length of survival or disease-free state, especially after diagnosis and treatment of malignant neoplasms (e.g. 60% 5-year survival rate).

Prolapse Protrusion or descent of an organ or part of it from its normal location (e.g. prolapsed intervertebral disc, rectal prolapse).

Psammoma (body)   Laminated calcified microspherule commonly found in meningiomas and papillary carcinomas of the thyroid and ovaries.

Pseudocyst   Cavity with a distinct wall but lacking an epithelial lining (contrast with cyst).

Pseudomembrane   'False' membrane consisting of inflammatory exudate rather than epithelium.

Punctum   Small orifice, especially where an epidermal cyst communicates with the skin surface.

Purpura   Small haemorrhages into the skin.

Pus   Creamy material consisting of neutrophil polymorphs, in various stages of disintegration, and tissue debris.

Pustule   Small abscess on skin.

Putrefaction   Decomposition or rotting of dead tissue due to bacterial action, often accompanied by unpleasant odours.

Pyaemia   Pus-inducing organisms in the blood.

Pyknosis   Shrinkage of nucleus in a necrotic cell.

Pyogenic   Inducing or forming pus (e.g. pyogenic bacteria).

q arm (of a chromosome)   Long arm (contrast with p arm).

Reactive (process)   Reversible response to an external stimulus.

Recessive   Characteristic of a gene of which both copies are necessary for the effect to be expressed.

Recurrence   Neoplasm growing at, or close to, site of previously treated primary neoplasm of identical type.

Regeneration   Formation of new cells identical to those lost.

Rejection   Damage to or failure of a tissue or organ transplant due to an immunological host-versus-graft reaction.

Relapse   Reappearance of the clinicopathological manifestations of a disease after a period of good health.

Remission   Period of good health prior to possible relapse.

Repair   Healing with replacement of lost tissue, but not necessarily by similar tissue.

Resolution   Restoration of normality.

Rhabdomyo-   Prefix—of striated muscle (e.g. rhabdomyosarcoma—malignant neoplasm of striated muscle).

Saprophyte   Organism deriving its nutrition from dead cells or tissue.

Sarcoma   Malignant neoplasm of mesenchyme (connective tissue).

Scirrhous   Of a scar-like consistency (i.e. firm, puckered) (e.g. scirrhous carcinoma of the breast).

Sclerosis   Hardening of a tissue, often due to deposition of excess collagen.

Secondary   1. Attributable to some known cause (e.g. secondary hypertension); 2. neoplasm formed by metastasis from a primary neoplasm (contrast with primary).

Septic   Infected.

Septum   Membrane or boundary dividing a normal or abnormal structure into separate parts.

Serotype   Classification of organisms according to their antigenic characteristics.

Serous   1. Serous exudate or effusion—containing serum or a fluid resembling serum; 2. serous cyst—containing fluid only resembling serum.

Sessile (polyp)   With a broad base rather than a discrete stalk (contrast with pedunculated).

Shock   State of cardiovascular collapse characterised by low blood pressure (e.g. due to severe haemorrhage).

Signet-ring cell   Neoplastic cell (usually adenocarcinoma) in which the nucleus shows crescentic deformation by a large globule of mucin within its cytoplasm.

Signs   Observable manifestations of disease (e.g. swelling, fever, abnormal heart sounds).

Sinus (pathological)   Abnormal track (tract) leading from an abscess to the skin surface and often discharging pus.

Spongiosis   Epidermal oedema causing partial separation of cells.

Stage   A recognised phase in the development or progression of a disease (usually a neoplasm); (compare with grade).

Stasis   Stagnation of fluid often due to obstruction (e.g. urinary stasis).

Steatorrhoea   Excess fat in the faeces, a manifestation of intestinal malabsorption.

Steatosis   Fatty change, especially in liver.

Stem cells   Renewable unspecialized cells capable of giving rise to specialized cell types.

Stenosis   Narrowing of a lumen.

Stoma   Any normal, pathological or surgically constructed opening between one hollow structure and another or the skin.

Strangulation   Obstruction of blood flow by external compression (e.g. strangulated hernia).

Stroma   Non-neoplastic reactive connective tissue within a neoplasm.

Suppuration Formation of pus; a feature of acute inflammation.

Symbiosis Close association of two living organisms that may be mutually or singly beneficial or detrimental.

Symptoms The patient's complaints attributable to the presence of a disease (e.g. pain, malaise, nausea).

Syndrome Combination of signs and symptoms characteristic of a particular disease, no one feature alone being diagnostic.

Systematic Concerning each body system separately.

Systemic Concerning all body systems as a whole.

Tamponade (cardiac) Compression of heart, and therefore restriction of its movement, by excess pericardial fluid (e.g. haemorrhage, effusion) or by pericardial fibrosis (e.g. post-inflammatory scarring).

Telangiectasia Dilated small blood vessels.

Telomere End of a chromosome (contrast with centromere).

Teratoma Germ-cell neoplasm in which there are representatives of endoderm, ectoderm and mesoderm; usually benign in the ovary and malignant in the testis.

Thrombophlebitis Venous inflammation associated with a thrombus.

Thrombus Solid mass of coagulated blood formed within the circulation (contrast with clot).

Toxaemia Presence of a toxin in the blood.

Toxin Substance having harmful effects, usually of bacterial origin by common usage.

Trabeculation Abnormal appearance of a surface characterised by ridges.

Transdifferentiation The ability of adult stem cells to differentiate into multiple cell types (also known as plasticity).

Transformation Process in which cells are converted from normal to neoplastic.

Translocation Exchange of chromosomal segments between one chromosome and another.

Transudate Abnormal collection of fluid of low protein content due to either hypoproteinaemia or increased intravascular pressure in capillary beds (contrast with exudate).

Trauma Injury.

Trematode A flatworm.

Trisomy Presence of three copies of a particular chromosome in otherwise diploid cells (e.g. trisomy 21, in which there are three copies of chromosome 21, is a feature of Down's syndrome).

Tumour Abnormal swelling, now synonymous with neoplasm.

Type (neoplasm) Identity of a neoplasm determined from its differentiated features or assumed origin (histogenesis).

Ulcer Full-thickness defect in a surface epithelium or mucosa.

Varicose Distended and tortuous, especially referring to a blood vessel (e.g. varicose vein).

Venereal Transmitted by sexual intercourse or intimate foreplay.

Vesicle (skin) Small fluid-filled blister.

Villous Characterised by numerous finger-like surface projections (villi) (e.g. villous adenoma of rectum).

Viraemia Presence of a virus in the blood.

Virulence (micro-organism) Relative ability to produce disease.

Volvulus Loop of twisted intestine.

Xenograft Transplantation from one species to another.

Patient's symptom	Possible pathological causes of this symptom	Page numbers
Abdominal pain, acute	Aortic aneurysm	278
	Appendicitis	397
	Cholecystitis	428
	Crohn's disease	385
	Diverticulitis	391
	Ectopic pregnancy	524
	Gastroenteritis	381
	Ischaemic bowel	390
	Pancreatitis	430
	Peptic ulcer	369
	Pyelonephritis	592
	Stones in bile duct – biliary colic	427
	Stones in ureter – renal colic	530
	Ulcerative colitis	387
Abdominal pain, chronic	Chronic peptic ulcer	369
	Crohn's disease	385
	Diverticular disease	391
	Endometriosis	514
	Fibroids	512
	Gallstones	427
	Hydronephrosis	533
	Ovarian cysts/tumour	514
	Ulcerative colitis	387
	Uteric colic	530
Abdominal swelling	Aortic aneurysm	278
	Colorectal cancer	395
	Enlarged bladder due to obstruction	547
	Fibroid uterus	512
	Gastric cancer	372
	Ovarian cyst/tumour	514
	Pancreatic cancer	431
	Polycystic kidneys	573
	Pregnancy	519
	Splenomegaly	616
Anorectal pain	Anal fissure	398
	Anorectal cancer	398
	Crohn's disease	385
	Perianal abscess	398
	Thrombosed haemorrhoids	398
Arm pain	Cervical spondylosis	758
	Myocardial ischaemia	297
Back pain	Ankylosing spondylitis	734
	Bone metastases	726
	Duodenal ulcer	369
	Myeloma	666
	Osteoarthritis	728
	Prolapsed intervertebral disc	735
	Pyelonephritis	592
	Renal stones	530
	Vertebral collapse due to osteoporosis	715

Patient's symptom	Possible pathological causes of this symptom	Page numbers
Blood in urine	Bladder tumour	534
	Glomerulonephritis	575
	Polycystic kidney disease	573
	Prostate cancer	539
	Prostatic hyperplasia	537
	Renal carcinoma	530
	Renal/ureteric stones	530
	Urethritis	547
	Urinary tract infection	533
Body hair, excess	Polycystic ovary syndrome	513
Breast enlargement, men	Chronic liver disease	415
	Hyperthyroidism	449
Breast lump	Abscess	474
	Breast cancer	481
	Cyst	475
	Duct ectasia	474
	Fat necrosis	475
	Fibroadenoma	479
	Fibrocystic disease	475
	Lipoma	481
Breast pain	Cyclical mastalgia	471
	Mastitis/breast abscess	474
	Pregnancy	472
Breath, shortness of, acute	Acute exacerbation of chronic obstructive pulmonary disease	338
	Acute left ventricular failure	291
	Asthma	340
	Diabetic ketoacidosis	462
	Pneumonia	327
	Pneumothorax	351
	Pulmonary embolism	334
Breath, shortness of, chronic	Anaemia	635
	Aortic valve stenosis	302
	Asthma	340
	Chronic obstructive pulmonary disease	338
	Congenital heart disease	308
	Congestive cardiac failure	291
	Recurrent pulmonary emboli	334
Calf pain	Deep vein thrombosis	288
Chest pain	Dissecting aortic aneurysm	278
	Gastro-oesophageal reflux disease	363
	Myocardial infarction	294
	Myocardial ischaemia	297
	Pleurisy	353
	Pulmonary embolism	334
Confusion	Cerebral haemorrhage	762
	Cerebral infarction	761
	Cerebral tumour	782

Patient's symptom	Possible pathological causes of this symptom	Page numbers
Confusion (continued)	Diabetic ketoacidosis	462
	Hypoglycaemia	465
	Hypothyroidism	452
Consciousness, loss of, episodic	Aortic valve stenosis	302
	Epilepsy	775
	Hypoglycaemia	465
	Paroxysmal arrhythmias	297
Constipation	Colorectal cancer	395
	Diverticular disease	391
	Hirschsprung's disease	378
Cough	Asthma	340
	Bronchiectasis	332
	Chronic bronchitis	338
	Left ventricular failure	291
	Lung cancer	347
	Respiratory tract infection	326
	Tuberculosis	331
Coughing up blood	Chest infection	326
	Lung cancer	347
	Mitral valve stenosis	301
	Pulmonary embolism	347
Diarrhoea	Acute infective gastroenteritis	381
	Carcinoid tumour	396
	Chronic intestinal infection	384
	Coeliac disease	379
	Colorectal cancer	395
	Crohn's disease	385
	Diverticulitis	391
	Drugs, e.g. antibiotics	384
	Ulcerative colitis	387
Dizziness	Cardiac arrhythmia	297
	Hypoglycaemia	465
Epigastric pain	Gallstones	427
	Gastritis	367
	Gastro-oesophageal reflux disease	363
	Pancreatitis	430
	Peptic ulcer	369
Eye, painful red	Acute glaucoma	796
	Acute infective conjunctivitis	795
	Acute irititis	796
	Corneal abrasion	794
	Corneal ulcer	794
Facial swelling	Hypothyroidism	452
Facial ulcers and blisters	Basal cell carcinoma	694
	Herpes simplex virus	687
	Impetigo	688
	Keratoacanthoma	696

Patient's symptom	Possible pathological causes of this symptom	Page numbers
Fever	Chronic pyelonephritis	592
	Leukaemia	655
	Lymphoma	602
	Rheumatoid arthritis	730
Finger clubbing	Bronchiectasis	332
	Lung cancer	347
Fits	Cerebral metastases	786
	Primary cerebral tumours	783
Flushing	Carcinoid syndrome	397
	Hyperglycaemia	462
	Hyperthyroidism	449
	Hypoglycaemia	465
Foot pain	Gout	736
	Osteoarthritis	728
	Verruca	687
Gait, abnormal	Intermittent claudication	272
	Multiple sclerosis	770
	Osteoarthritis	728
	Parkinson's disease	778
	Spinal nerve root pain	758
Haemoptysis	Bronchiectasis	332
	Lung cancer	347
	Pulmonary embolism	334
	Respiratory tract infection	326
	Tuberculosis	331
Hair loss	Alopecia areata	705
	Hypoparathyroidism	460
	Hypopituitarism	440
	Hypothyroidism	452
	Male pattern baldness	705
	Tinea capitis	688
Hallucinations	Cerebral tumour	782
	Temporal lobe epilepsy	775
Headache	Cerebral metastases	786
	Cervical spondylosis	758
	Intracerebral haemorrhage	762
	Meningitis	765
	Primary cerebral tumours	783
	Temporal arteritis	287
Incontinence	Prostatic hypertrophy	537
	Urinary tract infection	533
Infertility	Chronic salpingitis	519
	Endometriosis	514
	Hypopituitarism	440
	Uterine fibroids	512

Patient's symptom	Possible pathological causes of this symptom	Page numbers
Intercourse, painful	Endometriosis	514
	Pelvic inflammatory disease	519
	Vulvovaginitis	501
Itching	Head lice	689
	Hodgkin's disease	602
	Impetigo	688
	Jaundice, typically obstructive	408
	Lichen planus	690
	Pityriasis rosea	692
	Psoriasis	690
	Scabies	689
	Uraemia of renal failure	570
	Urticaria	689
Jaundice	Alcoholic cirrhosis	421
	Carcinoma of bile duct	429
	Carcinoma of head of pancreas	431
	Cholangitis	419
	Cholestasis of pregnancy	409
	Drug-induced cholestasis	409
	Gallstones in bile duct	427
	Haemolytic anaemia	645
	Primary biliary cirrhosis	419
	Viral hepatitis	409
Joints, pain, multiple	Osteoarthritis	728
	Psoriatic arthropathy	738
	Rheumatoid arthritis	730
Joints, pain, single	Acute exacerbation of osteoarthritis	728
	Gout/pseudogout	736
Libido, loss of	Hypothyroidism	452
Memory loss	Alzheimer's disease	779
	Cerebral infarcts	761
	Hypothyroidism	452
	Subarachnoid haemorrhage	763
	Traumatic head injury	755
Neck, lumps	Goitre	452
	Lymphoma	602
	Prominent normal lymph nodes	599
	Reactive lymphadenitis	599
	Sebaceous cyst	693
Neck, stiff	Ankylosing spondylitis	734
	Cervical spondylosis	758
	Rheumatoid arthritis	730
Nipple discharge	Duct ectasia	474
	Duct papilloma	480
	Intraduct carcinoma	484
	Mastitis/breast abscess	474
	Pregnancy	472
	Prolactinoma	441

Patient's symptom	Possible pathological causes of this symptom	Page numbers
Numbness/paraesthesiae	Cerebrovascular accident	761
	Cervical spondylosis	758
	Diabetic neuropathy	788
	Multiple sclerosis	770
	Peripheral polyneuropathy	788
	Prolapsed intervertebral disc	735
Palpitations	Hyperthyroidism	449
	Ischaemic heart disease	294
	Mitral valve disease	300
Pelvic pain	Ectopic pregnancy	524
	Endometriosis	514
	Ovarian cysts/tumours	513
	Pelvic inflammatory disease	519
	Urinary tract infection	533
Penile pain	Balanitis	543
	Balanitis xerotica obliterans	544
	Herpes simplex	544
	Prostatitis	536
	Urethritis	547
Penile ulceration	Balanitis	543
	Balanitis xerotica obliterans	544
	Herpes simplex	544
Periods, absence	Polycystic ovary syndrome	513
	Pregnancy	519
Periods, heavy	Cervical polyps	501
	Dysfunctional uterine bleeding	508
	Endometrial carcinoma	510
	Endometrial polyps	509
	Endometriosis	514
	Fibroids	512
Periods, painful	Chronic pelvic inflammatory disease	519
	Endometrial polyp	509
	Endometriosis	514
	Uterine malformation	506
Puberty, delayed	Hyperthyroidism	449
Purpura	Infective endocarditis	303
	Vasculitis	284
Rectal bleeding	Anal fissure	398
	Bowel ischaemia	390
	Colonic angiodysplasia	391
	Colorectal adenomas	393
	Colorectal cancer	395
	Crohn's disease	385
	Diverticular disease	391
	Endometriosis	514
	Gastroenteritis	381
	Haemorrhoids	398
	Ulcerative colitis	387

Patient's symptom	Possible pathological causes of this symptom	Page numbers
Vision, loss of, gradual	Cataract	796
	Chronic glaucoma	796
	Diabetic retinopathy	794
	Hypertensive retinopathy	794
	Senile macular degeneration	796
Vomiting	Acute viral labyrinthitis	799
	Appendicitis	397
	Gastroenteritis	381
	Hyperglycaemia	462
	Hypoglycaemia	465
	Perforated peptic ulcer	369
	Pyelonephritis	592
	Pyloric stenosis	366
	Stenosing gastric cancer	372
	Ureteric calculus	530
Vomiting blood	Acute gastritis	367
	Blood dyscrasia, e.g. thrombocytopenia	670
	Gastric cancer	372
	Gastro-oesophageal reflux	363
	Mallory–Weiss tear	363
	Oesophageal cancer	364
	Oesophageal varices	363
	Peptic ulcer	369
Vulval irritation	*Candida* infection	499
	Trichomonas vaginalis	499
Vulval swelling	Bartholin's cyst	499
Vulval ulceration	*Candida* infection	499
	Herpes simplex	499
	Squamous cell carcinoma	500
Weight gain	Hypothyroidism	452
	Oedema of chronic renal failure	570
Weight loss	Hyperthyroidism	449
	Untreated type 1 diabetes mellitus	462

Note: page numbers in *italic* indicate tables, those in **bold** indicate figures and those in ***bold italics*** indicate textboxes.

821

I

keratinocytes, 692, 699
  melanocytic naevi, 700
  pemphigus, 697
  squamous cell carcinoma, 695–696
keratoacanthoma, *694*, 696
keratoconjunctivitis, 795
keratohyaline granules, 692
keratosis, 806
kernicterus, 408, 653
KGF (keratinocyte growth factor), 111
kidney, 563–594
  acute failure, 570, 589, 590
  agenesis, 96
  amyloidosis, *143*, 144–145, 585
  autoimmune disease, 191
  carcinoma, prognosis, *256*
  chronic failure, 570, 576, 584, 587,
    719–720
  coagulative necrosis, **106**
  common clinical problems, **563**
  congenital diseases, 572–573, 574–575
  cystic disease, 573–575
  diabetes mellitus and, 284, 583–585
  function, 564–568
  glomerular disease, 570–572, 575–586
    post-streptococcal, *47*, **49**, 50, 185–186,
      577–578
  gout, 590–591, 737
  haemodialysis
    aluminium concentration, 139, *773*
    amyloidosis, *143*, 144
    cysts, 575
    encephalopathy, 139
    renal osteodystrophy, 719, *720*
  heart failure and, 291
  hydronephrosis, 533, 592
  hypertension, 281, 282–283, 284
  infection-associated disease, 586–587, 589
  infections, 592–593
  infective endocarditis, 305, 583
  investigation of disease, 568–569
  ionising radiation injury, 118
  multiple myeloma, 585, 668
  nephritis, 569, 573, 576, 590, 592
  nephrotic syndrome, 20, **176**, 179, 569, 573,
    576
  oedema, 569–570
  pathophysiology of disease, *563–564*, 569
  pregnancy, 568, 588–589
  proteinuria, *563*, 564, 569, 576
  pyelonephritis, 592–593
  structure, 564–568
  systemic lupus erythematosus, 582, 741
  transplantation, 193–195, 587–588
  tubules, 564, 566, 567, 568, 573
  tubulo-interstitial disorders, 589–593, 737
  tumours, 231, 531–532
  vasculature, 284, 564, 565, 566, 585–586,
    588, 589
  wound healing, 113
Kikuchi's disease, 601
kinin system, 205, **206**
Klinefelter's syndrome, 40, *41*, 94
Koch's postulates, 16
Koebner effect, 690
koilocytosis, 502, **503**, **506**
koilonychia, *621*, 639
Korsakoff's psychosis, 137, 774
Krabbe's globoid cell leukodystrophy, 772
Krukenberg tumour, 519
Kugelberg–Welander disease, 791
kuru, 768
kwashiorkor, 136, 773

L

labile cells, 75, 92, 108, 109
laboratory tests *See* diagnostic pathology
labyrinthitis, 799
lactate dehydrogenase, 61–62
lactating adenoma, 481
lactation, 472
Lambert–Eaton myasthenic syndrome, 782, 793
Langerhans, islets of, 462, **462**, 464–465
Langerhans' cell histiocytosis (LCH;
    histiocytosis X), 347, 601
Langerhans' cells, 682, 686
Langer's lines, 682
Langhans' giant cells, 217
language of pathology, 8
large B-cell lymphoma
  diffuse, 610
  mediastinal, 606, 615
large cell lymphoma, anaplastic (ALCL), 611,
    612
large cell undifferentiated carcinoma (LCUC),
    348, 349
large intestine *See* colorectal pathology
Laron dwarfism, 86
larva migrans, *54*, 689
laryngitis, 208, 326
laryngotracheobronchitis, 327
larynx
  inflammatory disorders, 208, 326
  laryngotracheobronchitis, 327
  structure and function, 320, **321**
  tumours, 121, *256*, 326, **327**
Lassa fever virus, *69*
latent intervals, 16, 245
LATS (long-acting thyroid stimulator), 451
LCH (Langerhans' cell histiocytosis), 347, 601
LCUC (large cell undifferentiated carcinoma),
    348, 349
LE (lupus erythematosus), 687, 689–690,
    704, 705
    systemic variant *See* systemic lupus
      erythematosus (SLE)
lead, 140, *773*
lectin pathway, *173*, 174, 175
left heart failure, 291, 292, 293
left ventricular hypertrophy, 81, 284
leg ulcers, 289, **681**, 698–699
legal issues *See* medicolegal issues
Legionnaires' disease, 330
leiomyoma, 745
  breast, 481
  nomenclature, *229*, 230
  oesophagus, 364
  stomach, 372
  uterine corpus, 512, **513**
leiomyosarcoma
  breast, 493
  myocardial, 315
  nomenclature, *229*, 230
  uterine corpus, 512
Leishmania sp., *53*, 688–689
leishmaniasis, *53*, 688–689
lens
  cataracts, 796
  uveitis induced by, 796
lentigo, 699–700
lentigo maligna melanoma, 701
lepromatous leprosy, 688
leprosy, *47*, 186, 688
leptomeningitis, 765
Leptospira interrogans, 48

Lesch–Nyhan syndrome, 129
Leser–Trélat sign, 693
lesions, definitions, 17, 30
LET (linear energy transfer), 116
leukaemia, 655–663
  acute, 607, 656–659, 664, 665
  adult T-cell leukaemia/lymphoma (ATLL), 611
  B-cell chronic lymphocytic, 608, 663
  bone marrow examination, 64
  chromosome abnormalities, *247*, 251, 656,
    657, 659, 663
  chronic, *247*, 251, 617, 655, 659–663
  joint changes, *738*
  splenic involvement, 617, 658, 661, 663
leukocytes, 624–627
  formation, 632, 633, 634, 655
  function, 635
    See also leukaemia; specific cells
leukocytosis, 212, 626, 661
leukodystrophies, 772
leukoencephalitis, acute haemorrhagic, 769
leukoencephalopathy, multifocal, 772
leukoerythroblastic blood film, 624
leukopenia, 627
leukoplakia
  oral, 358, 360
  vulval, 500
leukotrienes, acute inflammation, 205
Lewy bodies, 778, **779**
Leydig cells, 549
  tumours, 556–557
LH (luteinising hormone), 407–408, 439,
    507–508
libido, loss of, **435**
lice, 689
lichen planus, 687, 690–692, 705, 706
lichen sclerosus, 500, 706
lichen simplex chronicus, 685
lichenoid reaction, 691, *709*
life expectancy, 260
Li–Fraumeni syndrome, *244*, *248*, 249, 483
ligaments, 727
light microscopy, 5, 6–7
limb girdle dystrophy, 792
limbic encephalitis, 782
limiting plate, 405
linear energy transfer (LET), 116
lines of Zahn, 150
lip
  angular cheilitis, 639
  cancer, 360
  cleft (hare), 97–98, 358
lipid pneumonia, 331
lipo-, meaning, 806
lipofuscin, 264
lipolysis, diabetes mellitus, 463
lipoma, 745
  breast, 481
  cardiac, 315
  dermal, 706
  nomenclature, *229*, 230
  thymus, 615
lipoproteinosis, alveolar, 347
lipoproteins
  cell membrane, 104, 274
  metabolism, 274, **276**
liposarcoma, 746
  breast, 493
  nomenclature, *229*, 230
-lithiasis, meaning, 806
liver, 404–426
  acute injury, 409–415
  brain and, *404*, 408, 422, *773*, 774–775